kings of scotland (Alba)
and earls of northumbria (England)

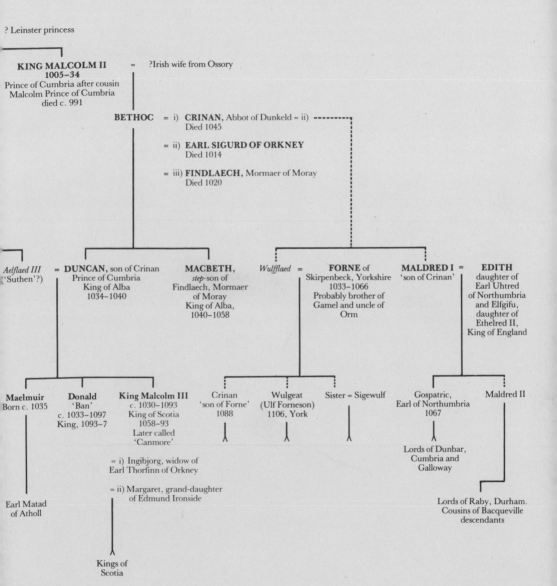

? Leinster princess

KING MALCOLM II
1005–34
Prince of Cumbria after cousin
Malcolm Prince of Cumbria
died c. 991
= ?Irish wife from Ossory

BETHOC = i) **CRINAN,** Abbot of Dunkeld = ii)
Died 1045

= ii) **EARL SIGURD OF ORKNEY**
Died 1014

= iii) **FINDLAECH,** Mormaer of Moray
Died 1020

Aelflaed III
('Suthen'?) = **DUNCAN,** son of Crinan
Prince of Cumbria
King of Alba
1034–1040

MACBETH,
step-son of
Findlaech, Mormaer
of Moray
King of Alba,
1040–1058

Wulfflaed = **FORNE** of
Skirpenbeck, Yorkshire
1033–1066
Probably brother of
Gamel and uncle of
Orm

MALDRED I = **EDITH**
'son of Crinan'
daughter of
Earl Uhtred
of Northumbria
and Elfgifu,
daughter of
Ethelred II,
King of England

Maelmuir
Born c. 1035

Donald
'Ban'
c. 1033–1097
King, 1093–7

King Malcolm III
c. 1030–1093
King of Scotia
1058–93
Later called
'Canmore'

= i) Ingibjorg, widow of
Earl Thorfinn of Orkney

= ii) Margaret, grand-daughter
of Edmund Ironside

Crinan
'son of Forne'
1088

Wulgeat
(Ulf Forneson)
1106, York

Sister = Sigewulf

Gospatric,
Earl of Northumbria
1067

Maldred II

Earl Matad
of Atholl

Lords of Dunbar,
Cumbria and
Galloway

Lords of Raby, Durham.
Cousins of Bacqueville
descendants

Kings of
Scotia

ALSO BY DOROTHY DUNNETT

The Game of Kings
Queens' Play
The Disorderly Knights
Pawn in Frankincense
The Ringed Castle
Checkmate

MYSTERIES

The Photogenic Soprano
Murder in the Round
Match for Murder
Murder in Focus

KING
HEREAFTER

KING HEREAFTER

A NOVEL BY

DOROTHY DUNNETT

ALFRED A. KNOPF

NEW YORK   1982

The author and publishers would like to thank the following for the use of small quotations from other sources reproduced in *King Hereafter:*

Sidgwick & Jackson *(The Viking Achievement* by Peter Foote and David M. Wilson); The Hogarth Press *(The Orkneying Saga* translated by Hermann Palsson and Paul Edwards); Penguin Books *(King Harald's Saga* translated by Magnus Magnusson and Hermann Palsson); Constable & Company *(Wandering Scholars* by Helen Waddell); Pelican Books *(The Celts* by Nora Chadwick); Penguin Books *(Njal's Saga* translated by Magnus Magnusson and Hermann Palsson). We regret that we were unable to trace the representatives of Alexander Burt Taylor, editor of *Orkneying Saga.*

Library of Congress Cataloging in Publication Data

Dunnett, Dorothy.
King hereafter.

I. Title.
PR6054.U56K5   1982   823'.914   81-48112
ISBN 0-394-52378-4   AACR2

Wealth dies.
Kinsmen die.
A man himself must likewise die.
But word-fame
Never dies
For him who achieves it well.

Wealth dies.
Kinsmen die.
A man himself must likewise die.
But one thing I know
That never dies —
The verdict on each man dead.

(Hávamál)

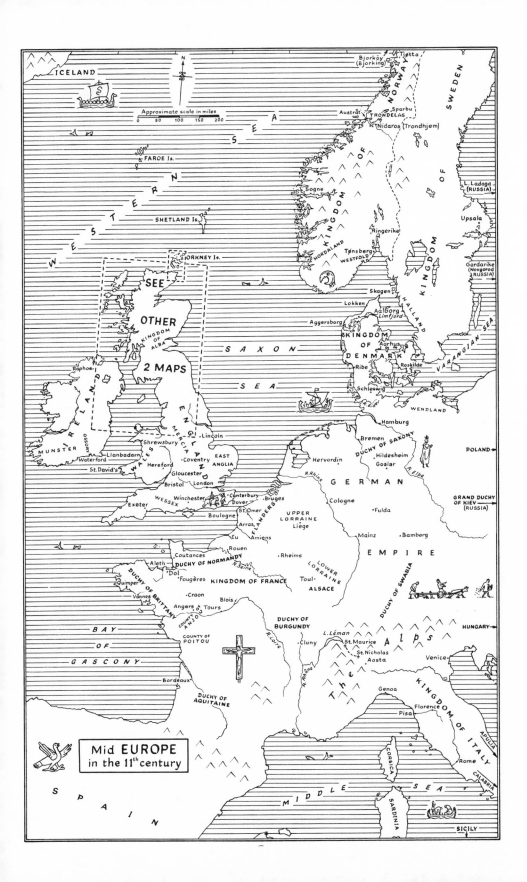

ICELAND

WESTERN OCEAN SEA

FAROE Is.

SHETLAND Is.

ORKNEY Is.

SEE OTHER 2 MAPS

KINGDOM OF ALBA

IRELAND

Raphoe

OSSORY

MUNSTER

Waterford

St. David's

Llanbadarn

WALES

Shrewsbury

Hereford

Coventry

Gloucester

Bristol

Exeter

WESSEX

Winchester

MERCIA

Lincoln

ENGLAND

EAST ANGLIA

London

Canterbury

Dover

Boulogne

St. Omer

Arras

Amiens

Eu

Rouen

FLANDERS

Bruges

UPPER LORRAINE

Liège

SAXON SEA

Skagen

Lokken

Aggersborg

Aalborg
Limfjord

KINGDOM OF DENMARK

Aarhus

Ribe

Roskilde

Schleswig

WENDLAND

Hamburg

Bremen

DUCHY OF SAXONY

Hildesheim

Goslar

Hervordin

R. Rhine

Cologne

Fulda

GERMAN

Mainz

Bamberg

EMPIRE

POLAND

GRAND DUCHY OF KIEV (RUSSIA)

Bjørkøy (Bjorking)

Tjøtta

Austrått

Sparbu

TRONDELAG

Nidaros (Trondhjem)

KINGDOM OF NORWAY

SWEDEN

Sogne

HORDALAND

Ringerike

Tønsberg

WESTFOLD

HALLAND

KINGDOM OF

L. Ladoga (RUSSIA)

Upsala

Gardarike
(Novgorod RUSSIA)

VARANGIAN SEA

Coutances

Aleth

Dol

Fougères

DUCHY OF NORMANDY

R. Seine

KINGDOM OF FRANCE

Rheims

LOWER LORRAINE

Toul

ALSACE

DUCHY OF SWABIA

HUNGARY

DUCHY OF BRITTANY

Quimper

Vannes

Craon

Angers

Tours

Blois

COUNTY OF ANJOU

COUNTY OF POITOU

R. Loire

DUCHY OF BURGUNDY

Cluny

L. Léman

St. Maurice

St. Nicholas

Aosta

The Alps

Venice

BAY OF GASCONY

Bordeaux

DUCHY OF AQUITAINE

R. Rhône

Genoa

Florence

Pisa

KINGDOM OF ITALY

APULIA

Rome

CALABRIA

CORSICA

SARDINIA

MIDDLE SEA

SICILY

SPAIN

Mid EUROPE
in the 11th century

Approximate scale in miles
0 50 100 150 200

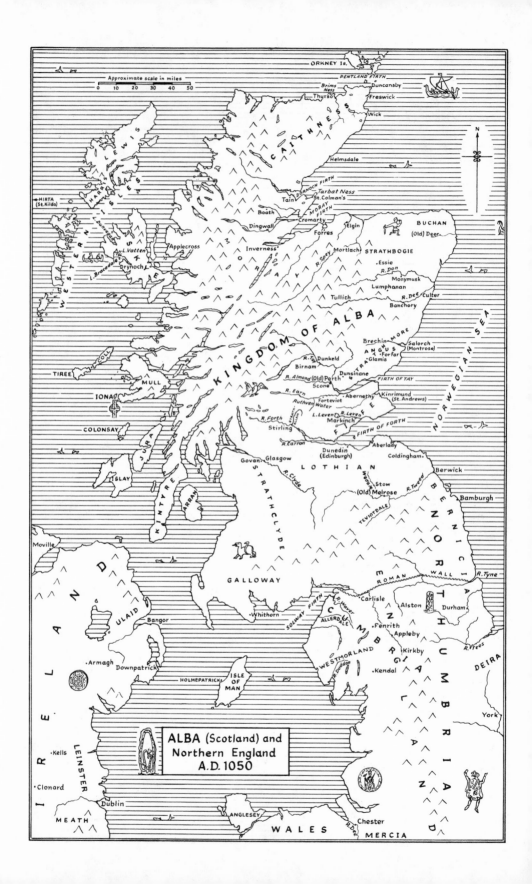

ALBA (Scotland) and
Northern England
A.D. 1050

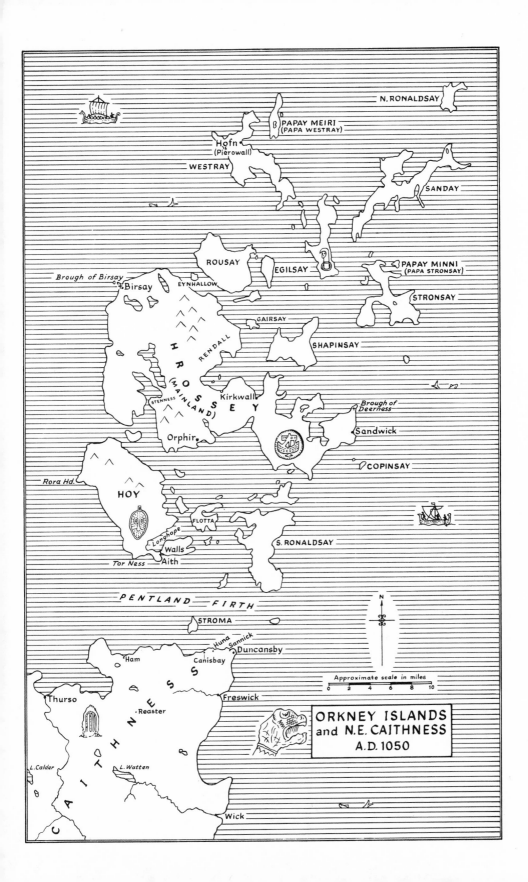

N. RONALDSAY

PAPAY MEIRI
(PAPA WESTRAY)

Hofn
(Pierowall)

WESTRAY

SANDAY

ROUSAY

EGILSAY

PAPAY MINNI
(PAPA STRONSAY)

Brough of Birsay

Birsay

EYNHALLOW

STRONSAY

H
R
O
S
S
E
Y

RENDALL

GAIRSAY

SHAPINSAY

(MAINLAND)

STENNESS

Kirkwall

Brough of
Deerness

Orphir

Sandwick

COPINSAY

Rora Hd.

HOY

FLOTTA

Longhope

S. RONALDSAY

Walls

Tor Ness   Aith

PENTLAND   FIRTH

N

STROMA

Huna
Sannick

Duncansby

Ham

Canisbay

Approximate scale in miles

0   2   4   6   8   10

Thurso

Reaster

Freswick

C
A
I
T
H
N
E
S
S

ORKNEY ISLANDS
and N.E. CAITHNESS
A.D. 1050

L. Calder

L. Watten

Wick

ᴘARᴛ ONE

NOW WITCHCRAFT CELEBRATES

What is this,
That rises like the issue of a king;
And wears upon his baby brow the round
And top of sovereignty?

—From hence to Inverness,
And bind us further to you.

ONE

WHEN THE YEAR one thousand came, Thorkel Amundason was five years old, and hardly noticed how frightened everyone was.

By the time Canute ruled England, Thorkel was nineteen and had heard as much about the old scare as he wanted, from the naked lips of men who might be able to read and to write, but who wouldn't know one end of a longship from the other.

He understood that folk had thought the Day of Judgement was coming, because a thousand years had passed since the White Christ was born, in that age when the Romans had conquered the world.

All the world, that is, except for the north.

The Romans had not conquered Denmark, or Norway, or Sweden. They had not conquered Ireland, or his own Orkney islands, or Iceland to his north. They had overcome England, beginning in the toe and pushing north until they stuck on the border of Alba and built their frontier wall there, stretching from sea to sea.

The barbarians who followed the Romans had learned all about the White Christ by the time that Charlemagne and the Pope had formed their big new Empire over the ocean. The Vikings who followed the barbarians liked the old gods.

Thorkel himself had always been partial to Thor. The priests had been amazed, so it was said, at the numbers who became tired of Thor as the year one thousand got nearer. Orkney declared for Christ overnight, followed by Iceland and all those bits of Norway the King could easily get at. Ireland and Alba, of course, had followed the Cross all along.

Alba, that men later called Scotland.

As a child, Thorkel Amundason had touched Alba often enough, on his father's trading-ship going to Dublin, or as part of a young man's crew looking for booty in England.

Alba he never attacked, nor did anyone else from Orkney or Norway. At the height of the Viking invasions, the King of Alba had found a way to buy peace. He had married his only daughter and heiress to the ruler of the Orkney islands, seven miles to his north, which long ago had been settled from Norway. And the baby born of that marriage he had made child-Earl of Caithness, his northernmost province, over which for uncountable years the Earls of Orkney and the Kings of Alba had squabbled.

The Orkney-Alban marriage lasted only six years. And when the Earl of Orkney was killed and his widow went back to Alba and married again, it was Thorkel Amundason who was chosen to train and protect the half-Orkney child, their only offspring. Thorkel was twenty, then.

Twenty, and ambitious. Twenty, and the only son of the greatest household in Orkney next to the Earls'.

For a while, the sight of Thorkel Amundason rearing a foster-son was the talk of Orkney. Girls who had good cause to know Thorkel's precise views on parenthood scoffed to each other over the dye-pots. Their fathers and brothers said less.

Then there came the day when one of the child's three older Earl-brothers died, and the other two suddenly noticed how openly critical Thorkel Amundason had become of their rule, and how keen to mention the rights of his fosterling, their half-Alban brother.

The joint Earls of Orkney did not like it. You might say that Thorkel Amundason was grooming the child for a large share of Orkney. You might even say that King Malcolm of Alba was abetting him. Without warning, Orkney became a dangerous place for Thorkel Amundason.

Thorkel removed himself and the child to Caithness and, from across seven miles of sea, continued his careful campaigning.

When he made his next move, he was twenty-five: handsome, eloquent, energetic—a born leader, men said. They admired the way Thorkel handled his foster-son, not chastising him as some might when the child ran off to Alba from time to time to visit his mother. In any case, Thorkel was not the man to upset the King, the child's Alban grandfather.

Thorkel's next move, everyone agreed, was a predictable one. He removed from life one of the joint Earls of Orkney. The chain of events which led up to the deed was quite complex, and the head of Earl Einar was cut off, in the event, by somebody else; but Thorkel assumed full responsibility, having long before weighed all the consequences.

Earl Einar's tax-ridden subjects, he knew, would hardly blame him. Earl Einar's surviving brother was not a man given to fighting. The King of Norway, Orkney's occasional overlord, had fallen out with the dead Earl quite recently and wouldn't be hard on his murderer, provided that Thorkel got to court fast and explained himself.

To do so, Thorkel Amundason duly slipped out of Orkney, consigned the boy to his mother in Alba, and took ship for the Norse court at Nídarós, two sailing days to the east, on the north-western fringes of Norway.

Of course, King Olaf of Norway was displeased with Thorkel Amundason. He showed his disapproval in a bluff way all that winter, and forced Thorkel to stay for two months at the home of some cousins before finally granting him guest-room at court.

The reconciliation, when it came, was no more than Thorkel expected. He had worked hard at being agreeable. His cousins the Arnasons were favourites of the Norwegian King. The late joint Earl of Orkney was not a friend the King would feel drawn to mourn. Yule was over and spring lay ahead, and a carefree sail back home, bearing a reprimand and possibly one or two well-chosen gifts to stiffen his loyalty and that of his foster-son, the child-Earl of Caithness and Orkney.

That was the plan, until the brat wrecked it.

TWO

UT FOR THE Festival of the Spring Sacrifice, it would never have happened.

You could also blame the native stubbornness of the people round about Nídarós. That is, while King Olaf and his court were intoning Easter Masses at one end of the sea inlet, the Festival of the Spring Sacrifice was preparing to get under way at the other.

Hints of forthcoming revelry had come to Thorkel Amundason's ears, but he ignored them. His Norwegian cousins might whisper, but it was no business of his. He had suffered the herring of Lent, and the watery wine and the boredom of Bishop Grimkell's Saxon Latin: atonement could require nothing more. Let the Arnasons whisper: they lived here. In two weeks he hoped to be gone: away from Norway and back to Caithness and his foster-son. Back to plan for the future in Orkney.

Who told the King about the Festival of the Spring Sacrifice Thorkel did not discover, but he suspected his cousin Kalv Arnason. Kalv was short, and red-haired, and had no discretion. Everyone knew what winters in the north were like. After six months with his wife, no man still in his senses would miss the chance of exchanging his longfire for a week of feasting and trading, carousing and horse-fights and wenching, at the host-farm at the end of the fjord. It did no harm and kept everyone happy. Provided the King didn't hear of it.

The King heard of it on his way into church for the first Mass of the day, when he was hungry. Following him with his retinue into the big timber building, Thorkel saw that something was wrong and hoped it need not concern him. Thorkel was ready to go home, although he had been well entertained and lacked for nothing away from the table. He had brought his own women with him, among the slaves of his travelling household, and had not had to lend them out more than he expected. He prided himself, too, on a little success with the wives of the court. Coming from Orkney, he was well travelled, and had better manners than some of their husbands.

A wife was something he had never troubled to acquire for himself. No marriage, no legitimate sons could vouchsafe him such power as might this cross-bred Earl he was rearing for Orkney.

At the end of Mass, the King got up like a fish on a line, and everyone rose. The King was thickset for a man of twenty-seven, and of no very great height, but he had been fighting since he was twelve years old and was still in the peak of condition. No one knew what his baptismal name had been. That had been given during his roaring Viking days in Spain and Friesland and Rouen until the dream sent him back: the dream that said, *Return, and you shall be King of Norway for ever.*

And he had been King for four years, and kept his name, Olaf: the name of Norway's first missionary king, who had done his converting, also, with an axe.

The King's guests, considerately attending Mass with him, had no idea what they were about to be let in for. Herded with the rest into the royal drinking-hall, Thorkel Amundason watched as the King strode to the steps of the High Chair and, turning, began to declaim. Then, with well-concealed resentment, he heard what the King had to say.

The King intended that very day, he announced, to mount an expedition of his loyal and Christian subjects against those pagans of Sparbu and Eynar and Vaerdal and Skogn whose devilish rites were an offence against the White Christ and himself, as their overlord.

'With your help, my good Trøndelagers,' said the King, 'and with the help of your friends, we shall launch a fleet of the Blessed against the heathen that will give Freya something to weep for.'

Those who didn't have metal about them reached up with their knife-handles and banged the shields hung on the wall. Thorkel applauded by kicking a barrel. Within a week of his escape, he had to risk his life and a blood-feud by helping King Olaf kill farmers at Sparbu.

Kalv his cousin was grinning. Kalv his red-headed cousin said, 'Why the frown, Thorkel? Everyone knows your skill with a sword. The late Earl Einar of Orkney could vouch for it. Enjoy yourself, collect some booty, and earn yourself King Olaf's favour. You may need it sooner than you might imagine.'

Hints from the Arnasons were as good as threats from anyone else. Thorkel said, 'What do you mean? I have the King's favour.'

'So you have,' said his cousin. 'But you don't know whose ship berthed an hour ago. He won't be expected to fight. But he'll be waiting here when the King comes back from Sparbu. Earl Brusi of Orkney is in Nídarós. You remember. You killed his brother last year.'

Thorkel smiled. 'In self-defence. Where is the crime? And with his brother gone, Earl Brusi is richer today by a third share of Orkney. I have no fear of Earl Brusi.'

The eyes of Kalv were round, pale-blue, and candid. 'Then why is he here?' Kalv enquired.

Because, thought Thorkel, *that hell-begotten boy has been up to some-thing. I should never have left him so long with his mother. I had to leave him or I should have been outlawed. I had to get King Olaf's pardon. I had to let*

*Earl Brusi settle down to enjoy his two-thirds of Orkney and come to terms
with his conscience. Brusi's not a short-tempered man: he'd never harm his
little brother in Caithness.* His little half-brother, Thorkel's foster-son. The
interfering young fool who, instead of leaving everything to his elders, had
done something stupid enough to bring Brusi here to complain.

'Why is Earl Brusi here? I can't imagine,' said Thorkel Amundason.
'Another wife perhaps, or a new swordsmith, or some timber? Some men
always keep low stocks in Orkney.'

As soon as he could escape from Kalv, Thorkel began to enquire about Earl
Brusi of Orkney. But men either knew nothing of him or were not prepared to
tell what they knew. When the horns blew from the jetty for muster, Thorkel
joined King Olaf's fleet of axe-armed crusaders, knowing little more than
Kalv's hint had conveyed. Trouble might await his return. While he could, he
should fight well for Olaf.

In the end, the Festival of the Spring Sacrifice had not even been started
when five ships, led by King Olaf's own *Charlemagne*, skimmed noiselessly
up the dark fjord and night-landed three hundred men to surround the great
farm-house of Maere in Sparbu while the guests slept and the beasts moved in
their pens and the wooden barns rustled with mice between the kegs of ale and
butter and flour, the barrels of pork and of beef, the crates of salt fish and
wadmoll and feathers, of seal oil and squirrel skins and all the other precious
goods that the people of the north brought to sell and to barter.

There was an old wooden statue of Thor inside a stone hut, with the timber
for a great fire built before it. King Olaf lit the pyre and led the shouting, so
that the guests and household of Maere jumped from bed with their weapons
and then shrank at the sight of the tightening ring of axe, spear, and arrow
about them.

Afterwards, it was said that every one was taken prisoner, and that King
Olaf ordered the execution of Ølve of Egge, the ringleader, and of many more
besides. Certainly, while the wealth in the barns was loaded on to his ships,
the King sent his men-at-arms abroad through the country to harry and
plunder wherever a friend of Odin might be suspected.

Kalv Arnason asked for, and was given, Ølve's rich widow to marry, with
her young sons and all her fine farmlands.

Thorkel Amundason took back to the ships a sword as red as the rest,
having fought with his usual skill, avoiding the eyes of those Maere men with
whom he was friendly. Nothing injured him, and he did not fail to congratulate Kalv before leaving.

He did not, like the rest of them, snore on the half-deck throughout the trip
back, full of pork and new beer, with gold rings on his arms. Neither did his
cousin Finn, Kalv's older brother. Finn said, 'Your little foster-son, the joint
Earl of Orkney. Tell me about the boy.'

Tell him about the boy. The oars handed back the cold April air, and
Thorkel elbowed his heavy cloak closer. 'Tell you what? You saw him last
summer when King Olaf sent for him. He's no beauty.'

'Does it matter?' said Finn his cousin. 'When his mother's a princess of Alba? Do you find the boy difficult?' The front of Finn's tunic was patched like leather with someone else's old blood, blurred where he had tried to scrub it away. He was the most straightforward, so everyone said, of the Arnasons.

Thorkel raised a neatly trimmed eyebrow. 'Difficult? Are your daughters difficult? They stamp their feet and your nurse lifts her hand to them.'

'I hear he is attached to his mother's third husband,' Finn said, his soft blue eyes round as sea-pebbles. 'The province-ruler she married in Alba. Does the boy really care about Orkney? Will he want his share when you have got it for him? You've fostered him for seven years, but you never trouble to mention his name. What is it? Thorfinn?'

'He's called Thorfinn,' agreed Thorkel shortly. A pagan name, like his own, but that was not why he didn't use it. With a boy like that, you had to watch your back as well as your front. Attaching a name to him wouldn't improve your authority. There were other considerations as well. He added, hearing the edge on his voice, 'You are asking what is my interest in fostering such a boy?'

The soft-focussed eyes considered his. 'Not really,' said Finn at length. 'No, that is not hard to guess. I only wondered if you were thinking that you had picked the wrong child to foster.'

Gulls squealed over the masthead. Near at hand, against the creak of wood and the rush of the sea there sounded the rap of thrown dice, and men's voices, and the harsh bellows-breath of the sleepers. Thorkel said, 'What other child is there?' But he knew. Of the boy's four older brothers, only one had had a son.

'Why,' Finn said, 'Rognvald, Earl Brusi's son. Ten years old and so pretty he could have fifty mothers to take the place of his own. He's here with his father. You know that Earl Brusi's in Nídarós?'

The youth Arnór Thordarson the song-maker halted beside them with a fan of hot smoking mutton on skewers, and Thorkel took one politely, as if the interruption were of no consequence. Thorkel said, 'You've seen Earl Brusi, then?' He bared his teeth for a bite.

'And spoken to him,' said Finn, watching him chew. 'He'd just had a talk with the King. Don't you want to know why Earl Brusi is here? You killed his brother. Or arranged for it.'

Thorkel gave his close attention to the meat. 'If you know why Earl Brusi is here, then I suppose you are going to tell me.'

Finn said, 'He isn't here because of the murder. He's here to complain to the King about your foster-son. Your foster-son Thorfinn, his little half-brother, who has promised him no peace, it seems, unless Brusi hands him half of Orkney.'

Despite himself, Thorkel's face grew red round his smile. As if he meant it, he said, 'It seems fair. Thorfinn and Brusi are the only two brothers left.'

Finn said, 'Brusi is a grown man with a son to look after, and Thorfinn is a child by a different mother. Earl Brusi claims both his own third of Orkney and the third willed him by the brother you killed. King Olaf agrees.'

'Does he?' said Thorkel. *Thorfinn*, his mind said. *Thorfinn, the stupid, half-grown, cocksure little fool.*

'Yes. The King promised, if need be, to support Brusi's cause with an army,' said his cousin Finn mildly. 'At a price, certainly. King Olaf doesn't give something for nothing.'

'Whatever the King wanted, I'm sure Brusi would give it him,' Thorkel remarked. The ship kicked to the current, and he flung the half-eaten mutton away.

'The King wanted sovereign rights,' said Finn, 'over all Brusi's Orkney inheritance. Overlordship of two-thirds of Orkney. Of course, Brusi agreed.'

'Kneeling?' said Thorkel. He laughed.

'Kneeling, naturally. That is why,' said Finn his cousin, 'I wondered if you hadn't picked the wrong princeling to foster.'

Successfully, Thorkel laughed again. 'You think I might have found the dainty young Rognvald more promising? But I should have had to kill his father Brusi first, shouldn't I? And what would be the use, with his land under King Olaf now anyway?'

Stupid, half-grown, cocksure little fool. Long after the conversation had ended, the oars beat the words through Thorkel's head. He hardly noticed the change in the stroke as the fleet came within sight of Nídarós, or the bustle about him, or the high, gilded profile of *Charlemagne*, berthed where the King had disembarked half a day earlier.

The first time Thorkel came from his thoughts, it was to find the boat docked and on the jetty an illusion; a nightmare; a grotesque and familiar figure he had believed to be safely at home, five hundred miles west of Nídarós.

Not the complaining Earl Brusi. Not the lovely young Rognvald his son. But a scowling juvenile, thin as a half-knotted thong, with a monstrous brow topped by a whisk of black hair over two watering eyes, thick as acorns.

It raised one arm and called. Its voice had not even started to break.

'Thorfinn,' said Thorkel, and the word itself was a groan. Here in Norway, here in Nídarós, here on King Olaf's jetty was the child-Earl of Caithness and Orkney. His foster-son.

Deliberately, Thorkel Amundason stepped ashore. Deliberately, he stalked towards the belligerent brat on whom for seven long years his hopes had been centred, and stopped before him. He said, 'Thorfinn Sigurdarson: if you have put a foot wrong, I will take you into a close-house and thrash you over the stool.'

He did not remember, just then, that Finn his cousin was behind him. He was concerned only, as so often before, to search the boy's face, looking in vain for what was his due in the unyielding, bellicose features, the half-grown nose, the wired lips, the challenging stare. The boy said, piping, 'Thorkel Amundason: I am nearly thirteen years old and of full age, and you are my servant. Who gave you leave to kill men in Maere for Norway?'

'My cousins,' said Thorkel. He took the boy's arm and turned him, walking, in the direction of the house he had been given. The boy shook himself free. 'I didn't notice,' added Thorkel, 'that you objected when Earl Einar's head rolled into the fire.'

'You mean you could have sewn it back on again?' the treble voice said. 'You did well there. Einar's share of the land went to Brusi, and Brusi ran squalling to Norway as soon as I complained. You wouldn't know. You weren't there. You ran off to Norway as well.'

'I thought you could wipe your own nose,' Thorkel said. 'I was wrong. You stupid fool: of course Earl Brusi ran to Norway if you threatened him. I told you to sit still for once and do nothing. *Nothing!*'

The steep, cobbled path between the wood-and-thatch houses was filling with yelling people and handcarts as the ships were unloaded. As the boy did not answer at once, Thorkel pushed him into a space between two wattled walls and said, 'So how did you threaten him? As if I couldn't guess.' Behind him, he was bitterly aware, Finn was lingering helpfully.

'I told him you'd come and pick holes in his wall-hangings,' the boy said in a mutter. He was tall for his age, the women kept saying, but put together in a ramshackle way that gave him no physical presence. In the draught between walls, his eyes were thinly watering once again.

Thorkel said, 'You told them you'd send your grandfather's army. You told them to hand over half Orkney or King Malcolm of Alba would attack. Didn't you?' Despite his level voice, he was breathing hard, and the boy's eyes flickered once and then stared back stonily.

'I haven't time to bother with that,' his foster-son said. 'If you think yourself my advisor, then say something intelligent. I've just come from King Olaf. He says if I don't give him overlordship of my share of Orkney, he will take it and put an Earl of his own to rule under him.'

It had become very quiet. '. . . And?' said Thorkel.

'And I said, of course, that I couldn't do him homage, as I was already an Earl of the King of Alba my grandfather, and his vassal.'

'And he said, *of course*, that such only applied to the Caithness lands you hold through your mother, and that the King of Alba had nothing to do with Orkney, which was by rights a Norwegian colony?'

'Yes,' said the boy.

'And then you told him to keep his hands off your bit of Orkney or the King of Alba would attack?' The yapping voice was easy to mimic. Any other boy would have been shamed.

'I said,' said the boy, 'that, being only young, I should like to go home and consult my counsellors before I gave him my answer. He said I couldn't go home, but he'd give me an hour to think it over. The hour is almost up.'

Thorkel said, 'What did you need an hour for? Your brother Earl Brusi became vassal for his share of Orkney right away.'

The boy's mouth opened. He said, 'I don't believe it.'

'Don't believe it?' said Thorkel. 'What else could be the outcome when you sent brother Brusi scuttling to Norway with the whole of Alba seemingly threatening his tail? He needed help, and King Olaf saw that he would pay the right price for it.'

The boy said, 'He can't use that weapon with me.'

'My God. My God,' Thorkel said piously. 'He doesn't have to, does he? He's got *you*. Brusi runs crying to Norway, and you run screaming after. All you've both done is make Olaf a present of Orkney while you two or some other friend of his runs it for him. Your royal grandfather won't attack Olaf. He won't attack him even if you never come back from Norway. He has another grandson with much more convenient attachments. And who in all Alba or Ireland or Cumbria would he find to set sail and battle for you?'

'I notice,' said the boy, 'that men will kill for money. Or power.'

'Well, your grandfather has little of either to spare,' Thorkel said. 'And now you have none either. Go back and promise anything King Olaf may ask. That way you'll leave here alive. Then go home and tell your mother's new spouse how his great plan succeeded. It was all Findlaech's idea, I take it?'

'No. It was mine,' the boy said. 'If I start taking other teachers, I will tell you so.'

That afternoon, the trumpets were blown for King Olaf, and men came to hear what news the King had, and to learn the terms of the settlement between the two Orkney Earls, Thorfinn and Brusi.

It was raining, and the mist had come down almost to man-height, so that most of the folk standing on the cobbled stretch in front of the king-house had their hoods over their ears, except when the intimations seemed to be veering towards trading-rights or harbour dues, in which case they were hooked smartly sideways.

The King and Queen Astrid were dry, being seated under a canopy in front of their hall, its carved timber and gilding glinting under the eaves and the wet, brooding row of royal pennants.

On one side of the royal couple sat Earl Brusi of Orkney, a mild man whose round, sulky face still reflected a recent exchange with Thorkel Amundason. His tunic and cloak, decently rich, echoed the clothes of his ten-year-old son Rognvald. In no other way did Rognvald resemble his father, being straight-backed and milky of skin, with lustrous blue eyes and yellow hair, satin-flat as if sheened by a glass-smoother.

Thorfinn, the twelve-year-old Earl, had a red cloak with a gold brooch like a dish on it, above which his neck appeared like a wick. Beneath the towering forehead, he possessed no other feature as significant as the short, charcoal line of his eyebrows.

The King rose and, using his sea-going voice, disposed briefly of welcome and courtesies and launched into the terms of the pact by which the brothers Brusi and Thorfinn, joint Earls of Orkney, had delivered Orkney into his, King Olaf's, hands and had pledged themselves to be his, King Olaf's, vassals. By which right, said King Olaf, he was pleased to announce the allotment of Orkney each could expect from him.

To Brusi, one-third of the islands. To Thorfinn, another third, just as he had

had before. And the third share, that of their dead brother Einar, he, King Olaf, now took in his keeping, to dispense in due course at his pleasure.

Beneath the canopy, Earl Brusi's mouth opened. That had not been in the bargain. Standing among the bonder, Kalv Arnason grinned, his arm round his new wife's neck, more to keep her from walking away than from any budding affection. Beside him, his brother Finn, with a child at each hand, peered at the king-house, for it seemed to him that under the thatch-drips the black-browed Thorfinn, the boy-Earl, was laughing.

However, when presently the younger Earl rose to follow his brother and kneel and promise homage to Norway, even Finn could see that the boy was not laughing at all, and that the look he exchanged with Thorkel, his handsome protector, was filled with venom.

Then the King called out Thorkel himself, as avowed slayer of Einar of Orkney, and decreed the amount he must pay to the two Earls to compensate for the loss of their brother. No sentence of outlawry was imposed on him.

So honour was satisfied, and so was King Olaf of Norway. Like Olaf Tryggvasson, he had laid the Orkneys under Norway again. The green, fertile islands with their mild climate and clever, boat-building peoples, with the rich, bounding blood of the Picts and the Irish, the Norse and the Danes and the Icelanders, to nourish their life-stream. Orkney, with its hundred small beaches and harbours: the crossroads where every merchant-ship rested, where every tax-boat and warship and supply vessel ran for shelter in the wild, open seaway between Norway and the Viking cities of Ireland; between Norway and her colonies in the western isles, the ports of Wales and the markets of western England, the wine road to Bordeaux and the Loire, the pilgrim road and the fighting road down to Spain and Jerusalem.

Everyone had to pass by the islands of Orkney. And only seven little miles separated Orkney from Caithness and the north part of Alba.

'So you see what you have thrown away,' Thorkel Amundason snapped at his foster-son later, in the cold, empty room of his guest-quarters.

Down at the jetty, the half-decks were already in place on the vessel taking them home, and all Thorkel's six months' of impedimenta were being thrown aboard quickly, with the meagre roll of his foster-son's baggage. It would be as well, had advised the Arnasons, to leave early rather than later.

The boy stood, his face lowering. 'My father paid taxes,' he said. 'Earl Sigurd my father used to send taxes to the old Earls of Norway before King Olaf arrived. My— They told me in Caithness.'

The door was open and the wall-hangings swirled. Thorkel said, 'Oh, yes. The Earl your father flung a bone to the dog now and then. But none in my hearing ever heard him called *vassal* after Olaf Tryggvasson died. It took his fifth and last son so to honour his grave. The blood of Alba, one supposes.'

It was unfair. Brusi had done the same. It was unfair, but Thorkel was past caring.

'Then you can suppose somewhere else,' said the boy shrilly. Outside the door, a yellow-haired child arrived and stood on the cobblestones, snivelling.

Neither of them paid any attention. The boy said, 'Go on. Take your things off my ship. If you write me a bill of promise, I'll even lend you the blood-fine for Brusi.'

Thorkel, who could not write, said, 'Why not? I'll do better here under King Olaf than under a vassal of his.' His voice stayed slow, but he was breathing fast under it.

'Go on, then,' said the boy. 'Find another minor to dry-nurse. Find another land full of heirs to be thinned out. There's Rognvald out there. He needs someone to wipe his nose. Look at him.'

The yellow-haired boy, noticed at last, took a step over the threshold. Tears still ran from the peerless blue eyes over the flawless skin. Losing grip suddenly of his temper, Thorkel said to Rognvald, 'And what's wrong with you?'

The son of Earl Brusi shut his lips, and his breath mewed behind them. He said, 'Are you going?'

'Yes, we're going,' said Thorkel shortly. 'If you've lost your father, go to Thord Foleson and ask.'

Earl Brusi's son gave a great sob and then shut his lips again. 'My father's going without me,' he said. 'He's going home to Orkney without me.'

In the silence, the shouts of the men at the wharves came quite clearly. Then Thorkel Amundason moved and, taking the youngster by the arm, led him gently into the room. There, one hand on his shoulder, he studied him. 'But why, Rognvald? Why would your father leave Norway without you?'

The pink lips trembled. 'Because the King says he has to. He says that if Father will be his good friend in Orkney, he can have the third share . . . King Olaf's share . . . the share that uncle Einar left to him. So Father will have two-thirds of Orkney, and I am to stay here as hostage. I don't want to live in Norway,' said Rognvald; and the tears ran from his eyes to his chin.

Kneeling, Thorkel smiled and took out his kerchief. 'You don't want your father to be a great Earl of Orkney?' he said. 'You don't want to grow up to be a fine war-leader and King Olaf's right-hand man? A brave young man like you?'

He knew, without looking, that Thorfinn had opened the door and walked out, his footsteps marching down to the waterside. He had time to wipe the child's eyes and begin another reassuring, sensible sentence before his cousin Kalv's voice said, from the doorway, 'Ah. I was looking for some lost property. I see it has found its way to the right market. So, my dear Thorkel, are you changing your mind? You would like to stay with us in Norway?'

'If it's safe,' Thorkel said. He straightened slowly. 'And if, of course, you will have me.'

'Oh, it's safe enough,' said Kalv airily. 'Provided you don't say very much and seem humble. Safer than it would be for your former menacing little nurseling. He'd be advised to get off while his skin's whole.'

'He's gone to embark,' Thorkel said. 'Don't you notice how quiet it's become? They'll be killing a sheep for him in Moray in a couple of days.'

Kalv was staring at him. The child, taking the kerchief from his fingers, blew his nose in it. Kalv said, 'You mean Moray in Alba, his mother's new home? Did he tell you he was going there?'

Thorkel Amundason put his hand on the golden head of the ten-year-old. 'He didn't need to,' he said. 'The whole stupid scheme was probably the ruler of Moray's in the first place. Findlaech. His mother's third husband. The first thing that boy Thorfinn will do in Moray is berate his stepfather for advising him wrongly.'

Kalv's mouth had opened as well. He said at last, 'Well, Finn was right. You and the boy are a pair to keep clear of. You've been with your foster-son ever since Sparbu. You were bear-leading him off and on for seven years before that. And he didn't tell you what happened before he left Alba?'

Thorkel looked down at the child Rognvald. 'Go outside,' he said. 'Go outside. I'll come in a minute.' And to Kalv, 'What, then?'

Kalv's face was rosy with pleasure. 'The boy's stepfather Findlaech was burned alive in his hall by two nephews,' he said. 'Thorfinn escaped with his life. Everyone else he knew died except the widow his mother, who was away at the time. The older of the murdering nephews is now ruling Moray and, of course, won't let Thorfinn's mother come back.

'Your Thorfinn has not only lost the lordship of his share of Orkney. He's lost his stepfather's Moray as well. All he has on the mainland is Caithness, with his two cousins prowling the frontiers. . . .

'That was why the boy fled here to Norway. To escape his cousins. And to try and claw half of Orkney out of Brusi his brother before people learned that he didn't have Moray behind him.

'We thought you had him trained to your heel,' said Kalv amiably. 'But I see times change. And this one is prettier.'

Because the tide had not yet turned, the longship with the boy Thorfinn of Orkney aboard did not put to sea as soon as she was loaded, but rode at the jetty while the provisions were properly stowed and the crewmen settled and the merchants and seamen took each other's measure. She was not an Orkney ship: merely a cargo vessel with a passage for sale. The boy, invisible beside the prow dragon, had not expected Thorkel to come himself to take off his luggage. When the smooth voice addressed him, he went white and got up slowly.

Thorkel's face was square as a four-cornered table. 'Lord,' he said. 'The King has laid on me a blood-fine to pay you.'

The black hair, tufted and burned, shook in the wind. 'The Earl Brusi you must pay,' the boy said. 'For Earl Einar's death you owe me nothing. I have told you. You may go.'

Thorkel's cloak stirred; and his hair; and his beard; but he did not move. 'The law requires,' he said, 'that a blood-fine be paid. If you do not wish the King's will to be done, you must impose one of your own. The King said that I might return to Orkney freely and enjoy all my possessions.'

'You may,' said the boy. 'If you want to.' It was a girl's voice. But the contempt in it was a man's. He sat down on his sea chest again.

'I want to,' said Thorkel. 'But, whatever you think, I am not a man who serves two masters. Therefore, since you dismiss me, I cannot go home.'

'Then serve Brusi,' the boy said. 'He has two-thirds of Orkney. There must be a living for you in that.' His colour had changed again. But the brows, in a straight line, had not altered.

'My father did not set me to serve Brusi,' Thorkel said. 'He set me to serve where I am neither liked nor am I trusted. My task is to serve you. I would finish it.'

'You don't want to stay in Norway?' said the boy. 'I have come into a fortune suddenly? What have you heard?'

'That you saw Findlaech your stepfather burn,' Thorkel said, 'when I was not there to help you.'

In public, *the boy* was what Thorkel Amundason called his foster-son, for only thus could he contain the knowledge that in this child was something he could neither outguess nor control.

Now he saw it confirmed yet again, in the willpower that would not break down into weeping, although the boy's mouth became small and the narrow throat twisted with effort. Thorkel Amundason said, 'Thorfinn. Grown men grieve for their kindred.'

Perversely, it worked, in that the boy plunged into speech. After a moment, he even dragged his voice into its usual pitch, although he breathed as if he had been running. He said, 'I mean to have Orkney. I mean to see my cousins burn as Findlaech mac Ruaidhrí burned. I shall see King Olaf into his grave before I become any man's vassal for what is mine, ever again. . . . What are you saying? Instead of the King, I must tell you what the blood-fine for my brother is to be?'

'You have the right,' Thorkel said. 'If you tell me never to come to Orkney again, I will obey you.'

He could see the boy's eyes, a dense and violent brown, trying to read him. Thorkel took a step closer and, with formality, knelt at his foster-child's feet. 'When you give a punishment, you must give it quickly,' he said.

'But mine is a very slow punishment,' Earl Sigurd's youngest son said. 'To come with me to Orkney. To defend the land as I shall do. To stay and serve me, and to obey me so long as we both are in life. Is that too much to ask?'

Long ago, this had been Thorkel's own dream. To be a wise and powerful counsellor, admired of princes, at the side of a willing and dutiful foster-son.

It was no surprise, now, to find the dream had reversed. He said, 'If you want it.'

'I need you,' said the boy. It was a cry of anger, not one of appeal. A cry born of a wave of frustration and fury that made him jump to his feet so that only skilful handling brought Thorkel Amundason upright also, and out of his way.

'For I am not grown yet,' said the boy. 'How long, how long before I am grown? And I make blunder upon blunder and mistake after mistake. . . . Why don't you stop me? You are a man. Make me think like a man. Make me act like a man. That is what I want you for.'

Nothing warned either of them, standing among the barrels and packs.

Moved by something he did not understand, Thorkel Amundason said, 'My lord, whatever you have need of, I shall try to find it for you.'

THREE

AND *that*,' said Kalv Arnason for the sixth time, 'is a bargain you must wish you had never made.'

He said it every year on his summer voyage when he saw his cousin Thorkel in Caithness. Sometimes, mercifully, Thorkel was elsewhere on the concerns of his stewardship: engaging tribute from here; putting a spoke in a blood-feud there; judging, correcting, advising. He had three good men to help him, and a body of housecarls, in case affairs took him south, within sight of the green lands of Moray in Alba, and a hunting party of Thorfinn's cousins showed signs of interest. Thorkel had no wish to be burned alive in his lodging like Findlaech, the last ruler of Moray.

This year, he was at Freswick on the east of Caithness when Kalv's fleet moved in past the broch and round Skirza. Thorkel left the big steading and walked to the shore with the Havardson reeve to see the crews settled under canvas, with a welcome of ale and fresh meat and barleycakes.

This was, naturally, why Kalv always stopped in the first place: it was a staging-post on the long voyage from Norway to the traders in Dublin. On the way out with the east wind, Kalv would lay down an offering of sealskins or soapstone or amber. On the way back with the west wind, it might be a jar of good wine, if he felt generous.

But seldom money. That, he used to say, was for his traders to worry about. He supplied the ships, and he protected them: what would he do with money at Egge? If he wanted some good Irish slaves or a sword, the traders would find them for him.

Somewhere at Egge, Thorkel was inclined to think, must be a stout wooden chest crammed with thin silver pennies and hacksilver.

There were eight merchants this time, including a man Thorkel knew well, married to one of Kalv's sisters. Kalv had also brought Siward, a nephew of his young wife's whom Thorkel had never met, and who looked quarrelsome.

Kalv was carrying, as a guest-gift, some of the finest beaver skins Thorkel had ever seen. Praising them, Thorkel placed them on a swept space on the hall floor. The next time he looked, Kalv's nephew, leaning back, had stretched out his heels on them.

Thorkel raised his eyebrows. Kalv, swearing, leaned forward and hooked out the bundle so that his nephew nearly slid after it. Siward sat sharply up. Although uncle and nephew, there was not much to choose between them in age; but whereas Kalv was spry and sinewy, Siward was built like a bullock. Then one of the prettier serfs put down a platter of pork, and Siward swung his knees in and stretched like a bow for the ale-horn.

Under cover of the eating and talk, Kalv said, 'So your foster-son is away. I am astonished. Now, *that*—'

'—is a bargain I must wish I had never made. When I decide to leave to fight Saracens, I shall let you know, Kalv, in time for your next year's arrangements. Naturally, the boy is away every summer. So are you.'

'On business,' said Kalv. 'What is *his* business? He should be learning to rule.'

The nephew Siward lifted a loaf and pulled it apart. 'According to gossip,' he said, 'Thorfinn's brother Earl Brusi is doing the ruling while Thorfinn roves about, spending his taxes. What's wrong? Has he fallen in love with his suit of rings and his axe? He does still own a third of Orkney, doesn't he?'

Thorkel Amundason shrugged and, smiling, passed him more bread. 'He likes adventure,' he said. It was true. Young men did fall in love with fighting. It was truer to say that Thorfinn's love affair had been with the sea ever since, at fourteen, he had got his first longship. Thorkel had no reason to think his foster-son backward in attaining the normal accomplishments with girl-serfs, but it was the vessel *Grágás* he had married.

It was not what Thorkel had foreseen when he saw himself lord in effect of the Orkneys. But he had Caithness and a third of Orkney to rule in the boy's absence, which for most men would be power enough. Remembering Nídarós, Thorkel said, 'And what of Rognvald in Norway? Homesick as ever? He must be sixteen.'

'Homesick?' said Kalv. 'With every courtman in Norway fighting the next for his favour? Rognvald, let me tell you, is the new Baldur. Cultivate Brusi's son and you'll never go wrong. Pity he isn't a girl. Marry him to Thorfinn, and their son would be master of Orkney.'

'Under King Olaf,' said Thorkel.

'What else?' said Kalv. His self-importance, as always, was maddening. 'I had the impression you were under King Olaf at present. The way things are, you'd better stick to him anyway. Canute isn't content with ruling England and Denmark, that's obvious. But for Olaf, you might find Canute overrunning Norway and the whole of Alba as well, right up to your Caithness frontiers and beyond, if he felt like it. And your uncle-burning neighbours in Moray won't stop him. The story goes that they've paid Canute homage already.

'I should worry about that, in your shoes. If Canute ever got a grip of Alba, the Moray cousins would push you out and rule the whole of the north. I suppose that's why they burned Thorfinn's stepfather. What are they called?

Malcolm and Gillacomghain? That's what I mean,' explained Kalv, stretching comfortably. 'You'd think, all things considered, that Thorfinn would be here, taking an interest.'

Thorkel Amundason shrugged, saying nothing. For six years he had waited, his foster-son's words in his head, watching him grow, and dreading the demand that was certain, surely, to come, but so far had not. *Thorkel Amundason, give me an army. I mean to drive Malcolm and Gillacomghain from Moray.*

Dreading it, because such an attack would be doomed. Moray was part of the kingdom of Alba. And if the King of Alba, the other Malcolm, had taken no steps to punish Findlaech's murderers, then it was not for Thorfinn his grandson to do so. The men of Caithness wouldn't support him. The men of one-third of Orkney wouldn't cross to fight for a child-Earl in Alba. And the sort of silver that would hire him an army was not within their resources.

Whereas it might well be within the resources of Malcolm and Gillacomghain, who had paid homage to King Canute of England, with the approval, one supposed, of Malcolm of Alba.

Stick to Olaf, Kalv was advising; and there was no doubt that he was right. Olaf was the only bulwark against Canute and his dreams of an empire of the north. Thorkel was surprised, indeed, that Kalv had risked going about with this fellow, his wife's nephew Siward. You heard of some district leaders in Norway who had already crossed to join Canute in England. He thought of asking Siward what his father was up to these days, and decided against it. In any case, Kalv was still pursuing something.

Kalv said, 'So you'd better look to your alliances, my friend, if you want to hold off King Canute and the Moray men. Thorfinn's eighteen. It's time you got him a wife. Only, if you'll take my advice, not an Irish one. I know he's got Ossory blood on both sides, but, believe me, you'd get nothing out of it.'

Thorkel did not mind being steered. He wondered how much Kalv was being paid. He said thoughtfully, 'You're right. What about an heiress from Dublin?'

Kalv's face changed, as he expected. 'Sitric's family? Well, they're Norse, and we trade with them, of course. But I ask you, who would marry the best town in Ireland to a lad with nothing more than a toe-hold in Orkney and the rights in a bit of the cold end of Alba? Unless he has attractions I haven't seen yet?'

'His father thought he was going to take over Dublin when he was killed at Clontarf,' said Kalv's nephew surprisingly. Kalv gave him a look, and turned back again.

Thorkel said placidly, 'It's difficult, isn't it? Who could Thorfinn suitably marry? You can't suggest a girl in your quarter? What about Finn's two little daughters?'

Kalv said cheerfully, 'Keep it in the family? If they weren't already spoken for, I'd say you couldn't do better. But there are a lot of other well-founded families in Trøndelagen who breed fast and might well be tempted. I'll try one or two when I get back, if you like. Don't marry him off till the autumn.'

Thorkel promised, and their ale-horns were refreshed, and emptied, and filled again. Kalv had achieved, it would seem, what he hoped for. Only once Thorkel himself brought back the subject. 'And so Finn's daughters are spoken for. Already? Who is Ingibjorg contracted to marry?'

Kalv did not shift in his seat, but by a small margin only. 'Oh, you know what contracts are,' he said. 'She's a child. Time enough to take it seriously when she's twelve. Till then, we're not making much of the news, although Finn, naturally, is pleased with the match. He's signed to marry his daughter to Earl Brusi's son Rognvald.'

So his cousins the Arnasons were backing Brusi and Orkney, and not Thorfinn and the cold end of Alba. Well, good luck to them. Thorkel Amundason smiled, and congratulated Kalv on his niece's prospects, and agreed yet again with Kalv's conviction that the hope of the north was King Olaf.

He believed it himself. Between the rival kings Canute and Olaf lay Caithness and one-third of Orkney, the land of his stewardship. Olaf surely would protect him in the interests of his own Orkney lordship. While Canute there in the south was already in league with Malcolm and Gillacomghain, his foes in neighbouring Moray.

He had never discussed with Thorfinn the present war over Norway, and how it threatened his lands. He never saw Thorfinn, except getting on to a ship or getting off it again. He had assumed that Thorfinn had lost interest in the management of his affairs, since Thorfinn showed none.

Until last week, that was. But that was something that Kalv here didn't know about.

When last week the envoy from Alba had arrived, it was pure bad luck that Thorfinn happened to be at home, having a shipload of cattle to land which came (he said) from somebody's tribute.

No one was ever impressed by Thorfinn. The envoy from Alba had taken one look at him and delivered his message, which was a demand from King Malcolm of Alba that his grandson should join him in Cumbria.

As a child, Thorfinn had sustained periodic summons to be viewed by his grandfather. Sometimes the inspection took place in Scone or Forteviot in the middle of Alba. Sometimes it brought him to Glamis, further east, where his mother had made her home now. Sometimes, as now, it required him to travel the full length of Alba and over the border to the land in the north-west of England that was not Alba at all, but was held by the Kings of Alba as vassals of the King of England.

Since the burning of Findlaech, Thorfinn had not seen his grandfather on any occasion, and his mother twice only. He preferred to stay at sea. If messages came, it was Thorkel Amundason who answered them.

As the envoy's speech drew to an end, Thorkel had wondered if he was meant to answer this one as well. Thorfinn, sectioned into a chair like a crane-fly, gave no impression of listening closely. In six years, nature had afflicted the boy with an extremity of untoward height, and made of the shapeless nose a flange like a rudder. Other changes were few.

The envoy had ended, and Thorfinn after all had replied. He said, 'I'll come.'

Thorkel Amundason could feel the shock and the rage again now. He had said, 'My foster-son. There are matters to think of.' And to the messenger: 'Does my lord King expect the Earl Thorfinn to stay long?'

'I think not. A day or two only,' the envoy had said.

'A journey such as that for a day or two only?' Thorkel had exclaimed. He had shown, he thought, no satisfaction. Now he would hear the reason.

'It doesn't matter,' Thorfinn had interrupted. 'It doesn't matter. I'll go.'

'The King your grandfather will welcome the news,' had said the envoy, damn him. Cumbria, where he came from, was full of Irish and Saxons and Norse, and his Norse was quite fluent. The envoy had added, 'Perhaps my lord Earl will come south with me?'

By then it was time, clearly, to take the matter in hand. Thorkel Amundason had said, 'Excuse me. I fear we go a little too fast. Tell me, sir. What does my lord King want with his grandson?'

But the chance of a straight answer was past. 'My lord, a family gathering, I would suppose?' had said the envoy. 'The King did not confide in me. But is it not natural, after all these years, for the King's two grandsons to meet in one place?'

And that was all he would say. He had left the next day. The only victory Thorkel achieved was to persuade the fool his foster-son to wait a few days before travelling.

He had tried, of course, to stop him going at all. He had tried until the last moment when, surrounded by boxes and barrels and sacks and the members of his sparse household, Thorfinn was about to wade out to his vessel. He had been in mid-tirade when the boy turned on him. 'Don't you know why he wants me in Cumbria?'

'To stick a knife in your back,' had said Thorkel Amundason shortly. Beneath it all, that was his fear.

'No. He needs me,' Thorfinn had said.

'*Needs* you?'

'It's the talk of the islands. King Canute has summoned my grandfather to do homage for Cumbria.'

'Then I suppose he will,' Thorkel had said. 'Cumbria is important to him.'

'Yes. But he might not be allowed to keep Cumbria,' Thorfinn had said, 'unless he can convince Canute his overlord that he can stop me from helping King Olaf.'

Around them, the routine of loading had gone on. Thorkel had said, after a while, 'But you are a vassal of Olaf's.'

'Not for Caithness,' Thorfinn had said.

His stare was unwinking. Thorkel had stared back. Malcolm and Gillacomghain had done homage to Canute for Moray. It didn't give Canute rights over Moray. It did give him leave to use the harbours and provisions of Moray in pursuit of his war against Olaf. Thorkel said, 'You think your grandfather will want you to pay homage for Caithness to *Canute?*'

'To allow Canute rights in Caithness,' Thorfinn amended. 'And perhaps even in my third of Orkney.'

'And will you?' Thorkel had said. It had sounded jocular, such was his alarm and despair.

'What do you suppose?' was all Thorfinn had answered. And, turning, had boarded the ship and sailed south.

That was last week, and Thorkel had heard nothing since. Of what had happened last week he had said nothing at all to Kalv Arnason. Now he was listening to Kalv, and half-agreeing to a Norwegian marriage, and wholly agreeing when Kalv said once more, as he did on departing, 'Tell the boy, wherever he is. Stick to Olaf and Norway. It's the best chance we've all got of survival.'

FOUR

ake me think like a man, the twelve-year-old Thorfinn had said to Thorkel his foster-father, and for a while, it was true, had taken Thorkel for tutor.

Make me act like a man, he had said also; and for that, his tutors were many and various, and the foremost of them all was the sea.

He had others, mostly men older than himself, whom Thorkel knew about and put up with. Most of them were on board with Thorfinn now as he sailed south to answer his grandfather's summons. First for fighting was Skeggi Havardson his father's nephew, twenty years Thorfinn's elder and his standard-bearer. First in mischief was a man older still: Eachmarcach, the nephew of King Sitric Silkbeard of Dublin.

On his way south to Cumbria, Thorfinn had diverged to take on board Eachmarcach, who spent his time sailing the western seas, looking for trouble. Learning where they were going, Eachmarcach laughed until he had to be slapped on the back. A broad, freckled man with a tightly curled ginger thatch, the heir of Dublin had little reverence for King Malcolm of Alba, Thorfinn's grandfather. And he could imagine (he said) King Malcolm's face when he saw himself, Eachmarcach, in Thorfinn's company.

Thorfinn, who could imagine it too, grinned but said nothing of moment, being doubled up in the midst of a wrestling-match. He had been a nuisance of a boy, and was growing up to be a nuisance of a man, it was obvious. The ragbag of crewmen who sailed with him found him amusing.

Arrived in no great haste at his rendezvous, Thorfinn left his ship and its crew on the coast and rode inland on the horses provided, taking with him Skeggi and Eachmarcach and such housecarls as an earl's train demanded.

That journey, too, was remarkable less for its speed than its eccentricity. When they reached the place of King Malcolm's Cumbrian camp, it was to find it all but deserted, apart from a waiting guard and a few hostages. King Malcolm's army had moved south to the Mercian border. King Malcolm himself, with his household and Duncan his grandson, was in Mercia, England, summoned there on short order by Canute to pay homage for his province of Cumbria. The Earl Thorfinn, ran the order, was to join him in Chester immediately.

'Will you go? I burned Chester once,' Eachmarcach said. 'At least, I burned some of the wharves up the river.'

'More fool you,' Thorfinn said. Mercia, south of the Cumbrian frontier, was one of the great English earldoms and its busy port Chester was one of Dublin's best markets.

'I didn't mean to,' said Eachmarcach. 'We'd captured some very strong ale. I wanted to marry the Lady of Mercia. You know. Leofric's wife. But the old Earl called out the guard. You've seen the Lady of Mercia?'

'Heard of her. That's her son over there,' Thorfinn said.

Eachmarcach looked at the hostages. Two were elderly. One was a raw-faced youth of fifteen with an unpleated shock of fair hair, playing some sort of game in the dust. None of the captives was shackled, and the guard stood about, watching. The youth talked and laughed all the time. He had a laugh like the flapping of crows' wings. For the son of a famous beauty, he was, as usually happens, nothing out of the way. Eachmarcach said, 'That's how to live to be eighty. Don't trust yourself into English hands without first asking for English hostages. Alfgar. That's what the boy's called. Alfgar, the sole heir to Mercia.'

The youth looked round, as if he caught the sound of his name. Eachmarcach grinned, since his nature was to be friendly. Thorfinn did not smile at all. Thorfinn said, 'He isn't very well guarded.'

In the town of Chester everything had come to a standstill ever since the King of England's army had marched up and camped itself a few days before on the opposite side of the river. From their homes of log and planking and wattle, and quite a few of cut stone, the citizens of Chester had watched King Canute of England and his household officers climb the mound to their Earl's timber palace and feast themselves at Earl Leofric's table while those talks went on which would end, you could be sure, in bringing no profit to Mercia.

And so, of course, it turned out. The first thing anyone knew, young Alfgar was on his way north to be held a hostage in Cumbria, and next the old King of the north had appeared at the gates, with ten unarmed men as he had promised, and had been led down to the riverside, where floated the canopied ship, with King Canute on board, upon which the two Kings were to hold their encounter.

Canute, of course, had his ten unarmed men also with him, but the oarsmen were Mercians and Earl Leofric was in attendance, as if he were the host and not obeying King Canute because there was no alternative. It was by no wish of Leofric's, you could be sure, that young Alfgar was now in Cumbria. A wild youth, some might say, and that corncrake of a laugh was a terror. But he was the Mercian heir; the only son of Earl Leofric and the Lady of Mercia.

The Lady might look placid enough, pacing down to the Dee with King Malcolm and waiting there on the bank with her women while the old King was helped into a boat and ferried into midstream for his meeting. Between the guards lining the river, you could see her chat to the King's grandson Duncan as if one youth were the same as another. But when the prince Duncan had followed his grandfather, it was to another boy that she turned, her son's best friend, the lad who was training in Wales for the priesthood. The gentle lad Sulien.

Striding up from the bank, the Lady was too smart to look anxious. But the boy Sulien did. You could see it as he hurried beside her. Learning to be a priest, he was, and Alfgar's very best friend. It showed you. There wasn't much wrong with young Alfgar.

'Slow down,' said the boy Sulien. 'My lady. Slow down. You would think the river Dee was on fire behind you.'

'Isn't it?' said Godiva, Lady of Mercia. 'It would seem no more than an appropriate judgement, when you consider the pack of designing men meeting there. Apart from Leofric, you understand. Not that Leofric doesn't design. But when he does, it's always for Mercia.'

As people did when with Sulien, she spoke as if to an equal, and not to a youth just a year older than her only son Alfgar. At the same time she slackened both her pace and her grip of her skirts, and the sunlit webs of her hair-veil hovered and sank to rest at her cheek and her shoulder as if to a dovecote. She was a very beautiful woman. Sulien said, 'Alfgar is security for the old King of Alba's life. Nothing will happen to him.'

Walking up to the fine, painted hall Earl Leofric had built for his Lady, with their attendants straggling behind them, Sulien of Llanbadarn had no sense of impending change, any more than had touched Thorkel Amundason in Norway six years before. His only concern at the time was for the Lady Godiva, whose house had been a second home to him from earliest childhood, long before her husband inherited one of the three big English earldoms.

Godiva had Breton blood, but Sulien was pure-bred from the duchy of Brittany, that part of the old Frankish continent that shouldered out into the Atlantic, divided only by the Narrow Seas from the south shore of England.

It was fashionable nowadays to speak of Brittany as a primitive place, full of unlettered savages. Its only fault that Sulien could see was that, in common with Wales and Alba and Ireland, it had fought too hard for its freedom. In resisting Roman conquest, it had forgone Roman civilization. Pushed to the western fringes of their land by invader after invader, pride as well as circumstance had seen to it that they spoke today the Celtic tongue of their forefathers and kept their customs.

Now, between Wales and Brittany and the north-west of England there existed a kinship, strengthened by cross-migration, by trade, by a common language, by a common church, that made it no more than natural that a branch of his own family should for two generations have been settled here in the north, between Cumbria and the land on the east. Or that when, among all his brothers and sisters, it had been a matter of choosing which should inherit the rule of their land and which the power of the church, he, already at home on both sides of the Narrow Seas, should be sent for his training to a Welsh monastery.

There had been three to choose from, all five hundred years old, but there had never been any doubt which his father would select. St David's might be the most famous, but Llanbadarn owed its name to St David's friend St Paternus, by tradition the first bishop of his father's own province of Vannes.

In the little time he had been there, Sulien had taken to the monastery on the river Rheidoe, although it was no longer the great teaching-house it had once been. That didn't matter. He knew what it was to be beaten to the book by the child-master in Brittany. He had learned church practice in the service of his own kinsman the Bishop of Vannes. He had learned good manners here, in the household of the Lady of Mercia. Free of childish matters, there stretched before him now the *cursus ordinum*, the long training, possibly somewhere in Ireland, that would return him to Llanbadarn as a man proceeding to Holy Orders.

It was an end he wished to attain, although the path that led to it was not entirely as he would have chosen. There were some games he was going to miss.

Meanwhile, he was only sixteen, and released for two days from the tyranny of the Office as temporary *clericellus* to one of the bishops down on the boat there. He talked to the Lady, seeking to cheer her as they came near her threshold, and hardly noticed until she stopped that her way was blocked by one of her own officers, newly emerged from the hall, who bowed, addressing her.

'Lady: another party has arrived to join the Kings on the ship. Led by the King of Alba's second grandson.'

The King of Alba was not at that moment a favourite of the Lady of Mercia. 'Who?' she said.

The house-steward glanced over his shoulder. 'If I have it right, the Earl of Orkney and Caithness, my lady. The prince Duncan, who is already on board, is the Earl's half-brother.'

'By his mother's first marriage. I remember,' said the Lady. She was watching the doorway, looking thoughtful. She added, 'I gather neither boy saw anything much of the mother. Her third marriage, to the man who was burned, ended in making her something of a recluse. I don't even know—'

She broke off as there was a movement in the doorway of the hall and a youth stepped out into the sunlight. Sulien said, 'What is his name? Do you know enough Norse to understand him?' They were speaking in Breton, one tongue the young Earl of Orkney would assuredly not possess.

'Norse and Saxon are not so unlike. His name is Thorfinn,' said the Lady of Mercia, and fell silent, watching the young man approach. Sulien followed her eyes.

If some men had a gift for seemly relations with space, and the ability to move gracefully through it, this was not one of them. The Earl of Orkney, little older than Sulien himself, was thin and tall as a ladder, and moved as if by external agency. His wind-burnished face was a structure of sinews and hollows in which eyes and brows were fierce accents above the shining, honed scythe of his nose. His hair, thick and tangled with salt, was of that black verging on brown that distinguishes the ruddy-skinned Pict from the swarthy blue-black of the Iberian.

Whatever looks could do for a man, he had missed, Sulien thought. He had neither the power to charm on first sight nor to horrify. He looked tiresome. He stopped and addressed his hostess.

'The Lady of Mercia?' The voice was an octave lower than Sulien had expected. Also, he had used *Domina*, which was clever. Of course, he could not be sure what language to speak.

Beside him, the Lady of Mercia inclined her head and assented. 'Godiva.' Her feelings towards any member of the King of Alba's family were not of the kind to encourage communication. As if he had been told, the Earl of Orkney studied her face and then turned and looked at Sulien. Since Godiva said nothing, Sulien resolved the matter by introducing himself. He chose Irish Gaelic, a Celtic language near enough to his own to allow him some fluency, which the other surely would have heard spoken at home in Caithness and in the house of his mother's third husband.

'I am Sulien of Vannes, studying at the monastery of Llanbadarn. The Lady has Breton and Saxon, and can understand Irish Gaelic. You are the Earl Thorfinn of Orkney, and you wish a boat to take you out to the meeting-place?'

Lashless brown eyes considered him. 'Not really,' said the Earl Thorfinn of Orkney. 'I've sent my cousin down to the water's edge to blow on his horn, and I imagine my grandfather will have a boat over quite quickly. I only—'

It was not in Godiva's nature, as her friends were aware, to be discourteous for long. Choosing the kind of slow Saxon a Norse-speaker might understand, she said, 'It would be quicker still if I arranged for you to take one of mine. Let me send a man with you.'

The Earl looked at her. 'Thank you,' he said. 'But Skeggi will manage. I'm not in a hurry.'

Mild understanding appeared on the Lady's face and, blending evidently with her conscience, produced—wrongly, Sulien thought—an invitation. She said, 'Perhaps then, if you come back indoors, I can offer you a refreshment. If you have time. Your grandfather was asking most anxiously for you.'

Disappointingly, she appeared to be right, and Sulien to be wrong. The Earl of Orkney showed no reluctance to turn and make his way back to the hall for a refreshment. He entered after the Lady and sat on a stool next to Sulien's, as she indicated. He said, 'It doesn't matter about the refreshments. I wanted to speak to you.'

'Oh,' said Godiva. Outside, Sulien could hear voices. Either cousin Skeggi had come back from the waterside or the rest of the Earl's party was arriving. It occurred to Sulien, and also possibly to the Lady, that not all of them might spurn her ale-barrels. She said, 'Of course we must have a talk. But should you stay now? We really don't want to upset your grandfather.'

Standing straight-boned and still, with a print of worry between her fair brows, she had never looked to better advantage. The Earl of Orkney returned her gaze tranquilly. 'Since we don't know one another,' he said, 'I can't tell whether you'd prefer truth to compliments. I'm in no hurry, because I don't like my grandfather. You may not want to upset him, but I do.'

The Lady drew a deep breath, but Sulien forestalled her. He said, 'At home, that's your affair. But you're in Chester now, and the Lady can't afford to provoke trouble. You may not know, but King Malcolm took hostages.'

'Well, of course,' said the Earl of Orkney, with an edge of impatience. 'That's what I'm here for.' He turned to Godiva. 'I came to say I've brought your son with me.'

She opened her mouth so suddenly that the linen creaked over her ears. '*Alfgar?*' said Godiva.

'Yes. We found him in my grandfather's camp. He said he wanted to leave.'

The Lady stared at him, and so did Sulien. Outside, as the disturbance came nearer, he could now distinguish Alfgar's voice shouting in Gaelic. The Lady said, 'You do dislike your grandfather, don't you?' She sounded breathless. Then the door was flung open and her son bounded in, followed by a stocky fellow with a grin and tightly curled ginger hair.

Sulien got to his feet. The Orkney Earl was standing already. Alfgar landed between them and hung there, an elbow on Sulien's shoulder and a wrist by the Orkney Earl's neck. 'Thorfinn of Orkney! Has he told you what he did? Eachmarcach of Dublin as well. King Malcolm will kill him! They walked in and . . .'

In the distance, a horn blew from the riverside. 'Ah,' said the Earl Thorfinn of Orkney.

The Lady of Mercia rose also and held out her hand to her son, who belatedly unhooked himself and bobbed his yellow head to kiss his mother's fingers and cheek. 'Yes, yes,' she said. 'I understand. I am quite overwhelmed by it all. Now stand still and stop talking while we think.'

From pale, her cheeks now were like carnations. To Thorfinn of Orkney she said, 'I am sorry. It was because of Alfgar.'

'Well, of course,' said the Earl. 'I think that was the horn.'

'But you won't go?' Godiva said. The smile had left her face. 'You won't cross to your grandfather now?'

'Why not?' Earl Thorfinn said.

The Lady of Mercia stared at him. 'You mean to cross to that ship and tell King Malcolm that you've disposed of the security that he arranged for his life?'

His hands dangling, the Earl Thorfinn gazed down at her, not unkindly. He said, 'What can he do? Underline his distrust of King Canute at the moment he is signing a pact with him? Offer the north as a prize for his friendship and demonstrate at the very same moment that he has no control of the north? Get rid of me and leave the north vacant for Norway?'

'. . . I see,' said the Lady of Mercia. 'But afterwards you and your friend might be well advised to leave before King Malcolm and your half-brother catch you?'

'Perhaps,' said Thorfinn mildly. His face was straight, but that of the Dublin man beside him bore a wide grin, and one could tell from Alfgar's chest that one of his laughs wasn't far away. Then Alfgar said, 'Why don't we all go on board? Father's there. Sulien's supposed to be with the old man from Llandaff. Thorfinn's entitled to at least one attendant: it's not everyone who can produce a Dublin king's heir for a friend. Canute won't complain, even if Malcolm does.'

'Why not?' said Earl Thorfinn. The mildness in the subterranean voice was still there. Here was a youth, it seemed to indicate, ready to fall in with the wishes of others. Sulien could not tell why, therefore, he became seized with the certainty that this proposal of Alfgar's was what Thorfinn had intended to do all along.

The Lady protested, of course, but to very little avail, although she took the trouble to walk down through the courtyard with them herself and, separating the young man Thorfinn, to give him, one supposed, a further piece of her mind. Sulien said as much to her when she turned to leave them.

He had expected to meet concern and exasperation. Instead, the Lady heard him with a kind of tolerance, behind which her own thoughts seemed shadowed. She said, 'I doubt if I could have moved that young man to do something he didn't want to at eight, never mind at eighteen. Anyone who tries would be wasting his strength. No. I had to give him some news. You and I were talking, when he came, of how a family can be split apart when the mother makes several marriages. Earl Thorfinn's mother died several weeks ago. No one had told him.'

Ahead, Alfgar had turned and was calling him; the other two were already at the riverbank. Sulien said, 'Was he upset?' Taking thought, it seemed to him that very little would upset the unprepossessing, self-possessed youth he had just met for the first time; and that even if it did, no one else would be likely to know it.

The Lady said, 'One can only guess. He did not answer at once, and then said only what was right for him to say. She was at Glamis, and he has been at sea most of the time. His foster-father brought him up. But the fact that his grandfather didn't trouble to tell him must have added fuel to that fire.'

Alfgar was calling again. Sulien said, 'Why tell him now?'

Sometimes—often—she surprised him. Her eyes on the river: 'He needed a shield, and I owed him something,' Godiva said.

FIVE

N BOARD THE conference ship, the interpreter had got to the word *immoderate* when the horn blew from the shore.

All the language so far had been polite, as befitted a meeting between a Danish King of eleven years' experience ruling the empire his father had conquered and a King of Alba some forty years older, with a lifetime behind him of controlling the shifting shapes and power factions in a piece of mountainous land, infiltrated through all its headlands and valleys by the clustered homesteads of different races.

No one had to tell Malcolm of Alba why he was here, or what King Canute wanted. Canute was on his way to add Norway to his empire of Denmark and England, and proposed, by threats or promises or the sword, if required, to stop interference from the peoples of this broad neck of land uneasily lying between his sure northern frontiers and Alba.

If Malcolm wished to keep his under-kingship of Cumbria and Westmorland next to it, so convenient for Ireland and the ports of Chester and the Severn, he had to satisfy Canute that King Olaf of Norway would find no support among the peoples who lived in these border lands and traded too with the eastern seaboard—with the half-Norse city of York and the rest of Northumbria.

Ten years ago, Malcolm had fought and defeated the Northumbrians for his rights on that side of the country. Today, no one in his senses would fight Canute for Cumbria. Therefore, Malcolm had to pay homage. He had to agree to hold Cumbria as King Canute's man, and to do nothing against him. Short of invasion and massacre, he did not intend to be forced to fight for him: that was for Leofric and Godwin and all the other Saxon leaders to do. Whether Canute would try to compel him, he was not yet able to tell.

The presence of his daughter's first husband had been inevitable, King Malcolm supposed. A clever man, benign in looks as the White Christ, with that beard and those eyes. There were Irish abbots as well as kings in my lord Crinan's busy ancestry.

Be that as it might, Crinan had managed to get one son on Bethoc, and had gone on, when that marriage ended, to others as fruitful. An able man, and now, someone told him, the richest dealer in England.

King Malcolm of Alba hardly remembered his own first wife, although he had a very clear memory of the Irish alliance he had needed at the time. She had been a weak breeder. All the boys had died young, and Bethoc his daughter was the only one who grew up. He had had to farm her out three times to different alliances, but she was a strong-minded woman, like himself, and had done well in each.

Not, of course, prolific; but he had reached the conclusion some time ago that a profusion of kinfolk was bad for a kingdom. He had had to clear his own way to the throne through a number of cousins and uncles. If such men lived, they subdivided the land or spent all their time and gear on slaughtering one another.

Bethoc had given my lord Crinan that single son, Duncan. This fellow here, round and shiny and smug as an apple. Then the purging in England had stopped, and Crinan went south to rich pickings just as the big northern alliance began to take shape. No King of Alba wanted to spend the rest of his life pushing Norwegians and Danes off his coasts: it made better sense to join them. If the Danes and the Norwegians succeeded in capturing Ireland, that was all right too. King Malcolm had plenty of kin over there who would see he got a share of the trade.

So when Sigurd of Orkney suggested a marriage pact, it made good sense to give him his daughter Bethoc. Generations of Orkney Earls had laid claim to the land north of Alba through marriages. Most of them got themselves killed, as had Sigurd. If Bethoc gave Orkney a son—and she did; just one, thank God—he could be made Earl of the disputed province, Caithness, and hold it in Alba's interest once and for all.

Which was what this young lout Thorfinn was supposed to be doing, except that the plan had gone wrong. All but one of his half-brothers in Orkney had died, and instead of being content with Caithness, the fool had laid claim to Orkney as well, which had provoked Norway into renewing its overlordship. And possibly into claiming the overlordship of Caithness as well, the next one knew.

To help prevent that very thing years before, he, Malcolm, had arranged Bethoc's third marriage to that fellow Findlaech, of the province that had Caithness for a neighbour. When Findlaech's heirs brought him word that Findlaech was courting Thorfinn and entertaining his grandiose claims to Orkney, he could hardly believe it.

Findlaech had had to go; and he, Malcolm, had made it plain that whoever achieved it had nothing to fear from him. He had made no stipulation about the fate of Thorfinn his grandson. Indeed, when he heard that the boy had escaped, Malcolm was not sure what his feelings were.

Thorfinn and Duncan were his only grandsons, but only Duncan had been reared as a prince. Duncan knew Saxon and both Celtic tongues, and had some training in affairs of law and of fighting. The other boy, one would expect, had learned little enough. They said he had been allowed to spend the summer on shipboard since he was fourteen.

What he had learned on shipboard, Malcolm could imagine. Enough to lead a plundering band of sea-rovers on cruises dignified by the description of tax-lifting. Enough to kill a few peasants and get a few serfs upon serfs. Not enough, it was perfectly sure, to hold Caithness against Findlaech's nephews and heirs without either King Olaf or King Canute at his back. And if he had chosen King Olaf, as he evidently had, it would have been better—far, far better—that he should have burned with his stepfather.

It was all at the back of his mind as he watched Canute speaking: a bulky, fair man in the prime of life, his preposterous crown making a wet ridge on his brow under the bilious green the Mercians had picked for the tenting. The interpreter had just said, 'My lord King, I fear, finds these demands quite immoderate' when the horn blew from the town side of the shore and the Bishop Lyfing walked over and parted the awning. Canute resumed what he was saying and Malcolm sat still, his damp beard spread on his chest. He could feel Duncan fidget beside him.

Because he knew more than anyone suspected of the English court's odd Saxon-Norse, the King of Alba grasped precisely what Lyfing was saying when the Bishop, re-entering, spoke quietly to Canute. 'Arrivals, my lord King, who wish you to send for them. The banner bears a black bird.'

The raven of Orkney. He had come. Thorfinn, the other grandson who ought to have burned, had arrived. And unless he was mad, prepared to be seduced from King Olaf of Norway, or to make a show of it.

The face of the old King showed nothing, but his foot bore down, hard, on the toes of Duncan beside him, who had taken the breath that was about to betray how well he, too, knew Saxon-Norse. King Malcolm of Alba said, clearly for the interpreter to hear, 'I do not consider these requests in the least immoderate. On the contrary, I have other requirements I have not even enumerated yet.'

At that, as he expected, the meeting was suspended until the new arrivals had boarded, and he took the chance, yet again, to go to the side, taking with him Duncan his grandson. To him he said: 'What will give this King pause is the prospect of an alliance, a strong alliance, between yourself and your half-brother Thorfinn. You will appear to know Thorfinn well. You will appear to love and respect him. You will, if necessary, defer to him.'

The apple had turned healthily red. 'I haven't seen him since he was eleven,' Duncan said. 'You sent for him. He broke my sledge with an axe.'

'Boys' play,' said Malcolm. 'Pay him out for it one day, if it rankles. But not today. By sheer accident, he has a finger-tip on the see-saw. Upset him, and you may lose more than your sledge.'

Skeggi the standard-bearer was not allowed in the boat, even though he was Earl Thorfinn's cousin: they could hear him complaining on the riverbank, all the way across to the ship. At first, it seemed that only the Earl Thorfinn and Leofric's son and the Dubliner were to be allowed over and then, by shamelessly invoking the name of the Bishop of Llandaff, Sulien got himself included. After all, he was temporary clerk to the Bishop, even though the opportunity for clerking was less tangible than the opportunity for watching King Malcolm's face when his hostage Alfgar stepped on board. Also, the Lady of Mercia had asked him particularly to report on the effectiveness of her awning.

The effectiveness of her awning was the first thing Sulien noticed, because it was lined with a dreadful green that accorded immediately with all he already knew about the Lady Godiva's views on this meeting.

Beneath it, Sulien was to find, the flow of mutual greetings bore the same tinge. Preceded by the Earl Thorfinn and his carroty royal friend from Dublin, Sulien transferred from the ferry to the conference ship. Alfgar, in a mood of dangerous hilarity, had elected to linger in the smaller boat, disguised in the ferryman's hooded cloak, stiff with soup-stains and salt. Sometimes Sulien had doubts about Alfgar.

Whether the Earl Thorfinn of Orkney intended first to pay his respects to Earl Leofric, his nominal host, or even to King Canute, who had summoned the meeting, would never be known. As he came to his grandfather's chair, King Malcolm's mottled face lifted to his, and King Malcolm said, 'You're late, boy. But welcome.' And so gripped his younger grandson's hand, Sulien saw that, short of wrenching apart, the Earl had no alternative but to kneel and kiss the knotted fingers, which he did, with deliberation if without an atom of grace.

Then the other grandson, Duncan, of the pink face and brown, feathered moustache, jumped forward grinning and said, 'Welcome, brother,' with his arms wide and his face in a flood of green sunlight. Between his neat brown crown and the Earl's towering head stretched a gap of between eight and ten inches.

Thorfinn of Orkney, on whose face Sulien had yet to see a trace of emotion, looked down, observed his half-brother's arms, and, with a nod, laid his folded cloak over them. Then, turning, he steered his ginger-topped friend to King Canute, before whom, without prompting, he knelt also. Earl Leofric, jolted into awareness, leaned over the King. 'The Earl Thorfinn of Orkney and Caithness, my Lord King. And . . .' He glanced at the other man.

The Earl Thorfinn, rising by stages like a siege tower, supplied the missing introduction. 'And Eachmarcach, nephew of King Sitric of Dublin. He trusts himself to you, my lord King, without surety.' He spoke in Norse.

It was not a language that Sulien knew well. He had to wait for the polite Gaelic translation before he perceived the kick in the last sentence. But even earlier he had caught sight of the anger in King Malcolm's eyes. Duncan, throwing the cloak on a stool, walked forward laughing. 'Have you forgotten your own tongue in . . . such a short time, brother?' He spoke in the language of Alba, Irish-Gaelic.

King Canute's head turned in his direction. So did that of the Earl, patient enquiry successfully imprinting itself on his face. The interpreter, his eyes on the King, was within a measure of offering to translate one half of the King of Alba's family to the other when King Canute addressed his reply to Thorfinn.

The interpreter translated in Gaelic. 'My lord King welcomes a man of honour who recognises another.'

Sulien, who had not been presented, sheltered in the lee of his surprised if affable Bishop and watched King Malcolm's pouched eyes travel from Canute to his grandson of Orkney. The King's brow, he saw, stood wreathed in veins, fat as the roots of a tree. It was inevitable that Alfgar should choose that moment to bound up from the ferry boat and, flinging back hood and cloak, stride calling to embrace his father.

Duncan's face became very red, and his grandfather's yellow. King Canute, his voice sharp, asked Earl Leofric a question, and Leofric, his arm round his son, turned, his eyes bright, and answered. Alfgar, detaching himself, skipped over and dropped to kiss King Canute's hand. He raised his head, his face smooth with touching humility, and drew breath to explain.

Immeasurably deep, rumbling over Alfgar's first words, Earl Thorfinn's voice spoke instead, addressing the King. And without translation King Canute answered and then, looking at the old King of Alba, added something again.

The Gaelic followed. 'My lord King,' said the interpreter, 'hears with pleasure that King Malcolm has seen fit to release Alfgar of Mercia, his former hostage. My lord King is of the opinion that the talks may now proceed with a freer heart on each side.'

King Malcolm placed his knotted hand hard on the cross on his breast and inclined his head. An old campaigner, he found words almost at once. He said, 'I have come to know with whom I am dealing. Certainly, let us proceed.' But he was breathing heavily enough for the noise to reach them all, and at Thorfinn his dear grandson he did not look at all.

The little lesson was over. From youth to age, as sharp a challenge as Sulien had ever heard one grown man give another in the field. A lesson Malcolm could do nothing about, although for a moment, blank surprise on his face, Alfgar seemed about to protest. Then Eachmarcach took him by the arm and sat him down, not far from Sulien.

Behind the Danish King, a well-made man with a cloudy brown beard and large evangelist's eyes had been watching Thorfinn from the moment he boarded. Prodded, Alfgar proved to know who he was. 'That's the lord Crinan. Merchant and mint-master. Duncan's father. Houses in York and Shrewsbury. My God, he must be thankful Thorfinn didn't get born to his wife.'

Crinan. The first husband of Earl Thorfinn's mother. In which case . . . Sulien said, 'You would think they might have something to say to one another.'

'Why? I don't suppose they've ever met,' Alfgar said. 'Thorfinn wouldn't probably know him.'

'But he knows which is Earl Thorfinn,' Sulien said. He thought of Leofric's face a few moments ago, and that of Alfgar's mother, before. Alfgar had called the Earl by his given name, without title; but they had been twenty-four hours in each other's company, and that was Alfgar's way.

What had been a confrontation of two kings, each with his circle, each intent on the business of extracting and offering safeguards, extracting and offering concessions, had changed. The opposing circles had blurred, and their intentions. Age and experience and cunning had united them in their own eyes as well as in Sulien's, isolating the three young men and discounting them, as Eachmarcach was isolated as a foreigner. Only Sulien observed that Leofric's son and the Dubliner occupied the real attention of the antagonists only briefly, whereas the Earl Thorfinn beside him now held the centre. It came to Sulien that he should have restrained Alfgar from coming here, and that he should not have come here himself.

King Canute was speaking, through his interpreter. He had a matter to raise, in Norse, with the Earl Thorfinn of Orkney. He would have his translator sit by King Malcolm. A grandfather would no doubt wish to know what his grandson was saying. My lord Thorfinn?

The young man got up. It was not easy to stand still on the deck before Canute, braced against the sway of the vessel. Earl Thorfinn was so tall that he could close his hand over the struts of the awning. In the sickly green light, his brow hung like a lantern, with his eyes lost altogether in the shadow beneath. King Canute said, 'I hear that you, Earl Thorfinn, are pledged a vassal of Olaf of Norway?'

Somewhere beside Malcolm of Alba, someone fidgeted. The Earl of Orkney neither shifted nor blinked. He said, 'Six years ago. I hoped to be given my proper inheritance of two-thirds of Orkney, just as Eachmarcach here hopes to become King of Dublin when his uncle should die. Unlike me, he has so far received no patronage and therefore has had no disappointments.'

'I am surprised,' said Canute, 'that, having received so small a return for your homage, you should not have thrown off the yoke.'

'I have done what I can,' said the youth thoughtfully. He swayed peacefully with a lurch of the deck, his skin boots squeaking a little. 'I have refused to join Brusi my half-brother in his attempts to deny food and shelter to those at war with King Olaf. With my stepfather dead and Moray denied me, I have no resources for more. I cannot defy King Olaf. I have little money. I have to sail every summer as it is, to bring cattle and corn for the winter, and I lose half of these to raiders. With the ships I have, I can defend nobody, not even myself. Eachmarcach is in the same case.'

'I know a little,' said Canute, 'of the talents of Eachmarcach. His uncle, as I remember, ruled Ireland for eight years after King Brian died. But of you, alas, I know nothing. I have here a letter from your half-brother Duncan which asserts he owes no homage for Cumbria since such is the right of none but English-born monarchs. He has since reconsidered, he tells me. But perhaps you in the north share his feelings? Perhaps you would prefer to be ruled by Norwegian-born kings such as you are used to?'

It was too fast for Sulien. The interpreter muttered in King Malcolm's ear, and, between that and his own poor vocabulary, he could do little but guess at the dialogue. But he heard that remark, and the pause that followed told its own story. Duncan's eyes, he saw, were fastened on the Earl's back.

Earl Thorfinn said, 'I am sure my brother's letter was written before he met my lord King. As for me, the Norse blood that I share with King Canute no more decides where my sword falls than his does.'

He was eighteen. No one laughed. Sulien swallowed. Canute said, 'And what does your Celtic blood suggest that I can rely on? You have been told, I take it, of the death of the lady your mother, whose tongue, it appears, is beyond you?'

He needed a shield, the Lady Godiva had said, and she was right. But for her, the news would have reached Earl Thorfinn here, with all the impact that Canute intended. You could see the King's eyes watching the youth; and behind him, unaltered, the vague, tranquil features of Crinan, the dead woman's husband. With some un-Christian pleasure, Sulien waited to hear her son cheat them of their expectations.

The Earl Thorfinn said, 'The Lady Bethoc is dead? Indeed, I am sorry to hear it. News takes a long time to travel these days and, as perhaps you will have gathered, I am little in touch with my mother's kin.'

There was a small silence. Sulien had heard men speak of a dead dog with more emotion. Then King Malcolm said, haste in his voice, 'Since the death of his other stepfather . . . Since the Mormaer of Moray was killed, the boy has had no settled home.'

His grandson's gaze did not move, nor did Canute's. Thorfinn said, 'Does that suffice for my answer? As others do, I take the path that will serve me best. And so long as it serves me, I will keep to it.'

Godiva had given him a shield, and he had turned it into a spear to injure his grandfather. The interpreter's voice fell into silence. The crown on the Danish King's head glittered green under the awning, and his features, heavy with thought, were shadowless as those of a man in a mist.

No one spoke, even Malcolm. The time for questions was past, and the time for debate, it was clear. Whatever King Malcolm's status in Alba, he was here as a vassal, and his two grandsons with him. What they were about to hear now from the monarch of Denmark and England was the passing of judgement.

Canute said, 'I address first my lord Earl of Orkney. Sit, and hear me.

'I can be a generous King, although you will have heard that I am not slow to act if those to whom I am generous do not respond as they should. Many magnates known to you in Norway, Earl Thorfinn, have become my men and are either awaiting the day when they may throw off King Olaf's rule or are already here in the west, ready to cross the sea with my gathering army.

'If you will be loyal to me: if you allow my ships what shelter and provisions they need on those shores of Caithness and Orkney which your steward controls, I undertake that, when I am ruler of Norway, you will hold beneath you the two-thirds of Orkney to which you say you are entitled.'

Over the beak of his nose, the Earl of Orkney's brows made a single black bar. 'Two-thirds of Orkney?' he said.

King Canute said, 'Your entitlement, so I understand. While Earl Brusi your brother still lives.'

There was another silence. Then Earl Thorfinn said, 'I agree.'

Sulien did not watch him accepting that invitation to murder; discarding his oath to King Olaf. He stared at the deck while King Canute, summoning Eachmarcach now before him, gave and received the same kind of promise: in exchange for loyalty to his interests, the King of the Saxons would support Eachmarcach's rightful claim as next ruler of Dublin. Only when, his tone altering, King Canute finally addressed the King of Alba and Duncan his grandson did Sulien bring himself to look up.

'My lord King of Alba and my lord Duncan of Cumbria. You have already told me that, except for service in war, you will do homage for these lands of Cumbria to me and to the monarchs who follow me as rulers of England, whatever their birth. I am prepared to accept your pledge on these terms, with one extra condition.

'Yours, my lord Malcolm, is not an easy country to rule, divided as it must be by nature and by its different races. Cumbria in the south you hold, as we have established, under myself through the lord Duncan. Caithness in the north is held by your other grandson who is also, in his own right, an Earl of Orkney. Alba, which lies between the two, is held towards the north by the brothers Gillacomghain and Malcolm, ruler of Moray, who owe allegiance to you, but act independently at times also. Of their friendship I have had to assure myself separately.

'South of Moray, the provinces are under their own leaders or mormaers, as you call them, who acknowledge yourself as their over-king. The heart of your kingdom, if it has a heart, is there in the centre of Alba, in Fife and Angus and Atholl where lie your principal palaces and your holy places, Scone and Dunkeld.'

He looked round, and back at King Malcolm. 'I have studied these things, for weakness in your lands, my lord, lays us both open to the intruder. I propose therefore that there should be returned to the councils of your kingdom the strong intelligence and good sense of my lord Crinan, your daughter's first husband, and that the abbacy of Dunkeld, vested in him on behalf of your daughter, should not be granted away on her death, but that my lord Crinan should enjoy its rights and its privileges, together with the duty to protect and foster this abbey for life. On that condition, and on those we have already agreed, do I offer you the peace that you seek.'

No one spoke. Outside, Sulien could hear the pooling sound of the river embracing the vessel, and the hiss and splash of plying small boats and skerries. Outside the awnings, the men of the ship and the servants of both Kings and the Bishops talked together in whispers.

More than fifty years since, on this spot, an English king had exacted obedience from his vassals as Canute was doing, and at the end of the conclave had had himself rowed for the oath-taking, with his vassal kings at the oars, to the church of St John round the river-bend.

The present summons to Chester, following that, had been an insult. The fact that Malcolm had come had told Canute all he wanted to know about the course of this meeting. So Malcolm, who had come to pay homage at a price, was being asked to pay more than he wanted. He was being asked to take into Alba one of England's great moneyers, Crinan the mint-master, whom accident had made the father of Duncan, but whose interests and acumen had led him to more lucrative regions long since.

The stewardship of the monastery of Dunkeld had never been denied him, nor a fair amount of its dues. But, formally installed in such a monastery at the head of the great waterway of the Tay, the lord Abbot of Dunkeld would hold for Canute a base in the centre of Alba from which all Alba might be controlled.

But a base, after all, surrounded by the armies of Malcolm. The veined eyes gave nothing away, but the old King's hands worked at the knees of his robe as he thought, assessing it all. Then he lifted the weight of his beard. 'My lord King, on that I shall agree,' he said; and the interpreter smiled at his master, repeating it.

It was over. The awning was drawn and men rose, saying little, watching approach the slim royal ferry that was to take the principals, as on that other occasion, to the church of St John for the service of thanksgiving and the ratification upon the altar-table of the new pact. Although this time, as King Canute said smiling, none would be required to labour for him at the oars.

SIX

ULIEN HAD NO special wish, this time, to be near his friend Alfgar or the Earl of Orkney or King Sitric's nephew as the transfer from the big boat to the shallower began to take place. He saw that Skeggi, the Earl's standard-bearer, was already in the longship awaiting his master. The prince Duncan joined him, crossing with unexpected agility. Even more unexpectedly, he turned and hailed his half-brother, Thorfinn of Orkney, whose cloak he held in his hand. 'Brother! Here is a seat for you!'

Forgetfully, he had used Gaelic. Gesturing belatedly to explain his meaning, Duncan brushed into the water his brother's neat, folded cloak. It lay blown on the waves for a moment, and then the river drew it away, the one exquisite brooch glinting as it swirled below and was gone.

Earl Thorfinn paused, saying nothing. Then he stepped down and sat by his brother, followed, despite his intentions, by Sulien. Such seats as there were, at either end of the boat, had been taken. Unnoticed, Sulien stood and listened to the prince Duncan, in the Celtic tongue, baiting his brother.

'Your poor, old-fashioned cloak with its cheap pedlar's brooch!' said Duncan cheerfully. 'How can you forgive me, you lout? You must let me buy you another. Two. And a Thor hammer for feast days. They tell me that's when you breed on the mares.'

There was no interpreter within earshot. Clearly, he thought himself safe. He waited, smiling up at his brother, preparing for some futile sentiment in the Norse language.

Earl Thorfinn turned his head. 'It's better, I suppose, than breeding on midgets,' he said in resonant Irish-Gaelic. He had good lungs.

Across the deck, King Malcolm's head made a small movement and checked. Near at hand, Duncan had, it seemed, forgotten to breathe. His eyes moved to where his grandfather was.

'Go on. Tell him,' said the Earl of Orkney. His expression was not unamiable. 'You don't have to be polite to me any longer. I have, I hope, made it quite clear that I don't belong to this family, nor do I propose to be adopted into it at moments of convenience.'

Now Duncan was breathing quickly, and there were spots of colour high on his cheeks. 'That's new,' he said. 'You kept running to us for help over Orkney.'

The Earl Thorfinn considered. 'Six years ago, yes. Don't you wish you had given it? I should hold all of Orkney; you would be my accredited ally, and we could both ask Canute for anything we wanted, and get it.'

'Or the promise of it. Do you imagine he trusts you?' Duncan said. 'The moment he fails to take Norway, you switch back to King Olaf. If you ever left him.'

'I should be a fool if I didn't,' said his brother. 'And so would Canute, if he didn't realise it. Get Crinan your father to explain it to you. He didn't have much to say in there, did he? Don't you get on with one another?'

'He remarried when I was two years old,' said Duncan. 'You at least ought to know that. He found he could make more money in England.'

'I've seen some of it,' Thorfinn said gravely. 'Doesn't he have a daughter? How would you like to have me in the family twice over?'

He could have been serious. Duncan said, 'I think my lord Crinan has a match a good deal more important than that arranged for Wulfflaed. Why not a thick Danish wife, or a fine, dung-smelling Wend? King Canute would find you someone suitable. Or maybe your Viking friend has a niece or a daughter in Dublin? What a pity,' said Duncan, getting reckless, 'that Sitric's mother is too old. She married everyone in Ireland in turn, didn't she? Even your father, if he hadn't got himself killed trying to win her. I wonder what our late mother thought of that?'

'What woman minds sharing her husband if he brings her the chance of a kingdom? The Lady Emma came back to marry King Canute on exactly those terms.' The boat bounced as it crossed someone's wake, and the glare of the sun on the red Roman walls doubled itself in the long, running furrows that spread to the bank.

Even out of his hearing, it was not wise to speak thus of King Canute. Sulien, glancing about, caught sight of the stalwart figure of Eachmarcach making his way towards the brothers as if he had heard them. They saw him, and knowing him for a Gaelic-speaker, Duncan fell silent.

It was Earl Thorfinn whom the Dubliner wanted. He called to him as he came. 'Skeggi says you can do Olaf Tryggvasson's trick.'

That, certainly, King Canute heard: his head turned. The other King sat without moving, impacted among the golden glitter, the silk and jewels of both royal parties. The longship, painted and carved and wreathed with silk streamers, overcame the next wake and then stroked smoothly forward to the pull of the oars. Both riverbanks were filled with people, talking or calling, who clearly did not know they were vassals. The Earl Thorfinn looked up at the Dubliner standing splay-legged before him. 'Sometimes,' he said.

'Prove it,' said Eachmarcach.

'Why not? On the way home,' the Earl of Orkney replied.

'On your own ship, with your own oarsmen? What sort of feat would that be?' Eachmarcach said. 'I'll wager my axe against yours that you couldn't do it on this boat.'

People were beginning to listen. At sea, by themselves, Sulien could guess how the matter would resolve itself. Here, a boy among peers on a day of imperial ceremony, the Earl of Orkney had to find another way to deal with his importunate friend. He said, 'Everyone knows that you are braver than King Sitric, and I am cleverer than Earl Sigurd, and Skeggi could run Freswick better than Thorkel. You don't have to prove it.'

'Look at them,' Eachmarcach said. He jerked his head towards the crumpled velvets and silks. 'They're rotten-soft. I want to show them.' Under the teazled, rust-coloured hair, his eyes glittered. Someone, somewhere, Sulien deduced, had a flask of wine under his robes and had been a little too hospitable. In the distance, King Canute spoke to his Bishop, and Lyfing, turning, began to thread his way aft.

'If they're soft, then you're drunk,' Earl Thorfinn said. 'In any case, here comes King Canute's veto.'

But Lyfing brought not a veto but a summons to explain to the King. Listening, in the crowd that gathered round Canute and Leofric, Sulien found Duncan, too, at his elbow. Related, the unspecified challenge sounded ridiculous. It was therefore to Sulien's total surprise that he heard the King turn to Earl Leofric, his nominal host, and say, 'If you will allow it, it would please me to see such a contest.'

Leofric said, 'My lord, I do not know what feat they speak of. But if it would give my lord King pleasure ...' Beside him, Alfgar his son was whispering noisily, his fair head jerking back and forth.

'It would,' Canute said. 'It is an exercise for the young. I have seen it done twice. Bid your oarsmen stop rowing.'

The oars lifted, dripping and parallel, and heads scraped round, among all the gold wire, to find out the reason. The Earl Thorfinn said in Norse, 'I have not agreed.'

'Yes, you have,' Eachmarcach said. 'Skeggi heard you. He is going to do it as well. And your axe is safe. Canute's offered a gold one, and prize-money. We're to run in pairs, one to each side. A knock-out contest, the axe to the winner.'

Alfgar of Mercia said, 'What *is* it? I want to do it.'

The Earl of Orkney looked him over. 'Can you swim?'

Seized with madness: 'He can swim very well,' Sulien said. 'And so can I.' He knew what it was, and he knew the feat was beyond him: was beyond all of them, probably. But Canute wanted it done, for a reason. He wanted to know what Canute's reason was.

Canute said, 'But that is only five. Good King Malcolm, lend us your grandson as well. Unless my lord Duncan is unable to swim?'

Duncan stepped forward. 'What have I to do?' he said. Despite his lack of height, he had good shoulders, and the round face with its fluffed upper lip was firm with resolve.

Earl Thorfinn, from the height of a thwart, bent down and unpinned his brother's bright cloak, which he bunched and threw to the gunwale, from where, swiftly, it slid overboard and then sank. 'Oh, the pity of it. But you won't be needing that,' Thorfinn said. 'I'll tell you what you have to do. You have to step over the rail and run across the oars of the ship, from the front to the back, while her crew are rowing her.'

'No one could do that,' said Alfgar of Mercia. 'Who is Olaf Tryggvasson anyway?'

'Was,' said Thorfinn. He was looking at Canute. 'His grandfather was one of the twenty assorted sons of Harald Haarfagre of Norway. King Olaf's called after him.'

Canute and the young man stared at one another. Then the King's eyes moved to Earl Leofric, who was speaking. Leofric said, 'These are men of high birth.'

'Then let them prove themselves,' Canute said.

There were six of them, brought up to lead and to rule. A boyhood of perpetual training, in games, at hunting, in battle, had given each of them balance and an accurate eye. They had all had to exercise judgement; to exert concentration; to defeat weariness; to push a task to completion in public, against odds. To all of them except perhaps Skeggi, their reputation and standing was the reputation and standing of their line, and at all costs to be upheld and defended. If they failed, they had to be seen to fail with courage and honour, flinching at nothing.

'Perhaps I may advise,' said Canute and, rising, looked to the oarsmen, fifteen on each side, who had lowered their blades and were keeping the vessel where she lay, in midstream, pointing up the shallow, fast-running river. Other craft, intrigued, had begun to hover before and behind.

Canute said, 'Clear the river ahead with the horn. Oarsmen, you will begin rowing on signal, in absolute unison, to the beat your master will give you. You will not falter, no matter what happens. If one life is lost because you do not keep beat, your master will know how to deal with you. The horn will tell you a runner has started. He will begin from behind you. You must listen, and be prepared to resist his weight as he passes, and keep the time of your sweep. If he falls, you continue to row.'

The Bishop from Llandaff said carefully, 'My lord King ... A blow from one of these blades could kill a man, or knock him senseless and drown him.'

Canute turned. 'I see,' he said, 'that you think we are asking too much. Your clerk is only a youth and my lord Alfgar, an only son, is still younger. You are right. I say that these two, if they wish, may withdraw.'

Alfgar looked at his father, a cry of protest half-escaped on his breath. The Earl of Mercia said stiffly, 'If the feat will give my lord pleasure, then of course my son will attempt it.'

My lady Godiva, Sulien thought. *Absolve him. He had no alternative.* Aloud he said, 'And I too, if you please.' He would make a fool of himself: that he knew. But he felt no doom-laden fear. He was agile and light and, when he fell, could keep out of trouble.

He knew Alfgar felt differently by the set of his jaw. Living in Godiva's house, he had early learned how good Alfgar was with the spear and the sword and the bow; how he liked to win at running; how proud he was of his splendid body. To fail would be a bad thing for Alfgar.

The Dubliner he did not know, or the man Skeggi, who was half an Icelander, he had heard. Older by twenty years than the rest, this pair had at least done this before, or attempted it, and had gained in cunning perhaps what they no longer commanded of suppleness.

There remained the two grandsons of Orkney and Alba. There was no doubt which had the build of a winner. Duncan was twenty, which meant he must have had battle experience. He looked self-reliant. And, for all he was short, he was compactly made, with a sturdy back and deep chest and well-turned, springy legs.

Nothing could have contrasted more with the lanky, half-shackled frame of his brother. But for a certain brightness of skin and the heavy, well-defined line of the eyebrows, the common blood of their mother had produced no physical likeness in her offspring. To the casual eye, the Earl of Orkney seemed little more than a miscellany of disengaged angles, occupied now in the poop with baring his shins and his feet and rebinding his short, baggy trousers to lie tight at the knee and the thigh. He had long, bony feet with knuckled toes agile as fingers.

What he was doing was undoubtedly sensible. Sulien pulled off his skin shoes and, untying his girdle, bound his serviceable robe between the legs with the wool, in a figure of eight. Smiling, Alfgar started to do the same with his tunic; but Duncan the prince did no more, it was seen, than unfasten his leggings.

Turning to make for the prow, Sulien wondered why men, looking forward, were grinning. Then he saw that Eachmarcach of Dublin and Skeggi the Icelander, with more common sense than sense perhaps of occasion, had simply set to and stripped themselves naked.

Whether for that reason or another, they made the run first. The signal for rowing was given, and a moment later, as the oars settled into their rhythm, the horn blew for the run. There was a double flash of brown flesh as the Dubliner on the port side and Skeggi on the other each handed himself over the side and paused, fist on rail, foot on gunwale, looking at the long, almond shape of the vessel stretching to the horizon, to infinity before him, the last of the oars drawn from view by the slow, perfect curve of the beam. At the fifteen shining shafts barring the water: rising flashing as one, reaching back, and gripping the river again. And below, streaming ahead, masked by sunlight, the body of unknowable water driving on to the sea.

The oars were seventeen feet long at the beam: longer where the shell swept high at the prow and the stern, and the holes that admitted them, small and snug, with a narrow slot for the blade, were pierced through the third strake down from the edge and the fourth up from the waterline. And since, for the moment of his passing, the weight of a man would have to be borne by each oarsman in turn, it was essential to find footing at the upper end of the shaft, where the movement would be least; and to pass quickly, before the rower's grip broke and the oar swung in his hands.

Then, as Sulien watched, Eachmarcach stepped down. His hand left the rail. His toes curled white round the shining wood of the oar just below him. And then, his arms crooked at his sides, he was off, his heels kicked flashing beneath him, his shoulders trimmed against the slope of the oars, settling no longer than a bird might on each. And every time bridging the gap right-footed as Skeggi, his head disappearing on the port side, must be using his left.

Everyone shouted. There was sweat coming through the cloth on the rowers' backs. They had not asked to play a leading role in this dangerous game, and if there was an accident, they would pay for it. Eachmarcach's shoulders were covered in ginger-white fur, and below that his skin was patchily red. He had got to the fifth oar, a third of the way gone. On the other side, Sulien could tell from the roar, Skeggi was moving as well.

On Eachmarcach's side, the seventh oarsman was not prepared for him; or perhaps, his concentration faltering, the Dubliner had lingered a moment longer than he should. The oar jerked and, losing its sweep, floundered and cracked against the neck of the blade just behind him. For a moment, between two and three oars at Eachmarcach's back were out of action, and, driven lop-sided, the gilded boarshead on the sternpost swung to the right. A cross-wave, kicking, ran under the keel, and a surge of noise on the other side of the vessel told that Skeggi had been shaken by it.

Then the even roar resumed, which would seem to tell that no fall had happened. But Eachmarcach, his attention caught by the shouts, turned his head for one fatal second as the oars, picking up, resumed their full power and he moved from the ninth to the tenth, to the eleventh.

Sulien saw the ginger head falter, half obscured by the swell of the beam, and then jerk. Two arms shot into sight. Eachmarcach yelled. Then, with an expert twist, he aligned his thickset, muscular body and dived, entering the river exactly between the shafts of two oars and gliding outwards, a pale, fishy shape underwater, until, grinning, spouting, and swearing, he raised his head far behind, beyond the digging line of the blades.

A skiff from one bank pulled off and set out for him. Sulien waved and turned, just as a roar louder than all the rest told him that, one way or another, Skeggi's trip, too, had come to an end. Then he saw a whinbush of grey-yellow hair and a scarlet face rolling inboard beyond the last of the oars and knew that the feat had been achieved, by one of them at least. And that it was possible.

He and Alfgar were next. Alfgar, smiling, was pale. He said, 'Did you notice the shaking just now? After the oars crashed?'

'They'll know better next time,' Sulien said.

'No. It wasn't only the shift of the boat,' Alfgar said. 'It's the tide coming in. I thought I'd better warn you.'

He had forgotten the Dee was a tidal estuary. He had forgotten to think what must happen when the incoming sea at the top of its flood met the down-moving flow of the river. He said, 'I expect it will be all right. This will be over in seconds.' For, of course, it would. But of equal certainty, it would take only one or two such cross-currents to unbalance them. He said, 'Anyway, it's good weather for a swim. See you in the water?'

'Perhaps,' Alfgar said.

They threw a coin, he found, to decide which side they should run on. It was one of Canute's, with *Lux, Lex, Pax, Rex* on the die. He did not look to see if the name of Duncan's father was on it as well.

'Take care,' said the Earl Thorfinn's cavernous voice. He was sitting, hugging his bound knees, on the half-deck beside him. 'If in doubt, put your hand on the rail and let them pull you in. It isn't worth getting wet over.'

He looked as a murderer and an oath-breaker ought to look. His expression, on the other hand, had somewhere in it a light or a shadow not evinced since his talk with Godiva. Sulien said, with austerity, 'It won't be the first time that the north has dragged Wales into her shiftless enterprises.' He waited to see, gratifyingly, the Earl's black eyebrows twitch and then went to the side he had been given, which was the same one from which Eachmarcach had fallen. The horn blew.

Not to look at the water, streaming like long wool beneath him. Not to look at the faces: the brimming boatful of faces, half turned his way, half to Alfgar. Not to look at the crowds on the shore. But to look only ahead, at the smooth white pine of the oars wheeling, wheeling in their small circles, and to keep, somehow, a sixth sense for the oarsmen, who were afraid, too, and on whom all his foothold depended.

Sulien said, just loud enough to be heard, 'I am coming—*now!*' And felt the wood, lightly warm, beneath one foot and then the other. 'And—*now!*' he said again, and passed through three feet of air, looking only at the rise of the next oar.

He did not hear the Danish King address Bishop Joseph of Llandaff. 'The boy is graceful. Find him a monastery by the sea.'

'He is at Llanbadarn, my lord.'

He did not see Canute turn to Earl Leofric and say, smiling, 'The young men do well.' Only Sulien, watching the Earl of Mercia bow, his eyes on his son, would have known what Leofric was thinking. *Too tense.* It was Alfgar's one mistake, to try too hard; to want too much. Not a bad fault in a ruler, but it should not rule his performance. Leofric had told him and told him until Godiva had stopped him telling him because, she said, it was making him worse. And seeing the muscles knot in the calf of Alfgar's right leg, his father had known, before it happened, how it was going to end.

None of that Sulien saw, for he was coming up to the seventh oarsman, the one who had faltered after Eachmarcach. The round shaft, coming out of its hole, rotated automatically, as if worked by a wheel, with no sign of trouble. Sulien said, in the same quiet voice, 'And—*now!*' and stepped on it lightly: one foot, both feet; and he was on the eighth, preparing to step on the ninth. His mind, in retrospect, seized the breath of a second to congratulate himself. His ears, dead to the particular voices, could not excise a shout, a roar of cheerful shock and of warning which was unmistakable in its meaning. Alfgar had fallen.

Sulien's foot slid on the beam, and all the resources of his body thundered in to his aid. A moment later and he could have steadied himself on the wood, but there was no time for that: already the timber was dropping under his weight. He was unbalanced when he launched himself at the next oar, and he hit it unevenly, the second foot as hard as the first, and then had to get off again. His balance this time was better: almost righted, although when his right foot took the wood, his knee started to tremble. There were five more oars ahead, and Alfgar had fallen.

His foot on the eleventh oar, Sulien thought of Alfgar and his mother Godiva. His second foot on the eleventh oar, he remembered what the Earl Thorfinn had said.

But the Mercians were too proud to save themselves. So was he, probably, to imagine he would finish. He wasn't going to, now he had allowed himself to think.

He missed his footing. Only his left foot reached the oar, at the wrong angle, so that he had to look down to see what room there was for his right, and so saw the violent water racing below him, and, ahead, the arrows that meant tidal currents flooding in at a pace faster than that of the slow-propelled vessel.

The water took his eyes with it, and the last of his balance. He fell, his shoulder striking the swinging oar just behind him, and the water drew him in with a great, splashing rush.

Then, one-handed and choking, he was up on the surface, and two heavy bodies flounced in beside him and had him under the arms, and a little distance off there was a boat with Alfgar in it, his face running with water and grinning.

So that everything was all right. Except for the last race, the race that was supposed to decide whether Skeggi, who had completed the run, was the winner, or whether he would have to run against one or both of the King's grandsons, if one or both of the King's grandsons should manage to finish. The last race, which in fact had nothing to do with that sort of competition at all, but had to do with the ruling of Orkney and the ruling of Alba.

Sulien said, when they got him into the skiff, 'I know we can't keep up with them, but what about rowing on, in case we can find out who wins?' But Alfgar, he found, had already arranged all that, and had even taken an oar himself, to make it faster. So that, although they had dropped far behind, Sulien could see by the black head that the Earl Thorfinn had drawn his side, the side that had had all the mishaps, and was lifting himself over the rail while his half-brother Duncan the prince did the same on the other side.

Had he been on board, Sulien would have found that the Earl of Orkney did not speak reassuringly, as he had done, to warn the oarsmen. That he didn't pause on the rail to remind himself to listen to nothing and look at nothing but the fifteen white oars soaring in front of him. That in fact the only thing he did was to look ahead at the running dark race of the incoming tide and, on the first breath of the horn, to lay one prehensile foot, at a grotesque angle, on the round, sticky surface of the first oar and then, without pause, to skip forward and set the other foot high on the next shaft.

His stern waggled. 'The bastard,' said Eachmarcach with satisfaction. 'I knew he'd do that.'

Behind in the skiff, Alfgar watched the dancing figure and said, 'I don't believe it.'

'They say Tryggvasson did it with one foot on each oar,' Sulien said.

'Well, that's hardly Tryggvasson,' said Alfgar rudely. 'That's—'

'I think,' said Sulien, 'that because he isn't well made, perhaps he practises very hard. This must be the work of a summer. Or more.'

'He's nearly there,' said Alfgar, his voice disbelieving. He caught a crab with his oar and looked back: a ridge of water bucked under their keel and plunged jostling ahead to where the longship had drawn away. 'And just in time. That's the flood-tide on its way. Where's the other boy?'

Boy? Duncan was twenty. The age Canute had been when he became King of Denmark and England. Sulien said, 'I can't see. They're all up at the other end, cheering on Orkney.'

Later, he realised that it was because they were all up at the stern cheering the Earl Thorfinn to his victory that none but the oarsmen saw the change in the run of the water; the change for which normally they would have altered stroke but could not, at this moment, under pain of death. And later, too, was given by others a picture of Duncan, sweat on his jaw, his shoulders firm, the tunic stuck to his thighs, copying with steady persistence the two-footed step, the concentration, the technique of Eachmarcach and Skeggi, hearing neither the roar of acclaim up ahead or the change in the sound of the water. As the Earl Thorfinn leaped from the last oar and, victorious, rolled aboard into Skeggi's hands and the welter of welcoming buffets and laughter, the stern of the longship rose and smacked, and then, pair by pair, the oars kicked and bounded.

Before Duncan's eyes, the line of looms broke in disorder. Then the shaft below him gave way and he was jumping, with nowhere to jump to. He must have tasted salt before he hit the water. An oarsman cried out, and wood clashed against wood as men dragged at the oars to keep clear of him.

They succeeded. The blow that felled him came not from the blades but the hard, oaken strakes of the vessel as the surge flung him drubbing against them. Those who were there saw him sink, and did not see him surface again.

From the skiff, they saw the longship shudder, and heard the thin ring of a command above the confusion of shouting, upon which the oars rose and changed pattern. The royal ship slowed on her course and then, held by back-paddling, returned and swung in mid-river. On her port side, visible now, there were two swimming heads in the river, and as Sulien watched, another man jumped over the side. All the swimmers were strangers. Sulien said, 'Duncan has fallen.'

'I fancy,' said Alfgar drily, 'that even Olaf Tryggvasson would have fallen.'

He did not stop rowing. And as they came close to the longship, Sulien craned to see.

Overloaded on the port side, the royal ship was low on that beam and rocked sharply, idling and waiting. Distantly, in her prow Sulien could see the heads of the two Kings standing on the half-deck: Canute speaking, and Malcolm held no doubt by pride, as well as by stiffness and age, from thrusting through to the side to watch the search for Duncan his grandson.

His other grandson was not there. The Earl Thorfinn of Orkney was, Sulien suddenly noticed, quite close at hand, by the high sternpost of the vessel. Undisturbed, it seemed, by the shouting and splashing from the other side of the boat, he was gazing peacefully into the water, his black hair over his brow. In front of Sulien, Alfgar lifted his oar, and motioned the boatman and Eachmarcach to do likewise. He said, 'They don't seem to have got him. He said he could swim, didn't he?'

The Earl Thorfinn continued to contemplate the river reposefully from the rail and gave no indication that he had noticed them. Sulien said, 'The prince could have been injured.' Beneath where Thorfinn was looking, you could just see something pale in the water. Sulien said suddenly, 'Row over there.'

'Where?'

'There. Where . . .' He broke off and pointed instead. 'There. There's something in the water.'

From the prow, Alfgar could see better than he could. He looked and then, seizing his oar, dug it in and looked again as the skiff bucked along nearer. 'It is!' he said. 'Go on!' And as the other two started to row, Alfgar twisted round, rising, and, cupping his mouth, roared to the longship and the two Kings and the knots of men, who, hearing, rushed to the rail. 'The prince Duncan is here! We've got him!'

Above on the stern, the Earl Thorfinn, sitting down, began at leisure to unwind the bands round his trousers.

The service of peace and thanksgiving in the church of St John the Baptist was kept short because it began late and because, naturally, the King of Alba was concerned about the health of his grandson Duncan, now being helped back to the Mercian palace. The other three submerged competitors all attended the service, in blankets. The final race, between the Earl Thorfinn and his cousin Skeggi, had been cancelled.

Sulien, his shoulder throbbing, kept away from the Earl of Orkney. Since they disembarked at the church, he had addressed Earl Thorfinn only once, and quietly, when no one was particularly near. 'You saw Duncan was there.'

'Yes,' the Earl said. He had been moved, his neck arched, to give all his attention to the upper frame of the church. He added, 'I knew you would save him. Or somebody.' Sulien waited, and then walked away.

He must have said much the same to his grandfather when the quarrel broke out at the altar-table as the service ended and they all gathered there to hear the treaty read and attested.

Beneath the voices of Bishop Lyfing and the interpreter came the murmur, subdued at first, of an exchange between Malcolm of Alba and his grandson of Orkney. Then the King's voice said something sharply and the Earl Thorfinn answered with insolence.

King Malcolm turned and, interrupting the Bishop, took the skin from his two hands and crumpled it. He said, 'I shall acknowledge no pact that offers more power to Orkney.'

The Bishop, his eyes narrowed, looked at his King. Canute said, 'I remind you. On this treaty depends your lordship of Cumbria. Is your dislike of one grandson so great?'

The rich cloak rose and fell over the old man's broad chest. 'He offends me,' he said.

The Earl Thorfinn had not spoken. Canute looked at him. 'He wants discipline, I agree, and his training leaves much to be desired. I, too, have been disturbed by what I have seen of him today. Perhaps there is a remedy that would suit both of us. My lord Thorfinn?'

Large though Canute was, the youth looked down on him, his hands loose at his sides, his tunic stained with salt and sweat from the run. The King of the Danes and the Saxons studied him, and then spoke.

'Earl Thorfinn. You swore to be the true vassal of King Olaf of Norway, and now you have made a like oath to me, King Olaf's enemy. The bond of the King your grandfather I have accepted: his territories abut on mine, and I can be just or generous, as occasion demands. For your conduct, I have no such surety. It seemed to me therefore, as this day progressed, that more should be demanded of you, and that you should lodge a hostage with me, in the person of Skeggi Havardson, your cousin.

'I have changed my mind. The hostage I require is yourself.'

Silence answered him. Beside the altar, King Malcolm's face did not change. Only somewhere in the eyes there was a gleam, perhaps of triumph, perhaps of disappointment, perhaps of perplexity. Thorfinn of Orkney went red.

King Canute said, 'If this were done, my lord King of Alba, would you feel free to ratify this agreement?'

'I should,' King Malcolm said. He cleared his throat.

'And you, my lord Earl of Orkney. If your cousin goes back with these terms, can your foster-father and your council hold to them until your return?'

'Yes,' said the youth. His hands still dangled in the folds of his trousers. 'Depending on when I return.'

'Did you think I would keep you for life? I have not so much time, or so much patience,' King Canute said. 'When I am King of Norway, you, my lord Thorfinn, may make your way back to your homeland.'

The youth bowed. Beside Sulien, the cousin Skeggi was watching open-mouthed while the Dubliner nudged him, grinning. At the altar, the voice of the interpreter had resumed and men were pushing their robes from their right arms while the clerk smoothed the parchment and dipped the quill, ready to hand it. An amendment, squeakily, was being written.

King Canute watched, his expression benign. On Earl Thorfinn's face there lingered the last of that sudden raw flush, and on either side of his aquiline nose his eyes glittered. It was not the face of a foolish youth condemned to a course of correction.

'Saint Paternus!' Sulien said.

'What?' said Alfgar.

'Nothing,' Sulien said. But inside, he went on repeating it. *Saint Paternus. Saint Paternus defend me. Of course the Earl Thorfinn isn't dismayed. This is what the Earl Thorfinn has been working for.*

It was while marking his cross that Canute of England remembered something his Norman wife had once said when she and her precious brother had asked him, for the sake of the duchy, not to fall out with Alba. Something about 'this youth with a barbarous name'.

It was true: it was barbarous. The boy's name ought to be changed. His had, from Canute to Lambert, when that fool at St Omer had baptised him. Salomon of Hungary had turned into *King Stephen*, by the body of God; and his own sister Estrith had been forced to take the name Margaret. While his wife Emma, of course, was supposed to be Alfgifu, but used her new name as little as he did.

Nevertheless ... Thorfinn was a heathenish name, and Emma would object. The King said, laying the quill down, 'I think, my lord King of Alba, that it might be seemly, since he comes to a Christian court, to baptise your grandson of Orkney. Will you, of your generosity, allow me to arrange it?'

Malcolm said, 'He is baptised.'

Canute said, 'Thorfinn? Thorfinn, surely, is a name recognised chiefly by pagans.'

The Earl of Orkney's voice was obliging. 'It is among pagans that I most often find myself. I have been baptised, my lord King: before the death of my stepfather Findlaech.

'Macbeth is what churchmen call me.'

SEVEN

THE NEWS THAT Thorfinn had defected from Norway to England was brought north to Thorkel his foster-father by Eachmarcach, whom he did not like, and Skeggi Havardson, who appeared to think it funny.

Then the winter closed in, which preserved him at least from the attacks, verbal and otherwise, of Earl Brusi and the Orkney-men loyal to Olaf, and from the longships which put ashore from Norway as his cousin Kalv once had done but, instead of putting up tents and calling for water, now found out his barns and his boathouses and tried to set fire to them.

Thorkel soon put a stop to that: he had men enough, as well as money. He had never seen as much money at one time as Thorfinn sent north from King Canute. Blood-money, which Skeggi, hilarious, helped him bury, and which he used himself, grimly, to mollify those in Caithness and Orkney who relished no more than he did being appointed to serve yet another king, and a Danish one at that. He called in the malt and meal for Yuletide early that year, and got his barns stored in Helmsdale and Duncansby and Freswick and Cromarty, and salt brought in good time for the cattle-slaughtering. He had timber, too, felled and well guarded, ready for when the longships would be drawn up to the nousts and the repairing could be done on the good days, and keels laid for new ships. It would be a bad winter. He could sense it.

Then the snow came, and persisted long after Yuletide, till at Lent, when one looked for the first softening in the wind, it snowed for three days and three nights without halting and the whole of Caithness became a board of ice-white set in seas of ice-grey. Shut in on either side of the longfires with his cousins and courtmen, with the Salmundarsons and the Havardsons and the Amundasons, they talked about the war until he had to forbid it, and then they went back to quarrelling about their women. When at last the wind veered and brought with it the Icelanders, always first into the sea, always first with the bad news, Thorkel hardly knew whether to be glad or to be sorry.

The merchants and the bards were allowed everywhere and brought tales from everywhere. The bards recited their news, some of it, and for a week of good cheer and brave songs and new bawdy stories were worth their fine lodging and the silver they expected at the end of it. It was from them that he got his first pictures of Thorfinn as chief of King Canute's housecarls, with a gold and silver inlaid axe and a house of two storeys in Winchester to sleep in. The King's chief wife, the Lady Emma, had made him her special care, said the bards, adding a phrase or two that Thorkel ignored. And he had gone merchanting with the Lady's ships, to Rouen and to Nantes and the Couesnon, and had been at the repairing of her fort at Exeter and the King's fort at Dover before the days grew too short. There was word of a woman or two they wanted him to marry, but so far they were all middle-aged widows, and he had said no.

It was well known, of course, said the bards, that the King of the Danes was preparing an army to invade and take Norway in the good weather, although he'd be lucky if he got as many as fifty shiploads of English to follow him. But of course, said the bards, young Thorfinn no doubt would be there in the foremost ship, with the Lady Emma behind him in some way or another, and about to make his name and fortune all over again.

Thorkel became sick of the bards.

Thore Hund sailed by very fast one day, going south, and did not stop. Afterwards, the tale came to Thorkel's ears: how King Olaf's tax-collectors had made Thore pour wine from the kegs on his ships to prove he had no money hidden, never noticing that the casks were double-skinned and the inside of them filled with a fortune in furs.

King Canute, they said, would appreciate the coming of Thore. And his son, the surly Siward, had escaped to England in the same ship, together with a few others everybody knew about: King Canute hadn't been mean with his money last autumn. And wasn't that a fine new suit of ring-mail, said the bards, that Thorkel himself had got since they saw him last? It was an ill wind, said the bards.

Thorkel threw the bards out, and his immortality with them.

Then full spring arrived, and Canute with his armada crossed the seas and, without a blow struck, made himself master of Norway. Thorfinn, they said, had not been with him, but guarding the havens facing Normandy at his back. He did not come home.

After a summer of vain counter-moves, King Olaf with his wife and son and the three loyal Arnasons left for Sweden and Russia, taking with them Rognvald, now seventeen, son of Earl Brusi of Orkney, and leaving behind them Erling Skialgsson, Haarek of Tjotta, Einar Tambarskelve, and Thorkel Amundason's cousin Kalv, who had changed sides even quicker than Thorfinn and was by way, rumour said, of being King Canute's new viceroy of Norway.

Money arrived from Thorfinn, with a gold arm-band weighing sixteen ounces. A third of the coins were silver pennies from Cologne, and among the rest there were three from Baghdad. There was no message, but of course Thorkel could not read anyway. He took the ingot-mould out to the furnace and melted down the arm-band himself. He was pouring the gold when the uproar began in the yard with the pigs squealing, and the geese hissing and flapping, and half the folk from the huts and the farmstead running to help a messenger with some axe-work on him and only enough breath to tell the news from the south.

The Earl Malcolm of Moray was dying: the elder of the two brothers who had burned their uncle in Alba all those years before. And Earl Malcolm's middle-aged brother Gillacomghain had gathered a war-band and, moving north, was sitting in Caithness, where he had laid claim to the ancient tax-rights of the Mormaers of Moray and Caithness.

Skeggi and his brother, up from Freswick, were among those who lowered the man from his horse, yelling for someone to go for the wise-woman while their faces were like new suns for happiness. Everyone had known that this was likely to happen, with Thorfinn away, as soon as the older brother started to fail. It promised a good war, with a lot of fine raiding, and they were well prepared.

It had to be said, of course, that Gillacomghain was well prepared as well, having been stockpiling Canute's pensions for even longer than Thorkel. And that Gillacomghain in this particular claim might have a backing that Thorfinn's birth wouldn't win him: the support, in men and weapons, of Thorfinn's grandfather.

For if Canute remembered his promise at Chester, the conquest of Norway would make Thorfinn a force to be measured: the owner of two-thirds of Orkney as well as the whole of Caithness.

It was a promise in which Thorkel placed little faith. But to Gillacomghain, as to Malcolm of Alba, the threat of it would be enough. In their place, there was little he'd stop at to check Canute's grip of the north through Thorfinn.

While Skeggi swept the heavens with cries about beacon-fires and horses, message-tokens and ships, Thorkel's mind was addressing his foster-son. *And where are you today, Thorfinn, in your house with two storeys, and your rich middle-aged widows who give you arm-bands to pass on to your door-keeper?*

In the event, it took a week of fighting to clear Gillacomghain and his men out of the Black Isle and back to the south side of the Moray Firth. In the course of it, Thorkel saw more than once the coarse yellow hair and stocky figure of Findlaech's nephew as he ran with his men, but among the men were few that he could recognise from Findlaech's day.

It was possible, then, that not too many of the farmers and fishermen of Moray had enjoyed the switch of masters when their old Mormaer, Thorfinn's stepfather, was burned. It explained why the present attack had been driven off with such speed, although his own precautions accounted for some of their luck.

A mixed blessing. Next time, Gillacomghain knew, he must look outside of Moray for the army he would bring over the firth. Perhaps to King Malcolm, who had been sparing of his support this time, it would seem. Or to the Irish mercenaries of the west, who would fight for the kind of silver Gillacomghain now had.

Thorkel commissioned a shipmaster going to York to bring him back three dozen Swedish axes, and sent Steingrim Salmundarson west on the tax-boat with an order to buy Frankish swords in Dublin—three of them, with their hilts on. He had some leather coats sewn, and rode round the coast on his garron to see how the new ships were shaping.

The ship from York came back with news of two marriage contracts. Prince Duncan of Alba had chosen a wife: a daughter of Ealdred of Bernicia, the land where Alba and England met on the east coast. With that marriage would come the inheritance of Ealdred's father, who once had ruled all Northumbria. And the even greater interests of Ealdred's mother, the only child of Durham's first Bishop-magnate.

It meant that, from the west coast to the east, the north of England could expect to see a good deal of the rulers of Alba. And it made one wonder if Duncan's marriage had taken place with or without Canute's blessing.

The second contract tied another knot between the same families. By this, Maldred, Duncan's half-brother, became wed to the same Ealdred's semi-royal stepsister. The stepsister was related both to Canute's chief wife and to his personal viceroy in Denmark. Which disposed of all doubt. Canute knew, all right. Despite the hazards, Canute was prepared to see Alba strengthen its stake in his northlands.

Thorkel Amundason forced the first axe-blade off its stake and weighed it in his hands, gazing after the shipmaster as he strode with his fellows back down to the jetty, and if Thorfinn had been there, might have been tempted to give him first trial of the edge of it. *What is he doing? What is the young imbecile doing now?*

Then Earl Hakon, the viceroy of Norway, sailed in and, barely observing the welcome-ale, mentioned that, being now lord of Norway, his uncle King Canute was pleased to fulfil the oath he had taken to make the Earl Thorfinn ruler of two-thirds of Orkney. The Earl Brusi had been informed, and had received land in Møre in compensation. Earl Hakon was glad to bear news so welcome and, time being short, would be equally glad to receive the taxes now owed to King Canute: namely, those for two-thirds of Orkney and Caithness.

Along the board, the Earl's men talked on, but Thorkel could hear how all his own had fallen silent. He said courteously, 'Being unaware of the great good fortune you mention, we have prepared for you the tribute for one-third of Orkney, as was usually paid to King Olaf, and as no doubt the Earl Brusi has already prepared for his double portion. As to the rest, the Earl Thorfinn owes nothing for the lands of Caithness.'

Hakon Ericsson, last of the great Norwegian Earls of Lade, was no great dissimulator, but at thirty-three knew the tricks of the conference table quite as well as did Thorkel. 'This I was prepared to believe,' said King Canute's nephew with an air entirely reasonable, 'until I learned that King Malcolm's tax-servants also have been recently menaced with weapons. If you owe no tax and no service to Alba, then Earl Thorfinn's agreement with Norway is valid and the tax is now owed to King Canute.'

It was then, after a very hard year and in prospect of another just like it, that Thorkel's self-control for a moment gave way. 'Then that is a matter, is it not, that King Canute must raise with Earl Thorfinn himself in England?' he suggested. 'Whatever agreement they come to, you can rely on me to fulfil to the letter.' And to himself: *He began it without me. Let him finish it, if he can*, Thorkel added.

He paid for two-thirds of Orkney in the end. He had expected to. Just as Earl Hakon had had no real hope of the Caithness tribute—as yet. The talk ended, of course, with a careful reference to the numbers of Trøndelagers who had deserted King Olaf for Canute, including Thore Hund of Bjarking, now in England with his son Siward. Earl Hakon thought he could find Thore land in Huntingdon. Siward preferred further north. Earl Hakon's own father had found much satisfaction in ruling Northumbria. Thorkel, of course, would have heard the latest news of Northumbria.

Thorkel had.

'Dynastic marriages,' said Earl Hakon, smiling. 'But the Arnasons aren't coming out of it all too badly. There is Kalv married to a rich widow. Finn got King Olaf's niece to wife, which no doubt is why Finn felt constrained to follow Olaf to Russia. And now his two daughters are placed.'

'Sigrid and Ingibjorg?' said Thorkel. Poor Finn, in Russia. Rognvald had fled to Russia as well. He wondered what Finn had done about Rognvald. He said, 'I thought the girls were too young. Or is it just a contract?'

'Thirteen and upwards, I should think,' Earl Hakon said. 'One of them is married, anyway. To my cousin Orm. The one with the long hair. Sigrid, isn't it?'

'There was one called Sigrid,' said Thorkel. They both had had long hair, so far as he could remember. 'What about the other one?'

'Oh, the other one should be across in the spring,' Earl Hakon said. 'You'll be interested. Of course, they broke her contract to the blond boy who's gone to Russia. Now she's signed to marry one of the two lords of Moray. Gillacomghain. The one who submitted to my lord Canute. Maybe,' said Earl Hakon, smiling, 'she'll persuade her husband to let you off with some of your taxes next time he comes collecting over the border? Or maybe you'd find it wiser,' said Earl Hakon, breaking this time into a laugh, 'to pay your tributes direct to King Canute instead? We must see what view your young lord Thorfinn thinks it wisest to take.'

There was no comment that he could possibly make, nor was there anything about it that he wanted to discuss with his council, although he ought to. The daughters and only heirs of Finn his cousin were being contracted to those favoured of Canute, whether by Canute's desire or because Finn despaired of ever returning from Russia. And, for whatever reason, Gillacomghain and not Thorfinn his foster-son had been offered the alliance.

That winter, Thorkel visited his home at Sandwick, Orkney, for the first time since Earl Brusi held it. Brusi himself stayed in the north. To be a vassal of King Olaf brought him no good now, with King Olaf in Russia and Rognvald, the bright, golden heir, gone also to that cold country over the mountains.

He heard later that Finn's younger daughter had turned thirteen and Gillacomghain had gone to Norway that autumn to claim her. Then the brother, Earl Malcolm mac Maelbrighde, had finally died, and Gillacomghain had had to leave his new wife in Norway and come back to Alba. After that, he kept economically at home in Moray till the weather got better. There were no raids for six months.

Child marriage, everyone said, was a killer for middle-aged husbands. How many cases did one not know? With cynicism not altogether unmixed with lower emotions, Thorkel awaited the news that Gillacomghain's little bride had crossed from Norway to join him.

In the event, he had the news before anyone, for Kalv his cousin brought the girl in the spring, calling on Thorkel in Caithness on his way to deliver her to her husband of six months in Moray. Leaving Kalv with his arm round a slave and his nose in an ale-horn, Thorkel went across to pay his respects to Finn's child at the women's house and found the little bride with Bergljot her royal mother.

The last time he had seen Ingibjorg was in the rain at Nídarós when Thorfinn had shrilled and vowed away the overlordship of Orkney. Then she had been about five, with long ox-blood hair and black brows over a gaze as clear and transparent and colourless as pond-jelly. Now she was thirteen and sat short-lapped, her small slippers dangling, so heavily pregnant that she might have been sitting a garron. He asked her jocularly what she had done with her hair, which was five inches long, and she replied in a polite, bored voice that she had cut it herself.

You had to excuse Gillacomghain's hurry, he supposed, when you remembered that there was no one now alive from that stock except Gillacomghain himself and Thorfinn, if you counted Findlaech's stepson. Had the child married Rognvald as was planned, the result would have been much the same, with a boy's hot blood to contend with. Daughters of the royal line were well aware of their fate: to cement their father's alliances, and to breed. Where one contract or one marriage failed, through death or another reason, then according to the need of the moment, the next was made in its place. The child she was carrying could have been Thorfinn's, had things fallen out differently. As it was, one supposed it would die like the rest of Gillacomghain's siring. If it was a daughter, Christian or not, he might very likely expose it. Gillacomghain was too old a man now to count on rearing and placing a girl-child.

The bride's spawn-like eyes made Thorkel uneasy, and he came out as soon as was courteous.

Outside, Kalv was waiting. Kalv backed him into a corn-strip where no one could hear, and said, 'You've heard what's happened? I was to be viceroy of Norway. Canute swore it. And now Earl Hakon his nephew has everything.'

'Maybe you should have stayed with King Olaf,' said Thorkel drily. It was no business of his if the Arnason family wanted representation on both sides in every battle. 'Where are you going to now, once you hand over the girl? To King Canute? To complain?'

'Do you *think*,' said Kalv, 'that I have been treated with justice?'

Thorkel let him go.

Gillacomghain's son was born in the summer and survived, as did his young mother. He was baptised Luloecen, which gave nothing away, as it was not a name known on either side of the family. Fatherhood, it seemed, restored Gillacomghain's energy. That year, the Mormaer of Moray made three punitive raids into Caithness and the Black Isle, in which Thorkel lost thirty men.

Kalv Arnason's stay with King Canute was a short one. He next sailed directly north, without calling at Wick or Freswick or Duncansby, and, after an unexpected descent on an acquaintance in Orkney, made his way back to Norway and Egge.

An order came to Thorkel Amundason from King Canute at Gloucester to pay Earl Hakon the required tax for all the lands held by the Earl Thorfinn under Norway. Caithness was included.

There was a piece of parchment as well as the spoken message, and Thorkel took it to the monks at Deerness, who read what was in it. It said the same, except that, underneath, Thorfinn had written *Do this* and added his name. Thorkel had seen the name written before, when Thorfinn had done it once as a joke, but this time it was much better formed, like a clerk's work. Someone in England must be teaching him.

Also on board were two kegs of wine which must have come from Thore Hund's ship, because there was an inner skin full of money. There was nothing to show whether it came from Canute or Thorfinn.

Earl Hakon continued to rule for Canute in Norway, and the Trøndelagen people were quiet. In the autumn, he crossed the sea to visit his uncle Canute and, sailing back, was diverted by bad weather to Orkney. No one ever knew whether he reached it or not, since his ship was next heard of in pieces, having overturned with the loss of all it carried.

In Egge, Kalv Arnason waited, throwing a number of feasts.

The news came that the late Earl Hakon's uncle Einar Tambarskelve and his son had visited King Canute and had asked, as the Earl's closest relatives, to be considered as the next rulers of Norway. Kalv Arnason stopped throwing feasts, hit his wife, and ordered two longships into the water, even though it was February.

The news came, before he could sail, that King Canute had refused to make Einar or Henry his son the viceroy of Norway. Kalv embraced the news-bearer. The messenger added that King Canute had announced that the next viceroy of Norway was to be the King's own son Svein, aged just thirteen. Kalv knocked the news-bearer down.

A man called Biorn, travelling very fast, left Norway for Russia with the news that Earl Hakon was drowned and Norway leaderless for the moment. The exiled King Olaf gathered an army and set out to recapture his kingdom with the three Arnasons, Rognvald Brusason and Harald, Olaf's fourteen-year-old half-brother.

It was the beginning of the year 1030. Norway, Denmark, Alba, England, and those parts of the north under the Earls of Orkney left the sowing of the harvest to the slaves and the women; and those who believed in the old gods made the old sacrifices, while nothing was spoken of or planned that had not to do with war.

King Canute gathered a fleet and an army and sent them north, but did not go with them. Instead, his forces were led by an experienced war-leader from Jomsberg, together with Svein, the young son of the King's lesser wife, whom he meant to make viceroy of Norway.

This time also, King Canute took thought, as he often did, without consulting his other wife, Emma. And after taking thought, he dispatched north with the fleet his noble housecarl and hostage, the twenty-one-year-old Thorfinn of Orkney.

EIGHT

NDER THE sun-warmed skies of high summer, Thorkel Amundason chose to await his fate on the sacred green prow of Orkney, the monks' cliff of Deerness by his father's homestead of Sandwick. Long ago, the Irish monks who brought Christ to Caithness had built their huts in the sun, above the terns and the seals, on this God-made tower of layered pink rock, chained to the gulleys and pools of the mainland by rotting spines of pebble and stone.

Now, the church was still there, and smoke rose through the thatch roofs of some of the round, lichened huts, but it was thirty years since an Irishwoman crossed the sea to bear sons to an Earl of Orkney, and no sensible abbot in Ulaid or Leinster would send monks to the Norsemen of Orkney for the sake of a few Irish slaves.

So beside him here on the headland, looking across the blue space of sea and of sky beyond which lay Norway and the war which would settle, one way or another, the fate of all Orkney, stood only David Hvita, the monk from Fair Isle, who lived here with his wife and his sons and a cousin or two who acted as helpers and who was paid by Thorkel's father to read and write for him, and teach his children, and give him advice, and withdraw discreetly when once in six years the Bishop Grimkell from Norway would come with the ships to collect King Olaf's tax and glance over the souls of his diocese.

Southwards, behind the low green-and-brown ridges, lay the sea channel that divided Orkney from Alba. There, Caithness was secure, but not only because it was guarded. All Alba lay quiet, as all Orkney lay quiet, awaiting the outcome of this war in the east. And it was to here, to Earl Brusi in his northern islands, that the first news would come, as fast as longship could bring it.

Because if King Olaf won: if the great combined armies of Sweden and the east, sweeping over the long mountain backbone and flooding down into the plains and fjords of west Norway, were to drive out King Canute's child ruler and the men of Nídarós who supported him, Earl Brusi would no longer have to cling to the outlands of Orkney, with the cold winds of the north for companions.

Two-thirds of Orkney would be his again, with King Olaf behind him. All of Orkney, if King Olaf recalled, as indeed he would recall, that Thorfinn, his other young vassal Earl, was not only an oath-breaker but a man cherished by Saxons.

It was possible—it was even possible, Thorkel Amundason knew, that the young fool was about to meet King Olaf head on in battle. Hanged for a rebel and traitor, what future would this fine Earl leave Thorkel his foster-father, and Thorkel's parents and family, here in Orkney? What could stop Brusi and King Olaf, together, from leaping those seven miles between Orkney and Alba and overrunning all Caithness?

At least that, said Thorkel to himself, his face twisting, would give our red-haired friend Gillacomghain something to think about. And Malcolm of Alba as well, squeezed like an old leather book-bag between Canute and Norway. No wonder, thought Thorkel Amundason, that Thorfinn took such trouble to cultivate Eachmarcach. There may come a time when we all need Ireland, one way or another.

The monk David said, 'Do you see something?'

There was something, far out in the haze. Thorkel looked down to clear his eyes, and studied the crab-claws and the shells on the tussocky turf, and the pink and paper-brown heads of the sea thrift, and, far below, the tranquil grey-and-white drift of the fulmars passaging on the airflow released by the spray and the rocks. Then he looked up and saw what the monk had seen: a single square sail, low on the horizon to the east. To the east, and not the north-east, where news from Nídarós might be expected.

He said, 'Another merchant.' He realised that he was hungry. Another merchant. Like birds before a forest fire, the flocks of aliens, the wandering craftsmen, the churchmen, the traders had risen and settled, wild-eyed and apprehensive, all over the east coasts of Orkney and Alba. It was the first time in living memory that Norway had been threatened by land. By sea, yes: when a dispute could be settled by the sword and the axe by men whose business was the sword and the axe. But a battle on land was another thing.

David said, 'I take leave to doubt it. The ship is covered in gold.'

He was right. With the sun behind him, Thorkel steadied his gaze on that far, moving speck and deciphered the pinpoint of brilliance as the sun caught the masthead and the prow. He forgot he was hungry, although it seemed a long time before the longship was near enough to see its great length, and the scarlet woven with gold of the sail, and, last of all, the banner that beat like a black bird of prey in the unclouded blue sky behind her.

In all the world, there were only two living men entitled to fly the black raven of Sigurd of Orkney, and one of them was here in Orkney as he was, standing no doubt on some headland watching. Thorkel said, 'It is the Earl Thorfinn,' and cleared his throat, and turned on the grass to drop down the steep path towards Sandwick, his home.

The monk David said, 'My lord, there is no need to leave. I don't know why, since they cannot possibly see us. But I think the longship has turned for this bay.'

Leaping down to the beach, with the little settlement emptying behind him, and the cliff-watchers, below, all beginning to run and call in his direction, Thorkel did not stop then to identify the glancing hurt he had felt, watching the longship turn and head for the promontory. And yet some time later, when an enemy used unwittingly a phrase of his mother's, he was reminded again of that moment.

Instead of a clean half-moon of blue pebbles, the beach was thick as a bere-field with heads: the cloth-bound heads of married women and the shining cloak-fall of hair of young girls, as well as the cloth and leather caps, the untrimmed hair and beards of the farmers, and the smooth chins and snake-moustaches of those who had travelled and fought and fancied a foreign style would make them sound wittier. The roar of talk, as the longship's prow, sixty feet high, cut towards them, grew to a storm, pushing back the kindly sound, the surfing lap of the waves.

The first thing that Thorkel saw was that the longship's flanks were unscarred, and that the shields ranged on the sides for her harbour-coming were not only unbloodied but new from the maker's. The second thing was that the prow-dragon, seen from afar, had been taken down for the shore landing. The third thing was that, among the glitter of silver and gold, a tall, bareheaded man was making his way forward among the helmeted throng and, as the ship was run up on the beach, took as his right the first foot on the gangplank and walked downwards slowly, his eyes drifting over the crowd.

The boy Thorfinn. The boy he had fostered, tall and loose-limbed, with the silken band of the *hlað* round his black hair, and a fine, long-sleeved tunic of wool above loose breeches gathered tight under the knee into soft leather boots. There was gold and enamel, fine as shell-work, on the scabbard of his sword and the sheath-ends of his belts, and the sword-pommel was deep-worked in gold like a king's. The high brow and the violent brown eyes were the same.

Then the crowd fell back, quietening, around Thorkel, and the boy saw him, and stopped.

Thorkel watched himself being studied: saw noted the grey in his hair and the scar on his neck where a Morayman's arrow had taken him. And, perhaps, the confidence and even the arrogance that two years of undivided power can give. Thorkel Amundason knew that he had ruled the north well, and that he had no need of a master. He also knew that on the deeds of this wealthy and self-willed young foster-son depended the lives of himself and his family. He said, 'You have news of King Olaf?'

The brown eyes turned to the right and to the left. 'An Orkney welcome,' the boy remarked.

The low wave of talk rose and fell, and half a dozen voices around and behind Thorkel called, 'Welcome, lord! Welcome!' to a rumble of scattered amusement. Orkney was reserving its judgement. Orkney was playing safe.

Thorkel said, 'Forgive me. We are glad to see you. But news of the war is of such moment to us all, as it must be to you, that we thought first of the greater issue.' The boy's accent had changed again. First, the sinuous Gaelic of his stepfather had infected it, and now in three words you heard the roundness of the colonial Saxon. Thorkel stood on the pebbles and hated him.

The boy said, 'I have news.' Behind him, the ship was emptying. Perhaps sixty men, well dressed and armed, gazing about them, jumped ashore or came down the gangplank and ranged themselves behind their master. Some of the faces were familiar: men who had left the islands in the last years to take service with Thore Hund, or King Canute and the chief of his housecarls. Two or three stayed aboard, with their weapons, and Thorkel realised, from a sudden thudding, that they had also brought horses. The boy said, raising his voice, 'I have news. Can you hear me?'

His voice rolled and boomed, even in that open space, as if it came from the cauldrons of the underworld, and along the beach, men replied with the voices of gulls. The boy stood, taller than any man there, and said, 'The war in Norway is ended. The men of Trøndelagen have won. King Olaf is dead. His half-brother Harald and Rognvald the son of Earl Brusi have fled back to Novgorod. King Canute is ruler of Norway, and I am defender of all Orkney and ruler of all but the isles of the north. Praise King Canute!'

The cheer that rose might be held to praise King Canute. Certainly the crewmen from the longship, joining in, might have had that impression. Thorkel said, 'King Canute defeated King Olaf?'

'The men of Nídarós defeated King Olaf,' the boy said. 'The news reached us at Vik as we were preparing to sail to do battle.'

Thorkel Amundason said, 'So King Canute took no part in the battle?' The boy and the men behind him bore no marks, not even a groove from an arrow.

The boy said, 'King Canute fought and won this battle without moving from Winchester. This battle was decided not with iron, but gold.' He raised his voice. 'Is there a welcome, then, for your Earl and his men, returned with news of victory?'

There was. Amid the roaring, amid the preparations to sweep the Earl and his men to the great hall at Sandwick, Thorkel Amundason stood back and said almost nothing, and on the march to the west, over the turf and cracked skins of the stone slabs, he let his father and kinsmen move to the Earl's side while he walked with his friends. Then, during the feasting that followed, he poured ale and wine into a stomach unfilled since morning until he had to leave the benches and empty himself under the moon, where the scythed hay rustled with voles in the in-fields, and a sheep moved cropping, and the salt tang and the hush of the sea drew him away from the heat and the noise, above the beach and along the high ground from where, looking over the ocean, he could discern the slivers of light from Kolbein's steading on Copinsay and, ahead, the glimmering fire on Deerness, a joy-beacon, dying now on the wind, to celebrate the death and defeat of a king.

If King Olaf had fallen, then Finn Arnason and all his brothers, it must be expected, would have died with him. So for Thorkel Amundason there was no kinship on either side of the sea that was not subject to the whim of a child: a child aged twenty-one years, being rocked in a cradle of gold by King Canute, his new foster-father.

The child's voice, just behind him and rumbling low as the breakers, said, 'I used to climb on Copinsay when I was small. It looks quiet in the moonlight.'

'It would make a good defence post,' Thorkel said. He did not turn. He had made sure, he thought, that no man's eye was on him as he left.

Thorfinn said, 'There is a boat down there. Do you suppose we could go over?'

The boat was his father's. 'It would only hold five or six,' Thorkel said. 'But call them out and see.'

He heard his foster-son move, and saw him against the sea, strolling to an outcrop of rock. He hitched himself onto it. Even so, his height was abnormal. The boy said, 'You have lost none of your cousins. Finn has gone back to Novgorod, where the child is.'

Thorkel said, 'I was wondering.' Enlightenment began to come. 'And Kalv?' he found himself asking.

The boy said, 'You know their habit. They always divided the family.'

'So Kalv fought against King Olaf,' Thorkel said.

'So Kalv killed King Olaf,' the boy said.

The fire on Deerness rose and fell, dusky red in the night, like the fire King Olaf had lit at Egge before he burned the god Thor and killed Ølve and gave his widow to Kalv. The boy had taken the dragon from his prow before landing today. The great monsters with their tongues of smoke and eyes of mountain-fire must not gaze on the land, lest the earth spirits be afraid and blight the bere in the field and the lamb in the womb. Thorkel Amundason said, 'There is a woman waiting for you at Duncansby. An old woman called Fridgerd.'

'Her foster-son is Arnór Thordarson the song-maker,' the boy said. 'He is in the hall there. She is waiting for him.'

Thorkel said, 'They call her a wise-woman.'

'. . . And I took the dragon from the prow,' the boy said. 'Call it superstition. Call it a requirement to look both ways, like Kalv. He wanted so very much to be viceroy of Norway. Canute will still appoint his own son, and Kalv will take his money and grumble. But there is no heir to King Olaf but the bastard son Magnús in Russia, and Magnús is six. You and I, surely, could manage that boat?'

Thorkel Amundason was empty as a dog-bladder and, ten minutes before, had walked chill and shaking in an unfriendly world. Thorkel said, 'Why not?' and ran down to the beach with his foster-son and pushed him brawling into the surf and was pushed in turn before they got the thing launched and across the channel of smooth, swelling sea.

Copinsay was a steep, turfy island girded with bird-ledges. They ran the boat up the shore, but avoided the farm. Kolbein had been one of the glittering retinue who had disembarked from the longships today. There would only be old women and babies in his house at this moment. So instead they climbed up past the barns and out to the right, to the south-eastern rim of the island, where the cliffs were. Round the rock-foot, the sea creamed in the dark, and the seals beaded the waves, rolling like puppies. The boy sang to them, long, bawdy songs, and the seals sang back, and Thorkel tripped on an old eider nest and had his hand scythed in a hole by a sea-parrot and laughed so much that his stomach went into spasms and had to be treated from a leather flask Thorfinn produced. They emptied the flask, and then went climbing.

The fowling-cliffs ran for a mile and were made of red flagstones, split vertically into geos and notches and chimneys, and layered across like a shield-maker's stackyard. From their green tops to the sea-shattered rocks at their base was a fall of two hundred feet. Thorkel, too, had spent summer days there with his friends, filling the egg-basket at the end of a rope, or lying at dusk while Kari silenced the guard-bird and all the slumbering cormorants were seized and throttled and thrown into the boats far below. He had never come unroped this way at night before, full of drink, behind a skipping black shadow that declaimed Odin-verses in Norse and sang love-songs in Gaelic and drinking-songs in Norman-French and Saxon and Wendish and raised the kittiwakes and the auks and the gulls and the fulmars in a screaming white cloud round their heads.

He enjoyed it. He said, clinging inwards to the sheaves of dark rock, 'I'm hungry.'

'Are you?' said the boy; and swung himself up to the clifftop. Thorkel slid down and sat where he was. When he opened his eyes, the boy was beside him again, with a stick in his hands. His fingers, spread under one end, supported and displayed a fine circle of black. When Thorkel touched it, he recognised the thin horsehair noose of the fowler. He remembered the horses on board and realised it had shared a pouch with the flask. A man of forethought, his young foster-son.

Then the boy wriggled along the thin ledge and began to work his way north, and Thorkel, in a bland, confused way, followed him as best he could, but couldn't remember the history of the stalking, the moments of trapping, or even the climb back to the top with a fat black-and-white auk in the breast of his shirt.

It was the boy who singed and spitted the birds and roasted them on a little fire he made in the lee of the cliff. Thorkel ate his down to the bones, and half Thorfinn's as well. The taste of fish-flavoured chicken brought back his childhood, and he talked a lot, and the boy listened. It was not until they had picked their way down to the shore, past the farmstead, now quite dark, that Thorkel's head began to clear and he realised how tired he was, and a number of other things as well. The boy said, 'Sit in the stern. I'll row,' and for a moment it appeared vital to refuse the service: to assert his leadership: to reverse the irreversible.

But he was too tired. He sat back and watched the smooth pull of the long, disjointed arms and Thorfinn's tangled black hair blowing in the sea-wind from the east. The moon had gone, and in its place was the grey northern half-dark of summer. Thorkel said, 'You're not a hostage any more, are you? Does Canute expect you to go back?'

'Hardly,' the boy said. He added, his voice patient, 'King Olaf is dead, and I have back two-thirds of Orkney.'

Thorkel found his eyes were wet. He could not think why. But he was hardly surprised when some time later, after no one had spoken at all, the boy said, looking past him at the sea, and the south sky above Alba, 'I wonder what Gillacomghain is planning to do now?'

Thorkel closed his eyes and shut out the future.

The next day, when he rose and went out to the yard, the first news they shouted to him, above the noise of the geese, was that the dragon-ship had gone.

It was from a fishing-boat, late in the afternoon, that he heard that she had sailed north, calling at a few of the islands before beaching at Westray with her dragon-head still on the prow. Earl Brusi had been at Westray that week, looking to his farms, and it was said that the half-brothers had had a short interview, in public, at which not very much had been drunk, and the dragon-ship's crew had stayed aboard the ship except for Arnór the song-maker.

They said that Brusi understood that King Olaf was dead, and that, being now a vassal of King Canute's, he could safely leave the defence of all the Orkneys, and hence the ship-levies and raising of war-bands, to Earl Thorfinn. As before, the produce of the northernmost isles would be his own, apart from any tribute exacted by Norway. But Thorfinn, who knew the regent Svein, King Canute's young son and his mother, had confidence that no unreasonable demands would be made, if indeed any were put forward at all.

From Thorfinn when he returned to Sandwick, with the dragon-head doffed, his foster-father heard almost nothing of this event, the boy being occupied with plans for taking up his residence across seas at Duncansby in Caithness, taking with him his dragon-ship, which, it appeared, had been a gift from King Canute. Two-thirds of the men had elected to stay with him. The rest were returning home to Norway and Denmark, well rewarded.

The Earl wished to know, quickly, the prospects for the harvest on both Orkney and Caithness and its southern parts, and about the state of the flocks and the hay crop. He thought he should be told about the families in all the settlements, and what sons there were of fourteen and over. He had forgotten the names of Thorkel's council men and would think it impolite not to know their ages and history. Who were the craftsmen these days? Where were the best ships being built? Were the markets still in the same place, and at the same time of year? What weapons did Thorkel have stored? What axes and spears, what swords and arrows and bows? How many men would have fighting-coats: jackets of plated leather; tunics of metal rings? When Thore Hund killed King Olaf, said Thorfinn, Thore Hund wore a reindeer coat sewn and charmed by the Lapps, so that the King's sword-edge only raised dust from it.

'I thought,' said Thorkel stiffly, 'that my cousin Kalv Arnason was the King-killer.'

'He took him in the neck,' said his foster-son, 'at the same time as Thore Hund's spear took the King through the belly. They could not say, it seems, which wound the King died of. If you are to be steward of Orkney for me, you will need a better hall, away from your father's. We shall require timber.'

'That is in short supply,' said Thorkel briefly. It was a long time since he had had to make an accounting.

'Then we shall have to get more. Outside Norway, the best,' said Thorfinn, 'I suppose, still comes from Moray?'

For ships, for shelter, for defences, they would need wood. He had always felled it in the south and the west, where it could be brought up to the mouth of the Ness. But the best and straightest trees, yes, were in Moray, and the rolling spates of the Spey would bring them riding out on their rafts to the sea. He said, 'You will challenge Gillacomghain now? In the autumn?'

'I shall cut my trees now, in the autumn,' Thorfinn said. 'And build my stockades and my ships through the winter. And be ready in the spring, when Malcolm and Canute and Gillacomghain have all decided what to do, and Gillacomghain challenges me in return.'

Thorkel did not go, either, on that timber raid, but he heard about it from the crewmen who brought him two shiploads from Duncansby: the smell of the resin came to him over the water as he stood on the jetty and watched them. They had felled the trees at night, in the first of the autumn rain that was to sweep across Europe and rot the barley and oats in the fields, so that the full barns of Caithness, of his provident storing, would pay for their own defence, and something over.

The Moraymen were farmers who raised flocks and grain-patches and fished, and had built no warships since the days of the great northern mormaers, the forebears of Gillacomghain and his uncle Findlaech, who had roved the seas of the north and ruled from Thurso south to the mountains of Mar.

Thorfinn and his woodsmen had loaded the timber and got it out as the rains fell and the land dissolved into quagmire behind them. Then, before Gillacomghain could be warned, far less get keel into water to follow them, the laden ships had set off for the north.

They offloaded at Cromarty and Tarbatness, at Helmsdale and Wick and Duncansby. There was oak, beech, and spruce; but, best of all, the long, straight lengths of pine needed for mast and for keel. They would cut more from their own woods, and they would buy more from Norway. But Gillacomghain had supplied his cousin by adoption with the nucleus of his new fleet.

The winter passed like no other Thorkel had known. This time, it was Thorfinn, not himself, who made the rounds of the district leaders on the horse he had brought from the south, with the long stirrups chequered with silver and copper, and a cloak lined with marten fur. His earl's band went with him, because he had mouths to feed and his dues were waiting, in meal and in butter, in malt and fish and in meat, to be eaten or brought back for storing. All the talk was of defence: how to preserve their homesteads, their flocks and barns from the passing raider and their young men and girls from the slavemen; how to fight off the dispossessed looking for good land to settle on.

He sent to Ireland before the winter closed in, and brought back threescore half-grown youths and girls of mixed Norse-Irish blood to work in the fields, in the farmhouse, on the shore, so that, no matter what the men of the house might be needed for, the work of producing food, of weaving and building and tending, would go on. He did all that his father Earl Sigurd had done for his people—or for himself, if you looked at it that way. For, no matter how much a man might wish to spend his days at his leisure, lying in his fleeces in winter with all the girls he wanted and an ale-flask at his elbow; or in summer sailing through the blue waters, hearing the sweet song of the axe; fighting one's friends and one's enemies and drinking and telling over long tales with them both, these would be nothing without hard work and vigilance: nothing but a cold hearth and an empty quern, a spear through your throat, and your girl in another man's blankets.

Of women in his foster-son's life Thorkel had heard no less or no more than of any other youth of his age. But of marriage alliances he had heard nothing. Tackled, Thorfinn was practical. It seemed to be his chief characteristic.

'In England, to tell you the truth, being unattached was my greatest profession.'

'And now?' Thorkel said.

'And now, of course, the land demands sons. What do you think? Between them, Crinan and Malcolm and Duncan have closed Northumbria and Cumbria against me. A Saxon marriage would be nonsense. About a Norman or a Breton one I am less certain. I have no intention of stretching my interests to the east, so I see no purpose in marrying in Norway, saving your presence. The Sudreyar, the western islands, might produce someone, except where my stepfather Crinan has interests. Perhaps best of all, there is Ireland. There are Irish blood and Irish tongues through all Caithness, and older stock still in Orkney. And how conveniently near it would be to south-west Alba, were we to find a reason for taking to the sea.'

'Who in Ireland?' Thorkel said. They were speaking beside the new hall Thorfinn was building by the haven at Wall, in Orkney, and he was cold and wet from a day in the saddle, and hoarse with answering questions. His name, he noticed, had changed nowadays. He was not Thorkel Amundason to anyone, but Thorkel Fóstri, Foster-father.

'I don't know—yet,' said his foster-son. 'I think I shall ask Eachmarcach again.'

And the next thing that Thorkel heard, he was off, in a spell of quiet seas in December, and did not come back until just before the January feast. All Thorkel could glean was that he had been to Tiree and to Ireland and had stayed some time in each place. So far as he could learn, the matter of marriage, if explored at all, had reached no point of conclusion.

In the spring, skirmishing began on frontiers between Moray and Caithness, and the district leaders, stocked with weapons and good earth and stockade defences and well primed on how to support one another, beat off the inroads with little difficulty and no loss beyond a weak cow or two and some hacked limbs. It was perhaps Gillacomghain testing his strength. It was in any case just what the border men on both sides had always done after the rigours of the winter, until the spring plenty or the spring voyages brought laden tables again.

Kalv Arnason visited Orkney. Thorkel heard a boat had come over from Duncansby and found the crew in Skeggi's house: he heard Kalv's voice raised in some tale of disaster before he lifted the latch. When he went in, Kalv stopped speaking. He looked cocky as ever, but there was a nervousness about him that had not been there before. He was soon picking up the thread of his story: how he had called at Duncansby to tell Earl Thorfinn what the new rulers of Norway wanted from him in tribute, and how Earl Thorfinn had told him that he was surprised to hear young Svein had expectations from him, and that he would be quite pleased to listen to him if he came here himself.

'Which, being a child,' Kalv said starkly, 'he is hardly likely to do, or his mother King Canute's lesser wife either. Don't you have any say these days in your foster-son's doings? You know, if he doesn't, that four of us fought on King Olaf's side. If Canute or his son don't get what they want out of Orkney, we are the ones who will suffer.'

'Surely not,' Thorkel said. He sat down on the bench, and after a bit Kalv sat as well. Someone gave him an ale-cup. 'Whatever the rest did for King Olaf, you were the one who dispatched him. I hear you looked after Finn and the rest after the battle. How is Finn?'

'In good health. Back at Ørland,' Kalv said. 'My brothers couldn't wait to escape from the tainted purlieus of Egge, once they were all better. You heard Finn tried to kill me after Olaf went down? Flung a knife at me and called me a nithing and an oath-breaker.'

'Finn believes in the White Christ,' said Thorkel. 'And I hear some very strange tales about that.'

'Oh, yes,' said Kalv. 'It has become a matter of treason to talk about the black afternoon and the failed crops as if they happened in every country and not just in Nídarós. There will be miracles at the grave very soon, mark my words. And if your idiot foster-son holds back his taxes, I shall be hanged for a devotee of the All-Father. So will he, I shouldn't wonder. Who's the old woman?'

Thorkel had been surprised, too, by the number of Icelanders in Thorfinn's household. 'You had better speak respectfully of Arnór's foster-mother,' he said. 'Second sight is a gift common to every indigent elder in Iceland.'

'I am told that when this one talks, Thorfinn listens,' Kalv said. 'You had better put it into her head that he will have to manage his affairs with more tact or we shall all have black afternoons, whatever the sun may be doing. Has it escaped his attention, do you think, that Gillacomghain is married to an Arnmødling as well?'

Skeggi, who was not an Arnmødling, said, 'Well, she'd better look out. A godly deputation has just come from Gillacomghain to Thorfinn. He is to send to Alba the tribute for his grandfather's Caithness or he will receive a call from Gillacomghain, the official collector.'

'What?' said Kalv.

Thorkel lifted his pensive gaze from Skeggi and, turning to Kalv, made the best of it. 'Gillacomghain wants to take over Caithness, and has got backing from the south to try and do it this way, by claiming tribute. Thorfinn won't pay, and Gillacomghain will take the excuse to invade and get rid of him. Don't repine. Your niece Ingibjorg may find herself queen of the north.'

'Margaret,' said Kalv. 'Everybody's wife is getting called Margaret these days. And I suppose Thorfinn will let himself be pushed out, just like that? What if he fights back and takes Moray?'

Thorkel looked shocked. 'Is it likely?' he said.

'Well, no,' said Kalv. 'But you don't want him over here in Orkney, do you? Tell him to pay up. Everyone has to. Everyone is a vassal to somebody.'

'You tell him,' Thorkel said.

NINE

HE INVASION CAME in the summer: an army of men from the south led by the lord Gillacomghain, and those men of Moray whose homes lay under his rule, and others who had owned land or had kinsfolk in the north, in those parts once ruled by the forebears of Findlaech his late uncle. There were also among them, it was said, men who did not live in Moray at all, but who came from further south and west. But if Duncan or his father sent them, they kept quiet about it.

Findlaech had been respected as well as feared. There were enough disaffected Moraymen in the south to make sure that good warning reached Caithness of what Gillacomghain was about, and enough divided loyalties in Gillacomghain's army to make sure that devastation wouldn't follow behind it. The beacons flared up through the north in plenty of time for Thorkel to set sail with his levies from Orkney.

Perhaps Gillacomghain saw their sails turn into the mouth of the Oykel. Without doubt his scouts, casting ahead as they crossed the Ness and worked their way north, brought back word of the landings, and then news of the army already mustered and waiting in Caithness. The army that proved exactly how Thorfinn had been spending his time in the Western Isles and in Ireland.

Even Thorkel, when he saw the tents and the numbers of men armed and waiting, felt ashamed that war had now come to this: mercenaries brought in with a Saxon king's money, instead of war fought in the old, heroic way, leader against leader and king against king. The loser died where he stood, as was right: he stood to gain most, and therefore lost all. And the men who had fought well on both sides went back to their farms and found another to protect them. As had happened to King Olaf and the Trøndelagers.

For a while there was nothing between the two armies but wading-birds in the marshland, and the scouts. Then Gillacomghain's army turned and went back.

Thorkel went to his foster-son's tent and said, 'Next time. Next time, where will the money come from? Canute's past bribes won't last for ever.'

Arnór the song-maker said, 'There won't be a next time,' showing that he knew as much as any skald ever did, for all the silver rings on his arms. He was not dressed, Thorkel noticed, for fighting.

'There will be a next time, and we shall have enough money,' said Thorfinn. 'You haven't heard that Gillacomghain had a nephew with him today? He hoped to plant him in Caithness. The boy's father, I'm told, is in business with Crinan.'

'So the church of Dunkeld is about to establish an outpost in Caithness?' Thorkel said.

'The church of Dunkeld in the shape of its abbot,' Thorfinn said, 'is of an adventurous turn of mind that likes to set up its tables and open its books anywhere where there may be a profit to be made. I am merely making a point. If there is any profit to be made out of Caithness, or indeed out of Orkney, I am going to make it.'

He did, too, employing the ships that carried the mercenaries home to bring back wine from Dublin which he sold to Haarek of Tjotta in exchange for a shipload of skins, with some bear furs and walrus ivories. Some of the walrus skins he had spiral-cut for ships' ropes and kept, because it made the best gear in the cold. The rest he sold in Tiree, and the profit came back in its own weight of money and hacksilver.

Thorkel Fóstri kept quiet and did, mostly, what he was told. In August, the news came that the late King Olaf was now a saint and his tomb at Nídarós the undisputed fount of miraculous healing. Kalv did not make a return visit, either that autumn or the following spring. Thore Hund, on the contrary, showed a lively interest in sharing the Lapp trade with Haarek and Thorfinn, and was to be seen often at Duncansby, which was more than could be said for his stocky son Siward, now well established in northern England at York.

In after years, Thorkel was to think of this interval after Thorfinn's homecoming as of the winter months of planning that went towards a long voyage a-viking. In all that time, he never saw his foster-son fight, or do anything other than work like a farm-manager or a usurer among his tenants or his associates on land or on sea. The boy was twenty-one years old when it began, and twenty-three when it ended and the vessel was launched, in bloodshed as the old gods demanded.

In that year, mocked and baffled, Gillacomghain applied for aid to the south, for the swordsmen and spearmen he would need to defeat this ungainly cuckoo, this cousin by marriage who sat in the north and defied his elders. Soon, if no one checked him, this half-Norse seaman might take it into his head to menace them all: himself, old King Malcolm in the south, and the prince Duncan, who ought to be looking towards his own future but who seemed only concerned, like his grandfather, with wealthy saints and their pickings.

The aid arrived in the form of the eminent merchant and moneyer Crinan, father of Duncan of Cumbria. My lord Crinan, making one of his regular visits to his lucrative abbey of Dunkeld, turned north out of the rivermouth afterwards and, from the monks' house at Brechin, summoned Gillacomghain south to confer with him. Gillacomghain came, with an armed escort larger than might have been accounted polite, and Brechin sheltered them both while they talked, below the pencil-tower of the Irishmen and its irritating bell-signals, rattling down spaced on the wind.

Worse even than that was the high, continuous voice of Gillacomghain's son outside the window. Luloecen was the only child he had managed to beget on Finn Arnason's daughter, and the boy was too valuable to leave where some friend of Findlaech could lay hold of him. The Arnason girl he could leave anywhere. If she got a child from some bedding, it couldn't be his, and he would be quite entitled to hand her back to her family, once he saw what way the wind was blowing in Norway. Gillacomghain didn't see how you could overlook the fact that her uncle had killed the only Norwegian anyone had ever thought worth canonising. Canute might not like that.

This man Crinan, who looked like a saint himself with his long, soft brown beard and large eyes, thought that King Canute would not hold that against Gillacomghain. He said it was well known that the men of North Norway were always ready to throw out a king, whether it was Olaf or Canute, and that a young man who found himself in as strong a position as Earl Thorfinn, with Caithness and most of Orkney under him, might well be considered a natural ally.

If Earl Thorfinn were to hold Moray as well, then King Canute would feel things had gone too far. He was sure, said Crinan, that King Malcolm his late wife's father felt the same. Not, of course, that attack would be easy. It was a matter of distance. The domains of King Malcolm and, of course, those of King Canute lay a very long way from Caithness. His own abbey of Dunkeld, he had no need to point out, had no men to support it other than a steward and those who worked the fields for the monks. Had Gillacomghain a plan?

Gillacomghain said that he believed it was for King Malcolm and the lord Crinan to promulgate a plan, given that they agreed that the Earl of Caithness should henceforth be his sister's son Maddan rather than King Malcolm's grandson Thorfinn of Orkney. As everyone knew, he had no resources to match those of Thorfinn. His brother Malcolm had left him nothing. And his wife's father Finn Arnason had offered only a hornful of silver for dowry, and that had been spent on the last expedition.

The lord Crinan, who had the gift of unlimited patience, and time to exert it in, heard him out to the end and then said, 'What you need is a fleet. My son Maldred has an uncle who will supply one for you.'

Gillacomghain did not care that the uncle in question was Carl the son of Thorbrand of York. All he needed to hear was that the fellow was rich, and had a trading-fleet, and could put twenty ships into the water at Berwick which could land an army anywhere on the coast of Caithness.

'How big an army?' said Gillacomghain, walking up and down with his sword banging in his excitement. 'It depends how big an army. Last time, this child potentate mobilised the whole of Ireland—the whole of Ireland, I tell you. That's the kind of money he has.'

Crinan's long robes stood on their furred hems on the beaten earth under his heels. 'Large enough, I believe,' he said. 'Large enough to send him running for Orkney. Unless he is young enough to want to stand and fight.'

Gillacomghain stood still. 'You don't suppose I'm going to take the north coast and hold it while he sits like a *madadh allaidh*, like a wild dog in his earldom, grinning at me over the water? He has to be killed, and Caithness conquered. I would say Orkney as well, save that I know Canute will have that for Norway.'

'Then if you want to trap him,' said Crinan, 'you will have to block his back door as well. Land an army in the south of Caithness, and another in the north, and seal off the havens with Carl's shipping. Thorfinn has only five vessels, they tell me, at Duncansby.'

'His watch will see the fleet coming,' said Gillacomghain. 'If he has fears of facing it, he will make off for the north and Orkney before we could get there.'

'His watch will see half the fleet coming,' said Crinan. 'And he will either elect to stay and fight such a small force wherever it may land, or make for the north and try to escape, as you say. He won't see the other ships till they arrive, because we shall send them straight north from Buchan Ness, so far out to sea that he can have no warning until it is too late. Then they will draw in to round Duncansby Head, destroy his vessels, and hold his own coast against him. Carl will do that. You and Maddan will land with the first ships and, if you are offered no battle, march north until he is contained between Carl's army and yours. I am no campaigner,' said the Abbot Crinan, crossing his robe over his waist and rising to his full height, 'but that seems to me to offer some prospect of success. . . . Your son seems to disagree.'

The howls of resistance outside made conversation all but impossible. Nevertheless, Gillacomghain laughed. 'Whatever he is refusing,' he said, 'it is not the kingdom of the north, and the long life and glory this day's work will bring to us all. Your plan, my lord, is all I could hope for. Set a time for it: that is all I can ask.'

Outside, he found the child had quietened: a young monk had set him apart from his nurse and was sitting cross-legged beside him, his hand at the boy's waist. The monk looked at Gillacomghain and the man from York and smiled and said to the child, 'Look: who is that?'

'Macdowall,' said the child. He spoke very clearly, for three.

'No. Look again,' said the monk. 'Who is the small man?'

'Kali Hundison,' said the child.

The monk laughed. 'No. It is your father. The nurse says it is your father,' he said. 'What is your name, my strange boy?'

The eyes, a clear, empty blue, took hold of his. 'Luloecen,' said the child. 'Luloecen it *was*. Who are you?'

For a moment, he could hardly remember, looking into those immense, clear blue eyes, who he was or why he had called at this monastery. Then he said, 'My name is Sulien,' and rose to his feet, still looking.

'I know,' said the child, and tugged his nurse's skirts to be lifted, and went off after his father without a backward glance.

*   *   *

The Abbot of Llanbadarn said, 'I know, my lady. It is a very strange message. Shipwrecked on his way to Ireland. On the east coast of Alba.'

'Only Sulien,' said Alfgar, 'could be shipwrecked on the east coast while travelling from the west coast further west. What about that Irish monastery he was going to study at?'

'He says that Earl Thorfinn has arranged for him to study at St Drostan's instead,' said his mother Godiva. 'I suspect the sound of St Drostan's. If there is more than one elderly hermit at this St Drostan's, I shall be surprised. Alfgar, did it seem to you that Sulien and Thorfinn were much attracted to one another when they met? You remember that dreadful race on the oars?'

'I wish they would hold it again,' Alfgar said. 'And next time I should leave my lord Duncan of Alba to drown. No, I remember no meeting of souls, but it's possible. Sulien likes nearly everybody, and Thorfinn is one to recognise worth when he sees it. He got on well with you. And everyone knows how he got on with the Lady Emma.'

'I don't know whether that's an indication of character or cunning or merely endurance,' Godiva said. 'But it certainly does show that he knows what is good for him. All the same, I don't want Sulien harmed, or I should never have . . . That is, Earl Thorfinn seems to have asked him to stay. The message is certainly odd: even devious.'

'Everything is devious about Thorfinn,' said Alfgar. 'Including the fact that he has offered the Icelanders, for a money advance, large tracts of standing timber in Moray that don't even belong to him. You know he has laid the Western Isles under him.'

'It's a good phrase,' said Godiva. 'Does it mean something?'

'It means,' said Alfgar, 'that he has reminded them that he expects to collect tribute from them in the same way that his late uncle did, and that when they forget, he sends a boat over to burn a few steadings until they remember. He's got a cousin to manage it for him, they say.'

'Moray,' said Godiva thoughtfully. She realised that the Abbot had dropped out of the conversation. 'Really,' said the Lady of Mercia, 'I can barely follow the import system of Lichfield, never mind the Western Isles, but I expect the church is quite expert in all this. How very good of you, my lord Abbot, to come to Chester yourself. And no doubt you will be writing to Sulien and giving him your news. Perhaps,' said the Lady of Mercia, 'if I can find a clerk who is not too busy, which isn't likely, you would take a message to Sulien from me as well? We must not lose sight of that charming young man.'

'Which one?' said Alfgar; and laughed when his mother landed a kick on his ankle.

As with any battle, the waiting beforehand was the worst of it.

In spite of the heat outside and the blinding flash of the sea, none of the five boat-companies could bear to stay inside the high, dark hall in Thurso where Thorfinn sat with those of his household who had not been sent away.

All the old people of Thurso had gone by now, and all the women and children. Through the low passes and the broad farmlands that led north from Moray, all that was valuable had been hidden and all who could not fight had gone to safety while Gillacomghain's army came marching up from the south. And now those who were left were still waiting: for the message from the west that would tell them that Carl Thorbrandsson's ships were sailing north towards Duncansby to block Thorfinn's back door.

Sulien said, for the third time, 'Five ships are not enough. He will have eleven.'

'Five ships of our kind will be enough,' said the Earl Thorfinn. 'Any more, and he would suspect something.'

There was no impatience in his voice, or even in his face, that Sulien could see. Landing on the jetty at Duncansby, sending up to the steading to tell Earl Thorfinn that Sulien of Brittany and Llanbadarn was here, he had wondered whether his tutors were right: whether his unshakable interest in people and affairs was a sign of an irresponsible nature, when all his soul should be committed to the vocation for which he was training.

Some of their anxiety, at least, was groundless. Wealth and power for their own sake held no attractions for him. He was young enough to despise those bishops who turned from the world of the spirit to fill an office of state or rule a province fit for an earldom. Saving souls was his concern, he told himself. So the chance encounter at Chester with this odd Earl of Orkney had caught his imagination.

He had seen men of power in Brittany who, by lifting a finger, could cause a town to be sacked or a countryside wasted. All that also was within the compass of this grim, self-contained Earl from the north, only two years older than himself, and making his way, as was Sulien, in a culture not wholly his own. Then behind the cool hostility he had sensed something else, and had ventured to appeal to it; and had been answered.

He might have thought himself mistaken, in the five years that followed, had not the Lady of Mercia brought his name up quite recently and, listening, agreed with him. 'Since he freed Alfgar, if for his own ends, you may feel free to canonise him, my dear Sulien. But no. I see you are serious. There is a person there, though a little astray so far: on that I agree. Also, there is wit. You found it.'

'I thought so,' said Sulien. He paused. 'The men about him don't seem of much use.'

'It does seem a pity,' had agreed the Lady Godiva. 'And, of course, intrigue against him everywhere. I heard only the other day from a shipman of some meeting to take place in Brechin. What about, I don't know, but the monks had discussed it abroad because the lord Abbot Crinan was coming. They needed cushions.'

Sulien had said, 'I hope you sold them some filled from your nettlebeds. I'm leaving soon to study in Ireland.'

'I know,' had said the Lady Godiva; and had smiled.

So that, because of the smile as much as his own inclinations, he had found himself stranded in Brechin in the course of a singularly erratic voyage to

Ireland; and, having heard what he had heard, had taken the logical step and brought his tidings here.

Of course, the Earl had no idea he was coming; had never heard of him in the intervening five years, unless Alfgar had gossiped. Might have no time for churchmen barely out of their teens who spoke Breton-Gaelic. Might, with justice, distrust anyone who broke a journey to Ireland by way of Brechin for motives which were not entirely evident.

In the event, it had been the same tall, black sparrow-hawk of a youth who had moved out of the steading at Duncansby and stood at a great distance, looking; and then had covered the slope to the jetty in a matter of seconds to stand before him, considering.

He must have looked apprehensive. 'It's all right,' said the Earl Thorfinn. 'We only eat Christians in Lent.'

He could feel the colour rush back to his face. Sulien said, 'Don't be deceived by the skirts: I got converted in Anglesey last week. I'm saved for the High, the Equally High, and the Third.'

'Then come in,' said the Earl. 'What are we waiting for? There's a Valkyrie longing to meet you. Or at least we can manage a Norn.'

'I know. Fridgerd Gamli's daughter,' Sulien said rashly, and hurried on without waiting. 'I want to talk to you. I have news, which I will give you, but I must make a condition.'

Then, of course, the Earl complained, walking him back to the house. But when they were in private and the condition had been outlined and met, the Earl did not utter a word, for Sulien told him all he had learned at Brechin from the voices floating out of the monks' little window.

What had taken him to Brechin in the first place, and what impelled him to betray Gillacomghain, Earl Thorfinn did not ask, either then or during all the weeks of planning that followed, through which Sulien stayed under his roof.

Why he stayed, he was not himself sure, although the ostensible reason was easy to find. He had made a condition, and the Earl no doubt thought that he would remain to see it carried out. There was a fascination, too, about watching a group of capable men preparing for war. He himself came from a family of warriors: anyone who had land these days could hardly, by definition, be anything else. He listened in on the councils, and had opinions to give when he was asked. He wrote to Llanbadarn, and to Ireland, to say that he would not be coming just yet, and someone from a little monastery in Deerness enclosed the note and sent it off in the next suitable ship, with a reassuring cross on the seal.

He took the chance also to mention to Thorkel the foster-father, of the appraising glances, that no doubt the Lord, Who had directed his footsteps to Caithness, would direct them away again in His own good time. Which baffled the good Thorkel, he felt, as it ought to.

Now the moment for battle had come, and he sat with Earl Thorfinn and his captains in the cool dark of the old hall at Thurso, awaiting the signal that would scatter them all. He was not supposed to fight, because of his calling. In spite of this, he had planned for some time to deceive the rest when the time came for him to follow the old and the children to safety. He had planned to hide himself aboard one of the warships and emerge into view when at sea.

Whether the Earl was a mind-reader he was unaware. But certainly something the Earl chose to say brought home the truth that in war the amateur who must be protected was a burden known to bring about the deaths of more first-class men than might the enemy. It had caused Sulien to change his intention.

He was thinking of it as the shouting began outside, telling that the message had come and it was time for the five vessels to leave for their appointment. He said to Earl Thorfinn, 'Well: here or hereafter, then,' and smiled, to make it casual; while Thorfinn's face produced the abbreviated expression he was coming to recognise as a contented, valedictory insult.

He waited until the ships had all set out, the square sails arched into the red evening sun, and then found his horse and rode off, away from the battle that was not his, to be shown for the first time, had he known it, a glimpse of the much longer battle that was.

TEN

IT WAS NEVER a handicap to the skald Arnór to write verses about a battle he hadn't been in.

He protested mildly when, having crossed the Pictish Firth in one of Thorfinn's five ships at no very great speed, he was dumped on the jetty at Sandwick; but only mildly, for the sails of Gillacomghain's friends were close behind, bright as a fresh twig of gorse on the cold, running waves.

They had chosen to make for Sandwick, Thorfinn said, so that it would appear that they were running for help to Thorkel Fóstri and whatever men he could muster. He would prefer it not to be known that Thorkel and the whole strength of Orkney were already on the mainland with the Caithness men, waiting to give Gillacomghain's army, in due course, the welcome it deserved.

Arnór watched the skiff go back to Thorfinn's ship with mixed feelings. If this battle went badly—and it was five ships against eleven—he would have to find a new master. He was only here anyway because this was where his foster-mother said he would make his reputation. So far in his life, his foster-mother had been generally right, but the gifts of wise-women do not last for ever, and he did not want to look a fool at Hitarnes because she had got some prediction confused. He just wanted to be more famous than his father Thord son of Kolbein would ever be, now that he thought more of his cows than his verses.

To the ships from Berwick, the state of affairs was quite clear: either some rumour had caught Thorfinn's ear in Caithness and he had made up his mind to escape, or he and his ships were merely crossing to visit his earldom in Orkney and had caught sight of the other fleet rounding the headland. He would not, perhaps, recognise the Northumbrian banners—or perhaps he would: he had been in York, they said, in his days with King Canute. But in any case a strange fleet sailing north in such numbers was not likely to be a friendly one, especially one packed with men as this was. Thorfinn could choose—to run for the shore and risk being overwhelmed and his five ships burned where they lay, before help could come. Or he could fight at sea, with the small chance that one ship or two might cut free and run in the confusion.

The crewmen on the Berwick ships had been warned to watch out for that.

It surprised them, as they got closer, to see how long and how low-built the Caithness boats were, taking the sea almost to the gunwales. Then the leading ship turned to the right, having dropped her passenger, and the sun struck red on the gold of her sternpost and lit the raven banner flown from her mast. Carl Thorbrandsson said to his shipmaster, 'She's going north-east round the coast. If we catch them before they round the point, they'll have to stand with the wind facing them and the sun in their eyes. Can we do it?'

'Unless they dump their cargo,' the shipmaster said. He had been through Orkney waters before, as most of them had for their trading; and there were drawings. He knew better, for example, than to cut straight across to Sandwick and intercept the Caithness men there. There were skerries opposite Sandwick, and more you couldn't see, under the water. He said, 'He's a young one, isn't he? You'd think he would have better advice than that.' They were overhauling the five ships very fast, with the wind behind them and the ropes taut and the men coming into battle-fever, with the noise rising, and the clashing of shield to shield, and snatches of chanting, bellowed from ship to ship, and laughter and the glinting of shaken spears and white teeth under the flash of the helms.

Ahead, the five ships turned, like haddock perceiving the net, and fled out to sea, the course of a madman. They held it for five minutes, during which the eleven Berwick vessels drove like harrows over the water. Then the Caithness ships stopped.

They stopped because, as if pulled by one hand, the sails of all five collapsed, leaving five rocking poles. At the same moment, like the limbs of an insect, thirty oars sprang from the near side of each ship and pulled her round to face the sun and the oncoming fleet from Northumbria.

For a moment, the five ships remained there, idling on the brisk waves, with the blinding sun lighting their prows as the southern fleet grew closer and closer. Close enough to see the men who rose to their feet, score upon score of them, in the five Caithness ships, with their spears held high and their axe-blades laid on their shoulders, with a ragged continuing yodel of derision that bounced off the waves. Close enough to see, briefly, the gold helm and red shield of the man they were fighting against, a tall, brooding predator on the bow. Close enough to see the raven banner above the man's head falter and flap and then, changing direction, begin to blow cleanly towards them.

The Northumbrians were good seamen, and quick. Almost before the wind reached them, the orders had gone singing out, and the oarsmen got to their chests while the sails came rattling down, flapping and swirling about them. The Caithness boats stood where they were, oars gently moving, and waited while the eleven ships of the enemy settled down to the long, hard pull against the new wind, across the space that separated them from their adversary.

Carl Thorbrandsson said, 'He knew the wind would veer at sunset. And by the time we reach him, the sun will be down. Who is this man Thorfinn?'

'A man King Canute wouldn't mind seeing out of the way, my lord,' said the shipmaster. 'If you remember.'

He could still make a man shrink if he wanted to. 'If I die,' said Carl Thorbrandsson, 'the ship goes to my sister's son. It is worth remembering.'

Then the arrows began to fall, shining seeds of a battle-crop, carried thick and fruitful on the enemy wind; while theirs hung spattered and kicking against the cold, moving curtain of air.

The Berwick fleet were well trained. They rowed forward against the wind and the arrows in the pink after-light of the sunset, stringing out, as they had planned, to encircle and smother the enemy. Only the enemy came at them, oars driving like whippets, and clear and distinct there were faces bearded and clean-shaven and moustached under the smooth helmet-cones, and words and syllables among all the shouting, and a stink of sweat on the wind that brought the hair standing raw on the spine. Then, like lampreys, the Caithness longships were there amongst them, their oars vanished as swiftly as they had appeared, and instead the crippling steel claws of the grappling-irons came shooting aboard and held fast to the timbers and tightened, until one by one every Thurso vessel was locked hard to another and the men were boarding, under the stubbed, whickering flight of their throwing-spears. Once aboard, the axes came out.

It may have been five ships against eleven. It was in fact nearly five hundred men against very few more. Five hundred men who knew to a moment how long the after-light was going to last, and when it would no longer be possible to tell friend from enemy in the well of a slim, rocking longship. Five hundred men who knew the tricks of the wind and the swirl and push of the current that very soon would take the locked mesh of ships and drive it straight for the shore.

The first to go was the Northumbrian vessel that had taken the brunt of the landing until, swept along its whole length by the boarders, the crewmen who were left had saved themselves by overrunning the ship next their own.

Now, ill-trimmed by the dead on her gunwales and bearing only her cargo of vanquished, she ran released into the grip of the wind, and the tide trapped and spun her across to the swerve of the current. The next ship rocked, and those who looked over their shoulders were dead men, and those who did not fell embracing the blades they were parrying. The sea washed white up the strakes, first on one side and then on the other, and slipped down again, frothing pink as the sunset; and helmets rolled in the water like quicksilver, until in time they filled and tilted and sank.

On the flagship, Carl Thorbrandsson had the pick of the men and in himself the best brain in the fleet. Under his rule, the first ship that attacked them was thrown off, ramming the sea; the grappling-irons slashed free; the darts and throwing-spears streaming after and landing in a chorus of loud, hollow voices and voices that were thick and timbreless.

A score of her crew were left stranded behind on the flagship. They made no play with their shields, or attempt to bargain for mercy, but, calling to one another, each leaped to a man he had marked and, twisting, hacking, and jabbing, accounted for twice their number before the last man was flung overboard.

Another Berwick ship swayed past, empty. Five at least had been successfully boarded: on three, so far as could be seen, the enemy had been repelled,
as on his own, and their bodies bundled into the sea. Carl Thorbrandsson
turned to leap to his stance on the stern-deck and so had the first view of the
enemy flagship, under oars once again, moving in from her kill and making
straight for his own.

There was time to have the warning blown, and then the louvred flanks
cracked together and, splitting wood into wood, held the two vessels side by
side as one ship.

The first pack of men who thudded over the side contained, in its midst, a
fellow who held aloft in both arms the raven banner of Orkney. Then came
the second wave, and the third, and the shouting altered as the thronged ship
fought for its life and the wind brought slaps of blood and snatches of cut hair
and the bottom-boards became spiked and pillowed with weapons and
bodies. Within his own circle of housecarls, the Northumbrian commander
fought as well as any, for he was a man used to battle, while searching again
and again for the golden helmet of the earl he had been paid to defeat. He said
aloud, breathlessly, to the shipmaster, 'If Thorfinn is dead, I will have the
retreat blown.'

'I should blow it anyway,' said the shipmaster. Except that the shipmaster
had exchanged his sharp voice for a rich one of abnormal depths, emanating
from a black, crane-like young man in a gold helmet, with a sword at the end
of each arm and his shoulder-joints working like a plough-ox's. Thorfinn
said, 'You're going to be left. Your men are running on to the next ship.'

It was true. He could see, as his war-band and the Earl's fought and
clattered around him, that the stern of the ship was already clear except for
the dead and the dying, and that the men of both sides, in an unsteady,
struggling mass, were closing up to the bucketing prow, where another of his
ships dodged and wallowed in the throes of the same prostitution. Thorfinn
said, 'Blow the retreat. I have no quarrel with you.'

Carl Thorbrandsson said, 'Tell your men to stand back. We can settle this
matter between us.' An axe came towards him, and he knocked the haft to one
side, seeing Thorfinn duck on his own account and then slash, each foot
taking the weight as the ship rocked. A man started to screech, both palms
open.

Thorfinn said, 'It *is* settled. I've won.'

He looked surprised, and even impatient. Carl considered a worthy reply.
Not until you've killed me, came to his mind. But that was Gillacomghain's
privilege, not his. He wondered what had happened to Gillacomghain.

The young man opposite shoved a thumb below the rim of his helmet and,
pushing it up from his eyes, said, 'Don't worry about crossing to help
Gillacomghain. If he got to the north coast at all, every other man of
battle-age in both Caithness and Orkney is lying there waiting for him. Tell
my lord Crinan when you go south. And anyone else who might be
interested.'

The ship was empty but for the men standing round himself, silent now, and Thorfinn's band, who had dropped back also. Carl Thorbrandsson said, 'A Northumbrian always knows—not when he is beaten, but when to take the sensible course. No doubt we shall meet again.' His trumpeter, responding to his upraised hand, was already blowing the retreat. Amid the confusion ahead, faces turned. He hesitated.

Thorfinn said, 'I think, by right of conquest, this vessel is probably mine. The longship ahead has not yet disengaged, if you want to join her.'

Carl Thorbrandsson made a kind of a bow and, guarded by his men, made what dignified progress he could down the empty boat, and up to the prow, and over to the next boat that belonged to him. Very soon after that, scrambling and fighting still, the men of both sides resorted to their own ships, and the vessels began slowly to part, the oars thrusting out in threes and fours until finally every ship still remaining was under way.

Eight turned south, into the night, and their sails, which they ran up directly, bloomed and dissolved on the black sea like foam. Two drove ashore and were later redeemed by David of Deerness and his family, who buried what they contained: the Northumbrian bodies in the turf and the brooches and arm-bands and finger-rings in the chapel, for the glory of God. The weapons and the ship-hulls and timbers they allowed the Earl Thorfinn to have, later, for a consideration.

The five ships of Earl Thorfinn and the flagship of Carl Thorbrandsson, from which he struck the banner, thereupon moved round to Sandwick, there to unload the dead and the injured, and to apportion what booty there might be. They lit fires on the shore and ate and rested while the longships were being set to rights, with Thorfinn moving about them, his long shadow roving over the shore, and their faces, and the turfy slopes up to the hall of Thorkel's father and all the booth-shapes round the big steading.

The women, come out of hiding, brought them bread in baskets, and new-slaughtered beef, and lard and cheeses, but only one cask of ale, for there was work still to be done. And although his cousins and friends shouted to their chieftain Thorfinn, and congratulated him and themselves, and made colourful boasts, it might have been seen that the Earl had come quite a long way from the ungainly boy who ran down the oarshafts at Chester and got an affectionate blow on the ear for it, mixed with insults.

To Arnór Thordarson, watching with the bright skaldic eye, it seemed that Thorfinn stood outside the camaraderie of common success, untouched, as he was untouched in the flesh. From fourteen, he had sailed and watched men kill and be killed: gathering taxes was no sinecure, and some said no legitimate business either. Boys travelled on all the longships and often women as well. You watched a youngster change from his first callow fears to the time when he strode into battle as a man should, tasting danger like salt, exulting in his own skills; ready if need be to find his grave in a place of courage and honour, knowing his fame would be sung by the skalds, and his sons would do no less after him.

Of the boy Thorfinn, he knew only what others had told him: of a silent, withdrawn child of few bodily gifts, but those worked upon like the dwarves

working metal, until he could hold his own in any of the half-homes or
half-wars he might find himself in.

His years with King Canute had broken that sequence. What his men saw
now was what they had to lead them, and they thought it adequate, Arnór
judged. But hardly the joyous, furious rogue, the rip-roaring Earl, the wild,
self-seeking, irresistible figure his father Sigurd had been.

In the middle of the night, when they were ready, Thorfinn sent round all
his men with word to go to the ships, and this time, when Arnór asked, he was
allowed to go with him.

The wind still blew in the right way for Thorfinn's purpose, and they all
knew the dark waters too well to miss the way, or mistake the currents, or be
swept into the Swelchie whirlpool, as they said had been Earl Hakon's fate.
They were making down past the islands of Orkney and across the firth to the
island of Stroma, where a beacon would be lit as they passed.

So Arnór knew. But still it was strange as they passed the low, black shape
of the island and saw, soft orange, the fire bloom on its slope and then, as they
left it behind, spooning its light in the wave-troughs, another smudge of
colour far ahead on the mainland. Thorfinn said, 'Gillacomghain is there in
Thurso. And Thorkel and his men are round them, hidden, waiting for us.'

'Prince,' said Arnór. 'I have made a verse.'

The youth Thorfinn did not look at him, or thank him, or express any of
those things due from an earl to his personal skald. 'Keep it,' he said, 'until we
have won more than half the battle. If we win it.'

'Lord, how could you fail?' said Arnór dutifully; and sent a curse through
the air to his foster-mother.

If it reached its destination at all, it was unlikely to disturb Fridgerd Gamli's
daughter, who in a long life had survived a good deal more than her
foster-son's petulance. In any case, her attention at present was on something
much more compelling: on a boy of twenty-one who had found his way, some
would say by her arts, some would say by no very great coincidence, to the
cluster of huts where the young and old of Thorfinn's household had taken
refuge until this day's work should be over.

To Sulien, nothing seemed out of the way. He had watched Thorfinn's ships
cross in the sunset to Orkney, and then had come here to find a spring he had
noticed, for he was thirsty and had no wish for the ale-horn. Then, as he
stooped to drink, a voice spoke. 'And good evening to you, Soulinus son of
Gingomarus, *y doethaf or Brytanyeit*. As it is a good evening, I hope, for your
friends.'

Wisest of the Bretons, she had called him: an old woman's mockery; except
that the little he knew of the wise-woman Fridgerd, sitting now, he dimly saw,
at the spring-side, had not led him to think her malicious. He said, 'I hope it is
a good evening for us all,' and bent to take his drink. When he had done, she
said, 'Sit, if you are in no haste. You are not needed yet.'

He was not sure what she meant. He said, feeling his way, 'It is not my
battle. Nor, I suppose, is it yours.'

'The blood of this land runs in Iceland,' she said. He saw she was smiling. She said, 'I have no quarrel with you, or your church.'

He was aware, then, of his youth, and of all that he had laid himself open to by his headstrong flight to the north when he might have sailed safely to Ireland. He said quietly, 'Did you cast the runes for him?'

She sat very still, her smile gone, her face kindly and serious. 'For the Earl Thorfinn? No. For myself, yes. They tell me that he will win half this battle.'

Sulien said, 'Did you tell him?'

'He did not need to be told,' Fridgerd Gamli's daughter said. 'Nor do you. There is no magic, either black or white, about that. I shall be here only a short time, but another like me will come. And when you have gone, there will be others to follow you. It is for you to remember that he finds himself in a land where people speak with two tongues and worship in different ways.'

'But he cannot follow two creeds,' Sulien said.

'At present,' said Arnór's foster-mother, 'he believes only one thing and thinks of one thing. But one day he is going to stand and look about him and wonder why he was born into two worlds. A small thing for a serf. A perilous thing for a clever man and the families he holds in his hand.'

She was wise. She had put into words his reason for coming. He said, 'There are monasteries here. I could find work to do for a while.'

Her hands relaxed, smoothing her skirts, dim in the dark as she made to get up. She was smiling again. 'Five years would be enough,' she said. 'Four, perhaps. You have seen your successor.'

He was still staring up at her as she rose and left him.

He must have fallen asleep by the spring, and was dreaming of a great noise, like a battle at sea or the public acclaim of a multitude, when he woke and heard the distant sound that had woven itself into his sleep: the noise indeed of a great crowd, but not one of acclaim. The sound of many men at death-grip with one another, filling the summer night sky over Thurso. And then as, starting up, he ran to the settlement, he saw the low clouds to the east take each to itself a tinge of brightening colour, hazed by a feathering column of smoke.

The trap had been sprung. The sleeping army of Moray had been surrounded and challenged.

Had Sulien been with Thorkel, instead of asleep by the spring in those hours, he would have seen him lying as he had lain all day with his men, out of sight of the bay, and of the big timber hall, the collection of cabins and stockyards and barns, the one or two steadings that made up the settlement known as Thurso, on the rising ground between the beach and the river Skinandi.

There, within the tall oak stockade round the Earl's empty hall and its grazings, lay Gillacomghain and his army, with his scouts posted around. The horses they had taken inside, and the animals they had collected to feed them, and the carts with their tents and their meal-bags, their ale and their weapons, dragged all the way from the east coast at Wick, where they had been landed. There were women with them as well: news that Thorkel had received with annoyance, for women involved in a battle caused nothing but trouble. He hoped, giving the requisite warnings to his company, that the other side would have enough common sense, at the least, to give them their own quarters.

Already, Gillacomghain and his men would have been moved to wonder, perhaps, at the empty house-steads in Wick and the lack of resistance; but, after all, the fleet had brought them in daylight and, thus warned, the Caithness people might not unreasonably have taken to their heels.

So Gillacomghain had marched unhindered to Thurso and entered it, and now could afford the luxury of a night's sleep, however dissatisfied he might be with the conquest. For of course he had found Thurso empty as well, and Thorfinn vanished: escaped to Orkney and gone to earth no doubt on his lands before the Berwick fleet had time to arrive and prevent it.

Perhaps Gillacomghain or his scouts had seen Carl's Northumbrian ships sail to Orkney before the light failed. He could not know how they had fared. But it must seem certain that, once escaped, Thorfinn would hardly bring back a handful of men to confront the whole army of Moray now in possession here. Gillacomghain might expect that his ally Carl, having chased Thorfinn to Orkney, might call here at Thurso before sailing homewards. More of Carl he could not expect. The land in dispute was not Orkney, and the overlords of Orkney had given no sanction for a landing here.

So might Gillacomghain think. But Thorkel, knowing better, watched the sun sink and counted the time during which, there to the north, the ships of Thorfinn and of the fleet from the south must be engaged. The night grew dark, and then a little lighter, and then, brought from man to man, the message he wanted.

The beacon was burning on Stroma. As he had ordered, on the opposite headland, another was glowing in answer. The man who touched it off would be able to see, by its light, the dim sails of Thorfinn's fleet approaching, with five longships or fewer, with Thorfinn aboard or left dead or injured at Sandwick.

In theory, it did not matter. In theory, it meant that the seaborne half of the Moray invasion had been defeated, and that the only enemy left was the one lying here, round the haven of Thurso.

When he might have been needed, Thorfinn had gone to the court of the Saxons. It was as well, Thorkel thought, that Caithness had a man of experience at hand for such battles as this. Whatever had happened at sea, Thorfinn's men had one success behind them and would no doubt be glad enough to see someone else take the brunt of the fighting next time. Indeed, there was no point in waiting.

He said as much to his second in command, who happened to be Skeggi, and naturally Skeggi agreed. So Thorkel rose and sent his fire-message round, and in no time at all the men were on their feet and dispersing, and the Moray outposts had been silently disposed of and the stockade approached and ringed by all the able men of Caithness and Orkney here under his command, to move at his order.

Then the well-paid man inside did what he was paid to do and, on the signal, drew back the bolts of the gateway, and the horns blew and brayed all round the army, and, screaming, Thorkel and his men hurled themselves in, shield upon shield, sword upon sword.

The hoot of the horns came over the water, and the shouting that followed.

Thorfinn stood, saying nothing, in the prow; but the other men in the dragon-ship crowded and pointed, and on the other ships as well, so that their course grew erratic and the captured vessel had to be thrust off with oars to avoid a glancing collision.

Arnór said, 'What has happened?'

'Thorkel has attacked,' Thorfinn said. 'It is a thing he does, when he is sure of being successful.'

By the time they got to the shore, the hall was on fire: a sky-running river of flame that became a golden ladder and gradually a collapsed heap of angles. The light made molten gold of the dragon-head as Thorfinn's *Grágás* slid up on the sand, and burnished his helmet and the rest of the gold on his person. Drunk with victory, the land army streamed down the seaweed and shingle towards him. His other ships, flocking to shore, were already half empty. Their crews, splashing into the water, floundered up through the sand, excitement colliding with excitement. In the middle of his men, on the higher ground, stood Thorkel.

The boy, as far as could be seen under the monstrous golden helmet, was unhurt. Thorkel said, 'Gillacomghain is dead.'

'Oh,' said Thorfinn. He sprang forward and stood looking down at his foster-father while the crowd called and jostled about them. He said, 'How?'

'In the hall,' Thorkel said. 'With fifty of his own men. We set fire to it. Only his household stayed with him. We let the Moraymen, the friends of Findlaech, come out if they wished. They're all there, penned in under guard with the rest of the army. They stopped fighting very soon. They stopped fighting at once, come to that, when they saw Gillacomghain was dead.'

The heat from the hall reached them where they stood. Thorfinn looked at it. Someone in the crowd said, 'You didn't let all of them come out if they wished, then. Tell him about the one whose head you cut off. The Earl of Caithness, he was going to be.'

Thorfinn looked away from the hall then. 'Maddan?' he said. 'Have you killed the nephew as well?'

'I killed everyone I knew of who stood against you, or might stand against you one day,' said Thorkel Fóstri. 'I thought Gillacomghain should burn.'

'You did it without me,' said Thorfinn. 'Why? Was it Sulien?'

What Sulien might have to do with it was beyond Thorkel Fóstri. Around him, he could feel the men becoming restive. They had done well and should have their due, even if he received none. He said, 'We thought we would save you the trouble. Didn't we, lads?'

And at that at least the boy came to his senses and began to say and do the things required of him, so that soon matters were as they should be and the ale-casks could be opened and the victory celebrated round the bright-glowing heat of the hall.

Thorfinn went to the Moraymen and spoke to them. 'Your Mormaer Gillacomghain is dead. I am the heir of his uncle Findlaech, whom he killed. Whom will you have for your Mormaer?'

There was a spokesman. There always was. He stood forward and said, 'We will have you, my lord.'

'Whom do you speak for?' said Thorfinn.

'For us all, my lord. We will swear, if you like.'

'I will take your oath in Forres,' Thorfinn said. 'When I come there to my stepfather's house. And you will come with me, to tell your friends what you have seen and what you have promised. What my stepfather did for you, I will do. Act to me as you acted to him, and no man will suffer.'

Sulien, arriving, caught that, and saw that he had come when the triumph was nearly over. There had been no shortage of voices on the way to tell him what had happened. The runes had been right.

Then Thorfinn turned and saw him and said, 'Your condition, as you see, has been obeyed to the letter.' For the first time, there was an emotion somewhere in the alarming, deep voice. Sulien saw that it was anger.

Then Thorkel Fóstri said, 'What about the women? We've put them over there.'

Thorfinn said, 'He had camp-girls with him?'

'Not only camp-girls. Some of good family, including his own. To make the point, I suppose, that he was settling here.'

The place Thorkel had indicated was a good timber-built house on the same rising ground as the hall. The family it belonged to had arrived there and were apparently trying to get in: the door had been barred from the inside, and an argument was going on. Thorfinn said, 'Go and eat, my foster-father. I'll see to the women.' Thorkel stopped, and then turned and walked elsewhere.

Sulien said, 'Can you manage all the women on your own, or shall I come?'

'Come if you like,' Thorfinn said. He got to the door of the house and spoke pleasantly enough to the folk outside. He knew them, and they gave him a hearing and after a while turned aside, grumbling, to find other shelter. Then he stood alone but for Sulien beside him and, raising his voice, gave a brief order.

'Unbar the door or I will burn it down.'

For a moment, there was silence. Then a woman's voice whimpered and was cut off; and another murmured. Footsteps came near, and there was a jarring sound of wood on wood from inside. Then the door swung slowly open.

Inside, there was a small fire. But the light from outside was much brighter, washing into the doorway and through the windows from the embers of Gillacomghain's funeral pyre. In its light, Thorfinn stood as he had come from the sea, with his face smeared with sweat and dirt, and his ring-mail dulled with other men's blood. He had given his helm to someone flattered to carry it, and its weight had left a circle of red round his brow and his flattened, salt-tangled hair. He was so tall that he had to bend to stare into the gloom of the house.

Faces appeared, underlit by the fire, pulled into unnatural shapes by fear and exhaustion and grief. Thorfinn said, 'Which of you is Ingibjorg, Bergljot's daughter, mother of Luloecen?'

A voice somewhere answered, 'I am.'

Sulien saw Earl Thorfinn turn towards the sound, but could not see, either, which of the women had spoken.

The Earl Thorfinn said, 'Ingibjorg, Bergljot's daughter, I have to tell you that Gillacomghain your husband is dead.'

A rustling ran through the group and then was stilled. From the back of the house, someone rose and picked her way forward to the light: a tall girl with uncovered hair the colour of ox-blood, not very long, and a tunic robe of dyed linen, creased and grimy with charcoal. There were circles under her eyes, which were colourless, translucent as pond-water. She said, 'Then I suppose I am your prisoner. Who are you?'

It was not a question he was often asked now. He said, 'I am Thorfinn of Orkney, Earl of Caithness.' The tone was the same as when he was addressing the shadows. It was, Sulien observed, perfectly courteous so far as it went.

There was nothing particularly critical in the girl's gaze either. She merely looked and sounded exhausted. She said, 'I see. Then you are going to hold me for ransom?'

'Ransom?' said Earl Thorfinn. He sounded surprised and a little impatient. 'No. I am going to marry you.'

ELEVEN

FOOLS THAT THEY were, Thorfinn's men of course thought that the great days of Orkney were back again, with a lusty young Earl who could thrash a Northumbrian fleet twice the size of his own and then throw his enemy's widow over his shoulder together with the province she and her son were heir to. She was, it was agreed, getting a bargain; for, although no one thought him a virgin, she would be the first of his wives and the senior one, at least for a while. And it might be that, after Gillacomghain, she could even teach him a thing or two.

Looked at sensibly, such a marriage was not only the natural but the sensible resolution of the feud between Thorfinn and the murdering rulers of Moray. Nothing could give more offence, wherever they might be, to the shades of Gillacomghain and his brother. It would put Thorfinn in possession of the whole of his stepfather's Moray. It would give him an Arnmødling wife kin to Thorkel Fóstri himself; one of the very girls he had considered long ago, in the days of Kalv's match-making. Of course, Thorfinn needed a wife, and the girl was an excellent choice. Thorkel Fóstri did not know, therefore, why he was angry, unless it was over this foolhardiness his foster-son showed in not taking counsel beforehand.

The Breton from Llanbadarn, Thorkel noticed, was as disconcerted as himself and, after coming away from Thorfinn's company with a red face later that day, had not come near him again. So all one could say, Thorkel supposed, was that the father's blood was coming out in the boy, as well it might; and that at least Orkney would have a man for an Earl when Brusi died, which seemed very likely to happen this year.

So Thorkel Fóstri told himself; but the situation still did not please him, and it was with divided feelings that he agreed to travel to Norway to see his cousin Finn Arnason about the drawing up of the marriage contract for Finn's daughter Ingibjorg, while his foster-son paraded off south and made himself Mormaer of Moray. Thorkel took with him the extra Northumbrian ship, freighted with the first threshing of bere, to sell up the fjord at Nídarós while he was there. In the event, he was glad to have a pretext for his voyage, since his cousin Finn Arnason, when he called on him at Austråt, proved far from inclined to invite attention to such an alliance.

In fact, Thorkel was disturbed at the changes in Finn. He had supported the losing side in King Olaf, of course, and had shared his exile in Russia. Returning he had fought for King Olaf again, even against his own brothers.

True, the family Arnmødling was famous for looking after its own, and the same brothers had taken care of Finn and the others after King Olaf died. But Finn, it was evident, could not get used to King Canute's conquest of Norway, and the canonisation of Olaf had hardly made matters better. In fact, there was unrest throughout Trøndelagen, where people resented the new Danish laws Canute's wife-regent had presented them with. And if there was to be a revolt, Finn Arnason's hall was the first place Canute would look for the culprit.

So Finn Arnason, who seemed to have lost weight, and who had taken to peering like a man very much older, welcomed his cousin Thorkel to his board, but said, once they were alone and Thorkel had explained his mission, 'So you wish your foster-son to marry my daughter. Is this wise?'

'It has nothing to do with me,' Thorkel said. 'I am nothing now but his marshal. I do as I am told.'

And at that Finn drew down his brows in the way he looked at everything now, and said, 'If that's true, you have chosen a fine time to abandon him. You would let him risk Canute's displeasure by a union like this?'

Thorkel admired the silver Herakles on his beaker. He said, 'The girl is Kalv's niece as well. Gillacomghain found that no disadvantage. Neither did Canute. But even if Kalv were to change sides again, Thorfinn would still go on with this marriage. It has nothing to do with us, or with Canute, or with Norway.'

'He *wants* the girl?' Finn Arnason said. 'That is always a complication.'

'If she walked into his house, he would have little idea who she was,' Thorkel said. 'He wanted Gillacomghain dead because Gillacomghain murdered his stepfather and stole his inheritance of Moray. But although his stepfather named him as heir, he has no claim by blood. By marrying Gillacomghain's widow, he will make Moray his beyond question, until her sons, by Gillacomghain or himself, are old enough to succeed. I tell you,' Thorkel said, 'he will take the girl, whether you want it or not.'

Finn said, 'I have no desire to fall foul of Canute because Thorfinn does.'

'Then withhold your consent,' Thorkel said. 'Men will hear of it. And, as I've said, it will make no difference. Your daughter will be rich, and the mother of powerful sons. I'm sure you have heard the news. Earl Brusi is dead. As the last living son of old Sigurd, Thorfinn is sole Earl of Orkney.'

'It is all I wanted him to have,' Thorkel said, and moved the cup between his hands. 'With Caithness, if he could keep it. Now he holds the mainland of Alba, from the Dee to the northernmost coast: the old kingdom of the north, that the kings of the north and the south have fought over ever since the Gaels came out of Ireland.

'He has no care for it. He has no notion of ruling it. He will treat it as a source of tax-gathering raids, as Sigurd treated Caithness and the Western Isles. But these are a different people, and he and Orkney may be sorry for it.

All this,' said Thorkel, 'the burning of Findlaech has done. There may come a day when Orkney wishes that Thorfinn had burned with him.'

Finn said, 'Every son, sooner or later, leaves his father. He may not be the worse for it. Nor may the father.'

Thorkel's hand closed hard on his beaker, and opened again. 'And daughters?' he said. 'Perhaps you should allow them some worthy proverb as well?'

By that time, it was not wholly correct that, had his intended wife stepped through the house, the boy Thorfinn would not have known her. In fact, the night after his foster-father departed, Thorfinn threw out her servants and bedded her, as was only prudent.

Her innermost views on the matter the girl Ingibjorg kept to herself: the days of hair-cropping were over. For two years, Gillacomghain had had nothing to bring to his marriage, and it would have been folly to risk bearing to anyone else.

This boy from Orkney was not a Wend or a Lapp, and had been reared by her father's own cousin. Her inheritance was rich, and the word *abduction* meant no more than this: that a man should lie with an heiress until he had got her with child, or to warn off other possible predators for one month or two until he could make a firm contract.

In this case, she supposed, the Earl of Orkney was making sure of her in case she or Gillacomghain's sole heir, her baby, fell into other hands between now and the foster-father's return with the settlement.

It irritated her that the night the youth had chosen should be the night of their arrival in Inverness, and that the sleeping-quarters she had shared with Gillacomghain should be those he invaded, sending the women squalling out to where, distantly, she could hear her son calling. Her new owner looked preoccupied and unkempt, as if he had been extremely busy and in half an hour would be so again, as soon as the present matter was over. He shut the door. 'The women say you have finished your courses,' he said.

She sat on the bed-blanket in her shift and watched him half-undress. He kept on his tunic and made no effort to coax her to take off her linen. She said, watching him untie his leggings, 'Or this would have happened to me a day or two sooner, on shipboard? What if I deny that this ever took place?' The distant cackle of the women made nonsense of the remark.

'Everyone knows it is happening,' said the Earl. Three days ago, he had had her husband burned alive in his hall. As he crossed to the bed, his height and the candle-shadows together plunged the room into black, wheeling troll-shapes. She drew her feet back on the mattress before he should have to lift them, and the mattress straw under her creaked and muttered under his weight on top of her own.

She tried to show neither pleasure nor displeasure; and he behaved as he should. Since there never had been any preliminaries, she did not miss them. Then, promptly, the business was over and he was dressing again. She felt bewildered, and then angry when she thought of the women out there, waiting. She said, 'And when will you have a spare five minutes again?'

In no way did that sound like a request. It came nearer, indeed, to an accusation. He had heard the women as well, and ought to remember she was Finn Arnason's daughter, and not one of the girl-slaves they supplied him with. He was sitting, a boot in his hand. He said, 'What need? Now I have a claim on any child you may find yourself with. Failing such an event, it is customary, I believe, to offer a widow the privacy of her bed for a year. You may count on so much. After that, should five minutes prove fruitful, there should be no doubts, at least, over the fathering. How old are you exactly?'

'Six years younger than you are,' she said. She sat up and pulled one of the woollen blankets over her shoulders. She was nearly seventeen.

'So there is plenty of time. Why are you angry?' said Thorfinn. 'I have been on your father's list of suitors and you have been on Thorkel's from the first years of our childhood. We might each have done worse.'

'Are there no mirrors in your house?' said Ingibjorg. 'If you stopped paying some of your Irish girls, one of them might tell you the truth. A boy's attempt is a boy's attempt.'

'I must confess,' Thorfinn said, 'that if that was an attempt, I should be wary of meeting with a success. If you consider your charms deserve better, then why not pour me some ale and entertain me, instead of accepting the traffic and then complaining about it?'

'The ale is over there,' she said. She left untouched the beaker he brought her. He took his own across to the stool he had occupied before and sat down and sipped. She said, 'Thorkel says your father had many wives.'

'He thought he needed many sons,' the Earl of Orkney said. 'But things went wrong, and most of them lived, while his land-holding shrank. My grandfather of Alba, on the other hand, tended to have one wife at a time and breed weaklings. There is a fine balance, not always easy to hit. Who looks after Luloecen?'

'Three women from Halfdan's household,' Ingibjorg said. She knew what was coming. Her grandfather Halfdan had been a half-brother of King Olaf and a grandson of Erik Bloodaxe. She said, 'It doesn't matter to me if you want different nurses. He has no special attachments.'

'Sulien said he should be brought up with men,' Thorfinn said.

'At three?' she said. 'Sulien is your young Breton churchman, isn't he? Hasn't he told you that if you are to hold Christian Moray you will have to pay lip-service at least to the Celtic church and call yourself by your civilized name, not your heathen one? It is years since anyone called me Ingibjorg here.'

'Let me guess,' Thorfinn said. 'You were baptised Margaret, and the family preferred Meregrota, so that at home and in the north you bear the good Nordic wife-name of Groa?'

'Someone told you,' she said.

'I hope they were right,' said Thorfinn. 'I should much prefer Groa to Ingibjorg. It takes less effort.'

'I am sure you have none to waste,' said the girl. She waited and then said,

'Thorkel says that once you have Moray you will have no idea what to do with it.'

'What need I do with it?' Thorfinn said. 'It will support me and my household, and I shall visit it from time to time. My home is a ship, not the mainland, and my hearth is in Orkney, not Alba.'

He left soon after that, and the women thought he had hurt her, because she was frowning and silent.

Instead of going back at once to what he had been doing, which was arguing with Gillacomghain's steward, Thorfinn went and found Sulien.

He was in the smithy, deep in talk with two other churchmen while the smith patched an abbot's sword and put an edge back on their knives. At the look on the Earl's face, the young Breton rose and, leaving his companions, joined him outside. Sulien said, 'Well? Everyone in the place knows what you have been doing. Did she scratch you?' He could not bring himself to smile.

Earl Thorfinn said, 'She's not a nun, you know. It'll be two months now before it's plain whether or not she is carrying, and no one else will try to take her till then.'

'I know all the arguments,' Sulien said. 'What did you want me for?'

He wanted the Earl to say that it didn't matter and to go away. Instead, Earl Thorfinn said, 'Have you seen that girl in daylight?'

'No,' Sulien said. 'She was under a blanket all the way here, because of the rain. Why? Even if she has two heads, I don't suppose it matters to anyone.'

This time, he was successful, and the Earl did turn and walk away. It was surprising, then, that Sulien found himself taking the trouble to catch up and fall into step beside him and say, 'Look. It's just that we are all human. Even young women.'

The black brows did not soften. 'If you say so,' the Earl answered shortly. After a moment, he added, 'If she had two heads, there would be nothing to worry about.'

'But she hasn't. So?' Sulien said.

Thorfinn stopped. 'So she's handsome,' he said. 'The handsomest girl I've ever seen in my life, and that includes Canute's court. How am I going to hold Moray with that running loose, turning men foolish?'

Sulien stared at him. For no reason that he could understand, a burden shifted. Laughter welled within him and spilled over. The Earl, he saw, was waiting patiently for him to recover. The Earl said, 'I know. The finest jest of the season. All I wanted was—'

'All you wanted was a reliable breeder,' Sulien said. 'I wonder what it is that you've got? Did she tell you that you needed a bath? Did she say what your face reminded her of?'

'She would have been unique if she didn't,' Thorfinn said. 'As to the bath, I have one on Saturdays. Saxons don't have them at all. Celts, I am given to understand, wade in up to the neck in cold rivers and stand intoning psalms. You don't approve of marriage?'

'On the contrary,' Sulien said. 'I propose to marry as soon as my studies are over. By that time, I shall know what to avoid. You have no idea how much I am learning.'

The Earl's face had relaxed. He aimed a blow at Sulien, which did not quite connect, and went off to find the steward and finish his argument.

Opportunities to study the reliable breeder were not lacking in the four weeks it took Thorkel to get back from Norway, for the girl Groa emerged from her bed-blanket to resume in every particular the life she had led when her husband Gillacomghain was alive, with the only difference that her son Luloecen's attendants had been sent off back home, and other nurses found, of the house of Findlaech. Thorfinn himself never came near her again, being mostly away with his housecarls cross-quartering Moray in the cause of removing any lingering doubts about who the new Mormaer might be. Some settlements were burned, but not many, and a few friends of Gillacomghain found themselves hanged. The weather was very wet.

Thorkel came back in September on a difficult wind, and bearing with him two messages: one containing the formal refusal of the bride's father to allow the marriage, and the other containing the informal assurance of the bride's father that if the marriage took place, no compensation would be exacted.

No member of the bride's family, as was natural, came with him to bless the union. The presence of the bride's uncle Kalv Arnason, on his way to collect a bad debt in Waterford, was purely coincidental. It was also bad luck for Thorkel Amundason, who felt he had troubles enough of his own without standing daily up to the knees in the undeviating stream of his cousin Kalv's complaints.

To find oneself unexpectedly guilty of murdering a saint was no doubt a sobering experience for any man. The effect on Kalv had been to make him gloomy but no less inquisitive. To look at, he was very little different from the agile young kinsman who had nipped ashore every spring at Caithness until Canute got hold of him, or even the Kalv of eleven years before who had helped King Olaf burn the heathens at Sparbu and witness the twelve-year-old Thorfinn swearing homage to Norway.

Kalv had not set eyes on Thorfinn since, but reckoned that with all that land he was quite a reasonable catch for Finn to have landed for a widowed daughter, especially through the back door, as it were, with Kalv himself doing all the unpleasant part such as going to the wedding. He then broke off to lament the miseries of life in Trøndelagen with the Yule-tax, and the fish-tax, and the tax on people who went to and from Iceland, and the new law that the bonder had to build the King's houses for him on all his farms.

Worst of all, of course, was the fact that no one could even leave Norway without Alfiva's permission. Kalv even recited the first lines of a little poem about Alfiva, which began:

> '*Alfiva's time our sons will*
> *Long remember; then ate we*
> *Food more fit for oxen,*

> *Shavings the fare of he-goats.*
> *It was not thus when the noble*
> *Olaf governed the Norsemen;*
> *Then could we all boast of*
> *Corn-filled barns and houses . . .'*

and then proceeded to some indecencies absent from the original verse, to do with King Olaf and King Canute's wife Alfiva, which were not only witty but even possibly true. Then, apparently cheered, he returned to the topic of marriage.

'Tell me: who is your foster-son Earl going to get for the wedding Mass? Grimkell can't do it, and I don't suppose Thorfinn wants to ask King Canute or his grandfather's bishop to oblige. I hear,' said Kalv, 'that there is a handsome young chaplain from Wales, or was I mistaken? And, of course, Gillacomghain had a priest.'

'Unfortunately,' Thorkel said, 'Gillacomghain's priest got burned with Gillacomghain in Thurso, and Sulien, who is not as handsome as all that, is only in deacon's orders. He'll get a prior from somewhere. I've told him to have it on the tribute-hill at Forres, where he can feast all the district leaders, at least from the north half of Moray. Then he'll need to take the girl south and display her.'

'I'll arrange the feast, if you like,' Kalv said. 'Ølve used to hold good ones, before he was killed.'

It seemed to Thorkel as good a way as any to get his mind off Queen Alfiva, so he left him with the ship's clerk, making lists. It occurred to him that for the first time for many years he had not been told that this was a bargain he must have cause to regret.

He saw the irony of it. For this year, for the first time, Kalv would have been right.

After that, nothing was as Thorkel Fóstri expected.

As the wind, relenting at last, let his ship sweep under sail towards the white stretches of sand that marked the mouth of the river Findhorn, he saw lying inland not only the blustered smoke of the wood-and-wattle settlement he remembered, but the gleam of new timber ringing the fortified hill of Forres beyond it, and within that, a long thatched roof he did not recognise, above which blew a flock of bright and unfamiliar banners. At the mouth of the river, there was a new building among the fishermen's huts, from which a couple of men put off in a skiff and, boarding, steered the helmsman round the skeined sandy course of the river. Below the hill, the old jetty at the crossing was already manned, and at its far end they could see a scattered party of men moving downhill from the stockade towards them.

Earl Thorfinn was among them. On the planks of the jetty, heaving in a familiar way beneath his feet, Thorkel said, 'You haven't met for a long time. Kalv, this is my lord Thorfinn of Orkney.'

He hardly needed to say it. The men round his foster-son were well dressed, but no one else wore a tunic of Cathay silk from the markets east of the Middle Sea, with three arm-bands of gold with dragons' heads beading their ridges, and a fur-lined scabbard netted with gold-work and embracing a sword-pommel of Saxon workmanship. Above it was the stormy, remembered face with the bright-coloured skin and blown sable hair. Thorfinn said, 'Welcome to White Ireland. You're smaller than I remembered.'

Kalv, who was not notable for his height, smiled and said, 'When we last met, you were crying and running about because your stepfather had died. I'm glad we meet in happier days.'

'Since Thorkel here killed Gillacomghain? Ah, he burned like a Trøndelagen man's conscience, I'm told,' Thorfinn said. 'And now I am to have you for uncle. You have a fine niece. Ever good to old men, ever good to young men, as Thorkel Fiflski said.'

Thorkel gazed at his foster-son. Beside him, he could feel Kalv pause and change mental feet, like a horse in mid-canter. Kalv said, 'I shall not be ashamed to own you. I expected to find you in pigtails, and your wife chewing limpets for ground-bait.'

'Until tomorrow,' Thorfinn said, 'you would be wrong to call her anything but a concubine, and barren at that. But after the morning-ale she will be living in wedlock again. Bring your shipmaster ashore and join in the merrymaking. There is a berth for your ship at Invereren, if you will send it back, and meat and ale on shore for your friends, and somewhere to sleep for the night. You yourself will want to stay with your niece, I make no doubt.'

The instructions passed to the ship, they had begun to walk up towards the hill. 'It is easily seen,' said Kalv, 'that you had word we were coming, when you have a sufficiency of meat and of guests to have your wedding tomorrow. I have no blessing from Finn to bring you: no doubt you know that also.'

'So long as you bring a *heimanfylgja* of sorts, even so small that it would fit under a fingernail, and I give you my *mundr* of the same order, the marriage is legal, they tell me, and assorts with the quality of her first husband better than any other bride-bargain I can think of,' said Thorfinn. 'There is her house. I will have you brought to the church-porch tomorrow. Kneel when other folk kneel and stand up when they stand: all I ask of you is that you put a cross next your name in the Gospel-page after, with the rest of us.'

'Who should stop me?' said Kalv. 'Will the child your stepson be there? I hear my niece and Gillacomghain made a sorcerer's maggot together.' He stumbled. 'What was that?'

Two eyes of a clear, empty blue looked up into and through his, from a child's face. 'He is Luloecen,' the child said. 'He will eat you; but not until you are dead.'

Kalv slipped his hand inside his shirt, to remember too late that he had put on his hammer pendant instead of his cross pendant today.

That was the fault of this Thorfinn, the half-heathen. He smiled, showing his teeth at the child, and turned to say something cutting to the Earl, but found he had gone off to the stockade gate, whistling. The maggot-child put up its hand, and he took it, carefully, and was led into the house of his niece its mother, the bride.

The long thatched building he had seen from the ship was indeed new, Thorkel found: a hall made of split oak trunks smoothed inside with an adze and let into an oak sill at the bottom. The sills and lintels were carved, and inside, the walls were covered to waist height by embroidered cloths dyed in scarlet and white. The upper parts, where the shelving allowed, were hung with shields, in shapes and colours Thorkel did not recognise. The hall was also full of strangers, or so it seemed to him at first. Then he began to see many faces from long ago, from Findlaech's day, when Thorfinn used to come with his stepfather and his mother Bethoc, King Malcolm's daughter.

He said to Thorfinn, 'I forgot you were taught to be an engineer, down there with the Danes and the Saxons. Did you invite your grandfather or your brother Duncan? They seem the only ones missing.'

'Of course,' Thorfinn said. 'I sent their invitation off this very morning.'

Thorkel smiled, and studied his foster-son.

The sense of untrammelled vigour which had struck Kalv in the face at their first meeting had caused Thorkel to wonder as well in these few minutes' walk into the stockade. A man's marriage-eve might account for this change, if the bride were to his taste and much wanted. But not to Thorfinn, with his bride picked and notched like a ewe and then set aside, on this night as on any other, to wait out the months in her widow's bed until the purified stock might be bred from. Thorkel said, 'It seems that Orkney is well forgotten for the land of the Irishmen. You don't speak to me in Norse any more.'

Thorfinn turned and looked at him, and said, 'You need to eat, and to drink, and to meet my friends, who might consider becoming your friends also. Has age taken your memory? You used to speak nothing but Gaelic when you were with Findlaech as well.'

Then Thorkel tasted auk on his tongue, and came to himself, and went to meet his foster-son's friends. Among them was a young Saxon from Mercia called Alfgar, who had the wildest laugh in the hall and was possessed of a fund of scandal, smoking-new, about public life in the chapels of Winchester as well as in Chester, mixed with a few things Thorkel had never heard of, occurring in Man and in Wales. He knew Eachmarcach of Ireland, said Alfgar, and thought he had the loudest laugh of anyone he had ever met.

Thorkel took Alfgar with him and introduced him to the kinsfolk from Caithness and Orkney, whom he began to see were there too, drinking hard but not so much as to be impolite to the Moray chieftains and their women, who had put on their best cloaks and pins and had dropped into the half-Norse half-Gaelic tongue usual on such occasions. Skeggi had brought some Icelanders, including a man Thorkel knew called Isleifr, who had hair all over his body like otter pelt. Isleifr was in talk with the young Breton Sulien, but they drew Thorkel into their circle, and soon Isleifr was holding the floor with some tale of joyous catastrophe, while Sulien was taken off by the Saxon boy Alfgar, who seemed to know him of old.

It came to Thorkel that his foster-son must indeed have found a priest, for he seemed to recognise not one but a dozen faces of churchmen he remembered from monasteries as far south as Kinbathoc. Then Skeggi said, 'Come and meet the foreigners and help Sulien talk to them.'

And so he went to the top bench, where Thorfinn also was signalling him over, and where he sat down, as indicated, between an abbot from Devon and a bishop from Brittany. Thorfinn said, 'I am not your brave sort of man who would enter into a marriage alliance without informing King Canute's Queen, the Lady Emma. When she is in her dower town of Exeter, there is no one she leans on more than my lord Abbot Ealdred here, who rules Tavistock and all the trading-ships moving from thereabouts over the sea, as far south as the river Loire—or am I exaggerating?'

'You are,' said the Abbot. He was young for the position, and fresh-faced and solid of build, with an air about him that Thorkel could not quite put a name to, unless it were one of success. If he were a favourite of King Canute's chief wife, of course, he would be in want of nothing. The Bishop, in an accent which would have been at home either in Brittany or over the border with the Normans, said, 'And what lies will you tell of me?'

'Bishop Hamon of Aaron's Rock,' said Thorfinn, acknowledging quickly. 'His bishopric of Aleth is the neighbour of the one at Vannes that Sulien comes from.'

The Bishop smiled, and then, his gaze shifting, smiled more broadly still. He said, 'My friend Macbeth, I think your bride has just entered the door with her ladies. You must go and greet her.'

It was true. The roar of talk and laughter, suddenly wavering, had taken fresh life as men moved back, shouting, from the doorway, taking their women-folk smiling with them. And through the free passage walked the bride of tomorrow as well as yesterday, Ingibjorg-Groa, with her women and Kalv her uncle beside her.

Thorkel Fóstri had not seen her since she was thirteen, except in a dark hut beside her husband's smouldering pyre, or huddled under a blanket on the long trip from Caithness to Moray. According to Sulien: *She's the handsomest girl I've ever seen in my life*, Thorfinn had said; which was probably true but, considering Thorfinn's record with slaves, not impressive.

Looking at her now, with a sinking heart, Thorkel recognised that she was the handsomest girl he too had ever seen in a much longer life than Thorfinn's. In fact, in the very poverty of the phrase, he could judge Thorfinn's panic that night. He had expected to marry a tax-source, not this tall girl with eyebrows as black as his own, and smooth dark-red hair uncovered by linen, and sleeves of pleated white silk under a long crimson tunic, fringed and belted with gold, and valleyed between her two breasts by the gold chains holding her casket-brooch and her purse and her trinkets. She had worn a fur-lined cloak as well, pinned by a brooch that Thorkel recognised from the treasure-chest of Thorfinn's mother. The women took it off, and she moved smiling between the people pressing about her, with Kalv pushing behind, his face red.

A surprise for Kalv, then, this wedding-eve emergence, as perhaps it was a surprise for Thorfinn. Not only to possess a beauty, but a beauty freely displayed, stalking into the hall as though she owned it, as indeed in a sense she had once owned everything. In Thorkel's ear, Sulien of Llanbadarn said, 'Why so shocked? Because the bride has made an early appearance, or because the Mormaer of Moray is called Macbeth MacFindlaech?' His Norse was fluent already.

'He is not Macbeth son of Findlaech,' said Thorkel shortly. 'He is Macbeth Son of Life, or Macbeth son of his mother. His baptismal name had to please two cultures. They chose it carefully.'

'It is the common fashion,' said Sulien, 'to call a man's heir by the name of son, even though he were only a stepson. I would think a foster-son closer still. Better, says the tomb saying, a good foster-son than a bad son. Why is Kalv your cousin also angry?'

'Because we are not all sitting round a dung fire chewing suet,' Thorkel said. He knew Thorfinn was behind him, but he didn't know how close until he spoke in Gaelic in his ear.

'Fair, clever women are listening to thee, with sharp grey knives in their hands and gold on their breasts,' the Earl said. 'If you will turn round, I shall present you to your cousin's daughter. It's three or four years since you met, isn't it?'

Nearly four years since a grotesque, pregnant child had passed by, on her way to join her elderly husband. And from that child had grown this red-haired girl with the light eyes and the black brows saying to Thorfinn, 'Kalv my uncle is angry, naturally, because the Arnmødling family are not supposed to be supporting this wedding and you have seen fit to invite two emissaries of King Canute.'

'Amazing though it may seem,' said Thorfinn, 'King Canute and the Lady Emma are two different people. Why wear red?'

'Because I was uncertain whether Thor or the White Christ had your devotion these days,' the girl said. 'I see that in the matter of hangings you have nodded to each side.'

'Why not?' said Thorfinn. 'The essence of the matter is simple. When you hear me addressed as Macbeth you wear white, and the rest of the time dress in animal pelt. If both names occur in the same sentence, you should wear whatever best suits you for running in.'

With irritation, Thorkel found his head swinging from speaker to speaker, forlorn as a bear on an iceberg. He said, 'Don't believe him. Orkney, as you know very well, was brought back to Christ thirty years ago.'

'Oh, there are a few priests living in corners where there is food to be had,' said Thorfinn carelessly. 'But should a devotee of Thor or of Odin or the Golden Calf, for that matter, turn up, I am sure there would be an accommodation. The Abbot tells me that a church to St Olaf is being erected in Exeter. You must visit it, Kalv, on your next trading-trip.'

Thorkel found that Sulien, grinning, had laid a hand on his arm. 'Withdraw,' said Sulien, 'from the assize-field. And bring Kalv as well. If there is a weapon handy, either Thorfinn or his lady will use it.'

It was good advice. With some trouble, Thorkel detached his cousin and took him away to a group of Duncansby men. Kalv said, 'What I should like to have seen was the first meeting between that hell-child of hers and his stepfather.'

'Why does that child disturb you?' said Sulien. 'Thorfinn and he have a perfect understanding. Thorfinn treats him as if he were five million years old.'

It was a good answer, and a correct one, Thorkel knew. What Sulien had not described was the moment of that first meeting, when the tall young man had looked down at the white-haired child of three, and the child had looked up, its eyes reflecting the sky, and said, 'Since one day I shall carry you, will you carry me now?'

He turned, and had his drinking-horn filled, and then went to lend a hand with the feasting-boards.

The wedding service took place the following morning, under an awning outside the south door of the small, plastered church that had always been there, with the priest's hut, and to which Thorfinn had merely added a coat of white lime. The Prior of St Drostan's of Deer, bringing with him the altar-silver and vestments which Deer already owed to the generosity of Findlaech's family, spoke the necessary words, but made no address to the people, and the chanting of the five or six monks he had brought with him hardly rose above the squeals of the seagulls and the barking of dogs and the crying of children from Invereren. What was taking place, patently, was the legalising of a marriage alliance created for the proper disposal of property. No one objected.

Early the following morning, when the fires had died down in the roasting-pits and everyone else at last was asleep or drunk, the bride said to her husband, 'I was always taught that a sober man was a coward. Are you a coward?'

'I always considered myself one,' the Earl said. 'Until I found out what I was marrying. Perhaps, since we are not expected to sleep together, we should mark the occasion in some other way. What about this? If you will agree to refrain from an attempt on my life, I shall give you the lands of Coulter to hold for your son as your *morgen-gifu*. More, I shall promise to respect your health likewise.' In the dark, his black brows were raised, but he was not smiling.

The lands of Coulter, on both sides of the Dee, were the southernmost limits of his mormaership. They were also the wardlands that protected the north-driving pass of Strathbogie: the route an army from Forres might take if it wished to march south without trusting the coast and its shipping. The route an army from the south of the same mind might use if it wished to invade Mar and Moray.

Sinna and the rest of her women had already moved ahead into the house. Light still came from the hall and the other buildings on top of the hill, but fitfully, and there was almost no shouting. Here, where the ox-spits had been, the air was heavy with the smells of hot beef and grease and the fumes of ale and mead and wine and other emanations of celebrating humanity. Then the salt dawn wind stirred as they stood there, and a haze of white sand lifted and struck them, like the cakes and the flowers that should have been thrown at their bridal, and had been at Gillacomghain's. Groa said, 'You tempt me. The lord Crinan would marry a rich widow of any sort who held the key to Strathbogie.'

'Then you see how much I should rely on your promise,' he said.

In her light eyes, the dying fire glimmered. She did not answer. After a moment, he spoke again, in a different voice. 'Very well. I know that without me you have no protector, and that Canute would not allow Crinan to increase his power at present. I don't think, either, that you see a place for yourself back in Norway. If you took Gillacomghain to your bed, you will take me, next summer. I don't, therefore, need to rely on your promise. Nor do you need to doubt mine.'

'I wonder,' she said. 'So long as you have Luloecen, you have Moray.'

In the purple darkness, her hair was Byzantine, touched with crimson where the light caught it; and the sand moved down her fine robe like silver. He said carefully, 'Luloecen is young. He might die. I shall need heirs for Orkney and Caithness. After you have paid your way with some sons, we might have this conversation again, with a priest present.'

She said, 'Save the price of it. Oaths never saved a man's life, or a woman's either. I will come on your progress. But I know these people as well as you do. When you plan your policies, I want to be there; or, one way or another, I will ruin them for you.'

'Policies?' Thorfinn said. 'Whatever policies there are to be made will fall to you and your council in any case: why do you think you have Coulter? I have no policies for Moray. I have told you before. My business is in the north, and so soon as this journey is over, I shall be going back there to look after it.'

'You were right. You are a coward,' she said, and did not wait to watch him walk back uphill, any more than he, turning, glanced back at her over his shoulder.

TWELVE

THE TWO SOUTHERN churchmen set sail the next day; and so did Kalv; and if a winged monster hovered over his head with a corpse in its plumage, there were none with heads clear enough to notice. Or so they said later. Sulien of Llanbadarn stayed, and so did Alfgar, the Mercian heir, who had no pressing business, it seemed, back in Chester.

After that, the ritual procession through the Earl of Orkney's new lands was over in three weeks, and towards the end the rain that had ruined the harvest began at last to stop, so that the deep mud started to dry beside the riverside settlements and there was blue sky behind the sheet-bronze of the bracken and the hill-shoulders brilliant with heather.

It was a good time to go, when meat was easy to come by because of the autumn killing, and food and hospitality would settle the tribute-score. Only, this time, their lord fed not only his retinue but the people themselves at the gathering-place for each district, and added ale and barleymeal from the wooden carts his oxen dragged behind him.

After a feast such as that, there was no trouble. The new Lady of Moray, after all, was the same as the old, and there was no one there who did not know Findlaech's stepson, who had in any case been this way before with his men, and had given the former friends of Gillacomghain something to think about. What was more, at the end of the feasting, Findlaech's stepson Macbeth stood up to his full height (and, God's Judgement, he was a very tall man) and said that since God had seen fit to send them bad harvests and those in Caithness and Orkney were good, he had given orders that the surplus meal in his barns should not be sent overseas, but should be kept to trade with the Moraymen for whatever the people of Caithness might need.

The first time he sat down after saying that, the Lady Groa, flushed and smiling beside him, addressed him under cover of the consequent noise. 'I didn't hear you telling my uncle that the Arnmødling family were to starve this winter?'

'If they ever make me King of Trøndelagen, I shall do what I can for them,' said Thorfinn-Macbeth. 'As it is, I've already bought the only thing the Trøndelagen had that I needed.'

Three people she knew came over to speak to her, and she talked and laughed with them. When they had left, 'If you mean me,' she said, 'I don't recall gold passing the way of my father, more than would buy him a comb-case.'

'Is it nothing,' said Thorfinn, 'that I have undertaken to feed, clothe, and shelter you for the rest of your life, whether the harvest fails in Caithness or not? That is, if other harvests fail, we shall have to think again. Smile.'

'I am laughing,' she said. 'Between you and Gillacomghain, I shall have that to tell that would earn my keep as an old woman at anyone's fireside.'

Then they moved on: to Deer, to Turriff, to Formartine, to Monymusk, for the chief meeting-place of each district was still the place where the monks had come first, long ago, and where most often there remained a small monastery or a collection of huts round a chapel dedicated to one of the familiar saints. And for their last visits of all, they made their way along the frontier of Mar, where the river Dee rolled down through its broad heath-lands from the hills where lay Coulter, the bride's dower lands.

There, because of the mire underfoot, they took to the river by barges, and for the first time there was peace to stand alone, and in silence, and watch the cloud-shadows move on the hills, and hear the thin, swooping voice of the curlew and smell the bog-myrtle hot in the sun. Then, round the next bend, they swept into the dancing curtain of gnats, and someone lit a smudge fire in a bucket, round which they crouched coughing and wrapped in their cloaks until they saw the smoke of Tullich in the lee of its hills in the distance and drew in where the boards had been laid at the mouth of the stream.

Five ways met at or near Tullich, including the pass that led north to the Don, and so it was a brisk little hamlet, with room for market-booths at the Dee crossing, and storage barns, and a good, well-built house for the toisech, the head of the family group, whom Groa knew. Gillacomghain had held this land himself, and until Luloecen was of age, his widow would have to appoint her steward for all these places, to see to their protection and their laws, their tributes and the things that made up their livelihood. She had been allowed to keep some of the men from Gillacomghain's council, whom Thorfinn thought he could trust, and in that she thought he was right.

For the rest, they would have to see. The land was full of young men, as was all of Alba, grown up since Clontarf and Carham took their toll, and the plunderings of sea-raiders, and the seasons when armed refugees would take possession of a ness or a beachhead and stay there, raiding, until they were thrown out. In the manner that the Earls of Orkney had taken Caithness until the King of Alba had been forced to regularise the invasion, by marriage.

The land was full of young men like Thorfinn, ready to plot, to argue, to kill for their rights. But men who knew who they were and what they wanted because they had learned it at the knee of their fathers, and would act as the blood of their race told them to.

Here was a half-breed whose nature was a meeting-place, like this township, of many different roads, with a guide to none of them. If killing

Gillacomghain had been necessary to bring to life Thorfinn's conception of himself, Gillacomghain was dead.

'What next?' the bride of Moray said to herself as the heat and the talking began again, and the smells of roast meat, and the squeak and hoot of the music, and the roaring chant of the songs, drowning the thud of heels on the bare earth as the dancing started under the stars. 'What next? He has done what Gillacomghain did, and next summer he will father his son, because so did Gillacomghain. Then, when there is nothing to prove, he will go to sea, because the sea gave him pleasure at fourteen. And he will be fourteen still in his soul when they lift him white-haired out of the ship, with the meeting-place nothing but dust again.'

The young Breton, whom she might have liked, said, 'You have been thinking solemn thoughts. May I ask you a solemn question?'

'If it has to do with my spiritual welfare, no,' Groa said.

'It has to do with your son,' Sulien said. 'Why did you give him such a name? You know what they would call him in Ireland?'

For a while, she was silent, thinking. She had not expected a Breton to know this. Then she said, 'I do. Gillacomghain was careful to tell me.'

'Gillacomghain chose the name?' Sulien asked.

'Or had it picked for him,' the girl said. 'He was told that he would be Mormaer of Moray, provided he so named his son. I call the child Lulach.'

'It is a better name,' said Sulien. 'If it were for me to say, I should call him that always. Suggest it to . . . your friends.'

'To the Earl Thorfinn?' she said. 'Does it matter?'

'Only if he knows what it means,' Sulien said. 'And he does.'

She did not answer, and he changed the conversation. And soon, anyway, it was time to withdraw to the house she had always used when she and Gillacomghain came here. As ever, Earl Thorfinn would stay till the end. He had energy, and he guarded his drinking better than most young men of his age; but the same could be said of all his friends and kinfolk and allies from Orkney and Iceland and Caithness.

When, therefore, lying awake in the dark, she heard the muted bustle later that night, and then the sound of crisp, quiet voices unblurred by drink, she knew she was listening to the Earl's companions even before she heard him speak himself. He said, 'How many? Can you tell?' and a voice she did not know answered, 'About four hundred, my lord, I should judge. And armed.'

Thorkel's voice said, 'You were wise to give two feast days to Deeside. They'll have had time to sober up at Banchory. I'll send the messengers out, and we'd better rouse what men we can here.'

'No. Wait,' her husband said. 'You say they are encamped? How well are they concealed? Do they have much baggage with them?'

The unknown scout said, 'They are not in an exposed position, my lord, but not unduly concealed either. And they have almost no baggage.'

'No smith, for example?' said Earl Thorfinn.

The man must have shaken his head, for one of the Duncansby cousins said,

'That doesn't prove anything. They're close to home. They might still mean to attack. Thorfinn, you should wake camp and send your lady home anyway.'

By then, she had her cloak over her shift and had pulled the door open. The dark knot of men in front of her broke apart, faces turning, pale shapes in the dark, and a flicker of light from a torch showed her Earl Thorfinn's bared brow and beaked nose and muscle-strapped shoulders. He was stripped to the waist, as he had risen.

The girl said, 'Before she goes or doesn't go, the lady would like to know the cause of alarm.'

'I would give you a report if I could,' her husband said, 'but we haven't decided whether to be alarmed yet or not. My brother has arrived in the neighbourhood under cover of darkness. With an army.'

'I thought Thorkel killed your brother in Orkney?' said his bride, puzzled.

'That was another brother. Thorkel: we should warn lower Deeside, but I don't want troops of men blundering in here. Can you round up what you can by daybreak and hold them out of sight, behind Culblean?'

'And if he attacks before then?' Thorkel said. 'Maddan's father was a partner of Crinan's. Duncan may want vengeance and Moray as well.'

'I,' said the girl tartly, 'am not marrying anyone else.'

'Duncan is married already,' said the Earl. 'To someone well-born and wealthy in Northumbria. I know he has reason to attack. I think he won't. I think we are being invited to make fools of ourselves. I think when he does attack, it will be with a lot more than four hundred men. If I am wrong, none of you will be left alive, I imagine, to blame me. Thorkel, take what men you need. The rest of us are going back to bed.'

'To *bed?*' said one of the Icelanders.

'You can sit up nursing your battle-axe all night if you want to. But until the scouts bring me worse news than that, bed is where I shall be.'

'And this,' said Groa, 'is warrior's instinct?'

'This,' said the Earl testily, 'is an excercise in the godly virtues of trust and forbearance. Who said woman was man's guardian devil? Go and pray somewhere. That's why I gave you a Christian wedding.'

'While you sleep?'

'I need to be fresh to be forbearing and trustful tomorrow. Good night.'

They were still arguing with him when she went in and shut the door.

The next morning, as the sun rose behind Culblean and whatever of armed men Thorkel had lying behind it, a showily dressed man from Appleby, lightly escorted, rode into Tullich under a jolting blue banner and announced that, with the Mormaer of Moray's permission, his lord Duncan, prince of Cumbria, wished to share his marriage festivities. Earl Thorfinn, in a tunic Groa had never seen before and all his arm-rings, accepted the greetings amiably under the flags and the awnings of the meeting-place, with his entourage, also polished, around him. There was not an armed man in sight. The messenger was presented with a gold buckle and a message of welcome; and in an hour the Earl Thorfinn's half-brother Duncan was with him.

They had not met for four years. Their last confrontation had been at Chester when the Earl Thorfinn had sat at ease on Leofric's longship, waiting for Duncan to drown.

Of the men standing now by the Earl, Alfgar of Mercia remembered that, and Sulien of Llanbadarn, who had helped lift him from the water. Since that day, living in daily commerce with Cumbria, both young men had had occasion to meet Duncan and his father King Malcolm of Alba. And because Gillacomghain had paid his Mormaer's tribute to Malcolm, his widow Groa knew Duncan as well, as did those men of Tullich who had been fit enough to rise from their mattresses that morning.

They knew Duncan, but all they knew of Thorfinn was that, in Gillacomghain's place, tribute would be required of him by his grandfather. And that he was neither paying taxes to Norway for Orkney nor tribute for Caithness to anyone.

Duncan said, 'Greetings, brother. Being old in years, our grandfather the King could not be present at your marriage, but bids you accept the wine that you see, and this cup as his bride-gift. . . . It has been my privilege once or twice before to embrace the bride. Do I have your leave?'

'If you can reach,' said Thorfinn of Orkney.

Her contorted face under Duncan's stiff one, the girl could only hope that he thought she was smiling in welcome. Whatever height King Malcolm had bestowed on his daughter, there was no doubt that her two sons did not share it. Thorfinn, son of Sigurd of Orkney, looked down on his half-brother Duncan, son of Crinan, lord Abbot of Dunkeld, whose head reached to his shoulder. Duncan was round-faced and russet, with fine brown hair and a thick, large moustache, soft as bran. His chin was shaved, as was the Earl's. It was one of the few things they had in common. Groa said, 'The cup is beautiful. I do not know your friends . . . Or . . .'

'You know one of them,' Duncan said as she hesitated. The moustache spread over the firm, coloured cheeks as he smiled. 'Your uncle Kalv's nephew Siward. His father is a great man in England these days, since he helped kill King Olaf. Siward lives in York now, where his wife is. He and I married sisters.'

More than the face, she remembered the broad chest and wide shoulders from her visits to Thore Hund's house long ago. The fur-trader's son was a big man, and older than her husband, she would judge, by quite a number of years. Earl Thorfinn said, 'I don't think we've met. How is Carl son of Thorbrand since his sea voyage?'

Siward opened his mouth. Duncan said quickly, 'You are talking of what happened to Gillacomghain. That is a matter we all want to forget, I am sure, especially with your lady present. We live nearer to King Canute than you do, and are not always free to act as we should wish. I have an introduction to make. My lord Crinan my father has sent you his daughter's new husband to wish you well of your marriage and Moray. This is my lord Forne.'

'Ah,' said the Earl. A man stepped forward, smiling, and Thorfinn addressed him. 'I thought once of marrying your wife, but I was told she was reserved for a union much more important. So you are Duncan's good-brother. And mine then, also.'

'I am glad,' said the man called Forne. 'I am to tell you from my lord Crinan that he bears you no grudge for the death of his partner's son Maddan. I act for him in Dunkeld from time to time, so we may meet.'

He looked like a man used to business; quietly dressed and clear-eyed and with hands not so hardened with weapons but that they might even have guided a quill-point. His speech had been Saxon bent to Norse, which they had all used, including Duncan; but when later they moved indoors to eat and drink with the Moraymen, talking of nothing, they all heard him speak Gaelic, of a sort, such as they used in the mixed races in Westmorland. Skeggi said to his cousin the Earl, 'Who is he? There is Norman there.'

'That is what I was thinking,' Earl Thorfinn observed. 'We shall find out soon enough. And I can tell you another thing, if you are sober enough to take it in. His nephew Orm is married to a third of those Northumbrian sisters.'

Alfgar had overheard. 'It's better than war, isn't it? An empire trussed up in marriage ties, from the west sea to the east across all northern England. I wonder who is the architect? Your grandfather King Malcolm? Duncan here? Or . . .'

Duncan, with Groa leading him, was approaching the board.

'The Abbot of Dunkeld,' Thorfinn said, 'I make no doubt, is a powerful man who, like the White God Heimdall, lies awake at night listening to the grass growing all over the world, and none of it under his feet. . . . When we have all drunk enough, my brother, no doubt you and I should converse.'

Something crossed the unchanging, apple-cheeked face and was gone. 'I brought Siward and Forne with me for that very purpose,' Duncan said.

'Then I suppose I had better take two of the serving-girls with me, to see to our wine, or the balance will fail,' Thorfinn said. Sulien, who was becoming used to his tongue, saw Alfgar staring. Sulien said, 'If there's any wine going, I don't think Thorkel would want to be missed. I saw him come in a while back.'

The bar of Thorfinn's brows lifted as he looked at his brother. 'Would you object to my foster-father? He's not as quick as he used to be.'

The bright skin was a little redder, but the smile was the same. 'Bring whom you like,' Duncan said. 'We are not going to quarrel.'

'I'm glad of that,' Thorfinn said. 'Will you lie down and let me walk over you here, or wait until we get to the meeting-house?'

Duncan's moustache spread in a brief, answering smile, but he did not trouble to answer. Thorkel arrived, laid a hand on his foster-son's shoulder, and said, 'Whether you want me or not, I'm coming in with you. Will you keep a leash on your tongue?'

'No,' Thorfinn said.

The ensuing hour took five hours to pass.

At the end of it, Groa, peering from the toisech's house amid the chatter of women and children, saw the neat wooden door of the meeting-house open and those conferring begin to come out. There were, reassuringly, five of them. She saw other heads turning sharply: those of Sulien and Alfgar, who had been doing nothing in particular with a group of men at the foot of the cross, and those of the Icelanders and the Caithness men engaged in their perpetual dicing.

The five men set off for the hall. Excusing herself, Groa left the women and followed.

There was a crowd in front of the door, including the prince Duncan and his friends, apparently on the point of departure. Duncan looked the same, except that he had a blue patch under each eye and his nose was pale. Thorkel had bags under his eyes as well. Earl Thorfinn and the man Forne were unaltered. She took part in a long, false-hearty muddle of leave-taking and, when the Cumbrian party was finally mounted, watched it ride off to the west, no doubt to join the four hundred armed men who had never been mentioned. 'Why the army?' she asked of Earl Thorfinn.

'It saved the prince asking for hostages,' said the Earl. 'And he reckoned he was safe anyway, when we were too drunk to respond, or too fearful. Would you like him for a husband? You would never end as a widow.'

'There are several ways of never becoming a widow,' the girl said. 'Two of them at least seem to be available to me without having to move to another marriage. Are you serious? Was he thinking of offering for me?'

'What do you think the attack on Thurso was all about?' the Earl said. 'If I had died and Gillacomghain had died, there was Moray sitting about in a hut waiting for Duncan or Maddan to marry it. He still wouldn't mind having you for his secondary wife, Danish fashion, if anything happened to me. If it does, you should accept the offer. It can be a profitable business. Look at Alfiva running Norway.'

'Look at Norway about to rise against her,' said Thorkel. 'I told you to keep your tongue off Siward. If his father and Kalv rebel and throw out Alfiva, you'll find the Earls ruling Norway again, with the Arnasons in the lead. Isn't that what we all want?'

'And you think the Earls could stand against Canute?' Thorfinn said.

'Maybe they can't. But what makes you think *you* can stand against Canute?' said Thorkel. 'You sat in there just now and promised the use of your fleet and your Caithness men to keep Malcolm's east coast safe against Canute's son Svein if war breaks out in Norway. Are you mad? Canute is your lord for all Orkney. Two of his churchmen have just been up at your wedding. He'll send the Danish fleet up, and you'll lose everything.'

'I don't think so,' said the Earl. He cleared a space on a hall bench and sat on it. 'Canute's having trouble in Normandy. He'll have his hands full if there's a rebellion in Norway. In any case, by offering to guard the coast, I've saved Duncan's face. I said I could pay him no tribute for at least a year, and he accepted it. I've also said I'll join him with longships to help clear the Norse out of Galloway.'

'Why?' said Alfgar.

'Because King Malcolm . . . or someone . . . wants sole possession of the western coast north of Cumbria,' said the Earl. 'Galloway and Govan and the old Glasgow churchlands, and Kintyre and all the islands next to Ireland that give a good base for striking, or trading, or whatever you may want.'

'I know that. Everyone in Mercia knows that. I meant, why join him?' Alfgar said.

'Brotherly feeling,' said Earl Thorfinn rebukingly.

Tullich had been their last visit. The following day, they all left in their various ways: Alfgar to the south and the rest by road and by ship to the northern reaches of Moray, to Caithness, to Orkney.

Groa was returning to Inverness, where Luloecen was. Her husband, it appeared, was taking a different, faster route north to Duncansby, and most of his band were going with him.

He came to say goodbye, and said it, in one word, cheerfully.

'Nothing else?' Groa said. Her red hair blew in the wind, and she held it down, gazing at him.

He thought. 'Until next summer,' he said.

ThIRTEEN

ON THE SUMMER of 1033, the harvests failed again all over Europe because of the rain, and travellers to Rome were killed and eaten, so report said. In Norway, a man calling himself the son of Olaf Tryggvasson tried to make himself king, but was defeated by the fleet of Canute's son Svein. The Trøndelagers, having other plans, helped neither side.

An Irishman whose land on the west coast of Alba had become a base for the Norse-Irish kindred of Dublin was attacked and killed by Earl Thorfinn of Orkney, who went on to drive out the Irishman's uncle from another stronghold in the south-west. The army of the prince of Cumbria played some part in the achievement.

A punitive expedition against the east coast of Alba was led from Norway by Svein's standard-bearer, on the advice of Svein's father, to discourage help for his rebels in Norway. The men of Fife, with the aid of the Orkney fleet, fought and defeated the foray. A force led by the prince Duncan arrived in time to play some part in the battle.

The Earl of Orkney allowed time to pass and then let it be known that, due to the drying climate of Caithness, there was a surplus of grain for barter, as he had promised. He became, by hearsay, mildly popular.

The unrest in the north of Norway continued to grow, not without some encouragement. At length, King Canute's lesser wife and her son Svein lost their nerve and, giving up Trøndelagen altogether, fled to the south, and from there out of the country.

Thus simply, thus foolishly, thus suddenly ended King Canute's Danish rule over Norway.

The Earl of Orkney returned to Caithness and paid attention to all the news that reached him from Nídarós. Then, with the onset of storms and security, he crossed the Pentlandsfjord and prepared to work through the winter restoring to order his neglected dominion in Orkney. To his wife in Moray he sent his regrets that he had not been able to see her that year.

'You did what?' said Thorkel Fóstri at Hǫfn, when he heard. 'Haven't you been to see her at all? Or the boy? You're going to lose Moray.'

'No, I'm not,' Thorfinn replied. 'She has a good, well-organised council of her men and mine, and the means to raise plenty of strength to protect her if Duncan or anyone else troubles her. And the whole of my resources to call on.'

'If she had the whole of your resources to call on, I shouldn't be worrying,' said Thorkel tartly. 'What if she goes to Duncan instead of the other way about?'

'He would send her back. He needs me. And she wouldn't stand for being anyone's second wife anyway. I rather suspect,' said Thorfinn, 'that she doesn't particularly care for being anyone's first wife either. Lording it alone in Moray is probably what she likes doing most, next to wishing she could be an abbess.'

'Lording it in Moray while you get yourself nearly killed fighting Duncan's battles for him,' said Thorkel. 'And who is supposed to hold the north of Scotland then?'

'There is another heir,' Thorfinn said.

Once, thought his foster-father, he could pin him down. Once, he could control him. Once, he could stop him. 'Who?' he said. 'Your four-year-old stepson? Caithness doesn't belong to Luloecen. Orkney doesn't belong to him. There is no way by which you could get Orkney to accept Gillacomghain's son, and so risk having the whole of the north in vassaldom to the King of Alba.'

'They risked it when they accepted me,' Thorfinn said. 'And as the King of Alba's grandson, I represented a greater threat than Luloecen would.'

'You were a grown man,' said Thorkel. 'Or old enough anyway to show what you meant to do. You fought for Orkney like a cur with a rat in its teeth, and you soon showed what your oath of vassaldom was worth.' He broke off, advisedly, and cleared his throat. 'You weren't seriously suggesting that Luloecen could follow you here?'

'No, I wasn't,' Thorfinn said. 'You've forgotten that there is another heir to Orkney of Sigurd's blood. Far away, like the Saxons' mysterious Athelings, but still alive.'

'*Rognvald!*' Thorkel had raised his voice. 'Rognvald, Brusi's son? The yellow-haired snivelling child we last saw in Nídarós?'

'The yellow-haired snivelling child you last saw at Nídarós,' Thorfinn agreed.

Warned, Thorkel looked at him. After a moment, he said, in a quieter voice, 'Rognvald has been in Russia for nearly four years—nearly six if you count the first time as well. Olaf is dead: Kalv killed him. You will never see Rognvald again.' And then, as Thorfinn did not at once agree, he said, 'Will we?'

'I am afraid we might,' Thorfinn said. 'I have just had word from Norway. There has been a meeting of the bonder. They have decided not to rule Trøndelagen themselves, in place of Canute or his son. They have decided—Kalv has decided—your cousin Kalv has decided to go to Russia in the spring and bring back King Olaf's young bastard Magnús to be the next King of Norway. And if Magnús comes,' Thorfinn said, and, throwing down the knife he was toying with, rose from the table,'—if Magnús comes, then Rognvald will come with him, to claim his father's inheritance, which is half of Orkney.'

They looked at one another. 'So?' said Thorkel slowly.

'So I am sending my regrets to my wife that I have been unable to visit her in the past year,' Thorfinn said. 'And I have said that I shall most certainly give myself the pleasure of a long stay in Moray in spring-time.' He spoke mildly. 'Would you like a daughter, Thorkel, if I have one? You would only have to wait thirteen years or so for her, and at least she would be a good linguist.'

'My God,' said Thorkel feelingly. 'With your tongue and her red hair . . . You should be prevented from breeding with each other. There must be a canonical rule about it somewhere. What will your sons be like?'

'Duncan, perhaps,' said Thorfinn. 'Soft and sly and stupid. We share the same mother, after all. You should have no trouble fostering that kind, if you have to. . . . I wonder how prolific Rognvald has been, or intends to be. It is tempting to hope that he has caught the Eastern sin.'

'Tempting from what point of view?' said Thorkel sourly, and left him sitting looking surprised.

They spent Yule in Orkney, where Thorfinn was fortifying the near-island at Birsay in the north-west and rebuilding some of the lodges he used when he moved through his property. He seemed to take pleasure in Orkney in the winter-time, perhaps because of the winds that dragged through land and sea like a scraping-board and flung the green waves and the white against the storm-beach at Skaill until the heathland was salt a mile inland and the night sky was cuffed with pale breakers.

Then, with the ships safely trussed in their nousts, the halls of his friends and his kinsmen opened their doors to him and to his household as was their duty as well as their pleasure, and the long roasting-fire would fling its light and its heat into their faces as the hot pebbles hissed and belched in the ale-bucket and the cauldrons swung on their chains in the noise and the laughter.

During the day, there were dangerous sports. They were all scarred from that summer's fighting. But they always collected their worst scars in the winter.

Word came from Moray that the Lady had received Earl Thorfinn's intimation that he would travel south to see her in the summer, and thanked him for it. The courier, one of the older Salmundarson boys, said that the Lady seemed to be well, and that, apart from a blood-feud and three districts laid low with a pest, Moray appeared to be quiet at the moment.

'And the boy?' Thorfinn didn't ask it, so Sulien did.

'I was coming to that,' said Starkad Salmundarson, who, no more than any member of his family, brooked interference. 'He's healthy. His hair's still white as a patriarch's, but he isn't a pink-eye. He wanted Earl Thorfinn to know that he didn't mind his name being changed to Lulach, but he has sent something so that Earl Thorfinn would always keep his proper name in mind.'

The something was a bare stick. They all looked at it.

'It had leaves on,' Starkad offered. 'They came off in my saddle-bag. I don't know what it means, either.'

Thorfinn turned it over. There were no runes on it anywhere: it was just an ordinary stick. 'Sulien?' he said. 'A message-token from an unknown land. Put it in your book-bag and tell me if it takes root. What else, Starkad?'

'Nothing from Moray,' said Starkad. 'But I heard something as I came over the Cabrach. They say the King your grandfather is low.'

'Lower than usual?' Thorfinn said. His grandfather must be over eighty, and had never ailed in his life. This was the moment brother Duncan had been both dreading and longing for, one supposed. He probably had his day-by-day instructions for the next five years by rote. The most weighty question facing himself, as another grandson, was whether it would be more dangerous to stay away from the funeral than to go to it.

Starkad said, 'He can't ride very much, and he's staying a lot with that old mistress he likes in Glamis. But he could hang on for a year yet, they tell me.'

'Starkad,' Thorfinn said, 'when we want to hear news upside down, we will stand on our heads as you tell it. Killer-Bardi is here: go and find him and get drunk somewhere.'

King Malcolm lived. The spring came, and with it the news that Kalv Arnason and Einar Tambarskelve were now on their way to Gardarike to offer the crown of Norway to the late King Olaf's bastard, aged ten. They had taken with them a large body of oath-taking Trønder and were expected to pick up Rognvald son of Brusi on their way back, at the end of the year.

Thorfinn, who could swear in five languages better than anyone Thorkel had ever heard, did so, and then said, 'They might even get the boy to come back at that. Einar Tambarskelve must be one of the only three men in Trøndelagen who didn't lay a finger on Olaf, and that ought to count. Thorkel, I want to see what is happening in Galloway, and then I'll leave you in Caithness and get down to Moray. Do you want to see what is happening in Galloway?'

'There's a rumour Suibhne's come back,' Thorkel said carefully.

'That's what I mean,' said Thorfinn. 'We go down there; and kill him; and perhaps look and see what is happening on Colonsay. Then I go to Moray.'

The Galloway campaign reached a satisfactory conclusion in June. On learning then that his wife had been for two weeks in Inverness, the Earl of Orkney sailed north with no particular haste, and rounding Duncansby Head, made for the wide arms of the Moray Firth, where the river Ness entered the eastern ocean. He did not happen to send word that he was coming.

Being troubled neither by news nor premonitions, Finn Arnason's daughter, in an embroidered robe with a train, was sitting under an awning on the wharfside with Sinna her woman and three of her housecarls, overseeing the noisy resolution of a misunderstanding, not to say an open piece of deception, to do with toll-payments.

Her hair and her neck, as befitted a married woman of nineteen, were wrapped in white linen, and she had brought her tablet-loom with her, unwinding its glittering ribbon over her skirts as the ivory placques clicked and clacked under her fingers. She said for the third time in Norse, 'We do not want fish. Put the kegs back on board. You can have no more timber until you pay in silver or wool, as we agreed. And you can have no more of anything until you settle for the dues on your last cargo.'

'I paid them,' the trader said, also for the third time. He was smiling.

'He didn't,' said Eochaid.

She had asked the prior of the monastery of Deer to find her a Norse-speaking clerk who understood business, and he had found this black-haired man Eochaid, a trained priest from Armagh, to help her steward.

He had proved quick-witted as well as skilful with numbers, and she hoped she could keep him all year, but it wasn't likely. To have a permanent trading-station you needed a town, with men who would do nothing but defend the town and its warehouses and keep order among the ships' crews. You needed goods to barter, regularly brought in, or a settlement of work-shops on the spot, with a surplus of food in the countryside big enough to feed the fighting-men and the craftsmen and the traders; and good roads to carry it all.

In Moray and Caithness, there were things to sell: hides and salmon and eels, squirrel and marten pelts and timber—and, God knew, there were things that they needed. But in all Alba there were no towns: there were only family settlements on the rivers and up the sides of the hills, on the drier land; and since the sea-raiding began and even before, the churches had dwindled to a handful of monasteries supporting a dozen or less in their huts, and a network of cells and chapels in which a monk might find shelter, or a travelling priest to baptise and shrive, bury and pray for his district, while losing even what learning once he had.

And so the fairs were lost, too: the saints' days on which the countrymen of a Saxon shire would at least know when to gather and bring their goods to market. Since she married Gillacomghain she had done her best to get to know the saints of Moray, but it seemed to her that an undue number of them had gone to their account without proper advice as to the date of the equinoctial gales.

The trader said to Eochaid, 'It's my word against yours. I'll fight you for it.' He was still grinning, and so were the fifteen men standing behind him. They all had either knives or axes stuck in their belts.

She could hear the housecarls breathing behind her, but they all stood still, as they had been told. She said, 'Didn't you see Sinna take out her kerchief a few minutes ago? You must think we are all children. Look up at the stockade.'

The Mormaer's hill was directly behind her, with her own house and all the service-buildings behind the log walls. On top of the log walls, by now, should be a line of throwing-spears and a row of elbows, cocked above arrow-heads. The ivory clacked under her fingers, and when she looked up, the trader had stopped smiling. 'Wool,' said Groa kindly. 'Or silver.'

He turned on his heel and walked back to the ship, and for a moment she thought she was going to get the fish as well, but he jerked a thumb over his shoulder and the fifteen men began rolling the kegs down to the quayside. Then the gangplank came up and the hawsers aboard, and the knörr moved off as soon as the first oars dug into the water, narrowly missing a longship skimming upriver, aiming for the same berth.

The Irish freedwoman Sinna, gazing at the near-collision in horror, flung her arms to the skies at the explosion of outrage and blasphemy that rose from both ships.

Her kerchief was still in her hand. Dutifully, the row of spearmen and archers on the Mormaer's mound released their weapons.

Sitting placidly under her awning, Groa saw, with surprise, that it was raining.

Then she saw that the rain was made of steel, and that it was falling steadily, with no very beneficial effect, on a dragon-ship bearing the black-raven banner of Orkney.

'Three killed and eighteen wounded,' Earl Thorfinn said.

The white-faced archers had been sent to their flogging and the screaming Sinna dismissed to her hut; the injured had been tended and the dead buried, and the Earl and his lady were now alone, in the hall-room of her house . . . of his house . . . on the hill. 'They were mostly from the other ship,' Groa said.

Under the crumpled mess of the elegant robe, her body shook like the skin of an idle horse bothered by flies. She had been shaking ever since she ran down to the riverside and her husband had stepped on shore like a man arrived to claim a very particular tax of his own, made up of lopped heads.

She had forgotten what he was like. He had flung his sword at her, pommel first, and she had just caught it, slashing her fingers. 'Try again,' he had said. 'Maybe you have better aim than they have.'

His face had been red and white, and his chest beating with anger.

She had explained. She had explained again, when she had been sent to do so, at the side of the ship. She would have done nothing for the trader under the circumstances, but Earl Thorfinn didn't want to hear about the circumstances. The trader's men were looked after equally with his own, and then sent off with as much gold as they might have had if she had given them a shipload of timber for nothing.

And now he and she were alone, and up and down his right arm was a stained envelope made from the lower half of Sinna's shift, held together by a cross-binding of tablet-made silk and gold ribbon of three months' making.

She ought to offer to see to it. She had no intention of going anywhere near him. She was married to him.

She sat down, letting him tower over her if he wanted to, and nursed her stinging fingers under their cloth. After a moment, he sat down, too, on the stool behind him, and leaned against the wall. 'Where is your steward?' he said.

'At Speymouth,' she said. 'He'll come here when I go south. Eochaid is here to look after the shipping, and he usually has two or three others to call on. One of them is inland supervising the felling, and the other chose to join you in Galloway. I used to do this when Gillacomghain was alive.'

'No doubt,' said Earl Thorfinn. 'I didn't hear whether or not he had the use of his right arm when we burned him.'

'I've explained,' she said. 'For the last time, I'm sorry. I'll make sure that it never happens again.'

'No. *I'll* make sure that it never happens again,' he said. 'You don't intend us to eat or drink today?'

'There's plenty,' she said. 'The girls are frightened to come in.'

'Then go out to them,' he said. 'And get your hand looked after. And bring back as much wine as you need to make you compliant and I need to make me simple-minded but eager. We have five minutes' work to do.'

She stood up. She did not even know him well enough to tell if he was playing with her. Her throat had closed and her heart was tolling like a dead-bell. He said, 'Unless it is the wrong time?'

'No,' she said.

'Well,' he said impatiently. And as she still stood, he said, 'Groa. I am here and you are here because I must have sons. Do you want me to stay any longer than I have to?'

Her knees gave way and she sat down again. Staring at him, she found she was rocking herself backwards and forwards in her anxiety. She stopped it. She said, 'Could we reconsider and make a fresh start tomorrow? After all, you've waited two years.'

He waited, courteously enough, until she had finished speaking, and then, rising, he opened the door and went out. She could hear him calling the slaves, and very soon he was back, with a spouted jug of wine in one hand and two cups in the crook of his arm. 'Now,' he said.

'I'll have both beakers,' she said.

Afterwards she reckoned that she had drunk at least two-thirds of the wine. She had a very vague memory of being helped into the bedchamber, and of the door closing. She needed hardly any undressing, and she let him steer her to the mattress and fold back her clothes. She lay with her eyes closed and at the end said, 'Four minutes. That was four minutes this time.'

There was a little silence and then he said, 'I'm beginning to find my way about.'

When she opened her eyes later, and the room had steadied, she found she was alone.

His blood was everywhere: her robe was covered with it, and the linen sheet they had sent her from Austråt. She did not feel any particular emotion, but lay quite quietly, with tears pouring into her ears.

'He's very practical,' Thorkel had once said. 'It seems to be his chief characteristic.'

She had time to remember it during the days that her husband spent on his back, with the herbalist monk from St Drostan's of Urquhart looking after him. He had known very well that his wound wouldn't let him take her next day, or for some time to come, for that matter.

In the event, his perseverance received its reward, although in no personal sense had he made any conquest, that night, of his partner. News of his progress, or lack of it, filtered through to the Lady from those attending her husband: that the wound was light, but that he was fevered with blood-loss; that the healing had become interrupted and a new ointment sent for; that he was better but weak. She felt no inclination to go and visit him, ailing or well, and receive more abuse for her share in his injuries. Sinna, she noticed, kept well clear of the sick-house as well. No one seemed to find her absence unwifely or surprising: she supposed they all thought she was frightened of him. In which they were perfectly right.

The Lady of Moray accordingly waited, pursuing her daily rounds warily, until, in the way of nature, it came to her that the means of absolution seemed to be at hand. In the privacy of her room, she wiped off the tears of wry laughter that sprang not entirely from hysteria and, putting on her best robe, went and rapped on the door of the sick-house.

Inside, she dismissed the slave sitting there and, surveying the low-lying bed and its inmate, addressed her husband.

'I have news for you. Unless deceived by the shocks to my womanly senses, I might be carrying.'

The yellow light from the lamp showed him unshaven. Above the black jowls, the nose and cheekbones had sharpened, casting black, jagged shadows. He looked grotesque.

Not a muscle moved round his mouth or his eyes. He lay and studied her. She said, 'You lost a lot of blood. Most of it over me.'

On either side of his mouth, two lines deepened a fraction. He said, 'I'll wager you had a headache next morning. However. There is a month, isn't there, to prove you right or wrong?'

His voice had not changed. Now she knew how he was taking it, she could meet him on the same ground. She said, 'Sadly, I realised that you might not believe me. It doesn't matter. Bound to my lord from the crown of my head to the soles of my feet, I shall be ready if needed; preferably with a different sort of wine. When can I expect Caw Revived?'

Undisturbed, the violent brown eyes studied her. 'I want to visit this steward of yours,' said Earl Thorfinn. 'And I have some things to see to in southern Moray and Mar for a week or two. Move to Monymusk, and I shall come there once a week.'

'Lulach is at Monymusk,' Groa said. Once a week? She could not read his face. 'And what about the wine?'

'I shall try, but next time you may have to suffer in ale,' said the Earl. 'As for Lulach, if he is to have a half-brother or -sister, he had better know who has fathered him or her.'

'Or them,' she said. 'If I have two at a birth, will you feel safe from Rognvald? Or will you never feel safe?'

'Not while you are about,' the Earl said.

He returned to Caithness in August, by which time it was public knowledge, confirmed by the women who knew, that his wife would bear him a child in the following March.

'Did you tell Lulach?' Sulien said.

'Lulach says it will be a son called Paul,' Thorfinn said.

Skeggi, who was frightened of children, let out a snort. 'I can see an Earl of Orkney having a son called Paul,' he said. 'Where in the name of Odin did he get that idea?'

'I rather think the whole thing is between the White Christ and Frey,' Thorfinn said peacefully. 'At the moment, I am not quite sure which is winning.'

FOURTEEN

N THE twenty-fifth day of November in that year of 1034, there died at Glamis in the thirtieth year of his reign Malcolm son of Kenneth, *King of Alba and glory of the whole west of Europe.* So reported the monkish scribes of the Irish, whose blood ran in his veins. To those of his own land who paid him tribute at his burial, he was a clever, tough, and unscrupulous man who had fought and killed to gain the throne and fought and killed to keep the throne, as had every ruler before him.

From the time when he seized the succession at the age of fifty, he had maintained his overlordship over the shifting races of Picts and Britons and Scots, the colonies of Norse and the colonies of Danes and of Irish long settled in the plains and rivers that ran from the Derwent in Cumbria to the border of Caithness in the furthermost north. Where fighting would serve, he had fought, to throw from his shores the Norwegians and the Danes, the armies of England when they harried his coast or marched inland in conquest or retribution, or tried to take for themselves the headlands and harbours they needed.

And where war would not serve, he used strategy. He swore fealty to Canute for Cumbria and for those fragments of Lothian he kept hold of; he gave his daughter and Caithness to Orkney; he let Durham keep her churches in the debatable south and did not harry the settlements in the long valleys between England and Alba which had owed allegiance once to Strathclyde or to England, so long as they paid him his dues.

An old man without sons, and with a son-in-law he secretly feared, Malcolm of Alba had turned in his later years, sensibly, from the northern mountains whose control was eluding him, and had bent all his energies on building for Duncan his grandson an empire of infinitely more wealth and promise: the sway over that neck of land—from Durham to Kendal, from Carlisle to Berwick—that lay between England and Alba. And furthermore, if he could get it, that other land next to Earl Leofric's frontiers: the lands deeper down into England that might, if he were fortunate, include the powerful city of York.

For that reason, he had established this network of dynastic marriages, which meant that his blood, however remotely, would run in every part of the country he coveted. It was now for Duncan his grandson to bring these conquests to pass. And it would be for the young sons of those marriages, growing up in all their ambition and vigour, to take and hold them, and to take and hold also the crumbling frontiers of the north which had fallen about the ears of that fool Gillacomghain and might make other barriers tremble. In his last days in Glamis, he had told Duncan over and over, 'Bring your armies here. Mass your troops here. Protect Angus.'

'I don't think,' Duncan had said, 'that you need trouble yourself over Thorfinn. He is spending all his strength running about keeping Galloway quiet for me. And when his nephew Rognvald comes back from Russia, they're bound to fight over Orkney. I shall be surprised if he survives a twelvemonth.'

'There is to be an heir, I am told,' his grandfather said.

And Duncan had smiled and said, 'You know I have two sons with the royal Saxon line in their heritage who can take care of any brat from that kennel, when they are older.'

And so King Malcolm died, frowning, they said.

Because it was winter, there was every excuse for his grandson of Orkney not to attend the funeral obsequies, which were rarely of great ceremony, there being a tendency among the kings of Alba to die suddenly in out-of-the-way places and frequently after a truncated reign.

The tradition was that burial should take place on Iona, the island from which nearly five hundred years since, St Columba had taken the God of the Celts to the Irish and Picts of the mainland.

A monastery to which kings came for burial, or even on pilgrimage, was likely to be very rich. Unerringly, the Vikings had found and sacked it, waited for the altar-silver again to accumulate, and sacked it again until, mournfully, the monks had packed their belongings and crossed the sea back to their saint's native Ireland, where the monastery of Kells opened its arms to become the new home for the church of Columba.

The men on Iona now were anchorites. The church was there, crumbling, and the wattle huts in which they slept and prayed; and perhaps a few sheep, but nothing else. A man going on pilgrimage had to take his own stock and servants to build him a cabin and furnish it. A man wishing to be buried there, such as a king, would require to import the abbot of the Columban mission from Ireland, with all his retinue, his plate, and his vestments, as well as his own bishop and monks from the mainland. And, whatever the season, would require to cross the sea twice, with a coffin.

'No doubt, one fine day, they'll row over a box with his liver and lights in it,' said Skeggi Havardson, who was not impressed by the White Christ in any form since the late Olaf had found himself canonised. 'You can't go, anyway. What about the proclamation of the new King? You shouldn't go to that, either.'

They were at Sandwick in Orkney at the time, preparing to hold Yule in the big hall that Thorkel Fóstri had inherited, now that his father had died. Outside, a rare occurrence, there was a powdering of snow on the field-strips, which the wind was lifting and throwing about like white grass-seed. Indoors, Arnór had just recited a new poem with something wrong with the last verse, and six men were helping him with it.

Thorfinn said, 'Why not? It's always held at the Moot Hill, and that's just south of Dunkeld. If he could get an army from Dunkeld to Tullich last year, you could get near enough to cut his throat if he kills me.'

'Two years ago,' Thorkel said. 'My guess is that, wherever it's held, they'll plan it for Easter.'

'You mean March,' said Thorfinn amiably.

'I mean March,' Thorkel assented. He could hear the sharpness of his voice.

'Well. Leaving aside the problems of March for the moment, let us consider,' Thorfinn said. 'There can't be anyone living now who remembers the last time they proclaimed a king. In fact, did Malcolm not just pick up a set of properly annotated gospel books and run?'

'I know what happens at a king-making,' offered one of the younger Salmundarsons. 'I've a cousin in Derry that told me once. They slaughter a mare—'

Three people groaned.

'—and bring her to the new King, and the new King makes . . . does . . . pretends that it's a mistress.'

Everyone groaned.

'And then they boil the mare, and he has a bath in the broth and then eats it. I told them,' said the Salmundarson boy, rather red in the face, 'that we stopped eating horseflesh thirty years ago when Olaf Tryggvasson said it was heathenish.'

'A good-luck custom. Why not?' said Thorfinn to the boy, through the ensuing uproar.

'That's what my cousin said,' said the boy quickly.

'All the same,' Thorfinn said gravely, 'I don't think I see Duncan embracing it. You'll probably find he merely marries a slab of rock: much less exciting. They'll still blame him if the crops go wrong.' He was shaving a piece of calfskin, and there were whiskers all over his knees.

The boy said, 'Why don't you go and be made king? You're a grandson of King Malcolm as well.'

There were some things now that no one said to Thorfinn: even Thorkel; even Sulien. No one spoke.

Thorfinn blew a drift of cowhair into the longfire, laid down the skin, and took up a whetstone. 'And what a very good idea nephew Rognvald would think that was,' he said. 'Or perhaps you think Brusi's son ought to have Orkney and Caithness to look after while I move down roughly in the direction of Winchester? I don't quite see how I could do it all otherwise.'

The boy, suddenly aware of the silence, looked at him, but said nothing more. Thorkel Fóstri, pitying him, said, 'Duncan is his grandfather's intended heir. Whatever the rights or the wrongs of it, you could only challenge him by going to war. And you might think, as Thorfinn says, that we have territory enough to look after.'

Sulien's voice spoke from the end of the hall, where he was grinding something in a bowl. 'None the less, he is within the royal derbfine, isn't he? Of the royal kindred within four generations from which the fittest man may be elected? Or is that Irish, like the horse-boilings?'

'No. Kings have been elected that way over here, or from alternate sides of the kindred. The Picts had a different way again, by descent through their women. For the past fifty years, the throne has been open to whoever among the kindred was strong enough to take and keep it. The last eight kings of Alba were all murdered. Half the battles Malcolm fought were to pick up enough booty to keep his electorate happy.'

Thorfinn, unexpectedly, had answered. He finished sharpening his knife and looked up, the blade glittering in his hand. 'I'm not up for election. You'll have to learn to like winters on Orkney.'

'All the same,' Skeggi said. 'I wonder if all the men who supported King Malcolm will find quite so much to admire in King Duncan? A war might not even be necessary.'

Thorfinn stood up. A further shower of cowhair fell into the fire and, sizzling, stank for a second time. He held up the pared skin. 'Do you see that? It will shortly be vellum.' He pointed to where Sulien was crouched. 'Do you see that? It will shortly be ink. By applying the one to the other, we are about to conquer ignorance and make war on stupidity. When you make a mistake, it doesn't bleed. When you have a success, it lasts not just till next week but for ever. Go and open the ale-cask.'

Thorkel Fóstri went, and the hall settled down to normal talk again. On the way back, he stopped beside Sulien. 'What was all that about?'

Sulien looked up. His hands were black. 'I'm not sure,' he said. 'But, at a guess, he has given us all the sensible arguments his head has already supplied. What the child in him or the god in him are saying is a different matter.'

Sinna, who always knew, said this baby was going to be early, and she was right.

Of all her lodgings in the province, Thorfinn's wife picked Lumphanan in the south to live in for the weeks before the child was due.

It was not a choice her housecarls thought much of, or her steward. It was too far south; it was less than secure; why not pick one of the islands now: what about Spynie? they said.

But she could see nothing wrong with Lumphanan, set in wooded hills between Monymusk and the Dee river, where the bridal progress had ended three years before. Surrounded by pools and by marshland, the rising ground by the small church was safe, and held within its stockade all she required in the way of buildings to serve herself and her household. And chief among her women was Sinna, who might not be very sensible when it came to flagging armed men, but who had been slave to Groa's mother and had delivered her in her time of both Groa herself and her sister Sigrid, now wed to a great earl in Norway, grandson to old Hakon himself.

She did not miss Sigrid, or her mother, a great deal. She missed Finn. Her father had always been courtly to her, even when she was small, and had tried to teach her the lessons about courage and loyalty that he would have taught to his sons.

Which was all very well for a man. But a woman, although she must have courage, had to make up her own mind about the meaning of loyalty. Emma, from Normandy, had married a Saxon king and then, after he was dead, had crossed the sea again to marry his conquerer. As she had done.

And Emma, who had had three children by her Saxon husband, had left the sons to be reared in Normandy, and the daughter to be married there, and now favoured above all the son Canute her second husband had given her. Which she, Groa, would never do. Never, and never.

In the last weeks, it was a trouble to move, but she felt better walking about the well-kept timber buildings on the higher ground, and down and over the causeway to the houses of the people who lived here all the year round with their flocks and their cattle, hunting and fowling and growing their patches of crops. Here they wove on their tall looms, and made their ewe-milk cheeses and malt, and brewed their ale, and collected their honey, and came out when the travelling packhorses came to the meeting of ways and set up their booths, so that they could buy new blades for their knives, and bowls from Shetland, and a pair of brooches or a chain for a dowry-gift.

And from the same houses, when the beacons were lit or the split arrow came down the pass, glinting in an upheld fist, would come the sons who would take their swords and their shields and go to fight for her husband.

They paid their dues to the toisech, the head of the chief tribe, and he stood to the district in place of its peace-maker and governor. And through the toisech they paid their dues to the Mormaer, who guarded the province and spoke for them to the King.

Except that the Mormaer of Moray was the Earl of Orkney, who had married the dragon-head on his ship.

She was watching the last of the old peats being brought up the slope from the covered stacks to the shed by the hall door, dry and crumbling in their strapped creels, when a mellow, meaty sensation drew her attention to the mound of belly under which were her feet.

The sensation thickened into a pang and then expired, like the retiring mud of a geyser. She said to Sinna, 'Why do I make wagers? You are always right. You may have the blue cloak.'

And after that it was quick, for although it was five years since Lulach was born, she was still barely twenty. Shamefully, she got excited again towards the end, when the pains rose, and blared like a bull-horn, with barely time for a breath in between.

Then there was one abrupt crisis of violence, and a paddling sensation, and a pause, and then Sinna held up a dark-coloured starfish with fair hair on its head and on its shoulders and halfway down its back.

Of its gender there was no possible doubt. 'Welcome thy coming,' said Sinna. 'Welcome, my heartlet. Thy mother has a prince in the very likeness of the Earl your father.'

And turned round, dismayed, as the girl, squealing, buried her head in her pillow.

On closer examination, however, she appeared to be laughing.

Towards midnight, she woke from the birth-sleep, lying on clean linen with a fresh robe about her. Beyond the door, a cat seemed to be mewing. Beside her was sitting Sinna, her hands folded and circles under her eyes. There was a satisfied look on her face.

At the foot of the bed stood Thorfinn of Orkney.

She was dreaming. The lamp flickered, and his shadow ran jagged over the beams, about to bring down death like his father's black raven. She dug her elbows into the mattress and felt her quiet body give a spurt of anger. The smug expression on Sinna's face altered and she said, 'Why, you're not to be alarmed. The Earl has come to see his son. Is that not—'

'Be quiet,' said the Earl.

He was plainly dressed but clean, with the single gold arm-ring she had seen above her elbow that night at Tullich. He showed no signs of dust. Groa said, 'Have you been waiting long?' Whether she had been sleeping for hours or for minutes, she had little idea.

'It seems like months,' he said. 'In fact, about two days altogether.'

'Not here,' she said.

'Up in the hill-fort,' said Earl Thorfinn. 'It didn't seem the best moment to introduce thirty good fighting-men into the establishment. They are here now, however, and will supplement your own housecarls after I've gone. Since you will choose to give birth to the King's nephew on the King's doorstep.'

She assimilated all that. Everything he said was an insult. What made her angriest of all was the fact that he knew the baby had come, and that it was a boy, and now she would never know what he thought about it. She said, 'I suppose you've seen him, too? It's more than I have.'

'I should have thought,' said the Earl, 'that you would have had a passing introduction. He looks like something very special from inside a mountain.'

'He's your very image, my lord,' Sinna said.

That struck Groa as funny, and she laughed quite a lot. When she managed to stop, she said, 'If it had been a girl, would you have had it exposed?'

'On the contrary,' her husband said. 'I had promised to rear her for Thorkel. They say you are well,'

'Not quite well enough to give you another as yet,' Groa said. 'But that will mend in a matter of weeks. Blow a horn when you are ready.' She paused and then said, 'What priest will sprinkle the water?'

'A bold one,' said the Earl. 'The Christian rites can, I think, wait. The child has already received his name: Sigurd.'

The air in her throat rose and set, like a bread-cake. He saw her looking at him and said, 'What did you expect? He will be the next Earl of Orkney. You must both appear there as soon as you can travel.'

'How can I refuse?' the girl said. 'It surprised me that I was allowed to bear him in Moray. Or do I smell policy after all? If Lulach were dead, the mantle of Moray and Orkney would fall on this child, wouldn't it?'

'He could claim them. But Lulach, I have just been reliably instructed by Lulach, is about to outlive me. I am taking him to Duncan's consecration at Scone. I know he is six years old. He will be safe. You may even want to come, too, if you are well enough.'

Her elbow jabbed the pillow again. 'Lulach is here! You haven't . . .'

'It may be,' the Earl said, 'that you cannot quite be first with everything, but I have kept for you the exclusive privilege of introducing Lulach to his half-brother. He arrived an hour ago with his household. Before I send him in, I have to ask you what gift you want from me. I believe this is usual.'

Transfixed on one elbow, she stared at him. 'What truck have we with what is usual? I have your handsome son. What else could I want? A saddle?'

'The good manners of your father,' said Earl Thorfinn, 'might not come amiss. What do women like? A pair of brooches? A ring? I shall send for whatever you want.'

'I will take whatever you give your slaves on such an occasion,' Groa said. 'Unless you think that, being your wife, I might ask for something more personal. For example, the band that you wear above your left elbow.'

There was a silence. Then he said, 'I am sorry. That is for a man, and the man it is destined for is already chosen.'

'Indeed,' said Groa. 'Tell me when he comes to give birth. That is a child of yours all the world will want to see.'

He made no comment on that, but only unstrapped his purse and, carrying it to her bedside, emptied upon her table all it contained. He said, 'There is what silver I have. When the goldsmith comes next, have him make what you want, and hone the two edges of your tongue as well, if you feel that they need it.' Then he went out.

Ten minutes later, Lulach was by her bed, his lint-white head inclined over the wrinkled scrap in her arms. 'Sigurd,' he said. 'I have heard of no Sigurd.'

'He is named after his grandfather,' Groa said. 'He was a man of many conquests, a great man. And Earl Sigurd's grandfather was called Earl Thorfinn; and Earl Thorfinn's grandfather was called Earl Rognvald, whose brother Earl Sigurd was the first Earl of Orkney, two hundred years before this. So you see he bears a very good name.'

'Better than Rognvald?' Lulach said. 'Or don't you know the answer? An old Icelander could tell you that.'

'Then you must find one and ask him,' said Groa. 'What do you think of your brother?'

The clear, pale eyes frowned. 'I know of no Sigurd,' Lulach said.

*   *   *

The birth-feast was held a week later there at Lumphanan, and was not large, for food was scarce and any that men had in store was required for the king-making next month. The chiefs of the district came, and some of those travelling south to Duncan's summons. By then, the fur had begun to leave the child's back and shoulders and the wild hair was shredding and rubbing off from his scalp, so that there remained only a fair-headed infant with Earl Thorfinn's acorn eyes and across his cheeks the small arrows of newborn dissipation.

Groa was surprised at the richness of the gifts men brought with them, until she realised that men pay to propitiate.

She saw her husband on the occasion of the feast, but at no other time. Two weeks after that, in a litter, and accompanied by the combined households of Moray and Orkney, she moved to the mouth of the Dee, where the infant would remain with his guard and his wet-nurse until she returned. Then, with Earl Thorfinn and her older son Lulach, she set out for the sacred hill in mid-country where her husband's brother was to be made King of Alba, and she, the Lady of Moray, would stand for the first time before all these alien peoples as the Lady of Caithness and Orkney as well.

Or, as Sinna had said, when the baggage-train came from the north with her clothes-chests and her horse-harness and her ornaments, 'He may be a troll with a troll for a son, but he is king of the north, my heartlet, and you are his lady. Show them what an Arnmødling is.'

Afraid, she thought. *And short-tempered. And lonely.*

FIFTEEN

TO THE DISAPPOINTMENT of some of his vassals, the new ruler Duncan neither ate, mated with, nor took a bath ritually in horse-flesh.

He did, however, fill the riverside haugh by the Moot Hill with newly built halls and service-huts to supplement the old booths and pavilions that men used when they met to pay tribute or argue for justice. The first thing that everyone saw, sailing up the wide river Tay, or travelling overland from the north or the south, was the little monastery by the ford in the distance, dwarfed by the new buildings and the hosts of brilliant banners. Flags flew also from the fortress of Perth on the other side of the river, where the new King was staying with his Northumbrian wife and her babies.

The Earl of Orkney and Caithness had brought his own canvas, above which fluttered the banner of Moray, alone. He and his household were barely installed when a message crossed the water from Perth, inviting the lord Macbeth and his lady to sup with his half-brother Duncan.

Notified, the lord Macbeth's wife dressed accordingly and was interested to see, when she presented herself to her husband, that he, too, had adopted Saxon attire. His eyebrows rose. 'Did you wear that thing when you came with Gillacomghain?' he said.

It had caused Sinna some trouble to keep the fine linen uncrushed on the journey so that the veil flowed down her back and swathed her cheeks and neck without blemish. Groa said, 'I shall do better than you with your tunic. The hall at Perth is famous for draughts. If you are Macbeth, what am I? Margaret?'

'Silent, if possible,' he said. If he thought it dangerous to trust himself unsupported in the stronghold, he said nothing of it. But Thorkel was left behind, and he took to serve them only house-slaves and Sinna, with a few of the well-born of Moray as escort and attendants.

The King's lodging at Perth was well built, as was that of Forteviot, a short ride to the south. Passing the confluence of the Tay and the Almond, one could see from the boat the height of the split-trunk stockade, and the thickness of the gatehouse, and the cone helms of men on the wall-walk. A smell of food and the crying of children drifted over the water.

The presence of old men and of children were the mark of any event of importance to a nation, for they were the memory-stream. But where were the old men of this nation? The last monarch had died in November, and gathered here now were the young contenders, with their brides swiftly married and swiftly made pregnant, and the children who would vie with each other in turn. In two or three days, Duncan would be consecrated as King of Alba because for twenty years his grandfather had proclaimed him as such, and for ten had made sure, by dint of his sword and his silver, that no rival lived who could challenge him.

Until the young men, like Groa's husband, grew rich. Until the children, like her two sons, grew up.

At the gatehouse, Crinan, Abbot of Dunkeld and father of the King-elect, waited to conduct them inside, and trumpets blew as they met. 'To warn them to get out their knives?' Groa said.

'To warn us to keep our mouths shut,' the Earl said; and, walking forward, greeted with apparent cheerfulness the lord Abbot with the soft brown beard skeined now with grey whose coins, they said, financed every war in England and Denmark and lined purses from Cologne to Pisa.

'And here is a change!' the lord Crinan said. 'I bear greetings from Canute to his housecarl, but am afraid to deliver them, so splendid have you become. The Lady of Moray is, of course, more beautiful than before, despite her company. You have a son, lady. May he be blessed.'

She inclined her head and smiled into the lord Abbot's eyes. From this man's schemes had come the fire that had killed her husband Gillacomghain. Through the kinsmen of his son, this man had tried to claim Caithness and had failed. Beside her, Earl Thorfinn said, 'We thank you. He has no teeth as yet, but they will grow.'

'Then when he is old enough, tell him to eschew bad advice,' my lord Crinan said. 'Or walrus-fangs will hardly avail him. Edith is here with her sons. And Wulfflaed my daughter, who has borne a son of my name. I have become a patriarch.'

'I hear my lord Duncan is also a father,' Groa said. It did not do to appear entirely dumb.

'Two sons,' said the lord Crinan, smiling. 'The elder named Malcolm after his dead grandfather. And his sweet wife is already near her time with a third. Dear Alba! Your air is sweet with the laughter of children.'

The hall door had opened, and the uproar within signified neither sweetness nor laughter. 'That is,' said the lord Abbot amiably, 'at times they also behave like their elders. My son, here is your fellow, the other fruit of your mother Bethoc, of blessed memory.'

Perhaps because of his round, russet cheeks: perhaps because of his lack of height: perhaps because of the smooth-bedded eyes, his youthfulness was always the first of the prince Duncan's characteristics. Even now, it came to mind first as he turned, despite the pale tunic deep-banded with gold and silver embroidery, and the gold glittering on his knife-sheath and buckle, and at the neck of his tunic, and from all the rings on his short hands as he closed them on the upper arms of his brother and then folded them tightly over the white veil of his brother's new wife while he kissed her full on the mouth.

It was an objectionable kiss, from which Groa did not draw back, although when he released her, she saw from the watching eyes about her that it had been marked and even anticipated. One of the observers, naturally, was Duncan's wife Ailid, whose condition perhaps accounted for a few things other than her expression of muted dislike. Beside her was a three-year-old boy with red cheeks.

At her side, Groa's husband had shown no concern while Duncan embraced her, and she had not sought to catch his attention. But now, presenting himself to Duncan's lady, the Earl neither gave her his hand nor saluted her, but merely bowed and remarked, 'And this is your young *pjokk*? He looks healthy.'

She was short, like Duncan, and had to look up a long way. 'I fear I do not know your language,' she said. 'This is my son Malcolm, the prince of Cumbria.'

The Earl studied her. He remarked, 'You might enjoy learning Norse. Malcolm will have to speak it in Cumbria. In Cumbria, they will call him *lang hals*, long-throat, because they think that is what *Moel col* means.'

'I am told,' said my lord Duncan's wife, 'that you have another name also when you are in the north. Do you worship Thor, that you are named after him?'

Black as a cockchafer, the brows of Earl Thorfinn were bent on her. 'When I am in the north,' the Earl said, 'there is an old polar bear whose health I am particular about, like Eirik the Red. When I come south, I tend to worship anything. There is a lady over there who could be your very twin. Is she your sister?'

'I have three sisters here,' said my lord Duncan's wife. 'One of them is married to a kinsman of your lady wife's. You will see him there, too. Siward, son of Thore Hund.'

Her uncle Kalv's nephew. Across the hall, Groa could see him now, a heavily built young man, with his head flung back, laughing. The last time she had seen him was at Tullich, when Duncan and Siward and Forne had come to one of her bride-feasts. Where she had heard the indiscreet words of young Alfgar the Mercian: *It's better than war, isn't it? An empire trussed up in marriage-ties, from the west sea to the east across all northern England. I wonder who is the architect?* And she remembered what, obliquely, Earl Thorfinn had answered.

It seemed likely, therefore, that Earl Thorfinn himself would not want to ask the next question, since it was important. So she asked it herself, with a degree of silliness she could see fulfilled all Ailid's expectations of her. 'Four sisters!' said Groa. 'Now, I know one of them is married to Forne's nephew, isn't she? Do I remember aright? But who has married the fourth?'

Behind her, penetrating the cloth over her ears was the loudest laugh she ever remembered. The owner's hand closed on her shoulder, and his other arm went round her husband's neck. 'Guess who?' said Alfgar of Mercia.

Beside her, Earl Thorfinn spun round with his hands up, and Alfgar's fingers slid from her shoulder as he jumped back, squaring up. There was an exchange of buffets, after which Alfgar, still laughing, dropped to a stool and lay back, his hands trailing the floor. 'You've grown another three feet. What's all this about siring a son?'

He was twenty-three, and had filled out in the three years since Tullich. Well-muscled and compact, with rough, fair hair and a young, uncut beard, he had the air, now, of an only son of a royal Mercian house. Eight years ago, someone had told her, Duncan's grandfather had seen fit to make Alfgar his hostage, and Earl Thorfinn had rescued him. If it was true, they must both have been children. Earl Thorfinn said, 'What's all this about marrying a wife?'

'That's her,' said Alfgar, pointing negligently. 'She's pregnant. They're all pregnant. That is, Siward's wife had her son a month ago: name of Osbern. There's another sister as well, wife of Ligulf, and she's pregnant, too.'

'It's well seen,' Earl Thorfinn remarked, 'that the Earl of Northumbria knows what to do with his daughters. He is, I hope, a generous grandfather.'

'After paying five dowries?' said Alfgar. 'In any case, I would have you know that we all married for love. All that the Earl leaves will go to his brother Eadulf. Including the earldom. Thorfinn, my father and mother are here. Will you go and see them before the enthronement?'

People were coming towards them. 'Godiva?' the Earl enquired. 'For Godiva, I could be ordered out of Paradise to the Pit Bottomless and never notice it. May I bring Sulien?'

'Never mind Sulien,' said Alfgar, rising slowly. 'It has just come to me, looking about, that I have not yet renewed my early acquaintance with the goddess, your countess. You wouldn't consider an exchange? Mine has many powerful sisters.'

'Mine has many powerful uncles,' said Earl Thorfinn, 'who think that boundary folk don't always know their own limitations. I shall bring her with me. Look, they are calling us to table.'

'They are calling you,' Alfgar said. 'Will you do homage for Caithness? That is all he wants to find out.'

'And so he will,' the Earl Thorfinn said. 'On the day of his consecration.'

The rest of that day had no particular pleasure about it, unless it were a pleasure to break bread with three plain women when you were less so. There was a hearty-spoken man with a beard called Dubhdaleithe, whom Groa fell into conversation with because he was Abbott of Deer, the Buchan monastery that one day soon, she knew, would supply Lulach with his first teachers.

Against her will, she found the big Irishman did not displease her. Born of a line of abbots of the monastery of Armagh in Ireland; great-nephew of an abbot of Armagh and Kells, he possessed a fund of harmless gossip about most of the churchmen present and some who had not yet arrived, such as the present Abbot of Raphoe and Kells, who was to preside at the enthronement. He then moved on to her husband's relatives.

'You'll have met the Bishop Malduin. That's him over there, the pink fellow, with his feathers ruffled because you've picked myself, an abbot only, to honour with that lovely face you have. Trained in Ireland and consecrated seven long years ago in York to look after the souls and ordain the new priests in Alba, but you'd be lucky, were you a would-be priest, to find him in daylight anywhere north of Northumbria. He's for civilised living these days, and not anxious to recall that he was brought up in the Western Isles, and his mother an Orkney earl's sister. He's your husband's full cousin.'

'I've never met him,' Groa said.

'Ah, he'd be worried what York and Duncan would say. You'll be all right now,' said Abbot Dubhdaleithe cheerfully. 'You'll be sitting next to him, I shouldn't wonder, for all the good it may do you. What is it they say? *These are the three that are hardest to talk to: a king bent on conquest; a Viking in his armour; and a low-born man protected by patronage.*'

'I see,' Groa said. 'And what are you waiting for me to say? That I have the knack of dealing with all of them?'

'The thing that is giving me joy,' said the Abbot Dubhdaleithe of Deer, 'is that I have no idea what you are going to say next. You'll set Bishop Malduin to gnawing the fork of his fist out of fear for you.'

She was too wise to answer with more than a smile, but what he said helped when she found herself sitting at table between that same Malduin, Bishop of Alba, and a man with a mild, noble face: the abbot mint-master who was King Duncan's father.

Terror, naturally, did not manifest itself in the neatly manicured person of her husband's cousin the Bishop, who appeared to have no more in common with her husband than a robin might have with a hen-harrier. Chatting of minor Irish-born clergy who lived and served the Celtic church throughout Alba, the Bishop's manner was a model of the kindliest tolerance. From time to time, speaking as man to man, he invited the opinion of my lord Crinan, across her. Later, as they took her measure, they each asked her the same questions, and she parried them, thoughtfully, in different ways.

Several places along the table, she could hear the Earl her husband doing the same, but more skilfully. She was getting used to the sound of his voice: half an octave lower than most men's, unmistakable whether speaking in Norse or Gaelic or Saxon, and inflected naturally for each. His face, she had learned, never changed either. All you could do was listen to what he said and apply your mind to it. She knew that an alliance between Mercia and Northumbria was a prospect no one in Moray had ever contemplated. Yet he had treated Alfgar like a brother.

To the King his brother at that moment he was saying, '. . . Why not leave serious affairs for serious occasions? When do you mount the Moot Hill?'

'When Kells and Raphoe condescends to arrive,' Duncan said splashily, and then repeated the sentence carefully. 'I told him to stay on in November, but no, he had to set sail. And look what happened.'

'What happened?' said Earl Thorfinn obediently. On her other side, Bishop Malduin asked Groa an encouraging question and she delivered the right answer, listening.

'What happened? Macnia's boat overturned. The Lector. The Abbot's brother. Drowned on the spot, and thirty men from Kells with him. Worse, they lost half the relics. They lost Saint Columba's book, and the canopy, and three of the swearing-relics of Saint Patrick. Grandfather was all right,' said Duncan bitterly. 'They let out the two girls who were keeping him warm and put the book on his chest, and he died shriven whiter than snow. But what am I to use for swearing-relics?'

'The two girls?' said Earl Thorfinn. 'Did they all drown, or did the Coarb of Columba struggle back to Raphoe and Kells?'

'I told you,' Duncan said pettishly. 'Maelmuire's boat got there safely. He was told when to come back. He should have come back days ago. If he's drowned, I shan't wait. Malduin can do it alone.'

Bishop Malduin, next to Groa, looked up at the sound of his name. 'It's all right,' Groa said. 'You have just been nominated to conduct the service of consecration if the Abbot of Kells has been shipwrecked. What relics do you use?'

There was a pause. 'We have St Fergus's head,' Bishop Malduin said. 'At least . . . Unless King Malcolm sold it.'

'Send to Emma,' said Alfgar cheerfully. 'Winchester is a charnel-house for Emma's relics: she has one for every day of the week. Who but Emma could cheat the Ascension and show you the milk-tooth of Christ?'

'Would a milk-tooth do?' said the Earl Thorfinn, turning to Duncan. 'It might produce some very small oaths.'

'What?' said Duncan.

Later, in their pavilion, the Earl spoke to his wife. 'Are you tired? It was hard work.'

'A little,' said Groa. Her women were waiting to put her to bed, and her body ached.

He said, 'Crinan talked a great deal. What questions did he ask?'

She found the end of her headdress and began to unwind it. Strands of red hair, in rat's tails, emerged from underneath. 'Was Lulach a healthy child, and did you propose to foster him,' she said. 'Did I think you would do homage for Caithness. Was the new child a healthy one, and did you propose to foster him. Did I think you would do homage for Caithness. Did my father in Norway favour the marriage, and what was his standing now that King Olaf was canonised. Did I—'

'—think that I would do homage for Caithness,' he finished. 'What did you answer?'

'I told them the truth,' Groa said. 'That I knew nothing of your affairs and, so far as I could see, was going to be blessed with such ignorance to the end of my days. Of my father, I said I had no news to give them, since I had seen none of my people for three years or more. When they asked me if you had other wives, I said I was sure of it.'

'Did you? Why?' said the Earl. Her women had come to help with the headdress, and he watched them.

'It is your children they are afraid of,' said Groa.

'Indeed?' he said.

Her headdress came off, and she jerked her hair free. Her cheeks tingled with risen blood, and then cooled. She said, 'Who is Godiva?'

'The Lady of Mercia? She is Alfgar's mother, the wife of Earl Leofric. Think of every woman you have ever admired.'

'No. You think of them,' said Groa. 'I am tired.'

The thirty-eighth Coarb of Columba and Adamnan, Maelmuire Uah Uchtain, Abbot of Kells and Raphoe, arrived next day, travel-stained and in no very good temper, with a retinue of forty laymen and monks, a book-shrine, and a casket of different relics. The chests of altar-silver and vestments filled a cart drawn by eight oxen and had their own guard of mail-shirted spearmen with crosses marked on all their weapons. It was easy to see how Macnia's boatload had sunk like a stone.

The ceremony was announced for the following day, and the Earl Thorfinn directed his wife to dress and accompany Sulien and himself to the tent of Earl Leofric of Mercia. She refused.

'Very well. I am taking Lulach,' he said. 'In ten minutes.'

In ten minutes, she was standing, dressed, by the pavilion door. A few minutes later her husband arrived with the boy and Sulien. 'You will need a child-minder,' Groa said, 'while your mind is on other things. What lies do you want me to tell for you today?'

'Ones that Lulach can't contradict,' the Earl said. 'Lulach?'

The white head came up. 'I don't know of this meeting,' Lulach said.

'You see? Perfect discretion,' said Earl Thorfinn to his wife. 'Now come and help me control Alfgar. And ask *him*, if you have the chance, why he's married Duncan's wife's sister.'

The white head came up.

'I know,' said Earl Thorfinn to his stepson. 'You don't know about that.'

'No, I don't,' said the child. 'Although it's very likely.'

'I'm glad,' said the Earl. 'So, I'm sure, is Alfgar, considering his wife is about to give birth. Lulach? The Chester sign is a boar. You will see it better if you sit on my shoulders. Now. Show us.' And so, white hair above black, they found the Mercian hall and were led inside to meet the Earl Leofric and his lady.

They were not there for long, and Groa did not even see her hosts at first, because Alfgar rushed at Sulien and knocked him to the floor, and they rolled over, shouting, while her husband in front of her swung her son to the ground. Then she heard a voice speaking Saxon, and saw an erect man in his early forties, in a furred coat, rise from a bench and come forward. Behind him came a lady who was clearly his wife Godiva.

She was everything that Earl Thorfinn had implied. Stately and slender, with a large-boned face of perfect proportions and yellow hair drawn back and knotted under a light coif of muslin. Her neck, bare like Groa's own, was a column of marble.

Lulach ran to her. She smiled down at him, ruffling his hair, and then stood him facing outwards, her hands on his shoulders. 'Now,' she said to Groa, 'I am jealous. What fool is telling the world that he married you for your province?'

'Not this fool,' said Alfgar from the floor. 'There, as the saying goes, stands a merry man as he twirls the ladle round in the bowl. He has a son, born within these three weeks.'

'And of course you are allowing his mother to stand,' said the Lady Godiva. 'Get off my adored Sulien and find servants to bring us some cakes and some wine, and then tell them to go. Thorfinn . . . What do I call you?'

'Perhaps . . . Macbeth,' he said. 'My wife's name in Gaelic is Gruoch.'

'My lord and lady of Moray and Orkney, you are welcome. Come to table. There are two men here for you to meet. Sulien, you as well.'

Gruoch. It was what they called her in Moray. She did not know that he knew it. She followed the rest to the table. Two men rose behind it: one strongly built in his thirties with a white scar of some kind on his clean-shaven jaw. The other was younger and bearded, with bright, narrow eyes and a heavy nose flattened from some early breaking.

'My lord Crinan brought them,' said Lady Godiva, 'from Brittany on some affair to do with Shrewsbury and the Marches, and had them accompany him north. I know their families. Perhaps you met them when you were with the Lady?'

It seemed unlikely. Then Groa recalled the years at Canute's court, and the time her husband had spent as Emma's man at Exeter and elsewhere, and the errands he had run, they said, over the sea to her homeland.

He did know one of them at least. Going forward, the Earl of Orkney said, 'Juhel de Fougères. Indeed, we met at Combour. But your friend from Normandy is a stranger.'

The scarred man smiled. 'A good guess,' he said. 'And half right. My name is Osbern de Eu. I am Norman-born. But Alan of Brittany is my cousin.'

'He has another cousin,' said Lady Godiva. 'In Normandy.'

'It is a great thing,' said the scarred man, 'to be able to boast of a kinsman called William the Bastard. What feat of arms could bring me more fame than my cousinship? Who am I? Cousin to William the Bastard, the eight-year-old lord Duke of Normandy.'

'I would rather say, nephew to the Lady Emma,' Earl Thorfinn observed. 'Even the fort of Eu was built—wasn't it?—by the Lady Emma's great-grandfather, who was an ancestor of mine, I might mention. So in a sense we are cousins as well. May we sit and investigate?'

'That is why you are here,' Godiva said. 'The Lady of Moray and I will sit and investigate by ourselves, on the other side of the room. Come, my dear.'

Groa followed. A seat was forthcoming, and some wine, both of which she required. She prepared to answer questions on the theme of maternity. The Lady Godiva said, 'Leofric has brought your husband here to give him some news. King Canute is ill, and may die before the end of the year. That is the reason for Alfgar's marriage.'

Groa looked at the open, intelligent eyes, and her brain cleared. 'Thank you,' she said. 'Thank you for telling me.' A further thought struck her. She took a breath, and released it.

'You should not tell me too much,' the Lady said. 'It is for your husband to do that. But I know a mission has gone to fetch King Olaf's young son back to Norway. I would expect the same reason prompted it. If the mission delays, it will be because it is waiting for Canute to die.'

Kalv. Kalv nobly struggling to Russia to bring back the rightful heir, with, as he would point out, all the risks that entailed. Kalv, staying all winter in Novgorod arguing, putting off time, hoping that news would come soon: *Canute the overlord of Norway is dead. It is safe to go back now with our child-king.* Groa said, 'Whatever Canute was as a youth, he has been a strong ruler, and not a bad one. I think I prefer what we have to what may come after. What will happen to Mercia?'

The Lady Godiva looked across the room to where her husband sat, wine in hand, busy in talk with the three Bretons and her son and Thorfinn of Orkney. 'We are not as large as we were,' she said. 'But powerful enough, as Northumbria is, to use our weight and play tactics. Sometimes we help to fight off the Welsh, and sometimes we league with them. Sometimes we encourage the Irish who come to trade with us, and at other times we warn them away. We have only one son, as against the host of young men struggling for power in Northumbria, and in some ways that is good, although a great deal depends on Alfgar. . . . I expect your husband needs a large family, soon, to hold all the land he has inherited?'

'It is necessary,' Groa said.

'It may be necessary, but it is not easy to be his wife in other things with dignity, as you are doing,' Godiva said. 'Even if you have nothing else, you have a partnership.'

Groa looked, in her turn, across the room. Thorfinn her husband was speaking, his black hair obscuring half his face. The deep voice, indecipherable, went on, mixed with comments from Alfgar and Sulien. She said, 'He must have been quite young when he came first to Chester.'

'He ran a race on the oars as my husband's boat passed down the river. Yes, young. Perhaps nineteen,' said Lady Godiva. 'But he knew what he wanted then, and he got it. I have often wondered if he thought it worth while.' She smiled suddenly. 'Am I insulting you?'

'No,' said Groa. 'I understand you. I don't know what he thinks. And that is the truth.'

'Perhaps that is safest,' the Lady said. The men were rising. She rose as well, and held out her hand to Lulach, who was crossing the room led by one of her slaves. Godiva said, 'He is a beautiful child. You didn't hear, by any chance, the discussion over my hair?'

Groa sighed and put her arm round the boy. 'No,' she said. 'Lulach, what did you say about the Lady Godiva?'

The clear eyes looked up. 'When I was Roger, I wrote about it,' Lulach said. 'Her long hair and white legs. Is your husband cruel to the people of Coventry?'

The Lady laughed. 'No, he isn't,' she said. 'And thank you for the compliments, even if they are only guesswork.' Earl Thorfinn had arrived. The Lady Godiva looked at him over the boy's head and said, 'Does he speak like this to you?'

'Yes,' said the Earl. 'He says you are a fertility goddess. I believe him.'

When they got back to their pavilions, Groa saw there was a man in spurs waiting outside the tent her husband used, with his men. She recognised him as one of the Amundasons from Helmsdale. He was covered with mud. When he saw Earl Thorfinn was approaching, he went inside the tent.

She knew Earl Thorfinn had seen him, but he said nothing of it, and left her at the entrance to her own quarters. After that, she did not see him for the rest of that day.

He had, of course, some acquaintances among the toisechs and mormaers and churchmen gathered here for the king-making, and doubtless there were many more whom he wished to meet. She had observed him already that morning, moving between one building and another, always with a group of men about him, talking.

There were some women she knew there also, from the days of Gillacomghain, and it would only be civil to seek them out again. She called Sinna and gave her instructions and proceeded to fill the rest of her own day, as it turned out, to her entire satisfaction.

Next day, standing in sunshine round the Mód or Moot Hill, the men of Mercia and of Cumbria and of Lothian and of a few places much further south watched the toisechs of Alba, from the Forth to the Spey, receive their new monarch.

Above the high cross: above the gold-fringed banners of Kells, fluttering before the porch of the little stone church of the monastery, rose the strains of the antique liturgy of the Gallician church of the Celts.

The threefold cry of the tersanctus, the Canticle, the Collect, and all the Eastern rituals, mixed with plainsong and organum and the long, unwinding scroll of the Alleluias, floated up and over the sky with the incense and ended. The banners jolted while the tonsured heads eddied, like floats round a rock, and the other heads, bare, mitred, or capped, worked through the crowd and settled, at length, into a slow-moving stream which made its way from the church and across and up to the Moot Hill.

'Credentia,' the Breton from Fougères said, 'is the other name, I am told, for this hill. How many hills of Credon do you know? I suppose it is practical. The hill where rights of credit are exercised by the seigneur; where tribute is brought at the correct seasons.'

'Some of them claim it means Hill of Belief,' said Osbern of Eu. 'It is part of the king-making. You must be practical in all directions. And it is a long time since the churchmen have had to present to the people a king. He cannot be known to them: the men of this country live in their pockets of rock as do seabirds and are hardly aware one colony of another, except to make war from time to time. So the king must be a symbol. So you see the sitting upon the stone, now, and the giving of the cloak and the wand. Then they will recite the names of his fathers, and he will take the oath of kingship, to protect and father his peoples. My lord Crinan explained it.'

'I heard him,' said Juhel de Fougères. 'What is important to you and to me is what follows.'

Among the royal kindred, like a pine tree over juniper scrub, the King's half-brother stood, his hands clasped behind him, his cloak pinned to one shoulder. The Breton said, 'There he is. A lapis-dyed velvet, you will note. How could the grandfather have been such a fool as to marry his daughter to Orkney?'

'Was he a fool?' said the other man. 'To his deathbed, he claimed overlordship of Caithness, and of Sigurd's other conquests as well. He could no longer hold them but he could claim them.'

'Then let us see,' said the Breton, 'what stuff his grandsons are made of, and who will claim, and who will refuse.'

From her place beside the Earl her husband, with the sun hot on her long, woven robe and her veil and her train, Groa saw the two men conversing. Beside her, Lulach was silent, as he had been through all the service: watching Duncan; watching equally his stepfather Thorfinn of Orkney with those clear, pale eyes as he moved without speaking through the ritual. Now, as the singing cut through the air and the robed figures clustered close about the short figure, square in its great chair under the canopy, she said in a low voice, 'When? When is the homage paid?'

'Now,' he said. 'Or soon. My cousin the Bishop will be first.'

'And then you?' she said. He spoke with absolute calm. A month ago, a week ago, she would have thought nothing of it.

'Probably,' he said. He was looking not at the ceremony in front or at the crowds down below, all around them, but beyond, as if searching for something. 'And then the feast?' she said. 'Lulach, you will enjoy that.'

'No. I have made my excuses to Duncan. After this we must leave,' said the Earl.

'Leave?' said Groa. Heads were turning, and she lowered her voice still further. 'But why? The messenger last night? Is there news? What is it?'

'Nothing troublesome,' he said. 'But there is really no reason to linger. And there is the baby. Thorkel, as you know, is not far away.'

If you need help, go to Thorkel, was what he was saying. Because if a crisis was coming, it would not save him to leave before the feast. This was one of Duncan's homes: here were his people: there, massed behind, were the men paid to defend him and his family. Here, Duncan could strike as he pleased, and vengeance, Thorkel's or anyone else's, would not raise the dead. She said, and did not realise how far her thoughts had carried her, 'And whom shall I marry then?'

'Duncan,' her husband said. 'Eventually. I imagine Raphoe and Kells would frown on a second wife, but the first one might always perish in childbirth. What do you wager that they'll call the new child Maelmuire? They won't let the Abbot over to Kells till he's baptised it, that's certain.'

The singing faded. The monks moved back. The steps cut into the grass of the Moot Hill were cleared, and the Abbot of Kells, bowing, came and removed from Duncan's hands the golden wand of his kingship. From two different parts of the mound, trumpets blared. Her husband said, 'I must tell you something.'

She had been scanning the meadow. It was true. Their pavilions had been struck. The flag of Moray was flying nowhere except here, behind the Earl's head. Then his words reached her, and she looked up into his direct gaze. 'What?' she said.

'Look,' said Lulach.

Children spoke, and one did not need to listen. Her eyes on Earl Thorfinn's, Groa said again, 'What?'

'Look,' said Lulach. 'A rider. A man speaking to the King's men.'

Earl Thorfinn turned, and did not turn back.

She therefore watched, too, as Lulach's rider dismounted and spoke: an envoy as bemired as her husband's man of the previous night, and as weary. Watched as the message went from one mouth to a second and then was carried under the canopy, to be slipped with discretion into the new monarch's ear.

Duncan listened, and turned red, and then pale. Her husband said, 'Lulach? Why don't I listen to you? You couldn't carry me yet.'

He looked different. Groa said, 'Is this solely between you and Lulach, or might I know what is happening?'

'Of course,' said the Earl Thorfinn. 'I am about to kneel to my brother in homage. There goes the Bishop. The hands. The promise. The kiss. Ah, well. *Ni heuir ni fedir*, as Sulien would say. No sowing, no harvest.' And as the Abbot of Kells stood before him, he gave him his hand and allowed himself to be led to the chair in the midst of the Moot Hill.

And in the event it was Sulien, whom he had invoked, who stood closest to the King's brother when he came to kneel, his cloak spread on the ground, before the High Chair; and Sulien's gaze, steady and searching, that rested on him throughout.

The Earl Thorfinn knelt, and Duncan looked down on him, his russet cheeks yellowed.

Silence fell. On the mound, those near to the chair could hear the King breathing. Then, slowly, the Earl lifted both hands, closed them palm to palm, and offered them as in prayer to his brother.

On the chair-arms, the short, ringed hands curled and uncurled as the two men remained, their gaze locked. Then, lifting his hands in turn, Duncan covered the passive fingers of vassaldom with the hands of the King. 'Make your oath. I will hear it,' he said.

From whatever caverns it came, the rich voice carried with ease: to the King's father and his wife and all her kindred; to the churchmen of Alba and Ireland; to the men who held their lands of the King and who would come in their turn to kneel and to submit. Her hands on Lulach's shoulders, Groa listened.

'I, Macbeth stepson of Findlaech son of Ruaidhrí, Mormaer of Moray, do accept thee Duncan son of Bethoc son of Malcolm as overlord for my lands in that province, and swear to defend them as the King would defend them from the enemies of Alba, and to pay what the King is due, as Findlaech my stepfather paid it. Further, my lord—'

He paused. Watching, Sulien saw that Duncan's grip on the closed hands had slackened, as his face had slackened. A little rustle ran over the mound and was gone. Everyone waited.

'—Further,' said the profound voice, 'I, Macbeth stepfather of Luloecen son of Gillacomghain son of Maelbrighde son of Ruaidhrí beg my lord King's permission to name my stepson Luloecen this day as my successor, to be Mormaer of Moray and its lands in Mar after me, and to become your man in his turn for these lands.'

'You have leave,' Duncan said. He dropped his hands.

Thorfinn of Orkney lowered his gently and, rising, drew something from under his cloak. 'This belonged to his great-uncle. It would do the boy great honour, sire, if the King's highness were to invest him with it now, in earnest of his forthcoming succession?'

Before Duncan had nodded, it seemed, Lulach was walking buoyantly up to the High Chair and was looking from his King to his stepfather. 'The ring?' he said. 'It's the ring, isn't it?'

Sulien didn't know what he meant. But Groa did, even before she saw the gold glimmer in Earl Thorfinn's hands, and then in Duncan's, and heard Lulach laugh because the big band would stay neither on his wrist nor above his elbow, but had to be held. Then the Bishop's voice quelled the rustle of comment and someone else was moving to kneel at the chair. Lulach dashed up beside her and, smiling, she put her hand over his mouth and then removed it to run her fingers admiringly over his ring. Then she removed them because they were shaking, and summoned her courage, and turned to her husband, returned to her side.

'You didn't tell me,' she said. 'About Lulach.'

'It was a surprise,' said the Earl. His face was impassive as ever, but his eyes seemed to have become a shade lighter. He said, 'It all depended on how Duncan felt.'

'And you didn't do homage for Caithness,' Groa said. 'Was that a surprise, too?'

'It was, to Duncan,' said Earl Thorfinn.

With difficulty, she weathered a reverent silence, then burst into whispers once more. 'Then why didn't he demand Caithness tribute? What made you think he'd grant favours?'

'Because he's just had some news and doesn't know what to do about it,' the Earl said. 'And my hope is that by the time he's made up his mind we'll be on shipboard.'

'News?' said Groa.

'Sad news. Remember all those Norse-Irish colonies I cleared out of the south-west for him? Perhaps you don't, but I did.'

'More fool you,' said Groa boldly.

'That's Thorkel's favourite comment. You must judge by results.'

'They came back?'

'They couldn't come back. They were dead. No. It's worse than that. A different lot of Irish-Norse have moved in and occupied all their lands.'

'So he wants you to clear them out all over again? I don't think you should,' Groa said.

'I don't think I should either,' said the Earl. 'In fact, I don't think even Duncan expects me to.'

At last, she became suspicious. 'Why? Wait a moment. Who are the new Irish-Norse? Who is their leader?'

'Eachmarcach,' said her husband simply. 'He's just used all Duncan's good bases to make himself King of Dublin.'

There was a long, long silence, during which twenty people offered to be liegemen to King Duncan and Groa heard none of them. At the end—

'You are clever, aren't you?' she said flatly.

'I married you. Otherwise—yes, I am certainly clever,' said Earl Thorfinn agreeably. 'It comes from living in Orkney. You will see when you get there.'

SIXTEEN

THAT SPRING, Kalv Arnason and the bonder of Trøndelagen sailed from Ladoga to Sweden as soon as the ice broke and by summer had crossed Kolan to Vaerdalen and Nídarós, accompanied by the late King Olaf's eleven-year-old bastard son Magnús. There, on the Eyrar of the river Nid, the bonder proclaimed Magnús the new King of Norway, and Magnús in turn declared an amnesty to all those concerned in his father's slaying of five years before.

It was further decreed that Kalv Arnason was to be regent during King Magnús's minority.

It was not proclaimed, because everyone noticed in any case, that wherever the boy-King Magnús might go, he was accompanied by his beautiful foster-brother: Rognvald son of Brusi the late Earl of Orkney.

The news came to Orkney with a trading-vessel and was brought by Thorkel Fóstri to Thorfinn, who did not swear this time even in Norse, but merely said, 'So it seems, brave Kalv, that King Canute is not expected to live.'

He thought. 'I seem to remember that Rognvald was once betrothed to my wife. Break the news gently to her, my foster-father—she may not be pleased to learn that she has married the wrong man.'

'And is that all you have to say?' Thorkel said. He knew now that he was not being told everything. It did not help to know that no one was in a better position. Since they came to Orkney, Thorfinn had taken no trouble to conceal the fact that he and his wife slept within separate partitions. 'Perhaps you have married the wrong wife,' Thorkel said.

'What are you saying?' Thorfinn said. 'Her uncle is regent of Norway, and her mother's cousin is King. By the way, I am taking eight ships to Dublin, not five. With all that going on, no one is likely to disturb us this summer except perhaps young Svein, looking for help or new subjects now that Magnús has deposed him. If he does, throw him out. Emma will like it.'

In the event, it was Thorfinn himself who came back from Ireland in time to sail south and show Duncan, in the throes of a minor invasion, how to dissuade Canute's oldest son from the idea of landing in Fife on the east coast of Alba. There were enough men at his rear to make sure that, while facing

Svein's spears in the front, the spears of his brother Duncan might not find their way through the back of his jacket, which had not been charmed by a Lapp. The well-known fact that he now held large parts of Strathclyde and Galloway in joint possession with Eachmarcach of Dublin and had just come back from establishing his interests in the Viking city of Dublin itself was not referred to by anybody.

By dint of collecting silver instead of heads from all the richer Danes he encountered, he returned to Orkney that autumn with a satisfied hird and a good deal left over to add to the shiploads he had already brought back from Dublin.

In November, King Canute died in Shaftesbury at a time that pleased everybody, since no one could go to war, and everyone could take time to sharpen their weapons and make allies and think what to do when the spring came.

It was the most interesting winter there had been for years.

Thore Hund, storm-stayed on his way back to Norway after his summer fur-voyage, remained part of the winter in Orkney with the Earl and his wife at their various halls.

He found a dozen others like himself, hemmed in by the gales and the currents and content to spend Yule as the guests of Earl Thorfinn, whose hearth and whose tables were always well plenished from the winter feast until spring-time, and whose generosity to the men who served him in Orkney and Caithness and to the stranger benighted at his door was already well known.

What the Earl gleaned from it all, in trade and news and future alliances, Thore Hund also began to recognise, as the feasting gave way to the talk, and the talk, sometimes when he was still there, to the planning. To Thorfinn's famous wife Groa, whose uncle Kalv had wed Thore's own sister, Thore Hund said, 'I am not sure where I have not seen something to match this before, unless it were a geyser, that time I was trading to Iceland. I am not a man who often feels tired, but Thorfinn makes me feel tired.'

'You have had a hard summer,' Groa said. They were at Orphir at the time. Because, in their fecundity, the Earls of Orkney had had so often to divide Orkney among numbers of sons, the islands were plenished in every quarter with Earls' halls, all commodious and built of good timber from Norway. And because the pasture was rich enough, except where the flagstones lay underground, the landed men, the *gaeðingar* of Orkney, were able to pay their Earl's winter tribute in food and malt from each ounceland which from quarter to quarter would keep the Earl and his *hirðmaðr* and his guests until the seas opened again in the spring-time. And if there appeared a shortage of anything, a boat or two sent on a calm day to Caithness would replenish the storehouse.

Since the Moot Hill enthronement, Groa had come to know Caithness as well as her husband's mysterious Orkney. Until then, she had seen it twice. Once, as a pregnant, mutinous child in a brief landing at Duncansby. And once, three years after that, when Gillacomghain had dragged her north to share in the war which was to place his nephew in Caithness, aided by that treacherous fleet from the south under Carl, son of Thorbrand of York. The strange little war that changed her life.

The burned hall at Thurso had been rebuilt. In the event, Thorfinn had not taken her there, but to a new hall set on the heights overlooking the wide sweep of sands on the other side of the river. She had also stayed briefly at Duncansby, at Freswick, and at Canisbay, where stood the most recent hall-house of all, on the high ground which looked down to the little thatched church of St Drostan's and the strand which ran along to the jetty at Huna. Two miles offshore lay the long green flank of the island of Stroma, with its snout pointing eastwards into the eddies.

The white shell-sand and the yellow sand of the rocks, the great broken headlands of sunlit red stacks circled with seabirds brought back, like the tide surging into a geo, the memory of all she had lost when she lost Austrât; and in the red cliffs and green turf of Orkney, she came face to face with her childhood itself. To her husband's young church-friend Sulien, when for the third night she had barred herself, weeping, into her box-bed, she had said through the door, 'It is nothing. I have come home, and among enemies.'

But she was not among enemies, because when, the next day, shame drove her to dress and to show herself, neither Skeggi nor Thorkel nor Starkad nor Arnór nor any of the argumentative host of her husband's immediate circle made any comment, nor, when she met them, did their women. Sulien, even-tempered as ever, was kind as she knew he would be, and made no overtures. Earl Thorfinn, who had been away fighting, they said, brought back with him the same unmoving face and the disrespectful, impersonal tongue that made her hackles rise and drove her to untangle her wits and put them to use quickly once more.

Lulach, under the tutelage of Sulien, and of the big Abbot Dubhdaleithe of Deer, was growing, she saw from time to time, like a wand. The infant, in the women's hall with his nurses, was fat and happy.

She was not among enemies: she had learned that, and she must not forget it. On the contrary. She was among people who did not hate their property, but conserved it and took care that no harm should befall it. She could hope to finish her days in peace and even in some sort of contentment, could she learn to think like a piece of good grazing-ground.

Even if you have nothing else, you have a partnership. What idiot had propounded that? The Mercian woman whom Earl Thorfinn admired. To whom, evidently, it was all too plain that there was nothing else in this marriage. And she had been wrong, at that. Nine months before that, there had been several intervals of four minutes each which might count, legally, as evidence of a union. Since then, there had been none.

From the time Sigurd was two months of age, she had prepared, silently, for the expected accosting; and none had come. Her husband had brought her to Caithness and then had vanished to Ireland, and from Ireland down to Alba, where he had stayed, or been kept, until autumn.

Thorkel Fóstri had brought her in his absence to Orkney and had been the first to introduce her to her husband's own lands. If, when Earl Thorfinn came back, he was told anything of her three-day retiral, she had no means of knowing. Only, after the feasting on the first evening of his return, he did not even spend the night in the same hall, never mind lift the latch of her partition. And it was the same the following night, and the next.

On the fourth day, they had moved north to the mainland at Birsay, and the hall there had no room for the women, but only one separate chamber at the end for the lord and the lady.

Like all her husband's possessions, it was well built and well kept, and rushes were already laid and hangings up before they arrived. Soon, the carts and the panniers of the eyki would be emptied and the hall dressed in readiness for the first of the feasts which would introduce to this district the child who would be their next earl, and his mother. She had seen the baby passed from end to end of the rollicking boards like a sheep's pluck during one of these feasts, and remembered Finn's tale of how the Wends served the young of their conquered, tossing them from one man to the next on their spearpoints. Her husband said, 'Are you cold? You are supposed to have a fur cloak for weather like this.'

For a minute, for two minutes perhaps if she were fortunate, they were alone by the bedchamber entrance. She said, 'Instruct me. Where do we each sleep?'

'Ah,' said the Earl Thorfinn and looked at her. 'Is this a conversation we should be having outside?'

'Since the subject is tenant-service,' Groa said, 'I suppose it might take place anywhere. Indeed, gather the elders round the thing-field if you wish.'

'Bring in the hammer the bride to hallow,' he said. 'All right. Let us make a pilgrimage round the graves of my fathers and see what the trolls have to say. Take my cloak.'

Round every house-stead there were burial mounds: some no more now than hummocks in the sandy turf. Before the priests came, a man's kindred were not driven far from their hearth-stones when their days on earth were finished, and you could get good advice, the wise-women said, by lying at night near the haugs, and good dreams by using their turf for a pillow. Groa said, as the wind caught her hair, 'You would hear that Fridgerd had died.' His cloak was made of wolfskin and lined with red wool, so heavy that the wind hardly lifted it. 'She went back to Iceland and ended her life as a nun.'

'I expect I ought to believe that,' the Earl said. 'After all, so did Gudrun, and how many husbands did she have? Four? And got rid of at least one other suitor. Did Arnór make a long, tragic poem?'

'He hasn't made any poems since he heard,' Groa said. 'Why didn't you take him to Ireland? He would have a harp-bag full of deathless eulogies to console himself with. Unless you ran from every battle?'

'As you see. What is it, then? You want me to act the husband? In fact, or just for the women?'

The wind whipped her breath away. She stopped and faced him. 'Indeed, I am suffering from no more than curiosity and a certain suspense,' Groa said.

'I understood there was some urgency in the matter. But if you have the pox or another wife, you may consider the enquiry withdrawn.'

'Good,' said the Earl. 'Then shall we go back? I miss my cloak.'

She did not move. 'Do you have another wife?'

'I thought of Emma,' said Earl Thorfinn, 'but she's fifty-three if she's a day, and I have nothing to offer her that she could make use of anyway. No. While your relatives are doing so well, I am quite content with the present arrangement. I was under the impression that you might be content with the present arrangement as well. We have a Mormaer of Moray and an Earl of Orkney in the making. It would be a pity to go to all that trouble again and produce a daughter for Rognvald to marry.'

'I thought that you had already promised the first girl to Thorkel,' Groa said.

'I had. Thorkel wriggled out of the arrangement,' the Earl said. 'I thought him chicken-hearted. I still think him chicken-hearted. He believed that you and I should be prevented from breeding.'

'In that case, he must be relieved at the turn of events,' Groa said. 'I don't suppose, since you no longer require me, that I might be allowed to take Sigurd to Norway and stay for a while with my parents?'

'I may have given the impression that I don't require you,' the Earl said, 'but I didn't invite you to take leave of your senses. The first act of Magnús's advisers would be to hold you and the baby as hostage.'

'Why? How could your plans affect Kalv?' Groa said. 'Or could I guess?'

'I'm sure you can guess,' Earl Thorfinn said. 'But don't act on it, that's all. As for the next generation, I feel we might review the matter, say, in a year.'

'You do?' Groa said. 'But is this the Thorfinn that Arnór sings about? What nations may fall to your axe before another year and nine months come to pass, and yourself all unprepared? Lulach and Sigurd cannot be expected to take care of everything. I must say,' said Groa, warming to her subject, 'that this must be the first time in history that a war-lord has planned his procreation to coincide with his strategy. What happens if you lose Moray and Orkney? You'll have a surplus.'

Jogging obstinately at his side as he strode back to the hall, she kicked the wolfskin, hitched it up, and stumbled again. Cross and perverse, she added, 'My lord Earl?' enticingly.

He stopped, and the sky was blotted out. He took hold of each of her arms, and even through the wolfskin he made sure that it hurt. 'You want my services, do you?' he said. 'You may have them. Tell me. I can make a beginning now, if you want. There are not so many people about. And from now on—am I right?—you want my unstinted duty, as often as you can accommodate me, through the twenty-four hours of each day and the seven days of each week until, I suppose, you become too old to conceive every year and take, like other wives, to finding and bringing home girls for me? . . . I agree. Over there is a place out of the wind. The ground is soft. What are you waiting for?'

Locked in half-mocking, half-bitter badinage, drunk with word-play, she had forgotten the mongrel he was. She had never known what his boundaries were. She had never known him at all. The fire sparked and the insults stung and glittered and it was all real, and she was standing alone in limbo with no guidelines at all.

Her body shook as it had at Inverness when she had brought the spears down on his ship and Sigurd had been conceived. She said, 'Let me go. Please let me go. I meant none of it.'

'You didn't, did you?' he said, and released the cloak, and walked off, alone, into the hall.

So now she talked with half her mind to Thore Hund in Orphir, and with the other half thought, despite herself, of what the Lady of Mercia had said. Even if you have nothing else, you have a partnership.

For the short time she had spent in her husband's company: for those two days at the Moot Hill, it had been true.

Now she again had his company, in public at least. And here was Thore of Huntingdon at her side, a grizzled windbag of grumbles and gossip and father to Siward, who had land in his father's shire and in York and had lost no time in marrying one of the five Northumbrian sisters whose kindred, hand holding hand, stretched from sea to sea.

The Lady of Orkney sat down. 'Never mind Earl Thorfinn and his energy,' Groa said. 'Tell me what you have been doing.'

The winter passed. When news came in, she made sure of hearing it.

The empire of Canute the Great, lord of England, Denmark, Norway, friend to Emperor and to Pope, was slipping bit by bit from the young, the greedy, the grasping and inept hands he had left it with.

Of the two sons of Canute's wife Alfiva, Svein at twenty-one had already shown himself a poor ruler in Norway, and had long since fled to the safety of his half-brother's kingdom in Denmark. Thirteen days after Canute's death, there met on the Danish-Saxon frontier at Oxford the Danes of London and the thanes north of the Thames led by Leofric, Earl of Mercia, who chose as king Harold Harefoot, Svein's nineteen-year-old younger brother, to guard all England on behalf of himself and his half-brother Hardecanute in Denmark.

After wasting half the day, rumour said, arguing against the decision, Earl Godwin of Wessex, Emma's friend, had been forced to bow to the majority, and had even found it in his heart, in succeeding weeks, to send one or two little gifts to King Harold. The Lady Emma, it was reported, had been allowed to retire to Winchester with her late husband's housecarls, and was entrenched there, awaiting the arrival of Canute's third and last son, her own cherished Hardecanute, from Denmark.

The year turned, and Hardecanute had not yet left Denmark. The Lady's mourning at Winchester was, however, tempered by a visit from her stepson Harold Harefoot. He relieved her of all her late husband's treasure-chest, and left quickly. Svein, his older brother, died suddenly without ever reclaiming

Norway. Magnús of Norway, now aged twelve, began to show every sign of waging war on the late Canute's Denmark.

They discussed it endlessly in Orkney over the boards, and Groa listened.

'What is Harold Harefoot like?' Sulien asked.

'Stupid,' had said Thore Hund. 'And greedy. He's meant to rule England jointly with his half-brother, but I don't trust Harefoot not to take the throne for himself, and then Emma will have to look out. She can't fly to Normandy now.'

'She may not need to,' said Earl Thorfinn. 'You forget the family she had by her first husband.'

'I'm not forgetting anything,' said Thorkel Fóstri. His face was red. These days, Thorkel did not like to be contradicted by Thorfinn. 'When Canute's father took over England, Emma left her two Saxon sons in Normandy. Edward and Alfred. They must be in their thirties, and Emma treats them as if they don't exist. Canute's son is to rule, not the Saxon boys.'

'Thank you,' said Thorfinn mildly. 'I was talking about Emma's first daughter, Goda. Report has it that Goda's husband has died, and that for her next, she may be looking to Flanders.'

They all glanced at one another. No one appeared to think elaboration was necessary. Blessedly, the skald Arnór said, 'Is that a good thing?'

'It's an interesting thing,' Thorfinn said. 'Especially as her mother Emma must be arranging it. The Counts of Flanders own Lille and are close to several places, such as Bacqueville-en-Caux, which serve houses of coiners and bankers. Has it occurred to nobody to wonder where Emma gets all that money from, and why it was removed so very quickly?'

Skeggi said, 'Canute's treasure. Thorkel said.'

'Well, we know he had treasure,' Thorfinn said. 'He had a great many lands which paid tax to him, and he had his toll-profits from the big ports, and the profits of justice, and all the rest of it. But, all the same, his spending was of the same order. So was Emma's. You are unlikely to find the body of St Florentine on a tree.'

Groa said, 'According to Thore Hund, Crinan's name is not on the new lists of moneyers. Not for Lincoln or York or Shrewsbury.'

Since she left Norway, there had not been a moment like it. Everyone turned and looked at her.

'Go on,' said her husband.

'Thore says that he gave up the dies for all three of his mints within days of Canute's death and withdrew his share of the silver before Harold Harefoot or anyone else could judge what it amounted to. It's probably somewhere in Yorkshire. Thore mentioned something else. There's a new moneyer appointed to Nottingham. Name of Forne.'

'Crinan's son-in-law. And next door, of course, to Lincoln. It used to be said,' Earl Thorfinn said, 'that one or two of the moneyers of Lincoln, with the blessing of the church, made a nice profit every year minting coins and forging weapons for less well-equipped lands to the east. Has Emma been planning, by any chance, to finance an invasion by Hardecanute?'

'You know her,' said Groa.

'Then I think she has, and probably still is, if she can get the money together. Perhaps,' said Earl Thorfinn thoughtfully, 'we should accord Abbot Crinan a moment's attention. On the one hand, he seems to have links with Denmark and with Emma, but he may have had to withdraw meantime from these. He does have connections, we know, with Emma's Devon and with quite a few powerful families on the borders of Normandy and Brittany. Are Crinan's interests banking, or trading, or usury?'

'Lulach calls him Banquerius,' Groa said.

'Bailiff: treasurer: tax-collector. I suppose he is all of these,' Sulien said. 'I know he has connections with Germany, but so have a good many churches, including my own. If they don't get shipwrecked in Scotland, you'll find Celtic monks moving all over Lorraine and the Empire. One die-cutter can serve Cologne and Metz and Verdun and Laon and Mouzon and Toul.'

'I knew about Cologne. I didn't know there were Irish in the Toul bishopric,' said Earl Thorfinn.

'Run by Bruno le Bon, the Emperor's cousin,' Sulien said. 'He's also cousin to the Bishops of Metz and Verdun, and both of them have Irish monks, too. Bruno's related to everybody. If Crinan starts using Dunkeld as a tool to get inside that network, he'd better watch out. He'll get his fingers burnt.'

'What do you mean?' Groa said. She had never seen Sulien excited before.

'I mean,' said Sulien, 'that, in most places, churches are the only buildings that have towers and strong walls and people who can read and count and make jewellery and money and organise food-producing and trade and be sure of protection and convenient hospitality wherever they travel with a regular basic income of contributions to do it all on. Therefore, the number and quality of a nation's churches are coming to matter more than the number and quality of her great lords, because the churches are united under their spiritual leader more than the great lords are, under their king or their emperor. And that if the power of the Roman Emperor and the power of the Popes should continue to amount to the same thing, then it will be very hard to prevent the churches that don't conform—the monastic settlements, the Celtic churches—from becoming like St Jacques and St Clement's and St Vannes and St Symphorien, a colony enbalmed in the stomach of a bishop's cathedral. On the other hand, if the churches don't take a lead—'

'We have had this conversation before,' the Earl said. 'I'm tired of it.'

'Canute wasn't in any doubt what to do about it,' Sulien said. 'His daughter is marrying the Emperor's only son this summer.'

'Canute had to think about his Danish frontiers, among other things,' Earl Thorfinn said. 'I don't have the Saxons and the Wends and the Archbishop of Hamburg and Bremen sitting on the borders of Moray: I only have Duncan. If you can't find enough monasteries to keep your writing-hand occupied, then you'd better finish your journey to Bangor.'

Sulien rose and went out.

Groa followed him. 'Tell me,' she said.

Sulien turned round. He was still breathing hard, but as she watched, he calmed himself and eventually produced a wry smile. 'No,' he said. 'This is between Thorfinn and me.'

She crossed her arms over her buffeting robe. 'He is fond of you,' she said. 'Of course you know that. And he is not stupid.'

'He is cleverer than any ruler this land has probably had, and yet he treats the place and its people as his father did,' Sulien said. 'The days of the Viking are over: the days when you spent the summer coursing the sea-ways and living off the produce of other men's hands. *Pay me and I'll protect you: defy me and I'll kill you.* Thorfinn studies Canute, who was born of two cultures as he was: who became King at twenty, and died Emperor of north Europe at forty. He doesn't see what else Canute was doing. . . . Thorfinn has a taste for intrigue, as an ox enjoys salt; that is all.'

'So you are giving up?' Groa said.

'I love him,' said Sulien.

And this time it was she who turned away.

That summer, Thorfinn did not move from Orkney, and Moray and Mar, Caithness and the Western Isles were ruled by stewards.

It had never happened before, and to meet the burden of supporting himself and his household, food was brought in from over the firth almost daily. Groa, with her women and the child Sigurd, crossed in one of the boats and spent some weeks moving from hall to hall throughout Caithness and Ross, making use of the summer tributes and talking, as she went, to as many of her husband's officers as she could find.

Sulien spent much of his time also in the south, at Deer or Monymusk, and had Lulach with him at intervals. There was no more word of his leaving, and Groa knew, without being told, that the matter which had occasioned the quarrel had never been discussed again. She listened to the news from the south with renewed interest.

The Saxon sons of the Lady Emma each ventured, she heard, to wrest England from King Harold Harefoot. The first attempt, by the son named Edward, was a dismal failure and he went home again. The second, by the son named Alfred, resulted in his capture, mutilation, and eventual death at the instigation, it was said, of Godwin, Earl of Wessex, once Emma's close ally. Emma's views no one reported.

Sigurd was fifteen months old and had not seen his father for two months. Groa found out where her husband was and, loading all her possessions into a longship, sailed from Thurso to Orkney.

The hall at Orphir was not full of beautiful Irish slaves, and Earl Thorfinn, when he came in, had not changed. At twelve, he had been an ugly boy; and at twenty-seven, he was an ugly man. She put the child down and let him walk, staggering, towards his father.

'To some god we should give praise,' said Earl Thorfinn. 'After all, he looks like you rather than me. I thought I asked you to stay in Caithness?'

She picked the child up and turned to the door. 'Sinna? Take him down to the beach and tell the shipmaster not to unload. We're going back as soon as the tide suits him.'

'And tell him those are my instructions as well,' said her husband.

Never for a moment had she expected that. Nor, of course, had Sinna. The older woman hesitated, and then took the child and went out. Earl Thorfinn said, 'You have six hours. Are you hungry? We eat only, I'm afraid, when we have time.'

'Time from what?' she said. It occurred to her that there were remarkably few people about. Of course, his hird was spread thinly, with the men he could trust overseas, looking after his affairs in the mainland. But she had been surprised to see, through an open door, how empty the barns were.

'From drinking and whoring and worshipping big wooden statues,' Earl Thorfinn said. 'How have you spent your summer?'

Sulien was not here. Whatever was wrong, she had to find it out for herself. 'Do you have time to listen?' she said.

'No,' he said. 'Why don't we get drunk instead? Have you ever been drunk?' He moved towards the high chair, and someone, at a signal, scurried up with a board.

Groa said nothing, and he turned and faced her. The servant stood, waiting for orders. Earl Thorfinn said, 'Ale for me, and water for my wife. Or whatever she asks.'

'Water will do,' Groa said, and sat in the other tall chair beside him. She said, 'You excel Gillacomghain.'

'No doubt,' he said. The ale came, in a cheap pottery cup; and her water, when it arrived, was in a vessel no better. She drew breath to comment, but he interrupted her. 'What made you decide to come at this remarkable moment? Only to see who I was sleeping with?'

She knew her colour was high, and could do nothing about it. 'Well, you didn't come to see who *I* was sleeping with,' she said.

'I didn't need to. I got reports daily,' he said. He had forgotten to drink from his cup. And although he was answering her, he was not, she saw, really thinking either of her or of what she was saying. In the distance, someone was shouting.

'I came,' she said, 'because we had not met for two months, and if we are man and wife in any sense at all, it seemed to me that it was wrong to live entirely apart. Or if you don't agree, I ought to know it.'

She ended, raising her voice against the bellow outside, and so did not hear what it said, but her husband, it was evident, heard both and understood both. He rose from the high chair, ignoring her, and then, finding the cup in his hand, he lifted his arm and hurled the thing at the board. It shattered in front of his wife, and the ale spattered her robe and slid down to pool in her lap. She raised her eyebrows.

And whether because of that or not, suddenly he came to himself.

With his stretched hand, he dammed and then swept back the flood on the table as people hurried with cloths. She took one to press over her robe and then stood up.

'The fault was mine. The fault was all mine. I am sorry,' her husband said. 'You will have to get your baggage ashore. But I expect you would want to unload and to change in any case, to prepare for our visitor.'

'Visitor?' Groa said.

'You arrived just after the first of the signal-lights. Evidently your sailing master didn't see it, or he would have turned back. His orders were clear.'

'Why?' said Groa. 'Who is coming? What is coming?'

'Three fully armed warships belonging to King Magnús of Norway,' Earl Thorfinn said. 'Manned and led by Rognvald son of Brusi, come to claim his father's share of the islands of Orkney.

'And to get them, most likely. I could fight Rognvald. I can't fight all Norway.'

SEVENTEEN

AFTER ROGNVALD, as after the little elf-wind that blisters, the islands of Orkney were never to be quite the same again.

No savage prows swept up to the strand below the great hall at Orphir: no grim hordes leaped ashore and began overrunning the land. Instead, watched by the entire population of Orkney, the three Norwegian ships sailed quietly north to the island of Westray, where stood the hall at Hǫfn, once the chief homestead of Brusi, Thorfinn's older half-brother and father to Rognvald.

Long before the three ships arrived, the steading at Hǫfn had been emptied and all those who wished had been taken off Westray. Peacefully, the foreign Earl's son took possession and, peacefully, he sent his first message south to his dearest uncle Thorfinn son of Sigurd.

In it, together with his warmest regards, he conveyed his apologies that necessity after an arduous voyage had caused him to quarter himself without invitation in his old childhood house-hall in Westray. It was, of course, a fact that the northern Isles, together with the east mainland and the island of Shapinsay—that was to say ninety-three ouncelands in all—had belonged to his father Earl Brusi and therefore were his, Rognvald's, by inheritance. He had, however, encountered some delay in occupying them and would have thought it impolite to arrive without warning, and thus upset any arrangements his uncle might have made, if in any way he could have prevented it.

As it was, he hoped his uncle would have no objection to himself and his friends making their way as soon as might be to all the property which was his, and he hoped to give himself the pleasure of calling on his uncle in Orphir, or wherever he might choose to be, in the very near future. Not wishing to impose on his uncle's hospitality, he would bring with him only two or three men to serve him on the journey. God's blessings, he was sure, would continue, as ever, to profit his uncle and all his family, whom he was hoping to meet.

With the message, he sent a Byzantine helmet made of gilded steel with an eagle and five plumes of crimson ostrich feathers on top.

'He has a sense of humour,' said Groa. 'And some courage, you will admit.'

'He can afford both,' said Thorkel Fóstri. 'The last time I saw him, he was weeping on the cobbles at Nídarós because his father was going away. Where shall we receive him?'

'Here,' said Earl Thorfinn. 'And since we are not having a war immediately, it would appear, we may as well restore all the furnishings, even if we have to take them all away afterwards.'

'Shall I be there?' Groa asked. She knew the answers to all the other questions. To fly back to Caithness now with the child would be unseemly. To invoke an army against Rognvald and throw him out of the northern islands was tempting but debarred by circumstances. To meet effrontery with effrontery was all that was left to do. She was sure her husband could manage it.

'You're his aunt,' said Earl Thorfinn shortly. 'Of course you will be there. You can discuss his jewellery with him. If this is a sample, he's probably wearing pendicles over his ears, if not earrings actually in them.'

Having already learned to tread very warily indeed, she did not answer.

Whatever else he might have brought from his long stay in Russia and points further east, the foster-brother of the King of Norway was dressed not in knobbed robes and cataseistae but in a plain linen tunic and narrow hose, whose bindings were, however, gartered in worked gold, which also adorned his belt, his purse, his knife-sheath, his reliquary brooch, his rings, his bracelets, his necklet, and the band which confined the pure silken fall of his pale yellow hair. The face within was that of an archangel worked by a master in ivory.

It was smiling, its blue eyes celestial. 'My dearest uncle and master,' said Rognvald gently, 'I kneel before you. For fifteen years have I awaited this day.'

'It even seemed for a year or two that you might not be coming,' Thorfinn said. 'I hope you will stand up: the dogs are a little excited. You know my wife, Finn Arnason's daughter. Indeed, I think we nearly shared her.'

The last sentence, if he heard it, provoked no answering riposte from Rognvald. Instead he smiled and, for the second time, sank with grace to his knees. 'Despite the dogs,' he said, 'I act as my impulses tell me. You were a child and I was little more when last we met. But from Kalv I had a picture of what you had become.' He rose and stood looking down at her, smiling still. 'His pigments were mud.'

'I am afraid, so are your knees,' Groa said. 'I am longing to hear about Kiev and Ladoga. We received your helmet.'

He laughed, and it was clear and musical, like his voice. 'It was, of course, for your dwarf,' he said. 'I suppose you keep several? I know you have bards. I got someone to sing one of the latest poems:

'From far Tuscar skerries
To Dublin the people
To a generous lord

Were subject. And truly
I tell men of Thorfinn. . . .

'That is something the rest of us envy you. There are no bards singing the praises of Rognvald.'

'I shall ask Arnór if he has a friend,' Thorfinn said. 'Here are some men you may know. And some wine.'

It was half an hour before he had finished greeting everyone, and another hour before the chatter at the board died away. He had kissed Thorkel Fóstri on both cheeks and given a gold ring, quietly, to the girl who brought his wine. At length—

'We have begun to know each other, dear Thorfinn,' he said. 'And that is good. But still there are matters between us that must be settled before we may be comfortable and love one another as uncle and nephew should. Should we speak of this alone?'

'There is no need. You have asked for the share of these islands that used to belong to the Earl Brusi your father. Indeed, you are settled there. You have a claim to them. I shall not dispute it,' Thorfinn said.

'How should you dispute it?' said Rognvald, smiling. 'You are my dear uncle and kinsman whom I trust, and I would not weary you by mentioning the matter, except to thank you for your stewardship over the years. I said as much to King Magnús when I told him I was yearning to hold my odal lands in Orkney again, and when he gave me my title of Earl and the three warships that perhaps you saw. I said that I had known you when you were young and knew your mind, and that you would return, willingly and freely, the heritage that was my father's, and also the second third of the isles, that King Olaf kept in fief, and which King Magnús has now seen fit to give me. . . .

'This is a hall my father loved,' Rognvald said, 'and I see you kept it as he had it, except for what the years may have done, here and there. But you have your other lodging, I know, in west mainland, for when you tire of your rich lands in Alba. You will not grudge your own kindred the means by which to make a living. I told King Magnús as much.'

His face, mobile and lovely, looked up wistfully into Thorfinn's black, impassive visage.

Thorfinn said, 'The wind gets noisier every year. Would you mind repeating what you have just said? You wish me to give you two-thirds of Orkney?'

An expression of sorrow flickered across Rognvald's face and was gone. 'King Magnús wishes it,' he said. 'Perhaps you don't remember paying homage to Norway in King Olaf's day, but Thorkel here will remind you. The northern third is mine, through my father. And the southern isles fell to King Olaf after the killing of my uncle Earl Einar, and he kept these in fief. My father had them in his lifetime, and King Magnús has given them to me his son now. Making one hundred and eighty-eight ouncelands in all. You still have west mainland and Rousay and Egilsay. You might even, for a consideration, look after Orphir for me. I would not have you deprived.'

'Thank you,' said Thorfinn. 'Do you know, of us all, my lady wife here turns out to understand you best. She said you had courage. And a sense of humour.'

Rognvald's smile became deeper. He had a dimple. 'As does everyone in this hall, I trust your wisdom,' he said. 'The men who follow you and me expect us to recognise what is fair, otherwise what are their prospects under us? Young as he is, even King Magnús strives hard to hold by this rule, now that he has attained his majority, with none to act for him.'

Finding that her eyes were stretched to their uttermost, Groa dropped her lids and unclasped her fingers. The meaning of all that was unmistakable.

Kalv is no longer regent. Don't expect him to be able to save you for your wife's sake. Even if you lose your head and attack me, your men probably won't follow. You are not as young as you were, and no beauty.

She considered her husband. That at least was true. And he was twenty-seven.

Earl Thorfinn said, 'Well, Rognvald, you put your case excellently. I think I see exactly what you mean. I shall send you my answer with as little delay as may be. Now, I expect you wish to get on your way while it is daylight.'

Being summer, it would be daylight for another five hours.

Rognvald said, 'Is there something you cannot understand?'

'No,' Thorfinn said. 'No, I can't say there is. But we in Orkney like to give proper thought to anything new. You will be told as soon as we have a reply for you.'

He got up, and so, raggedly, did his company. After an interval, Rognvald stood as well, followed by his three men. He said, 'I had expected to finish this business today. In fact, I can hardly halt my plans to move into this hall by next week.'

'Why halt them?' said Thorfinn. 'If we are still here, we are still here, and I am sure there will be room of a kind for everybody, although it might be uncomfortable for some. If you find there is no need to come south yet, of course, so much the better for both of us. . . . Here are your horses already. I cannot remember,' Thorfinn said, 'when I have seen such a fine pair of spurs. I hope you will remember not to use them too freely in Orkney. It is not Kiev, as you notice. There is small room for manoeuvering and a great number of big, harmful boulders. . . . An uncle's blessing upon you.'

Everyone could see the gravity in the delicate face as Rognvald listened to that. Then the white-toothed smile returned, and, without haste, Thorfinn's nephew made his farewells, gathered his men, and rode off.

'What . . . ?' said Thorkel Fóstri.

'I have saved my face,' said Thorfinn. 'And one-third of Orkney. If you think you could have done better, you are welcome to try. Otherwise you wait a week and then send a message complying. I shan't be here. I shall be in Caithness for the rest of the summer.'

He caught sight of Groa's face. 'I am sure you would prefer to stay,' Thorfinn said. 'If you do, I have not the least objection.'

*   *   *

By the time Rognvald got his reply, there had evacuated to Caithness from the south isles all those lendermen or others who had reason to fear a change of lord, or who wished for their own reasons to stay with Thorfinn.

On the west mainland, Thorkel Fóstri was already ensconced with a force of men three times the number of Rognvald's, with well-stocked farms and barns to feed them from. This was one-third of Orkney to which Rognvald was not entitled, and which, lacking Norwegian support, he was to have no opportunity to encroach on.

The arrangements for some of this were already made before Rognvald ever set foot on Orkney. The rest were launched that evening, almost before the hoof-beats of his horses had faded.

In them, the Earl Thorfinn's wife Groa took no share. Familiar with the domestic repercussions of failure, Groa kept out of her second husband's path on the evening of Rognvald's departure, and concerned herself with the disposal of her own household and servants. By midnight, when there were still other people's garrons in the field and light and noise in the hall, she decided not to return there, but to sleep with the women and Sinna.

It took her some moments, when she got there, to realise that Sinna was unwilling to receive her. 'What is it?' said the Lady of one-third of Orkney. 'Sinna, I'm tired.'

Sinna said, 'Lady: tonight is your place not with your lord?'

'Only when he's successful,' said Groa. 'I expect that you remember Gillacomghain?'

'It is still your place,' Sinna said. 'Thorkel Fóstri says so.'

'Thorkel Fóstri!' Groa stared at the Irishwoman. 'Then it is serious. Unless Thorkel Fóstri makes a habit of discussing his lord with you? He certainly doesn't with me.'

Sinna shook her head. She had made no effort to open the door any further. 'Oh, well,' said Groa bad-temperedly and turned and stalked back to the reeking hall. She had a very clear idea of how she had succeeded in sobering Gillacomghain, in the end.

She opened the hall door and an emanation of hot oil and sweat and smoke and ale fumes and foodstuffs struck her, together with the subterranean cadences of her husband's voice, undimmed in energy, remorselessly issuing instructions. She turned and made to go out.

As she feared, he had seen her. Ending what he was saying, he rose from the high chair, threw some final words to someone in a corner, and followed her out. 'Have I kept you from your bed? I'm sorry.'

She walked vaguely in the direction of the small stream that ran down to the shore; remembered another conversation at night, out of doors, and halted preparatory to returning, without evident haste, to Sinna's hut. She said, 'Not at all. I came to apply balm to your wounds at the request of the more tender-hearted of your henchmen. But you don't seem to require consoling or sobering.'

She realised she had let someone down as soon as she heard the tone of his voice. 'Who? Sulien?'

'It doesn't matter,' she said. 'Have you finished now for the night?'

'Then Thorkel,' he said. 'And thank you both for your opinion of me. Whatever I run crying from, it's not this.'

'Well, perhaps you should,' said Groa, caught on the wrong foot and cross in her turn. 'You've lost two-thirds of your earldom without a blow struck or a word raised in anger. You did the same thing fifteen years ago. Kalv told me.'

'I'm not sure,' said Earl Thorfinn, 'that I want to be reminded of Kalv at this moment. The inadequacies of a thirteen-year-old I can only apologise for. The bloodless game you saw played just now happened that way because the only alternative was full-scale war against Norway, including the Arnasons. To you that may seem a good idea, for, with Harold Harefoot busy nursing his throne and Duncan with his head in the ground acting buffer, I should have no help from the south, and, even throwing in Moray and Caithness, Magnús would overwhelm us with numbers.

'I don't want that, however poor a figure I seem to cut as a result. In fact, there has been time to prepare for it. Whenever there has been an over-strong King of Norway or a bad Earl of Orkney, men have simply slipped out of the islands to Caithness or the Western Isles.

'Magnús may not have a long reign. And although Rognvald has come at harvest-time, he has several hundred men to feed through the winter with no reserves to draw on such as we have in Caithness.

'Meanwhile, my fleet is safe, and still the biggest in northern waters. A few successful landings; a good summer's trade; a generous disposal of booty, and the popular opinion of me will rise.' He had come to a halt, speaking quietly, outside Sinna's door.

'At least you and Arnór haven't lost confidence in one another,' Groa said. 'He must make a song out of it. So I scuttle to Moray, and you turn pirate? Because of one blustering child?'

'Weren't you impressed? You ought to have been. Everything he said and did has been planned for a very long time. Even at a distance, you could see it taking shape. I could do nothing to prevent it, and he knew it. Whatever else he is, he is not a blustering child. He is, in fact, just two years younger than I am.'

He paused. 'It seemed likely that he would claim the south isles as well. I had prepared for it. And there are some prospects other than piracy. That was why we went to the enthronement. That was why there was more than one reason for cultivating Eachmarcach. I have land on the southwest coast, now.'

'I see,' said Groa. 'What you have had is a success. Allow me to congratulate you and wish you a very good night. If you have any bad luck, send for me.'

She had come, against her inclinations, to bind up his wounds, and he had none. Or if he had, he had found a consolation for them in a field which had already received the weight of Sulien's disapproval.

He has a taste for intrigue, as an ox enjoys salt, Sulien had said. The Earl of

Orkney had lost two-thirds of his islands and, for all one could tell, was enjoying it.

If anyone had told the red-haired Lady of Orkney that her husband's people would show they had missed her when she returned to her own lands of Moray, she would have been pleased but disbelieving: but so it transpired. What her husband thought about her reception, no one knew. Earl Thorfinn, whatever he was doing, set a pace of his own that was hard enough to keep up with, without trying to understand him as well.

In Orkney, matters settled. Rognvald made no effort to seize what did not belong to him, and was considerate to the bonder in the two parts of the islands which he had moved into. The only landowners likely to be resentful, as Thorfinn had predicted, were those who, like Thorkel Fóstri after Earl Sigurd's death, had had to leave their homes and property to begin a new life elsewhere. On the other hand, there was plenty of land, some of it already farmed by other branches of the same Orcadian families. And Thorfinn, as he had told his wife, had made sure that they would have little chance to repine.

The summer passed, and the winter. Magnús, King of Norway, sent his *gjaldkeri* to exact rents from both Earls of Orkney, which both Earls of Orkney paid without demur. Duncan, King of Alba, at his father's request, sent his father to Moray to collect what was due to him there. The lord Crinan did not see Groa, who was staying elsewhere, but received his rents from Thorfinn's steward and gleaned some interesting information about the situation in Orkney.

The Lady Emma began to store silver again.

In Norway, Kalv Arnason and his brother Finn fell out over the departure of Rognvald, which otherwise caused some general satisfaction, as removing a dangerous favourite from King Magnús's side. Although conscious of no immediate improvement in his status as demoted regent, Kalv threw himself with enthusiasm into the common occupation of harassing Denmark, and, as a result, the Lady Emma's son Hardecanute was prevented yet again from crossing the sea to attend to his late father's kingdom of England.

In England, Hardecanute's dilemma was noted. His half-brother and joint King, Harold Harefoot, settled into his throne, drew a long sprinter's breath, and informed his stepmother the Lady Emma that her presence in England was no longer convenient.

In Northumbria, the five husbands of the five daughters of Earl Ealdred continued to work hard at their communal interests in apparent amity and without public reference to the shifting power-groups into which the five frequently found themselves falling. The sole unaffiliated member, Alfgar of Mercia, was aware that the dominant brother-in-law was proving to be Siward of York, aided by Duncan of Alba, but could not find out what they were up to.

The frontiers of the large provinces lying south of the rivers Forth and Clyde in Alba became more confused than they had been even in the late

Malcolm's reign, as families from Cumbria or Westmorland or Yorkshire moved into new land, or land already held by their ancestors. Many of them were Norse and Irish in origin, and some could even trace their forebears back to the sons of the first Earl Thorfinn of Orkney who fought in York with Erik Bloodaxe.

Crinan, Abbot of Dunkeld, with his son's permission, spent less time in his houses in England and more in the vicinity of Dunkeld in Alba, where his son-in-law Forne already had a hall-house. He kept his houses in Shrewsbury and in York, as did Carl son of Thorbrand, whose first favour from the new King Harold Harefoot was a licence to operate the mint in the Lady Emma's former possession of Exeter.

Off the west coast of Alba, trouble developed among the friends and allies of Orkney.

Thorfinn's cousin Ghilander in the western island of Colonsay sent a cutter to Caithness asking for the support of Thorfinn's fleet; and at the same moment, and for the same reason, an identical appeal was dispatched by Eachmarcach, King of Dublin. Warned by the signals moving from beacon to beacon, Thorfinn got to Thurso in time to receive both, and within a day his fleet was in the water and heading west. 'Who,' said Arnór Earlskald, 'is Diarmaid son of Dunchadh Mael-na-mbo of Ireland?'

'Someone you're going to hear a good deal more about,' said Thorkel Fóstri. 'Call him *son of cow-chief* if you prefer it. His father was King of the Ui-Ceinnselaigh in Ireland, and his son has ambitions to be King of all Leinster, beginning with burning Waterford to the ground; and King of the Foreigners of Dublin, beginning with trying to edge Eachmarcach out of the post.'

Arnór looked alarmed. 'Dublin?' he said.

'I don't think,' Thorkel said, 'you are going to perish under the raven banner in Dublin, but you may very well have a difficult moment or two in the Western Isles. Diarmaid has been nipping at Galloway and the islands without much success so far, because Thorfinn has some ships there. But now Diarmaid's sent a good, strong force to take a few easily fortified places in the Western Isles and plunder the trading-ships as they pass up and down to Dublin. It's not the first time, you know. He and his family did the same to Gillacomghain.'

Thorkel had no objection to frightening Arnór. Speaking to Thorfinn later, it was different. Then Thorkel said, 'Listen, and tell me that I'm wrong. You haven't got enough ships to fight Diarmaid's whole fleet. You should have waited for the rest to come up from Galloway. There's a limit to what you owe Eachmarcach.'

'You're wrong,' Thorfinn said. 'I don't owe Eachmarcach anything. Every ship Diarmaid plunders is losing me a tenth of its cargo in tolls. From the Outer Isles he'll take Skye, and from Skye he'll move back into the west coast and Lochaber.'

'And you'll stop him with six ships against twelve?' Thorkel said. 'Success has gone to your head.'

'These days,' Thorfinn said, 'we seem to have only one topic. However. Since you are so obsessed with Rognvald, perhaps you would look over there and tell me if you agree that the three ships behind us are his?' His fastened hair, plaited for fighting, exposed the tall basket-brow to the sun, and the niche under each sharpened cheekbone from which sprang the unit of mouth and jaw; the single prominent lobe that lent his face its unremitting, saturnine expression, like the mask of a wolf-hound, and hid whatever he might be thinking, as now.

Thorkel looked behind. There was no mistaking the three ships, with their crane-necks and the blue-and-white netted sails bearing down from their rudder-side. And as they got closer, no mistaking the glitter of steel from within them.

They were full of armed men. Far more full than Thorfinn's longships, which carried only their normal complement. Three ships against six might seem harmless enough, but, crew for crew, it was the trick of Deerness again, but this time not in their favour. Thorkel said, 'The puppy's flying the raven of Orkney.'

'He has the right,' Thorfinn said. 'If he can keep it.'

Over their own ships, like a comber, had run a confusion of glitter and colour and sound as men seized their shields and spears and the steersmen twisted, taut, waiting for orders. Thorkel's arm began to rise and Thorfinn held it down. 'Wait.'

Thorkel said, 'You'll never have a better chance.'

He did not need to say any more. The leading ship was close enough now for an arrow-shot. It was more than close enough to see the single blond man, unarmed, standing alone in the prow with a white shield gripped at arm's-length above him.

'Kill him if he kills me,' Thorfinn said and, unarmed as Rognvald was, walked up to his own prow and faced him. The space between the two ships slowly vanished. The shouting in all the ships died. On the crane-ship Rognvald lowered the shield, and his hair, given back to the sun, blew transparent as Syrian silk about his bare neck. He was smiling. He called.

'My lord Thorfinn! Uncle! Am I welcome?'

'It depends,' said Thorfinn, 'what you bring.'

Rognvald was so close that they could see the design on his *hlað*. He was still smiling. 'Three hundred men,' he said, 'to fight the son of Domnall Ramhar, provided I have half of the booty.' The red tongue of his crane-head turned and lay side by side with the gold beak of Thorfinn's grey goose. The sea, surging between the two ships, slapped their sides.

Thorfinn considered his nephew, then lifted his voice. 'When you have an equal number of ships, you may have an equal share of the booty. One-third, provided your men bear their proper share of the fighting.'

'They are, for the most part, your men,' Rognvald said. 'And you should know therefore how they were trained. Man for man, you do us less than justice.'

Thorfinn shrugged. 'Did we invite you?'

'Very well,' said Rognvald. 'But when you do, it will be a different story. Have you a plan?'

'To round Skye,' said Thorfinn. 'I hear Diarmaid's nephew uses the broch and the fort-hill in Bracadale.'

'I have better news than that,' Rognvald said. 'I hear that he has a fort in Loch Dunvegan and is there at this moment. Give me a light boat and I shall go ahead and scout for you.'

'And rouse them against us?' murmured Thorkel Fóstri. He stared at Thorfinn agreeing, and watched, without speaking, the manoeuvres between ship and ship that eventually gave effect to the plan. Then it was over, and the cutter, the smallest and fastest of Thorfinn's fleet, was drawing smoothly away westwards in front of them while, behind, the three dragon-ships fell into line with their own.

Thorfinn, returning, stopped beside his foster-father and lifted the bar of his brows. 'I marry into your family. Why don't you trust mine?'

'Because I don't want to die at the whim of a knave and a madman,' Thorkel Fóstri said.

'One-fourth, they say, depends on the fostering. The rest,' Thorfinn said, 'comes from my native wit. Rognvald was hungry last winter. I saw to that. He needs cattle and money, not only now but so long as he stays on the islands. He will have to earn them.'

Against the noises of men and the sea-hiss and the creaking, there was silence. Then Thorkel said, 'I see. Then, of the two of you, I will follow the fourth that I fostered. As for the other one and three-fourths, you will have to excuse me.'

Rognvald did not betray them; but that did not save either side from what lay ahead. For although the son of Domnall the Fat, Diarmaid's brother, had posted some men at the rock of Dunvegan, which they took, the main part of his fleet was elsewhere.

'You were right,' said Rognvald to Thorfinn when uncle and nephew met, breathless and bloody on the weed-thick shore below the fortress. 'The main part of the Irish fleet is in Loch Bracadale. At least there is none here to warn them that we are coming.'

He had fought without restraint, and cleverly, for his body had the good proportions that make for perfect balance in every movement, and, as Groa had once remarked, he had courage.

'We had to clear out Dunvegan anyway,' said Thorfinn mildly. 'Take your crane-ship again and Thorkel will lead you south round Duirinish and into the loch. I had a fancy to try something else. Between the head of the loch here and the north of Loch Bracadale is not a great distance. Men could cut through on foot and be in Bracadale before the ships had cleared Loch Dunvegan. Men with fire-arrows, perhaps? The Irish fleet may be in the inner loch, but they also might be in Vatten or Caroy. If I take a hundred men, we shall come down the shore at their backs as you and Thorkel sail into the loch.

At the very least, we can find and get rid of their scouts and discover where the main fleet is. Will you follow Thorkel?'

'No,' said Rognvald. 'Highly though I think of him and his family. My ships are all large, but yours are not. I don't know the country, but there are men here who do, and you tell me the distance is short. Let me take the men across the neck to Loch Bracadale. And let me carry two of your ships.'

Thorkel had arrived. 'What?' he said.

In front of him, the immense, disjointed young man he had fostered gazed thoughtfully down at the compact body and fair, amused face of his half-brother's still younger son Rognvald.

'The idea has some merit,' Thorfinn said. 'Who can tell us about the path between the two lochs?'

'I can,' said someone; and described it. At the end, Thorkel shrugged his shoulders and looked at the others. 'So it can't be done. Let's get out to the ships.'

'I beg your pardon,' said Rognvald. His colour high and his eyes blue with excitement, he looked like Baldur come back to earth, and Thorkel hated him. 'I beg your pardon, but it *can* be done, if I do it. I don't speak from vanity. This is a matter much practised in Russia.'

'Of course,' said Thorfinn. 'I'd forgotten. What, then? Axemen for rollers. Fresh men to fight, as well as for porterage. A courier, who will signal to us from the point, and a set of agreed signals . . . It couldn't be done at nightfall? No, we want them on board.'

'No,' said Rognvald. 'And, in any case, noise would travel . . . Do you know, uncle mine, that I was beginning to find the summer dull? I begin to have some hopes for the future.'

'Why not take Arnór with you?' Thorfinn said. 'He has made up one verse for me already. Arnór, how does it run?'

Thorkel Fóstri swore under his breath, and Arnór looked from one to the other, sulking. 'Which one, my lord Earl?'

'Never mind. I shall recite it myself,' Thorfinn said, and did.

> '*O God guard the glorious*
> *Kin-Betterer of great Turf-Einar*
> *From harm: I pray show mercy*
> *To him whomm faithful chiefs love . . .*'

He broke off. '*Kin-Betterer of the great Turf-Einar?* Doesn't that apply to you as well?'

Rognvald considered. 'Certainly,' he said, 'Turf-Einar was equally my ancestor. The verse might refer to either of us.'

'It was intended for you. There is no doubt about it,' Thorfinn said. 'And all the time I believed it was a prayer for my own success, and even gave the skald some reward for it.'

He turned to Arnór. 'There is no question of it. You stay and cross the isthmus on foot with the ships and Earl Rognvald, who will give you a suitable present for your fine invocation on his behalf. The ring I gave you may be returned any time.'

The men already boarded thought there was a lot of laughter on shore and were keen to know the cause, but Thorkel, when he arrived, said shortly that he had no idea and if they were to get to their next battle in time, they had better set sail and be quick about it. Which, knowing Thorkel Fóstri, they did, looking inquisitively over their shoulders at the mob of men and the golden head still on the shore.

Late that night, the seven ships under Thorfinn stole their way into an anchorage and, making fast, lay locked together, gently rocking in silence while the men slept. Then the blackness around them turned to tablets of black and less than black and somewhere, a long way off, a blackbird announced a cherried sentence and the watch on each ship, stretching, began to move bending from man to man. The wind had dropped.

They entered Loch Bracadale with the sunrise, rose-coloured oars laying darkling folds on the rose-tinted pool of the fjord. A dusting of guillemots, asleep on the water, roused and dived with almost no sound, leaving pink and verdigris rings on the surface. A charcoal rock needled with cormorants became suddenly bare, and from the shore came the scalloped cry of an oyster-catcher, joined after a moment by others. Then the longships slid past, and the sounds died away.

With no sound at all, but with a glory that bludgeoned the senses, the furnace doors were thrown finally open, and the spires and pinnacles of the mountains of Skye stood suddenly stark before them, against mighty rivers of scarlet and brass.

On Thorfinn's ship, no one spoke. The grey goose flamed, and its shadow moved, shortening. 'On such a day,' Thorfinn said, 'it would not be a hardship to die.'

Sharply, Thorkel Fóstri turned his head. 'You have seen a sunrise before.'

The air could be drunk: fresh and cold, with a smell of peat-smoke and seaweed. Thorfinn said, 'Not like this one.'

The sea-loch with its green islands began to open before them. Thorkel Fóstri said, 'Was that the knoll?' and had hardly spoken when, from the rising ground on their left, a shield flashed once, and paused, and then several times more.

Rognvald had arrived at Loch Vatten, the ancient stronghold of Snaebjorn his grandfather's cousin. And the Irish flotilla of warships was still in the inner loch, the long finger of water that ran six miles inland to Drynoch. There were ten of them.

'Then they'll be at Loch Beag,' Thorfinn said. 'There's a fort just inside the entrance. All right. There's no hurry now. It will only be a matter of moments before their look-out wakes up, wherever he is. I thought you had a mail shirt?'

'It came undone,' Thorkel Fóstri said. 'And the smith has been too busy to mend it. Don't offer me yours: I couldn't stand the weight of it.'

'I wasn't going to,' Thorfinn said. 'You'll just have to fight better than usual.'

The shields were out now, and the spears, and the sun, high and yellow and normal, flashed on the bossed leather jackets and the polished cones with their tangs over cheekbone or nose, and the heavy barred gloves and grey ring-tunics. Arnór held Thorfinn's weapons: the gilded axe and the helmet from Canute, and the painted red shield: the good hide stretched over a framework that had once been Sigurd's, with a spiked and engraved boss in the centre that Sulien had told them was Breton.

The green island of Wiay lay ahead of them. From its rear, a square of blue sail appeared, luminous in the low sun. Following, crowding, were others. The wind had risen, and was against them.

Thorkel Fóstri turned and looked over the water to where, out of sight, Thorfinn's nephew Rognvald was waiting, with a hundred armed men and two ships, to burn the tail of Diarmaid's nephew. 'I have changed my mind,' Thorfinn said. 'I would rather Diarmaid's nephew died today. Let us go and arrange it.'

Afterwards, they said that the crimson sunrise, like the dark afternoon at Stiklestad, had been its own harbinger. Afterwards, the loch received heavier bodies than the black and white feathers of guillemots, and the water became red all over again.

The Irish ships, in the end, were destroyed. They fought, in their first confrontation, with an abandon the Orkneymen had neither expected nor experienced before, but found themselves slowly borne back towards Vatten. When the two ships of Rognvald closed in from the rear and attacked them, they went into a blood-frenzy that reminded Thorkel of all he had heard of the berserkers.

Yet these were Irishmen, men of Leinster, out for a roving life and some booty and to satisfy the ambitions of a dangerous kinsman just coming into the peak of his powers.

'They're terrified of Diarmaid. They must be terrified of Diarmaid,' yelled Thorkel Fóstri to his foster-son as he hacked, swearing, at the throng of big-shouldered men who had begun to find their way over his gunwales.

He heard Thorfinn snort something in reply and had the satisfaction of seeing the shield-wall of men beside him advance and push the invaders back into their own rocking boat before something punched him hard in the ribs and he turned round to fight it. Then he found that he couldn't turn round, because of the haft of the spear that was stuck in him.

Late in the afternoon, when the Irish ships were emptied and sunk and the land forts destroyed; when the Irish dead had all been buried and covered with stones, against the wolves; and their own dead and wounded placed on board the nine ships with their booty, Thorfinn had time to kneel by his foster-father where he had been laid in the stern. Rognvald was there.

That day, Rognvald had been everywhere. Without him, it was clear, their own losses would have been even greater. And while they sailed at their ease through the night, he and his men had achieved the porterage of the two ships that had turned the whole battle. Bit by bit, now that there was time, the scale of that endeavour had begun to emerge.

Sitting now beside Thorkel's quiet body, he said, 'I've been able to take the spear out. If he doesn't bleed any more, he might live. But the man who knew most about these things on my ship is dead.'

'And on mine, too,' Thorfinn said. Thorkel was yellow-white and breathing harshly, and the cloths over his side were stained red. Thorfinn said, 'We should get back quickly. How many have you lost?'

'Thirty men,' Rognvald said. 'Some of them yours. This will bring Diarmaid after us.'

'Us?' said Thorfinn. 'We have some men to ransom, and some stock from the forts, and a quantity of reasonable swords and belts and gear that will fetch money. But it seems little enough to make anyone eager for more.'

Rognvald smiled. His face was blackened with metal-dirt and smeared blood, and with his helmet removed, his hair clung darkened and dull to his head. 'Of course,' he said, 'I needed the booty, and wish it had been more. Nor would I hope for a battle of that sort more often than I deserve it. But yesterday I was dead, and today I am alive. You do not know what you have done.'

'Allowed you to take two-thirds of Orkney?' said Thorfinn. Squatting on Thorkel Fóstri's other side, he had not ceased watching the wounded man's face.

'And saw to it that if I needed food, I could not get it,' Rognvald said. 'It was a clever move, and I could have complained to King Magnús, as I would have done had you refused to move out of your trithing.'

'But you didn't,' Thorfinn said. 'He's too busy?'

'Don't you know, even yet, why I came back to Orkney?' Rognvald said.

Then Thorfinn looked up. Rognvald's gaze, waiting for his, took and sustained it. Thorfinn did not look away, but his face held no expression. Rognvald said, 'I am the dog at your heel. Everything I have ever done has been an attempt to be like Thorfinn.'

There was no one within earshot, and no escape either. Between them, Thorkel Fóstri groaned and was silent.

'What do you want?' Thorfinn said.

'This,' said Rognvald. 'I knew only one way to make you give it me.'

'To sail with me?' Thorfinn said. 'But surely—'

'But surely not,' Rognvald said. 'Your brother's son, the rival claimant to Orkney? You would never have let me within your doors unless I had forced you. I am not a bad fighter, on sea or on land. But if you find me an encumbrance, you can always tell me.'

'And you will go?' Thorfinn said.

'No,' said Rognvald, smiling again through the dirt. 'But you can always tell me.' He rose, and then sat down again.

'What is it?' Thorfinn said.

'Shall I be brave, or shall I make you sorry for me?' said Rognvald. 'I had an argument two days ago with a man with an axe, and he got the better of me for a moment, before I killed him. I have a cut on one thigh.' He leaned his head back against the bulwark and looked at Thorfinn. His skin, naturally fair, had turned pallid. Then, bending forward, he unfurled a stained cloth from above his right knee.

The wound was freshly re-opened, and so deep that Thorfinn could see the white bone. He said, 'You walked all night with that?'

'With an eye, naturally, to this moment,' Rognvald said. 'I inflicted the cut on myself, to tell the truth, but I hope you won't tell anyone.'

He was no fool. From no angle could he have produced so deep a gash by his own hand. And to prove or disprove his story, one need only question his men. He was rebinding the wound already himself, smiling a little. He said, his eyes on what he was doing, 'Have I persuaded you? Are we partners?'

'I suppose I might have expected this,' Thorfinn said. 'You are really fishing for Arnór.'

'No. You may keep Arnór,' Rognvald said. It was an assent, however oblique, and he knew it. He said, 'Thorkel won't like it. Nor will your beautiful wife.'

'I'm not sure that you will like it,' said Thorfinn, 'when you know what I have in mind to do. But if you will undertake to carry all of my ships whenever I find it convenient, I have no doubt that we will make a team to astonish the Empire.'

'Or Duncan?' Rognvald said.

EIGHTEEN

A s PREDICTED, Thorkel Fóstri did not like the new alliance, nor what he heard of its subsequent course, from his sickbed at Helmsdale. Nor, to begin with, did many of Thorfinn's hird, with the exception of Arnór, for whom a new world had opened.

> *Deeds done doughtily*
> *By my lord at Loch Vatten,*
> *By the Tester of Men;*
> *—I was with him in peril,*
> *Swiftly the warrior-band*
> *Bore up the shield-wall*
> *That Friday morning.*
> *The grey wolf was gaping*
> *O'er each bloody corpse.*

Thus sang Arnór Jarlaskáld, and the men who had been there applauded him.

When Diarmaid, over in Ireland, took time from his plundering of Waterford to send another and bigger fleet to attack Galloway and to reclaim and strengthen the bases he already had on that coast, Arnór was the first to jump aboard with Rognvald and Thorfinn and set out again to oppose him.

Thereafter there were so many battles that he lost track of them, but there was no doubt of the success of the combined sweep, and even Eachmarcach, who joined them for part of it, had to admit that his friend Thorfinn was earning all he possessed of rights in Dublin and on the headlands and fortresses of the opposite mainland, that had once been held by the kings of Cumbria and Strathclyde.

After a wet start, it proved a remarkably good season for acorns, and the ships they brought back with them were full of pigs. It had been, said Rognvald, as they parted in the firth to go their separate ways for the winter, a year for the *strand-hogg*.

Thorfinn came back to Caithness, but, it appeared, found difficulty in settling. There was, as usual, a spate of domestic matters requiring his attention, together with some news of the outside world that had escaped him during the long summer of flying over the seas, punctuated by explosions of battle and the bright counter-explosions of after-battle when one touched a shackle-free crest for a moment and held it, perhaps, for a night, with the brotherhood of one's friends.

The Lady Emma, said Thorkel baldly, standing with both hands on a stick, had been sent packing finally by her stepson King Harold of England, and was now in Bruges as guest of Baldwin, Count of Flanders, the young stepson of her niece.

'Oh,' said Thorfinn.

King Magnús of Norway (said Thorkel), on whose advice no one knew, had slackened his war on Hardecanute, Emma's son ruling Denmark, and a pact had been made between the two Kings whereby the survivor would inherit both Norway and Denmark if the other died childless. Magnús, as Thorfinn was aware, was fourteen years of age, and Hardecanute was twenty-two but had had no success with any girl he had been supplied with.

'Well, I hope at least he had some amusement trying,' Thorfinn said. 'Have some pork. It's the best you've ever tasted.'

Thorkel Fóstri lifted his stick, and his foster-son trapped its heel in his hand as it swept sharply down to his dish-edge. Thorkel Fóstri snatched a step to keep balance, and then, changing his hold, slowly lowered the ferrule as Thorfinn released it.

'I said, have some pork. I also said, perhaps, I am not over-interested at the moment in what you are telling me. I didn't say you could strike me and get away with it,' Thorfinn said. 'I have, I think, heard everything you have been saying, and also what you imply. My stewards in Caithness and Moray and Ross and Mar and Lochaber have all been working hard on my behalf, but are not likely to continue to work hard if I pay no attention to them and if I fail to resolve the difficulties that fall to be settled by an overlord. You also think I ought to visit my wife. When,' said Thorfinn, cutting some pork, 'I have been at home for more than twenty-four hours I may give the matter some thought, and I may even agree. But at the moment I don't want advice.'

'You are right,' Thorkel Fóstri said. 'And it is the last time you shall have it. If there's nothing more, I should like to leave for Helmsdale in the morning.'

'There's nothing more,' said Thorfinn. 'Unless you want some pork?'

It was an open winter, with just enough frost to stiffen the roads. From Helmsdale, some weeks later, Thorkel Fóstri heard that Thorfinn had moved from Thurso to Canisbay and then, bypassing Helmsdale, had moved on south to visit his lands on both sides of the Spey.

He had with him all his hird, barring the men he had left to control Caithness and Birsay; and with him was Rognvald.

Then he was back, and the summons came as usual for Thorkel Fóstri to come to Canisbay for the Yule gathering, which meant for most of the rest of the winter. After a sleepless night, he sent back the messenger, accepting. He had never thought the rift permanent. It was his own attitude to Thorfinn that he did not want altered.

In the event, the Yule was no different from the ones they had in Orkney, and Rognvald was not there, having returned with his own men to hold festival in his island of Westray.

Thorfinn himself greeted him as if nothing had happened and seemed unchanged. It was from his men that Thorkel Fóstri began to hear the tales of that winter passage through Speyside and Moray; of the hunting, the dicing, the horse-fights, and the wagers. Tales of the visit to Thorfinn's wife, which had lasted three hours and had not included any glimpse of his sons, who could not be brought in time from their foster-homes.

The Lady of Moray, said Thorkel's informant, had not been in the least put out, but had shown openly enough for a blind man to see her admiration for the Earl Rognvald. But where a lesser man might have objected, the Earl Thorfinn had placed his nephew's arm round his wife's shoulders and told him to entertain her while he went to see to his business. Being a well-bred man, the Earl Rognvald had, of course, removed his arm, but had stayed talking with the Lady until her husband was ready to leave. So Groa had been angry and shown it, and Thorfinn had retaliated.

Thorkel Fóstri said, 'And where was the Lady's son? The boy Lulach?'

'At his fostering, my lord. At Monymusk, with the clerk Sulien. We did not go there.'

No, indeed. And Sulien was not here, this Yule, for the first time. Without being told, he knew that Sulien would spend this Yule with Groa, not Thorfinn.

His side hurt, and he went early back to his house before the celebrations were over.

Afterwards, when the harm had been done, Thorkel Fóstri was wont to say that the year now dawning, of Thorfinn's twenty-ninth birthday, was the year when the three Norns laid their hands on the fabric of his foster-son's life and wove in the thread that was to run to the end.

Other men felt the torque first.

Ealdred, Earl of Northumbria, riding out of York on some business in the north, was set upon and killed by a small group of men who broke through the ranks of his retinue, slashed, and withdrew before they could be stopped.

The killers were led by Carl son of Thorbrand, who six years before had led a fleet against Thorfinn at Deerness.

Then, it had been a matter of obliging a friend; but this time, the object was vengeance. Twenty years before, on Canute's advice, Carl's father had killed Earl Ealdred's father, and Earl Ealdred had responded in turn by bringing about Thorbrand's death. He was not the first to desire it. Earl Uhtred himself had tried to get rid of Carl's father, even when he had Carl's sister to wife. There were no soft men in Northumbria.

Five daughters went into mourning, including the wives of King Duncan of Alba, Alfgar of Mercia, Siward son of Thore Hund, and Orm nephew of

Forne. The earldom of Northumbria, as predicted, went to none of their husbands, but to the late Earl's only full brother Earl Eadulf, half-brother of Maldred's wife and uncle therefore of Crinan's two grandsons.

Despite this sad fact, it was reported that the five husbands, with the possible exception of Alfgar, showed no signs of jealousy but, on the contrary, redoubled the care with which they cultivated that part of their wives' lands which fell to the middle and western sides of the country.

In this, Alfgar of Mercia would undoubtedly have taken his share had his attention not been distracted by some fierce raiding by the men of Gwynedd on the Mercian frontier which required prompt action by himself and his uncle Edwin. The opposition being stronger than either of them expected, they retired after a damaging success.

In Bruges, the Lady Emma considered the future of her son Hardecanute in Denmark and her stepson Harold Harefoot in England and decided that she would enjoy a visit from her oldest surviving son, the half-Saxon Edward in Normandy, now in his mid-thirties, unmarried, and with no occupation other than hunting, at which he was by now extremely accomplished, when he could afford it.

Edward's visit to his mother was short. She asked him to lead an attack against Harold Harefoot and he refused, directing her attention instead to her other son Hardecanute in Denmark.

It was a predictable reverse, but one she did not enjoy. After Edward had gone, she sent another courier to Denmark, bought the head of St Valentine, and through an excellent young man called Hermann of Hainault, whom her late husband had come across at the Flemish monastery of St Bertin's, commissioned the writing of her biography.

It was, she ruled, to contain no allusions whatever to her first husband King Aethelred, the father of Edward.

In other parts of Europe, young men stirred. In Sweden, Svein Ulfsson, nephew of the late Canute, listened to the news from Denmark and began, quietly, on his twentieth birthday, to make certain arrangements.

In Constantinople, a powerful twenty-three-year-old called Harald, half-brother of the late canonised King Olaf, shut the lid of his first chest of treasure and, taking his sword, went out thoughtfully to join Georgios Maniakos in Sicily and begin filling the next.

In Hungary, the vehemently converted King Stephen, alias Salomon, died in the arms of his Venetian nephew Peter, tranquil in the belief that his German widow Gisela would be maintained as she deserved by his nephew Peter when King.

Peter, who had no such intentions, was promptly embroiled in a national revolt by the Magyar nobility and allowed his aunt Gisela to starve without interference. What had happened to Stephen's protégés, the Lady Emma's two Saxon stepsons, hustled abroad during King Canute's reign after the death of Edmund Ironside their father, was a matter for speculation throughout Europe, especially as both boys should now have reached the age at which they might be expected to multiply.

The concept of a warren of royal Saxons flourishing under the care of some unknown and ambitious monarch was one that roused either goose-pimples or hilarity, depending on where it was being debated.

In Normandy, Duke William the Bastard attained the age of ten years. In Dol, on the Norman-Brittany border, the Archbishop Jarnegon died and, after many and appropriate gifts to Count Alan, was replaced by his former archdeacon Juhel de Fougères, who communicated immediately thereafter with his friends in Mercia, Devon, and Alba.

In York, Ealdred, the new Earl of Northumbria, suddenly realised that the history of thirty years since had repeated itself; and that the silver mines, the St Cuthbert's Cumbrian shrines, and the western harbours for Ireland had all silently disappeared from outside his control.

Emulating the history of thirty years before, he gathered an army and, marching west, proceeded to attack Cumbria, as his father Uhtred had done.

With remarkable alacrity, the five husbands of his five nieces all vanished before he got there, with the exception of Duncan, King of Alba and ruler of Cumbria. Which made the pattern complete, since it was Duncan's grandfather King Malcolm whom Ealdred's father had defeated so firmly all that time ago.

Whether because of this impending event or in ignorance of it, Thorfinn of Caithness, Moray, and Orkney took to sea with his fellow-Earl and all the ships he possessed and sailed west and south towards Cumbria. This time, he did not say where he was going, nor, as the weeks passed, had his people any idea what had happened to him or their kinsmen.

In the end, Thorkel Fóstri, who controlled his foster-son's affairs now on land rather than by sea, sent to Thorfinn's wife, who in turn sent for Sulien and her son Lulach.

Sulien had news to tell her. She listened to what he had to say, and did not try to stop him when he left for Caithness, taking Lulach and his servants with him. By fate or by coincidence, he arrived at Thurso as Thorfinn's fleet began to come in.

From Trelleborg to Tønsberg, from Rousay to Rodel, there could have been few boys of the age of nine who had not stood on the shore of their fathers and watched the boats of the kindred come home from their viking. When, at fourteen, they buckled on the sword their father had bought and carried their box up the gangplank, they knew the worst and the best, and were prepared for it.

To Lulach it was unknown. The horns blew for the longships' arrival, and Sulien, his robe crumpled still from the riding, his fresh face unsmiling, took the boy by the shoulder and walked him downhill from the door of the hall, disregarding the others, men and women, who left their houses and, brushing by, made for the beach and the jetty before him.

Thorkel Fóstri, rising, was moved to stop him, and then paused and, taking his stick, walked slowly down after him. For more than five years, the Breton had been friend and surrogate father to Lulach. Whatever Sulien's motives, the lad would come to no harm. Then the sails began to appear round the western headland and, like everyone else, he began to count. As the sails dropped and the figureheads were taken in and they began to work under oar to the beach, you could see the damage.

The grey-goose figurehead with the scarlet sail made for the rivermouth and the wharf, as Sulien had expected. He and the boy took the ford over the river to where the burned hall had once stood and the new building now looked down on the sweep of the shore. Far over the sea, the sun picked out the clear green of the Orkney island of Hoy, while here, behind the new hall, the eastern horn of the bay lay as if stitched in pink on the braided blue silk of the seascape.

Thorfinn's figurehead came down, bright against the stiff flaps of scarlet as the sail was roughly stowed. The lower strakes of the boat were foul with weed, and the timber above was chopped and shaved as if tooled by an adze. Three of the thwarts stood blank and empty, and the gunwales, with their careful gilding, were scuffed and gapped. The oars lifted on her larboard side and she slid to her place by the wharf, while a man vaulted ashore with a cable. Lulach ran and held out his arms for the prow rope, which someone threw to him, grinning.

On board, there was a lot of talk and laughter and other sounds. Someone screamed once, and then a second time. The gangplank came down, and Lulach came slowly and stood by Sulien, along with the dozen or two others who had joined them by this time. The first man, carrying another over his shoulder, steadied himself and began to come ashore.

There were sixty men on board, a third of them wounded in one way or another, and two who had died so recently that they had been brought home to be buried. They came ashore in various ways, according to their wounds and their natures: some shouting and capering; some limping but joyous, with a clinking sack and perhaps a fur hat over one eye; two had a girl by the hand. One man crawled down the gangplank, and three were dragged ashore on their boxes. A man with his youth well behind him hopped down on two makeshift crutches, with his white-matted chest filled with necklaces: of glass and silver and amber and cornelian and great beads of walrus ivory that glistened like butter.

The crowd opened and swallowed them with screams of dismay and delight and a great wave of laughter. Thorfinn came ashore, carrying Rognvald in his arms.

Lulach's eyes filled his face. 'Stepfather?' he said.

Thorfinn stopped. Rognvald's head lay over his arm, its mouth open. The long yellow hair, rough with salt, swayed and dangled.

Thorfinn's eyes moved from Lulach to Sulien and back to Lulach. Shifting the weight on his arms, he lifted Rognvald's motionless body and pitched it face down on to the grass by the quayside. It struck the ground with a sound that began like a grunt and accelerated. Rognvald raised himself a hand-span from the turf and, hair hanging, vomited into it, without opening his eyes.

'You've found an occasion to celebrate?' Sulien said. The smell of ale hanging over the ship was thick as wadmoll.

'Clearly, it was a mistake,' Thorfinn said. His gaze switched to Lulach. 'And who are you these days? Someone no one has heard of?'

The clear gaze showed disappointment, not disapproval. 'No. Or I shouldn't exist. What have you done?' said Lulach.

'Sailed here and there,' Thorfinn said. 'Visited friends. Sometimes, if I found my friends had guests they didn't want, I encouraged them to leave. Sometimes, if I found my friends had guests I didn't want, I encouraged them to leave also. It is the first rule a good landlord must keep to: to take care of his tenants and his property. Sulien agrees.'

His eyes were brown-black and glittering with what he had drunk. Sulien said, 'Go on. I brought Lulach so that he could listen to you.'

'I thought you had brought him so that I could listen to him,' said Thorfinn, and Sulien, struck silent, looked at him.

'Oh, come,' Thorfinn said. 'There must be something that you can say? I keep hoping between one visit and the next that I shall find someone who understands me enough to quarrel with. I forget that you and Lulach are children.' He put his arms lightly round both their shoulders and turned them in the direction of the new hall. The noise at the quay began to die away.

'I am not a child,' Lulach said.

'No, Luloecen the Fool, you are not a child,' Thorfinn said. 'Dead men do not frighten you, and you know Arnór's verses before he has invented them.'

'Not all of them,' Lulach said, and recited.

> *'One battle-shower*
> *Will the English remember.*
> *Ne'er was a greater.*
> *There with his warrior band*
> *Came the giver of Rings.*
> *The keen-tempered sword*
> *Bit the stout-hearted host.*
>
>   . . . . .
> *Upon England's shores*
> *The Earl bore his banner—*
> *Ever and again*
> *Reddening the eagle's tongue.*
> *The Prince bade them carry—'*

'Stop it!' Sulien said, and put his hand over Lulach's mouth.

They had got to the hall. There was no one there but some elderly slaves, whom Thorfinn sent running for tables. When they were seated, the three of them: 'No. Don't stop,' said Thorfinn. 'You came here for a purpose, and you will go through life bearing your failure unless you complete it. . . . We have committed every sin except that of dishonouring our parents, since some of us have none. We have cleared Diarmaid's men from my father's holdings on the islands and mainlands of Alba, and Eachmarcach's enemies from Anglesey and the Welsh coast, with the invaluable aid of Gruffydd ap Llywelyn; and installed Godfrey, Eachmarcach's nephew, to look after our combined interests in Man. We found the Severn channel and discouraged some rough men from interfering with the settlements on Caldy and Flatholme and Lundy. We discovered my half-brother Duncan battling to save his royal heritage in Cumbria against an unprovoked attack from his wife's uncle Earl Eadulf, and took the chance to clear a base for ourselves on the river Waver and the Hougan peninsula, with the discreet help of my third cousin Thor of Allerdale—'

'*You fool!*' said Sulien. 'You fool! You mounted a double attack with Eadulf against King Duncan in Cumbria? That was why you left so quickly? Don't you see what you have done?'

'Obtained two bases on the Hougan peninsula and the river Waver,' said Thorfinn. 'I didn't need to collaborate with Eadulf. He signalled his intentions with trumpet calls all over Bamburgh.'

'He's stupid, isn't he?' Sulien said. 'It amazes me sometimes that he has lived as long as he has. How long do you think his good fortune is going to last?'

'You mean which of the five husbands is going to kill him?' Thorfinn said. 'I am really too drunk to tell you. But somehow I don't think it will be Duncan.'

Sulien flushed. Slowly, he placed his two elbows on the board in front of him and pressed his hands into his eyes. He said, 'If I thought you knew where you were going, I could forgive you. Sometimes you make it appear that you do, but I think you are playing with us. . . . If you go where you are going by default, by drifting, by following other men's fancies, you will freeze in hell, and deserve it.'

Thorfinn leaned back in the high chair. The mark of the helmet was still red round the sun-browned dome of his brow, and his unshaven chin was dark under the untrimmed black of a half-grown moustache. With relaxation, his lids had grown thick. 'You won't be content until you have preached,' he said. 'So why not preach?'

Sulien dropped his hands sharply. '*Sêit mo srôin.* Blow my nose, says the leper. Is there no voice in your own head to listen to? There is a chance to spite Duncan and you take it, regardless of Orkney and Caithness, left behind you exposed to whatever may come. There is a peace pact between Norway and Denmark—have you heard it?—so that Magnús is free for the first time since he came back from Russia to look around his dependencies and correct anything of which he doesn't entirely approve. If a fleet had come, what could we have done?'

'Mentioned Rognvald's name, and asked them to number off and come in as invited,' Thorfinn said. 'You forget that we possess the golden talisman, the King's foster-brother. Also that I have had the good sense to wed an Arnmødling.'

It was a slip, although he realised it as soon as he had made it. 'Certainly,' Sulien said, 'you married Finn Arnason's daughter. It can hardly be long before her father or one of her uncles crosses the sea, I suppose, to ask if you think she is dead or rate her as a slave-girl, that you pay no more attention to her than to some painted wood on your ship's prow. Yes, look at Lulach. I brought him to hear what concerns him.'

'Have you finished?' Thorfinn said.

'I haven't even finished with Norway,' Sulien said. 'Do you never look at the west coast of Norway and see reflected in it the cause of half your own troubles: the sea inlets and mountains that cut off region from region, as they do also in Wales? No one can rule such a country until they find some common belief: a structure along whose veins the blood of nationhood can be made to run. . . . Olaf placed his hopes in the church, and Canute followed him, using English bishops and English abbots to fashion it.

'But now Harold Harefoot is King of England, Magnús must have his bishops consecrated elsewhere. Rome is far away. But the Archbishop of Hamburg and Bremen is always ready to dispatch his evangelists: to convert the heathen and open his lap to the heathen's tribute of bear fur and walrus tusks. Whether or not Magnús has designs on Orkney or Shetland or Iceland,' Sulien said, 'you may depend on it that Hamburg and Bremen will look to him to call in the black sheep to the fold, and then your vassaldom will really start. For if people learn to pay their dues and cleanse their souls in Orkney, will they not expect to do the same when they stay or visit their kinsmen in Caithness? And if there is one metropolitan and one church in Caithness and Orkney, what is Moray to do? Either Norway will take over your empire, body and soul, or your empire will break in pieces while you are sailing and drinking and encouraging rough men to move from one windy cliff to another.'

'I forget what your solution is,' Thorfinn said. 'Although, to be sure, I have heard it often enough. We join up the monk at Eynhallow with the group at Papay Minni; and the three men at Applecross with the other good and solitary souls at Lismore and Tullich and Dornoch and Kindrochit and Insh and Glendochart and all over the rest of my provinces, and make them all bishop-princes, answerable only to myself and the Lateran? They wouldn't enjoy it.'

'You surprise me,' Sulien said. 'I didn't know you had made an inventory of your soul-doctors. When do we look for the results?'

'You have seen them,' said Thorfinn placidly. 'Until recently, my conduct would have shocked you. You haven't an answer?'

'At least I look for one,' Sulien said. 'You talk of a dozen small houses, scattered over all your country. Perhaps you have visited them: I doubt it. But I can tell you that I have, because that is why I came here, to study and to learn. I have seen monasteries, yes: monasteries which struggle and fade, and are given another injection of monks or of money from a mother-house somewhere in Ireland, and who struggle on once again, with poor teachers or none; with the remains of a library, or a single book-satchel hung on a hook, with one dog-eared gospel inside it, and the prayers for the sick and the dying.

'Families who need to hunt, to fish, to tend the fields and the flocks, to go a-viking to please their overlord can't spare sons to enter the priesthood. How many priests do you think that you have, when the whole country can be served by an ambling bishop consecrated in Durham or York, with a comfortable living somewhere else?'

Thorfinn stretched out his legs and gazed at him. 'Would we fare very much better if we had seven bishops as Brittany has, and each of them the tool of some duke or other? In any case, I thought all our ills were to be cured by the Servants of God. Or have they stopped arriving?'

'You have seen them,' said Sulien. With an effort, he dropped and steadied his voice. 'Every group of Culdees lives like the next: a quiet life of prayer and isolation led by a group of old men under a prior. They are a well for spiritual refreshment. They are not the stuff with which to bind a people together and protect it from its enemies.'

'Without the Culdees,' Lulach said, 'where would a king die?'

Thorfinn looked at his stepson and did not answer.

Sulien said, 'Yes. You are right. Where does a king go when he wishes to lay down his sceptre, and the kindred are waiting to seize it? There is nowhere but a house of God. Of course, if you have the health for it, and the gold, you can go to Rome, as Eachmarcach's uncle did, and live out your life in a hostel.'

'There was a King of Alba went to Rome,' Lulach said. 'One cold winter, the ink froze at Fulda. There was a king of Alba who murdered his uncle and married his uncle's widow.'

As before, Thorfinn did not speak.

Sulien said gently, 'I didn't know that. Was it the same king?'

'I thought it was,' Lulach said. 'There was a king who got a child on the miller's daughter of Forteviot.'

'The same king?' Sulien said. His face, watching the boy's, was full of pity.

'His name was Henry,' Lulach said. 'How would I know what kind of miller it was? Stepfather, if everyone becomes a Culdee when he grows old, won't they all become earls and kings?'

'What a very good question,' Thorfinn said. He looked at Sulien. 'Well. Go on. If you don't want to make too much of the Culdees, what other spiritual means do we have to bind our indifferent peoples together? A brotherhood of the little saints? We have quite an assortment. Finnian and Machar and Torannan, Moluag and Triduana, Madan and Fergus and Ethernais, all with their cells and their chapels in strategic strong-points.

'There are dangers, of course. One could hardly make much of St Cuthbert without disturbing Duncan's monopoly, and he would be uneasy, I am sure, if we encroached on St Ninian and St Kentigern. What about our more promising alliances? Would Brittany's St Serf and St Gobrien lock hands with ours over the seas? Would Cornwall allow our St Drostan to nod to their Drostan son of King Cunomor, and Juhel de Fougères remind us of his sister's husband Triscandus? Would your St Brieuc and theirs remember his holy places in Alba? What about the other soul-friends of my new friends the Welsh? St Cewydd and St Tudwal and the others you are longing to tell me about? Come,' Thorfinn said. 'I have read your lecture for you. Don't leave me to end it as well. You must have some new thoughts to offer.'

The boy said, 'I am going,' and went.

'He has sense,' Sulien said. He was white. He said, 'You know it all. You know it better than I do, when you trouble to give it a thought. I can't forgive you for that.'

'So you have come to tell me you are leaving,' Thorfinn said. 'Or so I would gather, since I appear to have been given my penance.'

'Yes, I am leaving,' Sulien said. 'I have to study in Ireland. You knew that.' He paused. Thorfinn had not moved, but leaned back with his legs stretched, looking at him.

'Am I supposed to beg you to stay?' Thorfinn said.

Sulien's face coloured again, and then paled. He said, 'It is my fault. I spoke so that you heard a priest, not a friend. I have done nothing for you.'

'Then at least we are not in one another's debt,' Thorfinn said. 'Lulach will miss you.'

'Thorfinn,' Sulien said. 'Thorfinn. . . . you know what he is.'

'Yes,' said Thorfinn.

Sulien could hear the harshness in his own voice. He said, 'He has the name of a ghost. Luloecen the Fool. Luloecen of the Threefold Prophecy.'

Thorfinn stamped his feet and stood up. 'I know. I have told you,' he said.

They stood facing one another. And then Sulien knew.

'He has told you what is to come?'

'Long ago,' Thorfinn replied. 'Long ago, while you were exploring rocks and picking off hermits. *A dhùdan fhéin an ceann gach fòid*: its own dust at the end of every peat. We all have troubles.'

The silence lay heavy between them. 'Send for your wife,' Sulien said at last. 'Send for your wife, even though she offends you. If I ask you, will you do that?'

'The proverb,' Thorfinn said, 'says nothing about adding a second peat, far less a creelful. Tell me when you wish to leave and I shall load a ship for you. It is the least I can do.'

Sulien left; and did not know that Thorfinn did not at once go about the business of settling in, but stood in the empty hall, his eyes on the door he had left by.

When he spoke, it was to himself, and still in Gaelic.

'There is a girl in the house who surpasses the women of Ireland, with red flowing hair. . . . She is beautiful, and skilled in many crafts. The heart of every man breaks with longing and love for her. . . .'

He broke off. 'And so,' he said, 'you do not offer her dust, do you, Lulach?'

NINETEEN

O THE SURPRISE of all and the disappointment of many, Sulien of Llanbadarn left, and unbridled licence failed to break out. Only Thorkel Fóstri refused to recognise the phenomenon, observing tartly that if it had, no one would have noticed the difference. Starkad and Arnór and the rest, who knew better, grinned at him as they always did, and went back to where Thorfinn was planning the next summer's sailing.

Despite Sulien's warnings, Dubhdaleithe son of Maelmuire was allowed to follow the desire of his heart and, leaving his abbey of Deer, to settle with a group of disciples on a piece of ground by St Cormac's chapel on the shores of the Dornoch Firth, an inlet of the sea north of Moray. His brother Aedh was given temporary charge of Deer and of Buchan, and word sent to the Lady of Moray to that effect.

The Lady of Moray, in the absence of interference from the Mormaer of Moray, continued to move about her province, calling on her bailiffs and advisors, with whom she was now on excellent terms. In the course of four months, two family groups found themselves elevated to direct service under the Mormaer, and two further districts received the doubtful blessing of a steward from the north, for whom a new lodging had to be built. In time, Groa visited these as well, and on the whole approved her husband's choice. In return, the new stewards failed signally to tell her what her husband's private instructions to them had been.

Before the end of the year, despite all Thorfinn's planning, Eachmarcach got himself thrown out of Dublin by his cousin Ivar son of Harald and arrived at Canisbay half a stone lighter and with no more than two battered longships and their complement. He stayed for a month, during which Thorfinn and he shouted at each other every night for eight days, and Eachmarcach began to eat again. At the end of a month, Guthorm Gunnhildarson called, apparently by chance, and he and Eachmarcach went off to Eachmarcach's nephew on the Isle of Man until the summer sailing could begin.

In the spring, Sulien wrote a stiff note from Moville, Ireland, in which he mentioned he had met a young monk called Maelbrighde, whom he did not like. He hoped, he said, that Thorfinn and Lulach were enjoying one another's company.

The message came with a trading-ship bringing three dozen Frankish mail shirts, on Thorfinn's order. The shipmaster, who had also called at Tiree, said there was interesting news of a battle in Wales in which the King of Gwynedd had died and the throne been taken by Thorfinn's recent ally Gruffydd ap Llywelyn. In the course of the fighting, a brother of Earl Leofric of Mercia had got himself killed, and after the battle King Gruffydd's victorious army had lost their heads and destroyed Llanbadarn.

To the relieved delight of the hird, unbridled licence for once made its appearance that night, interrupted but not restrained by the arrival of Rognvald, Thorfinn's nephew. Rognvald, waiting patiently until he judged Thorfinn able to understand what he was saying, reported that Duncan, King of Alba, had just made the rounds of Moray with three hundred men, living in guest-quarters and consuming his tribute, as was his right of choice, instead of having it delivered. He had stayed a week with the Lady of Moray at Brodie.

They were in Thorfinn's hall-house at Sannick at the time, above the sandy sweep of the bay under the headland. Thorfinn, his hair wet because he had just stuck it into a barrel, said, 'How do you know all this?'

The dimple showed. Rognvald with the passing of years had only grown, at twenty-eight, more ethereal. 'I was visiting Groa,' he said. 'Your wife. I had found a pair of gerfalcons I knew she would like.'

'Gerfalcons from where?' said Thorfinn evenly. He looked, Rognvald noted, as if the founts of energy were less prodigal than once they had been.

Rognvald conveyed astonishment. 'From Brims Ness,' he said. 'I suppose you don't grudge your wife a couple of birds now and then. I knew it hadn't occurred to you that she'd like them.'

'And?' said Thorfinn.

'And what?' said Rognvald. 'After Eadulf's visitation, anyone could guess that your dear brother was going to be a little short of provender for his courtmen this year, and you were going to be the provider. I must say, however, he doesn't share your admirable restraint in the marriage-couch. If I hadn't been there, I don't know how your wife might have fared. You know, of course, that his own died of milk-fever. He is in the market-place.'

'Indeed. Do you think anyone will pick him?' Thorfinn said.

Rognvald laughed. 'Next time you say that, loosen your knuckles. He did say that I was to tell you that he was sending to ask Finn Arnason for his daughter in marriage, since you seemed to have voided the bargain. He also said,' said Rognvald, picking up a cloth from the floor and wiping, gracefully, the puddled ale from the board between himself and his uncle, 'that he wished to have a little talk with you about the tribute from Caithness. He's a simple fellow, isn't he?' said Rognvald, putting the cloth fastidiously down on the floor again. 'But I think perhaps you will have to give the matter some thought, if you want to keep Moray. Perhaps you don't.'

'Not if I'm going to lose all my gerfalcons,' Thorfinn said.

Rognvald waited. When nothing happened, he said, 'I suppose you know how much Duncan hates you.'

'Does he? On the other hand,' Thorfinn said, 'the Lord of Ossory is dying, I'm told, so that none of his Irish friends will be too anxious to leave home just at present, and of course Duncan's wife's uncle has just relieved him of half his strength on the border. If I were you, I shouldn't take it all too much to heart. Groa probably liked it.'

'Dear Christ,' said Rognvald simply. 'What offence are you waiting for, that you will swallow whatever this silly man offers you?'

'The one he comes and offers me out of his own hand and mouth and not other people's,' Thorfinn said. 'Have you ever climbed that stack out in the sea there? We were just making a wager on it.'

The golden hair shone and the eyes sparkled. 'No. But I'll wager I'm faster than you are,' Rognvald said; and a moment later they were down on the strand with twenty others and pushing off two of the skiffs.

A Salmundarson got his shield on top first, with Thorfinn just behind him, and no one hurt except a kinsman of Isleifr's who broke his leg in three places and never walked the same way again except on an incline.

They agreed that it was good to have Rognvald back.

Later, the extraordinary gales arrived, and swept cows off the headlands into the sea, and broke down sacred trees, and bowled wicker huts like birds' nests from end to end of the plough-rigs. At the autumn's end, Thorfinn came back from his sailing with two shredded sails in *Grágás* and three others dismasted; but in spite of it he had visited Eachmarcach in Man and cleared the sea for him, as well as re-establishing his victualling and repair bases in Cumbria and Galloway, and reminding Diarmaid son of the Cow-Chief whose land it was. His third cousin Thor, whom he happened to meet in the course of it, was glad to pass the time of day with him, and he even had occasion to pick up a little carrying-trade which gave him a profit on a brief trip to Exeter.

On the way home, he stopped off at the Dee estuary and sent a longboat up to Chester with a silk cloak for the Lady of Mercia, as a result of which her son Alfgar came out himself to bring him back to the hall.

In the boat, they talked business. In the hall, Thorfinn walked over to the Earl of Mercia and said, 'I came to tell you and your wife that the killing of your brother was by no desire of mine. I needed Gruffydd the year before and I may need him again, but not against you.'

'I am glad you told me,' Leofric said. 'But Alfgar here is your strongest advocate. We understand policy, and the need to adapt it. You are running the same risk as my brother. . . . Do you have news from the south?'

'Only what you have,' Thorfinn said. 'The Lady Emma has sent to Denmark, and her son there is gathering ships and an army. He may take them to Bruges, but won't attack England, they think, till the spring.'

He paused. His hair had been barbered, Godiva saw, for this journey, and in spite of the hard sailing, he was well and expensively dressed. He said, 'You probably know that the Hungarians have got rid of their latest king, Peter.

He's escaped to Conrad's son, the new Emperor of the Romans. Whether with or without the royal Saxons, the sons of Edmund Ironside he was supposed to be harbouring, isn't known.'

'But I'm sure you'll find out,' Alfgar said. 'Your exquisite kinsman of Orkney must surely have heard them talked of in Russia—not that I would expect you to discuss anything as prosaic with that princeling about. Duncan can speak of nothing but your nephew since he came back from Moray.'

'I heard,' Thorfinn said, 'that he had been sizing up the situation.'

'Are you surprised? My lord Duncan didn't like one of you sitting on his grandfather's north coast, and he likes two of you still less, especially now Magnús is growing a beard over there in Orkney. You know Duncan's wife died?'

'And I know the implications,' Thorfinn said.

Godiva said, 'Forgive us if we don't go into the implications. Have you had a message from Sulien?'

His face gave nothing away, but she knew she had been understood. 'There is nothing I can say,' he said.

'Come and eat, then,' said Alfgar. 'Did you hear about Llanbadarn?'

After a bitter winter, the King of England, Harold Harefoot, died at Oxford in March, aged twenty-four.

The news came to Bruges, where the Lady Emma waited in exile, with her son Hardecanute and sixty hired ships and an army. On its heels came the Bishop of London, to tell Canute's widow that her stepson Harold was dead, and to offer the crown of England to her son by Canute, Hardecanute of Denmark.

Emma's three years of exile were finished. In June, she returned to her household in Winchester, and her favourite son was crowned King of England. His first act was to have his half-brother dug up, his head cut off, and his body flung in the Thames.

Although hard to follow, it set the tone for the next half a dozen. Hardecanute announced a massive new tax imposition, and appointed as his regent in Denmark his young cousin Svein, son of the late Canute's sister Estrith or Margaret.

Svein, who had already decided he was wasted in Sweden, accepted humbly, and all over England the earls sat up and took notice, while Magnús of Norway sent King Hardecanute his congratulations and asked warmly after his health.

Groa, moving from Turriff to Deeside with her five-year-old son and her household, was overtaken and stopped by a fast-riding group of men led by Skeggi, whom she knew but did not approve of. With no preamble, he instructed the Lady of Moray to turn round her troop and accompany him forthwith to the community of St Cormac by Tain.

While excellent in his day at running across rows of oarlooms, Skeggi was less practised at handling young matrons.

'Lulach!' said Groa. 'What has happened? Something has happened to—'

'Not at all,' said Skeggi crossly. 'What could happen to Lulach? You've to go and join him, that's all. Earl Thorfinn's orders.'

It had been raining. Her garron shook its mane, and horse-smelling spray covered her face. 'My lord Thorfinn would like us in Tain? I wonder why?' Groa said. Out of the corner of her eye she could see Sigurd's cheek bulging where Sinna had fed a cake into it.

'I don't know,' Skeggi said. 'It's taken us two days to find you. Where's your man, and I'll give him his orders?'

'Never mind,' Groa said. 'I'm sure you are as tired as we are with riding. Come to the next lodging with us and tell me about it.'

Skeggi said, 'I've told you about it. Unless I get you back soon, he'll have my skin for windows.'

'And if you don't come with me, so shall I,' Groa said. 'Which is it to be?'

She had thirty men with her, to his eight. Her steward, trotting back to them now at her signal, was not a man he knew well. Skeggi rode to meet him and stopped him in the road. 'I've to take her up to Ross. Thorfinn says. She won't go.'

Groa, riding up, had no trouble hearing that. 'I don't recall refusing to go,' said the Lady of Moray. 'I do recall refusing to turn round and run at the blow of a whistle. Do we move on and talk at our rest-place, or do I tell Morgund to get his sword ready?'

Unfortunately Morgund, who looked after five districts, was no match for Skeggi, who spent eight months of every year fighting and the rest playing at fighting. 'I've got his sword ready for him,' said Skeggi prosaically from behind the captain, and indeed he had, with his hand at Morgund's neck and the point of his own sword pressing against Morgund's spine.

'Look, my lady. If I don't get you back fast enough, it'll be bloodshed, and if you don't come away now, it'll be bloodshed, and all for nothing that matters. Will you turn your horse and ride north, or are you willing to face Thorfinn over what's going to happen?'

His voice was plaintive, and if she didn't know her husband's hird, she would have thought it dangerous bluff.

Fortunately or otherwise, Skeggi didn't know how to bluff. If she didn't turn round, he would kill Morgund. And then, of course, the rest of her troop would kill him.

She said, 'I shall send your nail-clippings to a friend. And your master's.' Then she turned her horse round.

Skeggi withdrew the sword and held it out, patiently, to its owner. 'You'd have to find him first,' he said. 'And that's a task I'd not wish on a one-legged man.'

'He's not there?' Groa reined up her horse. 'All this rush, and he isn't even there? Where is he?'

'I told you,' said Skeggi patiently. 'I was to get you back fast. He'll find out soon enough if I didn't. And you'll find out where he's been when he gets back. Maybe.'

'If I'm still there when he gets back. Maybe,' Groa said coldly and rode on, in the rain.

At St Cormac's when she got there was a flamboyant welcome from Dubhdaleithe and a sweet one from Lulach. Earl Thorfinn and all the hird except Thorkel were missing. There was, however, a box of her husband's beside a group of new wooden cabins that had been built over the rise from the wattle huts used by the monk and his followers. On top of the box was a packet of neatly waxed cloth, and inside the cloth, when she opened it with no compunction, was a scrap of much-folded vellum written all over in Sulien's characteristic, flat-topped, beautiful script.

What it conveyed was no personal news, but merely two items from some monkish annals. The first said, *There has perished Donnchad MacGillapadraig, Arch-king of Leinster and Ossory and Champion of Ireland, who found death together with a prey. His successor is chosen.*

The second said, *There sleeps in Christ, Maelmuire Uah Uchtain, coarb of Colum-Cille, and the Fair of Teltown itself on the day after the Feast of St Germain.*

Afterwards, she wondered what Earl Thorfinn would have done if she had gone to Lulach's mentor to have the note read to her. At the time, she was merely mystified, and ashamed, and resentful because she was ashamed, and because her prying held no danger at all, since her husband was quite unaware that she could read in any tongue, far less Gillacomghain's Irish Gaelic.

She put the parchment back in the bag, and would have put it in the box to await the Earl's arrival, except that the box had been locked.

And that, too, she resented.

'Behave as you usually do,' Thorfinn had said impatiently to his foster-father before he sailed off so carelessly. 'What is the trouble? She can stay by the monk with the boys and her household, and you'll be at Dingwall. Go and see her from time to time. Get her what she needs. Answer whatever you like to her questions. But just keep her there until I tell you to move her.'

This, a man could do with a concubine or even with most married women Thorkel Fóstri had cause to know. But his cousin Finn Arnason's daughter, this infant bride, this widow, this tall, supple girl in her mid-twenties with hair like haws on the bough, and arched feet that sprang through the mosses of these northlands where she was exiled, was not anyone's wife, or even the Lady of Moray, but a sharp, buoyant mind, half freed to the winds by this brusque break from routine, half stranded alone in a thicket where pride and fear would not let her rest until she had discovered why she had been brought there.

The thought of Thorfinn tied to a woman was not one his foster-father had drawn pleasure from. But five years of neglect such as this was an offence to the girl's family—to *his* family—as well as to the young bride. Thorkel Fóstri resented her and was sorry for her at the same time, and the astonishing flowering of her physical beauty made it even more difficult, when he called on her at last, to obey his foster-son's casual edict.

With no state to keep, with no needlework to occupy her hands while she received complaints and gave orders and entertained visitors, she had left her fine robes in their boxes and dressed as her women did, in a strapped tunic of wool, bright-banded at the hem over gay short-sleeved linen tied with silk at her throat; and her dark red hair, knotted and ribboned, was lifted high from her white nape. She came off the hill to meet him, reluctantly, he could see, while below on the shore came the squeals of her younger son and the women, and Lulach's white head showed, and his brown, glistening arms, delving for shellfish. Groa said, 'Come and sit in the sun and tell me what war you are preparing for.'

From the knoll she led him to, its boulders scoured and glazed by the wind, you looked down on the broad, sandy flats of the firth, and the children. Thorkel said, sitting, 'What has Duftah been saying?'

'Is that what you call him? It's easier, I dare say than Dubhdaleithe. Lulach calls him St Duthac,' Groa said. She sat, her skirts falling over her bare feet. She said, 'Duftah hasn't told me anything. He didn't need to. It's like the waterfront at Nídarós on a feast day, with the ox-carts and the horses and the longships whipping up and down the firths on both sides.

'Magnús would attack Orkney if he had fallen out with Rognvald, which he hasn't; so it can't be that. It can't be Svein or Hardecanute: they've hardly climbed into their thrones. The truth is, I suppose, that Duncan has sent, demanding tribute for Caithness, this time with menaces?'

'Something like that,' Thorkel Fóstri said. 'It's as well to be prepared.'

'But Earl Thorfinn isn't here?' Groa said. 'So perhaps he isn't taking Duncan as seriously as you are. Did *you* send for me?'

Afterwards, he saw that he should have lied; but then he had not yet got her measure. 'No, Thorfinn did,' he said.

'To bargain with?' said Groa. 'Would you agree to that, without consulting me?'

'Bargaining? You are here for your safety,' Thorkel said.

'Then Earl Thorfinn is going to refuse payment again?' Groa said. 'Perhaps I should be even safer if he simply paid tribute for Caithness, even if he had to do it from his revenues out of Moray. I shouldn't object.'

Only a fool would take her up on that, although he saw clearly enough that one day Thorfinn would have to answer for it. Thorkel Fóstri said, 'It may not come to anything. These are only precautions. Duncan is embroiled in a concern of his own at the moment, and we are waiting to hear the results of it.'

Contemplatively, Thorfinn's wife was studying him. She said, 'Indeed. Duncan has been King of Alba for six years now, and has done nothing whatever except hold on to Cumbria and watch all his relatives creeping up on him. You mean something has pushed him into action?'

'Duncan is besieging Durham,' Thorkel Fóstri said. 'Does that make you feel better? Thorfinn's going to disown Bethoc his late mother, he says, and proclaim himself a bastard like the Duke of Normandy and King Magnús. Certainly you wonder how she came to give birth to this imbecile Duncan.'

'Lulach says—' said Groa, and stopped.

'Another fancy?' said Thorkel Fóstri, smiling.

Groa said, 'He has a string of birth-tales to do with my husband. One of them claims that the lord Macbeth's mother was beguiled by a tall, handsome man who turned out to be the Devil. When the half-devil son was born, the Devil made . . . promises.'

'The Devil was Sigurd,' said Thorkel, still smiling. 'And you could call Thorfinn half a devil at times, or even a whole one. But I promise you that Bethoc and the late Earl of Orkney were properly contracted, even though the church had to settle with Crinan first. From the bed of the Abbot to Orkney must have been quite a shock in one way. But Sigurd was a great man. Tell Lulach that. Before they went into league, he and Findlaech had many a match against one another, with little to spare on either side. Now, what do you need that I may bring you? I sent a cook. Have you need of a cobbler?'

'Not, I suppose, unless Duncan fails to take Durham,' Groa said. 'Where is Earl Thorfinn, and when is he coming back?'

'When did you know Thorfinn trouble to send word of his movements?' said Thorkel Fóstri. 'But he can't be far. And of course he will come to see you as soon as he gets back. You may be sure of it.'

Reporting the conversation three hours later to Thorfinn, who in fact was no further away than his headquarters at the Moot Hill of Dingwall at the head of the next firth, Thorkel Fóstri said, 'I don't suppose there is a chance that we are all wrong and Duncan will manage to capture Durham? We know he's got the Ossory men and Maldred's Ulidian uncles and of course Maldred himself and his tenants. And, whatever extra ground Eadulf may have won for himself the other day, Duncan can still draw on plenty of liegemen in Cumbria. He hasn't got the skill to break through into the bluff, but at least he can block the peninsula neck and line the riverbanks and starve Durham out. Don't you think he has enough men for that?'

'He's got enough men,' Thorfinn said. Someone had brought in three late gulls' eggs and he was juggling with them. 'He's even got some good advice. Thor from Allerdale has gone along with him, and his war-band.'

Thorkel looked at his foster-son in silence. Then he said, 'So that's what you were doing.'

'Well, none of Earl Eadulf's other four nieces is going to send her husband in to help Duncan,' Thorfinn said. 'I tried to convince Alfgar that it was a good idea, and he nearly sank the boat laughing. After all, Duncan was the one Eadulf attacked, and Duncan might as well take the risk. Eadulf is going to defend Durham to the death anyway. It was his grandfather who founded the place and set up the shrine of St Cuthbert there. It's rich: it's a great stronghold; it's got lands that would make a saint's mouth water, in Lothian as well as England. Whoever holds Durham and Cumbria has the north of England in the palm of his hand, and the south of Alba as well. And if you throw in St Oswald's head, you have the chance of a foothold in the Shrewsbury district to boot.'

'Bones of Christ,' Thorkel said faintly. He pulled himself together. 'So what about Crinan?'

'My guess,' said Thorfinn, 'is that Crinan is at this moment being saintly in Kells.'

'I brought you Sulien's note,' Thorkel Fóstri said. 'Was that what he suggested?'

'More or less. What he was saying,' Thorfinn said, 'was that we may expect to see Duncan's army on or before the third week in July. Unless, of course, someone kills him at Durham.'

'Such as Thor?' Thorkel Fóstri said.

'God's splendour, no,' Thorfinn said. 'I don't want Duncan dead. Hasn't it struck you yet that such is my appointed role in the life of Duncan's kindred: to get rid of Duncan so that they can step into his shoes? Think of Orm. Think of Ligulf. Think of Maldred. Think—if you have the fortitude—of Kalv's nephew Siward.'

'You're right,' said Thorkel Fóstri. 'Now you mention it. Give me Duncan to fight against, any day.'

Knowing Thorfinn, he waited and, when the three eggs came flying towards him, caught them quite deftly.

Despite the services of Thor his brother's third cousin, King Duncan of Alba was routed at Durham as his grandfather had been over thirty years earlier.

After the battle was over, Earl Eadulf, as was the family custom, engaged a number of women to groom the handsomest enemy heads and mount them on poles round the market-place. He paid them in cows, but they would have done it for nothing, such was the pleasure of combing the curly bronze hair and the long moustaches and the virile red jut of the chin-beards. That every trophy was Irish could hardly diminish the triumph.

Duncan's head, being still on his shoulders, was not among them.

The activity in and between the two firths that enclosed Groa's peninsula reached a peak of frenzied proportions; and halted. Women stopped milking the house-cow with their chins on their shoulders; and seals came back to the firth. Then, in a day or two, only the seals were there, and the monks, because everyone else had moved out.

Thorfinn rode to visit his wife.

Sinna saw him come, from where she sat in the sun with Sigurd outside one of the little thatched huts, talking to one of the slaves as she ground meal for their cakes in a hand-quern. Above the grumbling scrape of the quern you could hear, far off, the voices of the monks who looked after Duftah and studied with him, and overhead, distinct when the girl's hand fell from the handle, the buzz of a lark, very high, its wings beating fast and then still. Groa, in the wood house, heard the hoof-beats and came to investigate.

She had been braiding her hair, and the light took her head and her face like a gemstone. The same sun, as he came near, fell full on the face of her husband, etching its alps and its ridges.

Sinna pushed the girl, and she got up and ran to take the Earl's reins, while he sat where he was without speaking. Then he gave them to her and dismounted, but as Sinna made to follow the girl and the garron, he stopped her. 'No. I have come to ask you all to make ready to leave. There is going to be fighting, and I want you in safety.'

Between the huts there was a movement, and Lulach walked slowly across to his stepfather. He said, 'Who is coming?'

'Duncan has lost Durham,' Groa suggested. 'And since he can't hold the south, must protect the rest of his patrimony from you and Rognvald and, if he can, increase it?'

'Partly,' said Earl Thorfinn. He turned to Lulach. 'We are speaking of my half-brother Duncan, the King of Alba. He married into the Earl of Northumbria's family and hoped to add the east side of north England to the west, but he is finding the other claimants are stronger. So he has to look to the north.'

'To Moray,' Groa said. 'It isn't just Caithness, is it? Duncan wants you out of Moray in every way. He wants control of the mormaerdom. He wants me, and he wants Lulach. And if an Irish force came over to help him at Durham, he has, too, a bigger army at present than he could ever hope to scrape together again, even allowing for what the defeat may have cost him.

'So he is using it quickly while it is there, and while he and it can make common cause before the time for the Fair at Teltown—because that is where they choose the new coarb of Colum-Cille, isn't it: the new head of the Columban church of Alba and Ireland? And his father Crinan might be a candidate because of his family, just as Duftah might have a claim through his great-uncle of Armagh and Kells. So—'

She stopped, her hands at her mouth, and stared at him. 'And so,' she ended slowly, 'Duncan is coming for you; for me; for Lulach . . . and also for Duftah.'

There was silence. Lulach, his hand on Sinna's shoulder, said nothing. A snipe rose near at hand, the sun sharp on its striped brown-and-white eel-back, and lifted its call like a reed underwater. Earl Thorfinn said, 'Sulien's letter. Who else knows about it?' And then, at the half-smile in her eyes, he said, 'I beg your pardon.'

'She has been able to read for a long time,' Lulach said. 'Sulien could have told you.'

Her son was the same height, now, as Sinna. The old woman moved and took the boy by the arm as it dropped. The old woman said, 'You are at fault, Earl, in leaving us here. Where can we go now, so that no one will find us?'

'To Caithness,' said Earl Thorfinn. 'There is a ship waiting. You will be quite safe, whatever happens. If Duncan moves north of Tarbatness, you will have word, and the shipmaster will take you to Norway. If you wish to go.'

'Or Orkney?' said Groa.

Her husband looked at her. 'There, too,' he said. 'It is unlikely to concern me, either way.'

'Doesn't it?' Groa said. 'I thought you more possessive than that, even under the sods. . . . Sinna, go and tell them to pack everything. Everything we have. We are leaving nothing behind. We have . . .' She turned to Earl Thorfinn. 'How long?'

'You hardly need to tell them,' said the Earl. 'There have been thirty faces watching us ever since I arrived. You have three hours.'

'Three . . .' She stared at him. 'You left us here until Duncan's army was three hours away?'

'He is a good deal further off than that,' her husband said. 'I only want to make sure that your ship is out of sight. He believes you are here. He must go on believing it.'

Sinna turned the boy round and scurried over the pebbled grass, calling. Groa said, 'I don't understand. You have let Duncan come this far north without going to meet him? Through Moray?'

'He has no ships,' the Earl said. He brought his gaze back from the settlement. 'He was bound to march. He has some provisions with him, and he will find more on the way, and no resistance. Until he gets to Inverness, he is in his own land and will expect none. I am only his Mormaer there, and only that because I am Findlaech's heir and your husband. He would expect to find loyalty to you there and will find it. But he will meet no one anxious to fight him on my behalf.'

'He must think we have a strange marriage,' Groa said. 'When the Mormaer's wife and her people will let the invader enter and march through her province to make war on the Mormaer her husband.'

'He has already suggested to you, I believe, that our marriage is void,' the Earl said. 'He will know, surely, that you are only here because you were forcibly brought here to keep you out of his hands. He hopes to hold Moray still, under a new mormaer, when all this is over, so he will try not to harm it. He thinks I am in the west, cruising: the information reached him very convincingly. He knows Duftah is here, because he has been told that as well, and Duftah has told me that he will not leave. Once he steps beyond Eskadale, he is in my land with an invading army, and must face the consequences.'

'How big an army?' said Groa.

His eyes studied her face. 'Big,' he said. 'But badly led.'

'And yours? I do not question the leadership,' said Groa with irony.

'If things fall out well,' he said, 'it will be adequate.'

'But surely?' Groa said. 'I see you can't call on Moray. But you have all Orkney and Ross and Caithness and the Western Isles, and probably Eachmarcach's men as well. And hardened men, used to this country.'

'One-third of Orkney,' Earl Thorfinn said. 'But, as I say, adequate. I shall come back for you with the baggage-train. What else?'

She stood where she was. 'One-third of Orkney? Rognvald isn't helping you?'

'I haven't asked him,' Earl Thorfinn said. 'I think he is in Wales, plundering wine-ships with Gruffydd. And Eachmarcach is best uncommitted. He can join in when he sees which side is winning. What else?'

'Nothing else. Bring your baggage-train in three hours,' Groa said. 'Sinna and the boys can go to Caithness. I am staying with Duftah.'

That he should agree, after a bitter five minutes of argument, might have surprised anyone but his wife, who knew that he had sent Skeggi to bring her north with orders to let nothing stand in his way. If he had wanted her removed to Caithness, he would have had it done. If he didn't have it done, it was because it was no longer important.

When Sigurd clung to her, screaming, and Sinna, aghast, tried to step back on shore, Earl Thorfinn used all the force that was necessary to separate them and sent the ship on its way with her sons and her household.

If she died, Lulach would live to outface Duncan one day as the rightful Mormaer of Moray. And if Rognvald had his skull cleaved by an angry Welsh matron, Sigurd lived to become Earl of Orkney and hold his own in the north. Neither she nor Thorfinn was irreplaceable.

The monks were packing as well, ready to move to the safe place the Earl had found for them all in the hills a little way up from the estuary. A safe place, provided the battle went well. And if Duncan's men overran all the country, as good a place to die in as any.

The former Abbot himself showed no surprise at Groa's decision, nor at the evident fact that her husband had not reversed it.

'He is wise,' Duftah said. 'He knows that your place is by your husband and his place is by you. Would you have it otherwise?'

Smiling, he continued ramming blankets into a bag, and did not appear to notice that no one answered him.

TWENTY

THE IRISHMEN IN Duncan's army talked all the time; and there was a penance he didn't deserve, after six years of suffering in the wake of his grandfather's mistakes. They talked even at the outset, when the priest was blessing them for the great crusade they were launched on, for St Columba and Christ; or perhaps it was the other way round.

He didn't even know who the priest was, because Malduin, the Bishop of Alba, had refused to come and do the job after the fiasco at Durham; or at least had become promptly invisible, so that no superior of his at Durham in later weeks could tap him on the shoulder and take away his living in Fife and Northumbria.

Duncan might be High King of Alba, but he could do nothing meantime about that, nor about the Irishmen. It was only the vision of Viking gold in Thorfinn's strongholds in the north that was keeping them here as it was, after Durham.

He still couldn't believe what had happened at Durham. He had got his army there fast, a third of it on horseback, and had swept the country before him, from Gilsland along Tyneside to the banks of the Wear.

There must have been hundreds rushing into the fort-town ahead of him, and he let them go. All the more mouths to feed. He didn't intend to make an assault. Just to sit outside and wait while they starved, secure in the knowledge that neither Ligulf to his north nor Siward to the south would trouble him. And once he had Durham, so the theory went, he would have the whole of Bernicia from Teeside north to the Forth, and the control at last of the churchlands of St Cuthbert and Kinrimund in Fife and Lothian, whether Ligulf liked it or not. And of Westmorland and Cumbria as well.

Riding north with his shadow before him, and behind him the din of the Irishmen, Duncan recalled that it was Maldred who had stopped the three boatloads of ale from proceeding up the river to Durham, and who had failed to stop the contents from reaching the army. Afterwards, you might wonder who sent them. At the time, he was only thankful that there were enough sober to stay watching the high, rocky peninsula made by the loops of the river, so that nothing got in or out.

You wouldn't think anyone, even Eadulf, would be fool enough to spend the night weakening the whole line of his palisade across the neck of the bluff. Or not, anyway, until the whole thing fell suddenly flat and a line of steel appeared, glittering, and bore down on the sleeping camp, with twenty more lines behind it.

He would never use horses again. Horses take an army quickly where you want it to go. Horses carry it out again even faster. He had been lucky to escape with as much of the host as he had. He hoped their brass spires caught a fire-bolt and melted all over the Congregation of St Cuthbert. He hoped that St Cuthbert would, at a convenient moment, return his attention to eider ducks.

Maldred rode up and said, 'The Jura men have got wind of the plate in the monastery at Abernethy. They're telling the others.'

They were riding through Fife at the time. Because they shared the same father, he needn't like Maldred; and he didn't. But because of Maldred and his father, they had the support of the Athollmen, and they were going to be able to get rest and supplies at Crinan's abbey. He said, 'I told you to break up the files so that the Fife and Angus men hemmed in the outsiders. Go and do it. And tell them Thorfinn took the plate long ago.'

He didn't know if it was true, and he didn't care. Somehow he had to get them north without looting. There were, he believed, enough land-owning men with him to protect their own until they got to the limits of Angus. But he had not called out the men of Mar and Moray, even though as King of Alba he was their overlord. That was Thorfinn's territory, and before him his stepfather Findlaech had held it until his two nephews had killed him.

He didn't think Moray would stand against him. Maldred disagreed, but then Maldred had no royal blood and was only a half-brother. Bethoc had produced only two sons: Duncan himself and Thorfinn, whom his grand-father should have killed years ago. Malcolm had disposed of everyone else: every second cousin, every half-nephew who might have divided the kingdom had been destroyed with great skill and thoroughness.

The injustice of it all overwhelmed Duncan. He said to Maldred, 'The Abbot our father had plenty of chances as well. Why should it be left to us to get rid of Thorfinn?'

Maldred, who had just been abused by three men from Forfar, said coldly, 'It was your grandfather's idea. He preferred Thorfinn's stewards, he said, to the King of Norway. And it kept the Irish from getting a bigger stranglehold on Mar and on Buchan. You notice, of course, the great success of that.'

'I expect,' said Duncan, 'that he thought my lord Crinan might do something about it, other than counting his money while Dunkeld was burned.' In no sense other than the physical one did he regard the Abbot Crinan as his father. It was because of Crinan's neglect that Dubhdaleithe of Armagh and his brother had elbowed their way into Alba and might well snatch control of the Celtic church at the Fair of Teltown next month. Unless Duftah, as they called him, was got out of the way. Duftah, the monk who had been Abbot of Deer and was now, the most reliable couriers said, in the peninsula of Tarbatness with the Lady of Moray and her son and heir Lulach.

Duncan's army camped that night in the fields about Perth, and the next night found all the supplies they required waiting for them in Crinan's abbey of Dunkeld. But then, provisioning on this march had not been a problem. They carried with them enough to make sure that no one would starve, and all the way had been able to buy or barter. Although the bere was not yet in, somehow fish or cattle or game had been forthcoming—not lavishly, but to a degree that removed at least that care from his shoulders.

Then, when they entered Moray, they found matters better than he had dared hope. Half the houses on their march were empty—for days the beacons had been burning, and he had expected that. But those who had remained on their land watched them pass without interfering, and if they offered to buy, would sell something out of their barns.

The High King had passed that way already, and had been entertained in guest-quarters as was his right in each district. He did not impose on them now, but what he wanted they gave him within reason, and watched silently as the army moved past.

They did not love Duncan. But, it seemed, they loved Groa with circum-spection, and Thorfinn their absent Mormaer commanded from them no duty at all.

The Lady of Moray. Groa. His grandfather had been disturbed, Duncan remembered, when Gillacomghain had married her, about the time King Olaf had been thrown out of Norway and Canute had been up in the Tay, taking promises of allegiance from everyone.

His grandfather had sent him to Inverness, and he had seen this red-haired child with the black brows and the light eyes.

That had been another miscalculation of his grandfather's: the attack on Thorfinn that had ended in total disaster, with Gillacomghain dead, and Thorfinn in Moray and husband to the red-haired heiress.

She was young. She could bear ten children yet. After Gillacomghain and Thorfinn, any man would be welcome, he imagined, far less the King of all Alba.

And this time it would be the throne of all Alba he sat on. Not a boulder at Scone and an abbey at Dunkeld and a parcel of districts in Fife and Perth and Angus and Moray and Lothian.

Duncan was prince of Cumbria as his grandfather had been and, if matters went well, might remain so. To wrest more land from England, as his grandfather had done was, at the moment, beyond him. But if he ruled Alba from Carlisle to Duncansby, and put his own man into Moray as guardian of Lulach . . . and got rid of Forne . . . and forced the Bishop of Alba to stay in Kinrimund . . . he would be a greater king than Malcolm had ever been. With a red-haired wife.

The Irishmen talked; and Duncan, marching up the Vale of Strathbogie, heard them, and was no longer disturbed.

He was within reach of the sea, and his enemy.

*   *   *

Skeggi said, 'I don't like it. He's too confident. I've prayed to Jesus and I've prayed to Odin Lord of the Gallows and still the barley jumps on the hearth every time I cast a grain down. I don't like it, I tell you.'

'Who's too confident?' said Thorkel Fóstri. 'Thorfinn or Duncan?'

'Now you mention it,' Skeggi said, 'both of them. How can Thorfinn know what Duncan is thinking? All this plotting is worthy of Loki, but if Duncan doesn't do what Thorfinn says he's going to do, then Odin or Saint Peter are going to have to throw dice for me.'

'He said Duncan would let them light all the war-beacons, and he did,' Thorkel Fóstri said. They were riding east, and very soon would part company, Skeggi to make for the Tarbatness Point and himself to get down to his command at Alness. The parting was something he was looking forward to.

'That's what I mean about confidence,' Skeggi said. 'Dear Thor and Christ, you have to be confident to bring a host on foot into enemy land this far north and make sure that the enemy knows that you're coming.'

'Well, Duncan doesn't want to come all this way and find he's only wiped out half of us,' Thorkel Fóstri said. 'He can't hold a country like the Normans do, by putting his own men into forts. He hasn't got any spare men and we haven't got any forts. He's got to kill all the leaders and scare the survivors so much that they'll pay him tribute and supply him with fighting-men whenever he asks them.'

Skeggi, staring ahead, was thinking of something else. 'Three thirty-hundreds,' he said. 'That's what they say Duncan has. Three thirty-hundreds, and we're making a stand against them! Do you think we have a chance?'

Thorkel Fóstri halted. 'This is where I go south. I don't know what chance we've got. They've got more men, but they've also got Duncan.'

'And we've got Thorfinn,' said Skeggi. 'Of good stock, though I say it myself, but a shade too inclined to run risks. You brought him up. In your opinion, is he the man to conduct a war of this kind?'

He had never thought much of Skeggi, but the question cut too near his heart, in this moment, to be ignored. 'I don't know,' Thorkel Fóstri said. 'Once I thought that I knew, but I don't know any longer. All I can tell you is that if we are going to die, it will be in a blaze, and not in some sour, whining cranny.'

'In a blaze. Like Gillacomghain,' said Skeggi gloomily; and trotted off, with his men, through the bogland.

'I thought,' said the Lady of Moray, 'that men of religion were supposed to be in the vanguard of battle these days. But I can see the trouble, of course. It must be quite hard to know what language to pray in, and even what god to pray to, when you bless this particular army.'

Standing beside her in the trees, looking down on the glittering stream of the Averon, Duftah of Buchan and the Clann Sinaidh smiled through the rug of his beard and slapped a scarred hand on the hilt of his sword. 'If it will ease your mind, she'll be out of her scabbard soon enough, whatever your husband has to say. There is MacBeathad son of Ainmire, the chief poet of Armagh, and his namesake playing Armagh off against Kells like a man stealing a hen from two foxes. And I thinking that, once the Welshman had gone, we should all be comfortable.'

'We should be comfortable enough,' Groa said, 'fifteen long miles from Dingwall as we are. Provided that Duncan is stopped at Dingwall, of course.'

'Ah,' said Duftah, and expanded his great diaphragm, inhaling the scent of the fir trees. 'Now, that I should not entirely count on. I should not count on it at all. I am a humble man, as you know; but, like Modomnoc's bees, men strive to find me, no matter where I may conceal myself. . . . Does it seem to you, as it does to my stomach, that a bite and a sup might not come amiss before we settle down to watch these great lords shout at one another?'

The smell of food had already reached her from the charcoal-burners' houses behind, where his people and hers had found shelter. Without speaking, she turned and led the way through the trees. He followed her, chuckling into his beard.

'You would say, *Let the pig into the house and it will make for the kitchen*,' he said.

'I would say, *Big ships going to the bottom, and pails floating*,' said Groa. 'Come and bless the food. No doubt it needs it.'

At Forres, as Duncan had expected, the folk from the rath settlement and the river had all taken their beasts and locked themselves behind the palisades of the hall-mound. The thatched houses stood about, with a dog or two nosing inside them, but nothing else had been left, and when a group of Ulstermen broke into the little church, they found it also quite empty.

Duncan hanged one of them as an example, and set a strong guard round the mount so that no one could get out and carry tales, for this time it mattered. And then he walked down to the riverbank and stood, helmet in the crook of his arm, with his moustache ruffled by the afternoon breeze and his firm cheeks russet with pleasure.

The three ships were there. The round-bellied knörrs paid off by Hardecanute had been making a nuisance of themselves round the east coast, picking up bits of cargo here and there when he had found them at Berwick, and paid off the portreeve who was about to take them off to his lord, and sobered one or two of them up enough to explain what he wanted.

They had made a nuisance of themselves here also, he expected, drinking off the last of their pay and haggling over their cargo. But there was nothing to connect three hired ships with the advance of his, Duncan's, army, and by the time anyone realised it, the thing would be over.

He sent his scouts out, and they came back with the news he had been hoping for. Eskadale, on the next firth, was undefended. Thorfinn was coming down to stop him from the north, gathering men hurriedly as he came. But, however quickly he marched, he could not get them south, so they reported, in time to save the Cromarty peninsula. So the stance would be made further north, at Dingwall.

'You were right,' Maldred said, when he heard; and if there was a thread of astonishment in his voice, it was no more than his half-brother had come to expect. 'So we put the first plan into effect. I sail, and you march to Dingwall. Unless you've changed your mind?'

He had not changed his mind, because Dingwall was where Thorfinn would be. There he had the big hall and the Moot Hill by the mouth of the river Peffer, where the long sea inlet reached into the hills. To gain the Tarbatness peninsula, a marching army would have to pass between the sea and the mountains of Easter Ross, where Dingwall, the assembly-place, lay. Unless Thorfinn wanted to lose Tarbatness as well as Cromarty, he would have to stand there and bar Duncan's way.

Nor would Duncan have him wait there in vain. At a carefully chosen hour, say halfway between dawn and midday, this half-breed brother would stand among his hammer-struck heathens and see the army of his overlord fill the plain before him with its steel.

Perhaps he would turn tail. Perhaps, as they came nearer, he would be encouraged to think that there were fewer of them than he expected: a number much the same as his own, and far from their homeland. Duncan hoped that he would feel emboldened—even contemptuous. He hoped to be there when Thorfinn's expression changed—for at some point, face to face with his King and his Maker, Thorfinn's face, surely, would change. Until it was changed for him, one way or another. Eadulf had made a show with the heads of a few Irishmen. He, Duncan, proposed to take home the head of the Earl of Orkney on the masthead of one of his ships.

For the ships were his little surprise. He was sorry, in a way, that he was not sailing himself, but even if Maldred's performance was usually indifferent, the two leaders with him were good. Even if only two out of the three landings succeeded, that would be enough. And one of them surely would find the monk, and the woman. And, having found them, would move south to Dingwall to close in on Thorfinn's back.

In the Mormaer's hall at Dingwall, Arnór Jarlaskáld hung up his harp, shook his arm free of cramp, and said, 'They're all going to sleep out there. How can you let them go to sleep, with Duncan's army just over the river? They don't want to sing any more: they just want to go to sleep.'

'So do I,' said Thorfinn. 'And I'm going to, over there, with the lamps out, so the rest of you had better do the same. Otkel?'

'I'll wake you, my lord Earl, if there's news,' Otkel said. In the last year or two, a number of young men had appeared, serving the hird, Arnór noticed. He settled down beside Starkad and said, 'How many runners does he have? I passed one on his way out again as I came back to the hall.'

Starkad said, 'They're in relays across the peninsula. Don't ask foolish questions. Go to sleep.'

'I still don't know how he thinks it's safe to sleep,' Arnór said. 'And if that's a foolish question, I'd rather ask it and stay alive than the other way about.'

Starkad snored. A voice on his other side said, 'Arnór: it's to do with the tides. Now will you be quiet? You will have all tomorrow to think of your verses.'

There were, of course, men of war who knew nothing of tides, but no prince brought up within reach of the Tay or the Solway would fail to know how important they were, or to find the right man to tell him about them.

Maldred, whose ship would make the first landing, sat on a bale of raw fleeces with the master's lamp and studied again the bit of vellum with the drawing of the peninsula: a hatchet-shape jutting into the sea, with Tarbatness at the peak of the blade and his own landing-place, at Rosskeen in the estuary, under the notch of the axe-beard. On the same shore, fifteen miles to the west, lay Dingwall, with Duncan's army presumably now settled within reach and poised for battle.

To the north, across the thick of the peninsula, was the Westray shore, on which Muiredach of Ulidia would make his landing, fifteen miles west of St Colman's, where Archú's men would be dropped, just inside the point of Tarbatness. The numbers had been carefully worked out; for though the northern settlements were small, this was where, rumour said, Thorfinn's wife and the monk had their houses. There would be defences there, and in the vale of Ulladule, in the centre, and of course at Rosskeen, where he, Maldred, was landing. Thorfinn was not so simple as to expect his enemy to throw all his force against Dingwall when a crossing might be made here, by determined men with rafts or coracles, from one side of the firth to the other. There might be a hundred men hidden there on the shore, waiting, as they thought, to pick off an offshoot of Duncan's army as they paddled painfully across the mile of water that separated firth from firth.

A hundred men who would cringe when the first light revealed a cargoship looming up, with three hundred armed men leaping ashore to attack them.

Maldred folded the map just as the lamp toppled over and the prow bucked along the first of the ocean rollers coming up from the south-east. He began to fall. His palm hit the flesh of the sheepskins and saluted them, ending up over his head, with a fistful of sheep's grease and maggots.

He lay on the lurching thwarts, and his mouth watered.

Once, her mother had stayed waking through a night such as this. 'When men go on a journey of the grave,' Bergljot had said, 'it does not behove women to sleep.'

So Groa did not try, but left the little huts she shared with the people from the farm and the smith's house below, beyond the bogs of the river.

Somewhere a child cried, and somewhere there was a murmuring: others, too, found it hard to find sleep. The monks, she supposed, prayed, but if so, they did it quietly. Outside, by the hollow which had once been an old forge, the moon shone through the trees on a world of darkness and silence, and the only sounds were those of the wild, for the cattle had long since been driven up into the hills beyond the loch, with the dogs. From the edge of the little hill, she looked into the blackness east and south, and felt the wind lift her hair, and wondered what the morning would bring.

Duftah's voice said, 'A wise man said, *If thou loathest death, why dost thou love sleep?* . . . Do you need me, or not?'

'I might ask the same,' Groa said.

'Ah yes,' the monk said. 'It does not do to forget: you are well versed in the ways of the child, and so of the man. I think tonight we need each other.'

The wind blew, and the tree shadows moved in the moonlight. Groa said, 'The smith is away, fighting for Thorfinn. His wife says his smith-work is famous.'

'There is an old tradition,' Duftah said. 'There was a monastery once in Westray; and bog iron, and oak trees for charcoal, and the smith made cauldrons and ploughshares and rivets and ladles, and sometimes silver bowls and cast crosses. When the Norse settled, they kept the smithy for swords and harness and axes. . . . It will make crosses again. His sons are there, in the hut.'

She did not answer. After a while, he said, 'Is it the beauty of the night, or your sons? You would be right to weep for either.'

'My father is losing his sight,' Groa said. 'I have not seen him for thirteen years.'

She knew that he had turned towards her. 'My poor daughter,' he said. 'It is a very little bulwark to hide behind, but I shall join you there if you wish, till you find better refuge.'

'There is none,' she said. Surely . . . surely there were two shades of black to the east where a moment before there had been one? Surely the wind that stirred her robe was sharper, with the sea in it as well as the lost rumours of woodsmoke and peat, of grass and wet mosses and night-breathing plants. Duftah murmured in Gaelic, and she half-listened, expecting a prayer; and found that instead it was something different.

> '*I have a shieling in the wood,*
> *None knows it save my God:*
> *An ash-tree on the hither side, a hazel bush beyond,*
> *A huge old tree encompasses it.*

> '*Two heath-clad doorposts for support,*
> *And a lintel of honeysuckle:*
> *The forest around its narrowness sheds*
> *Its mast upon fat swine.*

> '*The size of my shieling tiny, not too tiny,*
> *Many are its familiar paths:*
> *From its gable a sweet strain sings*
> *A she-bird in her cloak of the ousel's hue.*

'*Though thou rejoicest in thy own pleasures,*
Greater than any wealth;
I am grateful for what is given me
From my good Christ.

'. . . When all seems lost, some things remain,' Duftah said.

Duncan said, 'When we make the attack, look for the gilded helmet. Thorfinn always wears Canute's helmet. I suppose it reminds him of the days when he learned to live like a lord. Where's the priest?'

The priest, in an unpriestly fashion, had been sleeping. Duncan had him wakened and brought to the tent. Confession didn't take long: in twenty-four hours in the field, there had been little opportunity to collect more than a minor transgression. After the ritual was over, he kept the priest by him, rehearsing the speeches he intended them both to make next morning, and getting his poet to write them down, in case when the time came he could not catch all the words. As morning drew near, Duncan realised, to his satisfaction, that he felt unafraid and quite happy.

With the move into the firth, the motion of the knörr settled down, and the three hundred soldiers she carried began to groan and sit up.

It was still dark, which was as it should be. They were to land, Duncan had decreed, when there was just enough light for a footing, and then to overwhelm whatever party might await them on shore, being careful to leave no survivors. One-third of the company would then strike northwards to Ulladule, there to rendezvous with the other two parties, while two-thirds returned to the knörr and sailed up the firth, there to land at a place called Clachan Biorach and attack Thorfinn's army from the rear.

In all these years of Saxon speech, Maldred had found little occasion to use his Gaelic and indeed had found conversation with Muiredach and Archú quite troublesome during the long wait at Forres. It was just as well that most of the men fighting under them were of their own race, as it happened. For himself, he found it a relief to talk to the shipmaster, who was Swedish, and whose tongue you heard any day in Northumbria. At least he knew the man understood him.

All the same, there was a confusion of purpose almost as soon as they began to sail up the inlet to Rosskeen—Maldred requiring that the knörr should down sail and row, and the master objecting on the grounds that the current was far too strong for the few oars that the cargo-boat carried. Which was all very well, but, as the diagram clearly showed, the channel up to Rosskeen consisted of shallow water running through swathes of flat sand, and demanded skilful manoeuvring. He got the vellum out again and tilted it towards the lamp and the vague pink light from the east that was beginning to suffuse the sky and the sea. The captain took the map from him, and the lamp, and carried both to the rear of the ship to show it to his steersman: the oarsmen followed him, peering.

In the prow of the ship, the spears and helms and shield-bosses glittered red, and so did the thin wash of waves, far away, running on to the sands of Rosskeen. Whatever knowledgeable eyes there might have been on board, none saw the glaze on the sea exactly halfway between ship and shore, or heard the lazy surfing of water that came not from the shore but from the sandbank immediately ahead of the knörr's painted snake-mouth.

From the masthead, someone screamed, 'Aft! Run aft! Quickly!' and to the best of their ability, three hundred men did. The knörr hit the sandbank and flew up it with the ease of a snow-sledge on runners.

Inside, the three hundred fell down, slicing one another, while the master and crew, including the man at the masthead, silently disappeared overboard. Righting themselves, bloodied and cursing, Maldred and his landing-party found themselves lodged, firmly and inescapably, on a large tract of sand completely surrounded by water beyond which was a beach, glimmering in the brightening light.

Set upon the beach, in a graceful half-moon, was a fence of linked wattle barriers.

And over and between the barriers, as they watched, rose a spray of glittering pink that began to fall arching towards them, bursting into familiar song.

Arrows; followed by spears; followed by catapulted balls of hay and pitch, blazing.

A third of them died in the first fifteen minutes, after which Maldred jumped into the sea, waving a shirt on a spearhead, and the rest swam and waded after.

The sun rose.

At St Colman's on the north, Muiredach of Ulidia made no mistake about his landing.

The knörr sailed as close as it could, and Muiredach's men jumped into the sea, dividing into sections as had been arranged, for there was a palisaded fort on the high ground above the sand and the rocks and the scatter of dark, silent huts.

They rushed the huts, one party covering another, but found them empty. The fort, when they reached it, was deserted, and the little church held nothing but the smell of dead incense to tell that someone had been there not so long ago.

It was not what they had expected, but simply meant that the monk and the woman must be in the west, where Archú's party would find and take them, or Maldred's men striking up from Rosskeen.

Meanwhile, their own plan of assault was quite clear. One small party, swords drawn, made its way to the east to scour the land between St Colman's and the point at Tarbatness. The rest, in troops of fifty, turned west through the bogs and the marshes that separated them from their fellows at Westray.

They were competent men, and there was nothing wrong with their planning. They had arrived at first light, and by the time they set out on the twelve miles they intended to cover, the sky was just bright enough to show the mottled green-and-pink mounds; the bright green cushions sporting the straw-coloured treacherous grasses that betrayed the bog, with its brown peaty pools and its cottongrass jerked by the wind.

It seemed at first like God's Judgement that, when they had skilfully steered clear of the marsh, the firm ground beneath them should start to give way.

They stood, half of that first party of fifty, and tried to draw one black-slimed leg after another out of the sucking grip of the mire, while their fellows marched on through the short, dry grass and heather and were hardly deterred until they, too, had felt the water close around their ankles. They were near enough to warn the second force, but the third and the fourth had to find out in their own way that someone had been before them, doctoring the line of march that any sensible hillman would follow. Then the arrows came, and the spears; singly and from different quarters, and began methodically to thin them out.

Finally, on three fronts, they came face to face with a line of armed men: fresh, fully equipped, and on ground of their own choosing. They fought well; and most of them died.

The last ship of the three rounded the point at Tarbatness, passed the beach of St Colman's, and made its way uncertainly west along the north shore of the peninsula towards Westray.

Uncertainly, because the steering-oar had broken and could not be mended, and the sail shackles had given way during the night, leaving the knörr to creep in under the power of her six pairs of oars.

It was not Archú's fault, therefore, that she arrived at her appointed landing-place when the sun had already risen and when the tide had receded to such an extent that the river Tain ran out to the firth over a stretch of pink sand that seemed to stretch shorewards to infinity. Since the ship could not come any nearer, they disembarked on the flat sand and had marched halfway across it before they saw, against the bright sky, the size and shape of the armed forces drawn up ahead of them.

Unlike their fellows, they fought a straightforward pitched battle, against much greater numbers; and lost.

South of Dingwall, the army woke at dawn and heard Duncan's speech, and the priest's, and knelt to be blessed. At the appointed time, which would take them to Dingwall by mid-morning, they set out to march round the hill-shoulder and down to the Moot Hill.

To the east, as they marched, they looked along the sun-touched avenue of the firth for the snake-head of Maldred's ship, but could not yet see it. Duncan was not unduly disturbed. Maldred's men might already have landed, and the knörr drawn off, as arranged, to lift them after the battle. Or it might arrive with a timing still nicer, when battle was already engaged, and shock Thorfinn into flight or submission.

They marched round the hill and there, like a storm-beach of steel flagged with banners, was the army of Ross and Caithness awaiting him, with, bright as a sequin in front, the gilded helmet of Canute on the alpine head of Thorfinn his brother.

Round Thorfinn the men awaited, and the sun shone through the white silk of the banner, so that the raven lay black on Thorfinn's helm and shoulders, and flapped its wings as if in omen: as if Odin had sent them Huginn or Muninn, Mind or Memory, and soon the dedicatory spear would be thrown over their enemy's heads: *Odin owns you all.* After which, there would be no quarter.

It would not be like that. But here they would have to fight, with none of the advantage of surprise that had been allowed their more fortunate colleagues facing Duncan's other landings through the peninsula. Thorfinn had made that plain all along, and had repeated it before them all that morning.

'The King has dispersed part of his forces beforehand through the peninsula; but so have we. He started with a far larger army than ours, and the difference between us is still in his favour. You will have to fight, and fight hard, at Dingwall. It is worth your while. Win this battle, and you will not have to fight it again. Lose, and the whole of the north will be a battlefield as Alba and Norway fight over it.'

And that was true, they all knew, and the men of the hird better than any. While Thorfinn held Caithness and Ross and Cromarty, he would defend them against every predator. He had called his brother *King*, and so he was, of Alba. But here in Ross he was no king of theirs, nor of Thorfinn's. What Thorfinn might owe him fo Moray was his own affair.

Nearly every man there, in one way or another, had fought for Thorfinn, on his raids, on his war-cruises, and most of them would claim to know him. None would claim to understand him, or the source of his energy. He was lucky, and in many things very successful. To stay with such a man made good sense. So, when the trumpets of Duncan's army glittered and blared, and the pennants jerked, and the clatter of men marching quickly changed to the jingle of men moving into the run, their spears and swords ready and flashing, the men under the raven responded smartly, as they had been trained.

The shield-wall came up. The spears rose, hefted, ready for throwing, and the smooth swords slid singing out of the scabbard. Then above them all Thorfinn's right arm rose, with the sword-blade barring the sun, written over with copper and silver. Then the long horns raised their thick voices and the air darkened as the birds of the land and the sea rose, alarmed, and circled.

The army were already shouting as they started to move. The shouting gained rhythm, and came to Duncan's ears in spurts and snatches as they drew breath until the two sides were close enough, above all the noise of both, for their cry to be heard.

They were calling his brother's pagan name. '*Thorfinn! Thorfinn!*' The hoarse double syllable ran from hill to hill and up to the peak of Ben Wyvis, until the southern army caught it and opposed it with a cry of their own. Then the spearpoints came ripping down on either side, and '*Thorfinn!*' and '*Alba!*' came mixed with their screams and the rapping of metal on wood.

The shock as the two armies met was like the tumbling roar of a landslide, with flesh and cloth instead of earth, and steel on steel instead of boulder on boulder. Each side clove through the other, man so close to man that the sword bit as it forced its way up and slashed as it found its way downwards again. In such a press, mail-shirts and helmets were hardly more use than the hide helms and metal-sewn jackets that most of them wore. Speed of eye and of arm were what helped a man live, not the weight of his metal in the rising August heat with the stench of blood and of ripped guts and of fright beginning to rise, with the ghosts of past wars; and the flies coming already.

The first climax came; and the first pause, with the golden helmet still flashing on one side and the white mask of the King on the other. Then Thorfinn's sword flashed again, and he shouted, 'Back! Back, my men! Back!'

The Irish on Duncan's side had recoiled. Sending to rally them, white with tension and fury, Duncan did not at first hear the call or realise what was happening. Then someone said, 'My lord! My lord King, they're retreating!'

For so long he had planned for this: how should he doubt it, now that it was happening? Duncan threw his head back and laughed. 'Of course!' said the King. 'Maldred's ship has arrived. The fools think they must fly or be caught between us. Where do you think Archú's force is waiting now, to rise at their backs? Eh? Where do you suppose Maldred's other men have been stationed, to give them the warm welcome they all deserve? Come, my stout lads of Alba. Forward, and thrash them!'

The sun reached its height, and hung, burning.

Far above it perhaps, in Valholl, the Hall of the Slain, with its six hundred and forty doorways, Heimdall the Watchman looked down and saw the northern army blown back like the keys of the ash tree, drifting into the thick of the empty peninsula, with the King's men like a whirlwind pursuing them.

A peninsula empty, at least, of the contingents of Duncan of Alba, which should have been drawn up in the appointed places, awaiting their triumph. The men of Alba who had landed with Maldred and Archú and Muiredach lay among the bog cotton, or corralled wounded in corners, or already laid helpless in the two big-bellied knörrs that should have been lying off-shore to take off their victorious master, but in fact were afloat in midstream, waiting for orders from under a raven banner.

Instead, the three troops of Thorfinn's which had vanquished them sheathed their swords and raced to join one another in the gentle green heart of Ulladule, with its church and its farmhouse, where the Strathrory river left its glen and wound down to the firth mouth. There, briefly, they waited.

Then men on garrons, who had run all day joining faction to faction, brought them word of Thorfinn their leader's arrival, and silently the triple company redeployed as they had been told.

Duncan's army swept through the heath crying victory, unaware that they were beating Thorfinn's host back into the sword-blades of men who were dead. And the army that rose at Thorfinn's rear and his flanks and behind Duncan's own charging host was not the supporting army of Duncan's triumphant Alba, but the angry men of the land they had invaded.

TWENTY-ONE

HERE BEING conventions in war, as in everything else, it was to these that King Duncan looked for succour when it came to him, finally, that this was a battle he was going to lose.

At first, he did not fully understand his plight, any more than did his leaders. His own army, pursuing, had lost some of its order, although the centre, with himself in the lead, was compact still. Thorfinn's army, retreating, had lost any pattern it once might have had, and the gilded helm of the Earl his brother flashed like marsh-fire, first in one quarter of the flying army and then in another.

It was an irritation to Duncan, who had expected a standing battle, man to man, of a kind that Thorfinn, despite the conventions, was unlikely to have survived. Or if no accident befell him in the first phase, then the men of Maldred or Archú or Muiredach would see to it in due course that the campaign received a clean finish, with no tedious aftermath of ransom or oath-taking to trouble about. When Thorfinn's army broke and ran, keeping so far ahead in their fear that the only fighting was peripheral, Duncan began to feel some concern for his plan, so well protected did Thorfinn appear to be. When Thorfinn's men began to break pace, in a confusion of yelling, and finally stopped, fenced about with a ring of clean steel, Duncan's first feeling was one of relief followed by a fervent prayer that vanity would drive his brother out from the centre and into the spearhead of a counter-attack, on which later his skald could produce some deathless battle-elegy. After all, northmen hardly cared how they lived, everyone knew, so long as they ended in glory.

Instead of ending in glory on Maldred's sword-edge, his brother Thorfinn seemed to have got the idea that he should reverse his army and stand to do battle with Duncan. Duncan had no objection. Urging onwards the spearmen about him, he found a grim satisfaction in the vigour with which his men flung themselves at the foe. Only when engaged and fighting himself did he see that the impetus shown by his host was due to an alien army risen from nowhere behind them.

He looked round for the banners of Maldred and Archú, and did not see them. Instead, answering his first desire, he saw the helm of Thorfinn his brother driving towards him. And behind Thorfinn, with every face to the front, a massive host, bigger by far than the one he had confronted at Dingwall. A host gaining momentum towards him, undivided in purpose, with no harrying armies at its flanks or its rear. A host of men who were all his enemies, as were the men enclosing his army behind him.

He had lost the battle. That was Duncan's first thought, even as he found himself fighting, as army crashed against army and his own bodyguard ran to protect him. He had lost the battle, and to save other men's lives and his own, he ought to surrender. That was the convention.

Someone thrust through the ring of men about him, and he used his sword again. Thorfinn was fighting, too: he could see his helm and his sword-arm thirty feet away in the mass of struggling men. To call his attention, he would need his trumpeter. His chain-mail creaked with his breathing, and the leather beneath scraped his neck. He turned his head and shouted, against the uproar, for his standard-bearer.

The priest was at his side, a reddened axe in his hand. The priest said, shrieking in his west-Cumbrian accent, 'My lord! Escape while you can! That pagan devil will kill you!'

Duncan stared at the priest. 'We're outnumbered,' he said. He frowned while he protected himself. He had never surrendered before. He had besieged Durham and, repulsed, had simply retreated. When raiders tried to land on his coasts, he had fought them and killed or driven them off, keeping the leaders to ransom. He had never been conquered in battle by an army larger than his own. He said, 'He is my brother.'

'Does he remember it?' said the priest. 'The prize is great, and he is not noted for piety. In his place, you might have been tempted yourself.'

One of his protectors, fighting about him, had heard. One of them said, 'We could get you out, my lord King, while the fighting goes on. Then the priest could go forth and call surrender. They'll stop quick enough. You'll save lives. There'll be no ransom to pay or oaths to keep. Quick. We'll come with you.'

He must have agreed, although he did not remember it, or taking off the mask helm that identified him. Someone found another and rammed it, bloody still, on his head as they fought their way to the edge of the battle. Most of the Irishmen were trying to do the same, and had no eyes for anything but the enemy. The last bit was the worst, and six of the twelve men with him had died before suddenly they were among trees and away. As they went, he thought he heard the noise lessen a degree in the centre, and fancied he saw a flash of white cloth. Then there was no sound but that of their own running feet and their breathing. Duncan threw the helm away.

They had thought to make for the ships, and had started in that direction when they came across another group flying, who told them that Thorfinn had taken the ships. And of course that must be right, for otherwise none of this would have happened. A little after that, they had the first luck that came from the day and found a garron grazing where its rider had been killed, and then a second one. He had seen the hoofmarks everywhere in the soft ground and understood now. So this was how it had been done.

He took one garron and two of his men took another, and they made for the hills, with four armed men at his stirrups. They made for the hills because they had no means to cross water, and the mountains showed the way to the west, where he might escape and be safe.

They also made for the hills because that was where the woman was, and the monk.

When they learned that, he knew the priest had been right and God was with him. For they had almost passed the man by who gave the news to them: a local man, early wounded and left in the heath, where they heard him calling, for he thought they were men of Thorfinn's. Before he learned they were not, he asked them to take him with them to where the monks were, at the smith's house. After that, hoping for his life, he told them the rest.

So, at the end of a day in which he had been tricked and tricked again, Duncan had at last been vouchsafed a truth; a morsel of information that might be more important than anything that had befallen him yet. For of course Thorfinn's wife would not be left to wander at will in the battleground of the peninsula; neither would Dubhdaleithe and his monks. If they were near at all, they could only be waiting there where the peninsula rose to the hills in the body of Ross. The glen of Thor's goats, the man said, where the river Averon ran down past the smith's house. Not so far from Strath Rory. Four miles, or five.

They would have her defended, and he had six men, that was all. But it might be enough to snatch Moray at least from the ruins of all he had hoped for. And if everything failed, and his enemies came after him, he would have a hostage beyond price in the woman, and a dead man, he hoped, in the monk.

There was a long view from the Druim na Caerdaich, and sharp eyes among the smith's children, so that one of his sons was the first to call out that there were horsemen moving on the other side of the river, and that they were making for the little cabins that made up his family's farm. Two horses, he said, and seven people, and them plunging in and out of the bog like men from chalk country.

'The monks will sort them,' his mother said.

The holy monk, the one who had been abbot, was behind the peat stack, and the others were in the rear of the bothies or crouched by the midden. The first thing Duncan knew was a hiss passing one of his ears and a yell from behind, followed by a thud as someone tumbled. He drew rein to wheel, and saw that he was surrounded, just within arrow-range, by a circle of men in brown robes.

The most powerful-looking of them all, a man with a beard like a mat, had emerged, still grasping his bow, by a peat stack. He lifted his voice. 'Duncan of Alba. If you would wear your helmet again, I suggest you and your friends step down from those ponies and stand in the middle, where we can see you. Is it a battle you're running from?'

'Dubhdaleithe Albanach?' Duncan said. After a moment's pause, he dismounted. 'Do you think me your enemy, that I bring six men to visit you when you have twice that number? I wished to speak to you.'

'You did?' said Duftah. 'Now, God forgive me if I have misjudged you. You are here to offer me Kells?'

Duncan smiled. His hair, flattened by the helmet, did not rise even in the wind. 'Of course,' he said. 'My father has long since fallen out with his cousins in Ireland. One day, your brother will die and you will be Abbot of Armagh. To be Coarb of St Columba as well would only be just: did your grandfather not hold both offices, as the great soul-friend of Ireland?'

'Indeed he did,' Duftah said. He let his bow to the ground and leaned on it. 'But here you are in the bog, with no throne about you that I can see. How could you make me Abbot of Kells when even Thorfinn will not raise a finger?'

'Thorfinn is afraid of the power of Columba,' Duncan said. 'As you very well know, men will bow to the heathen while he has them in his power, but they will turn to Christ as soon as they are free of him. Come south to Alba and I will show you whether or not I can make you Abbot of Kells.'

'*Is* afraid?' Duftah said. 'I made sure you had taken the head of him before you came riding for me.'

'I left that to others,' Duncan said. 'Is the Lady here?'

'Somewhere,' said Duftah. 'So you are saying that soon she will be a widow. Now, there is a lasting pity, and she so young. I would be sorry to think that you and your men would dishonour her.'

'Not unless,' Duncan said, 'you would think it dishonour to make her the wife of the King. I have long wished to make her my lady. Will you not bring her so that I can tell her?'

'Oh, she's here,' said the monk, astonished. 'Would you not have noticed her? The eager one over there, with my sword in her hand.'

He flicked a finger at one of the monks, whose hood, promptly tossed back, revealed a flag of shining red hair and a pair of shining light eyes under brows black as soot. 'It seems a small army,' said Groa, 'to take the north with; but no doubt most of them ran at the sound of your name. Did you wish to offer me something?'

'A king's hand in marriage,' said Duncan. 'And safe passage for your friends of Armagh, once they lay down their arms. My army is not far away, and I should not like to see them hurt.' He smiled. 'Is there a woman alive who would not want the title of Queen? Is there a woman alive who would become it better?'

'You're right,' said Groa. 'Except that I have, to my knowledge, a husband living.'

'What of it?' said Duncan. 'It is a marriage that death, or the church, can annul for you. Here is my horse. Let me take you away from this wilderness.'

The girl thought, digging the point of the sword-blade into the turf, both hands wrapped round the pommel. She raised it and leaned the flat on one shoulder. 'Well,' she said, 'at least you took thought to come, with all the other matters that must occupy the mind of a king at such times. There are some who take no heed how their womenfolk fare, from one year's end to another. . . . I will go with you. Or, at least, I shall when you have got the Earl Thorfinn behind you there out of the way.'

Duncan jumped.

So silently had his enemy come through the trees that neither he nor his men had heard a hint of them. So close had been his success: so near his moment of escape. And now, ringing the clearing behind him were thirty axemen or more, led by one of unnatural height with a face like the beak of a dragon-ship within his expensive gilt helmet.

Thorfinn of Orkney, his brother, put up a finger and thumb and eased off the helmet. His rumbling voice, like his height, was ridiculous. He said, 'I am afraid the question does not arise. There has already been a slight contest, which I have won. You, my lady, are still my wife, and the King here is now my prisoner.'

The powerful, handsome man beside Thorfinn disagreed with his master, it seemed. He said, 'Then you're a fool. The King came here to get rid of you. Kill him.'

'He doesn't want to die,' Thorfinn said. He walked forward, taking his time over it, until he was so close that Duncan could smell the sweat and the blood and see the battle-tiredness, like his own, bitten into his half-brother's face. Thorfinn said, 'Give me your sword.'

It would have been easy to make one savage slash, and Duncan drew breath to do it. Then his eyes ran round the men standing waiting, and he set his teeth and held out his sword. Thorfinn's companion, moving forward, disarmed the men who were with him.

Thorfinn said, 'I have paid the shipmasters to take the rest of your men back to Berwick. You may go with them. First, you will come with me and, in the presence of your men and mine, swear that as Earl of Caithness I hold all the land north of Eskadale free of any duties or tribute towards the High King of Alba. You will swear that I owe Alba nothing for Orkney. You will swear that as Mormaer of Moray I shall pay Alba what Findlaech my stepfather paid, with the same rights. And you will repeat the promise you made on your accession, that after me the rule of Moray will be invested in Lulach my stepson. All that you will swear.'

Again, the older man with Thorfinn interrupted. A man who spoke in pure Norse, and with a familiarity that identified him. This was Thorkel, one remembered: Thorfinn's foster-father. Thorkel saying, 'Of course he will swear it. And come back next year with a bigger army. Thorfinn, you can't do it this way.'

'There is no other way,' said Thorfinn shortly.

'Yes, there is. Kill him,' said his foster-father. 'Or if you're too nice for that, let me kill him. Or if that doesn't suit you, why not the traditional duel, the *holm-gangr*? We haven't got a holm, but I'm sure my lord your brother would prefer that to outright execution. If he kills you, I swear I'll release him.'

'What?' said Thorfinn's wife.

'This is murder,' said Duncan. He cleared his throat.

The foster-father went on interfering, and no one told him to be quiet. He said, 'It would be murder to let die all those who laid down their lives today, thinking to buy peace for the north, only to find that the whole war has to be fought again because Thorfinn couldn't face up to his duty. I'll fight him if you like, but you should. In a fenced ring, with no other helping, and with whatever weapons you please. It was how your father settled his people's quarrels, and your stepfather. If you had chosen it at the start, a lot of Caithness men would be living today.'

It was demeaning to appeal to a servant. If, as it seemed, Thorfinn had no will of his own, then it could not be avoided.

'It is murder,' said Duncan to the man Thorkel. 'Look at the difference between us. He said I could go. Do you doubt my oath? Of course I should agree to all that he asks. He has won the right, in fair battle. Let us go back to the ships. This monk can hear my oath on a Christ's book.'

His voice stopped, and no one spoke. Thorfinn studied the grass. The Lady said, 'Thorkel Fóstri is right. It should be a duel between you.'

Thorfinn lifted his head. 'And you would belong to the winner?'

'What choice would I have?' the Lady said.

'Then we fight,' said Thorfinn briefly.

They chose a stretch by the river and staked it, while the smith's family, with their belongings, came down the hillside and crossed the water and stood watching and silent. Through the trees, men were arriving, in twos and threes, as word filtered through to those few on this side of the peninsula. The man whom Duftah had killed was dragged out of the way, and the remaining five hung about beside Duncan, who had been given the use of a hut, and food and ale if he wished it.

He had jibbed at going into the booth, and Thorkel Fóstri had pushed him instead into the next one with the anvil in it, and the tongs and draw-plate and nail-iron and ladle hanging still on the wall. 'Try this one,' he said. 'Four stone walls. We can hardly burn it around you.'

Outside, Thorfinn sat on a log, with a leather flask in his hand, and Groa watched him. Duftah said, 'Speak to him.'

'Afterwards,' Groa said.

'And if there is no afterwards?' Duftah said.

'Then he will not know what he has missed, will he?' Groa said, and walked away. Then Thorfinn stood, and laid the flask down, and, sliding his sword from the scabbard, looked at it. Duftah opened the door of the smithy and spoke, and a little later Duncan emerged, walking stiffly.

For a moment, by the stakes, the half-brothers faced one another. Then the monk said, 'What you do, you do, each of you, for your peoples. May God indemnify both your souls. My lord King, will you enter on this side.' He waited. 'My lord Earl, on that.' Again he waited, and so did the two men, facing each other.

'*To action*,' said Duftah Albanach. And the sword of Thorfinn, like the flail of a reaper, swept down and cut the King through the right shoulder before Duncan had time to move.

Duncan dropped his sword. His spread fingers, clutching his shoulder, barely checked the spurt of the blood: soon all his arm and side was thick, shining red, and, gasping, his head fell forward and he dropped to his knees. Thorkel Fóstri said, 'You have won. Take his head.' The rope swayed as Duftah crossed and hurried over with two of his monks. Thorkel Fóstri vaulted over as well and strode up. 'Dispatch him! What are you thinking of?'

'That I should have managed it better,' Thorfinn said. 'With eight inches' difference in height, the least I could have done was to cripple him neatly.' There were four of them now on the grass beside the crouching figure of Duncan, and a woman, untying a bundle, was hurrying over with cloths. Thorkel Fóstri lifted his sword and cried out as Thorfinn struck his arm down with a blow from his fist.

'Kill him, and I will kill you,' Thorfinn said to his foster-father. 'The duel is over. Get a litter made, and find a gospel. The King has an oath to take before he sails back to Berwick.'

Groa turned to the nearest hut and sat down, and put her hands over her ears, and shut her eyes. After a long time, she heard someone come into the hut and found it was the woman who lived there, come to tell her that the monks were going back to St Cormac's and would take her with them. There was a garron.

She walked outside and stood looking.

The settlement had come to clamorous life, with women moving briskly from place to place, and children screaming and playing. All the armed men had gone. Down by the river, the stakes had been uprooted and only by the trampled ground and the blood could you tell that there had been a fight.

Not a fight. An execution. And not an execution either, for that would have been simple. A deliberate wounding, which perhaps had not taken quite the course the swordsman had intended.

She knew, from the women, that Duncan had been carried out by his men, under escort, on their way to the ships and the remnants of his army. Thorfinn and the rest of his men had left also, and in some encampment no doubt were engaged in the affairs that followed a battle: the celebrations; the gathering in of the dead and the wounded.

And now here were the monks, prepared to go back to their church and their houses as if nothing had happened. And as if nothing had happened, she was to go with them.

They were kind, helping her into the saddle. She said, 'Should I not go to the camp, where my lord Thorfinn is?'

Duftah was not there, but the muscular arms and the soft Irish voices reminded her of him. Someone said, 'The orders came from my lord's foster-father Thorkel. You were to go to St Cormac's, my lady.'

Of course, the women and Sigurd and Lulach were still away: someone would have to send for them, now that the danger was over. She left the settlement, and the stream, and the hills as if they had been no more than a break on her journey and travelled back with the monks to St Cormac's.

St Cormac's was empty. Like hers, the monks' servants had gone, and they had much to do, to get their baggage-mules unpacked and their hamlet in order. She did not want their help or even their attention: she was too tired to unfasten boxes and too tired to take any of the laborious steps that would bring her food and drink and bedding or even something to wear, now that she need no longer look like a monk.

She arrived among the last by the chapel, and waited only to learn that the bundles containing her gear had been left outside the empty houses she and her household had used. Then, deaf to well-meaning protests, she set off alone to find herself a cabin.

There was no danger: the new huts were almost within sight, just over a rise in the ground. She wanted no company. She did not know what she wanted. She stumbled, walking over the beaten earth and the grass, and her bones felt aching and weak. She topped the rise and saw below her the smokeless thatched roofs beneath which her sons had played and slept, and the well, and the peat-stacks, and the boxes and rolls, neatly piled where the monks had bestowed them.

She did not know how long she stood, her eyes resting on it unfocussed, before she realised that the space by the huts was not deserted. By a still-saddled garron, a man was standing there as if undecided: a man of ungainly height with a black, uncovered head who moved at last and began, slowly, to loosen the girths of his pony.

She did not need to see his face to know who it was, but none the less she stared, her breath catching. Thorfinn of Orkney and Caithness, victor of today's brilliant battle, was not with his army in Dingwall but here alone, without escort or harbingers.

She had learned not to trust impulse. She neither ran to her husband nor called, but walked steadily down to the huts, so that she was halfway there before he looked up and saw her coming. She saw him check, with a suddenness that seemed to suggest something more than astonishment. Then he simply stood, his elbow couched on the saddle, and waited until she stopped in front of him. He said, 'I thought you were at Balnagowan.'

'The monks brought me here,' Groa said. She wondered what Thorkel Fóstri was essaying. In the afternoon light, Thorfinn's face looked different, although there was no particular expression on it she could name, and the black brows above the dark brown eyes were unmoving. He carried neither helmet nor shield, and had exchanged his mail-shirt for narrow trousers and a loose tunic, with only his armlets and the linked gold of his belt to show his standing.

He said, 'Are all the huts empty?'

'This one is, and the two others. There hasn't been time to furnish them yet,' Groa said. 'Why? Whom do you want to bring here?'

He ignored that, and went into the nearest hut, leaving the pony.

Inside, she knew, there was only a beaten earth floor, and the roof was so low that he would have to bend all the time. He came back to the doorpost and leaned against it. 'It seems about the right height for children. Do you want to stay here? I shall get the monks to come and unpack what you need.'

'They are busy,' Groa said. 'It's all over there, in the boxes. I shall get it myself when I need it.'

He did not move. 'Oh,' he said. After a moment, he added, 'Do you think you could get it now?'

His voice, fathomless as the sea in a cavern, told her nothing through its inflections. Whatever that request might imply, she did not want to interpret it, or face it, or deal with it.

Then she remembered that he was accustomed to giving orders, to women as well as to men, and that for him explanations were unnecessary. She found a ring and hitched the garron where it could graze. Then, finding her way to the baggage, she searched for the box with her bedding, and with a mattress roll and an armful of rushes walked quietly back to the house. Sounds from over the hill indicated that the monks had withdrawn to the church, having no doubt made their own dispositions as to supper. The smell of roast sheep rose and lingered somewhere in the still air. It occurred to her to wonder if she would be sent to forage for food. She had not intended to return to the monks' hamlet till morning. Arrived, she laid her burdens on the threshold and pushed open the door of the rough wooden hut he had entered.

She could not get the door fully open, because he was lying behind it, his hand outstretched near the post it had been gripping. He did not move as she squeezed through and dropped kneeling, and when she turned his shoulder to look at his face, she found he had lost consciousness. Behind the unshaved stubble his skin stood, pallid and glistening, over all the peaks of his face; and under the shut eyes, the hollows were brown as oiled leather.

She had never seen Gillacomghain struck down by pure exhaustion, but she could recognise it in another man when she saw it. She pulled the Earl's shoulder until he rolled over, his shoulders and cheek on the earth, and only then saw the blood he was lying in.

His eyes opened, and he turned his head and saw her.

'It's all right. The monks will help,' Groa said.

His hand caught her robe, but could not hold it. 'No. They gossip.'

His breathing altered. He was angry, possibly with her: certainly with himself and whatever had brought this about. He said, 'Not the monks. Go away.'

Not the monks. Not the hird: that was why he was here, so that no one would know he was vulnerable. Someone knew: Thorkel knew—that was why she had been sent here, but without the Earl being consulted. The single desperate stroke at Duncan was now explained. It had been Inverness all over again. He had had to make the first blow do all the work; there might have been no chance of another.

She said, 'No monks. All right,' and waited until his eyes closed again. Then she set about dealing with the matter.

*   *   *

He wakened to darkness, and the slow, stammering hush of the sea, and a little steatite lamp glowing green-grey in a corner. He had been asleep far too long, for his muscles were stiff from the boards of his sea-chest, and he could hear no sound from the men. He said, 'Rognvald?'

A hand lifted the steatite lamp and brought it over. Set down, the glow burned through a hanging of deep crimson silk. He could not remember whose bed had such a curtain, and could only deduce that, since he could not be on board his ship, there must have been a landing he had forgotten about.

Then the curtain brushed his hand, and he lifted his fingers and let the fringe of it trickle between them. It was warm.

When it fell away, he closed his eyes, feeling the lamplight still on his lids, and seeking still, without haste, to distinguish where he might be.

Rognvald had not replied. Rognvald always replied, or threw himself upon him, or launched him into some boisterous game. He said aloud, 'Not Rognvald.'

No one answered. Certainly not Rognvald, then; and not Arnór, for he would have come rushing over; and not Thorkel, for if it was time to wake, Thorkel would have wakened him, a little roughly, long before now. And if Skeggi or Killer-Bardi or Starkad were here, he would hear them, for, like children, they could never stay silent for long.

Findlaech his stepfather had been a silent man, unless he was stirred to anger. Silent but thoughtful, and kind. If the day had been too much for you, he would know it, and would let you sleep.

But he had had this dream a great many times before, and had learned to scotch it at the start, even in sleep. Findlaech was dead. His mother, that busy, practical womam, was dead. Sigurd, the great roaring Colossus at whose knees he had walked, had gone before he could come to know him: Sigurd his father, from whom came the Norse blood in his veins. . . .

Duftah. Duftah, who had so much ambition that one day certainly he would be a saint: Duftah would have made his presence known, gently but firmly, by now. Sulien . . . Ah, Sulien. That had hurt, and hurt still. Sulien would sit quietly like this and let him think, but Sulien held no truck with crimson silk hangings and in any case was no longer here. . . . He had once come across a verse, just after he met Sulien. He tried it aloud, stopping to think.

I used to be young. I journeyed alone, then I lost my way. I thought myself rich when I met someone else. Man is man's delight. That was it.

His thoughts wandered, until in time he remembered what he had been pursuing. Sulien. Sulien was in Ireland. So where was he himself now?

A pillow under his head. A sack filled with chaff under his body, stripped to the waist. Round his arm and his side, clean wrappings skilfully bound. And under his arm a fine sheet with embroidery he had seen before. Once. In the course of six . . . four minutes . . .

And then he knew where he was, and who was with him.

A long time afterwards, he opened his eyes, well prepared for the face he would see in the lamplight, and said, 'I rise, a corpse already wept, and live. I thought I asked you to go away? It's my good fortune, I see, that you stayed.'

Her face was Greek in the lamplight, with its rounded classical jaw, and its brow broad and pure above the dark wings of the eyebrows. Her lashes were wet.

'You wanted Rognvald,' Groa said. 'I'm sorry.'

He lay looking at her. Perhaps it was true. Yes, it was true: he remembered dimly speaking his name. What else had he said? She had risen and was bringing him water. She put her arm behind his shoulders, and her hair fell forward again, brushing his skin.

He drank, and she slid her arm out, letting him sink to the pillow. He said, 'I thought I was on board ship. I am sorry, there is blood—' He stopped abruptly.

'—over the sheet again,' said Groa serenely. If she had been weeping, the reason was not now visible. She said, 'Don't be afraid. I won't take advantage of you.' She pulled, smiling, a wry face. *'Man is man's delight.'*

Why was he so tired? Why could he not deal with this: make her laugh; make her angry; please her; reward her for her care of him; protect himself, as he always did, from the probing, inquisitive mind? He drew a breath and said, 'What an unfortunate night you have had. What an unfortunate night I have had, if I have to interpret all my ravings. I seem to remember dreaming of Sulien, who is your friend as well.'

'You said, *It hurts,*' Groa said. After a pause, she said, 'It is two nights since you came here, not one.'

He sat upright; and the protesting pain in his side barely registered. 'What!'

'So I had to call the monks in,' Groa said. 'I'm sorry. But someone had to send word to Thorkel, and see to you from time to time. No one knows that you are hurt: only that you are busy with some crisis in Caithness. You've opened the gash again. What was it? An axe?'

'I don't know,' he said. 'What about Duncan? The ships?'

'They got away safely. Half your own men have finished their work and gone. A longship called, and was sent north to bring Sinna and the boys back to me. We assumed that was what you want. You will tell us, I suppose, where you want us to go.'

'Skeggi is dead,' Thorfinn said. 'I remember now. Thorkel told me.'

She touched his shoulder. 'Lie down. It was a fine campaign. You should hear Arnór's verses.'

Then the doors of his mind stood wide open. He said, 'You must be tired as well. Why not put the lamp out and lie down and sleep?'

She looked at him and obeyed, without questioning. There was another pallet against the wall: she lay on it dressed as she was, and blew out the lamp.

Then silence fell; and he could begin at the beginning and plan the war, and fight it, from the very first day to the moment when he brought his sword down on his half-brother's shoulder.

It ended: and he became aware of the force of his own breathing, and of the complaint in his arm and his side, and the fact that someone was holding him. Groa's voice said, 'Please . . . please . . . Keep some pity at least for yourself.'

Her weight was beside him; her arms under his shoulders, her hair on the pillow beside him. He put up his hand, and a tear fell on it, then another. He touched her wet cheek. 'What is it?' he said 'What is it?' A river of tears fell into his palm and he felt her lips part as she gasped, and gasped again. He lifted his other hand and cupped her face and held it. 'What is it?' he said for the third time.

Perhaps the firmness of his hold calmed her. He felt her hands withdraw from beneath him, and a moment later she caught his wrists and lowered them from her face. She turned his hands over and he knew from the sound of her voice that she was sitting now, her eyes lowered as if she could see them. She said, 'Compassion. Nothing you would recognise.'

If she had not been so near, he would not have betrayed himself. But his hands were in hers, and her fingers on the hammering vein in his wrist: nor by any exertion of will would the run of his breath return to anything approaching normal. He said quietly, 'I would recognise compassion. Is it compassion?'

She let his hands go. Sitting still, she said, 'No.'

'Let me light the lamp,' Thorfinn said. He moved before she could stop him, and found his way, limping, to where her pallet was, and picked up lamp and flint and tinder. Suddenly, his fingers were steady. He lit it.

She sat where he had left her, with her hair on her shoulders like poppy, and her eyes opened wide in her white face. He walked over and set the lamp down, and then sat down gently beside her and lifted her hand in both of his and held it between them. 'No,' he said. 'Compassion would be a very great thing, but I think . . . I am beginning to think . . . I am beginning to wonder if we may not have something greater. Is that what you wanted to say?'

She did not speak.

He said, 'What is it? Do you not know that I love you?'

She stood up, her hand wrenching from his, and stared at him.

He stood, too, but slowly. 'Or am I wrong?' he said. 'If I am wrong, tell me. Tell me quickly. You will lose nothing by it.'

He did not know what she could read in his eyes. He only knew that the shadows melted from the face opposite him until it was luminous as the soapstone of the lamp.

She stood before him, her hands loose in her robe, and said, 'I thought if ever you spoke those words to me, I would know you were lying, or if you were not, there was no way that I would ever be sure of it. I knew if ever I spoke those words to you, that you would take them for a nice courtesy and might even thank me. I cannot tell what has come to us, but I look at you and I believe you. If I tell you the same, will you believe me? I love you. I have always loved you . . . even through the six minutes . . . even through the four minutes . . . whatever distance there was between us.'

He looked at her. She said, 'Can you not accept, even yet, that something good may befall you?'

The lamplight burned on her hair. She said, her face uplifted, her hands on his breast, 'Could you bring your mind to it, I am prepared to be embraced. If it hurts to bend down, there's a box I could stand on.'

He could not only bend: he could lift her. There were, it seemed, a great many other things he could do that an hour before would have been beyond his strength if he had even thought of them. But he took infinite care in the design of them, moving from harbour to harbour in the voyage of the night with a care one would keep for a child; for a virgin; for something unbroken of rarest fragility, which remained still where it had always lain waiting, in the girl who had borne a child to an old man at fourteen; in the girl who had known nothing since except rape at the hands of her husband.

Through the night, he taught her joy, with patience; and received it.

In the morning, men rode into the settlement, shouting, and banged on all the doors, and thumped on the Earl's door, finding it shut, until Groa, gowned like a monk, jerked it open.

Thorkel Fóstri stood on the threshold. He said, his eyes on her and then sliding past her, 'Thorfinn! Is he here?'

'He is asleep,' she said, and came out, shutting the door behind her. 'He is better, but he ought to sleep. What is it?' She paused. 'Is it the children?'

'The children? No,' said Thorkel Fóstri. He looked at her hair, and her bare feet, and then back at her eyes. He said, 'You will have to wake him. We have just heard from Moray. Duncan is dead.'

'Dead? In Moray?' she said.

'I don't know how. They had a rough voyage. I suppose the wound wouldn't close. They tried to save him by putting him ashore at the mouth of the Lossie. They found some monks near Elgin who would look after him. But he died.'

'Yes. The Earl will have to be wakened,' said Groa.

'Not only for that,' Thorkel Fóstri said. 'There is more to the story. Duncan died, and there were the rags of his army about him, with none of the gold he had promised them, or the booty. Thorfinn paid the ships to carry them safely to Berwick, but the shipmasters saw the chance to unload all of them instead at the Lossie and sail quickly for home with their money.

'The Irish, those that weren't killed, made their own way home west through the hills, as you probably know. The men from Angus and Atholl and Fife and from Duncan's lands further south were soured by the war before ever they landed in Moray, and now found themselves leaderless, without ships, without transport, and the whole province to pass through before they could all reach their homes.

'Would you expect them to mourn Duncan and file off homeward with their hands folded, chanting? They are putting your Moraymen to the sword, and stripping the land of all they can eat, or drive before them, or turn into money. Tell Thorfinn he will have to leave his bed and march south and fight, unless he wants his kingdom gone before he can claim it.'

'His kingdom?' said Groa. Behind her, she heard a door open sharply.

'His kingdom,' said Thorkel Fóstri grimly. 'With Duncan dead, what other grandson of Malcolm's is living?

'Thorfinn is not only Earl of Orkney and Caithness. He is King of Alba. He has only to take it.'

PART
TWO

OF DIRE COMBUSTION AND CONFUS'D EVENTS

He is already nam'd, and gone to Scone
To be invested.

— Who was that Thane, lives yet;
But under heavy judgment bears that life
Which he deserves to lose. Whether he was combin'd
with those of Norway, or did line the rebel
With hidden help and vantage . . . I know not.

ONE

e is King of Alba. He has only to take it, his foster-father had said. And if Duncan had died at his brother's hand by the smith's houses, it would have been true. There, with the beaten army of Duncan under his heel, Thorfinn could have called his friends together and made his decision.

Then, a little thought would have told him what the last years should already have made plain. Ruling as Earl Sigurd his father had done, he could not even expect to hold what he had. If he wished to add Duncan's land against the advancing shield-wall of the lesser kindred in England, he would not only face a life-time of battle, long or short. He would have to change.

What his choice would have been there at Tarbatness could never be known. The opportunity to make it was lost, and with it the treasure of one night. The news from Moray reached him, and by noon he and the best of his men were at sea, on the two ships he kept within signal-range, while the rest of his fleet was summoned to carry the remainder.

He came back to the hut for his sword just before he left St Cormac's, and Groa lifted it for him. There was nothing to say. To mention his wound, to express dismay or anguish, would have been childish. On his order, Moray had stayed silent and watched Duncan's army march north. No ruler worth his salt, far less Findlaech's stepson, would stand aside now and watch Duncan's army ravage it on its way south.

He said, 'Stay with Duftah. I shall leave you a guard. When it is safe, I shall send for you.'

She could not speak, but she smiled.

He hesitated, then, raising one hand, lifted the hair from her neck and let it fall. Then, with his hand on her shoulder, he kissed her lightly and left.

After that, the news came quickly enough of what he was doing.

That he should meet slaughter with slaughter was to be expected. Landing in the wake of Duncan's men, he had tracked them from hall to barn and from house to church and from field to fold throughout Moray, mutilating where they had mutilated and burning where they had burned.

Then, as they ran stumbling before him, with their red swords and their heavy pack-trains and their stolen cattle, he crossed, as they had done, out of Moray and south to their own lands of Angus and Fife, where their own barns and malt-houses and halls and houses and churches were to be found. And these he burned, too, and killed their people as they had killed his people of Moray. And again. And again.

Sulien the priest was in the scriptorium at Clonard when the news came, painting God talking to Noah under a rainbow.

Because he had been grinding gold, the flies were all over him, drawn by the scent of the honey: they crawled over the three Persons of the Trinity with the Enemy crouching at Christ's feet, and flicked up and down the figures of David harping, with Ethan, Iduthin, Asaph, and Eman in gaiters beside him.

Then the Abbot, in person, stood at Sulien's elbow and said, 'It would not cross your mind, I know, to leave us before the Psalter is finished, and it already paid for by the Bishop of Crediton, but I brought the messenger to you myself, just in case.'

Afterwards, when he was packing and the Abbot was threatening him, as he took it, with excommunication for forsaking Bishop Lyfing's commission for the benefit of a horse-eating berserker, Sulien stood silent and then said, 'This is a baptised prince, as you are, who sustained me in his lands for five years. He has a right to my friendship.'

'He lets his friends burn Llanbadarn, and then expects you to run when he snaps his fingers?'

'He does not know I am coming,' said Sulien briefly.

In Chester, Alfgar took the best news, as always, to his mother.

'Have you heard? Thorfinn has murdered his brother and taken the kingdom. They say there's hardly a man of Duncan's left living.'

He was twenty-eight years old, and marriage had done nothing for him except perhaps modify the quality of his laugh. Godiva sat and looked at him.

Her son grinned. 'All right. Duncan attacked him and lost, and Thorfinn chased his army all the way down to Fife. Orm and Siward and the rest will be puking all over Northumbria, wondering what he's going to do next. They thought Duncan would get himself killed at Durham and we'd all walk in before Thorfinn noticed.'

'He may go back north,' Godiva said. 'Could he rule a kingdom?'

'You wouldn't say so,' Alfgar said. 'On the other hand, this is how Canute started, by chopping off the assorted limbs of the populace; and he ended by walking barefoot to Durham and ruling half northern Europe. Thorfinn admired Canute.'

Godiva looked at him without seeing him. 'Yes. The Lady Emma, too, might find it quite convenient to have Thorfinn to deal with, instead of your wife and her sisters. What is your Aelflaed saying?'

'That three children is enough,' Alfgar said. 'When she draws breath to say anything else, it's to complain that Siward and her sister are much richer than we are. Which is probably true, since his father went off to the Holy Land and didn't come back. I wonder who has the Lapp fur-trade now.'

'Haarek of Tjotta's son Finn,' Godiva said. 'The Lady Groa's first cousin. As you would know, if you paid more attention to what goes on down at the wharves. He made no mistake, that young man Thorfinn, when he married an Arnason's daughter. One day, Magnús of Norway might well claim England as well as Denmark.'

'My sweet lady mother, you are getting old,' said Alfgar, and came and sat at her feet. 'It was an Arnason who killed Magnús's father, don't you remember? The golden child in Norway is Rognvald, Thorfinn's little nephew. If Magnús becomes King of Norway and Denmark and England, then Thorfinn had better look out.'

The Lady of Mercia looked down at the merry face of her son. 'What you are saying,' she said, 'is that it is not by chance that Thorfinn has overrun all the lands of Duncan his brother, and that he may well make himself King of Alba?'

'What I am saying,' said Alfgar, 'is that Duncan's sons were at Dunkeld, and that Thorfinn has driven out every man of Duncan's in the neighbour-hood and put a ring of steel round Dunkeld that would defy a good thought to get past it. Does that look like the work of an innocent savage?'

'No. But it looks, at last, like the work of a king,' Godiva said. 'Except that it would upset your father, I would suggest that you go to Fife and see if you can talk to Thorfinn and find out what he is going to do.'

'Would you believe it,' Alfgar said, 'but that is just what my wife's sister was saying?' He laid his handsome head in his mother's lap and twisted round to look up at her, grinning. 'What would you give to go in my place?'

Godiva thought. 'Your wife, and your wife's sister, I believe,' she said.

Wearing all his arm-rings, and with his golden hair combed, Rognvald went to Tarbatness and called on his uncle's wife.

He found Groa gone, and only the monk there, and her two sons, and forty armed men under the command of Killer-Bardi, who would not let him land.

Rognvald called him up to the skiff, and gave him a twisted gold finger-ring, and patted the bulwark of the other man's ring-mail shirt, pensively. 'Would I ever blame a man for following orders? Tell the prince that the Earl his nephew congratulates him on his good fortune in the south. Should he be held there by affairs, he can rest assured that the Earl his nephew will take good care of the north in his absence.'

The words did not please Killer-Bardi, nor the fact that the young Earl, when he uttered them, was clearly sober.

The Earl Thorfinn of Orkney, they said, had taken over the guest-quarters of the monastery of Kinrimund, on the east coast of Fife, next to the hall of the Bishop of Alba, who was absent.

So the lord Crinan, father of the dead King Duncan, was told when he found himself barred by armed men from access to his own monastery of

Dunkeld, on the river Tay, where his three young grandsons had lived since their mother died.

With a hardihood characteristic of all his long career since the day when he married King Malcolm's only daughter, Crinan of Dunkeld took his excited son-in-law Forne by the arm, turned him round, and proceeded with his sober retinue of some thirty riders to follow the course of the river Tay south to the borders of Fife, and then across to the coast where Thorfinn and his army had halted.

The path Earl Thorfinn had taken was not hard to follow. Smoke still lingered among the burned houses, and the scavenging birds were about, jostling in glistening crowds on the ground, rising screaming with anger at each interruption. They passed cairn after cairn of freshly piled stones, some already scattered by wolves.

Apart from Forne, the men he had with him were his own, and seasoned. They rode straight-backed and silent: they had seen this before. When Vikings were defied, or cheated out of their protection money, they behaved in just this way: in Ireland; off the Welsh coast; in Man. They left behind them blood and legends. Already the bardic verses were being sung, celebrating the death of his son and the Earl's victory:

> *A keen sword at Tarbatness*
> *Reddened the wolf's fare.*
> *The young Prince wielded it . . .*
> *Thin swords sang there . . .*
> *There fought with Scotland's King*
> *Our valiant lord . . .*

They were yelling that at the camp outside Dunkeld when he left, and it had upset Forne.

It might be that Forne was right. On the face of it, the appearance of thirty unarmed men with an abbot could offer no threat to the victor of Tarbatness in the midst of his hosting. But the victor of Tarbatness, pitchforked out of Orkney into this particular arena, might well have lost his head. Or at best, he had Viking stock to impress: was of Viking stock himself. The signs, as they began to ride, were not good.

On the other hand, instructions of some kind had been left at Dunkeld. No one tried to stop them departing, although they were offered no boats. And although there were Thorfinn's men at the first ferry-crossing on the Earn, they were not stopped there either, although they were asked their business. The leader, Crinan judged, was a Caithness fellow; but there were at least two Gaelic-speakers among the small group of men, perhaps trained in Moray. After a short consultation, one of these joined Crinan's party to act as guide and to save him annoyance, it was suggested.

It seemed likely that he, Crinan, knew the way to Kinrimund better than they might do, but he made no objection, and when they reached the first of two armed camps they passed on the way, he was clearly expected. Indeed, the well-dressed man in charge asked politely if he might have the services of my lord Abbot's priest for two of his wounded, and Crinan let the man go readily, and told him to take his time, while he sipped ale with the leader and engaged in conversation which told him very little.

The beasts he saw penned by the camp were only enough, he judged, to feed the company for a couple of weeks, and there was no sign of other plunder. When they left, he watched as they moved out of the woods and across the planked bogs and the beaten earth of the heath-paths, and saw more than once the tracks of cattle disappearing up into the high ground between the Firth and the Leven.

The hill-forts were occupied, and Thorfinn had not yet marched to clear them out. Or perhaps, since they would be full of leaderless cottagers and their families, he did not think it worth while. So the cairns belonged to the chiefs and their followers who had gone to his son Duncan's hosting and had survived Tarbatness to fall to the same enemy here. It had been one of his fears that a hundred of Duncan's men might at some point jump out of a spinney, slaughter his unwanted guides, and demand to be led on some hopeless crusade. It was, in part, the reason why he had made every man lay down his arms before they got to Dunkeld. Weapons were no defence under these circumstances, nor were hordes of panicking men.

Only careful negotiation was going to get them out of this, if anything could. Provided that somewhere at the end of the journey there was a young man able to negotiate.

On the sandy banks of the Eden, looking across to the smoke of Kinrimund, Forne said, 'Well, you were right. He didn't have us killed at Dunkeld, so we have been allowed to pass through and see him. I forget what you said about getting out afterwards.'

Crinan did not reply. His son-in-law said, 'I thought you said this place was small.'

'It's a Pictish monastery,' the Abbot said. 'Or was once. The place was called Cenrigmonaid. On a headland between two good beaches. What you see is the smoke from his men's cooking-fires. Are you hungry?'

They had made camp themselves the previous night, for fifty miles in a day was more than he now cared to travel. He had slept well. He knew that Forne was afraid and disconcerted. Forne was an able man, unlike his own late son, and it would do him no harm to be shaken up. Without waiting for his answer, Crinan led the way down to the ford and splashed over. On the far side, as they approached, a mounted escort moved up, awaiting them.

It seemed that someone had broken into the Bishop's store-room and perhaps even his tithe-barn. There were woven hangings with Saxon designs running along three of the four walls of the biggest apartment of the timber-built palace. In front of the Release of Peter was a carved oak chair, painted and gilded, with nobody in it, and nearby on the rushes another chair and some stools with velvet cushions on them. The wainscoting under the hangings was carved, and so was the board at one end of the room, on which were set candles and a pitcher, together with a number of handsome goblets. There was an embossed silver plate.

A clerk, writing in a corner, laid down his quill and rose, with no undue haste, lifting his wide sleeve-corner over the desk-stand. 'My lord Abbot; my lord. I trust you have had a good journey? . . . Allow me to offer you wine. We serve ourselves, being in camp as you see. The Earl hopes to be with you directly.'

The late King's father smiled and said the right things, aware that Forne had glanced at him. If Thorfinn was using his old title, it only meant that he was giving nothing away. As only living grandson of a king, he could already lay claim to a greater, as his bard at least knew.

It was not that, but the presence of the house-priest himself that was significant. Crinan received his cup, smiling, and said, 'And you are of the Bishop's house, my friend?'

A subterranean voice from the doorway said, 'He is from Deer monastery. Thank you, Master Eochaid.' And as the clerk smiled, bowed, and prepared to leave the room, Thorfinn of Orkney walked in, crossed to the carved chair, and seated himself with deliberation, his empty hands on its arms. Then he waited.

The silence did not disturb Crinan. He examined his stepson as he knew he was being examined, and noted the changes.

The height was there, as he remembered, but now filled in: the great muscles of chest and biceps and shoulder had knitted across so that there was a compactness lacking before. Now Earl Sigurd's son moved better: stood better; sat better—not, he would guess, as a matter of practice but because sinews trained to war will keep their suppleness for every exercise.

He looked at the young man's face. Any man, if he acted well enough, could conceal his uneasiness. No man whom he had ever known could hide the signs of a leader stretched beyond his capacity. A cough, perhaps; or an irritation of the skin; or the fine play of the muscles by the eye or by the lip that no physician he knew had been able to conjure away unless he took the man's office with it.

Here was a half-bred kinglet from the north in enemy country, with blood on his hands and the father of the dead man confronting him. What could he make of it?

In the face opposite, he could see no tell-tale signals as yet. The eyes studying him in turn were brown as a Spaniard's; the weathervane of a nose unstirred by irregular breathing; the mouth closed and perfectly still. Where it clung to his neck and his temples, the black hair was wet, as if the prince had been moving quickly through the heat of the campfires and the September sunshine, but his linen tunic-robe was fresh: the gold arm-bands glittered under the short sleeves, and gold flashed from the links of his sword-belt, which he had not taken off.

Crinan waited a long time at ease, sipping his wine, while Forne sat breathing quickly beside him. Then Crinan said, 'I am here because I need your help, and because I think you need mine.'

'Not the bereaved father?' Thorfinn said.

'No more than the bereaved brother,' Crinan replied. He knew precisely what had happened to Duncan: there had been no shortage of people to tell him. It interested him to know why Thorfinn had not finished off both his stepbrother and his stepbrother's army, and what had prompted him to send Duncan south by sea, with his men. You would say that a more experienced commander might have guessed what would happen. You would then wonder how experienced Thorfinn might be.

This was not the time to probe that, but to avoid it. Crinan said, 'I don't have to tell you the importance of Cumbria. In return for my wife's interest in Dunkeld, I made it possible for both my son Duncan and his grandfather to rule there.'

'I am sure you are right. If I have occasion to see Hardecanute, I shall remind him of your good offices under his father. Meanwhile,' said Thorfinn, 'your grandsons will do as well under my care at Dunkeld as they would in Cumbria. Perhaps better.'

'I think,' Crinan said, 'that the world will expect of you a little more candour than this. Alba is without a king, and there is no one of the royal kindred left alive, save yourself and these three boys. In two years, Malcolm will be twelve, and his own man. If you claim him for fostering, you must release him then. If you claim him as hostage, then you claim the throne also, by implication. Is that what you want?'

'Do I need to claim the throne?' Thorfinn said.

Crinan continued to smile, but would not have cared to admit how much skill it needed. The brevity of these responses was upsetting, and also the weight of knowledge behind them. He had learned not to expect shouting, but he had expected aggression.

Instead, neither Teltown nor Duncan's death had been mentioned; and now this. What Thorfinn had implied was true. Legitimate or bastard and of whatever line on the opposite side, the kings of Alba had to fulfil only three requirements. They had to be of the royal blood within four generations; they had to be whole and without physical blemish; and they had to excel, in strength and in leadership, any one of their rivals.

Children, therefore, were debarred until they had grown to manhood; and so had developed the tradition by which first one branch of the royal line and then another would take the throne.

Sometimes several branches would flourish and the choice become a matter of war and contention between them. Sometimes a king would do as Malcolm had done, who had destroyed all his rivals until there was none left to follow but his two grandsons Duncan and Thorfinn.

Duncan to hold Cumbria and add to it Alba, when the time came. And Thorfinn to act as a buffer in Orkney and Caithness against the ambitions of Norway, and later, when this became inconvenient, to be killed or returned safely to the confines of Orkney by the attentions of Gillacomghain.

But then Thorfinn had killed Gillacomghain and, by taking his widow, had extended his rule to Moray as well. An aged man, within two years of his deathbed, Malcolm had been able to do nothing about that. Or perhaps, studying Thorfinn's nature, he had reached the conclusion that nothing need be done about Thorfinn. He had employed him to help defend his coasts, and had lost some coastal bases in the process, which he might have thought fair exchange, having no fleet of his own.

As for the rest, Thorfinn had shown no particular interest in Moray, never mind in expanding his landholding southwards. Sailing, fighting, and roistering in his patrimony in Orkney were all he asked from life, it would appear; and once the handsome Rognvald appeared, he had ceased to take any interest either in his young wife.

So what had happened now, you might say, was an accident, unforeseen by anyone. Malcolm's careful dynastic marriages in the north of England had become not a holding of hands but a barrier erected in front of his dear grandson's face. And, baulked in the south, Duncan had made this inept attempt against Thorfinn, which had failed. And, more than failing, had brought Thorfinn headlong south to this point, where he sat among the blood and the dust, wondering which path to take.

Or not wondering. Nothing he had said or done so far had committed him to any one course of action. He had Duncan's sons, but had not killed them. He had injured Duncan himself, but had not dispatched him. Now he asked, 'Do I need to claim the throne?' knowing that there was only one answer.

'No,' Crinan said. 'The throne is yours by right, if you want it. No doubt you have a stout army of Orkneymen. Can you hold the whole of this country from Cumbria to Orkney single-handed? No one has done, so far. Malcolm had a Findlaech to hold Moray and a Sigurd to hold Caithness, and these you don't have, for the lines of both end in yourself. Can you hold Cumbria against Ligulf and Siward? Can you even hold Fife and Angus and Lothian without Malduin the Bishop? York consecrated him, and York wants Cumbria and Lothian as well as the rest of the north. I offered you a joint rule. I did not think I would have to justify it.'

'I have nothing against joint rule,' Thorfinn said. 'Indeed, I have it already. With Rognvald.'

The heat rose, despite himself, in Crinan's face. 'Rognvald has no claim to the throne!' he said sharply.

'Neither have you,' Thorfinn said.

They looked at one another. Then Crinan rose, and Forne followed.

'On the matter of Cumbria,' Thorfinn said.

Crinan stood still.

'On the matter of Cumbria, there may well be something we should talk about, later on. I shall send you a messenger.'

'I shall be at Alston,' Crinan said. 'Unless the Mercians have other plans. Perhaps you could ask Leofric, should you have occasion to see him also.'

He caught Forne's eyes, and they began the process of leave-taking, with brevity. Thorfinn did nothing to delay their departure, and gave them an escort out of his territory, together with a set of fresh horses. No doubt they belonged to the Bishop and were easily come by.

Forne said, 'Is it play, or is he in earnest?'

Crinan looked at him. 'I think you have to hope,' he said, 'that he is in earnest. A man like that, who does not know, or does not care, what he is doing, would be a threat I could not contemplate.'

Sulien watched them depart under the blue-and-gold flag of Dunkeld, and then, taking his leave of the priest from Deer, whom he knew well and with whom he had been chatting, walked across the cobbles and in through the door of the Bishop's palace.

Thorfinn was still there, alone in a carved chair with his head propped on one hand, and his fingers masking his face. As the door unlatched and then fastened shut, he opened an eye between finger-tips. Then he said, *'Sulien!'* and half-lowered the hand, its palm open.

Sulien walked slowly forward. 'Father Eochaid says you are an obstinate bastard with wound-fever,' he said. 'I was passing, on my way from Ireland to Wales. You've had visitors.'

'Alfgar yesterday. Crinan today,' Thorfinn said. 'Now you. An infestation.'

'And Groa tomorrow,' Sulien said. 'She sent for me.'

'An infestation,' Thorfinn repeated.

'You have a decision to take. I suggest,' Sulien said, 'that you take it when you are fit.'

'You want to make it for me,' Thorfinn said.

'Of course. Doesn't everybody?' Sulien said. 'Can you walk, or do we have to carry you like the Pope?'

'I didn't know the Pope was carrying me,' Thorfinn said. 'But indeed I may have to ask him to, before all this is finished.'

It was merely a quip, Sulien thought, to cover his condition. Later, with terrified admiration, he saw that it was something quite different.

The next day, the Lady of Moray arrived, and from that moment, you would say, the poison appeared to leave the Earl's wounds and they healed. Or so Arnór Jarlaskáld would have it, who, faced with superior competition, had ended by ceding first place to the Earl's wife and his favourite from Brittany. What Thorkel Fóstri thought, no one knew, but the formal politeness he had always used towards the Lady was now, everyone saw, of a different dimension.

The actual meeting between the Earl and his wife no one witnessed, and indeed at any time they were observed together afterwards, they appeared to be having words, so that the transformation, to the uninitiated, seemed all the stranger.

For a week, nothing happened that the watching world could lay a finger on. The holding-camps in Fife and Atholl and Angus remained, and so did the guard at the crossroads and the ferries. Experimentally, one or two of the hill-forts began to empty, as people crept back to their steadings and began, furtively, to resume daily life without being attacked. In two places, independently of each other, a toisech of Duncan's army emerged from hiding and, rallying all the men he could find, attacked the nearest encampment and tried to drive Thorfinn's men out. In both cases, the leader was killed and the men who had risen under him mostly died in the fighting. September waned, and the harvest was fully in, and the time for tribute-paying drew near, with no King to receive it and no King to protect anyone in return.

In Durham, the Earl Eadulf of Northumbria sent for the Bishop of Alba, whose modest hall beside the half-finished church had been held in uneasy tenure ever since the late King Duncan's attack.

Twelve years as bishop, first to the ageing Malcolm, and then to King Duncan his grandson, had done nothing for the worldly advancement of Malduin Gilla Odhrain, sole Bishop of Alba. The tightrope he walked in the service of his various masters had already been frayed to a thread by Duncan's ineffable siege of Durham.

Bishop Malduin had been in Durham when Duncan attacked it, and that had saved Bishop Malduin's skin, for the moment. The best policy, it appeared, was to stay in Durham while Duncan marched north to seek out his half-brother. And now Duncan was dead; and Thorfinn was not only in Fife, but sitting, so the Bishop understood, in Kinrimund, in one of the Bishop's chief halls, and enjoying the land that supported it.

The Bishop and this marauder Thorfinn were strangers. But men of eminence would not fail to recall that Thorfinn was the Bishop's first cousin. No one could fail to recall save Thorfinn, who had walked into his hall and was eating his rents without a thought for his cousin's very special position, or how matters would look to his masters in Durham. A man gave his all to God's work, and this was the sort of reward he got. There was no justice anywhere, and life was merely a fight for survival in the face of the betrayals you received from your own heathen-worshipping family.

The summons from Earl Eadulf came, and Bishop Malduin presented himself with black rage in his heart, prepared for any sort of iniquity.

With Earl Eadulf was his nephew Ligulf of Bamburgh, and they were both smiling.

'Well, Bishop,' said the Earl agreeably. 'It seems that your family contains a surprising number of quarrelsome people. Here is a man who seems to think he can kill a king and then require bishops to scamper here and there at will. Your cousin Thorfinn has sent to beg the comfort of your spiritual advice in your own hall of Kinrimund. My first impulse, naturally, was to return his messenger's head to him to rebuke his presumption. But, on second thoughts, it would be un-Christian, as I am sure you would agree, to deny an opportunity for repentance to any man, however blackened his soul. I think you should go.'

Of all he had anticipated, nothing had been as appalling as this. Bishop Malduin said, 'My lord Earl, I wish nothing to do with this man. He is beyond redemption. I would humbly suggest that there is no place for a bishop in Alba until the new King is proclaimed, on which I should willingly accede to any instructions you may see fit to give me. But in the meantime—'

He broke off, because the Earl and his nephew were both frowning. He might have known it. They were getting rid of him. They had never supported him. They would involve him in Thorfinn's disaster, and he would die in Alba.

Earl Eadulf said, 'Meantime, you will also, if you please, accede to my instructions and go to Earl Thorfinn in Alba. When you get there, you will act very carefully in accordance with some information that my lord Ligulf will now give you. You will stay with your cousin until it is clear what he is going to do. You will then return and report on the matter, if he will let you. If he will not, you will be given the means to send messages.'

He raised his eyebrows. 'Is this such a great thing to ask? Do you not forget, my lord Bishop, that, unlike the rest of us, who stumble on our given way in faint hope of redemption, all that you do is under the shining banner of Christ, with at the end God and His angels awaiting you?'

Bishop Malduin bowed. What was awaiting him was a tall, black-browed war-lord who sliced people's backs and pulled their lungs out from under their shoulderblades. With the home life of God and His angels it had nothing in common.

'You're a wild fool,' said Groa. 'You should never have sent for him. He'll find out all he can, and the next thing you know, the Northumbrian army will have taken over Alba in the name of Duncan's children.'

'*Whiter than the snow of one night was her skin, and her body appearing through her dress.* Why are you so beautiful,' said Thorfinn, 'and talk so much?'

'Because,' said Groa, pulling clear, 'the Bishop of Alba and his officers have been waiting for you in the hall for all of ten minutes while you have supposedly been changing from one tunic to another. It's going to be like being married to Edgar, who had to be found and dragged off a mattress halfway through his coronation.'

'What coronation?' said Thorfinn, and rammed the last buckle home, and went out, just failing to close the door sharply. After a moment, his wife shook out her dress and followed.

What lay between them was as dear to him, she knew, as it was to herself. But at this moment its purpose must only be to support him, not to compete with the decision that had to be made.

For the decision would be taken: they all knew that now. He had risen, clear of his fever, and had not issued the orders that would have ended it all; that would have sent his northerners back to the borders of Moray and allowed Eadulf and whoever so pleased to march in and take the unsettled, leaderless land.

She thought that he might have done that, after the slaughter, if Sulien had not come. Not that Sulien, she believed, could ever drive Thorfinn into a course he did not wish to follow. But he could make him pause; and consider.

The results of the consideration had been quickly apparent.

For a week now, the district leaders of Alba had been coming in, sometimes in groups, sometimes singly, in answer to the message Thorfinn had caused to be passed among them.

At first, only the toisechs who had not fought for Duncan had arrived. Then, gradually, had come some of the leaders in the families that Tarbatness had decimated, and sometimes a priest, taking the place of more than one widow and her children.

To them all, Thorfinn had said the same thing. 'This is your country. I do not want it, but you have no other protector in Alba. South of Alba, there are many men who would gladly govern, in the name of King Duncan's children, for the ten years it would take for King Duncan's heir to gather and lead his own army.

'The choice is yours. If I rule, I rule as king, by right of royal descent, not as tutor to the sons of my half-brother. If you wish to give Alba to the Earls of the south, I shall return to Moray, and to my own Caithness and Orkney.'

And the bolder of the chiefs from Angus and Atholl and Fife and Strathearn replied in the same way. 'If you were to rule, prince, who would be your mormaers? Men of Orkney?'

To which Thorfinn's answer, too, was identical. 'The men of the north belong in the north, and have enough business there without looking further. The mormaers who ruled under King Duncan would remain, if they so wished, to rule under me. The mormaerdoms fallen vacant would be filled by their toisechs and by me, in consultation.'

The first time he heard it, Sulien had stood before Thorfinn as he came away and said, 'You would accept this burden, if they agree? You would accept it?'

And Thorfinn, no expression in his face or his voice, had said, 'What Viking did you ever know to refuse an offer of such land and so many riches? Study has made you foolish.'

She had married a very great man; or a Viking. She did not yet know which.

Within a week, Bishop Malduin was back in Durham, muttering replies before the surprised rage of Earl Eadulf.

'He would not hear of my staying. My lord Earl, I had no alternative. I was unarmed, in the camp of a war-leader. He insisted on sending me home.'

'And your errand?' Earl Eadulf said.

'He is holding Alba at present by force,' Bishop Malduin said. 'There are armed camps everywhere, and the people are muttering.'

'And his intentions?'

'Those he has not yet announced. But he is asking all Duncan's men which they would prefer: rule under himself, or rule by you or your friends, my lord Earl.'

'What!' said Earl Eadulf. 'But you told him, I hope, what I asked you to. You told him that I had no claims to press against Alba other than those I already held in King Duncan's day, provided that I might take Cumbria off his hands.'

'I told him,' said the Bishop. 'And he thanked you for the offer concerning Cumbria, which he would have been delighted to accept . . .'

'Would have been?' Earl Eadulf said.

'. . . but for the embargo of King Hardecanute, whose leave he had asked, and who would by no means countenance the passing of Cumbria into your hands, my lord Eadulf. I regret,' said Bishop Malduin, 'that under the circumstances I could not obtain the assurances my lord Earl was anxious for. It was not my fault.'

'*Emma*,' Earl Eadulf said. He looked the Bishop of Alba up and down. 'Does your cousin know Emma? The Lady? Does he?'

'He was her husband's housecarl. Yes. I thought you knew. Yes, he knows the Lady Emma,' the Bishop said. 'But that is a long time ago. The Lady Emma has not seen him for years. But his recent visitors have included Earl Alfgar. And my lord Crinan, the late King Duncan's father.'

'I wonder,' Earl Eadulf said, 'that he did not ask you to stay to adorn his new kingdom. He knows now, if he has exchanged greetings with Winchester, that while Hardecanute is King I cannot take Cumbria or send an army further north: as far as the Lady Emma is concerned, I am too strong here already. So there is little doubt, is there, what ruler Alba will choose?'

Bishop Malduin did not answer, for this was his opinion as well, and he saw no need to make matters worse by confirming it.

In Alba, as the time set aside for consultation drew to its end, the small doubt there had been was no longer evident. Beneath the gloved hand of Thorfinn, the country lay silent, sullen, and waiting. Seated in his carved chair before an empty desk, by a stand-desk that was also empty, the Earl of Orkney looked at his foster-father with something like anger and enquired, 'Well?'

'You have only to lift your hand,' Thorkel Fóstri said. And after a moment, 'What else were you born for?'

'Why not happiness, like other men?' Thorfinn said.

'You have that,' said his foster-father. 'But if you try to trap it, it will change. Why do you resist? It is your right.'

'I resist because it is no use resisting,' Thorfinn said. 'Do you not think that is unfair? I shall be King because I was King; and I shall die because I did die; and did I remember them, I could even tell what are the three ways it might befall me.'

He stood up and walked round the desk, and turned, facing Thorkel Fóstri. He said, 'Prepare your men and mine for marching. You will lead them to Caithness. The Moray men, and the Moray men only, will go with me to Scone.'

Thorkel Fóstri looked at him. 'Then you will take the throne?'

'If they offer it,' Thorfinn said.

'They will offer it,' said his foster-father. He paused. 'I would gladly be there.'

'No,' said Thorfinn. 'You are of Orkney.'

TWO

AT TRIBUTE-TIME, in October, the new Abbot of Kells crossed from Ireland and was given a princely escort to the monastery at Scone by the man who had summoned him, the lord who was half-brother to the late King Duncan of Alba.

To the monastery or to Perth, or to the guest-quarters about both, came other churchmen, including the Abbot Duftah of Tain, and his brother the Abbot of Deer, and the Bishop of Alba, returned once more, rebelliously, at the behest of both his masters.

But, most important of all, there came to the Moot Hill that October the men of Alba, with their tributes, in sufficient numbers to put beyond doubt the decision of the tuaths. In the absence of another natural leader—in the absence, indeed, of any leaders at all—they were prepared to accept the heathen, the foreign grandson from the north, and remain to give their silent endorsement to the brief ceremony that made him so: the truncated Mass held within the church, the walk to the Court Hill, the robing and oath-taking ritual upon the stone on which Duncan had sat six years before.

None made jokes this time about a ritual marriage with mares, for the hird, his closest friends, were absent: Arnór and Thorkel Fóstri; Starkad and Eachmarcach. No man from Orkney or Caithness saw their great Earl Thorfinn become Macbeth, King of Alba. Only the men of Alba, with among them Sulien of Llanbadarn, and Lulach his stepson, standing tall and white-haired and watchful, and his wife.

Sulien stood, his hands folded together, and watched chieftain after chief step up the hill and, kneeling, take the vow of allegiance, his hands between the hands of the tall man who, twelve years before, had come to Chester, nervous, obstinate, gallant, to tackle King Canute and his grandfather both and outface them, somehow, with the newly freed Alfgar gambolling about him and Duncan watching, apprehension on his face.

Now there was the face of a man, instead of the bony, flickering features of youth; and instead of the hlað, there was a thin band of gold confining his hair, for Alba's kings wore no crown. And in place of the cloak sunk below the waters of Dee, the silken robe woven with gold that had crossed many lands to be made into a vestment fit for a king.

The ceremony was to be no pagan shout of triumph: it was, of design, quick and quiet.

The feast afterwards told a different story.

Even Sulien, who knew something of Thorfinn's possessions, caught his breath when he entered the hall with the rest and saw the hanging lamps, with their scented oil and golden twined beasts, and the glistening silk of the hangings, and the burden of glass and of silver and gold on the woven cloth of the long boards, set Saxon-style with the cross-table at the far end.

There stood the chair Malcolm had used, and Duncan after him, with its posts foiled in gold and wrought with pebbled stones of different colours. 'He keeps fine state, for a berserker,' someone said, as Thorfinn stood there, with his wife and his stepson, and then sat, so that all could sit.

Not Thorfinn. Macbeth. For evermore now, his baptised name, even if it seemed to be no part of him. Sulien wondered if either he or his wife had heard that remark, and knew that if they had, it would seem no more than just. Even Groa, before the day began, had said, thinking of all her husband must do, 'Well, Sulien. At least his Gaelic is good; or so it seems to me after all I learned in Moray. Do you think so?'

And he had looked at her and said, 'My lady, he is almost pure Gael: have you never realised it? Of his four grandparents, three were from Alba or Ireland, and the fourth was a quarter-Gael by descent. I don't know who my lord Crinan's mother was, but I doubt if Duncan could claim as much. Remind him.'

'Remind him that he and I come of different races?' Groa had said.

'You are here, alone of his friends,' Sulien said.

'I am here as the widow of the Mormaer of Moray, and Lulach as his son,' had said Groa flatly.

And it was true. She was there to remind the men of Alba that their new King was not only an Earl of the north but already, for eight years, had taken his place at their side as Mormaer of Moray. The churchmen were here to reassure the devout: the faithful would not be required to sue Odin or eat horseflesh or expose their latest-born children. The gold and the silver were there as a reminder of material things: with a simple oath of allegiance they had bought not only a man but a fleet, an army, a wealth of moveable riches.

Abbot Duftah of Tain, smiling, was sitting beside him. 'I have just heard a man say,' he said, 'that in England they pay Danegeld to make the Danes go away, and here in Alba we pay them to come. Nevertheless, he does well, I should judge. What of Cumbria?'

'The question of Cumbria,' Sulien said, 'was settled at the Feast of Teltown. Were you disappointed that none of your line became the new Abbot of Kells?'

Duftah laughed. 'Would I be human if I were not?' he said. 'But it takes the sting out of the disappointment, I will say, to find that Crinan's house failed to supply the post either. He is a good man, Abbot Robhartach, and there's a justice about the affair that you've maybe not noticed. It was the Abbot's own father Ferdomhnach that ousted Crinan's line from the abbacy thirty years ago. So friend Crinan is feeling the cold?'

'I would guess so. At least he offered Thorfinn joint rule of Cumbria so long as he could have access to Dunkeld and stay Abbot there.'

'I see,' said Duftah, 'that you have the same difficulty as myself. Thorfinn. It is a name I shall miss, though Macbeth is a better. Son of Life, it means, or of the Elect. Well, that you might say he now is, whether the trumpeter angels have observed it or not. Ah, praise God. The food.'

The food came, in profusion. The drink, when it came, proved to be wine, not ale, and was served with a more careful hand. The aim, clearly, was to encourage the guests to relax, but not to render them either quarrelsome or incapable of listening to what their host wished to say to them when the time came.

Malduin, Bishop of Alba, ate with both hands and watched everything from his high seat not far from his northern cousin, who had exchanged his thunderbolt so easily for the cross and the symbols of kingship.

After the tension of the ritual and what preceded it, the present comfort, the Bishop saw, was already bringing relief. There were few women present: no man had been certain enough of this gathering to risk wife and family unless it might be more dangerous to leave them at home. But each man at least knew his neighbour, and though talk at first was subdued, so that one could hear plainly the sound of the harp, and then of the flutes and some stringed instrument playing out of sight somewhere, shortly there was a little laughter and some louder exchanges. Presently, when the tumblers came in, and then a man who sat on a stool and sang a long, reflective ballad about a number of people they knew and did not like, the occasion almost began to take on the colour of a celebration.

In any case, he, Malduin, must make the best of it, for this time he would not be going back. That had been made quite clear by Earl Eadulf. If his cousin took the throne, he was to stay at his side and act in the best interests of Durham while (it was implied) depleting the treasury of his cousin and not that of Eadulf.

And since this time he had not been asked to leave, he supposed that he would have to obey. Down the board, he saw the faces of the monks he had brought back with him beginning to brighten a little now when they saw that there was good food about, and no shortage of silver. Beside the woman Groa, the new Abbot of Kells was laughing heartily, his tonsure red with the summer's sun. He was probably right to be merry, with full tithe-barns behind him after his first progress round the Columban churches in Ireland and the dues of Dunkeld still to come, with whatever the new King cared to give him as his enthronement-gift.

The new King, whose hair was not the red-gold of the Celt or the straw-white of the Norseman but black as that of the Picts who had ruled this land two hundred years ago. Whose nose and cheekbones and jaw might have been chipped out by a chisel underneath the tall brow, round as an egg below the gold band and the thickness of his hair. His cousin Thorfinn-Macbeth, who was rising to speak.

He spoke in Gaelic, beginning, as was the custom, with a toast to the church and the Trinity. Much of what he said after that had already been affirmed on the Moot Hill, and had to do with the undertakings he had made: to see justice done; to protect and foster their interests. He touched, to end with, on other matters.

'I will not bring men from Orkney or Caithness south to hold your mormaerdoms. They have their own frontiers to guard. Therefore, if we are to defend this country, I shall need your help.

'I do not propose on your behalf, either, to claim more land than my stepbrother Duncan held, and my grandfather before him. Lothian will, as before, allow the dues of its churches ruled by St Cuthbert to go to St Cuthbert. Cumbria, as before, will be held under the King of England and ruled on his behalf. I have the promise of the late King's father, my lord Crinan, that I shall have his aid in this.

'Those of you who are concerned for the future of the Christian church need not fear. As you see, the Bishop of Alba is returned among us, and we have the care once more of the church of Columba. Christianity in Orkney is only fifty years old, but long before that men had freedom to worship as they pleased, and this will continue. I have taken one step already to help with the cure of souls in Fife, which has long, through no fault of Bishop Malduin's, been without pastors. With the leave of the Loch Leven hermits, I am causing the monastery there to be rebuilt, and a group of monks, led by Prior Tuathal, will settle there.'

He paused. They were not, Sulien saw, greatly stirred by the new church, except to wonder what land or dues it might require of them. They were, however, interested in weighing up what they had got for a king. So far, they had accorded him silence, and the atmosphere at least was not inimical.

Thorfinn said, 'It is usual at these times to talk of the succession. I am doing so only in order to tell you that the next King will be chosen by you on my death, and not beforehand. My stepson Lulach, who is here, is eleven and will soon take his place as the future Mormaer of Moray. My only son Sigurd is a child of five, and will be Earl of Orkney and of Caithness when the time comes, whatever else the future may hold for him.

'There remain the three sons of my late brother. They are at Dunkeld, since to send them south now would defeat the purpose that prompted you to ask me, and not the men of Northumbria, to become lord of Alba.

'In two years' time, the eldest, Malcolm, will be twelve and the youngest, five. The future of the youngest might be best served by leaving him at Dunkeld. The abbacy is at present in his family, and may well fall to him one day. If, at the end of two years, the other two wish to leave, I do not mean to stop them. Today, you have made me King of Alba till my death: they have no claim on the throne until then. If they fall into the hands of another power, as they may well do, then at least this kingdom will have had two years to prepare, and to settle. I have to learn to know you, and you have to learn to know me. There is one last matter.'

His voice had changed, and the murmuring that had run round the room stopped. Thorfinn said, 'I spoke of justice. You enforce it among yourselves, and when your power fails, you call on the King's. To give us all security, I also must enforce it. When the army of Duncan my brother marched through Moray, the leaders, for their own ends, despoiled the country and slaughtered those who resisted. Most of those concerned have paid for these acts, but not all. I am told, by the men of Moray who are here, that two of these leaders have been seen on the Moot Hill and in this hall. Have them stand.'

Duftah said, 'What is he doing?' Tapped on the shoulder, two men in different parts of the hall rose slowly and stood, pressed awkwardly between bench and table and glancing round, anger on their faces.

Thorfinn said, 'Thank you. I am further told that since we began to gather here, a rising occurred in Fortriu, where two former henchmen of the late King gathered men from a hill-fort and launched an attack on the men of Moray as they set out to join me here. The leaders, it is said, are the same men.' For the last few moments, his gaze had moved only between the two standing there in their places. Now he said to each of them, 'Do you deny this?'

One was silent. The other said, 'He won't speak to a brother-killer, but I will. So would every man here, if he had the stomach for it. They may eat your food and stuff your gold in their purses, but do you think they want the kingdom of Malcolm and Duncan to lie under a Norse heathen who'll let in the hordes from the Frisian Sea to scour our grain-barns when the crops fail in Norway, and, when we can't pay the dues they wring from us, will land and burn us to the ground and carry our women off to get slaves on in Orkney? We all know what you are. They may lie down under you now, but you will need to keep your sword at your bedside from now on, and your place warm beside Odin in the next world, for neither Christ nor Christ's people want you in this.'

No one spoke, or breathed. Across the tables, Sulien saw how white Groa had become, and waited until, her eyes meeting his, she remembered her friends. The silence stretched on, while Thorfinn studied the man who had spoken and the man, breathing hard, stared back at his face. Then Thorfinn said, 'I do not think that all the men here believe as you do, or the oath they have each taken would go for nothing, and the God in whose name they made it. But if any man does, I say only this. If in the days to come, or in the years to come, I or any man in my charge behaves as you have described, then he is released from his oath and his allegiance, and free to end my rule in any way that he can. Indeed, if I were to act as you say, I could not survive.'

He paused. 'You have spoken, and I have heard you. Any man is free to speak, and for that you will not be punished. But your acts you must stand by, and for these you are now being judged. For the lives you took among your own people in Moray, and for your inciting of a rebellion on the eve of this assembly, you and your fellow must accept the due penalty, which is death. Take them out and behead them.'

Still no one spoke. No one moved, save a group of helmeted men who marched from the door and laid hands on the condemned men in silence.

There was a brief struggle, during which the spokesman again lifted his voice in a scream. 'You cowardly fools! Will you sit there and let him take me? He has sent his men north. There he is! Run at him!'

The guests at either side looked away. Along the tables, a man shifted on his bench, and then another, till each, finding himself alone, subsided and became very still. The howling of the two victims travelled along the hall and through the door, and dwindled, and stopped, with precision.

Be it courage, be it bravado, they had let him do it.

Sulien drew a long, shaking breath and saw Duftah's hand uncurl beside him. At the cross-table, Groa still sat immobile, her chin high in its swathes, her eyes open. And Thorfinn, standing unarmed beside her, lifted his eyes from the board and drew breath, slowly, to speak to his people.

His words never came. They were forestalled by a young, high voice calling in Norse from the furthest extent of the chamber.

'Uncle! Thorfinn, my dear disciple of Odin! Hardly the wand in your hand, and you have to teach your new vassals manners! If you need some help, there are men I could send for.'

Rognvald. Rognvald, whom Sulien had last seen carried drunk off a scarred Viking longship, among the wounded and the dead and the plunder. Rognvald, lovely as Baldur, with the golden hair lit by the sun from the doorway, and the blue eyes filled with hilarity, and in his uplifted arm a sword, down which a river of fresh blood was streaming, from the severed head stuck open-eyed on its point. The head of one of the two condemned men they had watched leave the hall a few moments before.

Of all those round the table, the King's nephew was known to no one except perhaps a few Moraymen, and few could understand what he said.

It hardly mattered. He spoke to the King familiarly in Norwegian, using the pagan style he had abandoned and the name of the god he had repudiated. No one could mistake that, or the cheerful contempt in his voice, or the triumph with which he held aloft the fresh-hewn head of one of their fellows.

The roar was in their throats when Thorfinn spoke: so quickly, in that immense, deep voice that was all he had of physical beauty, that it filled the hall before other sound could be heard. He said calmly, 'This is a cockerel from Norway who needs to be given a lesson. Take his sword, and what is on it.'

He was looking not at his own men who had returned panting to the doorway, but at the men sitting nearest to Rognvald. Realising it, they glanced at one another and then, as Rognvald angrily took a step backwards, threw themselves upon him, gripping him, while a third wrested the sword from his grasp, and its burden.

'What!' said Rognvald, and wrenched at the fists holding him. 'What are you doing?'

Thorfinn looked not at him, but at his own men. 'Punishment does not include indignity. Take what he brought in, and give it what burial the man's kindred would want. And since my nephew has lent a dead man his sword, it may as well furnish the living. Keep the Earl Rognvald's sword and send it to the dead toisech's family. As for the Earl Rognvald my nephew . . .'

They could hardly hold Rognvald now, so violent was his resistance, and there was blood by his mouth and the marks of handling springing red along his jaw and the tanned skin of his arms. He said, 'You are using me. You are using me to raise your credit with a herd of sheep-milking Irishmen.'

He had spoken in Gaelic. In bad Gaelic, but with some words there at least that men would understand.

Thorfinn answered him in the same tongue.

'With the wand newly in my hand, as you say, I am punishing misconduct in this realm, whether committed by a man who owes me allegiance or a man who is of the blood of my family.' He turned again to his men. 'Take him out and thrash him.'

'*What!*' said Rognvald.

Sitting still at the tables in their separate places were the two men who had half-risen when the sentence on the executed men had been passed. That Thorfinn had noticed it had been apparent to none. Now he turned and, looking from the one to the other, said quietly, 'It may seem to you that this order will not be carried out. I should be obliged, therefore, if you would both accompany my nephew and witness his punishment.'

They stood slowly, first one and then the other, as he was speaking. At the end, they glanced at each other and quickly away. Then the nearest said grimly, 'Yes, my lord King,' and, leaving the bench, walked to the door, pursued by his fellow. Rognvald stopped struggling.

He had never looked so to advantage, Sulien thought, as now, standing straight and slender and defiant, with his head flung back and his bruised arms at his sides, facing his uncle.

Rognvald said, 'You have thrown away Orkney for a straw-death among peasants.' And, turning, walked out, with armed men about him.

They watched him go, and then all the eyes in the hall returned to the cross-table.

'I suppose,' Thorfinn said, 'the making of a king is rarely done without pains. We seem today to have had more than our share. On the other hand, perhaps there are some things that it is better for all of us to know now, rather than later. I have confidence in you. I hope you will have cause to have some in me, in time to come. Meanwhile, there is food still on the tables, and wine to which, having listened to me, you may now feel you require to apply yourselves and which, having spoken, I am now happy to have served to you in whatever abundance you wish.'

He sat, at last. The rumble that answered him had the echoes of amusement in it, and did not die away, but altered to the sound men make when they are discussing matters too delicate to shout aloud but too momentous to leave to a better occasion. Then, as the wine went round without stint, louder talk came, and laughter, and normality, hesitating, settled in and took charge.

Sulien said, 'I want to be sick.'

'The trouble with you,' said Duftah cheerfully, 'is that you forget to pray.'

*   *   *

They left, most of them, before nightfall, but long before that, as was seemly, Groa had left the hall. She did not expect Thorfinn to come for a long time, and so stayed with Lulach and her women for a while before withdrawing to the inner chamber she shared with her husband. For two hours, she paced backwards and forwards, the breath from her night-robe stirring the brazier embers and bending the flames of the candles, until she heard his voice outside, and someone replying. Then the latch rattled and lifted.

Because she had learned to read the unreadable, she knew, as he stood with his back to the door, slowly pressing it shut, that at this moment she was not his wife, but one more person to face.

She had prepared, in two hours, the words that on this day she should speak to him, and the things she must do. Discarding them all, she said, 'The bed is there. Could you sleep?'

'Probably never again,' he said. It was meant, she thought, to be amusing. Latterly, he had taken off the silk robe: it would be at the monastery, with the wand and the gospels. Bound above his black brows he still wore the gold band, and would always wear it. He said, 'I have just come from Rognvald.'

With that said, she could not move. The inner eye of love knew that beyond him was a jar of wine, and a pitcher, and that he had drunk nothing as yet. She said, 'What happened?'

'He forgave me,' he said.

With irony? With thankfulness? It was impossible to tell. And, not knowing, what could she say? He understood, far better than she did, the implications of everything that had happened since the moment Rognvald walked into the hall. He knew Rognvald better than she did: he knew, as she did not, how close the links between Rognvald and himself might be, and how personal. There was nothing whatever she could say except, 'Once he came in, there was nothing else you could do.' And that he knew already. It was not that kind of reassurance he needed.

He must have been watching her. He said, 'You are longing to cross to that jar and make me as drunk as possible, as quickly as possible. But then I should have to forfeit my conjugal rights, and I am sure that would be bad for the kingdom. Doesn't the barley rot on the stalk, should the King of one day fail to display his fertility?'

'Then come here,' Groa said. Her body, listening, started to tremble.

He left the door. 'Where?' he said, and, lifting the robe, slipped it from her shoulders. His fingers also were unsteady, and his eyes, watching what they were doing, were more black than brown. He lifted his hands to the white, marbled globes of her breasts and cupped them, his fingers moving over the soft, darkened aureoles, over and over so that her bones melted.

Then, slowly, the caress stilled and Thorfinn looked up. 'Groa?'

She smiled, holding his eyes, but did not answer. His free hand, slipping gently downwards over her skin, reached her waist, and then her belly, and rested there.

'In a month,' she said, 'there may be something to see. It is a little early.'

He let both hands fall and stood back a little, so that the light from the candle fell on her face. 'The King's fertility,' he said, 'has already manifested itself?'

'In Tarbatness,' Groa said. 'I am awed. Since you were not present either through my first child-bearing or my second, how did you know what to look for?'

'There is no secret,' Thorfinn said. 'In every Norse camp, there are slave-girls who are carrying.' He drew a soft breath, quick as a gasp, and got rid of it. Then, moving forward again, he lifted his hands and settled her robe once more on her shoulders. 'Wine,' he said. 'Is it not an occasion for wine?'

Her thoughts on the unborn child, she was slow, this time, to read him. 'Sit,' she said; and as he threw himself down on the mattress, she crossed the small room and found two beakers and filled them. 'I suppose,' she said, her back turned, 'it will be a son again, since that seems to come easily to you. And you will name him Erlend as you wanted, after your great-great uncle, Skull-splitter's brother.'

She turned round, the wine in her hands, and then stopped. He still sat, elbows on knees, as she had left him, but now his two fists were raised to his brow, flesh rammed against flesh in immobile violence, his eyes shut, his lips open and rigid.

She set the cups down, and did not know what to do.

Without moving, he spoke. 'I am so thankful. It is news above any other I would have wished. It is only that I am tired.'

Then she said, 'Thorfinn!' quickly, and moved to him; but had hardly got to his side before he loosed his fingers and thumbs and plunged them down to the mattress like spear-points.

'No! Macbeth. Macbeth. *Macbeth!*' The name reached her like sling-shot.

Groa said, 'They are the same man. I should know. I married both.'

The candles flickered; and the aromatic twigs mewed in the brazier and dispatched a milk-blue twist of smoke to spiral between them. His eyes opened, and she thought, *What have I said that is as important as that?*

He rose; and when he spoke, it was after a long interval. 'Then . . . Whom you love, I should cherish,' he said. He came and stood before her, his face grave but no longer leaden. He touched her cheek, and then put his arms closely around her, drawing her head to his shoulder and brushing her hair with his lips.

'Be thou alone my heart's special love: let there be none else save the High King of Heaven. . . . It shall be Erlend. He was fathered by Thorfinn upon Groa and will be born to Macbeth and to Groa, who alone can make one man whole. Can you make me sleep without wine?'

'I can try,' she said.

THREE

MAN OF JUST over thirty might be held to be at the height of his
powers, but not necessarily of his wisdom. To acquire a kingdom of dissident peoples with no towns, no money, and a number
of different languages, with few and indifferent roads, and with
frontiers so vague that their demarcation virtually did not exist,
would have been a daunting task for a man of that country trained
for its kinghood.

That it was left to a man from the north was not a measure of the country's
despair, because the country had no voice to speak with. It was evidence only
that, of the assorted families who carried most weight in all the separate
corners of the kingdom, many had now lost their leaders; some were so placed
that one overlord was as good or as bad as another; and some, weary of
generations of coastal fighting, were prepared to place themselves in the
enemy's hand, provided he had a fleet and fighting-men to defend them.

Long before this, Sulien had thought of these things, because it was his
nature to look ahead, and he had accepted what Thorfinn would not accept:
that only Duncan's life stood between him and the throne. When he left
Ireland to go to Thorfinn at Kinrimund, it was in the face of black despair, for
he knew his own limits and thought, whatever he found, to face a country
destined for ruin and a man who would be his enemy henceforward.

It had not been like that, for, whatever disorder circumstances had brought
about in Thorfinn's life, it was not one of the intellect.

He would not make the decision whether or not to take the kingdom: not
until the last moment. But what he had done, with meticulous clarity, was to
think through what that decision, either way, would entail.

When Sulien found him, Thorfinn already knew what the greatest difficulties were, and what might be done to solve them. In the brief time they had
together after the fever broke, Sulien sat and asked questions, and Thorfinn
answered them.

From the bottom of his soul, Sulien believed in the Most High; and he saw
this as God's will, that a man, whatever his blood, brought up to be a
warrior-merchant of the north, should stop to turn every gift to preparing

himself for such a burden, should the charge be vouchshafed him or not.

But it had been allowed him; and before he left, late that autumn, Sulien saw come to pass all the things that Thorfinn had spoken of, lying there in the Bishop's house, with Alfgar, with Crinan hammering at his doors and requiring to be dealt with.

'About Alfgar. If there is an enthronement, then it will have to be quick and simple, and even then there will probably be trouble. So, no eminent visitors. We send them a messenger later with the news that a new King has been proclaimed, together with some expensive trifle.'

'And Crinan?' Sulien had asked.

'The boys would have to stay at Dunkeld, and Crinan at Alston. There is no reason why he couldn't remain officially Abbot, and his rents would be collected on his behalf and used to maintain his grandsons. After Malcolm was old enough, one would have to think again. But he couldn't be allowed into Dunkeld at first. In any case, Dunkeld would be useful. I would bring some of the ships down to the Tay.'

'The Bishop of Alba?'

'Poor Cousin Malduin. He would have to come back for the king-making, and I should have to ask the new Abbot of Kells to come over. You will have heard that neither Crinan's house nor Duftah's was successful in the election, but that won't stop the abbots from making war on one another. Kells and Downpatrick have been burned already. I suppose one of the lessons the Irish church learned from the Vikings was that you can set fire to altars and the Trinity pays no attention.'

'I think—' Sulien had begun.

'That I should spare you such blasphemy. Very well. Bishop Malduin is a liability, but I couldn't dismiss him without stirring up trouble over Lothian and the St Cuthbert's churches, which I couldn't yet afford to do. So he would stay, but in Alba, not Durham, and would be kept on a very short tether.'

'There are some holy men you can trust,' had said Sulien. 'You talked once of the Culdees. There are Irish monks like them all over the Rhineland, all with friends accustomed to trade.'

'I thought of it,' Thorfinn said. 'A carrying-trade might be possible. There is no surplus that I can see to support anything else.'

'Then what about these?' Sulien had said. The coins of Sitric, Eachmarcach's uncle, were not quite the Byzantine replicas that Sitric had aimed at, and you would guess from the spread hands on either side of the alarmed silver face that the pendicles of the Ottoman crown had unexpectedly puzzled the die-maker. But it was coinage, the mark of a civilised country.

Thorfinn had picked one up and flipped it. 'It must make Crinan weep for his profession. But at least it's their own. We use other folks' silver up north; you know that. You need money when you hire mercenaries or when you pay off attackers.

'Duncan got Irish troops to come over for silver, and for what they could get out of it: he possibly promised them tracts of Moray and Angus, once they had got rid of me and a few of the toisechs. But I couldn't call in the Irish, except the Irish of Dublin, and I wouldn't call in anyone else. So, to begin with, everything I did would have to be paid for by my own trading in the north, in the ships that the people of the north build and furnish for me. The rest of the country would have to keep me in food-rents, together with as much of a hird as they will let me have, and enough stored to sustain men on campaign and exchange for their fighting-equipment. Under no circumstances,' Thorfinn had said, 'would it appear that we are likely to indulge in the sins of the rich.'

'You spoke of the hird,' Sulien said.

'It would need another name. For the first winter, I should have to stay in the south and have none of my own men about me. Thorkel Fóstri, of course, will keep Caithness, and Moray has managed fairly well so far with the leaders I gave it, under Groa. Lulach should go there now and begin to learn his trade, whatever happens. No. The difficult part would be drawing together the courtmen of Alba when it has never been the custom for men to leave their families and their farms except for battle. It may be impossible. I might not be able to feed and maintain a household such as that. They may not have slave-labour or rents enough to let them leave the land and engage in affairs. I might be able to do no more than move between Glamis and Forteviot and Perth and Kinrimund and the rest, as old Malcolm did, using my own family as my officers.'

'That way,' had said Sulien, 'you would be less of a burden where you happened to stay. That way, few people who mattered would know what you were doing until you had done it.'

'That is the way Malcolm ruled,' Thorfinn said. 'And Duncan. And they could not hold what they had.'

'Because they ruled alone, without the protection of the hird?' Sulien said. It was unfair. But he had to find out.

'You are changing your ground,' Thorfinn said. 'But I suppose I have to answer, if I am to pass whatever test you are setting me. In a country as far-flung as this, they could not know the minds of their district leaders, or carry them in their own policies, unless they talked together and saw each other more often than the winter weather and the bad roads allow. In Orkney, it is easy: we are all within reach of each other in winter-time, and all at home. Even in Caithness, people come for the feasts and stay many months, and then there is the companionship on the sea.

'The bonds welded there make it easy to know whom to trust, and men do not often move from faction to faction, but stay with their kinsmen and those whom they know. Before the men of Alba could face a common enemy, they must know each other, and how long will that take, unless they are helped? The men of Lothian don't even speak the same tongue as the men of Fife over the estuary, and the men of Cumbria and Strathclyde are different from both.'

'And beyond Moray, different again,' Sulien said, and waited, but when Thorfinn continued, it was on another tack. And soon the discussion had ended.

The name of Rognvald had never been spoken at any time on that occasion. Then the time came when the enthronement was over and the chiefs of Alba, what was left of them, had ridden thoughtfully away, and Sulien found, going to the pavilion of Rognvald, Earl of Orkney, that there was nothing there but flattened grass and dead embers.

As with Groa, the scene in the hall the previous day had filled the Breton with horror. Unlike Groa, he could at least do something about it. As soon as the tables were drawn and the leave-taking over and the hall freed of all the concourse that had filled it, Sulien had hurried out to find Rognvald and had found instead the newly made King standing in front of him. 'If you are seeking the brilliant Rognvald, I am told that he is in his pavilion. If you wish to come, I am about to go and see him.'

And so Sulien witnessed the scene, the essence of which Thorfinn was to describe in three words, with perfect accuracy, later that night to his wife.

And indeed there was nothing more to say of it, unless you told of the smell, which was that of a flesher's stall, or the sight of the straight-nosed, delicate profile sunk in the pillow, its skin bruised and stained under the disordered gold hair. And below that, the shoulders and back, pink and red, with the margins still crossed like reed-shadows with fine scarlet lines.

There were cloths on a board, and a bowl of red water, and a phial of ointment, and a man in a black gown who drew back, and a group of men in the kind of tunic Thorfinn himself wore at sea who did not draw back, although one of their number said softly, 'My lord Rognvald. King Macbeth has come to speak with you.'

And Rognvald had opened one swollen eye and looked up, a little, at the dark face of his uncle towering over him.

For a long time, they gazed at each other, until the corner of one red lip curled and a golden eyebrow lifted in raillery. 'Tell King Macbeth,' said Rognvald, 'that, naturally, I forgive him.'

That was all. And next day, he had gone.

At last the thirty-ninth Abbot of Kells and Raphoe departed, with his great train, weighed down with gifts. Sulien did not ask him how he would make his way back to Ireland, nor what part he would play or had played in Duncan's funeral obsequies, in Elgin or Iona. Thorfinn had said nothing of Duncan, although Lulach, walking with him one day, had suddenly said, 'If Donwald and his wife killed the King, why do they blame my stepfather?'

Sulien stopped. 'There was a Donwald,' he said. 'But he and his wife killed Malcolm Duff. Another king. Not King Duncan.'

'Duncan, King of Cumbria,' Lulach said. 'I could have told you that when I was Simeon. There never was a King Duncan in Alba.'

'Now you are back,' Sulien said, 'I want your stepfather to have peace. He has much to his hand.'

'If he wanted peace, he would have chosen it,' Lulach said. 'What is peace? When a wicked man dies, those who are left behind enjoy peace. St Moluag never killed a living thing, and when he died, the birds wept.'

Sulien left for Ireland just before Yule, and the King did not try to restrain him. 'Go back, then, to your skin hoops and whelk shells,' he said. 'And leave me to my board games.'

'Am I so transparent?' Sulien said. 'You should take heart that I am leaving you.'

'You are satisfied that this is not merely a board game?'

'I know what it is better than you do. It is the black gosling seeking the black goose,' Sulien said. 'And there will be no peace for you or for any of us until you find her.'

With the profusion of youth and the purse of a man who has just raised £34,000 in taxes, Hardecanute, King of England and Denmark, proclaimed that his hird in future would be fed four times daily from his tables instead of once, as was usual. Thus rendering himself secure for the moment, he left them behind him and, taking only a small retinue of a dozen, rode to Winchester to visit his mother Emma, the Flower of Normandy.

At fifty-nine, the Lady Emma was no longer quite the ravishing heiress who had married King Aethelred of England, or even the beautiful woman who fifteen years later had married the late King Canute of Denmark, who with his father had by that time conquered England. Nor had her three years of exile in Flanders brought back those years of imposing beauty. Handsome, however, she remained, with her big frame and strong, regular features. Handsome and intelligent. Intelligent and powerful. Powerful and perfectly ruthless.

Hardecanute entered the room and she said, 'I hear you have been buying the smiles of your hird with the grain-barns and byres of your subjects. How old are you?'

He kept smiling. 'Twenty-two, lady mother.'

'If you want to eat four times a day, stuff yourself in a chamber. Do it for your men and they will take you for a fool. What's this news about Northumbria?'

'But you have to tell me how you are. Your leg. How is your leg? Is it better?'

'It is the same as it usually is. You may sit down, if that is what you are after. Now. What about Eadulf?'

Hardecanute sat, with relief. 'There have been several quite reliable reports. He has been negotiating alliances in the hope of adding Cumbria to his own lands.'

'Negotiating? Who with? Your father's mint-master? Crinan?'

'No. With the new King you were so pleased about. Thorfinn. Macbeth. What did he send you? He sent me a dagger. Look. German-made.'

'He sent me a reliquary. Never mind that. Earl Eadulf went to Alba to see the new King Thorfinn-Macbeth? When?'

'Not himself. He sent the Bishop of Alba. Macbeth sent him back with a refusal, and then invited the Bishop to come back for the crowning. He's still there, they say.'

'Not the crowning. They don't have a crowning,' the Lady said. To correct was automatic. 'The Bishop would go for the ritual anyway. It doesn't mean that the new King has given up Cumbria.'

'Whether he has given it up or not,' Hardecanute said, 'it looks as if Eadulf is preparing to take it. We could raise enough men in the north to stop it. The Mercians would help.'

'Four meals a day! You would think men and spears sat about in tithe-barns as well,' the Lady said. 'There is no need to be wasteful. Send to Earl Siward at York. You know Earl Siward?'

'The Norwegian? His father held Huntingdon,' Hardecanute said boldly.

He had been lucky and got it right. His mother said, 'He is connected by marriage with the Arnason tribe. His father helped to kill King Olaf: the family will never go back to Norway now. But, principally, the man Siward has married one of the five nieces of Eadulf and so has quite a legitimate claim on Northumbria himself. If Earl Eadulf were to resign the vital breath in the near future.'

As always, Hardecanute felt hollow in the presence of his mother. He thought of something to say. 'You wouldn't mind an alliance between Siward and this new Macbeth?'

'An alliance? They are Vikings. They will face each other, snarling and snapping, one would confidently hope, for many years. And meanwhile the prospect of Earl Eadulf in possession of the whole of northern England is not one that I could entertain, on your behalf or my own. Is this all sufficiently clear, my son? Do you understand me?' said the Lady.

'Of course,' he said. 'I see now that your idea is an excellent one. I shall put it into effect as soon as orders can be issued.' His chest heaved, and he coughed.

'You have coughed before,' his mother said. 'It is a sign of weakness. Control it. I shall have a posset made up and sent to you.'

'Yes, mother,' he said.

The winter passed, and people thought it good riddance; it had been an unlucky twelvemonth for weather, with poor grapes abroad and the prospect of sour wine at home; and wheat had gone up to fifty-five pence a sester, for those who were so great that they had to buy it.

With the first spring wind from Norway, Kalv Arnason sailed to Freswick and called, as he had been wont to do years before, on his good cousin Thorkel, foster-father of the new King of Alba.

He came in a single ship, for it was not a trading-voyage. With resignation, Thorkel listened to the women cackling overhead, crowding the loft window, and then the shouts of his men as they ran round from the strip-fields over the beach. It was Kalv's banner, there was no doubt about that; and he had put out the red-and-black shields for coming into the beach, so that they could get the pork, if they had any, over the roasting-fire and hang their axes back up on the wall.

At forty-six, one did not go running down to the jetty for a man who was five years younger, even though the years had put no more on his belly than on

Kalv's, as Thorkel observed with faint regret. The trim, agile figure of his cousin was the same, and the neat auburn hair and the sympathetic blue eyes with the merest trace of sauciness still remaining, after all that had happened, in the corners.

'Well!' said Kalv from the doorway. 'Do you work hard enough at a patch, it will produce a good crop in the end, as they say. And how does it suit you to have your finger on the golden *skid-sledi* of one of the kings of the Western world? What has your foster-son Thorfinn taken out of his treasure-chest and given you, since you put him on his throne? I seem to see nothing here but the old bowls and hangings. Are you saving the silk and the gold for a visit from the Emperor's longship?'

'I don't know how it is,' Thorkel said, 'but I can always tell when things are going badly with you. Come in and sit down and have some cheap wine in an old wooden cup. Then you will feel better.'

When the story came, in due course, it was much as he expected. Now fully sixteen, King Magnús of Norway no longer had need of a regent, and had taken to going about with men of his own choice. Kalv was being neglected. He was no longer even quite so confident of the amnesty Magnús had proclaimed on his return from Russia those four years since.

'What are you saying?' Thorkel Fóstri said patiently. 'You have just been complaining that Einar Tambarskelve stands higher in Magnús's favour than you do, and he gave as many promises to King Canute as anyone.'

'It's true he didn't support King Olaf at the Holy River battle,' Kalv said, leaning his chin on his hand and frowning. 'But he didn't swing the blade that killed King Olaf either.'

'This is nonsense,' said Thorkel. The girl who had just come in with the platters was the prettiest slave he happened to have, and not really thickening yet. He signed to her to serve Kalv and make a fuss of him. He said, 'What's wrong with your brother Finn? Why can't he help you? He stayed with King Olaf through thick and thin: the King must owe him something.'

'You might think so,' said Kalv. 'Although Finn is not getting any younger, and there are some days when he is not sure whether it is a cow on the beach or two stout men lifting a cooking-pot. The mistake poor Finn made was to marry his daughter to your foster-son.'

Thorkel leaned back. 'What's wrong? Thorfinn paid his scatt for Orkney, and so does Macbeth. With Rognvald there, King Magnús surely has no fears for the islands.'

'Ah, Rognvald,' Kalv said. 'Well, you know how Rognvald is dear to King Magnús. I won't say they shared a bed on the way home from Russia, but no doubt it would have come to that. Is that girl bearing to you? I don't know how it is with you, but two days at sea is a long time.'

'When you've finished talking, you can have her,' said Thorkel. 'About Rognvald. Go on.'

The girl walked out, and Kalv wiped a hand on his side and stretched for his cup. 'Everyone has heard what happened, of course, at the enthronement. I've just come from Orkney. King Magnús wanted to know how things were.'

'And how were they?' said Thorkel. He had heard: he was well in control of his third of Orkney. But he wanted to know what tale Kalv would take home.

'Oh, I was lucky to see Rognvald at all,' Kalv replied. 'He was just going aboard for the spring sailing—to the western isles, he said. He was quite himself, too: laughing and joking. He said he had grown tired waiting for his uncle to get off his throne and come sailing at the usual time, and if he forgot sometimes which were his rents and which were King Macbeth's, the King could not blame him.'

He paused, shooting a glance at Thorkel from the pellucid blue eyes. 'He has got a new dog, called Sam after the one Olaf the Peacock gave to Gunnor, and has taught it this trick. He says *Thorfinn* to its face, and the dog replies by snarling and barking. Arnór Jarlaskáld has made some new verses about it.' He broke off, a little abruptly.

Thorkel knew what Arnór wanted of Rognvald. He said, 'And you think King Magnús will punish you for that?'

'For that and what my nephew Siward has done,' Kalv said. 'Thore Hund's son. I brought him here once. You remember.'

The hulking youth who had stretched out with his heels on his father's furs, and had followed his father to lucrative exile at the time his father, with Kalv, had killed King Olaf.

'What has Siward done?' Thorkel asked. He did not relish the kind of news Kalv always brought.

'Nothing to benefit you or me,' Kalv replied. 'He has killed his wife's uncle. Eadulf, the Earl of Northumbria. Killed him, and taken Northumbria in his place, with Hardecanute's full blessing. Now he has York under his hand, and his wife's sister's husband in Durham and Bamburgh, and, now Eadmund of Durham is going, the gift of the bishopric to dispose of, to the highest bidder, or the most convenient one. He has brought his other woman back and, for all I know, is preparing to install a third one. At first, King Magnús hardly knew what to think; and then Einar Tambarskelve told him. Now he knows it was a plot.'

'A plot?' said Thorkel Fóstri.

'Between my nephew Siward and my niece Ingibjorg-Groa,' said Kalv. 'To take over the country from the Orkneys down to the Humber, pushing out Rognvald. A joint rule between Siward and Thorfinn his cousin by marriage.'

'Macbeth,' said Thorkel automatically. He said, 'It isn't true, but I suppose it is no good just saying so. But consider, at least. If there had been the slightest risk of that happening, Hardecanute would never have allowed Siward to take over Northumbria.'

'Could he have stopped him?' said Kalv.

'Yes, he could. In the same way as Thorfinn . . . as Macbeth will stop Siward if he so much as trails the thong of his boot on land that wasn't Eadulf's before.'

He swung his legs over the bench and clapped Kalv on the shoulder. 'It won't happen, and when he sees there's no danger, King Magnús will forget he ever worried about it. Meanwhile, what else do you want? You have a good wife, and a rich farm, and a girl over there, waiting for you. Or had you forgotten about her?'

He had. He stared out of the open door at the swept yard, and the river glittering in the sunshine, and the houses of Thorkel's kinsfolk and his serfs, and the farms that stood here and there over the bay, and at his own ship tied to its post on the sand, with the sea-edge like white tortoise-shell running layering in.

It was a good bay, although open to the weather, as his fjord at home was not. On the other hand, there was always Canisbay and the long sands to the east, or Thurso, if the wind blew another way. He said, 'And where will Thorfinn . . . Where will Macbeth look for a chief lenderman in Caithness and Orkney when you have stormed into the arms of the Aesir?'

'To his family,' said Thorkel agreeably. 'A stepson and a son, with another on the way. Indeed, unless the girl you saw has caught your particular fancy, I see I ought to set her aside and pick you another. I have done my share towards supplying the hird of the future, but you are right: I should not risk marring her business. Who knows what need there will be for good men in Caithness and Orkney in times to come?'

There was a middle-aged woman he was quite fond of, whom he brought out instead, and indeed the way Kalv led her off, anything else would have been an extravagance. And if his own girl was disappointed, she had the sense not to show it.

Erlend, the son sired by Thorfinn but born to Macbeth, arrived at the King's house at Forteviot, just south of Perth, where his father had lived for a month awaiting that moment by the side of his wife; and not, as on another occasion, behind the walls of a hill-fort.

This time, the birth was easy, for the child was not large, but middle-sized and wiry, with a loud voice that was heard right away. As soon as it was seen that it was a son, Thorfinn let it be told what name it would be known by.

To all but Groa, the choice seemed at first an eccentric one. Erlend son of Earl Einar of Orkney had fought and died some sixty years before this, at the side of Earl Erik Bloodaxe. It was no name for a Christian king.

Second thoughts demonstrated that therein lay the grounds for its choosing. It was not the name of a Christian king, but the name of a future joint Earl of Orkney. Whatever the future might hold for him, the christening water was claiming no kingdoms.

Like his stepbrother Lulach in Moray, like his brother Sigurd in the nursery, he offered no provocation and should have no rivals of Alba breathing over his shoulder. It was a clever choice, men said, and showed that the new King carried Norse wits at least where his Celtic heart ought to be.

So said all but Groa, who had remembered that the name Erlend means *Foreigner*.

Kneeling by the bed, Thorfinn said, 'He is a *sglumach*. Do you know what that means? A fine fledgling.'

'Indeed!' said Groa. 'I thought it was less complimentary.'

He looked the better, she thought, for the enforced stay of the last few weeks. Until it became too hard for her, they had moved incessantly in the seven months that had passed since the enthronement: from Glamis to Perth to Inchaffray; from Forteviot to Kinrimund; from Monifieth to Loch Ore or Loch Leven, where their hall was on an island, next to the new island-monastery of the Culdees. And gradually men were coming about him, and not only their servants and Eochaid, her former clerk who acted as house-priest, or the toisechs who knew him from Moray.

A singer had been found who could make verse in the Irish style, because in no way at all could Arnór Jarlaskáld be brought to a sense of what was required. Down from Caithness and Orkney floated the verse he was making already, in praise of his master:

> *'The Man of the Sword,*
> *Seeking Scotland's throne,*
> *Ever won victory.*
> *Fire flamed fiercely,*
> *Fast fell the Irish host,*
> *And flower of Welsh manhood.'*

So sang Arnór:

> *'Humbled the homesteads,*
> *Burning in Alba.*
> *Red flame from smoking thatch*
> *Shot high; for that day*
> *Dire danger failed not . . .'*

If ever a skald wrote himself out of office, it was Arnór.

And now Arnór was with Rognvald. Thinking of it, she was moved to speak to her husband as he watched the child in her arms. 'That was the first winter you have ever spent out of Orkney. This is the first spring you have never taken your longship to sea. How do you feel?'

'Deprived,' he said. The infant had closed a fist round one of his fingers, and he left it there.

After a moment, it must have occurred to him that she might take him seriously, and he looked up. But she was smiling.

With infinite care, he held that year to the course he had laid out for himself, accepting the news about Orkney, accepting the formidable change in Northumbria and moving slowly onwards, having embraced them as best he might in his plans, as tree-wood might grow over a canker.

He thought to have the better part of two years before both Crinan and Siward became restive, and he had to attend to Lothian and to Cumbria and prepare for the moment when Duncan's sons left his grasp.

At no time had he been under any illusions about that. He either killed them or he released them to go wherever they wished, when the eldest was of age. He had been to Dunkeld once to see them, and to satisfy himself that they were being well taken care of by the monks and the lay men and women who served the monastery.

He had found Malcolm a ready talker, fresh-faced and brown-haired like his father, with the promise of stocky power behind the skinny awkwardness of an eleven-year-old. Donald, at nine, was fair and sullen, and Maelmuire at five, more interested in a ball he wanted to play with than a man his nurse called *the King*, but who turned out not to be his father.

Malcolm talked and laughed, his eyes flickering; and it was easy to see that he knew just who this King was and what he had to do with his father. By questioning, his uncle found that he would like a bigger horse, and a helmet, and not to have to eat seal-meat and blood-puddings.

His uncle, who had well-defined views about bribery, agreed to the necessity for a horse, indicated that he would have to earn the helmet by good behaviour, and said that he did not often eat seal-meat himself, unless there was no other choice, but he had an uncle who did so frequently when taking part in a seal-hunt and had even been known to try bear-flesh.

As for blood-sausages, they were a favourite tit-bit among Icelanders, and he supposed that you would be glad of them if there came a bad year for the hay and the grazing and there was little else to do but slaughter what you had and eat it down to the toes and the tail. 'In Alba,' he had said, 'that is not necessary, nor in Caithness or Moray or Orkney.' Then Malcolm had asked, with animation, to hear about seal-hunts.

'Poor boy,' Groa had said when she heard. 'He knows, of course, that his father set out to attack you, and died as a result. You won't overcome that in a moment. Loyalty alone would forbid it. In any case, he probably thought you would come in with an axe and make ropes of them.'

And Thorfinn had replied, 'Certainly I felt he entertained a few doubts about the nature and extent of my upbringing. His family are a difficult lot. There was the Fair in Mag Muirthemni, to which the Ulstermen would bring in their wallets the tongue of every man they had killed. After that, why object to a blood-sausage?'

'Would you like me to visit him?' Groa had said. 'Or Lulach? There is a year between them, but Lulach would be careful.' She did not need to add, 'And he is not your son but Gillacomghain's.'

'I feel,' said Thorfinn, 'that Lulach would only confuse the issue. No. There is no remedy. You could read in their eyes what Duncan has said of me. You could see in Malcolm's face that he already saw himself King, and a better one than his father. They have nothing to cling to but hatred.'

'Until Crinan gets hold of them. Or Siward,' Groa had said.

'Crinan is a man in his sixties whose business is finance, not leading war-bands on behalf of children,' Thorfinn had said. 'As for Siward, he has taken Northumbria, but I don't see him issuing any challenges to Harde-canute as yet. He has to set about making Eadulf's shoes fit him first. And, however wealthy he might be, he can't be as rich as Emma. She will keep him in check.

'We have a year. We have at least a year to find our own feet in Alba before anything happens.'

They had less than a year. That autumn, when the coughing would keep him walking the floor every night, and blood ran coiling into his ale-cup, King Hardecanute went to see his mother at Winchester.

A day later, the Lady Emma summoned her closest friend in the world, Bishop Aelfwin, and directed him to carry certain messages to her middle-aged half-Saxon son Edward in Normandy.

The Bishop returned; and in due course another embassy left Winchester, this time of a much more imposing sort, and carrying with it the younger sons of a number of people hoping for continued favours from the Lady, who were left as hostages with the hosts of her son Edward. And when that deputation returned, it brought with it Edward himself, Hardecanute's half-brother, with a retinue which of design was not large but which consisted entirely of young, strong, bright-eyed Normans.

In June 1042, King Hardecanute died, aged twenty-four: the last of King Canute's family. And Emma's sole remaining son Edward, from dividing the glory and wealth of England with his half-brother, was left King of England, with no other rival.

For some days, the Lady Emma received no one. Then she sent for and kissed her son Edward, and gave him a ring, which he later had valued, and presented rolls of cloth to Ralph her grandson and to her nephew Osbern, who had come from Normandy with him.

To Bishop Aelfwin, who had stood behind her chair throughout, she gave the head of St Valentine, for her dear son Hardecanute's redemption.

'What now?' said Groa.

'Now,' said the King of Alba, 'I go sailing with Rognvald.'

FOUR

T HORFINN!' SAID ROGNVALD; and his dog Sam, which was of the small kind that kills rats and frequents badger-holes, barked and barked.

'That is,' said Rognvald, 'my lord King, you are welcome. The lack of ceremony I must apologise for. It crossed my mind, when I saw the dragon, that it was Thorkel Fóstri again, with his sour, miserly face, come to nudge my beam in case I collect the wrong rents. But I see it is yourself.' He looked down and Arnór Jarlaskáld, within his arm, looked up and smiled. Rognvald said, 'Or perhaps you have come to ask me to take care of your third of Orkney? We all notice you have little time for it now.'

Although he had spoken of lack of ceremony, there were forty men standing around him on the beach-head, and he had raised his voice just a little so that all he said could be heard.

The King his uncle did not interrupt him. Behind Thorfinn on the jetty stood only Starkad his standard-bearer, although there were others in the skiff that still bumped in the water. The longship he had come by stood off in deeper water. This time, it was not *Grágás*, but the great dragon presented by Canute, its shields and banner announcing beyond all doubt the presence of the King of Alba. When Rognvald had finished, the King said, 'I have my own rents to collect, and thought we might sail in company. Also, there is some trouble in Kintyre and Galloway where Eachmarcach's brother's son seems to have forgotten whose land it is. I have promised to call for Eachmarcach on Man and see what can be done about it.'

'With one ship?' said Rognvald. 'I have to tell you, my uncle, that if you are asking me or my men to come and help you, it would seem that you presume a little too much on the warm feeling I have for you.'

'I have eight more ships waiting off Saviskaill,' said the King. 'Do you wish to come? I should like to leave on the next tide.'

Rognvald dropped his arm, and beside him Arnór stood looking from one of his masters to the other. On Thorfinn's face nothing could be read, and Starkad behind was as impassive. But in the skiff, the faces watched, grinning and eager: Orkney and Caithness faces known to them all.

Thorfinn's men, then, would still fight for him. And if he, Rognvald, took every ship he could spare, he would still be outnumbered.

Rognvald smiled. 'How well you know me,' he said. 'Of course I will come, provided there is a proper agreement about the booty.'

'I thought I told you,' said the King. 'We are rent-collecting.'

'Of course,' said Rognvald. 'But I am sure Eachmarcach's brother's son has some goods that don't belong to him and that he isn't likely to have need of very soon; and there might even be some men of Diarmaid's about with a ship or two low in the water: I hear he has made himself King of Leinster at last. There is only one matter that pains me.'

'Yes?' said the King.

'There is the dog. He has just got into my ways, and I shall have to leave him behind. Or, as you see, he would kill himself barking at vermin. You will come to the hall? And your *merkismaðr?*'

'Why not? *Guð borgar fyrir hrafninn*: God pays for the Raven, they say. It is only fair that you should find the price of the ale. Arnór, what verse have you been making?'

Arnór opened his mouth.

'Indeed,' Rognvald said, 'up to this moment I have to tell you that he has been too busy to put nail to harp-string. But now, perhaps, that will change.' And, laying his slender hand on the King's arm, he walked him up the slope to the hall.

After three weeks, Groa could bear it no longer and, taking Lulach with her, set sail from the Tay to Caithness, where she joined Thorkel Fóstri at Canisbay.

Thorkel Fóstri was angry with her. 'What are you afraid of? If Norway is going to push its claim to Denmark and to England, now that Hardecanute is dead, it will need all the friends it can make. Magnús isn't going to fall out with a man who is not only King of Alba but holds Caithness and a third of the Orkneys as well. And Rognvald is too shrewd to cross Magnús.'

'That is not what I am afraid of,' said Groa flatly. 'Although I think you are wrong. It's my belief that when Rognvald looks at Thorfinn, he sees neither a king nor a kinsman, but a man two years older than himself by whose orders he was publicly thrashed. And what Magnús wishes or does not wish is not likely to enter his thoughts.'

Thorkel Fóstri stood, his arms folded, and looked at her. 'Rognvald never forgets what King Magnús wishes,' he said. 'But if not that, what do you fear? The fighting? Thorfinn is a master, and he doesn't let his skills rest between battles: they cost him too much. Or . . .' He hesitated, and then evidently decided to speak. 'Or is it Rognvald himself? There is nothing you need fear there, now.'

Now. She said, 'It seems I am being foolish. But I should like, now that I am here, to wait for the ships coming back. Lulach does not know Caithness or Orkney.'

Thorkel Fóstri hesitated again. Then he said, 'The King said, if you came, that I was to ask you not to make the journey to Orkney. He will explain, he said.'

She smiled and nodded and walked away slowly, leaving him to his embarrassment. The dear and prescient lover or the clear-sighted King: one or other had guessed what she would do, and probably why. She would not go to Orkney.

After that, the wait was a long one, but she did not waste her time. From Thorkel Fóstri she borrowed half a dozen of his shaggy, big-headed garrons, and with these and one of her younger women, and sometimes with Lulach, she rode from one group of steadings to the next along the coast, and sat with the womenfolk, and walked out with the children to the shore.

East towards Duncansby, she stood on the broken, glittering shell-sand, white and lilac, of Sannick Bay and spoke of the ailments of geese, and the making of tallow from sheep-fat, while the fulmars rose and fell with motionless wings in the salt airs round Duncansby Head, and she thought of another grey goose, but did not speak of it.

They were repairing fish-nets at Huna, beside the grooved block of slate where the fish-hooks and the needles were rubbed, and the knives and swords, at a pinch, to keep them brilliant. At Huna, she stood with her back to a hurdle of dark trunks of seaweed and looked at the long dolphin shape of the island of Stroma, with white spray breaking and breaking under its neck, to the east. But she did not ask to be taken over, for the steward of Stroma was an Orkney man.

Then she rode west to where the biggest headland of all stood dark red against the afternoon sky, and set her pony up round the lochans and bogs to the top, where she tied it to a rock and climbed to where the pony could not go but a man or a woman could lean on the wind as into the bosom of God and look upon the whole sunlit world of green grass and blue sea, from the land's edge that lay towards Norway to the smudged snow-capped peak of Ben Loyal, far to the west, pointing to the way her husband's ships had sailed.

There was nothing now on the sea but a trio of fishing-boats, and a wide merchantman hurrying west, and the birds. And to the north, Hoy and Stroma and Ronaldsay, of the forbidden Orkneys.

Her skirts jerked and tugged and the wind boxed her ears with soft woollen hands while her hair wrapped itself round her throat. She pulled her shawl over her head and forced her way down and back to her garron.

Below the headland was the beach the fleet most often used, and she took Lulach there, where, two miles long, the olive-brown wave-shadows moved in, one after the other, towards the unbroken sheen of the sand.

That night, in the field, helping Lulach lift the saddle from the wide, unkempt back of his garron, Thorkel Fóstri said, 'Luloecen, I would ask you something.'

The white head came up, and the clear eyes. 'Luloecen?'

They were alone. Thorkel Fóstri stood with the saddle between them and said, 'What did you say to your stepfather? What did you tell him that brought the King and your mother together?'

The pale eyes were steady. Lulach smiled. 'They were married,' he said.

'He had to have children,' Thorkel said. 'You made him your prophecy, and he knew what he must do, and what he must not do. Then, at Tarbatness, he allowed this to happen. Why?'

'Can't you guess? I told everyone,' Lulach said, 'when I was Snorri. I told him her destiny. He is a great man, but only a man.'

'What did you tell him?' said Thorkel, and started back as the boy snatched the saddle from his arms and, hugging it, circled him.

'It's written,' said Lulach. 'But you cannot read, can you?'

Next day, the sun-signals began to run all along the coast from the west to tell that the Earl's fleet had been sighted, and by afternoon all the King's friends were in Thurso, waiting. Those folk who ran out to the headland saw the longships approaching in convoy: fourteen coming in where fourteen had set out; and then the five ships of Earl Rognvald altering sail to make for the east mainland of Orkney.

The rest turned for the beach, and the rivermouth.

Four years ago, Thorkel Fóstri had let Lulach go down to the wharf for this sort of home-coming, and Lulach had watched the Earls come drunken home and had been present at the encounter afterwards, whatever it was, that had ended in Sulien's departure.

This time, leaving both the Lady and Lulach in the hall, Thorfinn's foster-father went down to the shore himself to see the King's dragon come to her dock.

This time, there was a difference, of course. She had been away for little more than a month, not for a season. She had been, in the main, collecting her dues from those lands in the west which owed tribute, therefore she and her fellows were little marked, although a sharp eye could see a hack or two that had not been there before.

But the chief difference lay in her mode of arrival. To commands that hardly carried over the water, her sails dropped. As she rowed her way into the rivermouth, with the same regulated efficiency, the larboard oars lifted as she slid to her berthing. The decks were clear of clutter, and the men, when the plank was down and they began to lift their boxes ashore, shouting and talking, were the leave-taking crewmen of a royal fighting-ship, not a horde lurching home from its viking.

The King came down the plank quite soon, talking to someone. His helmet under his arm was sea-tarnished and his open hide jacket stained with salt, but otherwise he could have stepped straight to a council-board, you would say. Then he turned to Thorkel Fóstri, and his foster-father saw how his brown skin glowed, and how the clear, far-sighted look had returned, so familiar that he had never realised until this moment that it had been missing. The King said, 'We have lost no one, not even Rognvald, and have had a successful voyage. The Lady is here?'

'With Lulach. In the hall,' Thorkel Fóstri said. 'Before you go in, I have news for you.'

'Well?' said the King.

It was not easy to speak. As the ships emptied, those whose steadings were here, over the beach, or along the riverside set off whistling for home; but the rest were already making their way to the hall, where by custom the home-coming feast would be spread, with their hands sluiced and their beards combed and their boxes on their backs, to put where they could see them.

Thorkel Fóstri said in a low voice, 'Word came this morning from Dunkeld. A trader sailed up the Tay to do business at Perth, or so he claimed. He landed a force somewhere out of sight. They marched to the monastery, and forced the gates, and took away Duncan's two older sons, Malcolm and Donald. They have gone, no one knows where.'

The King listened, his head a little bent. His foster-father said, 'I left men on guard on that monastery, and on the riverbank, and at the ferry. I shall have them all hanged.'

'No,' said the King. 'No. I told them myself that it was likely to happen, and if it did, they were not to make more than a show of force, since the thing was being done secretly and not in proper fashion. I said that when Malcolm was twelve, he could choose whether to stay in Alba or not.'

'He has made no choice,' Thorkel Fóstri said. 'Someone has taken him, who means no good to you and perhaps none to the boys either.'

'Now, that is foolish,' said his foster-son. 'The boys would be of no use to anyone dead, that is obvious. No. I know where they are.'

They had reached the door of the hall. 'How can you know?' Thorkel said.

'Because I have just come from Crinan,' said the King. 'I told you we had a few pirates' nests to smoke out for our own good and Eachmarcach's. At least his brother's son will trouble him no more: Rognvald stormed ashore and came back with his head. Then, while they laid about Kintyre, I took my ship into the Waver and saw Thor and Crinan.'

'So that's where they are,' Thorkel Fóstri said. 'With their grandfather.' Drawing to one side, he stood under the eaves and thought about it.

'You might have thought so, but Crinan doesn't want children on his hands, or to trouble with war,' the King said. 'He would like his rents from Dunkeld, and I have told him they will be sent to him, but that Dunkeld is still closed to him, as it was before the boys left. The youngest is still there, and has to be paid for.'

'And the other two?' Thorkel asked.

'Rumour had it, said Crinan, that Forne his son-in-law hoped to get hold of them. If he did, they were to go to one of their aunts. Crinan's guess was that it would be to Kalv's nephew, the new Earl Siward of Northumbria.'

Thorkel thought about Kalv. He said, 'He will rear them in York, a permanent threat to you. Did you expect that?'

'I suppose so,' the King said. 'It was always likely. Nor is Crinan quite innocent, of course, of his share of plotting. Eachmarcach says that Maldred has been canvassing freely in Ireland for someone to take the younger boy, Donald. His guess is that the boy will go to Downpatrick, and not to Siward, thus halving the risk. Siward, after all, can't be sure yet that the new King

Edward will let him keep Northumbria. And Malcolm is still very young: he might sicken and die. I am rather pleased, indeed, that, whatever fate overtakes my poor nephews, it won't be under my roof.'

Inside the hall, it was too crowded even for benches, and men were coming out into the sunlight, talking, with a filled ale-horn in one hand and a piece of roast meat in the other. The noise, already deafening, intensified into a roar of welcome as men saw the King was entering. They made a passage for him through the long room, banging on the posts or the wall-shields or their platters and cups with their knives.

From the doorway, he had seen his wife's red hair burning beside the high chair, with the boy's white head next to her. He reached his lady and kissed her hand and then her cheek, leading her to the other tall chair next his own, and ruffling the boy's hair as he moved. Then someone called for silence and he spoke; and at the end there were cheers and the noise broke out again. Someone brought him wine.

Groa said, 'According to Lulach, you have a new name. Walter, son of Fleance. That is, if you killed someone named Makglave. Did you?'

'Now you come to mention it,' Thorfinn said, 'I have his head somewhere. As to names, I am at the moment far from impoverished, but if Walter appeals to you, then by all means appeal to me by it.'

'Forne had a grandson called Walter,' said Lulach. 'And a son called Alan.'

'I'm not surprised,' said the King. 'Who will tell me news of my family, or have you all done nothing but grow two feet taller, as I observe?'

They told him the news, broken into, as he allowed on such occasions, by the overtures that came from the men standing about them, by way of observation or question or merrymaking of some sort. There was no way of avoiding it, and no way of shortening it. With the discretion he now knew was part of her, Groa introduced only the lightest of topics and, in the course of the long evening, asked only three questions, harmless in themselves, that showed him her mind.

The first time, she said, 'Where is Isleifr? He went with you?'

He had watched her search for the big Icelander who, since Skeggi's death, had acted as his standard-bearer when Thorkel was absent. He said, 'Isleifr continues to bear a charmed life, but in Ireland. I have sent him to Sulien. If you can guess why, I shall give you the Lombardian earrings a merchant sold me in Ramsay, if I can get them back from the girl I gave them to. Lulach, you are not allowed to reply.'

'Isleifr in Ireland? I didn't know of it,' said Lulach placidly. He was a tranquil child, and stirred to light laughter by the smallest things. All his mother's guesses, of intent, made him laugh, and when they all failed, he listened, smiling, to his stepfather supplying the answer.

'Isleifr wants to be a priest,' said the King. 'As his father was a leader and a holy man in the old faith before he was converted. And since Isleifr has set his heart on it, I thought that Sulien could best find him a place to begin his studies. He will come back, I hope. Meanwhile, we shall look after young Gizur and Dalla until she has her new child, and then send them to join him.'

'To Ireland?' Groa said, and her eyes scanned his face. 'But if he wants to serve in Iceland, and I suppose he does, won't he have to look to Bremen for some of his training?' She paused. 'You've thought of that.'

'It wasn't difficult,' Thorfinn said. 'He can study in Saxony later.'

'Of course,' Groa said. 'I see it. Softened by Celts, at least he will have a foot in both cultures, and a child brought up in each. Poor Dalla.'

Then she changed the subject, a little too quickly.

The second time, when the noise had risen and men's attention had started to slacken, she said, 'Did Thorkel tell you the news?' And when he nodded, she said, 'We hear that cousin Siward has arranged a new Bishop of Durham much to his liking. Called, I think Aethelric.'

'Now, there,' said Thorfinn, 'is a victory of faith over sin. The family has come a long way, I must say, since Ølve's pagan feast at Sparbu. A spiritual tutor for cousin Siward. Six strokes for indenting with the teeth the cup of salvation. I wish him well of the entire affair.'

'Do you?' said Groa. 'I'm glad.'

And the third time: 'Why can it be,' Groa said, 'that no one is quoting Arnór Jarlaskáld? Did his invention fail him, with two masters to serve?'

'I would blame his courage rather than his invention,' Thorfinn said. 'Indeed, he left his harp at home, for fear one of us should demand a panegyric and the other would kill him. When he saw there was no trouble between us, he took to the ale-jar out of sheer relief.'

He looked at her, and his voice faded. He said, 'It won't be long now.'

It was long. It was night before the hall was empty of all but the young men who slept there and Thorkel Fóstri waiting to speak to him. The boy had gone to his sleeping-quarters long since, and Groa to the hall-room they shared, where she would look at him presently and judge whether or not he wanted to talk, or whether or not he required to talk, whether he knew it or not.

He did not think he did. It was too confused and too delicate. Where her questions had tended, they both very well knew: the one that mattered most had been about Rognvald.

There had been no trouble between them: there he had spoken the truth. For the first few days of the voyage, Rognvald had toyed with him like a wild-cat: all gleaming eyes and soft fur and fine-needled pricking, now from teeth, now from claws.

It was a game he had no objection, himself, to taking part in, and he had played it. The trick was to take the barren exchanges and develop them into a different sort of competition and then, with luck, into something each could tolerate and even enjoy.

Rognvald had been at sea every year, as Thorfinn had not, and was in any case a man created by gods for feats of skill and endurance. What Rognvald might lack was ingenuity, although he had cunning. What he certainly had was vanity, and that, played upon, might produce the ends one desired.

So it had been, in many ways, a nightmare voyage, although a satisfactory one. The business with Eachmarcach had been genuine enough, and the threatened south-west needed attending to. But before that, there was little enough reason for what he and Rognvald had done.

In the days of Thorfinn's childhood, his father's sister Svanlaug had lived in the western isles and her husband had kept order there for Earl Sigurd. Then he had died, and his son Malduin had found softer quarters as Bishop of Alba, with no ambition to exchange them for a longhouse on Tiree and a trio of fast cutters that would rarely find themselves out of the water.

Instead of Malduin, the western isles were in the care of his phlegmatic half-brother Ghilander, who got on well enough with the Norse and Irish and Icelandic folk who populated the isles and paid their tribute to Orkney. It was only when Diarmaid or someone like him swept down with a tight fleet of fighting-ships and scoured the shores, herding off cattle and women alike, that the lack of a strong chief could be dangerous.

So it was sensible to go out to the isles, and to take the tax, of course, that was due, but also to clear away the unauthorised settlers and frighten off a few more who had thought of it, as well as show cousin Ghilander that kinship wouldn't count for too much if the Earls were to tire of his laziness.

To go to Tiree by way of the island of Hirtir was, of course, an unusual thing, Hirtir being as far out to the west as you could get without overtaking Leif Ericsson.

The wager, however, was made on the way to North Rona, which was not an island on the way to anywhere either, although the hermit had been glad to see them, and they found that someone else had taken the seals the previous year and who it was, so that in due course the matter could be dealt with. Then the south-east wind started up, which was excellent for a long, fast passage by sail to the west, but meant that when they got to the main island of Hirtir there was a swell running into the bay enough to lift all their ships to the top of Conochair and drop them thirteen hundred feet down into the sea again.

Since a race to the top of Conochair was the wager they had had in mind, they simply replaced it with one of total madness: Rognvald challenged his uncle to climb to the top of Stac an Armin and leave his ship's weathervane there, which his uncle agreed to do, provided that Rognvald would then bring it down again.

Stac an Armin was a whitened tower of rock over six hundred feet high, rearing out of the sea by the shores of the next island, Boreray. It could only be approached by ship's boat, and it could only be landed on by leaping from the gunwale of the boat at the top of a wave and clinging to the jagged sides like a cat on a pine tree. The breeding-ledges were filled with straw heaps and the questing white goose-heads of gannets, and a pair of skuas came screaming down to the attack, beaks raking before the boat had well reached the stack.

They had both made the climb. He remembered the red fingerprints he made on the guano-skin of the rock, planting the vane, and that, looking down on the wrinkled sea, he could not see the boat for the moving white carpet of geese wheeling in the draughts far below him.

That was when the change in Rognvald had begun. The mischief, even the vicious mischief, was still there, but without the glitter that had made it so hard to handle. Rognvald had been afraid himself, mortally afraid on that climb, and its achievement had altered his mood.

So, too, had the King's readiness to accept the challenge. After that, it was still a duel, but Rognvald never again suggested anything quite as dangerous, and usually the men came with them, boat vying against boat as if every day were a feast day and the world was a playground again, made of blue dolphin sea and green islands, in which to run and to climb and to swim, to leap and to fish and to hunt. When the fighting came, it was no more than an extension of it, and a dead Norse-speaking Irishman, speared out of a boat fleeing from the big bay of Erik's isle, was no more than a deer to be dragged out of the sea for the stripping.

Last night, making their last camp on shore, Rognvald had taken him down to the sea-edge, where the waves moved towards them like rods, black dimly slotted with white. Rognvald's cobbler had made him gannet-neck shoes, soft as down on the inside, and his hair was as light and soft, and his skin river-fresh. He said, 'What is the magic, uncle, that charms your life? Perhaps I should pay more heed to the White Christ. What did Hallfred Troublesskáld say?

> *' 'Tis heavy to cherish hatred*
> *for Frigg's divine husband*
> *Now that Christ has our worship*
> *For the skald delighted in Odin.'*

'*More* heed?' Thorfinn had answered.

'Indeed,' had said Rognvald, 'I have been thinking serious thoughts about religion lately, and I have in mind going to see my foster-brother in Norway one day soon, to see what can be done for these poor souls in my care in Orkney.'

'In two-thirds of Orkney,' Thorfinn had remarked.

Rognvald had smiled and then looked up, his face ghostly in the night-sparkle of the soft, bursting seas. 'As I was saying. What charm do you bear? I meant to come back with all Orkney. You knew it.'

'And now?' It was like being on Stac an Armin again, exploring by touch and by intuition.

'I had forgotten,' said Rognvald, 'what you were like; and you reminded me. Of purpose, of course, and so I should discount it. I cannot do that, for what you are is what I am also. Do you not feel it?'

Red prints on the rock, and the sea, far below. 'Yes,' he had answered. And then, 'There is one kind of love I will not give you,' he had added.

There had been a long pause. Then, 'I know that,' Rognvald had said. 'But you may receive it, may you not?'

Rognvald's touch, light as thistledown, fell on one shoulder; and as Rognvald stretched up, his breath came warm and sweet, just before his lips found one cheek and pressed it. Then he was no longer touching, but only one pace away, the bird-skin noiseless on the sand. 'If it is given from the heart, and without thought of reward,' Rognvald had added.

You were of his blood. You were only two years older. You were the King. He had turned to Rognvald and said, 'Give me trust, and I will return it to you. That is all I ask.' And Rognvald had smiled, and he had felt, for one terrible moment, that his hands had slipped from the rock, and that the white flocks were parting, and that he was falling and falling into the slow, wrinkled sea.

Thorkel Fóstri said, 'What is wrong? We have been waiting for you in the hall.'

He was in Thurso and the voyage was over. The King said, 'I am sorry. You wanted to talk to me.'

'There is no need now,' said Thorkel Fóstri. His voice sounded grim, as it often did now. 'I have heard all that you have been doing, and more.' He paused. 'Your wife was afraid. I thought it was because of Earl Rognvald.'

'No,' he said.

'No,' said Thorkel Fóstri. 'No. I realise that now. And Rognvald?'

'Is tamed,' he said. It was an effort to speak, he was so tired.

'And then?' Thorkel persisted. It sounded harmless: a minor conversation. Words were useless. What he was saying was, *What are you?*

'And now,' said the King, 'I really must get back south. I have sent Bishop Malduin to the new King of England, asking when I may travel to Winchester to offer him homage for Cumbria.'

In the darkness, Thorkel's eyes glittered, and then he turned away. 'And not before time,' he said. 'The King in Caithness is all very well, but who will look to the farms if the lot of you are playing pirates all summer? Homage for Cumbria?'

'Think about it,' Thorfinn said, making it brisk, and turned to the hall. What waited for him there was the innermost part of his life, without which the rest could not go on. She had been afraid, and he must still her fears; and also conceal from her that his fears had been greater yet; and still were.

FIVE

N THE FIRST day of Easter, it being judged that no invasion from Norway was imminent, Edward son of Aethelred was officially crowned King of England at Winchester by the Archbishop Eadsige of Canterbury and, before all the people, was duly instructed as to his duties as King and his responsibilities to his new nation.

The ceremony was not a success, and neither was the banquet afterwards, at which the King's mother found herself seated staring across two tables at the young King of Alba, who had the good sense to stare woodenly back. He was sitting, she saw, next to his wife's cousin the new Earl of Northumbria, a well-intentioned and calamitous provision by Edward's well-intentioned and calamitous seneschal, whom she must get rid of forthwith.

Three seats along from her, she could hear the King her own son forgetting Anglo-Saxon names, as he had been forgetting them for a year now. So much for last night's session with herself and Aelfwin, trying to teach him, yet again, the names of his English courtmen from outside London and Gloucester and Winchester. Sitting there in the church, you could sense the derision as the Archbishop ranted on about Christian succession, and not only because the old man was making a mess of it, either. Anyone who had been with Edward or knew of Edward during all those years at Rouen must be perfectly well aware that in forty years he had never managed to father a child, despite every encouragement; and all the doctors had done for him, it seemed, was convince him that he now knew more about healing than they did.

Her younger son Alfred had been popular, but she had known from the day she left him in Normandy, thirty years since, that Edward was stupid, with the stupid man's timidity that occasionally—very occasionally—could burst into hysterical action. She had always prayed that Edward would never have to be brought in to fill Canute's shoes. She could control Edward. But she couldn't lead armies, and since he couldn't either, the power was going to lie with those who did.

Godwin, Leofric, and Siward. She could see them from where she was sitting, in their embroidered robes and gold belts, their thick rings glowing with colour in the candlelight.

Leofric of Mercia, whose brat Alfgar was a grown man now, and as sharp and energetic and ambitious as his father, you could be sure, as well as possessing a mother who clearly meddled with some Breton arts she had better leave alone, since her looks had never changed in twenty years. And there was energy there as well, the kind of special edge that these Breton-Caux marriages brought, like the Norse-Irish ones she had come across. Leofric and his son would take some watching.

Then Godwin of Wessex. One could say it like that, as if he were merely another powerful earl, and not one of her oldest and once dearest friends, who had fought side by side with Canute and had—almost certainly—brought about the death of her son Alfred. Godwin she no longer could trust, nor feel near to, although the past lay there and could not be ignored. Nor could those links with the past that might promise trouble in future. Godwin and Canute's sister had married sister and brother. Godwin's wife was aunt to Svein, whom her son Hardecanute had put in charge of Denmark, and whom Magnús of Norway had just succeeded—for the moment—in pushing out.

Now England was under a Saxon King, Denmark was no longer the motherland. If Godwin were to be disappointed with the new England, he and his sons did not have far to seek for a different ally.

And, lastly, Siward, sitting next to the boy from Orkney who had once been Canute's housecarl, and about whom she must do something as soon as the meal finished. Siward, who had taken the hint and promptly slaughtered his wife's uncle Eadulf, whose empire-building in the north had been too blatant for comfort. She remembered suggesting it to her other son, her dear son, and he at least had seen the implications at once. *You wouldn't mind an alliance between Siward and this new Macbeth?*

He had been her dear son, but he was young, and he didn't know northmen as she did. She had known that the Orkney boy would never take Siward into partnership, and she had been proved right. And now, her agents said, the fellow Siward had raided deep into Alba and got hold of two of his three nephews, Duncan's sons.

The Orkney King might have no pretensions to Northumbria. But, with Thorfinn-Macbeth killed or rejected by Alba, there was no doubt now who would have the pickings of Alba in the future, as the mother's good-brother of two helpless children. And Edward's fool of a seneschal had placed the two men side by side at the banquet table.

She must certainly do something about that, and tonight. For, given Alba, this gross Norwegian Earl would be stronger than either Godwin or Leofric, and that would be bad. For only by keeping these three great Earls equal, and equally at each other's throats, was she going to be able to push Edward the way he should go.

The King of England's musicians, who were experiencing the same language difficulty as the King of England, had trailed to a halt, and had been followed by the King of England's tumblers, whose antics at least were understood by all his subjects. In the reduced din that followed, the King of Alba opened tranquil conversation, in his subterranean voice, with the Earl of North-umbria sitting next to him.

'I am sure we are intended to speak to each other. Did they know you were here, I am certain Thorkel Fóstri and my wife your cousin would send loving greetings to you and your family. How are the boys?'

All the men of Thore Hund's line grew to a great size. Beside Earl Siward's father, the Lapps with their furs had looked like squirrels, and beside Earl Siward even the man they now called Macbeth, King of Alba, had no advantage of height and was half the other man's width. The bullock Kalv Arnason's nephew had grown into the bull, rough-haired, rough-bearded, and quick in temper, who was now ruler over half the north of England, as well as the great merchant-city of York.

So, although Siward was Earl to the other man's King, the difference in rank did not concern him. Siward was pure-bred Norwegian: the son of a rich man who with his own hands had brought down a king—as could his son if he chose. And this King was a half-bred fifth son, born to an island colony, and nearly ten years younger than himself.

Siward took his time about turning his shoulder and answered when he was ready. 'The boys? Osbern is young yet, but as good with his sword as he needs to be. My other child is Ranveig, a girl.'

'I am sure her husband, when you pick him, will be a fortunate man,' the King said. 'I was referring, however, to the nephews we have in common and you have in fact. How are Malcolm and Donald?'

The cliff of Siward's brow lifted. 'Duncan's sons?'

'Duncan's sons,' affirmed the King. 'By all means, let us leave the subject if it makes you uneasy. I merely wished to enquire after their health. I am really quite relieved that you felt you could support them. I had rather, on the whole, that they sickened and died while under your roof than while under mine. The monks tell me the younger one takes to his bed every time he eats fish. You will have noticed.'

'I have no knowledge of King Duncan's sons,' Siward said. 'I am sure, however, your late brother would be as surprised as am I to see you so eager to kneel with your tribute. As I remember, Canute had to take an army north before Duncan or his grandfather would produce one vat of mead or a barrel of butter for Cumbria.'

'If you are thinking of some flamboyant gesture of defiance for North-umbria,' the King said, 'I don't really recommend it. Canute and his army gave Duncan and my grandfather such a fright that they had to summon me and invoke the King of Norway to save their skins, and you can't do either. That is, if you summoned me, I'm afraid I wouldn't come; and you can't really invoke the King of Norway since your father and Kalv killed his father. How, incidentally, are you proposing to reconcile the honest traders of York to the fact that your progenitor slaughtered a saint? You'll have to build a church to St Olaf.'

It was already half-built. The fellow knew it. 'Perhaps,' said Siward. 'These matters take money. If I set out like my forefathers and killed poor Christians and sank trading-ships, no doubt I could outfit my followers in silk tunics and gold-hilted weapons, and even pay all my tribute in silver; but these are not the ways of the White Christ.'

In the beaked, solemn face, the eyes stood like bronze pennies, and moved, scanning his face. 'Now I must give you some news that will strengthen your faith,' said the fellow from Orkney. 'The gold-hilted weapons you see, and the tribute in silver that King Edward was pleased to accept from me came from no other source than the White Christ himself. The White Christ at Dunkeld. The White Christ and, of course, my lord Crinan, the Abbot whose care had amassed it. You would have been surprised at the amount,' said the King, 'had you called for the boys a little sooner. But, of course, they were expensive to feed. Especially since one cannot eat fish. Someone wishes to call your attention.'

It was as well, because Siward could feel his fists clenching. The messenger was the King's new chaplain, Hermann, from Mons in Hainault, whose accent at least could be followed. While he was listening, Edward of England got up, as a signal that the banquet was at an end, and so Thorfinn was saved as well from returning to the foolish conversation he had been trapped into. Siward walked away from the boards without troubling to look back at his cousin's husband.

The chaplain Hermann watched him go, and then, lifting his chin, caught King Macbeth's attention and delivered his other and very different message.

The King of Alba had been given a hall for himself and his retinue just off the market-place, and it was there that Earl Siward of Northumbria sought him an hour after that, striking the door with his fist until the King's steward opened it, so that he could see within the nobles from Alba he had been speaking of, with their gold-hilted swords and silk tunics, looking up from their dice and their laughter.

Behind Siward were a dozen of his own men with their swords, and he was too angry to care about lowering his voice.

'My lord King is not here,' said the steward, and opened the door wider so that this could be seen. 'I do not know my lord's whereabouts, but no doubt he will sleep here. Perhaps the Earl and his men wish to enter and wait?'

Even one glance through the door showed that Thorfinn had more men here than he had. And the noise in the road behind him and the glint of royal badges reminded him that he was in the King's Winchester and disturbing the peace.

He left. To Ligulf, when he got back to the pavilion they shared, he said, 'I told you what he said at table. He is behind it. I know he is behind it.'

To Ligulf, his dark and powerful brother-in-law who held Bamburgh castle, the matter was as important as it was to Siward, and he was short of patience. 'Well?' he said. 'You saw King Edward? What did he want?'

Siward's strong teeth showed among the thick, springing whiskers. 'Custody of Duncan's two boys,' he said. 'Just that. He thinks it more suitable that the boys should be given a courtly rearing. He considered handing them to their grandfather, but my lord Crinan is not now of an age to take kindly to the training of young children, and the King, of his generosity, was therefore willing to undertake this burden himself.' Spray fell from his words.

Ligulf watched him. 'You told him that Donald was in Ireland?'

'He accepted that. He may have suspected it. He wants Malcolm forthwith.'

'Will you send him?'

'Do you want me to defy him? The King? He has only to ask Godwin or Leofric and we are dead or exiled, the lot of us.'

'And so?'

'And so we have lost Malcolm. But we still have access to Donald,' said Siward. 'And when Rognvald and Magnús of Norway move in to tear Thorfinn to pieces, this Norman fool of a King will see that he picked the wrong man to favour today.'

From the banqueting-hall, the priest Hermann led the tall King of Alba through the crowds to the lavish guest-quarters that bore the banner of Mercia.

Of design, Leofric of Mercia himself was not there: a wise precaution in any family having dealings with Emma the Queen Mother. Instead, waiting for them was Godiva his wife and his son Alfgar, now a tough and sinewy thirty-year-old with watchful eyes as well as a hearty laugh and a strong grip of welcome. Godiva said, 'Thorfinn!' and then changed it. 'No, Macbeth. We must remember. We are in the invisible presence of the Lady Emma, who did not think it wise to meet you herself at this juncture. You are to talk instead with Master Hermann here, and with the Archbishop. I think you know each other.'

From his cushioned seat at the back of the small room, Juhel, Archbishop of Dol, rose and came forward briskly, and his bright eyes observed many things.

The Mercians made way for him. The association between them and this King from the north was of old standing and ran deep, the Lady Emma thought. The Mercians would learn of these discussions anyway. To allow them to observe and to share merely made a virtue of necessity.

Archbishop Juhel gave his hand to the King, and saw the other man's eyes glance at his broken nose, which was as good as a badge and would remind him of the last time they had met, at King Duncan's enthronement, when he was not yet Archbishop.

Now, Juhel de Fougères made the right responses, not forgetting to ask after his young compatriot Sulien. They sat talking. Alfgar and his handsome mother spoke occasionally, but were mostly silent. Hermann, whom the Archbishop knew very well, was taking a polite share in the exchange, but was also watching and judging.

Feeling his way, slowly, to the business of the evening, the Archbishop watched and judged also.

'He is of your own age,' the Lady Emma had said. 'And has spent most of his life in the north. But do not underestimate him.'

Himself, Archbishop Juhel did not underestimate the Queen Mother either. Everyone dealing with trade and with money in Bruges and Arras and Rouen, in Mont St Michel and Tours, in Chaourse Flanders or Cahors Aquitaine, to the Count of which Emma sent, every year, some expensive trifle—everyone knew about Emma, widow of two Kings of England. And now, with Norman mercenaries becoming Norman dukes in Italy, everyone had a cousin or two where it mattered in Lombardy, and the network was becoming complete.

Nowadays, money was something all men had need of. The church required it, to pay armies to push the Saracens back in the Mediterranean; to fight off the heathenish tribes of the Baltic; to establish churches and send her missions abroad. Kings required it, to bribe their enemies and to pay their friends for services rendered where land was wanting or inappropriate; to hire fleets with, and foreign fighting-men; to buy the luxuries that their status demanded.

And since not every country could make money or, having made it, could protect the place where it was kept, a trade in money was always there: money that did not go rotten or stink or require great ships to carry it backwards and forwards, or fail altogether if the weather was bad or some tribe of ignorant savages wiped out the seed and the growers. Money which grew of its own accord: in Exeter, in Alston, in the Hertz mountains where the Emperor Henry had made his new palace.

Money, which was power, which was the wheel upon which ran Emma the Queen Mother's heart.

Ten years ago, hiring himself and his ships, Thorfinn of Orkney had wanted adventure perhaps as much as money, if not more. He had his household to pay, and those men who, building his ships, had to raise their crops and herd their beasts using serf-labour. Now, as Macbeth of Alba, it would seem that riches lay to his hand within his new provinces and he had no call to look further to England or further south over the sea.

He, Juhel, had said so to the Old Lady. And Emma had replied, over the coif-draped shelf of her bosom, with her jewelled stick quivering close to her hand against the carved arm of her chair-throne: 'Rubbish. He can expect grain from Caithness and timber and salmon from Moray, but his new lands are Irish and primitive, and those regions that are not are either dangerous to tamper with yet, such as Lothian, or require money to guard them, such as Dunkeld and Cumbria. He is living off Crinan's money now, and I doubt if Crinan will complain: they need each other. But he has to protect old King Malcolm's realm and his own with nothing like old King Malcolm's resources.'

He remembered demurring at that, which was always a mistake with the Lady. 'But you depended on Malcolm of Alba to hold Cumbria for you? He must have had men to fight for him—the same men his grandson Thorfinn now possesses?'

'He had Leinstermen to fight for him,' the Lady had pointed out with impatience. 'You ought to know that, at least. Leinstermen, the present King's enemies. And Crinan his daughter's husband to keep the rest of Cumbria quiet. The Alban kings have always had to use landless Irish or northmen to fight with. What else have they? The land provides for nothing but small families of mixed Pictish and Irish and Brittonic blood, crowding together the better to scrape a living from their herding and hunting and grain-patches.

'They survive. They will even rise now and then: they burned Dunkeld when the King's daughter died. But that is rare, as it is rare in the north. The household leaders will hand over tribute and sit in the council of their tuaths and bring home a gold arm-band or a roll of fine wool now and then for their wives, but it is the lord and his kindred who order the provinces and hold the wealth in their hands.

'So the Earls of Orkney and Caithness have always ruled. So this one will rule in Alba. And so he will need money and fighting-men. And if he can't get fighting-men, or if the Viking spirit is not what it was—for there is nothing like kingship,' had said Emma, 'for making a man look to his name instead of his weapons—then he is going to have to buy peace; and peace is the most expensive commodity of all.

'Have no fear,' Emma had said. 'Go and talk to him. He will listen.'

'Let me guess,' said Thorfinn, once of Orkney and Moray, who, it appeared, had been watching him as he looked into his cup. 'You have come to talk about the Celtic church.'

Juhel de Fougères looked at his Flemish friend Hermann, who was already smiling, and allowed his own smile to broaden. 'Alas,' he said. 'You use sorcerers.'

'Always,' said the tall man, 'when dealing with Bretons. Sprung from the stock of the Druids of Bayeux, and tracing your hallowed line from the temple of Belenus.' He spoke, without apparent trouble, the kind of Gaelic they still spoke in Cumbria and south-west Scotland, and parts of Lothian, and Wales, and Brittany. But then, he had been Sulien's sponsor and friend.

The Archbishop said, 'If you know I am to talk about the church, then obviously you also know why.'

'Obviously,' said the King. 'For the same reason that my nephew Rognvald of Orkney has lately begun to show a novel concern for the souls of his people. We are all talking, I take it, about King Magnús of Norway and his claims upon Denmark and England?'

'You may take it,' said the Archbishop, 'that we are all intended, at least, to be talking about exactly that.'

'The point being,' said the King of Alba in the even, rumbling voice that defeated all interpretation, 'that if Magnús is at war with both Denmark and England, his church will now look towards Saxony. His immediate spiritual lord will be the Archbishop of Bremen. Its overlords will be the King of Germany and the Pope. What do we know of Pope Silvester?'

'That he wants to abdicate and marry his cousin,' said Godiva. 'Or so run the rumours in Chester.'

'And in Thurso,' said the King. 'And what do we know of Henry, the new Emperor of the Romans and King of Germany?'

'I feel sure you want me to tell you,' said Edward of England's chaplain Hermann agreeably, 'that the Emperor Henry is a young man of deep faith and some acumen, who is not likely to leave the nomination of the next Pope to the counts of Crescenti and Tusculum as heretofore. An active Pope of his choice might feel impelled to do what no Pope with his whole heart has yet done since the heathen hordes overwhelmed Rome. He might seek to draw all the north, including Norway and her colonies, fully into his flock, and to extract the same obedience from those Celtic churches which have so far remained autonomous from the earliest Christian age—'

'Namely, those of Alba, of Ireland, and of Brittany,' the King said. 'Or no. Ireland is wild Irish with oases of Norsemen, and too complicated to administer. But you and I, Archbishop Juhel, would undoubtedly receive a kindly summons from the Coarb of Peter. That is, if there were to be an active Pope. And we should then have to choose whether to remain as we are, with pastoral missionary-priests and roving bishops with no see and no pallium; or pay our dues to Rome and be granted the structure of diocese, writing-office, and local administration; or enter, with Norway and her friends, under the benevolent care of the Archbishop of Hamburg and Bremen.

'A third choice that you in Brittany, Archbishop, are spared, but which would offer us some advantages. A Saxon mother-church with no harsh requirements in dues; a common tongue; a common understanding; and, for me, the prospect of uniting divergent people from Orkney to Cumbria under one efficient spiritual leadership, well taught and well able to bring my country into better prosperity. Would you blame me if I were to choose as Norway chooses?'

Alfgar of Mercia said suddenly, 'Thorfinn. Macbeth. You know who is Archbishop in Hamburg now?'

It was interesting that Alfgar of Mercia should know. It was even more interesting that the King should reply without hesitation, 'If I didn't, I should hardly be here. The stories about Adalbert were already going the rounds when he was only a well-born sub-deacon at Bremen ten years ago. Now he is in the Archbishop's seat, with looks, authority, money, and power. He will have Magnús tucked in his sleeve, and likely Denmark and Iceland as well. And who likes Adalbert can count on the Emperor Henry.'

In the harsh-angled face, the brown, slotted eyes moved, and Juhel de Fougères found himself under tranquil scrutiny. 'And what,' said the King, 'can the Lady Emma offer that would serve me better than that?'

'You are imprecise in your equation,' said Archbishop Juhel. 'Alba would not accept the spiritual guidance of a German archbishopric. If you tried to impose it, you would split your kingdom in two. You have two choices only. You stay as you are, which I do not think you can afford to do. Or you extend the paternal authority your people and mine already recognise in the Pope, and accept also the services, the structure, and the dependence that the Roman obedience imposes.'

'Would you do this?' said the other man.

'I may have no choice,' said the Archbishop. 'We have stayed worshipping our small saints, as you have, for five hundred years: many of them are the same. But although my people are the rough children they have always been, the world outside our frontiers has changed. Anjou is about to come into new hands, and that means the old Breton lands by the Loire may now be beyond our reach even for trade. And the Emperor has seen, too, where the money lies: he sent Bruno of Toul last year to arrange him a new wife. He has picked Agnes, Aquitaine's daughter: a stepdaughter of Anjou and the descendant of Burgundy and two Italian Kings.'

'But Popes always need money,' said the King.

'So will you,' said the Archbishop. 'And you have two valuable assets: your fleet, and your loyalty.'

'Provided the churches of Alba remain innocent of any master save only the Pope,' the King said. 'If that is the proposition, then I think this time *your* equation is at fault. I can ally myself with Norway without placing my priests under Archbishop Adalbert. In fact, I am not tied to any decision beforehand. If someone happens to want my fleet, they may always ask for it. If someone wants my loyalty for a certain occasion, then I am always ready to listen. My character has altered for the better, you see. There was a time when I would promise anyone anything.'

In his place, it was precisely what the Archbishop would have replied. As the Lady was keeping the balance of power among England's three leading earldoms, so this man was acting towards all the nations that threatened his borders. It almost looked, as the Lady had hinted, as if he intended to rule, rather than treat Alba as a Viking base to be held under threat for its tribute. And if he did, he had a long task ahead, because he had to find and nurture leaders from the Gaelic lands he had taken over who would cleave to him, and would work in amity with his chieftains and kindred in the north.

Archbishop Juhel, studying the man opposite, slowly reached a conclusion. He said, 'That, I take it, is what you wish me to tell the Lady Emma, and I shall do so. If you are going to knit the two halves of your kingdom together, I suppose you have already come to the conclusion that neither the Pope nor the Archbishop of Hamburg and Bremen is likely to serve you as yet. Our mutual friend Sulien of Llanbadarn spoke of the Culdees, the small monasteries of holy men following their own ascetic disciplines, that are all you have, he said, of a common church, but at present act independently of each other. You could not build a state upon them, he said, unworldly as they are, but you could unite a people.'

'A charming notion of Sulien's,' the King said approvingly. 'I was drawn to it. We all were, until we looked to the example of Dol and saw how well business may flourish under prince-bishops who know what they are about. My own Bishop Malduin would tell you the same. He is a strong supporter of a policy you haven't yet mentioned: that all the churches under his pastoral care should be ruled from Earl Siward's York. Also a charming idea, but with some disadvantages.'

Juhel de Fougères smiled. With Siward in control of York, only lunacy would dictate that particular resolution, and this the other man knew as well as he did. The Archbishop said, 'I see there is little an outsider can do, except wish you luck in your deliberations, and success in your eventual course of action. Indeed, all I could with profit offer you, were you ever as far south as Cumbria, would be some considerations on matters of trade. You have referred to it, and I will not contradict what you said. We are knowledgeable.'

'So I have observed,' said Thorfinn of Alba.

'Well? Are you satisfied?' Alfgar said, when the Archbishop and the chaplain had gone. 'Juhel is able, and ambitious, and will use you, just as much as he will try to use Emma, for his own ends. So long as you know it, you are quite safe to meet him in Cumbria. He won't tell Emma anything that doesn't suit him.'

'So I judged,' said Thorfinn.

'You are using the Culdees, aren't you?' said Alfgar. 'Crinan said Archbishop Malduin was weeping into his wine-cup because you forced him to give up some of his churchlands to support them.'

'What else is Crinan saying?' said Thorfinn.

'He dislikes being barred out of Dunkeld. And he objects to Siward holding his grandsons.'

'He doesn't hold them,' said Thorfinn mildly. 'Edward of England is taking one into fosterage, and the other's in Ireland.'

'What!' said Alfgar. His eyes glittered. 'When?'

'It was arranged this evening,' Thorfinn said. 'So you may tell Crinan that Siward is not going to lay hands on Cumbria yet. In fact, unless he miscalculates badly, my lord Crinan may well find himself reunited one day with his abbacy. His third grandson is still there. And it would save me the trouble of protecting it. It will depend, I suppose, on how much influence Siward has over Maldred and Forne.'

'And on how much regard my lord Crinan has for his son and his son-in-law,' Godiva said. 'Don't you agree? I have been waiting for half an hour to say something perceptive.'

'You don't need to say anything,' the King said. 'But it's a delight when you do. Maldred's a nonentity, I'm told. But Forne won't cross the border, if I can help it. My lady of Mercia, if I drink any more, I shan't be able to board ship tomorrow.'

'You're going home?' Godiva said. 'I hoped—Why? Have you had word of some trouble?'

'Not yet,' said the King of Alba. 'But broken promises always take their toll, or so the priests say. Instead of enjoying your company, I am supposed to be sailing the seas with Earl Rognvald my nephew at this moment.'

'He will understand,' said Godiva. 'It was a matter of state.'

'He will understand,' said the King of Alba. 'And he will act accordingly.'

SIX

B Y THE TIME Thorfinn returned to his kingdom, his nephew Rognvald, as he feared, had set out alone on his sailing.

'So what will you do now?' said his wife Groa.

'Foster my toisechs. Cultivate Eachmarcach. And spend the winter in Orkney,' said Thorfinn.

'Which you don't want to do,' Groa said.

'No, I don't. Yes, I do,' said her husband.

That autumn, led by King Edward, there rode to Winchester the Earls Siward, Godwin, and Leofric. There they called on the King's mother Emma and removed her private fortune, carrying off gold and silver, they said, without measure. The choicest box, when forced open in Gloucester, proved to harbour the head of St Ouen.

The Lady Emma, they said, wept and raged, but not as much as she might have done had a well-filled ship not left for Bruges beforehand.

Canterbury, worthy custodians of the rest of St Ouen, launched a long, gentle campaign that disturbed the King's healing-powers through Advent.

That winter in Orkney, the King of Alba's beautiful wife had cause to mourn, also, for the talents of a different kind that were being squandered.

The Rognvald who returned from his plundering cruise had been an enemy, as had been the Rognvald who had returned humiliated from the enthronement. And what Groa saw enacted around her through Yule and beyond, although she did not know it, was Stac an Armin all over again.

The harsh, bold contests, the extravagant feasting were what a daughter of Finn Arnason knew and expected, and in her, too, vibrated the chords of memory and of love at the warm brotherhood that opened to receive their own kind: the good fellowship and the song and the laughter.

This was part of Thorfinn: the loss of this, she knew, was the highest price he paid in his self-imposed exile. So she knew, too, as the drinking grew out of all bounds and the play became lethal, that a war was being fought and, however it ended, the sport would never be the same again, or the ground it was played on. At times, too, she thought that Rognvald himself was being swept by the tempest of his own making into a direction he had not meant to follow.

It was a hard winter, rare in Orkney; so that they slid Norse-style on wood from one hall to another, Rognvald's company and Thorfinn's company: one from two-thirds of Orkney and one drawn from only a third, and so weaker; and so more belligerent. For the men, too, opposed one another as the Earls did, and if one was traced of a morning only by the blood spider-pink in the snow, another died somewhere else before the next day was out, by the hand of his fellows.

Then Rognvald turned his attention to Groa herself.

Already, she had learned, as all the women had, when to disappear. To stay at home when the horse-fights took place, with the wagers higher and higher, from which Thorfinn came home cheerfully pallid with a displaced shoulder that had been knocked roughly back into place again. Or the day when the cry had gone up: '*Whales in the bay!*' and every man and every boat and every weapon had taken to sea to drive ashore the great shoal, and each shift of wind from the blood-reddened sands had brought the smell of the killing, and the sound of squealing and drumming from the half-slaughtered beasts. Then, for days, the hot, fishy reek of the rendering blubber, and the night-clouds glaring red over the fires of the fishermen.

From that, some men never returned, and most of the rest, including Thorfinn, brought back gashes of some sort, from their own spears and tridents or another's.

This time, he dealt with his ripped forearm himself, and she only found out about it the following night. Throughout, he made nothing of what was happening, and neither, grimly, did she; for she understood all the reasons. For most of the time, she knew, he was more sober than he appeared; for some of the time, against his intention, he was not; and that was a danger no one could protect him from except himself. For Rognvald, never quite sober, never quite incapable, was ready to turn to his own ends every weakness.

So, during the horse-play after the feast, when the whale-oil had been casked and put into store to bring winter's light and good silver for all their hard work, Earl Rognvald found out his aunt, his beautiful aunt who was four years younger than he was, and dragged her into the capering circle round the flute-player and there, before them all, locked her tight in a long, sucking kiss that was broken by Thorfinn's nudging shoulder and Thorfinn's heel in the back of the knee, so that before Rognvald knew it, the girl had gone dancing off in her husband's arms, while he rolled like a fool on the trampled grass of the yard. And when he started after them, a knot of Thorfinn's men happened to be in his way, and Thorfinn himself and his wife had vanished indoors.

Indoors, Thorfinn locked the door of the room they shared, and turned. Groa said. 'That was foolish. Or no. The foolishness was mine, for allowing it to happen. You could do nothing else.'

He said, 'I should never have brought you.'

'You had to bring me,' said Groa. 'He has to accept you, and your kingdom, and your wife. I am not going home.'

Thorfinn said, 'It will happen again.' He turned from her and dropped to his heels before the little, scented peat-fire that warmed the room, its blue smoke rising to the wattle and thatch just above them. His interlaced fingers were hard as the wattle.

'I can stay indoors,' Groa said. 'He only wants to provoke you in public.'

'I could handle him without you,' Thorfinn said. 'I have to find a way of handling him *with* you as well, or there will be no peace. I can't go south and do what I have to do with all this vindictiveness let loose behind me. If I am to rule at all, I have to tame him. If I can't tame him . . .'

'You have to kill him,' said Groa. 'That is what Thorkel Fóstri told you, isn't it?'

'Thorkel Fóstri's solutions,' said Thorfinn, getting up, 'all tend to a certain uniformity. The sons of Muspell cannot be expected to solve every problem. If I set my men to guard you, it will look either as if I am afraid of him or that I cannot trust you. On the other hand, there are some fairly fierce beldames in Sandwick and Skeggbjarnarstead, as I remember. If you were surrounded by these, it would make it a little harder for Rognvald to get at you.'

'But might look equally as if you didn't trust me?' Groa said.

He looked at her. 'You would rather have Rognvald than the old women?'

'Infinitely,' Groa said gravely, and waited as, with equal gravity, he crossed to where she was sitting.

They had reached no conclusions, for there was nothing in the situation that they did not know already, and if there was a way out, it was not at present obvious. He had troubles enough. And her role was not to discuss them, but to help him escape from them.

It took a week to prove them both wrong. A week to realise that, whatever Rognvald's intentions had been before, now they were perfectly plain. Vicious sport was no longer enough to take the edge off his hunger. Now he wanted to kill.

Every day, Groa watched Thorfinn leave for his rounds, his councils, his hunting, his feasting, and every night when he returned, the sound of his voice on the threshold brought the tears of relief to her closed eyes. After a week of it, she took half a dozen men and her sledge and her horses and went to Thorkel Fóstri at Sandwick.

Since his wound at Loch Vatten, his leg would stiffen at times, as it had done this last week, and instead of watching over his foster-son, as he had done all his life, Thorkel Fóstri had to sit at the fire listening to his women quarrelling over the spinning, and cuffing the latest brat or two out of the way, until the pain and his bad temper lifted and he could get back to the boy's side again. The boy whose destiny he once had thought he had in his hand. The boy he used to curse for his presumption, and whom he had nearly abandoned for Rognvald.

The years had taught him their lesson. He had reared Thorfinn, but had not had the making of him. And time had brought Thorfinn other friends. He had learned to accept them, as he had learned to come to terms with the girl, the beguiling girl who had taken for herself that part of Thorfinn's inner thoughts that his foster-father had never had.

So that it was with no bitterness towards her but only anxiety that he heard her out, and then said, 'You are right. It must not go on. It can only end fatally if it does. You both go home, or you bring it to a head.'

'I can bring it to a head,' Groa said. 'But if I do, they will fight. And Rognvald will fight to the death.'

'He won't win,' said Thorkel Fóstri.

'You can't be sure. No one can,' Groa said. 'If he doesn't kill Thorfinn, he could still leave him maimed for life. And if Thorfinn kills him, it may undo all he has spent this devilish winter trying to bring about. He could lose the goodwill of all Rognvald's men, and Orkney itself, once King Magnús heard about it. Rognvald is Magnús's foster-brother.'

'And is that worse,' Thorkel Fóstri said, 'than losing your husband, until the day he appears belly up in the sea, buoying a fishing-net? If Rognvald has his way, death in a fair fight is not how Thorfinn will finish.'

For a long time, she was silent. Then she said, 'Thorfinn thought he could tame him.'

'It is the Celtic in him,' Thorkel Fóstri said. 'You would do well to help him root it out. He thought he could tame Erlend his brother, and would have found out his mistake soon enough, had I not had the good luck to cut off Erlend's head. No doubt he would have tried to serve Gillacomghain the same way. Would you have been glad if he had?'

She flushed and then lifted her chin. 'I suppose you may say as much to Thorfinn, if he will let you. I do not think you have the right to say it to me.'

'No,' said Thorkel Fóstri. 'You are right. He needed a woman: I had not realised it. And, as it has turned out, he could have found none better.'

'On the other hand,' said Groa thoughtfully, 'if he had spared Gillacomghain, he might not now be having such trouble with Rognvald. So it is hard to know, isn't it, which of us is at fault?'

He was being played with, by a girl, as once long ago he in his turn had amused himself with his cousin Kalv Arnason. He began to be angry, and then came to his senses and smiled. He said, 'I never met an Arnmødling lacking in courage. Will you do it, then? When? I will come back tomorrow, if they have to lay me on the sledge.'

'Yes. Come back,' said Groa. 'We shall both need all the help we can get.'

In the event, she had to do nothing, for Rognvald caught her after sundown one afternoon as they were travelling in torch-lit cavalcade from Birsay to Orphir.

They had been later setting out than they intended, but the snow was not deep and the ground hard and good for the horses and the sledges packed with their possessions, for they would be at Orphir for three weeks at least before moving on. With them were all of the hird who were not in Caithness, as were Sinna and her young sons: perhaps fifty riders in all. And with Groa in the sledge were three of her women.

They had passed Isbister when they saw the dancing flares to the east, beyond Beaquoy, which grew larger and plainer and lit, finally, the faces of Rognvald and a great party, come from the east mainland, to command his uncle Thorfinn's hospitality at Orphir for one night, or perhaps more.

The hall at Orphir was big, and there was food in plenty. Also, having belonged to Earl Einar, the lands of Orphir, strictly speaking, fell within Rognvald's claim, although he preferred, it seemed, to see his uncle there meantime, rather than in his stronghold of Birsay. Thorfinn therefore acceded, agreeably enough, and the two parties fell into line and picked up a gay, jogging pace while the sound of voices and laughter and the jingle of horse-harness fled with their shadows over the sparkling night-fields of snow, and Rognvald edged his horse to trot by Groa's big sledge. 'And greetings to my lady aunt,' he observed. 'I heard that your husband had tied you to the stock of the bed lest you and I continued our half-finished business.'

Groa looked up. The winter-fair face looking down at her, with the coils of yellow-gold hair straying over his furs, had the bloom of beauty that Rognvald never lost, no matter what he might do, and the torchlight danced in his eyes. He said, 'I suppose there is no room in the sledge for a nephew?'

The sledge she had chosen was one of the largest they had, drawn by two good horses, with a man from Buckquoy riding one of them. 'I don't see why not,' said Groa; and the next moment, laughing, he had flung his reins to his own nearest man and, kicking his feet free of the stirrups, had vaulted lightly down among them as the sledge sped beside him. The runners dug into the snow, and it swerved, causing the rider ahead to look back. Groa raised a hand to reassure him, and then made room for Rognvald beside her. He put an arm round the fur of her cloak and smiled; and she said, 'I wanted to talk to you.'

His smile broadened. 'How disappointing,' he said. 'I wanted to kiss you. But let me guess. Thorfinn is frightened, and has asked you to beg for him?'

The women were staring at them. 'Is it likely?' said Groa.

'Then,' said Rognvald, 'it must be, after all, that your wishes and mine are the same. Why do we need to go to Orphir? Tell your driver to turn east.'

'We are going to Orphir,' Groa said. 'And on the way there, I am going to address you like an aunt. What are you thinking of? I would not allow a child of mine to behave the way you do. Here you are, at thirty-two Earl of Orkney, with silver and ships and men to follow you, and you think of nothing but wasting Thorfinn's time and your own with this stupid feud. You hold two-thirds of Orkney, which in my view is twice as much as you should have, but Thorfinn has not tried to take it away from you, as he very well might have done.

'He has not tried to harm you. If you left him alone, he would be where he ought to be, looking after his lands in the south, and you would be able to order your life as you please, with no rival in Orkney but Thorfinn's steward here in the west. What is the sense in trying to injure each other? Either you lose your life or, if you succeed in killing him, you make yourself hated by all his people, and lose your sport anyway.'

She ended breathlessly, and with some apprehension, which she hoped was not obvious. She had had no idea he would let her speak without interruption, but he had been silent, smiling, all the way through.

Now his dimple became deeper still. 'As you say. I should lose my sport—some of it. But I should gain the whole of Orkney, shouldn't I—and a great deal more, as stepfather of your two little sons?'

He had slipped his hand, still smiling, under the rug that covered their laps. She thought her responses were quick, but she had barely flinched when there was a sudden crack and Rognvald, with a hiss, snatched back his bared fingers. Unna, the oldest of her three women, smoothed the rug again over their knees and sat back, her silver knife-case gripped still in one hand. Rognvald, staring at her, had lifted his arm.

'You are going to strike an old woman, are you, Rognvald?' said Groa. 'Your men will burst with pride. And do you really expect me to believe that any of this has to do with me, or with my sons, or with Orkney?'

'Fortunately,' Rognvald said, 'in this world, women have only one simple function, and what they believe or do not believe is of no importance to anyone. I have decided to take you to the east mainland. Tell your driver and the women to get out, or I will throw them out.'

The sledge slowed. 'They are going to get out anyway,' Groa said. All around her, men were drawing rein and the other sledges, too, were running down to a halt. Ahead, the night had become brilliant with fire: a ring of flares ended beside a vast bonfire that lit the low walls and barns and sleeping-quarters and drink-hall of a big steading. 'And so am I. And so are you. The Loch of Stenness has frozen, and the family at Brodgar have invited us to an ice-feast. No doubt,' said Groa, 'they would welcome you, but if you do not care for it, there is no reason why you should not ride straight on to Orphir.'

For a moment, she thought he would try to force the sledge out; but by now it was safely surrounded. Rognvald said, 'You knew, of course, that we were nearly at Stenness when you asked me to join you. How prudish you are. And of course it won't save you in the end, or your grotesque bedfellow. I will stay.'

And then Thorfinn was beside her, and lifting her out, and did not leave her all through the feasting.

At the end, when the big, savoury cauldron on the fire was nearly empty, and the horns had been filled and refilled from the vat, the others bound the polished bones on to their boots and pushed off on to the loch with their double sticks.

Rognvald was among them, and all his men, on skate-bones lent from the household. Watching them skim flashing past the flares as the bat-games and the races began, you remembered the years he had spent in Russia. The men he had with him now were his own special hird, who, like himself, had fled from King Olaf's death-battle to Jaroslav's court in Novgorod.

Like him, they had thrown off their furs, and the bright-dyed stuff of their jackets glowed and dimmed like fruit on a vine as they amused themselves after the contests, weaving and interweaving across the white field of the lake that vanished west into darkness while, to the north, high on the ridge between lakes, the great ring of monoliths whose makers' race had known Wessex and Brittany, too, lent its nearer stones now and then to familiar fires.

Then a spray of cold slush slapped their faces, and Rognvald, halting before them, said, 'I declare, uncle, you are shaking. Is it fear for yourself, or your wife, or the figure you cut on the ice? A silver cup says you won't race with me. A golden cup says you won't win.'

'A fairly safe wager, under the circumstances,' Thorfinn said. 'But if you are in such sore need of a cup, then who am I to refuse you?' And Groa, silent, watched him bind the bones to his feet and pick up the sticks and step out into the noise and laughter on the lake and did not stop him, for it took courage to stand, a king and a leader, and pit the practice of one or two frozen winters against his enemy and the skill of six years. But on the ice, surrounded by men of both factions, nothing more than humiliation of a humdrum kind could come to him, which no doubt he would pass off. And so long as Rognvald was on the ice, she was safe.

In the event, a score of them took part in the ensuing race to and from the row of boulders, half swallowed in darkness, which was their makeshift boundary mark. The woman of the farmstead, her face flushed and smiling, swung the tallow-dip that gave them their starting signal and the skaters set off, in a whooping, uneven row, their backs brilliant in the firelight.

It was not to be expected that, drunk or sober, at war or at sport, any man of such a group would dream of pinning all his faith on his natural gifts. Shoulders and knees, elbows and hips and the pointed ends of the skating-sticks came into play instantly, until the receding line, bunching as it progressed, looked less like a contest of skaters than the crews of two longships that had just had a head-on collision. They receded, roaring, with one man at least among them traversing the ice on his shoulders, and Groa, laughing, shook back her hood and talked across the fire with the other women where they sat at ease on the shore on the heaped, straw-stuffed hides.

She watched, as long as she could, the ducking, swaying head of Thorfinn, who was demonstrating, it would seem, that the balance required of a youth skipping on oars at nineteeen can serve him just as well in other ways fourteen years later. Then she could distinguish nothing but a dark line on the ice which became a mound which became, in turn, part of the darkness. The shouting continued.

Having reached the boundary, the contestants did not return as quickly as they had gone, but, held in woman-talk, Groa was not unduly concerned. Not far away, one of the passenger-sledges had been turned, and a pony brought down from the horse-lines was being clipped into its harness: someone feeling the cold, no doubt, had decided to make for his warm bed at Orphir.

That there was a connection between the two did not cross her mind until a pair of hands closed on her arms and jerked her upwards. She gasped, kicking and wrenching, but the man behind her, whoever he was, did not let go, although one of the women shouted and picked up the big ladle and two more were running towards her. But he was too strong for her and too quick. Before he could be stopped, he had thrown her into the sledge and held her there while a dark figure vaulted on to the pony's back and, seizing the reins, flung the horse and the sledge into motion.

The man holding her down dropped his hands and jumped back. The rider ahead, whose back was all she could see, raised his whip-hand and brought the thong coiling down, so that the garron kicked up its heels and, ears flattening, lengthened its pace. The snow began racing below her. Already it was too late to jump. Already the black bulk of the steading was blocking the flames of the fire, and the cries of the women were thinning, overlaid by the hiss of the runners.

Then the rider ahead, whip and reins in one hand, twisted round, smiling, and looked at her, his teeth dimly white below the black circle of fur he had pulled over the bright, gilded hair. 'Why not jump?' Rognvald said. 'I don't want you. I only want Thorfinn to follow me.'

The sledge swerved. The horse was running wild. Rognvald paid no attention, twisted round, smiling, with the reins lying loose in his fingers.

Groa said, 'I am not getting out.'

'You are hoping for rescue?' Rognvald said. 'I have told my men not to come after me. Thorfinn will come, of course: he will follow the tracks. My guess is that he, too, will come alone. He knows that in a duel one does not need companions.'

The sledge lurched, and he half-turned and, looking ahead, took the reins in both hands again. He was still smiling. They crossed a ridge of bared rock, and she gripped the sides of the sledge as it bucketed. He was steering straight, she saw, for another. She took a short breath and called. 'If he finds me in the snow, he won't come after you.'

This time, he did not turn, but she could just make out his words, although the wind snatched his voice. 'He won't find you, my beautiful aunt. I shall make quite sure of that.'

There was a mound ahead, one of the great burial mounds that shouldered out of the snow-covered turf all about them, only just blacker than the cloud-covered sky overhead. She saw him guide the horse to its slope and flung her weight to the right just as the runner on that side mounted the incline and ran jumping, striking sparks from the half-submerged stone-work. Then it thudded down to the level and the sledge was running evenly again, for the moment.

'Do you think,' Rognvald said, 'that the stream will be frozen? It runs very fast. A skin of ice, perhaps: not much more. It isn't, of course, a very broad stream. Any horse could leap it. What the sledge will do, there is no telling, is there, until we find out?'

She knew the stream, and she knew what the sledge would do. It would overturn. And in that icy water she would not drown. But unless taken quickly to warmth, she would die.

Which was what he wanted. Not to rule Orkney as stepfather to Sigurd and Erlend. Not even to rule Orkney, two-thirds or all of it. But to stand in the centre of Thorfinn's world so that he had no world that was not Rognvald his nephew. Then her eye fell on the two thick, plaited cords that joined the sledge to the yoke of the horse, and she remembered the knife at her belt.

She had little time, and the use of hardly more than one hand, or she would have been thrown from the racing, bucketing sledge as she laboured. But, bracing herself as best she could, she began work on the thongs, sawing quickly, first on one side and then the other, for if one were to part prematurely, the sledge would scythe round under the galloping heels and nothing then was likely to save her. She must so work that the last strands would give way together and, evenly balanced, the sledge would merely run gently on, losing momentum.

Then Rognvald would turn as his horse ran free of the weight, and, coming back, would bend over her. And she would still have the knife in her hand.

She had the thong half through when the first cry came from behind, and at that second she stopped what she was doing, because Rognvald turned, scanning the darkness behind her. Then he lowered his gaze. 'Do you play board games? It was a risk I took, that your husband would bring his friends with him. I believe he has brought one. How unfair. I must point it out to him.'

Then she looked round as well, and saw, far behind, two galloping horses, their torch-flares streaming like hair-stars. Unencumbered, they were gaining ground fast. Then Rognvald laughed, and she turned and made out, dim black on dim grey ahead, the line of the brook he was making for.

This time, she did not heed whether he saw her or not. She grasped the front board of the sledge and slashed the ropes through, one after the other.

The sledge kicked. Like a towed skiff severed at sea, its nose swung wildly, first to one side and then the other, and the harsh saw of the runners alone would have told Rognvald what had happened, without the sudden stumble and peck of his horse. He began to wheel round. Then his eyes lifted to something behind her. He laughed a second time and, leading the reins in an arc, turned his mare back again and pressed her into a trot. For a moment, Groa could see horse and rider black against the grey of the snow. Then there was nothing but the sound of muffled hooves drumming as Rognvald rode off, spurring from trot to full gallop.

The snow turned from grey to pink, and her shadow flickered before her, ahead of the maundering sledge. The runners ran to a halt, and two fur-cloaked horsemen overtook her in a flurry of snow.

One was Thorkel Fóstri. The other was Thorfinn, who was out of the saddle before she could stand, and was holding her, her face deep in the warmth and the softness between glove and shoulder. She began to shake, and he tightened his grip. Then he said, 'Groa. Will you ride back with Thorkel Fóstri?'

She lifted her head, without looking up at him. 'Let him go. Please. Thorkel Fóstri?' She made to twist round, but Thorfinn's grasp only tightened.

Behind her, she heard the swift jingle as Thorfinn's foster-father dismounted, and then his quick breathing, and Thorkel's voice saying, 'Go back with her. I'll see to it.'

Then Thorfinn's hands dropped. He said, 'That isn't what she meant. Go away, both of you. Rognvald has to be dealt with.'

'He's waiting for you,' Groa said. 'He knew you would follow.'

Thorfinn said, 'My foster-father: you will neither track us, nor will you look for us until first light.'

'As you say,' said Thorkel Fóstri.

'On the hilt of my sword,' said the King.

Thorkel Fóstri said, 'He may give you promises. They mean nothing.'

'That is for me to judge,' said the King. 'How much does your promise mean?'

'That is for you to judge,' said Thorkel Fóstri harshly, and, dropping his hand on the cross-guard, took the oath asked of him. Then, turning, he faced Groa and, holding pommel and reins, offered her his help to spring into the saddle.

The flare in its socket showed her the fire-haze round Thorfinn's black hair, and the two tongues of cheekbone and jaw, and the predatory nose, lit bright as the gold of a weathervane. His eyes, deep as cup-markings, brimmed with shadow. He said, 'Quickly. I shall come,' and stood waiting until she was in the saddle and Thorkel mounted behind her, the reins in his hand. Then, as they turned to go, he put foot to his own stirrup and was off.

Her hands round Thorkel's hide coat Groa watched, chin on shoulder, as the flare disappeared into the darkness and the sound of hooves faded, going fast but not so fast that he could not read the trail by the light of his torch. It would not take long for him to catch up with Rognvald, since all Rognvald wished, and all he had worked for, was to be caught.

What happened then was fated to happen, and only a faint heart would put it off from day to day or year to year. Only a faint heart like hers.

SEVEN

THE TRAIL WAS indeed easy to follow, for by now it was late, and deep cold had crisped over the snow, so that the hoofmarks of Rognvald's horse were like ink on a piperoll, or like the marks of an Arabesque poem: alluring picture and message at once. Down through the shallows of a fast, icy stream he was led, and up and over a rise, and then wheeling down to the flat, frozen face of another loch, where his horse found ice and staggered briefly, as he saw from the scars the other horse also had done.

Then the trail looped round again, and for a moment he saw far away and a little below him a circle of flares in the darkness, masked and unmasked by the black moving figures of men, and a single light, travelling swiftly, making towards it.

Thorkel Fóstri had obeyed, then, and taken Groa to safety. At a guess, he would not return. The oath on the sword-hilt might give him pause, but not very much. More than that was the knowledge that he could not return, anyway, in time to alter the outcome. And that someone had to stay at Brodgar to control Rognvald's men and his own when both sides came to guess what was happening.

Thorfinn knew Rognvald's hird-leader, a hard-faced man from Westray called Styrkar who had escaped to Russia with Harald Sigurdsson. He was sensible enough, one would hope, to realise that extra bloodshed was useless, and to persuade his men to let well alone and camp by the lake for the night. No one, he supposed, would leave for Orphir now.

The trail turned east. The dash-marks made by the whipping harness had gone: Rognvald had taken time to pull it up, free of the galloping hooves. When she cut it, Groa must have had no hope of rescue. He wondered what she had meant to achieve, and then remembered the knife.

She was an Arnmødling, and pure-blooded Norse. They both owed their upbringing to the Norse way of thought, overlaid and changed in its turn by the time they had spent, both of them, among the Picts and the Gaels of the province of Moray—he for six years with his stepfather Findlaech, and Groa for four with Gillacomghain her husband. She would have made

Gillacomghain a good child-wife: grimly obliterating from her consciousness that part of their personal lives that she found repugnant, and building
upon what was left, until she had made a place for herself, organising, guiding, advising the people less capable who looked to them.

As the first Lady of Alba, she had no such sinecure; no well-defined niche;
no well-defined people, only a vast land of river and mountain and forest
which offered two courses only to its ruler and his lady. They could take its
tribute, and use it to make a life for themselves where they chose, free of any
care other than guarding it. Or they could look further off than their own
lives, or the lives of the races within it, and consider what might be needed to
bring such a land into order.

He now knew which he wanted to do, and he knew that it was the decision
Groa had expected of him. That, too, lay behind her fear of Rognvald, and her
contempt for him; that the road that stretched before him should be blocked
at the outset by a single spoiled youth.

But that was too simple a view. Rognvald was not a child. He had fought
and fought bravely in Russia. At Stiklestad, as a boy, he had dragged the
wounded Harald from the battlefield. He could have stayed in Norway as the
King's foster-brother and found great honour there. But he had chosen to
come back to Orkney, the land of Brusi his father, and seek the Thorfinn
he remembered, the other Earl of Orkney, the son of his grandfather's old
age.

It might have worked. There was so much that was good in Rognvald—his
courage, his vigour, his imagination, the stylish grace he applied to most
things—that it would have worked, had he found the Thorfinn he remembered, unencumbered by marriage; lord of part-Orkney and Caithness alone,
and not also of a great province and now a kingdom which would take him
south, away from the hearth of his kindred.

And now the imagination, the sense of mischief were being employed
against him. He had been afraid of it on the lake when it came to him suddenly
that Rognvald was no longer with them. And when, not very long after, he
was thrown to the ground by Rognvald's men and held there, in a series of
movements that could have appeared accidental, he knew that it was part of a
plan, and that the plan must involve Groa.

They had released him quite suddenly: as soon as Starkad, hearing his name
called, had begun to come to his help. But by the time he had raced to the
shore, Rognvald was off in the sledge and there was nothing he could do but
run for the horse-line, shouting to Starkad as he went. Only after he was
mounted did he discover Thorkel Fóstri, also mounted, beside him.

But all that was now far behind, in the stadir country, the land farmed by
his hirdmen. Thormod's steading had been passed, and now he heard the dogs
barking from Geirmund's, but saw no blazing lights: with a feast going on at
the loch, there would be no one there in any case but a few slaves and the
children. The trail swung wide, and he went on, through the bitter white
night, in his circle of blustering torchlight: on to the east away from Stenness
and Orphir. On into the dale country of frozen marsh and low hills where no

farms were to be found, only the mounds of the dead where the *haug-búi* watched.

Not the family mound of one's ancestors, where, unless one forgot to pay due respects, the walker after death would lie quietly. But the mounds they said the first settlers from Norway had found, two hundred years since: the tombs of the giants who had built the great rings of Kjallar, of Odin, whose monoliths, men said, might walk every Yuletide down to the water to drink and which, if you stood in their way as they came rumbling back, would slake the last of their thirst with your blood.

He had seen, racing after Groa, the marks of the hooves and the sledge-runners heeling over just such a mound, and now there were more, all about him. So Rognvald did not fear Odin, whatever they had taught him at Novgorod. It was more than he could say, despite Sulien. Or perhaps the White Christ also employed his Norns, and the name of one of them was Luloecen.

Then, as if the name had called it into being, a casting-spear flashed, once, in the light of his torch.

There had been no least sound of warning, and it was brilliantly thrown. Thorfinn flung himself on the neck of his garron, dragging the horse's head round, and as he did it, felt for and hurled the torch from him.

It did not go out. It arched through the black air and lay, spluttering, thirty feet off. Its light sparked on the spear vibrating in the ground under his horse's trampling feet.

A second spear glinted, hissed, and sank, with a thud, full into the garron's broad chest. The sky wheeled. The broad foot-rest of the stirrup, swinging, trapped Thorfinn's foot. The horse fell, with Thorfinn under him. He felt the ringing blow as his shoulder and head struck the ground. And then, with its scream still half-voiced in the air, his horse's weight, like one of the monoliths, fell across him and he heard, before he felt it, the bone snap in his leg. He lay still, and someone laughed.

Not the walker after death. But Rognvald, still mounted, picking his way delicately from the further side of a grave-mound to its top, from which he looked down, smiling at his uncle, the distant torchlight glimmering on his fair face and the hands busy below it, stringing his hunting-bow. Then, taking his time, he reached for an arrow and fitted it, smiling still.

There was time to see the silver chasing on the little weapon, and to observe that Rognvald still shot Tartar-fashion, with the shaft to the right of the bow. He was the best archer that Thorfinn had ever seen. He could aim and hit the hooves of a horse galloping immediately in front of him. He would have his sport, without doubt, before he killed him.

Thorfinn said, without very much breath, 'You'll get the same results, without any more bloodshed, if you leave me. My leg is broken.'

The arrowhead did not waver. Rognvald's even teeth gleamed. 'But,' he said, 'think of the pleasure I'd miss. They might still track you. And, alas, there is the arrowhead in your horse to betray my share in it. I am afraid there will be bloodshed between your men and mine, whatever I do. . . . Let me see. I am, I'm afraid, a little lacking in practice.'

The wind had dropped. In the stillness, the arrow came with the sound of a gnat and, burning down the skin of his neck, sank into the snow by his shoulder. 'No,' Rognvald said. 'It seems I still have the knack.' The second arrow was already fitted.

He would have twenty, perhaps. His horse would spoil his aim a little: it was surprising, in fact, that he had not dismounted. But presumably art demanded that he should bestride the mound on his horse—beautiful, golden, deadly as Alexander—and teach fear to an ugly man who was his only rival. The second arrow came, and struck through his hair; and the third, and pinned him to the snow by the skin of his shoulder.

He was using, Thorfinn saw, trefoil barbs, each with three cutting-edges, not one. The pain was as nothing compared with the pain of his leg. The pain of his leg was as nothing compared with a sense of tragedy born of nothing so trivial as this, his death in the snow. He said, 'You will plunge Orkney into war, and perhaps Alba. Rognvald. This is child's play.'

'No,' said Rognvald. 'You, an old man's mistake, clinging bumping and crying to the cross-axle of some foreign kingdom: that is child's play. I am performing a favour for you, as well as Alba.'

Thorfinn said, 'Siward will take Alba. Then Orkney.'

'If I let him,' said Rognvald. 'I imagine Siward and I will have quite a lot to say to each other, once you are dead.' And the fourth arrow came, scoring his wrist and burying itself in his *roggvarfeldr*. He sank his palms in the snow and tried again to pull himself free. The snapped bones ground in his leg, and the snow round his hand began to turn black. His head swam and he stopped, breathing quickly. 'Keep awake,' Rognvald said, and, fitting the fifth arrow, his teeth gleaming, turned it delicately so that the barb pointed at the other man's loins.

If it hit, he could not keep silent. On the other hand, it was a difficult shot. His shaggy cloak, his *roggvarfeldr*, lay in folds over what was exposed of his body, and the bulk of the horse shielded him from the waist down from the distant, dancing light of the torch. Rognvald would not know whether he had made a hit or not until he heard him scream.

Then he would scream. And it would not be unexpected after that if he fainted. And after that it would not be surprising if, baulked of his sport, Rognvald decided either to come down and rouse him or come and finish him off with his own hands. But, at any rate, to come down . . .

The arrow sparked. There was a tearing thud as it drove through the fleeces. He had screamed before he had time to know whether or not it had hit him. And then he felt the shaft hard against the inside of his thigh and knew it had not. Then he screamed again with the full power of his great voice, and on top of the mound Rognvald's horse, alarmed, suddenly trampled.

He heard Rognvald swear, and saw his thighs close and his wrist furl the reins. He saw, without surprise, that Rognvald's horse was not going to rear, or throw him, or do anything useful except dance a little until it felt the whip on its haunches. He saw, with stupefied disbelief, Rognvald's horse suddenly buckle and, bowing its neck, begin to roll over and over to the foot of the mound, where it lay silent and then began, rhythmically, to squeal. And he saw Rognvald drop from the saddle with a cry that became suddenly hollow, then stopped, for no reason that he could see. For he could not see Rognvald, either: only the unbroken white globe of the mound, and the threshing black bulk of the horse at its foot.

Silence fell. The injured horse rustled and grunted intermittently. The horse across his legs was growing cold, and so was he, despite the cloak. Soon, lying no doubt where he had been thrown on the other side of the mound, Rognvald would come to his senses, and then it would begin all over again, but at close quarters. Before that he must, if he could, get his legs free.

He was just strong enough, he thought, to do it. The handicap was the pain, which threatened his senses. After the third attempt, he could hardly see for the sweat and blood pouring into his eyes, and his arm was wet from wrist to shoulder where he had pulled himself free from the arrow. But he had got one knee up just a little, and in a moment the weight on the broken leg might be eased. There was no sound from Rognvald.

There was still no sound from Rognvald ten minutes later when, free of the carcass, Thorfinn lay with his eyes closed, an easy target and, at that moment, an uncaring one. Then, at the foot of the mound, the horse again started to scream, and, lifting himself, Thorfinn got to a knee and then to one foot, his weight on the strong wooden shaft of his scabbard.

Using it as a crutch, he groped his way slowly to the base of the mound and then subsided, out of reach of the thrashing hooves. The horse was alive, but would not walk again. He drew his sword and, waiting until it took breath, cut its throat. If Rognvald heard, he might guess what had happened. Or he might, with luck, think merely that the beast had collapsed.

Thorfinn sat and looked up at the mound. There was no sound, and nothing to be seen. Rognvald, then, must still be unconscious. It was odd, because the thickness of the snow, you would say, would have saved him from the worst of the fall. Nor was it very likely that he was lying in ambush just over the brow of the hill. He had the arrows: Thorfinn the sword. It was very much in his interest to shoot before Thorfinn got too near. He wished, too, late, that he had thought to leave his cloak beside his dead horse, thus deceiving Rognvald at least for a moment into thinking he was still there. But already the cold and the loss of blood were making him shiver, and soon the torch would lose the last of its light and Rognvald would see nothing anyway. Meanwhile . . .

Meanwhile, here were reins, and Rognvald's whip in its socket, and with the edge of his sword he could fashion himself some sort of splint, as quickly as may be. And that done, there remained only one course of action that appealed to him. Somehow, he must edge his way up the slope of the mound to the top. And, somehow, find out what had happened to his half-brother's son who was trying to kill him.

He had pulled himself halfway up, his hands gripping the heather under the snow, when he heard the sound, so short that he could hardly detect whether it was the voice of a man or of an animal. Then, when after a pause he resumed climbing again, he heard it once more, and for longer.

The first time, it had appeared to come from the other side of the mound. This time, it came from within it.

Whatever god belonged to the mound, it had saved him once. Or rather, you might say, looking about, that there was nothing odd about the accident to Rognvald's horse. You could see, from the black crevices under the turmoil of hoofprints, how uneven the mound-top was, under the snow. The horse had caught a foreleg, clearly, in one of these and had lost its balance, throwing Rognvald as it fell.

Thorfinn pulled himself a little higher and looked about. Yes. There, strewn about like straws in a salt-pan, were Rognvald's arrows, scattered as he dropped. There was a cleared place in the snow where something heavy had fallen. And here another, so black in the whiteness that he could not tell what lay underneath: heather or rock.

He drew back just in time.

What lay underneath was neither heather nor rock, but sheer space. What had tripped Rognvald's horse was not a twist of heather but a crevice in the ground. A crack beside many others into which all the top of the mound was seamed and broken and all of them, it seemed, surrounding something that was not a slit but a hole large enough to take a man's body. Thorfinn moved, bit by bit, to the edge and looked over and down.

Blackness, and no sound of anything living. He lifted his head. The torch was still burning, but far away on level ground, beyond the other side of the grave, and none of its light touched the cavity. He turned back, putting his weight on his good side, and felt for the purse at his belt, in which he always carried kindling. His hands were cold, but at length the spark came, and a strip from his shirt made a spill for him. He held it up, and looked down.

Fifteen feet below him, Rognvald lay, his eyes closed, his white face turned upwards, in a nest made of white bones, like a charnel-house.

It *was* a charnel-house. The bones about him were human but light and brittle as chaff and must have greatly broken his fall, violent as it had been. Then Thorfinn saw the way he was lying, and the glitter of blood from the great wedge-shaped rock slab beside him. He held the light low, seeking a way to let himself down, and saw that there was none. Then his small light went out.

He sat back on his heels. How long to daylight? Eight hours, at least. Perhaps more. He knew exactly where he was. There were no farms within shouting distance and no reason for anyone to pass here at night. He could reach no one by fire that he could not reach as well by his voice, so that there was little object in trying to set fire to the saddles, as he had thought of at first. It would, of course, give him warmth for a bit, but it would do nothing for Rognvald lying there, injured and coatless. He would be dead of cold by the morning.

Perhaps he was dead now. Or shamming. Turning back on his elbows, Thorfinn considered both ideas and dismissed them. He had been in too many battles to mistake what he had seen. Not dead, certainly, although perhaps shamming unconsciousness. And from the way he was stretched, and the little whine he had heard, climbing the slope, it might be a hurt to the chest: at the very least, to his ribs.

Which meant that, even awake, he could not possibly climb out. And of course he himself could not lift him. Even the harness, if he could collect it and join it together, would not stretch from the nearest horse down to the tomb. And his own strength at this moment was not all that great.

What, then? Perhaps, after all, he should try to collect the saddles and fire them. He could throw his coat down. That would give Rognvald a little warmth. He tried to think, rubbing his hands, which he couldn't feel any longer, and something fresh and cold touched his cheek. He lifted his head.

Snow. It seemed then that tonight the gods had withdrawn their favour. He could not sit out coatless in snow while the fires died. And no one would come, now, before daylight and probably a long time after, for all their tracks would be long since covered.

Thorfinn sighed and then, tightening his lips, made the long crawl down to Rognvald's saddle-bags. Inside one was a knife in a sheath, which he drew out and slipped inside his own jacket, under the cloak. In the other, blessedly, was a leather flask of something that, when he unstoppered it, proved to be very strong wine. 'Well, Rognvald my nephew,' he said. 'Let me sign the cup to you twice, once for Odin and once for Olaf Sigurdsson's god, and we shall see what comes of it.' And he drank.

He rested there only a moment, till he felt the warmth of the drink take effect. Then he stoppered the flask and buckled that, too, to his belt before starting the long drag uphill to the hole again. There he lit another scrap and looked down.

Rognvald lay as he had left him, save that this time he could see, gleaming beside him, a shard of the small embossed bow. What he mostly examined, before the light went out, was the disposition of the stones which provided the stepped roof of the beehive. If he could cling to one of these and it did not give way, he might manage to hand himself down, partly at least. He had marked where to fall, away from the boulders that seemed to litter the chamber, and away from Rognvald himself.

The last thing he did, before he began, was to unbuckle the scabbard that had served him so well as a crutch and lay it, with his sword still inside, where he thought the snow might not hide it completely, at the mouth of the hole.

Everyone in Orkney knew the Earl's sword: it would not be taken. And if by chance someone came and saw the dead horses, they would not immediately ride away before searching further. He did not want, on the whole, to make his last resting-place here, with the *haug-búi* and Rognvald, away from the sound of the sea. And that they would both be alive when they were found was unlikely. Once he climbed down here, his fate would be Rognvald's. Which, he supposed, was what Rognvald had wanted, one way or the other, all along.

In the event, he did not have to drop the whole fifteen feet, but the fall was bad enough, when it came, to make him gasp high in his throat as his leg struck the litter below.

Then, with the wisdom of experience, he rolled, and Rognvald's sword, meant for his throat, buried itself in the rubble where he had landed, taking Rognvald's body tumbling after it. Thorfinn heard him land and cry out in his turn and, his head swimming, nevertheless flung himself somehow towards the sound. His hands struck Rognvald's back as Rognvald was attempting to rise, and he felt the damaged ribs give way beneath them. Rognvald gasped, and dropped. All movement halted.

For a moment, the pain from his leg filled Thorfinn's world. He began to shiver, and then tried to take hold of himself. First, the sword to be found and got out of the way. Then, Rognvald's state to be distinguished. He had been able to sham unconsciousness, looked upon from above. Close at hand, it would be a different matter. Thorfinn put out a hand, groping cautiously through the rickle of disjointed bones and, touching a sleeve, snatched back his fingers. But the arm did not stir, even though he ran his fingers down it, and at the end he found Rognvald's hand, fallen open, and then the flat steel of his sword, very near it. Thorfinn felt his way to the pommel and, grasping it, felt for the wall by which he might draw himself up.

The opening in the roof was hardly visible at first. Then, as his eyes grew more used to the blackness, he could see, here and there, the grey glimmer of driving snow up there in the outside world. He lifted the sword and balanced it, judging the trajectory. It would be, to say the least of it, foolish if he threw the thing and it merely came back to his hand, point downwards this time. But when he swung his arm and let it go, it spun quite neatly up and out through the roof-gap to land—from the sound of it, not very far from his own. So, unless he had another knife on his person, Rognvald would have to get rid of him with his bare hands, if he still wanted to, and still could.

A wave of pain washed over him, and Thorfinn sat down. After a moment, he found his flint and tinder again and, coaxing a little light, turned to where he had heard Rognvald fall.

In the blackness that surrounded them, he had forgotten the charnel-house. It was not that, of course: just a burial chamber built of mighty squared blocks, with high wall recesses leading to side chambers. The block of stone that had caused Rognvald's injury had been the block-door to one of these chambers, tumbled aside centuries ago by the first robbers.

Whatever they had taken from the graves, it had not been the men and women who lay there in the recesses and in this, the main chamber, and even in the passage that he saw ran out, low and narrow, under the hill to one side. As later burials came, the earlier bones had been swept aside, mixed sometimes with bones that, he saw, were not human at all. Wild animals fallen through, once the roof breach had been made, and then trapped. Or the beasts of the dead, sacrificed and put there to serve them. Or later sacrifices, perhaps, in the days when someone had a farm nearby, and the wife of the household would come at certain times of the year, or at some turning-point in the life of the day, and offer a brace of fowl, or a stoup of milk, or a shank of meat to the *haug-búi*.

They spread all round the other man as he lay, the snub-nosed skulls and slender arm-bones and fretted pelvises, and the dust of them drifted into the wet yellow silk of his hair. Rognvald's eyes were open and looking at him. Thorfinn said, 'Where are you hurt?'

Rognvald collected his breath. 'Does it matter?' he said.

Thorfinn watched, with regret, his strip of cloth begin to burn itself out, and tore off and added another strip to it. There seemed to be nothing else around them that would give them light or heat, and he would prefer to keep what clothes he did have. He pulled himself over to Rognvald, who did not move, although his hands tightened.

There was no knife tucked in the other man's belt, or anywhere else that he could see: even his Russian lizard-skin purse had gone, as had the fur hat. Thorfinn leaned on one elbow and, hauling out the flask, unstoppered and proffered it. 'Don't thank me: it's your own. But I expect we'll both need it before this night is over.'

Rognvald took the flask slowly and then, thrusting it to his mouth, drank greedily in short gulps, punctuated by shallow breaths. His eyes all the time watched Thorfinn. Once, his gaze flicked down and rested on the unusual angle of his uncle's left leg, no longer held straight by its makeshift splint.

Thorfinn said, 'I told you. It broke when the horse fell on it. As you say, it probably doesn't matter, but we might as well do what we can. What about you? Ribs? Collarbone?' The light was going. He took back the flask and drank from it briefly.

'Ribs,' said Rognvald. 'You fell through the mound, then, as well?' His face, despite the pain, had suddenly cleared and his eyes, returning to Thorfinn's, had begun to sparkle. He said, 'I always have luck. You can't get back, can you? You're imprisoned here, as I am. You're going to die, too.'

'Possibly,' Thorfinn said. He knew a little about bones. He added another piece of shirt to the light and, untying Rognvald's jacket, began to explore with gentle hands. Rognvald's breath hissed through his teeth, and, sitting up, Thorfinn began to unbuckle Rognvald's belt and his own. Then he bent to untie the tangle of harness which hung round his leg. 'Sometimes strapping can help. I'll see what I can do before the light goes. I can do my own in the dark. Did you strike your head as well?'

'I suppose so,' said Rognvald. His eyes were still bright, but he was frowning. He said, 'You aren't wearing your sword.'

'No,' said Thorfinn. 'I left it by the opening, in case someone passes. Can you lift yourself?'

Rognvald pushed himself up. '*Left* it?'

'Oh, don't be a fool,' Thorfinn said. 'How often could I have had you killed in the last few weeks, if I'd really wanted? Because you had gone off your head, there was no reason for me to forget that we are kinsmen. In any case, I couldn't walk, and it had begun to snow. Your tomb looked quite inviting.'

The light went out. He finished by touch what he had started, and cleared the ground beneath Rognvald's shoulders and settled him. Rognvald's hand when he touched it was cold. Thorfinn said, 'Although I don't know why, in the midst of all the elaborate plotting, you didn't have the common sense to keep your cloak on. Here. Pull mine over you.'

He dragged it from under himself and flung it over, but did not hear Rognvald move to adjust it. At the moment, in fact, he did not much care what Rognvald did. He was cold, and the pain and the concentration had given him a headache, and he wanted to get the splinting over before he either lost his senses or was sick. Rognvald said, 'Thorfinn?'

The broken bone, sickeningly, would not stay together. He could hear himself wheezing, and when Rognvald did not speak again, knew that it must be apparent what he was doing; and that Rognvald, unable to help, was at least refraining from intruding on his struggles. Then he got the thing in place, and the splint, and began to do the strapping by touch. The flesh-wounds had long since stopped bleeding, but the sweat was running, again, into his eyes. When at last it was done, he lay back more suddenly than he intended to, and the nest of bones cracked in his ears as he sank back into them. He thought of what would amuse Groa. 'It was St Winwaloe,' he said, 'I think, who slept upon nutshells.'

Groa didn't answer and all the lights had gone out, so he thought he might as well close his eyes and go to sleep.

He woke because of the nature of a dream he was having; and because he was cold. Not bitterly cold, but the sort of cold one might feel in winter, on a campaign night in the open. The smell under his chin was the familiar campaign one as well, of his old, shaggy cloak, and another man, clearly, was sharing it, although he did not remember inviting anyone. But there was nothing of challenge or provocation about the body pressed close to his own, in whose arms, indeed, he appeared to be lying. It lay only as one man might shield another for warmth, and he was grateful for it. Thorfinn moved a little, and a throbbing pain in one leg seized his senses. He opened his eyes.

Above was not the dark wooden ceiling of any hall he had ever owned, but a pattern of peculiar grey shapes, the biggest nearly circular, and all breathing cold air down on him. By his head, when he looked to see where he was lying, were broken piles of disarranged human bones. And on his other side . . .

But this time he did not turn, because he knew whom he would see on his other side. He lay still, thinking and looking up at the sky, which told him that it was just past dawn, and that the night was over, and that they were both alive. Then Rognvald behind him withdrew his arm quietly, and shifted so that they were no longer quite together, and said, 'You fainted. But I think it turned to sleep. What do you feel?'

'Relief, largely,' Thorfinn said, and turned his head. Rognvald's face, dimly seen, was smiling a little. It could be deduced that he had suffered a good deal more pain than his uncle, and had therefore had rather less sleep. But there was a kind of calmness about him that had not been there before. Thorfinn said, 'I might even say I was grateful if I didn't remember that, but for you, I should be whole, happy, and in bed at Orphir. *He was not a stone in the place of an egg, and he was not a wisp in the place of a club; but he was a hero in place of a hero.* What about your bones?'

'There is still flesh on them,' said Rognvald. 'And that, under the circumstances, is what matters. If you are looking for your knife, it is by your hand. It fell from your jacket last night.'

Thorfinn turned his head. The knife he had taken from Rognvald's saddle-bag was indeed there, where his fingers could grasp it in a moment. He opened his lips and Rognvald said, 'I know it is mine. Keep it.'

Thorfinn picked it up and laid it where either of them, at need, could obtain it. There was no need to say anything. Unwittingly, he had given the other man the ultimate proof that he meant him no harm. Last night, he had disarmed Rognvald, but had made no attempt to use his own weapon, and instead had done what he could to ensure that he would live through the night. And Rognvald for his part had done as much for him when he was no longer conscious.

Thorfinn said, 'The flask was yours, too. I have a feeling that, if we were careful, we might get a breakfast each out of it. And then, if you have nothing better to do, we might throw dice for a while. I have a pair in my purse, heavily weighted in my favour.'

Rognvald laughed, and then got rather pale and grinned carefully, his hand to his strapping. 'Tell me no jokes, and I don't care what your dice do. Thorfinn?'

Thorfinn unstoppered the flask. 'Yes?'

Rognvald said, 'I envy you Alba. It is no secret.'

Thorfinn drank, and then held the flask out. He kept his voice level. 'There is nothing I can do,' he said. 'I have set my hand to it. I would turn back now for no man: not for my closest friend.' He hesitated, and then said, 'If you want to see me often in Orkney, all you have to do is make trouble and we shall meet, but as enemies. I would rather be your friend. But I cannot come often.'

'I have no one else,' Rognvald said. He smiled again. 'Are you not sorry for me? Why don't you tell me to go home to King Magnús or Harald Sigurdsson?'

'I can't think why not,' Thorfinn said. 'Unless it were that you would at once suspect me of wishing to have back the rest of the Orkneys.'

'And don't you?' said Rognvald.

'I did have them once,' Thorfinn said slowly. 'And of course it is hard to give part of them up. About the disputed third, we should likely never agree, but, as you know, I have never tried to take it from you. But your father's share belongs to you: about that there is no doubt at all. I cannot think of anyone else in the world who could have taken those northern isles with my agreement, and I cannot think of anyone else I should ever share Orkney with, to the day of my death. Once, we might have ruled jointly, but now it is different. You are Earl of two-thirds, and Thorkel Fóstri will rule the rest for me, and be your good friend so long as you are his. And when I come north, we shall meet.'

'I think,' said Rognvald, '. . . I think you have probably given me what I deserve, if not something rather better. I shall reconcile myself, in your absence, to Thorkel Fóstri. I shall not, however, share a cloak with him.'

He laid down the now empty flask and, clearing a space on the flagstones between them, picked up the knife and proceeded to scratch out a gaming-board. 'All right,' he said. 'What shall we play for? Love? Or money?'

'Money, I feel,' Thorfinn said, 'would be safer.'

When the rescuers came three hours later, the rattle of dice still proceeded from inside the mound, half drowned now and then by an outburst of arguing voices.

The voices sounded entirely amicable and proved, on investigation, to belong to two men, one fair and one dark, sharing a cloak on the floor, far below them. By the side of the fair man was a small pile of what appeared to be chicken-bones. By the side of the dark was a still larger. 'Thorfinn!' said Thorkel Fóstri; and the dog Sam, who had brought them there, jumped about in the new snow and redoubled his barking.

'I told you he was a magnificent tracker,' Rognvald said, throwing the dice.

'Indeed you are right,' Thorfinn said. 'The baying of the great hound Garm, who belongs to the present and the future. I could almost forgive him for other things.' Above, Thorkel Fóstri called again, and the dog's yapping rose a note higher. Showers of snow fell from the opening. Thorfinn threw, his eyes on the board, and raised his voice. 'Do you mind? If you stop calling, we might have peace to finish the game. Is Styrkar there?'

'My lord?' It was the voice of Rognvald's chief officer.

'Oh, Styrkar,' Thorfinn said. 'Your Earl wishes to borrow from you a considerable sum of money. What do you have?'

There was a pause. 'My lord?' said the same voice. 'I have a little hacksilver, of course. And my arm-rings.'

'I hardly think that will be enough,' Thorfinn said. 'Rognvald? Shall we count the bones here, or take them with us and let the clerks do it?'

Beside him, he knew Rognvald was grinning, in spite of the pain he was in. The stupefaction above was nearly tangible. They could hear murmured talk, and some busy tramping, but even when the ropes came, and then the help they needed, no one asked how they came by their injuries, either then or when they were got somehow on horseback for the ride back to Brodgar.

In fact, the ride was the worst part, for it ended in public by the frozen lake, before both hirds and the folk of the steading, where the men had stayed overnight, crammed into barns or in front of the big fires in deerskins. In Groa's face, the first he saw, Thorfinn saw reflected his own disarticulated appearance. Rognvald, he was happy to see, looked rather worse when he came, cautiously, to take his leave. 'We shall go straight back to the east. You are a sledge short. I am leaving you one of mine, with a rider. He can bring it back when it's got you to Orphir.'

He knew the sledge Rognvald meant. It was smoother-running than any remaining to him. And it was true, he could not have ridden to Orphir. He said, 'And you? They found no ribs missing when they looked at you in there? I thought that pile of bones was higher than it might have been.'

'I hope, all the same, that Styrkar satisfied you,' Rognvald said. 'You can keep the rugs in the sledge. If you don't want that stinking cloak, I could take it for Sam to sit on.'

Thorfinn picked the cloak up from the bench where they had put him. It did smell, now, and they had brought him another one. He held it out and, when Rognvald came, gave him the cloak and the light clasp of his two hands under it, as Rognvald stood over him. Thorfinn said, 'What shall I wish you?'

In the pale face, the handsome eyes were too large and too bright. 'Just peace, I believe,' Rognvald said, and smiled, and walked away.

Thorfinn was not a small man, so the sledge would not take Groa as well, but she rode at his side during the short journey to his own hall at Orphir, and if he did not remember quite all of it, it was not surprising, as his night's sleep had been fairly sparse.

In fact, when he did open his eyes near the end of the journey, he thought at first they were arriving somewhere quite different, for he did not expect to round the hill and see spread on the shore not only the buildings of his house-stead, implanted between here and Swanbister, but six strange longships drawn up on the beach, and tents by the score set up on either side of the stream and halfway up the hill.

He looked up, to see Groa staring down, frowning also. He said, 'Thorkel!' and his foster-father, riding ahead, paused and turned. Thorkel said, 'I don't know what it is either, but there's Bardi riding uphill to tell us. You look terrible.'

'It was worth it,' said Thorfinn. The snow was beginning to melt, and the sledge bumped and grated. Killer-Bardi got closer, and Thorkel Fóstri touched Rognvald's driver on the shoulder so that he slackened pace, and the sledge ran to a halt. Killer-Bardi, arriving, stared down at the King and said, 'What's happened?'

'Nothing,' said Thorkel Fóstri. 'Whose ships are they?'

'They came at daybreak. He's waiting for you in the hall. Kalv Arnason,' the steward said. 'The Lady's uncle. From Norway.'

'Let's go down,' said Thorfinn abruptly.

He had built a stockade round the main buildings last year, but the gates were already open, and the riders swept in, half the hird going ahead of him. The sledge drew up at the door of the hall, Groa dismounting beside it, and before he had begun to think how to get out, Kalv was striding out of the doorway and up to them. He said, 'My little niece!' and kissed Groa lavishly. He looked as if he had had a bad voyage, and his hair was greying. Then he turned to the sledge.

'Well, Kalv?' said Thorfinn.

Kalv, at least, noticed nothing wrong with his newly returned host. 'My dear boy!' he said. 'Or should I say my lord King these days? I hardly expected to find you in Orkney, the heel-end, as it were, of all your kingdom. Why should a man stay in Orkney when he has the milk and honey of Alba there for the taking?'

'Why should a man leave Norway when he has the milk and honey of King Magnús for the taking?' Thorfinn replied. 'Why the visit, Kalv?'

'Visit!' said Kalv. His smile stretched wider. 'This time, nephew, I have more to offer you than a barrel of herring on my way out to Dublin. This time I have come to stay, with six of the finest warships you ever saw, and three hundred champions to man them.'

There was a little silence, during which Thorfinn heard Groa catch her breath. He said, 'You have? Then let us go into the hall and hear about it. Thorkel?'

From staring at the late regent of Norway, Thorkel Fóstri turned slowly and looked at his foster-son. Then he said, 'I'll get you a chair,' and strode away, calling to someone. Which was not helpful, since to leave the sledge promptly was, at that moment, the first necessity in Thorfinn's mind.

He said to Starkad, 'Give me your arm,' but even as the standard bearer started forward, Kalv said, as if no one had spoken, 'Why am I here, do you ask? Because of the ingratitude of kings' sons, that's why. Did I or did I not take a party to Russia, paying all my own expenses, to beg King Magnús to come back and rule us, instead of Canute's son? Have I not been King Magnús's guardian and friend all the years of his boyhood? Did he not give me and everyone else the fullest amnesty—'

'For killing his father?' Thorkel Fóstri was back, although without the promised chair. He said bluntly, 'What is it, Kalv? Has Magnús thrown you out?'

Kalv went pale, and then red. 'He has broken his word,' he said. 'Retracted his amnesty. Threatened all those who had anything to do with the death of his father. I had to fly for my life. I never mean to go back. I wouldn't go back if he begged me. You'll need someone to look after Orkney for you, and keep that young wastrel Rognvald in order. He might as well learn that in this part of the world he'll never cheat his way into the ruler's real favour: he'll always be an oath-breaking foreigner who is holding a nice piece of land he isn't entitled to. You've been too slack with him. Leave it to me. These six longships there will see that you get back your lost third of Orkney, if not all of it.'

Too late, the chair had arrived. With Thorkel's hand on his wrist, Thorfinn pulled himself out of the sledge and, using his good leg, reached for and captured the chair-rail. There, without sitting down or answering Kalv, he twisted to speak to the sledge-driver.

Before he had fully turned, the horse had started to step, and before he could speak, the equipage was moving off, gathering speed over the snow as it made for the gateway.

'Well!' said Kalv. 'He was in a hurry to get to his supper.'

'He was in a hurry to get to Rognvald,' said Thorfinn, and sat down and let them deliver him, finally, to his hall-house at Orphir.

EIGHT

AND SO, MY dear Malduin,' said Siward, Earl of Northumbria, 'it seems that your young cousin is having a little trouble in Orkney, and that Alba will have to do without him for the rest of the winter at least. I ask myself what I can do to help matters.'

The Bishop of Alba, sitting opposite in a cushioned chair, pursed his lips and continued, for the moment, to draw off a fine pair of sewn gloves he had just collected from his York lodging on the way here. He might not be dressed in his ceremonial robes, but some respect was due to his rank, and the son of a fur-pedlar ought to remember it. Also, he objected to the sudden summons from Fife. It was a long way to travel in winter, and Elfswitha his present wife was never slow to suggest what the markets and workshops of York might provide to make life in Alba more bearable.

Not that he found it untenable. When this fellow Siward killed Earl Eadulf, Malduin's household had been upset for weeks until matters settled, for, after all, if the new Earl of Northumbria were to make war on the Bishop's cousin Thorfinn of Alba, the Bishop wished to choose the right side. Then he had had his interview, like this one. Earl Siward wished him to continue serving the King of Alba, as before, from his hall in Fife.

He had done so and, since Thorfinn his cousin troubled him very little, had succeeded in creating for himself, with industry, a way of life very nearly as convenient as the one Earl Eadulf had disrupted. And after fifteen years in office he had acquired, also, a certain authority that allowed him to forget, unless he must absolutely remember, that his father Gilla Odhrain had married the Earl of Orkney's sister and that his half-brother Ghilander still sat like a peasant among the black ewes in the Hebrides.

Now he laid the paired gloves with precision on his lap, folded his hands, and bent a confessor's gaze on the son of Thore Hund. 'According to my information,' said the Bishop, 'King Magnús of Norway has had nothing to do with what happened. The Earls fell out, and the King received an injury of little importance. Your minions, surely, have informed you of this.'

The Earl's fingers, flicking over and over through his beard, did not falter, nor did his gaze move from the Bishop's. 'And so,' he said, 'you expect your cousin Thorfinn to come south in the spring?'

'He will have his tributes to collect,' said the Bishop. Behind him, footsteps crossed the boards. In front of him, Earl Siward dropped his hand from his beard.

'Ah, Ligulf,' said the Earl. 'You remember Ligulf of Bamburgh, I am sure, Bishop Malduin? He and I married sisters. Ligulf: the Bishop has been singularly deep in prayer this winter, and appears to know very little of what is going on in Orkney. For example, have you not heard, my lord Bishop, that six shiploads of refugees from Norway have been given shelter by your cousin of Orkney, thus renewing the skirmish between the two Earls? And since the boatloads include women and children, your cousin has had to give them land on which to live, rather than add them profitably to his hird?'

'It is as well, perhaps,' said Earl Siward, 'that all this escaped you, my lord Bishop, or you must have been concerned for your brother in the Western Isles, who might well have been swept aside to provide a living for this fugitive Kalv and his crew. But, of course, neither the Western Isles nor Orkney itself, one supposes, would be free of harrying by Earl Rognvald, so the Norwegians have been accommodated in Caithness.

'A welcome accretion, I am sure, for the people of Caithness. And even more welcome news, I am certain, for King Magnús of Norway, when he hears. But, as you say, it need not concern the King your cousin. He will be in Alba this summer, collecting his rents.'

Ligulf pulled up a stool and sat down. A sallow man with a narrow face, his long black moustaches moved, like crow's wings, with his smile. He said, 'My good brother found the Christmas crown-wearing somewhat trying. The Lady Emma has not yet forgiven the loss of her resources, and she has some local support. Carl Thorbrandsson is wealthy enough to do as he pleases, and so is the family of my lord Crinan, for all they are kinsmen by marriage. We are waiting, indeed, with a little anxiety to hear what my lord Crinan in particular will do.'

The Bishop of Alba noticed, to his annoyance, that one of the gloves on his lap was unaccountably teased out in one corner. He smoothed it flat again and, folding his hands once more, said, 'Gossip, I fear, does not come within my province. If you wish accredited news, I can only tell you what I have heard. The King's foster-father has been restored to his old command in Orkney, which means, I take it, that the King himself is thus free to travel south. On the second matter, I understand that couriers have already been sent to Cumbria to invite my lord Crinan to return to his abbacy at Dunkeld, with his family if he so wishes.'

'What!' said Earl Siward. His flat cheekbones above the springing beard had turned red under last summer's burning. 'Where did you hear that?'

'Between prayers,' said Bishop Malduin calmly. Then, as the Earl continued to stare at him, 'My clerk brought the news from Dunkeld. The church in Alba is a poor thing, but I pursue what duties I can. It is as well to see that the young child your nephew is cared for. He is, of course, King Duncan's youngest son, but still the throne might one day be his.'

Ligulf said, 'My lord Crinan . . . To return to Dunkeld with his family?' He looked at his brother-in-law. 'Forne. And Orm and Maldred, no doubt. You said he was clever. I believe you.'

'You refer to my cousin Thorfinn?' said the Bishop. 'He is an opportunist, yes. From your point of view, of course, it is a pity that Magnús of Norway should at present be so preoccupied with his war against Denmark. It would take very little to push Thorfinn's foster-father out of Orkney now, and there would be an excellent excuse for invading Caithness while the rebels are there enjoying Thorfinn's hospitality. Without fighting-men from the north or from Ireland, Thorfinn could not possibly retain hold of Alba.'

The crow's wings parted on Ligulf's face again. 'What are you saying? That King Magnús of Norway should be invited to rule the Orkneys and Alba? I rather think the King of England might object.'

With a bang, Earl Siward of Northumbria struck both arms of his chair. 'But the Lady Emma might not,' he said. 'With the King of England a simple-minded eunuch and Svein of Denmark beaten into a corner by Norway, what is there left?'

'The Saxon Athelings?' said Ligulf. 'The Russians are selling off daughters: the Emperor Henry himself refused one the other day. The babies that Canute sent to Hungary can't possibly be there still, with revolution after revolution taking place. If they're not in Germany, they must be in Russia.'

'Forget the Athelings,' said Siward. 'While Emma lives, you'll never hear of them; or if you do, her assassins will be there first. And you can dismiss the Normans' young bastard as well. He has a council about him that would throw Emma out of power the moment he took over England. But with Magnús . . .'

The Bishop of Alba cleared his throat languidly, in the fashion that arrested unwanted chatter on the occasion of his more ghostly dialogues. 'No doubt,' he said, 'speculation is interesting; but the facts remain that the King is still in possession of Caithness and Alba and part of Orkney, and Abbot Crinan and his friends are in possession of Dunkeld, and, moreover, Norway is, as you pointed out, fully occupied at present with her claims upon Denmark and, presumably, England.

'So far as I can see, there is little you can do about any of these matters. If it interests you, the object of establishing my lord Crinan back in Dunkeld is less one of strategy than one of trade. Dunkeld is, like York here and London, at the head of a tidal estuary, and under Crinan enjoyed a considerable trade of a certain kind with the merchants of Norway and Denmark and also elsewhere in the Baltic. I am told that the King plans to turn the Abbot's undoubted skills to the benefit of himself and his new kingdom. He will certainly have to find them riches soon; and with Earl Rognvald on his tail and a new kingdom to rule, he will not pick them up so readily on the high seas. In this new policy, there may lie no threat to Northumbria at all.'

Ligulf of Bamburgh slapped his palms on his thighs and sat, elbows akimbo, smiling at the Bishop of Alba. 'How shrewd,' he said. 'And how penetrating. Indeed, you have thrown light, as your calling requires of you, on many places of gloom and obscurity, and have made them all plain. Siward, am I not right?'

'Eh?' said Earl Siward. He continued to stare, brows knitted, into the fire-basket.

'I said,' said Ligulf of Bamburgh, 'that perhaps the Bishop would welcome a dish of mutton and a cup of our wine before he has to go?'

'Oh,' said Siward. 'Yes. Send for them, will you? Perhaps Osbern would join us. How old is the boy?'

He was looking at the Bishop. 'My stepson?' said Malduin. 'No. You mean—'

'King Duncan's son. The boy at Dunkeld. How old is the boy at . . . ?'

'Ah, yes. He is eight, I believe, Earl Siward. A little family sadly sundered. The oldest, Malcolm, is still with King Edward?'

Siward did not reply. His brother-in-law, already risen, said, 'He is being fostered in the south, yes, my lord Bishop.'

'And the second son? Donald? Is he still in Ireland?'

But this time even Ligulf did not hear him, and the Bishop was forced to get up, collecting his gloves, and walk to the other room.

He left very soon after that, picking his way past the Earl's handsome new church as he rode thoughtfully back to his lodging.

Walking on either side of him, his men-at-arms were splashed up to the edge of their cloaks, but it didn't matter: he had already called on the Archbishop, taking him the little magnifying-glass that Crinan had got for him eight years ago.

Aelfric had been gracious, for him, in his grand residence beside St Peter's, with the bullsheads of the Sixth Legion built into the walls. He had received the magnifying-glass with a quip about old age, in Latin, that Bishop Malduin had been tempted to cap in Greek, except that it was unwise with a Saxon who had not had the advantages of a training in Ireland. The Archbishop had been wearing silk, and his house was full of servants, and Malduin had been given wine in a cup made of glass, and afterwards had been permitted to keep the glass as a gift. It was in his saddle-bag now.

His wife of course would be delighted, and so was he: no one in Alba had such a cup. It was perhaps churlish to feel that something of a less domestic nature, a psalter perhaps, would have been more flattering from one high bishop to another.

He was still in the good quarter of the town and passing the well-kept house that had belonged to Crinan and now, one supposed, to his son Maldred, unless all the college of coiners kept the property in their own hands. When Crinan was there, there had been no need for the Bishop to go to the Jews outside the walls, or to send his man down to the workshops on the Fosse or to the wharves, as he had done today, to find out what was for sale and bring it to his lodging, together with some merchant he didn't know. In the summer, he used to enjoy going down to the jetties himself to watch the knörrs coming in from the Baltic or further afield, with cargoes that might run from honestone to elephant tusks and silks from Cathay or Italy.

Now, in winter, there would be nothing much at the riverside but barges of brushwood and clay, too late, as usual, for the flood embankment, or a boat in through the rivers from Lincoln, full of those grey bowls and pitchers that his half-brother's wife used to treat as if they came from Charlemagne's table.

You could smile, for, living in the Western Isles, she had never seen a town except perhaps a glimpse of Dublin, and certainly never one with eight thousand people in it. They said only London was bigger than York. He had been in London once or twice. He liked cities. Except that it riled him to be summoned, he was pleased to be here and not sitting hunched over his brazier, listening to the drone of illiterate farmers' sons trying to train for the priesthood. Although in Fife the hunting was good.

He reached his lodging. The merchant with the amber had not yet arrived, but someone else was waiting for the Bishop as he shook his cloak off and walked in. A man he vaguely recognised from the past. A tallish man with broad shoulders and coarse, straight hair exactly between red and yellow, who wore on his shoulder a Pictish buckle, the twin of one he had seen his cousin Thorfinn sometimes use. A kinsman, in fact, of Thorfinn, whose line had kept a toe-hold in the region when all the Norse kings of York had finally fled, and had returned from Dublin, quietly, in later years to settle and spread: first in Westmorland, and then back in the York region itself. The man whose eager helpfulness, on the occasion of King Duncan's campaign against Durham, had largely contributed to the failure of that campaign.

The Bishop of Alba said, 'Thor, is it not? Of Allerdale?'

'There, now,' said his uninvited guest, in Gaelic. 'I wore the brooch in the hopes that you would remember the twin of it. And there is not the least need for worry: I kept my hood over my face all the way here, so the Earl will have no cause to imagine that you and Thorfinn and I have a plot in it. Are you well?'

It was more than time to recover the initiative. 'I am well, I thank you,' the Bishop said. 'But pressed for time, I am afraid. Perhaps it is something you could leave with my clerk?'

When he smiled, the man's colouring became positively vulgar. 'Cumbria?' he said. 'I'll leave it with your clerk if you wish, but I should have thought, my lord Bishop, that you would have wanted the least taste of it yourself, to begin with.'

'Sit down,' said Bishop Malduin shortly, and did so himself, with his gloves on.

Later, he was in two minds as to whether he had done the right thing or not. It was hard enough, as he complained from time to time to his Maker, to have Cousin Thorfinn and the Earl Siward both to serve without meddling with the balance of power between them. Naturally, with the lord Crinan and his family reinstalled in Dunkeld, Thorfinn's intentions for Cumbria became of instant importance both to Siward and to men like Thor here, who owned land throughout northern England. He was worried himself, come to that.

Whoever controlled Dunkeld was not unlikely to meddle with the interests of Fife and even of Lothian, at present mainly Siward's concern. And Crinan was not only a powerful dealer; he was abbot of a Columban church rooted in Ireland and subject to influences York and Durham knew nothing of, not least of which were the vagaries of Irish tribal politics.

He did not know, therefore, if he had been wise to listen to this fourth-generation exiled Orcadian with the three languages and the air of undeviating jollity. All that was required of him was inaction, that must be said. He was under no obligation to his cousin Thorfinn. The land he had been given in Fife had mostly belonged to the men who had gone north with Duncan and paid for it with their lives. Nobody lived on it now but slaves and cottagers and widows: someone had to look after it. And the rest, such as it was, he had been told he could reclaim for himself from the marshes.

He didn't owe anything to Thorfinn, and the Columban church had nothing to offer him, even if his interests had not been tied firmly to the lowlands of Scotland. There, in the Anglian churches, the churches dedicated to St Cuthbert, lay the promise of rich shrines and the rewards of friendly alliance with the powers of Northumbria and the King further south. Whatever measure of control England let fall under the Kings of Alba, she could never afford to allow it to become absolute, so that the small line of ecclesiastical strong-points fell asunder, and the neck of land between the Forth and the Clyde became a thoroughfare for the Norse of the east to reach the Norse of the west: a thoroughfare and a base from which they might overwhelm all England.

No. He did not relish being ordered about by the fur-trader's offspring and his minion the new Bishop at Durham, nor yet by the sword-happy war-lord who sat in the Archbishop's throne at York; but there were compensations. It did not do to cross one's fate. Particularly when there was nothing to do but do nothing.

It could be said that the man Thor and he had reached a reasonable understanding. He had been quite surprised when, on parting, the fellow had lifted his cloak and taken from under it a small marquetry box, which he laid on the table and opened.

It was full of amber. Not Whitby stuff either, washed up on the beaches and then worked in some local shed. This was Baltic amber, carved where they understood such things. He picked up a pendant, and the thing shone like honey over a flame.

'It appeals to you, so?' said the man Thor. 'Then you will give me the pleasure, surely, of presenting it to you and the lovely girl you have waiting there at home for you, I have no doubt. All I ask is that your two lips stay shut. If it got about that Thor mac Thorfinn was selling his amber for nothing, it would be the ruin of me.'

He might look and sound like a goat-herd, but it did not do to forget that he was a merchant-coiner as well, with licence to strike in London as well as here with his brother in York. Hence the land he owned. Hence the army he could bring, fully paid for, when his interest was engaged, or attacked.

In retrospect, the Bishop saw, he had done the right thing. He had nothing with which to reproach himself. He had a glass cup and an amber pendant and a conscience as unblemished as either.

Since news has a way of travelling wherever there are waterways, the tale of Bishop Malduin's summons to York moved north in due course and entered the river Tay and, passing the King's hall at Perth, arrived with the last of the salt water at the sprawling monastery of Dunkeld, where, on the rising ground looking to Birnam, the lord Abbot Crinan had now made, at last, his permanent home.

It amused him to be back in the kingdom whose heiress he had married forty years before.

Bethoc. A tough-minded young woman who had attended to the affairs of the marriage-bed as he might one of his tally-boards: had produced their son Duncan and then, when the King and policy both required it, had removed herself north and placed herself, with equal briskness, at the disposal of Earl Sigurd of Orkney.

He, Crinan, had been brought to Alba because he had had to fly, temporarily, from his Saxon masters and because he had something King Malcolm needed.

A head for business and the means to supply silver was part of it. Easy movement between one trading-centre and another was another part. At the height of his power, his ships had carried him anywhere he pleased: to Denmark or Norway, to Friesland and Germany, to Normandy and Brittany and south to Aquitaine. He had bought Moorish silk in Spain, in his day. But most of the work was done, of course, with his small, folding balance and the weights he still carried, native to the inside of his shirt as his heart was.

He went everywhere because merchants in money or in goods went everywhere as churchmen did, under licence to kings who lived only to kill each other. Sometimes, as with churchmen, the safe-conduct failed, and that was the end of it. But in the meantime the King of Norway sent you his gold to have new regalia made, and the portion of gold that was yours for your trouble you lent, at interest, to the King of Denmark to pay for the new ships he needed for his next war on Norway. And of course, because you moved freely from court to court and baron to baron, men gave you secrets to carry.

Two or three years in Alba had been enough, and he had given the troubles of King Malcolm little more than a passing thought in all the years that followed, save that he collected his rents from Dunkeld and brought his boats into the Tay and supplied good advice and fighting-men and silver, for a consideration, when it was needed. Latterly, as he withdrew more to his lands in Cumbria, he had been able to watch and to weigh up his royal son, and to find no reason to disagree with the general opinion: that when King Malcolm went, this youth of modest gifts was not likely to stand up to King Canute for long.

You could say, of course, that it would do no one any harm, and himself least of all, to allow Canute the satisfaction of increasing his empire by the dimensions of Alba and Orkney. But sometimes kings died young, and he had little confidence in Canute's heirs.

Then, at Chester, he had seen Bethoc's other son Thorfinn.

In a long and successful career, he supposed that there, on the royal ferry, he had experienced his only real moment of regret: that the extraordinary, ramshackle youth sitting on deck winding back his leggings should not be his son, and that the fool on the riverbed, drowning, was not the son of Bethoc and Sigurd.

But Thorfinn was not his son, and self-interest had not prevented him from executing the neat little plan to send Gillacomghain north to oust his uncle's stepson, together with Carl Thorbrandsson. At the same time, it had been no accident that Carl Thorbrandsson was one of his own brotherhood of coiners and, in particular, ran the Lady Emma's mint at Exeter.

Behind Emma's dealings with young Thorfinn lay something a trifle more than expediency. The Lady all her life had looked after her north-born family, to its remotest members. And, in an odd way, you could say Thorfinn was her family. Orkney and Normandy, after all, had been settled by kinsmen. Emma and Sigurd, Thorfinn's father, were second cousins of the half-blood. And he himself stood between them.

So Thorfinn had survived to inherit Moray; and now he had Alba, with Rognvald hampering him in the north, and the five husbands of those five Northumbrian sisters and their adherents staring hungrily at his borders on the south. A situation that would tax a man strongly based as Malcolm had been in the middle and south of his kingdom, with his own adherents and Ireland to call upon. A situation full of peril for an interloper from the north, as men must see him, with no great families who had known him from childhood and who for his benefit and their own would follow him into war; and no Irish to call upon except the exiled Eachmarcach.

It had been wise of Thorfinn to invite himself, Crinan, to return, and to bring Maldred with him if he wished. It would be even wiser of Thorfinn to make use of him, now he was here. The observer always saw the heart of the game. He had counsel to offer, and it would be worth the price he would exact for it.

The summer passed, and Thorfinn did not come to see him, although every man who arrived in Dunkeld had a different story about his doings in Alba: how long he had stayed in each part, and what meetings he had held, and how he had set people to look to the marsh-passes and bridges, and clear and re-lay the most useful paths, and how he had even gone up to the hill-shielings to count the stock and look at the condition of the hay, and into the turf huts to see what there was in the way of good tools for ploughing and reaping and cutting and even for slicing the peat.

In some parts, he had stopped men from felling their own timber, which had not pleased them very well, and in others he had set them to cut it, even though the pains of dragging the logs had never seemed worth the effort. And when the timber was there, it was put into store for their own use, or the King's. Instead of butter, this year he wanted wagons, and instead of malt, next year he wanted ships.

And that was a matter of complaint as well, for there was a big difference between the good summer you could have, when you felt like it, down at the shore with the other fisher families knocking up a new boat for the season, and the kind of ships that traders and fighting-men had. Men who knew about these things had to come and live beside you, and eat your food, and expect you down at the sheds most mornings, unless you could show a good reason why.

The King had promised to install no hierarchy from Orkney, and to that extent he had broken his promise. On the other hand, the day-to-day ordering of the districts was, four years after he had taken the kingdom, in the hands of the best-respected families in each district, and as the roads improved and hence the markets, and the movement of surplus food from one part of the country to another, men could come to him in increasing numbers and stay, as his hird in Orkney had done, and both advise and be advised, as well as provide the strength at the centre without which there could be no central justice; or none that could be enforced.

Already, Crinan knew from report that Thorfinn had men with him who were not only servants, free or unfree, but had lands of their own in Angus and Moray; about Perth; in the lands leading southwards to Cumbria; and inside Cumbria itself. A small court, but one which seemed a good deal bigger by now than a self-seeking nucleus, and which, to exist at all, must already have faced up to or conquered the barrier of language. If he had men from Strathclyde and Cumbria in his entourage, then Cumbrian was being spoken as well as Gaelic, and very likely Saxon as well. And if he had Cumbrians with him, Siward must know of it.

That, to the skilled observer who sat at Dunkeld, was one of the perils in what Thorfinn was doing. There were many others. Every week from the north came different jokes about the blood-feud in Orkney: the skirmishing that daily beset Thorkel Fóstri, the King's steward there; the disasters that overtook any ship of Thorfinn's that came within his nephew Rognvald's reach on the sea or laid up, collecting its tributes.

The men of the north, it appeared, had been instructed to deal with it, and they did. It was not easy, for they had their own farmlands to see to, and the rents to collect, and twice Thorfinn had sent them down the west coast to clear the Irish-Norse out of his headlands, and once to support Eachmarcach in an attack.

For a year perhaps, they could do that, if the bere ripened well and the winter was mild and the vital balance was struck, and preserved, between food-raising time and all the other things they had been set to do. For a year, too, their regard for Thorfinn, even in his absence, would carry them through much that was unpleasant, and in particular the unwanted presence in Caithness of the kinsmen from Norway: the colony of Kalv Arnason and his friends that had dropped like a plague on the land and was stretching its resources to the limit.

They had been fed this year. They would have to be fed again next. And the hird, as was its right. And the new court, here in Alba, as well as the King himself and his personal household of chaplain and servants and officers.

When, therefore, Crinan, Abbot of Dunkeld, looked from his window high over the Tay one fine morning in September and saw moving slowly towards him the glittering prow of the longship *Grágás*, he smiled within his grey beard and reached for the fine, furred robe he wore in other people's writing-offices for business. 'So, my stepson,' he said to the window. 'You have remembered the in-field that has not yet had a spade put to it. I wonder what you want most. My counsel or my money?'

Then, very soon, he and Thorfinn stood face to face in his receiving-hall and Crinan was conscious, in his critical survey, of only one thing: that this was the man he would have wished for his son.

He looked, now, like a king. It was mainly, perhaps, a matter of dress. In Alba, men expected the royal house to appear in the Saxon tunic with its heavy worked hem and wide oversleeves: there was no room here for barbaric gold arm-rings and waistcoats of pelt. Thorfinn's ankle-boots were not made on any last his stepfather had seen in London or the Rhineland in recent years, and his inlaid belt one would guess was an heirloom from some Irish king's treasure-house. The ribbon of gold confining his hair was less novel: it simply replaced the *hlað* which he had always worn. And his dark, solemn face with the steady brown gaze was, it seemed, changeless. He looked as if nothing had disturbed him and nothing could.

Crinan said, 'You mentioned a meeting four years ago in Kinrimund.' He chose Saxon, of intent, and then saw, by the amusement in the other man's eyes, that he could expect no ascendancy there.

Thorfinn said, in the same language, 'I am known for keeping my appointments. Do you regret leaving Cumbria?'

'What!' said Crinan, sitting. 'Did you think I would take root in Dunkeld? I am in Cumbria as often as here, and further afield where there is need for it. It is the only way to keep one's friends, when one is old. I have seen your kinsman Thor twice in the Cotentin; once at Valoignes and once in Bayeux. Do you suppose that your cousin Bishop Malduin is aware of it? You know that he was summoned to York in the winter?'

'If you had gone to Fougères,' said Thorfinn, seating himself also, 'you would have heard my name mentioned at least as often. You may take it, therefore, that I have not come here because I have need of money, and, further, that I take a cousinly interest in all that Bishop Malduin is doing. Indeed, that's why I'm here.'

'You think,' said Crinan, 'that Earl Siward is going to take over Cumbria? I suppose he might, while you are so heavily engaged in other places.'

'I am not sure,' Thorfinn said. 'I am not sure, indeed, if I have done you a disservice in inviting you back to Dunkeld. It all depends on the daughters of Ealdred. There are only four of them left, but they and their husbands might still prove very troublesome. And I cannot spare men to protect Dunkeld in perpetuity.'

Abbot Crinan said, 'Are you by any chance inviting me to return to Cumbria? I imagine I should receive even shorter shrift there, if one of the daughters or her husband come to regard me as one of your agents. In any case, I challenge your arithmetic. One of the daughters is married to Alfgar of Mercia, and he is unlikely to harm you, unless you have offended him recently.'

'Which leaves three,' remarked the King. 'One married to Earl Siward, whose intentions we are discussing. One married to Ligulf of Bamburgh, who has a double interest since his own family married into Earl Eadulf's. And one married to Orm.'

'Whose uncle married my daughter. You are asking, in fact, whether I can trust my son-in-law and his nephew?' the Abbot said. He was smiling. He did not smile when alone, thinking of this very same problem.

'I am sure, since they are here with you, that Forne and Maldred your son both have your confidence,' Thorfinn said. 'Excluding Alfgar, whom I have not to my knowledge offended, that leaves Ligulf and possibly Orm to help Earl Siward with whatever conquests he may care to attempt. None of them has land in Cumbria at the moment, but, on the other hand, none of them may be quite prepared to find himself face to face with Mercia.'

'So you think they may march north and busy themselves with Dunkeld?' Crinan said. 'I am moved by your concern, but I can't say that I share it. Would they take so much trouble to retrieve my youngest grandson? He is nine—you possibly saw him on the way in—but in no sense a remarkable child, and he has two older brothers, one of whom at least is well within Earl Siward's grasp. Or my son Maldred? It is true that he is married to a daughter of a previous Earl of Northumbria, but he has laid no claim to the earldom, and by moving north has made his renunciation quite clear. In addition, his wife is a niece of King Edward of England, and one would credit Siward with enough sense not to offend there. No. I am grateful, as I said, for the warning. I do not see the danger.'

Thorfinn said, 'I cannot protect you. I cannot, either, have Dunkeld turned into an armed Cumbrian camp, however agreeable I find the individual members of your family. Your entourage may run to two hundred men, but not more.'

'I understand your difficulty,' the Abbot said. 'I sympathise, indeed. We little thought, either of us, four years ago that, far from enjoying joint rule with your nephew in Orkney, he would be bleeding you dry of the ships and the men you now need so badly. Why do you allow it?'

'What do you do with a badly reared child?' Thorfinn said. 'He is jealous of my Norwegian colony. It will pass.'

'It won't pass if you continue to support Kalv Arnason,' the Abbot said. 'I have wondered if, in retrospect, you did not wish you had sent Kalv instead to his wife's nephew Siward of Northumbria. With one stroke, you would have pleased your nephew of Orkney and embarrassed the Earl of Northumbria while sparing yourself a great deal of hardship and expense. But perhaps your lady wife Kalv's niece was insistent.'

'My lady wife Kalv's niece felt as you do,' said the King in the deep, unhurried voice that brought all his answers. 'But Kalv, I have reason to know, is a true son of Norway who would do almost anything to get back his wife's farm at Egge. I felt that he and Siward and Magnús would have a pact made in a trice which the Lady Emma might like, but which I should not.'

Canute had thought his way like this into an empire. Crinan had felt no pleasure like this with anyone since the days of Canute. And he had no time at all in which to extend it, for already Thorfinn was showing signs of wishing to leave. Crinan said, 'I seldom give advice for nothing. But I will tell you again what you know already. Borrow nothing that you cannot be sure of repaying. And take back Orkney. While that canker exists, you can do nothing lasting with Alba or Cumbria.'.

He learned nothing more; for the King merely made some non-committal reply and proceeded, as he had guessed, to make the first moves towards leaving. It was, surprisingly, on their way down to the river wharf that he made the only personal remark of his visit. 'We do not know each other well,' Thorfinn said. 'But my mother spoke of you.'

'You remember her?' Crinan said. He, too, had met Bethoc once or twice after her next marriage to Sigurd was over. She had never mentioned Thorfinn. But then, she had hardly spoken of her first son, of Duncan. She had been a practical woman, and a strong help-meet to each of her husbands without allowing herself to become deeply engaged, he imagined, with any of them. Certainly, there had been no trace of grand passion in the marriage she had shared with himself. It would have been most inconvenient if there had been.

Thorfinn said, 'I was nineteen when she died. Latterly, we saw little of each other: she was living in Angus and I was at sea most of the time. I remember her best in Moray when I was young and my stepfather Findlaech was alive.'

'And what did she say of me?' Crinan asked.

The glimmer he had learned to be wary of entered his stepson's solemn gaze. 'That, were it possible to combine the virtues and vices of all of her husbands, you would have a man capable of ruling the world,' Thorfinn said. 'Your business acumen had her bewitched. She was not a woman, of course, who depended on the softer emotions.'

Now, why did you say that? Crinan wondered. They had arrived at the riverside, and, halting, he looked at his stepson's face and thought he knew. An old hurt lay there, and not a hurt caused by any resentment against mother-neglect. Thorfinn had loved his stepfather, and his mother had not. It was as simple as that.

And in all that lay one danger he had never thought of, and one he could not warn the King against, although, obliquely, he could try.

Crinan said, 'She was a woman who had learned the only thing a well-born woman must know: that she cannot survive, nor can her husbands in the work they have to do, unless the softer emotions are expunged from her life. As you know, it is also true of men in high places. If you give yourself to anyone or anything, the enemy will move into the unguarded space and cripple you.'

'As you suggest I should do with Earl Rognvald,' Thorfinn said. 'My stepfather, I must leave. You will think over what I have said about Cumbria.'

'I shall think more of the friendship that brought you here,' Crinan said, and smiled; and watched the King board, amid the swift, orderly preparations for rowing downriver, and the good-humoured faces of his men.

He had tried to warn him and, through him, Gillacomghain's widow his wife. But, clearly, it was already too late.

In that, he was right. But, for all his passionless acumen, he failed to observe that the wheel which this year had turned so inexorably for his stepson was turning also for himself, and towards a destiny about which he, too, had received his warning.

He made his own dispositions, as his conversation with Thorfinn and his own intelligence dictated, and after the turn of the year he began, with discretion, to remove what goods he still possessed in Cumbria and transport them, bit by bit, to the monastery of Dunkeld and his storehouses. It was on one such trip, in the spring, that he disembarked with his goods and his men at the riverside where eight months before he had parted with the King his stepson.

The silence at the monastery should have warned him. The absence of his own men-at-arms there and on the pathway up to his hall finally did; but by then it was too late, and the cataract of steel was already pouring down the hillsides towards him.

He saw the banners before he died; and died, characteristically, with a mild imprecation on his lips, not against his murderers but against himself for having been so foolish.

NINE

THE NEWS REACHED the King at Inverness, on the northern-most confines of Moray, where he had come not to rest from his labours but to turn to the general benefit the sixteenth birthday of his stepson Lulach.

The man who had the enjoyment of breaking it was Kalv Arnason from Trøndelagen, now resident in Caithness and invited, as was no more than his right, to his great-nephew's celebration. The messenger he intercepted on the outskirts of Inverness could hardly have gone any further anyway, and it was worth all the trouble to see Thorfinn's face when he told him.

He had stood still, on the crowded, garlanded knoll overlooking the river, and said, 'Crinan is dead, and Maldred his son? Who else? His daughter's son Forne?'

'He was south, in Nottingham. And of course they got the boy. Maelmuire. Duncan's youngest. But they killed every man Crinan had. Nearly two hundred, the man said. Dunkeld is clean. Dunkeld is your own at last. I told you,' said Kalv, 'that no man in his senses would have let that double-dealing banker into the finest port in the kingdom. They got all the gold, of course. That was your other mistake. Take his harvest from such as Crinan, and within a year it will be worth reaping again. The Lady Emma, they say, was the same. You ought to have thought of that, too.'

It was worth it, at any rate, up to that point. And then, just as he was finishing what was left in his drinking-horn, Thorfinn had picked it clean from his fingers and said, 'You must advise me again when your thirst will allow you. Where is the man who brought this news?' And when Kalv, with some coldness, had told him, had gone striding off without speaking further.

Kalv turned to Groa his niece. And she, in turn, signed to a slave, who dipped another horn in the cask and brought it to him, while Groa said, politely as was only right, 'I didn't hear. There has been an attack on Dunkeld? By Earl Siward?'

'Not by himself. No. The English King wouldn't put up with it. But by Ligulf and Orm, two of his kinsmen. The boy Maelmuire is their nephew as

well, you see. That was the excuse, or one of them. And they say that the
Bishop of Durham's flag was there as well. Malduin's master. A churchly
rebuke to an overworldly abbot, if you stretched a point and forgot that
Dunkeld was in another kingdom. They'll send the boy to Ireland, I expect,
where his brother is. And with Maldred gone, Siward is now sure of
Northumbria.'

'Maldred had sons?' Groa said.

'Children. No threat to Siward. He'll foster them.' Kalv emptied his horn,
shook the drips from it, and looked up, grinning. 'That's an abbacy Thorfinn
will need to think about filling.'

'I am sure,' said Groa, 'he will take the best advice. Your horn is empty. Let
me have it.'

And after that, the day was more the sort of festival it ought to be, with
more food than anyone could eat, even though it was May, and sport and
music and dancing and all the things men do, from custom and affection, to
tease a youth who has become of full age.

Kalv had met fools who were afraid of Groa's son, or claimed to see
something other-worldly about him. For himself, he had always taken him for
what he was, a simpleton with no harm in him, and had treated him as he
would any other boy, on the few occasions he had had to do with him.

When, as now, Sigrid his wife was there, he kept clear of him. It was hardly
his fault she was barren: if Ølve had got two sons on her, he wished he had
asked him for the trick, before he killed him. It had been no help in his career,
either, that she should blame King Magnús's father for the death of both her
sons, and keep saying so.

Latterly, she had taken to pointing out that the slaves of Egge were the only
ones in the whole of Trøndelagen to stay childless until they were old enough
to go to market themselves. And when she had caught him bidding for a
red-headed man for the goats, she had laughed herself silly.

Groa said, 'You did very well. Myself, I think I should have done with his
horn what the sheep-farmers do.'

'Kalv?' said Thorfinn. 'No. But I miss Thorkel Fóstri. Is that Lulach?'

'I let him come here to sleep,' Groa said. 'Otherwise he would have no
peace. You don't mind?'

Outside the window she had just shuttered, it was dawn, and still the hall
and the yard and the sleeping-quarters were full of guests and singing and
talking. It had been her suggestion to take some rest now, while they could,
and Thorfinn had needed so little persuading that she knew that he had
thought of little else all that day but the news from Dunkeld. He sat down
now beside Lulach's slumbering form and moved his hand gently over the
thick, silvery hair. 'No. He enjoyed his day, I believe. He has a kind heart. You
can see how Sigurd worships him.'

'He calls Earl Siward the Dragon-slayer,' Groa said. 'Perhaps you heard
him. Some Siward, it appears, drove out a dragon that had been ravaging
Orkney, and then went to kill another in Northumbria. . . . You will have to

think of a marriage alliance for Lulach one of these days.'

'Do you want to see him married?' Thorfinn said. He did not look up.

'One must think of the future. But it might destroy his power,' she said. She paused. 'At least, his strangeness. It is hardly power.'

'It is power,' Thorfinn said, and drew the cover over the boy and looked up. 'Don't be afraid. It does me no harm. Should you be standing there?'

This spring, she had lost a child, hardly three months on its journey, and his care for her had been like a lining of silk under all that he did. She smiled and said, 'I look worn and frail. Thank you,' and came and sat in the circle of his arm.

'No. But I shall have to go to Dunkeld tomorrow,' he said. 'Rognvald, what am I to do with you? This should never have happened if I had had the trained men I should have by now.'

'You warned Crinan,' Groa said. 'They were *his* kinsmen, not yours.'

He released her and stood, his chin supported in thought, his head bent, as always, because of his height. He spoke, frowning a little, to the floor.

'How could he have been so blind? Crinan used to know better than any man living what was going on behind closed doors. The Godwin family marry a daughter to King Edward: surely that was a danger signal? We know it doesn't mean heirs, but it does prevent other alliances. So that throws Siward and Mercia into one another's arms, or as near as Leofric can bring himself.

'And meanwhile Emma is busy. The Bishop of Ramsbury died last month and the job has gone to Hermann, the little chaplain from Hainault whom I met in Winchester, while Osbern's nephew Alfred has settled in as sheriff of Dorset, next door to our friends from Dol. And that means an alignment of the trading and money interests that won't go ignored, especially as England has just bought off Denmark with some sort of specious promise that if King Edward dies, Svein can expect to cross over and sit on his throne. . . .

'All straws in the wind. But they should have warned Crinan. I'm vulnerable to Magnús of Norway, now he is no longer threatened by Denmark; for all England knows, I might have offered my services to Magnús already. He's made one alliance in Saxony and it's certainly known that I've done business, too, in Arras and Mont St Michel. An attack on Dunkeld offered nothing but profit to Siward's family: the death of Maldred, the removal of Crinan from the race for power; the acquisition of the last of Duncan's three sons, not to mention the silver. But even then Siward would hardly have risked it without the profoundest encouragement from other quarters. I should have dismantled the foundry.'

'Whose foundry?' said Groa. She sat up. 'Crinan's? Crinan had a furnace at Dunkeld? Who was he striking for?'

'Anyone who would pay him. Norway, I expect,' Thorfinn said. 'It was in the stone building they used to keep books in. You could smell the hot metal from the waterside. I sent some men to look about while I was talking to him. It's common enough, of course, for a monastery to melt down its offerings, but this was something much more. And these things are hard to keep quiet.'

'And now?' Groa said.

'I shall complain to the Archbishop of York, and to Earl Siward, and to King Edward, and much good it will do me. I shall have a long talk with the Bishop at Kinrimund. And from somewhere I shall find a new abbot for Dunkeld, which brings me up against a whole field of thistles whose traversing I had hoped to postpone until my other tenures were a little more secure. I don't know my sons and I hardly know my wife, these days. Are you sick of me?' said Thorfinn suddenly.

'Yes,' said Groa. 'That is why I am sitting here listening to you, instead of lying in Rognvald's arms.'

Till she was better, they could do nothing but talk, and she knew it was hard for him, and that he was thinking aloud now for that reason as much as any other. But then she smiled up at him, unthinking, and the candles wavered; and from standing he had laid himself silently at her feet, with his head resting, heavy and warm, against her knees. She touched his hair, as he had touched Lulach's, and moved her fingers through and through its thick softness.

She said, 'I had some news from Kalv. He has been receiving messages from my father. The Grand Duke of Kiev has given one of his daughters in marriage to Harald, St Olaf's half-brother. And there are rumours that, after fifteen years of fighting the Saracens, Harald is about to cross back from Russia and claim a share of the throne from King Magnús his nephew.'

Beneath her fingers, Thorfinn had become very still. Then he gave a sound that might have been a laugh. '*True prince of the awning of the sun, help the mighty Rognvald,*' he said. 'That's from Arnór's latest poem. He has invented some splendid pieces, I'm told, in honour of King Magnús as well.'

He moved a little, resting his weight against the side of the bed, and she lifted her fingers. He said, 'Arnór's third cousin is Harald's marshal. I used to get all my information through him. Does Kalv have any idea what this means?'

'He's excited, of course,' said Groa slowly. 'It might be good news, or it might be bad. Harald fought at Stiklestad too, although he was only fifteen. He saw Kalv kill his half-brother. But he may need men like Kalv to get back his inheritance.' She paused, and then said, 'Kalv will do anything to get back to Egge. You know that.'

'So that,' Thorfinn said, 'if I have to settle the matter of Rognvald, I should do it soon, while King Magnús is concerned about the prospect of dividing his kingdom, and before Harald Sigurdsson arrives and I have to contend with the war-hardened leader of the Varangian guard?'

She said, 'I can't tell you what to do.'

She knew he was smiling: something rare, that he kept only for her. She felt, again, the warmth of his head at her knee.

'*I know,*' he said, '*that it is no nickname to call thee the Ever-Blooming, because of the excellence of thy shape, and because of thy intelligence, and because of thy family. And it is no nickname to call you the Favourite, because thou art the beloved and desired of the men of the whole world, for the splendour and lustre of thy beauty. . . .*'

He moved from Gaelic to Norse, and she felt the change in him as one stream of blood ran into another. 'I know,' he said, 'that you will never tell me what to do about Rognvald. I only weep, as a man, for Rognvald, because when I have done it, he will not have you waiting, as have I, to carry his head on your knee.'

Towards the end of August, there arrived off the island of Westray in Orkney two strongly manned ships led by Thorkel Fóstri, the King's foster-father.

The last time Thorfinn had sent a messenger to his nephew Rognvald, the messenger had returned tied to a sledge with his hands cut off, and nearly dead from an old, hairy cloak bound tightly over his face.

This time, Thorkel Fóstri said what he had to say with fifty axemen behind him and more on the shore. It was Earl Rognvald's steward he spoke to, since Earl Rognvald sent word that he was busy, and that if a man sent his nurse instead of coming himself, he could hardly expect another man to do more.

The same steward brought back the reply, half a day later; and Thorkel Fóstri sailed with it to Sannick in Caithness, where Thorfinn had gone to settle a new dispute between Kalv Arnason's men and the old settlers. There, he took his foster-father to the guest-quarters he was living in and heard him out in silence. At the end:

'Well,' said Thorfinn, 'barring the insults, which are more imaginative than I have heard before, the reply seems to be what we expected. Find Kalv, and we shall tell him about it.'

As was to be expected, on being told the news, Kalv became extremely disturbed. His face became as red as his hair still was in places, and his hand wiped at his belt where his axe used to be. He said, 'I want you to tell me again. You have sent demanding of Rognvald the third of Orkney that King Magnús elected to give him, and since, naturally, Rognvald refused, you have begun to raise an army to take it?'

'You have it,' said the King. 'Although I doubt very much if the army will ever see action. Rognvald's men at least will be very aware that he has only the resources of two-thirds of Orkney to fight me with, if as much, whereas I have all Caithness and Moray and the Western Isles, with as many from Alba as I might coax to follow me.'

'Alba?' snapped Kalv. 'Alba won't fight Orkney battles for you, and you're a fool if you think so.'

'I don't,' said the King mildly. 'But Rognvald's men are unlikely to realise it.'

'So,' said Kalv. 'You expect Rognvald to give up his uncle's land without a murmur and sit tamely in Westray while you take the southern isles and East Hrossey from him? He won't, you know. You know what he'll do? He'll complain to Magnús of Norway, who is sitting over there biting his nails to think of an excuse to invade us. It's the end of you, and of me.'

'If Magnús wants war, then I agree with you,' said the King. 'But does he? The attacks on Denmark were costly. And although he may guess that Alba won't fight my battles, he can't be sure what England would do. Also, he may need all his resources if there is to be a quarrel over his own kingdom. It seems very likely that Harald Sigurdsson is on his way back.'

'Guesswork,' said Kalv. 'You're laying down cheese at a bear-hole.'

'It may therefore turn out,' said the King, 'that Rognvald will be persuaded to make the best of things and go back and settle in Norway, where his foster-brother the King may well have need of him. Does that not seem likely?'

'No,' said Kalv rudely. 'And from the look on cousin Thorkel's face, he doesn't think so either. It's a pity he's afraid to say so. I never thought, when I saw him beat you for your mistakes, that one day I would watch him licking your boots while you made them.'

'Indeed,' said Thorfinn. 'Now you come to mention it, my boots were remarkably clean on the day you came begging for shelter. I know what Thorkel Fóstri thinks about this. I know the dangers. The matters you point out have all been thought of. If you dislike my way of doing things, you have only to move out of my guest-quarters.'

Kalv got up. 'Oh,' he said. 'It is easy to insult a man who is down on his luck. There is valour in that, and all the good breeding that mixed blood is noted for. You are saying, I take it, that either I fight Norway for you or starve.'

'If I fight Norway and lose,' said Thorfinn agreeably, 'then you may discover a fate worse than starving, for if King Magnús changes his mind, still Harald Sigurdsson may find it hard to overlook what you did to his brother. That is for you to decide. I have not asked you to fight for me, nor, if I ever do, shall I abuse you in any way if you refuse me. That is because you are an Arnason, and because of your niece my wife and your cousin Thorkel Fóstri, whose kinship you may well be thankful for. I think we have finished what we have to say to one another.'

Throughout this speech, Kalv's chest moved up and down, and it was not at all clear that he shared this opinion. At the end, he stood in silence for more than a moment, without replying. Then he turned on his heel and walked out.

'So?' said Thorkel Fóstri.

'So now we watch,' said the King his foster-son. 'And see if Rognvald sends to Norway or goes there himself. And then we watch to see who or what comes back. And meantime we pray—should we write to Sulien?—we pray that Harald Sigurdsson arrives very soon in his nephew's kingdom of Norway and proves to be as rich and as aggressive and as belligerent as report makes him out to be.'

'He may be so much all these things,' Thorkel Fóstri said, 'that he sails to help Rognvald at the head of a war-fleet.'

'True,' said the King. 'In which case I have made a serious mistake. And it is wholly your fault for not having beaten me sufficiently.'

For four weeks, Earl Rognvald made no move, and Thorfinn remained in the north, waiting. Then, as autumn moved towards winter, four longships left the harbour at Hǫfn and set sail on the west wind for Norway. Leading them was the flagship, with Rognvald aboard.

Reporting, Thorkel Fóstri was matter-of-fact.

'He has dismantled his halls and taken the hird. You could walk into the whole of Orkney at this moment, if you wanted. The story is that he has gone to ask Magnús for an army.'

'And do his people think Rognvald will get it?' asked the King. He had been interviewing two of his men from the south all that morning, and Thorkel Fóstri knew that there was trouble in Alba. But it couldn't be helped. He said, 'Magnús has the men to spare. And there is no sign of his uncle coming as yet. Report has it that Magnús will try to persuade Rognvald to settle in Norway, but that Rognvald sets too much store on this feud to agree.'

He stopped, eyeing Thorfinn. 'He's a brave man, I'll say that for him. He could do nothing against you with only the men he has in Orkney. So he threw everything he possessed into the game. Orkney abandoned, in the hope that when he returns, it will be with the whole of Norway behind him.'

'The winds will be against him now,' Thorfinn said.

'Oh, he won't come back this side of winter,' said his foster-father. 'By the spring, we should know what is happening. Not all my cousins are sitting here at your table.'

'I'm not sure whom to thank for that,' Thorfinn said, 'but I do, every day. I must depend on you, as with everything else, for that warning. And meantime it is a matter of ships and more ships.'

'You hold to that?' Thorkel said. 'You won't move into Orkney? You could win them over, in a winter.'

'They would fight to the death for me, I am sure,' Thorfinn said. 'So would the people of Caithness and parts further south, excluding, of course, Kalv and his kinsmen. I prefer, if an army is coming, that it makes no landings at all. Or, if I can't prevent that, at least Rognvald should meet no resistance in his share of Orkney, and little in mine, if I am not there. Next to losing Orkney, it would be short-sighted to turn it into a desert.'

'Oh, yes,' said Thorkel Fóstri. 'There is a great deal to be said for the long view, provided that it won't take three generations to show the returns for it. I'm getting old. I'm fifty.'

'You are fortunate,' Thorfinn said.

There followed a winter that none of Thorfinn's household took lightly, although he himself showed nothing of either concern or apprehension, but merely expended on Alba the torrent of energy that had been pent up in the north through the autumn.

With him moved his household, including his wife and his stepson Lulach and his older son, who was now eleven; and under the eyes of his young courtmen and his sons, he set about repairing the damage that even a few months of absence had done to his hardly established command of Duncan's country. They were present at the interview he held in Fife with the Bishop of Alba, from which the Bishop departed sallow of face; and at the boisterous exchange with Alfgar of Mercia in Cumbria, who had burst in with a tick-bag full of gossip and precious information, indiscriminately mixed.

Always, Groa enjoyed Alfgar's company, even when the extravagance of his compliments forced her, laughing, to put her hands over her ears; but she envied, too, the equanimity with which Thorfinn sat through the unsparing account of what Swegen of Wessex had done to the Abbess of Leominster before asking, mildly, what the news about Harald Sigurdsson was.

'He's still in Russia, so far as I know,' Alfgar said. 'Married to Jaroslav's daughter; but not because her seven brothers would like him in Kiev. If that fellow takes over Norway, England will have to look out. So will you. Unless, of course, you become his vassal for Alba as well as Orkney. That would give everybody something to think about.'

'Including your father,' Thorfinn said. 'Alfgar, to everybody but you, the passing years seem to bring a certain accession of tact. Tell your father that I have no intention of either allying myself with the King of Norway or becoming his vassal for Alba. If I have to, I shall deliver a nod on behalf of Orkney, but no more than a nod. In return, I expect you to tell me if Earl Leofric has been seen hunting from time to time with Earl Siward.'

'They never hit anything,' said Alfgar. 'You'd hear that the Bishop of Durham got a sharp reprimand for meddling with other people's churches, but Siward had him reinstalled almost before he had crossed the river. You want to watch,' Alfgar said, 'and not get defeated by Norway. If the English think that King Magnús is going to get a foothold through you in the north, they'll back Siward to do anything he likes, including marching straight into Alba. You know he's trying to get one of the boys back from Ireland?'

'No,' said Thorfinn. Then he said, 'One of Duncan's sons . . . Of course. Donald must be twelve; perhaps thirteen. Where *is* the boy?'

'That's what's puzzling Siward. It's a pity,' said Alfgar, 'that you didn't persuade King Edward to take over both boys. And now the third one's in Ireland, isn't he? What does that look mean?'

'It means that I have that matter, at least, in hand,' Thorfinn said. 'I hear you have a daughter as beautiful as your mother.'

'I've got a new boy as well,' Alfgar said. 'With the same wet-nurse Edith had. It was worth all the labour to get her in the household again. I don't believe in quick weaning. Was it you who said that both my sons had noses like Lapps'?'

'Yes,' said Thorfinn. 'But then, so have you. Ask about it some time.'

Alfgar's laugh rolled over the wall-hangings. He shook his head at Groa. 'He will sit there making jokes instead of looking to the storm-beach he calls a kingdom. Tell him, can't you, that the rest of us will begin to find life very difficult unless he makes some effort to take the thing seriously? The days for playing at Vikings are over.'

'Nonsense,' said Thorfinn. 'They have only begun.'

Later, he said, 'What is this? Groa, what is it? It was only Alfgar.'

And through the tears that, amazingly, had broken down all her self-control she said, 'It isn't that. Or not only that. I heard the news that came this afternoon.'

'Ah,' he said. 'Well, yes. Magnús is raising a levy in Norway. It seems that he has offered Rognvald both a fleet and an army to chastise me with in the spring. But we knew that was likely.'

'And Kalv?' Groa said. 'Magnús has offered him back all his lands and his status in Norway, provided he supports Rognvald against you. That was in the message as well, wasn't it?'

'What do you do to my messengers that make them tell you all their secrets?' said Thorfinn. 'My love, my love; O glory of women; smile at me. It is a time for making jokes, and laughing at them.'

'Time to take Lulach from Moray so that he may see, as he may never see again, how a kingdom should be ruled,' Groa said. 'Time to try to teach Sigurd the same lesson, although he is only eleven. But Erlend, at five, has to be left with his nurses. You were five when your father died. What do you recall of him? Anything?'

'Then we should talk,' Thorfinn said. It was a gift he had, that he would not fight against the inevitable, but listen to it, although not necessarily to surrender. And, recognising it yet again, it stole the words from her.

So he said them instead. 'If you are left, you will hold Moray. For Lulach, it would be best to look for a marriage with the lands about Moray, to knit his interest to whatever king may take Alba. It does not sound desirable, or even profitable; but Bishop Malduin has a young daughter, as well as a family claim to the mormaerdom of Angus, and Lulach might do well to bind himself there. For you, you will also have to think of a husband.'

The sound she made, had she been a human being, would have been a denial. He took it as such.

'What we have is ours, and dies with us. You have sons. Even if they are offered Orkney, it will be many years before they are old enough to hold power, or to lead. A man must do it, and a man you can influence. You sheared your hair to the roots, but you married Gillacomghain. You saw him burned by my men in front of your eyes, yet you married me. What we have should make the chain stronger, not weaker,' said Thorfinn. 'Crinan tried to tell me that soul-friendship between a man and a woman must be a mistake. I will not believe it.'

She said, 'You are telling me to take to husband the man who will kill you.'

'You say that,' he said, 'as if it cost me nothing. O Befind, whose fair body is the colour of snow: smile at me.'

And from his courage she took courage, and smiled.

TEN

AS HE HAD done twenty-five years before, a beautiful child on the jetties at Nídarós, Rognvald of Orkney took his hurts to the man he thought would best help him. And, though he had his own troubles, the King of Norway kissed him and promised him a well-equipped army, although not the largest, and a well-found fleet of war-ships, although not the greatest, with which to chastise the swaggering bully who thought to defy the King of Norway's own partition of Orkney. Enough, with luck, to wrest Orkney whole from Thorfinn. Enough, perhaps, to land on Caithness and annex it to the Norwegian crown.

Or at least so Rognvald, returning the embrace with tears on his cheeks, allowed him to go on believing. And indeed, with the ships and the men he would gather in Shetland and Orkney to add to these, such a feat might well be within his grasp.

He sailed late in the spring on a light easterly wind, and by the time he reached Hǫfn and found it empty, the armies of Thorfinn, lying patiently waiting in Caithness, knew the quality of the enemy's fleet and its number; and stirred and quickened, like seed well fed and watchfully tended to which the hour of springing has come.

For three weeks, Thorfinn had husbanded them while the real grain had grown unregarded round empty houses and the flocks and the herds had all gone, barring what was required to feed the men who lay under awnings round Thurso bay: the three thousand men who would sail under his banner; the two thousand who fed them and served them, who acted as guides and as runners, and who would augment, at need, the forces already deployed in small numbers at all those points where a landing might be made.

In small numbers because, from the beginning, Thorfinn's battle-plan had depended on a conviction that nothing could shake.

To Thorkel Fóstri, expostulating, Thorfinn said, 'Whatever he has told King Magnús, Rognvald wants only to kill me. That he can only be sure of doing at sea. It is a sea-battle he wants, and a sea-battle we shall give him. At the end of it, winner or loser, he might fall on the shore of Caithness, but I promise you that he will be in no state to attack it.'

It had pleased the Caithness men, and the Orkney men had made no demur. Long since, anything of value had been removed from the Orkneys, including food. Rognvald's newly arrived army would require a day, perhaps two, to rest after their journey, but after that their attack wouldn't be long delayed. They could support an army only with what they brought with them.

Copsige, a man of enterprise, watching from Cornholm, had carried the news of Rognvald's ships. 'Only thirty of them, my lord Earl, but great ships: as great as *Grágás*, all of them, and filled with men. As many men as your sixty will hold. My lord, the armies are even.'

Thirty ships against sixty: that was the second strand in the battle-plan. Thirty tall-sided ships who would seek, therefore, to use their advantage by grappling and who, once lashed to the enemy, would require steady water under the keel. Which led to the third strand: the sea.

Between the scattered islands of Orkney and the long, rocky coast of Caithness lay the most dangerous passage of waters ever known about England or Alba, whose tidal current could run twice as fast as a longship, and whose waves could rise two hundred feet up the towering cliff-faces and overwhelm islands.

Once, fighting Carl Thorbrandsson, the Orkney fleet had been able to put to good use the tricks of current and tide. Now, as one Earl of Orkney set sail against another, the sea was the ally of neither and the potential enemy of both.

Thorfinn said, 'He's in Westray. He can't come down the east coast to attack: that way he'll enter the eastern neck of the firth and either be swept into the tidal race through the passage or be swept out of it with my fleet pursuing him. So he will come down the west side of Orkney, with open sea on his right and the Caithness coast ahead, across the western neck of the firth. Are we agreed?'

There was no dispute. Thorkel Fóstri said, 'He will know you are here. In Thurso Bay.'

Below them, side by side on two miles of white sand, lay the longships, gold-tipped, embracing the foam like a necklet. As their spies had reported, so would Rognvald's. As he sailed south from Westray to Hrossey to Hoy, his prows would point straight towards Thurso, and each fleet, whatever it did, would be in fullest view of the other.

'So we sail out to meet him,' said Thorfinn. 'Which he will expect. If we're lucky, we get warning from the beacon on Hoy. If we're undeservedly lucky, the wind will change and allow us to meet him under sail high up on the west coast and out of the firth. If neither of these things happens, we shan't see much of him till he's off Rora Head, and we might have to row part or all of the way to meet him, which puts us all in the thick of the tide-race.

'If we engage there and the tide is making, we all get swept eastwards and into deep trouble. If it's on the ebb, Rognvald may well find himself pushed westwards before we meet up with him, and we should then bear down on him with the tide, plus the wind, which would be most enjoyable from our point of view but not from Rognvald's.

'Therefore, if the wind doesn't change, Rognvald is likely to time his arrival off south-west Hoy at slack water. Or just before. That means a lot of lurching but no real punishing current for an hour anyway, and even then only a mild one, with the wind to cancel it.'

'If the wind stays easterly,' Thorkel Fóstri said.

'If, of course,' the King said. 'Who's the expert on winds? Otkel?'

Everyone looked at Otkel, Thorkel's nephew, who had once taken a longship round Duncansby, gale-force wind against tide, and lived to tell of it. Otkel said, 'Variable. But it looks set for twenty-four hours at the moment. You can take it that the Earl will aim for slack water, no matter what the wind, and a quick kill before the flood starts.'

One of the Salmundarsons said, 'No matter what the wind? He won't row down against a southerly, surely, even if he has to keep his men starving till it changes.'

'No,' said Thorkel Fóstri. 'But winds have been known to alter. And although he knows the currents as well as we do, his ships are full of Norwegians.'

'As ours are full of Irishmen,' the King said tranquilly. 'But Earl Rognvald will spread his hird through the fleet, as I shall spread mine. Don't underestimate their seamanship. Everything I have said, Rognvald will have said also. It is the wind, in the end, that will have the last say. The wind, and those with the quickest wits to deal with it. So. The next slack water is when? Five in the morning?'

'It would mean sailing all through the night from Westray,' Thorkel Fóstri said. 'He won't ask them to do that so soon after crossing from Norway. But tomorrow afternoon. That is possible. Before the wind changes.'

'I think you are right,' the King said. 'Tonight, we sleep. Tomorrow, we shall keep them all active but not too busy. By mid-afternoon or before, we should know if the fleet is coming. Meanwhile—Otkel?—I am to be told of any change in the quality of the wind. And if it changes, this is what we must do. . . .'

Later, looking back on it, it seemed to Thorkel Fóstri that nothing had been left undone that could be done beforehand: nothing had been left unsaid that should have been said before that battle came that was to decide the fate of Orkney, and that was to decide the fate, for all time to come, of the far greater country called Alba. Only, they were men. And wind, they said, was the breath of the gods.

It was the beacon on Hoy, after all, that gave them their first warning, followed very soon after by the smoke from Easter Head and from Holborn as the flash of gold, far to the north, told of the Norwegian fleet rounding the west point of Hoy with Rognvald's banner flying above it. It was three hours after midday, with a steady easterly breeze, and a fitful sun white behind cloud-haze.

Before the smoke had dispelled, the sixty ships of Thorfinn of Orkney and

Alba were in the water, borne out by a black, living carpet of men, the steel on them glinting like sand-flies.

They left the bay under oar, with *Grágás* in the lead under the rippling black-and-white flag of the raven, and her flock of long, slender goslings combing the white sea behind her.

Today of all days, Thorfinn had made sure that he would stand in every man's eye. Standing high in the stern by his steersman, he wore a tunic of scarlet under his ring-mail to match the scarlet, Thor's red, of the flagship; and fingers of bright scarlet ribbon quivered and blew from the crest of Canute's golden helmet. Only his profile looked unfamiliar, rendered Greek by the tongue of the nose-guard and the metal curve at either jaw. So far as could be seen, he looked unworried; and certainly, as he scanned the boats of his fleet and saw the fierce, lusty faces and heard the shouts and the snatches of chanting and the wild, bronchial belling of war-horns, he must have known that he had performed his task well and his crop was ripe and ready for cutting.

The sail was not yet up when the look-out called down from the masthead. 'My lord? The smoke on Hoy. It's changed direction.'

'I see,' said Thorfinn. The smoke had changed. Overhead, the fretted weathervane glinted and swung. The pattern on the water ahead, pale grey on dark, blurred and brightened and blurred again as gusts of random air passed across. Then, lifting its voice, the wind walked from the east to the south-east, to the south, and as sail upon sail, rattling up, opened its throat to receive it, began to impel Thorfinn's fleet through the last of the ebb towards Hoy.

David, the priest from Deerness, said, 'Did I not know you tongueless in prayer as an Irishman's bell, I would say you had made God an offer. Or are we sinking after all?'

'That's the headland east-going current,' said Thorfinn blandly. 'We hit the west-going ebb in a moment. But if it's any comfort, at the rate we are going, we'll meet the other fleet somewhere off Hoy, and not in the tide-rip at all. If, that's to say, the wind stays in the south.'

'Tell me what to pray for,' said David, 'and I'll do my best. Do you know Arnór's on board?'

Two weeks before, on the last of the ferries from Orphir, Arnór Jarlaskáld had appeared, silently, at the great camp at Thurso and had made his way, silently, to Thorfinn's hall.

For the hird, and for the landed-men and the mercenary leaders from the Western Isles and from Ireland who were then with Thorfinn, roistering, it was a joyous moment, pregnant with disaster. Everyone there had tried his hand at one version or another of Arnór's verses in praise of Thorfinn's enemy Rognvald and his other verses in praise of Rognvald's foster-brother King Magnús. If Thorfinn did not appear to have heard either the originals or their parodies, it still did not mean that he would take kindly to the return of his promiscuous bard. Especially since everyone there knew precisely why Arnór had left Rognvald for Thorfinn.

It was, therefore, a great disappointment when Thorfinn neither had his

skald hanged nor his harp-fingers cut off, but merely greeted him mildly with
a remark or two that seemed harmless enough till you thought about it, by
which time Arnór's neck had turned red and he looked fit to weep. But that
was all, and afterwards Thorfinn's manner had been to him just as it was
before Rognvald had wooed the silly man to himself, and before Kalv
Arnason, changing sides for reasons much less romantic, had come to take all
Rognvald's attention.

You would think, knowing Kalv's record, that his friends would hardly be
astonished to find that Kalv had abandoned Thorfinn for Rognvald, once
King Magnús entered the feud on Rognvald's side. Certainly, considering the
words he and Kalv had already exchanged, Thorfinn could not have been
much surprised, although he said little when the news first arrived.

It was through Arnór that Kalv's former host learned that Kalv's six ships
were now in Orkney, with the two hundred fighting-men Kalv had quartered
so neatly on Thorfinn in Caithness. It was further through Arnór that it was
discovered that Kalv and his ships were not at Hǫfn with the rest of
Rognvald's fleet, but had sailed south to Longhope, on the south-east of Hoy,
for reasons unknown but easy to guess at. *My lord, the armies are even*,
Copsige had said. And so they had been until Kalv's men joined Rognvald.

It might be thought, then, that Thorfinn would have no objection to his
fickle Arnór's presence on board to share whatever fate held in store and, if he
survived, to sing of it. That Arnór had been ordered to stay ashore had been a
surprise to them all: that Arnór had disobeyed the order was a greater one.
And now here was Thorfinn, clearly angry, summoning the poet before him
and lashing him, briefly, with his tongue before consigning him to the lower
reaches of the longship, under someone's spare shield. It was true Arnór
would do little good in a battle, and was as likely to behead you on the
backswing as he was to cut down the enemy. But at least, if he was there, he
could be thinking up verses.

The wind held, and the sixty ships of Thorfinn's fleet, jolting, began to cross
the open firth from Caithness towards Hoy in Orkney.

From the thwarts of the longship, nothing of Rognvald's fleet could be seen.
From the masthead, the last sighting had shown that, facing into the wind, the
enemy fleet had downed sail and were now moving south under oar: a slow
business with the drag of Hoy Sound to pull against. Nor would they pull
hard, for Rognvald needed fresh men to fight with and would be better
pleased the further north Thorfinn came. It looked as if western Hoy, after all,
would see the encounter, with the firth and its race far behind them. The wind
sang, the ropes creaked, and Thorfinn walked down the mid-passage of his
twenty-roomed ship, with laughter breaking out where he spoke, and joined
his voice, on one beam and then on the other, to that of Thorkel Fóstri, of
Bardi, of Starkad and Steingrim and all the other shipmasters whose eye he
could catch: to collect their attention, to remind them, to prepare them. In ten
minutes, or fifteen, they would be within arrow range, and then casting-spear
range.

And after that the oars would come in and they would board and fight with sword and axe, as if their feet were on land, for the sea would be rafted over with ships, and blood-greedy.

Although prepared for great ships, no man in that Caithness flotilla took lightly the first sight of Rognvald's fleet at close quarters with its snarling jaws ringing the sky, while the wind drove the longships like leaves towards the big vessels and under their bellies. Then, according to plan, the sixty sails thundered down and from each galley the oars swung out on their grommets and began to spoon through the waves. Tumbling sea came into view in widening lanes between every ten longships until instead of one fleet there were six, flying shallow and spume-misted over the slack, aiming each for its prey. And behind the moving backs of the oarsmen gleamed the helmeted heads of the fighting-men, standing balanced in ranks, with spearpoint and arrowhead glinting.

Then they were within range, and the grey of the sky was meshed with shimmering steel, upborne on the roar of men's voices.

Rognvald's men threw against the wind, and Thorfinn's men with it. And above the roar then came the screams, with the hiss and whicker and whine of arrow and spear arching above it like harp-music. Then, with dead and dying on every ship, the two fleets crashed together and the low vessels, cutting through, sought to segregate the high vessels of Rognvald's fleet and, having done so, to mob them like starlings.

Long before, planning it all, Thorkel Fóstri had said to his foster-son, 'Of course you will make straight for Rognvald. *Grágás* is the best ship we have to match his, and, man for man, there is no doubt that yours will fight better. Get rid of Rognvald, and the attack will collapse.'

'So Rognvald will reason,' Thorfinn had said.

For some reason, it had made Thorkel angry. 'You know him,' he had said. 'All right. What will he do?'

And Thorfinn had been silent for a while, and then had said, 'Ship to ship while both of us are fresh: that would be too risky for him. Besides, he wants to kill. He would like to see the hird destroyed as well, and all the men who follow me. It must ruin my reputation as well as end my life, this battle. *Grágás* will become the main target, that is certain. But not of Rognvald alone. In his place, I should assign two ships, or perhaps even three, to stand off and do what damage may be done with the bow and the spear while the rest of the fleet make sure that no one can come to the rescue. Then, with all the smaller ships crippled, he should grapple *Grágás* and board her from each side, with other ships standing by to put more men where they are needed. That should be his plan.'

'And yours?' Thorkel had said.

'Split his fleet. Confine each group with a ring of small ships, including the group with Rognvald's ship in it. We should coax them to throw what they can before we get to close quarters. We have as many men as they have. While they are leaning over, dealing with one ship, the crew of another will be climbing to board at their backs. And I shall be there to give them cover.'

'All of them?' Thorkel had said.

'*Grágás* has eighty oarsmen and height. I can see where I am needed, and I can get there. And, with luck, keep away from Rognvald's grappling-irons.'

'With luck,' Thorkel Fóstri had said.

And luck was what, at first, it seemed they would have. From Thorfinn's flagship, all the crew could see how the enemy fleet had been herded into five groups, the taller mast-poles rocking and scything within the lesser pole-ring of the longships. Confined with them was Rognvald's flagship, painted white as Thorfinn's was red, and with Rognvald himself, small and clear and distinct in the prow, in a tunic of hide studded with glittering metal.

With the bravado for which his men loved him, he wore no helmet, but could be picked out by friend or by enemy by the bright silken hair, braided clear of his face and bound over his brows by a *hlað*. He stood looking across the water to where Thorfinn stood, and seemed to be laughing. Then he moved down and back, and was hidden.

It was clear, by then, which of Thorfinn's boats were receiving the worst of the battle, and, to his orders, the oars of *Grágás* dipped and she cut through the sea to the rescue. Then, for all of them, the fighting began, and went on for longer than it seemed human endurance would last.

Later, in such a fight, you found the wounds you had no recollection of. Later, with your ears deadened and aching, you recalled dimly the violence of the noise: the thunderous sound of timber crashing on timber; the searing din of metal on metal and the hollow drumming made by the shields, and the stamping of feet in the boat-shells; and the soft thud of axe and of sword-edge as they sank into cloth, into hide, into flesh. And always, at sea, the swinging shadows of gulls, so that the cries from above and below were as one.

It was the change in sound that first warned Thorkel Fóstri. At that moment, he and Thorfinn were on the same Norwegian ship, having overwhelmed it from two sides and cut the cable that bound it to its fellows so that none could cross to its rescue.

He saw, across the uneven axe-fighting that was all that was left, that Thorfinn had looked suddenly up; and a moment later he, too, was free to look about him. Distinct as writing, the sounds of the battle came to him, clear in every element; and hard upon that another change: a change in the motion of the stained timbers under him. He said aloud, 'The wind has dropped,' and saw that Thorfinn, too, had called something to those men fighting nearest him, and that he was returning to the attack, quickly, to clear the boat of the last of the enemy.

Swinging his sword to do the same, Thorkel Fóstri glimpsed men running: Thorfinn's men, sent to cross back to their own ship. A moment later, between strokes, he saw the oars swing out on *Grágás* and realised why. Already, the red cliffs of Hoy were closer than they had been: the little stream that had surfed in blown spray from the turf at the top was now falling straight to the sea in a film of silver, and the boulders at the cliff-foot were vanishing under slow-breaking waves.

The wind had dropped, and the flood-tide was under way, driving them all south and east, against the cliff-face of Hoy and, ultimately, round and into the east-running race. And the ship they were on and Thorfinn's ship, lashed to it, and his own longship, grappled also below, were on the easterly fringe of the battle and all three about to drive on the rocks unless the oars on *Grágás* could hold them.

Then Thorfinn was beside him, shoulder to shoulder, with his shield up, saying breathlessly, '*Enough! said Ferdiaidh, and he fell dead at the ford.* Could you man this boat?'

'No,' said Thorkel Fóstri. A man came at him, fighting left-handed, and he drove at him with his sword.

'Then call your men back to the longship and cut free. Have you time?'

The cliffs were very close. 'I think so,' said Thorkel Fóstri and, ducking, lifted his horn. As he blew, he saw that Thorfinn was already fighting his way back to *Grágás*, the rest of his men with him. And that, on the way, they were slashing and flinging overboard all the Norwegians' oars. Then he himself was back in his longship with the last of his crew, and the grapple freed not a moment too soon, as his own oars came out and began to pull against the drag of the tide and away from the cliff.

By then, he had less than twenty-five men, many wounded, so that, although he took an oar himself, the longship hung without responding for long beats of time. It must have been then, on the other side, that Thorfinn cut *Grágás* free of the Norwegian ship on his beam, and, oarless, the foreign ship lurched and swung and began to drive cliffwards.

The men remaining on her were in no two minds about what to do. As the red cliffs hung over their prow, they jumped and swam: some to be thrown on the rocks of the shore, some towards Thorkel Fóstri's longship with its low freeboard, so easy to grip and to mount.

It was the end of Thorkel's vessel. Either he allowed himself to be boarded, or his men abandoned their oars and fought back. For a while, they rowed at half-strength while Thorkel himself and the rest hacked and slashed at the hands and heads and shoulders fringing his gunwales. Then, borne on the tide, the beam of the abandoned Norwegian ship swept past them and with her undertow caught the undermanned longship and bore it, too, faster and faster to the cliff-side. Then there was nothing for it but to jump into the water, alongside the enemy, and fight the sea, and the men in it, for what was left of your life.

The rending crash as the Norwegian ship struck and the lesser one as Thorkel's longship in its turn broke its back on the rocks were hardly heard by the remnants of each crew as they struggled in the littered, buffeting water.

They had been seen. Thorkel Fóstri did not know until later that when *Grágás* loomed at his side, ropes trailing, she had arrived there dragging with her the enemy ship whose grappling had caused Thorfinn to return in the first place. He did see, however, the second Norwegian ship that, cutting itself free of the longships assailing it, moved slowly towards him and the other men struggling in the water, and bringing forward its bowmen, began methodically to pick off all those men who were recognisably his and Thorfinn's. Then they were within range of *Grágás*, and the direction of the barbs altered.

His hands about another man's throat, Thorkel Fóstri held on until he felt the enemy slacken, and then, plunging for Thorfinn's flagship, seized a rope and got himself aboard with his axe safely still at his belt. Then he saw the Norwegian boat already lashed to Thorfinn's other beam, and the dead lying under his feet, and, snatching somebody's shield, set himself grimly to weather the curtain of arrows falling from the second enemy ship, and to collect what men he could to repel a second boarding while the red cliffs he had escaped once began to come nearer and nearer.

At his shoulder, someone said, 'They're mad. They'll have to disengage and row, or we'll all crash.'

It was Arnór Jarlaskáld, white of face but apparently unscathed. 'In verse,' Thorkel Fóstri said, panting, as he hefted a newly come casting-spear, aimed, and flung. 'In verse, mighty Grettir-battler. That's what we pay you for, isn't it?'

But of course Arnór was right. He could not understand the enemy's purpose. That three of the great ships had been able to concentrate on *Grágás* meant, he knew, that the longships of their own fleet must have suffered desperate losses. The dead on Thorfinn's ship alone showed what his self-imposed task of monitor must have cost him. It was true, as well, that until the solid flotilla now spanning the sea took care also and began to pull westwards, movement away from the cliffs was almost impossible.

Then, over his shoulder, he saw bare masts moving and realised that part of the fleet at least was disengaging and rowing out of the current. At the same moment, *Grágás* swung, and an outbreak of hoarse cheering behind him suggested that one attacker, at least, had been repelled and cut loose. He could do no more than guess, for the enemy ship now close on his side had deployed no oars to hold its position or to escape the current, but was allowing the tide to fetch it nearer and nearer while bringing to bear on them, with smooth efficiency, the crushing assault by missile that was the preface to boarding.

And around him, men were dying. He threw back what weapons he got, for by this stage in the long battle it was clear that Thorfinn had no reserves left, of casting-spears or of arrows. For a moment, indeed, the fighting was so hard that he thought he was fainting, for his eyes blurred, and the prow of the enemy ship for a moment seemed wreathed in smoke, as if its dragon had come to life and the golden-haired demon at its neck, laughing, was a thing of white flame and sulphur.

Then he saw the reason for the suicidal attack, and why they need look for no withdrawal. The enemy ship reaching their side was the flagship, and the man in the prow was Earl Rognvald.

Thorfinn's voice said, 'I can't bring any more to help you. We've cut loose from the other ship, but she's still there, and there's a third coming up on the stern. The mist may just save us.' A spear, flashing across, glanced off the bright rim of his shield, and he swore under his breath as his hand on the strap took the jolt. There was blood on his neck, and his sword-hand was thick with it.

Thorkel said, 'Mist?'

'Rognvald will drive his ship on the rocks if he has to, but the rest won't. When it gets to mast-height, they'll disengage and start rowing. Otherwise, the tide-race through the firth will simply swallow them. Look. It's catching us now. Whether we row or not, we're setting to the south of Hoy.'

'White Christ, protect us,' Thorkel Fóstri said. 'Tor Ness is down there. All right. The rest will make westwards. But Rognvald won't. Rognvald will follow you.'

They spoke in gasps. It was as much as he could do to risk a tearing glance over his shoulder. But Thorfinn was right. It was mist, and coming down fast, with swathes already lying between ship and ship, and a strange white light on all their faces. Behind, a sudden brightening told that the enemy ship lying there had veered off. A moment later, the vessel astern had begun to move also, oars glancing with light.

Thorfinn's voice rolled over *Grágás*. For a moment, on Thorkel Fóstri's side, there were no defenders at all. Then, on every second or third two-man thwart there was an oar thrust through its slot, and the hazed golden prow was swinging slowly and cleanly away from the white-swaddled red of the cliffs and into the shadowed white curtain that had stolen the place of the sky and the sea.

Behind, on Rognvald's white ship, there was a glint of gold and a glint of silver and a voice calling, cutting in contempt and in anger. This time, Rognvald was not laughing.

Then the mist came fully down, and he and his ship hung on its wall for a moment and then disappeared.

Thorkel Fóstri sat down.

The roll of the ship roused him. That, and Thorfinn's grip on his arm, and Thorfinn's fist with a horn full of strong liquor in it. The golden helm set aside, his foster-son's face was smeared with blood and dirt, the black brows a single bar under the disordered black hair.

'Drink,' said Thorfinn. 'We're rounding Tor Ness, or so Otkel swears. I'm trying for Aith.'

The bay of Aith, a notch in the south coast of Hoy, was past the next headland, and the next headland at flood-tide was a killer. Thorkel Fóstri lifted the horn from his mouth and said, 'You're rowing blind into Aith on the flood? You're crazy!' and meant it, for round them the whiteness was absolute: even the horns of the prow and the stern had vanished into the mist, and rowers three benches off were barely visible.

A good man in a calm sea might circumnavigate Tor and Brims Ness by the kick of the eddy and the hiss of the breakers. Roaring down on the tide, lurching, juddering through the cross-currents, hammering into the fall-back, and squealing and grinding as her timbers and rigging complained, *Grágás* deadened the ear with her clamour, so that the screams of her wounded hardly registered, and the voices of helmsman and look-out, crying to one another, had to be carried repeating like elixir from prow to stern and back again.

Thorkel Fóstri said, 'And you've lost your freeboard. You're shipping water. What's pulling you down?'

'We're carrying seventy dead,' Thorfinn said. 'Only half of them mine.' He shouted something to someone, and they replied: he turned back, holding on with both hands. 'But still not enough to fight Rognvald with. He thought I was escaping him.'

'And, my God, aren't you?' Thorkel Fóstri said. Aith Hope, bad as it was, offered some prospect of shelter until the mist lifted, by which time the easterly flow would have weakened. There was an eddy, if you knew how to catch it, that ran from mid-firth doubling back into the shore this side of Easter Head. Take that, and they might find themselves safe back in Thurso before Rognvald came hunting. Or run through the firth and turn southwards for Moray. With more dead than living to crew him, Thorfinn could expect nothing at Rognvald's hands but the vilest of deaths.

On the other hand, out there to the west were the remains of sixty longships, interleaved with the great ships of Rognvald's command and rowing blind in the mist to hold their own against the sweep of the flood and avoid being sucked through the neck of the firth to destruction. Those who were fully manned still might just manage it. The rest would end, dead men and timbers, in the rocky jaws of the passage. Then the mist would rise, and, baulked of his principal victim, Rognvald and his ships would turn on the longships amongst them and make sure that before they died, their crews cursed their King who had left them.

He waited, then, for Thorfinn's rebuttal, which meant his death as well as Thorfinn's, and was confused when instead Thorfinn said, 'Temporarily, there is no doubt. But have you forgotten the six ships at Longhope?'

'Longhope?' said Thorkel Fóstri. It became impossible to sit any longer with dignity, and so, slowly, he stood, legs spread, one hand on the rigging. Then he said, '*Kalv Arnason?*' The longship rolled, and righted herself.

'As you say,' Thorfinn said.

'But he's on Rognvald's side. He crossed to Rognvald.'

'Did you see him fighting for Rognvald just now?' Thorfinn said.

Thorkel Fóstri said, 'He doesn't need to. He's been promised his farm back in Norway. He has only to stay out of the fighting. He'll lose Egge if he helps you. He won't.'

'Maybe he won't,' Thorfinn said. 'But it would only be civil to give him the chance. He owes me something.'

'He owes you his skin,' Thorkel Fóstri said. 'But then, so does Rognvald. That night in the *haugr*. You had only to walk away.'

'On my broken leg?' said Thorfinn.

'Don't be a fool. He would have killed you.'

'Perhaps,' Thorfinn said.

'Well?' said his foster-father. Now that he felt stronger, the full force of his anger was rising.

'Well,' said Thorfinn. 'I don't think Kalv would care, personally, to drive the knife in my back. But even if he did, there is the matter, isn't there, of Uncle

Harald's forthcoming arrival? Magnús may well present Kalv with Egge, but Harald may not be pleased to let him keep it.'

Thorkel Fóstri stared at him. 'You are relying on that?'

'Partly,' said Thorfinn placatingly. 'For the rest, we must depend on Kalv's strong sense of family. Remember? You used to complain of it again and again.'

'O Body of God,' said Thorkel Fóstri, and gripped the rigging as the timbers heaved and jolted under him and the whiteness hid what was ahead.

To six dragon-ships, fog-bound in a harbour, the ghost of another approaching is a matter for drumbeating and horns, and also for standing to arms, since the newcomer might be an enemy or, even worse, in the hands of a cousin.

To Kalv Arnason, alert on the prow of his longship, it was therefore a matter of relief that the newcomer, far from approaching, merely slid to the side of the little anchorage and there let down her anchor, following this trusting action by lowering two of her skiffs. Watching these, as they passed and repassed to the shore, it appeared to Kalv Arnason that they were unloading something, in quantity, but the mist was too thick to see what.

He sent a man to his furthermost ship to see what a swimmer could make of it, and the swimmer came back, sullen and dripping, inside one of the skiffs he was observing, with two men rowing and a third man, tall as a tree, in the bows.

He knew who it was even before the skiff arrived, bumping gently, and the tall man stood up and said, 'We have been unloading dead men, eighty of them. And twenty wounded. How are you, Kalv? My wife your niece sends her greetings, and so does your cousin Thorkel Fóstri, who is with me, there on *Grágás*. Are you going to ask me on board?'

'Thorfinn,' said Kalv Arnason, with the least flatness in the ebullient voice, and the least pallor in the healthy face. He said, 'I have not the slightest objection, of course. And I am glad to see that you yourself have taken no harm. But is it wise? With Rognvald behind you, it would be prudent to prepare to make over the firth at the first lifting of the mist. It disappears, as you know, often as fast as it comes.'

'Then,' said Thorfinn, 'since good advice is always worth listening to, and you have not the least objection to my boarding, will you let down your ladder before your fenders take harm, and give me more of it?'

And so, despite himself, he was sitting presently beside Earl Thorfinn drinking ale under his own stern shelter, with the horn cracking under his finger-bones as he gathered the strength to look into that tranquil, battle-marked face and defy it.

'Did it seem to you,' Thorfinn said, 'when you swung the axe that killed King Olaf, that his half-brother Harald was pleased or otherwise? Naturally, you will have given this problem much thought, since if Rognvald wins, the King of Norway may still have to deny you that dear homeland of Egge that your wife brought you when you killed her first husband. But then, even so, no doubt you have discussed with Rognvald what part of Orkney he will give you to farm under his rule when he is vassal for all the islands to Norway?'

Kalv Arnason took a quick drink, and his jaw set in the obstinate line that his cousin Thorkel would have recognised. 'Under you, my dear nephew,' he said, 'I had a pittance in Caithness.'

'Naturally,' Thorfinn said. 'With one-third of Orkney in my hands and my nephew Rognvald to battle against, I had nothing to spare. With all Orkney behind me, it would be different. I should owe Norway nothing. And especially I should need a strong man I could trust in the Western Isles.'

'The Western Isles?' said Groa's uncle.

'To gather the tribute and see it well guarded. The man I have at present is worthless. There are plenty of pickings in the islands,' Thorfinn said. 'And good land. As good as Egge, I believe. It might,' said Thorfinn, 'be worth considering, if a quiet life appeals to you. Because if an accident were to befall me, I don't know who would worry you most: King Olaf's kinsfolk or Thore Hund's son, your nephew Siward of Northumbria . . . ?'

Grágás had finished unloading by the time the skiff came back from Kalv's ship, and the mist was thin enough to see that Thorfinn was in it. Infuriatingly, he neither signalled nor said anything of significance until he was fully aboard and standing beside his foster-father, with the fifty men he had left crowding about him.

'Well?' said Thorkel Fóstri. 'Is he for you or against you?'

'Why, for us,' said Thorfinn. 'Did you ever doubt it? And if you will give him time, there are thirty men crossing over to fill up our row-benches so that we shall have no trouble in catching up with Earl Rognvald, once we see him. And by the look of the mist, we may not have so long to wait. . . . Have you drunk all the ale?'

Of the ninety ships who had met in conflict that afternoon off the west coast of Hoy, perhaps half survived the fight and the mist to be revealed one to another when, five hours later, the south-east wind lifted again and began to blow the vapour away.

They lay broached-to on the waves, scattered over the seas to the west, with the wreckage of those in collision and those overturned floating abandoned between them. The battle had cost them lives. But the exhaustion laid on them all by the sea hung over every ship like a shroud, so that, even when vision returned, the oars barely moved more than was required of them, and men looked about them sluggishly, with their hands empty of weapons.

Then, from the smallest ships, the cheering began, ragged and scattered, but enough to make Earl Rognvald pause from where he strode from bench to bench on the white flagship, joking, laughing, insulting, encouraging: stirring his hird to collect their fleet and prepare for battle again. He leaped to the prow and looked at the longships and where they were pointing.

Then he saw, as they had done, the six clean, striped sails skimming taut-bellied round Hoy towards him, led by a sail he saw in his dreams, sewn with patterns of silk in gold and scarlet and white, with before it a high golden prow he knew as well, above the flash of red strakes at each curtsey.

The cheer, from Thorfinn's men, was for Thorfinn, who had not deserted them. The silence he felt all around him was the silence of recognition and fear; for all his men knew the Arnmødling colours.

Kalv, the turncoat, had turned again, or been made to turn, by the disarming tongue, the schooled face, the unschooled eyes that had been his own downfall, or nearly.

Seven fresh ships against his weary ones, which were still more than twice that number. Odds good enough, surely, to make certain that, out of all those seven ships, one man at least should not live out the day.

Rognvald gave the order to row, and, signalling, drew his flock again under his command: some to join him, and the rest to move quickly against the lesser ships, and the weaker, before they could unite.

It was eight hours after midday, and the east-going tide, feeble now, squabbled under the wind, so that the oars dug into the waves and men lost their footing, a minor nuisance. Battle had begun. And there were two hours of daylight left, to see it finished.

All Rognvald's men knew the Arnmødling colours. It was by no accident, then, that the six ships led by Kalv made straight for the longships that held Rognvald's men and, with their strong bows and bright casting-spears, began to beat them into surrender.

From where they were occupied in their slaughter among the small ships of Thorfinn's scattered flotilla, the big vessels from Norway noticed, and began to signal uneasily, one to the other.

Grágás, the King's flagship, paid no attention to any other ship on the sea, but, sail down, rowed on a ramming-course straight for the white dragon of Rognvald.

His heart eased, his eyes bright, Rognvald watched Thorfinn coming and saw, this time, that the black head was bare as his own, for no man there on either side could fail to recognise the two Earls, any more than any man there would lay a finger on either. As if magic enclosed them, they were sacrosanct, united by blood, and by the unique right of the kindred to kill its own members.

He saw Thorfinn's prow turn, showing the carving, as it prepared to slide by and grapple for boarding, and he leaped, with his men, to their positions, and laughed aloud with the joy of it. It seemed unfair, then, that Thorfinn had used his encounter with Kalv to advantage, and that, just before the ships closed, a grid of cast steel should fall on Rognvald's ship, clearing the first line of men and killing half of his oarsmen.

Because his discipline was good, and his planning, it took seconds to drag down the dead and replace them. But in those seconds another whickering cast scored the clouds, falling this time on their shields, but piercing as well, so that he had to raise his voice over the screaming and draw off, instead of clenching fast, as he'd meant, with the grappling-irons.

And even drawing off was hard enough, for the other boat, rowing freshly and well, let no space grow between them, but threw its own irons over his gunwales, so that he had to have them cut or uprooted and flung back.

The men on Thorfinn's ship were jeering, and he let them. When he was ready, he would fight and they could mock him if they wished, from wherever their heads happened to fall. When he was ready, he shouted, and his men shouted in answer, and blew their horns as, this time, the two beams drove together and the cables flew, crossing from Rognvald's side to Thorfinn's and vice versa. Then, as the ropes landed, so the men jumped aboard with their axes and swords, some on one ship and some on the other, and opened the first steaming wounds, and caused the first dead man to clutter the footboards with his shield and his helm and his scabbard.

Smiling, Rognvald vaulted down from the stern and began to wade forward, cutting and hacking and looking half at what he was doing and half to where, more slowly, Thorfinn stepped down in his turn and, axe in hand, was crossing his vessel. 'Well, uncle?' said Rognvald. 'Does your third of Orkney look good to you now?'

Thorfinn had stopped. 'Only justice seems good,' he said. He was frowning.

'Justice?' said Rognvald. 'Then why not see justice done? Put it to the test. Why have you stopped? Three paces more, and we shall have a field of justice all our own. Don't be afraid. My men will not touch you.' Pushed by the struggle about him, he staggered a little. He was splashed with other men's blood.

Thorfinn said quickly, 'There is no need. It is clear who has won. Look about you. The Norse ships are leaving.'

Brusi's son stood, smiling still, for he did not believe it. It was his men who looked round, in the thick of the fighting, and who began calling, so that at last Rognvald looked swiftly over his shoulder.

It was true. It was unbelievably true. The ships he had been given by Norway, the ships that had fought all afternoon at his side, had given up before the onslaught of Kalv Arnason and one by one were twisting out of the fighting, were laying inboard their oars and scrambling, were raising the sail that would help them run north, out of trouble.

Rognvald had seen only that when, with a crash, Kalv Arnason's flagship hurled itself grappling against his opposite beam and the first of Kalv Arnason's men began to throw themselves into his vessel.

Printed with longing, Rognvald's face turned once towards where Thorfinn stood unmoving in the midst of his own men and watching him.

There was no leap that would take him to Thorfinn's side. There was no weapon made that would reach him. With hate and fury and still that unspeakable longing marring all his fair face, Rognvald threw what he had, his father's great golden axe, towards the black, towering figure outfacing him, and then, with a gasp, wheeled and, killing and slashing, began to drive back these second invaders.

He meant, after that, to turn and renew the battle. It was his men who, against all his threats and his orders, cut the shackles on either side and set themselves, with oar and then sail, to escape northwards after their fellows.

Kalv saw no reason to stop his assault, or to fall back, or to let his prey walk out free from so dainty a trap. It was Thorfinn's instant disengagement that first drew Kalv's startled attention, and then Kalv's anger, and then Kalv's stubborn back, until, racing in Rognvald's wake, he became aware that *Grágás*, flying alongside, was firmly heading him off, and that he was not the only shipmaster giving play to his fury.

It was brought home to him, indeed, in a moment: when, with a whine and a thud, the golden axe of Rognvald's father struck by his foot, thrown with venom by Brusi's half-brother.

And across the darkening sea, as Rognvald's ship fled on the tide and the wind towards freedom: 'Sail where you will,' said Thorfinn's echoing voice. 'Catch whom you can. But Rognvald is for me or for no one.'

'And my thanks?' Kalv Arnason bawled.

'There is his axe,' said Thorfinn. 'And it not in your head. Be contented.'

ELEVEN

ENTLY ...' SAID the King; and his wife laughed, and slackened her grasp.

'Was it such a celebration? Yes, I can see that it was. Is that better?'

'It is a little,' said Thorfinn, 'like Mael Duin's voyage to the thirty-one islands: revolving ramparts of fire, through which beautiful people move to haunting music. Yes, that is better. And yes, it has been rather a long celebration. But with cause.'

They were alone in their chamber at Orphir, so that she could look at him, tracing the new scars with gentle fingers, and ask the questions one did not ask newly arrived on the jetty, with excited people about her, and her sons. She said, 'So Rognvald is safely back in Norway, having lost most of the force he was given, and with no hope of another? And Kalv and his people have left for the Western Isles, and Eachmarcach is King of Dublin again? Now I think of it, I'm thankful to find you so human in your rejoicing. Otherwise, I should have feared for you.'

'Oh, fear for me,' Thorfinn said. 'But not because I am less than human. What does Lulach say of it all?'

'You know he never speaks when you are in danger,' Groa said. She glanced at him. 'He has taken to calling you the King of the Jutes. A new fancy.'

'There was a famous prince everyone knows,' Thorfinn said. 'A mere six hundred years ago, give or take a decade. That one?'

'His uncle. You never had a brother's son of the same name as the prince?' enquired Groa. She smiled.

'The only brother's son I have is called Rognvald, and is living quietly in Norway, far from where he can cause anyone harm. We have talked about him enough. Come and tell me how you are faring.'

'I have come. I am telling you.' She could hardly be closer.

'But without so many warm garments between us,' explained Thorfinn patiently; but his fingertips were not being patient at all.

After ten years, the Orkneys were his again. Rognvald's hird, the men who had been with him in Norway and Russia, had gone back to Nídarós in his company. The mercenaries, the dead, and the injured had been hunted for all through the islands the day after the battle, and, once found, had been killed or ransomed, nursed or buried, according to their destiny.

In a very short time, even then, Thorfinn knew that Brusi's men would serve him in the end; and that very soon he could sit in Westray, as Rognvald had done, and men would come to him for advice and for justice, as they had come before Rognvald returned.

Rognvald had been a young god, full of magic and mischief, whom they had loved to lead them overseas to high adventure. But the sun had set on the Viking, or was setting. What remained was still high adventure, but of a different kind.

One tried in vain to teach as much to Arnór Jarlaskáld, whose verse on the recent occurrence even the scarffs on the rocks were repeating:

> *Straight and sure,*
> *True service to one's lord—*
> *Unwilling, this one,*
> *To war with Brusi's son:*
> *Awkward our choice*
> *When Earls are eager*
> *To fight—friendship*
> *Is far from easy.*

> *I beheld both my princes*
> *In Pentland Firth, hewing*
> *At each other's men.*
> *Deep grew my sorrow.*
> *Blood streaked the sea,*
> *Blood fell on shield-rim—*
> *Bespattered the ship.*
> *Black blood oozed*
> *From the yielding seams.*

Sitting on Aith Hope, where he had been forcibly placed with the dead and the wounded, Arnór had used his time well. Without a skald, the deeds of a war-lord would die. It was Arnór's bad luck, and his master's, that men should wish, now and then, to celebrate something in their lives other than battles. With a lesser poet who peddled his verses like bits of robbed-out foreign mosaic, one might throw the hearth-stool away and close one's door on him. But, rare of his breed, Arnór gave love with his *kvaedi* and hoped for love in return, even from enemies. And if the love remained, and not the verses, it would be equally a judgement of sorts.

At the great feast that night, at which he had no need to drink because Groa was there and the boys, she said to him, 'I can feel happiness all around you, like the warmth from a burning wax-light. You will stay in Orkney all winter, till you are sure of your people again?' And when he nodded, she said,

'You know you have been drunk on sea-water, not ale. Can you ever be so happy anywhere else?'

Thorfinn said, 'Was Canute happy? I suppose he was. About King Olaf I don't know: he was my age when he died. If you are apprehensive, I suggest you watch what happens to your great-uncle Harald in Norway. He'll persuade Magnús to give him half the throne soon, when he has finished exhibiting how awkward and how powerful he can be. And then we shall see a King of Norway who has spent half his life with the Orientals. They say Jaroslav's father in Russia had eight hundred concubines. And seventy years ago *his* father went about with his head shaven, save for a lock on one side, and long moustaches, and a ring in one ear. Yet in their turn they all come from the northern islands, as you and I do. Will Harald be happy?'

'He is not a Celt,' Groa said.

'Then he will be happy,' said Thorfinn. 'And now that I think of it, so will Rognvald, with any luck.'

The child they wanted was conceived that night in Orphir, and because her health came before everything else, Thorfinn made her stay at the hall, as soon as they knew of it, and rode about Orkney on his own, with the hird and with their older son Sigurd, who was eleven, and to whom he was God. And she did not grudge him it, but stayed with Erlend and with Sinna and her women and discovered that David the priest was good at board-games, and that Thorkel Fóstri, on the days he preferred not to ride, would tell her things about Thorfinn that she did not yet know.

It was to be a hard winter, when wolves ran on the ice between Norway and Denmark, and forests froze round Cologne. By October, the first signs were there already, and men travelled less, but returned to their steadings to see to their barns and to make all snug for the harsh weather to come, before feast-time arrived. The couriers that came back and forth, when they could, from the mainland of Alba, stopped arriving and Thorfinn came home with only those courtmen who belonged to his household and restored Sigurd, who could not stop talking, to his mother, and tossed Erlend in the air and asked after Lulach, who was staying at Deerness with Thorkel Fóstri.

The air of contentment was still there, although tempered, when he held her, with a restraint she knew he did not enjoy. Until this child was safe, they slept in different beds. So he kissed her, complaining, and she said, 'Ah, the black-headed fighting-men the fifty islands will see, come next July.' She hesitated, and then said it. 'I have never seen a son of yours by another.'

His face did not change, but she turned scarlet under the brown, velvety gaze.

'At twenty-three,' he said, 'I cannot recollect having so many. And after that, of course, I was forced into marriage.'

'So?' she said sternly. She knew that her colour was high, but she had no fears now.

'Is there a question?' he said. 'There is this Druid. I ask him what the present hour is good for. And he says, *for begetting a King on a Queen.*'

'I have met him?' she said.

'Surely,' said Thorfinn. 'He sits on your pillow. And, that being so, what chance do I have, and myself exhausted?'

Those nights, she went to bed early, when the tables were cleared and the rest of the women withdrew to their sleeping-quarters. Lying on her down mattress, she could hear Thorfinn's voice, low and rich through the timber wall, and the exclamations and rejoinders of his men, as they sat talking and drinking.

Masculine talk. The mild, austere voice of her father remonstrating with his hot-headed brothers, persuading Kalv into moderation, explaining to Thorberg and Kolbiorn. The hoarse, lewd voice of Gillacomghain her husband boasting of his prowess to his brother. The good-humoured roughness Thorfinn used with the hird when he was handling them, stirring their interest in something he wanted. If Thorfinn had ever had personal exchanges with anyone, man or woman, apart from herself, she had never heard them. But he must have had: with his foster-father; with Sulien, she imagined. With other women, she did not believe, despite the question she had made him answer. His nature was otherwise.

She did not know, therefore, as she drifted into sleep, how long into the night Thorfinn talked, or how long he sat with his hands round his horn, saying nothing in particular, with the two men or three who still stayed with him when the rest had crossed to the wall-benches and rolled, stretching, into their skins and drawn the covers over them as the long centre fire glowed and glimmered on the axes and shields, and the painted carving on the pillars and beams. Nor did even Thorfinn know that on such nights men took turns to sit with him in silence while he thought, for toleration and acceptance had grown, a long time since, into something else.

On such a night, it was Sinna, kept awake by a wriggling Erlend, who realised that a great cold had come suddenly, and that the tapers burned still in the hall, where there were no slaves awake to see to the fire. For a while, she stayed where she was, grumbling and muttering. Then, because what disturbed her girl Groa was to her also a matter of moment, she rose and found another blanket to put on the bed and, having tucked up the boy, pulled her old sheepskin cloak over her robe and opened the door of her sleeping-hut.

Orphir lay still on the slopes of its hill, hut after hut black on the grey, save only the long shape of the drinking-hall with its amber rectangles of flickering membrane. She could hear the stream that ran down to the shore, and the breath of the sea washing the shores of the Flow, and sense rather than see the low black islands that lay out there over the water: Cava and Flotta and Huna, with Ronaldsay lying behind. And to the west, unseen, the ramparts of the island of Hoy, outside which such a terrible carnage had been wrought five months before.

Then she saw a longship on the beach which had not been there at dusk. And as she stood, staring, a hand gripped her over the elbow and another palmed her over the face, so that she could neither breathe nor call out, and the voice of Rognvald, Thorfinn's nephew, said, 'Be still, little woman, or I will feed your bowels to my dog.'

Then two men tied her and threw her gagged in a corner, where she had to watch what all the others were doing: the others who came up from the beach with great bundles, which they stacked man-deep round the walls of the drinking-hall before melting into the darkness, steel glinting, to where the sleeping-quarters lay silent.

There had never been a guard posted at Orphir until the struggle between the two Earls began, and the first thing that Thorfinn had done after the battle was to remove him. Magnús of Norway could never give Rognvald another army. That everyone knew.

He had not given Rognvald another army. Rognvald had one ship, with the men needed to sail her. It was all he required, when his only purpose was to kill his father's half-brother.

Sinna saw it all happen: saw the hall-lights glint gold on the Earl's silken hair as he passed and repassed, and willed in vain that Thorfinn within would rise, would extinguish the lights, would open a shutter, would send a man into the yard . . . anything to avert what was going to happen.

But nothing averted it, and she watched as the brand was kindled that Rognvald stretched to the darkness round the hall door, as his men did on each of its long sides and its ends. Watched as, stark-lit by the ring of bright fire, Rognvald threw back his fair head and called.

'Hallo there, my uncle! Are you cold? Come out! I have kindled a fire for you, and my aunt, and your soul-friends. Come and warm yourselves at it!'

Groa was so deeply asleep that the shouting in the main part of the hall did not fully wake her at first, and it was the smoke, oozing thick through the timbers and catching her throat, that roused her at last.

There was enough light in the chamber to show her where her cloak was, and that Thorfinn's bed was empty still. Then she saw why the light was orange and red, and what was making it. She was halfway to the door when it opened and Thorfinn's hands stopped her, gripping her shoulders. Behind him Sigurd stood, pressing hard at his father's back. When she flung out her arm, he ran to her.

Thorfinn said, 'Rognvald has set fire to the hall. Take Sigurd and walk out. He is letting go all the thralls and the women and children. Sigurd, take care of your mother.' He had flung her cloak over her shoulders and, dragging rugs from the bed, pushed them into Sigurd's arms. 'Quickly. I'll follow.'

She didn't move. 'Erlend!'

'He's safe. All the huts are empty. The women are safe. They're waiting. Quickly. Groa, *run*.'

The door to the big hall hung open. It was full of Thorfinn's men, half dressed, steel in their hands. The main door to the yard stood empty, outlined in brilliant orange. Very few slaves slept in the hall. By now, they had gone. Thorfinn said, 'Groa: I cannot fight till you go.'

She said, 'He'll kill the boys,' on something like a scream, and he shouted back at her, so sharp was his anger. 'Rognvald will never do that. You will kill

Sigurd yourself if you keep him.' And, taking their son by the arm, he flung him into the hall, while she ran after. She saw Thorfinn drag the rug over the boy's head and shoulders. Then, '*Run!*' he said. 'Run. And hide if you can,' and pushed the boy through the fire and into the open.

Then Groa felt her husband's hand on her back and caught his arm with her own. 'You cannot fight, with me or without me,' she said. 'Can you? You burn, or you run through the door and they kill you.'

He said 'Groa—' with the lie on his lips, and then the wisdom he had came to his rescue and he was silent.

She said, 'Give me this gift,' and in all the uproar there was a splinter of silence between them. Then he said, 'Shoes. Cloak. Rugs in the water-butt. Wait in the chamber.' And was gone into the swirling smoke of the hall, where the tapers glared on black, moving billows, and on the edge of an axe; on a man's arm moving quickly; on a group of blundering shadows that masked the doorway and stood screaming and then fell, so that the flames on the threshold sprang flattening like sheaves and then roared upwards again. She heard, as she thrust her feet into her shoes, as she plunged the rugs into the butt, the thuds and cries as other men hacked their way out of the building and died of the steel Rognvald's men threw at them.

Rognvald's men were all round the hall. She could hear them yelling and taunting because Thorfinn lacked the courage to come and meet death with his friends, but would rather let himself die in his dung while his wife stroked his hand and younger men taunted and spat on him. She heard the words they used.

You could not see if there was anyone left now in the hall. The hangings had gone, and the lines of flame caulking the timbers had spilled over, one log to the next, so that the great inside wall of the building stood like a cascade of tumbling fire, with a bush of fire like a stork's nest on every pillar, and the roof-beams brilliant with light as a sunset.

And the walls of the chamber she was in had caught now, too, and the bed she had lain on.

He had said to wait; and she waited; and he came; but by then she could not see how he looked, for her swollen eyes were closed, and she could not breathe very much any more, and her fists were raw where she had tried to beat the flames from the hem of her cloak and her shoulders.

But then she felt him between her face and the heat, and his arms round her body, lifting her. Something burning touched her bare ankle and forced her lids open. Her cheek rolled on his shoulder. A small dazzle tormented her eyes, and she put out a blundering hand and it stopped as a lock of her own hair, smoking, seared into her palm.

Then there was a series of terrible movements where she cried out to him to loosen his grip because he was gouging the flesh from her bones. There was an explosion of light, greater than anything that had gone before, and of heat like the heat of liquid brass pouring over her body.

And then it was dark and there was nothing.

*   *   *

To help a child in a panic, you must first stop it screaming. To stop it screaming, you call it by name.

A child was trying to scream, and someone was calling its name, over and over, steadily, softly.

'Groa. Groa. Groa? Don't cry. It's all right. Groa. Groa . . .'

The beautiful voice was Thorfinn's. The crying child was herself. The head and limbs brushed and tinselled with pain; the hips and stomach and groin through which pain was rolling, solid as tide-water: rolling, collecting, exploding, and ebbing bodefully back, to begin the whole flood once again: those were hers, too.

She knew what was happening, and what had happened, and cut off her cries with a gasp and opened her eyes.

Darkness. Darkness, of course. In October, in Orkney, the nights were long.

Darkness, and cold open air, and the noise of sea and strained timbers, and the shuddering hardness of wood underneath her, helped a little by something yielding and harsh, and something softer but damp. Heather and rugs, spread in the well of a boat. A small boat moving fast with the pull of two oars. A boat rowed by Thorfinn, who was only a voice, and at whose feet she was lying. He said, 'Can you bear it? Can you try to bear it, thou bravest of brave? We mustn't be heard.'

She could hear him apportion his breath: to the words; to the oars. The boat kicked and slid, and the oars dug and stuttered and then resumed their straight sweep.

Orphir. He was rowing from Orphir. It was a strong tide round Graemsay. Who would hide them on Graemsay that Rognvald would not discover?

The boat veered again, and she heard him catch his breath.

He knew where he was going, and he didn't need questions. The weight of pain in her body moved, ground to its peak, and began to recede, and the freezing air licked at the sweat on her wrists and her forehead. She said, 'I can bear it. When is dawn?'

He said, 'We shall be safe long before dawn. I love you. Have I said so?'

'Not today,' she said, and when she began crying again, did not know it.

The family who lived in the turf hut on the rocks above Ham in Caithness were freed slaves: Bathrik, the son of an Irishman, made his living mainly by gathering kelp, and his wife had the Norse name of Gyrid.

It was one of their two unmarried daughters who heard the geese snort and hiss just before dawn the next morning, and, lighting the lantern, saw that all three of the birds had come out of the barn and were standing, sunk on their pink clumsy feet, with their thick, scaly necks lifted seawards. Then she saw, as the first faint greyness of day touched the water, that there was a boat there, far down on the mud, half in and half out of the tide-edge, and something moving, it seemed, at one end of it.

She ran and shook her father and brother, and found their boots, and an axe. Then, after the menfolk had gone, she and her mother and sister stood at the shutter and peered through the darkness till they heard by the sound of ordinary voices and the bob of the lantern returning that there was nothing out of the way about it all.

And in that they were wrong, for when the party returned, it was her brother who carried the lantern, and her father who bore a seal-woman in his arms: a beautiful thing, fast asleep, with long red hair and a strange-blemished face and long, fine clothes, all wet with the sea.

Then her father Bathrik stooped and brought the seal-woman into the light, and it was to be seen that she was not sleeping at all, but very sick, and that the marks on her face seemed to be burns, and that her robe was not only wet with the sea, but dyed and sodden with blood.

Gyrid started forward, and between them they laid her on the bed-straw while Bathrik straightened, panting with news much more than with labour. 'It is the Lady of Orkney. The Earl is there. She is ill. It is woman's business. Gyrid, you must find out what to do, and set to curing her. They want no one to know they are here. No one. No one at the hall even, or the fisher-houses. The Lady is to stay here until she is able to be better hid. The Earl will lie in the shed, with the peat and the fish. Straw. Klakkr, put straw in the shed. Malmuru, give a poke to the fire and hang the pot on. Gyrid—'

Gyrid, kneeling, paid no attention. 'The poor young one,' she said. ''Tis a baby she's lost. Malmuru, come quickly.'

'And if she dies?' said Bathrik's son. 'Who will get the blame? Or is she the Earl's wife at all, skulking at night on the seashore? She will be some man's whore in trouble.'

'You fool,' said Bathrik. 'Do you think I don't know Thorfinn when I see him? You saw him yourself. Ten feet tall, and black, and nobody's fool. If he wants to hide, it's for a good purpose.'

'I saw nothing,' said his son. 'You took the lantern. Where is he, then? We don't know where he is, far less where he's come from.'

'He was behind me,' Bathrik said. He picked up the lantern.

'I am still behind you,' Thorfinn said from the doorway. 'How is my wife?' He did not come into the light.

Gyrid made a token movement, but did not halt what she was doing. 'We'll have to stop the bleeding, my lord. But she's warmer already. Never fear. We'll care for her.'

'Whatever happens,' the Earl said, 'you won't suffer. There is my purse. Smash the boat. There may be blood . . . and footmarks to cover. We are not here. We have never been here. Can you do this?'

It was the son who spoke up. 'I dare say we can, my lord Earl. But if you came from Thurso Bay or Canisbay in the dark, your unfriends can come twice as fast in the daylight. There may not be time for all these fine contrivings.'

'There will be time,' Thorfinn said.

Then Klakkr's sister caught the lantern and held it up higher, so that it lit the Earl's head and shoulders, his body, his arms, and his hands.

The girl's throat closed on itself. Then, like a stuck door punched suddenly open, her air-passage cleared and filled, whining. Even Gyrid looked round.

The Earl's lips moved and the salt glittered everywhere on the tattered black skin.

'If,' said Thorfinn, 'you will show me the shed?'

Gyrid rose.

'Not to touch me,' said Thorfinn, 'would be best.'

And waited patiently as they came to him slowly and anxiously, as might birds of the wild, save for the look on their faces.

The storms began after that, with sleet and continuous rain, so that the short daylight hours were almost as dark as the night, and if Gyrid did not bring her spare eggs round the settlement, it was no wonder; and everyone knew that Bathrik and his son were no good to anyone once the meat was salted and the ale-cask had been broached.

Besides, by then the news had come about the burning of Earl Thorfinn in Orphir.

The first man who told it was scoffed at, for no ship would cross from Norway in winter, and Rognvald had been sent off only that summer, truly whipped, as half Caithness was aware, who had fought with Thorfinn in that battle. Thorfinn the Mighty. His tents had been pitched there, and he had ridden round here, and he had said this or that to your cousin's boy, joking, while he held off two kicking Trøndelagers with his left hand and drove his sword through a third with his right.

Thorfinn, the first Earl of Orkney to become King of all Alba also, could not be dead. A murdering death, without battle. And by his own kith and kin: a man whose life he had spared over and over.

And the red-headed Lady. Now, that was a pity.

But if Thorfinn was dead, who was Earl of Caithness? And what of the friends of Thorfinn still living, who had lands in Caithness and Orkney?

The toisechs murmured together in the big settlements and made their own discreet enquiries, while the little townships, like Ham, closed their shutters and kept themselves to themselves and said nothing, waiting. You had to look to yourself. If a woman wept, she was thrashed for it.

They did not have to wait long. Before November was out, Earl Rognvald crossed from Orkney to Thurso and sent a party of horsemen round the country, telling them who their new Earl was to be, which was himself. He took the chance also to look here and there for the friends of Thorfinn who might have slipped out of Orkney and found a friendly house to plot sedition in.

Rognvald's horsemen were very thorough. They came to Ham almost at once, and took the tribute set aside for the dead Earl, and asked for news of the dead Earl's two sons, whom someone seemed to be hiding, and of his friends, but not as if they expected an answer. Then they set to searching themselves.

And since one did not argue with bare swords and spearpoints, the people of Ham let them look where they wished, including the open stone huts where the food dried, and the byres and the sheep-pens and the grain-lofts, where there were any, and even the vats and the cauldrons they used for the milk and the malt and the cheeses. They thrust their spears through the peat-stacks and the thatch, and tossed the hay, and the heather-piles for the rope-making.

There was nothing they didn't look into: even the well-bucket at Bathrik's, so the story went. The toisech, watching his wife's chests being tumbled, asked later how they had found things at Bathrik's, and Earl Rognvald's man had said the boy had been cheeky as usual, and the three women tiresome, and Bathrik the worse for drink, and wanting to know how often they were to change earls anyway, and what if a new King of Alba came next, hunting Earl Rognvald.

To which, evidently, Earl Rognvald's man had replied that there was no problem in that, since the next King of Alba had already been chosen by his uncle Earl Siward, who now ruled in his name in the Lowlands. And that there was nothing the King would like better than to have Earl Rognvald take Caithness and the north off his hands.

It was the first anyone had heard of a new King of Alba and caused a good deal of talk, until the next gale came and they had to see to their roofs again. And Earl Rognvald's men, having found nothing, went away and did not come back. Only up at the toisech's house, men looked at one another and began, quietly, to sharpen their weapons. For it seemed to them that, whatever claim Rognvald might have on Orkney now his uncle was dead, he had none on Caithness. And that there might be enough of Thorfinn's fighting-men left, somewhere or another, to put forward this viewpoint, given encouragement and a little time. Especially if Thorfinn's two sons could be found.

Somewhere about November, it began to seem as if Thorfinn might live.

It was not a matter on which he had an opinion, having left the conscious world in the doorway of Bathrik's hovel in Ham and never yet having shown any desire to return to it. Indeed, when at last he moved, fractionally, of his own volition, and caught his breath and then, slowly, opened his eyes, Gyrid screamed, and his lashes dropped again, a long way, into dark caverns.

When they lifted again, Groa was there. Out of the new, marbled skin, pink and brown, the brown eyes were the same, within their singed charcoal lashes. Her tears fell on the blankets, although she was smiling. After a long time, he said, 'Don't grieve. We shall have others.'

It was all he said before he left her again, and she had not been able to speak at all.

The next time he awoke, Malmuru was at his side, and he was afraid and bewildered.

She said, 'Your wife is sleeping. She sat by you all night. There is your friend.'

He looked at Malmuru, and not at his friend. He remembered who he was, and then what had happened. If he could not lift his hand, it was because he had been ill, not because he was bound. He had expected to see Groa because he had seen Groa once before when he had wakened. Groa was safe.

When, once before, he had seen Groa, there had been someone, a man, on his other side. The same man, perhaps. The freed slave at Ham who had taken them in.

A friend?

Thorkel Fóstri said, 'Look at me. Child: child, look at me.'

Then Thorfinn turned his head.

Thorkel Fóstri said, 'Don't blame Bathrik or his wife. They were afraid. They thought you would both die. They heard I was somewhere in Caithness and managed to get word to me. No one else knows I'm here. . . . Dear son, your boys are safe, and your wife. You have only to get well.'

To Groa, an hour later, Thorkel Fóstri said, 'I think he heard me. He is sleeping again. Now you must go.'

Groa said, 'You are in danger, too.'

And Thorkel Fóstri said, 'Which of us do you think he would rather see killed? Rognvald's men might think of returning. And next time they may remember the earth-houses.'

Thorkel Fóstri was right. Thorfinn could not yet travel to Moray, where the boys were hidden, as she could, weak though she was. Nor would he want to. Rognvald, some day, would have to be dealt with.

She said, 'He does not even know that his throne has gone.' There was no way now of recovering Canute's golden helmet, lying blotched and mis-shapen in the ruins of Orphir. Or the circlet of gold that had burned its way through his brow and his hair before he had dragged it off and thrown it into the furnace. It marked his skin still: the permanent fillet of kingship.

The willpower that could drive him to stand in that furnace of Orphir waiting; waiting for the moment when the roof should cave in and the loft-floor would give him the footing he needed to break out unseen: that was not the temper of the refugee or the exile. Or the willpower that had brought him to cross the Pentland Firth alone at night while she lay at his feet, and the black skin and grey flesh and white ooze of his hands wrapped the looms of his oars and froze there.

'He has lost neither his earldom nor Alba,' Thorkel Fóstri said. 'Trust us. We shall do nothing until he is well. But then you shall hear of us.'

She kissed her lord as he still lay unwitting, and left while she had the courage.

After that, it was Thorkel Fóstri who ruled the régime that brought his foster-son back to full consciousness and then, methodically, to recover his strength. It was Thorkel Fóstri, also, who answered his first low, savage questions.

'They are fools to have told you. It's true. As soon as news of your death got about, Siward invaded in the name of Duncan's second son Donald. . . . It's nothing, Thorfinn. A thirteen-year-old boy who hasn't yet left Ireland? Siward will hold the eastern part of the Lowlands, which was his in practice already, and perhaps the north shore of the Forth, but he can't afford to keep an army in Alba, not with all the power-struggle now going on with Godwin and Mercia in England. When you are well, in the spring, and they hear you have Orkney again, they will melt like the snow.'

Thorfinn said, 'I am not a child, although I lie here like one. Get me on my feet in two weeks and I shall have Orkney in two weeks. Keep me longer and I shall have you hanged, even though you are my foster-father, and the man of this house made a slave again.'

Thorkel Fóstri got up and went out.

Later, when Thorfinn had wakened again and the women were feeding him, his foster-father came and stood in the shadows in the little turf hut they had cleared for a sickroom, and waited until they had finished their fussing and gone.

Always, Thorfinn slept after this, for he spoke to the women and made them laugh, and it tired him out. Now, without letting him sleep, Thorkel Fóstri said, 'I have found a place in Reaster for you. I will take you there in four days. The smoke here is beginning to be noticed. I have told them at Freswick and Duncansby, and warned Odalric and one or two others you can trust. They will need to know, if you plan to attack this side of Christmas. I have made a list, too, of the men who have escaped from Orkney and the men who are still there but can be relied on. I got David to write it for me. Otkel my nephew is coming to Reaster and will work with you until you can hold a sword. I shall be at Canisbay gathering weapons. If you want me, send word.'

He had meant, then, to walk out. He did not know why he didn't, for Thorfinn said nothing, but lay throughout open-eyed, listening; and at the end neither stirred nor moved his gaze. Now the sun-tan had faded, the burnt parts of his skin figured brown on pure white, like the hide of a cow.

Thorkel Fóstri said, 'At Inverness . . . Was that how you escaped?'

The white skin could not become whiter, but he knew what he had done. Then Thorfinn said, 'Findlaech showed me. But he was too heavy for the loft-floor.'

Thorkel Fóstri said, 'Every year, Rognvald goes to Papay Minni for his tribute of malt. It is a small island, and he can only take a few with him.' He paused, and then said, 'You will burn him, then, as he did you and the Lady? . . . Thorfinn, as long as men live in wood houses, this is how they must kill.'

'I shall burn him,' Thorfinn said. 'And then we shall build houses of stone. It is too late, but it is better than nothing.'

He stopped speaking, but his eyes remained open, saying something quite different.

Thorkel Fóstri said, 'Your father was never as stubborn as this. Where does it come from? Why do I not hang myself, before you do it for me?'

And because he felt a fool, weeping, lowered himself to the bedside, where the rugs muffled his face and where Thorfinn's ruined hand, already stretched, touched his head and his cheek.

Then it stilled, and he looked up and saw that Thorfinn slept, which for some reason seemed a greater grief than anything that had happened before.

*   *   *

Before Christmas that year, all Earl Rognvald's friends had agreed how important it was that the Earl should be kept cheerful, in view of the difficult time he was having, with the whole of Orkney and Caithness to look after, and no help to be looked for from Norway. It was also well seen that Earl Siward, though glad of the chance to move into Alba, would readily allow Earl Rognvald to succumb to any misfortune that might overtake him; especially as no one knew what Harald Sigurdsson would do once he had persuaded King Magnús, as seemed likely, to give him half the Norwegian throne. For King Magnús at twenty-two years old was a man, but not a very experienced one, while his uncle Harald at thirty-one was rich, experienced, and ready for anything, including taking over Orkney and Caithness and Alba, once he felt like it.

When, therefore, Rognvald announced that he was going over, as usual, to collect the Christmas malt from the monks at Papay Minni and needed thirty men to crew the cargo boat who could also swim from Ramberry to Quanterness and back at low water, there were forty of them and more who jumped into the sea, although less than thirty came back and he had to make up the numbers later out of his courtmen.

At that time, with Hǫfn fallen into disrepair and Orphir burned down, Earl Rognvald had moved his household to Kirkwall, where there was a stream and the stumps and gravestones and midden of an old monastery. There was also a good enough harbour, except in north winds; and a back door to Knarston and the Flow that was not to be sniffed at, besides deep bays like Inganess and Deer in the south where you could beach a flotilla if you wanted to.

Best of all, of course, the new hall was Earl Rognvald's own idea, and had none of the pawmarks of the kindred on it. As the feeling of ownership grew on him, he had even begun to have a church built by the stream, and meant to dedicate it to St Olaf, which ought to please King Magnús and his uncle King Harald.

There were of course other advantages also, as Siward of York had been among the first men to recognise. Now there were three churches to St Olaf in or about the Saxons' big trade-town of London, they said, and one in Dublin. Whatever the standard-bearers might be doing, you had to think of your trade.

But that was for spring. In December, there was the Yuletide feast to prepare for, and the welcome they got at Papay Minni was always the first sign that the year's labours were over, and you could eat and drink and rejoice with your friends, for the sea was your lock and bolt, and the weather your shield. Of the thirty men who rowed round Huip on Stronsay, and through Papa Sound, and into the monks' little jetty, there were, on occasion, a bare twenty sensible enough to ply the oars on the way back, and it took almost as many men, sometimes, to carry Earl Rognvald as it did to carry the malt, with the dog Sam to nip at your heels, whom you kicked at your peril.

This year, the cold had steadied the sea and there was little wind to pull against, which was just as well, in an open boat, for the incoming splatter froze tight on your beard and your furs and there were reefs you would know all about if the night fell before you were ready for it.

The island itself was a scrap, and the beach little but streaked sand and boulders, with a few nousts built above the tide-mark, and above that, the strip-fields of the monks with their neat dry-stone edging. The soil of Papay Minni was rich, and grew thick crops of bere, and some oats, so that the monks hardly troubled with grazing, save for a milch-cow or two and a half-dozen ewes. They got the cloth for their clothes from the big farm on Stronsay, and a share of feathers and oil, and kept bees, and did their own fishing. And if it was a wonder, sometimes, that they ever found time to pray, no one troubled, least of all their young, handsome Earl and his men so long as they breathed in the warm, mothering smell of the malt as they pulled past the kiln, and saw the familiar faces there on the strand, with bright torches flaring in the murk, and strong hands ready to help the Earl up to the eating-chamber that the monks had built themselves, a dozen years since, to hold themselves and their guests.

Built well and stoutly, of timber.

For all the years the young Earl had been to the island, no man there could remember the match of the pleasure-frenzy that possessed him that night. Even before the drinking became as heavy as it did, Rognvald hurled himself into the mouth of the evening like a man bewitched. His fair face white, his blue eyes brilliant, he was first in the roaring of battle-songs, and the telling of battle-tales, and then tales that the monks, intoxicated themselves, might have shut their ears to, but that there could be no harm in such laughter.

Then the competitions began, that every man who lived with Rognvald half longed for and half dreaded, for in the nature of them some man or another would lose his life, or end it a cripple. But for those who won there was the prize of Rognvald's excited attention, and his praise, and if you wanted such a thing, and knew how to attract it, perhaps something much more.

That was when, as now, the night was half worn through and the men who had rowed through the day slipped down, despite themselves, on the bench or laid their arms on the table, while the monks slept through their duty in a thicket of ale-fumes and the men still seated with Rognvald round the dying longfire spoke in different voices and laughed in a different way from the drinking-hall manners they had been using before.

Then the man sitting next to Rognvald shifted in Rognvald's arm and said, 'Look. The fire is low. Shall I get turf for it? Perhaps, my lord, you could show me where it is kept.'

But Rognvald was sleepy, and said, 'Why go out? We shall be old enough when this fire burns out.'

'Old enough?' The favoured one smiled, teasing him, keeping him awake.

Rognvald looked down at the other man, smiling. His hand, moving up, touched the speaker's neck, and his ear, and caressed it. 'Did I say old? I meant warm. I corrected King Olaf, my foster-father, once, when he made a slip of the tongue.' His finger and thumb, gripping the flesh of the ear, twisted lightly and began, gently, to increase their pressure. 'He told me that if ever I made such a slip of my own, I should not expect to live long.'

He smiled into the other man's face and the man smiled back, with watering eyes. 'My lord,' he said, and then gasped as Rognvald's toying hand made a swift movement.

'That was at Stiklestad,' Rognvald said. 'So you see, my foster-father King Olaf barely outlived his error.'

The ear was bleeding. Rognvald withdrew his arm, laughing, and the men still round him laughed as well; even the sufferer, through his tears. 'Perhaps it means my uncle Thorfinn is still alive,' Rognvald said, and laughed very loudly this time, so that he did not at first hear what was said to him by a man at the far end of the hall.

'My lord? My lord Earl. I smell smoke.'

Then he heard, and stopped laughing, so that the voice of the son of hell outside could be heard quite plainly: the beloved voice saying,

'*Hallo there, my nephew! Are you cold? Come out! I have kindled a fire for you and your soul-friends. Come and warm yourselves at it!*'

He did not come out, or even move, at the beginning, so that the long-hundred of men surrounding the hall in the darkness had nothing to do at first but stand and watch the ring of firewood catch and blaze round the base of the long timber building and against the shuttered door of the hall.

Then Thorfinn lifted his great voice again and the monks, offered their lives, began to appear dazed and half-awake at the upper half-door, already barred by red flames, and Thorfinn's men helped them out, with a wary eye to the smoke-filled spaces behind them. A spear did fly out, and then another; and then three or four men who were clearly not men of the church tried to scramble over the half-door at once and were killed before they got past the wood-pile. Another monk, weeping and coughing, clung to the door-post.

Thorkel Fóstri said, 'Rognvald is inside. The priest says so.'

Thorfinn did not answer.

Thorkel Fóstri said, 'He will come out. Whether your axe takes him or not, I promise you mine will.'

The flash of white at the half-door told them, again, that a churchman was coming, and for a moment they saw him quite plainly in his linen clothes, bent and racked with coughing.

There was a pause. Then Thorfinn said sharply, 'Make way for the deacon!' and those men detailed for the task jumped forward to help the fellow over the threshold.

He waited till Thorfinn's men were quite near; then they saw him fall back, as if overcome. They were pressed round the doorway, or as near to it as they could get, when he came at them in a rush and, setting his hand to the door-bar, vaulted clean over it, and over the men there.

The white robe flashed through the light, and, white and gold, the face of the deacon. Then he landed, in the smoke and the darkness; and they heard a sound that might have been a laugh, or a groan, and saw that he had gone.

'*Rognvald!*' said Thorkel Fóstri.

'Who else do you know,' said Thorfinn, 'who could have done that?' Then he said, 'You had better go after him. I shall keep half the men here.'

Thorkel Fóstri said, 'Odalric will see to the hall. Go back to the boat. You have done enough.' His men were setting off already, dividing as they went, in the direction that Rognvald had taken.

'If Rognvald can jump,' Thorfinn said, 'I can stand.'

Then Thorkel Fóstri began to run, for the noise of the flames and the screams from the hall were drowning out the footfalls of his party. At the edge of the light, something occurred to him. He turned and shouted.

'The dog! The dog will track him. He had the dog in the hall.'

Thorfinn's deepest voice answered him drily. 'He had thought of that. He had the dog under his arm when he vaulted.'

From north to south, Papay Minni measured less than a mile, with no buildings on it save the monastery. No man could hide on Papay Minni once night was over.

From three points on the island, an active man could swim, with ease, to the neighbouring great isle of Stronsay. But although Thorkel Fóstri's search parties made their way first to those points, it was in the knowledge that no man, unless perfectly desperate, would try to make that crossing in the night sea of December, with nothing of succour or warmth to welcome him on the far side.

If Rognvald were to make his escape, it must be by boat: one of the small boats of the monks, drawn up in their stony nests on the beach to the south.

Although, therefore, Thorkel Fóstri sent his men over the island, neglecting no reef or boulder elsewhere as they laced the cold night with their torches, he himself led the way to the landing-place, where the sea slithered in and pattered on ribbons of ice.

Except where the boats lay, the shore was bedded with water-smooth boulders below which, on summer nights, the petrels churred and hiccoughed and buzzed so that all the beach seemed to prickle with secretive sound.

No man could hide there at this moment. But since the vessels were empty, as his torch showed, and none was afloat or could have been run out so quickly, the reef looming dark over there and the stack of boulders over here, barely reached by his torchlight, were the only spots on this beach where Earl Rognvald could have concealed himself.

It was midnight. Thorkel Fóstri stood with his back to the sea and looked at the reef and the stack while Otkel and the rest of his men gathered round and the brands flickered gold on their sword-blades.

Above the black silhouette of the islet, the sky stood red as sunrise, with a glory that bludgeoned the senses; and against mighty rivers of scarlet and brass, the smoke hung like spume, white and black, and moved lazily upwards.

Far behind, under that light, his foster-son, Thorkel knew, would be standing and would stand, whatever it cost him, until he learned that the night's work was done. He had given the orders that had to be given, and had flinched only once that Thorkel had seen. Now, whatever he felt, nothing could alter the outcome.

It had been Thorfinn's will that Rognvald be sought out and slaughtered. Face to face, perhaps his resolution would again falter. One would never know; what strength he still lacked had, in the end, prevented Thorfinn from joining the hunt. And Thorkel Fóstri, the King's surrogate father and chief huntsman, had no thought of bringing a live man back to justice. A lissom, golden-haired man with a face full of laughter and longing.

Thorkel Fóstri set himself, foursquare and firm, between the reef and the stack, and men saw his arm swell as he tightened his grip on his weapon. Then he drew a long breath and called aloud, ringingly, as if invoking a god. Called aloud, like a slogan of war, the name of the one man who could not hear him, and in whose cause, as through all his life, he was acting.

'*Thorfinn!*' cried Thorkel Fóstri. And among the rocks of the stack, a well-taught dog barked and went on barking wildly until Thorkel Fóstri strode over and lifted his axe and brought it down on the neck of the master, and the neck of the dog.

PART THREE

PURE AS SNOW

How he solicits Heaven,
Himself best knows

—Ourself will mingle with society,
And play the humble host.

—And sundry blessings hang about his throne,
That speak him full of grace.

ONE

'AND SO,' SAID the Archbishop of Hamburg and Bremen, 'this man Thorfinn, you say, now has the whole of Alba and Orkney and the isles to the west, including also a good share of Ireland. Is he likely to keep it?'

He walked between two little trees, and his robe caught. His entourage eddied, vying to be the first to free it. One of the bishops—Bovo, Ascelin, he didn't see which—not only freed it, but carried the hem until they reached the paved part of the orchard. Bishop John, whom he had addressed, remained trotting unperturbed at his right hand.

Bishop John said, 'He has a large fleet, and I don't see that he has anything to fear from England at present. There was an attempt to take the country while he was in the north, but the claimant's supporters withdrew even before they were attacked. He has pacified Norway. The word from Ireland is that he can expect to keep the throne now.'

Bishop John was Irish, which was useful, and had been ordained and spent all his early years in the bishopric of Toul in Lorraine, which was more useful still.

Archbishop Adalbert said, 'His fleet may keep out invaders, but how will he rule? Half the country is Norse and half Irish.'

'He has the Celtic church,' said Bishop John. 'If he decides to employ it. Small monasteries, stocked for the most part from Ireland. The standard of literacy is not high and the mode of worship is antiquated, as my lord is aware.'

Everything flooded round Bremen, but sometimes the apples were good, although the best came to the Archbishop's table from his father, Count Frederick of Goseck. The Archbishop snapped his fingers, and someone—his brother Dedo this time—broke a piece of ripe fruit from the bough and gave it to him. The Archbishop said, 'Then what will our barbarian monarch choose to do? Ignore the church and rule by elevating the ablest chiefs of each region, who may then become power-greedy? Or will he, in his wisdom, invite the church to help him, and if so, which church? The Celtic church, to which you refer? Or the church of Rome whose power is vested in Canterbury in England? Or the church of Rome that serves Norway and all the pagan lands of the north through my own humble endeavours—and yours, my dear son. And yours, my dear sons, of course.'

The apple was covered with dust. Since the walls had came down and the basilica been started, everything was always covered with dust. One wondered how one was expected to uphold here in Saxony the standing of the greatest empire the world had ever known, and that of God into the bargain, with workmen who took so long over their task. To entertain the Emperor, as he had last week, had almost brought about a state of collapse: he had beaten every man in his household when it was over. The Emperor had asked him if he had had second thoughts about his refusal to occupy the Throne of St Peter and he had replied that such a thing was beyond his powers, unworthy wretch that he was.

The right answer, of course. But a grasp of diplomacy did not guarantee an easy life, or a comfortable one. The Archbishop threw the apple away, frowning, and his brother dropped back. Bishop John said, 'The King has been baptised. My information is that he plans to use both secular and spiritual help, with a bias so far to the Celtic church.'

'Thorfinn?' said the Archbishop. He stopped, and so did everyone else. They formed a neat circle. He said, 'Hardly a civilised name.'

Bishop John said, 'His baptismal name is Macbeth. He has just had his elder son renamed Paul.'

Paul. The Archbishop raised his eyes to the wide, cloudy sky. Next to St Stephen, it was no secret that Paul was his own preferred saint. One had to remember, however, St Paulinus of York, and even St Paul Aurelian of the Batz Islands. He said, 'Why has he named his son Paul?'

'My lord, I do not know,' said Bishop John. 'Except that it was through a Paul Hên, I believe, that the ancient saint Serf or Servanus performed his ministrations in Orkney. The missions bringing the first Christian witness to Orkney are, happily, of the deepest interest to this King. Already, relics have passed between two shrines to St Serf: one in Alba, and one near Aleth, in Brittany. Other apostles of the Orkney Isles are to be favoured: St Brendan of Culross and St Kentigern of Culross, Wales, and Glasgow, on whom the King has commissioned a history.'

Bishop John hesitated, and the Archbishop waited. Bishop John said, 'You will recall, my lord, that St David of Wales was closely connected with Léon in Brittany, and was himself brought up by Paulinus, the pupil of St Germanus, to whom there is a chapel in Cornwall.' He paused again. 'That is what I meant when I said the King was displaying an interest in the Celtic church.'

Archbishop Adalbert gazed at the Irishman, his expression kind. The Irishman turned red and looked at the other bishops, all of whom were gazing elsewhere. The Archbishop said, 'I must give you the benefit of the doubt. You do understand what you have been saying?'

'Yes, my lord,' said Bishop John. 'That is, I hope so. I think so.'

'It was for the sake of my health, in that case,' said the Archbishop, 'that you wasted ten minutes in wandering chatter while withholding the sole cogent item? I seek to add lustre to God's shrine in Bremen. Now you tell me of a monstrous, an unequivocal move to unite the primitive church in those places where, so far, the hand of Rome, the hand of Cluny, the hand of Canterbury or of Bremen, has stretched but has not yet been taken?'

His voice calmed. 'You do understand what is happening in Brittany?'

'My lord, yes,' said Bishop John. 'But this alliance may be no more than temporary. To acknowledge Rome, the King must acknowledge England or Norway.'

The Archbishop walked forward and the circle opened, quickly, as it always did. Because his gaze had brushed the doors of his palace, these, too, now stood ajar, waiting. He said, 'I have no difficulty in comprehending the position. You said, however, that Norway was friendly?'

'A surface peace,' said Bishop John, 'I greatly fear. Also, there are rumours that King Magnús's health is not good. Should he expire, his uncle King Harald would make a formidable enemy for an Earl of Orkney who was also King of Alba.'

'Then it seems to me,' said Archbishop Adalbert, 'that the first step this church should take is to remove that fear. Norway and Alba shall be led, as free peoples, to worship side by side at the same precious altar. Two letters.'

The bishops kept silent. 'From the Pope?' said his brother Dedo.

The Pope was in Pesaro, dying and writing rambling letters—*my soul-friend, my sister, my wife and my dove*—to the stone face of his sweet church of Bamberg. The Archbishop knew Suidger through and through from his Halberstadt days: well enough to push him into the papal chair he himself didn't want. To the end, Suidger had rained privileges on him, with letters styling him *vos*. Suidger wouldn't write the sort of letter he wanted written now. Nor, perhaps, would the Emperor. But neither of them would know about it until it was done.

The writing-clerk had come, with his boy and the materials. Indoors, the Archbishop sent the company away, including Bishop John, and seated himself on his down cushion and had some apples brought. He chose one, conscious of the impeccable taste that had led him to buy its impeccable platter, and bit into it while he thought of his letter. When he began to dictate, it was without any hesitation at all:

Adalbert, Archbishop, servant of the servants of God, to Harald, King of the Norwegians, greetings and benediction . . .

Afterwards, he walked to his window and stood for a long time, considering the walls of his magnificent half-built basilica on its little eminence above the distant, gentle flow of the Weser.

Svein of Denmark. William the Bastard in Normandy. The Emperor Henry and his namesake, the monarch of France. The young, ambitious men now growing up and seizing office in Brittany and Anjou, in Wessex and Mercia in England. Macbeth, the King of Alba and Orkney; Harald of Norway, the former war-lord of Byzantium.

Suddenly, Europe was full of young princes, standing, looking at one another.

It would be a pity if, among those who toiled in God's vineyard, some profit was not to be had from it all.

The day before the wedding, Finn Arnason sat on his favourite bench outside the door of his fine hall at Austrat and called to his daughter's husband Thorfinn.

'So! What do you think now of Harald, King of the Norwegians? Do you suppose that Archbishop Adalbert intended this when he set out to meddle between you?'

'Of course,' said his daughter's husband placidly, from his shady seat opposite. 'Why else turn down the papal tiara? When the forthcoming war has destroyed Byzantium, Russia, and Norway, whom will you discern in the dust but Archbishop Adalbert, the new Eastern Patriarch? . . . What, as a matter of interest, has King Harald done with his first wife while preparing to marry an Arnmødling?'

'Sent her back to Russia, if he's wise,' said Finn Arnason, and grinned broadly at the blur under the leaves.

An extraordinary man, as Groa had said: tall as a mast, with this cavernous voice. Sixteen years she had been married, and since he was twelve years old Thorfinn had been to Norway only once.

Finn said, 'It will break Kalv's heart to miss seeing his other niece marry a king. But King Harald hasn't forgiven him, any more than Magnús did before he died. And at least, things being as they are, it is safe for you to visit Norway at last. And that, I take it, was part of the Archbishop's purpose.'

'Well,' Thorfinn said, 'I hope your niece Thora bears no grudges for the way it has been achieved. Does she mind being made second wife?'

'Thora?' said Finn's wife from the doorway, her arms full of pressed linen. 'To get away from Giske and her Erlingsson uncles, she would marry a soap-boiler, far less a man whose gold would tax twelve men to carry it. Did you see the robe King Harald sent to Sunnmøre, and the jewels? Besides,' said Bergljot, retreating into the house and addressing her daughter Groa, whose arms were full of garments also, 'the Russian wife has only two daughters, and if anyone will make sons, it is Thora, who is not my idea of a womanly woman. There. That is the last of it. The girls have done all the rest. I tell you, I should not care to dress this family for a royal wedding every day. Sit down and talk to me. You are happy?'

Over the years, the Lady of Orkney and Alba had exchanged messages with her parents in Norway, and twice in recent times Finn or Bergljot had managed to cross the German ocean to see her, but not her husband, for friendship with Thorfinn was too dangerous. So Groa already knew that her mother's fair hair had faded, and that the fine skin was marked just a little, and that her tread had more weight. She knew that her father's pale blue eyes, so like those of Kalv his brother, saw you clearly when you stood close at hand, and hardly at all at a distance.

She had forgotten, though, through the long years getting used to Thorfinn, how serious they both were. She said, 'Yes. Very happy.' She glanced through the sunlit square of the door and beyond to Thorfinn's solemn face. Of its own accord, her mouth smiled.

Her mother said, 'He looks well, your husband. He has recovered?'

'Of course. It was more than a year ago,' Groa said. One did not want to go into all that. Rognvald's funeral at Papay Minni; the hunting down of his men at Kirkwall. The day she found Thorfinn gone and realised he had set sail for Norway to confront King Magnús and force him to pardon him.

He had come back from that with his life—just. And when Magnús had died, it seemed possible that the whole trouble would flare up again, now that Harald was fully King. A rich and powerful war-lord, and ambitious. And cruel, people said.

And now had come this summons. King Harald proposed to take to wife her cousin Thora, and his great-niece the Lady of Alba and Thorfinn her husband were both warmly bidden to the marriage-feast.

Homage for Orkney had not been mentioned, but she well knew that it would arise before the visit was over, and that Thorfinn, accepting, had made his dispositions, which so far appeared to possess only negative qualities. He had brought two longships only, and a retinue such as would not disgrace a king on a visit of state but would pose no threat to his host-country either. He had brought Lulach but not the two heirs to Orkney. He had brought her, without the guards that might have been expected, for, after all, the King was to marry an Arnmødling, and to harm an Arnmødling would rouse the whole of Trøndelagen against their new King.

Her mother said, 'He is well, and you are happy, but you have no more sons?'

Groa brought her gaze back. 'I thought I told you,' she said. 'We lost two.'

Her mother said, 'Children are lost every day. That does not make you barren. I shall send a woman to you.'

'I have seen women,' said Groa. 'And men. If you think it will help, of course I shall see whom you like. Otherwise, there is no need to concern yourself. It is better sometimes that there should not be too many royal children.'

'You quote your husband,' said Bergljot. 'And you? You are content to have only three men to follow you, and no more than two of them whole?' She noticed Lulach then, in the corner, and flushed, for she was not an unkind woman.

Groa smiled at her son, who smiled back. 'Lulach doesn't mind,' Groa said. 'He says he would sooner have a saint for a nephew than a king for a brother.'

'A nephew?' said her mother. 'It is his stepbrother, it seems to me, who has been given the name of a saint. Why let your husband change the good name of Sigurd to Paul? There are none of that name in our family.'

'Nor in his,' Groa said. 'But if he thinks it is wise, then I have no objection. To change from Ingibjorg to Margaret caused me no trouble. I forgot to tell you: Kalv sends you his love.'

'Kalv!' said her mother. 'That fool! But he saved your husband's life, I am told, in the fight against Rognvald. I expect he did the right thing. Magnús might have invited Kalv back, but I don't think he would have lived long at Egge. And now he is a great man in the Western Isles?'

'He is rich enough,' Groa said. 'He controls all the Sudreyar and collects tribute, and goes sailing with Thorfinn and with Guthorm and with Eachmarcach of Dublin when the pirates come raiding. . . . You know Eachmarcach is King of Dublin again? It doesn't stop Kalv complaining.'

'When Kalv stops complaining, he will be dead,' Bergljot said. 'And what, I wonder, will King Harald make of your husband tomorrow? As you know, Halfdan my father was a tall man. But I have never set eyes on a man to equal Harald in stature before. I doubt if the King my uncle is used to a man he cannot look down on.'

Outside, the men were rising, and Groa got up, too, signing Lulach towards her. 'Then tomorrow,' Groa said, 'should provide a useful experience, should it not, for both of them?'

The wedding between King Harald of Norway and Thorberg Arnason's daughter was marked by a feast in the royal hall at Nídarós that lasted three days and three nights.

True, that of the King's other wife Ellisif had gone on for a month, but the Greek style of worship was different, and the Grand Duke Jaroslav had in any case two other daughters whose gifts he wished to impress upon bystanders.

In the course of it, as predicted, the King of Norway and the King of Alba met for the first time face to face and discovered that, unique for each, their eye-level was the same.

'Ah,' said the King of Norway, standing before the High Seat in Magnús's old timber hall by St Olaf's. 'The Earl of Orkney, I believe. Had your nephew killed you, I was going to marry my great-niece your widow.'

'Indeed,' said Thorfinn, 'I expected it.' He bowed to the bride, a thickset, freckled girl covered with jewels, who smiled broadly in return. 'In fact,' said Thorfinn, 'your great-niece my wife was studying Russian until the very last moment. I have brought a trifle for you both as a memento of . . . Orkney. We are honoured to be under your roof.'

That was all, for others were waiting. Afterwards, Thora and her mother Ragnhild got to the storehouse where the gifts were guarded and found Thorfinn's chest and had it unshackled.

Inside was a woven gold headdress, and a silk over-robe of many different colours, embroidered with pearls. Ragnhild said, 'We must show this to Harald at once.'

'No! I shall wear it!' said Thora. 'Today the silk robe from my husband, and tomorrow the gift of my cousin's husband of Orkney.'

'Are you a fool?' said her mother. 'Have you listened to nothing I told you? He is the King of Alba, not merely the Orkney husband of your cousin, and this is sent to remind you. Harald's silk robe was Greek. This is from Cathay. Harald's jewels were set by Byzantine craftsmen. This headdress is Saracen.

Such a gift brings with it a message. *I have gold. I have a fleet. I have rich friends on the Continent.* We must show this to Harald at once.'

'*Then* may I wear it?' said Thora.

Her mother gazed at her. 'He will either rip it to tatters,' she observed, 'or he will have you wear it at once. Perhaps you can influence him one way or another, if it means so much to you. You are his wife. If you don't listen to me, still instinct must count for something.'

Then the contests began.

Seated with the rest round the wide, grassy space beside the half-finished church, Groa said to her husband, 'The dress Thora is wearing. Isn't that the one you gave her yesterday?'

'Yes,' said Thorfinn.

Since Rognvald, things were different with him. Groa waited, and then said, 'You thought she might not put it on. It means that Harald has taken no offence?'

'It means,' Thorfinn said, 'either that your cousin Thora surprised him last night, or that I am going to have to fight my way through half these contests.'

Then the horse-battle came to an end and a shadow stood over them, belonging to a man of King Harald's sent to suggest that the Kings should try the first throw in the wrestling-match.

Thorfinn stood up, and Groa jumped to her feet.

'She didn't surprise him,' she said. 'Shall I go and sit by her?'

Thorfinn surveyed her. 'I shall fight for my throne,' he said, 'if I must. But pay for it with the customs of my marriage-bed I cannot yet bring myself to do. If you give her any news that will make Harald's pleasures one iota stronger or sweeter, I shall divorce you and buy in four concubines.'

Finn Arnason, waiting for her to sit down again, wondered why his daughter was laughing so much, and then wished she were closer, for he thought, before she lifted her hand to her cheek, that he saw the glitter of tears on it.

The wrestling was the first of the contests between the two Kings. Challenged or challenger, each of them fought in every competition that followed, on that afternoon and the next, and men said that, in all the time kings had been married or buried in their day, Trøndelagen had never seen anything like it.

Because it was sport and not war, the trials were reasonably short and the weapons were reasonably blunted. It did not prevent men being hurt, or even being killed, but it helped one family take its prejudices out on another without being called to law for it, and it made men merry, and it beggared some and made others rich men for life with the wagers.

The Kings were not immune. At the end of the first day, after exercise with spear and axe and sword, with horse and with bow, Thorfinn's dark skin, when he pulled off his tunic, was suffused with weals and bloody contusions, and the King of Norway, smeared with unguents by his loving bride, alarmed her by lying back on the mattress and smiling in quite a new way from between the long flaxen moustaches that lay with his beard on the blond, matted fur of his chest.

'Tonight,' said King Harald, 'I am tired; and you will do all the work.'

By that time, it was already clear that, physically, the two Kings were equally matched. And the following day, although they still took part in all the games that took place, it was apparent that no dramatic conquest was about to take place and neither King was going to help his reputation one way or another by continuing. Then, after the feast, King Harald challenged the King of Alba, in public, to a game at the tables, with dice.

It had been a long banquet, and the women had already been given leave to retire, including, at length, the bride Thora, who today had displayed all the lethargy that men had come to admire in a consort of Harald's. Groa said, 'Shall I stay?'

'No,' said Thorfinn. 'And take your father away.'

She smiled, her hand hard on his shoulder. 'What are you gambling for?'

'Nothing small, you may be sure,' Thorfinn said. The tone of his voice said something, and she answered it with her hand and smiled again, leaving.

The quarrel broke out very much later, when there were only a hundred or so men left in the hall, all of them Harald's and most of them drunk.

Drunkest of all, you would say, was King Harald himself, whose great frame, through all the evening, had been dealt horn after horn of French wine, followed, as his taste started to blur, with ale from the casks in the corner.

An ordinary man would have succumbed. Harald would pick up the dice, throw them, and call; then, lurching out to the yard to make water, would plunge himself bodily into some trough and take his place five minutes later, hair and beard streaming like straw, water pooling the floor and the board from the squelching remains of his finery.

The last time, standing holding the bench, he put up his hand, swearing, and ripped the clogged silk from his shoulders and chest, down to the underlinen over his hips. Then, stepping out of the mess, he sat down, naked but for his leggings and ankle-boots, and looked at Thorfinn.

'What are you afraid to show, cousin?' he said. 'The knife you have under there, or the tool you haven't?'

Thorfinn looked up, the coin-brown eyes sparkling under the bar of his brow. He said, 'It is, of course, the privilege of a host to ask his guests to strip, whatever their sex. However, the fire is burning low. And I would point out that, although the game is exciting, I am not yet wet.'

Thorir of Steig, a cousin of Harald's, bent over Thorfinn and said, 'The King sits naked before you. Where are your manners, that you keep on your coat?'

Thorfinn looked round. 'Alas!' he said. 'Are you telling me of a new custom? You must forgive me. It has not yet reached the hovels of Orkney. When the King strips, we all strip. Cousin Harald, there are a hundred men of yours here. Where shall we all put our clothes, to be sure of finding them in the morning?'

No one moved. Behind Thorfinn, Ulf Ospaksson, Harald's marshal, put a finger and thumb of each hand to the top of his royal guest's collar. Thorfinn said, 'In any case, there are more important things to speak about. The King has been cheating.'

Then, men moved.

Thorfinn looked round. He said drily, 'In Norway, it seems, there are good grounds for suspecting a man who will not take off his clothing.'

Harald watched him. Thorfinn stood, shaking off the grip at his collar, and around him steel moved and sparkled. Thorfinn lifted his hands and slowly and carefully took off his tasselled jacket, and the belt and light tunic under, and his linen. He said, 'Although I have a bow and arrow in each, I should like to keep my boots on.' He waited, and when Harald jerked his head, he sat down. He wore, it could be seen, a bracelet on each arm.

Thorfinn said, 'Now I shall say it again. Your dice are doctored.'

'I find this tedious,' King Harald said. 'And the sight of you is not as amusing as I thought it would be. You won the second game with dice of your own choosing, and I did not complain. Either you finish this match or you cede Orkney to me in any case. Choose.'

'Why trouble to finish the match?' Thorfinn said. 'Prove to me that your dice are fair, and you can have Orkney now.'

Harald rose to his feet. Browned by the suns of the Middle Sea, his skin bore upon it the white scars of all the long years of his fighting, and in the set of his head you could see, without being told, the strength of physique and of character that had made him the greatest of the Varangian chiefs. He said, 'I have been insulted enough in my own hall. A guest may miscall my honour once, or even twice, if he is related. The third time, he forfeits his immunity.'

'Very well,' said Thorfinn. 'Provided that, before I am struck down, you appoint one of your men to make public test of your dice before anyone leaves. You have won the Trøndelagers by your marriage. Show them that they can also trust you to lead them in truth and in justice.'

There was an axe hung on the wall. Harald looked at it.

Orm, who had married Finn Arnason's other daughter, said, 'My lord King. What my brother offers is just. Moreover, there are men in Caithness and Alba who might seek vengeance for such a deed.'

Harald took down the axe.

Thorfinn said, 'My dice are on the floor, in my belt-purse. If Thorir will lift them to the board, I shall offer them to test as well.'

Harald turned, the axe in both hands, and Thorfinn rose and stood before him.

Thorfinn said, 'For mine were loaded as well; and he might as well have the testing of both of them.'

Harald screamed, and the fumes of it rolled through the room. He lifted the axe, scattering the men who stood around him. He swung it round and let himself spin with it, so that his waist wore a circle of silver. He let it go, and it flashed over heads and out through the door into darkness. He flung himself forward and caught Thorfinn's neck with one elbow, while with the other fist he fetched him an underhand, vicious, and crippling blow in the soft lower part of the belly.

Harald's laugh howled through the room, and his blood-veined eyes, dancing, raked over the company. 'What are you waiting for?' he shouted. 'Here is something to celebrate! A man who will risk his life to divert us. A man who will gamble with an axe on the wall to amuse Harald of Norway. What can your verses do, Arnór, that can match that?'

He roared with laughter and, staggering back, sat down heavily. '*For your dice were loaded as well!* Drink! Drink! My cousin is overcome! Bring us something to drink!'

The beakers were brought, amid uproar, and Thorfinn took his and straightened. Harald said, 'A boon. A jester is worth the whole expense of his master. You must name what you want, and I shall give it to you.'

Someone had banked up the fires. Sweat ran down their cheekbones and shone on the faces and throats of the men yelling and drinking about them. Thorfinn said, 'There is no such thing as a fee between cousins. It would be agreeable, to be sure, to have your confirmation that Orkney for all time is mine, and will be asked to pay nothing to Norway.'

'Is there any question of it?' Harald said. 'Two-thirds were always rightly yours, and since Rognvald's death, I can think of no one better to take over his share and his father's.'

He drank; and cold blue eyes gazed into cold brown. 'It will disappoint the Archbishop,' Thorfinn said.

'Adalbert?' Harald laughed, and the ale drenched the mat on his chest, and his thighs, and discoloured the kid of his boots. He said, 'Adalbert is Denmark's confessor, not mine. I wish him well. But it won't take him long to find out that none of my bishops will come his way for consecration, and if he wants your trade, my friend, he will have to seek it through Denmark or England. Will he get it?'

Thorfinn considered. 'Compared to Orkney,' he said, 'what have Denmark and England to offer me? Apart from money, that is.' Several men, laughing, blundered into them, and Harald pushed them off. Arnór the bard was asleep at his feet.

'I wonder,' Harald said. The blue eyes smiled. 'Thora's mother is cousin by her aunt's marriage to this man Siward, Earl of Northumbria. And Edward of England, I am told, is somewhat weak.'

'I am sorry to say you are right,' said Thorfinn. He drank again, his colour restored. He said, 'He is, however, surrounded by other strong earls, and there is an even stronger army of kinsfolk waiting in Flanders and Normandy. Also, his treasure-chests, I am told, almost equal your own.' He bent and, picking up his tunic, prepared to pull it over his head. He said, 'As you see, I am not easily offended, myself. I think you may find it useful, as well, to keep whatever friends you may have.'

'Agreed,' said Harald. He watched the other man dressing. He said, 'Then we have made a bargain?'

Thorfinn fastened his belt and stood up. No one paid any attention. He stirred Arnór with his toe and, when he did not get up, walked away from him.

'A bargain? My empty purse hasn't noticed it,' Thorfinn said; and wound his way out of the hall.

Groa was awake. 'Thorfinn?' she said.

'Half of him,' Thorfinn said. 'The wrong half, unfortunately.'

She sat up. 'What?'

'It's all right,' he said. 'I was making a joke, before I forgot how. Orkney is mine. He won't interfere meantime. He's too uneasy about your dear Trøndelagers.'

'What about my father?' Groa said. 'And Thorberg and Arne and Kolbiorn and the rest? Will they be safe, now he has married Thora?'

'I don't know,' Thorfinn said. He stopped pulling off his footgear and, without undressing any further, lay back on the sheet as he was. He said, 'I have a feeling the first wife is not too far away. They say the Empress Zoe doted on Harald. Perhaps it was the moustaches. I made an expensive mistake when I shaved.'

'You had to. It all got burned off,' Groa said. She added quickly, 'In any case, what conquest were you planning on?'

'None,' said Thorfinn. 'I hoped for a small service, perhaps. There was a time when I could barely stop you from undressing me.'

Her face relaxed. She said, 'I thought you were only half a man?'

'That's why I don't want to undress myself,' Thorfinn said. 'Tell me. When we leave, will you find the parting too hard? You missed your father.'

She untied the tasselled jacket and laid it open. 'Yes,' she said. 'But there are other things I should miss even more. There was a time in Moray when I would lie weeping for the sunsets of Austråt.'

'And now?' said Thorfinn. His fingers touched her and drew her softly down to his side.

'Now we lodge in Alba,' Groa said. 'And it is the sunsets in Orkney that I weep for. And if *I* do . . . Thorfinn, can you do it? No man has done all this before.'

'I have an idea,' Thorfinn said. 'I shall give you up. And with the strength I have left, I shall take over the Empire.'

TWO

·

AN YOU DO it alone?' Thorfinn's wife had asked. And, naturally, he had been guarded in his reply.

Afterwards, she realised that he had set himself a studied programme, as once before, when first he found himself on the throne, and that it was intended to occupy all the four seasons that followed the wedding of her cousin Thora in Norway.

In Orkney, Thorkel Fóstri ruled with all the powers of an earl, and the men of Rognvald's lands had long since recognised Thorfinn's renewed overlordship. In Caithness, the land lay peacefully under Thorkel's kinsfolk and all those other families which now had ties on both sides of the firth. And in the isles and the fjords of the west, the island communities and the scattered farms were protected by Kalv.

In Alba, because of the King's long absences on Rognvald's account, much of his previous work had to be looked to again. But, on the other hand, a new generation of young men was growing which had no close ties with the old house of Duncan and Malcolm.

Her own son Lulach was now of an age to take his inheritance of Moray and, with Morgund and the other good friends she had left there, to begin to learn what a mormaer's work meant. She knew the world's opinion of Lulach, but as a man he had learned how to subdue the fancies that his kinsfolk found so disconcerting. And beneath it was an excellent and unimpaired brain.

Since Duftah had left two years before to become Lector of Armagh, and since Aedh his brother had died, the community of monks at Tarbatness had reshaped itself, and Deer and Buchan were now in the hands of Duftah's cousin Mael-Isu.

In the south-west, the lands that had once been Strathclyde and the lands of Cumbria lay under the attentions of Thorfinn's man Thor of Allerdale.

The rest of the land that had been Alba, from Cumbria north, was now Thorfinn's primary concern. He had soon put his print on it. With Eachmarcach, newly restored, as his agent, Thorfinn recovered the boy Maelmuire from Ireland and restored him to the care of the Mormaer Cormac at Dunkeld.

*   *   *

News of her husband came to Groa in Fife, in the dower lands Thorfinn had given her when Lulach had come of age to take Moray. Since the slaughter of Duncan's adherents, the King and the Bishop of Alba had held between them in Fife all that was not bog or stony wasteland.

So that the Culdees of the province might begin to play the part that he planned for them, Thorfinn had already given Prior Tuathal some of his land, and forced the Bishop to do likewise.

As his wife, Groa had needed no forcing. It was the first time she had seen her name with its title, the title that the Lady Emma used, Thorfinn said, on her charters: *Gruoch Regina*. And Thorfinn, as he must be in Alba, was again *Macbeth*, the name Lulach had remembered, on parting, to call him.

'But not Macbeth, King of Orkney,' Groa had corrected. 'Macbeth of Alba.'

The clear blue eyes mocked her, gravely, from under the feathered white hair. 'When I was Caradoc of Llancarvan,' said Lulach, 'Macbeth, King of Orkney, is what I called him. Do you want to argue about it?'

'No! No!' she had said, laughing, and pretending to ward him off as he returned her laughter. She shut the door.

'Now no one will hear me,' said Lulach.

Through the winter, she stayed in Fife, as once she had done in Moray, and served the country as was its due from an officer of the crown, woman or man. Of what was happening elsewhere in Alba she knew only the surface. Food was not plentiful: as Christmas approached, she saw nothing like the great stores that men were used to in Caithness and Orkney. Since the wars, there had been no slave-employing landowners in these parts, and few enough left in the farms to look after the beasts and the crops.

She worried about Thorfinn's retinue. The hird were in Caithness and Orkney. Here he had a king's train: of some younger sons from Ireland, some men of birth from the landed families in Alba and Cumbria, all of whom had to be supported or else given land on which they could support themselves.

In Alba, there was no land to spare except forest and waste that had not yet been brought into cultivation. Nor could he maintain a great household for long on the cheeses and malt, the sticks of eels and firkins of honey, the grudging flitches of bacon and the sparse sacks of wool that were all the farms had to spare. So he had to buy what he needed.

Hence, of course, the visit to Norway and the chestloads of silver he had wrung from it. So he had to have silver. But when the silver one day came to an end, he must depend on the north to serve Alba, and that could not continue or it would split the kingdom before ever it had united.

From the ships in the Tay—the constant passing and repassing of longships from the north to Dunkeld, where Thorfinn's clerks where—she gleaned the news, as Thorfinn must be doing, of the course of King Harald's husbandly interest in Trøndelagen.

It did not look promising. King Harald was greedy, men said, and overbearing, and beginning to insist on more than his legal rights from his farmers. He had made some friendly overtures towards England, and when two of his wife's uncles took a fleet of twenty-five ships to Sandwich and pillaged all over Essex, selling the booty in Flanders, he disclaimed all responsibility at once.

Groa's mother sent word that no one was to be disturbed, as they had plenty of stout hearts as well as weapons in Nídarós. In the same ship was a box from the King of Norway to the King of Alba containing a set of ivory gaming-pieces, a gold cup, a roll of Russian furs, and a bag of silver pennies minted mostly in Lille.

At Yule, Groa joined her husband in the new feasting-hall at Perth, where she found Lulach waiting, along with many of Thorfinn's chief landowners.

Her other two sons she did not expect. Since he turned seven, Erlend's place had been in Caithness with his foster-parents; and Sigurd, who was now Paul, lived with Thorkel Fóstri, as his father had done, but at thirteen had no call to sail friendless to Norway to outface a king in pursuit of his heritage.

They were honest, good-hearted boys: fair, now, as her mother had been, and would be seen by the people of Orkney on this feast day to be what they were: the future joint Earls of a flourishing country.

Future Kings of Alba she did not see there, and was not sorry.

At Perth, she and Thorfinn worked together, as they were accustomed to do, upon the various natures of their subjects and guests, and there were few moments of privacy. But, steady and constant, the river ran as ever below, from which she drew all her comfort.

He brought Lulach to her. 'We have been discussing,' said Thorfinn, 'the thorny question of marriage. We have also surveyed Bishop Malduin's daughter and concluded that on no account could we risk a closer acquaintanceship with her.'

It was a matter on which she had been, privately, apprehensive. 'I am glad to see,' Groa said, 'that your good taste in the matter of women has not wholly deserted you. Is there anyone else?'

'I have another proposal,' Thorfinn said. 'Sinill, a cousin of Bishop Malduin's, has a daughter whom Lulach seems to think may be harmless. Sinill had a claim to Angus, as Malduin has. There is the added advantage—'

'—that Sinill's daughter might just conceivably be the daughter of the late King Malcolm?' Groa said.

'Did you hear that? I thought I was keeping you too busy at the time,' Thorfinn said.

'Then you have a very short memory,' Groa said. 'No. Everyone knew your grandfather spent all his last years at Glamis. Lulach, what do you say? You know how these things must be arranged.'

His bright lips smiled, and his eyes were clear as rainwater. 'No one knew who she was,' he said. 'Of course, arrange it as you wish. She should be pleased. She will have thirty years of life for her dowry.'

Over his head, Thorfinn looked at his wife, the boy's mother. 'She will be pleased,' he said.

*   *   *

And the next day, Arnór Jarlaskáld came home.

'Well?' said Thorfinn. The times they had spoken together since Rognvald's death had been few, and when the hour had come to leave after Thora's wedding, Arnór could not be found. Later, they heard some of the verses he had made for King Harald.

'I have news,' Arnór said.

'It must be bad news,' Thorfinn said, 'to bring you home from the laden tables of King Harald. Unless Thjodolf Arnarsson the poet is a son of yours we haven't heard of? How did his last verses run?' And, gazing at the rafters, Thorfinn quoted melodiously:

> '*Subjects of King Harald*
> *Must show their subjection*
> *By standing up or sitting*
> *Just as the king wishes.*
> *All the people humbly*
> *Bow before this warrior;*
> *The king demands obedience*
> *To all his royal orders.*'

Arnór had flushed. 'He is no relation of mine,' he said. 'We are on the best of terms, King Harald and I. I was about to tell you. He has married my third cousin Ulf, the marshal, to Jorunn, his wife Thora's sister. So that your wife, my lord, and Ulf are now cousins. As it were.'

'My lady?' Thorfinn said. And as Groa turned: 'Come and greet your third cousin Arnór, newly landed from Norway. He will enlighten you in a moment, when he has told us the rest of his news. There is more?'

'My parents?' said Groa.

'They are well. They send greetings. They are all well.' Arnór looked from Thorfinn to Groa and back again. He said, 'You'll have heard that Isleifr came back from Hervordin. A priest now, can you imagine it? He came to see us at Nídarós, but left after the troubles began. They say he is back in Iceland again.'

'Arnór,' said Thorfinn. 'There is a bench. Sit down and tell us. What troubles?'

Which was how the news came to Alba of the killing of Einar Tambarskelve and his son Henry. Einar, who, courted by Canute, had still become reconciled in the end to King Olaf. Einar, who, with Kalv, had brought young King Magnús back from Russia. Einar, who, spearhead of the stubborn Trøndelagen opposition to King Harald's heavy measures, had been struck down and killed in a darkened room by King Harald's men, with his son.

Groa said, 'Trøndelagen will rise against Harald. Einar's widow has half the Lade fortune since her two brothers died. All Einar's friends will support her, and the Lade grandchildren. Svein of Denmark is married to one of them.' Her sister Sigrid was married to another. She did not need to say so.

Thorfinn said, 'Would Trøndelagen rise against the Arnmødling family?'

They looked at one another.

Arnór said, 'There is no one in the whole of Norway so respected as Finn Arnason your father, my lady.'

'After Christmas,' Thorfinn said, 'we ought to be thinking of a spring feast for Paul's fourteenth birthday, and in any case by March food is not always so plentiful in these parts. I can leave Alba for a month. So can you. I shall tell Thorkel Fóstri to expect us at Canisbay.'

She said nothing, for there was nothing to say. He could not interfere. But he would be within reach when the snows melted in Nídarós.

They melted, and brought with them to Canisbay not the flying wrack of her family but a housecarl on his way west to the Sudreyar, bearing messages from Finn Arnason to his exiled brother Kalv.

Groa knew the man, and he told them his news while he ate. Then she sped him on his way, her eyes on Thorfinn's face. He said nothing.

The courier took a day to find Kalv. The day following that, Kalv himself sailed into the river below the great hall at Thurso and bounded up the hill to greet Groa his niece and her husband. 'You will have heard! Now, where is the man who says that patience in hardship doesn't bring its own reward!'

He flung his arms round Thorfinn, scrubbed him with his whitened bristles, and then did the same to his niece Groa, kissing her roundly. Pushing fifty now, he had developed a little belly from his two years in the isles west of Alba, and the tuber of his nose hinted at the closeness of his acquaintance with the Dublin wine-wharves.

Kalv said, 'Perhaps, good friends that you are, you sent a message to Queen Thora? *Here, rubbing his back among swine in the Sudreyar, is the Viking leader your uncle, who saved the Earl of Orkney's life against Rognvald his nephew, dear though the boy was. What can we do for him?* And what has Queen Thora done?'

He laughed, so that those members of the farm and household who were standing about the hall entrance, looking busy and smiling, were able with justification to turn round and smile more broadly still.

'She has given me back all my lands!' Kalv exclaimed. 'Egge is mine! I am on my way home to Norway again!'

'Come in,' said Groa, 'and tell us all about it.'

She did not look at Thorfinn. For he knew, as Kalv did, that the concerns of Queen Thora his niece carried no weight with King Harald, who had lost no time in recovering his first wife with her daughters from Tønsberg and placing them in the new hall he was building at the top of the fjord east of Ringerike.

Kalv's years of exile were ending because Finn his brother had struck a bargain.

For Kalv's sake, Finn his brother had called a meeting in Nídarós, and had persuaded his friends not to rise in revolt because of the murder of Einar Tambarskelve.

Because men trusted Finn, the threatened rebellion was over, and his brother Kalv had been invited back home to regain all his estates and his revenues.

'And Sigrid your wife?' Groa asked, when she judged that Kalv had talked enough, and perhaps drunk enough as well. 'And your household? When do they follow?'

'In the spring,' Kalv said. 'In the summer. In the autumn, with any luck. You know women and the things they think they have to pack. And it will take as long, I suppose, to call back my men from whatever little farm they have found for themselves over the winter. We shall be taking new blood back to Egge, Thorfinn, mark my words! Egge will have more cradles with black-headed children than you two have managed to fill, I can tell you!'

'Kalv,' said Thorfinn. 'I have here a horn full of wine I was keeping for a very special occasion. See, hero that you are, if you can finish it all in one draught.'

Presently, turning Kalv on his side: 'Half as much,' Groa said, 'would have sufficed.'

'There are some things,' said the King, 'that I prefer to be sure about.'

Kalv Arnason died in battle in Denmark that summer, killed in an attack on Fyn island to which King Harald had promised his support but failed to give it.

The news came to Thorfinn in his chamber at Perth, and the man who brought it, a trader-cousin of one of the Salmundarsons, was of the opinion that Kalv deserved all he got.

'Any fool,' said the trader, 'could tell that Harald isn't the man to forgive anything, far less the murder of his own saintly half-brother. If he invited Kalv back, it wasn't because he married an Arnmødling, I can tell you.'

'How can you be sure?' Thorfinn said.

'How can I be sure? He sent the great warrior Kalv to command the attack, and then held back his reinforcements until Kalv's spearhead had been slaughtered. It was plain enough to satisfy Finn Arnason, anyway. Thirty years of service to the royal house, and he'd been tricked by King Harald into luring back his own brother. Now Finn has left Norway. So should I in his place. Your lady wife ought to know. Her father has left Norway for Denmark.'

Thorfinn said slowly, 'Finn Arnason has taken his family to serve under King Svein of Denmark? When?'

'Just before I came away. The tale is that Svein welcomed him like a brother and gave him Halland, the earldom opposite Aalborg, to defend against Harald. He'll do it, too. And many a Trøndelager will sympathise with him.'

He paused. 'So I hope King Harald of Norway owes you nothing. You won't see it now.'

'I think,' said Thorfinn, 'that it is rather the other way about. Did you see my wife on the jetty?'

'My lord King,' said the trader, 'there were about forty men on that jetty, watching the horses step ashore and trying to stroke them. You'll have paid more for these than a peat-carrier would take in a day. Will you fight them?'

The door opened, and the Lady of Alba came in.

'Now,' said Groa, 'I have seen everything. In the whole of Alba, there are to my knowledge two stretches of firm, level ground where those Koran-worshipping creatures will neither break an elegant leg on the stones nor sink up to the ribs in a morass. You have horses from Ireland and Moray and Iceland and Galloway and your grandfather's stud farm in Angus, and I never heard a word of complaint. Have you gone out of your senses?'

'I hear there were forty people down at the jetty,' Thorfinn said.

'Oh, yes,' said Groa. 'You would think a new sort of woman had arrived. As for harness, anything less than goldsmith-work is going to look like penury. I beg your pardon.'

'This is Hogni from Iceland. He is just leaving to eat in the hall,' said Thorfinn. To Hogni he said, 'You will be asked for your news. There is no need to conceal it.'

'What news?' demanded Groa, as he knew she would, the moment the door closed on the trader.

And so he told her.

When he finished speaking, she raised her hand and drew the linen slowly down the curve of her hair until the folds fell and were stilled by her fingers. Over her down-bent lids, her brows were as black as his own, but shapely, and sheened with light, like the smooth purple-red of her hair. He never tired of looking at Groa.

She said, 'You couldn't have stopped Kalv going back. No one could.'

He never tired of her thinking. He said, 'Your father had no real choice either. He couldn't have denied Kalv the chance. Finn is safer in Denmark.'

'Fighting against his friends?' Groa said. She pulled down the rest of her veil and began, slowly, to unpin the brooch at her breast. She said, 'No more boxes of new silver pennies. I wonder what Harald will do. You need peace so badly. You must have peace to do what you have to do.'

'I'm not in any present danger from Harald,' Thorfinn said. 'As you say, no more chests of new pennies. But Denmark is not proving easy to swallow, and now he has Finn's friends in Nídarós lying waiting to pounce at his back. . . . Peace? There has been peace in Alba ever since I came to the throne nine years ago. Only I didn't know then what to do with it.'

'You spent seven years of it fighting for Orkney,' Groa said. 'Paul and Erlend are not going to tell you that you were wrong.'

'Neither would Siward of Northumbria, were you to ask him,' Thorfinn said. 'The fact remains: the united kingdom of Orkney, Caithness, Cumbria, Moray, and Alba is two years old instead of nine. Do you think Sulien might come to Lulach's wedding-feast? I shall have to construct my excuses.'

'I have observed,' Groa said, 'that at moments of self-doubt Sulien is always present to watch you take the wrong turning. You want to see Lulach settled soon? August, in Glamis?'

'September, in Scone,' Thorfinn said. 'Unless you and he have any grave objections. The girl, I take it, will do as she is told.'

'I've been to see her,' Groa said. 'She laughs a lot.'

'Introduce her to Alfgar,' Thorfinn said. 'I see that, like me, Lulach counts not the cost where the state is concerned.'

'I don't recall laughing a lot,' Groa said. 'Except at Inverness, when my men speared you. You won't remember. I did it quietly.'

'I remember,' said Thorfinn. 'And how I stopped it, as well. I must tell Lulach.'

Then he took her into the hall and the hall became warm, as if someone had carried a brazier into it.

There were gale-force winds blowing in Scone in September, and a strong smell of fish, and of money.

The priest Sulien of Brittany and Llanbadarn did not arrive, unsurprisingly, for Lulach's wedding Mass. 'I hardly know why,' remarked Dubhdaleithe, Abbot of Armagh, looking about him. 'You seem to have invited half the churchmen of the northern world: is there a flaw in the marriage contract? Groa, you get handsomer as this fellow gets uglier. What are you? Thorfinn or Macbeth?'

'Macbeth, for the moment. I hear you've hardly stopped fighting since you left Tarbatness. Ireland must be breathing a sigh of relief this day, with Duftah abroad.'

'Oh, the church is in a desperate state in Ireland,' said Duftah blandly. The mighty beard and scarred hands were the same, and the voice that had comforted on the night before Thorfinn had fought his half-brother Duncan for the throne. 'The holy relics are jumping from altar to altar at a price you wouldn't believe, and some disciples of the Lord you and I know are not above thievery. I see you still depend on Kells for the occasion. Robhartach's looking his age.'

'If you forget,' said Thorfinn, 'that your great-uncle was once Abbot of both Armagh and Kells, you'll find that Robhartach suddenly looks younger. We've had timber halls put up instead of pavilions. You'll find your kins-people easily.'

'I noticed,' said Abbot Duftah, 'that someone seems to have come by a fortune. Also, there's a strong smell of fish.'

'That's Isleifr,' said Thorfinn. 'You remember. Gizur the White's son from Iceland who left me for Ireland and Westphalia to train as a priest. He's on his way back to Saxony. Go and see him.'

'Where?' said Duftah.

Groa said, 'You said there was a strong smell of fish. Follow it.' She smiled at the Abbot's expression and looked after him as he turned and strode through the crowds, moving from building to building under the banners.

Thorfinn said, 'Should I have warned him?'

'No,' said his lady wife. 'But I shouldn't give the same advice to Bishop Malduin your cousin.'

'If you look a little more closely,' said the King, 'you will note that the prelate who has just joined Abbot Duftah and is making his way to Isleifr's is none other than Bishop Malduin my cousin.'

*   *   *

Inside the priest Isleifr's booth, the bride Finnghuala ceased screaming for a moment when the door opened, and then continued from where she lay on the ground. Far from going to her aid, Lulach her bridegroom of the next day sat weeping and hugging his knees on the far side of the booth. Maelmuire, his fifteen-year-old cousin of the half-blood, lay beside him, beating clenched fists on the ground, while Paul and Erlend, the bride's young second cousins, were clinging together, the elder attempting to comfort the younger, who, bawling with fear, was sitting shut-eyed on the ground.

The noise, the smoke from the fire, and the astounding aroma of fish at first disguised from both Dubhdaleithe and his fellow churchman the full horror of the occasion. Then the Bishop, leaving the doorway, cried, 'That is the voice of my niece!' and rushed through the fog towards the bride.

It was natural that he failed to observe, crawling on all fours in his path, the naked hindquarters of a small yellow man with black hair. And that, falling headlong over this obstacle, Bishop Malduin should only then perceive, hanging before him, the little creature's discarded clothes, racked on the wet, shining teeth of a white Greenland bear-cub.

In a flurry of red-and-white wool and gold braiding, the Bishop landed full on the bear, and the bear, confused, responded according to the promptings of nature with its teeth, its claws, and its bladder.

The stench of fish sprang freshly thickened into the tainted atmosphere, and the bride, squealing with uncontrollable mirth, sprang to her feet and dashed from the booth, dragging her hooting bridegroom behind her.

The three boys followed, the youngest still tremulous.

The small yellow man stood up yelling. The cub shoved itself free and sat up. The Bishop lay on the ground. The Abbot of Armagh sank on his knees by the Bishop, put out a hand, and drew it back again.

The priest Isleifr, emerging stocky and practical from the obscurity, exclaimed, 'Dear, dear. What a girl you have there! You'll have to forgive her. High spirits, no more. She stuffed some fish up his . . . No harm done, I assure you. Teeth small as a kitten's. Bites that fade in an evening . . .' He came to a halt and looked down. 'It's a pity about the robes,' Isleifr said.

It was a good, hearty wedding, and the marriage feast was without parallel in the experience of any man visiting Alba, as were the guest-gifts each received on departure.

On the second day of the feast, Lulach led his bride from their chamber, kissed his mother, and said, 'How could I fail with such a pedigree? Lulaig mic Gillacomghain mic Maelbrighde mic Ruaidhrí mic Morgaind mic Domnall mic Cathmail mic Ruaidhrí mic Aircellach mic Ferchair fhoda . . . My wife was overcome. I could hardly persuade her from her knees.'

'You are happy,' said Groa.

'Finnghuala is happy,' said Lulach. 'When this night's work brings me a son, I think I should call him Snaebjorn.'

It meant Snow-bear.

'If you wish your uncle by marriage to expel you from his communion,' Groa said.

'Then Snaekolf,' Lulach said. 'I had a forebear called Snaekolf. Or was it Melsnati?'

Groa was seldom disturbed by her son. She said, 'Whatever it was, I suggest you borrow some other name from your pedigree until Bishop Malduin is with *his* forebears, white or otherwise.' And waited, smiling, while the bride laughed and laughed.

On the last day of the feast, Sulien of Llanbadarn walked into the hall, saying, 'It seems that no marriage feast has taken place in Alba worth mentioning, for all anyone is talking about is some tale to do with a bear. Have you a married son here or not?'

It was nine years since his last, brief visit to Alba, when he had stood beside Thorfinn's sickbed at St Andrews and his throne on the Moot Hill of Scone. Now he was thirty-eight, but the slight, buoyant carriage was the same as when, a boy fresh from Brittany, he had run on the ship's oars at Chester, and his tonsured hair was still dark. Only perhaps in the seamed brow and dark-lidded gaze, the eye of a friend could trace the weight of thirteen years of exile and study.

He had made an entrance, and so men looked at him. But all those who knew Thorfinn best looked nowhere after that first glance save at the High Chair.

Aware of it, Thorfinn showed nothing except perhaps by his stillness. Sulien also, though his smiling glance swept the King's, brought his attention to rest solely on Lulach, the boy of twenty who had been his care and his foster-child, and who now rose, white hair silk above the bright bridal silks, clear face untroubled and empty as the face of the sky, and said, 'Come and meet my wife, who will tell you.'

In the space made for him between Thorfinn and Lulach at table, Sulien said, 'I missed the wedding Mass. It was a grief to me.'

'We all know,' said Thorfinn, 'that a sense of direction is not your strongest point.'

Sulien said, 'You gave me plenty of warning. But to finish the work of so many years in a few weeks is not easy. I could not fail my abbot.'

Thorfinn said, 'You are not returning to Ireland?'

Sulien's eyes moved to Groa, which was answer enough, for those who knew him. Then he said, 'I have been asked by the Bishop of St David's to come back to Wales to teach. I have accepted.'

'Your dream?' said Groa. 'You will be bishop one day. We are happy for you.'

'Part of my dream,' Sulien said. 'The rest has been realised.'

Thorfinn said, 'I am sorry for the man who has to deal with your pupils. I have a few of them here already complaining about the lack of equipment.'

'You will have more,' Sulien said.

And from that moment, to Finnghuala's simple pleasure, it became an occasion of quite singular gaiety: indeed, the most inventive feast day of them all, so that she was almost sorry when day dawned at last and the young prince her husband lifted her up in his arms to carry her to their chamber.

Almost, but not quite. All the girls she knew had told her that Lulach was not like other men.

But he was.

Long before that, Thorfinn had taken Sulien off, and Groa was moved to nothing but thankfulness when the bed beside her stayed empty until long after she woke.

From what she saw of the King during the leave-taking, as the halls and the booths slowly emptied next day, she judged that he had slept not at all and that it had done him no harm. Sulien, accustomed to vigils, was unchanged.

Only later, when she found Sulien packing, did Groa say, 'But you have only just come! You must not leave us!'

Thorfinn said, 'He has to go to Rheims. The Pope is holding a Michaelmas synod, and churchmen are flocking. Twenty bishops at least. And Emma is sending a trio from Somerset.'

'The new Pope? Pope Leo?' said Groa. 'I thought they'd only just managed to get him to Rome.'

'Bruno le Bon, the Emperor's second cousin. He's back in Toul again,' said Thorfinn, 'after five months in Rome and Apulia and a good read of Peter Damian's Book of Gomorrha. He's back, says Sulien here, to reform France and Germany, or to drum up money, or to keep an eye on the Emperor, or because no one came to his Lateran synod, or because he likes Toul and doesn't like Rome and Apulia. Take your pick.'

'Don't listen to him,' said Sulien. 'Bishop Bruno was a clever and courageous leader of men. He was also a good man. As Pope Leo, he is still all of those things.'

Groa looked at Thorfinn. She said flatly, 'You are going to Rheims with him. Or to Wales.'

'Nonsense,' said the King. The bar of his brows rose and descended. 'Why should I do that? Sulien is going to Rheims, and then he is going to bring all his news back to Denmark, where you and I shall be visiting your mother and father.'

No one spoke. Sulien smiled.

'You mean it,' said Groa at length.

'I mean it,' said Thorfinn.

Slowly, Groa sat down. 'You can leave the kingdom?' she said.

'I can leave it,' said Thorfinn. 'I have been working for two years to make it safe for hands other than mine. Norway cannot afford to attack, and England won't, while Cumbria is mine and Mercia friendly. While the fleet is there, goods and silver will flow and the coast will be defended. Besides, Lulach says that the peace will not break for four years.'

'Then I am reassured,' said Groa. Her face was pink.

'And I shall see you both in Denmark,' Sulien said. 'You can guess what it is. I have promised to bring him a copy of Peter Damian's Book of Gomorrha.'

'To correct,' said Thorfinn.

THREE

A T AALBORG, THE girls were giving trouble again.

For any King of Denmark, it was sensible to move to Aalborg when caught in a long war with Norway. Aalborg sat on the Limfjord, whose waterway stretched from sea to sea across the north of Jutland. Fleets could sit in the Limfjord, and armies could lie, and did, at Aggersborg on the north shore. From Aalborg, ships could sail west to England and Normandy, or east to Halland and Sweden and Russia beyond.

Finn Arnason and his wife had crossed the eastern sound from his earldom of Halland last week, and today every man who could be spared was busy finishing the new hall that had been built to house this man Thorfinn-Macbeth and his suite. An hour ago, the Jammerbugt bailiff had sent to say that the ships from Alba had arrived in Lokken as directed and were being escorted round to the fjord, having landed their party.

There were horses for fifty people waiting at Borglumkloster, and the ride to Aalborg would take three hours, one could reckon, added to whatever time his bailiff managed to promote for a landing-feast and a rest. Meanwhile, the King of Alba, as was well known, had only one wife and she was an Arnmødling, so that it behoved the King of Denmark to get the girls out of the way, or at least to relegate them to the women's quarters, where they would be in no danger of pushing themselves into the seats at the feast table beside the legal Lady of Alba and her father and mother.

As soon as Kalv Arnason had been killed and Finn his brother had defected from Norway to the Danish court, it had occurred to his new employer that a message of friendship and goodwill to Alba might have interesting and even profitable results.

He had only half-expected a reply to his invitation to spend the winter in Denmark. An acceptance within the month had given him what might be termed alarmed satisfaction.

Satisfaction because, by bringing his court openly to Denmark, the present opponent of Norway, Thorfinn-Macbeth was certainly making a statement if not actually issuing a challenge to Harald of Norway, to whose forebears Orkney had for so long owed allegiance.

And alarm because, evidently, the King of Alba was strong enough to do so with impunity.

Ragna, the girl he liked best when she wasn't talking, said, 'The King will think that he has a child to deal with; or that you smell. If you wish to impress him, why don't you offer him a trader's peace and take his wife to your couch, while I show him what Svein of Denmark expects of a woman? He will respect you after that, I assure you.'

He cuffed her then, and had the other two in after his morning-ale instead; but the Irish one sulked and the other spent all her time, when she had the breath, hinting that what he needed was another wife.

King Svein of Denmark had had enough of wives. The German mirror in his chamber showed him at his prime, so far as women were concerned: middle-sized and fair; not so bulky as his uncle Canute had been, but with his uncle's thin, crooked nose with the high ridge and more than his uncle's fertility: five sons and two daughters to date, and all healthy, unlike Canute's clutch of weak, stripling kings.

As he was healthy. He was thirty-one years old and, with any luck, now able to get what he wanted—in every direction—without having to marry for it.

One wondered, therefore, if the tales they told about Thorfinn were true. He knew (everyone did) about the red-haired beauty, Groa his wife. Svein had been in Sweden, in tedious exile with his mother, when Groa made both her marriages. She was about his own age, he had heard. And had been married to Thorfinn for seventeen years.

Of course Thorfinn would hold on to her, an Arnmødling. Anyone would. He, Svein, didn't need an Arnmødling: he had Finn Arnason himself serving under him. But after seventeen years, a woman might well be bored: a man might have found himself other diversions.

King Svein, touching up his hair with his comb, wondered if, after all, that little horse-fly Ragna had been uttering nonsense. There was sometimes more to an alliance, these days, than the bishops wrote down on their parchments.

'And what,' had asked Groa two days before, 'is the nature of King Svein of Denmark?'

Sailing in *Grágás* and another, larger ship of whose building she had been unaware, she and Thorfinn and their train had broken their journey to Denmark at the only part of the Norwegian coast at which they could be sure of a welcome: at the fjord by Dale in Hordaland where Orm and Sigrid her sister had lands.

Orm's cousin Gunnhild of Lade had been the first wife of King Svein of Denmark. 'Lusty,' said Sigrid, Groa's sister.

'So said Gunnhild?' Groa enquired.

'So say I,' answered Sigrid austerely. 'You will be lucky to get through your first night unmolested. Whether or not your husband will protect you, I suppose you know best. A barren woman has few defences.'

'Thorfinn?' Groa called. 'Will you protect me from King Svein's advances?'

'I never saw any harm,' Thorfinn called in reply, 'in a little rape in the autumn. Svein has seven concubines, Guthorm says. He wrote the names down for me.'

'Is he joking?' Sigrid said. 'He does not smile.'

'Thorfinn never smiles,' said the Lady of Alba. 'Perhaps King Svein of Denmark is a merry man, of the kind a woman can warm to.'

For three weeks after the King of Alba's arrival in Denmark, the Danish court feasted its eyes on the red hair of the Lady of Alba, lit by the October sunshine of the day and the wax lights of the night at the banquet table.

During that time, no business was discussed nor any untoward approach made on either side. At the gates to Aalborg, King Svein had ridden forth to meet his guests and, taking the hand of the Lady, had chastely kissed her, according to custom, on either cheek.

The flawless face had not escaped his observation. Neither had the brown, unwinking gaze of the King of Alba, or the fact that the magnificent horses he and the Lady Groa were riding were certainly not from the stables at Borglumkloster and must therefore have sailed here from Alba.

The only exchange between himself and the Lady had occurred at the doors to the guest-quarters, where she had paused, glanced about, and remarked, 'Is there not a strong smell of fish?'

To which King Svein had replied quickly. 'In your own quarters, no. In fact, they have been newly built for that reason. The odour elsewhere will, I am told, disperse before very long.'

And had broken off because the King of Alba, looking down at his wife, had said forbiddingly, 'And because of the niceness of your senses, must complaint and contumely attach itself to the simplest of functions? Isleifr has passed through, that is all, with his bear. King Svein welcomes everyone, yourself included.'

Smiling a little, King Svein led his guests to their residence.

He had been right. Seventeen years evidently blunted the appetite, even for luxuries: for fire and sweet fruit-flesh; for deep wine and honey. And there was no haste, for in some things he liked to think of himself as an artist, and this Lady would sleep here all winter.

Such was still the pattern when in November the priest Sulien and his servants rode into Aalborg with his baggage and two mule-loads of red Pingsdorf stoneware full of good Rhenish wine.

Groa was absent from the guest-quarters, staying at the hall set aside for her parents. Sulien paid his respects to the King, proffered his gift from the vineyards of Germany, and, on being allotted both a welcome and a guest-house, found his way at length to the hall of Alba, bearing a spouted pitcher and two matching beakers.

The hall was full of men: well-dressed chieftains from Orkney and Caithness, stalwart landed-men from Moray and Angus and Perth, from the hilly land to the south, and from the Cumbrian beaches and mountains, mixed with young hirdmen of Svein's, of their own standing and calibre.

The Bishop of Alba was not present, and Sulien saw only two priests:

Eochaid, now Prior of Scone, who had been with the household since the
killing of Duncan, and Tuathal, the man Thorfinn had made Abbot of the
Culdees of Loch Leven. Arnór Jarlaskáld, he noticed, was not of the party.

Then Thorfinn saw him and, waiting for him to approach, said, 'You don't
look any different. You have come from the Pope's synods at Rheims and at
Mainz? Bishop Walo returned three days ago, travelling cross-country riding
his crozier. There has been a lot of whispering.'

'The Pope and Archbishop Adalbert spent a lot of time talking of Denmark.
I have enough wine for two,' Sulien said.

'Then unless you want two other people to have it, you had better come
into my chamber,' Thorfinn said; and about him, men smiled: even men from
Angus and Perth.

In the chamber, Sulien said, 'They appear, poor fools, to tolerate you. I
didn't think it was possible.'

'You would be surprised,' Thorfinn said, 'what money can do. All right.
Tell me about Bruno. Or I shall tell you. Military, forty-seven, and not averse
to using his head. Warms the Lateran chair for five minutes, and then marches
north from Rome into Germany and, with the sword of anathema, helps his
cousin the Emperor put down rebellions in Lorraine and Flanders. Tours
Alsace; honours, at a price, the churches of kinsfolk; keeps a promise to
consecrate the church of St Remigius, Apostle of the Franks; and throws in a
synod that demands the presence of all good-living French bishops just when
their liege lord King Henry wants them somewhere else fighting for him.
Whose bad planning?'

'The Pope's, if you like,' Sulien said. 'He's apt to follow an impulse, and he
hasn't got his household together yet and won't until the Lorraine business is
safely over and he can call in some of his relatives from that quarter. The
fund-raising was sensible enough. He's got rich brothers and sisters and
cousins he can milk all over Rhineland and Burgundy and the Vosges, and he
needs money if he is to begin to do anything. Apart from pilgrims' offerings,
he's got virtually nothing else. Between them, the Saracens and the Greeks
and the Normans have overrun the papal lands in south Italy, and the princes
of the Roman Campagna have whipped away what the church used to have
there. The mistake, I think, was in holding the synod in France.'

'The King thought he was poaching?'

'The King agreed at first, and then someone persuaded him that he would
lose face and authority if he let the Pope come in and harangue his bishops. A
two-day fever and a discreet cancellation would have saved everyone's face.'

'But instead?'

'But instead the synod was called, with excommunication for any French
bishop who chose to march instead to King Henry's battles. Which, naturally,
most of them did, since their livelihood depends on King Henry and not on
Pope Bruno-Leo. Thorfinn, why are you so interested in Pope Leo?'

'Because I enjoy listening to a Breton scion trained in Scotland and Ireland
and about to join a major Welsh monastery discoursing on the troubles of the
Coarb of St Peter. What else happened at Rheims?'

'I'll tell you if you tell me what you're doing in Denmark. And without Bishop Malduin,' Sulien said.

'Do you want your wine back, too?' Thorfinn said. 'I shall do what I can.'

It was no longer so simple as once it had been; but it was not difficult. Sulien said, 'We are very autocratic, of a sudden, for a half-breed pretender on a precarious throne? Go on. I doubt if Groa hears quite everything. You have to talk to someone.'

The sound of singing, muffled, came through the wall, and of talking and laughter.

Inside, the fire-basket glowed and flickered between the two men, and red light sank through the beaker in Sulien's hand and glared on the King's jagged profile: the cheek-knob, the scimitar nose, the globe of the brow beneath the Indian-black hair. 'If I began, I should never stop talking,' Thorfinn said. His eyes did not lift. 'So tell me what happened at Rheims.'

Sulien studied him. Then, smiling a little, he lifted his beaker, drained it, and, setting it down, folded his arms and leaned back.

'Two things you should know about,' he said. 'Or perhaps three. Make sure, when you become king of the Western world, that your servants know how to control the enthusiasm of your subjects. The crowds for the consecration of St Rémi were such that the brethren could neither get into the church nor the Pope leave his house, and the relic, which the Pope at first carried on his own shoulders—'

'Weeping?' said Thorfinn.

'Weeping, as you say—caused such a surge of the population that a fair number were trampled to death when it issued, and the bearers finally had to pass the saint's body into the new church by way of a window. . . . Do not underrate, in your calculations, the hunger that poor men feel for spiritual comfort. The people stood in the open all night, their torches burning, and sang.'

'One must worship an oak if one is to live under it,' Thorfinn said. 'What do you want with my knife?'

Sulien finished the nimble movement by which he had drawn it out of its sheath, and turned its blade so that the runes, small as they were, sparkled red. 'To live under two oaks,' Thorfinn said, 'doubles the duties, but also imposes a sense of proportion. You said there were three things I ought to know about.'

'There appear to be more,' Sulien said. He laid the knife down. 'The Pope spoke against simony, and altars served by laymen, and incestuous marriages, and the abandonment of legitimate wives for adulterous unions; against monks and clerics abandoning the habit or making war; against thefts, injustices to the poor, sodomy, and various heresies. The churchmen present were then asked to declare on oath that they had never bought or sold holy office. But you don't want to hear about all that.'

There was a short silence. Thorfinn said, 'I have never seen you so angry. I thought it was with me.' He waited, and then said, 'So, he spoke against all those things, and then he acted in a way you did not like. Tell me. He may still be a good man.'

'He *is* a good man,' Sulien said. 'He excommunicated, of course, those bishops who obeyed the King of France and failed to attend, including Beauvais and Amiens, strong adherents of Boulogne and Flanders. He denounced Geoffrey of Anjou for imprisoning a bishop of the opposite faction and Theobald of Blois for setting aside his wife, whose family also opposed Anjou. Two counts were excommunicated for incest, both of them sympathetic to Flanders. Geoffey of Coutances, whose kinsman Nigel-Constantine led a revolt against Duke William of Normandy, was allowed to keep his expensive bishopric, but the Archbishop of Rheims, Primate of all Gaul, was accused of simony and told to report to the Easter synod at Rome, having also relinquished a monastery the Pope thought should properly belong to Toul, his own bishopric. Does this mean anything to you?'

'It means something to *you*. Go on,' Thorfinn said.

'This time you are *my* confessor?' Sulien said. He drew a steadying breath. 'You must judge. The Bishop of Nantes has been deposed and is to be replaced by the abbot of Hildebrand's monastery in Rome. That offers control of the mouth of the Loire, where the King of France, you will remember, is lay abbot of St Martin's of Tours.'

'That, I imagine, is going to unsettle a lot of people, including Eachmarcach,' Thorfinn said. 'And so I expect he also said something about Dol.'

'The Pope,' said Sulien, 'entertained a serious complaint by the clerics of Tours against Dol in Brittany. Archbishop Juhel has been likewise commanded to appear at the synod at Rome to defend himself. I can see, now, that you are listening.'

'I am listening. Is there anything more?'

'Trifles. He forbade Baldwin of Flanders to marry his daughter to Duke William of Normandy, who is descended, as she is, from Duke Rollo.'

'Is she?' said Thorfinn. 'Matilda?'

'Through Adela, the wife of her great-grandfather,' Sulien said. 'Their children would be idiots. The Emperor is suspicious of Normandy and Anjou. The Emperor is quelling a war with Flanders and Lorraine. The Pope is acting accordingly. You should meet him,' said Sulien. 'You would get along famously.'

He regretted it as soon as he said it. But Thorfinn only grunted and, rising, collected his beaker and refilled it and his own. 'No one likes to be wrong,' Thorfinn said. He brought the wine back and set it down. 'I tried to tell you that board-games are inescapable. Since Charlemagne's time, the Emperor of the Romans has protected the Pope. Bruno has to consider his interests or lose any power for good he may have.'

Thorfinn moved away and sat down again. 'Anyway, the picture isn't as one-sided as all that. The Pope is opposing Lorraine even though they are closer in kinship to him than to the Emperor. Geoffrey of Anjou is stepfather to the Emperor's wife. In continuing the case against Dol, the Pope is doing the French King a service. You said the English legates to Rheims were all of Emma's faction.'

'I'm sure Walo told you who they were,' Sulien said. 'All three are related; all three speak Bruno's dialect. The two abbots work together closely for trade and have mint-rights all over England, and especially in Somerset. The Bishop of Wells, also in Somerset, used to be Canute's priest. Is there anything else I can tell you?'

'Now *I* am the person you are angry with. You know why I am in Denmark,' Thorfinn said. 'Now Norway is cut off by war from the Archbishop of Bremen, I am free to consider what the church of Bremen can offer me. I know Walo argued a case for Denmark at Mainz, but what happened no one, naturally, is likely to tell me.'

'What happened at Mainz? A confrontation between Denmark and Archbishop Adalbert of Bremen,' Sulien said. 'They've been testing each other's strength ever since Svein came to the throne. Now Svein is demanding an archbishop of his own so that Denmark can rule its own church; and Adalbert doesn't like it.'

'Svein would need a lot of new bishops,' Thorfinn said. He looked thoughtful.

'Which either Adalbert or the Pope would have to consecrate. Therefore, deadlock exists at the moment,' Sulien said.

Thorfinn continued to look thoughtful. He said, 'What is higher than an archbishop? A patriarch? How many of those are there?'

'Constantinople, Jerusalem, Antioch . . . five, I should think,' Sulien said. 'No, that's impossible. For Adalbert to make himself into a new patriarch, he would have to seed the north with archbishops like dandelions.'

'I don't think,' Thorfinn said, 'that I could come to care for archbishops like dandelions. A few modest bishops is all I require. Now Duncan's sons are growing up and Bishop Malduin is still paid and supported from York, I need lettered men I can rely on, to train our own young men and ordain them. You know all that. For generations, we've taken them from Ireland. It worked, in a way, because the same families ruled in both countries, but it gave Alba no chance, in bad times, under bad rule, to develop a strong church of its own. The result has been poor husbandry and rank ignorance. Germany has monks who speak both our languages.'

Sulien said, 'Germany could devour you and what is left of your culture.'

'That, I gather, is King Svein's suspicion,' Thorfinn said. 'Indeed, we have a lot in common, which is why I am here. To observe, and to learn. Do you blame me?'

'I am afraid for you,' Sulien said. 'I am afraid for your country, if you lose your way. Where is all this money coming from? The ships and the horses they tell me about; the clothes your hird wears; Groa's jewels . . . Where is Groa?'

'Money?' Thorfinn said. The bar of his eyebrows rose and fell again. 'Booty. Regular bribes from King Harald and Emma. Protection payment from Llanbadarn and practically everywhere. A toll-chain across the Pentland Firth. Money offers no problems, I assure you. As for Groa . . .'

'They said she was at the hall of her parents,' Sulien said. 'But when I called there, she hadn't arrived.'

'She will, later on,' Thorfinn said. 'At this present moment, I rather imagine—I told you we had a lot in common—she is in the private quarters of our host, the divorced Svein of Denmark.'

FOUR

H, AN ABLE man!' said King Svein of Denmark. 'An able man and a fine huntsman. Look at his record today. A man after my own heart. But to pay no attention to the needs of his wife: that I cannot forgive him. I married twice, as you know, but neither lady, if I say it myself, had any cause for dissatisfaction. Gytha—the Lade heiress: your sister married her cousin—Gytha died of poison, a tragedy. And Gunnhild, of course, has been torn from my side because of a so-called Swedish alliance. What has love to do with a Swedish alliance?'

'There are consolations,' the Lady of Alba said. She was given to saying things like that. She sat in a man's chamber with her light eyes and her dark brows and her knotted red hair, pulsing womanhood, and said things like that. Also, she brought her woman Sinna, who was half asleep in a corner.

King Svein of Denmark said, 'A man will seek, yes, when he is free and has no wife to dishonour. But why, do you think, does your husband the King send you each day to the house of your parents, and debar you from his couch when you come back at night? These things are known and talked about.'

She lifted one hand, and the spike-lantern glowed on the great necklace of gold and cornelians and amber she was touching, and on the rings of her fingers. 'He gives me these,' she said. 'And feeds and shelters me.'

Svein settled back in his chair so that the lamp could catch, too, his square head with its glossy yellow hair that all his women said was irresistible; the short patrician lip and rounded chin, each with its tailored thatch of light gold. 'It seems to me,' he said, 'that for some weeks now that privilege has fallen to me. And I, too, have seen bracelets of mine on your arms, although you are not wearing them tonight.'

'Perhaps,' said the Lady of Alba, 'Your concubines are accustomed to displaying their jewels to their parents. My father is Finn Arnason, whom Harald of Norway would welcome, should Denmark displease him.'

'And if Alba should displease him, I wonder what your father would do?' King Svein said. 'I told you that a foreign court offers many temptations to men of mixed blood. Is it so hard to persuade your husband to travel?

Hamburg is a busy town, Bremen a rich one. The Archbishop would welcome him. And you could stay here. With your parents.'

At last, the old woman had fallen asleep. As on every occasion, the Arnason daughter had seated herself not on the settle but in the high-backed chair that would not admit two. Her overskirt was embroidered with rolled metal thread, and the robe under it had a border of pearls like a reliquary. There were pearls beading the twists of her hair, wound among smooth copper roulades, each turning through amber, and crimson, and a lustre the colour of grape-bloom.

He slid from his chair and said, 'Look. I will ask you again. On my knees. Persuade your husband to go to Bremen. You said you could.'

The pearled hem slid from his fingers just as he raised it, and he moved his hand barely in time, as she stood. She said, 'I have stayed long enough. I told you. I can persuade him. Eventually.'

The old woman had wakened. Svein stood up, too. He said, his voice carefully low, 'Who is he with while you are here? And do you think he has done no more than touch the hem of her dress?'

She smiled. 'It would take a great deal to make me believe that,' she said.

'But if you found it were true?' King Svein said. It always ended like this. His shirt was sticky with sweat.

'Even if I found it were true,' the Lady of Alba said. 'While he is here, I could do nothing.'

He took her out himself, and confided her and the old woman to the care of their servants.

Ragna had not yet returned. When he was told, Svein sent the messenger staggering with a cuff and an order and turned into his chamber to pour himself wine, for his hands were trembling.

When the Irish girl came, he took her on the straw on the threshold of the room before his chamberlain had even left. He didn't care. They were both men. They had seen it all before.

But the Irish girl never satisfied him as his favourite did even when, as tonight, Ragna came late, and from another man's bed, and had to drag into being the joyous, sinewy lust that was his everyday portion.

Later, she fell asleep and he shook her awake, angry, and said, 'You were late.'

She opened her eyes and looked up through the mesh of her hair. 'I had to wait until the priest went.'

Weeks ago, he had been flattered when she had resisted his order to go and lie with the Alban King and had continued to weep and refuse until he had pulled his knife out. Women in Italy, he had been told, found flaxen hair fashionable. Should he choose to crop her locks short at the scalp, would it not provide a fine wig for a Tuscan woman?

She had obeyed him sulkily then and, after the first night or two of the foreigner, had stopped complaining.

If anyone had cause to complain, it was himself. He had taxed her with losing her looks, but for a girl serving two masters she did what she could. It was not her fault but the fault of the red-haired Queen that he still had to come hungry to bed, with an edge to the hunger that a fine woman's presence made all but insupportable.

Meanwhile, he made sure of one thing: no foreign king could lay legal claim to a child begotten on Ragna, for everyone knew where Ragna spent the rest of her time. And, conversely, nothing would suit King Svein more than to sire a child—a son—on the Arnason woman; for everyone knew that she and her husband slept in different quarters. Kings came to grief in battle or died of a sickness, and other kings married their widows. He had done it himself once already.

'And so?' he said to Ragna, and shook her awake again, smiling quite fondly.

'Does he please you, this Thorfinn from storm-ridden Orkney? Is he vigorous? What words do you speak? What services did he demand that surprised you? I want you to tell me.'

'He uses me hard, as you do,' said Ragna, and winced. Then she put her arms round his neck. 'But all the time it's: *Show me again, do you do thus with King Svein? Does King Svein really do thus and thus? And how often? I cannot believe it! Is he a god?* he will say. And some things I show him. But some things I do not,' ended Ragna.

'But why not?' said Svein. 'Look. Here is something I have just thought of. It is to show you that I forgive you for sleeping. I will do it, and you will tell him tomorrow.'

The next day, a ship arrived from Orkney, for the weather remained open, and delivered falcons, a gift for King Svein, as well as sundry crates and writings for Thorfinn of Alba.

It was not the first so to make its way from the Pentland Firth or the Tay. The journey, after all, would take less than ten days. Thorfinn from whatever distance was still, it seemed, keeping an eye on his kingdom.

They went hawking later that day, and the Caithness birds exceeded all King Svein had heard of them. The following morning, he arranged a full day's hunting over the heathlands and patches of forest, and in the afternoon they changed horses and raced along the edge of the sea, sand and spray in their faces and the courtmen cheering them on, until all they could see were the ruddy faces and furs in the light of the flares and the ghostly waves from the Barbarian ocean, rolling over and over.

They moved to Aarhus at the end of December, and to Viborg for Christmas, for the seas had closed; and Harald of Norway had turned his mind from raiding to the building of his new town on the Foldenfjord, where he had established a sanctuary for the corpse of his cousin St Halvard and a hall of Russian splendour, so they said, for his Russian wife Ellisif and her daughters.

King Svein noticed that his guest Thorfinn of Alba paid attention to such items of news and always took the chance to sit next to the envoys, the guests, and the couriers that came to the Danish court from Germany and the south.

He wondered if he had been wrong in deciding, this year, not to cut himself off from the continent by spending Christmas at Roskilde; and bit his nails when word came in from Bremen that the Archbishop was not expected back in his diocese for several weeks.

Returned from the side of the Pope, the Archbishop of Hamburg and Bremen attended the Emperor Henry at Christmas in Frisia, after which the Emperor left for his palace at Goslar.

From Goslar, a courier rode without haste to Bremen and then continued to Viborg, where he remained for some space with King Svein.

Returning to his chamber, King Svein called for his concubine Ragna and, pulling down the taut cloth from her shoulder-clasps, observed with an experienced eye how the sharp, tender breasts had become squat.

He smiled, although she had been the best he had ever had and he knew, also from experience, that she would never be as exceptional again.

'What a pity,' he said. 'But now, really, it hardly matters.'

That night, they had some music, and one of his three skalds intoned a long poem in eulogy of the King's brother Bjorn, who had been murdered that year in England by the King's half-English nephew Swegen Godwinsson, who had coveted his lands and even possibly his position in the line of succession.

Swegen was now in exile in Flanders. King Svein looked not dissatisfied, sitting in his high chair listening to the poem. He approved of the Emperor's war against Flanders.

After the poem, there was a discourse by Bishop Walo of Ribe, for, naturally, this was a Christian as well as a civilised court; and the King of Alba's bard sang to the harp, amid shuffling.

When he finally ended and the tables had been drawn, King Svein decided, since it was a merry as well as a civilised court, to select one of the shufflers to pay for his inattention.

For safety, the women were sent to their quarters. King Svein escorted the Lady Groa himself and petted her hand, which he had not permitted himself to do for a week. Returning to the cleared hall, he settled himself lavishly beside the King of Alba his guest, saying, 'You must not mind the delay. First they have to bridle the heifer, and then they have to shave bare his tail. He is wild, you understand.'

'I'm not sure that I do,' Thorfinn said. 'But I rely on you to instruct me.'

'Arnketil understands,' King Svein remarked. 'It is not everywhere that a young man transgressing good manners is allowed to redeem himself so, and even to better himself, if he has the ability. You will note the shoes Arnketil is assuming. They have been greased.'

'So I see,' Thorfinn said.

'And, further, when you see the heifer brought in, you will note that its tail has been smeared with grease also.'

'What next?' said Thorfinn. 'The slave-girls?'

Svein was in a mood to humour everyone. He laughed. 'Another time, perhaps we shall try it. When you and I are on our own. No. My men will make a ring with their shields. The heifer stands in the centre. My bard begins a poem: it is not one for the ladies' ears: you will recognise it, no doubt, when you hear it. Arnketil takes the floor in his greased shoes, and seizes the beast by the tail while another man, with a whip, goads the heifer. If Arnketil contrives to hang on to the beast till the end of the poem, the heifer is his.'

'And if not?' Thorfinn said.

'Then he pays a fine for his misbehaviour. It is good sport,' King Svein said. 'You have enjoyed your stay? You feel at home in my country? My people please you?'

The young men were lining up in the hall, laughing and pushing one another, with their shields shouldered up in position. Thorfinn said, 'Is this a host indicating to his guest that he has outstayed his welcome?'

King Svein swept up a hand in a signal and turned, smiling broadly. 'It is a host,' he said, 'who so values his guest that, were he to stay in Denmark ten years, he would never grow tired of his company. Except that, for such a delight, he would have to compete with a personage greater by far. After the play, we shall talk of it. There is the heifer.'

'So I notice,' the King of Alba remarked.

The heifer, an active animal hitherto proud of its tail, darted into the hall and stood with its feet splayed, swinging its head at the noise, the lights, the smoke, and, last of all, the man standing before it, a whip in his hand.

The man raised his hand, and the heifer backed, paused, lifted its naked, glistening tail, and, rumbling, emptied its bowels on the boards.

'As a protest, I admire it,' said Thorfinn. 'But I feel it was a tactical error.'

'My fool is hesitating,' said King Svein. 'In battle, does a man hold back when offered an advantage? Lefsi, have your men clear the dung from the floor. If Arnketil wishes to keep his feet clean, we shall not hinder him.'

He waited. His verse-maker, a man from Sweden, stood beside him. 'Now!' said King Svein to the bard, and the man opened his mouth; and the gentlemanly Arnketil laid hold of the tail of the heifer.

Through the uproar: 'Do your men practise on ice?' said Thorfinn. The heifer galloped past the dais with Arnketil skimming behind it, his legs opening and shutting. The heifer slowed down, and Arnketil shot to one side, described a tight circle, and returned in a crouch with his knees bent.

He revolved.

The heifer, unused to having its tail wrung, kicked out sharply and, turning, charged in the opposite direction, where weeping men braced their shields to receive him. With a squeal of greased skins, Arnketil followed it. His feet danced of their own volition, flipping from heel to toe and once or twice crossing one another so that his chin swept through the air and his locked hands slid down the tail until, with a snap of the knees that all but struck fire, he surged up the beast's rump and took a fresh grip of its lathered appendage.

By the time the bard had reached the third verse, the heifer had impaled half a dozen shields and three men, and had learned how to bat Arnketil from end to end of the shield-bearers with a pleasing effect like a drum-roll. Very soon after that, it positioned itself for a clear run, cleared the length of the hall with its hooves hardly touching the ground, and stopped dead.

With the tail tight in his hands and his feet together, Arnketil whistled under the beast's belly and, feet first, up the screaming ranks of spectators, where he hung for a moment, suspended on shoulders and elbows. The tail was still in one hand.

On the floor, the heifer stood, looking confused. The bard, halfway through the fourth verse, paused and looked at King Svein, who was crying into his sleeve. King Svein said, 'The decision rests with my lord of Alba. Thorfinn, what do you say? Has he won or lost?'

The black, lowering gaze surveyed the floor.

'The heifer has certainly lost,' Thorfinn said. 'So, by the same token, I would say that your man Arnketil has certainly won. There is a ring of mine I feel he also deserves, if you will allow him the heifer. You spoke of a personage greater than Svein. Does one exist?'

King Svein stood, raised his arms to signify a judgement in Arnketil's favour, and gave Thorfinn's ring to his steward to convey, with the heifer, to the hole in the crowd that was Arnketil. He sat down again, ignoring the ensuing upheaval. He grinned at Thorfinn.

'Even Canute,' said Svein, 'acknowledged one man's power to be greater than his own in the Western world. Henry, Emperor of the Romans, has sent to invite you and your company to his palace at Goslar, in Saxony.'

He waited, wishing he could read the other man's face. He had been surprised to be accosted thus in public, but, on the whole, the moment was well chosen: in this uproar, they might as well be in private.

He could not think that there would be any doubt of the man's reply. Everyone knew that the King of England was childless and that he, Svein, was the heir with the most likely claim. Canute had been his uncle. Earl Eric of Northumbria had been his wife's uncle. His cousin Edith was Queen of England. Other kinsfolk had ruled the Severn mouth and still did. Emma, the Queen Mother of England, was his aunt by marriage and had shown him long ago, by her attentions, that she regarded this man Thorfinn as someone to watch.

She had been right, as usual. With all the north in tribute to him, from Cumbria through the Irish shores to the Orkneys, Thorfinn was a power that Norway now had to reckon with and no doubt would, if freed from its present engagement with himself.

So he and Alba needed one another against the threat of Norway, and the fact of Thorfinn's long stay was public witness, as it was meant to be, to an alliance.

Further, Thorfinn required to be on good terms with England, for the Godwins' power was great, as well as Emma's, and someone in England was fostering two substitute kings, the sons of Thorfinn's half-brother.

It was only common sense therefore, to make the bonds tighter: to seal the alliance by extending it to the friends and allies of himself and England: to the Metropolitan of the church in the north, to whom Norway no longer adhered; to the King of Germany and Emperor of the Romans, whose first wife had been Svein's first cousin and who had chosen the Pope, whom the Metropolitan had to obey.

Traffic with women played a large part in King Svein's life, but he never engaged in it against his own interests. The besieging of Thorfinn's red-headed wife would have been necessary even had she not proved, as she had, tempting enough to drive him mad over the winter.

Thorfinn had two churches to rule and had not yet made up his mind, it would appear, whether to risk one by indulging the other. The arrival of the priest Sulien had alarmed Svein. Already resistant to drawing closer to Bremen, Thorfinn might well turn and go home to please his Celts and their hermits.

On the other hand, should Thorfinn choose to travel, he was not short of silver. Why, then, not open doors further afield that he might find more irresistible than those of Bremen?

Thorfinn said, 'Goslar, in the Harz mountains? They say the hunting is good.'

'Even in Lent,' King Svein said, 'I hear the Emperor keeps an excellent table.'

'My wife,' Thorfinn said, 'would be distressed to part with her parents.'

'Why not leave her with them?' said King Svein gaily.

As a good host should, he accompanied Thorfinn to his frontier when, along with eighty men, skeins of baggage-mules, and several wooden-wheeled vehicles, the King of Alba shortly set out for Saxony.

Sulien the priest did not accompany them, although Tuathal the prior and a dozen courtmen at least were still in evidence. The grace-feast offered, as was the custom, to King Svein by his departing guest had been more than lavish, and the exchange of gifts generous to the point of absurdity. All had been done that was seemly. And the farewells between Thorfinn and his wife had been, Svein was content to see, stoical.

To the river Eider, where Jutland joined Germany, was a ride of four days. At Schleswig, Canute's old Bishop Rudolf would be waiting to assume the task of conductor: from the frontier to Hamburg, the Archbishop's officers had already received their instructions: to provide mounts, escorts, hospitality, and whatever else the King of Alba might require on his way to the Emperor.

From there, it was a hundred and fifty miles to Goslar, across the flat, pink-earthed plains and through the forests of Saxony, handed from one guest-quarter to another. Ascelin of Hildesheim would take care of the last stretch, and would not be backward in reciting the needs of the new church as well as the cathedral.

King Svein said, riding into Schleswig, 'I doubt if the Archbishop of Bremen will be in his diocese, but you must admire his accumulation of treasure and forgive his officers if they suggest that you add to it. In Adalbert's case, I rather suspect that the Lesum gold and the rest will get itself melted down one day soon in order to buy Bremen a comté. On the other hand, Hildesheim has an expensive pair of bronze doors still to pay for.'

'The same thing happens at home,' Thorfinn said. 'Some monk is always explaining that he needs a new pair of shoes. Don't be concerned. I understand a hint when I hear one. And before we meet with the Bishop, there is another matter we should speak of privately. You have a concubine, a young woman called Ragna.'

King Svein refrained from smiling. The cavalcade was slowing down.

'She is one of those who serve me. Yes. As a rule,' said King Svein, 'I do not keep a girl very long.'

There was a pause.

The King of Alba said carefully, 'You would not object, then, if the girl left your service and passed to another?'

This time King Svein smiled, because he could not prevent himself. 'Why,' he said, 'not in the least, as soon as she is delivered of whatever brat of mine she is carrying. Who finds her so much to his liking? I will make him a gift of her.'

'I am sorry to tell you,' said the King of Alba, 'that the man in question has taken the gift before it was offered and, indeed, has been sharing her favours for so many weeks that it is a question whether the child may be his rather than your own. On his behalf, may I beg your forgiveness?'

Stretching across, King Svein pressed one ringed hand on his royal guest's arm. 'How could I refuse? Of course,' he said. 'And the girl, too. I bear no grudges. How could I? Anything under my roof that pleases you is yours: I told you that at the start.'

'And the girl?' said Thorfinn.

'Is yours to do with as you please, so soon as the child is delivered. She will not suffer: I promise it, on my honour. I shall give her a new robe and three marks for herself when she joins you.'

'Then I shall get my cook to send for her in the summer,' Thorfinn said. 'He will be overjoyed, even lacking the baby. And the girl, from what he says, seems to find him very much to her taste. Indeed, they both have real cause to thank you.'

'Your cook?' said King Svein.

'Over there. The large man with black hair. I believe,' said Thorfinn, 'that, to begin with, the young woman thought she had found her way to *my* bed and was quite frightened when she learned otherwise. But he has a way, my cook, of persuading a girl that there is nowhere she would rather be than attempting some new feat on his mattress. If the child has black hair, you had better send it to be taught of an acrobat.'

Such was his emotion that, after the leave-taking, King Svein covered the ground back to Viborg in three days. Instead of seeking his hall, he made straight for the quarters of Finn and Bergljot Arnason.

The building was shuttered and empty, since Earl Finn of Halland, his wife, and the Lady Groa their daughter had long since left it to travel to Aarhus.

King Svein had enough dignity still to quell the impulse to set off straight after them. He sent a hirdman instead, who duly reported. The Arnasons had found a good wind and had left the rivermouth in a hired ship for Halland.

King Svein needed the Arnasons: he could do nothing to harm them.

He needed Thorfinn of Alba: he could not pursue Thorfinn's wife across oceans.

He had promised, in public, to do no mischief to the girl Ragna, his former concubine.

On the other hand, there was a good sale for blond hair in Tuscany.

King Svein sent them some.

FIVE

HAT MARCH, THE Emperor of the Romans took to his bed with his usual ailment and cancelled his proposed attack on the dukedom of Poland, thereby releasing upon the Saxony plains a large quantity of assorted militia, all riding in different directions accompanied by food, drink, and arms for three months and a full-blooded potential for mischief.

That no one thought of baiting a tight-knit cavalcade under the flags of Hamburg and Bremen was a tribute to the absent Archbishop, as much as to the chain-mail and steel of his officers. And by the time the Hildesheim escort took over for the last leg of the journey, the countryside was almost clear and it looked as if the Emperor's heathen guests from the pimple on the chin of the world were about to be delivered intact to the Emperor's bedside.

There was a moment in the approach to Goslar that impressed every visitor from a flat country: when the green, level grassland ahead released from its horizon a surf-line of mounded blue hills that mounted the sky until at last one drew rein above the invisible hollow and looked at the mountains fully revealed, green and blue, full of gods and of demons.

The Harz mountains, with the Emperor's new palace on their lower slopes, the eastern sun on its face, and the towers of the new church and the old, and the spilling of wood and stone buildings that had spored in the hollow to serve the hunting-lodge and frontier fortress and citadel that, with Tilleda and Werla and Pöhlde, had seen kings and Emperors halt and move on for a hundred years since the first Henry.

Except that the third Henry had shown in ten years a tendency not to move on, having consumed his dues of fat pigs and cattle and malt and honey and corn, but to dwell rather longer than was convenient, given that there existed elsewhere in Saxony alone twenty imperial manors also waiting to nourish the Emperor. But it was to Goselager, the place on the Gose, that he looked for long days of sport and of leisure with his Empress-Queen and his priests, and where he had erected this vast double salon, big enough for the entertainment of Popes, and most likely for the choosing of them as well.

And opposite the palace, the shining, three-towered spread of the cathedral built to house the travel-worn bones of SS Simon the Zealot and Jude Thaddaeus the Apostle, spared from his hoard at Toulouse by the Queen's brother William of Aquitaine.

Foreigners, it was to be assumed, had little interest in this. It was best to halt, admiring the view, and then to lead the way down into the basin, past the basilica of St George and its discarded residence, through the muddy market-place, and up to the King's Bridge over the Gose, running narrow and clear over its pebbles, where the Emperor's guard stopped them again, but only as a formality: the Bishop's harbingers had done their work properly.

From the bridge, you could see the cathedral at the top of the rise: yellow-white against the blue sky and green hills. And as you reached the cathedral, there opened up on your right the great slope of busy, paved courtyard, enclosed with haphazard building, that ended in the new palace.

It stood printing the sky like a piece of horse-harness, engraved in pale gold and black with arched windows, and the banners on the long, plunging roof flew and chattered like jungle-birds.

There was a strong smell of fish.

'Can I help it?' cried Isleifr of Iceland.

Scarlet with joy, he thrashed in the King of Alba's iron, one-handed embrace, and a seam opened with a ladder of sound across his priestly black shoulders. 'Look, you'll have me in rags. It's six months since Lulach's wedding in Scone. Can I help it if men follow my bear as if they have come into season? Do you know what I have suffered? Can you imagine how much a Greenland bear can grow in six months? He has eaten his keeper and torn up three Germans already.'

'Not the Emperor?' said Thorfinn, releasing him. 'I heard he was poorly. Isleifr, why bring a bear to the Emperor?'

'Because I wanted him to remember me,' Isleifr said. 'And I'll wager he'll remember me when the visitation from Alba has gone from his memory. In any case, you'd better get out of your travelling-clothes. They'll send a deputation to summon you any minute, and I've had enough trouble educating them over Iceland. They thought I'd wear goatskins laundered in cow-piss.'

'Compared with stale fish,' Thorfinn said, 'that would be tolerable. A deputation to meet the Emperor?'

'Are you nervous?' Isleifr said. 'I'll sell you a Frankish phrase book. *Altdeutsche Gespräche*, it's called. *Erro e guille trenchen*, id est, *ego volo bibere*. So long as you know Latin, it's simple.'

Irony was a new thing for Isleifr. He stared at Thorfinn, his face even redder. 'Am I shouting? It's because you speak my name the right way.'

'I must remember not to,' said Thorfinn. 'And we'll talk later. In the meantime, whom shall we see?'

'Not the Emperor,' Isleifr said. 'He's got Roman fever and won't be up for three days or a week. No. The Emperor's easy, so long as you look holy and timid. You'll wish you had to deal with the Emperor before this night is over.'

'You alarm me,' said Thorfinn. 'Then let me guess. We are in the new cathedral's guest-house, under the beneficent protection, daily approaching, of the bones of SS Simon and Jude. But the Bishop of Osnabrück, whose care it should be, has vanished, and the Bishop of Hildesheim, who shares his duty, has gone home. So who is left to act host? Who in Saxony, my saintly Isleifr, can be as dangerous as your smile seems to suggest? Your Greenland bear?'

'No. Very nearly. The Archbishop of Hamburg and Bremen,' said Isleifr soberly.

'But no music,' said Archbishop Adalbert of Hamburg and Bremen, smiling at the King of Alba, who was wearing a robe whose folds clacked against his own whenever either of them moved in his chair-stall.

'No music, which, I hold, arrests conversation. Sanctioned by God and agreeable to Man: such are good talk and hospitality.'

The Archbishop gave a second agreeable smile, and his servants lost some of their terror. For the evening entertainment of the King of Alba, the mule-carts had been sent to the Archbishop's own lodge in the mountains, and the eating-hall of the cathedral, barely finished, had been hung with the Archbishop's famous silks with the elephant cartouches, and the tables laid with his silver, and the kitchens packed with the white bread, the wines, the delicate fish from the vivarium, the plump birds and fine, scented meats from his storehouse.

All had been done, and in time. So now the Archbishop gave that agreeable smile, addressing his guest. 'You have noticed the elephants. You know their history?'

'I am dazzled. Tell me,' said Thorfinn. On his other side, the Provost of Goslar gave a cough which almost extinguished the snort that preceded it.

'You will have heard it. How, fifty years ago, the Emperor's great-great uncle opened the tomb of Charlemagne in Aachen, the second Rome, my dear Mak Betta. And there sat the great King in his jewels, with one glove, pierced by his fingernails, holding the sceptre. A sight to inspire awe. The Emperor received reverent attention. He was laid in silks from this bale, among elephants, and the tomb was resealed. Look at them. Look at my elephants. Are they not a wonder, with their black Eastern eyes and their toenails? From the imperial workshops of Byzantium to Svatioslav, and from Kiev as a gift to the Emperor.

'The Rhine,' said the Archbishop, 'is where you will still find the best compound twills. In Mainz or Cologne. We buried my old friend Pope Clement three years ago in Bamberg in a length made in Thebes, as fine as any I have ever seen: Provost Anno will remember. I sent a bale very like it the other day to Edward of England.'

'As a hint?' said Thorfinn.

His handsome face composed, the Archbishop considered the remark.

Then he laughed. 'The King supported us with his fleet shortly thereafter, in the Emperor's chastisement of the Duke of Lorraine,' he said. 'If that is what you mean.'

'I expect,' said the King of Alba, 'that is what I meant. I am glad, at any rate, that the Emperor's ailment has proved less than serious.'

'He is better. In a day or two, he will receive you. And the Queen. A remarkable woman. She has taken the greatest interest in the gift of our friend Isleifr here. Along with, of course, the delectable doves, her little daughters.'

Someone removed Thorfinn's platter and put down another, of silver.

'I believe,' said Thorfinn, 'that the Emperor's oldest daughter, the niece of King Edward, is Abbess of Quedlinburg, very near here? Perhaps Duke Casimir plans to visit his kinswoman.'

On the Archbishop's other side, the pallid cheeks of the Duke of Poland paused in their exercise and then continued. Archbishop Adalbert said, 'He hears you, but his grasp of Saxon is uncertain at times. Of course, his father was a cousin of King Canute, Beatrice's grandfather. I had forgotten. You knew King Canute well, I am told, and even as a young man served the Lady Emma in England?'

He held out a dish with his own hands to his awkward guest, having side-stepped the matter of Quedlinburg. His own mother had been brought up in that convent, and for a child of eight to be appointed abbess was only natural when the child was royal and the place the stronghold that it was. He wished that Casimir, having received the imperial forgiveness, would stop sulking, take the Emperor's gifts, and go home, preferably before the end of the banquet.

Casimir said, in excellent Low German, 'Perhaps I should call on her. Perhaps I should call on the Abbess and tell her how Bratislav took our church treasure, and carried hundreds of Poles off to slavery, and seized the bones of the apostle Adalbert. Have you no interest in the bones of the apostle Adalbert, Archbishop Adalbert?'

The Archbishop laid down his dish and turned patiently, releasing a scent of rosewater that betrayed, insidiously, that he had had his uncanonical daily cold bath. He said, 'Matters for the council chamber have been disposed of in the council chamber. We must think of our guests from afar, who are tired and wish to be entertained.'

'*I* am tired,' said Duke Casimir. 'Tired of being treated as a child because I have a German mother kin to the Emperor. I am Polish. I do not wish to sit with you any longer.' He stood up.

The Archbishop rose as well. 'You have a touch of fever. I can see it,' said the Archbishop kindly. 'Here is the Provost, who will see you to your quarters, and I shall send my own physician to attend you. A bath of hot salt, I always recommend. I know that some are against it. But for the Emperor, as you see, it works wonders.'

Smiling, he sat down, arranging his wide-skirted gown, as the company half-rose and sat again, and the Provost of Goslar got to his feet with no great alacrity and the Duke of Poland, after staring for a moment, turned on his heel and stalked out.

'I am a great believer in salt,' said Archbishop Adalbert to the King of Alba.

'. . . They tell me,' said the Archbishop of Bremen, 'that your peoples north of Alba prefer to call you Thorfinn, the pagan name of your forefathers. Old beliefs are hard to uproot, I know, and old practices; and both Orkney and Iceland have had little more than fifty years of Christian witness. What backsliding there has been among the barbarians here, I need hardly tell you, or what pockets of sin still untouched. The Estonians adore dragons and birds, and sacrifice slaves to them. You have seen, sanctified in the church here, the altar to the Saxon god Krodo, made within this last year. In Uppsala, horses and dogs hung with men in their sacred groves until very recently and unless we have care, may do so again.'

'That Christian witness may falter is known to everyone,' the King of Alba said gravely. 'Or perhaps I should put it differently. A people cannot be converted until it learns to stop killing its missionaries. And sometimes that is something that only a temporal power can do.

'Olaf Tryggvasson offered Christ to my father in Orkney on the point of a sword, and sent his priest, steel in hand, to baptise the father of your good priest Isleifr there, and through him convert Iceland. In later years, King Olaf the Saint similarly persuaded his countrymen. The end of each, you perhaps know. To those of us who are but common clay, it offers small inducement to multiply churches and found bishoprics. Should the throne weaken and totter, the pagan will return a hundredfold. As threatens in Norway.'

'Because the church in Norway is weak,' said Archbishop Adalbert. 'Because its bishops are consecrated no man knows where, in booths and on carpets, and its priests fly to their homeland like hares as king succeeds enemy king. In Germany, the King and the church are brother and sister.'

'But,' said Thorfinn, black-browed face pensively bent, 'Germany is the market-place of the world, and has rich lands with which to clothe and nourish its sister. Alba and Orkney are poor, and have to spend the little they have to defend themselves.'

'Forgive me,' said the Archbishop of Hamburg and Bremen, 'but, in your modesty, you would have us ignore both your own effects and the more than seemly attire of your courtmen. Either you are richer than you care to boast, or you wear the skins of your countrymen on your backs.'

The King of Alba, it seemed, never smiled. The tall brow lifted itself and fell again. 'The rings? The brooches?' said Thorfinn. 'The horse? That came from Spain to Ireland, and was a gift from the King of Dublin for services my fleet had rendered, and tribute owed me. The rest came mostly through trade, which is dwindling as tolls and taxes abroad become higher. The silver that paid for our clothes and the ivory triptych I placed on the altar at Hamburg came, before we fell out, from King Harald of Norway. I hesitated to bring you the triptych, but thought that in the bosom of Hamburg, fruitful mother of peoples, it would come by no defilement. It was plundered, as the inscription makes plain, from the shrine of St Olaf at Nídarós.'

'King Harald should take heed,' said the Archbishop, and the full, shapely lips pressed together. 'King Harald should take heed, lest we visit him with the rod of correction and claim from him the obedience of a man who has offended the Lord. I hear King Svein bravely withstands his grievous assaults upon Denmark.'

'King Svein asked me to help him,' said the King of Alba. 'But of course I refused.'

'Refused?'

Thorfinn looked apologetic. 'How can my fleet ply for silver if they are fighting? Already, the Norwegian trade is lost to us. Slaves are expensive. The tilled land and the pastures are still producing far less than they should, and there is no money for roads and for bridges that would join market to market, and allow workshops to flourish, and provide myself and my priests and my governors with an income from taxes and tolls. I cannot offer a hand to an ally. I cannot offer, as I should, even a son's welcome to Mother Church.'

'So you say,' said Archbishop Adalbert. 'But I wonder if you have considered what Mother Church may offer you? The services of seasoned farmer, of scribe, and of steward: the repository of wisdom in all those places where it may be wanting in the matter of tax-collecting and justice and government. Such things are unknown or unheeded in the innocent and unworldly sphere of the Celtic tribes, and while their hermits may pray for your souls, they will not tell you how to order your bodies, which are the temples and defence of your spirit. Nor are we harsh to the humble flocks who have just crossed our thresholds. The church of Ribe pays no dues to Bremen. None. And yet all our wealth, both of earth and of heaven, is at the disposal of King Svein. It could be yours as well.'

'It's working,' said Odalric of Caithness. 'At least, Thorfinn's just drunk off his wine, which ought to mean the worst bit is over.'

'You mean,' said Leofwine in his Welsh-Gaelic, 'that the Emperor is to waive harbour and market dues and see that all river shipments are toll-free on Thorfinn's boats in future?'

Ferteth, the Dunblane toisech, said, 'Be careful. The place is full of monks who speak Irish.'

'No, it isn't,' said Isleifr. 'They're all at Bishop John's, supping with Tuathal and Eochaid. You haven't known Thorfinn for very long, have you?'

The Dunblane toisech was sweating. He said, 'He's fond of money. It's natural.'

'Oh, he's ambitious,' said Isleifr. 'You don't start life as the fifth and last son of an island earl and finish it as head of a kingdom without hacking a long, bloody furrow. He's ambitious and heathen, and Adalbert is ambitious and holy. But Thorfinn has got something that the Archbishop wants.'

'The same way that King Svein wanted something that Thorfinn had,' said the Atholl man, Cormac.

'The Lady?' said the Moray toisech, and grinned. 'That was a game. This is serious. The Archbishop wants to be patriarch of the north, and Thorfinn can help him. Or the Archbishop *thinks* he can help him.'

'And is the Archbishop mistaken?' said Otkel of Orkney. 'Or perhaps half mistaken? I should rather like to know. Ferocious wolves take large bites. I don't think I'd like the Archbishop for my enemy.'

SIX

N HIS LODGING near the King's Mill and under the knoll of St Mary's, Bishop John, the saintliest man in Goslar, was innocently tiddly. The wine which, being Sunday, he had been able to serve along with a reasonable meal was only one of the causes. The other was the sound in his ears: the joyous sound of five Gaelic voices vying with one another in the accents of Ireland and Alba.

There had been a point, earlier in the evening, when the noise had made him apprehensive. This was what Abbot Ekbert complained of in Fulda, and Archbishop Pilgrim had found so disturbing in Cologne that he had tried to dismiss Abbot Ailill of St Martin's and St Pantaleon and his brisk communities of Irish monks.

But Abbot Ekbert was not here, and Archbishop Pilgrim was asleep in Christ these fourteen years, and the present Archbishop of Cologne, in whom ran the blood of Popes and Emperors, had things on his mind other than the conduct of the Irish monks in his diocese. Other things, such as un-Christian dislike of Bishop John's own lifelong hero, Adalbert of Hamburg and Bremen.

Thinking about it, Bishop John cried a little, and Abbot Maieul, his friend and Ailill's successor from St Martin's Cologne, patted his hand without faltering in the conversational duel he was conducting with the King of Alba's prior over a cryptogram.

Everyone knew, of course, that the King of Alba was important because he had a fleet; and it was to be expected that he did some trading. It had been a surprise, however, to find his two priests so congenial. The Prior, Eochaid, was a lettered man, as you would expect of anyone trained in Armagh. The visiting Abbot, Tuathal, had studied in Swords, and for several years, it would appear, he and Abbot Maieul had been exchanging riddles and acrostics and even secular verses, one of which they were now chanting together. It sometimes seemed to Bishop John that the happy nature of Maieul of Cologne led the Abbot alarmingly close to frivolity.

Bishop John looked up, his eyes refilling with tears, and Prior Tuathal, who was holding his other hand, leaned over and explained the import of the last two lines of the secular verse, which were so unexpectedly witty that Bishop John swallowed his tongue and had to be given drink and banged on the shoulderblades.

His fourth and fifth guests, who had come with Abbot Maieul from Cologne, watched, smiling with rueful affection. The younger, who had the good Irish-Breton name of Muiredach, said, 'If you give him any more, he will fall asleep.'

Muiredach mac Robartaig might be the son of the Abbot of Kells, but he was only sixteen. Bishop John said, 'Is it for the guests, now, to advise the host what he is drinking, and the mouths of them wet with the hospitality broth?'

'He said something,' said Sigurd. Bishop John heard him quite clearly. It was unlike Sigurd to be obtuse. Sigurd had been sent especially from Cologne to join the brethren at Goslar and tend the workshops. The Archbishop's welcome had been cool, but that was because he did not yet know Sigurd as Bishop John did. Bishop John said, 'Was I talking to you? It was Muiredach here whose manners need watching.'

'I don't know what he's saying either,' said Muiredach. 'Give him another drink.'

They gave him another drink, and because arguing made him tired, Bishop John went to sleep.

When they had made him comfortable, 'We don't often breed saints,' said Abbot Maieul of Cologne. 'Let us make sure this one comes to no harm. Tuathal. Your King is here to obtain Bremen-consecrated bishops. Why, I wonder? Merely to promote alliance?'

'You are half right,' said Tuathal. The acumen that had led Thorfinn to place him in Fife, the storm-centre of his new kingdom, was there to be seen in his sharp eyes and thick, pock-marked face. 'We need alliances because we lack organisation, except at sea. We need Frankish-trained men, with Gaelic as one of their languages.'

'For Orkney?' said the Abbot of St Martin's. 'And what of Malduin, the Gaelic-speaking Bishop of Alba you have already? I do not see him here.'

Tuathal said, 'Bishop Malduin was consecrated at York. And York means Northumbria, whose ties to Norway are strong. As for Orkney, Celtic monks have had a stake there and in Caithness from the earliest times. In theory, Irish bishops could serve there. . . .'

'But Irish bishops don't know how to organise?' said Abbot Maieul.

Eochaid answered. 'There are other objections. The Bishop of Dublin is consecrated by the Archbishop of Canterbury in England. The Welsh bishops, too. For Canterbury, my King has nothing but respect. But in England, since the time of Gregory, the souls of the northern peoples are held to be a matter for the churchmen of York. And that, as I have explained, holds its dangers.'

'I fear it is true,' said the Abbot of St Martin's. He glanced to the pallet where Bishop John, his fur robe tucked around him, was sleeping musically.

'Is it mannerly, do you suppose, to summon the servants in the absence of one's host and request a little more wine? Sigurd, you are more of this establishment than anyone.'

'His name is Sigurd?' queried Prior Tuathal as the man thus addressed, with no reluctance, sprang to his feet and departed.

'He is an Irish Norseman from Dublin, trained at Kells. His name in Christ should be Jon, but we do not use it here. Muiredach and I thought you would like him. He does not enjoy the prospect of working at Goslar close to Archbishop Adalbert. . . . Ah, Sigurd. The wine.'

Pouring the wine with his powerful hands, the priest Sigurd, it could be seen, wore a half-smile. Tuathal said to him as he sat down, 'So you have been here a week. How do you like Goslar?'

'As well as any battle-field,' Sigurd said. A burly man in his forties, his crucifix shone like a mirror and his tonsure had been drawn with a compass. He added, 'They tried to get me dictating in the scriptorium, till they discovered my stutter.'

There was a pause. 'I was not aware,' said Abbot Maieul, 'that you had a stutter?'

'You should see,' said the priest Sigurd amiably, 'the thirty-two copies of Livy that thirty-two monks are rewriting in half the number of pages. There are other things I'm better at.'

He rummaged down at his girdle and laid a silver disc on the table. Half an inch in diameter, it bore the legend HERRENNUS EPS, COLONIA URBS.

'Producing those, for example. They brought me here to run the Goslar mint. You know about the mines in the Rammelsberg? Silver, copper, and lead. That's how Goslar came to be here at all.'

Tuathal said, 'We have silver in Cumbria.'

'But no coins?' Sigurd said. 'We had coins in Dublin.'

'The Vikings had,' Tuathal said. 'But the tribes don't use coin. They've no roads or bridges to pay toll on and they do their own fighting. They don't even expect coin for their prisoners: the Irish fight to kill, not to ransom.'

'But the Irish,' said Abbot Maieul, 'as we have just said, are not organised. Isleifr wished, I think, to see the furnaces to compare them with those at Hervordin, and one of your noblemen—Leofwine?—professed an interest also. It may be that the mine-workings would interest your King Macbeth as well.'

'Macbethad. A fine Irish name. Son of Life,' said Bishop John thoughtfully. His guests turned.

The Bishop, his eyes on the painted wood ceiling, smoothed the fur over his chest with one gentle, ringed hand. 'The leader of his king's forces in the north—was it not so? Regent for his king in the north, and he fought his master and killed him. So barbarians take the throne. King Olaf. King Canute.'

Eochaid flushed, but Prior Tuathal only smiled and, leaning over, drew the fur robe a trifle higher. 'King Olaf has been made a saint,' he said. 'And it was after a fair fight that King Duncan met his end.'

The soft eyes turned. 'But he is a king,' said Bishop John. 'Do his people follow him?'

'Yes,' said Tuathal. He drew back.

'In adversity?' said Bishop John. 'A man needs a God-fearing king, a shriven king, in adversity.'

Abbot Maieul came over and knelt. 'Cease to concern yourself,' he said. 'King Macbeth is here because he knows what his nation needs, and is preparing for it. And how better to look for salvation than through the church of Bremen and Archbishop Adalbert?'

Bishop John's eyes were closing. He smiled. 'Indeed,' he said. 'There is Christ risen again, one would say. But for the ablutions. Save him, Mary, Mother of God, from the sin he has, of resorting to so many ablutions.'

'. . . Dreams,' Archbishop Adalbert said. 'Dreams and their interpretation. I think, with the Greeks, that they have much to tell us. Bishop John (who, I trust, is entertaining your Irishmen adequately) would not agree. The Greeks are pagan, he says. But sometimes the Lord speaks through strange instruments, and in any case the Greeks are pagan no longer. My new church at Bremen, which you have not yet seen, is built as a compliment to the church at Benevento. The beauty of its ritual, of which you may have heard, is meant to echo the glory of St Sophia, that struck the eyes and ears of the Russian and drew him forthwith from other gods. Who interprets your dreams?'

One cold winter, the ink froze at Fulda. 'In Alba,' Thorfinn said, 'matters are slightly different. Other people have the dreams, and I interpret them. Or should if I knew Greek. There is a disturbance?'

It was only reasonable that the fellow should draw attention to it: the shouting had been going on outside for five minutes. The Archbishop felt himself paling with anger. He had wished to talk about dreams. He turned and snapped his fingers.

From the doorway, a man ran towards him.

A second man, entering uninvited, melted discreetly to the end of the table, where sat Isleifr with some of the King of Alba's companions. Isleifr said, 'Oh, Christ and Odin.'

'What?' said Odalric, who had the quickest wits. Then he grinned. 'Christ and Odin? Isleifr: the bear?'

The Archbishop stood up, brilliant as Charlemagne, two hundred years dead against the elephant silks. He said, 'The Greenland bear has escaped. Men with weapons are running to find it. Until it is killed, none should leave the church buildings.'

Thorfinn's face, wholly bland under the level black bar of his eyebrows, looked across at Isleifr. He said, 'Where will it go?'

'Oh, Christ and Odin,' said Isleifr, whose vocabulary, it seemed, had suffered some impairment. 'There's a vivarium, isn't there? You know where he'll go, then. He'll make straight for the Emperor's fishpond.'

'It seems a pity to kill him,' said Thorfinn. 'Can't you catch him? You would need a few men who can swim, and poles and forks and a fishnet.'

Isleifr said, 'I told you. He's eaten his keeper. No one swims at this court.'

'*You* do,' said Thorfinn. 'I've seen you. So do Odalric and Hlodver and Otkel. So do I.'

'Holy Christ,' said Isleifr, laying hands in extremity on a variant. 'My bear kills the King of Alba while he's under the protection of the Emperor of the Romans, and what's my life worth?'

'You'd better come and protect me, then,' said Thorfinn, shaking himself free of his over-robe. He turned at the door. 'If my lord Archbishop permits? An occasion such as tonight does not deserve to be marked by death and disaster, even to the Emperor's fish.'

'It rather seems,' said Abbot Maieul, 'that our host has entered upon his night's sleep. I am sure he will not mind if we disperse quietly. Or as quietly as we can. There seems to be a great deal of noise going on outside. Who is that at the door?'

'Gillocher of Lumphanan,' said the face at the door, which appeared to be lit from within like a lantern. It said, 'Tuathal, can you or Eochaid swim?'

'*Swim?*' said Abbot Tuathal. 'No. Why?'

'I can swim,' said Sigurd the Dubliner unexpectedly. 'Why?'

'Follow me,' said Gillocher of Lumphanan, and disappeared.

They followed.

When Bishop John woke, the room was empty.

His robe was creased, and his ring had bitten into his cheek. There was a channel of wet running from the corner of his mouth. He did not feel very well.

He sat up.

The servants would have to be spoken to once again: he would get Bovo to help. Last night's supper lay uncleared on the table, and the candles sat in their pools, hoary as marsh-spirits. They had all gone, without leave, to the ceremony.

He could hear there was a ceremony. The cheering came through his half-shuttered window, and the blaze of lights: they must have lined the whole courtyard with torches.

If there was a ceremony, then the Archbishop would be in charge of it.

If the Archbishop was presiding over anything, his court of churchmen, including his bishops, ought to be present.

He, John, had forgotten something, and the Archbishop was going to be, rightly, very grieved.

Bishop John rose stiffly, wiped his face, shook out his gown, smoothed his hair, and walked carefully out of the room and along to the doorway of his lodging. He opened the door. Light and noise burst upon him.

It was, near enough, as the square looked at tribute-time, when the ewes crowded in, rearing and jumping, with their knuckles on each other's shoulders, and the heifers blundered, mouths open, and swerved, sending younger beasts rolling, and from each braying head the yell of protest made itself heard: a various, unceasing uproar that sped, rising and falling, from wall to wall of the square.

Except that these were not sheep or cattle or goats, but men he knew, making their way in shrieking dispersal down the great slope from St Mary's.

He saw faces he knew. Abbot Maieul, laughing. He had been talking to Abbot Maieul—hadn't he?—only recently, and the Abbot had said nothing of an engagement. Two monks from the cathedral, with a basket of fish— fish? At this hour of night?—swinging between them. Servants and noblemen of the court: plenty of those, and behaving no differently from the others. Three men whose faces he vaguely recognised as belonging to the train of the King of Alba. They, it seemed, had been fishing also.

And there . . . There, walking alone, shaking off with a gesture of irritation two or three men who appeared to wish to serve him, was his own master, the Archbishop of Hamburg and Bremen, making his way, very erect and not laughing at all, to his quarters in the halls of the cathedral.

If he, John, had been remiss, then the sooner he confessed and made his peace the better.

Bishop John left the doorway and ventured out into the courtyard. A number of people called to him, and he smiled cautiously in return. As he drew nearer to the new church, the crowd thinned and he found it easier to keep the Archbishop in view. Indeed, as if God had laid a path for his feet, a carpet of silver, it seemed, unrolled between Bishop John and his master.

Bishop John followed the silver carpet. It led through the great doors and across the inner yard to the suite set apart for the Archbishop. Bishop John tapped on the door and waited a very long time, making patterns on the silver carpet with the toe of his slipper. Then it came to him that perhaps he had not really tapped at all, and he did so again, rather loudly.

The Archbishop's voice, also loud, answered crossly. Bishop John opened the door.

The Archbishop stood in his chamber, naked but for his breeches of linen; and the water of his uncanonical ablutions ran from his hair to his shoulders and chest, and from his underbreeches over his knees to the floor.

Tears welled into Bishop John's eyes. He lowered his head.

'My lord, my lord. I shall pray for you,' said Bishop John, and sadly turned, and walked back to his lodging.

'Who pushed him in?' Thorfinn said. 'Can't one of you cretins stop laughing? Isleifr?'

Isleifr wailed, and choked, and wailed again, holding his ribs. Tears poured down his face. Malpedar of Buchan said, 'It was one of the monks. I saw him. But I don't think the Archbishop realised it. My lord, you swam like a fish, getting him out.'

'That was the bear,' Thorfinn said. 'It was holding me by the ankles. Is it all right? Isleifr?'

'The bear,' said Isleifr, whining a little, 'is in excellent order. The King's fishpond is a different matter. Thorfinn . . .'

'What?' said Thorfinn. He continued with what he was doing, which was wrapping a band of white cloth round a missing strip of brown flesh on his forearm.

Isleifr said, 'You came here to get the Archbishop's goodwill, and the Emperor's. Has this harmed you?'

Thorfinn looked up, a strip of cloth in his teeth. 'Do you think I am doing this for amusement?' He finished tying the cloth and lay back, soaking a number of cushions.

'What you mean is this: we have turned the Emperor's court into a barbarian sports-ground, as he would expect of King Svein or King Harald.

'He knows now that I am not St Columba: angelic in appearance, graceful in speech, holy in action. But neither am I Harald or Svein, or the kind of leader that lurks in forests with robbers, stealthily eating mare's flesh off a wooden griddle. Now he knows that as well.

'I have no objection to this Emperor or this Archbishop perceiving that the men of Alba have blood in their veins. You did well. We all did rather well. And when the Archbishop has had time to think it all over, his conclusions will do us no harm either.'

Cormac of Dunkeld blew his nose, wiped his eyes, and, resting his chin on his arms, looked blearily and lovingly at his master, the monarch of Alba.

'My lord Thorfinn,' he said. 'We have had a vote, all of us in your court. We think you should be King of Vinland as well, and take us with you.'

'Perhaps. Come to me,' said Thorfinn, 'when you can swim.'

On the third and last day of their stay, when the Archbishop of Hamburg had gone, and the Archbishop of Cologne had arrived, and the Emperor had recovered sufficiently to give the promised banquet of state, the King of Germany and the King of Alba met at last, as had been intended, face to face in an antechamber of the great salon.

'His conclusions will do us no harm,' Thorfinn had said; and in that he had been proved right. Beginning on the morning after his soaking, gifts had appeared, and delicacies from the Emperor's table. Wealthy courtiers took the King hunting, and officials of the mines and of the mint conveyed the King, as he desired, up the great hill of the Rammelsberg, against whose cheek the King's palace rested. A tailor begged an appointment, and a tunic, abbreviated in the French style, arrived to take the place of the one drenched in the fishpond. With it was a floor-length gown, tight-sleeved, of yellow taffeta sewn with flowers and tendrils, to wear at the banquet; and a mantle cut like a cope and trimmed in bands and lozenges with goldsmith's work.

Prior Tuathal said, 'You look like the Pope. Or Archbishop Adalbert. What did you give the Emperor?'

'The Arabian horse,' Thorfinn said. 'Among other things.'

On the day of the banquet, he wore the robe and the cope and, passing uphill with his men in procession between the Emperor's guard and the trumpeters, made his way to the terrace and through the arch under the audience balcony. At the top of the stairs, the Emperor and his Queen stood awaiting him.

Despite his French wife, the French mode of the bare chin had not commended itself to the Emperor. The thin nose and narrow face, pallid still, tapered to its conclusion in silky black hair that feathered also his upper lip and curled a little over his ears, under the jewelless band of the Patrician of Rome. Not for today, it would seem, the hinged octagonal crown, half laurel wreath and half helmet, with its queer graven enamels nearly a hundred years old: King David as the symbol of Justice, King Solomon as the symbol of wisdom.

The Emperor's wife, small, firm, precise as a bird, wore her crown over her veil: a gold filigree band two inches deep, set with designs of pale stones— amethysts, aquamarines, rock crystals, pearls. She had Lombard eyes and her cheeks and lips were coloured a little. As she smiled and spoke in greeting and lifted her mantle to lead the way to the banqueting-hall, she showed ankle-slippers all sewn with sirens and gryphons, with needle-fine toes and soles of perfect neats' leather.

The hall, the *Aula Imperialis*, was a hundred and fifty feet long and, along that length, clothed with Bohemian lions and one-headed imperial eagles in scarlet and rose-purple silks. The throne, in open-work bronze surrounded by cage-walls of heavy worked marble, stood against the wall-hangings and looked to the row of six triple windows piercing the opposite wall and giving entrance, in their midst, to the balcony.

Through the windows, beyond the sunlit slope of the courtyard and the trees and the rooftops of the cathedral lay the little hill of St Peter, and to the south the green wooded horizon also rose gently, to the slopes of Hahnenberg and great Rammelsberg itself.

The tables ran lengthwise, with that of the Emperor on a dais, where he sat not on his throne but on a high, cushioned, carved chair beside those for his Queen and his guest Macbeth, King of Alba.

The Queen had been watching her guest, the King from the north. As they turned to their seats, she spoke to him gravely. 'You look at our hills and think of Alba, whose hills you have left?'

He made an answer with equal gravity, but not the true one. *I look at your hills, and I think of the sea, that I have exchanged for a fishpond. I look at this hall, and I think of the chamber at Orphir with my wife Groa in it.*

The two hours of the banquet passed quickly.

There were familiar faces and strange ones: Anno, Provost of Goslar, with his tassel-hair and his scowl; Abbot Maieul and his superior, the Archbishop of Cologne, with his famous crucifix in which Christ wore the piled hair and blue and classical features, carved in lapis-lazuli, of the Empress Livia. The Archbishop's sister Richeza of Poland. The Queen's young kinsman Robert le Bourguignon, great-nephew of her mother, with whom she had shared her childhood.

They asked the King of Alba what he thought of William of Normandy and of Earl Godwin's oldest son Harold, and he answered with perfect truth that he had not met either of them.

They asked the King of Alba who were his heirs and what rivals they had, and he named them. They asked him whether he expected the sons of his dead brother Duncan to fight for the throne on his death. He replied that such a thing was quite possible; as it was possible that one or all of the four claimants to the throne of Edward of England might have to fight the sons of Edmund Ironside, wherever they might be hidden.

They discussed the weather.

Then the banquet was over and they listened to music by the Emperor's court musicians, and a rendering of exceptional quality by Cadou, the King of Alba's household harpist, of a song to the happy virgin Odile, the blind patron saint of Alsace, which Archbishop Herimann applauded with deliberation, his large white hands beating together so that his rings flashed.

The private audience followed.

This time, the room held ten people but only two chairs. In one sat the Emperor, with the Archbishop of Cologne and the Provost of Goslar standing closest behind him. Opposite sat the King of Alba, while at his back Eochaid's well-formed, tranquil head and the scarred and folded face of Prior Tuathal appeared embossed in the lamplight, like the one-headed eagle with its chevronned breast and striped wings on the hanging behind them.

In his hand, Thorfinn held wine in a goblet of gold moulded between walls of thin antique glass. On a table nearby lay a cushion on which rested the Arabic sword of Charlemagne, with its curved fishskin handle and its steel blade flowering with bright gilded copper.

The Emperor said, 'An agreement has already been reached, as you know, between our officers. To make the way safe for merchants and pilgrims was a care King Canute also took upon himself. You have asked my Archbishop of Hamburg and Bremen to help you spread the word of God in your country, and to send you bishops to train your priests and ordain them. He has received your supplication with joy, as have I; and I shall make it my task to see that His Holiness hears your request, and that he instructs that it should be forthwith fulfilled from the ranks of whatever good men may be suitable.'

'I ask this with diffidence,' said the King of Alba, his eyes round and unrevealing as bronze pennies. 'One day, God willing, my people will be united in prosperity, but to sustain a levy is at present beyond them, and the land I could offer any man of the church is of little worth. Also, such men would require the gift of tongues.'

The Emperor turned his head on his shoulder. The Archbishop Herimann said, 'What do your people pay already, my lord, for the services of baptism and confirmation and burial, for the visitation of the sick and the dedication of altars and the ordaining of men to holy orders? From pagan times, priests have grown greedy in these matters and, without order, may well take more from the needy than Mother Church with her tithes could ever do. But, as the Emperor has said, we understand that northern nations are not as others, and that a fixed see and a fixed tribute may not at first be possible. We should be poor Christians if we debarred any man from Christ on those grounds. His Holiness, I am certain, will give his consent.'

The Emperor turned his head gently. At thirty-three, the composure of long training gave him an air of maturity and even of saintliness. His private life, as was well known, was without blemish, and negotiations and policy-making, battle and journeying for the sake of the Empire and the sake of his church filled all but the least of his days.

He said, 'His Holiness will require of us, naturally, an assurance that any bishop or bishops sent you will have the support and respect of a King whose own life is a worthy one in the eyes of the church and of his subjects. Your confessor stands behind you. But your peoples are diverse, as you say, and your father was not a Christian born. Has it never seemed to you that the ancient Christian peoples over whom you now rule may falter sometimes in their allegiance, unsure of your faith? Has it ever occurred to you that a purpose might be served, beneficial to you and to the peoples you lead, in presenting yourself for absolution to His Holiness himself at Rome?'

Prior Tuathal's mouth opened.

'How would this be possible?' the King of Alba said.

The Emperor lifted a finger, and his wine-server brought forward a pitcher. 'The present Pope has revived the custom of an annual synod at Rome after the celebration of Easter. It takes place this year at the end of the month of April. Princes of the northern nations are made welcome in Rome at this time, and the Icelandic priest Isleifr has a writ with my seal, as you may know, to enable him to travel there through my dominions. Two bishops from England, Ealdred and Hermann, are going from Flanders, I hear.' He glanced again at the Archbishop of Cologne, who nodded.

The Emperor sipped, and continued in his dry voice. 'Provided, therefore, that there is no other difficulty—that your presence is not immediately required in your kingdom; that your resources permit; that such a step is within the compass of your spirit—the matter is simply arranged. My messengers ride daily to Rome: the Archbishop will acquaint His Holiness of your intention. You may even have company for most of your journey: the Pope's kinsman and mine, Adalbero, Bishop of Metz, is to attend both the Easter ceremonies and the synod and, were I to warn him, would await you with pleasure at Strasbourg.'

He smiled. 'Does such a prospect interest you?'

'Who would not be stirred,' Thorfinn said, 'by such a mark of the Emperor's thoughtfulness? It is also true that I have no call to speed back to my country, having intended to linger in Bremen and Denmark. I am much moved to do as you say.'

'You would not regret it,' the Emperor said. 'The ceremony of the golden rose, alone, is a wonder men yearn to see. Nor will you lack common ground with His Holiness. Was that not an address by the Pope to his ancestress that your gifted young bard sang just now? Those who passed through Altorf and Hohenbourg in the Pope's train last November brought back two such songs he composed there.'

'The Emperor recognised the source. I am gratified,' said the King of Alba. 'If, then, I may presume to act upon your imperial lordship's generous proposals, my churchmen and the officers of the Archbishop of Cologne might examine the details?'

The Emperor laid down his goblet with gentle care, glanced at the door, which opened, and rose unhurriedly to his feet. 'You will go from here to Rome? I congratulate you on the decision. The Archbishop, I know, will do all he can to smooth your way for you. And, were there no other reward, the blessing you will receive at the Tomb of the Apostles will be as a light to the end of your days.'

Everyone stood. The Emperor's guests, bowing, moved forward to leave. The Emperor said, 'Archbishop Herimann tells me that five Irish kings have taken the pilgrim's road to Rome in the last twenty years alone. As Bishop of Toul, the present Pope crossed the Alps annually, and my wife's father also travelled every year either to Rome or to Compostela. But, to our knowledge, Mak Betta, you will be the first King of Alba to present himself at the Throne of St Peter.'

'And the first Earl of Orkney,' remarked his guest; and departed.

Two days later, in brilliant spring weather, the retinue of the King of Alba set out for Fulda, banners waving, mounted on eighty good, local horses supplied by the Emperor of the Romans, and accompanied by an armed imperial escort and a large train of sumpter-mules bearing the King of Alba's neat baggage and the Emperor's gifts.

The Emperor, in a scarlet mantle, raised his hand as the cavalcade passed under his balcony, and among the glittering throng of his courtiers the Queen laid back her blue veil and raised her hand also, her other hand restraining two jumping small girls.

Her salute was returned by the King; and also by a middle-aged man in priest's clothes riding behind him, whose cowl could not hide the fact that his cheek was marked with a tear.

'*Isleifr!*' said Odalric of Caithness, jogging beside him. 'He ate up his keeper and the whole of the Emperor's vivarium.'

Isleifr's face hitched in a sniff, but Isleifr's dignity, it was plain, was not going to permit him to answer. Odalric looked round and caught someone else's bright face and laughed aloud.

'*Rome!*' Leofwine of Cumbria had shrieked when, two evenings before, Tuathal had left Thorfinn's side to bring his followers news of the journey. '*Pope Leo!* No one told me I was going to meet Bruno le Bon!'

Prior Eochaid had glanced at Tuathal and sat down, opening the neck of his gown where it had become a little too tight in the course of the evening. 'He did tell you to expect a long trip. We should be home by midsummer, as we anticipated.'

Malpedar of Buchan had said thoughtfully, 'Ceremony of the Rose? That's a coincidence. Do you remember that iron box that arrived when we were at Aalborg?'

Ferteth had said, 'A lot of things arrived while we were at Aalborg. Wait a minute. Cadou, who taught you that song?'

Eochaid, Prior of Scone, said, 'I did. And in my turn I got it from Sulien of Llanbadarn, at the King's suggestion, in Denmark.'

'Wasn't Sulien also at Scone?' Gillecrist had said. 'Come to think of it, what a lot of churchmen there were at Scone, Prior Eochaid. Including the Abbot of Kells, that lad Muiredach's father.'

'And don't you remember,' had said Otkel of Orkney, 'something else that Sulien mentioned? The Archbishop of Dol has been summoned to Rome to appear at this synod.'

Silence fell.

Morgund of Moray said, 'He's had this planned since Lulach's wedding.'

Prior Tuathal said, 'He's had this planned since he made up his mind to work us into becoming a nation.'

'God forgive me. I like this King,' said Morgund of Moray.

SEVEN

THE FIRE AND the chill of many temperings go to the fashioning of a nation. The kingdom of Alba, you might say, was forged in one sense as the cavalcade of young men who were its heirs moved past the engraved milestones of Agrippa and took the royal road south to Rome the Golden.

And every day the future was fixed to the past as they came face to face with the ghosts of their ancestors: the blue-eyed, ruddy-haired Celts who fifteen hundred years earlier had begun to move west and north from their cradle of iron and salt. The Celts, who treasured their enemies' heads embalmed in cedar oil; whose own carved almond heads looked up from the earth or down from some coign wherever their feet had trodden. Heads in gritstone, in sandstone, in limestone, in granite, glared with ringed, pebble eyes at their children: the harrowed bands of their pates caught the flickering light in dim churches: their slit mouths and wedge-noses stamped the stone with exclamation-marks of indignation and horror.

In Payerne, where the Emperor's father had been crowned King of Burgundy, the close-set, gooseberry eyes and fringed hands belonged to the Prophets Jeremiah and Isaiah, Daniel and Ezekiel, and to the Evangelists who crouched on their shoulders.

Four men upon four: it was a tradition old already in Ireland when Colgu Ua Duineachta taught Alcuin, who bore it to Tours. In the church of St Sebastian in the Barberini vineyard at Rome, the Prophets and the Evangelists, new-painted over the apse, supported one another and waited for the footsteps of their kind while they offered their tithe to the long, silent choir of the centuries.

Also on his way to Rome, although a week or two later, Bishop Ealdred of Worcester, whose affinities were not Celtic but high-born Anglo-Saxon, discovered quite early in whose footsteps he was following.

'Thorfinn!' said Bishop Ealdred. 'Or rather, Macbeth. He'll want to be called Macbeth now. We must remember. But how interesting. How very interesting. So there *is* something going on. I thought so. I wonder why he made such a long stay at Woffenheim?'

The Pope's parents had built the abbey of Woffenheim; the Pope's aunt was its abbess, and the Pope's nephew was the abbey's advocate. 'I can't imagine why,' said Bishop Hermann of Ramsbury, Wiltshire. He was ten years younger than his fellow-envoy, and three stones lighter, and, in eight years of doing business together, had never ceased to enjoy the spectacle of Bishop Ealdred conducting an intrigue; or to rejoice when the result surprised Bishop Ealdred.

Bishop Ealdred said, 'Use your brains. If he wants the Pope's favour—and he does—he ought to have kissed the shrine and got out, leaving behind a nice box of something on the altar. However. If he's run short of money, the stay at Romainmôtier'll have put new heart into him. A mule-load of almonds a year: that's all the Pope wants from the monks in taxation.'

'I don't expect,' said Bishop Hermann, 'that they grow almonds in Alba. I suppose eels would travel.'

Behind him, young Alfred giggled. A sheriff at twenty-two, Alfred might be frivolous, but was by no means unintelligent. He was also well-connected. For example, Osbern of Eu, who captained one of the new Welsh frontier forts in the service of Edward of England, was his uncle by marriage.

Bishop Hermann dropped back to ride beside Alfred. He said, 'Wasn't your uncle Osbern in Alba for the last King's enthronement? Has he had many dealings with this one?'

Alfred grinned. As with Duke William, bastardy caused him no inconvenience. The Breton blood showed itself in the brown, knowing eyes and black hair, and the Hainault in the short, stocky build and powerful calves gripping his gelding. He said, 'If there's money in it, you'll find Osbern there. He and Juhel did a lot of trading with Orkney, but I can't see Osbern giving up Bordeaux wine and Welsh girls for the snowy mountains of Alba. Our friend Macbeth ought to feel at home here.'

'Rubbish,' said Bishop Ealdred. He stood in his stirrups to shout an order to the pack-mule driver ahead, and his horse belched and slid in the slush. He sat down again.

'I was there in the north when this fellow made his Norwegian marriage. September, and you'd get the same weather in Hereford. Except for the wind. East-coast wind. Knocks you over. Makes them into good seamen, though.'

'He was trading,' shouted the monk Goscelin de Riveire, the fourth of the party. The wind here, too, could knock you over. It had pursued them ever since they left the north shore of Lake Leman. It had whirled from behind the tall, icy spires and wrenched and tugged at their furs when they came out of St Maurice, and now, as they climbed up from the monastery at St Pierre, it came scouring behind like a broom, so that the wet on their path trembled and scurried uphill before them, between the high, moulded mountains of snow.

Ealdred said, 'Well, there would be little sense in coming all this way without trading. Give your horse its head: it knows how to pick its way better than you do. What's wrong? Your fingers won't freeze.'

Hermann smiled abstractedly. Goscelin was second cousin to Alfred, but had none of his impudence. Goscelin was worried about his hands because he held a pen with them. Of course the agents of Alba would take the chance to trade on this journey, as the English party had done. Not for nothing did Bishop Ealdred's diocese include Bristol, one of the five great English trading-ports. And anyway, a visit to Ghent was part of their mission: to deliver the dues from the church's holdings in England.

Hermann had kept Goscelin out of the delicate bargaining, for Goscelin had no head for business: only a fevered compulsion to write about other men's lives, from devotion.

For that, he, Hermann, was to blame, who had advised the Lady-Dowager Emma that her history should be set down at St Bertin's on the border of Flanders and Normandy.

He was not to know that the Abbot Bovo would go mad, or that the writing of Lives—almost anyone's Lives—would become the enduring concern of the monastery.

Or of two of the monks, anyway. Since he got hold of both English emissaries at the synod of Rheims, Fulchard, for his sins but certainly not for theirs, was launched on the careers of the saintly brothers Adelulf and Botulf. Goscelin, breathing on his fingers beside him, was disputing with the same Fulchard the right to embark on a Life of St Bertin from Luxeuil, one of the monastery's founders.

It was, of course, the right time to do it, with an Alsatian Pope, and the trade running as fast as horseflesh could take it along the path beaten out by history: from the mineral springs of Luxeuil to St Riquier and St Bertin's, and from St Bertin's to the mineral springs of Bath and Wells, re-stocked by monks from St Bertin's a hundred years since. And between Bath and Ghent the cloth trade, with its roots further back even than that, in the days when Alfred the Great refounded Bath and married his daughter in Flanders.

The old route for cloth, and for doctors, and for biographers who spoke Norman-French and Alsatian-German and were protégés, as he was, of the Queen of England and the King's mother Emma of Normandy.

That day, they reached the top of the Alpine pass of Mount Jupiter, eight thousand feet higher than sea level and free, since King Canute made his complaint, of the bandits that used to plague it. Just before King Canute was born, Saracens had held the passes, brought in by some fool of a French-Italian monarch. Now, from Augustus's road, where the ruins of the Roman temple still stood, rose the smoke of a group of bright wooden buildings, their warmth greening the snow all about them.

They were new. The previous spring, the Archdeacon Bernard of Aosta had brought his monks and his workmen from the Italian side of the mountains and had built the hospice of St Nicholas, whose guestmaster stood on its threshold, and whose hot soup and great fires were soon warming them.

'The passes are open. It is well. We have food,' the guestmaster said. 'When there is a synod in Rome, the Bishop makes special provision. Some men are more used to mountains than others. We had a party from the north of the world, from Alba, two weeks ago.'

'On all fours?' said Alfred. 'In animal pelts?'

'Like you or me. You would notice no difference,' said the guestmaster kindly. 'They tell me they have seen Roman cities.'

'Anyone who has seen York or Winchester, or Bath or Chester or Exeter, has seen a Roman city,' said Bishop Ealdred. 'The Romans were in England for five hundred years.' He blew his nose, which was dissolving in the heat.

'I wonder where the King of Alba will stay,' Bishop Hermann remarked.

It was a matter of more than ordinary interest. Secular Rome and its republic of senators was not free with its hospitality. Since the time of Constantine the Great, only two Roman emperors had ever lived in the city, and in living memory the young half-Greek Emperor Otto had been besieged in his house on the Aventine. Notoriously, every coronation ended in conflict between the imperial troops and the Pontiff's militia. Charlemagne himself had had to lodge over the river, in what was now the Leonine City, the Borgo, the suburb where all the foreigners and their monks set up their hostels.

The English hospice was there. 'Not in the English hospice, at least,' Bishop Ealdred said. 'The King of Alba a pensioner of King Edward's? No. Not the figure he would wish to cut. I wonder.'

'What do you wonder?' said Hermann. He remembered a little exhibition in Winchester, mounted by Emma, in which this man Thorfinn had performed, along with Alfgar of Mercia and young Alfred's kinsman the Archbishop of Dol. It struck him that after a week or so more of Ealdred's company, he might be quite ready to have the King of Alba staying at the English hospice.

Ealdred said, 'I wonder why he stayed so long in Woffenheim.'

Within the golden dunghill of Rome, the Pope came back from Siponte as the fourth week of Lent drew to its close and the theatre of the city began to draw back its curtains for Easter.

The box from Woffenheim had arrived. Like Pope Leo himself, his aunt the Abbess was particular about dates. That Sunday, Laetare Sunday, he rode, as was the tradition, from the basilica of Constantine, his home on the Caelius Hill, eastwards to the Sessorianan Palace, once Constantine's also.

For eight hundred years, the central hall of the palace, converted into a church, had held the fragment of the True Cross brought to Rome from Jerusalem by St Helen, Constantine's mother. The church was called Holy Cross of Jerusalem. His parents' abbey of Woffenheim was named after the Holy Cross also. It was fitting that as he rode the short distance under the banner of St Peter, with the great cross from the Lateran flashing before him, and the steel-lined causeway before and behind him crammed like a flower-filled river with colour, with scent, and with song—it was fitting that the rose he bore in his hand, the golden rose scented with balm and with musk, the emblem of Christianity, should emanate from his family, the family of Bruno of Nordgau.

Seated in his ivory chair below the half-dome of the apse, he listened critically to the Introit: *Oculi mei semper ad Dominum,* and felt the hand of Constantine again on his shoulder. Constantine the Great, who had recognised the Pope as Christ's Vicar on Earth and had made over to St Sylvester the imperial palace of the Lateran, where he now lived, beside the basilica now known as St John's. At this altar, Pope Sylvester had died while saying Mass: died *in Jerusalem,* as had been prophesied.

Rome was full of churches built by Constantine, most of them in need of repair. He had pointed them out to the bishop from the other Constantine's city, Coutances in Normandy, who had shared his expedition to Italy. To build a new church in Coutances was admirable. But to save the souls of his unfortunate kindred, Bishop Goisfrid might not find it unwise to invoke the aid of Saints Peter and Paul in their basilicas outside the walls, into which the roof tiles were leaking.

There was a voice of some stridency in the choir. Pope Leo frowned and looked up at the rafters, whose gilding showed no sign of dampness. He had given the returns from this monastery, only last year, to Richer of Monte Cassino, sitting over there unmoved, apparently, by any defect in the praises.

Richer had admired the rose in the Pope's hand. It was not, of course, the rose his aunt the Abbess had been instructed to send, although it encompassed it. What he held was a wand wound about with rose leaves and half-open roses. In the centre was the golden rose, weighing two Roman ounces, that he had stipulated as Woffenheim's annual tribute.

With the wand, his aunt had sent a note of explanation. The smithwork on the rose he recognised. It came from Essen. The wand, he fancied, was English. Soon, showing it to the people, he would be required to discourse on it.

So that Rome might have roses for pious use, Constantine had provided Pope Mark with a rose-farm. He, Leo, did not propose, in the present state of unrest, to encourage the throwing of roses from church roofs. But of the symbolism of the wand he could make something. Aaron's rod, bringing forth blooms in the tabernacle; signifying God's chosen race, set aside for the priesthood.

A clever, even an inspired implication. The name Constantine, he seemed to remember, was not unknown among the monarchs of Alba, although he had a feeling that Bishop Goisfrid might be nearer the blood-line than the emperors of Constantinople or Rome.

Nevertheless, the gift implied a certain degree of education, a familiarity with the ways of the church, and a desire to please.

The Holy See should respond.

Beneath the unwelcome sound of the next choral offering, the Pope spoke to the Archbishop of Sicily on his right.

'When the rose has been blessed, I intend to dedicate it. Prepare the Prefect to ride at my right hand to the Lateran. And I have a message for the Chancellor. I wish to know when the harbingers of the Archbishop of Metz approach the City.'

'The Archbishop of Dol, Holiness?' said Humbert. 'It is arranged. You will be told as soon as he arrives, or any of the disaffected from Brittany.'

The Pope had great hopes of Archbishop Humbert. He had brought him from his own diocese of Toul and given him Sicily, which was, of course, still in the possession of the heathen. But through the power of the Apostolic spirit, along with Humbert's Greek, all might soon, God willing, be altered. Meanwhile, Archbishop Humbert ought to remember that this Pope was no child, or decadent princeling with his mind on his food or his women.

Leo said, 'The word I used was Metz. He is bringing the King of Alba to Rome. Pray attend to what you are told.'

He watched Humbert go and slip back, under cover of the singing. The singing had changed.

'I have conveyed your message, Holiness,' Humbert said. 'Also, I have advised the chorister with the sore throat not to harm himself by trying to sing in your presence.'

He sat down, returning his attention to the service, a little flushed; and the Pope leaned back, caressing his rose. The voices sprang, strong and pure, bright as jewels, to the ellipses of light and silver and wax that blossomed through the haze of the incense and sparkled on the gold on the altar, and the sheen of the hangings, and the hundreds of ruddy faces, lifted rapt and waiting towards him.

The Pope remembered all the other reasons why he had brought Humbert to Italy, and was moved. When he began to speak, the rose in his hand, it was to be seen that there were tears in his eyes; and by the time he had ended, they were running quite freely into the bright, carroty strands of his beard.

As directed, the Prefect, secular governor of the city of Rome, rode from the church at the side of the Pope, and through the crowds up the slope to the Lateran. There, on the steps of the palace, the Pontiff turned and, drawing his churchmen about him, made formal gift to the city of the golden-rose wand supplied by his aunt the Abbess, in its setting provided by the King of the country called Alba.

Later, one of the deans followed the Prefect to the Castella to obtain his written receipt, at a fee of one silver penny.

'I will tell you a truth,' said Gillocher of Lumphanan, toying with a moustache-end. 'It was in me that this man had overreached himself and I should never get to Rome, save as much of me as birds should carry out in their claws. Eighty-eight bodies they found in that inn-keeper's hut in Châtenay. And that's no more than a minute ago.'

Odalric of Caithness grinned tolerantly without turning. 'So the eighty-eight various pilgrims didn't ride with the Archbishop of Metz. An uncle with connections in Basle. A niece married in Montbéliard and another the wife of the Marquis of Tuscany. Not to mention enough armed men to scare off the Valkyries. Aren't we supposed to be talking in the Italian tongue?'

Cormac of Atholl, standing by the wide shutters, consigned the Latin tongue to another destination and continued without turning either. 'When

Thorfinn overreaches himself, I dare say you will know it, but I doubt if he will. What's that tower? Where is Thorfinn, anyway?'

'In Rome,' said Thorfinn behind him. 'The conscience and confessor of Metz has just removed himself to his own house elsewhere in the Borgo. Will this do?'

He came to the window and they made way for him, but only a little, for his height gave him a better view than most. When they closed about him, it was with no particular care, although it might have been noticed that none pressed against him or incommoded him in any way.

They went on talking. Fourteen vigorous men who had come a long way since they left Alba six months before. Fourteen men of mixed race who had found nothing remarkable in the country of Denmark, for to some of them it offered the language and nature of home, while to others it was a land of aliens with whom one learned, as had one's fathers, to consort without quarrelling.

From Denmark to Goslar, the circumstances of their journey had been little different. There were towns, but none of them were large. There were rich churches, but they had seen churches before.

From Goslar to the Vosges, from the Vosges to the Alps, from the Alps down through Italy to the rolling plain of the Roman Campagna and the dark, honey-comb slabs of a road two thousand years old that had led them to this spot—that was another matter entirely.

They fell out with one another. That had not changed. They were a self-opinionated and disparate group: it was for that reason that they had been picked. One was full-blooded Norse and two, from Orkney and Caithness, were Norse of the half-blood. Ten were of Irish descent, and one was Cumbrian, with all that implied of Breton-Welsh in the strain. Two were priests: Tuathal from beside Dublin and Eochaid of Ulidian descent. While a third priest, who had joined them at Goslar, was Isleifr the Icelander, who, alone of them all, had lived in the Roman Empire and had already embraced its canons.

So they fell out with one another and not infrequently with their King, but did not notice perhaps that the grounds for dispute were not quite the same as they had been, or that now and then they noisily made common cause over quite a few issues.

Whatever they did, Thorfinn's treatment of them, naturally, had undergone no improvement. It was like being propelled by a brief, battering wind that smacked your ears and kept your brain in a turmoil. On some wax tablet somewhere, Thorfinn's energy was no doubt being made into a proverb. Saddle-weariness never afflicted the wayfarers from Alba: their brains got more worn out each day than their rumps did.

And now they were here; and Thorfinn said, 'Will this do?' and Cormac of Dunkeld, who was little and peppery, said, 'I suppose it will have to, failing the Elysian Fields. It's the Emperor's palace, isn't it?'

'You should have listened,' said Thorfinn, 'to your latimer. You are outside Rome, in the foreigners' suburb over the river. Where you are standing now was the Circus of Nero, where St Paul met his death, on the slopes of the Vatican hill. The big church with the bell-tower outside is built over the tomb of St Peter. To pray there is why most pilgrims come here. Hence the schools and churches and hospices, built all around us. Eochaid, there is St Cecilia's, as I told you.'

His voice echoed; and he glanced round, as if reminded of where he stood. The hangings glimmered and footsteps, crossing a floor just beyond, clacked light and clear on the marble. Outside in the afternoon sun, the leaves of spring glittered, bright as embroidery.

Thorfinn said, 'Herimann the German Arch-Chancellor has rooms here, and so has the permanent Imperial Commissioner, who is our host.'

'The Emperor pays our expenses?' said Otkel of Orkney, who had a profound interest in prices, particularly when paid by other people.

'The Pope allows Archbishop Herimann the dues from the church of St John of the Latin Gate. It probably dates from Pope Victor's exile in Germany. Now,' said Thorfinn, 'I imagine he can use it for the Emperor's guests or his own. It is for you to remember that we are guests. We don't go out unattended, nor do our servants. That is, you are free to walk as you wish in the Leonine City. But to enter Rome, you must be invited.'

'You can't see the river,' said Eochaid the priest, his voice a shade flat. He had understood the interpreter and the guide. Down there beyond the laurels and oaks flowed the Tiber, and the drum fortress called the Castella of Cencius marked the bridge into the city, *Felix Roma.*

Rome. Its seven green mounds lay over the river before him, and beyond them, low blue hills ringed the horizon: the hills of Tusculum, of Prenestina, of Tibur. He said, speaking to no one, 'It looks like a walled garden created for angels.'

It was true. Terracotta and white in the sunlight, the slim columns stood; the reeled arcades, the thumbnail arches, the delicate boxes of brick, cross-pleated with staircase and portico. The triangles of pyramid and pediment. The assiduous tooth-comb of the aqueducts, bringing the rivers riding on triumphal arches. The domes; the campanile stalks; the tablets of fluted clay tile or chalked bronze with their feet in drifting blue smoke from the other, invisible roofs of reed and of wood.

Angels holding a ledger of glass, regarding the appointment of kings.

Thorfinn said, 'We attend a thanksgiving Mass for pilgrims in two days' time, here at St Peter's. After the ceremony, we make our official entry to Rome and I have an audience with Pope Leo. Or so says the Count Palatine of the Lateran Court.'

'The man with the two gowns with gold braid on them?' said Kineth of Angus.

'The man we gave the first vase to?' said Hlodver cheekily. 'I don't like it. The money'll never last out. We'll have to travel on foot like King Ratchis. And they say there's never enough food in the city at Easter. As for Lent, no wonder the Pontiff likes travelling. One mule-load of fish from the church of St Basil; one boatload of wood from the bishopric of Ostia . . . You'll enjoy your audience in a freezing cold room over a fish-head, I shouldn't wonder.'

'After Dingwall, an outrage,' said Leofwine. 'My lord, there are matters to attend to.'

'Yes. The unpacking, first,' said Thorfinn. 'Then the steward will offer us food. If it consists solely of fish-heads, you may apportion your share to the poor. If you wish to examine the Borgo, remember that there will be beggars and pickpockets and men of many races not above picking a quarrel. Also that, because of the pilgrims here for Easter, prices are bound to be high. I don't expect to walk home, but I don't expect to carry you, either. Tuathal, Isleifr, and Eochaid, we should have a talk later.'

The three priests looked at one another, but only two of them turned to walk out of the room with the others. Eochaid, keeping his place by his lord at the window, said, 'My lord King. I have to go to St Cecilia's?'

'Don't you want to?' said Thorfinn, without turning round. Over the river to the south-east, one could glimpse the Baptistry of St John with its cupola, and behind it, the atrium and bell-towers of the Constantine basilica, the mother and summit of all churches. The glittering roofs beside and behind that were those of the papal palace and monastery.

His attention drawn to something else, Eochaid said, 'Shades of the pillar saints. But there seems to be a tower over there with a man on it.'

Thorfinn moved his eyes. 'I suppose,' said Thorfinn, 'he might be mortifying the flesh; but he's more likely to be a minion of the princes Crescentius or Frangipani. The triumphal arches and obelisks make good forts and watchtowers. . . . Tuathal is in a condition of efficient ecstasy: that is why he is here.'

Tuathal, prior of a humble group of Culdees on an island in Fife, was master of every shade of statecraft in Fife and, for that matter, the rest of Alba as well. Tuathal's faith was a tool, like his pen-knife, and it, too, he kept shining and clean. Eochaid understood Tuathal and respected him. He did not understand Thorfinn, for all their ten years together as King and master of the writing-chamber. The King was Sulien's business. From time to time, Eochaid or another had the name of his chaplain, but if he had a soul-friend, it was Sulien, present or absent, and no one else.

All that Eochaid recognised. The turn of this conversation he did not recognise at all. He said, with composure, 'It is plain that it is your element as well. I am here because I understand music.'

'But you knew what to expect?' Thorfinn said. When he turned, the glossy brown eyes travelled all over Eochaid's face.

Eochaid smiled. 'Let me reassure you,' he said. 'Even Rome cannot disturb my beliefs. I shall not be a hindrance to you; neither will Tuathal or Isleifr. And in lay matters you can count on the others.'

'Can I?' said Thorfinn.

'You think I flatter you?' Eochaid said. 'Certainly you have worked with them in Alba. But until this journey they were as strangers in a market-place, eyeing one another. That is why they, too, are here, I take it.'

'You leave out the question of why I am here,' Thorfinn said.

Eochaid kept his voice level. 'I should not presume to ask,' the Prior said.

'When in private audience with the Pontiff, one is expected from time to time to diverge from the subject of money,' Thorfinn remarked. 'It will be assumed that, like other men, I have been guilty of sin; and, like other kings, I require, for the good of my land, to be shriven.'

It was better to be straightforward. 'You did not discuss this with Sulien?' Eochaid said.

'Sulien is not here. You will be there at the Lateran with me. So will Tuathal. You know the concessions I want. If I get them, I can work towards a uniform rule from Orkney to Cumbria. Until I have uniform rule and uniform Christian observance, the whole weight of the kingdom will continue to rest on my shoulders. A wet autumn, an outbreak of St Anthony's fire, and men will whisper that even the Coarb of St Peter could find for me no fitting penance. What is it they say? *For it is the prince's falsehood that brings perverse weather, and dries up the fruit of the earth. . . . Against his sons, his crimes will be retained, men's faces will be turned, men's hearts will be closed. Not welcome, all will say, are the sons of that prince: evil was your father's lordship before.'*

Prior Eochaid walked to a stool and sat down. He said, 'You are saying, I think, that the mystery of kingship is something you lack that this Pope can give you. That is true. You are saying that you are a man of sin, as are we all; and that, for your soul's good and that of your country, you must ask to be shriven. That is natural. What else you are saying is unclear. Are you not aware of your sins? Are you asking me what to confess to? Have you never taken the life of a man?'

Thorfinn remained standing. 'The Pope himself has fought wars,' he said. 'Most bishops have killed.'

Eochaid said gently, 'But the Holy Father has not caused the death of his brother's son, or his two brothers, or the husband of the woman he married.'

'No,' said Thorfinn. 'I will not defend myself, to you or to anyone else. But if I confess to these deaths, I shall be charged with them.' He paused, and then added in a reflective voice, 'I shall be charged with them anyway.'

Eochaid looked at him. 'Then do not be specific, except in your afflictions. For what do you need the Pope's blessing? For many years, your marriage has been barren of children.'

He was a courageous man. He bore the long silence that followed, knowing that he had stepped a second time on forbidden ground.

He did not expect Thorfinn to say eventually, as he did, 'You know my stepson Lulach?'

A loving and sweet-tempered youth. Eochaid had heard the rumours and did not believe them. He said, 'You are lucky to have him, and your other sons. But life is fragile, and the royal line and your Queen's health are worth praying for, surely?'

Somehow, he could tell, he had misunderstood. But Thorfinn only said, 'Yes. Well, whatever fate must befall the heirs of my line, I suppose it will do no harm to let the Pope take the blame for it. Very well. I shall claim intercession for fruitfulness, and ask forgiveness for any misdeeds of mine in the opposite sphere. . . . How are the linguists coming along?'

The subject of conscience, it seemed, had been closed. Eochaid said, 'Those of us trained in the priesthood have no trouble, and Leofwine has a natural gift for language. The rest have some phrases, that's all. You and Cormac and Leofwine are still our only exponents of Norman-French. I'm told even the Pope has to use Halinard of Lyons when he goes to Apulia.'

'It's the way,' said Thorfinn, 'you can identify our commercial souls. Which reminds me: the contingent from Dol has not yet arrived. But if you hear of the envoys from Tours, I should like to know where they are staying. A matter, of course, of the wine-trade.'

'Of course,' said Eochaid. He felt unhappy. He said, 'You asked about St Cecilia. Of course, I shall be glad to do what I can. In every way. In every way possible.'

'If I didn't know that,' said Thorfinn, 'we shouldn't have had this conversation. . . . Come. I have a feeling I should oversee the unpacking. Otkel will have sold all the oblations, Kineth will have smelt out the most exquisite market, and Hlodver will be driving Morgund to complain to Odalric, who will pretend not to understand Gaelic. You are right. A miracle has happened. We are brothers. We are pilgrims. We are Athletes of Christ, learning to fight on our knees.

'Whoever we are, we are in Rome, and therefore next door to Paradise.'

EIGHT

WILL TELL YOU another truth,' said Gillocher of Lumphanan, 'and that is
how glad I am that the chief of us is the one with the strongest belly. It
comes from being a seaman.'

'He told you not to drink the water,' Otkel said.

'I haven't. Christ knows what would be happening if I'd drunk the
water,' Gillocher said. 'I would never leave the building at all. How the
lions and the gladiators ever got out to face one another is past my understanding.'

It was the day on which history was to be made. The day when a ruler of
Alba and Orkney would enter the city of Rome for the first time in the
seventeen hundred years of its existence.

The previous two days had made history, too, in the velocity with which
Thorfinn had deployed his complaining courtmen through the Borgo. From
what they discovered, he learned that the envoys of Dol and of England had
not yet arrived. And he himself, calling to deliver gifts and take refreshment at
the house of Archbishop Adalbero of Metz, whose company from Strasbourg
he had so lately enjoyed, had one encounter of note. That is, he found himself
trapped in the presence of sub-deacon Hildebrand, the Pope's financial
expert, and subjected to a thorough discussion on the tax referred to as Peter's
Pence.

Hearing, Leofwine said, 'Oh, my God. Cormac and I should have been with
you; or Tuathal. What did you say?'

'There was no difficulty,' said Thorfinn. 'I simply took off my boots, and
there were my toes.'

'Well. I'm sorry,' said Leofwine. 'But you did put the question of accounting into our hands. I hear he's a Jew. Hildebrand.'

'He could be descended from one. His father was Tuscan, of no particular
standing, but his mother's brother was abbot here of St Mary's, the Cluniac
house. He has no time for our friend Adalbert of Hamburg and Bremen.'

'In that case, I like him,' said Leofwine. 'So he proved to be sharp, and you
enjoyed scoring points off one another.'

'He was sharp,' Thorfinn conceded. 'He had the Pope's golden rose in the bag with his parchments. He went to school at the Palatium with the Prefect Cencius. We discussed how poor Alba was.'

'And he remarked,' said Leofwine, 'that England had been paying Peter's Pence to the Apostle of God for victory and life eternal with all the saints without end for three hundred years without visibly declining into beggary, and should we not enjoy the same favours?'

'He said something of the sort,' Thorfinn agreed. 'Which goes to show that he hadn't really considered whether life eternal with Offa was an inducement. He was disappointed to hear that the only money we had was in shipping.'

'Wait a moment,' said Leofwine. 'Hildebrand and Pope Gregory . . . Wasn't it Pope Gregory who—'

'Bought his papacy with the proceeds of the papal tribute from England? Yes. That's what they deposed him for. So Hildebrand, having been Gregory's private chaplain, is not in the strongest position to demand your money or mine. It occurred to me, indeed, that the Apostle of God might be relieved to be spared a dilemma. Some day, England and Alba might be at war, and both entitled to win.'

Leofwine laughed. 'Don't expect too much for your money. Nowadays, the tribute goes to light the churches of Peter and Paul over Easter. It buys the saints' beneficent protection but no particular promise of victory. If the Mother Church is pitch black at the weekend, you'll know the English haven't arrived.'

Leaving Thorfinn, Leofwine felt quite light-hearted. It was, however, the last time he laughed for a while, for the next day was the day of the entry.

Spectacle was the business of Rome. It was six hundred years since the barbarians had overwhelmed this, the capital of the world, and three hundred since the Pope, threatened by a Lombard invasion, had asked Pepin the Frank, for the love of St Peter and the remission of his sins, to protect them. Fifty years after that, with the crowning of Pepin's son Charlemagne in St Peter's, the Holy Roman Empire had begun, of which Henry in Goslar was now the Caesar.

In the interests of the city, the church, and the people of Rome, the King of Alba rode the short distance between the state palace and the basilica of St Peter's on a white palfrey, flanked by the Count Palatine of the Lateran and by Hugo, the Cardinal-deacon. Before him, singing, walked the clergy of the basilica, and behind him, also on foot, followed the file of his courtmen and servants, led by his confessors.

The retinue wore, uniformly, cloaks of velvet the colour of wine-lees over tunics of dark blue wool. Their faces were uniformly grim and uniformly pallid, and one of them bore a tuft of floss on a freshly cut chin. The King, supported no doubt by the dutiful stomach envied by Gillocher, looked composed and controlled his mount discreetly in the narrow path cleared between onlookers.

There were a great many onlookers; and the nearest of them, as the procession approached the high, galleried portico of St Peter's, had an air of having been there all night.

The attraction, of course, was not only spectacle. Largesse was required by Rome of her visiting children, and the greater their standing, the greater Rome's claims on their charity. A Pope could expect to dispense five thousand pounds in alms at his inaugural procession: an Emperor probably more.

As with everything else, Thorfinn had made it his business to find out about that beforehand; and if he had not, there were Adalbero and Hildebrand ready to tell him, and the money-lenders passing the time of day at every corner. The honour of a ceremonial entry carried a penalty-clause all of its own.

The thought of it could sour, a trifle, a newcomer's appreciation of the colour, the scent, and the music. At St John's, it was said, they would consume two hundred pounds of balm at one Easter evening of baptism. The chandeliers here at St Peter's each required thirteen hundred wax candles to fill them. Candles and oil were for sale in the markets beside the platea. The candles, once bought, did not always burn.

Thorfinn dismounted at the steps of St Peter's, climbed them, and, passing into the forecourt, knelt between the pale, painted pillars.

The doors before which he paid homage were of deeply worked silver. They shot strange lights into the shadows beneath his bent knee, and the fall of his cloak, and the formal tent of his supplicant's hands. The mosaics on either side of the door stamped their myriad hatches on the Deity's luminous Greek face and dress, and on his long hand of blessing, thumb and third finger joined. Below, the Emperor Otto slept in his borrowed sarcophagus of figured white marble.

Thorfinn rose, and the silver doors opened, followed by the rays of the sun, which Constantine chose to admit into all his basilicas, built for the worship of God and the celebration of Sunday, *the great and venerable day of the sun.*

Inside, Thorfinn knelt again with the Cardinal on the *Rota Porphyretica,* the single red stone in the patterned black-and-white glaze of the flooring. Then, led by the priests and the choristers, he moved up the long nave between the eighty-six marble columns under the silvery blaze of the lights, and towards the gold of the High Altar and the Confessio. The voices rose, and fresco and mosaic gave them back. Gold sparkled and winked through the mists of burned spices. Above the baldaquin of the altar, above Thorfinn's head, a crown hung, made of jewels like flowers.

The Cardinal spoke; and Thorfinn answered.

Below the liquid eyes of the Prophets, among the clear peacock wings of the angels, his men stood behind in the aisles and forgot who they were and where they came from.

Later, returned to the same basilica steps, Leofwine opened the satchel at his side and took from it a bag, from which he filled the silver cup Cormac held.

Neither remarked on the fact that Leofwine's hand was shaking. Neither, in fact, spoke at all. Then the King took the cup and emptied it, in a drift of bright, spinning coins, into the crowd packed below him.

The procession re-formed.

At Nero's bridge, where the Prefect and senators awaited them, Kineth of Angus at last found his voice and spoke softly. 'How can Thorfinn do that when he doesn't believe?'

Isleifr turned round. 'What do you mean, he doesn't believe? Constantine, who brought Christ to Rome, must have believed. But he had a statue made of himself as Apollo the Sun God just the same, with pieces of the True Cross and the Nails of the Passion built into it. When they talk of Christ in Iceland, in England, in Saxony, they are thinking of Christ the young leader, the Odin . . . *Stripped himself then the young hero that was God Almighty, strong and brave . . . Mighty King of Rome, who sits in the south at the Well of Urd, and rules over lands of the mountain kings . . .* What of it? If all paths lead the same way, does it matter if they are made differently?'

'We are moving,' said Odalric. 'Be calm. Save it for later.'

Before they stepped from the bridge into the city of Rome, the news of their coming, of their style, and of what they had laid on the altars was known to the Pontiff's most skilful advisor, the sub-deacon Hildebrand at the Lateran palace.

Pagan princes were encouraged to come at Easter, since this was the time of baptism and the Pope would assuredly be in the city.

Unbaptised princes now were rare. Kings and envoys were pagan only in the original sense: that they came from remote lands outside the city, and city customs were unknown to them.

One did not, however, make the error of underrating them. Did those barbarians who adored Sidonius Appollinarius adore him still when they heard his verses bewailing their attachment?

> *They do not come to you at dawn*
> *Breathing out leeks and ardour:*
> *Great, friendly souls, with appetites*
> *Much bigger than your larder . . .*

No. The merchant who knew the wood-and-wattle markets of Dublin and Birku and the Dnieper had usually paid his respects in his time to the sweating pillar in Constantinople, and in Rome would encounter Domitian's *meta sudans* with no sense of wonder. As the Saracen knew Leptis Magna and the Greek columns of Paestum and Taormina, so the Frank came from the amphitheatre of Autun to the Flavian Colosseum without trepidation, as the Wend leaving his marshes saw the Forum and walls of Colonia and, travelling, learned from the milestones.

Nevertheless, crossing the bridge, they would experience wonder. The avenues were still broad, although meaner buildings encroached on the symmetry and wadded the dancing arches, the white, fractured temples, as if prescribed by some physician whose herbs mended marble.

Despite the fortress and the Ghetto beside it, the Campo dei Fiori was still imposing, and the church of St Mark kept its beauty two hundred years after its last restoration. No man could fail to be moved by the ruins of the Imperial Forum, and the Tullianum, where St Peter, it was said, had been imprisoned and where Caesar, it was certain, had left Vercingetorix to die. There was the Senate House of Rome, converted to the church of St Adrian. There, they would be told, were the columns of the Curia Pompeii, where Caesar was murdered. There was the Roman Forum, and the triple arch of Septimus Severus celebrating the Conquest of the East with, close by it, the site of the Golden Milestone, the column from which once led all the roads of the empire.

From there, pagans followed the Sacred Way. From the Arch of Titus and its story of the capture of Jerusalem to the mighty, dismembered cylinder of the Colosseum. Then past the basilica of St Clement to the first glimpse of the octagon and dome of the Baptistry and the huddle of booths, and then the quadrangles, opening up with their tiered roofs, and the long north wall of the basilica showing behind them.

And then, lined with people, its basalt blocks swept for the procession, would appear the platea, the space before the eastern front door of the Lateran with its graveyard of monuments, brought here to proclaim that this spot, before the Mother of Churches, bore witness to the greatness of Rome past as well as Rome present.

Blocking the sun, its shadow striping the square, would stand the bronze equestrian statue of Constantine, wearing the tight-curled hair and long beard of Marcus Aurelius, his right hand outstretched. Below its plinth, Romans themselves stood to marvel at the other memorials. The vast bronze hand holding a globe; the gleaming face with its curled nostrils that might belong to the tyrant Nero or to the Sun God, or to both. The pig-like wolf with open mouth and inscribed Assyrian coat, giving suck to the founders of Rome against the painted wall of the Patriarchium.

The great square, then, to cross. And then before the visiting pagans, the portico of Constantine's basilica, made and remade but still essentially that built seven hundred years ago on the tract of land owned by the Emperor's wife, where once the Laterani family had had their palace and cavalry school.

The procession was coming. Hildebrand could hear the noise from where he stood among the archives close to the Holy Staircase.

The windows here were of oiled linen, so that he could not look out, but he knew what to expect. This amicable roar was occasioned by the throwing of small money by the chancellors of the visiting monarch, and reflected the fact that the money had been efficiently dispensed and was not yet exhausted.

He was not surprised. The conflict that had already taken place between himself and the King of Alba at Adalbero's house in the Borgo had given him an idea of the man's capacity; and he had advised the Pope accordingly. Alert and sharp-minded himself, Leo was, he thought, not displeased to be having this encounter. Unlike poor John Gratian, Hildebrand's last master, Pope Leo was not so deeply embedded in the toils of the spirit that he did not perceive that spiritual armies must be led and manoeuvred like any other. He, Hildebrand, was lucky at thirty to be permitted to stand beside these great princes, the Emperor Henry and Pope Leo from Alsace, and learn from their mistakes.

Meanwhile, there was no hurry. The Pope had already left to walk down to the basilica from his apartments on the second floor of the Patriarchium, along with three of the cardinals, Halinard of Lyons, and Humbert of Marmoutier. Whatever self-control still remained to their guests from the country after the pitiless trial of a Roman welcome would now meet a greater opponent by far: the power of the Mass, the Word of the Lord, to steal the soul and cow the spirit.

Of course, much had been lost to the basilica. Beyond the cedarwood doors, these worshippers would not look down the nave and see the great ciborium of beaten silver with a silver Christ, onyx-eyed, seated among his Apostles. The golden lamp with its eighty dolphins no longer burned oil of spikenard in front of the altar. The coloured glass windows, bought with Charlemagne's money to rival those of Haghia Sophia, had also long gone.

But not everything could be carried away. Christ in mosaic looked down from the deep golden shell of the apse, and the arcades were still encrusted with Pope Sergius's silver; the brass columns of the presbyterium had been dressed with veils of wild silk embroidered with glittering crosses, and the altar wore cloth of gold all covered with jewels, flanked by curtains of Byzantian purple woven with eagles and basilisks.

Down there, stunned by the glory, the voice of God speaking from caverns of unimaginable beauty, none would make an accounting.

Except, perhaps, the chieftain. The extremely ill-favoured man who called himself King and indeed, by whatever means, had come to rule a collection of lands large enough and well enough placed to attract the Empire's attention.

It would be interesting, thought Hildebrand, to see what change St John might have wrought in that rumbling voice and unmoving presence.

If the answer was none, then he would be even more interested. For you cannot lead your men into battle unless you have spotted the enemy.

The King of Alba, whose only enemy was a prophecy, rose when the Pope rose, and waited while the Pope left the basilica and the basilica emptied; and, without even looking, was aware of the resentment in the eyes of the men of Alba grouped in silence about him. Resentment that all life was transformed save for the rumbling voice and unmoved presence of their leader.

Then came the summons to the papal chamber, and he walked out of the north door before them, and up the marble steps to the Leonine wing and a long room lined with bright windowed alcoves. In the centre, water sparkled and whispered in a great porphyry basin, and columns of porphyry and white sculptured marble attended the doorways, their heads and bases fashioned with lilies.

At the end, before a heavy white table, was set a canopied throne upon which the Pope had seated himself. Behind, the ranks of his cardinals and advisors, in red and white, black and brown, glinting with bullion, repeated the curve of the apse.

Nine Roman palms tall, the Pope who had been Bruno of Toul was straight-backed and vigorous, with raw cheeks and a long, stalking nose and strong eyebrows. The red hair of his beard met the red furze circling his head, on which was bedded the tall cone of the papal tiara, encircled with gold. The pallium with its submissive crosses wandered across strong thighs and knees on which were planted swordsman's hands, handed down from generations of counts of Nordgau. Jewels boxed in gold hemmed the robe at his sandal, the cuffs, close and wide, of his sleeves, and flamed in pastilles of colour at his muscular neck.

The party from Alba, halted two-thirds of the way along the room, began one by one to be presented. Moving forward, first of them all, under the uniform Latinising voice of the Chancellor Peter, Thorfinn could feel on his back the distraught gaze—the hatred, even—of his followers.

He knew without looking that Hlodver and Gillocher had been weeping, and he had been prepared for the withdrawn silence of the three priests who would now sustain with him the burden of this interview. The thickened voice of Cormac of Atholl had taken him by surprise, on the way up the stairs. 'You will be asked to prostrate yourself,' Cormac said. 'I take it you will?'

He had not replied. He waited now until the very end of the Cardinal's introduction before he moved. Then, managing his height and the weight of his robes in the only way possible, he laid himself flat before the throne, brushed the gilded slipper with his lips, and rose, as swiftly and silently as did the churchmen. The man he had spoken to at Adalbero's house, the sub-deacon Hildebrand, came forward a little and said, 'The Pope bids you welcome, my son. You will remain, with your priests, after your companions have been presented?'

Which was as expected. He stood and watched critically while the material embodiment of Buchan and Strathearn, Moray and Angus and the rest, performed, with varying success, the same movement. Otkel of the iron nerves stood on his cloak-end on rising and only just caught his great brooch as it ripped from its moorings. Eochaid looked ill, which was a pity, as he would be needed before very long. As Thorfinn had felt their distrust, so he felt their anger and foreboding as one by one they bowed themselves out of the room, leaving him alone with Eochaid, Tuathal, and Isleifr. The Pope spoke, and Hildebrand said, 'His Holiness knows that you speak several tongues. He asks if you wish an interpreter.'

Italian was only Latin spoken familiarly, as the Legions had spoken it before they left England. But Thorfinn was not fluent in it, although he could understand all that was being said. He said, 'My Saxon is different from the tongue of the Vosges, but I think I can make myself understood, if His Holiness will forgive my lack of skill.'

'On the contrary. I compliment you, my son,' said Leo. It was, thank God, the accent he had been led to expect. Four low stools appeared and were carefully placed in a row facing the throne.

'Be seated,' said the Pope. 'And tell me if it is true—I have been led to believe that it is true—that one of you has mended Pope Gerbert's steam organ in St Cecilia's?'

Behind Hildebrand, Sicho was fidgetting. Airard, whom Hildebrand was to succeed at St Paul's and whom he did not like, gave a great yawn. The rest of the Pope's entourage, with the exception of the Archbishop of Sicily, stood silent. Audiences, in their experience, were seldom as lengthy as this one.

The Archbishop of Sicily was not among the silent because he was locked in four-part verbal combat with the two Irish-trained priests and the Holy Father on the subject of the flattened note in the Irish musical scale. Occasionally, from among the wagging heads, a vocal example from Egypt, Servia, or Wallachia would float piping aloft and jettison itself against the unmusical branches of a Jesse tree.

Sub-deacon Hildebrand did not interfere, nor did anyone else. In the hands of this Pope, the power of music to enliven injurious mourning, suppress foaming rage, soften bloody savageness, and incite the indolent and weary was not only exercised but extended into areas where Cassiodorus had never ventured.

The tranquil, black-haired priest from the place called Scone might think he was talking solely about the purity of Greek music in the Roman church of seven hundred years since, before the wave of antiphony from Syria drowned it, but the Pope's response, instant and candid, went on to embrace with perfect ease the subject of early Irish unorthodoxy on the dating of Easter and the fashion of tonsure, long since corrected, with happy results for both Rome and those churches which adopted the customs of Ireland.

Of course, he said, smiling: as with the flattened note, antique customs persisted, such as the way Irish churchmen still mixed the chalice, and the Greek method of arranging the breads in cross-form for feast day, the Lamb in the middle.

Indeed, said unexpectedly the subterranean voice of the King of Alba at that point. Indeed, one could not praise too highly the famous tolerance of the Holy See when Constantinople, as he had heard, was denouncing the Latin church as Jewish because of its unleavened bread, and found rude and ignorant the Latin habit of shaving, and of eating strangled beasts, and of forbidding priests to take a wife.

The church, remarked the King, was of course already established in Ireland and Alba when the great Pope Gregory sent his mission to England and at the same time performed his unparalllelled service to the music of the Western church. Passing through Basle, said King Macbeth, they had been lost in admiration for the song composed by Pope Leo, a second Gregory, in honour of his great predecessor.

He wished, said the King, he had also managed to hear the response of nocturnes Pope Leo had also composed for the Abbot of Gorze, to serve the feast of the martyr whose relics St Chrodegang of Metz had sent him. The men of God—the Culdees, one might almost call them—who followed St

Chrodegang's Rule in Alsace and Lorraine and then in Ireland were, he supposed, men of the sort Pope Gregory thought of as *golden-mouthed*, the true upholders of Christianity.

That was so, assented Leo cheerfully, nodding; and even glanced round at his relative Frederic of Lorraine, who nodded briskly as well. Although, said Pope Leo, his orange beard spreading again, was it not Pope Gregory's sensitive conscience that detected something subversive in the Blessed St Columba's views of the Holy Trinity, as exemplified in the hymn *Altus Prosater Vetustus?*

'They all hummed a few bars, the priest Eochaid in harmony.

Of course, said the Pope, there was much to admire in the early church of western Europe. Its austerity. The authority of personal rule, as invested in its early missionaries, who, like the travelling ministry of the Apostles, brought the Word to the north. Such had been the custom of the Mother Church itself for two hundred years, until each town had its sufficiency of churches and those churches came under the rule of a bishop who was himself subject to authority and of uniform learning with his fellows.

'We have no towns,' said the priest Tuathal. The King Macbeth had not intervened.

Leo's good mood continued. No more had St Benedict, he said, when in his cave he had promulgated the way of life that had commended itself to all the Western world outside those placid waters of the antique church. From the deserts of Egypt, mankind had moved into cities, and the church must so arrange herself that she might minister to them.

The King of Alba must know, said the Pope, of that place on the banks of the river Loire where the bones of St Benedict rested. The King had a fleet. He sustained his people by trade. He must have observed, said the Pope, the animation, the good sense, the orderliness of the men of business in Tours and in Nantes when compared with those more primitive lands of the north whose tenets were full of prejudice and whose loyalties were confused.

And that, thought Hildebrand, was dangerous ground. All very well to hint about Brittany. But anyone who had heard the rumours could retort that they were breeding heretics in Tours and Angers these days, and the Bishop of Nantes had been no saint either.

On the other hand, this little group of men also knew what they were about. There was the slightest pause, and then the Culdee Prior broke in to congratulate Archbishop Humbert on the metrical responsaries he and his Holiness had written together for the Feast of St Columbanus. 'For,' said Prior Tuathal, 'all churchmen of the older condition remember what that great Irishman replied when accused by the Franks of a different manner of worship: *Let Gaul, I beg, contain us side by side, whom the Kingdom of Heaven shall contain.*'

He then questioned the Pope on a matter of mixed intervals in the later responsaries, and the Pope answered by singing the appropriate portion and inducing Prior Eochaid to accompany him.

The names of John and Theodore, Moengal, Notker, Hogar, Huebald,

Ratpert, and even John Scotus Erigena came up in rapid succession, followed by that of Tuathal's namesake, of whom it was said that the Frankish Emperor cursed whoever had made such a man a monk.

They sang, briefly, *Hodie cantandus*.

They touched lightly on acrostic sermons, and the dialogues for soloist and chorus composed by Romanus for Constantinople, which the Culdee Prior had off by heart in their entirety.

They came, at last, to Guy of Pomposa and the new system now taught in the Lateran choristers' school, coupled with the song the Pope was this week composing for the saint-bishop Hidulphus's memory, in advance of his proposed autumn visit to Trèves. The Pope sang, in his extremely melodious voice, several extracts. The priests, their eyes shining, applauded, and so, after a moment, did the entourage standing behind, with the exception of Hildebrand himself, who thought that enough was enough.

The King of Alba, who evidently felt the same, said, 'How can we thank you sufficiently, my lord Pope, for your generosity, both of your time and your wisdom? Of your glorious music, it is useless for laymen such as we are to speak.'

It had been a long session, and ceremonial garments were heating; but the warmth that suffused the Pope's face owed something to personal satisfaction as well. He said, 'Men do not make the long journey to Rome to discuss nothing but music. They come for advice, and this I have given you. All episcopal order inherits the power Christ first granted to Peter, and this order you must now reinstate, if your people are not to walk as aliens in the error of blindness. I have considered the candidature of the priest Isleifr, and when the time comes, I shall instruct the Archbishop of Bremen to consecrate him as Bishop for Iceland.

'Alba has one bishop nearing the end of his office, and no other consecrated by any recognised authority. I have advised that you end this state of affairs, and you have accepted my advice. When two priests have been found who will meet with your requirements, both as to language and the nature of their training, they will be sent to you. As the church in Alba strengthens and flourishes, you hope, you say, to train their successors and fellows yourselves. From the priests you have brought with you today, I should say that your hope is well founded.

'You also look forward,' said the Pope, 'as does King Svein of Denmark, to the time when the number of bishops may justify the appointment of a metropolitan of your own, and you express the wish, also expressed by King Svein, that such an archbishop or even archbishops should be directly responsible to the Holy See, and not to any intermediary.'

He paused, and Hildebrand did not blame him. This had emerged in the early minutes of the audience, closely entwined in a matter to do with the use of the Magnificat at Matins, and although the name of Adalbert of Bremen had never been mentioned, it had performed an antiphony of its own behind every sentence, along with the unspoken name of Archbishop Herimann of Cologne.

The Pope said, 'I have decided that the Metropolitan of Alba, when the time comes, should claim the pallium from the Apostolic See, and should regard himself as responsible to the Apostolic See in all things, including such dues as the kingdom of Alba may then contrive to afford from the prosperity with which the protection of St Peter may well endow her.

'There remains the matter of your spiritual welfare. I came barefoot to Rome. Bearing scrip and staff, King Canute himself came here thus and traversed the paths of due pilgrimage. This, I have told you, I expect of you all. You who are priests will have no more required of you. You who are monarch of your people, and who have sinned as mortal man must, will come to me here at my chapel after the purification of your pilgrimage, to learn what further atonement God may demand. For the King, so your old records say, must be without blemish; and so must he who expects to receive an Apostolic Blessing under this roof. . . . You may leave.'

Transported, they prostrated themselves with inhuman deftness, and left.

'I thought,' said Sub-deacon Hildebrand to the Pope, 'that you might have considered a final chorus before letting them go?'

It was a liberty, but he spoke in a murmur, as the Pontiff was rising, and he thought that to strike a note less than serious would not go amiss.

'It was necessary,' Leo said. 'You were right. I have seldom seen such application.'

'A man like that could clear Calabria for you,' Hildebrand said. 'If his brother hadn't died, you might have tempted him, like the Normans, into profitable exile. As it is . . .'

'As it is,' said the Pope, 'he may well be travelling in the opposite direction. I have invited him, with his priests and his noblemen, to the Easter procession and banquet. The Archbishop of Dol ought not to be present. Macbeth of Alba should then have audience of me and leave, before the opening of the synod. Let him be advised.'

It was a privilege indeed to observe the great, and to learn. Archbishop Adalbert of Bremen, it was said, was building a house for himself in the Borgo. It would be interesting to know if, in time to come, he would ever occupy it. It would be interesting to know whom, in time to come, he might have to sell it to.

Down in the platea of St John, the nobles of Alba awaited in silence the return of their King from his audience.

It seemed a long wait. Here and there, a horse trampled, shaking its bit, and the officers of the city wards and the escorting senators fell into conversation among themselves and rubbed their sleeved arms against a little spring wind.

Then at last there came a small bustle glimpsed between pillars, and a splash of red, and another, followed by the glint of gold as Thorfinn came down the steps, followed by Isleifr, Tuathal, and Eochaid. With their escorting deacons, they began the traverse of the courtyard.

Kineth of Angus said, '*A' Ghaoitha*. My God, they've bungled it. Look at Thorfinn. He looks like a thunderstorm.'

'He always looks like a thunderstorm,' said Morgund. 'What about the three priests? Can you see them?'

The procession came nearer, and he could see them.

'*A' Ghaoitha*, they're weeping,' said Kineth. 'He's excommunicated them.'

Thorfinn was within earshot. He turned and surveyed Isleifr, who was red-eyed, and Tuathal and Eochaid, whose cheeks were not dry.

'No,' said Thorfinn. He switched to Gaelic. 'It's something worse. I've promised to kiss them all when we get back to the Ager. And then to sing them a song.'

'A song? What sort of song?' said Kineth of Angus.

Thorfinn took his leave of the churchmen, fitted himself into the procession, and gave the signal for the departure. He looked back at his inquisitor.

'An address to sore feet,' he said. 'Eochaid is just composing it. Tell them about it, Eochaid.'

And Eochaid did.

NINE

O MORE THAN the next man did Ealdred, Bishop of Worcester, England, enjoy the rigours of travelling. But in the art of arriving he was matchless.

The cavalcade which on Easter Eve swept up to the gates of the Leonine City might have missed the morning audience, overrun the beginning of the baptismal ceremonies, left barely enough time for a quick change and a meal, and none at all for a dash to the sulphur-baths, but there was not a mark or a wrinkle on those bits of its clothing it was not sitting on; and its horse-harness, its banners, its baggage-mules, and the helmets and spears of its escort were of the same impeccable order.

The opening of the gates, the struggle through the belligerent hordes of the Borgo, the broken-down Schola Saxorum with an apologetic and over-worked deacon in charge were, as the Bishop expected, the impoverished sequitur, but that could not reduce the achievement.

England had made its entry in the style with which it should be synony-mous. Its forthcoming march to the Baptistry, albeit with a few hundred thousand other pilgrims, should not either do it dishonour.

The good mood persisted for as long as it took them to divest Bishop Ealdred of his robes, and for the over-eager lad Alfred to return from his necessary errand.

'Well, they got here all right,' said Alfred, vaulting across to his box and grabbing the fresh shirt held out by his servant. 'There is no doubt they got here. They're at the papal palace.'

The Bishop's arms remained in the air, but his face sank.

'*Archbishop Juhel?*' he said. '*In the Vatican palace?*'

Goscelin looked round, and Bishop Hermann.

'No,' Alfred said, from inside his Holy Saturday tunic. He pulled it down. 'Macbeth of Alba and his men. No one knows where Juhel is. Macbeth of Alba and his men are lodged in the Vatican palace. And wait,' Alfred said, ''till you hear why he stayed so long at Woffenheim.'

It was, naturally, a matter of minor irritation only. The implications, however, were not minor; and from the moment that Bishop Ealdred, with his entourage, passed through the Porta Castella and crossed the bridge into the city of Rome, he found that his mind tended to return to them.

Riding beneath the triumphal arches and past the Temple of Concord, Bishop Ealdred was not overwhelmed. Before Lyfing had died four years ago, Ealdred had extracted from him all he could learn about Lyfing's visit to Rome with King Canute.

Macbeth of Alba, he was aware, would know at least as much, and from the same sources. As Thorfinn of Orkney, he had joined the English court as a housecarl immediately after Canute's return. And as Thorfinn and as Macbeth, he had been favoured of Canute's wife Emma.

To deliver one's tribute, for example, one had, as now, to force a path away from the crowds which poured towards the high, gilded dome of the Baptistry with its clutch of oratories huddled about, their doors glinting copper and silver, and equally from the other stream that swirled on round the square double wings of the Patriarchium and up to the portico of the basilica.

Struggling through to the door of the Camera, he glimpsed the Constantine horse, from which a Prefect of the City had once been hung by the hair by one Pope, and to which, in his turn, another Pope had been dragged and left naked.

No wonder the Chair was less than popular. No wonder Lyons and Bremen had refused it. There were other ways of exercising power.

The clerk of the Camera was talkative. He had not himself met the King from the top of the world, but two of his nobles from Alba had called. Civility itself, they had been. And well advised in their gifts to the Camera. For instance, this book. And these vestments.

It was an Evesham gospel, with smith-work by Mannig and Godric. The embroidery was harder to place, but, from Hermann's face, Bishop Ealdred thought it Shaftesbury needle-work.

In the name of the holy and indivisible Trinity, Father, Son, and Holy Ghost, the King of Alba had paid what was due to the Lord God and the Holy Apostles. It did not do to forget that the King of Alba was still Emma's protégé.

'And furthermore,' said the Archarius, lifting the vestments away, 'the King presented the white palfrey he was riding, together with its horse-cloth and harness, for the use and benefit of the Abbot of Cluny.'

It did not do to forget that the King of Alba was a man with a number of very good ideas of his own.

As Bishop Ealdred had suspected, it was rather unpleasant in the Baptistry, once the novelty of the handsome little room had worn off: the shallow cistern ringed by porphyry columns upholding their eight-sided galleried entablature; the plated floor; the walls encrusted with mosaics and marbles; the two-tiered cupola that lobbed back the cries and the chanting and the gushing and slapping of the Claudian waters so that, even standing in the outer-ring passage, one felt the ears deaden while the head filled with fumes from the incense.

The Pope administered the sacrament of baptism three times on Easter Eve, and he was now embarked on his third and last service. Water as well as noise and perfume seeped through the doors from the inner room. Soaked and tearful figures in white robes stumbled out, passing the original great porphyry urn with its gold lining, but not the seven silver deer pouring water, or the silver statues of Christ and St John, with the golden lamb standing between, which now lay converted into earrings and bracelets in some pagan grave.

Lands in Africa and in Sicily, in Gozo and Cephalonia, had once supported this room with their tribute. Before the coming of the Saracens, before the Eastern Emperor showed his greed, twenty-five thousand gold solidi each year came to the papal curia from Sicily and Calabria. No wonder this Pope would do anything to get the Normans out.

After the Washing of Regeneration, they witnessed the ceremony of Consignatio in the chapel of the Holy Cross next door, passing the closed doors of the oratory of St Andrew the Constantinopolitan and the oratory of St John the Baptist, whose dalmatic, boxed in the altar, could stop floods or bring rain and ought, said Bishop Hermann, to parade twice a day in the Baptistry.

They attended a Stational Service at the Lateran and rode back with their entourage through the crowded, torch-lit streets and over the Tiber to the hospice.

Supper was found to be over, and the little fish that was left lay like horn on the plate. 'I wonder,' said Alfred, 'what they're eating in the palace. They've done their penance; you heard?'

How a young man of this cast of mind could become Sheriff of Dorset, with its mint at Wareham, its proximity to Emma's great port of Exeter, might have been hard to understand unless you knew all his antecedents in Flanders and Brionne and Brittany.

Bishop Ealdred said, 'I take it you are speaking of the King of Alba and his retinue, and, further, that you are surprised that, having come to Rome, they have also troubled to purchase spiritual favour. Why do you suppose that they came?'

'Why did *we* come?' said Bishop Hermann. He leaned back against the wall and stuck his feet out. A good businessman, but a trifle too smug: about his wit; about having been chaplain to the King of England. He was only from Mons, after all.

Bishop Ealdred said, 'Both Alfred and Goscelin know very well why we are here. The King vowed to visit Rome in thanksgiving for his return from his long exile in Normandy. However, his counsellors would not allow him to leave England, things being as they are.'

'The Godwin family being as they are,' Alfred said. 'What penance do you think the Pope will lay on King Edward? Thorfinn has been on bare feet round all the churches.'

'Macbeth,' said Bishop Ealdred automatically. He added acidly, 'Round not quite *all* the churches, surely. There has hardly been time.' He could feel his patience leaving him, as it often did when he was hungry. There was bread and cheese and some wine in one of his boxes: he had sent for it.

Bishop Ealdred met Hermann's knowing eye and frowned irritably. When he, Ealdred, had his audience with Pope Leo, there were a number of topics to be aired that had little to do with King Edward's spiritual future. Topics to do with the future of Edmund Ironside's descendants, wherever they might presently be. Such as in Passau, with the widow of Stephen of Hungary? Topics to do with the confirmation of new and worthy bishops much loved by King Edward, such as Ulf, the King's former chaplain, who had been expelled by his flock and was on his way to the Pope to complain personally.

'Why has Alba come?' Bishop Ealdred said. 'Vanity. Superstition. To gain merit in the eyes of his people. To emulate Canute. As a bulwark against Norway, which has quarrelled with his wife's father. To please Emma the Lady-Dowager, who he seems to think is going to live for ever. What else is there?'

'The food, I suppose,' said Bishop Hermann.

Asleep later on his uncomfortable mattress, mollified with bread and cheese, the Bishop of Worcester did not hear the brief conversation between the oldest and youngest of his companions.

'*Women?*' said Bishop Hermann. 'In the name of Christ, Alfred. It's Easter.'

'I'm not in holy orders,' said Alfred. 'I don't care if it's the day of the Immaculate Conception. If I have to wait more than thirty minutes, I'll go in and corrupt Goscelin.'

'It's almost worth it,' said Bishop Hermann, 'to refuse you. And I don't know why you think I should know. But if I were to guess, I'd say . . .' He paused and thought. 'Try the sulphur-baths.'

The Pope's banquet took place on the following day, and Macbeth of Alba's departure feast was held two days later.

The envoys of England were at both, although their initial encounter was of the briefest.

With all the foreign princes and churchmen in Rome, they took part in the great procession that marched from St Peter's to the Liberian church of St Mary, where solemn Mass was to be heard. The icon painted by St Luke and finished by angels led the way, followed by the Cross, the Deacon, the Primicier, the militia with their red banners and cherub-topped lances, by the notaries, advocates, and judges, by the choir, and by the sub-deacons led by their prior.

After the foreigners came the Roman abbots and the Cardinals with their white horse-cloths. The Pope came next, on a great horse with a scarlet mantle and horse-cloth that battled with the brighter orange-vermilion of his hair and his beard. Two cubicularii carried a baldaquin over his head, and beside him and after him rode the prefect and senators, the nobles and captains and officials from the Campagna, together with the Pope's personal servants bearing his robes for the rain, and a silk bag containing all he would need for the Mass.

It did not rain. The bells rang, against a great deal of chanting, and incense eddied about, followed by sneezes.

An immensely tall man with black hair, whom Bishop Ealdred did not at first recognise, leaned over and said in Saxon, 'Lights in St Paul's. You got the money in, then?'

Languorous behind Bishop Ealdred, Alfred giggled.

Bishop Ealdred said, 'My lord King. Forgive me. Although it is a long time since we first met in Forres . . .'

And then broke off, for ahead was the looming bulk, six hundred years old, of the Basilica Liberiana, the church of St Mary of the Snow on the Esquiline Hill.

Inside, the church was immense, with pillars of Pavian marble and a jumble of thin, unmatched bricks from some ancient pillage. The Magi wore Persian costumes and the Virgin Mary, Mother of God, appeared as an Empress of the East in diadem, earrings, and pearls.

Under the wingless angels, the priest Eochaid was emboldened to say to his King, 'What is it? The audience tomorrow? You have nothing to fear.'

'No. Yes. I think you should come with me,' Thorfinn said.

Eochaid waited. When the singing began, he said, 'If you take anyone, I think it should be Tuathal.'

There was a silence. Then Thorfinn said, 'If you think so.' He did not look round.

After a while, Eochaid said, 'We came here on pilgrimage. It is the Easter service.'

The choiring voices rose, stage by stage, like a fountain. The Pope's voice, sonorous and impassioned, flowed from their midst.

'You didn't tell me the legend,' Thorfinn said. 'About the magical circle of snow.'

'That fell in August? The sort of weather we have in Scone. That's why they built the church here. I didn't think you'd be interested,' Eochaid said.

There was a long interval. Then Thorfinn said, 'It is a theme in my family. In my stepfather's family. Lulach's son will be named Mael Snechta.'

'Isleifr's priest-father was named Gizur the White,' Eochaid said. 'It is the same idea. The man of magic. The Druid. The White Christ.'

'I suppose it is,' Thorfinn said. 'Tomorrow, I must remember. My oath must carry real conviction. Not to sacrifice to demons. Not to drink the blood of animals. Not to celebrate Thursday. And not to masquerade in the skins of beasts on the Kalends of January. Although it can be chilly in Scone.'

The priest Eochaid was rarely angry, but on this journey he had learned to know when anger would serve him. He said, 'On this day and in this place, wounded vanity is not the best orator.'

'On this day and in this place,' Thorfinn said, 'my grandfather's grandson would agree with you, even if my father's son had reservations. I think we should be quiet. Bishop Ealdred is looking annoyed, and I want him in a good humour.'

*   *   *

At the papal banquet that followed the service, Bishop Ealdred was in a good humour, for reasons which, to do him justice, were not wholly due to the skill of the Lateran kitchens.

This feast the Pope had chosen to give in the Triclinium, the hall where, two hundred and fifty years previously, another Pope Leo had received Charlemagne. Garlanded on the apse was Leo's monogram, above the handsome mosaic of Christ, piecemeal in brown against a mathematical blue sky. About him stood the Apostles, and below his feet issued the quadruple rivers of Paradise.

There was mosaic, too, on the flat walls on either side of the apse. On the left, a seated Christ gave keys to a kneeling Pope Sylvester and a banner to the Emperor Constantine, beardless in Frankish costume. On the right, a seated St Peter offered a Roman standard to a kneeling Charlemagne, bearded in blue with bands round his legs; and a pallium to the miniature, folded figure of Leo himself.

The present Leo, minium only in colouring, presided at his table under the mosaic, with his priests and cardinal-bishops seated at the board on his right, and the cardinal-deacons on his left at another. Before him, down the length of the hall, ran the long lines of tables, ribbed with the glowing faces and reaching arms of his princely guests and lesser churchmen. Heads of every shade and fashion of barbering and faces clean-shaven or with beads forked or flowing or close; with moustaches uncut or wholly absent, or trained Saxon-style to droop like parched corn over the dog-teeth.

And tunics and robes, also, from the weaving-sheds and workshops of many lands, in all the colours of the mosaics: oyster white and dull gold and carmine, salt green and earth red, azure and violet, figured with foliage and medallions and writing, flowered with pearls and emeralds, garnets and sapphires, encrusted with gold.

From each of these men, he, Leo, would extract his due, because the society known to the missionary saints no longer existed; and without money the church would collapse, and with it all order.

For himself, little sufficed. To feed and clothe his followers as well as himself, he had kept his bishopric of Toul. The gold chalice on the table before him, with its trumpet foot and gemmed filigree bands, had been made for St Goscelin of Toul, his predecessor, and was here because little else of silver or gold remained in the Lateran treasury.

Of the rest of the plate on the table, most had been given by the Emperor Henry. Like his own, Henry's faith he believed to be deep. Like himself, the Emperor knew the self-abasement of the whip and would lead armies, weeping. Not for himself the busy halls of Michael Cerularius in Constantinople, inhabited by the dyer, the artificer, the confectioner, the render of spices, filled with the pneumatic melodies of silver blackbirds and golden blackcap warblers. Not for the Emperor the rising throne, the mechanical lions of Constantine VII that roared and beat the ground with their tails. He and his protector lived moderate lives. On days of penance, he slept on the floor, his head on a pillow of stone. He would be surprised if Henry did not do the same.

And yet—that very alliance between Empire and Papacy that the mosaics in this room commemorated was presently his greatest concern.

Humbert, dear Humbert seated there, shining and talkative between the two priests from Alba, had been brought to Rome not for his music but for his Greek. Some day, when diplomacy could do no more, force might have to be used to drive the Normans out of Italy, and he might have to send an envoy to the court of the silver blackbirds to ask the Eastern Emperor to lend the Western his aid.

And because he would depend also—did depend—on the Emperor, he must have regard to the Emperor's interests in all his dealings: with Baldwin of Flanders and those he was sheltering; with his own family of Lorraine; with the King of France and his enemies and his allies. The sword of anathema, you might say, was in his own hand as often as the sword of physical destruction was in Henry's.

Simony, heresy, incest. They must all be stamped out, and without such grounds he would never excommunicate. But the truth was that sin was everywhere. If he were not to lay flat the internal structure of the church and render helpless those laymen who supported it, he could only proceed by choosing here and there a churl of substitution, a scapegoat. It was the policy that dictated the choice of scapegoats that he wondered, through the night, if he would be forgiven.

The large, well-dressed Saxon over there, deep in talk with the Bishop of Coutances, would come to his audience tomorrow primed with penitential messages from his master the King of England. But somewhere in the conversation there would emerge a reference to England's recent support in the Emperor's wars, and England's consequent suffering through the excommunication of both her trading-partners in Flanders and Boulogne.

For the irregularity of their unions, Eustace of Boulogne and Ingelram of Ponthieu deserved to be excommunicated. Equally, the Count of Anjou had imprisoned a bishop and could not be forgiven. Brittany and Nantes were a matter of pain, and he did not want to think about them.

Because of a letter that had reached him today, he must call before next week's synod a man he admired, Lanfranc, the brilliant Prior of Bec in Normandy.

It was, there was no doubt, his very brilliance that had entangled him in religious dialogue with this heretic Bérenger. But it must be stopped. That was what was important, not the fact that Lanfranc's friend the Bishop of Nantes had been deposed, thus admitting a chain of vacancies which would give Hildebrand there possession of the church of St Paul's here at Rome.

It was Hildebrand who had suggested the restoration of the traditional Easter synod. Without Hildebrand, he sometimes felt, they would all be lost.

It was Hildebrand who had suggested placing the King of Alba between Prior Lanfranc and Hugh of Semur, the new Abbot of the great Burgundian foundation of Cluny, beloved of Hildebrand and of the Emperor and his lady, and the most energetic centre of reform since St Benedict pointed the way to salvation.

He had asked the King of Alba, on the occasion of his first audience, about the raven on his banner, it being in his mind that the Blessed St Benedict himself had been guided by three such birds to found his monastery, cradle of the faith, at Monte Cassino.

The answer had not been entirely satisfactory, but he had not been displeased by the rest of the discussion. He understood, from his last conversations with the Emperor and Archbishop Adalbert, the importance of the lands this King now ruled over. As his dear Toul, *Leucha civitas,* was the key of Lorraine, so Orkney with its fleet and its boatbuilding peoples, its strategic position in those waters which, they said, congealed in winter into meadows of salt, was the key to the dominion of the north.

To this, the man Macbeth had added Alba. As did Olaf and Harald of Norway, so this seafaring adventurer, it seemed, was now prepared to adopt a pastoral country and accept responsibility for it.

A man who could do such a thing was not without gifts as well as ambition. It was seen that he was acquainted with the world and observed the courtesies. He could exact proper behaviour from his servants and from his noblemen, comporting themselves with decency there at the table.

It did not, of course, alter the understanding that the visit should end very shortly. With the opening of the synod, accommodation, of course, was at a premium. But, more than that, Leo knew how familiarity altered the pagan: how respect lessened as he found his way from the Sacred Highway to those parts within the walls where the buildings had not been restored or the roads cleared of refuse, and where, in winter, the wolves came to howl. When he discovered also the market for women, and drink, and the useful offices of the money-lenders. When, sick of a place where the corn-strips were covered with marble and the rivers with refuse, he assuaged his longing with riot and violence.

The Pope talked, and ate with animation, but those closest to him observed that his eyes, beneath the weight of the tiara, were red-rimmed and damp.

TEN

ETWEEN THE POPE's banquet and the King of Alba's, the English party hardly took respite.

Deploying his mission about their duties in the city and out of it, Bishop Ealdred received their reports and digested, in the efficient curia of his mind, all their implications.

Wherever they went, it seemed, the officers of the King of Alba were already in evidence.

Some of the activity, naturally, had to do with the homeward journey, and with the banquet. It was amazing, however, how often Hermann or Goscelin would return with an account of how they had seen the man Leofwine of Cumbria at this goldsmith or that merchant's, or the big, fair Norseman Otkel down at the wharves, with the priest Isleifr translating for him; or the little brown-bearded man Hlodver sitting on the edge of a tumbler's mat, his arms full of cabbage-leaves crowded with dates.

Alfred called on the Bishop of Rennes and found no less than three of the King of Alba's men with him. The Fougères half of Alfred was related to the Bishop of Rennes. Alfred was related to everybody. Bishop Ealdred, receiving his account, said, 'And what did you learn?'

'Well: I asked them how they enjoyed exchanging the smoky roofs of Tours for the gilded roofs of Rome, but they weren't very amused. It seems everyone says that.'

'How disappointing for you,' said Bishop Ealdred. 'And what else did you gather?'

'The Irishmen have been up to the Palatine again,' Alfred said, 'visiting the grave of Cairbre Ua Coimhghillain, who died twelve years ago. They didn't find anything.'

'Except their deceased Irish friend, one would imagine,' said Bishop Ealdred. 'What a pity. It seems that they are going to leave Rome with half their mission uncompleted. And nothing else?'

'No. They were nervous,' said Alfred.

'They were probably expecting the Archfiend,' said Bishop Ealdred.

'Clearly, you met him on your way out. The continuous aura of sulphur is, I must tell you, a little disturbing. Ah. Hermann.'

The Bishop of Wiltshire moved from the threshold and sat down carefully. 'It's the water,' he said. 'I don't blame him. I've just come from Lanfranc's. Thorfinn was there. Macbeth. They're everywhere, like the mosquitoes. I never saw such energy. Orkney water and Rome water must possess the same properties. You need bronze piping to put up with it.'

'Indeed,' said Bishop Ealdred. 'Well, no doubt, if you try, you will find some on sale in Rome somewhere.'

On the day of the King of Alba's banquet, his last engagement in Rome, the Pope gave two audiences: one to the English delegation, and one to Thorfinn, attended by Tuathal.

Both took place in the Oratory of St Sylvester, approached through an arch beyond the long council chamber on the Patriarchium first floor.

Profoundly moved by his encounter, as well as rather pleased, Bishop Ealdred rehearsed it immediately afterwards while Goscelin wrote it down, word by melodious word.

Likewise Thorfinn, whose audience had been somewhat longer, returned and conveyed briefly its contents to his assembled company. Nothing untoward had happened: the outcome was as they expected; the farewell gifts proposed by the Pope were of very great value and represented the high opinion the Pontiff held of the conduct of the men of Alba on this, their first visit to Rome.

He then disappeared, to make arrangements for the transport of the Pope's boxes from the Archarius to the Borgo, taking with him Prior Tuathal, who did not look very well.

By the time his first guests arrived for their repast, Thorfinn was back and ready to greet them.

The meal, served in the large room of the Vatican palace, was satisfactory, and well cooked by men everyone knew they could trust. The Prefect and senators, the cardinals, the bishops with whom the party from Alba had shared the life of the Borgo brought good conduct with them and maintained it. There was music and a little tumbling and sleight of hand, which no one protested against. And through all the talk there was the spectacle, through the sapphire-blue windows of night, of the city of Rome, hung in the darkness over the river like a votive diadem of glimmering light. Rome, the mistress and centre of the world, that tonight was real and tomorrow would be lost in the marshes of memory.

'And your meeting?' said Bishop Ealdred to the King. 'I take it your audience went well? Got all you wanted? The Holy Father was in generous mood?'

'Indeed,' said the King of Alba. 'A happy triumph in Christ, with Satan trodden under the holy feet. We have been overwhelmed with attention. And you?'

'Naturally,' said Bishop Ealdred. 'A privilege. A pleasure, of course. My

King will, I think, have cause to be pleased with the results of my work this morning.'

'King Edward has been excused his vow of pilgrimage?' said the King. 'I trust the cost was not more than will be convenient?'

'Should absolution be cheap?' said Bishop Ealdred. 'I have undertaken, on behalf of my King, that he will dispose of his intended outlay to the needy. He is also to reconstruct and endow a new abbey. On the island of Thorney, on the outskirts of London.'

Bishop Ealdred paused. 'Perhaps, in the light of your own undertakings, such an exaction may strike you as trivial.'

'I rather think,' said the King of Alba, 'that we have been weighed on the same scale. I, too, have undertaken to build and endow a cathedral. On the island of Birsay.'

'Indeed,' said Bishop Ealdred. His eyes flickered. 'A cathedral?'

'Should absolution be cheap?' said the King of Alba.

Later that night, when it was over, Eochaid of Scone found his way to the room he shared with his fellow-priest Tuathal.

'Do you suppose,' Eochaid said, 'that our friend Bishop Ealdred has heard of the island of Birsay?'

'Does it matter?' Tuathal said. He threw some footgear into a box and began carefully to wrap up his packet of sand and his whetstone. 'If the marsh of Thorney serves London, I imagine he thinks Birsay is Thorfinn's metropolis. Which, I suppose, it is. It's also an island half a mile long off the west coast of Orkney. It's just as well the Pope doesn't know the chin of the world either.'

The tone of voice, for a moment, matched the look on Tuathal's face when he had come back with Thorfinn from the Lateran. Eochaid said, 'So you heard the cock crow.'

Tuathal stopped and looked at him.

Eochaid said, 'That is why I told Thorfinn to take you, and why he agreed. I knew if he was asked a direct question, he wouldn't evade it. . . . He wouldn't lose anything either, of course. The Emperor needs him. Here is a king of the north taking positive steps towards Rome. The fact that his own faith is wanting will be treated as a matter for injunction and penance. He will build a church on Birsay. But it was a shock?'

Tuathal the business-like, the practical, sat down. 'He was honest,' he said. 'He said, since he was asked, why he found it hard to choose his faith. If you don't know, I can't tell you.'

'Only Sulien knows it all,' Eochaid said. 'But if you are to serve him, it is right that you should understand. So you will leave?'

'I gave my word not to talk about what happened,' Tuathal said. 'It would undo his work. I can see that.'

Eochaid said nothing. After a moment, he too sat down, and waited.

'The runes,' Tuathal said. 'He wore runes even there, on a chain round his neck. Leo leaned forward and snapped it, and Thorfinn said, "It makes no difference."'

Still Eochaid said nothing.

Tuathal said, 'I don't care all that much. I want success for him: success for the country. I thought I knew what was going on, precisely. I thought I knew where I was with him. I don't.'

Eochaid said, 'You don't speak of what lies ahead for him if he is not saved?'

Tuathal looked up sharply. He said, 'No. It would have been your first thought; and Sulien's. It must have been, when you found out. But, whatever you both have said to him, it has made no difference. Oh, he is aware. He is aware, and he carries his own despair about with him.'

'What did he say?' Eochaid said. 'You were bitter afterwards; and what did he say?'

'What did he say? He answered in the words of the serpent; the manipulator; the creature of no belief who prepares other men for their doom. He answered in Irish. I shall go to my grave listening to him,' Tuathal said.

'I know,' said Eochaid; and spoke in his musical voice.

> *''Tis I that outraged Jesus of old;*
> *'Tis I that robbed my children of heaven;*
> *By rights 'tis I that should have gone upon the Cross.*
> *There would be no Hell; there would be no sorrow;*
> *There would be no fear, if it were not for me.*

'Will you leave him?'

'How can I?' said Tuathal.

The King of Alba and his people departed.

On the twenty-ninth day of April of the year 1050 there opened in Rome the Easter Synod of the Holy Catholic and Apostolic Church.

During the three days of its deliberations, it was attended by fifty-three archbishops and bishops, including Halinard of Lyons, Humbert of Sicily, Adalbero of Metz, Ealdred of Worcester, Herimann of Wiltshire, Geoffrey of Coutances, Main of Rennes, and Hugo of Nevers.

After a short dispute in which blood was shed, Guy, Archbishop of Milan, sat on the Pontiff's right side.

Peter, Cardinal Archdeacon of the Holy Roman Church, proclaimed the agenda, after divine service before the high altar of the Lateran, on which were placed the golden reliquaries containing the heads of the Apostle Peter (broad, so men said, with a hairy beard of black mixed with white) and of the Apostle Paul (long, and bald as to the crown, with a red beard and hair, said those who knew those who had seen it).

The Pope announced that he intended to canonise his saintly predecessor, Gerard, Bishop of Toul, and would visit Toul to that end in October. The synod (*Fiat! Fiat!*) chorussed agreement.

The Pope caused to be read aloud a heretical letter from Bérenger, Archdeacon of Angers and Scholar of Tours, to the Prior Lanfranc of Bec, who was then required to stand up and prove his faith, which he did, to the satisfaction of both the Pope and the synod. The heretic Bérenger was excommunicated in his absence. The present synod (*Fiat! Fiat!*) concurred.

The Pope referred to the renewed complaint by the clerics of Tours against Juhel, Bishop of Dol, who, with seven suffragans, had defied the authority of the Metropolitan of Tours and himself taken the title of Archbishop. This was an error of long standing which ran counter to ancient edict.

The legates of the bishopric of Tours were now present in Rome and should stand forth to be judged. The Bishop of Dol and his suffragans should do likewise.

There was a stir, and Richer of St Julien, Tours, stepped forward, with three priests behind him.

There was a long pause.

'Holy Father,' said Cardinal Peter. 'The Bishop of Dol does not seem to be present, or his suffragans.'

'Let them be called,' said the Pope. 'On the part of God, and on the part of glorious Peter, Prince of Apostles, of whom we the Vicar are present.'

The Archdeacon called the summons, and repeated it twice.

'Let them be searched for,' said the Pope; and the Cardinal Archbishop of Porto, with John of Civita-Vecchia and Bernard of Padua, left the basilica.

The synod returned to its business. Time passed. The three envoys returned and were admitted. The Pope called them forward.

'Holy Father,' said John of Porto. 'The Bishop of Dol and his companions have escaped. That is, they have left the place of their lodging without leave and are nowhere to be found.'

The Pope's face did not change, nor his great robe tremble as he stood to rehearse the sins of the absent Bishop: his presumption in disdaining the Metropolitan; his conduct that embraced, so men informed him, the pollution of simony.

The Bishop of Dol might, if he wished, attend in person and plead his case at the forthcoming synod at Vercelli. Until then, by the authority of the Father, the Son, and the Holy Ghost, of St Peter, and of himself, the Universal and Apostolic Pope, Bishop Juhel of Dol and all his suffragans were hereby excommunicated.

'*Fiat! Fiat!*' responded the Pope's Easter synod in chorus.

'*Fiat!*' said Bishop Ealdred of Worcester slowly, all by himself.

Hermann, he noticed, was not quick enough to say even that.

Far from Rome and his discreet detention in the Cluniac monastery of St Mary's, Juhel, Archbishop of Dol, paused for the first time in his headlong flight to await and finally to receive the man to whom he owed his freedom.

'Well, thank God,' said Archbishop Juhel on greeting him. 'We thought you had been stopped among the eternal snows and martyred, like St Maurice, for failing to persecute Christians. Do you suppose, *Domino cooperante*, that I'm excommunicated yet?'

'I would say,' said Thorfinn of Alba, 'that if you're not, we've had a lot of trouble for nothing. Is the food better than on the Aventine, or do you want to return?'

Juhel de Fougères laughed and shouted back, through the din of arrival and the uproar of welcome. 'Come in and find out,' he said, 'before there's a rock-fall.'

Rock-falls were not unknown at the monastery of St Maurice at Agaune; or worse. Here the Alpine road from Rome to Geneva, topping its crest, plunged winding down to find itself locked in a towering gorge, with the torrent of the Rhône, white and snow-green, its only companion.

Where the river debouched from the gorge to flow through green, flooded meadows towards the next defile had been recognised by many races as a place of command, a place to live, a place of sanctuary in which to rest and pray. The Celts had called it Acaunus, from the slender white spires that rose behind the great mountain bulwarks that shut in the valley.

The Romans had built there an imperial customs-house, and a shrine dedicated to Mercury, and another to the nymphs of the spring that marked the bluff closing the north-western neck of the valley. There a Roman legion had camped, brought back from Thebes in Upper Egypt to help drive back the attacks of the Alemans, and there Maurice, its Christian leader, had been killed with his companions because he spared fellow-believers.

Or so the legend ran. During the subsequent seven hundred years, tales of martyred Theban legionaries proliferated and were believed. But the kings of Burgundy, keepers of the Lance of St Maurice, thought it good to take special care of the little basilica built on the spot where the nymphs once had their shrine, and where pilgrims, soldiers, merchants and churchmen, emperors and their officials, Popes and their legates passed on their way to and from Rome. Whose chief glory, so it was said, was the singing of psalms day and night, without cease, in praise of the Lord Who sent the spring as well as the snows.

The Roman Emperor Henry was now King of Burgundy, and St Maurice Agaune was his, which was why, having escaped in the King of Alba's advance baggage-train, Juhel of Fougères had found here a refuge in which to await the arrival of the King of Alba himself.

'But I wondered,' said the Archbishop inside the hospice, 'if I had made a mistake, or if you had. Then I heard your men singing.'

'I thought I had stopped them,' Thorfinn said, 'before anyone could make out the words. And these are your companions? I know the Bishop of Aleth.'

'Bishop Hamon: of course,' said Juhel of Dol. 'He was at your marriage in Forres, with Ealdred, and then there was the matter of the relics of St Serf. How percipient, one must allow, the Lady Emma has always been. Now let me introduce the rest of my suffragans. For they certainly know you, both through me and through your charming friend Sulien.'

They were sitting by then at the long boards inside the main room of the hospice, with soup and bread and cheese on the table, and flagons of ale.

Earlier, they had taken wine with the Prior himself, poured from the golden ewer of Charlemagne, with its medallion of lions and gryphons, its slender neck-strips, smoother than satin, of enamel-work peeled from some Sassanid sceptre. Upon the slab of the altar, engraved with odd Celtic whorls, Thorfinn had placed a dish as Greek as the carved sardonyx vase that stood there already. When the Pope called to celebrate the Feast of St Maurice in September, he would see and no doubt recognise it and perhaps even redeem it, at the cost of some land or some privileges.

Introducing his five Breton bishops—Adam of St Brieuc, Dudic of Vannes, Salomon of Léon, Guy of Tréguier, Orscand of Quimper—Juhel said, 'Most of them, as they will tell you if I do not, are naturally also the mactierns of their regions, or at least of the blood of the ruling house, as your abbots are. Indeed, Brittany and Alba are two halves of the same picture: a collection of parties who are not always content to acknowledge a common leader. Did your noblemen not fear, also, that they would incur the Pope's wrath and even his excommunication?'

'The risk seemed remote,' Thorfinn said. 'And then when at the Pope's banquet I was seated between Prior Lanfranc and Hugo of Cluny, it vanished altogether.'

'So you knew that I was at the Cluniac monastery,' Juhel said. 'But you kept going to the other St Mary's. They told us. They were amused.'

'Perhaps you would rather have been freed by the English party?' Thorfinn said. 'It seemed to me, however, a little unwise, so I forestalled them. Is Sheriff Alfred quite the nuisance he appears? He is related to you?'

'He's my uncle of the half-blood. Being with Ealdred probably brings out the worst in him. There is no one quite so undiplomatic as Ealdred when he is not being diplomatic,' Juhel said. 'Alfred is, as you will have noticed, half my age, but has had relatives in England since the time of King Canute. I assume you know that also. You know his uncle Osbern. You know Carl of York and Exeter.'

The bishops were talking among themselves as they ate, and so were the men Thorfinn had brought with him, rather loudly. They were, of course, on their way home. Their manners were better polished than those of their counterparts in Brittany would have been. And these were youngish men: not the mactierns, the mormaers, the chiefs of each region whom Thorfinn had taken to Winchester. Thorfinn had brought to Rome not the men who ruled his districts, but the next generation.

He had also, it would appear, weighed up the situation in Rome with remarkable accuracy. He had deduced that the Pope did not want a confrontation. That it would defeat all his hopes of reform in Normandy as well as Brittany if the Archbishop of Dol, publicly instructed to bow to the Archbishop of Tours, had refused, and had thereby incurred something more drastic than excommunication. In engineering his escape, Thorfinn had saved Archbishop Juhel from the Lateran prison.

Thorfinn said, 'Tours will go on complaining. What will you do?'

'Prevaricate,' Juhel said. He rubbed his bent nose and grinned. 'After all, they haven't heard my side of the dispute. All they can accuse me of is not appearing to present it.'

'And if one day you must?' Thorfinn said.

'Then,' said Archbishop Juhel, 'it so happens that I have this excellent two-hundred-year-old letter from Pope Adrien to King Salomon of Brittany conveying the insignia of authority to Festinien, his elected Archbishop of Dol. I would have brought it with me, except that the ink isn't dry.'

'*Vera Bruta Brittanica,*' Thorfinn said. 'What chance has the Sovereign Pontiff against it?'

'You learn guile,' Juhel said. 'We are surrounded by Main and Anjou and Normandy. You by England and Norway and Denmark. We are all treading a dangerous path. The protection of St Peter can be costly.'

'Sometimes,' Thorfinn said. 'St Peter doesn't seem over-anxious to protect his vassal King Andrew of Hungary against German invasions. It must worry Hungary. I gather the Archbishop of Colocza himself is on his way to converse with the Pope.'

'Ah,' said Archbishop Juhel, and buried his face in his ale.

'To beg the Pope's interest in halting the Hungarian wars,' continued Thorfinn. 'What else?'

'What else, indeed?' said Archbishop Juhel. 'But I should wager that, by fair means or foul, Ealdred and Hermann somehow get to that meeting.'

'Or Bishop Ulf of Dorchester,' Thorfinn said, 'racing so slowly to beg the Pontiff to confirm him in his enormous see.'

'And the Pope will do it,' Juhel said. 'Bishop Ulf may even be allowed to shift his seat into Lincoln, which is what he really wants. After all, the un-Saxon Leofric was allowed to take over Exeter. And Hermann isn't content, of course, with Berkshire and Wiltshire, any more than Ealdred is happy with only Worcester. What's more, they'll get what they want. The Pope will give every encouragement. He thinks these changes are progress; that the bishops, Roman-fashion, are coming in from the country. The bishops in fact are stepping aside from the earls and preparing to make themselves into princes.'

'That is the other danger of bishops. Archbishops are worse. . . . Tell me,' said Archbishop Juhel, 'what was the fee for your shriving? Did you promise to erect a bishop's seat in a city? The opinion on the Aventine was that you had, in return for St Peter's somewhat distant protection and a bone of St Andrew. . . . Why should I lower my voice? I thought the Fool for Christ had already crossed to your shores?'

Thorfinn removed his hand. 'There is a place called Hexham,' he said, 'that I should prefer to have a monopoly of St Andrew until the spiritual boundaries between myself and Northumbria are a little more clearly defined. I've promised nothing I shan't carry out. I shall build churches. I shall accept bishops. But there will be no Roman system, yet. Not until we have towns.'

'Hasn't Sulien told you?' Juhel said. 'Towns corrupt. For towns, you must have rules.'

'The early church was pure and free, with few rules,' Thorfinn said. 'But the desert offers no protection to the young and the old and the sick. . . . You have heard it all before.'

'I know it better than you do,' said Juhel of Dol. 'The heathen overran Europe, and the Celtic church stayed through the centuries the loving guardians of faith and of learning. But now the lands and the peoples they served are beginning to change. . . . When Emma invited you to Canute's court, she planned to use you and your people as mercenaries, the way King Salomon used the Norse, and your grandfather used your father's men and the Irish.'

'I know that, of course,' Thorfinn said. 'A mercenary is what I was.' His voice was neutral.

The Archbishop glanced at him, and went on. 'We talked of the dangers of vassaldom. The Lady-Dowager is still using you. Everything that happens in England today has to do with this childless King and his possible heirs. You know that. The Lady Emma is still using you, to counterbalance the power of Norway, as well as of Mercia and Northumbria in the north.'

'*Emma* is using *me?*' Thorfinn said.

They looked at one another.

'Is that all you wanted to know?' Thorfinn said. 'That when Emma dies, my policies will be the same? Then you had better learn that they may not remain the same, but they will remain mine. They have always been mine.'

'Good,' said the Archbishop of Dol. 'A man I can't move to anger is a man I'd rather not deal with. What and who you are is important. To me, and to many people. You know that. You have just put it to the proof. You were represented to me, when I first heard of you, as a half-pagan jarl with a collection of Christian lands from which he took tribute.'

'And now?' said Thorfinn. 'The plaything of princes? I am willing to be flattered, but I do not intend to lend you any more money.'

'Now, Macbeth of Alba,' said Archbishop Juhel. 'Now you are a king with a kingdom. Perhaps a great king, about to make a great kingdom. What is it like up there on your pinnacle?'

He was not expected to answer. He had no intention of telling the truth. He did not dislike his pinnacle; except that it was land-locked, and noisy.

ELEVEN

SUSPENDED LIKE BUTTERFLY wings in the haze, under banners of white marked with gold, the dragon-ships of the pilgrim King of Alba moved into the mouth of the Tay, and on either side of the river the first bonfires shimmered into the air.

They were expected. By merchant-ship, by mule-train, by courier; there were ways, however leisurely, of passing news between Alba and Rome. A king requires to be assured of the safety of his kingdom: a kingdom requires to know the exact whereabouts of its king. An envoy of Archbishop Herimann's, riding relay-horses, had borne the message that summoned Thorfinn's ships to meet their lord at Cologne. And before the King himself reached the city, the news was on the high seas and on its way home.

Behind it, the cavalcade of the King swept northwards almost as swiftly, escorted by song and clamour and laughter; by contests solemn and ludicrous; by endless talk and at length by argument: argument with Thorfinn himself that went on day and night in the way to which his hird were long accustomed.

But three-quarters of these men were not of his hird, and until this journey he had been a stranger to them. Also, they were landsmen who recognised but could not share the sudden liberation of the spirit that the sea bestowed on her exiles.

From the Rhine to the Tay, Odalric, Otkel, and Hlodver sailed the ship with their souls, and occasionally, out of goodwill, joined Thorfinn and the rest in the well, where the talk was still good and the laughter burst out when it was calm, and still, in the skirl of the wind, the brassy bugles of triumph were ringing. Then land rose out of the sea: the cliffs and meadows and beaches of Alba; and they stood in silence, holding the rigging, for whereas men of the north could recall the summer hosting and the long months of raiding and fighting with perhaps a winter abroad at the end of it, laid up with a broken ship, or a wound, or a girl, men of the land seldom left their wives, or their parents, or their children for long.

To them, the tranquil investment of the broad estuary was a thing that caught at the throat, personal as a bereavement. The sand-flats on either side moved slowly closer, and the turf and the trees and the low hills behind became greener, and the scattered cabins and their fields more distinct. The smell of wood-smoke came over the water, and of cow-dung, and bracken, and honey; and instead of rafts of small birds and seaweed, there were swans floating through amber reed-beds, and nets on the beach, and small jetties.

Somewhere over a ridge, a lamb issued grating complaints and dogs had started to bark, the sound knitting from shore to shore with the voices of people. First one or two, and then a great many, running, and moving in groups, and calling, their hands hooding their greetings.

Their faces were rosy, and some of them wore coloured clothes. A rowing-boat put out from one bank, and then two or three from another. They came round three sides of the dragon-ships and settled there, more and more of them, like fish at the trawl, rowers calling and smiling to rowers.

Ahead, the river wound glittering over its meadowlands. On their right hand and on their left, and ahead in the mountains of Atholl, joy-fires flamed, gold against the blue sky, like a garland.

'My lord King,' said Eochaid. 'Your people are making you welcome.'

There were flags flying from the citadel of Perth, and from the Hill of Tribute and Eochaid's monastery opposite. The flickering colours were the first things to catch the eye as the dragon-ships with their flotilla rounded the deep bend of the Tay above Earnmouth. Then you could see the shadows of them dancing on the thatched and slatted roofs of the new hall and its huddle of buildings about it, and coloured cloths, red and yellow and green, hung over the shining palisade of timber that crowned its green mound.

Below that, the land to the water's edge, where Almond joined Tay, was packed with folk, tight as a mussel-bed. The river beyond was hedged with small boats, and at the long wharf an awning had been raised, bright with streamers, to protect from sun or from rain the King's lady with her sons, and his mormaers standing about her.

An impartial eye, had there been one, would have noticed that on board the King's men stood, their faces shining, in a packed knot about him, while on shore Ghilander and his company waited apart from Thorkel Fóstri and Starkad and theirs; that Mael-Isu and Thor of Allerdale claimed each a different stance on the quayside, and that the King's stepson Lulach was surrounded by his people of Moray, as Maelmuire, the King's young nephew, held a separate place with the Prior of Dunkeld and his family.

In the centre waited the Queen, jewelled and still as an icon in her straight robe, with a fillet binding her brow over the pale gauze that lay close round her face and her shoulders. On either side of her stood the King's sons. Paul, to whom the year between fourteen and fifteen had given his father's nose and something of his height, together with a diffident fairness that came from another quarter. And Erlend, short and flushed, whose straw-coloured hair parted, whatever he did, on each side of his nine-year-old ears.

Then the ships began to swing in to the shore, and the shouting, that for the last mile had never stopped, but had become part of the sky, like a migration of geese or of bees, heightened and became suddenly intimate.

It was Morgund, stiff Morgund of Moray who had viewed his Queen's marriage with nothing but disapproval, who raised his hand and shouted first, smiling at Lulach and then at his Queen. And Lulach, his face satin-brown beneath the glowing white hair, smiled his open, affectionate smile and then transferred it, deepening, to his father.

To those who knew Thorfinn, the response was there, in his eyes. To the people, under the white banner given by God's own apostle, stood a man half a head taller than the tallest, in a blowing, brilliant cloak, on a golden galley lined by glittering shields, above which laughed the faces of his oarsmen and his friends.

The oars lifted; the beam of the galley touched wood; the ropes fore and after were thrown ashore and the gangplank laid through the opened gunwale, the crowd running round it.

It dropped at the feet of Thorkel Fóstri, and he started forward. Behind him, the Breton priest Sulien raised a swift hand to restrain him, hesitated, and then dropped it, at the Queen's smile.

First of all the King's subjects to greet him, Thorkel Fóstri boarded *Grágás* as if in battle again, and took in his grip the twelve-year-old boy with burned hair who had defied him at Nídarós. For the rights of a king's wife and king's sons are not as the rights of a father.

On shore: 'I shall begin with the youngest,' said the King, standing under the awning. 'Erlend, what do you wish for most?'

'A helmet?' said Erlend.

'I have brought you one,' said the King. 'Paul: how is my Orkney?'

'In good order, my lord,' his son said. His voice, rumbling through the thin frame, came from his feet. The King said, 'Then you have done well. I am pleased with you. Maelmuire?'

Cormac of Atholl, one arm round his wife, was ruffling the boy's hair with the other. He gave the youngster a little push, smiling, and Duncan's son went to his uncle.

'You are keeping Dunkeld, as your grandfather did. Is it safe?' asked the King.

Although he, too, was fifteen, Maelmuire's voice still betrayed him now and then. It did so now and he blushed, but recovered as the King paid no attention, and spoke for the well-being of Dunkeld, the warmth still round his shoulders where the lord Cormac's arm had gripped him.

'Then I am pleased with you, too,' the King said. 'And now, the lord Lulach?'

'I am here,' said Groa's son, smiling beside him. 'My lord King, I have to tell you that Moray is in good heart, and so are we all. And that as from last week you have a grandson.'

For the first time, the King paused. Then he said, 'In Rome, men showed me a church dedicated to St Mary of the Snow after a miracle.'

'Mael Snechta is the name of my son,' Lulach said. 'Bishop Malduin is not here, and so has not been able to object.' His eyes were dancing.

'Then,' said Thorfinn, 'I have brought you a blessing, which is perhaps more than you deserve, considering the nature of your labours, but which I shall certainly give to Finnghuala. It is news fit for trumpets, and you shall have them. . . . My lady?'

It seemed that until then the King had hardly looked at his wife where she stood, behind her three sons and her nephew. Now they faced one another.

Within the gauze, her face was pale as tinted enamel. Her eyes, searching his face, were light as quartz under her black brows. Then the King placed his hands lightly on his wife's shoulders and kissed her on the mouth.

It was a formal embrace, before crowds, with sunlight and shadow tumbling about them from the tossing awning, and the roar of the continuing welcome thundering still against the ears. Their lips met and drew apart, and no one could have guessed at the unguarded moment of oblivion that came to them both, or the wonder of recognition that followed it.

Then the King said, 'There is no story, they say, without its song following it. You have carried my shield for six months. Now lay it down: for from today I shall take all your burdens.'

The Queen said, with no less formality, 'Your mormaers bore your shield. Here are the others, waiting to welcome you. And Sulien.'

The voice of Erlend said, shrill with eagerness, 'Father, he's married! Sulien is married!'

'Ah,' said the King, and turned to his soul-friend.

Sulien smiled, saying nothing.

'The girl I know of?' said the King.

'Yes. We are happy. She is with child, so I have left her in Wales,' Sulien said. 'And here are your mormaers. Your lady thought—'

The Lady had thought that the King, as custom required, would sup in hall with the reunited officers of his kingdom before the latter dispersed to their families over the river, there to await the banquet of state and the public accounting.

The people thought otherwise. The people surged forward as the formal greetings came to an end, shouting questions to which, drunk with emotion, the voyagers began to attempt impossible answers. Tuathal, his arms in the air, surrounded by excited, purposeful faces, looked at Odalric, who caught the eye of Malpedar, who looked at Hlodver, who attracted the attention, jumping, of Otkel.

As if endowed by divine locomotion, Thorfinn, King of Alba, rose in the air and, chaired to the brink of the river, embarked on a boat that, followed by dozens, deposited him on the opposite shore. From there, levitated likewise among the throngs of his people, he arrived at the Moot Hill, where, ten years before, he had been elected as King, and where, again brought by his people, but this time by common as well as by noble, he was set and, gathering breath, proceeded to address them.

It was not the address that three days later he would give in his great hall of Perth to the men who led the tribes of his kingdom. It spoke not of trade or of planting, or of timber, of shipbuilding and the making of roads; little of the building of warehouses and the spinning and dyeing of wool, the improvement of tanning and the better breeding of garrons, the keeping of bees and the fencing of parks, and the training of scholars and scribes and of artificers, craftsmen in wood and iron and leather, gold and silver, whose work could make Alba great and envied of peoples.

He told them instead that St Peter the Apostle of Christ had taken them under his protection, and the Emperor of the Romans, his friend. He told them of the churches that would be built to revive the Word of God as men had known it of old, from Orkney to Allerdale. He reminded them of the old saints, of Servan and Drostan and all the rest, who had once interceded for the ancestors of every man present, and who once more would intercede for them as a people. And he showed them, chief of all the priceless gifts the Sovereign Pontiff had given this kingdom, the banner blessed by the Pope, and the gospel, bound in gold and in gems, that would lie now and for ever in this their church of Scone.

Then Tuathal, standing there in his travel-stained cloak, read from the book and Eochaid, raising his voice, led the praise: the noise of hundred upon hundred strong, untrained, lusty voices addressing the Lord, as did Constantine in his half-pagan innocence, while the Sun, His vehicle, sank in a glory of flame in the west.

Gillocher of Lumphanan turned to Malpedar of Buchan and smiled through the veils of his joy. 'We convinced him,' he said. 'All those arguments, but we convinced him, in the end.'

Then there followed the supper.

When the speeches were over and the mormaers had gone, on the heels of the King's pilgrim-companions who survived, in the teeth of their various needs, barely more than a couple of hours, the King rose and, as the company stumbled to its feet, made at last for his chamber.

Groa was there.

The room they shared was quite large, opening from the small hall where his servants slept, and where hers were within call. Inside, the walls were reeded with timber, against which light cloths had been hung, woven with pictures, and the floor had been strewn with flowers, over the herbs. There was a window, but it was shuttered.

In the half-hour since she left table, she had been disrobed and dressed again, in a stiff gown with long, open sleeves, tied from neck to hem with tassels of silk between thickly worked braiding. Her hair remained twisted and pleated as it had been under her veil. Where she sat, on a little low stool with her head resting back on the wall, it burned and flamed in the glow of a little gilt lamp set in a bracket above her. Her skirts lay about her like petals, and her face, as on the shore, was clear and pale as enamel.

Then the door opened and closed, and Thorfinn was standing there, his shoulders against it, motionless in the rosy gloom. His face was in darkness and he did not speak, or she could not hear him above the hammering of her heart.

She wondered what his inner eye saw. Not a wooden hut whose earth floor was clad only in rushes; whose light might be a taper or fulmar-oil; whose window was an open space between bark; whose bed was a board padded with down packed in linen. Not a wife who was an earl's daughter from Norway and had never in all her life trodden floors of mosaic or marble, or worshipped amid silver and gold in the footsteps of hundreds.

It did not help to know that Thorfinn's men during the supper had most likely, in their euphoria, been exaggerating. It did not help to suspect that they had not.

And yet . . . Ninety-nine men out of a hundred would have said, 'I am home. For you, I have achieved such and such. Now I am beyond belief tired. Comfort me.'

He had said, *You have carried my shield for six months. Now lay it down, for I shall take all your burdens.*

He had said: *There is no story without its song following it.*

Groa rose and walked across the room and, standing before him, slid her hands through his arms and rested them flat on the door at his back, where his own hands were spread, keeping him upright.

'Take your shield back tomorrow,' she said. 'There is nothing to tell you. There is nothing to ask you. Tonight is for sleep.'

Thorfinn said, 'I failed nobody else.'

'Must you be perfect?' said Groa. After a moment, she said, 'If you fail, you should fail with your lovers. Findlaech. Thorkel Fóstri. Sulien. Lulach. And me.'

He turned his face away. 'And that should be your reward?'

'The gift of your absolute trust? Yes,' said Groa.

She released his hands from the door and, bringing them forward, held one on each of her shoulders. 'I am your crozier. Where shall I take you?' she said.

Thorfinn said, 'To your knee.'

In the end, she took her seat again under the lamp and sat for a long time, her fingers at ease in the thick of his hair, breathing the scent of bruised spices. After a long time, the lamp flickered, the oil growing low; and he stirred and lifted his head under her hand.

'Your hair,' he said. It was still pinned in its coils.

'I shall do it,' she said. There had never been a time when they were together at night and he had not unpinned her hair and let it down, like a robe in his hands.

'No,' he said. 'I have something for you.'

Something had revived. He rose of his own accord, who so lately had needed her crozier, and, crossing to the first of his boxes, drew from it a casket, and from the casket something burning with green and crimson and gold that he brought, cupped in his hands, to the lamp.

'It was worn,' he said, 'by the Empress Irene. But you are not dressed for it.'

'Am I not?' She looked down.

'No.'

Carefully, using one of his hands and two of hers, the cords of her night-robe were opened, from her neck to her throat, and the robe sank like a sheath, first from her shoulders and then, as her arms were drawn free, like a calyx framing the stem of her waist, and the white skin above and below, finely marbled with veins.

'That is how she would look,' Thorfinn said; and did not move for a long time. Then he stepped forward and clasped the necklet high round her throat.

It was heavy. She stood very straight, cuffed in gold while the fine almond jewels glowed and blazed in their network and trembled among the spurs and fringes of gold that trickled over her breasts and between them.

Thorfinn drew a long breath.

'Now,' he said. 'Now the hair should come down.'

But only half was ever unpinned. It fell sweetly, smothering the gold of the necklace and cradling the sphere of one breast, touched to life by the warmth of its coil. Then the leisurely, unpinning hands were there no longer, or the space between them, or pity, or thought itself. Against his cheek, when her lips were free, she said, 'If you wish.'

And from Thorfinn, who never laughed, there came a sound that might have been a laugh.

'Thou gem of valour,' he said, 'and princess incomparable. You hold a fool in your hands who has strength for the business of six minutes, or perhaps only for four; and who will do nothing for you, for afterwards sleep will carry him off as if to the grave. And if that is true failure, and it is, I still cannot spare you it.'

He was right. Of all the vast energy of which for nine months he had been the everlasting torrent and reservoir, there was tonight nothing left but one last golden coin, sent spinning into the air for six minutes, or perhaps only for four. But because she was already attuned to the moment, she, too, caught the flash of the coin at its zenith: the brief explosion of light before darkness came, and peace, with her husband asleep in her arms.

For six months, this bed had been her own, as had the beds in all her lodgings. The lamps in each were to her liking, and the place where her robes lay, and where her mirror and comb were to hand. The manner in which her girls and Sinna and Unna attended her followed the path that pleased her best, and that everyone knew.

For six months, lying here unencumbered on the coolness of linen, with the shutters pulled wide to admit the soft airs and noises of night, she had tried to see with Thorfinn's eyes and think with his brain and share the common experience of his uncommon journey: the daily assault of exchange and confrontation, of decisions to be taken and problems to be passed on or dealt with.

Then, insensibly, her mind would pass instead to the problems she herself would face with the dawn, and the decisions she would have to make or unmake, and the men whom she must court, or check, or pacify. And she would find in the quiet order of her chamber a solace that itself disturbed her, because one day she must relinquish it.

Today. And tonight she knew that she would have lain on a moorland, with the wolves at her back, provided only that, of all the souls in the world, one ugly man lay sleeping like this at her shoulder.

Towards dawn, his breathing quietened and changed. Then, very lightly, for he thought her asleep, his fingers began to trace on her body the subtle pattern, the overture to a journey he had created over the years, drawing on arts that had nothing to do with his Nordic blood, and which was the presage of not four minutes or six, but long, slow combers of joy with only the sun and the moon for their hourglass.

So, last of the travellers, Thorfinn himself found his release. As a tired blade, tempered over and over, will regain its value and lustre, so, between dawn and rising, he took his refreshment.

And then, upon rising, he took up the shield of his kingdom.

TWELVE

A S IN THE time of Hakon of Norway, who came to power *at mun banda*, with the goodwill and to the pleasure of the gods of his sanctuaries, the Lord of the Apostle Peter was, it seemed, content with his homage, and blessed Alba and Orkney both with peace and with fruitfulness.

None remembered a year such as followed. Whatever shadows fell on the countries about her, Thorfinn's land seemed untouched.

At home, the growing-season was cold. But because of the new tools and the new kilns and the new warehouses, there was food in Alba where corn and milk and fruit were wanting in Ireland.

Overseas, the great Finn Arnason, the Queen's father, had proved his loyalty and his worth to King Svein and was favoured above all men; while the King of Denmark himself continued to be neighbourly to the Archbishop of Hamburg and Bremen, as was his wont, but did not delay in sending a ship full of rich gifts to Alba, whose mission to Rome had been attended by so many benefits.

With the ship, King Svein sent a crop-headed young woman called Ragna, who the previous month had been delivered of a large purple infant with a shock of black hair. It proved to be a daughter, so King Svein sent the baby as well, assigned to the King of Alba's personal cook.

In Norway, Harald the King spent part of his time with his Norwegian wife Groa's cousin and part with his Russian wife, the sister of the Queens of France and of Hungary. The rest of his energy he deployed in wars against Denmark that left no time or money or men he could trust to enforce his claim to the lordship of Orkney.

In Ireland, Eachmarcach, King of Dublin, was feeling his age, and sent Thorfinn the tribute owing for the lands he had conquered, without troubling to visit in person, which had a lot to commend it. The islands and Galloway, left to Thorfinn to order, were quiet under his mormaers.

In England, every man's eye was turned to Wessex, where the Earl Godwin and his family were improving their stranglehold on the kingdom against the growing ill-will of Leofric of Mercia, of Siward of Northumbria, and of King Edward himself. Leofric's noisy son Alfgar, now pushing forty and father of four children ranging in age from fourteen years to six months, dashed into Forteviot and out again, having cast in Thorfinn's direction his congratulations, a gift from his mother, and the latest rumours from everywhere.

Thorfinn learned that Bishop Ealdred was back and renewing diplomatic relations with his kingly master and all three competing Earls, as befitted a man whose diocese included Worcester and Bristol.

Bishop Hermann, it seemed, had also returned, laden with parchment, and had picked up the threads of the various businesses now rolling briskly between Herefordshire, Dorset, and Devon, Normandy and the Breton coast, Flanders and points further south in the Rhineland.

With a smugness he had noticed elsewhere, Alfgar made pointed mention, Bishop Ulf had made his way from Rome via Besançon, and was now re-ensconced in his splendid diocese of Dorchester. It had, according to opinion, been a near thing, as the synod at Vercelli had been tempted to break his staff for incompetence, until introduced to a greater temptation. ('By whom?' said Thorfinn. 'Ask my father,' said Alfgar.)

Personally, Alfgar said, he didn't enjoy having Godwin's son Harold so close to his borders, however competent he might be in fighting the Welsh, but at least it occupied the attention of Thorfinn's old friend Siward of Northumbria and kept his heavy hand out of other people's affairs. Perhaps Thorfinn had heard that Siward had got another son from his wife at last, although by this time her figure had spread so much giving light to daughters or mishaps that neither she nor anyone else could tell whether she was carrying or not.

No doubt Thorfinn's Bishop Malduin, who had been absent sick in York for nearly a year, had been a comfort to them all.

And of course Thorfinn's nephew Malcolm was still in the south with Edward's court, although hardly raising his voice over a whisper in view of all the intrigue with the Godwinsons. Alfgar himself would, however, rely on Bishop Ealdred to keep matters from getting too ugly. It didn't do to forget that Ealdred had the blood of Aethelred, however emulsified, in his veins, and that the Godwin family knew it. And so what was the news from Germany?

'You mean Hungary?' said Thorfinn.

'I mean Germany,' said Alfgar. 'That's what I came for. Go on. I've paid for it. The two grandsons of the late King of England are in exile, and the wife of one of them is related to both the Pope and the Emperor. If anyone would find out what was happening, you would. You and Ealdred.'

'And Bishop Ulf,' Thorfinn said.

'Oh,' said Alfgar thoughtfully. 'And so?'

'And so one son of Edmund Ironside is dead, and the other suffers from indifferent health and has sired two girls of whom the oldest is five. I should not, I think,' Thorfinn said, 'allow that information to filter through to the Godwinsons or Earl Siward. The King, of course, will know.'

'How does it feel,' said Alfgar, 'to be God?'

He had been asked that, or something similar, once before. He refrained, as once before, from replying. The last man to miss silence was Alfgar.

It remained noisy, not to say clamorous; but every week, it seemed, some new achievement was made and there blew through the kingdom the gaiety that comes with success.

The mormaers of the regions received back to their hearths, not always with pleasure, the heirs or kinsmen who had represented them in Rome, and endured, not always willingly, long days and long nights of assertive monologues, followed now and then by outright disputes.

Thorfinn went nowhere near them. When, in due course, it became apparent that his mormaers wished to confer, he called a council at Scone to which he invited them all, from Thorkel Fóstri in Orkney to Thor of Allerdale in the south.

When they came, as they did, he set them round a table and listened. Then he spoke to them.

Most of them, now, were acquainted with Saxon. But he spoke in Gaelic, with which every man was familiar, for uniformity was the theme of the meeting.

Uniformity of justice, with the same rules enforced by the King's authority through the King's agents everywhere from Fife to the Hebrides.

Uniformity of worship, so that men might be baptised and buried and shriven on the same terms in the same way, and be taught the same practices, and have ready to hand a source of aid for the poor and the sick and the traveller; a source of education for new entrants to the church; a source of learning to be drawn upon in matters of record or dispute.

Uniformity in the way land and rights and property were held and changed hands, so that the rule in Gowrie and the rule in Orkney should for the first time be the same, and both the rights and the duties of a landowner be known; for if the church were to serve, it must be paid its due in rents or labour or offerings, and the king and his law-bands likewise.

Uniformity of aims and ideals, so that no region should plan independently of its neighbour, but each should look towards the rest, as brother to brother, and to the King as to a father. So, as in Alba of old, men had brought their token of earth to the Moot Hill of Scone to signify unity, so each region would bring its own excellence and bind it into the country that was neither Alba nor Orkney, but men had begun to call Scotia.

When Thorfinn spoke in that fashion, he was answered with thoughts as well as words, and with deep speech that achieved many things before it ran shallow.

Halfway through, Thorkel Fóstri took his eyes from the High Chair and said to Tuathal, 'It sounds well. But if all law is to be uniform, how do we decide which laws are best?'

'It has been decided already,' Tuathal said. 'On the road back from Rome.'

In September, a merchant ship rowed into the mouth of the Tay flying the banner of the Archbishop of Hamburg and Bremen.

Word had reached Abernethy, where the King was. Before the visitor rounded the bend of the river, Thorfinn was on the jetty below his castle of Perth with Prior Eochaid and his courtmen about him, and the booths at the wharves were being prepared to receive seamen.

Then the broad, well-kept vessel berthed, to a sequence of quiet Saxon orders, and the gangplank came down, with two oarsmen to hold it steady.

Of the two men who disembarked, one was clearly the master of the vessel and, very likely, a trading-officer of the Archbishop's household.

The other was neither tall enough nor grand enough to be the Archbishop. His thickset form was smothered in a coarse, hooded cloak, and of his face nothing could be seen but a heavy, clean-shaven chin with a glint of gold chain beneath it.

Then he lifted one hand, and the ring on it flashed as he pushed back his hood, revealing a big, lively face with a nose on it like an elk's, and above it the ellipse of a pink, marbled tonsure, precise as if drawn with a compass.

A face one had last seen at Goslar, plunging about the Emperor's fishpond in its small-clothes.

'Father Sigurd! No, I see . . .' said Thorfinn.

'Bishop Jon,' said the same Irish-Norse priest from Dublin who had poured the wine at his namesake's little party at Goslar. 'Newly consecrated by the noble Archbishop himself, who thought a stutter in Gaelic would hardly be noticed, were I to embark on a dictation of *The Intoxication of the Men of Ulster* in honest cross-vigil outside my cave. So, I am, for want of a better, your Bishop for Orkney.'

'Now, there is a coincidence,' Thorfinn said. 'I have a cave handy here, with your name on it. But the question is, can you endure it?'

'I am a great man for co-operation,' said Bishop Jon. 'The three hundred swords of the family of Kinvard, the three hundred shields of the family of Kynnwyd, and the three hundred spears of the Coelings: whatever enterprise they undertook together, they never failed in it. They were all my cousins, and that is on my Irish side only.'

'And the Norse side?' said Thorfinn, leading the way to the hall.

'Ah, well,' said Bishop Jon. 'Likely enough, it would be the Norse side they were fighting.'

Later, when he had recovered from the experience of meeting Groa and the shipmaster had been taken off, leaving the King and the Irish priest Eochaid, whom he already knew, the new Bishop for Orkney asked sober questions and listened carefully to sober answers.

Thorfinn was plain. 'You have been consecrated Bishop for Orkney because Archbishop Adalbert is responsible for the northern isles, and since Norway cut herself off from Bremen, Orkney and the north have been without spiritual aid.

'Orkney, of course, needs attention. But so does all the rest of this country. For many years, there has been only one bishop in Alba, and that bishop has been consecrated at York, and devoted to Northumbrian interests. For the last year, our Bishop Malduin has been sick in York. Perhaps it is a genuine sickness. Perhaps, now he is older, he will feel less impelled to fight for exclusive rights over his territory, or would not at this moment receive support from York if he did. The fact is that for the last year no priests have been ordained, no new churches have been built, and those few that exist have been neglected, despite all that good men like Mael-Isu and the rest have been able to do.

'What I am asking of you, therefore, is that you should be a Bishop for Scotia: for the north and for Alba as well, travelling as you can to every cure in the country. If you agree, I shall take you riding with me as soon as you are rested: I have to talk to my mormaers before winter. Then, also before winter, I shall call a council and you will be introduced.'

'This is what I understood,' Bishop Jon said. 'Although not quite perhaps what the Archbishop understood. And if your Bishop Malduin recovers, or receives encouragement from his superiors to return?'

'As I have said, he is older now,' Thorfinn said. 'There are regions where he has never troubled to travel and probably never will. It should be possible to keep out of his way. Indeed, I was hoping you would have a companion before long. It is too much for one man.'

'There is a priest called Hrolf,' Bishop Jon said. 'We've worked together. Archbishop Herimann thought he could reasonably be consecrated for the Sudreyar. No doubt Man and the rest of the islands could benefit from an occasional visit.'

Father Eochaid smiled. Thorfinn said, 'The name of Archbishop Herimann, though great in Cologne, is unknown in this country. We should prefer to keep it so.'

'Ah,' said Bishop Jon, and gave a great sigh of pleasure. 'The particular deviousness of the Dublin man: that is what I missed the most, back there in Cologne. That is not to say that there is no intrigue in the Empire: far from it. But it is of very modest dimensions, much to do with simple forswearing and an access of assassination now and then. I knew,' said Bishop Jon, 'that, did I get to fathom you, I would find a place where a plumb-bob would fall in a twist.'

He studied Thorfinn, his jaw meeting his lips. 'You'll need a rest, come the winter.'

The dark face was unsurprised. 'I'm taking one,' Thorfinn said. 'In Orkney. The mormaers here will have seen enough of me. I have an heir with a sixteenth birthday to celebrate. And the lendermen will require to see their new Bishop.'

'You want me to come?' said Bishop Jon.

'Of course,' said Thorfinn. 'We have a cathedral to build.'

The winter came: a sparkling winter of pleasure; and Thorfinn was God without noise: in merriment but also in silence.

Instead of sailing, he rode north with his wife and Bishop Jon and their servants, gathering familiar faces as he went—Ghilander and Kineth,

Gillocher and Morgund—to attend the baptismal feast of Lulach's first son at Forres.

He knew from an earlier visit that the Shaveling of the Snow did not share its father's brilliant hair, but was dun-coloured, like Finnghuala the white-shouldered, its mother. But Lulach regarded his son and his wife with the same untroubled affection he gave to all the world, and from the warmth of men's looks in his hall, and the teasing of their wives, it was easy to see that he had found his place and was well able to fill it.

From there, the King took the north road again, sharing the company of Malpedar and Mael-Isu for a while, and then met in due time by Hlodver and by Odalric, each with his party of welcome at the boundary-stone of his region.

The change from autumn to winter came on the journey, when, to start with, the hillsides were clothed to the top with coloured tree-plumes, coarse-stitched with the black of the firs. Then, one morning they awoke to a powder of snow, white and grey and grey-white on the hill-shoulders, and later, high in the passes, looked up to mountains cloaked with grey conifers, stiff as winter fox fur on a robe.

There were no icy peaks, blue and white, like the spires by the Temple of Mercury, nor did the rivers boil at their sides, jade-green from the snow-caps of summer. As they reached the northernmost point of the mainland, the land became one of low, gentle contours, fostering the snow-thatched longhouses and cabins of small communities. Houses with the mud paths beaten round them to the spring and the close-house, the peat-stack, the barn and the byre and where, fitted into the wall, did you open a door, was a broody goose or a piglet, or a breathing heap of new pups, rump on paw, their slit-eyes fastened in slumber.

Because the cavalcade carried the raven banner, not the white one, it was recognised all the way, and people ran out to greet them, to ask questions, to make a complaint to Odalric and the King, who would listen and promise to make answer. If a woman brought new-laid eggs, Thorfinn would take and carry them himself, as he would knock on a door himself, on the rare occasions they sought water or news that was not to be had for the asking.

Then he would fold his great height down on a bench and talk and listen for a while, and, rising, would leave what he thought they would accept from the King who was still the Earl of Orkney. And then would bring Bishop Jon in to bless them.

Once, Groa thought to apologise to their new Bishop, fresh from the comforts of Cologne, for the slowness of the journey.

'Ah, no,' said Bishop Jon. ' 'Tis the missionary spirit. Thus were all the great saints, from Patrick onwards. The skills are the same, whether it is the kingdom of heaven or one of this earth that you are offering.'

Because it was late, the Pentland Firth was as stormy as she had ever seen it, but, like Thorfinn, Bishop Jon appeared to possess a stomach made like a wolf-trap.

Then they were home.

That night, Thorkel Fóstri gave a great feast for them in their own hall at Orphir, and the next night in Sandwick. Then, as each door was flung wide for the Earl, returned hallowed from Rome with his Bishop, the old friendships burst into flame and were renewed, and deepened, and new ones were born of the next generation. And with the little hills and the lochs, the turn of a road and the rise of a mound, the unrolling of a rocky inlet or the disrobing, new-bathed, of a shining quarter of sand, the familiarity made itself known that was as old as the understanding of hunger, and of the haze of light on the breast, and of the smiling face over it.

After two weeks of it, when there was no one they had not seen, Thorfinn rode out one morning and did not come back, either that night or the next.

Then, when, despite her knowledge of him, Groa worried, reports began to come in: he had been seen on the island of Sanday; he had borrowed a boat from a different beach and had set out to sail her from island to island, alone.

A week afterwards, he came back without explanation, as he had gone.

Once, after Rome, he had disappeared in the same way, but only for two days; and even those had caused a stir, as no doubt he had known.

Then, it had not been enough, and he must have realised that also. This time, a different person came back, blessed at a different altar, and hallowed by the power of the sea, and the salt air, and silence.

That night, he said, 'I meant to tell you. The Emperor has his son. After three daughters, Agnes has borne him an heir.'

He had unpinned her hair and was letting it fall through his fingers. Groa said, 'I thought you had noticed.'

His hands continued their slow task. 'It is always the right time, isn't it?' he said. 'Groa. No child is worth another illness of yours. We have enough.'

She turned and, detaching his hands, held them in hers. 'I did want you to have a last son,' she said. 'But I am barren.'

His eyes changed; he sat quite still, his hands clasped in hers. Then he said, 'You are saying that I may love you when I wish and there will be no illness?'

She could not see his face through the haze. 'So they say,' Groa said.

'What gift have you given me,' he said, 'that can compare with that?'

Soon after that, from their old hall on the shore opposite Birsay, they walked across the causeway to the island with Bishop Jon and their sons and half a hundred high-spirited friends with a great deal of advice to give, and inspected the low walls that were all that could be seen of the old Pictish chapel and its boundary-stones.

Bishop Jon was analytical.

'Well, now,' he said. 'Thinking back to Sceilg Mhichil and Inishmurray and Inishbofin of the early Fathers in Ireland, what you have here is surely a site fit for a King of Companies, with a cooked, crisp pig in the meat pot, and a vessel of mead on the table, with its goblets beside it. Do you want my opinion in the Norse language?'

'If I can understand it,' Thorfinn said.

'It will serve,' said Bishop Jon shortly.

In the event, the church that was to be known as the *cathedra*, or bishop's seat of Christ Church in Birsay, occupied a good deal of the King's time that winter in Orkney. Arnór Jarlaskáld, arriving for a circumspect visit at Yule, found the evening talk round the longfire, of drainage gulleys and flag-setting and the cutting of sandstone, too technical for his liking, and asked the Lady, when he could get her away, about the broad, nimble Bishop with his spruce assembly of tongues that clacked their way through his speech, turn about like a weaving-shuttle.

Groa explained. 'They're rebuilding the church of the old Pictish monastery. And now they have the feel of it, they've decided to knock down part of Earl Sigurd's hall and build a better one. With heating-flues, and a water-channel, and a bath-house outside. Some of the houses are being rebuilt as well, and they are to repair the slipway. Bishop Jon,' said Groa reflectively, 'says that in the old days, to pay a builder to put up a wooden oratory with a stone church and round tower could cost thirty cows.'

Arnór, whose tongue had become sharper in his years in Norway and Iceland, said, 'Thorfinn will have to decide whether he wants an engineer or a cowherd, it seems to me. Or, better than either, a land full of vassals who will sweat gold for him. It is well seen that churches come expensive. Should Isleifr come back with such plans for Skalholt when he goes to Bremen to fetch his bishopric, I doubt his fellows may not let him into Iceland.'

'It may be,' said Groa, whose tranquillity these days nothing could disturb, 'that you should have talked to the Pope yourself, Arnór, about all these things. I am sure that, despite his expenses, you will find Thorfinn as open-handed as he used to be when you sing us your verses. I hear King Harald is a poet himself?'

'You are wondering,' Arnór said, 'nor do I blame you, how a man like myself can stay with a King who dealt so harshly with your uncle Kalv Arnason and caused your father to desert, against his noble will, to King Svein of Denmark. It is hard,' said Arnór. 'But an artist has a responsibility to his art, as you will concede, and things are difficult enough, considering that King Harald will not even hear your father's name spoken, although I'm glad to say he has nothing against those members of your family who elected to stay in Norway. You will have heard that Earl Siward of Northumbria is pressing for his daughter to marry your cousin John, son of Arne Arnason who fought for King Olaf?'

'No,' Groa said. 'No, I hadn't heard of it.'

'It is well, then,' said Arnór, 'that two lines of the same blood should have a friend who can pass between them with news. You were asking about King Harald's verse. I should not care to repeat it.'

'Rats would fall dead from the roof. Is it so bad?' said Thorfinn, coming in, fresh and cold from the rain.

Arnór jumped. 'My lord. No. Not to say bad, for one whose trade is quite other. But—'

'Then recite us some,' Thorfinn said. 'And then, to sweeten the after-taste, give us some of your own.'

And so, his jauntiness fully returned, Arnór recited.

> *'Now I have caused the deaths*
> *Of thirteen of my enemies;*
> *I kill without compunction,*
> *And remember all my killings.*
> *Treason must be scotched*
> *By fair means or foul*
> *Before it overwhelms me:*
> *Oak-trees grow from acorns.'*

'I suppose,' Thorfinn said, 'the Archbishop of Hamburg and Bremen must be quite thankful that King Harald is taking his spiritual business somewhere else. Now we want you to compose something suitable for Paul's festival that the Bishop will also find to his taste. They are both across on the island should you want them.'

They were always across on the island. The seamaster's ability in Thorfinn that had lent itself so readily to his early training in Dover and Exeter had found its way to his elder son, and that, together with the seawater of Orkney that ran in his blood, set him at the feet of Bishop Jon, who knew more of engineering than any of them. 'Although,' he would add, 'you need Hrolf. Hrolf will teach your masons. Wait until Hrolf comes.'

In turn, Paul himself came under scrutiny, as became apparent when Yule was over with its joyous anarchy: its blend of *haustblot* and Christian festival that the new Bishop from Viking Dublin and from Cologne conducted without a mistake. Then, as the day of Paul's manhood drew near, the Bishop said to Thorfinn, 'You hold this feast in Orkney. This son, therefore, is not your heir for the whole kingdom?'

That week, they were in Orphir. What had happened once in Orphir the Bishop knew; or if he did not, could have guessed from the charred timber that showed sometimes among the new, when a chest was pulled from the wall.

He knew also of the other fire, on the mainland, that had made the Queen, Groa, a widow with a young son. The white-haired son Lulach, whose child he had baptised in Moray.

Thorfinn said, 'My sons were reared in Orkney and Caithness, in the expectation that those were the lands they would rule. My stepson was brought up in Moray for the same reason.'

Bishop Jon sat down and inflated, as was his wont, the thinking cavities of his face. 'But,' he said, 'you fell heir to Alba. They were still young. You must have made plans.'

Thorfinn lifted and brought across the yew gaming-board that would preserve them from interruption and sat down opposite, with the bag of pieces in his other hand. He tipped them out.

'Orkney was my skin, and Alba my coat,' he said. 'I accepted Alba in tutelage. But until four years ago, I was contending for the earldom in Orkney. I secured my line here, for it needs a strong rule to hold it. And Lulach was the rightful heir of the Mormaer of Moray.'

'I understood from your wife,' Bishop Jon said, 'that *you* were the rightful heir. Findlaech your stepfather was the Mormaer, she said. But never mind. It is your move. So the future of the rest of Alba did not matter? Or not until four years ago?'

Thorfinn made his move. 'Four years ago, I governed a collection of tribes,' he said. 'I thought perhaps it could be done in my lifetime. I thought one could expect no more than that, and not even that if war came.'

Bishop Jon picked up a piece. 'But now,' he said, 'you look like having a kingdom. And if it is not to break up when you die, the people must be able to look to the future. The King of England is childless, and the contention is pulling his kingdom apart. You have sons.'

'You are winning. What was the stake?' Thorfinn said. In his turn, he picked up another piece and put it on the board. He said, 'After me, there must be a strong Earl of Orkney. It cannot be held from the south. Paul is a man, and has been reared for the task. He knows little of the world outside Orkney, and wants to know less. And the people know he is theirs.'

'So Paul stays. And Erlend?' said Bishop Jon.

'A boy of nine, who worships his older brother, and speaks mainly Norse. I planned that they should rule the north together,' Thorfinn said. 'If I were given ten years of life, and brought him south now, the people might come to accept him. You have won that piece also.'

'But they accept Lulach now,' the Bishop said. 'He has Gaelic and some Norse; he holds Moray now and is popular; he is known in the south both for himself and as your stepson, and he shares what your people are coming to feel for you and for your lady wife. What I am saying, and what you must also have recognised, is that Lulach your stepson is your natural heir for Alba, and perhaps for all Scotia as well. Why not, then, announce it? Your sons of Orkney will not surely be hurt? Your wife surely does not object?'

'She knows,' Thorfinn said. 'So does Lulach himself. Be satisfied. Your church will continue. You have won the game.'

'So I have,' said Bishop Jon. He looked down. 'Did we decide what we were playing for?'

'Time?' said Thorfinn. At which Bishop Jon laughed. For although he would have preferred a little more candour, he supposed, from Thorfinn's viewpoint, that it was quite an amusing remark.

*　　*　　*

'It sounds,' said Groa later, 'like one of your less successful conversations. I hope you paid him for winning, in something you could afford.'

'It was unavoidable,' Thorfinn said. 'Although it wasn't particularly pleasant.'

'I thought you were rather pleased with him,' Groa said.

'I was. I am. Always remembering that, but for the Emperor and Archbishop Herimann, the amiable Jon would not be here at all. They are bound to want to know who the next King of England will be, and therefore whom we are supporting. And what I do in Cumbria will tell them that.'

'But Alfgar advised against sending Erlend to Cumbria,' Groa said. 'You remember. He doesn't get on with Thor of Allerdale.'

'What Alfgar suggested,' Thorfinn said, 'was that we send Erlend to him for the rest of his fostering. Or to his parents Godiva and Leofric. It's the same area. Erlend will use the same languages. If the south-west of Scotia were to fall to him, he would know as much as Duncan ever did about it.'

Groa said, 'Alfgar's wife and Siward's wife are sisters.'

'And so are or were the wives of Duncan, Ligulf, and Orm. I haven't forgotten,' Thorfinn said. 'Perhaps, after all, our intentions will appear less than blatant. You can rely on Godiva to see that nothing happens to Erlend. And to be parted from Paul won't be a bad thing for either. For one thing, Paul must marry soon.'

'Must he?' said Groa. 'Whom would you elect to have a grandson in Orkney?'

She saw him consider the point, and concede it.

'I can't imagine. An elegiac poet with very poor connections, possibly? So we mustn't marry off Paul. Did I ever mention,' said Thorfinn, 'how much I dislike having my conjugal rights interfered with by your unfeminine taste for debate?'

The circumstances of the discussion, as it happened, had arrived at a condition that robbed his words not only of sting but of any relevant content whatever.

'No,' said Groa, with difficulty. 'But if you will start all over again, I could try another approach that might please you.'

THIRTEEN

THE GOLDEN MONTHS continued to pass.

This time, when the King moved from Orkney, other men from the north journeyed to Atholl and Moray and Fife in his company, for now they had acquaintances there, and prospects of business, for the isolation of the north had been broken.

With them also travelled the King's younger son Erlend, on his way to Mercia. He was conducted not by the King or his mother, which would have made of the journey an act of state, but by Odalric of Caithness, whose family had reared him for two years already.

The boy Erlend was quiet, but did not show his fright, for these things happened to every person of rank, and an Orkneyman should not behave with less dignity than other princes. So the Lady Godiva, Alfgar's mother, receiving him, respected that dignity and neither consoled him nor commented on his red eyes of a morning, but provided for him light-hearted days filled with new friends and new occupations.

Accordingly, the youngster who greeted his father that summer when Thorfinn paid his first visit to Bromley was brown and bright-eyed and cheerful and had some new words of Saxon to show off already.

Thorfinn stayed with his son and Godiva for three days, and then, acquiring a courtesy escort, set off further south still, to find Alfgar.

Alfgar, when discovered, was unaccountably jumpy.

'You've seen Erlend? A good boy. No trouble. My two eldest are a bit beyond him, but Edith is about the right age. I didn't know you were coming to Coventry,' said Alfgar.

'Well, I'm hardly likely to cross into Mercia without sanction from the Earl your father,' Thorfinn said. 'I thought he was here, with Sheriff Aethelwine.'

'Yes. No. That is,' said Alfgar, 'they were here, but they're away for a day or two. Are you staying long?'

'Evidently not,' Thorfinn said. 'I think it's going to rain.'

'Oh. Please,' said Alfgar. He snapped his fingers, and the steward waiting at the door sent forward the two grooms standing beside him and disappeared himself inside the priory guest-house. 'Please come in, and bring your men.'

'If it's convenient,' said Thorfinn politely, dismounting. 'Are we going into the hall? I thought, if your father and the sheriff had gone, that the meeting must be over.'

Alfgar stopped, causing other people to stumble against him. He waved them irritably on into the hall and remained where he was on the threshold, staring at the unmoved face of his visitor. He said bitterly, 'I might have known my mother would tell you.'

'That there's a conspiracy afoot against the Godwins of Wessex? Every swineherd knows,' Thorfinn said. 'Earl Siward, I'm told, left here the day before yesterday, and the wise-women with the cauldron and the spells vanished only this morning. I have a bone to pick with you, Alfgar.'

His voice rumbled over the yard, and all the lines resident in Alfgar's ruddy face, between the resplendent fair hair and the beard, became abruptly apparent. He said, 'For Christ's sake. All right. My chambers are over there.'

Thorfinn stood still. 'You offered to take Erlend, and I accepted your offer,' he said. 'There was no word then of Siward of Northumbria sharing the same house.'

'It was only for a day. Nothing happened. Siward came straight on from Bromley to Coventry. Do you think I would let a son of yours be killed or captured under my roof?' Alfgar snapped.

'It isn't your roof yet. Your father Leofric wants an alliance with Siward. Siward is uncle to the late Duncan's sons, and even uncle of the half-blood to mine. I understand,' Thorfinn said, 'that Northumbria and Mercia are disturbed by the growing power of the house of Earl Godwin, but I will not have my sons used as decoys.'

'With Godiva there?' Alfgar said. 'Don't belittle your powers. What could happen to you or your sons so long as your women are there to protect you? In any case, we didn't need to offer the lavish bribe of your youngest son. If we had needed to buy Siward, we had something better to offer.'

He gave Thorfinn no time to reply. Instead, striding off to his quarters, he flung open the door and waited until his guest, at a more moderate pace, had caught up with him.

'Go in,' said Alfgar. 'Since you have decided to call, you and my other visitor might as well take time to become acquainted.'

The inner door was closed with a tapestry. Pulling it aside, Thorfinn walked into the room, gloomy after the daylight save where a lamp glowed on the woodwork, and the rushes, and the chest and stools and wall-benches set with deep cushions.

On one of the benches, a figure was lying, now perfectly still; although a misplaced cushion and a dying rumour of sound hinted that, a moment before, matters had been otherwise. There was no one else in the room.

Thorfinn, standing quite still, looked at the occupant of the bench.

'I have disturbed you,' he said. 'Alfgar tells me we know one another.'

For a little time, nothing happened. Then, turning its head, the recumbent figure raised one languid arm and, tucking it under its neck, subjected the

King in the doorway to an unhurried scrutiny that would have been insolent in a much older man, never mind this lad of just over twenty, with the shaved hair and clean chin of the Normans, against which the angry, mishandled spots of his puberty stood out like molehills in winter.

'Well, my uncle,' said Duncan's son Malcolm. 'What smell of quick profit has tempted you south from your mouse-hole? Are you still building cathedrals? They said you were silly with age-sickness.'

'So the King has been here,' Thorfinn said.

Behind him, blocked from his own doorway, Alfgar fidgetted. 'Malcolm rode with him from Gloucester and decided to stay for a day. There is no question of Siward being allowed to take Malcolm north yet: don't misunderstand me. In any case, Malcolm wouldn't want to go. He enjoys Edward's court. Don't you?' said Alfgar to the bench.

The boy Malcolm ignored him. Eleven years had passed since his father King Duncan had died at Tarbatness by the hand of this man who now ruled his kingdom. For eight years now, Malcolm, once prince of Alba, had lived at the English court as guest, as hostage, as refugee with King Edward, separated from his youngest brother Maelmuire at Dunkeld, and his younger brother Donald in Ireland.

Up to the age of ten, he had been the oldest son of a king. Not, it was true, much of a king. He soon came to know that men thought his sire stupid, and, indeed, shared that opinion. It was not enjoyable to hear Duncan talk of his subjects and then find, issuing simple orders oneself to those subjects, that the kingdom so airily claimed included only this land and that, and an overlordship or two of the most intangible nature, not to mention one or two lands where the natives openly laughed if he tried to assert his rights.

He would not, when he came of age, allow any people to laugh at him.

Nor did they now, for his reply to finding himself a penniless lodger at a French-Saxon court had been to rival his betters at least in the skills he could perfect: to become a better man with the sword, with the spear, with the axe, with the bow, than any of them. He had spent two summers learning how to run on the oars of a longship.

So, when he was insolent to men of his own age, he rarely paid for it. As for men of power, he was careful not to offend. One day, this King Thorfinn-Macbeth his uncle would die, and his two sons by the red-haired woman were far younger than he was, and only interested in the north.

There was a time when he had wondered, when the returns from his miserable estates were even smaller than usual, whether or not to leave England for Alba and persuade Thorfinn to accept him as heir. He was of the blood; he had all the skills; he was the right age. He could win over the dissaffected who might still blame Thorfinn for his brother's death. And in return, surely, Thorfinn would shower him with riches.

It had seemed, briefly, a good idea. But Edward of England and the Lady Emma when they came to hear of it, had been quite outspoken in their condemnation of it, and of him, and it had taken him a long time to regain their favour, such as it was.

He had not tried again. And as time went on, he saw how childish he had been. If Orkney had been promised to the children, then the overlordship, in return for Arnmødling support, would be promised to the stepson Lulach, who was a grown man with an heir of his own. Crossing the border was not the way to position. It was, more likely, the way to ambiguous death.

So now he said to Alfgar, 'But the King my uncle hasn't replied to my question. Doesn't he understand the Frankish tongue? Shall I try Saxon? Really, I forget what people say to one another in the north.' He had made no effort yet to rise from the bench.

'In the north,' Thorfinn said, 'children speak when they are spoken to, and rise when their elders enter a room, whether ailing or not. Failure to rise, indeed, will often settle, one way or another, any doubts on the matter of age-sickness.'

There was a pause; and then Malcolm smiled. He had a small mouth lined with bright rose-colour, and his lashes were so fair that his eyes appeared without rims. 'Whatever happens in Forteviot,' he said, 'it is not usual in Winchester for an uncle and nephew to be seen brawling on the floor of a priory. My lord King, I am happy to see you.' He rose. 'When are you leaving?'

'I thought you and I might have a talk,' Thorfinn said. 'If Alfgar would excuse us.'

There was a pause.

Alfgar said, 'Must you? They are serving food in the hall. It will be over in a few minutes.'

'Then should we not go?' Malcolm said. 'Courtesy would seem to require it.'

'So thoughtful a guest,' Thorfinn said. 'Indeed, you are right. When you sit down, convey our apologies.'

The silence this time was a brief one.

'Indeed, I shall,' said Malcolm shortly, and walked forward. Thorfinn and Alfgar stood aside and watched him leave the tapestried door, and the main one, and make his way over the yard.

'So easily scared?' said Thorfinn.

'What were you doing at twenty-one?' Alfgar said. 'No. What a stupid question. Fighting. And honing the edge of your cunning. We are alone, so that you can draw me into telling you all about the plans against Godwin. So much I understand.'

'Well, you'd be a fool if you didn't,' Thorfinn said. 'Edward is courting popularity. Edward has paid off some ships, and rescinded some taxes, and now is showing some interest in curbing the power of Wessex. But Edward is an idiot, and Emma his mother is nearly seventy and not what she was. You might not get East Anglia. You might lose everything.'

'Sit down,' said Alfgar. 'Indeed, lie down, if you're going to dictate to me, and then I won't be tempted to knock you over. Emma may not be what she was, but she is still capable of pushing Edward where she wants him to go.

The Godwin Queen hasn't produced a royal heir, so the four candidates for the succession are natural supporters for any scheme to oust the Earl and his sons.'

'The four candidates?' Thorfinn said. He sat down where his nephew had lately been seated and, lifting his booted feet to the cushions, crossed them and lay back peacefully, his arms folded over his tunic.

'As if you didn't know,' Alfgar said. He sat, with vehemence, on a low stool and shoved his hands on his knees, his back stiff. 'Harald of Norway, your wife's cousin's husband. King Svein of Denmark, nephew of King Canute and also of Earl Godwin's lady. Any one of the Godwins: the Earl himself or one of the Queen's older brothers: Swegen, Harold, or Tostig. And Count Eustace of Boulogne, the vassal of Flanders, to whom Emma has just married her middle-aged, once-widowed daughter.'

'You've missed out one contender,' Thorfinn said.

'I've missed out dozens,' said Alfgar rattily. 'The world is full of second cousins who would like to be King of England. What matters is whether or not they have the backing. Who do you mean? Not yourself? You don't seriously imagine . . . ?'

'I don't seriously imagine,' Thorfinn said. 'I meant William of Normandy.'

The shutter creaked. A cart rumbled into the courtyard and began unloading staves for barrels. A monk in a brown gown wandered out of a doorway and crossed to it, his sandals crunching the dust.

Alfgar said, 'You bastard. You difficult bastard. What do you know? What are you meddling with now?'

'Nothing,' said Thorfinn. 'Duke William is two years older than Malcolm. His pimples and his barons are going to settle down some day.'

Alfgar said, 'Is it true that you are in the money-market? That you picked up Crinan's network? They say you're exploiting the Alston mines, and Winchester never sees a penny of mineral fees.'

'And how much money does the Wardrobe see of your salt-taxes?' Thorfinn said. 'You were talking, I think, about Eustace.'

'Before you caused a diversion,' Alfgar said. 'Of course, he's the likeliest candidate. Norway and Denmark are at one another's throats, William can hardly hold on to his dukedom, and Edmund Ironside's surviving son, I seem to remember you telling me, was in failing health with only two daughters to follow him. Boulogne and Hainault and French Burgundy are all currently in one another's pockets, and there is nothing Count Eustace would like more in this world than to have control of both ends of the shortest crossing between England and the Continent. He wants Dover and Folkestone, and if the Godwin family weren't there, Emma his mother-in-law would have presented him with them, if not the whole Kentish coast.'

'Would you say,' Thorfinn remarked, 'a high price for getting rid of the Godwin family? What did Siward say?'

'Siward has York to trade from. We have Chester. With Harold Godwinsson out of the way, we should also have Bristol. We're not greedy,' said Alfgar with virtue.

'Would you have Bristol? Earl Ralph holds the Hereford border. And he is Count Eustace's stepson,' Thorfinn said.

'On the other hand,' said Alfgar, 'as you seem to have forgotten, I have spent rather a long time cultivating the friends of Earl Ralph and of Eustace. Osbern of Eu. Alfred of Marle. The Bishops Ealdred and Hermann and Leofric . . .'

He halted.

'That took a long time,' Thorfinn said.

'You couldn't have foreseen that,' Alfgar said. 'You couldn't have known that Edward and Emma were going to make a marriage alliance with Boulogne and . . .' He stopped again. 'Did you come across a man called Robert le Bourguignon on your travels?'

'Yes,' said Thorfinn. 'Adèle of France's young and numerate offspring. The brother of Tonnerre and Nevers and the husband of Hadwise of Sablé. Lulach talks of him. Why?'

'Lulach?' Alfgar said. He waited, and then said, 'Well, thank God there's something you don't know. There's been a battle at Credon, or Craon. The place by the Loire. The winner was Geoffrey of Anjou. He's made your friend Robert le Bourguignon hereditary seigneur of Craon under his lordship.'

Gratifyingly, Thorfinn sat up. 'Which links both parts of Burgundy with Anjou; with the Aquitaine; with the Cotentin; with the Pays du Caux; with Coucy and Marle, Cambrai and Lille . . . Alfgar, you will make a *very* intelligent Earl of Mercia,' Thorfinn said.

Through the years, Alfgar had become at least intelligent enough to recognise that questioning Thorfinn about his machinations was perfectly useless. He said, following his only lead, 'Then what does Lulach say?'

Thorfinn said, 'Lulach says that because of a nephew and a great-grandson of Robert the Burgundian, there sprang a new line of kings for England and Scotia, and some love-songs.'

Alfgar leaned forward and embraced one hand with the other. 'Then it's a marriage?' he said. 'You're making Lulach your heir?'

'He also says,' Thorfinn continued, 'that because of Robert's great-nephew, the seats of Lulach's descendants were occupied by Jerusalem, although against the monks of Loch Leven even Jerusalem failed. . . . A marriage? Perhaps. My heir for Scotia? I have not yet declared him. The kings that are to come? They will not spring from me, nor from Lulach. Does it matter? I have trouble enough with the problems I have. How do you expect to get rid of the Godwin family?'

Alfgar let his hands slip between his knees, where they dangled frustratedly. 'I don't know,' he said, 'how you have patience to hear out that rubbish of Lulach's. I could find you an old woman any day who would be more entertaining, and even capable of a shrewd guess now and then, if you must dabble in that kind of thing. The Godwin family? Well, the King's made a start against them already. That's what the meeting here was about.' Alfgar's skin had turned pink. 'Thorfinn, I can't tell you the details.'

'Then don't,' said Thorfinn unemotionally. 'Just tell me which of his heirs the King has invited to visit him. And when.'

'Eustace of Boulogne, Emma's son-in-law. In September. A visit to his stepson in the West Country.'

'But since Godwin is strong in the West Country, that is not where he will meet his challenge. May I guess?' said Thorfinn.

'My God, no,' said Alfgar, getting up. 'You know too much already. I only told you because I was sure Emma would find a way of sending a hint. You ought to be warned.'

'No. Eachmarcach ought to be warned,' Thorfinn said. 'When you own the whole of central England, from the west coast to the east, what will you do with it?'

'Divorce my wife,' said Alfgar. 'Do you still want yours? You could marry my mother.'

'There must be other remedies,' said Thorfinn. 'You might send to King Svein. He always has some girl he is trying to get rid of. At the very worst, they could teach your wife a thing or two. I don't know how he or King Harald find the energy to make war on one another. It is, I suppose, lucky for Eustace.'

'Married to Emma's daughter?' said Alfgar. 'I don't think even Dover—'

He stopped.

'Now you are going to worry,' said Thorfinn kindly. 'Perhaps I should get on my way before you drop any more secrets. Would a cup of wine be too much to expect?'

Shrewsbury was not much out of the way on the road to Alba from Coventry, and Thorfinn had a troop of armed men and a safe-conduct.

Sulien, who was waiting for him, needed neither. In a little chamber lent by the abbot, he said, 'Yes. I shall let Eachmarcach know. Be careful. Leofric and Siward are not a good team, and the King can only reflect Emma or react against her. You have a good man in Bishop Jon.'

'I thought so. The other one, Hrolf, should be there by the time I get back,' Thorfinn said. 'With any luck, we shall keep them. Do you hear much of Thor of Allerdale?'

'Nothing to worry you,' Sulien said. 'You can't put a bishop in Cumbria yet. But at the same time Thor is far too interested in power and money to strike up a friendship with Siward. I should say, however, that you might expect your Bishop Malduin to make a recovery soon.'

'I thought of that,' Thorfinn said. 'Siward needs to know what is happening. How annoyed Malduin is going to be. Rival bishops: alienated land and dues. Even priests who, now and then, may know more than he does. His wife will hate it even more.'

'From which I gather that you feel you can handle it,' Sulien said. 'I'm glad. The air of gloom, I suppose, was because Alfgar had been discussing money.'

'Conversation with Alfgar always turns on money,' Thorfinn said. 'His parents have been endowing churches like jackdaws. I don't like Llanbadarn in the middle of this. Not with a wife and young family there. Why not bring them north to me in September?'

'Alfgar will look after us,' Sulien said. 'He is wise six inches deep, and loyal eight inches.'

'Well, if he becomes dead nine inches, come to me,' Thorfinn said. 'And don't mistake me. I am fond of Alfgar.'

'Did I belittle him?' Sulien said. 'I beg your pardon, and his. What is it, Thorfinn?'

'I don't know,' said the King. 'There is nothing wrong that I can see. Conditions change every day, and I deal with them. I enjoy it.'

'So you have much to lose. It's a common experience,' Sulien said.

Later, he stood in the grounds and watched Thorfinn and his men ride round the curve of the river until the bulk of the town in its loop hid them from him. He wished Bishop Jon were not, to his recollection, quite so business-like; and that Bishop Hrolf, of whom he had heard, were not quite so practised an engineer.

He wished Bishop Malduin were dead, and enjoined on himself, quickly, an act of contrition.

Whatever lay ahead for this kingdom, the presence or absence of Sulien was not going to alter it.

'What do you mean,' Groa said, 'his laugh isn't loud any more? Is Alfgar ill?'

'No. Only growing tired of his wife. Don't you notice,' Thorfinn said, 'how soft my laugh has become lately? What do you make of Bishop Hrolf?'

'Large, powerful, and given to practical jokes. He is an expert on drainage,' Groa said. 'And he has a loud voice and no wife. Should we do something about it?'

'No,' said Thorfinn. 'He might lose his interest in drainage.'

The summer waned, profitably.

The Irish masons, fresh in from Govan, reported that the vineyards of Gaul had suffered in the unfortunate squabble between the seigneurs of Neustrie, and Eachmarcach was importing wine from Cologne and Wissant this year. They began to build a round tower at Abernethy and repair another at Brechin in Angus, and took the ladders inside with them at meal-breaks so that they could give Eachmarcach's purchase the attention it merited. Then Bishop Hrolf climbed up a rope with his crucifix, and the masons all emerged with the ladders and crept down them, crying.

An Icelandic vessel trading wool cloaks and pumice and sulphur delivered a smith and three carpenters with their families from Totnes and Guernsey, and reported that you could hardly walk past St Paul's church in London for the brawl going on between the new Bishop's men and the men of the Archbishop of Canterbury, but that the Archbishop of Canterbury seemed to be winning. The King, they said, had stalked off to Gloucester.

The smith set up a furnace and forge next to the blooms of iron Thorfinn had brought back from the Rhine and began to make a number of objects, including plough-shares. The carpenters went further north, smacking their wives' heads when they complained.

A man collecting hides and unloading bolts of cloth and holy-water pots at the mouth of the Dee said that all the pigs about Winchester were being killed ahead of time for the feast the Lady Emma was giving for her daughter's new husband and the army of courtmen and servants he had brought from Boulogne. He rolled down some salt he had forgotten, and remarked that everyone would have square heads and thick accents in England soon at this rate: had they heard that Earl Godwin's son Tostig had got himself married to the sister of Baldwin of Flanders?

A clerk from Abingdon, delivering books, gold thread, and a present of two velvet cushions from a heavily armed pack-train, said that the King's nephew Ralph had taken his stepfather round all the new castles on the Welsh border, and that Count Eustace had been able, so they said, to spare him a few experienced men to add to the excellent officers who had crossed the sea to man them already. Bishop Ealdred, who had failed to drive off that nasty attack by the Welsh only the other day, would no doubt be thankful.

'Will he?' said Prior Tuathal. 'He lost a lot of men in that attack and nearly got himself killed. I wonder if Bishop Ealdred is losing his touch?'

'For conciliation or for running?' Thorfinn said. 'That's Harold Godwinsson's country. The Bishop can't be nice to the Welsh and stay friendly with Harold. And anyway it's been a bad summer and the cattle are fatter on the Saxon side of the border. When's the lead coming?'

Exactly on time, the lead came in from Cumbria and was unloaded at Scone by men with oyster-catcher beaks fastening their jackets. The shipmaster and his clerk, taking ale at the priory, were unsurprised to find the royal consignee there, as well as Prior Eochaid and the man Cormac of Atholl.

That was great news, then, said the shipmaster, for those that didn't like foreigners, although how the fools thought you got in your wine and your pepper and your sword-blades without them was a different matter. A great brawl there had been on the south coast as that fellow Eustace of Boulogne had come to take ship across to his country. Some said it was over the question of where his men should sleep for the night. Some said, since he married the King's sister, he expected the King to let him take over the castle of Dover. In Earl Godwin's country! Of course, the men of the town were in arms in a moment, and so were Eustace's men. Twenty killed on each side, and Eustace back raging to Gloucester to ask the King if this was how he treated his kinsmen.

Well, that's been known, said the shipmaster; and everyone knew what kind of answer they'd get from Edward. Or thought they knew. But, Mary, Mother of Christ, not this time. This time, King Edward called Earl Godwin before him and told him straight to his face to go off and harry his townspeople of Dover for the harm they'd done to his sister's husband.

Did Godwin agree? Could his lordship *see* Godwin agreeing? He turned on his heel, said the shipmaster, and went off and collected an army. Held it fifteen miles out of Gloucester, with young Harold and Tostig, and challenged the King to send out Count Eustace and all his men and turn out the foreigners left in the castle.

'*I don't think,*' said the King, '*that I can bear it. Could you tell me the rest of it quickly?*'

Oh, if there's that much of a hurry, said the shipmaster, two words will do it. Wessex isn't England, though some think it is. The King sent horsemen out, and before you'd know it, armies from Mercia and Northumbria and even from young Ralph his nephew in Hereford were there at Gloucester, nose to nose with the Godwinssons.

Those that don't like their landlords, said the shipmaster, were all for letting them flatten each other and giving us all a fresh start. But the bishops got preaching, as usual, and the upshot was: hostages taken on both sides, and the Godwinssons to come to London to answer charges in front of the council.

More than which, said the shipmaster, weighing the bag in his hand, he could not be expected to say, the meeting in London not having been held yet.

He left.

'*Poor Edward of England. He's bungled it,*' said Cormac of Atholl.

'*He thought the south coast would accept Eustace. How unfortunate,*' said Thorfinn.

'*They might get rid of the Godwinssons,*' Eochaid offered.

'*They might. But without Eustace, they'll be back. One contender dismissed. When, do you think,*' said Thorfinn, '*ought we to expect Bishop Malduin to forsake York and be drawn to his needy pastoral cure in Kinrimund?*'

'*When the Godwins have gone,*' said Cormac of Atholl. '*Give him a month.*'

FOURTEEN

ND SO,' SAID Thorfinn affably to Bishop Malduin of Alba, 'the Godwin family have got themselves outlawed, and you are fit and burning once more to respond to the call of your office. So bad deeds are balanced with good. I hear the Queen of England, Earl Godwin's daughter, is in a nunnery?'

'That is correct. Earl Godwin himself, with three of his sons, is in Flanders, which is, of course, the home of Tostig's new bride. And Harold and one of his brothers have, I believe, made their way to Ireland from Bristol.'

'Pursued slowly by Bishop Ealdred, who reached the quay too late to wave. And my lord Siward is pleased?'

The Bishop said, 'The King called out all the militia. That of Northumbria formed only part of the force.'

Whatever his cousin of Orkney said to him, Bishop Malduin was not going to make an issue of it. Talking with Thorfinn always unsettled him.

Listening to the Archbishop of York and Earl Siward, he found the nature of the King of Scotia simple to understand, if not easy to like.

Face to face with the man himself, Bishop Malduin was aware, of course, with every word spoken, that here was a smart-witted Viking greedy for riches and power, and to that end equally ready to sue either God or the guts of an animal.

Such a man, my lord Siward said, would take even the Pope as his spiritual overlord, rather than acknowledge a superior closer at hand. Would the Pope see a tithe of the dues being raised in his name? The produce of his churchlands? The returns for the services of his priests? The offerings brought by the faithful?

No, said my lord Siward. And neither would Bishop Malduin. Or if any reached pious coffers at all, they would be those belonging to the two Bishops sent by the Pope's favour so that they might report and keep the King's face before the eyes of the Pope and the people.

'Go and see what he is doing,' had said the Earl Siward. 'And I shall pray in my church of St Olaf's for guidance as to how I may help you.'

Face to face with the man, therefore, it should have been simple. But they talked of the flight of Earl Godwin, and, without warning, the King changed the subject and it was not simple at all.

'You are wondering what I am doing,' said Thorfinn, 'about the division of our spiritual labours, now I have, as you must know, three bishops in the place of one. I have an idea about that.'

'Indeed,' said Bishop Malduin, 'I have to congratulate you, my son, on your hazardous voyage to the Tombs of the Apostles and an audience, I hear, with the Holy Father himself. I heard that he had offered two churchmen to sustain you during my illness. They speak, I believe, both Irish and Norse? So gifted?'

'You have been reviving your Norse?' the King asked.

'What need?' said Bishop Malduin. 'Now that Earl Siward, as doubtless you have heard, is to marry his daughter into your wife's family . . . or at least,' said Bishop Malduin with smoothness, 'that branch which remained loyal to Norway? Norse bishops have always served Orkney, and will be happy to do so again. Your Irishmen may leave their cold northern cabins and retire with a clear conscience to Goslar.'

'I have this difficulty,' said Thorfinn, 'with my cook. Do you ever hesitate when taking your broth? Does the smell of a sauce ever disturb you? For five years, I have had the same cook, and no one, to my knowledge, has ever died at his hand. An attack of nausea, yes. But death in agony, no. I should not like to lose him.'

He had lost Bishop Malduin. Bishop Malduin thought of the lord Siward's great, lowering bulk and the lord Ligulf's friendly smile, printed about by the caret of his silken moustaches, and gritted his teeth.

'Your cook, my son?'

'King Svein of Denmark sent my cook his best concubine. My cook likes King Svein of Denmark,' said the King of Scotia. 'He doesn't like King Harald of Norway at all. There is the dilemma.'

Along the tracks of Bishop Malduin's mind, obliterating the Latin of Psalm, the Latin of prayer, the Latin of ritual, sprang words of coarse country Gaelic: words from his boyhood in the monastery school in Ireland, used by one crude country boy when another was teasing him.

Bishop Malduin said, 'You are pleased, my cousin, to amuse yourself. It is not a pleasant thing, at my age, to find my cure has been usurped by others. It is not pleasing, either, to those who consecrated me as Bishop for Alba. In the past, the whole country served to supply no more than a modest living. What can I expect now?'

'Indeed,' said the King, 'I should be a poor kinsman had I not already thought of your plight. More than that, as I said to the Holy Father in Rome, have I been concerned with the plight of the poor folk who lie to the south of us, between Fife and Bamburgh, and who have had scant attention from the Bishop of Alba or the Bishop of Durham since the Lothians became a matter of dispute between the Earls of Northumbria and King Malcolm my grand-father. Who, these days, is concerned for the cure of souls in Abercorn and Aberlady, Hailes and Cramond, Coldingham, Melrose and Tyningham? Good provider that he is, Bishop Aethelric does not forget to collect from the lands of St Cuthbert all the tributes due to the shrine of St Cuthbert at Durham, but, in return, what pastoral care do the people on these lands enjoy?

'The Pope himself,' continued Thorfinn gravely, 'confessed concern. I reassured him. In the Bishop of Alba, I said, we had a man practised in Saxon as well as Gaelic; a man who understood the Angles south of the Forth from long sojourn with Earl Siward of Northumbria; a man to whom Earl Siward and his friend the Bishop of Durham would without doubt be happy to allot the revenues which at present disappear to the south, in return for his services among the poor and the deprived people of Lothian. The Holy Father's contentment,' said Thorfinn, 'was such as to gladden the heart. He sent you his blessing.'

Bishop Malduin sat without movement, encased in the stifling mould of his anger.

The lands of the Bishop of Alba had never been large, and old Malcolm, liberal enough in time of war, had never been slow in time of peace to win back the property he had allotted so freely. Then had come this marauder his cousin Thorfinn, making free with the Fife lands of dead men or the young he had orphaned, and forcing the Bishop to spare from the little he had to enrich the shrines of St Serf and St Drostan.

Dunkeld and Kinrimund had always worked together in Malcolm's day, and the lands of Crinan ought by rights to have come to him, but had they? He had claim by descent to the lands of Angus, but who collected the revenues there now? That fool Gillocher and his power-mad cousin Kineth of Brechin, who had come back from Rome with his head turned.

Rivals stared at Bishop Malduin everywhere. Lulach the royal stepson, ensconced in Moray with his confessors. Eochaid, the new Prior of Scone, who had taken a faster grip on the place than the absent Coarb of St Columba ever had, and who was always in the King's household. And now the biggest threat of them all, Tuathal of St Serf's in the middle of Fife, his own precinct.

You weren't supposed to run a group of Culdees like a mint-master. You weren't supposed to run a kingdom like a Cluniac market. Enrich a shrine, yes. From the gold in your coffers and the returns from your lands, you could support the clergy who served the shrine, and the priests who would starve otherwise on the little their flock could afford.

But to teach men to manage their land; to encourage strangers to trade; to take an interest in shipping: how did that benefit the church, how did it improve the spiritual welfare of a country? Trouble, that was what it brought. The kind of trouble the Earls of Northumbria struck with the foreigners and the kindred who had been allowed to grow too powerful.

Thorfinn was trying to build York in Alba. He and his minions would fail. Or else the minions would swell and obliterate him. But meantime, was he himself, twenty-three years a bishop and no longer young, to end milled between magnates and living off herbs in the Lothians? He said, 'My son, what the Holy Father desires must command attention from us all. But if, despite this, the Earl Siward should refuse to allow the revenues from the

Lothians to be alienated, how then should I live?'

'Is it possible,' said the King, 'that he would refuse? Why, then, you must live as all the Bishops of Alba have done. From your lands of Kinrimund, and upon my expense as an officer in attendance on my household. The other Bishops, being much to the north, cannot do this.'

The man was wicked. Everyone knew how far the King of Scotia's household had to ride, and how often. Forty miles a day, every day for a week, was not unknown. Even the favoured Eochaid and Tuathal, he had heard, complained sometimes. Bishop Malduin said, 'My son, you are speaking to a man who is no longer young.'

'. . . Or there is retirement,' said the King. 'Perhaps you should consider retirement? The Culdees, I am sure, would accept you, and we should find a convent for your wife. I should be disappointed. The deprived people of Lothian will be disappointed. But the decision, my cousin, must lie with you. Tell me when you have made it, and, one way or the other, we shall write to Earl Siward together.'

'So what happened?' said Lulach.

'To Bishop Malduin? He's gone south to try and persuade Earl Siward to give up the church-tithes from Lothian. You don't know about that.'

'No, I don't,' said Lulach cheerfully. 'But I don't mind conjecturing with you. Isn't this a bad time to issue a challenge to Siward over Lothian, now the Godwin family are out of his way and he has a new alliance with Norway?'

'It would be if the English succession was settled,' Thorfinn said. 'But it isn't. Eustace is no longer a favourite, and Godwin is banished, but there are still two strong runners left to occupy the attention of both Siward and Norway. I think Siward will agree.'

'Agree to give up his church dues in Lothian? You're mad. He's mad,' said Groa to Prior Tuathal. They were all, for once, on her own lands in Fife south of Loch Leven, and it was dusk, which meant that Tuathal would stay overnight rather than try to get back to the island once the geese had landed. From Iceland they came, the flocks of thick-beaked Vikings, darkening the sky after the first full moon of September, and from dusk to dawn the shores and isles of Loch Leven were theirs, to disturb at one's risk. The older monks knew them by sight, as each dropped, year by year, to his familiar roosting-place, and some of them came to the hand, as did the priory birds.

One could live, winter and summer, on a lake such as this, ringed with low, pretty hills; full of life, as were the other small lochs about it. During winters in Orkney, she felt like that. When age blew on one's cheek instead of winter, life in such a place was not hard to contemplate.

But this debate was not about peace, but about consolidating the south-lands of Alba. And her role was not to applaud, but to provoke. 'He's mad,' said Groa again of the King her husband. 'With the Godwin family exiled, Siward has conquered his greatest rival for power in England. Now all of England outside Wessex is divided between Siward and Mercia.'

'I suppose you could put it like that,' Thorfinn said. 'On the other hand, since Alfgar has been given the Godwinsson lands of East Anglia . . .'

'What!' said Groa.

'Didn't I tell you? Alfgar's an Earl. His wife will love it. And it means that he and his parents now hold the whole of central England from sea to sea, south of Northumbria on the east coast and of Cumbria on the west, leaving Siward with as much as he can retain of Middle Anglia and the eastern lands north of the Humber. I think,' said Thorfinn, 'that we might spend Christmas in Cumbria this year. We never have.'

'We've never dared,' said Tuathal bluntly.

'I know nothing of it,' said Lulach cheerfully.

Christmas in Cumbria was hard work.

Advancing in cold and blustery weather from the princely guest-house on Carlisle's southern outskirts to the royal hall maintained by Thor, the King's distant cousin in Allerdale, and proceeding eastwards from there to the palace between Penrith and Appleby where, led by Leofwine, the whole of East Cumbria was assembled to welcome them, Bishop Hrolf felt it his duty to instruct, to learn, and to entertain his fellow-travellers.

His fellow-travellers, who were saving their energy for the extremely cautious festivities which were taking place at each halt, were not responsive. Bishop Hrolf, who liked to spice his learning with a little jollity, rallied them out of their apathy by tying their leg-bands together while they were sleeping, or by emptying some ale-horn and refilling it swiftly from a small bag of sawdust. Bishop Hrolf became the largest cross that the King of Alba's Christmas cavalcade to Cumbria had to bear.

Bishop Hrolf loved the Romans. His Celtic blood, much diluted, did not prevent him from wishing, from time to time, that the Emperors in their day had crossed to Ireland and there established a Bremen, a Goslar, a Cologne: a city of mighty stone churches over which Bishop Hrolf could preside.

Instead, the Romans had reached, here in Cumbria, the northern limit of their English conquest, marked by the line of their Wall. Four hundred years ago, the walls and fountain of Luguvallium had still stood, when Carlisle was given by the King of Northumbria to St Cuthbert and there was a house of nuns at its gates.

The Roman roads were still there. They were riding on one now: the great highway from Carlisle to York. And the settlements they were visiting were still to be found where the Roman engineers first had made their selection: at the great crossroads and the fords, at the points guarding the few awkward highways from this principality ringed with hills and wedged between Alba and Mercia.

Once, this land had been lived in by Romans and by Britons, speaking the language they now spoke in Wales. It was the tongue St Kentigern of blessed memory would use when he came south to preach and establish his church. It would be known to St Cuthbert of (he reminded himself) not quite such blessed memory when the Celtic church was dismissed from Lindisfarne a hundred years later and he found refuge in Carlisle and the Solway.

Then, of course, had come those other refugees when the Viking raids had started. Refugees from the Viking kingdom of York. Refugees from Ireland: Gaels at first, and then those of mixed Norse and Irish descent.

To preach in Cumbria, as to preach in the island of Man, you required four different tongues. It was one of the reasons, they said, why the Bishops of Alba had had little to do with the area. And why the Bishop of Durham, who would ordain a priest or two in an emergency, had shown no interest, either, in rebuilding the churches and monasteries.

Not, of course, that the Bishop of Durham had any rights here, since, a hundred years before, the King of England had ceded to Malcolm of Cumbria all the land from the Firth of Clyde south to the river Duddon and Stainmore.

Or so ran the theory. In practice, Bishop Hrolf gathered, it was not uncommon for a good, Celtic-trained bishop much involved with the Anglian part of his cure to obtain consecration from the Archbishop of York in addition to the simple ceremony required by his native church, to make his teaching more acceptable. And when the Bishop of Alba was called further north, to his flock or to his king, it was natural that his brother of Durham should see to urgent business, such as the examination and ordaining of young men serving God near his area.

Harmless in itself. Dangerous when the Bishop of Durham and his brother, as now, were the friends of a powerful and ambitious Earl Siward at York. For the temporal lords, as well as the lords of the church, had an interest in Cumbria.

The lands of St Cuthbert had once been wide and rich, and nowhere more so than here, long divorced from their parent shrines in the east.

For a hundred years, Cumbria and Northumbria had lain quarrelling side by side, each greedy to swallow the other. Intermarriage had led to claims on each side already: this King's brother had already tried, as had his grandfather, to take Durham. Any such claim from the east would surely begin with a pious endeavour to revive the claims of St Cuthbert to the wide, scattered lands that had once been the province of the Prince-Bishop of Durham.

To forestall this, Thorfinn had offered Bishop Malduin the care of Lothian. To minimise this threat, he had raised a thicket of other saintly men who now slept in the Lord. Bishop Hrolf had read about St Serf and St Kentigern in the Life of St Serf which this King had commissioned. He had even seen, in some recent epistle, a suggestion that St Kentigern and St Columba had had, on one occasion, a pleasing encounter.

To his recollection, the normal life-span of man made such a meeting unlikely, but he had heard no rebuttals, and Robhartach, the Abbot of Iona, was silent on the subject: that is, he had been absent in Kells on the two occasions on which Bishop Hrolf had called on him.

On the other hand, the Columban church, whatever its past, had no great hold on this district, although one could not say as much for the church of Armagh. Shrines to St Patrick were the first thing one noticed in Allerdale. He and Prior Tuathal, of whom Bishop Hrolf had a high opinion, had had an interesting talk on the subject.

Reminded of his rapport with Prior Tuathal, Bishop Hrolf urged his mare out of the column and began to drop back in the Prior's direction, while assembling a theory he intended to propound about the monetary policy of the Emperor Hadrian.

When he arrived at the rear of the column, however, it was to find that the Prior Tuathal had seemingly vanished. The Bishop glanced about for a bit, and then, dismissing the matter, set about lecturing two of the men-at-arms in a kindly fashion for their over-indulgence in mead, while contriving to unfasten their girth-buckles during the ensuing approach to a river-ford.

Thus, he told them smiling on the far bank, they had been sobered once and baptised twice, at any rate.

And so, smiling in a less spontaneous way, they agreed with him.

'On drains,' said Thorfinn in the guest-hall outside Appleby, 'on drains he is unparallelled. Why fuss over trifles? Bishop Malduin would be worse.'

'I know what the Lady means,' said Tuathal thoughtfully. 'Bishop Malduin might ill-wish you a colic by demons, but he wouldn't strap up a pig in your battle-shield. However. God, I feel, is competent to relieve us of this difficulty. Hrolf is a good engineer.'

'God, I feel, might need a little encouragement,' Groa said. 'The priest at Dacre said he could hardly get through the vigil, he had been talked at so much. Which reminds me. For a Christmas feast, I have seen better tables.'

'They will be happy you noticed,' said Thorfinn. 'They have got into the habit of paying their taxes in silver, and don't keep storage-barns as they used to. It's time they were reminded. A bad harvest can be worse than a royal visitation. At least Leofwine is still friendly.'

They had kept away, this time, from Crinan's lands about Alston, but the halls they were occupying were served by peoples who remembered the other princes of Cumbria, Thorfinn's brother and grandfather, and who thought of Thor the merchant-coiner of Allerdale as their immediate protector and leader, rather than as the kinsman and representative of the Orcadian Earl who had fought Duncan of Cumbria and taken his place.

Gillecrist of Strathclyde, an impulsive man who loved fishing and fighting in equal proportions, said, 'Leofwine hasn't altered since Rome. But Thor is restless. He was asking me who owned the lands that used to belong to the see of Glasgow, and what your plans were for Lothian.'

Groa looked at the King. 'Thor helped you in the past. You got your base on the Waver with his men. He didn't do overmuch to help Duncan at Durham. He kept Malduin on more than one occasion from troubling you. And against Diarmaid mac Mael-na-mbo he has always been your staunchest ally in Galloway and the Sudreyar. He is not of the temper to enjoy having an overlord, but you are his third cousin.'

I am the dog at your heel. Everything I have ever done has been an attempt to be like Thorfinn.

'It's fourteen years since I cleared Diarmaid's fleet from the Sudreyar. But you're right. If Thor objected to threatening gestures from Northumbria or

Ireland then, he is not likely to suffer them now. Which is just as well, with Diarmaid sheltering Harold Godwinsson.'

'Is that true?' said Tuathal.

'So Thor says, and I believe him. While Earl Godwin and the rest went to Bruges, Harold and his younger brother made for the Severn estuary and Ireland. The Severn sees most of the trade in the west—far more now than Chester did. Harold held it, and will want it back, but he will need help against Emma's nephew and the Norman outposts, not to mention King Gruffydd of Wales. My guess is that Harold went to Ireland to complete a bargain with Diarmaid of Leinster.'

'What sort of bargain?' said Groa. 'Against Eachmarcach?'

'Perhaps,' said Thorfinn. 'Eachmarcach is not a young man, and he has been King of Dublin on and off now for seventeen years. What will happen to our interests in Ireland and Man if Dublin falls into unfriendly hands has been something I have been giving a lot of thought to. On the other hand, Diarmaid is fighting-mad and has been ever since he claimed Meath. He wants to make Turlough Ua Brian King of Munster, and the present incumbent is giving him trouble. He may recruit Harold and his men to help him attack Munster instead.'

'He may recruit Harold and his brother and get them killed, which would be best of all,' said Prior Tuathal with un-Christian firmness. 'For, while King Edward won't mind a west-coast alliance excluding the Godwin family, Harold wouldn't like it at all, if he ever came back from exile. After all, it was to prevent such an alliance between the Welsh and the Mercians and the Cumbrians, presumably, that the Kings of England farmed out Cumbria in the first place. They couldn't hold it. Cumbria was self-supporting and too far from Wessex to benefit from Wessex protection. Now it's different.'

'They're still self-supporting,' said Groa, 'except at Christmas. And not any nearer to Wessex. What's the difference? A friendly Mercia to make a bridge between Wales and Cumbria?'

'That and other things,' Thorfinn said. 'Once, the only way you could hold such a country was by clearing it through mass slaughter and planting it with your own people. Unless, that is, you had control of a fleet that could exact regular tributes under threat.'

'As you did in Ireland. But the productive areas of Cumbria tend to be inland. So they must either ravage the country or what? Ah,' said Groa, who enjoyed keeping ahead of everybody and always hoped, one day, to find herself ahead of Thorfinn, 'you're thinking of the Norman forts. The defence works on the Welsh border. With a few of those, you could hold a country.'

'Don't tell Thor,' said Thorfinn. 'And it's a long time since I sailed the Irish coast collecting tributes under threat.'

'I know. Eachmarcach does it for you. Thorfinn,' Groa said. 'If you lose Eachmarcach from Dublin, you may well lose Man and Kintyre, and Galloway and the Cumbrian bases will be none too easy to hold. What will you do?'

'Put to sea in the spring,' Thorfinn said. 'I've talked to Thor about it already.'

They all looked at him, their thoughts in their eyes. A show of force. Preventative war. But still war.

Groa said, 'Diarmaid may go for Munster. The sons of Godwin may decide not to help him, or be killed, or be allowed to return. You don't know.'

'No,' said Thorfinn. 'But I know someone who probably does.'

He had not unpacked fully, as she had. He had not unpacked at all, nor had his servants. Groa said, 'Whom are you going to see? Sulien?'

There was a glint in his eye. 'No,' said Thorfinn. 'This year, I felt I should make a gesture. Such as offering a token payment for Cumbria to the person who would most appreciate it.'

It was Gillecrist, across Tuathal's silence, who said, 'My lord King . . . A state visit to Edward of England?'

'No, my friend of Strathclyde,' said Thorfinn. 'A private visit to the Lady Emma at Winchester.'

FIFTEEN

ON HER GREAT, velvet-draped chamber above the stone undercroft, Emma sat erect in a bed built like a coffin, its back carved and gilt like a dragon-ship.

With her were three of her ladies, all of them Norman women married to Saxons, which was her preference. Beside her stood two of her Winchester churchmen: Stigand the Bishop, her ancient crony and ally, and Odo, a sparer, wilier version of Ealdred his brother who had led the English King's recent mission to Rome.

There were, on the bed and underfoot in the room, seven or eight lapdogs, of which one was dyed blue.

Thorfinn entered the room and stood still as the usher retreated. No one spoke. The door closed behind him. The eyes of the dogs shone; then after a moment their ears dropped and they subsided.

The Old Lady, the Lady-Dowager, the widow of two Kings of England sat and stared at her visitor.

He wondered how clearly she could see. Her eyes, colourless as glass powder, were watering, and a sickle of hair had escaped from her head-veil, still royally pinned by its fillet. Like a tired parchment bag, her face hung from the hook of her nose.

He had seen women of ninety who did not look like that. Emma was old, but not so aged. Emma was ill, and probably dying.

She said, 'As a trader of furs, you have my safe-conduct to pass from your ship and back to it again, without digressing. Otherwise, you are here at your own risk.'

Her voice crackled from lack of air pressure, but was otherwise firm. No one rushed to correct her. Therefore, she knew who he was.

He said, 'Thank you, my lady. I know it. I wished to see you without commitment to either of us.' He did not look at Bishop Stigand, who was a friend of the exiled Godwin family as well as of Emma's. He had seen one of the women, Thola, once, in the company of Archbishop Juhel. He wished Hermann had been present, instead of Ealdred's brother.

Part of the parchment bag creased and sank, as if pulled from behind. The air was thick with balsam and heat, overlying the smell of the dogs and a lingering, nursery odour of sour milk and urine. Emma said, 'How long do you think you would last outside these doors if you and I had this talk unattended? How old are you, Macbeth of Alba?'

Ten years ago, he had attended the crowning of her son here at Winchester, and she had arranged for the child Malcolm his nephew to be removed from the power of Siward and fostered instead here at court.

More than twenty years ago, younger than Malcolm was now, he himself had been brought to the English court, a guest, a nominal housecarl, a hostage, and had learned how kingdoms are run. He said, 'I am forty-two years old, my lady Dowager, and I have come to see how you fare, and to offer you, if you wish to send for it, some silver from Cumbria.'

Again, her face seamed and shadowed. Her knuckles, joined on the thin quilt before her, were hedged with rings like the shields on a longship. 'With your homage, of course?' she said. 'With your fealty? Now that you have seen how I fare? Or do you expect King Svein of Denmark to be here to receive it by then? I hear you share the same mistresses.'

He knew the games that she played. He said, 'Judge, then, of my surprise when my lord Eustace arrived from Boulogne. It must have been as great as King Svein's.'

On the quilt, the row of shields tilted and flashed. She said, 'A man who cannot match Harald of Norway is no King for England. Eustace will learn.'

'Who will teach him, I wonder?' said Thorfinn. 'Not King Svein, you think. Then King Svein's cousins, the sons of Earl Godwin? No, no, of course not. It was over my lord Eustace's visit that Earl Godwin was exiled.'

A miracle happened. The narrow bed became not a coffin but a chair of state. The figure straightened. The rows of shields parted company, and one of them, lifting, effected a bestowal of the stray strand of hair, a straightening of the head-veil. Emma sat up.

'My good lords,' she said. 'Is the King of Alba, is the King of Scotia, to be denied a seat in the house of his overlord? Thola, give him a chair. My good Bishop Stigand, you have business elsewhere, and whatever of note King Macbeth has to tell me, your colleague Odo will apprise you of later. Ladies, you may leave Thola with me. My lord King, stand no longer.'

So simply, in a moment, Thorfinn was seated and alone in the room with Emma and Odo and Thola. He said, 'The succession of England, you are about to tell me, is a matter for argument in each common ale-house, and you have had enough of ignorant speculation. I agree with you. I say only, when you have picked Godwin of Wessex, or found Edmund Ironside's son, or decided to offer the apple to William of Normandy, where will you find a successor for Emma of England?'

'Is my son dead?' said Emma. 'I was not aware of it. Naturally, I shall accept your tribute of silver, which is overdue. In exchange, I am happy to confirm what you already know. Edmund Ironside's son is a man who enjoys indifferent health and has never led an army or seen one led in his life. Until his daughters become marriageable, he does not exist.'

'Or until he has a son,' Thorfinn said. 'Barter, however, was not in my mind. I wished merely to ask, since the King, God be praised, is in his prime, how I may serve him? My lands, as you know, are not wealthy. But so long as I hold the seaways, and the ship-stations I require in the isles of the Sudreyar and in Ireland, I may continue to defend Cumbria for you against any ambitious earl or alien landing.'

'I should hope so,' said Emma. 'Since such, I believe, are the terms upon which you hold Cumbria and stir your finger in Cumbrian silver. Am I to believe that Macbeth's fleet is impotent against two exiled Saxons and an Irish bully? If so, Cumbria ought to be in better hands.'

He had brought her money, and she had paid him. She had warned him. All that he said in this room would be transmitted to Stigand, and thence to the Godwin family. He said, 'My fleet is preparing already,' and left it at that. The warning would reach Harold Godwinsson. With the way the rain fell in Ireland, none of the roads would bear an action till spring.

'You are fortunate that Tostig, Harold's younger brother, did not go to Ireland,' Emma remarked. 'My son Edward has never forgiven Earl Godwin for his brother's death, but he favours Tostig. A young man to watch, in my opinion. Should the family ever return.'

Between Ealdred's brother and the woman Thola, a glance flickered. With Emma, one did not show surprise or consternation, or ask alarmed questions. Thorfinn said, 'Could the Godwin family endure life in England with your son's many close and noble officers from over the water?'

'I hardly think so,' said Emma. A trickle from one unwinking eye drifted over the parchment bag, infusing all its seams. The woman of the chamber leaned forward and dried it with a square of fine linen. Emma paid no attention. She said, before the hand had left her face, 'Our Norman friends, no doubt, would be required to leave, in that event. Not an irreversible tragedy. They are good mercenaries. At present, of course, you draw yours from Ireland.'

It was made in the form of a statement, and Thorfinn was in no haste to answer it. She thought the Godwin family would return. Given the backing of Flanders, it was not impossible. So Eustace was out of the running, and Svein of Denmark. . . . He supposed that Godwin could claim the throne by right of possession, but little else; he was married to King Svein's aunt; his wife was King Canute's sister-in-law; his daughter was Queen. Until he had had Emma's son killed, he could have counted on Emma for anything. All the south-east coast of England, at the very least, would support him.

Emma said, 'What are you thinking? You were one of the ugliest boys I have ever seen, and you have not changed. If you had been a handsome man, would you still be Earl of Orkney and Caithness and nothing more?'

'Canute was a handsome man,' Thorfinn said.

There was a pause. The shields lay still. The scarf-ends on her chest rose a little. 'His nose was crooked,' said Emma. 'But he conquered England at an age when you were still learning how to give orders in Dover.'

'He was a great King,' said Thorfinn. 'But he fell heir to his father's ground-work in conquering England, and he inherited Denmark from his brother. Norway he took but could not hold, not because of King Olaf but because of the Trøndelagers. I do not know why he wanted an empire, unless it was because it is in the character of men of the north to care little for their posterity so long as their own names will live. To be known in one's time and after it can be inducement enough.'

'Fame? Is that all you want?' Emma said. 'You fought for Orkney and Caithness: that was your heritage; that was a matter of pride. Perhaps Moray was a matter of pride also: you took it back from the man who slew your stepfather. But Alba you need not have touched. It belonged to your grandfather, yes. But you could have left it in Crinan's hands until his grandchildren grew; or let the Northumbrian Earls have it. But you took Alba and Cumbria and added the islands and Ireland, and now, my lord Siward says, you have your eye on Lothian and maybe the rest of Bernicia. You deal with Popes and with kings, but I do not see a great dynasty rising to follow you. Is that all you wish? A name that men will remember? And if your enemies take from you, bit by bit, all you have conquered and you are left in your old age with no more than your father Sigurd possessed, will you die an embittered man? For it may happen.'

Sulien had said that to him once, but no one else; not even Groa. He answered with the truth, as he had answered Sulien, because it could harm no one and she was dying.

'His name is all a Viking expects to leave, and he hopes to make it a glorious one. Reared in obscurity, among a pack of kindred, the drive for renown and the drive to annexe one's rights are probably equal. Until my brother the King of Alba died, the pattern was, as you say, probably simple. And I didn't want his kingdom. It was too big to hold for tribute in the only way I knew.'

'I thought I had taught you otherwise,' Emma said.

'I learned a great deal from England,' Thorfinn said. 'Including respect for the damage Northumbria and Mercia could inflict. Without a fleet and without my grandfather's allies, Alba had no defences. Crinan had very little interest in Alba, and no following. His resources were elsewhere. He would leave at the first sign of trouble, and Alba would be fought over until it became a lawless wasteland, like the pagan lands of the Baltic. So, in turn, my northlands on its borders would be threatened.'

'So,' said Emma. 'You made of Alba a buffer for Orkney. Then you realised that it could not be relied on to do even that unless it could be induced to unite its disparate regions, to find a common object in feeding and defending itself. Perhaps you looked at other countries, at their farms and their towns and their way of life, and felt shame that the land of your grandfather should be so backward?'

'Perhaps,' said Thorfinn. He paused. 'Also, being so vulnerable, it required outside support; it required colonies to sustain it. A strong Alba could dispense with the Isle of Man and with Ireland. It should have a trading-fleet of its own, and not one built in Caithness and Orkney. It should survive, no matter what happened to me.'

'And you would be content with that as your monument?' Emma said. 'A land for others to rule?'

Thorfinn looked at her. 'Wife and mother of kings,' he said, 'forgive me if I remind you that we come from the same stock. What kings may follow me I do not know, and I do not care. When my day is ended, it is ended. But, as with you, on some book my name will be written.'

'Even if, as with me, you have to pay twice its worth to have it done,' said Emma equably. 'You have not thought to ask my lord Odo where his brother the Bishop Ealdred has gone.'

Thorfinn turned, and Odo of Winchester closed his mouth and straightened a little. 'You wish me to tell my lord of Alba?' he said to Emma.

The pillows had dragged the veil once again a little askew, and her shapeless face was bracketed by the long hoops of hair. Through it, her dignity and her contempt burned unimpaired.

'Naturally,' said the Lady-Dowager. 'Or I should hardly have mentioned it. Are you afraid that this King will run with a trumpet to Norway? Norway knows.'

'The succession?' said Thorfinn. 'In its remoter provisions, as we know— the King your son being in his full vigour.'

'You're no fool,' said Emma. 'Ealdred has been sent to Normandy. To invite Duke William the Bastard to take the throne of England when Edward dies.'

She stared at Thorfinn, and their eyes held.

'It would hardly be a game,' Thorfinn said softly, 'without all the men competing.'

Emma of England sat back. She smiled. She rested one sleeve on her pillow and extended her hand, a little, towards her visitor. The fingers trembled. 'I know I can rely on you,' she said, 'to do the right thing. You came on a Swedish ship?'

'Yes,' said Thorfinn. He rose and went forward and, taking the hand, kissed its wrist, and placed the kiss of peace also on her cheek, lukewarm as dried apple. He stepped back.

'Tell the master next time to bring me some sables,' said Emma, 'now I have silver to pay for them. If I am dead, Edward can wear them for mourning, in case his frame of mind is not otherwise perfectly evidenced.'

Thola opened the door for him, leaving. More than anyone of her age perhaps, Emma had been hated. But, without her, the world was about to be a less intriguing place.

She lived only till March, and was gone before the sables had time to arrive that would signal to the world whether or not her son Edward mourned her.

Ralph her grandson saw her buried, with his mother Goda, Emma's daughter, whose new husband Eustace remained tactfully behind at Boulogne. Earl Leofric attended the funeral Mass with his son Alfgar, and all the Normans and Bretons who in the past fifty years had joined the households of the two Kings she had married, and of her royal stepson and sons, as well as that of her own.

William, by the grace of God Duke of Normandy, did not witness the obsequies of his great-aunt; nor did the King of Scotia, whose blood-link with her was even more tenuous, and who had turned from her deathbed to face, without her, a new landscape whose ghost she had drawn for him.

No doubt, as the Lady Emma designed, the warning reached King Diarmaid in Ireland, and the Godwinssons: Attack Dublin in the spring and you will face Thorfinn of Scotia, who has made himself Eachmarcach's protector. A warning she thought sufficient to deter Diarmaid from attack.

She was wrong. Her wits blunted by age and by sickness, she misconstrued Diarmaid's temper, which would have taken such news, had it reached him in time, as no more than a challenge.

In fact, hungry for war as he was, it never reached him at all. Despite the rain and the roads, the combined forces of Leinster and the sons of Earl Godwin marched upon Eachmarcach with winter still on the land, and before any fleet of Thorfinn's could take the water against them.

Before Thorfinn himself had returned, the news passed from Galloway to the Clyde, and from there to Groa and his courtmen, waiting for him in Perth.

When his cavalcade was seen moving up from the south, Groa remained in the hall with Cormac and Tuathal while the rest ran out to the gates and the shouting and barking of dogs mingled with the distant horn-blowing of the King's servants. It was not her place to give him such news. What it meant to him, she would know when she saw him.

When she saw him, she knew not only what it meant to him, but that it had been no news; for his hand as he entered the hall was on the shoulder of Erlend their son.

She held out her hand to the boy, smiling, and, when he was within her arm, looked over his head to her husband.

'You have heard the news from Ireland,' she said. 'Diarmaid has driven Eachmarcach and the Norsemen from Dublin and made himself King.'

'I've been in Chester and Man,' Thorfinn said. 'Eachmarcach is on the island with what is left of his men, staying with his nephew Godfrey. I left Bishop Hrolf with him. Diarmaid was clever to move in the winter. And Eachmarcach is not what he was. . . . Godiva says she can't keep Erlend in food any longer and perhaps we would send him back in the autumn when the new harvest is in, if it's a good one. I've told him he can join Paul in Orkney when the weather allows. I'm hungry.'

There had been peace for too long. She'd grown used to it.

She had forgotten what it was like to wait like this in her chamber after the meal while her husband brought his men round to his way of thinking, patiently talking, discussing, explaining, until when he finally reached her, jaded from the long, heavy travelling, he could only say, 'I brought Erlend back as a precaution. The rumour is that Harold Godwinsson is only lingering till better weather before making a bid to get back to England. The

King is bound to oppose him, supported by Siward and Mercia. It may well be the end of Earl Harold. And then we shall see what my fleet can do to put Eachmarcach back where he would like to be.'

Groa said, 'And if Harold of Wessex prevails?'

'It will shake us a little,' said Thorfinn. 'But it will shake Siward and Mercia more.'

Thorfinn was probably right. But it was the end, meantime, of the other plans he had been making for the spring and the summer. The councils he held had to do more with the raising of levies and the supply of ships and of equipment, and less with the new forest-clearing and ploughing, the new ditching and trenching and the laying of paths and marsh-bridges and all the matters of efficient spring husbandry.

He held meetings and he moved, incessantly, from end to end of his kingdom. When the news came that Harold Godwinsson and his brother had sailed south from Ireland, Thorfinn was in Orkney, climbing about three half-made longboats and talking, with sawdust and salt in his hair.

Thorfinn came south to Inverness, where news might be more quickly received, and Lulach and Tuathal met him there.

They knew nothing more, either of Harold's destination or his intentions. Discussing the matter, Tuathal said to the King what Groa had stopped herself from saying. 'You say if Earl Harold is killed, you may be able to reinstate Eachmarcach. But Eachmarcach is old, and there is only Godfrey his nephew left of his line. Godfrey can hold the island of Man for you, but could he keep Dublin once you put him there?'

Since Rome, the association between the King and the Prior of St Serf's had become a firm, working partnership, at the core of a team of which Eochaid and Sulien were the soul, and men like Thorkel Fóstri and Cormac and Odalric the capable craftsmen.

So, roving up and down before Tuathal's pock-scarred, enquiring face, Thorfinn spoke as to a colleague. 'Do you imagine I'm going to plunge Alba into a war for all I can get out of Ireland? My father thought he had a claim to be King of Dublin, and the Brian war killed him. No. A friendly trading-port, some extra fees, and a reserve of men I can draw on for two or three years until this country can stand on its feet: that's all I want. And there is a limit to what I will pay for it.'

It contented them all for the moment, Groa saw. He did not allow them to forget Diarmaid, the potential enemy: half his fleet lay among the Western Isles and their inlets, in case of attack from that quarter. But the news of the exiled Godwin family, she well knew, was what he was waiting for.

At the end of June, it arrived. The outlawed Earl Godwin had sailed from Flanders to the south coast of England and, having roused half the land in his cause, had joined with his son Harold's nine ships from Ireland. The combined fleets, it was said, were moving to threaten the King's ships at London.

Thorfinn received the news and did not comment. His Queen, in desperation, launched a trial commentary of her own.

'*Emma, where are you now?*' said the Lady Groa.

'*Married to God?*' Thorfinn suggested. '*Emma's grandson Earl Ralph is about to receive the first dove of war in religious history. Poor Alfgar, in Harold's East Anglia.*'

'*Poor Earl Ralph in Swegen Godwinsson's Herefordshire. Poor William, by divine grace Duke of Normandy. I thought,*' said Groa, '*that you thought that Emma planned the offer to Duke William to provoke the Godwins into trying to return.*'

'*Emma liked boiling pots,*' said Thorfinn.

'*So do you,*' said the Lady Groa.

He had said nothing, she realised, because there was nothing worth saying. Or not until they knew the outcome of the battle, if there had been a battle. And who was now heir to England, or even King of it.

The household of Scotia moved south to Moray in time for the next news, which came from the west side of England, not the east, and was not about the Godwins at all.

With characteristic opportunism, Gruffydd ap Llywelyn, for thirteen years King of North Wales, had made another successful attack on his English neighbours, culminating in a pitched battle outside Leominster in which had died many Saxons as well as Normans from the castle garrison.

'*What castle?*' said Groa.

'*Hereford?*' said Thorfinn. '*Earl Ralph would be away fighting the Godwinssons. The Godwinssons hated the Norman castlemen. They're supposed to prevent the Welsh raids, but all they ever did was sit there and eat up the countryside and watch the Godwinssons. Osbern of Eu has a castle as well. Alfred keeps his money in it.*'

'*So Gruffydd was hoping for booty?*' said Groa.

'*He got it. Bags of silver and clothing, a lot of good-looking slaves, a herd of cattle and some fine breeding-mares, and all the food and wine he could carry. Eachmarcach helped him.*'

'*What!*'

'*What do you expect? Stuck on Man with a failure behind him and time on his hands. Guthorm Gunnhildarson went with him.*'

'*But not Bishop Hrolf?*'

'*Well, hardly,*' said Thorfinn. '*I expect he went to escape Bishop Hrolf.*'

They made light of it, since it was over and the news conveyed no hint of tragedy.

It was a week before they learned of the aftermath. Leaving Rhuddlan, Eachmarcach of Dublin and Guthorm his ancient ally had fallen out while dividing the plunder. In the violent clash between factions that followed, Guthorm fought as his uncle King Olaf would have wished him, and carried the day and the booty, leaving Eachmarcach and his exiled Dubliners dead on a profitless field.

The messenger who brought the news to Thorfinn came from Sulien. He was heard in silence, and in the same silence ended. 'I was to tell you, my lord King, that Bishop Hrolf will stay on the island of Man with King Eachmarcach's nephew until you order otherwise. The Archdeacon Sulien wishes me to say that Diarmaid of Leinster is installed in Dublin in strength and will not be lightly dislodged. Also that Godfrey of Man is not a great warrior.'

Thirteen years before, Thorfinn had made an alliance with Wales, and on the heels of it, Gruffydd had ravaged Llanbadarn, the school of Sulien's youth, and of King Alfred's great scholar Asser. Now Sulien was attempting again to build in Wales a retreat, a citadel of art and of learning, even while the spears and axes flashed about him. And he still cared what happened to Alba.

Groa said, 'Sulien has a wife and two children now. How safe is he?'

'As safe as he wants to be,' Thorfinn said.

Eachmarcach was dead, and Ireland was lost, as his father had lost it.

The year, the twisting, dangerous year, moved on its way, and still there was no news of a battle for England, or a conquest, or a pact, or a surrender.

Then, in September, word came. The town of London had declared for Earl Godwin of Wessex, and on opposite sides of the Thames there stood in challenge at last King Edward's fifty ships and his foreign friends and his levies, against the combined fleets of the men of Earl Godwin.

'What will happen?' said Groa. They were, for reasons she could not fathom, in one of their seldom-used lodges in Teviotdale, with a clutter of pavilions outside containing Gillecrist of Strathclyde and a number of men from north Cumbria.

'Did you imagine the King would fight Godwin?' Thorfinn said. 'They'd merely lose the best men from both sides, and the foreign heirs would move in for the pickings. My guess is that the King will hold a public gemot, a council, and will receive the exiled Godwin and friends to his bosom. It is Emma's power that they have been bidding for. Emma's power, not the throne of King Edward. You should hear tomorrow, or the next day, what happened.'

'*I* shall?' said Groa. She looked at her husband. 'What messages have been passing between you and Chester and Sulien? Thorfinn?'

'I'll tell you when I come back,' Thorfinn said. 'Wait for me. I'm only going to the Mercian border.'

'I'm too simple to understand why?' Groa said. 'Or you don't know what you are doing in any case?'

'I don't know what Emma was doing,' Thorfinn said. 'But she seemed to have everything planned, and I don't mind playing the pieces for her. What is it?'

'What would have happened,' said Groa, 'if you and Emma had married each other?'

'I should be a widower, and free to marry you,' Thorfinn said. 'And Eustace of Boulogne would be your stepson. He and Lulach would pass through a world of horror together.'

As always, he left her laughing; but it was different when he had gone, six months after Emma's death, to do Emma's bidding.

*   *   *

Thorfinn of Scotia, with a king's escort, pitched camp at Kirkby, the agreed spot on the north Mercian border, and had been there only a matter of hours when, below the birdsong and the chatter and rattle about him, there came the vibrating thud of many hooves and the rumble of wheels and finally, into distant view between trees, the banner of Mercia, followed by other, unknown banners jerking behind it.

The standard-bearer bore Leofric's badge, but was unfamiliar: presumably a minor official of Leofric's household performing the office of safe-conduct.

The long column of cavalry and footmen behind looked foreign as well as unfamiliar as they came near the brink of the boundary-stream. That is, the hooded chain-mail tunics were commonplace, but the conical helms with their nose-guards were Norman, as were the circular haircuts and shaven napes of the stirrup-servants running beside them.

Then they began to traverse the stream, the advance testing the bed for the wagons lumbering behind, piled with boxes and gay with the head-veils of women. The sun shone on the water, and on the long harp-shields with their gilded bosses, and on the bright spears and horse-harness; the tips of the bows and the crowded, filigreed quivers; on the worked heads of sword and of axe and of dagger in silver and gold. The spurs, rowelling the horses over the stream, reflected gold into the muddy water, and a footsoldier, with a shout, held up a lance on which a live fish flashed and curled, silver against the blue sky.

So Edward of England, it appeared, had forgiven the Godwinssons. And before the ill-will of the Godwinssons, Emma's friends and the boyhood friends of her son were in flight.

Thorfinn could hear his men counting. For the moment, numbers mattered less to the King than did the identities of the leaders, of whom there were more than a dozen. Then they came closer, and he began to distinguish the faces.

Some of them, as he expected, were those of war-leaders of reputation and birth from the duchy of Normandy: men such as the triumphant Godwin family were unlikely to suffer in England. Others were more surprising: an exiled vicomte, an excommunicated bishop he remembered, and, with them, an even more powerful abbot, all of whom, one had to suppose, had found themselves trapped in England when Earl Godwin was reinstated.

Among the younger faces was one remarkably like that of Goscelin de Riveire, the junior interpreter-monk whom he had met in Rome with his second cousin Alfred of Lincoln and Dorset. In fact, surveying the party, there was hardly one noble lord to whom the south-west coast of England was not as familiar as the halls of power in the Norman shores opposite them.

The second last man to arrive, with irony behind the formality of his greeting, was Carl Thorbrandsson, landowner in twelve English counties, whose life Thorfinn had spared once on the deck of a longship off Orkney.

The last was the scarred and powerful figure of Osbern of Eu, whom Thorfinn had first met nearly twenty years before at the enthronement of Duncan his brother. Osbern, uncle of Sheriff Alfred and nephew of the late Queen Mother Emma.

It came to Thorfinn that every landed man he could see, with perhaps one exception, was related to the late Lady Emma. But then, the ducal blood ran throughout Normandy.

'My lord King,' said Osbern of Eu. 'I see that you are a man of your word. So am I.'

'We have enemies, each of us; and in time to come, no doubt we shall have more. Here is my arm and my sword to protect you and yours. I ask in return only that we and our countrymen over the water may think of you, as we have always done, as a friend and an ally.'

'If it were not so, you would not be here, nor should I,' said Thorfinn. 'Be welcome; and come to the camp.'

'I won't say no,' Osbern said, 'not now I smell what you're cooking. We haven't stopped to eat for eight hours. Did you know the Godwin brothers picked up your young nephew Donald in Ireland? Found where Siward had stowed him after his invasion failed, and brought him back, screaming and kicking . . .

'My God, what a lot we've got to tell you,' said Osbern. 'We match well, you and I. Wait till we start campaigning. Then you'll know what it's like to live again.'

PART FOUR

WHAT IS THE NIGHT?

*. . . Untie the winds, and let them fight
Against the Churches.*

*—and now a wood
Comes toward Dunsinane.*

—So shall I, Love.

ONE

O, AS THE Saxons to England, and the de Hautevilles in late years to Italy, the fighting friends of Duke William of Normandy entered the federation of lands known as Scotia; and the Norns were seen to smile.

The King of Scotia, ignoring the smile, set his intellect and his energy to handle the flamboyant newcomers.

First, he delayed their arrival in the north until they had lost their belligerence.

It was not difficult. They were tired from the swift journey from Hereford, and sore with defeat.

Since Earl Godwin had challenged King Edward in London, everything had turned out as predicted. Faced with a large and threatening army, the King had offered a mollified ear when Earl Godwin laid his axe by the throne, knelt, and begged for forgiveness.

He received it, to the cheers of the populace. To rather more violent acclaim, the Archbishop of Canterbury and the Bishops of London and Dorchester were proclaimed outlaw, together with all those Frenchmen, said the council, whose bad laws and advice had led the King into error.

Exception was made for the elderly, the wholly inefficient, and the friends the King wanted to hunt with. These included several horse-marshals and sheriffs, two half-Bretons, the chamberlain, the chancellor, and several people satisfactorily tied into English property, such as Bishop Hermann of Wiltshire, Dudoc of Wells, Leofric of Exeter, and Alfred of Lincoln and Dorset. Ralph the King's nephew remained because he was brainless, occupying still the Hereford earldom of Godwin's son Swegen, who had gone to Jerusalem, not before time. Richard, the sheriff who had raised the fortress at Overton, the most exposed quarter of the Welsh border, had been allowed to stay because he was a good administrator and no one else would take the job anyway.

Ewias castle, under Osbern of Eu, had been different. The English of the southern march who grew the castle's food and suffered from the high spirits of its garrison had made no effort, like their lord Swegen, to disguise their fear and resentment of the foreigners planted in their midst, and the resulting failure of the castlemen, lacking proper co-operation, to keep out the Welsh had only embittered them further.

Ewias, on its steep escarpment ten miles south of Hereford, was, with its garrison, the one sure target earmarked by the returning Godwin family for destruction. The other Normans who had incurred the Godwin displeasure were equally aware of their danger.

The south coast, gateway to Normandy, was sealed off by Godwin's ships and Godwin's adherents. Without waiting for official dismissal, or for the five days' grace to which they were entitled, the Archbishop of Canterbury and the Bishop of Dorchester with their friends fought their way out of the East Gate of London and fled north to Essex, where Ralph, one of the favoured half-Bretons, had his castle, and where the Abbot of Ramsay, which had supplied so many bishops to Dorchester and which had already sheltered a Bishop of London, kept a fishing-boat or two at Eadulf's Ness.

They escaped, because of their speed and the unexpected direction of their flight. The rest of the Normans, debarred from the south and the Severn, rode west to the temporary shelter of their fellow-countrymen at Ewias castle and, from there, north through Mercia.

'You were lucky. You were lucky Earl Leofric gave you a safe-conduct,' observed Thor of Allerdale, riding into camp at Thorfinn's invitation to renew old acquaintanceships and hale them away, as it turned out, for a bit of boar-hunting. Thor, to whom the years of authority had brought a broader waist and a drift of sand through the fiery starkness of his hair and his beard, was full of hearty advice to the men, with most of whom, over the years, he had done some kind of business or other. His son Dolphin, made in his image, was with him.

Osbern of Eu, who saw Thor's kind every day, said, 'He didn't run much of a risk. Alfgar's going to lose East Anglia to Harold again anyway, so they'll let Leofric make his gesture. He wouldn't give us shipping.'

It had been Thor's first concern: to discover which of the refugees, if any, were merely waiting to take ship back to Normandy, and which intended to stay. He had seen them all now, and identified them. There, for example, was Hugh de Riveire, whose family had helped fortify Emma's Exeter. And hence also, one supposed, Carl Thorbrandsson, who had once run the Exeter mint.

They were all pretty well related. You could say that much. But you couldn't say there was any clear pattern of loyalty, to Duke William or against him. Maybe Thorfinn was merely seeking a safeguard against whatever might happen south of his frontiers. Maybe he was simply protecting his trade. And maybe Osbern of Eu was doing the same. His nephew Alfred was still there in England, nursing his lands in case the Godwin family ever got kicked out again. And if they didn't, here was Alba, all ready to be exploited under Thorfinn. Or over him. Or instead of him.

Thor of Allerdale said to Thorfinn, 'It's wonderful, isn't it, how business alters partnerships? I suppose you and Carl have met a dozen times since Crinan, of blessed memory, evolved his great plan to take over Cumbria and Northumbria and persuaded Carl and your wife's first husband that the north would be safer without you. But of course you killed Gillacomghain and took over Moray as well, which meant that Duncan, being of limited talents, was doomed. I often wonder how clever my lord Abbot Crinan really was.'

'Clever enough,' said Carl Thorbrandsson agreeably. A short, springy man now in his fifties, he had no need to speak otherwise: every sensible man in Alba and England treated him with the respect due to his record. He said, 'If Duncan died, Crinan still had his son Maldred or his son-in-law Forne to promote. Remember the five daughters of Ealdred, and the network of power across the north? Crinan wasn't to know that my lord Thorfinn here would spare my life. Or that the husbands of two of the daughters would come to Dunkeld one day and kill him.'

'Why talk as if it were all in the past?' Thor of Allerdale said. 'You still have your lands in Yorkshire, haven't you? And Siward is still there, and Forne and Ligulf and Orm. Only Alfgar is close to inheriting Mercia, and Duncan is dead and two of his sons now in England. You heard that, Thorfinn? Donald has been brought out of Ireland again. What do you think the Godwin family will do with him and Malcolm?'

'Groom them for the earldom of Northumbria?' Thorfinn said. 'They have equal claim, you might say, with Siward's son, or Alfgar's three, or Ligulf's two, or Forne's two, or Orm's only male heir. The idea should keep Siward quiet for a while, anyway.'

'While you annexe Lothian?' said Thor of Allerdale, and laughed adroitly. 'You'll have Bishop Malduin back shortly, won't you, now Siward sees which way the wind is blowing?'

No one rose to the bait, to his disappointment, and Thorfinn was not even listening, but answering someone's query about boar-nets.

In any case, it was unwise to probe. Thor of Allerdale got up, found his son, and flung himself, with enthusiasm, into the business of sport, while making a private resolve to send Leofwine soon to pay a short visit to Alba.

Leofwine's ideas of policy were rubbish, but there were times when his defects were useful.

Bishop Malduin came back at the beginning of winter, when the Normans were all safely ensconced in their temporary quarters in the great timber camp round the Moot Hill of Scone.

That, too, had been effected smoothly because Thorfinn's second step, on arriving home with his vastly more amenable guests, had been to call a council of his own magnates in Perth.

Because he had taken the precaution of testing the views of the more important beforehand, some of those with furthest to travel, including Thorkel Fóstri and Lulach his stepson from Moray, were in Perth already.

It was therefore before a large gathering of leaders from all parts of the country that Thorfinn introduced one by one the men who had escaped the vengeance of the Godwin family in the south, and affirmed that, for the good of the kingdom as well as by reason of friendship, he had offered harbour to any who wished to remain in the country.

Because of the weather, he spoke to them indoors, in the big timber hall above the river, and his voice filled it without difficulty, against the rustle of rain on the roof and the hurrying, orderly turmoil in the yard outside: the rap of horse-hooves and the rumble and thud of wood being unloaded from wood, and the voices of men from the jetty, impatient to get in from the wet. A profound smell of seething meat unrolled from the door-jambs and made common cause with the smell of hot ale that lingered from the welcome-cauldron.

To his mormaers and abbots and bishops, to his clerks and his toisechs, including those men who had been with him in Rome, it was familiar, and they gave him a reasonable hearing, for a man of reason was what they had found him to be.

'Many of them,' said Thorfinn, 'are friends and associates of yours already, as well as of mine. They would have me tell you that they are not here as beggars. What they have brought with them will feed them for a long while, and will pay their way for longer.

'What they require after that, if they remain with us, they have offered to pay for with services.'

He broke off and allowed the change of air that followed his words to become a murmur half heard, wholly heard, and then silence again. Thorkel Fóstri, standing with the rest, saw his King wait and draw breath, and felt ashamed because still, after all these years, the admiration in him should have to fight with the envy.

Thorfinn said, 'You know what has happened in Ireland. You know that our western shores are now at risk, whereas in the last years we have had peace to repair the damage latter wars have done, and to prepare for prosperity. I would have you know that I am not prepared to throw away all that has been done in these years in a bid to reclaim my rights or the rights of my father in Ireland. The laws and the programme I have laid down will continue. But if danger should offer, from whatever source, we now have a shield: the men you see with me, and their followers.'

How old was Osbern of Eu? In his fifties, Thorkel Fóstri calculated. The scar on his face, serrated now as he smiled, was an old one. Not young, but in full fighting vigour, and the veteran of God knew what campaigns, in Normandy or out of it. The newest tactics, the newest weapons: Osbern of Eu and his friends would earn their keep, all right.

Thorfinn was speaking again. 'In two or three years, I hope, we shall ourselves be restored, and armed, and ready to defend our country against any aggressor. Until then, we owe the best living we can offer to those who share our burdens. The force is, as you see, presently in winter quarters here at Scone. In the spring, it will disperse. The west coast is the source of greatest concern, and especially that part nearest Ireland and furthest from Orkney. Tribute-hills and gathering-places exist in every quarter and will provide a temporary encampment, but fortifications will have to be built, and lands allotted to feed the defenders and house them.

'All that will be done with as little disturbance as possible, and with the advice of the leaders of every community. I am also proposing,' said the even, formidable voice, 'to make available to some of our friends lands in the valleys south of the Forth and the Clyde that are at present under the supervision of no one and have been neglected since the time of Malcolm my grandfather. In this way, our guests may be supported without depriving any existing household of its livelihood. They have agreed to this. They have also agreed that, for the length of their stay, they will put themselves under the law and the leadership of this land, and will accept and subject themselves to our justice.'

He ended, and surveyed them all. Because of the height of the dais, he had remained seated, as had his companions, and, like them, he wore only the heavy tunic and wool cloak of riding-length, not the long robes of ceremony. He said, 'I accept their word, and am satisfied with this arrangement. But I will not impose it against strong views to the contrary. Is there any disagreement?'

No one stood up and said, as Killer-Bardi had when the idea was first mooted, 'I don't know what you want to bring in strangers for. We've always been able to defend ourselves without any trouble.'

Bishop Jon had scotched that, in his odd Scandinavian with the strong Irish accent. 'True enough,' had said Bishop Jon, 'when there were twenty sons to a family, and all a ruler required was enough land to feed himself and his concubines. But Christian observance, I would remind you, is putting a stop to that, and the practice of lifting someone else's cattle whenever it's mealtime.'

And Thorfinn himself had made the other half of the point. Alba had always had to call in mercenaries. And would have to get help where she could, until she could grow enough and earn enough to keep her own sons to fight for her.

So, although a few people cleared their throats, it was only Leofwine of Cumbria who finally stood up and said, 'My lord King ... I mean no disrespect, but over a matter of land, all of us want to be careful. In Alba and Strathclyde and Cumbria, there's waste land, and undrained land and uncleared land enough to feed any number of families; but to reclaim them needs time and labour. Meantime, when their resources are done, these men will have to live off something, and if they're fighting, they'll have no time for harvest or sowing. So, at the best, they'll have to be helped from ready-made land.'

He paused. 'There are ways round that,' Thorfinn said. 'And in good years, they can be paid in food anyway. But, of course, care will have to be taken. Was that all your point?'

'Well,' said Leofwine, and hesitated under a row of blue Norman eyes. He said, 'My lord, they have land, surely, in their own country, and battles enough to satisfy any man, whether for Duke William or against him. What's to prevent them taking a man's land here and then putting it under a caretaker while they rush back to Normandy when their own property is under attack or they see a prospect of extending it?

'We may get nothing out of this bargain. We may even lose our young men, if they get tired of clearing woodland and fancy going back, instead, to fight with Viscount Nigel in another Val-ès-Dunes, or with my lord fitzOsbern in another Domfront, or with Anjou in Maine, for that matter. Then you lose everything.'

'I will answer that,' Thorfinn said, 'and then, if they wish, our guests may have more to say. Firstly, the men you see here who are landowners in Normandy and also head of their houses will remain here for only one winter. While they enjoy our hospitality, we shall have, I hope, an exchange of mutual profit, and in the spring they will return home. The Normans who remain in England and the Normans who remain here must be drawn from those who have forfeited their land overseas, or who are of a cadet line and have none. As long as the House of Godwin is in power, it is hardly feasible for a man to own land and manage it on both sides of the water.'

'But they will go back in your ships,' Leofwine said. Discomfort had turned his face scarlet, but he spoke up loudly none the less. 'And I can think of a few younger sons who may go back with them.'

'So can I,' Thorfinn said. 'And our Norman friends in their turn have already told me of kinsmen of theirs who want to come here and join us. There is always a traffic in young fighting-men. You cannot halt it. And, provided they come back—and I think they will—I don't object to seeing the Alba of my sons in the hands of experienced men who have learned leadership at the flank of an expert. I think it worth trying. Is there anyone who still does not?'

Because the smell of food seeping into the hall was growing stronger, and because Bishop Malduin had not yet heard the news and been dispatched on his furious mission from York, no one had anything of moment to add, beyond a disarming speech of thanks delivered by Osbern of Eu. Thus ended the second stage of the planned Norman influx, without causing grievous offence to any one of Thorfinn's present subjects barring the one he had omitted to tell in the first place, which was Groa his wife.

She did not tax him with it. The thing was too trivial, and he was too busy.

So was she. She had taken upon herself the settling of the womenfolk of the Norman castlemen, who included cheerful Welsh bedfellows as well as resentful if legitimate Norman ones. Flodwig, the only son of the last Archbishop of Dol, who seemed to have been their principal interpreter in Herefordshire, performed the same office now, and the transition from Cumbric to Gaelic she herself could now manage with small trouble.

It seemed a long time since, a girl of seventeen, she had run Gillacomghain's household and then Thorfinn's with the aid of one steward, who would handle the stores and the incoming tributes and oversee the managers of the land that was farmed, while she saw that the cloth was woven and bought, and that the sewing and shoemaking were done, and the supply of men and girls and skilled women was always enough for the household's needs in cooked food and service. If no one else was there to do it, she bought new oxen herself and hired smiths or leatherworkers, and herself settled a case of wife-stealing or theft, or herself complained to the miller about badly ground bere.

Now it was all too large, and growing larger. The changing group of mormaers and men-at-arms who advised and attended the King had to be fed, and his churchmen and scribes as well as his household, quite apart from the special councils and feasts. There were always envoys or other visitors.

To accommodate all that, the lands held directly under the King, providing for his sheep and corn and swine and cattle and horse-breeding, his hunting and his fisheries, had had to grow also, for the ownerless lands of Fife that had come to him after Duncan's death had not proved enough. Now, if a holding fell vacant through death or misdemeanour, Thorfinn would often choose a man of his own to run it under the Crown.

All that was beyond the scope of one steward now. Every aspect of daily life, from the upkeep of buildings to the itinerary of the household, from the maintenance and making of arms and of tools to the building of ships, the felling of timber, the care of the horses, had to be in someone's hands, usually those of a man who was either a mormaer or a kinsman of one. Men who already had land, or access to it, and who, so far, could be rewarded with excitement, with companionship, and with silver.

So far. But Thorfinn must remember how, once in Orkney at least, once in Alba at least, rulers had bought the swords of their subjects in time of crisis by offering them in free gift the lands they had hitherto maintained as tenants. And how, later, necessity had forced the ruler or his descendants in every case to take back the gift.

In allotting more land to these Normans, Thorfinn was offering a hostage to fortune. For his own men in time to come would look for advancement; and to provide it, the food-barns would have to be full, and the chests of silver, locked in Dunkeld there.

On the other hand, if she had thought of it, then Thorfinn undoubtedly had also. And, despite everything, had gone ahead.

To Lulach, who had stayed at Perth for several weeks after the council meeting, Groa one day broached the subject obliquely. They were alone in Thorfinn's quarters in Abernethy, between the hills and the broad water-meadows of the Tay, and Thorfinn himself was absent in Angus.

Once, he was never *absent*, for wherever he was, there was the kingdom, and herself at his side. But for years there had been no methodical progress from region to region of the kingdom, hearing complaints, meting out justice, consuming tributes in kind.

Or no, that was wrong. Of course the household had travelled, incessantly. But the moves were not so frequent. Instead, Thorfinn himself made of each resting-place a base from which, day by day and week by week, he rode from place to place, wherever there were people, with a band of picked helpers. Fast and tirelessly mobile, he went where the household was too cumbersome to go, and where his presence was demanded. Between one move of the household and the next, he could be in Orkney and back.

She did not ask to go with him, and he did not invite her. The reasons were obvious. She was no more than in her mid-thirties and could ride as long as he did. But the household needed her presence, and the kind of business he was transacting, the kind of relationships he was establishing with these his subjects, did not.

He needed her to help him rule the kingdom. But it was a long time since he had needed her personally, as on the day he had come back from Rome, strained beyond his resources by months of meticulous work with the powerful men he was wooing, with the young courtiers he was training. Since that occasion, he had not turned to her for help or understanding. And even then the comfort she had given him had been of limited duration. The open air and the sea had been his real need, and his salvation.

So to her son Lulach, who had spent a serene morning hawking and seemed to miss neither his wife nor his new-born daughter in Moray, Groa said, 'I wonder what sort of court King Malcolm kept in his day? Full, I'm told, of Norse-Irish women and no wives. And yet he could hold off the Vikings and defeat the English in pitched battle.'

'I don't think Thorfinn has any Norse-Irish girls,' said Lulach dreamily. 'In fact, I'm sure he hasn't.' Steam rose gently from all his clothing, and a strong smell of horseflesh. His hair, against the wood of the settle, was pink as dawn snow in the firelight.

'Well, that's good,' said Groa with some irritation. 'Don't you know how Malcolm ruled?'

Lulach tasted the mead in his cup, drank from it, and set it down once again on the floor. He said, 'He didn't have Normans, if that's what you mean. He had his daughter's husband to call on whenever Vikings were needed, and his mother's people in Ireland whenever Vikings ran short. His household, I suppose, was like that of any Irish king of his day with no sons. He fought for his people in return for his keep. You don't have to run a very big household for that. . . . Didn't Thorfinn tell you the Normans were coming?'

He always got to the root of the trouble, and it was always painful. You had to be very even-tempered to live with Lulach. Groa said, 'I think it's a little dangerous.'

'But at first,' Lulach said, 'weren't you surprised by his cleverness? I think he wanted you to be surprised by his cleverness. You are the only person whose opinion really matters to him.'

Her eyes flickered, and she bent to pick up the gold spool she was working with, turning away from the heat of the fire. The linen cord in her lap was half-covered with bullion already, with a speck of blood on it where the fine wire had opened her thumb. Lulach said, 'Do you want me to speak to him?'

Her eyes cleared. 'No,' said Groa. She looked up. 'So long as nothing is wrong. You didn't tell him anything new?'

'He doesn't want to know, any more,' Lulach said. 'And it wouldn't make any difference. Don't grieve because he isn't brought low with doubt, or with pain, or despair. When he does call on you, it will be for something even you will find almost impossible to give. Save your strength for that day.'

The wire fell from her lap and leap-frogged in thin golden coils over the flags and into the glowing red core of the fire. 'Because of the Normans?' she said. 'Lulach, I think I want to know.'

Lulach's perfect teeth showed in his slow, charming smile. 'Then you should have read my account of the Normans,' he said. 'Hugh and his friend Osbern Pentecost flying north from their castles to take refuge with King Macbeth. Pentecost, someone said, was God's answer to Babel, but we seem to have more languages now, don't we, than ever we had? . . . I wish you wouldn't cry. It doesn't change anything.'

'Next time I say I want to know, *don't tell me anything,*' Groa said. 'And meantime, whom do you know who would like gilded firewood? The ultimate decadence. As we sink into financial chaos, men will look down on our ruins and murmur: *Like Egypt, like Rome, like Byzantium, these men of Scotia went down in their glory.* Yes, what is it?'

She wondered if she had been overheard. But the man of her chamber who entered was much too engaged with his own news.

'My lady, a harbinger has arrived. The Bishop of Alba is on his way here, hoping for an audience with the King.'

Before she had drawn breath, Lulach was on his feet beside her. 'The King is on his way back from Angus. I'll meet him. My lady will be happy to see the Bishop and entertain him until the King comes.' He turned to Groa. 'If that is right?'

He could change so quickly. It was perfectly right, and the course of action that, given time, she would have propounded. Lulach left while she was still giving orders for the guest-quarters to be made ready, and the Prior sent for.

It was some time later, when changing her robe in the hands of her women, that she realised to the full her position. Whatever she thought of the Normans, she now faced the prospect of excusing their presence to the man whose superior in York had just abetted the return of Earl Godwin, the Normans' chief enemy.

It appeared that there were ways in which she could help her husband the King after all. She let them pleat her hair and knot pearls into it, and then selected with care the objects to hang at her girdle: enough to outmatch York but not enough to make her walk like a draw-bullock.

Then, having delegated the Prior to offer the Bishop an opportunity for rest and refreshment, Groa sat back with her ladies and waited, thoughtfully, for the Bishop to present himself after his supper. After (she had impressed on the Prior) his excellent but somewhat lingering supper, with no lack of generosity in the matter of wine.

Bishop Malduin was aware, flushed in the heat, that the table of the pure and humble brethren of Abernethy had undergone a transformation since his last truncated visit, and put it down, with accuracy, to the presence of a royal hall and a greater sophistication in the matter of how to handle a bishop.

And the King Thorfinn, or Macbeth, was not present.

The Bishop's stomach, wizened with the burning tokens of apprehension, began to whine and cluck its way into neutrality, and then on to appetite. Instead of water, to which, facing the King, he would have confined himself, he allowed himself a little wine.

Not too much. He had the Lady to see, and no doubt she would find some way of summoning up a new, tough mormaer or even a usurping bishop to try and shake his confidence before the King arrived.

A little wine, however, would do no harm. He had never been better prepared for any encounter with this upstart kinsman and his acolytes who had turned his comfortable bishopric into a badgersett. Forne and Gamel, Ligulf and Orm, Earl Siward himself, over and over again, had discussed the matter with him, so that he fully understood everything that was at stake.

His wife had understood, too, when he told her. His wife who had inherited a nice bit of land about York, and who had married him because he was once a nephew by marriage of the heiress of Scotland and had been promised a bishopric.

He was not, like some other men, in danger of killing himself with his own cunning, or a hulking bully fit only for the battle-field. He was not, he admitted, a man of his unsavoury times. But it had seemed then that he could not fail. If King Malcolm or his grandson Duncan took Durham, then the Bishop of Alba their kinsman would surely become Bishop of Alba and Durham as well, with the lands and the tributes of the whole of the church of St Cuthbert in his keeping.

Or if, as the cynicism of King Malcolm and the quality of his grandson King Duncan emerged, the dice fell in the opposite direction, the Bishop of Alba was still there, discreet, well trained, helpful to his superiors, to enable an Earl of Northumbria to add the lands of Cumbria and Lothian to the lands of St Cuthbert he already held and appoint the Bishop of Alba over them all.

In all the years of their association, Siward had never in so many words promised Bishop Malduin the bishopric of St Cuthbert's town of Durham, but he had taken it for granted that, sooner or later, it would fall into his obedient lap. The present Bishop was in trouble over money matters: everyone knew that; and the one before that had bought his cross and his ring quite openly from King Hardecanute; while Bishop Aldhun had become richer and more powerful than anybody by marrying his daughter to Earl Uhtred, who had been killed by Carl Thorbrandsson's father, and whose granddaughter Earl Siward had married.

None of these attractive things had so far happened to Bishop Malduin, and, while waiting, his daughter had been forced to make a marriage of only modest prospects, and his stepson Colban, whose clerical failings still marred the book-rolls in York and in Durham, was now spreading equal despair from the desk of Ghilander, his own half-brother in Angus.

None the less, he had never given up hope. He could never make a friend of Siward, this fur-trader's bullying son from the mountains of Norway. The Orkney strain in the Bishop's blood, tamed and muted by years of study and civilised living, recognised nothing familiar there. But Siward, year by year, was growing stronger and richer, and the new Archbishop of York, they said, was as eager to get his hands on the northern diocese as Siward was.

Hence the disbelief with which he had heard his cousin Thorfinn's ultimatum. *Persuade Earl Siward to allot you the living of all the St Cuthbert churches in Lothian as well as your charges in Alba, or I will make life in Alba so unbearable for you that you will have to retire.*

In effect, that was what Thorfinn had threatened, and that was what the Bishop had told Earl Siward and his wife. He had dreaded his wife's response even more than that of Earl Siward, and with reason. His wife had had time to make her attitude very clear in the weeks of waiting that followed his report to Earl Siward.

The weeks of waiting, he now believed, had a lot to do with the progress of Earl Godwin's bid to return to power after his exile. The subsequent delay was due, he knew very well, to the extraordinary, the outrageous news that had arrived from Cumbria.

Thorfinn of Alba had given shelter to a troop of powerful Normans escaping from the authority of the Godwin family in the south. And was proposing to settle them, among other places, in the lands south of the river Forth. In Lothian.

The thought of it made his mouth dry, but he sipped very carefully. He was not a big man, and he made it a rule never to appear unsteady or dishevelled. Every detail of his appearance should be correct and was, from his clean-shaven chin to his pointed slippers, with his immaculate robe tailored smoothly over the little pot-belly kept firm by hunting. He hardly noticed how Thorfinn's wife looked when he finally entered her chamber: he was wondering at the time whether she knew enough to put a proper value on his fur trim, and had noticed the new ring Earl Siward had sent him as a little present on leaving.

The Lady rose, as she should, and said, 'Oh, dear, you have some beef on your squirrel. Anghared will bring a cloth while you sit down. So tell me your news. Your wife has chosen her convent?'

You forgot what these people were like. The blood pumped through his head as he compressed his chins, hunting for the invisible stain. He came up for air and met an invitation to suicide. He said, smiling, his hands poised in mid-air, 'You are mistaken, my lady. My wife is not entering a religious house.'

The woman attendant came back with a cloth and a bowl, and began to dab at a bit of sleeve that the woman Groa . . . the Queen pointed out to her. He was not quite in time, himself, to inspect it. The Queen said, 'But of course that is good news. She is coming back with you, then, to my husband's court? He will be delighted.'

He smiled again, deprecatingly. His right arm, obeying the jerks on its sleeve, wagged steadily up and down. He said, 'That is a matter for negotiation, my lady. It had better await the King your husband's arrival.'

'What a pity,' the Lady said. 'Don't you have a friend who would negotiate for you? I would do it myself, but I don't know your wife very well.'

They seemed, irritatingly, to be at cross-purposes. He said, 'It is not a matter of negotiation between my wife and myself, my lady. It is a question of whether my lord Macbeth will accept what is best for the church as a whole.'

'You mean,' said the Queen, 'that it might be best for the church as a whole if you did not come back? Surely not.'

Bishop Malduin, finding that he had recovered sole ownership of his arm, took it down and gave an irritable smile and a nod of thanks to the woman Anghared as she took her bowl and departed. He said, 'The Pope will have to be advised, my lady, that my cousin your husband in his search for political leverage has importuned the Holy See for the appointment of two bishops whom he cannot support unless I, the present incumbent, am asked to run about in attendance as his household priest.'

'I thought,' said the Lady Groa, 'that the bishopric was to be supported by the dues from the churches of Lothian?'

Bishop Malduin did not like argumentative women and, outside his home, dealt with them firmly. 'Unhappily,' he said without undue regret, 'the Archbishop cannot see his way to allowing the lands and dues of St Cuthbert to be alienated from the shrine of St Cuthbert.'

'The Archbishop?' said the Queen with interest. 'I thought the Archbishop was outlawed. By Earl Godwin.'

'The Archbishop of York,' said the Bishop. He removed the sharpness from his voice. 'The Bishops of Durham are the concern of the Archbishops of York. There is a new one. Cynsige.'

'I see,' said the Lady Groa. He doubted if she did. She said, 'Then I suppose what you are suggesting is that Bishop Jon or Bishop Hrolf join the King's household, and you go to Man or to Orkney?'

'No, no,' he said. 'Really, I think we had better leave these things until your husband arrives.' He repaired his vehemence with a laugh. 'Indeed, that *would* be a matter for negotiation between myself and my wife.'

'I thought your mother came from Orkney,' said the Queen. 'But you surprise me. In fact, I think it's shameful. After all the help you have given him, and the position of your wife as one of his tenants, Earl Siward won't let you enjoy the church dues of Lothian? They're not even his to withhold, are they? I thought old King Malcolm fought the Bernicians for his rights in Lothian thirty years ago, and got them.'

'And lost them again, as any right-thinking person would realise, through his and his grandson's insane attacks against Durham,' said Bishop Malduin shortly. 'I have, of course, been honoured by Earl Siward's offer of the cure of the churches of Lothian. But under the tutelage, as it should be, of Durham and the archbishopric of York, to whom the churchlands and the rest of the dues rightly belong.'

'I haven't offered you any wine,' said the Queen thoughtfully. She rose herself and walked to the chest upon which lay the cups and a pitcher and poured with a capable hand. She said, 'Of course, it would make a good living. The dues from the Kinrimund lands under the King of Alba, and the dues from the Lothian churches under the Archbishop and the Earl of Northumbria. Where would you live?' She returned and handed him a cup.

He took it. 'Oh, in Durham,' said the Bishop. 'My wife likes it. It's within reach of York on one side and the Lothian lands on the other. A competent steward could look after Kinrimund. I have a good one there now. It was always out of the way.' He sipped and smiled up at her. 'You come from Norway and you look surprised? Half the people of Scandinavia are looked after by missionary churchmen. Grimkell doesn't forget Norway when he comes back to be Abbot of Abingdon. Siward was joint Bishop of Uppsala at the same time as he was Archbishop of Canterbury. Alwyn, my predecessor, was a Saxon and was consecrated, as I was, by the Archbishop of York. I can look after Thorfinn's good people from Durham.'

The Lady took her cup and sat down briskly, holding it with both hands. 'That,' she said, 'should certainly restore Christian life to the churches of Lothian, with Thorfinn's Norman friends all about them, to garrison and protect them.' She lifted her cup in salute. 'A compromise, but a good one. Let us drink to it.'

The Bishop did not drink. Through the food, through the warmth, the wryness of his stomach made itself felt. He said, 'Thorfinn's friends have no place in these churches. These churches are English.'

'Oh, come,' the Queen said. 'Did the Archbishop of Canterbury man the churches of Uppsala, or a King of Ireland send armed troops to Bobbio? Earl Siward cannot expect to keep troops in Lothian unless he claims Lothian. So far, you have mentioned only his rights to the churches of St Cuthbert.'

The Bishop was silent.

'Does he claim Lothian?' said the Queen. 'Or do you need time to think about it before my husband arrives?'

'Of course he claims Lothian,' said Bishop Malduin. He set down his wine, and some of it jumped on to the table, and the cloth of his sleeve. He was marked: defiled by manipulation and aggression. He said, 'Show me the parchment that says it is not his. Does your husband dare to dispute it?'

'Candidly,' the Lady said, 'I don't think he needs to, while Earl Godwin is taking up so much of everyone's time and Mercia is being so sensible. It's well known that Thorfinn is no friend to Norway, and I can see that it might be quite to England's advantage to have a string of church-forts across the Lothian neck in the hands of someone who won't be tempted to lease them to an enemy.'

'And your Norman friends?' said Bishop Malduin. 'They, I suppose, are comrades of England as well?'

'At the moment,' said the Lady, 'they seem to be about half in favour of Duke William and half against him, so that I don't suppose they seem much of a threat even to Earl Godwin, so long as they don't interfere with the running of England. I don't suppose Earl Godwin worries much about the running of Northumbria, except when he looks at the number of sons he has to provide for.

'I can't, of course, speak for my husband,' said the Lady, 'but I'm sure, whatever the outcome of this little quarrel, he wouldn't wish a bishop to suffer. If Earl Siward won't change his mind over the Lothian churches, we shall always welcome you and your wife back to Kinrimund. It isn't, I'm afraid, quite as attractive as Durham, but the hunting is good.'

He had lost the Lothian churches. He had lost Lothian, not that he had had any hopes of that particular embassy. He had been ground between magnates, as he had dreaded, and there might well be no place for him in the end but Kinrimund, for the Earl, in conveying his magnificent ring, had made it jocularly clear that he could expect to live idle on the charges of Durham no longer.

The woman and her husband his cousin Thorfinn had prepared for this: had planned to belittle him. When Thorfinn arrived, he would hear the same story, but openly offensive this time, without the woman's pagan cunning. His own wife at least was predictable.

His own gown smelt repulsively—unnecessarily?—of wet squirrel. Bishop Malduin got to his feet, his lips tightened, just as the door opened without so much as a knock and a man came in.

The Queen, who had been rising as well, became suddenly much more serious, and her light, foreign eyes under the black brows stayed wide open, like those of a kestrel wondering if it has seen a vole, or a stone.

The newcomer was the cousin his King, muddy from travelling but lacking, it must be said, the traveller's usual aura of wind-blown dampness and cold.

Thorfinn of Scotia smiled at the Bishop, and then at his wife.

'Forgive me,' he said. 'Had I known you were coming, I could have stayed to welcome you, or even forestalled your visit, for you must know from my wife by now that I could never countenance the right of Earl Siward and the Archbishop of York to defend and garrison the Lothian churches, and Earl Siward, I am sure, has reached a similar conclusion about our new friends the Normans. Am I right?'

'You are correct, my lord,' said Bishop Malduin. 'That is the sum of our conclusions. I am gravely disturbed about it.'

'No need,' said Thorfinn. 'You will report to Earl Siward—or, if you prefer, I can dispatch a reply for you. And then what? Can we persuade you to return to your see here in Alba? Kinrimund is not such a bad place.'

'Just what I was saying,' said Groa. Her voice cracked.

'You are persuasive,' said Bishop Malduin austerely. His legs quivered with tiredness. He said, 'I have had a long day, as no doubt have you, my lord. If you would excuse me, I should prefer to discuss final conclusions in the morning, when we are both fresher.'

'Why, of course,' said Thorfinn. 'Let me take you across to your quarters. And how is your lady wife . . . ?'

When, for the second time that evening, the door opened and closed behind her husband, Groa was alone. Thorfinn said, 'Now he'll allow himself a little drink, and sleep like a log.'

'Where were you listening?' said Groa.

'In the next room. I was just riding in at the gate as Lulach rode out to find me. He told me you were worried about the Normans,' Thorfinn said.

'And you still let me talk to the Bishop alone?'

Thorfinn said, 'It was one way to make you think it all through. I knew that, once you had, you would agree with me.' He had flung down his stained cloak, which was dry, and was looking round for some means of taking his boots off.

Groa said, 'I'm not sure that I do, but I am a good deal less in accord with Earl Siward and your dear cousin Malduin. How did your father come to have a nephew like that?'

'It was his sister,' said Thorfinn. 'She had no initiative either. Didn't even know when to help her husband off with his boots.'

Groa walked to her seat and sat down gently, crossing her ankles and folding her hands on her lap. She smiled at him. 'Tonight, I did the King's work,' she said. 'Now you do the Queen's.'

'Well, I'll try,' said Thorfinn. 'But with my boots on, it isn't going to be comfortable. You may wish you had nothing to worry about but the Normans. Don't be disturbed by what Lulach tells you. He can't always be certain.'

'Do you suppose I listen to him? When you talk all the time?' she was saying; when his embrace, unexpectedly harsh, extinguished both her lies and her laughter.

TWO

WHEN, IN THE way women will, Groa railed against the Fates that had allowed them to live all this time in golden security and now seemed to have left them, Thorfinn was amused, but not sympathetic.

Looked at sensibly, what he said was quite true. Nothing stood still. In the affairs of all the powers on whom their own welfare depended, there were tides and currents as well, sometimes colliding with theirs, sometimes making for peace.

They still exchanged gifts and trade with the Emperor; they still had the interest and friendship of Pope Leo, even though for a year the Pope had been not in Rome but in Germany, caught by the cry for a mediator between attacking Germany and defending Hungary; pressed by the fighting in Italy to beg help against the triumphant Normans.

Still, the Emperor and the Pope were the two greatest forces in the west, and because of them and Thorfinn's comradely relations with Svein of Denmark, because of England's weakness at sea and because of her terror of Norway, neither King Edward nor the House of Godwin was likely that winter (said Thorfinn, with justice) to trouble Scotia.

And without the backing of Wessex, Earl Siward wouldn't now move. For a vacant Northumbria was not only prey for the sons of Godwin and for Mercia. There were those among the remaining husbands of the five daughters of Ealdred who would like nothing better than to see Siward perish in an effort to plant a few Anglian soldiers and a bishop in some crumbling old forts in the Lothians.

A message, therefore, of patient good sense had been sent by Thorfinn to Earl Siward, and a request that Bishop Malduin's wife and household should be sent to join the Bishop at Kinrimund, where the King would be pleased to defray their expenses pending an agreement on the sponsorship of the Lothian churches.

As for the Lothian lands in lay possession, Thorfinn's message explained, there certainly seemed to be some confusion as to where the frontiers lay, and to which overlord, if any, the present owners should pay service and dues. He proposed to draw up what could be learned of the history of this area, and hoped that the Earl of Northumbria would ask his old men to do the same, when a meeting might be called to their mutual benefit.

In the meantime, said Thorfinn, since the western portion of Lothian adhering to the lands of Strathclyde and Cumbria and the old see of Glasgow had never, as he understood it, been in dispute, he intended to dispose of the land there as he thought best, with such fortifications as he considered necessary to preserve order.

To which effusion Earl Siward of Northumbria made no response whatever, although he must have received it, since Bishop Malduin's wife was with her husband in less than two weeks. Their words on greeting each other were not recorded.

By then, in any case, Thorfinn was in Scone with Osbern of Eu, drawing maps and discussing strategy. War-talk for night after night as the lamps burned in the hall, after days spent in sport and hunting and exercise. War-talk or defence-talk. It was the same thing. The young men about Thorfinn were learning Norman-French and listened, their eyes shining, to what Duke William did, and Humphrey, Tancred's son in Apulia, and Count Geoffrey in Anjou. It was a surprise when, just short of Christmas, Thorfinn decided the weather was good enough to take his wife and personal household north to join his two sons in Orkney.

'And leave the Normans and their disciples?' said Groa. 'You'll never get back. They'll install King Osbern in Scone come the spring-time.'

'You can't trust anyone, can you?' Thorfinn said. 'There they are in Jerusalem with armed deacons round the True Cross, they say, to stop pilgrims biting bits off when they kiss it.'

He was not disturbed. He knew, of course, his own power over his men. And now the Normans would know it.

In a sense, they did not leave the newcomers behind. There was only one topic, it would seem, in the staging-posts they passed on their way, in the halls of Kineth of Angus and Gillocher of Mar, of Malpedar of Buchan and of Morgund of Moray, before the fires of Hlodver at Dingwall and Odalric of Caithness, and finally at Birsay in their own hall on the shore, with Otkel leaning forward asking questions, and Thorkel Fóstri and Killer-Bardi and the rest sitting silent, listening, with the Earl's sons and his wife.

One topic: William of Normandy. Because fighting-men are always eager for details about a new fighting-leader, the questions began, and continued. And Thorfinn gave to them his considered answers, as ever.

Listening to him, Thorkel Fóstri wondered, as he had at Scone, what Thorfinn thought of this, the first of the next generation of rulers. Norway, Denmark, the Empire were in the hands of men of Thorfinn's own age, at the height of their vigour. Such also were most of his friends: Sulien and Alfgar of Mercia, for example. And Siward of Northumbria, whether counted as kinsman or enemy, must be nearly ten years Thorfinn's senior.

But the sons of Earl Godwin and the sons of Thorfinn's brother Duncan and this young great-nephew of Emma's were the men who would see Europe and perhaps guide it, some of them, through the second half of the century. William of Normandy, in his mid-twenties, was already married to Matilda, the daughter of Baldwin of Flanders, flouting Pope Leo's injunction, linking him not only to Lille and Bruges and Ghent, but to Tostig, the son of Earl Godwin who had married Judith of Flanders, Matilda's aunt.

In the field, William had shown himself both brave and resourceful. Somehow he had survived the attempted assassinations, the palace revolutions of his childhood, and was beginning to gather about him men who were willing to gamble their fortune with his, as well as others who were still not committed, and yet others who might, before he grew any stronger, take any chance that presented itself to push their own claims.

He was inventive, in his tactics, in his use of equipment. He was harsh: his brutality in the taking of Alençon was such that the war against him collapsed and men's lives, you might say, were thereby preserved in the end. Canute had done that, in his earliest days, when he mutilated the Saxon hostages confided to him. Then had entered upon a wise and just rule, marked by church endowments and by pilgrimage.

As Thorfinn had done at the start of his reign, in Fife. And had followed the same pattern afterwards. It was a standard sequence of conquest, and not confined to pagans. Only that year, the Emperor had hanged Manichee heretics in Goslar, so Isleifr had told him.

So there was much to admire in William, bastard son of Duke Robert of Normandy, whose ancestors and Thorfinn's were the same. What Thorkel Fóstri wished he knew was whether Thorfinn admired the new Duke, or whether he felt as he, Thorkel Fóstri, had once felt and still sometimes did, looking on a younger, able, ambitious man with all his future before him. He wished he knew, because, sooner or later, for the sake of his country, Thorfinn was going to have to choose.

Eventually, they talked themselves out; or at least the talk became overlaid by the preparations for the Christmas feast, only two weeks away, and those matters of business that had been laid aside for the Earl's attention: the visits he had to make, and the people he had to see. Paul, at seventeen, had begun to take his share in the running of the islands under Otkel, and his father the Earl must be shown the results and discuss them; with Erlend, a silent eleven, listening avidly.

There was the building on the island of Birsay to visit, with Bishop Jon to explain the niceties of the church and of the hall, both of which were roofed and full of carpenters attempting to produce a cathedral and a palace in time for the celebration of Yule.

It would have been inconsiderate of the King and his wife to spare them their self-imposed task; to dismiss the sweating craftsmen to their homes to enjoy the feast-time in front of a longfire with their wives and children, or drinking with the Earl in his comfortable timber hall, well fired and warmly hung, on the opposite shore.

It would have been inconsiderate, and the possibility was not discussed, although Groa, moving from hall to hall with her husband, took the chance to pack a few extra boxes with thick clothes and blankets, and spent a little time during her last call at Orphir studying the crucifix Bishop Jon had pinned over her bed and wondering whether or not it would be Christian to pray for a wind.

Just a small wind; for a small wind was all that was needed to make the passage between the shore and the island of Birsay difficult for a large number of people. A wind large enough to make it certain that no Yule feast could be held, and small enough to allow the workmen and their womenfolk and the hall people who were over already to cross to the shore and spend Christmas with a clear conscience at home. . . .

It was perhaps less a prayer than a wish, in its final form; but by the time the Queen went to bed that evening, it looked almost as if she had been heard.

That day, Arnór Jarlaskáld had made one of his erratic descents upon Orkney, and the talk in the hall was worth listening to, as was the singing, but it was as well that the women should know when to leave. Preparing for bed in the new wing that was not now a new wing, after the fire that seemed so long ago, Groa heard the chorussing and the laughter, muffled through two walls, and smiled.

In two hours or a little less, it would end, and Thorfinn would come in, a little drunk or more than a little drunk, as he could afford to be only in Caithness and Orkney, and so deliver himself, briefly, into her charge.

God knew she did not want him lowered by doubt, or by pain, or by despair, as Lulach had once seemed to accuse her. But, now and then, she wanted to be at his side when his mind was still and there was nothing there but the sweetness within the forbidding exterior; and the love.

She awoke to a door banging. All the doors of the hall and its adjoining chambers were fitted with strong latches, and were closed at night; to find one left loose was unusual. She lay, half asleep, listening to the blustering wind outside her shutters, and then, satisfied by the sound of steps somewhere outside, and the decisive snap as someone shut and latched the loose door, she went to sleep again.

The next time she woke, it was to the slamming of the same door and the thud of two others further away. In her own room, the door was still latched, but was rattling, with a rhythm she could hear repeated outside in the strong, irregular fluster of a wind from the east, with the hiss of a roused sea behind it.

The bed beside her was empty, but there were men in the yard: she could see a glimmer of light between the shutters and hear a flotsam of voices now and then, when the wind died.

They would be securing the boats, and perhaps some of the stock, and looking to the hay and peat-stacks. Orkney lay on the track of the Atlantic winds: every bush in Orkney was wind-pruned; every hill was marked and terraced with wind-stripes. Everyone knew what to do. It lacked five days to Christmas, and it might be, with a good wind and a following swell, that they might not have to spend Christmas at Birsay. She went to sleep, smiling.

The third and last time she was wakened that night, it was by the voice of her husband saying, 'What it is to have a clear conscience. My Queen, there is a gale and a high tide coming together, and the general view is that the women and children might be better off up in the hill-houses.'

She surveyed her husband. She had heard of storms great enough to flood some of the booths near to the shore, but never one that had thrown more than spray on the walls of the longhouses. The inland sea at her door might be seven miles across, but it was enclosed on three sides by islands.

Beside her, the lamp suddenly rattled and she felt her hair lift. Behind Thorfinn, the door slammed shut with a force that made her bed jerk. He said, 'Come.' If he had drunk anything at all, it had left him.

He had a lantern lit by the time she had dressed, wrapping herself last of all in the big, hooded cloak she had brought for Birsay. He said, 'Have you a basket? Take your jewel-box. And these.'

What he pulled out and flung on the bed were garments of his own: a thick jacket and breeches and boots. He said, 'In a high wind, the cloak will pull you over. Now come.'

At such times, you did not disobey Thorfinn or even talk to him. She saw the weight he had to exert to drag the door open. And that was an inner door. Then she was in the empty hall, with all the candles blown out and only some lamps guttering here and there. And finally Thorfinn laid hands on the outer door and began to move it, fraction by fraction, as if it were a gravestone, until she could force her way out. Literally force her way out against a baffle-wall of inimical air that leaned against her, pressing unevenly. It sucked out the air in her head and her lungs, and she twisted her head sharply, snatching breath from the folds of her cloak. Then she felt a hand on her elbow and the voice of Bishop Jon said, 'I'll take you.'

Then she was battering her way at his side, thrown by her cloak, along the stout southern wall of the building and then hurled free round its corner and sent, propelled by the wind, at a staggering run up the hill that led inland, with Bishop Jon, in leggings and jacket as Thorfinn had been, with his arm locked in hers, acting as drag-anchor and lantern-bearer at once.

She could not look round. But behind her she could hear, all over the bay, the scraps of men's voices shouting, and the rumble of rollers as the ships were drawn up to safety, and the lowing and bleating of animals being driven uphill. Once, a dog squealed and went on squealing in pain, and a flying plank, grazing her shoulder, reminded her of what a high wind could do.

They had nearly arrived at the first of the longhouses scattered over the hillside, belonging to the families who stayed in Orphir all the year round and cared for the land and the hall on behalf of the Earl. Bishop Jon said, 'Sinna and some of your own women are there already. They will be glad of your company. And all the men, you understand, will be needed to make things secure. High tide is at seven in the morning. It will be dark, which is troublesome, but the wind hasn't been blowing so long. It may spend itself before the next one.'

He did not remember, perhaps, that she came from Trøndelagen and knew about the sea. Whether the storm blew itself out quickly or not, the seas it moved took longer to reach their height, and longer, too, to die away. The next high tide, twelve hours after this one, was the one they had to be afraid of. The vigil in the longhouses was going to last for a day, and perhaps for part of the next night at least.

He took her to the biggest house, whose womenfolk she knew well. On the landward side, they had opened a shutter a little and she could see inside. It was packed with women, young and old, and with children. She could see Erlend, looking angry. She said, 'Have you enough men?'

He stopped, his back to the wind. 'My lady,' said Bishop Jon. 'We have enough men for what is needed down there, but not enough to stand guard over the longhouses; not until after the tide. All of the houses are in good shape, and there should be no trouble. But if trouble comes, it's able-bodied people with a head on their shoulders like yourself and your friends that will be needed.'

At the door, she stopped for the last time. 'It's a south-east wind, isn't it? What about Deerness and Copinsay and Sandwick? What about Sanday and Stronsay? And the Pentland Firth? Thurso?'

'Do you think,' said Bishop Jon, 'that your husband and his forefathers have never seen storms before and don't know what standing orders to give? He's just taking precautions. Arnór will make a verse about it tomorrow.'

Someone had made a pronouncement on it already. *The Gods are never so dangerous as when they wake from sleep.* She opened her mouth and then closed it again, because, whatever she said, he would have a patient answer. St Columba, too, had been nice to his importunate gardener. *'Ah, beloved! 'Tis thou should be lord of this monastery!'*

'Leave it to me,' said Groa. 'We'll be all right. Go and do what you can. And be careful.'

Then as he turned away, she went to the door already opening for her.

'I don't see,' said Paul, 'why Erlend had to go to the houses. He's strong. And he's sensible.'

It was the first time he had spoken to his father since the crisis began, although he had never lost him to sight, not for a moment. It was the first time that he had seen his father do anything but ride about and talk to people and sail boats and race and jump and swim and lay wagers at horse-fights on feast days and drink. He was good at sports, and he could handle a boat better than any of the other men's fathers. But he never seemed to go to war, as other men's fathers did. He never even settled a quarrel by fighting. He seemed to like the easy life down there in Alba, or feasting with Popes and with Emperors further south.

People spoke of the great times when he fought sea-battles all over the Sudreyar and further south, in England and Ireland and Wales, but he, Paul, had not been there and didn't remember them. He didn't remember much of the fighting in Orkney, even, when the man they called Rognvald, who must have been his cousin, was killed.

Men spoke of that as if it was a heroic thing, but it was Thorkel Fóstri, he found, who had done the actual killing, and his father wouldn't speak about it at all.

He was proud of his father, who was an earl and a king, but he wished his father stayed in Orkney all summer, as Otkel did, who had taken his son fighting once, when pirates tried to take over Foula. Because Earl Thorfinn wasn't there to give permission, Otkel had not taken Paul with him, although Paul had begged. He had been fourteen years old. His father had been given *Grágás* at fourteen, and had gone with Thorkel Fóstri raiding the tribute-lands.

Since then, his father had told both Thorkel and Otkel to take his son Paul with them whenever there was prospect of fighting, but there had never been anything worth speaking of, except an Icelandic trader who hadn't paid his toll and had to be stopped in the Firth, or, once, a small flotilla of ships from Ireland that had fled when they saw them. He was well trained. He had had mock fights enough, and some of them pretty dirty. But he had not been able to show anyone, yet, that he was anything but what his father now was: a rich man who did what he liked because he was King and everyone was polite to him.

It surprised him, therefore, that his father should be here, in the thick of the night and the storm, helping with the heavy, difficult work as well as directing it.

With his height and arm-span, of course, his father had an advantage. When the horses, being bridled to lead them to safety, panicked and lashed out in the dark, threatening to do worse harm to the buildings than the wind would, it was his father who forced his way between them and dragged out the pair who were causing most trouble. When the roof of the cooking-stores threatened to blow off, it was his father who held a mat over it, wooden shingles spurting and whirling about him, until the thing could be bound down and weighted.

They lost the spices. 'Innocent of pepper as Paulinus's cook,' said his father cheerfully. 'Most of it up my nose. Erlend? He's too light on his feet. The wind would bowl him over. He'll be a good man to help the women.'

Which was satisfactory. Erlend, six years younger, needed someone to speak up for him, sometimes.

His father's face was bleeding a little, and there was more roofing coming down somewhere. A spray of trotter-bone pegs hit the ground and bounced into the darkness, followed by the crack and snap of thin flags flipping and breaking. A handful of what he thought was heather thatch caught him in the face, but it wasn't: a corn-stack had been pushed over and some of the netting had burst. He ran to help and found that, instead of repairing it, men were thrusting what they could into carts, still under its netting.

The carts rocked as they worked. As soon as they were taken from shelter, they began to slide on locked wheels over the yard, and then to tilt. The door came off a shed full of tools, and spades, even, were turning over and over; while a flock of rods kept for wattling thrust through the air, cruel as arrows.

One of them put a man's eye out. It was the first of the really bad injuries, and Paul saw it. He was looking at the man, screaming without being heard, blood coming from between his fingers, when Paul himself was attacked by something thin and cold and slippery that whipped round his neck and stayed there, tugging, as if it wanted to pull his head off.

He put up his hands and found it was a long strand of seaweed. Lokki-lines, they called them, the older people. Seaweed torn from the beach, all that distance away. There had been shore-foam on the beach yesterday. The old people had a name for that as well. The Draug's vomit, they called it. They said it meant death.

'Got a new collar?' his father yelled. 'Look. There are some sacks over there that wouldn't go into the barn. They're well pinned down, but it would be a pity to lose them. Can you get some of them into the hall? And the stuff from that shed. The torf-skeri and shovels.'

He disappeared and Paul, leaning on the wind, began work on the bags. They were full of wool. It was hard to hold them and pull the hall-door open, and every time he did it, the row of shields on the wall clapped about, booming like gongs, and the wind-path swept through the rushes grew broader. They had the malt-sacks in there already, he saw, and heaps of oars, nearly as high as the tapestry. The fire had roared itself out and the ash in the centre flushed up grey with each entry and lay over everything.

Each time he went out, there was more seaweed flying about, and great handfuls of sand, slapping into your face or your clothes. One of the sacks was ripped from his arms as he struggled yet again with the hall-door, and the soft tufts of plucked wool, black and brown and light brown and milky, flowered into the air like a dandelion clock and were blown away just as quickly.

His father's voice roared, 'Leave that! It's time to go.'

Paul looked round. There were still a lot of men about, and a few lanterns, so that you could see dimly. A knot of men came from the shore at a staggering run, carrying another who was crying. He could see men coming away now, too, from where the ships had been put: the first job, and the heaviest he had shared with his father. The noise from the shore was much greater: a familiar hiss and booming he had heard often before with a big tide on the make, but muffled now because of the deafening sound of the wind. He shouted, 'When are *you* going?'

'When the yard is clear,' his father yelled back. 'See you up on the hillside.'

'I'll wait,' shouted Paul.

He saw his father's palm come up in acceptance, and then his father disappeared again, blundering forcefully into the wind, checking the groups of men coming inwards towards him. Paul could hear, intermittently, the resonance of his voice through the noise in the throat of the wind, and the roar from the shore that was becoming louder and louder.

How close was the sea? As a good leader should, his father was making sure that no one was left in its path; that no man, taking a last wistful thought to a neglected fishing-boat or a skiff or a hoard of nets he had forgotten, should dash back and drown for his folly.

But a tide could come quickly, and no one was there now on the rocks to watch it advancing.

It came to Paul that he could watch it advancing from the roof of the hall. He knew the footholds. He had often helped with the thatching.

He hurtled round the end of the building, into the cross-draughts and eddies of its sheltered side, and started to climb.

He thought he knew the force of the wind. He had not observed that, from the gale it had been, it had risen through level after level of violence to a power that no man living on Orkney had ever experienced or was to experience again.

He reached the top of the wall and, lying flat on the thatch, pulled himself quickly upwards until his body lay slanting just under the spine and, by raising himself a fraction, he could look over the roof-tree and down to where the beach lay.

The gale, pouring over the roof, caught him before he had even started to make his next movement. It lifted him for a moment before it threw him down, so that for a second he saw what he wanted: that the sea had already overrun the beach and the rocks and the shingle and was advancing like a black wall rimmed with white over the slipways and grasslands of Orphir. He saw men scurrying over the yard, their faces white in the lantern-light, leaning back into the wind with their knees and legs taking the strain as the storm behind tried to bowl them over.

None of them saw him. The wind grabbed him under the arms and flipped him outwards and back as it had the torn raven banner already. It was the folds of the banner, lying thick and cold in the shelter below, that saved his life, but not his skull from the blow that deprived him of consciousness.

Paul Thorfinnsson woke to find himself lying, his hair whipping his face, in the arms of someone who was running. For seventeen, he was big and heavily built, but the man who carried him was so tall and held his weight so easily that there was no doubt who he was. Only for a moment did he pause and face the buffeting wind with an effort, and Paul recognised in that moment his own struggle with bales of wool before the same door. Then the door of the Earl's hall slowly yielded, and his father carried him in and laid him on the same bales.

He moved as he was placed there. His father's voice said sharply, 'You're awake? Where are you hurt?'

He did not know himself. He moved and felt dizzy. 'My arm. My shoulder. I could walk.'

'It's too late.'

It was. There was a rapping noise at the shutters, as if someone had thrown a handful of pebbles against them. He said, 'The others?'

'Up the hill. I told them not to wait. Or to come back.'

'They will,' said Paul. They loved his father. He knew that now, and was proud of it.

'I told them I'd be safe in the hall. Whether I found you or not. Paul.'

'Yes?' he said. The wool was soft under his shoulder. Out of all Europe, out of the whole kingdom of Alba and Cumbria, out of all Moray and Caithness and the myriad islands of Orkney, his father was here, only here, and alone with himself.

'Don't worry,' said Thorfinn. 'At least, listen. If the shutters burst, the bales will float for a while, and there will be oars and benches moving about to take hold of. Do you hear me?'

It hurt to fill his lungs, but he said loudly, 'Yes!' The shutters rattled and clattered under another onslaught of stones, and yet another. The yard must be full of water, the first probing lines running ahead of the oncoming battalions and bringing their debris. First pebbles, then big, rounded stones from the storm-beach, bounding and pounding against the timber walls and the planks of the shutters.

He sensed that his father had moved away and guessed what he must be doing: fortifying the boards with the heaviest things he could drag: the sack of provisions, the bench-boards, the high chair itself.

The hall became a sounding-board. Within its shaking beams, there was nothing to be heard and nothing to be felt but the scream and roar of the wind, and the clattering percussion of objects striking the walls and the shutters, and the thunder of water outside, becoming louder and louder under a chattering ground-base of discarded boulders.

Then the main wall of water struck the building, and the shutters burst inwards like reeds, and the salt water rushed white and green into the hall at Orphir, thrusting obstructions aside, while a slap of water, heavy as lead, fell on the thatch and through it, to pour foaming down on the deepening sea on the hall-floor.

The bales under Paul moved, but he was kept from slipping by his father's hand, firm on his good arm. Behind the King's back he could see the white-flecked water still flooding in; then it dwindled. He wondered what would have happened if the thatch had opened over their heads. His father said, 'All right. Pressure inside and out. The walls will stand.'

He could hear him better because the noise was less between waves. His father made no attempt to mend the wrecked shutters. His father had been shielding him from the stones coming through. The bales knocked together again, but the fall from the roof-breach had dwindled, and so had the rush from the windows. The wind, seizing on the hole in the roof, tugged and groaned, and spewed wet straw down over his hair and into the water. His father said, 'Now, that is a problem. Or we'll have the roof off.'

He spoke as if playing a board-game. Paul said, 'The sea? My lord?'

His father adjusted the bales, splashing about, and took a grip of his arm again. A faint radiance, investing what remained of the roof, indicated that, whatever happened, dawn still intended to come. His father said, 'Either the sea comes to stay, or it attacks and runs off. We seem to have been at the end of its reach on this occasion. I think we'll find that it is drawing back.'

Now, for the first time, he felt the real fiery ache of his arm and his shoulder;

but he would not be less nonchalant than his father. 'There's another high tide this evening,' he said.

'Indeed there is,' Thorfinn said. 'Well, you can stay for that one if you like. I'm going to be busy.'

In the cold dawn, with the wind pushing them so that they could hardly face each other, the King and his wife met on the slope above the battered hall.

The sea had receded, and the yard and the grasslands were a wilderness of sand and mud and wriggling fish, of stones and pebbles and seaweed, of driftwood and shellfish. Half the buildings between the hall and the shore had disappeared.

Thorfinn's face was hollow, as hers was. Only Erlend, drunk on the night and the excitement, jumped up and down, swinging on his mother's arm.

Thorfinn said, 'Paul's arm is broken, but he is all right. They've taken him off to a dry house. How did you manage?'

'The roof came off!' Erlend said. 'The roof came off a woman's house, and we all helped to save what we could. The milk-vat ran away. And I saw a hen get killed. It got blown against a thatch-stone and got killed. And her loom fell about and got broken.'

'They said you were in there with Paul,' Groa said.

'He looked after me very well,' Thorfinn said. 'But we can't really invite anyone there until we've lifted the codfish out of the tapestries.'

'How much longer?' said Groa.

He turned and faced into the wind.

Above, the sun shone: a disc of pale, hazy yellow in a milky grey sky, below which unrolled a waste of glittering white.

Like melting ice, it dazzled the eye. The sparkle of spray, the glassy mist hanging over the water were pretty enough to taste on the tongue. Now and then, as they rolled, you could see the flanks of the waves, swollen fawn with sand and with mud, or pale green gorged with half-consumed white.

She said, 'They say a south-easterly can last for a week.'

'Taliesin had a riddle,' he said. '*Figure who it is, created before the Flood, a mighty creature without flesh, without bone, without veins, without blood, without hands, and without feet. . . .* It will last no longer than you can bear. That I promise you.'

No one who really knew him would ever let him down, she thought. But sometimes a man's best would not be quite enough. She said, 'Thorfinn. Where are the rest of the ships?'

And knew, by the fact that he did not turn, that she had guessed right.

'When I know myself,' he said, 'I shall tell you.'

The storm lasted five days, and to ride over Orkney after that was like riding through a great field the day after beggars had left it.

There were no trees to overturn, as happened in Ireland or Moray. But seaweed and stones lodged in the uprooted bushes that littered the low hills and meadows; beehives were found where they rolled in the bed of a stream;

fish lay silver in farmyards, and drowned sheep on the shore. Dead birds were to be seen everywhere, and live ones, in quarrelling flocks, feeding on the burst stacks and blown seed-corn; stabbing the cheeses that shone in the short winter grass; pecking at the dried skeins of fish; fluttering trapped beneath torn scraps of net.

Three farmsteads were nothing but black, glittering wood and a column of smoke where a vat of fish-oil had overturned into a brazier, or a roasting-fire got out of hand, or a guttering candle caught hangings.

On the west, they said, the waves had ranged a hundred feet high up the cliffs, scouring the bird-ledges clean and breaking through bridges and tunnels of rock where no gap had existed before. The ships at Sandwick had been lost, *Grágás* with them.

In the Pentland Firth, they said, the waves had overrun the island of Stroma from end to end, piling fish and wreckage on the top, and destroying the steading and boats of Thorfinn's steward. At Thurso, the long beach had disappeared into the sea, and the tide had swept over the grassland behind it, taking twenty drekar and pinnaces with it.

At Birsay, no boat left in the nousts had survived. The big ships, those drawn up far on the shore, had tumbled together, smashing one another to powder. The new slipway to the island was broken with rocks, and the tower of its new church, its mortar still wet, had staggered and fallen.

The rest of the fleet was in the Sudreyar, wintering ready for defence or for trade in the spring-time. For two weeks, while he worked with his people to patch up his earldom, Thorfinn heard no news he could trust. Then the seas settled a little, and a boat came, carrying a crew he recognised and a Skyeman he knew well, but who would not meet his eye.

Which was how Thorfinn of Orkney and Scotia learned that the wind had achieved what neither Rognvald nor Norway had managed to do.

Two-thirds of his fleet was wrecked or missing.

And until he could replace them, he was crippled.

THREE

T MIGHT BE supposed that the loss of his ships, with *Grágás* his flagship among them, was the greatest single blow that a sea-lord such as Thorfinn might receive.

That he appeared to treat it philosophically, as he had accepted and dealt with the reversal in Ireland, the death of the Lady Emma, the restlessness on his southern borders, was therefore partly a matter of pride, but also the mark of what had become his nature.

His Norman guests, from whom he made no effort to conceal what had happened, were inclined, on his return, to admire him for it.

Being Normans, they had spent the winter in relative cheerfulness, bedding women, hunting, and exploring those parts of the country unknown to them, in the absence of the winter wars they were accustomed to. Against the advice of their hosts, they ventured into regions of mountain and marsh that occasioned difficulties never encountered in the well-drained chalklands of the Pays de Caux, and returned with an altered view of the country in whose service they had placed themselves.

Whereas in Normandy the boundaries between region and region were artificial, imposed by conquest and maintained by fortifications, here they were geographical. Some areas here were almost empty: settled only by herdsmen and fishermen, and hardly feeding themselves, never mind raising corn to feed others, or a surplus of men to defend themselves.

Other regions were much richer in cropland and pasture, with good timber and fisheries, and there people prospered and multiplied, or had been doing, it was clear, under this King's guidance. But for the whole country to flourish, the richer regions must yield all they could spare to help feed and develop the poorer; and the manpower, too, must be deployed where it was needed to defend the vulnerable harbours and pirate bases of the north and the west, with all the consequent problems of travel in that wild land of mountain and river.

Hugh de Riveire, a man as able as his older cousin Osbern of Eu, considered the changed circumstances over the fire in the privacy of their quarters at Scone, and reached a conclusion.

'We know the country as a whole can't be wealthy. Therefore, most of the King's resources must have been bound up in those ships and the various uses he could make of them. So what now?'

Baldric, well informed through long dealings in Flanders, said drily, 'You would be surprised what he could do with those ships. But he still has some left. And they are expert builders.'

Osbern of Ewias grunted. 'You've seen what the gales did. In Orkney, they take extraordinary precautions, and yet look what happened. Here, everyone was ready for the winter storms, but not for what they got. It'll be a long, long time before anyone in Orkney or Scotia has the time or the heart for shipbuilding, and if the King's stupid enough to force it on them, they'll defy him, or starve. On the other hand, he's got money.'

'That's true,' said his cousin. 'He could commission ships: Svein of Denmark has built for him before. And buy in food, if he has to, and if anyone has a surplus to sell and wants to sell it to him. But money won't last for ever, and in the meantime, people may have taken their business elsewhere.'

'So long as he still has silver to pay us with,' Flodwig said.

'That he'll find,' said Osbern of Eu. 'Until he gets the kingdom on its feet, he's going to need all the allies he can get.'

It was to be a spring, it seemed, of repairs.

In Scotia and in Orkney, the work went on as fast as resources would allow, and more speedily than it might once have done because of the cleared roads and the stations of help that now existed through the newborn network of local churches and local leadership.

In England, the rents torn in the fabric by the departure of the Normans and the return of the Godwin family were being mended also, without overmuch trouble. Ulf, the bishop whose capabilities had so little impressed Bishop Ealdred, had disappeared from view and been replaced at Dorchester by a Saxon, Wulfwig, who was known to be on good terms with Leofric of Mercia.

The Bishop of London stayed abroad for a while, and then discreetly returned and was found to be in office again, and so effectively that no one troubled to make an issue of it.

The outlawed Archbishop of Canterbury made a successful appeal to the Pope, who at once denounced all those who had taken it upon themselves, without papal advice or authority, to outlaw an archbishop. He dispatched a legate to Winchester conveying his reproaches and anger, and excommunicated Stigand, the Bishop of Winchester, whom the King and Earl Godwin had appointed Archbishop of Canterbury in Robert's place.

The appeased Archbishop of Canterbury left the Pope's side and returned to await events in his former abbey of Jumièges, where, unhappily, he was taken ill and subsequently died. His land in England, together with that of Bishop Ulf's, was divided between Harold, the eldest son of Earl Godwin, and his sister the Queen, who had been retrieved from her convent. Tostig, the brother of Harold and Edith, was not a beneficiary.

In the absence of any Archbishop of Canterbury other than the excommunicant Stigand, a stream of newly promoted churchmen, including Archbishop Cynsige of York, took themselves to the Continent to be consecrated. They were lucky if they caught the Pontiff. After a busy Christmas of bargaining, the Pope had finally traded the temporal claims of Bamberg and Fulda for the town of Benevento among other possessions of the Empire in Italy. More importantly, Emperor Henry had also agreed to send an army to help throw the Normans, once and for all, out of Apulia.

When the Emperor changed his mind and recalled his forces, the Pope determined to march south without them. Seven hundred Swabian infantry joined him, raised by Frederic of Lorraine, the Pope's chief lieutenant. As soon as he began to march south, German mercenaries and then men from the non-Norman states came to offer their services. Not everyone was a friend of the de Hautevilles. So mighty was God, there was even a promise of help from the Greeks.

Trailed under the four-pointed flags by anxious English abbots, Pope Leo took time to ratify a bull defining the privileges of the great metropolitan church of Hamburg and Bremen over the Swedes, the Danes, the Finns, the Norwegians, and the Baltic Slavs, and over Orkney, Iceland, and Greenland, *to take the place of the Pope in these regions, and to ordain bishops for them, as brought into the fold of Christ.*

To Archbishop Adalbert himself, Leo confirmed the honours of the pallium, the use of the Roman mitre, and the privilege of a white horse-cloth and pearl caparisons, as the Pope himself used. Then he replaced his white-and-gold helmet, caused the horns to be blown, and proceeded south once again with his army.

In Scotia, which had not been mentioned as part of the Archbishop Adalbert's spiritual kingdom, a few members of the Norman party left at short notice, to be more than replaced in the next week or two by friends and kinsmen who wanted their posts. Viscount Nigel-Constantine and the elderly Bishop Hugh of Lisieux waited until the agreed time and took ship, with decorum and in an atmosphere of surprising goodwill. Carl Thorbrandsson went south with the Abbot of Mont St Michel, the late Emma's cousin, who had business to transact in Cornwall. Both the agreements and the plans drawn up between the King of Scotia and the Normans at the start of the winter began to be implemented, and the camp at Scone became empty.

In the spring, the news arrived that Swegen, the eldest of Earl Godwin's family of seven sons and four daughters, had died on pilgrimage. In a swift readjustment of his property, Somerset and Berkshire were reunited with the earldom of Wessex, and Oxfordshire and Hereford went to Earl Ralph the King's confused nephew. Tostig, Earl Godwin's third son, received nothing extra.

In April, Earl Godwin died of a stroke, and his eldest son Harold became Earl of Wessex while Alfgar, son of the Earl of Mercia, was restored to his still-warm earldom of East Anglia. Tostig, Earl Harold's second brother, was not made noticeably better off; but he did, of course, possess certain lands and was married to Judith of Flanders.

In Ireland, Diarmaid, King of Dublin, made two attacks on Meath along with the King of Ossory, and, noticing that there were few Orkney ships these days in the water and no Orkney attempts at interference, decided it was time to look for some easy weapons and cattle and money, and maybe even a harbour or two.

It was more of a wish than a plan, so that when he observed that all the best places for landing were growing spears instead of whinbushes these days, with Norman helmets, would you believe it, on some of the hillsides, he made a smooth withdrawal without ever getting the axes out. The levies cheered, and the Normans returned to watching the Irish Sea with one eye and the goings-on in England with the other.

In June, the vast papal army in Italy came into contact with the smaller Norman army, led by the Hauteville half-brothers and their kinsman the Count of Aversa. The papal army was beaten, and the Pope extracted from the town of Civitate, from which he had witnessed the battle. The Normans escorted the Pope and his retinue, with care, back to Benevento and detained him there, with care, as their prisoner.

In July, Siward, Earl of Northumbria, sent a small embassy north to his kinswoman's husband Macbeth of Alba, requesting the courtesy of a meeting to discuss matters of moment between them. He suggested an open-air site on the boundary-lands, with no more than twelve unarmed men on each side. Unarmed, to avoid misunderstandings. Where he thought the boundary-lands might be, he did not indicate.

The time for repairs, it would seem, was about to give way to the time for offence, if not injury.

In the end, they met among the monastery buildings at Melrose, on its river-girt promontory thirty miles inland from Berwick.

The third Abbot of Melrose, founded from Lindisfarne and Iona four hundred years previously, had been St Cuthbert. Resident in that fact was a potential profit; but it would, clearly, have to be worked for. The palisaded earthwork that once lay across the neck of the promontory, beside which they foregathered, was beaten half flat; and the huts, once the two parties of principals had made their way inside, were mostly empty and ruinous.

The largest intact building, erected beside the small church, was occupied by three resident monks, a lay servant, and a group of men from Berwick, who, under the supervision of a black-robed clerk, were carrying out and setting up before the building a trestle table with a stool for each end, and a couple of benches. The table was remarkably clean and had a patina that suggested an acquaintance with money rather than supper-plates.

The sightseers on the banks of the river, who, sensing something afoot, had been gathering for a few hours, dodged about, seeking a view between bushes. They had already witnessed a spectacle: the sight of the two cousins (Norwegian, surely? You never saw a black Irishman that height), tall as two abbeys, arriving in cavalcade, one from the north and one on the Roman road from the south, and dismounting and greeting one another.

Then the men-at-arms under the two banners, the King's and the Earl's, had waited outside, and the rest had got round the gate and walked talking inside: the King Macbeth with less meat on him, like a man who fed at sea, and Siward of Northumbria the way he always was, with his chest round as a shield under his tunic, and only his hair and beard greyer than you would think for a man not much past fifty.

Living where they did, everyone could identify Earl Siward's party. It was more a family, really, than a deputation, excluding the Bishop, of course: Aethelric of Durham, whom the monks had wanted to disown after that business eight years ago, until he had had to go to Siward and slip him a bit of St Cuthbert's best to get him reinstated.

Aside from the Bishop, it was what you would expect. Osbern, the oldest son and the hope of the family, if a bit wild as yet. Siward of Warwickshire his cousin, who was younger and worse, except in front of the old man. Ligulf of Bamburgh, the Earl's brother-in-law, whom no one crossed at all and even the Earl didn't swear at. And Forne, merchant of York, who had been a master coiner at Nottingham now for years, and had thought his fortune made, no doubt, when he married the sister of Duncan—King Duncan, the last one to rule Alba and Cumbria. There was a young boy with him, who would be one of the sons.

The native denizens of the no-man's-land they called Lothian, between the Firth of Forth and Northumberland, then turned their attention to the six figures walking behind Macbeth of Alba, but, except for Bishop Malduin, who was easy to recognise because of his embroidered robes and his doubtful expression, the three middle-aged men and the two young ones were unfamiliar.

The local overlords, the magnates of the neighbourhood, who had spent a frenzied few weeks petitioning and being petitioned by their would-be superiors, had not been invited and therefore sat at home, drinking behind closed doors and not available to enlighten their countrymen.

Thorfinn said, 'Now that we all know one another, perhaps we should sit down?' and pulled out a stool at one end of the table for Earl Siward, as a host might, before taking the other end himself.

Tuathal of St Serf's, sitting down on one side with Cormac and Eochaid, saw Lulach smile and shot a brief glance to warn him. Thorfinn would have his reasons for whatever he did. But they needn't be underlined.

Already, he thought, Siward had suffered a little in the opening moves. He had brought with him the Bishop of Durham, which was mandatory, and which of course Thorfinn had matched by bringing Malduin, flashing an expensive ring of unknown provenance.

But of Siward's remaining small group, three were youths, and one of them, Crinan the son of Forne, not only took his name from his grandfather but looked, with his soft brown hair and tranquil gaze, remarkably like Thorfinn's stepfather.

The message was plain. *This is the new generation, who will run Lothian and maybe all Scotia when Macbeth is dead.*

If he understood it, Thorfinn gave no sign, greeting Crinan. On the other hand, Siward could not quite conceal his moment of stillness when Cormac of Dunkeld, bustling up, had drawn forward the boy standing beside him and said, 'And now, my lord Siward, may I have the pleasure of introducing you again to your nephew. Maelmuire. Maelmuire, of course, of Atholl, Duncan's son. You met him . . . Well, after a fashion, you met him ten years ago or so. He was eight. If you remember? I'm sure you wouldn't have known him. Maelmuire, your uncle.'

Maelmuire, Duncan's youngest son and the only one still in Thorfinn's keeping, whom Siward had already tried to capture once. And whom, casually, Thorfinn had now brought south from his fastness to greet his uncle.

Maelmuire has nothing to fear from you now, nor have I. What was that you were saying about the next generation and where and what they would rule?

Oh, yes, one might smile inwardly. But not openly, yet.

It had been a hot summer, and dust rose from the rough flags as they settled. Thorfinn, looking down the short length of the table to his wife's cousin opposite, said, 'I heard about your wife. I'm sorry.'

He did not specify whether it was the mother of Osbern or the mother of the baby Waltheof who had died. The omission meant, Tuathal knew, that he had not yet found out. Like most people of Scandinavian blood, Siward sometimes troubled with gospel-marriages and sometimes didn't. The property-deals were always carefully documented.

Earl Siward said, 'I thank you. I have heard about your ships. I am sorry. They are not so simple to replace, are they? And the work of reproduction less enjoyable.'

'I can't say,' said Thorfinn, 'that I've ever bedded a ship, but I'll take your word for it. We still seem to have some left. You wanted to talk about Lothian?'

It was hot. The sun shone equally on them both: their shadows, enormous and jagged, covered the ground between the table and the eating-house, and waves of heat beat on the tonsures of the Alban priests.

Tuathal, who knew that thoroughness was the secret of success, had long since extracted from Thorkel Fóstri all that he could tell about Earl Siward of Northumbria, and had deduced a good deal more. The hulking nephew of Kalv Arnason had been only a youth when King Olaf had killed his uncle Ølve at the spring feast at Sparbu and had given to Kalv his uncle's rich widow in gratitude.

Then, Siward's father had submitted to Olaf, but before ten years had gone by, his father had finished his dialogue with Olaf's enemy Canute, tucked the Lapp fur-monopoly under his belt, and shared with Kalv the blows that killed King Olaf at Stiklestad.

The son's reward had been a comfortable living in England, both before and after his father's death. Siward was probably already one of the richest men in Scandinavian York, as well as a useful war-leader and a forthright advisor to Canute and his heirs by the time it occurred to the Lady Emma that she might do worse than encourage him to take over Northumbria.

There had been no difficulty about that. Siward had merely killed his wife's uncle, as Carl Thorbrandsson had already killed his wife's father, and had joined thereby the bloody brethren of kinsmen whose lethal manoeuvrings had kept him busy for the twelve years he had now held the earldom.

Did he regret his exile? Had he envied Kalv, turning his coat so adroitly over and over, and at least buying back some years at Egge?

'Envy? He despised Kalv. Kalv was a fool,' Thorkel had said. 'There was only one man he envied.'

'He hated Thorfinn? Always? I suppose he must have done,' Tuathal had said, thinking aloud. 'Or the Lady Emma would never have risked making Siward her buffer between the rest of England and Scotia. But then, what if Siward had tried to take over Scotia?'

'Twelve years ago? Against Thorfinn's manpower, and his money, and his fleet? Even with England and Denmark behind him,' had said Thorkel Fóstri with scorn, 'I doubt if he would have got a levy over the Forth. And England wouldn't have backed him. Magnús had Norway then, remember, and half a foot in Orkney already through Thorfinn's nephew Rognvald. England would rather have had Thorfinn in Scotia, I can tell you, than Siward or Norway.'

And that, thought Tuathal, was still true. Despite Thorfinn's present weakness, it was still, thank God, true. He had said, 'And Thorfinn? He's used to dealing with princes these days. Does he resent being forced to barter with someone . . .'

He had paused, having caught Eochaid's eye, to rephrase the question, but Thorkel Fóstri's voice, at its most sardonic, had taken him up. 'Someone like me, from the barbarous north? Haven't you noticed yet that Thorfinn is prouder of being Earl of Orkney than he is of ruling Scotia? He fought for Orkney and won it, against men just like Siward. His own kind. He knows them too well to despise them.'

His own kind? Thorfinn was three-quarters Celt. They were not his own kind. Tuathal had said, 'So it's just another negotiation? Thorfinn neither likes nor dislikes Kalv's nephew? I find it hard to believe.'

To which Thorkel Fóstri had answered in a way he had not expected. 'When did you ever know whether Thorfinn likes or dislikes a man? He takes them for what they are, and deals with them accordingly. It's the secret of his success. You don't fight the sea by getting angry with it, or persuade it to be kinder by loving it.'

The bitterness was plain for all to hear. Eochaid had got up and left, and he, Tuathal, had asked only one or two questions more.

He was not embarrassed. It merely appeared to him a paradox worth someone's attention: how a man such as Thorkel described could inspire what Thorkel undoubtedly felt for him.

Prior Tuathal pulled his hood absently over his reddening crown and sat, his chin in the sun, bending his sharp intelligence to the exchange between the Earl and the King by which all his theories were about to be tested.

Siward's shoulders were massive, and his beard sat like a cushion between them. The hair on his face was untrimmed, and his nose had spread with drinking, but the weather-hard skin was not the skin of a drunkard, and if the hair on his temples was thinning, you could not see it for the leather fillet he wore. His eyes were bright blue. He made Thorfinn look like an Arab.

Earl Siward said, 'You can't blame churchmen for getting it wrong. We can settle this face to face. I know your position, and you know mine. Earl Godwin died, and now young Harold of Wessex sees Welsh and Irish and Norsemen behind every curtain and is looking to Mercia to protect him. Leofwine's been made Bishop of Lichfield. Alfgar's cousin Leofric's been given Coventry now as well as Peterborough. And Alfgar himself, of course, has got East Anglia again, so Mercia stretches from sea to sea south of us both, and cutting us both off from Wessex.'

'I had noticed as much,' said Thorfinn. 'So an alliance against Mercia is what you are proposing?'

Siward said, 'I'd be a fool if I did, seeing that you and Alfgar have been cultivating each other for thirty years. You're better off than I am. You've lost your ships, you've lost your friends in Ireland, you've lost the Lady Emma and the active support of the Pope, but you're still strong enough to stop Harald of Norway from using you as a base, and you're no threat to Wessex so long as you get rid of those Normans.'

'Ah,' said Thorfinn. 'You're proposing that you and Mercia and the Normans and I invade Wessex and drive out the Godwinssons again? Mercia wouldn't agree to it. And Duke William, they tell me, is being kept too busy hanging on to his dukedom to worry about the crown he's been promised.'

The Earl dragged his fists back from the table and, opening his shoulders and mouth, stretched his sinews, as if parting Philistine pillars. Then he exhaled through his nose and laid his fists, with care, back on the table. 'You feel no call,' he said, 'to treat these things seriously?'

'Not if getting rid of Osbern of Eu is going to be the point at issue,' Thorfinn said.

'He's a cousin of William of Normandy,' said Earl Siward. His nose had begun to shine in the heat, but his eyes were wide open and calculating.

'So am I. So are you, probably, in the widest sense. I could throw them out and replace them with Bretons,' said Thorfinn. 'But *they* are all cousins of Duke William as well. And would also require land in the Lothians.' His skin, polished brown below the thin, short-sleeved tunic, showed no change with the heat. Above one elbow he wore a thick gold band of Norse design that Tuathal had never seen before.

Of his own kind. A man not incapable of irony, Thorkel Fóstri, it seemed, could not necessarily detect it in somebody else.

Earl Siward drew breath. Thorfinn forestalled him. 'I thought—am I wrong?—that you were one of those who voted for Duke William as heir. In which case you are right: you are worse off than I am. For whereas my wife's family is discredited, you have just married a daughter into Norway. Wessex may not trust you or even want you. What if Mercia and I were to take over Northumbria?'

One of the young men, the son Osbern, glared and turned to his father.

They all had to learn. Siward's beard relaxed. He said, 'I wish you meant it.'

'It was an interesting thought,' Thorfinn said. 'I'll give you another. I want the land west of Wedale and the south bank of the river Forth to do with as I please. I also want the rights to all other churches in the Lothians, now existing and to be established, which are not and have never been in the past dedicated to the shrine of St Cuthbert. The remaining Lothian lands and the remaining churches you may retain.'

Silence fell. Even after Tuathal started to breathe, Earl Siward still remained motionless. Then Siward said, 'And the Normans?'

Thorfinn said, 'The land I have described is my land, and I shall place on it whom I please.'

'Your land?' said Siward. 'Your grandfather had Danes and Norwegians attacking both coasts and a Scandinavian earldom threatening to move up from Northumbria. Your father was dead. Your grandfather had lost the support of the Orkney fleet. He had to fight for Lothian. But after that, there was old age and an incompetent grandson and vassaldom under Canute and then a King of Alba who did half his ruling from Orkney. What makes it your land?'

'Take it from me,' said Thorfinn.

Silence fell, briefly, again. To look at the six faces opposite was difficult. One looked from side to side, at the two speakers, or else down at the table or, fleetingly, at one's own side. The boy Maelmuire, who had started with a high colour like his father Duncan's, had gone very pale. His first experience of the conflict between two powerful men, tossing between them the idea of war. Two men who were his own uncles.

Cormac beside him was nervous, Tuathal thought, for the boy's sake. Eochaid was watching Thorfinn, as if hardly noting what was being said. And Lulach and Bishop Malduin, sitting side by side, might have belonged to different worlds: the Bishop grave and faintly uneasy, his eyes flickering across the table to the men of York and Durham and Bamburgh whom he must know so well. And Lulach, his face clear-textured and open, reflecting the sky and the sunlight and an untouched innocence: the innocence, Tuathal had long ago decided, that does not know what responsibility means.

Then a new voice spoke up. Bishop Aethelric of Durham, in the harsh Saxon they were all using, said, 'Will my lord King allow me to speak? You make no claim on the churches of St Cuthbert?'

Thorfinn turned and looked at him. 'On those east of Wedale and south of the Forth estuary? No,' he said. 'I offer these with their privileges freely to the diocese of Durham. The remaining churches would be Bishop Malduin's concern.'

'From Kinrimund?' said Bishop Aethelric.

'From whatever part of Alba he wishes to take as his lodging,' Thorfinn said.

'I have no quarrel with that,' said Bishop Aethelric; and glanced at his Earl quickly, and sat back on his bench.

'And Bishop Malduin?' said Earl Siward thoughtfully.

Probably because of the heat, Bishop Malduin's face had assumed a motley of different colours, like a majuscule in a saint's gospel-book: blue and pink and yellow and red and a little white, here and there. He opened his mouth and then said, 'It seems to me, my lord Earl, my lord King, that the churches of St Cuthbert should be indivisible. It seems to me an insult to the saint to divide them.'

'Oh,' said Thorfinn. 'You mean I should have offered Dunedin also to Earl Siward? And the rest of the churches to the north?'

'No!' said Bishop Malduin. 'That is not at all what—'

'But why not?' said Ligulf of Bamburgh. 'The land and the churches both belong to Bernicia. And how can the rights of churches be divorced from those of the lands they occupy? How can a farmer in the south of Lothian pay his land-dues to one overlord and his church-dues to another? The wealthy will train priests of their own, as they do now, and your churches will be empty and useless. I say the churches belong with the land, and all should be under Durham and York.'

'Poor Bishop Malduin,' said Thorfinn gently.

'Who consecrated Bishop Malduin?' said Ligulf. 'When he dies, where will you get your next bishop? The Pope is a prisoner. Adalbert of Bremen claims to be spiritual overlord of the Orkneys and Norway: do you want to set a precedent there?'

'It is a difficulty,' Thorfinn said. 'You must feel it yourselves, with one of your archbishops excommunicated, and the other newly appointed and barely back from his own consecration. He did manage to reach the Pope before the Normans did?'

Siward cleared his throat loudly enough to make Ligulf glance at him and then sit back. But his voice when he spoke was quite gentle. 'Archbishop Cynsige has the pallium and the power to consecrate bishops,' he said. 'He turns a father's eye, naturally, on Bishop Malduin's work. But you do not require his services at present, and I see no point in discussing them. As I understand it, you offer me a fraction of Lothian, and war if I do not accept?'

'I offer you a division of Lothian that ought to suit us both,' Thorfinn said. 'Have you any other suggestion to make?'

'The limits of the Forth lands?' said Siward.

'We have drawings. You will be shown them,' said Thorfinn.

'And the churches Ligulf spoke of? All the churches in Lothian were St Cuthbert's at one time.'

'I do not offer you all the churches,' Thorfinn said. 'I offer only those which belong to his shrine by reason of direct dedication or association with the saint. And these are, for that reason, the richest. The rest will remain, under Bishop Malduin, to be pastors to their flock.'

The Earl Siward of Northumbria lifted his arms from the table and folded them. 'I do not think,' he said, 'that my brother-in-law Ligulf is satisfied. Or my son or my nephew, who are not used to dealing with ultimatums.'

Thorfinn said, 'I am not dealing with your brother-in-law, or your son, or your nephew. Your Bishop seems satisfied.'

'And so is one of his brothers-in-law,' said Forne. 'My son is rather young to speak with authority, but I believe that if his grandfather his namesake were here, he would agree, too. The proposal has come from Scotia, but might equally have come from this side. We are both apprehensive of strong forces and we are both under necessity of taking precautions. We have nothing in common with which to make an alliance except some frontier ground. Let us each take what we need, if we can agree upon it, and save our fighting-resources for when real danger threatens.'

'Your wife's father,' said Thorfinn, 'always had a high opinion of your good sense even if it didn't save him, in the end, from the rest of your family. My lord my cousin, have we the basis for an agreement? In which case we might move into the shade and partake of some wine?'

'We have,' said Siward. He rose. He said, 'There was a time, my lord my cousin, when you preferred axes to ink. I liked you better.'

The boy Crinan and Lulach strolled from the table together.

'Don't you have a sister called Edith?' said Lulach. 'Earl Alfgar has a daughter called Edith. Three Kings, two Ediths, and the House of the Grey Sandal-hose. How proud your grandfather Crinan would have been. Does the sun give you a headache?'

'I know you're glad to see me back,' said Thorfinn. 'But I can't breathe. What is it? I wasn't in any danger.'

His wife released him. 'Of course not. That's why you meet Siward on the border instead of in the more usual way, such as in one another's houses. You heard them outside. They thought you were lucky to get back as well.'

'I don't mind,' said Thorfinn. 'But, really, assassination wasn't going to solve anything. Assassination only works—I don't really have to explain?—when the victim's people were sick of him anyway and ready to let in the new man without overmuch fuss. Or are you trying to tell me that the mormaers think Siward would laugh at their jokes?'

'They weren't all that sick of Duncan,' said Groa critically. 'But they let you walk in and take his place before they even knew that you never laugh at anything, even if it's funny.'

'Yes. Well, I had the whole of north Scotland from the Orkneys to Moray, and Siward has only those bits of Northumbria that Ligulf and the rest haven't written their crosses on. I knew I wasn't in any danger. He had to bargain,' said Thorfinn.

'I'm surprised Ligulf and the rest let him,' said Groa.

'Are you? Then amuse yourself in the long autumn evenings,' said Thorfinn, 'working out what bargain he made with them before he came north. If the pact even stands till the autumn.'

'How long do you give it?' she said. She wished she hadn't started the conversation. She was glad she had, because she forgot sometimes how extraordinary he was.

'Not long. Long enough to let me do what I need to do in Lothian. What's wrong?' he said. 'I like not being able to breathe.'

FOUR

'Wait till we start campaigning,' Osbern of Eu had said to Thorfinn, 'and then you'll know what it's like to live again.'

A lamentable remark, if you took it seriously, and fit for the Thorfinn of twenty years earlier. At the time, he had shrugged without answering.

But when the portents continued to gather that autumn, and ruling the kingdom grew further and further from the planned exercise it had been and more like taking a fleet out in freakish, untoward weather, there was a change in Thorfinn as well: the extra swiftness, the finer edge, the sharper zest created by danger.

It struck sparks, flint against steel, from the bright fighting trim of his mercenaries. The Normans, that summer, began to mesh into the fabric of the new, alert life of the country. The west-coast defences given a structure and a system of manning, they moved inland to the key sites at crossroads or ford or defile where, usually, there had long been a hill-fort or an earthwork of some kind. Sometimes they supervised the repair of what they found. Sometimes they made a new fort, throwing up a ditched mound with a palisade on the crown enclosing a timber citadel, with a defensible yard at its feet. It could be done in less than a week by men working with vigour, and mostly they did, for their own new lands looked to the forts for protection and warning. Ewias had performed that service for Osbern, and he did not forget it.

Then, having settled their men and their stewards and their womenfolk, if they had any, they moved eastwards to do the same for themselves and for others along the course of the Forth, and to drift, with an inquisitive eye, through the hills and croplands that lay southwards in Northumbrian hands.

Their seniors attended Thorfinn, moving in rotation, so that he always had Osbern or Ansfred his son or Baldric or Hugh de Riveire or Flodwig or Salomon of the Val de Saire or some combination of these in his company, as was the rule with his mormaers and their leading men. From wherever they lodged, the couriers raced in and out, carrying orders and relaying messages.

The wounds left by the gale were sore to mend. It was well into the summer before the clang of the forge or the thud of mallet and axe meant anything other than repaired houses and fencing and barns: new scythes and spades instead of weapons; new bridges and malt-vats, new sledges and jetties, new creels and baskets and thatching instead of new ships. Then the land had to be cleared of its debris for the sowing and pasture, and the forests cleared of their tangle, and the journeys made, of necessity, to bring in new seed and new livestock.

By late summer, the nousts and the sheds had been mended in Orkney, and there were keels in them, waiting for the harvest to finish. The ships that had survived were divided, some to continue with the trade that was their life-blood; the rest thinly spread through the Sudreyar, including Man, where Bishop Hrolf cultivated his souls and his fortifications with equal exuberance and had received from his smith on Holmepatrick, in his scant leisure from illegal coining, a custom-made tunic of chain-mail with the cross of Christ on every ring of it.

Thorfinn sent to Svein of Denmark, who seemed no nearer to ending his war with Harald of Norway, and obtained an undertaking that, if the terms were right, Svein would get him ships somewhere, although not before spring. After a brief, acid interval, the terms became right and the bargain was struck.

Bishop Jon, after a punishing excursion in Thorfinn's company to Buchan, rode south to Brechin to bathe his feet and get rid of the dust in his throat and found Prior Tuathal from Fife already there, with the Abbot and Malpedar the Mormaer.

Tuathal, it seemed, had come north from the Forth estuary, where a new church to St Serf was being raised beside the traditional shrine of St Kentigern.

'Indeed,' said Bishop Jon, ''tis to be hoped that the two saintly souls got on well together in life (if so be that they ever met at all, which I take leave to doubt) now that the lord King has made a packet of them, so to speak, for posterity. He had a good eye for a defensible site, had St Kentigern.'

He lifted one dripping foot from its basin and his servant, kneeling, dried it. The foot, like Bishop Jon, was large, well formed, and perfectly manicured. He added, 'I also hear that Earl Siward has lost no time in equipping all his churches of St Cuthbert with four stout walls, a ditch, and a garrison. Will you hand me my sandals? Only God, the cherubim, and the angels were ever meant by the Lord to be seen with bare feet. Were you and I walking on clouds, we'd be upsides with them.'

'In some respects,' said Prior Tuathal, his pigskin face agreeably blank. 'A week after the pact, Stow and Melrose filled up with soldiers. It allowed us to do the same, if we wished, with our churches.'

'The fountain of rightful possession. Well, of course,' said Bishop Jon. 'And our good friend Bishop Malduin has been helping?' He nodded, and his body-servant got up and retired.

'In every way possible,' Prior Tuathal said. 'Except, of course, in any direction to do with fortifications or the requirements of war.'

'The devotion that's in it!' said Bishop Jon abstractedly. 'Like Paul the hermit, alone like a bird on his rock, naked except for his hairs. Although I did hear he had a lad or two with him. Malduin, that is to say.'

'Two young Fife men. That's right. Fothaid's father was blinded and

Cathail's killed in the year King Duncan died. They've both been brought up in Ireland and the Bishop has taken them into his household.'

'And their fathers' lands?' Bishop Jon enquired.

'The King apportioned them between the monastery at Kinrimund and the priory at St Serf's until the heirs grew from childhood. What happens next will be his decision.'

'Well, does he want a home for the priest, I would take him with pleasure,' said Bishop Jon, 'and no doubt you could find room for the other if called on. D'you still send those terrible cryptograms?'

'How else would I know what was going on in Cologne?' said the Prior blandly.

'I hardly like to suggest,' said the Bishop. 'But when my hat is on, you'd hardly notice the notch the Emperor clipped in my ear. Have you heard the news of the Athelings yet? King Edward's nephew that was exiled to Hungary?'

Prior Tuathal's clever eyes opened. 'He's dead?'

'He's frail, but a good stone's throw from death,' the Bishop said. 'His third child, they say, will arrive at any moment, God protect them. And with the Holy Father a prisoner and the Emperor in uncertain health, the situation of that little family must be arousing a host of eloquent prayers this minute. And the heir with only two little girls so far, and no great prospect of life.'

'You've told the King?' Tuathal said. 'What did he say?'

'You could write it without fraying your pen. *Pray for a girl,* was all he said, to my recollection. He had just heard about Baldric and his party leaving, and was speaking entirely in the vocative. I left before I found myself dispatched to Teviotdale,' said Bishop Jon. 'There is a dangerous rising afoot against Duke William in Normandy, and half my lord Osbern's relatives have gone to the aid of the Duke, the flesh-seeking spears in their hands. My lord Osbern himself is still here.'

'Until when?' said Tuathal.

'Until, no doubt, he sees who is winning. I wish him and his friends no evil,' said Bishop Jon, shaking down his book-satchel and peering into it, 'but it's a difficult thing to make plans for your country with them sitting there, their heads switching from this shoulder to the other, and so sleek you would think it was a cow that licked them all. Do you have a prayer for a caementarius on you? I have to bless this tower before it falls down or the masons perish of liver-rot.'

'I'm never without one,' said Tuathal. 'If I suggest to the King that he spends Christmas at Scone and attends special Masses of Supplication for the continued well-being of his country, would you support me?'

'He has already proposed it,' said Bishop Jon. 'He has, you must agree, a remarkably clear idea of policy, if the topography of God's Kingdom at times eludes him a trifle. Here is a blessing for bells. It will do admirably. Is there a bell?'

'I'll go and look,' said Tuathal.

*   *   *

The Masses were held at Christmas, and at Scone instead of the newly finished cathedral at Birsay, for the King did not go to Orkney that winter. They were held in the open, before a portable altar, and three bishops were present, in gold and crimson and purple and white, as well as all the churchmen who could contrive to be there, and several thousand people from Fife and Angus and Lennox and Strathearn and even further away. Afterwards, Thorfinn gave a great feast.

Osbern of Eu and his companions attended, in splendid humour because of the good news the King had brought them from Cumbria.

The King had ridden everywhere that autumn, but he had spent longest with Thor and Dunegal and Leofwine in Cumbria, where he had gleaned the first tidings of Duke William's victory against his rebel kinsmen.

Everyone knew that Duke William still had his hands full with Anjou and Aquitaine, but a victory was a victory, and the Normans drank deeply that Christmas, but not so deeply, as Osbern cheerfully assured his employer, that they would not be able to defend Scotia against anyone who tried to interfere with it.

'And if Duke William calls?' had said Thorfinn calmly.

It was the real danger, and it turned Eochaid cold to hear Thorfinn speak of it openly, as if it amused him. At least the Normans enjoyed the way he dealt with them. Perhaps they knew, as Thorfinn did, that the Pope was learning Greek, there in his imprisonment in Benevento, so that he could the better engage the help of the Eastern Emperor to throw the Normans out of their new lands in Italy. If he ever got out. If the Byzantine Empire would ever bring itself to unite with the Empire of the West.

But Eochaid kept his counsel, as Tuathal did, about everything except what Thorfinn had to know.

Like Tuathal, Eochaid had been in the saddle all autumn, mostly at the King's side, until he had had to return to his own Scone to prepare for this Christmas.

He had made another visit as well, about which he had not told the King. While in Cumbria, he had obtained leave from Earl Leofric to ride south through Mercia and spend two days in the quiet of Oswestry with Thorfinn's *periglour* Sulien, who had travelled from Llanbadarn to meet him.

A young man of twenty-one, Sulien had talked music and manuscripts in Moray with Eochaid. Now, more than twenty years later, the Breton presbyter had lost none of his grace or his repose. He listened, saying nothing, to all the Prior had to tell him and, at the end, strolled in silence beside him, his hands lightly clasped at his back.

They had left the church and the low huts behind, and the sun was warm, and the soft air off the hills. Sulien said, 'You are concerned about Lothian. You are right. But don't mistrust the King's judgement. Whatever he did or did not do, Earl Siward was going to make trouble in Lothian. With his kinsmen and the Godwin family hounding him, and Mercia threatening to overwhelm him, he had to extend north, or else clear his rivals out of Northumbria. And no one was going to help him do that. What Thorfinn did was earn a breathing-space, and the right to lodge some sort of defence in the area. Earl Siward can be a nuisance. But, alone, he can't be a threat to the nation.'

'I wanted to hear you say that. And the Normans?'

Sulien smiled, walking still. 'Do you want my expert opinion? I don't see much of my homeland, but my brother is married into the kindred of Osbern of Eu, and I saw Osbern at Ewias. He's a good fighting-machine, and honest. I should have invited him, as Thorfinn did, but only time will tell if he was right. It identifies him with the Norman cause and the Norman heir, which becomes a threat if Duke William is successful. On the other hand, if Duke William *is* successful, Thorfinn has a sponsor as strong as King Canute or the Lady Emma ever was and, one supposes, guaranteed security for Orkney with no Norwegian overlord. How are matters with his wife's family?'

'We hear from Denmark from time to time,' Eochaid said. 'Finn Arnason holds Halland for King Svein, but his sight is worse, and he is never at court, although he can still fight on shipboard and the young men respect him. His kinsmen in Norway don't seem to have suffered. His niece Thora has given Harald an heir, and still shares his bed with the Russian. His nephew John has married Earl Siward's daughter, but there is no sign of an alliance between Earl Siward and Norway. It was what Thorfinn feared.'

'But England and Wessex would never allow it,' said Sulien. 'Is Thorfinn afraid?'

There was a long silence. Then Eochaid said, 'No. He is like a man riding a dolphin.'

They walked. Then Sulien said, 'But you are afraid. Of what?'

'Of fowl-pip,' said Eochaid. 'Or a bad harvest.'

Sulien stopped. 'So he hasn't given in,' he said. 'Even after all these years. Even after all you and I and the others could do. Even after Rome. You would think, if you didn't know better, that Lulach was right: that he was the son of the Devil.' He broke off.

'He's the son of Earl Sigurd,' said Eochaid. 'You're talking about something I've never been told about, and I didn't come here to find out. Tuathal knows more than I do. He heard Thorfinn answer the Pope's questions in Rome. And, despite what he answered, Pope Leo gave him absolution. He walked barefoot to three shrines, and he returned shriven, and has done more for the church than any King of Alba before him. Nor could anyone know that he had reservations; that he didn't feel as we all did, treading that ground. But . . .'

Sulien began walking, slowly, again. 'No one can know, but they sense it. Is that what you are saying?'

Eochaid said, 'It hardly matters. Even if he had brought his kingship pure and intact back from Rome and launched a holy crusade such as apostles dream of, two years is not enough to sew a kingdom together.

'Moray and the north will always be his, and the rest would have joined them in time with no more than what he was offering: equal rule, equal justice, equal worship. But with the peace breaking, he had to bring in help.

And now old churches are acquiring palisades and fortified towers faster than gospel-books, and new churches appear where a Norman baron sees the need for a fortress. The mormaers agree with his policy now. But they are not unshakable.'

'And the young leaders?' said Sulien. 'The men who went to Rome?'

'For them, Thorfinn can do no wrong,' Eochaid said. 'But will the people follow them? The conduct of the nation means nothing to those who live in clay huts. If Odin does not bring them peace and good harvests, then it is the duty of God and the King. If either fails, it is the fault of the King, since God is without blemish. A diverse people in time of hardship need a priest-king. The English know that. Edward is anointed with holy oil: he has the power of healing, they say; he loves his chaplains and worships daily, prostrate, where he can be seen. The Emperor submits to great fasts and to flagellation.'

'While Thorfinn builds,' Sulien said. 'With nothing but common sense in the mortar, and a tongue that can adjust most problems and people to scale, and an arrogance that will not connive at pretence, even if pretence is of the essence of kingship. There is nothing I can do.'

'Nothing?' said Eochaid.

'Even if Lulach did not exist, there is nothing I can do,' Sulien said. 'If you are wise, you will not even say we have met, for he would be troubled for your sake and mine, and he will be troubled by other things soon enough.'

'We are in good heart,' said Eochaid. 'It may pass. We only need peace, and events may so turn that we receive it. He may ride his dolphin to shore. I have never yet seen him lose courage.'

'He will do his utmost for you,' Sulien said. 'You can trust him for that. He will need you when he turns against Lulach.'

The breeze rattled Eochaid's springing black hair over his ears and pulled at the ends of his lashes. He said, 'I'm sorry. You said—'

'I said what you thought I said,' Sulien replied. 'There will come a day, sooner or later, when he will not want to see Lulach. Lulach will understand. But Thorfinn will be at a crossroads he cannot leave without help.'

Eochaid said, 'If he sent for you, would you come?'

Sulien said, 'He will not send for me.'

Before the Christmas rinds had been thrown to the pigs, Osbern of Eu had gone, in one of Thorfinn's remaining ships, and twenty men with him, in seas as ready to rob them of life as the war they were joining in Normandy.

For two months, while the fighting swayed back and forth overseas, Bishop Hrolf, released by the same storms from sentinel duty in the islands, took it upon himself to oversee the defences of the more vulnerable parts of the mainland. He asked everyone who had been to Denmark about the barracks at Trelleborg and Aggersborg and Fyrkat. He enquired about the uses of ancient hill-forts, and discoursed on the adaptation of antique buildings for military purposes—to wit, the Colosseum in Rome and the amphitheatre at Arles. He pointed out the aptness of Roman strategic sites for present-day purposes, exemplifying Cramond on the river Forth and Cargill by the river

Tay. He had reason to believe, he said, that the Normans in Herefordshire had made good use of the Roman building-materials ready to hand, and there was no reason why others should not do the same. He walked all over Lyne picking up blocks of red sandstone ashlar and pointing out the old grooves and cramp-holes. He found the quarry they came from. He quoted, to the irritation of his more sensitive colleagues, an Irish poem on the subject of forts:

> '*The fort over against the oak-wood*
> *Once it was Bruidge's, it was Cathal's.*
> *It was Aed's, it was Ailill's,*
> *It was Conaing's, it was Cuiline's,*
> *And it was Maelduin's.*
> *The fort remains after each in its turn*
> *And, the Kings asleep in the ground.*'

There were times when men went and made confessions to Bishop Hrolf, to stop him talking about engineering. Finally, the only one listening to him was Thorfinn, who listened to everybody, usually while doing other things, disconcertingly, at the same time.

He had good reason, of course. Olaf of Norway was not the only sea-lord, veteran of countless shipboard battles and raids, to find a straightforward land-conflict beyond him. And if he required a tutor, Thorfinn could have found none better than the Normans, natives of a crowded, belligerent duchy full of strong young barons fighting for power.

Such was not the condition of Scotia, whose disparate regions, lacking the same resources and manpower, had begun to knit together under a King whose descent embraced them all. In recent years, all her wars had been frontier battles, fought round her coasts to repel raiders and oust alien settlements. Of a massive invasion such as England had suffered under Canute and his father from Denmark, or such as Duke William was resisting now from the King of France and Geoffrey of Anjou, Alba had no experience.

That the kindred of Osbern of Eu and the kindred of William fitzOsbern with their friends had succeeded in carrying Duke William to a resounding victory against the invasion of his combined enemies was therefore news of more than ordinary importance. It came in the spring, when men's minds were occupied more with the new wave of cattle-fever than with wars far overseas.

To that, also, the King had given a great part of his attention, but when, late in the spring, word came of the sighting of ships from Normandy in the Clyde, he left his wife and household at Perth, where they had stayed a full week, and rode with a small retinue westwards to meet them.

He came back without warning, overriding his own harbingers and flashing through the opening gates and straight to the hall, heralded only by the flag streaming above him. The hall-door slammed.

Groa heard it, emerging from the dairy with her steward. Of the few men with Thorfinn, she had recognised Osbern of Eu and the Riveire boy, and the sallow face of Gillecrist of Strathclyde. As the rest of the retinue began to come, straggling, into the yard, Groa dismissed her steward and went to her rooms at the other end of the hall, where Anghared, Ferteth's wife, was sewing stockings and talking to Eochaid's sister Maire, who was teaching one of Sinna's girls how to embroider.

They stopped talking when Groa entered, and she could feel their eyes on her back as she stood at the window, watching.

The yard was full of movement: of boys leading the incoming horses off to the stables, and bringing fresh ones. More men entered the hall by its main door, and several times someone came out beckoning and stood on the steps, issuing orders. Three horsemen left, members of the armed household, and someone of greater consequence accompanied by three or four servants on garrons but no pack-mules. It could have been Tuathal.

Through it all, she could hear, as probably no one else could hear, the ground-bass of Thorfinn's voice through the heavy timbers in the hall. Not raised, for that would be unheard of. But speaking shortly, as in the hunting-field.

She was not needed, so she did not interfere. A serving-man, sent to the kitchens, reported that they were already busy, having had their instructions, and in due course she and the women attending her ate where they were, in the chamber. By that time, many more men had arrived, swirling up through the yard to be sucked into the hall, as if it had become the quiet, humming centre of some whirlpool of power. The yard was still noisy with jangling harness and talk at dusk when the women had gone and the bracket-torches below the fiery sky to the west glowed like running water dyed red.

Much later, when it was dark and the yard was quieter at last, the door from the hall opened, and then her own, and Thorfinn came in.

The anger of his arrival was gone, beaten underfoot by hard work, like men treading cloth in a trough. There lingered perhaps an echo of grimness, and an echo of something else: an expression she had seen on the faces of men who have just loaded ship for a voyage. There were no overtones of distress, and none even of weariness, although she was a better judge of these things than most people.

She finished what she was doing, which was pouring wine, and carried a cup to him in silence, since any enquiry seemed pointless. He waited until she was seated, and then said, 'Precautions, that's all. King Edward has let young Malcolm go. He's been sent north to Northumbria to join his uncle Siward.'

'Why?' said Groa.

'Opinion varies. Duke William's success? It looks as if he is going to hold Normandy. Also, there's news from Quedlinburg through St Omer. Edward Atheling has a son, heir to the English throne if Edward dies. And Pope Leo is ill, and not expected to live.'

'In prison? He's dying in prison?' said Groa.

'No. He's been freed by the Normans in return for full recognition of all their conquests to date in Italy. He wrote to Greece: *I look forward to the day when by the Eastern and Western Emperors together, this enemy nation will be expelled from the church of Christ and Christianity will be avenged.* But Constantine didn't answer.'

'All your work,' said Groa. 'All your work in Rome.'

'Oh, there is always work,' Thorfinn said. 'Only the picture changes, and one's work must change with it. We are not dealing with Emma. We are dealing with Earl Harold Godwinsson of Wessex, who has quite different ambitions.'

'Including infanticide?' said Groa. 'Does Earl Harold know where Edmund Ironside's new-born grandson is? Do you know?'

'What you can be sure of,' said Thorfinn, eluding the question, 'is that the Pope and the Emperor Henry both know, and that one is dying while the other enjoys indifferent health and has only a three-year-old son to succeed him. If I were Harold of Wessex, which I'm glad I'm not, I should send a polite embassy soon, preferably under Bishop Ealdred, to extract the child before someone else has a better idea. As his guardian, Harold would have fifteen years before the boy became anything to be reckoned with. And it would encourage Duke William to forget any silly ideas about the succession that King Edward put into his head.'

Groa said, 'If you were Harold of Wessex, I might get some direct answers. Why has he sent Duncan's eldest son north, after he has been kept at court all these years? Isn't Malcolm a rival for Siward's earldom?'

'Nearly everyone you can think of is a rival for Siward's earldom,' Thorfinn said. 'But, without a faction behind him, he isn't much danger, although I suppose he could combine in time with a cousin or two. An outbreak of strife in Northumbria would suit Harold very well, I imagine, especially if Siward got himself killed in the course of it. They could appoint English-trained Malcolm as Earl and steer him from Wessex. And if Malcolm got killed, they always have Donald. An inexhaustible supply of Duncanssons. What's Maelmuire like? You've seen more of him than I have.'

She paused, collecting her thoughts and studying his face at the same time. It gave nothing away.

'Religious,' she said. 'In spite of Cormac, whom he loves. Nineteen, with a big appetite and nice manners: Cormac again. Takes a long time to learn anything new, but perseveres. All his friends are younger than he is. He doesn't like girls, but is fond of reading and has to be summoned by relays of hand-bells from his chief joy, the herb-garden.'

'He doesn't like single girls. What about you?' Thorfinn said.

'We are friends,' Groa said. She searched his face again with her eyes. 'The tact did not pass unnoticed. Why should this topic matter? You talked about everything else as you usually do. Why should I feel Maelmuire is important?'

'I don't know Duncan's other sons,' Thorfinn said. 'That's all. Stop trying to think. You'll grow wrinkles.'

It was said with no expectation of diverting her, and she paid no attention accordingly. She said, 'So the precautions are in case Siward decides to promote Malcolm as King in your place? Is that likely?'

'No,' said Thorfinn. 'Or not very. We have, I admit, been less vulnerable in the past than we are now, but Northumbria alone could never expect to overrun Alba. And Siward knows that the moment he steps from his chair, a family friend will do his best to replace him. If Siward had been strong, Harold of Wessex would never have sent Malcolm to him. Harold wants Northumbria for the Godwin family, not an inflated Siward or a Scotia so weak that Norway could step in and settle there.'

'But you are sending round to put everyone on his guard, just in case. In the spring, when they're busy,' said Groa.

'It'll take their minds off the cattle-fever,' said Thorfinn. 'Cease to concern yourself. My herb-garden, like Maelmuire's, is being looked after by others. My sage will flourish without you: my pennyroyal and rue, my mint and poppy and southernwood, my parsley and radishes. Like Strabo's gladioli and lilies and roses, I keep you for sweetness' sake only.'

She smiled at him, accepting the love and the irony both, and allowed him to end the discussion.

So it was serious, whatever it was.

And, for the first time, he was not going to tell her.

He went to Kinrimund at the end of the month, on the heels of two silly clashes between troops from the new church-fortresses in Lothian and their opposite numbers in the property of St Cuthbert.

The results might have been worse: a number of cattle lost from one side to the other, some barns and carts burned, and half a dozen women held hostage and returned in other than mint condition.

Between feuding families, almost a normal occurrence. Among edgy garrisons, with military pride an ingredient, something to be squashed immediately. With Osbern of Eu and a group of his own leaders and their following, Thorfinn had visited the Lothians and made his views known to the offending bands with frightening precision.

That was when, without awaiting Rogation Week, the air over Alba became filled with the smell of split wood and turned earth and the dank odour of freshly laid mortar as men carried out the King's orders and places of refuge and defence were repaired and strengthened from the west side of the kingdom to the east. From Glamis, her home for the moment, Groa moved about her concerns with the farm people and tried to ignore the rumble of wagons taking felled timber to the palisade, or men with pickaxes and shovels on their way to Dunsinane, where the old ring-fort below the watch-station had received new stone-and-earth walls, and shelters for folk as well as animals.

It was coming close to midsummer, and a time when every man had more than enough work on his own land; but Bishop Hrolf, rendered pentecostal amid the dusty glory of his chosen element, dispensed his rota of tasks with a bone-clear, indisputable justice that only the hardier ever disputed, and then under plain fear of excommunication.

It was to Bishop Hrolf, indeed, arriving unexpectedly that evening with

Prior Tuathal behind him and a string of riders as hot and soiled, though not as cheerful, as he looked himself, that Groa expressed her surprise.

'Of course you are welcome. Breasal will show you where to go, and then you must come back to the hall. You will know: the King has left for Kinrimund. I thought he meant to take you both with him.'

Wood-flour clad the heated planes of Bishop Hrolf's brow and cheeks and gloved the powerful crag of his nose save, endearingly, for the double fingermark where he had blown it. Tuathal, in a leather helmet borrowed from someone, had wiped his face, seamed with infilled pock-marks like a well-repaired amphora.

Bishop Hrolf said, 'Ah, Kinrimund. Very wise. Enough is enough. No, my lady. The King is better advised to deal with this himself. A pity. For myself, a great pity. But no one can say Bishop Malduin has not received latitude. Every courtesy and consideration. But there are temporal rights as well as temporal privileges, and a kingdom must be ruled. Excuse me.'

Groa looked after the Bishop as he retreated. Prior Tuathal, also watching, remained at her side.

'He's embarrassed,' said Tuathal. 'After all, he and Bishop Jon were brought in because Malduin wasn't doing his job. You know, probably, that Malduin wouldn't have anything to do with the fortifications in Fife and the Lothians, and would only release his land-workers when under a direct order from my lord your husband.'

She knew. At Abernethy, when she had teased Bishop Malduin over his squirrel, the confusion of allegiance from which he was suffering had been very plain. He was Thorfinn's first cousin, and his very revolt against his heritage had driven him into the arms of Siward and Durham. Now, with this new drive of Thorfinn's, when the adherence and co-operation of every man was important, it was a matter that must be resolved, and seen to be so.

Groa said, 'If that's what he's gone to Kinrimund for, then I wish I'd known. I would have said a charm over him, against the shot of gods, elves, and witches. Except that if the Bishop's good wife is there, she'll probably have said it over the Bishop already. What is the worst that can happen?'

'That the King should lose his temper,' Tuathal said.

In the event, it was Bishop Malduin who lost his temper, as he might not have done if Elfswitha his wife had not been sitting draped in white cloth in the corner, with her large, shallow eyes fixed on himself, even when the King was starting to speak to her. Her household utensils glittered and clanked in her lap, keys against scissors, knife against comb and spirtle and needle-case. Hitched to her girdle, a battery to be respected, as many a junior, including Colban her son, had discovered.

Now the King said, 'I am sorry to say as much before your lady, but it was by your wish that she stayed. I repeat, however: I do not think we face war. But Earl Siward's acts are not those of a friend, and I must take steps to protect myself. The union between the regions of Scotia is recent, and must be bolstered in time of stress. A bishop who cannot make up his mind which side he is supporting is inconvenient. So I must ask you: Will you come to Scone and make it publicly known that this kingdom is your prime care? That, in war and in peace, you will strive, with your prayers and with what material aid you can summon, to work for the sole weal of Scotia? And that if, God forfend, a state of war should exist between this kingdom and England, or any conflict should arise between this kingdom and Northumbria, with Earl Siward or with the Bishops of York and of Durham, that you will choose to support this kingdom and no other?'

In the ensuing silence, Elfswitha's weapons clanked once and the shallow eyes stared.

The Bishop stood up. 'It is an insult,' he said. 'My service is to mankind. My only master is God.'

'You are Bishop of Alba,' Thorfinn said.

'A land without priests and without churches. Where Irish monks preferred not to come. Nevertheless,' said Bishop Malduin, 'I did what I could. I have found young men and trained them. I have ordained those who were fit. I have performed all the offices that my calling requires, whatever the discomfort. Even when what few benefits might exist were pre-empted over my head by two strangers. That is the duty I owe to my cloth. But engage in warfare, no. Encourage young husbands and fathers to walk out to slaughter—again, no. Not to save myself from your anger, or my body from whatever punishment you may choose to inflict on it. It is against my beliefs as a man of the church,' said Bishop Malduin.

The King did not rise. Standing alone in the room, with his wife's glare enshrined on his right and the King, in riding-trousers and tunic, occupying the whole of a high-backed chair on the left, made Bishop Malduin feel isolated and unsure. Once, stepping out to read before twenty-four pairs of eyes, he had been sick in front of twenty-four porridge-bowls.

The King said, 'It has its attractions, as an idea. Unique, of course. I can't think of anyone, from my lord Pope down to Bishop Ealdred, who would agree with you, but attractive, for all that. If you were a hermit or even a monk, you would have little trouble indeed in implementing it. Unfortunately, on becoming a bishop you forfeit your right to that particular principle. If you do not help your people, or allow them to help themselves, they may all die, and take you with them. If the master you rely on for your temporal well-being has not dealt with you, that is, already. What is the fate of false coiners? *Genitalibus et oculis privatus?* Their wives do not, I'm sure, like it.'

Elfswitha clanked twice.

'You threaten, my lord,' said the Bishop.

'Not unless you are a false coiner, as well as a greedy and cowardly man. You quote principles. You have no principles,' said the King. 'You have no guiding rule save self-interest. Yet you are my Bishop and you can, as you say, fulfil the spiritual calls that men make on you. I have to tell you that you must also fulfil the other obligations you have to your people if you are to remain in this kingdom. I shan't place an axe or a flag in your hand. But if I and mine prepare to defend the kingdom, you and yours must do the same. Choose.'

The Bishop's legs trembled with anger. 'Abuse will not serve you,' he said. 'I join the martyrs, punished for what I believe. What does Peter Damian himself say of the Pope's illness? That it is due to the wrath of the Lord against a militant prelate. Shall I fear your anger when that other might be my fate?'

'Sit down,' said the King. He half-rose and the Bishop, looking round, found a chair higher than his wife's stool and sat on it.

The King said, 'Let's be plain. You want Durham. You won't get it now. If you go to Siward, he'll make you fight, too. You had better, therefore, resign yourself to it. The only difference would be this: In Alba, you would have a see. In Northumbria, you would not. Which is it to be?'

The Bishop wished he had remained standing. He drew himself up in his seat, preparing for martyrdom. Elfswitha's voice, from the corner said, 'We will stay. You give us no alternative. We will stay in Alba.'

The Bishop looked at his wife.

'And co-operate in every way?' said the King. 'In the encouragement of your people against their enemies? In the provision of labour for attack or defence?'

The shallow eyes delivered their message. 'You leave us no alternative,' echoed the Bishop. He looked at the King. 'You compel us.'

'That is my right and my privilege,' said the King. 'And my power. For all of that, no doubt I shall answer, as you will, to an authority other than Peter Damian. I have made myself understood?'

'You have,' said the Bishop with stiffness.

'And you agree to remain on my terms and proclaim them?'

'I do,' said the Bishop.

'Then, since I am busy, as you are,' said the King, 'there seems little more to be said. Such words between cousins should not have had to be spoken. I am sorry. I will not ask for your blessing. Only think, when you pray, of your people. Whatever lies between you and me, they should not suffer.'

He saw the King to the gates and, coming back, heard the clangour of Elfswitha's malevolence before he arrived at the door of their chamber.

Whether struck down by the Lord's retribution or by his failure in Italy or by the neglect of his sponsor the Emperor, the tenth Pope Leo, Bruno de Nordgau, died in April in the city of Rome, far from his beloved Toul and the Vosges of his family. The Alpine snows closed over his militant steps, and the sinners he had excommunicated for one reason or another turned their thoughts from irregular union or simony, if they had ever been on them, and peered into the mists of what promised to be a very long vacancy. In the home of Hildebrand, gathering dust, lay a long, padded box containing a golden rod entwined with roses.

The news came to Perth on the day of the King's special council, and was brought to Thorfinn by Bishop Jon as he prepared to leave with Prior Eochaid for the Moot Hill.

Bishop Jon, a warm-hearted man, had been weeping, and even Eochaid, remembering, found himself moved near to tears.

So to end all that endeavour. And what, now, of Adalbert of Hamburg and Bremen, the Metropolitan of the North, and his white-and-pearled caparison, and his iron ambition? What of Isleifr's white bear, uselessly rampant in Goslar, while Isleifr waited in vain for his summons to consecration? What of Juhel of Dol and his careful and simian plotting to keep his suffragans out of the grasping fingers of Tours?

Bruno of Nordgau had been fifty-one years old when he died. Ten more years of his pontificate might have set both the church and the statesmanship of western Europe in a different direction. He had snapped the circlet of runes from Thorfinn's throat. But the Norns had smiled, and lifted the shears in the end.

Of what he felt, Thorfinn's face gave no sign. Perhaps Bruno's death, long expected, had already been consigned to the past. It was part of Thorfinn's philosophy: the Viking philosophy that lived afresh each coming day. There was the imminent council to think of, and the fact, of which everyone was aware, that Bishop Malduin had not so far arrived to confirm his allegiance as promised. And that the ships had again been delayed: the long-awaited new ships commissioned from King Svein of Denmark, about which King Svein of Denmark had been so apologetic.

Lost in thought, Eochaid did not at first hear the shouting outside, or see Thorfinn thrusting his way through the crowd to the door until he had almost gone.

Something about the note of that call, something about Thorfinn's manner as he stood in the yard listening to the stammering rider who stood grasping his saddle and speaking into his ear made Eochaid's shaven scalp tingle, and his body shrank, for a moment, from its clothing.

Then Thorfinn looked up and, catching sight of the Prior, walked to his side as eager helpers swarmed to the messenger. The King said, 'Come to my room. I have sent for Tuathal and Osbern.'

The texture of his voice was unfamiliar, and his face, when Eochaid glanced up, was drained with some sort of force which Eochaid suddenly saw was consuming anger.

He followed the King into his chamber, and Thorfinn in silence walked to the window and stood there, looking outwards. Almost at once, the door behind Eochaid opened, and Osbern of Eu came in, looking heated, and followed by Tuathal, his thick face enquiring and grim.

The door closed.

The King said, without turning round, 'That was a message from Lothian. A clerk of Durham, collecting church-dues with an armed escort from Melrose, came into conflict yesterday evening with an equally large party of Normans under Flodwig of Dol, and a running battle ensued. Several farms were burned or devastated in its path, with some consequent deaths. Of the opposing parties, a score of men lost their lives or were badly hurt on each side. Among the Northumbrian dead was counted Osbern, the only adult son of Earl Siward.'

The King turned; and even Tuathal flinched.

The King said, 'My lord of Eu, you and your countrymen have brought this nation to war. I hope, when Siward comes with his army, that you find the field as easy to quit as it has been to enter.'

FIVE

O AVENGE THE death of a son is not hasty work, if he is to be honoured.

To raise major levies, King Edward's leave would have to be sought by Earl Siward. To muster an army would take time—but not too much time, for men were hard to come by at harvest. In high summer, provisions were plentiful, but would have to be gathered and loaded. Auxiliary shipping was not unlikely, to carry reinforcements and food and extra weapons and take off the wounded. York's ships were mostly trading, in summer-time. To collect a small fleet would take a week or two.

So Norse mind interpreted Norse, as Alba moved, prepared by her King, from the state of armed defence to the state of imminent war.

Those were the weeks when the minutes were measured like mancuses of purest gold. When Thorfinn was never to be seen in one place for more than a few hours, and when he no longer looked like a man with a fleet ready loaded for sea, but like a man already on board and lifting his ship to meet the first swell of the storm.

The first wave, and the next, and the third. The news that Kinrimund was empty and Bishop Malduin, his wife, and his household had vanished, no one knew where.

The news that the Bishop of Alba was in York, and that two young Fife men, Fothaid priest-son of Maelmichael and Cathail son of Dubhacon, had travelled there with him.

The news, received much later in silence, that Ghilander also had fled, with Colban the Bishop's stepson, and that Kineth of Brechin had gone with them, leaving Angus leaderless.

The secret news from Dunegal of Nithsdale, using a name that only Thorfinn would recognise, that Thorfinn did not talk of at all, at least before Groa.

His energy, she saw, was not abated, or his confidence shaken. In place of zest, there was determination, that was all.

She moved into Fife to be near the Forth estuary, where Thorfinn was oftenest to be found. He visited her there one evening, Bishop Jon and Eochaid in tow, and the three men talked without ceasing, before food and through food and after it, Bishop Jon making notes in his own hand on a slate with a stylus that squealed. Then he ceased to make notes and listened, his clean-shaven jaw sinking lower and lower until, with a small thud, the slate dropped to the floor and Thorfinn, turning, saw that he was asleep.

'Don't wake him,' said Groa. 'Morgund will be here soon anyway. He arrived this afternoon and I sent him off to rest. He had Lulach with him.'

'Lulach?' said Thorfinn. 'I didn't send for him.'

'You are calling on Moray to fight for you,' Groa said.

'I shall be calling on the northern fleet, such as it is, to fight for me,' Thorfinn said. 'But I expect Thorkel and Hlodver and Odalric to stay where they are and look after my interests until I tell them otherwise.'

Somehow she had ruffled him: a rare occasion indeed. Otherwise, he would never have referred to the only point upon which he and his advisors were at odds.

At no time since the earliest plans were drawn up would Thorfinn consider drawing men from the north to fight on land in Alba.

With his ships, he had been liberal. Only one fighting-ship remained off the island of Man, and two of moderate size further north in the Sudreyar. Six were at sea, on the business of trade—an act of faith that he might have cause to regret. The rest were on the Caithness coast, refitted and waiting, with men of Orkney and Caithness to man them.

If the new ships came from Denmark, the Caithness flotilla might not be needed. If the new ships did not come, the handful now in the north represented the only sea-force Thorfinn could lay against any fleet Siward might bring.

Few as they were, they might be sufficient, for the men in them would be seasoned seamen and raiders who would brawl for the love of it, on shipboard anywhere; who would defend their own northern lands to the death, on land or on sea; but who would never march south in cold blood to throw away life defending a foreigner's ground. One day perhaps, but not yet. There had not been time to teach them. That Groa understood, even if Thorfinn's southern council did not.

He had carried the day, of course, for although in fourteen years he had made himself supreme King in Alba, he was born to the north, and from Moray to the northernmost island of Orkney he was the leader men trusted and knew.

One day, when he was gone, they would turn to Paul, and to Erlend when he was old enough. It was to safeguard Orkney that Paul was being left there at this moment. It had hurt him, Groa knew, that his father did not need him at his side now, in the first hour of real danger since Rognvald had tried to claim the north seven years before. But he had been reared to rule Orkney, and he would keep his place.

There had been little dispute about anything else Thorfinn had wanted to do since the day he was told of the fighting in Lothian. That evening, pacing the floor of his chamber before the most able of his mormaers and his churchmen, he had said, 'What would I do if I were Siward and I had just lost all hope of my heirs ruling Northumbria? And he has, make no doubt of it. The only other son is a child, and his nephew will have no better chance than the rest of his brothers-in-law and their offspring against the brethren of Wessex, once Siward goes. What would you do, my lord Prior?'

And Tuathal, whose authority Groa had watched advance through the years, had said, 'I should make for Wedale straight off, and every fortified place with Normans in it. And I shouldn't leave Lothian until I had killed every Norman I could find, and all the families who were supporting them. I should destroy the crops and burn every building, and flatten what wouldn't burn.'

'How well you know Siward,' Thorfinn had said. 'But would he do that all over Lothian, or only in Wedale? The St Cuthbert churches elsewhere are his, you must remember, and their lands and their people. The rest of the churches are mine, and the fringe of land south of the Forth estuary, but there are not necessarily Normans in all of them. Also, my share of the Lothians has been in the care of my cousin the Bishop of Alba. They may have come to share his lack of discrimination.'

He had put into words what they all knew. It released the voice of Osbern of Eu, his colour still high from the interview that had preceded this one. He said, 'These fortresses can pin down a countryside, but they won't stand against an army mustered for war.'

'But an army mustered for war would overrun friend and enemy alike,' Cormac of Atholl had said, 'And Earl Siward has allies—hasn't he?—to placate with land when this is all over, and rivals who would be better off settled in Lothian than snapping at his heels for a bigger share of Northumbria.'

'I agree with you,' Thorfinn had said. 'To blacken Lothian would do him no service. He must attack Wedale, yes; and the Norman lands to the west and any fortresses near. But he'd be wise to leave the rest to be taken at leisure, and make positive use of his friends in the Lothians. Call them under his banner. Use them as signalmen between his army and any ships he has on the coast. Because if he's going to take Lothian and settle it, he's going to need all the friends he can get.'

Bishop Hrolf, hands on knees, was considering. 'This man Siward: how can he hope to hold Lothian, so far from York and from Durham, with a strength such as yours massed to the north of him? He cannot, unless he destroys your strength first, or converts it into one friendly to him.' He sat up. 'I say he must either wreak his vengeance on Wedale and retreat, or he must go further and seek to destroy you and your whole power.'

'Again, I agree,' Thorfinn had said. 'Where? Will he expect to find us massed against him at Melrose?'

'Hardly,' said Tuathal. 'With disaffected Lothian behind you, and possibly sea-borne troops as well, by that time. But he might expect you to trust your estuary lands more than you should, and give him battle west of Dunedin, where he would have you between his ships and his army. Unless he knows more than we do about how soon your new longships are coming.'

'I wonder,' Thorfinn had said. 'Can he rely on his fleet? He must know that I shall bring down some vessels from Orkney. He must know, at the very least, that a great many more are coming, through Svein, with men in them who are fighting for money. If he is unlucky, then there will be a battle at sea, and the best he can hope for is that none of our sea-borne army manages to make a landing. Consider, therefore. If you invade Alba through Wedale and, say, Tweeddale and you have no supporting ships, what do you do?'

No one answered, for there was no need to answer. Without ships, there was only one way to cross the river Forth to Fife and Strathearn: one key to the royal lands by Loch Leven; one way to strike north between the low hills to Forteviot and Perth and Scone; to strike upriver to Dunkeld, or across river to Angus, where lay Glamis and Forfar and Brechin. And that one way was the bridge and causeway at Stirling, the rock fortress on the river forty miles inland from Dunedin.

Then Cormac of Atholl had shifted in his place abruptly. 'You would win a battle at the Forth crossing. But what if you are wrong? What if Siward has no interest in settling Lothian, but only in vengeance and money?'

Thorfinn had said, 'To get to Dunkeld . . . to get to anywhere that matters, he would still have to sail up the Tay or march north by the Forth crossing. Our ships will have instructions. They will guard Taymouth as well as the Forth.'

'Are there enough of them?' said Bishop Jon.

'No. But their seamanship is excellent, and they will have coastal signals to help them. The alternative is to divide our forces. I am not in favour.'

And they had accepted that, too, although to Groa it had been a questionable decision. By the time Siward's army had reached the plains by the Forth, it would have marched a very long way, and suffered fighting, and would be drawn, in any case, only from those regions Siward was master of, for neither Wessex nor Mercia, it was sure, would waste men on extending Northumbria's empire. And against this jaded, depleted army would be the whole resources of Thorfinn's kingdom, from Moray south to the Forth, fresh and waiting. It was a small risk, surely, to deploy some of them, as an insurance, to Perth.

But that, after all, was the only discussion at which she had been present, and many conclusions, clearly, had been come to since then. Among them, and the reason for Thorfinn's presence in the south-east, was the resolve to clear Lothian. When and if Siward of Northumbria and his army made their way to Wedale, they would find there neither Normans nor loyal families on which to expend the grief and fury of loss.

They were tired, then, these men sitting here in her chamber; tired enough, like Bishop Jon, to fall asleep. But to stretch himself to the limit should be the pride and destiny of every man, and she shared, in that part of her being that was not maternal, Paul's disappointment at being excluded from such a brotherhood.

Whereas Lulach had come, and had not been welcome.

He knew it, she thought, the moment he entered the room and sought his stepfather's face, although he greeted Thorfinn, clearly, with light affection as he always did, and Thorfinn, distanced now from the moment's irritation, showed no desire to hector him.

After satisfying herself to that end, she rose presently to give them a chance to be together, and to allow Bishop Jon to awaken without embarrassment. The toisechs' and mormaers' wives and daughters and sisters who always moved with the court would be waiting, and eager for news. It occurred to her, not for the first time, what a large part of her life was spent among women, now that the kingdom had changed. It had many advantages. She liked being with women she was fond of. But not perhaps quite so often.

She did not observe Eochaid, therefore, as he sat quietly watching the King with his stepson, or hear Lulach say, smiling, 'You would like to shoot an apple from my head, like Palnatoke, and perhaps miss. It is natural. If Paul or Erlend or I were to die at Siward's hand, you would feel as he does. Yet Siward, too, must have looked at his son Osbern sometimes and seen nothing but another man to sit in his chair.'

There was a pause, as if Eochaid's presence had made itself felt, and the impending arrival of Morgund. Bishop Jon breathed gently, the stylus in his scrolled fingers voyaging up and down on the buoy of his abdomen. Thorfinn said, 'I think I can look my successor in the face, provided I have even the illusion of free will. Whatever happens, you are not to blame.'

'Yet you kept the rod,' Lulach said. 'The bough with leaves I once sent you. It came from Birnam.'

'I kept it,' said Thorfinn, 'for a *hlauttvein*. A blood-twig to sprinkle and hallow with, after the sacrifice. I thought that was why you sent it.'

'And you thought of it again when *Grágás* was lost,' Lulach said. 'It was a storm like that, wasn't it, that sent down the *Bison?*' And, smiling, he quoted softly:

> '*It was Thor's giant-killing hammer*
> *That smashed the ocean-striding Bison.*
> *It was our gods who drove*
> *The Bellringer's boat ashore.*
> *Your Christ could not save*
> *This buffalo of the sea from destruction.*
> *I do not think your God*
> *Kept guard over him at all.*'

Bishop Jon yawned. 'The *Bison?*' he said. 'Thangbrand's ship. Thangbrand, Willibald's son. As bloody-minded a missionary as any I ever heard of, and if his ship went down, it was because God and the Aesir were pushing together.'

He opened one eye on Eochaid. 'It's his pleasure,' he said, 'that figure of mischief over there, to blow any piece of rubbish out of his mouth and challenge me to return it. Have you caught me out yet? Young Lulach?'

'Bishop Jon,' said Lulach, with laughter in his wide eyes. 'When you are awake, no one can catch you. Come and see me off. I am going back to Moray before the excitement begins.'

He could not have known. But he had barely been gone for an hour when there came the signal that Thorfinn had been waiting for.

He did what had to be done, and then went to find Groa.

'Pack,' he said. 'And leave in the morning. Siward has called in his levies and has begun to march north.'

In the mouth of war, the names of honour, for three long days, were those of the signalmen.

Pinnacled above an empty land into which, hour by hour, a torrent of steel was being inducted, they sent the tidings from Soutra and Pentland, from the hills south of Traquair and east of Penteiacob to where Thorfinn waited with his army.

The Earl Siward and his Northumbrian army have crossed the river Tweed.

They have moved through the moors, burning all they can find, and are spreading north and west through all the passes, leaving no living object behind them.

They are between the hills and the Forth and are sparing nothing in Lothian, from the east coast to Dunedin. They are making no haste, and suffering no losses that matter.

But for its refugees, Lothian and its southlands are dead.

Cormac of Atholl said, 'We were wrong. We thought he would court Lothian. We thought he would pass straight through Wedale to the north.'

'I was wrong,' Thorfinn said. 'Outside the churches of St Cuthbert, he is allowing his men to ravage and rob where they wish, and at leisure. He has five thousand men, no more than we have, and Malcolm is not with him.'

'Who is with him?' said Cormac. 'Has anyone caught sight of banners?'

'Most of those who love us best,' Thorfinn said. 'Ligulf of Bamburgh, with the Bernician strength. Siward's nephew of the same name, whom we met at Melrose. York and Durham, perhaps even in the persons of Aethelric and Cynsige, with the armed power of the church. My brother's nephews Gospatrick and the second Maldred. Our friend Forne, who married my stepfather's daughter, with Wulfgeat. Brand of Peterborough, and Leofnoth and Ulfcetel, since someone has to look after the army's treasure-box. And, last but not least, my cousin Bishop Malduin of Kinrimund with, no doubt, his stepson Colban. Kineth of Angus, it is said, was seen with them.'

'I dare say,' Cormac said. 'Good for troops to see men changing sides before battle. After it, if he's any sense, Siward will execute the whole brood, including your cousin the Bishop, begging your pardon. So they are all there, kicking our teeth in. Is that all they are going to do?'

The summer breeze blew in his face. Waiting for the King to speak, he could hear the gust claw through the heather behind him and set the flowering whin, silk and tinsel, rubbing together, bough against bough.

It was because the moment of decision was approaching that they were up here on the hill of Dumyat, six miles from Thorfinn's muster-point at

Dunblane, and half that from the crag on the Forth beside which, on one side or another, Thorfinn would take his stand against any Northumbrian advance out of Lothian.

Below them, from right to left, the river Forth ran to the sea: a silver inlay of zig-zags in a great plain chequered with corn and green mosses and the harsh buff and sliced resilient brown of peat-beds. Beyond the river, the plain married into wandering uplands where the low Lennox hills banded the horizon, a ridge thrusting eastwards above forest and hamlet to merge with the west Lothian hills and the Pentlands, and to end far to the left, where sea and sky met, with the crag, small and clear, of Dunedin.

Today there were no boats and no fishing-nets in the river. The cabins of wattle and clay, of timber, of turf packed with stone, showed no smoke from the woven-reed thatches, neat as favours for children, that mushroomed everywhere on high ground, and on the slopes of the rock-citadel opposite. No mill-oxen dragged by: no cattle stood in the marshes or sheep, lately shorn, walked with their lambs on the hills.

Sound had vanished as well: of the blows of a wood-axe and the shout of a drover, of children calling and the crow of a cock; the beast-sounds from the byres and the fields; the groan and clank of a winch at a well; the clack of loom-shuttles and women's voices chattering over them; the brazen voice of a meat-cauldron being scoured and the squelch and fizz of cloth being pounded at the washing-stones in the side streams.

The women and children and old people had gone. The men fit for fighting were moving down there, in thick leather jackets and helmets, with their spears and hunting-axes, their clubs and their knives and their bows, with satchels packed by their wives with barley-bread and some lard, a goatsmilk cheese and a bit of dried fish and mutton, with a few onions, fresh-dug, for savour.

Their toisech would greet them, in his cone helmet with its metal nose-guard and his tunic of ring-mail over leather, and would lead them to the wing of the army commanded by my lord Ferteth, their Mormaer, and my lord Gillecrist, the Mormaer for Lennox and Strathclyde. And there they would greet the men that they knew, and collect what news they could, and visit the cess-pits more often than they would like to admit, while turning all the time to look up here, where the King their leader was deciding what was going to save them from the army of Northumbria.

At least once in their lives, most of these men would have met Thorfinn: more perhaps than had come face to face with King Duncan in the six years of his reign and before, when he had been prince of Cumbria in the shadow of Malcolm his grandfather.

The men who had marched north with Duncan to dispose of his dangerous half-brother at Tarbatness had mostly died in that battle. The young men who had grown to manhood in the past fourteen years had had no experience of war, and little of fighting, other than the kind that might break out between neighbours, or the kind they saw during their service at court, when a raid on coast or frontier had to be repelled, or the King's justice enforced.

Whereas Siward, as a direct vassal of England, had appeared on every battlefield with his Northumbrian levies and knew their strength, as they knew each other's.

But it took more, surely, than fourteen years of moderate peace to erase the fighting instinct that had served a race through two hundred years and more of Viking attacks, through the civil onslaughts that led to the fusion of Pict and Scot, of Scandinavian and Gael; the wars of royal cousin against royal cousin as the descendants of Kenneth MacAlpin fought for the throne.

Against invasion, such people would always fight, with all the skills of a hard daily life, with bow and spear and axe to aid them. What they would not yet do, and what Thorfinn had not asked them to do, was to fight as a nation, north beside south, no matter what the threat.

Between them, Canute and his sons had achieved it in England. They had had to farm Cumbria out, but Siward was England's man, fighting England's enemies. The difference, Cormac thought, was that under Emma's care Northumbria had never been allowed to become a threat to Wessex. Whereas, under Thorkel Fóstri, under his sons of Orkney and Moray, Thorfinn might well command the north to come to the aid of Alba the south and might well be obeyed. But the south, witnessing the brilliant array of fighting-men that the north could so amply provide, and their foreign tongue and alien ways, might well think their better safety lay with the enemy.

In the distance, the smoke lay over the land like a corpse-veil. Over the river, the banners glinted red over the fort, and the long line of its shadow began to creep down its rock to the east. Thorfinn said, 'He's arrived at the coast and judged our numbers. He ought to muster and start south before nightfall, if he's going south.'

The Norman Hugh de Riveire, hands on his hips, moved from his view-point to the King's and studied the skyline. 'Is he a man who would punish and run, this Siward?' he said. 'Even with equal numbers?'

'He is not the man to punish and run,' Thorfinn said. He turned, and the flash of his movement drew every eye within range. 'Nor is he the kind to come north at all without a very sure chance of success. I don't think our strengths are meant to be equal. I think he has come to a rendezvous. In which case, we don't wait. We cross the Drip ford at nightfall and attack, or provoke an attack as soon as there is light enough.'

The Norman said, 'What rendezvous? No second army has come into Lothian. I have heard your couriers. Not even a ship has been sighted. And if it were, there is your fleet waiting out in the estuary to welcome it. Your excellent ships. Ten, did you not say, in the Forth and two held back, waiting at Taymouth? A small fleet, but no smaller then Siward's will be, considering what manpower he has. The reinforcements will never land.' Polite reason vying with impatience made his French quicker and more idiosyncratic.

He added fretfully, 'Your own new ships will come sooner, that you have purchased from Denmark. You fight now, and perhaps you throw away your biggest advantage.'

'I had thought of that,' Thorfinn said. Only once had he ever lost his temper with the Normans. His eyes rested on de Riveire's face. 'There was a danger that allies of Siward's might approach him from the south-west. There is no sign of them so far. But we would be as well to take no risks. The Danish ships have taken too long already. They may well arrive when this is all over.'

'From the south-west?' There was coming anger as well as puzzlement in de Riveire's face. He frowned at Cormac.

'My lord of Atholl has been told,' Thorfinn said. 'And my lord of Eu also. We had no wish to spread alarm. We hoped that, in time, our fears would prove baseless. We still have no proof. But Earl Siward's delay is inexplicable otherwise. He also must know that my ships from Denmark might arrive at any moment. It is wiser to attack while we can.'

'From the south-west?' the Norman repeated. His brow had cleared. Given a military problem, Osbern of Eu and his men resembled nothing so much, Cormac thought, as a starving man with a knife set before a belly-piece of fat pork and an ale-horn. He was smiling at the King with something that, under normal circumstances, might have been admiration. 'More of your cousins or your brothers marching against you, my lord? We have the same trouble in Cotenville.'

'A third cousin, merely,' Thorfinn said. 'But, unluckily, he could bring the power of Cumbria with him. His name is Thor of Allerdale.'

It still had the power to turn the stomach, that whisper of shifting allegiance that Thorfinn himself had picked up weeks ago, and that Dunegal of Nithsdale's hurried warning of danger had seemed to confirm.

Dunegal of Nithsdale had not come to Thorfinn's standard, nor had any of the men of Dumfries and the western lands of St Cuthbert. Absent also was Leofwine, who had taken Thorfinn for King as Cormac had, or so it seemed, on the glorious journey to and from Rome, and who had stood trembling as Cormac had on the steps of St Peter's, one of a brotherhood that had seemed to promise a future none of them had so far dreamed of.

They were not here, nor was Thor of Allerdale himself; but, after all, it was strategy such as this which had kept Allerdale free despite the wolves at his frontiers. And the wolves had not all come north. The banners gathering there on the banks of the Carron on the other side of the Forth did not include those of Orm or Gamel, the kindred of Siward's wife, or of Osulf her cousin, whose father Siward had killed, or Copsi or Carl Thorbrandsson or Archil, all powers in York.

They did not include the banners of Edward of England, or the Fighting Man or the Dragon of Harold of Wessex. Whatever else they had sent, the south of England had not supported Siward with an army. Some of the magnates of York had not shared his ambitions either, one had to believe. Not every thane had been left behind to act as a watchdog.

But some had. And with Northumbria there, even half-manned at her borders, Cumbria had to keep guard.

So one might argue. But the arguments did not convince. For, as Thorfinn had said, his royal nephew Malcolm was not with his uncle. And without Malcolm, the excuse for conquest had gone.

Thorfinn said, 'The night will be short enough. The men should have a good supper and rest. Let us go down.'

They strode down and found more news already arriving. The enemy, having mustered at Dunedin, was not turning south. Instead, it was marching west, six thousand strong, along the opposite bank of the river towards them.

At the door of his tent, Osbern of Eu looked at the King.

'You are not disturbed?' he said. 'Therefore, there is no danger of an attack during the night?'

'No,' said Thorfinn. 'He'll manage twenty-five miles or so by nightfall, and that will bring him to the stream over there called the Carron, with a dozen miles of forest and boggy ground between himself and the main river-crossing. He'd never traverse that in the dark, and his men will be tired. He'll probably take them over the Carron and put them into the *coille torr*, the forest there, for the night.

'By morning, we ought to be on the same side of the Forth as they are, and facing the open space to the west of the forest. There's a Roman road there, and some firm ground if you know where to look. Bishop Hrolf will tell you all about it in a moment. Unfortunately, Forne and the Fife and Angus men will know of it as well.'

'If they are waiting for reinforcements,' remarked Osbern of Eu, 'they will be in no hurry to fight in any case. Then what?'

'Then we send an invitation,' said Thorfinn. 'A pressing one.'

SIX

A T FOUR O'CLOCK, nearly an hour before sunrise, the first black-bird began to sing and Thorfinn moved from light sleep to full awareness a moment before Klakkr son of Bathrik, his body-servant for many years, touched him on the shoulder and gave him the sentry's report: no movement from the enemy in the wood.

The familiar Scandinavian-Irish of Caithness was linked, as his sword was linked, with the high, cold brilliance of the moment. The dawn waking to battle, with his friends sleeping about him. The strong hand of Skeggi, still half-laid on his axe. The warm hair of Rognvald, shining like eglantine among the crushed bracken.

Odin, Father of Victory, said the runes on his own Ulfberht axe. It lay over there with the gold helm made in Germany to replace the helm of Canute's that had blown in pearls to the wind, beading the ashes of his forebears' great hall at Orphir.

A new helmet he owned, and a new circlet of gold, and a white scabbard marked with a cross, and a white shield bossed in steel with a great silver cross studding the cow's hide. And white gloves with a tunic of silvery mail, lying there in a tent that was empty but for himself and Klakkr.

Last night, the newest bard, who was called Lorcáin, had sung: a song to God, and one to the King. Every arm of his host had its priests, and the two Bishops, Jon and Hrolf, had moved quietly among them once they were settled. Sometimes, above the noise, one voice or another could be heard: *Deliver, O Lord, the souls of thy servants. . . . May we all reach that Kingdom. May we deserve it. May we inhabit it for ever and ever. . . . The blessing of God come upon us. May the Son of Mary save us. May He protect us this night.* Or a scrap of Norman-French: *Pro Deo amur et pro Christian poblo et nostro commun salvament. . . .*

Last night, he had listened to prayers, but had prayed to no one, for that had never been his habit. With the same instinct that had sent Bishop Jon, he noted, to pare his nails and perfect the glossy ring of his tonsure, he on the eve of battle came cleansed from a hot bath: the ritual *laugardagr* observed once a week by his forefathers, of which the other Bishop John in far-off Bremen would so have disapproved. Despite all his years with his stepfather Find-laech, despite the life he had made in Alba, the Norse came first to his tongue, always, in a matter of war.

Soon, the army outside his tent would kneel to receive the sacrament, himself beside them. Alone of them all, he had been shriven by the Pope—the Bishop would proclaim it yet again—and yet felt no different from the man who had stood on shipboard beneath a sky turned to flame and faced death with no fears and no doubts, for on such a day it was no hardship to die.

No different? That wasn't quite true. The wild elation had gone, with his early youth and his comrades. Still, the Normans were his kind. Like Tuathal, they liked puzzles, but in steel. They liked solving them, as he did, for the sufficient reward of achievement; but also for power, and to compel the respect of their fellow-men, and to earn a name for skill and for courage.

Such a nature had carried him into his tortuous business of ruling, where he had found himself responsible for people who owned neither ships nor battle-gear, nor skill, nor health, nor ability. People who needed a God and a leader as he needed his sword. People who lived if their leader were successful, and who bled and died for each of his mistakes.

So, now, war was different; but he did not know what to do about it.

He suspected that Bishop Jon, who guessed, and Tuathal, who knew, had long discussed how to lead him to the state of proper sanctity in which a king should dwell. 'Pray to Brigit, why not?' had said Bishop Jon encouragingly only the other night. 'Goddess of poetry, healing and smithcraft, if she takes you that way; and if not, enough saints of the name to see you out of any small predicament. *Mise dol a mach orra shlighe-sa, Dhé* . . . There's a fine prayer, now. It should appeal to you.'

While Klakkr brought him ale to drink, and water to splash on his face, Thorfinn ran the lines through the echo-chamber of his mind:

> *I go out in thy path, O God;*
> *God be before me; God be behind me; God be in my tread.*
> *The knowledge which Mary made for her Son, Brigid breathed through her*
>   *palms.*
> *Knowledge of truth, without knowledge of falsehood.*
> *As she obtained her quest, so may I too see*
> *The semblance of that which I myself am in quest of.*

It pleased him. He consigned the thought, as a gift, to one of the two he held most dear.

To the other, he had already quoted Alcuin. 'Death? An uncertain occur-rence; an unavoidable journey. Ceres; sorceress; if it comes, you must wear the royal helmet. You must endure, as a daughter of Eve. That it should all go for nothing: that would be a cheap death indeed.'

Before his people, ten minutes later, Thorfinn said, 'Every group of families appoints its protector and, when its protector is challenged, must choose which contender to follow.

'You have chosen to follow me, as your fathers chose to follow my grandfather against the same enemy. I think you are men, as your fathers were, who will not lightly see your homes burned, your women shamed, your cattle driven off, your children taken for slaves. Let us show Northumbria what they have wakened.'

He stood, resenting the fate that had forced him to declaim, while they shook their spears and cheered him.

At Tarbatness, his name had been the battle-cry. Now he heard, roared for him, the war-slogan of Duncan's doomed men: '*Albanaid! Albanaid! Albanaid!*'

A hand fell on his arm.

Eochaid of Scone, friend, priest, and secretary, said, 'My lord King. There is news.' His fingers and thumb were stained with ink still, from the long hours with the quill that had assembled there at Dunblane the cartloads of tenting and weapons, of beef and pork and ale-kegs and mattocks, of campaign cauldrons and ovens, of sacks of charcoal for the blacksmiths, of meal for the griddles, and of oats for the couriers, horses, and the toisechs' garrons, and the powerful mounts that the Normans, alone among Western fighting-men, were accustomed to ride into the battle itself.

In battle, too, Eochaid would stand with the Bishops and the King in the van. For, as Prior of Scone and its guardian, he bore round his neck the Brecbennoch, the little silver reliquary casket of St Columba which was all the Celtic church could bring to any battle while its Abbots of Iona and Armagh and Kells disputed with one another in the turmoil of Irish battle, Irish famine, Irish plague, demanding the grace of St Columba and first claim to the aid of his relics.

Eochaid said, 'It is good news from Fife. Earl Siward's ships were sighted south of the estuary two hours ago. Six only, and two of them small. The eight ships you left waiting had already moved across to intercept them.'

'Siward's fleet has the wind,' Thorfinn said. 'But one of my ships has Killer-Bardi in it. And even if my eight have sunk to the bottom, it is too late for anyone to interfere with this battle now. Although, as you see, Siward is not anxious to fight. Should we tell him the news, do you think?'

Eochaid smiled. The early sun, striking up from the silver, made patterns on his cheek, and on his throat with all the music in it. He screwed up his eyes and said, 'We should have the sun against us for a bit. But I can find a spokesman for you, if you like.'

From side to side of the field, the army buzzed, like a harp strung with horse-hair, and the sun rose higher ahead above the black forest of pine mixed with alder and birch that closed the battleground at its far end, and within which the Northumbrian army was waiting.

'Send a priest,' Thorfinn said. 'I would go myself if I thought it would serve any purpose to be killed before a blow had been struck. He'll have to be quick. They'll be out of that wood very soon.'

He saw the man Eochaid picked, and watched him ride out to mid-field with two unarmed monks and the biggest cross they could find, drawing men's eyes from Thorfinn himself. It was as if a looking-glass had been diverted. He used the moment to check on his leaders.

Holding the men of Lennox and Strathearn on his left, on the edge of the boggy ground that ran to the river, were Gillecrist and Ferteth, with Bishop Hrolf, encased in crosses and relics, between them.

On his own right, on the rising ground that led to a wood, and then to the moors and hills that rimmed the horizon, stood Cormac and Gillocher with the men of Atholl and Mar, and the church-banner of Tuathal, holding firm those men of Fife who had chosen to follow the King rather than Bishop Malduin, his acolytes, and his family.

The men of Buchan and of Moray, who knew him best, he had kept in the centre under himself, with Morgund and Mael-Isu. Among these also stood the men of Angus, deserted by Kineth, with Malpedar from Moray to work with their own leaders and the presence of the Moray men to stiffen them. Above them, overshadowing the rippling wicker-work of personal banners, floated the white standard blessed by the Pope, in the care of Bishop Jon.

Behind him was the rock-fortress of Stirling guarding the bridge, the narrow crossing over the Forth. Behind that, among the bogs of the river-plain, was the wide crossing that led to their station last night and then, further north, to Dunblane, where their base was.

The horse-lines and baggage were over the river. Siward's were in the forest ahead, along with six thousand men far from home and greedy for booty. An hour ago, all you could see was the sparkle of steel in the blackness under the trees, and the falling ray of an arrow when one of his men moved too near, having a look at the ground.

Now the trees were fenced with armed men standing shoulder to shoulder: brown, featureless faces above scales bright as fresh-landed fish. In the centre, taller and broader than any man there, his greying head bare, stood Siward their leader, Kalv's nephew. Siward, son of that rich Norwegian fur-trader who had found more profit in England than in the uncertain fortunes of Norway. Siward, the man who had planned in his turn a fair dominion for himself and his offspring, and had seen his son die in the land of his rival. Siward, the man who, had he, Thorfinn, been standing under that cross and issuing that challenge instead of a priest, would have had no hesitation in ordering his best marksman to smite him dead with his bow or his javelin.

As he would do to Siward, given the chance.

Bishop Jon said, 'Will you listen to that? I never heard the fellow so eloquent when he was blessing the butter. "*What hope has your fleet against the fleet of Macbeth? They have met, and your ships have sunk. What hope has your army against an army blessed by the Pope? Throw down your arms, and we will spare you. If your men are afraid to fight, as we see, and also afraid to surrender, place yourself in our hands. You will be an honoured hostage, and to your underlings we shall display our lenience.*"'

'I told him what to say. You don't have to repeat it,' Thorfinn said. A flashing ripple passed through the distant trees and struck an answering glitter from his own side. Then Siward, his arm raised, had his men under control, and in a moment the sound of his voice could be heard shouting his rebuttal.

Throughout, Thorfinn kept his horse motionless. It didn't matter what the words were. He had had no expectation of doing more than exasperate, and supply a distraction. He looked round again and collected the eyes of his leaders. He had drawn his sword and held it, not yet in challenge aloft, but where the naked blade could just be seen by men on horse-back.

Only the leaders were mounted, and even that would not last long, although there were horse-boys behind with replacements. Siward's army would be the same. A man used to wielding an axe fought best on foot, and preferred the round targe with its cutting-edge and ramming-spike to the long, harp-shaped shields of the cavalry.

Above the trees, a frieze of white smoke rose into the blue morning sky and hung unremarked under the sun, thickening a little. On either side of Thorfinn, there was a rustle and clash as men shifted. The priest, standing in front of them, was relaying Siward's message, which contained words he thought he had forgotten.

Over the forest, the smoke looked like newly plucked wool, with darker tufts here and there, and glints of orange, bright as sunrise on spear-blades. A shadow passed over the empty battle field: then another. The voice of both armies changed. The rumour of noise from under the trees became spaced, punctuated by sharper sounds and sometimes by a subterranean crackling, like distant footsteps in frost. Then the sun started to darken, and the orange spear-tips melted together to form one mountainous band, and the spaces under the trees flashed and shook with leaping men and torn shouting.

Thorfinn said, 'He will either send back a fire-party and advance with the rest while he still has them in order, or he'll abandon both his carts and his cover and bring them all on to finish us.'

'I think—' Tuathal said.

'Yes. Good. He's bringing them all. Let's go,' said Thorfinn, and stood in his stirrups.

Every face was already turned.

The pleasure he felt, and the calmness, and the determination burned as clear as the trees in the forest. He smiled—the unknown, rare smile, as if it were his wife he was going to meet—and, lifting his glittering sword, thrust it upwards and forwards.

The answering roar blenched the flames back and cleared the face of the sun for an instant. The trumpets blew on both sides. Then, in a long, jolting line, Northumbria marched from the flames of the forest with Siward in the van, mounted now, and buckling the straps of his helmet before taking his gloves and his shield.

His voice, shouting commands, hardly ceased. It was not necessary to hear them. As they approached, the Northumbrian army began to divide, until it, too, was formed in three blocks across the limited ground, to match the three advancing rectangles of Alba.

The horses wanted to break out and canter. Thorfinn held his big gelding hard-reined, and saw the mormaers doing the same. The marching-pace had to be held even and steady. He wanted Siward's army over the centre, and also over the bright, narrow vein of the deepest of the many rivulets that seamed the field, running down to the Forth. He also wanted to see who was opposing him.

Cynsige of York in the centre, with Siward. The power of the church that consecrated the Bishops of Alba against the power of a dead and discredited Pope.

On Siward's right, the standard of Siward his nephew and of Forne, who surely had no great experience behind him, and the great banner of Durham. Bishop Aethelric, this time, against Bishop Hrolf, the nominee of Cologne and Bremen and Goslar. Gillecrist and Ferteth should manage the nephew and Forne. Bishop Aethelric, he had heard, was accounted able even in Peterborough, and ruthless into the bargain. But he had not, perhaps, been taught overmuch about the battle-tactics of the Romans.

Siward's left wing, though, was of a kind that spelled danger. Ligulf of Bamburgh against Atholl and Mar. Hard fighting-men all of them, and Ligulf with a reputation equalling Earl Siward's own.

And with Ligulf, the banner he would rather not have seen. The flag of Kinrimund, with, under it, Malduin, Bishop of Alba, and his men, and Kineth, his lost Mormaer of Angus. Tuathal's Fife levies would be opposed by their own flesh and blood. And the men of Angus, here in the centre, would be close enough to their fellows under Kineth to make it easy for them to falter or abscond.

All riddles could be solved. Including this one.

Siward's men were over the stream. Watching, Thorfinn could feel the eyes of the trumpeter beside him burning into his skin. 'Yes. Now,' he said, and lifted his sword again, spurring suddenly as the trumpet blared, followed by those on either flank.

Now he was riding clear in the front, and so, on each wing, were Cormac and Ferteth, their shields held before them. The exposure lasted only an instant. A spear, too spent to hurt, struck his own shield and found no room to fall to the ground, for by then men and shields were packed close around and behind him, and the three wedges had formed the *svinfylkja*, the pig's snout, the secret of Odin that he hoped fur-traders' sons had not been instructed about.

Thorfinn spurred, and the wedge of men behind him and behind Cormac and behind Ferteth broke into a pounding run.

To the Northumbrian army they must appear as three arrowheads with a thousand barbs each, roofed and armoured on either side by the heavy, scaled ranks of their shields. The risky moment was the first, when they made impact. But his horse was from Normandy, brought up through Wales and trained to kill with its hooves. And once it went, he would be in the thick of it with all his weapons and a better chance than most.

He aimed for the centre, where Siward's helmet flashed and dulled as the smoke wavered over the sun. He was conscious of a gust of warmth, brought by the wind, and of a sprinkle of white ash, gentle as snow. He hoped, an instant before the impact, that the gambit of the fire was not going to spoil the gambit of the Normans, and saw from a distant glitter far on his right that it was not. The shields of his men broke bows against the shields of his enemies, and the shouting that had been going on all the time rose to a shattering yell. Steel flashed. He lifted his sword and slashed, one, two, three, at the men between him and Siward and then found himself hurtling beyond him, pushed by the momentum of his own men screaming behind and on either side. He serrated the air with his sword and used his shield as a wall and a battering-ram. Like sod sliced by the share, or sea by the bowsprit, butchered meat in its clothing reeled back on this side and that, and as men fell behind him, they were replaced in the *svinfylkja* by others. It was the same, he could see, on either side.

He knew what Siward would be thinking, behind him. Let a dart enter the body so far, and the body will give way and encircle it. He wondered when Siward would glance to the wood on the rise. When he would see the glitter transform itself into a body of fully armed horsemen thundering down to cut his army in half, just ahead of the three driving wedges. And then, having cut it in half, turn again and again at the charge to carve it, neatly, for Thorfinn's well-placed and well-protected infantry to engulf and slaughter.

The Norman cry was '*Dex aie!*' Coming from eighty throats, it swept with them down from the wooded foothills and made them sound like a flock of scavenging birds disturbed from their carcass. He saw the flash of Osbern's teeth before the struggling mass all around him was rocked sideways by the shock of the cavalry; of live men flinging themselves out of its pathway and of dead men thrown after them.

He could feel the fighting around and behind him slacken. His horse had taken a dozen blows and was weakening. Thorfinn lifted himself in the saddle and saw men's heads turn, and the flash of a spear to be deflected. He was the only man still mounted, apart from the Normans, and the Normans had seen him. Siward, taller than anyone else, was behind him and to the left. Thorfinn drew a great breath and roared, '*Albanaid!*' and was answered by a shout that drowned that of the Normans. Then he shook his feet free of the stirrups and, lifting his horse for the last time, sent it rearing into the enemy mass to crash and sink amongst them. His pristine shield with the glittering cross was scarred and broken by blows of which he had no recollection. He threw it away and, transferring his sword to the left hand, felt at his belt with the right and pulled out the big Ulfberht axe. Tuathal, unexpectedly beside him, screamed, 'My lord!'

The wedges had served their purpose. It was time to disband all three and convert them instead to small killing-groups, easy for the Normans to recognise. Already, on the side nearest the river, Osbern had reformed his men and was driving back again at a different angle. Thorfinn shouted to the men about him; and again, over a mass of heads, to Malpedar with a knot of Angus men at his shoulder. He had seen Mael-Isu drop a little time back, and the Strathclyde pennant had suddenly gone.

Tuathal said, 'My lord, news. News! Your fleet is coming.'

Someone saved him from a blade he had not seen, and he killed the man who wielded it and began to fight his way back the way he had come, towards Siward, still calling orders. His fleet, whether it had sunk Siward's or not, was twenty-five miles out in the estuary and its arrival was irrelevant.

Tuathal said, 'My lord! Your new Danish fleet. Twenty-five sail.'

He said, *'Are you sure?'*

And Tuathal said, 'Scandlain told me himself.'

Twenty-five ships, and a thousand mercenaries in them. More than could ever come to Siward's aid, no matter where he sent for them. That they, too, were out of reach at the moment was of no importance. He could afford to wait for them now, if he wanted.

Tuathal said, 'Siward's trumpets. They're regrouping.'

Again, an unmistakable slackening: a foundering of noise as well as action. Thorfinn said, 'No. They're withdrawing. Let them.'

He had seen one trumpeter killed. Another, a younger man, had been at his elbow ever since. He turned to speak.

Tuathal said, 'You have them beaten?' A spear squealed on the rim of his shield and he lifted his sword. A man thrust past, dragging another, and, seeing the King, stopped and lifted his axe, hatred in his face. Before it came shoulder-high, Thorfinn killed him and saw him drop bleeding over his friend. The axeman wore the first beard of a boy and had big ears that stuck through his hair. For a moment, he was a person and what had happened to him was death. Then the moment passed.

Thorfinn said, 'Why should we lose men?' and had the signal blown: to pull back and allow the enemy to withdraw.

Osbern of Eu, ignoring it, led his column of horse, hardly impaired, in another thundering drive through the streaming Northumbrians and pulled up above Thorfinn's head. His horse fretted, its haunches nudging its neighbours, and flayed the air with a hoof. The frog was thick with what it had galloped through.

'Herding them into the fire?' Osbern called. 'But the wind has changed.'

It had moved to the south-west, isolating untouched the stretch of forest between the high road and the marsh of the river. There, the Northumbrians were running. Thorfinn saw, to his regret, the banners of Durham and Kinrimund. He said, 'Let them go. They'll surrender. My big fleet from Denmark has been sighted.'

'So the saints have heard us,' said Osbern. He turned and yelled at Hugh de Riveire and his men, who had launched on a private war at his back. He turned back. 'You have tides in your blood. When will they come?'

'Not for a while. My own ships will lead them in and show them where to land. Till they do—'

'I knew it. You want us to lie east of the forest with the fire in our faces and cut off Siward if he tries to make his escape. How will your mercenaries know we are friendly, if they come from the east?'

'Killer-Bardi will lead them. Take some Moray men. They know him.

Excuse me,' said Thorfinn. 'It is not usual for a king to be left alone in the field at the end of a withdrawal. That battle was yours. Celebrate when the reinforcements come.'

It was more than time to cross the field back to his starting-point, along with the wary groups of his van dragging their wounded. One of them shouted. 'My lord King! Is it true that a great army is coming, and the war has ended?'

Thorfinn was walking backwards, Tuathal and the trumpeter at his side, looking across the trampled mess of earth beaten with turf and heaped with dark shapes like cattle resting on dung.

He was not interested yet in the dead, who would have to be cleared and identified later. He was interested in how far Siward had taken his men back into the untouched part of the forest, where the clearing kept for the highway from Dunedin to the Forth crossing had encouraged the fire to turn to one side, helped by the slight change of wind.

There, the forest was not so thick, and lay close to the bank that sloped down to the bogs by the riverside. Had the disengagement happened in any other way, it would have been worth sending all his army, Normans included, crashing through the trees to clean them out while the fighting-power was still in them and Siward's troops were disorganised by the sudden descent of the cavalry. Siward himself must have wondered why he abstained. The way the battle was going, another half-hour would have seen the Northumbrian army beaten to shreds.

The heaps of dead reclaimed his interest. They were out of range, most of them, of the forest. He shouted back to the man who had spoken to him, 'Are you tired of fighting? Reinforcements are coming. The Northumbrians will keep till they get here.' To the trumpeter, he said, 'I want the dead on both sides counted quickly. Find Prior Eochaid. I saw him a moment ago. And get him to take out a party.'

He had reached the white standard, with Bishop Jon standing, arms folded, beside it. Bishop Jon looked at Tuathal, and Tuathal answered the look without speaking. There was no point in appearing to notice. Alba was empty enough of men to govern and serve, without throwing them away to no purpose. Thorfinn said, 'Is there more news from Scandlain?'

Scandlain was the chief of his mounted body of couriers and signalmen. Scandlain could get a simple message from one end of Fife to the other in a matter of minutes. For greater detail, they would have to rely on a chain of fast horses aided by signals, and no one could expect miracles. But sometimes Scandlain could achieve them. And the messengers would come all the time.

Bishop Jon said, 'Report says that Killer-Bardi's flotilla had locked horns with Siward's when your new fleet made its appearance over the ocean and changed course at once to join your ten ships from Orkney, with what sad effect on Siward's ships is not yet clearly known. Does that man not have a Christian name?'

'Killer-Bardi?' said Thorfinn. 'He's called Lawrence. It doesn't suit him.'

'Oh, you're elated,' said Bishop Jon. 'I'm sure I don't know for what act of yours the Deity has seen fit to bless us with mounted Normans, and shiploads of mercenaries, and woods that burn in a trice, but you must have dropped a word somewhere that commended itself.'

'We declared a trading-peace, heaven and I,' said Thorfinn. 'I saw Mael-Isu. Whom else have we lost?'

'Gillecrist of Strathclyde is dead,' said the Bishop. 'And Morgund and Gillocher have had a *minutio*, but nothing serious. You've lost a ring or two of your curtain, I see. You'll be stiff tomorrow. Is your helmet not frying you?'

'It is,' said Thorfinn. 'But it's also identifying me. I'll walk through and tell them what's happening. Tuathal, they can eat, but serve the ale as if every pint of it cost you a toenail. The standard can go back in its socket. Bishop, you and Hrolf and the physicians ought to be busy. Eat in relays.'

'And you, my lord?' said Tuathal. Eochaid, approaching behind, looked drawn, but did not walk as if hurt. There was a splash of blood on the roof of the Brecbennoch.

Thorfinn said, 'The venison of the Naas, the fish of the Boyne and the cresses of the Brosna are the due of the High King, but devil a man of you will have stirred himself over it. How many?'

'Seventy of ours, and over four hundred of my lord Siward's,' said Eochaid. 'But you have lost two mormaers.'

Odin the Leveller. 'We shall not need to use that formation again,' Thorfinn said, and saw that the forest was quiet and the scouts had nothing to disturb them before turning to walk to his men.

They had heard the news of the new fleet already. They were high-hearted and noisy with success; bright-eyed still with the plunge through the wedges, that excited crash of the cavalry ringing in their ears. They were warm under the sun and full of vigour hardly drained in the short battle and soon flooding back. They wanted to drink, failing a quick thrash with a woman, and then tumble back into the field and race shouting into the forest to make the kill of which they had been unkindly baulked. Thorfinn could hardly get a hearing, at first, for the shouting. He simply stood still saying nothing until the cries died away, and then told them what they were waiting for, and that he expected little more fighting.

Someone shouted, 'But there's booty in that forest that hasn't been burnt. And it was us that did the fighting.'

'Then see that you are there,' Thorfinn said, 'when the booty is shared at the standard-pole. The mercenaries fight for their hire; and I fight for Alba. Are you satisfied?'

They cheered him and themselves, and discovered, at the uncovering of the food, how hungry they were. He saw that they kept in their lines, with their helms and weapons in reach, and went back to the awning his servants had raised with a bench under it, and some saddles. Their shields, reversed, served as boards on light trestles. Klakkr, he saw, had brought out a second shield, also silver on white, and was already cleaning his sword. He took off his helmet, his sweating brow cold in the air, and wondered who was lying outside the pavilion, wrapped in wool cloaking. Then he saw the broken string of a relic-bag and realised it was Mael-Isu of Deer.

He ignored it. The secret of a long day of battle was fitting the components together: the state of caution; the state of preparedness; the state of uncaring action; the state of elation; the state of waiting; so that each stage matched the others in sureness and strength, with every thread of body and mind strung to its finest pitch ready to sing to the touch, from one night's sleep until the next, or until death itself.

So he did not wish greatly to eat, although he did, and he kept the same singing pitch running through his being as he talked quietly with Tuathal and Eochaid and the others about what was to be done; which meant what Siward would do.

What a man like Siward would do, who was hiding a second time in a forest and had blown the withdrawal within minutes of the Normans' arrival.

'You would almost think he had heard the news as well,' said Morgund of Moray, who had a round red bruise from a spear-butt in the middle of his forehead and had blunted his axe on six men.

'Could they have learned it from us?' Thorfinn said.

Tuathal said, 'If you mean, did any of our Fife men defect, then the answer is yes, but I killed them both. We were opposite Malduin. He said his prayers aloud all through the fighting, but no one from our side ever got near him.'

'More's the pity,' said Malpedar. 'And the Angus men, I can tell you, were too busy to do more than yell insults at the other Angus men. In any case, if Siward knew fresh forces were coming, you'd expect him either to gather his forces and try to reverse the battle quickly, or to muster them in the forest and get away before the rest of the enemy could arrive.'

'He hasn't done that,' Thorfinn said. 'And wasn't even trying to when I posted the Normans behind him. When is the next message due? Whoever brings it—Ferteth?—see that the messenger reaches me without having to walk through the camp. I should like to know this time before the horse-boys do.'

It was unfair, because last time he had been in the thick of the fighting when the message came, and Tuathal had fought to be beside him. It was unfair, but that was the least of it.

The next messenger was Scandlain himself once again, and he was seeking to avoid the encampment even before Ferteth arrived to conduct him. Nor would he say anything at all until he was before Thorfinn under the awning.

So Thorfinn gathered from Ferteth. To Scandlain he said, 'Sit. There is some ale. The six of us here will all attend to your news, but you will tell it with your back to the men, and you will not expect to read what we think on our faces. What have you to say?'

'You speak as if you knew,' Scandlain said.

Under the awning, it was very quiet. The fringe flapped in the little wind, and eddies from over the field brought the resinous warmth of the dying fires and another powdering of silvery ash mixed with charcoal. It had settled already on the mounds still lying heaped on the field, white as quicklime; flesh not yet cold and consigned already to ashes; bone, juice, and fibre still consuming its fuel, deflating from its last action; sponging off the last image and led already to dust.

'The fleet from Denmark?' said Thorfinn.

'The fleet from Denmark,' agreed the signalman. 'Twenty-five ships. I told you, my lord. It appeared in the estuary. Your old ships, my lord King, were already engaged with the ships of Earl Siward and getting much the best of it. Two of the Northumbrian ships were on fire, and one broken-masted and drifting. The other three turned to fly up the estuary, which was stupid, as the tide was against them and they lost the wind.

'My man could hear from his hilltop the cheering from the Orkney ships, my lord, as the twenty-five new ships sailed into view. Dragons they are, with twenty-five thwarts apiece and maybe seventy-five men packed between the gunwales. Fighting-ships, as you ordered. They identified your ten ships right away and cheered back. The leading ship raised a raven flag to the masthead, and Killer-Bardi ran up another. It was like boys from a priest-school on a feast day, my man reported.'

'And then?' Thorfinn said. Under the heated steel rings and leather, his shirt was wet enough to wring water out of, and his skin shivered with cold.

'The twenty-five ships from Denmark got up to the Orkney ships,' the signalman said, 'and surrounded them. The men in them were mercenaries, maybe Swedish: at any rate, they spoke the same language, you could see. They were shouting over the sides as the ships came up close, exchanging nonsense and laughing.'

'And then?' Thorfinn said.

'And then, my lord King,' Scandlain said, 'every man in the dragon-ships jumped to his feet with a spear in his hand and cast the spear through the heart of a man in the Orkney ship next to him, and, after that, threw aboard grappling-irons. Then they followed the irons and boarded, axes in their hands, and more spears, and killed every man on the ships, but for two that broke away and fled north.

'Then the twenty-five ships from Denmark sailed over to Siward's ships and took aboard the men from the wrecked ships, and greeted the ones on the three ships that were not damaged, and, led by the three ships, set sail across the mouth of the estuary.

'Twelve ships, led by one of Earl Siward's unloaded nearly a thousand men at the mouth of the river Leven and then turned and sailed out. Thirteen ships, led by two of Earl Siward's, continued north past the estuary and were last seen setting round for the mouth of the Tay.

'All twenty-five ships have broken out my lord Siward's colours. No other banner is flying. Killer-Bardi is dead. While you sit here, my lord King, pinned by Siward, foreigners in Siward's hire are invading the heart of the kingdom.'

No one spoke. Then Bishop Hrolf of the stentorian voice cried in a whisper, '*Mo dê brot!* And where is the Lady?'

'On the Tay,' Thorfinn said. 'At Dunkeld.'

SEVEN

SVEIN OF DENMARK had betrayed him with Siward. Why, was for later.

This was not only vengeance for a lost son, but an invasion.

Not an invasion by Denmark, or five hundred ships would have arrived. An attempt, therefore, by Siward to possess not only Lothian but a divided Alba itself. With England's blessing, but without England's material support.

Without, it seemed, Thor of Allerdale. (But Gillecrist, who might have advised him about that, was dead.) And without, it seemed, his nephew Malcolm to tinge the conquest with legality. But perhaps Malcolm had refused to come.

Lacking ships, the Forth crossing here was the only sure access to Perth and Scone and Dunkeld, Forteviot, Glamis, and Forfar. For those who were sea-borne, the river Tay led, a royal highroad, to them all.

An invading army would find no resistance. Two watch-vessels at the mouth of the estuary who would fly, if they were wise. Fifty men left as insurance at Forteviot.

Having taken his strongholds, his wife, and his wealth, such an army had only to march thirty miles south to trap him here, with two thousand enemy mercenaries at his back and Siward before him, triumphant.

Siward, who had done his best to delay. Who had fought only when driven to it, and withdrawn as soon as he could. For whom the news of his ships, far from mortifying, must have signalled the approach of the far greater fleet he was awaiting. For he would know, as the nine men watching him knew, that unless Thorfinn defended the Tay, he was lost. With part of his army or with all his army, Thorfinn had to withdraw.

It crossed his mind that an hour earlier, receiving this news, he could have cut off Siward's escape from the field and forced him to finish the battle. Instead of seventy dead, it might have cost him five hundred, a thousand, to destroy Siward's army so that it could neither attack him nor follow him.

But then he could have turned north to the Tay in safety. With a tired army. But with an army twice the size of the one awaiting him.

One hour. So small a margin.

He wondered how long he had been silent. A short time only, for no one had spoken. He said, 'All right. Over nine hundred have landed at Leven-mouth. Any horses?'

'None,' Scandlain said.

'You're sure?'

'My man was quite sure.'

'And how long ago? Two hours? Tuathal, how many garrons could they pick up in Fife?'

Gillocher broke in. 'None. Fife is empty. We have all the garrons at Dunblane.' His voice shook a little.

Thorfinn said, 'Empty? This army will pass through Markinch and Scoonie. How many garrons could Malduin's friends hide? A hundred?'

'Not much more,' said Tuathal. 'But I see. If some of the nine hundred got horses, they could ride north ahead of the foot and meet the fleet as it came into the Tay, in time to protect the main landings.'

'If they have horses,' Thorfinn said, 'they'll be at the Ochils by now, and at Tayside with two hours to spare before the fleet gets into the river. They may take Abernethy, or leave it for their foot. They would certainly have time to get to the river Almond and cut off any interference from the garrisons there at Perth and at Scone, even if they can't overwhelm them. They'll probably try to do the same at Forteviot. It's on the way here.

'A courier, then, to Forteviot, Scandlain. Of the fifty men at arms there, thirty to get inside Scone, ten to Perth, and the rest to stay with the household. No fighting on the way. No sallies once they get there. Just hold these three strongholds until they are rescued. And the scout to return and tell us what he can find. Two—another man to go quickly and quietly round the burning part of the forest with word for the Normans. My lord Osbern to come here immediately. The rest to round up all the horses they can find and bring them back here, unseen if they can. I take it the signals are lit?'

'Yes. Tayside knows trouble is coming. My lord,' said Scandlain, 'I don't know if any courier can get to Forteviot before mounted men from the Leven.'

'I do. He can. And you and he will win this day for us,' Thorfinn said. 'Quickly . . .'

He watched Scandlain go. The courier might even do it. The mercenaries had to get hold of their horses somewhere in Fife, and there were always distractions. Bishop Hrolf said, 'I've lost count. How many landing on Tay?'

'Thirteen longships, including two guide-ships of Siward's? About eleven hundred fresh men,' Thorfinn said. 'They'll come on the flood past Earn-mouth but not any further: the banks are too conveniently close for assailants, and we trust there will be assailants. They must, clearly, try to take the main citadels, and especially Scone. Then they should turn south past Forteviot and march against us. By that time, the rest of the army landed at Leven should have reached Tayside by foot and joined with them. A total of two hundred foot and a hundred horse in possession of all central Alba by nightfall, and ready to march south and fall on us tomorrow morning.'

Ferteth said, 'We could thrash Siward by then.'

'We could at a price,' Thorfinn said. 'We began evenly matched. His losses are small. If we fight now, it will be a fight to a standstill and, no matter who wins, the slaughter will be crippling. If we killed every Northumbrian, we should still have fresh troops coming against us, and Scone and Perth would have fallen.'

He drew a long breath, keeping it clear, keeping it steady, keeping it low. 'We can't afford to wait and let the northern army join with Siward. We can't afford to run north. We couldn't outdistance Siward. We should have to fight all the way, and arrive too late to save anything. We have to split our force and deal with both invasions. Remember, the one in the north is arriving in stages, beginning with a small group of horsemen from Leven who will be unsupported for at least two hours after they have arrived at the Tay. And we have five hundred horses in the lines over the bridge here.'

'If you detached five hundred men now and sent them north? What could they do?' said Malpedar.

'No: I see,' said Eochaid. 'They might get rid of the Leven men, for a start, and help the places already being attacked. And once the ships came, they could hinder the disembarkation and delay the eleven hundred in their march, wherever they may be making for. From Earnmouth to the Almond is eight miles. To Forteviot, ten. I should like to go with them, if I may.'

The Prior got up. He had wiped the blood from the reliquary and only a little remained, stuck in the filigree of its thick little roof-disc. Back in Scone were the embroidered vestments, the golden book-shrines and chalices, the great painted gospels which could be replaced one day, precious though they were. Back in Scone were the monks, Eochaid's family. And the Stone of Inauguration, upon which the Kings of Alba were enthroned. And the long, jewelled box containing the rod, without roses or leaves, that was the wand of his kingship.

Of all of these, Eochaid was the guardian. Thorfinn said, 'You and Ferteth and Cormac will go, with five hundred Strathearn men. In a moment, I shall tell you how.'

Cormac of Atholl said, 'Can you beat Siward with five hundred men gone?'

Thorfinn said, 'I think we can beat him with two thousand gone, provided the Normans remain. We shall have to. You and your horsemen will be facing four times your numbers by the time the foot-army from Leven has joined up with the eleven hundred from the ships. But less than three hours after that, fifteen hundred footsoldiers of ours could be there, provided they start within the next half-hour.'

Cormac said, 'They'll arrive having marched thirty miles.'

'The Leven army will have come just as far. The ship-borne army will have had five hours of marching and fighting. With your help, and that of the Forteviot men, the main citadels may still be standing. And with what we have left here, we can stop Siward's army from joining the others.'

Tuathal said, 'We shall only have two-thirds of Siward's force. Less. But we can certainly hold them up.'

'Don't you see?' said Bishop Jon. 'They'll want to be held up. The longer he thinks he's pinning us all down here, the better chance, surely, Siward thinks he is giving the fleet to take Perth and Scone. Cormac, O hound of feats, you'll have to steal those horsemen away the equal of an army of angels for silence.'

'About that,' said Thorfinn, 'I shall have something to tell you. Then I shall speak to the men. Then we shall move. There is no time to say what should be said. But this is a matter for concern, not a matter for despair. Siward is fighting from greed, whereas we fight for our homes. We will win.'

He had not mentioned Dunkeld. No one had mentioned Dunkeld. Dunkeld, which would be attacked: nothing surer. But, first, Scone and Perth had to fall. And twelve river-miles and three hours of marching lay between Scone and Dunkeld, Crinan's monastery, Cormac's monastery. Where Groa was.

'Bottom pudding!' said Siward of Northumbria. 'Do all the cooks come from Bamburgh? Take it to Ligulf and bring me some meat. What d'you see?'

Forne of Skirpenbeck took away the bowl, although that was not his business, and came back with a leg of pork, the burnt seaweed still sticking to it. He said, 'They've got the news, on the other side. Bishop Aethelric saw the King addressing the army, and some sort of movement is starting.'

'Is it, by God!' Siward said. He got up, taking the meat, and, setting his teeth in it, walked to the edge of the forest. His cheek-hairs moved as he chewed, and his beard glistened with fat.

He swallowed. 'Aye. They're trying to cover it, but they're mustering. They're withdrawing men to go north. But how many? What would you do if you were Thorfinn?'

'Retire to Orkney with my red-haired wife and forget about Alba,' said Ligulf, strolling up. 'He's withdrawing a lot. Look at that. Mind you, I've seen better-managed secret dispersals.'

Forne said suddenly, '*Is* he withdrawing a lot? Look more closely.'

Everyone peered. The two Maldredssons came up, and the fool Malduin, who had, however, made all this possible. Siward said, 'I can see the Normans already in line, and a lot of foot behind the banners and awnings.'

'A lot of foot, with a lot of spaces between,' Forne said. 'It looks a good many at first glance, but I doubt if there are five hundred men there ready to leave. Could Thorfinn be tricking us?'

'Could Thorfinn be a Norseman?' said Ligulf. 'If you think half his army has withdrawn, you're going to attack him, aren't you? And what a shock you're going to get when you find his full army there, all but a hundred or two.'

'Hence the apparent poor cover. He's right,' said Forne. 'The scouts say it looks at first glance as if thousands are leaving. It's only five hundred. We shouldn't attack.'

'Of course we shouldn't attack,' said Siward. 'So long as you give me something better than bottom pudding, I'm willing to sit here till nightfall if need be.'

'He'll try to provoke you,' said Forne.

'Personally, it seems,' Ligulf said. 'He's coming himself, a bishop on either side, to address you from mid-field. Or no. Before mid-field and out of bowshot, more's the pity. I can't quite hear him, but the gutturals sound very insulting. He seems to be speaking Norse.'

He was speaking Norse, and it was more than insulting. Earl Siward's tunic creaked with the force of his breathing. Thorfinn had not even troubled to wear his helmet. On either side of the black ridge of his brow, the soot-black plaits were looped, Viking-style, under the leather band of the *hlaŏ*, confining his hair in case his head became bared in battle. His father had been killed in the Brian war when his helmet-buckle had been slashed apart.

He was still speaking. Siward jerked his head, and a hail of arrows and javelins sped rustling from the forest on either side of him and thudded, in sufficient reply, into the ground between himself and Kalv's nephew by marriage, who had won a kingdom and thought he was no one's vassal yet.

The King waited a moment and then turned back, his bishops following. Earl Siward made a joke that was barely repeatable, even when changed into Anglo-Saxon, and pushed past Bishop Malduin into the forest, laughing and biting into his pork. It would be entertaining to see what the fellow would try to do next. It would teach him. It would teach him to strut about Lothian and Cumbria, treating Siward like some English underling.

He needed a lesson for that. For the death of Osbern his son, he needed another lesson, which he would receive also.

The next hour was, of course, highly unpleasant. Although there was no question of rising to it, the means of provocation were ingenious. Shield-hung hurdles were brought out into the field, and bowmen and slingshot-throwers behind them began to shred the trees with a descending curtain of missiles. He had to put archers and javelin-throwers of his own up all the climbable trees before he had them on the run, and lost a dozen men to no purpose.

The heat and the gnats were the next burden. As the sun rose into clear skies and burned down on the plain of the Forth, you would say the exposed army opposite would have the worst of it, despite their shields and their awnings.

But there in the open air they escaped the shimmering body of heat from the blaze on the other side of the highway. And since the wind changed, the smoke, once so unwelcome, had drifted north-east; and the armed hosts native to the wood had arrived in their thousands to attack the armed host that was not.

The army became restive. The army wanted to get out of the trees. The army wanted to slake its thirst and, rightly, was not prepared to believe their Earl when he quoted the number of ale-casks destroyed in the fire. A group of men who had come with Leofnoth found a broached cask and began to drag it out of the rear of the wood, and Siward had three of them hanged. He noticed that someone had moved the few horses they had managed to round up, and sent two men to find out where they had been taken. A shout from the front of the wood called him back to the edge of the field, where men were watching a group of the enemy busy with spades on the high ground to his left, near the wood where they stationed the Normans. Supervising the diggers was a large man he recognised as the Irish-Scandinavian bishop from Saxony whose name be believed to be Hrolf.

Forne said, 'They're diverting the stream to come through the wood.'

'Then shake your fist at them,' said Earl Siward, slapping his neck. 'For, by God, they don't know it, but they couldn't do us a better service. I'd send out and help them if it wouldn't spoil everything.'

It was only a little after that, and before the damming had got very much further, that Ligulf said, 'Siward?'

The Earl of Northumbria objected to the way Ligulf addressed him. He said, 'Well?'

'Send a man up to look at that part of the army,' Ligulf said. 'Is it as thick on the ground as it was?'

His best climber was standing by. Earl Siward snapped his fingers, and the man darted off. Siward said, 'Where? I see. They've shifted them.'

'Where to?' said Ligulf. 'Look along the line.'

'It looks the same to me,' Siward said. 'The banners are all there.'

'They would be,' said Ligulf. 'Here's your man.'

'Well?' said Siward. *Could Thorfinn be tricking us? Could Thorfinn be a Norseman?*

'My lord Earl,' said the climber. His chest was heaving. 'The men on the right wing and the men on the left have lost half the ranks behind them, although they're spread out and from the front it looks just the same. My lord, fifteen hundred men must have gone.'

'*What?*' said Siward of Northumbria.

'What a pity,' said Ligulf his brother-in-law. 'And we have wasted all this time resisting provocation, which was just what they wanted. But now, my dear Siward, I think the time has come to be provoked.'

'God blind him!' Siward said. 'Is Thorfinn still there?'

'Yes, my lord. I could see his helmet,' said the scout.

Fifteen hundred men on their way to the Tay. No, two thousand altogether, including the horsemen who had already left. But fifteen hundred whom he had time to catch, provided he finished this business quickly. Against him, after all, was a force now only two-thirds of his in size, and lacking the Normans.

He said, 'Prepare the men to give battle. To form up as before, but this time quietly. This time we shall surprise them. This time, they will not dream that we are coming until they hear the trumpet and see us marching upon them. In half an hour we shall be riding north, victors.'

In the event, however, the victorious half-hour expired and Siward of Northumbria was not even aware of it. For the army of Alba, it seemed, was not at all unprepared for the sudden emergence of the enemy from the wood and only waited politely, as before, for the troublesome stream to be crossed, together with a number of novel earthworks of Bishop Hrolf's devising, before throwing itself in neat but different formation against Siward's lines.

In the van, as before, flashed the white-and-gold helmet of Thorfinn, towards which Siward spent all his great strength in fighting. It was with anger and astonishment, therefore, that he found, confronting that royal figure at last, that the face under the helmet was the minatory one of Bishop Hrolf.

He would have had no hesitation in sending the Bishop back to Saxony by celestial transport, save that at that moment the Normans emerged again from the wood.

He had seen them leave with his own eyes. Ligulf had seen them, too. It was all Ligulf's fault.

The half-hour went by, but neither army, killing and being killed, was aware of it.

Under the same sun, Thorfinn of Orkney and Alba had crossed the river and was riding north with a handful of men and a fresh horse collected, with all else he required, at Dunblane. He led them round the range of the Ochils and swept through the strath down which the river Allan poured on its way to the Forth far behind him. In due course, he would meet with the Earn, flowing north and east in the opposite direction to add its waters to those of the Tay eight miles east of Scone.

Also behind him were fifteen hundred of his own men on foot, with Bishop Jon leading them.

Ahead, it was easy to see where Eochaid and the five hundred horsemen had already passed, leaving churned earth and dung on either side of the cart-wide stones of the road. All the steadings the King went by were empty, although hearth-fires still burned; and there was no one at the little monastery of Dunning. Eochaid would have taken the monks with him for safety, and those of Muthill as well. Or perhaps they had gone with their people to comfort them.

Then, just short of his hall at Forteviot, the King came across the first group of injured. Not men-at-arms, but a lad of eleven and another not much older, supporting an elderly man. He stopped.

They recognised him, or perhaps the gold band round his helmet. The man sank to his knees, but the boys were too excited to care. A group of thirty horsemen had come against Forteviot from the east an hour before, and had tried to set fire to it with burning arrows, and strike down the defenders with slingshot and spears. They were getting the best of it, too, for there were only serving-people left and a few armed men, since the rest went off north with the courier. But then my lord Prior of Scone had appeared like a miracle, with a great army behind him, and had killed every horseman. You could see them for yourself, past the next bit of wood. And they had been asked if they wanted to stay in the fort, since more soldiers had now been put into it, but they thought, since they couldn't fight, they would rather go and hide with their people.

Tuathal dismounted and helped the man up, and the King himself bent over and spoke to him, for that was all there was time to do. Then he spurred on to Forteviot. Men would always fight for Eochaid, and Ferteth and Cormac of course were their Mormaers. Men, it seemed, were ready to fight for himself, as well.

At Forteviot, he went no further than the gateway to pick up more news. More than a hundred enemy horsemen had arrived from the Levenmouth landing two hours before noon. Thirty had cut through Glen Farg straight to Forteviot. The rest had overrun Abernethy and crossed the Earn higher up, by the last ford before it flowed into the Tay.

There the intruders had divided. Fifty had continued upriver, on a course that would take them to Perth and to Scone opposite. Fifty had remained where they were, on the Tayside meadows called Rhind, where the estuary narrowed to river.

'So that is where the landings will be. What look-outs do we have?'

'Plenty on the north side of Tay, my lord. I doubt we'll have lost our man on Moncrieffe Hill.'

'We'll put another there. And Prior Eochaid?'

'Has gone to Scone, my lord, with fifty horsemen. He said that was all he would need. My lords of Strathearn and of Atholl have taken the rest of the horses to Rhind. It'll be four hundred and fifty of them against the fifty enemy horse waiting there, and easy enough, you would think. But they say there's a fleet coming upriver, and it may get to Rhind before they do.'

'It won't,' said Thorfinn. 'And, in any case, there are fifteen hundred men marching behind me. Can you hold out until they get here?'

'Of course, my lord King,' said the captain of Forteviot. 'They'll have this hall only when we are all dead.'

The words followed Thorfinn as he flung his horse away from the gates. Confidence was a great thing. Under that roof, Erlend had been born. Behind him, Tuathal's fractured voice said, '*Marching behind us?* They can't get here for five hours.'

'Oh, they might manage it quicker,' Thorfinn said. 'If Siward is chasing them.'

Tuathal said, 'I don't suppose you mean that, but I'd prefer not to have heard it.'

'Save your breath,' said Thorfinn. 'And start to think how best to welcome fifteen enemy ships who want to offload an army.'

The longships were beautiful, and worth all he had paid King Svein of Denmark. The only thing wrong with them was that they flew the Northumbrian flag, and not his.

They were already in sight when Thorfinn with Tuathal behind him rounded Moncrieffe Hill and dashed into the flat plain of Rhind, where the Earn joined the Tay. Distant in the big river, the line of vessels threaded the sandbanks, the sinuous pattern of poles moving past the green northern slopes of the estuary. Their wells were crammed with cone helmets and glittered with shield-hoops and the faggoted filaments that were spears. They looked like vessels infested with hornets.

In front of the King, the marshes and mud-flats of Earnbank were already filled with struggling men as his own dismounted vanguard disposed of the last of the fifty intruders from the Forth landing. He sent someone to round up loose horses and looked for Cormac and Ferteth. Knots of horsemen, as far as the eye could see, were moving along the banks of the Tay, firing the jetties that were not already broken, and two ferry boats crowded with men were in midstream on the Tay, hazed with smoke as they struck tinder into their torches.

Cormac appeared and said, 'These horsemen were Swedish. Some Northumbrians and three Fife men. They're all dead. I can only get forty over the river before the ships come, and they won't have horses.'

'They may discourage a landing on the north shore,' Thorfinn said. There were bits of cornland and thatched buildings all over the firmer ground and the slopes of the hill behind him, some of them fired by the early arrivals but many intact. He said, 'There's cover. Let's get the horsemen out of sight. And the bodies. They'll want to land on this side anyway. It's where they'll be expecting the Levenmouth army to arrive in two or three hours to support them. They may not even know of the bogs.'

'Ghilander and Fothaid are with them. They do,' said Cormac; and plunged off, shouting orders.

Ferteth at his elbow said, 'I heard. I told the men along the banks not to come back, but stay to harry the march between the hill and the river. They'll hide.'

Thorfinn said, 'If the landings take place on the north side, they'll have to look for more boats upriver and get themselves across till we can come.'

'I'll tell them,' said Ferteth.

'No. Send someone. I need you,' Thorfinn said. 'It's here, as they land, that we'll need all the ingenuity we can get.'

It was hardly past noon and in a few moments eleven hundred fresh fighting-men would be stepping ashore. Against them were five hundred men, less the fifty Eochaid had taken to Scone. Men who, since sunrise this morning, had fought in Siward's first battle and had ridden thirty miles and more to arrive here, with two further skirmishes.

They looked, as he felt, high-hearted and tireless. It would not last. But it was another moment, another gift from life, to put with the others.

He had orders to give, and he gave them, swiftly making his rounds, and was ready when the first dragon-ship turned its baleful golden jaws to the land and ran towards him.

The dragon-ships had been promised no opposition.

They had expected some throwing of stones and worse from whatever straggle of peasants ventured down from the hills to the banks, and that they received. They were not even disturbed by the burning jetties, or the waiting batons of flame and black smoke that fenced the narrowing river beyond them. They did not intend rowing so far. Where they would land on the southern bank of the Tay was a spit of fine, shoaling sand lifting to watery meadows. Longship keels had no need of jetties, except to unload dry-shod merchants and unwieldy cargo. The springing swan-bows, neck by neck, would slide homing into the sand-flats like silk.

They were surprised to see leather helmets and the glitter of ranked steel among the rock-throwing denizens of the north bank and to receive several arrows, harmless in the teeth of the wind, as they began to swing round to the south shore to accomplish their landing. Bows and arrows being the staple of every river vessel's equipment, their archers shot back, with the wind, and had the satisfaction of seeing a few men and youngsters impaled.

On the south bank, on the other hand, all was as it should be. Drawn up waiting for them were their friends: the men landed early that morning by their companion ships at the mouth of the Leven. The helmets and the shields were the same: they had designs you could hardly forget if you wanted to. And some of them were already quelling the fires on the landing-stages.

The men on the shore cheered, shaking their swords and their spears, and the men on board the two leading ships cheered as well, as the seamen leaned forward, swinging the seventeen-foot oars for the stroke that would lift the prows safely home to their beaching.

A valance of stones appeared in mid-air and fell, knocking oar blades and oarsmen.

A fringe of arrows, whistling, followed it, thudding into wood, flesh, and leather. Men screamed. The leading longships, interrupted in mid-stroke, swung helplessly, half on and half off the shore-bank and fouling the ship close behind them. Archers and men-at-arms, knocked off balance, thrust and twisted and swore in both ships. In their sterns, men jolted over the gunwales found themselves swept away, sinking in midstream. Off the prows, the first man to jump knee-deep into the water clutching a mooring-rope met three feet of good German steel.

The fifty men on the shore, whose shields were not now familiar at all, were in the water before anyone else, and started boarding. Following them was another double line of fifty, risen from nowhere. And then more and more, running from all directions. And there all the time, a line of kneeling archers, letting fly from behind their ranked shields.

Each ship carried seventy-five men, closely packed, with little room to swing sword or axe against roaring trolls high on the gunwales, who walked on men as on a highway and brought steel, thick and thin, hissing down, cleaving and searing. The fighting groups overbalanced into the shallower water and continued struggling there, ignoring the arrows beginning to fall from the following ships of the line, swinging up, oars flashing to fill the breadth of the river. The fighting spread from the two helpless ships to the third rammed behind them, now cramped fast with a grappling-iron and rocking with incomers from the two dying vessels ahead.

A trumpet blew on the land. A fourth and fifth longship, shipping oars, slid to the rear of the third and locked, pouring fresh men over its stern. The dragon-ships of midstream, abandoning the dead in the first and the second, thrust forward and, turning rapidly in, ran up on shore further upriver and began to land men fast, under a renewed fall of arrows. On the bank, the

trumpet twittered again, and the water became full of spray and hurtling bodies as shoremen left their attack and threw themselves back on
the sand.

Some of them, racing in from the river, met and clashed with running
parties of mercenaries, cutting straight from their landings to intercept.

Horns from the fleet drew back the mercenaries. To shouted commands,
they threw up their shields and ran to take up defensive formation. Soon,
behind a barricade of shields and of steel, the helpless ships were drawn off,
and the rest of the crippled fleet began to come in, two by two, and make their
proper landings.

The misleading welcoming party with its treacherous shields had quite
vanished, but for the dead and the wounded in the three leading ships and on
shore. As the disembarked men were being lined up to march, a detail of
mercenaries went from heap to heap, spitting those who still lived and
removing what valuables they could discover.

It was when, on their leader's orders, they went to search the huts and
hovels and woods beside and ahead of them to find signs of retreat or of
ambush that the news they brought back seemed to unsettle their leader and
the noblemen from Northumbria and from Fife whom he conferred with.

Indeed, he gave the Northumbrians a taste of his temper.

'Four hundred horses,' he said. 'My men say there are traces of at least four
hundred horses. The men who attacked us just now all have mounts.

'They will not, therefore, have retreated. They lie ahead, and since they can
travel at twice our pace, we may be sure that for all the length of our march we
shall be subject to ambush. I was not told, when we left, that I should have to
fight a running battle with four hundred horsemen. I was told that a band
from Levenmouth would be waiting, with a further support from the same
source in three hours. I was told that your Earl Siward had the army of Alba
immobilised in the south, and expected to overwhelm it. What has
happened?'

But the men from Northumbria and from Fife did not appear to know. And
so, black with anger, hot for revenge, the nine hundred invaders, who had
once been eleven hundred, marched, sword in hand, towards Scone.

A third of the way towards Scone and when the running fight with the
marching shipmen was at its hottest, the good news came to Thorfinn.
Eochaid and his fifty horsemen had overcome the special detachment from
Leven and were safely inside the monastery.

Two-thirds of the way towards Scone, Thorfinn withdrew what was left of
his horsemen and, leaving the damaged nine hundred to continue their march,
raced on to Scone himself, with all the men he had left.

He had sent word to Eochaid, and the gates opened. Around him in the
yard, his men made water anywhere and, long-throated, poured down the
mead and the ale and snatched bread and cheese while the monks clustered
over the wounded. Eochaid said, '*My lord!*'

'It's other men's blood,' Thorfinn said. He caught a towel and, dragging his helmet off, scoured his face and his neck. He said, 'They're three miles away; about eight hundred and fifty. Did you get horses?'

'Forty left of our own, and thirty of the besiegers'. They'll be fresher than yours.'

'Yes.' Thorfinn tipped the ale-jug into his open mouth, and his throat became his own again, and the rest of his body. He said, 'Give me the ten Forteviot men, mounted, and the best horses you have in exchange for our worst. That gives Cormac three hundred mobile men outside to harry them with, once the shipmen settle down to besiege you. Then the foot-army from Forth should be here to help you in about three hours from now. Do you want Ferteth to come in beside you?'

'You'll need him. You have your own Perth to guard, over the river. We can hold out for days. You know that,' said Eochaid. 'Is there any news from the Forth?'

'We know the fifteen hundred got away and are coming. Bishop Jon sent word. We don't know how Siward's battle went. We should have news any moment. Look. Arrows and throwing-spears. We pulled a handcart off one of the ships.'

'Keep the arrows,' Eochaid said. 'My flock aren't archers.'

Thorfinn had already noted that among the fighting-men and the monks and the household there were women, and boys with clubs in their grip, and old men with axes. Not everyone had taken shelter in the hill-forts. He said, 'They have been fighting beside us, too, all the way along.'

'You sound surprised,' said Eochaid. 'These are their brothers and sons who are riding with you. And don't you remember your home-coming from Rome? Do you think they don't care who protects them?'

There was nothing, it seemed, that he was able to say. Eochaid lifted his hands to his neck and began to unfasten the chain of the Brecbennoch. Behind them, men were hurrying and horses trampling and snorting as Ferteth and Cormac prepared to withdraw. Eochaid said, 'Why not take it? We have faith enough here. We shall save Scone if God wills it. And the invader will reach Dunkeld only over our bodies.'

The chain was warm. The little relic-house, five inches long, hung from his fist. Thorfinn said, 'It deserves better than I can give it. I shall take it to Tuathal.'

'Take?' said Eochaid. His fresh horse was waiting, with the King's saddle on it.

Thorfinn said, 'There are friends of Malduin's with the ship-army. Fothaid and Ghilander. We cut out a Fife man and made him tell us the plan for the men they dropped on the Forth. The foot-army from Levenmouth is coming up through Glen Farg and expects to cross the Earn at the nearest main ford and march to their friends here at Scone. They would double the numbers against you. They won't be allowed to. I've sent Tuathal with a hundred horse to catch them in the ravine at Glen Farg.'

'A hundred against nearly nine hundred?' said Eochaid.

'He won't stop them all. But he might hold the rest at the Earn until our fifteen hundred come up from the south.'

'And you are going to help him? Alone? There are still twenty Forteviot men here,' Eochaid said. 'And horses for them. Take them. I shall expect to see you back with your new army. You and Tuathal and Bishop Jon.'

'In this world, it is a possibility,' Thorfinn said.

It was time to mount. For the first time that day, he felt the ache of loss, and without real reason. He gave the only gift in his power and, removing his eyes from Eochaid's, dropped on one knee.

Eochaid's hand, still marked with ink, touched his hair, and he received Eochaid's blessing.

Then he rose quickly, and mounted, and turned his horse with his knees while he fastened his helmet and the Forteviot men collected behind him.

Then, without looking back, he left Scone.

It was seven miles to the river Earn ford. He crossed the Tay from Scone to his fort of Perth on the opposite side and transmitted encouragement, he hoped, to its captain. After that, he turned south, on a fresh horse, with twenty fresh men beside him and the afternoon sun hot on his right.

He had been fighting, one way or another, since just after noon. He had been fighting or riding since three hours after sunrise this morning. And there were six hours to get through before sunset.

The toisech among the men with him wanted to talk, and he was sharp with him, because he had to think. Later, he relented. To think was one thing. To shut his eyes as he rode was another.

Three and a half hours after noon, he was close enough to the Earn to hear the shouting and deduce that the army landed that morning at Levenmouth had completed its march northwards through Fife and even its struggle, harassed by Tuathal, through the defile of Glen Farg, and was now here, on one side or the other of the Earn crossing. Then, rounding a hill and thundering over the plain to the river with goat-dung flung from his hooves, and smashed heads of ripe barley, and mussel-shells, he was able to see what was happening.

Tuathal had crossed the Earn and was on this side, strung out with what remained of his hundred horsemen.

On the opposite side were the men who had marched up from Levenmouth. More than eight hundred mercenaries, but not in battle order. Or only those detailed to keep guard against any hint of attack from Tuathal's side of the river.

Behind, the remaining hundreds lay on the grass; or sat chewing, their satchels open beside them and their leather flasks between their dusty cloth knees. There seemed to be a lot of wounded. Tuathal had made a good job, then, of his ambush.

After that, of course, Tuathal had had to drop his attack and race to be first over the river, since he could not face eight times his number in the open plain between the Glen and the crossing. And the mercenary army, logically enough, had taken full advantage of the respite. Whether to care for their wounded or because the men had rebelled, tired from the long day's march and from the fight in the defile, they were being allowed to eat and to rest.

After all, they must expect to see very soon traces of the hundred of their number who had found garrons and arrived here before them. They would expect to learn of the success of the Tay landings, and to set off on the seven miles that would take them to the central strongholds of Alba, already besieged by their fellows.

Behind them lay Fife, tamed or docile or empty. Further south lay Lothian and the plains of the Forth, in the grip of Earl Siward's army. They would not expect the taking of Perth and Scone to be easy, and night would fall long before they could send back to clear out Abernethy and Forteviot, or before they could press on the further twelve miles to Dunkeld. There was time to rest. By their lights, it was sensible; even necessary.

It was an unheard-of stroke of good fortune. The longer they stayed, the more chance it gave Bishop Jon's army to arrive. The fifteen hundred men who had set off north from the Forth directly after the first struggle with Siward and who must be less than two hours away at this moment, marching up Strathallan by the way he had come himself, passing Dunblane and Forteviot.

Tuathal, spurring up to him, said, 'You see. We tired them out.'

The Prior had taken his helmet off. He looked the way all the Forth army looked now, with brown keel-marks under his eyes and his riddled skin beaten like metal. Then he asked, 'Eochaid?'

His eyes were on the casket. 'Triumphant in Scone,' Thorfinn said. He unclasped the chain and signed to the toisech, who was hovering, to lead his men to join the rest on the riverbank. The relic came free, and he held it out.

'You are to have it,' he said. 'I am merely the messenger. Scone is invested, but there are three hundred horsemen of mine in the neighbourhood to keep everyone unhappy. Have you heard from Bishop Jon?'

'No,' said Tuathal. 'I was hoping you had. Neither of my couriers came back.' He took the chain and held it. 'You should have this.'

'It will be safer with you,' Thorfinn said. 'You will fight harder, but I am the target. Anyway, I have my axe.'

Tuathal's sharp eyes relaxed. He said, 'What will we poor priests do when you conquer, against a double invasion and your own new fleet turned against you?'

Thorfinn put his horse in motion, walking beside Tuathal's down to where their own men waited on the riverbank. In relays, they, too, were resting. The wind brought the smell of sweat and horses and metal and beaten grass and sweet clover. Also, the sharp odour of food. He said, 'If we conquer. It depends on the south.'

He dismissed from his mind, because it was of no concern at this moment, the fate of the army he had left fighting Siward. He had weakened his own side by subtracting two thousand men. But he had left them the inestimable advantage of the eighty Normans on their strong horses.

Face to face, these two armies would have to fight one another to a standstill, for neither could afford to give way. He knew what the losses might be. He knew that Siward, finally, might have just enough extra power to prevail, upon which his men had their orders: to give way; to appear to fly; to cross the Forth somehow at the wide ford, having got rid of the bridge. And to stand at the ford as long as humanly possible, denying the Northumbrians the crossing until they were forced to give way.

By then, very likely, there would be nothing much of an organised army left on either side, and both sides would be exhausted. He would expect no man, having come through that, to set out to march thirty odd miles to the Tay, this side of nightfall. Equally, he was safe from any remnant of Siward's army on foot.

He had thought that perhaps Osbern or some of his friends still on horseback might have got through, provided the fighting was over. That none of them had could be a bad sign or a good.

Meantime, all that mattered were the fifteen hundred marching men who, however tired they might be, would still be able to save them. He said, 'Your couriers didn't come back. Send two more. Send two of the Forteviot men: they'll ride faster.'

He saw from the look that crossed Tuathal's face that he was understood, even before he himself tossed someone his reins and, dismounting, walked down through the men, rallying them; stopping to talk to the wounded; lifting from the food-baskets some bread and a piece of mutton in passing. The look that recognised, no matter what their hard fighting and their successes so far, that all the future hinged on the army they were now waiting for. And that if that army did not come, the invaders would very likely prevail.

Half an hour passed. He remembered it afterwards as the oddest part of the day. In the heat of the afternoon, both armies lay quiet, somnolent after the long hours of nervous exertion and the effects of the warmth and the food. Thorfinn sent Tuathal to sleep for ten minutes and, when he returned, dropped in his place on the bare earth of an old wattle barn, asleep before he stopped moving.

Seven miles off behind him, Eochaid and Ferteth and Cormac were fighting to save Perth and Scone from the army besieging them; and here, motionless under the sun, were a hundred men who could help them. Except that if they moved away, there would be nothing to hinder the army couched over the river from crossing and flinging their full weight against Scone before his own men from the south could arrive.

One made one's decisions and stood by them. And when there was a chance to rest, one did not waste it.

Tuathal wakened him just after four. 'The other side seem to be stirring. Ours are standing to arms.'

No courier had come from the south. However fast the army was marching, the Forteviot men would take an hour to reach them, and another hour to come back. Unless, of course, they met an incoming messenger on their way.

Patience.

He talked to Tuathal and then to the toisechs as he put on his mail shirt again and took up his helmet. The golden fillet and the richness of his dress and his harness were all he carried that would identify him, for his banner was on the Forth and his pennant had long since gone. But, with his height, it was enough. When he appeared, riding, and the sun flashed on the gold, his own men turned as they stood with their spears and called to him, '*Albanaid!*'

He raised his sword and answered them with the same word. It did not, now, bear the stamp of Duncan on it. Nothing did.

The men across the river marshalled themselves into lines and raised their banners.

'Cathail macDubhacon, fighting in Siward's hired army. May he go to hell with his pains, as he deserves,' said Prior Tuathal.

Thorfinn looked at the banner. 'Osbern had a favourite saying. *La laiterie ouverte rend les cats friaunds*. Alba, I agree, is not a dairy. But still, I should prefer Cathail and his friends captured, not killed.'

'You expect too much,' said Tuathal.

'I used the word *prefer*, not *expect*,' Thorfinn said. 'Why do you suppose they are moving like that? To try the next ford upriver?'

'There's no advantage in that,' Tuathal said. 'Our horse would get there before they do.'

Thorfinn said, 'They're not dividing their forces, either. But they might. Why don't we send half our force forward, parallel to theirs? We can soon send on the rest if we have to.'

The men, revived by their rest, were excited and restive. Leaving a toisech in charge, Thorfinn rode on with Tuathal and the advance group. After a moment, he said, 'They're striking away from the river, and south. It's Forteviot.'

'Can you be sure?' Tuathal said. He had put a sleeveless tunic over his shirt of mail, and the Brecbennoch clung to it, undisturbed by the pace of his horse.

'I can't be sure,' Thorfinn said. 'That's why they're doing it. If we gallop on and pack ourselves into Forteviot, they simply turn and race for Scone, crossing the river unhindered. If they turn all their power on Forteviot, we either have to do nothing or cross the river ourselves and give battle. We should not only lose, against eight times our numbers, but we might well tempt the Forteviot garrison to come out and rescue us, and the fort would be taken.'

Tuathal said, 'If Bishop Jon's army is near, this little force will walk straight into its arms. It can't be far off. It can't be far off.'

'Whistle up your other half, then,' Thorfinn said. 'All we can do is keep pace on this side until we see what will happen. By Forteviot, we can cross the Earn anywhere, if we have to. If Bishop Jon and his stout men arrive, as you say, we shan't have to.'

The other army, obscured now by scrub and by trees, continued to move gently south, nor, said the scouts, was there any diminishing of its numbers. Tuathal said, 'They're taking their time, aren't they?' and broke off.

'They were,' Thorfinn said. 'That was an order by trumpet, repeated twice. And that, my lord Prior, is a jog-trot. They're in a hurry now, all right. And they're still making south. So they haven't heard of Bishop Jon and his army. So if they run fast enough, they'll run into its jaws, and Bishop Jon can say a prayer over Cathail. Let's keep up with them.'

Behind him, the horses moved to a trot, and he could feel the wariness giving way to disbelief, and the disbelief to the first stirrings of a dazed expectancy.

Everyone knew they were riding towards Bishop Jon's army. And so was the enemy. Above the rustle and thud of the hooves, he could hear the voices of Tuathal's riders behind him calling to one another, quipping breathlessly, their voices still surprised. Without anything said, Tuathal turned in the saddle and held up a flat palm for silence.

Silence was not in fact necessary. But open jubilation or even jeering might be unwise. Perhaps this was merely a ruse to trick them into a crossing at Forteviot.

Perhaps it was not. In which case, the less the other army suspected, the better.

It seemed a wise edict, if a bit over-cautious. The band of riders obeyed it sufficiently. Battle-excitement was something no one would expect to extinguish. When, far in the distance, a familiar rider was seen approaching on their side of the river, and then behind him another, the wise edict found itself swept aside, and the men behind Thorfinn gave a snatched cheer, and then went on cheering.

The riders were the Forteviot men. The men sent south an hour ago to bring back news of Bishop Jon's army.

Tuathal said, 'It's too soon. They must have got news at Forteviot.'

And then, 'They're . . . O Mary, Mother of Christ. Keep them off.'

'Not now,' said Thorfinn.

It was too late. Whatever news the couriers had to tell, the men behind would have to hear it. They had stopped cheering and calling already and, instead of speeding, the sound of their hoof-beats had slackened.

The galloping men in the distance came closer.

White faces: cracked voices shouting. These were not the outriders of a large and powerful army sweeping to join them: an army visible, if they rode hard, in half an hour.

These were men unmarked by battle who screamed indistinguishable news as they rode, so that over the river and through the trees you could glimpse the turning masks of grinning enemy faces, while on this side of the river the King put up his hand and Tuathal and his men came to a halt.

Silence fell. The horses pawed, shaking their manes and switching tails, and harness jangled. Faced with that band of silent men, the two riders' headlong rush veered and slowed, and one of them dropped to a loiter. Everyone saw him slide suddenly from his horse and bend, retching and whistling, into the grass.

The other rider rode up and stopped.

The other rider said in a whisper, 'Save yourselves.' His eyes were fixed on Thorfinn.

Thorfinn said steadily, 'We will. Tell us what you know. Bishop Jon's army?'

'Cut to pieces. The Normans, too, that escaped Siward and joined them. Forteviot's burning. Do you see the smoke now? They do, over the water. They're going to strip the bodies and finish the killing. . . .

'It was the surprise, you see,' said the Forteviot man. 'Not the numbers, although there were enough of them. They were waiting at Ruthven Water. By St Cathán's church and the monks' houses. Bishop Jon and my lord of Riveire and the rest came marching up, suspecting nothing. My lords, save yourselves, there is nothing any man can do there.'

'Who was waiting at St Cathán's?' said Thorfinn. He put all the skills he had ever learned into the timbre of his voice.

The man drew a long breath and spoke clearly.

'A great army of men, my lord King, splendidly equipped with many banners, and two of them gilded. One was the flag of Thor of Allerdale. The other was the royal standard, they say, flown by my lord Malcolm, King Duncan's eldest son.'

He choked, and his chest leaped. 'My lord, the kingdom is lost.'

Thorfinn said, 'Fife is not Alba. Scone is Alba, which can be rescued. Dunkeld is Alba, which is still safe.'

'My lord!' said the Forteviot man. 'Dunkeld fell early this morning. Allerdale's army came from there. And a thousand men stayed, they were boasting, to level the church and the hall and the monastery and then leave to do the same to Scone and to Perth.

'My lord King, there is nowhere to go. Alba has fallen.'

EIGHT

unkeld fell early this morning.

To weep would solve nothing, or to fall into panic, or to obey the heave of the belly, the sudden gripe of the bowel, that came not only to messengers.

But above belly and bowel was a controlling head, and a tongue that could ask the other, necessary questions. Then Thorfinn turned to the swarm of stamping horses about him, and their sallow-faced riders.

'Any survivors of the battle at Ruthven Water would do best to lose themselves among the hills until I can call them again. You may wish to do the same. I don't know how far the south-west has risen for Allerdale, or Angus for Kineth, but Moray is safe, and the coast down to Salorch and further. There should be ships of mine waiting there, watching the English off Monifieth. If any of you reach them, have them wait. There will be other refugees like yourself. And if you reach Moray, by sea or by land, go to my stepson Lulach. He will tell you what to do.'

'And you, my lord?' said Tuathal. His marled face had not changed at all. Only the skin round his eyes was wet, as if from a cold wind.

Thorfinn said, 'I am going to Scone. You heard the report. The army at Dunkeld split in two. Half left early to come here. But the rest stayed to destroy and to plunder, and did not plan to march downriver till later. If they did not leave till three hours after noon, or even two, they won't have reached Scone as yet, or Perth.

'I am going to warn them. There are three hundred horsemen of ours there already, with Strathearn and Atholl. We'll put a gate of armed men across the Tay north of Scone and give them the kind of welcome we gave to the shipmen. Then we shall join Prior Eochaid in Scone. It is our sacred place, our shrine: the casket that holds the heart of this kingdom. I will not leave it. And besides, if Bishop Jon and our Norman friends know their business, it can stand a siege longer, perhaps, than Allerdale or King Duncan's son are prepared to give it. Does anyone want to come with me?'

Death and life are in the power of the tongue.

They followed him, every one, barring the man he forced to ride for the Tay to cross and reach the coast and his ships.

He did not close his eyes this time, thundering back north the seven miles he had come, with a hundred men more than twenty.

So boldly one spoke. The Normans were the best fortress-builders he knew, but Forteviot had fallen; Dunkeld had fallen. But Thor of Cumbria had not learned the lesson of the Hereford marches, and of Normandy. A strong fortress changing hands can pin down a region on behalf of its conquerors. A fortress destroyed is no use to them.

Malcolm must have been in Dunkeld, where his young brother was. That would, of course, be why Dunkeld had fallen. A mediocre nineteen-year-old, content to hunt and fish and tend his herb-garden: how could he resist the dashing older brother whom he had not seen for twelve years, with his sword and his banner and his Saxon jewels and accent?

My herb-garden is already cared for. I keep you for sweetness' sake only.

She had gone to Dunkeld because, as his friend, she had thought to keep Maelmuire strong.

And he had allowed her because, as at Tarbatness, her forfeit in any war was different from his.

He gambled his life. She risked no physical harm. Only capture, and the exchange of one marriage-bed for another. As had already happened.

It meant that she would continue, if he did not. And, surely, that was what mattered. To go on. To go on, however with honour was possible.

> *The halt can ride,*
> *The handless can herd,*
> *The deaf can fight with spirit.*
> *A blind man is better*
> *Than a corpse on a pyre.*
> *A corpse is no good to anyone.*

Tuathal said, 'My lord?'

And Thorfinn said, 'Something amused me, for a moment. You have, no doubt, made the sad calculation. If Earl Siward and his chief officers have joined Thor and Malcolm by now, along with the Normans' horses, we may expect them within the next hour behind us. It's even possible that Allerdale's whole army could reach Scone from Ruthven by sunset if he whips them enough.'

His horse stumbled. He collected it and closed up to Tuathal's again. 'Perhaps I should have mentioned it before.'

'It would have made no difference,' Tuathal said. After a bit, he said, 'The men who betrayed you were not your men.' The silver box on his chest thudded and thudded.

'I know,' said Thorfinn. 'I have exculpated both God and the Pope.'

*   *   *

Shortly after that, they all saw a fresh cloud of smoke mount into the air ahead of them and spread, thickening, and he thought it was all over: that the Dunkeld army had arrived and, joining the shipmen, had taken both citadels. He was quite near before he saw that the flames sprang from the new buildings at the place of assembly and the outlying cabins and barns on both sides of the river. Over Scone and over the fortress of Perth, his own banners flew still.

So there was still a little room to manipulate fate.

By now, both places would be tightly invested by the shipmen. But by the time his force joined with Cormac's, they would have a good band of horsemen between them. Say the Cumbrian army from Dunkeld was still several miles off, marching south. Say, for the sake of argument, that they brought their prisoners with them—well guarded, of course.

Even a thousand marching men, if laden with booty, if full of food and good plundered wine, would stagger under the impact of four hundred horse. And the shipmen, abandoning Scone and hurrying, as they would, to the rescue, might well arrive far too late, if at all. And might leave the way free for the skilful, in their turn, to race back and into Scone with their prisoners.

It was a good plan, and it might work if the Dunkeld army were only far enough off. Up to now, there had been an answer, a possible response to every disaster. He would find one for this.

The answer he found was not that one.

Because both forts were under siege, it was hard to get over the Tay. He found the horsemen on this side were leaderless, since Ferteth was dead. Then Cormac, over the river, created a diversion, and they crossed to the Scone side and streamed into cover, to Cormac's incoherent welcome.

It was taken for granted that the King came in the van of an army, and he had to collect them and break the news quickly. But first he told Cormac, who had reared Maelmuire, and whose wife was at Dunkeld with Ferteth's wife, and with Groa.

He waited until the anger came, and then outlined his plan. Then, on the barest heels of their scouts, they mounted and streamed north at once, on both sides of the river, spreading out as they went through the smoke and the trees, counting every furlong a gain before they should find themselves at grips with the Cumbrian army.

It struck Thorfinn to wonder whether Thor his third cousin or Malcolm his nephew would be with the Ruthven banners or whether they might meet him face to face here. He did not share, now, Cormac's tempestuous fury with the men he thought of as traitors. Affairs changed, and policies had to adapt to them: his as well as other men's.

Nothing yet.

The horse-ford lay ahead, through the trees, by which they would cross back over the Tay to take the Dunkeld road that was shortest and firmest. He could see, flashing bright through the leaves on the other side of the water, those of his men who had been at Perth with Ferteth riding parallel with them.

Shallow-draught boats used the river, so he kept it scoured, as Crinan had in his day, and men on foot used boat-bridges or ferries or walked down the right bank to Perth, where there were crossings all the time.

Because of the woods on either side, and the booths at the crossing, there was not a long view. There were always sheds of a sort by fords like this one. When the river was high, travellers sometimes preferred to sit and wait, rather than cast about for a crossing. And then the man with fat ducks to sell, or some ironmongery, or a piece of cloth or a basket of berries, would find a customer, or the husband of one.

The Cumbrian army might come down either bank, but it was likelier, now, to be the one they were joining. If he was wrong, the scouts would warn them, and on horses they could always get back.

Today, of course, the booths were empty, as were all the farms they had passed. He watched the scouts make sure, however, and then wade over and search on the other side before he gave the sign to start the crossing. He led it himself, and had just thrust his horse down and into the water when he caught sight of the new stake driven into the banking, and the rope round its neck that ran sagging under the water.

Thorfinn flung up a hand in warning, and halted.

On either side, too late to stop, horses slid and splashed into the water, and others, pressing behind, pushed lop-haunched into the turmoil. The water, thickened with mud, slapped and surged, and a pair of wood-pigeons exploded, gay as pudding-time bladders, from the forest ahead. One of the Strathearn men over the river gave a short cry.

Every head turned. The river chattered over its selvedges. Their feet soft in the mud, the horses nipped one another. On the other side, a man fell slowly down the flank of his garron until the haft of the spear in his throat met the ground.

Thorfinn roared, '*Back!*'

And then, deep in the woods on both sides of the river, the trees stretched, and walked.

A memory plucked at the warp of his stomach. 'Lulach?' said the King; and Tuathal looked at him.

Then anyone could see that the razored leaf-blades and whorled metal boles were no more than human: a party sent to secure a crossing for wains and horses and perhaps even some of the army. And sent, for better concealment, with twigs of oak and birch and hazel thrust in their harness. From what forest, it could not matter.

They had been unwise to make themselves known, for Thorfinn's band greatly outnumbered them. As the first throwing-spear whipped past him and the first arrow made its hit, he shouted the dismounting order and flung himself with the others out of the saddle. Across the river, his men collected themselves and surged into the light, open woodland, steel flashing. On Thorfinn's side, his main party behind in the trees were already engaged on either flank, sword against sword, with the Cumbrians who had already crossed.

He joined them, catching Tuathal's eye again as he lifted his sword. Their scouts had been deceived, and it might have been a disaster. Instead, a unit of the Cumbrian army had been delivered into their hands.

He met a fist with steel in it and swerved, slashing. The feel of the hand-grip, filling his palm, reminded his muscles of the fighting already behind him, as did the jarring on shoulder and wrist through the blows on his shield. The noise-curtain of shouting and battering steel was deafening. Green and red, sheared flesh and sliced boughs tumbled together, and lobes of honeysuckle stuck to the mesh of his mail, along with faggots of truncated hair.

The smell of blood; the smell of sweat; the smell of ordure; the smell of bruised green things. The smell of battle on land.

Battle on land, where land hid your enemy. Behind this advance guard was Allerdale's army. How far behind? Their scouts ought to warn them. But scouts made mistakes. And got killed.

No screamed warning came from the riverbank. From the glimpses he contrived, the fighting on the further side, as on this, appeared to be going his way. It began to seem as if most of the Cumbrian party had already crossed to this, the Scone bank, before his band arrived. Then, hearing him come, had hidden and let them through.

In which case, why give themselves away as they had done? And why, outnumbered as they were, make a stand as stubborn as any the shipmen had countered with?

An axe bit into his shield between the studs, but he was backing already. He wrenched his sword out from flesh and leather and turned on the axeman. In the distance, above all the noise, a trumpet blew with his own warning-call.

It was what he had been waiting for. Except that the alarm came from his own side of the river, behind him.

The Allerdale army, then, was approaching. It had crossed the Tay already, upriver. Trap or accident, this crossing was secondary. And its leader, whom he had been fighting towards, had engaged and held them, knowing that the main army would arrive at their backs.

The men over the river were safe. There was no time for his small army to cross now. 'My lord?' said his trumpeter at his side.

'Mount and retreat,' said Thorfinn. Tossing their heads, the horses would be waiting under the trees, nervous camp-followers, distant spectators of every battle. There were few enough men left to oppose him. He saw the leader's mouth open, under the nose-piece of his helmet, and guessed he, too, was ordering some sort of deployment, but could not hear what he was shouting. A moment later, a sudden concerted movement told him. The remaining Cumbrians were dashing to cut them off from their horses.

Whoever he was, their leader was good. But Thorfinn's men, too, were well practised, and there were more of them. He saw Cormac already in front of them, a line of men waiting; and, calling to those nearest, Thorfinn, too, forced his way through the lumber of battle to attack the little band on the flank.

Between Cormac's men and his own, the Cumbrians had no hope of escape and fought as men fight who have nothing to lose. The group round the leader were the last to die, and there was room in Thorfinn, as the leader turned, for regret that it was no normal campaign in which he might give quarter or take prisoners. Then he saw the bright-stubbled jaw under the helmet, and the determination in the bright eyes, and the uplifted arm with an axe in it, and realised that Thor of Allerdale had sent his son Dolphin to lead the van of his army.

The axe came down, clipping the mesh of the King's shoulder and hacking leather and flesh as Thorfinn flung himself sideways. His own sword was already descending through the flank of the other man's face and into his neck and chest, clean as slicing a steak from a mackerel.

It was a death-blow: so quick that as the boy fell they saw him stamped in the meat of his cheek by the volleyed rings from Thorfinn's splintered tunic. Then Cormac said, *'My lord!'* and, through the trees, the King saw the first lines of the main Cumbrian army running towards them.

A horse appeared, pulled by Tuathal, already mounted, and Thorfinn vaulted wrong-sided into the saddle, letting his shield drop. Then, streaming through the trees between the whistling barbs, the Alban horsemen began to force their way back from the river, round the nose of the Cumbrian army, and, using what cover they could, into the hilly country behind, out of reach of footsoldiers from either Scone or this oncoming army. Out of reach only for the moment, and within range of anyone else's mounted scouts.

As soon as he could find a fit man, Thorfinn sent off a scout of his own to report the size of the new army, and whether the women from Dunkeld were with it. By that time, he knew that the wound in his shoulder was a bad one, and that he had taken others, worse than the cuts and bruises and gashes they had all borne from early morning.

It was true, he saw, of everyone. By now, none was as quick as he should be, and their numbers were a good deal depleted. He had left wounded in the wood, as well as dead, and men who could not find horses in time, although some of these would hide and escape. On the other side of the river, the survivors, too, ought to save themselves with any luck.

What he had to decide now was whether he had enough fit men to launch the flank attacks he had planned to weaken the advancing Cumbrians still further, or whether he should send all he had back to Scone to arrange some sort of diversion and try to get most of the party inside.

Scone, the heart of the kingdom, and fortified as well as they knew how. But, of its nature, not as amenable to the work of Bishop Hrolf or the Normans as would be a rock-citadel or a simple fortress of mound and bailey and ditch. And even of these, Osbern of Eu had made no promises. *They can pin down a countryside,* he had said. *But they won't stand against an army mustered for war.*

They would see about that, when they got inside. Meanwhile, they drew breath, counting, assessing, while the wounded were attended to in a heathery hollow, and those who had ale-flasks shared quickly what they had.

He spoke to them briefly, commending the fight, warning them that the respite would be of the briefest. Then he dismounted, rather abruptly, on the side furthest away from the company and found Tuathal arriving already with his knife and a helmet of water and a lad carrying an armful of torn cloth and moss.

He sat, his right arm looped through the reins, while Tuathal hacked away broken mail and got a dressing in and began to bind it tightly enough to stop the bleeding. The sun shone full on Thorfinn's face, but coldness visited him with occasional fingers. Old and familiar warnings. Loss of blood was a serious enemy. You never ignored it. He said, 'How long till sunset? Three hours, perhaps less? Siward and Allerdale and Malcolm with the Normans' horses could be at Scone by now.'

'I sent a scout that way as well,' Tuathal said. His neck was scarred and his hand bleeding, but his colour was still high. He said, 'The Lady won't come to harm.'

In action, you felt almost no pain at all. Out of action, you did. Thorfinn said, 'What does that mean?'

Tuathal's hands did not pause. He said, 'That you can probably either retire to Scone or escape up Strathmore without affecting that issue.'

'Or, being disabled, I can safely surrender?' said Thorfinn.

Tuathal finished his work and looked up. 'You're not crippled,' he said. 'But a lot of your men are, and Cormac has a leg-wound. Most could ride well enough to escape to the north. This fight held us up just a little too long. You may get inside Scone. But getting inside Scone may not save it.'

Thorfinn said, 'It is the centre of Alba.' He rose to his feet and looked down on Tuathal, his arm on the saddle.

Tuathal said, 'I understand all it implies. But would it not be a gesture as great to take the remains of Scone's people north with you to fight in consort with northmen to take back the kingdom? Instead of losing everything, you might find in disaster the unity you've been striving for.'

'And Eochaid?' Thorfinn said; and saw Tuathal's colour become higher.

Tuathal said, 'With you, that is not a consideration. And against me, a dishonest weapon.'

True. Thorfinn said, 'Do my promises have any value?'

'No doubt,' said Tuathal, 'you will make up your own mind. You said you would never leave Scone. You didn't say you would kill everybody trying to get into it.'

Thorfinn said, 'If you listen, you will hear me say in a moment that anyone wishing to escape to Strathmore has my full leave to do so. . . . *Here!*'

It was the first of the scouts, looking for them. The fellow dropped, gasping, from his horse, and all round the hollow, men stood up. 'Eight hundred men, my lord King. Marching for Scone in close formation, shields outermost.'

Cormac, mounted, was at his side. He said, 'We expected a thousand or more.'

Thorfinn said carefully, 'We killed a hundred or more at the crossing.' And next: 'Could you see any women?'

'My lord, I could see,' said the man. 'There are no women.'

His body had dissolved, leaving a wintry filigree of half-empty veins.

The man said, 'My lord, there's more. I saw a man ride up shouting. He said Earl Siward and a hundred horse were at Scone.'

'A trick?' said Thorfinn.

The scout shook his head. Had he been less tired, it would have been vehement. 'They didn't see me. I'm sure of it. And anyway— Look! He'll tell you!'

The scout from Scone, who did not dismount at all, began shouting as soon as they saw him. The message was the same. The shipmen were tight around Scone and Perth, and now a hundred horse had joined them, under Earl Siward and my lord Malcolm and my lord Thor of Allerdale. Most of the horses he recognised as belonging to the Normans. The rest must have been Siward's own.

Tuathal said, 'My lord King, you cannot get into Scone.'

Cormac said nothing. His wife, too, had been at Dunkeld. Thorfinn said to him, 'How bad is your leg?'

'Well enough to ride to Dunkeld,' Cormac said. The sun sheened the sweat on his face. He said to the scout, 'Was my lord Maelmuire with the Cumbrians from Dunkeld?'

'There were no colours of his,' said the man. 'My lord, I thought Dunkeld was levelled.'

Tuathal said, 'In less than two hours, Allerdale's foot-army will be at Scone also. My lord, whatever harm we do now to this Cumbrian army, we cannot save Scone, neither can we get into it. Nevertheless, it is for you to say. This is your kingdom and we here are your people. What do you want us to do?'

The resolution, as with most problems, was clear enough. He worked through to it in the time it took him to leave his horse and stride to the highest part of the knoll. He looked down at them all, standing, faces upturned, under his shadow.

'No band of men I have ever known could have fought better. We set out to fight one army and found ourselves invaded by three. We tried to save Scone. Now Scone must fall. It is the heart of the kingdom, but it is not the whole kingdom. So I repeat what I said on the Earn. Angus may still be ours. Moray is certainly ours. Save yourselves, therefore. Take the valley to the north-east and the coast. Get to Lulach my stepson. Whatever the Earl Siward may take, he will not be allowed to hold it for long. God be with you.'

'And you, my lord? My lord King, where do you go?'

The shout came from the thick of the crowd, loud against the looser cross-talk of the others.

Thorfinn said, 'Somewhere between here and Dunkeld there must be a party with the Lady of Alba, and my lady of Atholl with her. Perhaps Dunkeld is not burned and they are still there. Before I leave for the north, I mean to search for them. I need no company.'

'You have it, however,' said Tuathal. 'Do you imagine Cormac or I will leave you with that task?'

It was odd. It was Earnside over again, with every man who could ride fighting for his attention. To ride, searching. To stay with him, for whatever purpose.

He must have worn an unaccustomed expression, for Tuathal suddenly smiled and said, 'You see. You see how greatly your lady is loved.'

He did not want to speak again, and it was Tuathal who discarded the wounded and chose escorts for them and mustered the fit men, mounted and ready to leave. Cormac said, 'My lord King,' and stopped. Cormac's face was grey, and the brown wash over his horse's flank was overlaid with fresh red.

He said nothing when they eased him from his horse and laid him down. Thorfinn said, 'Rest. The others will help you to move when you can. We shall find them and bring them back safely.'

Cormac said, 'Maelmuire.'

'What could he do?' Thorfinn said. 'It was his family. I shan't harm Maelmuire.'

He saw the relief, and left quickly, for there was nothing more he could say. He had two hundred men, and Tuathal and the Brecbennoch; and somewhere out there, within half an hour's ride under the evening sun, was what was left of Dunkeld and a party of valuable women, strongly escorted, making—one would expect?—a leisurely journey to Scone in order to arrive there when all the fighting was over and the citadel had surrendered and the flag of Malcolm or Siward would greet Groa, entering, and not that of her husband.

If Groa were still alive.

No man of standing would harm her. Her value, as bride or hostage, was priceless.

Of the two thousand men Thor of Allerdale had brought against him from Cumbria, it might be that one or two had no particular standing, but had reputations of other kinds to maintain. And for some mistakes there was no remedy other than destroying the evidence. It happened on strand-raids as well. There was really no remedy.

They had split into groups. Being who he was and what he was, he applied his mind all the time he was riding, marshalling the facts as he knew them, judging as best he could the immediate effects of what had happened, and then those of more lasting potential. Without that, he could hardly counter-plan. And although he might guess Malcolm's motives, or those of Thor or of Siward, he did not yet know for certain. About escape he did not think at all, for he had already reviewed the possibilities and could do nothing further.

The observing part of his brain combed the low, tumbling landscape of bog and hill, copse and spinney, for signs of a detachment of riders, or a few riders surrounded by foot. He had sent a small party of mounted to cross back over the river to the rear of the marching troops from Dunkeld, in case the captives were taken down that side. They had been given a trumpet, to use in extremity only, for the horsemen at Scone would be riding this way soon enough, once they knew the King of Alba was here.

For the same reason, all Thorfinn's search at the outset was confined to the land stretching between Scone and the riverbank, for at any moment Siward's horse might arrive. They quartered the ground, keeping just within each other's view, to render horn-signals unnecessary. Thorfinn himself took the river, from above the crossing up to the grass-grown Roman fort at Cargill. If they came down towards Scone on this bank, any party would expect to cross the Tay hereabouts.

This, at least, was the way the Cumbrian army had come, clearly marked by the swathe of its trampling. Below Cargill, he saw something dark by the riverbank, and beyond it another: a wooden rectangle half-embedded in reeds. Rafts, hewn upriver and brought here to form a rough bridge. Hewn perhaps from the trees that had already provided the leafy disguises. *Lulach, I know; I remember. I pay the lip-twisting eyrir. I blame neither you nor the Norns, but only myself. My life is my own, and I will not surrender.*

Unless he kept a clear head, he would not have a chance to surrender. Thorfinn brought his horse to a halt and studied the river. On the far side, another raft had been left, not this time afloat but conveniently high on the far bank, at a place where the crossing was easiest.

Waiting for someone?

He held up his hand, and the twenty men with him slowed and surrounded him. He spoke. One spurred off to talk to the group under Tuathal. Then he and his men cast about and, finding what cover they could, dismounted and lay full length, waiting.

The horses, led out of sight, walked slouching, like beaten stallions after a horse-fight. Thorfinn lay behind a spread of low gorse and propped his brow on his hand, forbidding his eyes to close. He wondered how many of his men, lying like this, would not wake even if a group of horsemen came over the low ridge on the other side of the river and began to make their way down to the raft. He wondered how, if the waiting lasted too long, he was ever going to rise. With a rustle, Tuathal slid down beside him.

'We can see a party approaching from the other side of the river. I've called some men back and put them lining the bank on this side. Do you want us to cross?'

'No,' said Thorfinn. 'It might be anyone. If it is the women, the escort might have orders to kill. I want them on this side, and close.'

He made himself play out the moves like a battle-game on a slab of scratched stone. The sound of hooves in the distance: how many hooves? The rising of a dark, moving body of people against the sinking sun on the low horizon. How many people? How many horses? And as they came closer: twelve footsoldiers, with shield and with spear, surrounding a group of three horses, each doubly laden. And walking beside them and behind them, six horses bearing men in mail shirts, fully armed with swords and with knives . . .

Two of the horses spurred ahead and, with the help of some of the footsoldiers, had a raft launched and ready before the laden garrons came up.

The double burdens were women, their cloak-hoods pulled over their faces and their cloaks pinned beneath. From their skirts below, you could tell they were women, but nothing showed of their age or their quality or their comeliness. If one was Groa, he could not guess which.

Getting the party across, there was a lot of talk among the men, and a lot of exertion. The horsemen were senior, by the sound of them, and nervous enough to make bad jokes now and then. The footsoldiers were sullen: afraid, perhaps, of missing their share of the pillage.

On the near bank, a quarrel broke out as the raft came to land, and the two horsemen who had forged over already turned back, speaking sharply to deal with it. The women, unaided, began to scramble ashore, their skirts floating and tugging, while behind them the other riders took to the water, the spare horses with them.

The first of the women appeared, alone, at the top of the bank.

Thorfinn waited. He waited until all six prisoners stood on the grass, and the horsemen, and the wrangling footsoldiers.

Only one man stood near enough to threaten the women. Thorfinn swung his right arm and let fly with his axe.

It fell, cleaving through helmet and skull, and the dead man was expiring still when arrow and spear struck his fellows. Thorfinn ran forward and snatched his axe as he ran.

His men sprang for the soldiers still living. He made for the women. For the tallest and slimmest, who, from the way she fled to him, was not anyone's serving-maid, or Eochaid's sister, or Ferteth's widow.

He slowed and stood, the sobbing tale of relief in his throat, and found dragged ajar the dangerous door that led back to the things that were normal and dear. He realised suddenly how he must look, weary and dirty and covered with blood. And what she would already have endured on his behalf, through the long day of treachery and betrayal.

So he stood, with, no doubt, ruefulness of a kind on his face, and waited as she came, light as air, to their meeting; and flung back her hood; and, raising her hand, drove the knife in it straight for his throat.

Even when tired, he was quicker than most men. He took the stroke twisting into his shoulder and killed the soldier in skirts with his own knife, wondering, as the blood flooded warm through his shirt, if it was the last thing he was to do. The other masqueraders, he saw, had already flung off their cloaks. Three of his men fell to their steel, but only three. He killed two of the skirted assassins himself.

Then the shouting in his ears was overtaken by the shouting further off: a great deal of it. He heard his own name, and his battle-cry rising thin and disorganised into the air from the hilly ground over which all his horsemen were scattered.

The other noise was quite different, although it came from men's throats also, to rouse and to rally. A cry that was not scattered at all, but rose from men in their ranks who could now be seen sweeping towards them. Men advancing as this party had done, from over the banks of the river. Men driving down from the north and herding his horsemen before them. And men

from the south and the east, from the direction of Scone, who were not on foot
at all, but on horseback, and who bore streaming among them the banner of
Siward of Northumbria.

Tuathal said, 'Here is your horse. Can you? Or with me?'

A twice-burdened horse would never escape. He said, 'Get me up.'

And, once in the saddle, he spoke again. 'Strathmore. If not, Dunsinane.'
Then his horse was galloping, north and east, and the others coming after
him.

At first, the footsoldiers were the danger, for they threw spears, although
there were almost no bowmen. One could do nothing but ride low and slash,
like the Normans, in passing. His sword slid from his hand and was lost,
which was a pity, but he laid his axe over the pommel and bound it to his wrist
with the slack of his rein, over and over. Then he slashed the reins, and his
horse, feeling the jerk, tossed its head as it raced. He could control it with his
thighs. It was as tired as he was.

Then his enemies were riding towards him. Men he recognised from half a
lifetime ago: from the field by the Forth just that morning, when he had toyed
with Siward, setting alight the forest about him; leaving his army, taunting, to
cover his retreat.

He recognised, too, the sturdy horses Osbern of Eu and his friends had
ridden north from Ewias castle to Kirkby, where Thor of Allerdale had visited
him and been made welcome.

Like that of his mount, the horses' heads were lowered with tiredness. As
with his men, Siward's were bloody and blackened. He glimpsed Siward
himself in their midst, the helmet deep on his brows and his face leaded black
upon red with sunset and weariness.

Between Siward's army and the Cumbrian detachment sent to trap them,
there was a gap that did not lead to Strathmore. He did not need to call his
men, even had he been able. They streamed to him from all over the moors:
towards him and the gap.

Wherever Groa might be, he could not reach her. He could not break
through to Scone, or to Perth, or to Dunkeld. He could not take the road
through Strathmore to the coast and to freedom. All he could do was cling to
his horse and guide it to the gap before it, too, was closed. The gap that led to
the nearest hill-fortress, and the only refuge he could reach before his enemies
did. The path that led to the hill called Dunsinane.

He sent no acknowledgements this time to Lulach. He sent no appeals to
the Deity of the Pope or the Deity of his axe. He dismissed from his mind all
that was irrelevant, including pain, and led the way up the long, rough
approach to the hill to the great ditch and the tall, newly rebuilt walls of the
ring-fort, whose gates were already opening.

He had had no idea there would be so many people inside. They laid the
timber bridge over the ditch for him, since it was not a jump he cared to make.
Tuathal was already within, flinging arrow-bundles into baskets and shouting for archers. By the time the last of the riders was putting horse to the
hillside, there were men outside covering their entry, as the foot of the hill

grew a dark girdle of footsoldiers and the arrows and throwing-spears started to flash. The gap had closed.

He waited until they were all in and the gates were shut, and then turned to look round.

Not the massed populace of the district, as once you would have found. With the advance of armies of thousands, these had dispersed further north, taking their children and livestock along with them.

But some country people there were: older men and young boys and even women, with bloody bandaging, some of them, to show the wounds taken when fighting beside him along the Tay, and later.

These and other familiar faces: of men still in leather and mail moving quickly towards him. Wounded men standing in the doorway of the fort's timber shelters, calling to him. Familiar faces of men—Gillocher, Morgund, Malpedar—whom he had last seen, not by the side of the Tay or the Earn, but early when the day was young and fresh and promising, between the rock-fortress and the forest on the river Forth. The men who had escaped Siward and had escaped, also, Thor of Allerdale's ambush at Ruthven Water. Some of the fifteen hundred of whose massacre he had heard nearly five hours before.

He did not dismount as they crowded round him, for he could see them better that way, for one thing. He said, 'Now let's show them what we can do. Listen to Prior Tuathal and do what he says. You must be quick.'

Then Tuathal's voice broke in immediately, speaking fast, and men dispersed, running. All the way here, Tuathal had planned it, calling to him, in case Allerdale's men rushed the hill as soon as they entered. It was clear, from the flags, that half the surrounding army at least was Allerdale's, or Thor commanding Siward's own advance troops. It didn't matter.

He listened to Tuathal shouting and thought that perhaps there wouldn't be an initial attack at all, until Siward came up. Then he realised that he was still surrounded, and mostly by women who had been speaking to him, although he had not answered. His horse began to move, drawn by the cheekband towards the nearest building, and he saw pallets through the open door, and a man coming out, apparently to greet him.

His face was familiar, too. Bishop Jon said, 'D'you know me, now? *A Diá*, there was an enemy of Patrick was peeled like an onion come every seventh year, and you have the very look of him. I have a legless fellow somewhere called Cormac would like a word in your ear in a moment. Meanwhile . . . Can ye walk at all?'

'I can even talk,' said Thorfinn. 'If you'll get me down off this animal.'

'Ah,' said Bishop Jon. The perfect tonsure of the previous night was clouded, Thorfinn observed, with fine bristles. The Bishop said, 'Should we take that thing out of your hand first?'

He had forgotten the axe. Bishop Jon unwound the reins and took the haft out of his hand. It had stuck fast with blood and had to be tugged from his palm, which reminded him of something, he couldn't think what. Then he was down, with the ground under his feet, after a fashion, and his ears assuming the office, it seemed, of his eyes. Bishop Jon said, 'Have you had a morsel since morning, I wonder? It's food you need, and a good cup of something, the moment we've got you cleaned up. Or else—'

'Or else what?' said Groa.

His eyes settled, like muddy water, and allowed his brain through.

It was Groa. He had never seen so much dirt on her face, or such pallid skin under it. Her unplaited hair, crimson-lit, dangled like hawsers. She made a movement to touch him, and checked it.

'Or else his wife will send him back where he came from. A man who doesn't know when he is beaten: that I admire,' said Bishop Jon. 'A man who doesn't know when he is killed is another matter entirely, and will need a new page in my psalter. Have I time to shave, or are you going to kiss her?'

Her tears came during the kiss, and made an island of it. He said, 'No, beloved? We have a long way to go,' and watched the control of years coming back.

He knew no one like her. There had never been anyone like her.

> *He spins you as a bubble spins on the water,*
> *He grinds you as a mill grinds dried malt,*
> *He pounces on you as a hawk pounces on a titmouse. . . .*

'Sulien,' said Thorfinn to himself. 'Sulien, hear me. Sulien, soul-friend. I hate thy God.'

NINE

ORD GOD ALMIGHTY,' said Siward of Northumbria. 'Lord God Almighty, what are they doing? They've let him get to the hill. They had the man twice. They had him trapped twice, and he bested them. Perhaps he didn't even have to go to the fort. Maybe he found all Strathmore free to escape through.'

Ligulf said, 'That he did not. Thor of Allerdale is between him and Strathmore, with the news of Dolphin's death in his ears. If Thorfinn rose straight in the air, the crows would come down and tear him at Thor's bidding. . . . We're through into Scone, and they'll have Perth in an hour. My God, did you see the stuff they took at Dunkeld?'

'Never mind about Dunkeld. What about Scone?' Siward said. 'I thought I told you to stay in Scone until the treasure was safeguarded?'

'Forne and the princeling are looking after it,' Ligulf said. 'Don't worry. You won't lose a pearl from the altar-cloth. That was a transformation, wasn't it? The boy has discovered blood-sports. You should send him to join Allerdale.'

'Which boy?' said Siward. His bones ached under the mail, and now, due to incompetence, a nightfall of struggle lay before them instead of a clean success with the Orkney King wiped from the accounting for ever. 'Which boy?' He was over fifty, and the earth was cluttered with boys.

'Well, not Maelmuire,' Ligulf said, 'who has hardly stopped vomiting since he left Dunkeld. I was talking of his brother Malcolm. You may be going to find Malcolm a handful.'

Siward of Northumbria paid no attention. He disliked Ligulf. He disliked all his brothers-in-law and their kin, with the possible exception of Forne.

Dunsinane. They knew all about that hill-fort from the Angus Mormaer, but hadn't been able to overrun it in time. He could see the steep face of it now, as he rode between low hills towards it, and steel glittering red, damn them, on the top.

Like eyebrow over eye, this range they called the Sidlaws lay north of the Tay, beginning behind him at Scone; and Dunsinane rose in the west of it. Not the tallest of mountains: the one they named the Black Hill overtopped it beyond, with only a knife-split between them; and beyond that, there was a higher one still.

But high enough, at six hundred feet above ground, to warrant the attention, centuries ago, of the old races who built the great circular forts with their concentric ditches and walls. This one, so they said, was over two hundred feet wide. Big enough to take a whole tribe and its beasts in time of danger, and subsequently built into something even safer than that. And on the knob at its summit, another fortification had been made, matching a similar one on the Black Hill.

A good place to defend. A good place for a signal-fire. A good place for a watch-station, with its northern slopes overlooking the rolling moors of Strathmore, patterned with plough-strips and homesteads and grazings, and dwindling to the line of high hills on the skyline. To the north-west ran the seam of the Tay, with Dunkeld and the mountains beyond it. And to the south, where he was riding, they could see him, as he could see them, together with all the hill approaches, save where on the west the bulk of the Black Hill blocked their vision. And behind him, the low, swelling folds that ran green to the Tay, and the Tay itself, in glimpses, and the hill-ridges lying beyond.

A commanding viewpoint in daylight. But now the sun was going. And soon Thorfinn and what he had saved of his men—one hundred? two?— would be alone on his hill in the dark.

Siward said, 'How badly wounded is he, do they say?'

'Thorfinn? Macbeth? Well, he can ride,' Ligulf said. 'But he was pouring blood, so it's said. I doubt if there's any fighting left in him. But he could still command their defences. They've got a long, gradual slope on the north side over there. He'll throw a line across there, I imagine, and draw the rest up inside the walls. Some of the cottagers who held up the shipmen seem to have taken refuge there already, and a handful of wounded and others who couldn't keep up with the fighting. He'll have more than two hundred to defend it with. And maybe some cattle. And, by all accounts, a good spring of water as well. They could hold out for a while, unless he dies of wound-sickness or a blood-burst.'

Above, the sky hung, changing colour like fine China silk, with homing birds on its surface like powder. Here, emptied by space of all texture, men's voices spoke and called and were thrown back from hill to hill, as every channel glinted with spears and with acorn helmets of dulled steel or leather and shields like shells on a necklace. Behind, when he twisted round, he saw that the black smoke obscuring the sun had been joined by another burst, this time of pure flame, rising over the river. He said, 'It looks as if Perth has gone. I was saying. We have enough men to do whatever we feel like. But we could lose a lot up that slope before we get to the walls and then over them.'

Siward grunted. He said, 'I wouldn't mind.' He felt, with satisfaction, Ligulf's annoyance.

Ligulf would like him to embark on a long siege. It would suit Ligulf . . . it would suit a lot of people to have Siward of Northumbria held up in Alba with most of his forces. He wished again, bitterly, that the fools who served him had managed to get rid of this half-bred seaman in daylight.

Ligulf said, 'Will they obey and storm the hill anyway? It's certain death.'

'The mercenaries will,' Siward said. 'So will the rest. I haven't shared out the booty as yet.'

'Then an appeal to surrender?' Ligulf said. 'Send someone to parley. He must know he's beaten, one way or another, unless he means to spend all his life there. What about Malduin?'

'That fool?' said Siward. Malduin of Alba was the only Bishop he had left. Aethelric, Bishop of the Holy Confessor Cuthbert and his Ever-Victorious Flag, had left after the second battle of Forth, and Cynsige had fallen sick and departed soon after. Siward said, 'Faced with Malduin, Thorfinn is more likely to hold out till the loosing of Satan. Unless . . .'

He stopped, because he could hear hooves pounding behind, above the jingling thud of marching men. The scout from Scone. He drew in his horse and waited.

It was Gospatrick, Malcolm's cousin. 'My lord Siward, Perth has fallen.'

One should hope so. But he said something approving. The boy's face was green. The boy said, 'My lord Siward, there is bad news as well. Your nephew . . . the young lord Siward was killed in the fighting.'

The Earl said something or other and, after a moment, put his horse in motion again. Osbern gone. And now his sister's son. And every other brat dead that that fool of a woman had ever thrown, except for a baby.

He was going to be the last. After he went, there was going to be none of Thore Hund's blood in Northumbria except the pink-faced issue of his God-blighted brothers-in-law.

But he hadn't gone yet. Not by a long, long way. By God, he wasn't going to go, either. In sixteen years, Waltheof would be a man, and Northumbria would be here, waiting for him. Northumbria and Lothians also. And more, if matters went right.

Ligulf prompted. 'You were saying? About an appeal by Malduin?'

'Ah, yes,' said Siward. 'Ah, yes. I was about to say that, while Bishop Malduin might not encourage our friend to surrender, his nephew young Malcolm might manage it. From what you say. And also that, while they are doing it, there are other possibilities that you and I might with profit explore. One cannot trust quite everything, after all, to churchmen and youngsters.'

Ligulf was smiling. The black moustaches opened like pincers. 'No indeed,' Ligulf said. 'So what were you thinking of?'

And smiled all the time that he listened, so that Siward thought the moustache-ends would be hooked on his ears.

The sun had set, and the hill of Dunsinane had been fully invested for an hour when the trumpet for parley blew at its foot and the banners of Kinrimund and of Malcolm son of Duncan stirred beside it in the afterglow.

Within the stout shelters of the ring-fort and the citadel on its peak, a light, Spartan orderliness had been attained, and nothing had been neglected.

Those in need had received food and drink, encouragement and solace, and their wounds cleaned and bound. Weapons and arms had been looked to, and damaged harness repaired, while all the dispositions for defence and for siege had been made as practice demanded. The only thing they were short of was rest, and only the badly wounded had leisure for that.

Even the women worked, for it kept their minds busy as well as their hands. Among them were those who had left Dunkeld with Groa: Anghared, who knew now how Ferteth had died; and Maire, Eochaid's sister, who stood with the Lady's hand at her shoulder and watched the smoke that fouled the western sky and the sunset. The smoke of burning Scone, of Moot Hill and monastery, of Stone and Rod and all that formed the core of Alba. The smoke of Eochaid's pyre.

No one knew yet quite how the women had made their escape from Dunkeld. To anyone who asked, Groa merely said vaguely that they had contrived to get out. Only to Cormac, lying paralysed in his hut, with Thorfinn and his wife kneeling beside him, did Groa say, 'Maelmuire helped us. They would kill him if they knew. He is a good boy.'

She had not heard how Thorfinn had come by the dreadful wound, which she had never quite seen, and he did not tell her. Perhaps, having found Groa and the rest missing, the Cumbrians had merely tried to turn the disaster to what advantage they could. Perhaps not. Malcolm, it appeared, had some little cunning. And Maelmuire's, it seemed certain, was a mind easily read.

With the mess cleared away, and the bleeding stopped, and some food inside him, Thorfinn found it possible to move about, with discretion, and at least people had ceased to look at him with horror. He felt extremely cold but quite clear-headed.

They were lucky to be where they were, but no one could say it was ideal. Pared of all possible cover, the hill still presented the attacker with great folds and bluffs and pockets in which he could lurk, unseen except from the highest point up above.

The outlook-tower and fortress built on the topmost knoll, above the ring-fort itself, took care of most of that, and was protected by the fortlet on the Black Hill beside it, across a narrow and plunging ravine.

He had a dozen men across there, but although they could protect him, he could do nothing for them if someone cared to climb the Black Hill on his blind side. Similarly, there were earth-and-stone bulwarks on the slopes under the walls of the big fort, which had already served to shelter the archers covering the entry of the last of his company. But that was an asset that, in the wrong hands, could become another danger.

Their supplies were good, but for Siward and Ligulf and Allerdale and the rest they would be nearly limitless. Already, at the start of slack water, Malpedar's sharp eyes had noticed the thin, moving blur of a longship rowing upriver between hill and hill on the dim, shining stretch that was the Tay.

Moving upriver with food and weapons and pavilions, no doubt, for the leading noblemen of the invasion. A smaller vessel, one of Siward's, had forced her way up against the tide some time before. It was the quickest way of getting men from one side of the river to the other. No doubt, in time, more of the twenty-five would come upriver, too. There was no opposition now. No one to throw firebrands and missiles. No one to harry them. They held both banks of the Tay from its mouth to Dunkeld.

Then the trumpet sounded, and he climbed the inner wall steps of the ring-fort, with Tuathal and Malpedar, the fittest, beside him, and the other two Mormaers behind: Gillocher with his broken arm strapped and Morgund with the bruise of the morning purple now between his scarred brows. Bishop Jon was already up on the wall, at another part.

They waited, hearing the shouting, thin from below; and then the louder voice of their own man outside, in his niche by the furthermost ledge, from which he could climb still in cover to safety.

In a moment, he appeared with his message. Bishop Malduin wanted to speak with the King. He would have with him the King's nephew Malcolm, and they would both come unarmed, provided that the spot where they met was outside the range of both armies.

Bishop Jon pursed his lips, and his face inflated at two of its angles. He said, '*Wide thy road with traffic of hundreds, O lucent land of grass and wagons.* You tell me you killed Allerdale's son.'

Thorfinn reflected. Then he spoke to the messenger. 'Tell my lord Bishop of Alba that in ten minutes' time I shall come to speak with him and my nephew by the yellow rock he will see halfway between the ground and the walls of the fort. I shall have Bishop Jon with me, and neither of us will be armed.'

Tuathal said, 'My lord?'

'I know,' said Thorfinn. 'But they're going to attack the Black Hill sometime, and we might as well encourage them to do it while there's a modicum of daylight left. I've just sent over another fifty men, but they'll need time to get through the ravine. Bishop Jon, I didn't ask your leave.'

'Neither you did,' said Bishop Jon. 'In fact, as I recall, I was busy refusing it as you interrupted me. I'll go if you assure me that there are archers behind all those barricades.'

'Of course,' said Thorfinn. 'And Allerdale has his archers in all the rough ground between there and the bottom. The balance is still fairly even.'

'In a way,' said Bishop Jon. 'But I offer you a thought. There is not a man out there but wants to get rid of you, for one very good reason or another. And, on the other side, there is hardly a man out there who cares very much what happens to either Bishop Malduin or your gallant young nephew, God rest their souls. In my view, the balance is not even.'

'Just what I was thinking,' Tuathal said.

'All right,' said Thorfinn. 'If you were Malcolm and that idea had struck you, too, what would you do about it?'

'Ah,' said Bishop Jon.

'Exactly,' said Thorfinn. 'Come along. We have ten minutes in which to make ourselves immortal.'

The voice that had rung over the fishpond at Goslar had no trouble making itself heard in darkening night on a hillside in Alba.

'It is our King's desire,' said Bishop Jon, firmly planted on the designated yellow rock, 'that this meeting should be conducted by churchmen. Above me, you see the banner blessed in Rome by the Holy Pontiff himself. The reliquary of the Blessed St Columba lies at my breast. Guided by God and His angels, let us therefore proceed to our business.'

Since he spoke in Latin, there was no immediate reaction whatever, except in the breast of Bishop Malduin, facing him. The usurper on the yellow rock held the Pope's banner himself, its white folds plain in the opaline after-light and the distant ruddy flicker from torches at the top of the hill and the bottom. You could even see the spark of the Brecbennoch on top of the long cloak the other Bishop was wearing. His cousin Thorfinn, standing below him, was also cloaked, but his features below the ringed helmet could not be distinguished.

Bishop Malduin was glad. Hate directed against Malcolm and the rival banner of Alba beside him he could understand. He disliked Malcolm himself. But it had been no part of his plan to be thrust into open war against the King his first cousin. And it was no fault of his that it had happened. If Thorfinn had seen fit to accept the established solution—the solution that suited everyone else—and unite the ministrations of Kinrimund and Durham, none of this need have happened. The man at his side jabbed an unmannerly elbow into his ribs, and Bishop Malduin announced stiffly, 'I speak for my lord, equally. But not in Latin, if you please. It is not understood.'

'Do you tell me, now?' said Bishop Jon in Irish-Gaelic, and with just enough astonishment to rile Malduin further. He then proceeded, still in Irish-Gaelic, to repeat, with good-humoured patience, all that he had just said.

Bishop Malduin said, 'That tongue is not understood either. I assume you have Saxon?'

He had Saxon, all right. It was the kind they spoke in Saxony, and, at the accent, Bishop Malduin felt his stomach twist. There was no point in extending this comedy further. He delivered, in the Northumbrian Saxon that his own side, at least, would understand, the ultimatum of Siward and Malcolm.

The Earl Siward had found King Macbeth and his men brave opponents, and regretted that such slaughter had been necessary. Now, however, the King would wish to take thought for the gallant few who had suffered with him and now shared his vigil on this hilltop.

For them, there was no hope except in surrender, and Earl Siward and his nephew the lord Malcolm were glad to offer them their lives, provided they threw aside their arms and came down from the fortress.

As for the King himself, they understood that he had taken such wounds that his future could not be robust. It was time to look at the facts. Lothian had never been his, and the Norman usurpers he had planted it with were gone, either dead or taken prisoner, and that part that had always belonged to the see of the west was Cumbrian once again.

Fife was empty. Two-thirds had followed himself, their Bishop, and their young lords. The rest had been led by Prior Tuathal to their deaths.

Atholl had fallen. Dunkeld was razed to the ground, its Mormaer dead or helpless, and Maelmuire, rightful heir to the abbacy, had joined my lord Malcolm his brother.

Scone likewise had been levelled, and the King's manors of Perth and Forteviot, and the Mormaers of both these countries, he understood, were now dead. Strathmore, they could see, lay before them occupied, and half Angus had risen to follow its Mormaer his kinsman under the banner of Kinrimund. The rest, he had no doubt, would follow.

Bishop Malduin paused, and no one interrupted him. Side by side, Thorfinn and the usurping Bishop stood watching him, and the little wind of the evening did not stir the folds of their cloaks any more than the cloaks they on their side were wearing. Bishop Malduin said quickly, 'It might be said, my lord King, that greed brought you down from your lands of Caithness and Orkney and impelled you to lay hands on a kingdom that was not for you.

'We are not greedy. We have the kingdom of Alba, all but Moray, and we do not seek to wrest that province from your stepson Lulach, any more than your grandfather King Malcolm sought to take it from Lulach's father Gillacomghain. Under the new King of Alba, he may keep it, provided that we may be assured of his loyalty.

'He has been brought up with your sons, my lord King. His lands abut on your own to the north. It seemed to my lord Siward and my lord Malcolm that the only way to ensure peace in Moray was by asking you to place yourself in our custody.

'I have to ask you therefore, my lord King, to step down now and throw yourself on our mercy. My lords will treat you with honour. You will keep your life, as will all those of your men who follow your example. It is even possible that, out of the generosity of your captors, Orkney and Caithness may be returned to you. The alternative is defeat and death on this hillside. And that this army marches on Moray and takes and kills your stepson Lulach also.'

Silence. Opposite, the Bishop stirred on his rock. He said, 'I hear you, now. It was a long speech, and I'm not sure that I remember all of it. May we confer?'

'Assuredly,' said Bishop Malduin. The light was going. The voices of men hung near and far in the air, like the murmur of marsh-geese at nightfall. A thickening of the sound, far up the hill of Dunsinane or even behind it, was probably only imagination.

Bishop Jon turned. He said, 'The King's lady is also here. What assurance of safety would she have?'

Virgin Mary, Mother of God. They might be going to agree. Bishop Malduin, his voice not quite firm, said loudly, 'The same.'

Bishop Jon paused. He said, 'You speak of mercy. It seems to the King that if he trusts himself to your honesty, he must test that honesty first. My lord Malcolm beside you is cloaked. Bid him throw back his cloak and his hood, and let us see whether or not he is unarmed, as was the condition.'

There *was* a layer of noise, high on the hill, that had not been there before. Bishop Malduin ignored it. He had stripped the young man of weapons himself before they set out, so that he was perfectly confident as he turned to him.

It annoyed him that my lord Malcolm was moving away, hissing something, and was making no effort to open his cloak.

Bishop Malduin did it for him, pulling the edge back so severely that the clasp broke and the whole cloak, hood and all, tumbled backwards.

The man who stood cloakless and glaring was not the young man whose weapons he had apologetically removed a short time ago. It was not my lord Malcolm at all. It was a mercenary, fully equipped with shirt of mail and sword-belt and waist-knife, with an axe in the hand that was not dropping his banner.

He lifted the axe. Bishop Jon flung himself off his rock with a remarkable clank. Bishop Malduin clung to his flagpole. Behind every boulder in front and behind, steel appeared. A stentorian voice—Earl Siward's voice—bellowed, '*Stop!*'

For Bishop Jon, instead of turning to fly, had taken his King by the arms and pulled back his cloak as Bishop Malduin had done.

And under the cloak was neither the mail shirt and battle-axe of perfidy or the weaponless negotiator of the parley conditions. Under the cloak were the long red hair and bright, jewelled dress of the Lady of Alba. The Lady Groa, whom no would-be ruler of Alba or Moray would dream of harming.

Mercenaries with bows and with spears were not necessarily of the same mind, and Bishop Jon was still in view. It was only chance that precisely at that moment the top of the mount burst into flame and the sounds Bishop Malduin had heard became suddenly the din of unmistakable battle, taking place on the crag with the black, stony crest that overtopped the highest point of Dunsinane.

He had understood that part of the Allerdale army was going to attempt something of the sort. Bishop Malduin peered up the hill. When he brought back his gaze, the Irishman and the woman were no more than running shadows under the walls of the ring-fort, their retreat masked by a curtain of spears and of arrows. And rising on either side of him, Siward's soldiers were throwing themselves forwards and upwards, sword in hand, to chase the enemy out of their hiding-places and sweep, struggling and fighting, up the slope to the fort.

Bishop Malduin did not wait to see that, or to see the counter-attack from the walls that forced Siward's men back and down, until torchlight showed the slope empty of all that was living, and tenanted only by the angular humps of the dead.

Long before that, Bishop Malduin was back with his friends, having abandoned with his plea his dignity and even his banner.

The flag of Malcolm had already fallen, and lay beside the body of his pretender, prostrate now on the heath with a dart in his throat.

In a little while, when he had recovered himself, Bishop Malduin took his courage and, leaving the anxious company of his kinsmen, made his way through the confusion of a newly settling encampment to look for Earl Siward, his leader.

Siward's pavilion was lit, and someone was shouting inside. At the entrance, Bishop Malduin turned and looked back at Dunsinane. The top half of the hill was lost in grey smoke, and you could not see where hill and sky met, save for the volcanic glow tinting all the curdling clouds above the highest citadel, where the seat of the blaze ought to be.

So that, at least, had succeeded. Bishop Malduin passed the guards and walked into the tent, where my lord Siward was informing his royal nephew Malcolm son of Duncan that he was a pampered, white-bellied parasite who, if threatened by a four-year-old goatherd from Bjarking, would undoubtedly piss himself.

My lord Malcolm, white with fury, got his sword out. None of the grinning men in the tent, Malduin saw, made a move to stop him. If he thought he could outmatch Siward with a sword, there might be some agreeable sport in the offing.

On the other hand, Siward might have lost his head, too. Bishop Malduin said, 'Does it matter? Their King didn't come either.'

Siward turned. 'You might have thought it mattered, if our men hadn't taken the Black Hill when they did and made a distraction. Thorfinn had men planted in every nook on that hillside, and they were angry. You would have got an arrow in the throat the next minute, and not only the greedy simpleton this fellow paid to dress up in his place.'

Malcolm's sword flashed in his hand. Siward turned on him. 'Do you realize yet? If Thorfinn had come, we would have lost him.'

Whether King Duncan's son Malcolm was easily frightened or merely prudent, Bishop Malduin did not know. It was true that, brought up in the south, his speech and style were not those of Northumbria, and still less those of Norway. If anything remained of his childhood in Cumbria, nothing Scandinavian about him would remind you. Earl Siward had recognised the necessity of bringing him, but Earl Siward had little time for him. However courageous or otherwise he might be, there was no doubt that the younger man's situation was solitary. And precarious.

He showed no awareness of it. He looked from Earl Siward to Malduin himself and gave a laugh. 'You mean he would have got away alive from that hillside?'

'He might have surrendered,' said Bishop Malduin. 'Does it matter?' Half the army, he imagined, must be within earshot by now. It was not good practice to make these things public.

The young man stared at him. Then he turned to his uncle. 'Well, my lord,' said Malcolm and, lifting his sword, drove it home in its sheath. 'It seems that to some men it appeared even possible that, with the King in your hands, you would spare him. If Thorfinn thought the same, then, I grant you, my absence might have made a difference. But Thorfinn knew you, didn't he, as well as we do? And sent his wife.'

Anger rose in Bishop Malduin's breast. It made his voice shake, addressing

Earl Siward. 'I spoke for you in good faith,' said the Bishop. 'You invoked the name of God and His church. You offered honourable captivity, and in the church's name I promised it.'

Siward said, 'Don't be a fool. You didn't know. Whatever happened, it would have been our blame, not yours. Look at the Irish fellow they had. He practised deception and knew it. Anyway, we'll have him tomorrow.'

'Tonight,' Malcolm said.

Siward sat down and made a sign, and men began to bustle about with boards and platters. His body-servant knelt, picking up the bits of clothing and arms he had discarded. Siward looked up. 'My men have had a long day,' he said. 'And so have I. We've tried one attack in the dark, and it failed. At first light tomorrow, we'll think of the next one.'

Malcolm stood where he was. 'I know the men are tired. But so are Thorfinn's. He lost men in that attack. He'll have lost more in the fire, and some of his arms, with any luck. The men who've taken over the Black Hill can harry them all night long, even with something as simple as stones. Surely now is the time? Now, when we know that the hill below the ring-fort is clear?'

Siward plunged his fists into a basin. Blood and dirt from his hands spread murkily into the water. His muscular forearms were pelted with hair, grey as his beard, and there was a gleam of gold over one elbow. The fur-trader's axiom. The gold in your purse is for luxuries. The gold that you wear is your life-line.

Siward did not even look up. He said, 'Have I said I want to stop anyone else? If Allerdale's men happen to be fresh and rested and wild for the honour of bringing down the last stand of Alba, I for one would do nothing to stop them. Ask Thor if you like. Do what you want. Only keep out of my way. I'm going to eat. And then I'm going to sleep.'

Malcolm looked at him. Then he turned and walked out of the tent. He did not look at Bishop Malduin as he passed, but Bishop Malduin saw that he was smiling.

Thor of Allerdale, it would appear, was of Malcolm's mind, for the first of their assaults on Dunsinane took place within the next couple of hours. The climbing of the hill was accomplished in silence, and the first crash of the conflict came to the occupied vales all about as the attackers came to the wall and flung poles and ladders against it.

So much the watchers could deduce, but not much else. The tumult went on for a long time, and the observers far down below could only glimpse the thickets of glittering steel that clustered here and there on the walls, and the bursts of sparks that were spear-shafts, lit by the glow of the fires. Above the hoarse breath that was shouting there played the virtuoso instruments of war: the sound of the trumpet, and of the human voice screaming, and of the chiming of smith-work, sweeter than any.

It went on for a long time without much variation. Then those who were connoisseurs of such things could tell that the ground-bass of shouting was increasing steadily. It continued getting louder and louder until it exploded in a fierce roar that rang all through the sleeping valleys. The roar of '*Albanaid!*'

Then there was silence.

The watchers set by Earl Siward ran to his tent as instructed and, as instructed, wakened him.

'My lord! An attack on Dunsinane has failed. They are counting the casualties. My lord Malcolm and my lord of Allerdale are unhurt.'

The Earl groaned and, turning over, grunted dismissal. They went back to their posts.

This time, they waited only an hour before Malcolm and the Cumbrian army launched their next attack; and the shouting began long before the tide of running men had come within reach of the walls.

This time the measures used on both sides could only be guessed at by a new pattern of incendiarism, and by a new quality in the noise that filtered down to them. It sounded, this time, as if some of the attackers were inside the fort. And, whatever was happening there, it made Earl Siward's observers thankful to have no part of it.

This time there was no victorious shout of any kind. Only, after a very long time, the noise seemed to die away, bit by bit, and men began to come down the hillside.

The watchers gathered what news they could and ran to wake the lord of Northumbria.

They found him not only wakened already, but apparently dressing, in a high temper, and speaking sharply as he did so to two men from his household who had not been there before. Before the watchers could even open their mouths, the Earl's body-servant came running with his boots and his cloak, and three more people pushed in the doorway and joined the others, looking half-slept and wary and as bad-tempered as they dared.

'Well?' snapped the Earl, looking up, and the senior of the two observers jumped and gathered his wits. 'They tried Dunsinane again, my lord, and got in. But they didn't manage to take the place and eventually got driven out, with a lot of wounded and dead. They don't know how many of Thorfinn's men they killed, but they say there can't be so many left. Thorfinn himself is still alive, so they say. My lord of Allerdale and my lord your nephew are both wounded, but say they would try again if you give them men from our army. Theirs won't follow them again.'

'Bring them here,' Siward said. He stood up.

'We *are* here,' said Thor of Allerdale from the doorway.

You would not at once recognise the big, carrot-haired man who had run Cumbria so long and so shrewdly under his various masters. Weariness had bleached him to neutrality, and all that was left was a masking of blood and sap-smears and peat, and an arm that dripped red down his breech-leg. He said, 'Next time, we bring you his head.'

Malcolm behind him did not speak. Siward looked at him. 'You got spitted?'

In the fleshy face, the cheekbones jutted unnaturally between the hollows below and above, and the small rose-mouth was a double white line. Malcolm said, 'Our men are tired, or we would have had him this time. Give us two hundred. Two hundred, that's all.'

'I told you,' Siward said. 'Wait till morning, when your men are rested. You've lost a lot, and upset them. It doesn't do any good. Try again tomorrow. I've got to go.'

Spoken like that, it could have meant anything. That he wished to visit the wounded. Review the battle-terrain. Inspect the state of the horses. Visit the easing-pit, even.

Malcolm said, 'My lord, before you go, will you not change your mind? There are still four hours to dawn. The honour of taking Thorfinn should belong to the Northumbrian army.'

Siward picked up his helmet. 'You have it,' he said; and rammed the thing on his head. It had a boar carved on top, to safeguard him. It had worked pretty well in this campaign. He said, 'By the time this dawn breaks, I expect the Northumbrian army and the rest of us with it to be off the Ness of Fife on our way south. I'm for York. I've done enough. I've taken the country for you. There's Scone. You can have yourself crowned there, if you can find enough people to do it.'

'It's levelled,' said Malcolm. He frowned.

Allerdale's exhaustion was of a different order. He said, 'You're *leaving*? My lord? Why? And on the ships?'

'They're all upriver, waiting,' said Siward. 'We have seven miles to march through the valleys there. The men won't mind. I haven't shared out the booty as yet. You have what belongs to your army?'

Malcolm said, 'I don't understand. You say you've taken the country. Maybe you have. But you haven't taken the King. And how can you keep the country unless you leave an army? You're removing the Northumbrians. And if all the ships are going . . . Are you taking the men from the Danish ships, too?'

'I hired them,' said Siward. More men had come in, including lord Ligulf, also, you would say, in a temper. Siward said, 'My army can look after Lothian and help Allerdale from time to time with any trouble he may have in Cumbria; but Northumbria is its business, and when there is trouble there, that's where I'll be.

'Allerdale's men are still with you. You're supposed to be the new lord of Fife and Angus and Atholl, so I suppose Bishop Malduin and his kinsmen and the young lords from all these parts might be expected to stay behind also and help you populate your new kingdom. As for Thorfinn, he doesn't sound to me like very much of a threat. If any of them up there are still alive in the morning, it won't take you very long to get rid of them. Or if your men have lost heart, sit about till they die.' He examined his sword and shoved it into the sheath, turning.

Malcolm said, 'You said you would see me King of Alba. The King wished you Godspeed. You got money from Harold of Wessex.'

Siward said, 'The King wished me Godspeed. The King wanted this war because he agreed with Earl Harold. Thorfinn of Alba was playing too great a part in the affairs of the nation and would be better got rid of.'

He heaved a laugh. 'And, as you say, Earl Harold gave me money. Earl Harold wants Northumbria for his young brother Tostig. My son is dead. My nephew is dead. Tostig will have it if I am killed on campaign in Alba, or if my kinsmen waste their time and their claims on slaughtering each other while I am away.

'I am going back to prevent that now. If, with a kingdom placed in your lap, you cannot pinch out the man on that hill and then rule it, I doubt very much if you were of the stuff that makes kings in the first place. I must go.'

Ligulf said to Forne, 'What?'

And Forne said, 'A messenger from the south. Osulf, Orm, and Archil are mustering. He's right. If he doesn't get back, he'll lose York.'

They stood and watched Siward stride out of the tent, and his nephew follow him, speaking still, with the man from Allerdale at his side.

Forne said, 'Which King would you rather have, if you came from Alba?'

'What?' said Ligulf. He brought his attention back. 'Ah, yes. Your wife's father had a leaning towards our man on the hill. Well, I tell you this. I sympathise with friend Malcolm. If I were friend Malcolm and carried just a little more weight with my allies, I would get between Siward and his ships and dare him to abandon me before Dunsinane were mine. For whoever plants his banner in Scone, there can be only one King of Alba while Thorfinn is alive.'

A woman's voice said, 'No, don't. Don't rouse him yet.'

And another's, close at hand, said, 'We must. Morgund will, anyway.'

Thorfinn opened his eyes. The third attack then, so quickly. But, of course, it would be. He lifted his head from his chest and said, 'I'm awake.' He had thought Morgund died when Malpedar did.

Cormac's wife said, 'Not another attack. But some sort of movement down below.'

She looked composed, the way women could in the midst of disaster. The dying fire from the citadel glimmered on the bandaging on her arm. Neither Groa nor the other two women had suffered much hurt so far, except the pains of loss and exhaustion, and those would be worse later on. The firing of the citadel, though, had been a mixed blessing. It showed them their attackers, but it also silhouetted the defenders against the blaze.

The besiegers had cut Tuathal down by its light, although he was still alive. He had heard Bishop Jon's voice somewhere, too, although he knew the Bishop could not walk any more than Cormac, who had done valorous things propped on the wall. If this was Morgund coming towards him, then he and Gillocher were the only two uncrippled leaders.

Of men, he supposed they had lost a hundred dead, and nearly that number of wounded. Their only success had been with the Black Hill, where his extra defenders had managed to extinguish Allerdale's attempt to take over the crest overlooking them.

Instead, he still had a few of his own men over there, and by firing the citadel had gulled both Siward and Allerdale, so it seemed, into thinking the Black Hill was now in friendly hands.

That way, they had managed to smuggle across some of the worst of their wounded, and then the country people. They could not get off the hill, for Allerdale's people ringed it, and Siward held the vale to the south, between the Sidlaws and the hills and braes that led to the Tay. But when Dunsinane fell, they might have a chance of escape.

The thirty or so who were left with him now were all men whose business was fighting, and his friends their mormaers, and his own wife and the mormaers' womenfolk, who would not leave and who had been their mainstay, with food and weapons and the binding of wounds.

He saw Groa kneeling by someone now, her short, ragged hair whipped by the wind. Somewhere out on the hill, a long red flag blew cold on the bushes instead of lying warm on her breast, or on his. And beside it, the torn gown he had worn in the foolish masquerade which had still brought Jon and himself back to safety and earned enough time to make the Black Hill defence finally possible.

The pity of it was that Malcolm had been determined enough, or stupid enough, or obstinate enough, to launch attack after attack, no matter how many men he might lose, instead of embarking, as one had hoped, on a long, peaceful siege. One wondered just how much encouragement he had received from Thor or from Siward, and what the reasons of Thor or of Siward might be. Siward's men, at any rate, had taken no part in either attack after the parley. Siward had more sense than to throw away men when he could attain the same end simply by waiting.

Except that now he did not appear to be waiting. Propped in his corner of the turf-and-stone wall, wedged into it like a piece of the masonry, Thorfinn watched the campfires blink and blink as men and horses passed and repassed, and listened to the rising hum of men bestirring themselves, ready for action.

On their side, there was nothing more they could do. He and the others were as ready for action as they could ever be, resting where they would fight. The great outer ring of the fort was long since beyond them to hold, even against a force as circumscribed as the Allerdale one. They had retired first to the inner ring, and now to the crown of the lower hill, where there were buildings behind a stout palisade. The ideal spot, of course, would have been the watch-tower on the knoll higher up, but that was burning still. And the heat, if it kept them away, would at least prevent the enemy also from occupying it.

As Morgund came over, Thorfinn said, 'All right. Here are your orders. This time we spit on them.'

The planes of Morgund's face, dim in the torchlight, looked puzzled. Thorfinn said, 'No. But I don't think boiling water will do much good this time. Leave the vats full, that's all. They'll fire the palisades.'

Bishop Jon's voice, from somewhere on the ground, said, continuing a suspended discussion, 'And the holy nuns there, tending the heavenly fire at Kildare: what would they say now, to hear you miscall our sweet Brigit like that?'

'Very well. In time of trouble, where was she?' said Thorfinn. Trumpet-calls now, and orders; and a movement in towards the foot of the hill, hidden even in daylight by the fall of the ground, and now quite invisible. Somewhere above, there should be a moon. At present, there were not even stars. After the clear July day, clouds had come in from the sea, and the breeze had stiffened and turned away the lingering heat of the ground. Now the heat of the fire, too, was dying, and there was no part of his body with warmth in it.

Bishop Jon said, 'Are ye dead or alive?'

'Let me think,' Thorfinn said. He saw Groa come up, and greeted her with his eyes.

'Alive,' said Bishop Jon crossly. 'Thanks to the Blessed Brigit. And am I dead or alive? Alive, I say; and let him deny it with an oath of three twelves who says otherwise. As to Tuathal here, I cannot tell.'

'I prayed to the Trinity,' said Tuathal. He sounded drowsy.

'Traitor!' said Bishop Jon. 'Are they coming yet? Ah, the music and harmony of the belly-darts, and the sighing and the winging of the spears and the lances. What about the Brecbennoch?'

'Keep it,' said Thorfinn. Lines of torches moving towards the foot of the hill. Other brands, higher up, held by horsemen. Of the lighted snippets that were tents, groups had darkened.

Morgund said, 'They won't harm the Lady.'

In the darkness, you could hear Tuathal's smile in his voice. 'A woman hung with a relic of the saint who would not so much as acknowledge a dairymaid? *Where there is a cow, there will be a woman, and where there is a woman, there will be trouble*, said St Columba. I keep to the Trinity, myself.'

The moon came out, and Thorfinn could see the look on Groa's face, and then one by one the others, lying in their shadows against the wall. She said, 'I have another cloak,' and knelt, letting the weight of it fall to the ground before she drew it over him. He did not ask who had died.

Eochaid's sister said, 'My lady,' and Groa touched his hand and rose quickly and went.

Then Gillocher said, 'My lord?'

'Yes?' said Thorfinn. The foot of the hill was still hidden, but in the new silver light he could see that files of men were indeed marching out of the tumble of moor they had occupied. And the tents had not merely darkened. Half of them had disappeared.

Unbrushed since morning, Gillocher's moustaches stuck up like tightly curled wool. His eyes were round. He said, 'The ladies are right. The Tay is full of longships. And men are marching.'

'I see them,' said Thorfinn.

'You see them on this side,' said Gillocher. 'But, my lord, they are on the other side of Dunsinane as well. Marching southwards.'

Thorfinn said nothing. Bishop Jon, his voice nearer and stronger, said, 'Did

I hear you aright? Earl Siward's men are marching round the foot of this hill and off southwards?'

'Towards the ships?' Thorfinn said. He spoke softly, not to disturb the sweet idea that had entered what was left of his mind. He said, 'What other banners do you see?'

Gillocher's head moved backwards and forwards between them. He would never lead an army to glory or out of it, but he made a good job of ruling Mar. And who else did he, Thorfinn, know who had led an army to glory? Or out of it?

Gillocher said, 'My lord Siward's flag was in the van. And then the flag of Bamburgh. I'm sure of that.'

'But not Thor of Allerdale, or Malcolm,' said Thorfinn, his eyes on the glinting shadows below. 'For there they are, I think. Moving round to take up Siward's positions, but more thinly spread. And there's a new tent with someone's flag going up. Whose? Morgund? Anyone?'

'It's Malcolm's,' said Groa. 'Thorfinn?'

They were all looking at him. He had nothing to give them but hope, and conjecture.

'Suppose,' said Thorfinn, 'that there is trouble down south and Earl Siward has had to withdraw his forces to deal with it. They seem to be withdrawing. And there are the ships. And I'm willing to believe it's not an elaborate trick. They don't need one.

'Suppose that, the ships having gone, my nephew Malcolm and my third cousin Thor remain behind, no doubt in outrage, to deal with us. Will they deal with us tonight?'

'With all that confusion below?' Groa said. 'And with the wounded they'll have? Unless he's more irresistible than he seems, I doubt if Malcolm would get Allerdale's forces to follow him. I think he'll wait now for morning.'

'I think so, too,' Thorfinn said. 'Which means, if all our guesses are right, we ought to try to get off this hill before daylight.'

'Now, then,' said Bishop Jon. 'Why did we not think to do that before?'

Tuathal, it seemed, had grasped it. 'Because Allerdale and Siward between them had us surrounded,' he said. 'But look. Allerdale's men have only got round to the north and the east, where they've always been. They don't have the Black Hill, although they think they do. They don't have the cleft between the Black Hill and the knoll here, although they think they do. We can't get up Strathmore, because they're guarding that. We can't cross the Black Hill and get down the east of the range, because we know they're there as well. But the south is open. It's full of Siward's men on their way to the river, but there's no cordon resettled there as yet. In the dark—'

'In the dark, we could climb down the steep side and mingle with them,' said Thorfinn. 'If we could walk. If we could pass as Northumbrian soldiers. If my understanding of what is happening is not wholly and extravagantly baseless.'

He paused. They all watched him: the dying, the disabled, the exhausted. He smiled. 'I don't think it is. Let's do it.'

He saw their faces warm in return; and then the moon vanished.

'*A Brigit bennach ar sêtt.* I told you so,' said Bishop Jon.

The sound of his voice, talking, was the chief recollection most people there brought away from their last moments on the hill as the numbers dwindled and dwindled, and the fit men and the women, bundled in tunic and trousers, made their way down the precipitous slopes and set off through the crowds in the dark.

The theory, it seemed, had been correct, and the slim hope had been realised. Whether through the offices of the Blessed Brigit or not, the moon stayed under cover. Those who were disabled or too ill to walk were left to the last, Thorfinn himself being of that number; and Tuathal and Bishop Jon remained with him.

Soon after the first women left, Cormac died, and Thorfinn sent Groa off with his staunch little widow. She went swiftly and without demur. The task of taking the sick down the hill would be heavy and specialised work. She could only hinder.

There was a wait, at the end, while they tried to improvise something on horseback. By then, it was later than it should be; nearer the hour when the sky would start to lighten. Already the bustle below them was lessening. Consciousness came and went, escorted by Bishop Jon's voice.

'Plague, tempest, and death, and men languid. Well, what saved us this day we shall never know,' said Bishop Jon. 'For, as you are aware, the Pope that blessed the banner is dead, and St Columba and St Brigit and even the Holy Trinity may have their prejudices; especially when faced by a man who has runes on his axe. If we owe this deliverance to the Aesir, all I ask is that you never inform me.'

'Who are the Aesir?' said Thorfinn, blandly.

'You don't know. Naturally,' said Bishop Jon. 'The whole army leaps into battle thundering *Albanaid!* save for the howl of the King hooting *Knyja's.*'

'An invitation to move on,' said Thorfinn. 'Memorise it.'

Tuathal said, 'If you had allowed yourself to surrender when that fleet sailed into the Forth, this would never have happened.'

'If Bishop Jon had allowed himself to surrender at St Cathán's, this would never have happened,' Thorfinn said.

'Then there was the fleet in the Tay,' Tuathal said. 'And the Cumbrian army from Dunkeld. Do you never feel you've wasted a day?'

They were resting quite close to one another, but he was too cold to answer. Tuathal's fingers, a little warmer than his own, touched his wrist and then closed on his hand. Bishop Jon said, 'The jokes you are listening to, such as they are, arise, you should know, from a profound sense of inadequacy, and even of awe. I have seen men overcome obstacles such as these out of pride, and out of greed, and even, be it whispered, from belief in the power of the Almighty. But what brought you to this place, from sunrise this morning? Apart from a most God-given valour.'

A leaf. A twig. A rose. A rod. A prophecy.

TEN

ALL THAT AUTUMN, while Thorfinn slept, the red-haired lady of Alba and Lulach her son ruled with the voice of the King, moving from hall to hall in Mar and Moray and Buchan as she had done when Gillacomghain had been Mormaer there, and Thorfinn after him, and sometimes into Cromarty and Caithness, as she had done also in the years before King Duncan died.

The place to which she always returned, however hard the journey, was the monastery in whose care the King lay, and those others who had also failed to recognise when to surrender.

Monymusk had been Lulach's choice, and she thought Thorfinn would have approved it. Its little stone church and the hall and hospice and cabins on the banks of the Don stood buttressed by the low hills of Mar, safely north of the borders of Angus, whose loyalty was as yet unknown, and south of both Deer and Mortlach, whose doors stood open to receive him if danger returned.

During the weeks when Thorfinn did not open his eyes, or did not know her when he did, no danger stirred. From Dunkeld to Stow, the country lay in its blood also, emptied of life.

Siward and his Northumbrians had gone, and the overseas mercenaries along with him. If Malcolm or Thor of Allerdale, finding themselves tricked, had attempted to drive their Cumbrians north, that bruised army, already far from home and glutted with booty, must have baulked. The first sure news of the Cumbrians was that they were marching off west, where their ships were waiting.

Leaving Malcolm stranded, naturally, in his tents beside Scone, protected only by the ranks of the disaffected: Ghilander and Kineth and Colban, Cathail and Fothaid, their friends and their kinsmen. And, of course, Bishop Malduin.

Thorkel Fóstri, the first of the northmen to arrive, with Paul and Erlend galloping behind him, was also the first to invoke the peculiar powers of the northern gods against Malduin of Alba, against Thor of Allerdale, and against King Svein of Denmark and all their lovers and kindred.

She had prepared the boys for what they would see in Thorfinn's chamber. They came out silent, Paul with his hand at the neck of his young brother, and she spoke to them, and then let Sinna take them to the little hall outside the monastery, where Lulach and Morgund were, and her women.

Then Thorkel Fóstri came out, and paid no attention to the men in the four occupied beds, or to the brother moving about them, or to herself in her plain lay-helper's robe, but sank down on a stool in the doorway and, dropping his head in his hands, burst into curses.

Groa said, 'The monks are fasting. For him, and for the others.' After a bit, she said, 'We may all feel like that, but you know that he doesn't. He accepts that people alter their plans all the time, and believes the art lies in being prepared for it. He will take all the blame for this upon himself. Cursing his kinsmen won't help anybody.'

Thorkel Fóstri flung his hands down and glared at her. His eyes were wet, but he paid no attention to them, fanning his anger. He said, 'Svein of Denmark isn't his kinsman. I thought your father was his war-leader in Halland? It was a waste of time, wasn't it, the months he spent with the foreigners, courting Svein and Adalbert and the Emperor, cajoling the Pope? The Pope's banner and the Pope's bishops did nothing to save him. And Svein took his silver and then resold all his ships to his enemy.'

It might have occurred to him, you would think: the agony she had gone through, trying to divine what had happened in Denmark, and her father's share in it.

It had occurred to him. He was only, in his misery, pulling her down beside him. Because, perhaps, she seemed composed. Because she had been there when it happened, and he had not. Groa said, 'I'm sure my father didn't know what was happening. I can only think that someone persuaded King Svein that Thorfinn was planning a secret alliance with Norway. Someone like Harold of Wessex. He's King Svein's first cousin.'

'So's his brother Tostig the Frog,' Thorkel Fóstri said. 'But why strengthen Siward, if Wessex wants into Northumbria?'

'It would get rid of Thorfinn,' Groa said. 'Without the extra power, I don't think Siward would have risked leaving York. And once he left York, he might not have got back, even if he lived to get out of Alba.'

Thorkel Fóstri's eyes were drying. He said, 'I heard there was a rising and Siward had to return. So Wessex fomented it?'

'They meant to,' Groa said. 'They probably tried to. But someone else got in before them. There are a lot of dissatisfied merchants in York.'

Thorkel Fóstri said, 'You speak as if you knew who it was.'

'Is it likely?' said Groa. 'Three hundred miles north of Siward's capital? It failed, anyway. Earl Alfgar was telling me. He was here two days ago, hoping to talk to Thorfinn.'

'To *talk* to him?' said Thorkel Fóstri.

Groa said, 'I gather that, in Mercia, wounds however dangerous would by now be invisible and a magical spring of new blood have restored what is deficient.'

She was being unfair. At that bedside, even Alfgar had been silent, looking down at the closed eyes and the brown, naked body, dressed only in wood and pulped herbage and bandages. That humming centre of energy, suspended on eider-feathers, blank and pliant as wax in its mould.

She wondered if Thorkel Fóstri understood what she was saying.

It seemed that he had. He said, 'You spoke of alliance with Norway. Was that Alfgar's idea?'

'Perhaps,' Groa said. 'He didn't say. Chiefly, he came to see how Thorfinn did. I thought it best to tell him that there was no chance of an alliance between Alba and Norway so long as Thorfinn was alive. He said he would come back.'

'None?' said Thorkel Fóstri. His eyes scanned her face, as if reading the weather. In Thorfinn, unless you knew him, the dense brown eyes gave nothing away.

She said, 'For the same reason that he would not let the north fight for him. You know that.'

'The north fought for him,' Thorkel Fóstri said. 'Killer-Bardi is dead, and the men from eight ships along with him. They tell me you lost six mormaers.'

Mael-Isu and Gillecrist. Ferteth and Malpedar. Cormac and Eochaid. Lorcáin the Bard and Klakkr the young body-servant. Hugh de Riveire dead, and Osbern Pentecost and all his men slain or taken prisoner. Missing: one hard-working, exuberant bishop called Hrolf. And killed in the field, three thousand men who had fought for Thorfinn of Alba.

She said, 'We have you and Lulach. And Gillocher and Morgund. And Odalric and the rest in the north. That is why it was wise not to allow them to fight.'

She did not mention Prior Tuathal or Bishop Jon because they lay before him, in two of the beds in this room, with the same chance of life that Thorfinn had.

Alfgar had been brisk, bending over them. Alfgar had said that never, in his long acquaintance with hard men, had he ever come across such a stiff-necked trio as her husband and these two, and if it so happened that they did not intend to leave their beds for a bier, he did not see who was going to succeed in making them.

He had also said something about being inclined to have a short discussion with Thor of Allerdale, except that he owed him some money.

When, now, Thorkel Fóstri said, 'What can I do?' she gave him the answer she had given Alfgar. 'I have spoken to Lulach and all the people who know Alba best. Winter is coming. There seems no immediate danger. The way we are, to think of revenge or retribution would be crazy. And, in any case, it is for Thorfinn to do what he thinks necessary, not anyone else. His reputation is not so weak, nor is ours, that we have to rush to prove anything. We shall all know, soon enough, what he wants to do.'

'Shall we?' he said.

'Lulach says so,' said Groa.

He stayed for some days, talking to the others, until he satisfied himself that what she had told him was true.

Earl Siward was not going to return: had not even shown any wish to resurrect the forts of the Lothians and stamp with ownership of a sort the smoking desert he had made of most of it.

The broken buildings, the burned and trampled crops of Fife and Strathearn presented Malcolm likewise with a problem in Scone. As the days grew cold, it became clear that there was insufficient food and shelter for the numbers that alone would guarantee him some kind of safety.

The men of Angus who had followed Kineth and Ghilander and Colban, and the men of Fife who had followed Bishop Malduin and the new young lords Fothaid and Cathail had families in Bernicia to think of, and hearths of a soldier's kind, and only temporary, but at least better than this, with the cold river overflowing its banks and nothing to eat but salt stores and what you could slaughter. And even that was sometimes suspect; tainted with the murrain that afflicted the cattle that autumn, so that any beasts they had found, that Siward's army or Allerdale's had not eaten or driven away, or that the owners had not herded up to their invisible grounds in the mountains, were half carcass already, and were for burning, not eating, half of them.

In the spring, it would be different. In the spring, all Malcolm's loyal men, all those who had struck a blow for the sole and rightful Bishop of Alba would come back, with their wives, to receive the land that was to be their reward. So Malcolm's uncle Thorfinn in his time had taken war into Fife. So Thorfinn had usurped for the Crown, for himself and his Queen and his stepson, for the Prior of St Serf's and his party of penmen and property-managers, the lands whose owners had died, leaving a line behind them that had lapsed, or whose heirs lay as yet in the cradle.

In the spring, they would come back, and would be forbearing with the thralls and the little farmers who had found their way back to their land from Mar and Moray, wearied with living in earth-houses and cabins and tents, and with relying on meal and ale given in charity. A family liked to sow its own seed and till its own land, come the spring-time. Some of them would be allowed to come back. For the rest, there were peasants enough in Bernicia and west of Bernicia to work their land for them, if need be. Slaves were easily got. And with the booty they had, they could pay for them.

There was a risk, of course. If Earl Siward had stayed as he should, and sent his ships back and forth with proper provisions, they might have got some buildings up now, and enough of a garrison, here and there, to make quite sure that their hard-won land was not snatched from them. It had wrecked their plans, that retreat of Earl Siward's. There had been a time when, urged by Bishop Malduin, Malcolm had all but struck tent and marched off south after him. With Siward and Allerdale gone, and the King still alive, all the pains of conquest, it seemed for a moment, might have gone for nothing.

But of course that was not true. Most of the fighting-men of Alba were dead, as were most of their leaders. The flag blessed by the Pope had proved worthless. The King himself was struck down. If Thorfinn lived, would anyone follow him? And if he raised an army tomorrow, how far could the tatters of Alba hold Scone, never mind Atholl, Angus, and Fife, and Siward's Lothians and Allerdale's Cumbria?

It was not hard to guess what Malcolm must be thinking, and all the reports that came north went to confirm it. Before Thorkel Fóstri went home, it was clear beyond doubt that the few thousand men who had gathered at Scone were not going to stay there, a wintry outpost in a deserted country.

And so it proved. By the time Thorfinn was rousing, at last, from his journey, Malcolm and Malduin and all their army had gone.

As perhaps he would have wished, the hour when Thorfinn came to awareness was private to himself, for both his wife and his stepson were absent, driven elsewhere by the endless cries for help, the ceaseless battle to deal with the ravages of what had happened.

The brethren at Monymusk, too, were hard-pressed by the needs of the sick and the dying outside the monastery as well as in it. The monk who, entering Thorfinn's chamber at night, found the King lying awake and himself again thought it enough to run with the news to his fellows, and in the morning to break it in triumph to the two patients still in the outer room.

When he had gone, the Prior of St Serf, the morning bristles fringing his pock-scarred face, swung his legs to the edge of his pallet and said, 'I'm going to see him.'

Bishop Jon, being from the waist upwards wholly restored, was shaving himself. He said, 'I agree as to the necessity, but I can't say I'm impressed by your chances. Your legs look like ribbons.'

'Faith will uphold me,' Tuathal said. He put his feet on the rushes and his knees creaked. He said, 'I quote, in the teeth of you, St Brigit, who could hang her cloak on a sunbeam.'

'It's snowing,' said Bishop Jon. 'Ah, why am I worrying? I see you would hardly let down a thistle for swiftness and lightness.' The scum from his half-naked jaw dripped unnoticed on to his towel, and his brow had creased in three directions. Tuathal limped quickly over the reeds and knocked on the jamb of the inner door.

'Come in,' said Thorfinn's voice. And Tuathal pushed the hanging aside.

There was nothing in the room but the bed, and a stool and table beside it, and a crucifix on the wall. No longer uncovered since the fever abated, the King lay with a decent quilt drawn to his waist. Above that, the white cage of bandaging still covered his shoulders and neck and his upper arms, holding his elbows close to his sides. His hands and forearms, which were quite untouched, were folded across his chest in the only manner, probably, that was open to him. Even the battle-swelling in his right hand had gone, that showed he had fought the last hours of the day using only his axe. Tuathal had seen Norsemen on raids plunge their right hands in cold water, in the course of a long killing, to restore them.

Above the bandages, the beaked face with its tall brow had acquired no beauty from the strictness and pallor of illness. His hair, bundled black on the pillow, met the black, bristling line of new beard clothing his jaw and the shelf of his lip. And under the single black hedge of his eyebrows, his eyes stood open within the black, stocky line of his lashes: lashes so short and so scattered that you would say nature had excelled, yet again, in the economy with which she had made him.

Tuathal said, 'My lord King . . . How are you?'

'Brooding,' said Thorfinn.

From the other side of the curtain, Bishop Jon heard his fellow-churchman utter a sound which was not a cry of alarm, but could almost have passed for a laugh. The murmur of voices, which had only just started, broke off; and then the King's voice said something again, speaking quite normally although not very loud; and Tuathal replied in the same tone.

After five minutes, the curtain stirred again and Tuathal, walking with a little more ease, limped his way back and dropped on his bed.

'Well?' said Bishop Jon.

Tuathal said, 'I wonder why he was denied comeliness?'

'So that people will listen to what he has to say,' Bishop Jon said. 'He spoke to you, then?'

'He knew how we would think before we did,' said Tuathal. 'He remembers very clearly what happened, and has used the night to contain it. I should like, were I not a Christian, to inflict as much on that fool of a monk.'

'I see,' said Bishop Jon. After a moment, he said, 'And physically?'

'I would say his life is secure. His weakness is something again, and the scale of his wounds. It will be a long business. He knows it.'

'Will he stay apart in his room?' said Bishop Jon.

'He spoke,' said Tuathal, 'of joining us in here for Christmas, if there was going to be a Christmas this year.'

Shortly after that, the Lady returned, and for the space of half an hour Bishop Jon read steadily aloud to Prior Tuathal from the writings of the Blessed Augustine, with whom he did not always see eye to eye, until the erratic conversation in the next room had given way to cadences of a more normal kind. By the time Bishop Jon shut the book, conversation itself had been replaced by what sounded like a public gemot.

After an hour of answering questions, the Lady, with good sense, clearly prescribed an interval and emerged, flushed and smiling. Seldom in its ceremonial coif, her hair since its lopping was most often wrapped in a folded napkin of silk, from which dark red strands looped and waved. Whatever Thorfinn's deficiencies as another Apollo, there was no doubt that he could bring those about him to bloom, one way or another.

When she returned, after a long space, she had Morgund with her. It was a pattern that was to become familiar to the incapacitated churchmen in the outer room as, morning and afternoon, friends were ushered in: magnates of the north as well as the remaining mormaers of Alba, who entered the inner room reluctantly, to emerge thoughtfully, later, with a different look and a different step.

Occasionally, observing the presence of the two invalids propped on their pillows, one would call a greeting or cross to make an enquiry. Pumped, they had no revelations to make that gave any inkling of what Thorfinn was thinking, beyond the fact that they felt better for seeing him.

The Prior of Monymusk, appealed to on his daily visitation, rebuked his patients for their curiosity and recommended that they think of nothing but getting well, whereby they could serve their King when he was ready for it. Since Prior Ruadhan's familia now included not only the Culdees of Monymusk but the refugee monks of Muthill, Dunblane, Abernethy, and Monifieth among others, the Bishop at least realised that there were times when even a prince of the church should be seen and not heard, and ceased asking accordingly.

The Lady, who came and went all the time, except when there were sickroom matters afoot, was not much more forthcoming. The King, it appeared, was slowly mending. As to his mood: 'How can one tell?' said Groa, looking them in the eye. 'Resigned? No. Nothing so Christian. How does he look?' she said to her escort of the moment, who happened to be the lord Lulach.

Her son considered. 'Grim, but calm,' he said. 'Would you say?'

And with that, they had to be satisfied.

The Feast of Columbanus had passed: a landmark in the calendar at Cologne and Luxeuil. Bishop Jon had at first been surprised to find the bears of Columbanus over here until he remembered the imprint of St Finnian of Clonard on all the churches hereabout, and the Irish strain in Angus and Mar that had brought the name Sinill into Bishop Malduin's family.

The lord Lulach, married to Sinill's daughter, had attended Mass on that day, Prior Ruadhan had observed. Whether the celebration of the Eucharist had taken place in the inner room also, he did not say. If Thorfinn were not yet quite himself, the chances were, thought Bishop Jon, that it had. He wondered if the Responsaries had been sung to the setting of Pope Leo, and further wondered why, when he mentioned it, Tuathal withdrew into thought.

Then he remembered Eochaid had been with the Prior at Rome. Eochaid, who had died at Scone and whose casket, perhaps, had brought the rest of them here. The Bishop said, 'There was the decapitated head of Donn Bo, that turned its face to the wall and sang sweetly all night. The music survives.'

'I suppose so,' Tuathal said.

Then the Feast of St Finnian himself was upon them, and everyone withdrew to the church save themselves, weaklings that they were, and the occupant of the inner room.

With the curtain drawn back, the King's voice could now carry from his room to theirs, and for some days now they had established in this way a simple form of dialogue, consisting largely of greetings and the occasional question or comment. Since the first time, Tuathal had not attempted to return through the doorway, feeling that the traffic, for a sick man, was already heavy enough.

On his side, Tuathal's limbs were so much stronger that he was able each day to work himself up and down the small room, and even on one occasion out into the yard, which had proved more exhausting than he had expected.

Bishop Jon, with a festering spear-wound to contend with, spent his days propped on the pillows, reading, gambling in a judicious, clerical way, and talking in his mellifluous voice about everything except the terrestrial future. Only in his prayers did he draw Tuathal with him in remembrance of those they had lost; and, for that, reserved all the passion so carefully blanched from his daily habit, that their dead might be waked with psalms and hymns and canticles wherever there were voices to pray.

Today, undisturbed by ministering footsteps, lay or clerical, the two men rested in silence as over the roofs of the monastery there floated the rich, strenuous voices of the monks, raised in psalmody.

The ring of it overlaid the lightest slur of the rushes, so that Thorfinn's voice, close at hand, shocked with its suddenness.

'This is not altogether the lunacy it may appear,' it said. 'But more an affirmation to the populace that their monarch is in vigour and ready to lead the other half to slaughter any time they may wish. There is an empty bed here?'

The King had come through the doorway. Adhering in suspended motion to the boarding of the little room, he was robed from neck to ground in the heavy grey wool the monks wore, showing none of his injuries. Above it, his face was clean-shaven again, and made out of white laths.

Tuathal flung his sheet aside. 'There are two,' he said.

'No,' said Thorfinn. 'Or if anything goes wrong, they'll blame you.' He took two more steps round the wall and stopped again, measuring the open distance to the nearest bed. Because of the cold, both the door and the shutters were firmly shut, but the room was bright with candlelight and the glow of the fire, burning on its hearth at the end of the hut instead of the centre, where it might incommode the service between the two pairs of beds. A burst of singing rose again, fierce as a dog barking, and the rosin bubbled and fizzed in the moss-candles. Thorfinn said, 'Can't we afford wax any more?'

Tuathal said, 'You get used to the smell. Look, it won't serve any purpose if they find you—'

'—prostrate on the floor, reciting the formula of perseverance? They won't,' said Thorfinn and in three steps reached the central pillar between himself and the vacant bed.

'It's a remarkable style you have, though,' said Bishop Jon. 'Like a man walking on scaffolding. Friend Tuathal—'

'I've got him,' said Tuathal. It was half true. In fact, he had made of himself simply another pillar. Thorfinn could neither grasp nor be grasped. He stood still.

After a while, Thorfinn said, 'Don't let me keep you, if you want to do anything else.' And then, at last, 'All right. To the bed. Then get back to your own. I shan't need you. If I can't get over this, I can't hope to hold councils.'

Bishop Jon said, 'Judgement of God!'

Tuathal moved with the King to the empty bed, and the King let himself fall in. The beds were built like coffins, boarded in to the floor to keep out rats and dogs and the draughts. He stood, and the mallet-thud of the King's breathing studded the singing. Bishop Jon said, 'Does he bleed, can you see?'

Tuathal shook his head.

'Then leave him,' said Bishop Jon. 'It is his achievement. He has to begin somewhere.'

It was an achievement. It was what the men outside needed to know: that their King was walking again, and had strolled from one room to the other that morning, to chat with his friends. The surprise on Prior Ruadhan's face when Mass ended and he and the Lady went across to the hospice had been worth seeing, everyone said. And the surprise on the Lady's face, to find the King leaning back on his pillows, listening to Bishop Jon against the opposite wall discoursing on Predestination.

'St Lucy, painted with the balls of her eyes in a dish. You look astonished,' said Thorfinn.

'Good,' said the Lady. *'What I feel is something I shall tell you later. I suppose we have St Finnian to thank that you have enough strength back to talk with at all?'*

'Feast days,' said Thorfinn, *'always bring their own special blessing.'*

That was December. By January, the kingdom of Scotia in its changed world had been skilfully reconstituted, and the inner council of three convalescent men who brought it about had been joined by a fourth.

He came a week after the King had transferred himself into the company of Bishop Jon and Prior Tuathal, and his coming was heralded by a confusion of barking and shouting unusual even in the thronged community that the King's presence had made of Monymusk. Tuathal, who had been making a speech, interrupted himself. 'What's that?'

'They're practising what Archbishop Juhel used to call *Les O of Advent*,' suggested Thorfinn lazily. '*O Sapientia*... It's perfectly plain. Are you deaf to wisdom this morning?'

'I wish I were deaf to ... They're coming here,' said Prior Tuathal, the crossness fading out of his voice as the noise swirled outside the shut door of the hospice.

The door opened, and Ruadhan, the Prior of Monymusk, stepped inside, his face pale with emotion.

'My nephew Malcolm has arrived with an apology?' said Thorfinn. 'My wife's cousin's husband has appeared off the coast with a fleet of three hundred, come to pay a courtesy call?'

'My dear lord,' said Ruadhan, and stood aside to give others entry.

From the arm of the man who was helping him: 'There was word,' said Bishop Hrolf, 'of a free bed in here. But if you are particular about your company, I can find another.' Then, his eyes finding Thorfinn and resting on him: 'Oh, my lord King,' he said.

'Can you feel your welcome?' said Thorfinn. 'We cannot speak it. There is a bed beside me. Bring him here.'

He came limping; no longer the man who balanced on half-finished towers and climbed palisades to put ferrets inside the leather of an erring man's sleeping-bag. His big-featured face, free of sawdust, was pale, and although his shoulders were broad as ever, the hands he stretched out as he came were too big for their wrists.

Thorfinn took them in his own, and dismissed both the helper and Prior Ruadhan with a sign as Hrolf sank to his knees. The door closed. Thorfinn said, 'That is an attitude for me, not for you. Your God can relent, after all.'

Warned by nothing in the King's face, but by some instinct of his own, Bishop Hrolf released Thorfinn's hands and, grasping the edge of the free bed, drew himself to sit uncomfortably on its edge. 'Sometimes,' he said. 'And so can men. You can thank Thor of Allerdale for looking after me.'

Thor, who with Malcolm had stormed Dunsinane again and again, regardless of cost, to try to kill Thorfinn his kinsman.

Tuathal said, 'You were his bishop. We heard you were lost by the Forth, in Siward's battle.'

Hrolf turned. To Bishop Jon he said, 'I heard you had fallen at St Cathán's. It's only a week since I learned that you were alive. It was a party of Allerdale men who found me and kept me for ransom, and when the fighting was over, Thor took me back to Cumbria himself, to be nursed until I could travel north.'

He turned back to the King. 'He made no trouble, either, when Alfgar helped to get the Norman families out of the country. He bears no animosity to anyone, now his purpose is achieved. Siward had promised him land in the border vales and in Lothian and even in Fife if he would help him. Now the way is clear, and in the spring he will take what he wants. He believes that there is no way that you or I or anyone left now can stop him. My lord, I have prayed for you.'

Thorfinn said, 'Something has upheld me, I am aware, that is not my own virtue. Tell me something. Would it dismay you if we were to disappoint my relative Thor in his expectations?'

Bishop Jon's voice from across the room said, 'That isn't possible. I keep telling you. That is too much to hope for.'

'In the long term?' said Thorfinn. 'Then let us try again. Would it give you concern if there were to be further conflict in which Thor of Allerdale would be on the opposite side?'

The big Bishop's face had changed. 'Then you are not going to leave Alba to Malcolm?'

'Do you think I should?' Thorfinn said.

'That's hardly the question,' Bishop Hrolf said. 'The question is can you do otherwise?'

'That,' said Thorfinn, 'is just what we were considering. Perhaps you would care, once you feel fit, to debate it with us? Unless, owing your life to Allerdale, you feel debarred from it?'

'I owe my life,' said Bishop Hrolf, 'according to your way of thinking, to the good chain-mail that twisted the spear in my side, and the smith at Holmepatrick that made the rings, and to the cross of Christ that he stamped on them.

Because of what Thor of Allerdale did, he will go to an easier accounting than he might have done. I owe him no service more.'

He yawned. 'If my lord King would excuse me?'

'Rest,' said Thorfinn, and signed to Tuathal, who stretched his hand for the bell that would bring the lay brethren running. But Bishop Hrolf had already slipped back into bed and, crossing his muddy boots on the coverlet, was allowing himself to slide into slumber.

And so the rebuilding began; for the next morning, in one searching exchange, Thorfinn and the best of his advisors gleaned all they needed to know of the rest of their situation: what was occurring in the world outside their borders.

They gleaned it with difficulty, for rest had restored Bishop Hrolf's appetite. When, washed and tended, he awaited the first tray of the day, he was heard to enquire of his fellow Bishop what the feeding was like.

'Need you ask?' said Bishop Jon, pumping air into and out of his face. 'The fruit and fat of the land, and the gifts of the sea in abundance. Here it comes.'

The bowls arrived, and were placed before the four men. Bishop Hrolf peered into his. 'You were saying?'

'A small collation of gruel,' said Bishop Jon blandly. ''Tis a low diet for us poor, bed-ridden mortals. You were saying?'

'I was saying that I rode twenty miles only yesterday,' said Bishop Hrolf. 'Had I known I would starve for it, I would have ridden in a different direction.'

'What would you enjoy?' asked Thorfinn.

The tone was enough. Bishop Hrolf turned, with suspicion.

'Yes?' said the King.

Bishop Hrolf gazed at the rafters. 'A bit of venison, maybe, with apples or leeks and some bread. Fish and eggs—there should be eggs. And not even wine: I should be content with ale, provided it's well brewed and seasoned. Now, would that be a sin? Even a small bird took bread to St Paul and St Antony.'

'Your small bird will serve you,' said the King, 'when you have finished talking.'

'You want to know whom you can trust?' Bishop Hrolf said.

'Who could afford that luxury?' Thorfinn said. 'No. I want to judge something much simpler. What, in their own interests, are all my fellow-rulers and would-be rulers likely to want to do next?'

Bishop Hrolf's powerful lips scoured the spoon. 'Thor of Allerdale? I've told you about him. The death of a son was not a thing he took lightly, I believe, but he is a man who cuts his losses. Leofwine and Dunegal of Nithsdale would not march against you, but they couldn't prevent their men joining Thor, which they did. Nor are they likely to refuse the land Thor could give them, which he will. They have a difficult time of it in Cumbria, with Siward stretching his eyes towards them, if not towards you, and Thor had little choice. I would expect Wessex to get a good share of the Alston silver from now on, which is what they wanted. And I would expect our friend Earl

Siward to be surprised at the reply he gets from Allerdale if he tries to act the overlord in those parts.'

'Even if he claims to be acting for Malcolm the son of the prince of Cumbria?' Thorfinn said.

Bishop Hrolf sent down three more spoonfuls of gruel. 'If he does that, Thor will be ready. He'll send an appeal for aid straight to King Edward of England, his one true overlord. Anyway, Thor thinks there's not much to fear now from Siward. Siward's hands are too full.'

'With the rising in his own Northumbria? We heard rumours,' Thorfinn said.

'If you heard it was Alfgar meddling, then you heard right,' Bishop Hrolf said. His spoon droned round the bowl, scouring it, like a man bruising mustard. 'Not openly, of course. Yet. But his claim to Northumbria is as good as Siward's. It was only his bad luck, I gather, that the Lady Emma chose Siward thirteen years ago to get rid of the previous incumbent.'

'But the attempt failed, and Earl Siward is still in charge. Suppose Earl Alfgar were to try again. What would Thor do?' said Thorfinn.

Bishop Hrolf dropped the shining spoon in its bowl and planked both on his table. 'Now, that does worry Thor,' he said. 'So far, he and Alfgar have got on reasonably well together, but Harold of Wessex is now favouring Mercia, and if Alfgar adds Northumbria to his father's empire, Cumbria will be nothing but an isolated pocket between Mercia and you, with all Thor's shipping threatened from Chester.'

'So in Thor's place,' said Thorfinn, 'you would look further up the west coast, wouldn't you, to our lands on the river Clyde? It's where Thor landed the force that took Dunkeld.'

'You're right, of course,' said Bishop Hrolf. 'Allerdale has begun moving men up into that part of Strathclyde already, with no real opposition. And Siward is letting him, whether he planned to or whether he has no alternative. So that at present no one power holds the land crossing between the Clyde and the Forth. And further north still, the west coast is held by your men of the north. It could be worse. But, meantime, you are cut off from Mercia and your ships have no sure anchorage between the Western Isles and the harbours of Mercia and of Wales. I'm dying of hunger.'

'Not yet,' said Thorfinn. 'England? Germany?'

Bishop Hrolf sighed. 'A Failure of Bread. The plight feared most by mankind. Very well. England. Harold of Wessex is flexing his ambitions daily, but has competition from young brother Tostig. Germany. The Emperor is at Goslar, trying to find a new Pope with Hildebrand's help after a little passage of arms against Baldwin of Flanders. The Emperor has also been feasting Bishop Ealdred and Abbot Alfwine, the rumour goes, as lavishly as if they were Godwinssons, and has encouraged Archbishop Herimann to do the same.'

'How Ealdred must be enjoying it,' Tuathal said from across the room. Putting down his bowl, he swung his legs out of bed with an agility increasing daily. 'Six months in Cologne? I wonder what he is buying? Psalters, chalices, statues, ideas for new churches . . .' He stepped across and, lifting a spoon from the rushes, cleaned it on a sheet-corner and restored it to the board òn Thorfinn's sheets. Tuathal said, 'I take it that Ealdred's mission has as much to do with the Pope-making as it has with trade and the return of the Athelings?'

'Thank you,' said Thorfinn. 'You may also take it that I can manage the rest by myself.'

His bowl was still half full. Tuathal, finding Bishop Hrolf's eyes upon him, turned aside and stepped back to his own bed. Bishop Hrolf cleared his throat. 'Of course the Pope-making matters. The Athelings are the Saxon heirs to the English throne and enjoyed the protection of the Emperor and the late Pope, but how might another Pope feel? One could imagine what use Duke William might make of the exiles in Normandy. He was, after all, promised the reversion of England himself. Also, a Pope of Hildebrand's choice might share Hildebrand's distaste for Archbishop Adalbert.'

'But the ultimate choice of Pope will be the Emperor's,' Thorfinn said. 'And, so far, he has always chosen wisely. The trouble lies in finding someone brave enough to accept. What else?'

'Some Irish gossip,' said Bishop Hrolf. 'Kells and Armagh, it seems, are at one another's throats again.'

Thorfinn's collation, too, was finished. He left the bowl on its board and leaned back, slackening. 'It's a pity,' he said. 'But we never could look for help from there. Now Eachmarcach has gone and Diarmaid is still successful, as I suppose he is, all we can hope for is that every faction remains absorbed in killing another.'

'Your hope,' said Bishop Hrolf, 'is being realised. But, in some quarters, Mercian rosettas are making a difference.'

'Alfgar's money? Alfgar is recruiting in Ireland?' The immense voice, for a moment, lost a little of its compression. 'He's a fool. Harold of Wessex supports Diarmaid. If Earl Harold finds out, there'll be trouble.'

'It depends,' said Bishop Hrolf. Since the incident of the spoon, he had made no further reference to food. 'If Alfgar wins Northumbria, he will be a force even Wessex will find it hard to withstand. And, what's more, he's followed your policy. He's cultivated both Bretons and Normandy. While he's excommunicated, Archbishop Juhel can't do much but amass money, but that he is doing with the greatest success. And Duke William's attention at the moment is held by the wars with Mayenne and Anjou, so that he won't be anxious to lose any more fighting-men overseas, but that may change.'

'I didn't know there were any Normans left,' Thorfinn said. It was the first sign of real tiredness. Then he said, 'So what is Siward doing to protect himself? He hopes to move north, I suppose, in the spring, and take over Lothian and as much to the north as he can be sure of keeping. But he can't afford to leave Northumbria empty of loyal followers.'

'He's kept the mercenaries,' Bishop Hrolf said. 'Or as many of them as would stay with him. And a great many of them did, so they said in Allerdale, when they were offered double rates for the winter. They're all in camp outside York with the rest of the men Siward thinks he can depend on.'

He rolled out a lip and sent his nose down to meet it. 'I've never been in favour of holding large numbers of men in one place. The Romans could do it. The Romans had drains. But come the warm weather, there will be camp-sickness, and it could jump the wall into York in a night.'

'Good,' said Thorfinn. 'You said you were hungry?'

Unspoken messages crossed the room and altered Bishop Hrolf's answer. 'Hungry?' he said. 'And how could I be, with my fine bowl of gruel stranded there in my belly like a ball of thread in an old, empty sack?'

'All right. I kept the best question to the last,' Thorfinn said. 'What is the gossip about Denmark?'

'That you were a fool to trust Svein to get your ships for you, but that you had no alternative,' Bishop Hrolf said. 'It's thought that Svein's cousin Harold had something to do with changing his mind, but that it was largely a matter of money. King Svein was paid twice, once by you and then by Siward, for the same fifteen ships. And with Siward and Wessex on his side, he felt you couldn't retaliate.'

'Really?' said Thorfinn.

'Well, that was the view of the moderates,' said Bishop Hrolf. 'The rest thought that Svein only agreed to do it on condition that they brought him your head. Otherwise, he would drive you into Norway's arms, and, even with Wessex and Siward, he would be in danger of going under.'

'Now that, knowing Svein, I find very convincing,' Thorfinn said. 'So how worried he must be, to find Siward back in York, Thor back in Allerdale, Malcolm sitting in a hole in the border somewhere, and myself alive and no doubt about to make a firm alliance with my wife's cousin's husband in Norway. Can we turn it to account? What do we need most?'

'Ships and money,' said Tuathal from the opposite side.

Thorfinn looked across at him. 'Ships we shall have, of our own building, in time. Money, I agree, is wanting. We've lost the silver mines, and we've lost all the treasure in store from Dunkeld southwards. On the other hand, while there isn't a Pope, Adalbert is all-powerful in the northern church, and anxious to expand his future patriarchate, while Svein is equally anxious to have Adalbert's support and, of course, the Emperor's in his conflict with Norway.'

Tuathal said, 'Oh, my good Lord. No.'

Bishop Hrolf, less well acquainted with the mind of the King, took a fraction longer to guess it. 'You mean to send King Svein a complaint?' he said.

'I mean,' said Thorfinn, 'to send him a demand for double the money I paid him for the fifteen ships I didn't get. Or I shall make an alliance with Norway against him. You, when you are well, will be my ambassador.'

Bishop Hrolf gazed at him. Bishop Jon, from the other side of the room, said, 'My lord . . . I thought an alliance with Norway was out of the question.'

'Of course it's out of the question,' said Thorfinn. 'What has that to do with it? That will settle Denmark. And tomorrow, when the others arrive, we shall decide what we want to happen in Scotia. There. Do you hear them outside, my lord Bishop? Here comes the rest of your repast.'

The door opened. Smells of undreamed-of allurement filled the bright room.

'We thought you might be hungry,' Thorfinn said. 'But a little drowsy after, perhaps. The delay was also to punish you for inflicting your absence upon us. Don't let it happen again.'

'Except when you send me to Denmark,' said Bishop Hrolf. His face had flushed. To his shame, saliva also swirled down his throat.

'In Denmark,' said the King, 'you will be feasted as never man has been feasted before. King Svein won't dare do otherwise.'

Later, when the food had gone and the lay brothers were there in a bustle of linen and bandages, Tuathal crossed and sat on the board-edge of Bishop Hrolf's bed.

When he wanted, the stentorian voice of Bishop Hrolf could be very quiet indeed. 'His hands?' he said.

A screen of men divided them from Thorfinn. Tuathal said, 'The strings of his shoulders are cut. He makes trial of his arms and his hands all the time, and the power is coming back slowly. He makes little of it, nor do we. He has his life.'

'Is it known?' said Bishop Hrolf.

'There was no need. He will make sure he is well enough before he leaves here.'

Men moved, and Tuathal smiled and drifted away from the bed.

Bishop Hrolf lay back and closed his eyes in the slothful wake, it might seem, of his meal.

So many weeks, and a spoon would not stay in his hand: what of a sword? What of the people, for whom the King must be unblemished, *dianim*? What of the country, whose only hope was to nurse this intelligence, so that it might steer them all out of chaos and avoid the war against which they had no men and no leader?

He lay unstirring still, as if sleeping, save that now and then his lips moved a little. And, watching him, two at least of his friends understood, and in their hearts added their prayers to his.

ELEVEN

THE YEAR CHANGED, and then began to unroll, like a wheel in turbulent country; like an unreeling ribbon of Groa's weaving that once, long ago, he had spoiled with his blood. A spinning ribbon in which, peg by peg, the device switched without warning, producing a new assortment of patterns, a new set of boundaries, a new line of direction, a mischievous disorder of design that tested his strength to the limit through the most powerful tenet by which he lived: Adapt and survive.

It began with the conferences he held after Bishop Hrolf's arrival, by which time he could hold a knife and cut with it. There followed the day he was strong enough to leave the hospice and take his proper place in the hall outside the monastery, where he took back the sceptre from his Lady's warm fingers, and from the cool hands of Lulach, whose eyes he met levelly because the inclination to avoid them was so very strong.

Lulach, who said, 'You cannot really envy King Canute, who was six years younger than you when he died? Who said, *I command you not to wet the feet or the robe of your lord!* I told you, when I was Henry.'

But that day was his first in his own hall, and he envied nobody. When in the evening the time came to shut the chamber-door on them all and turn to Groa, he said, 'I like your hair short. It does not, as on another occasion, constitute a protest?'

'My lips are bruised,' she said. 'I am protesting. Where did all this strength come from?'

'Well, not practice,' he said. '*Virgo corpore et virgo mente,* I'm told it's called. It's much overrated.'

'Yes. But gently,' said Groa. She looked like a far sea in sunlight. She said, 'Not all at once. You can't—'

'Yes, I can,' he said. 'I'm very agile. I've been playing my harp with my feet like Gunnar in the snake-pit. There's nothing I can't do. Several times over.'

And he proved it, until she looked and became to him like a sea in a summer storm, to be conquered in triumph and delight, and then to sink beside, in the dreaming sway of the after-seas.

Late that night, the tide of her sorrow came, too, and he lay, caressing her cheek on his breast, drenched in the flood of her tears.

It was a luxury from which, like trust, he was debarred. He guessed that this was the first time Groa, too, had given way. He knew why she wept, but there was nothing to be gained by putting it into words. He stroked her hair until she fell asleep and then fell asleep suddenly himself, as if the relief he had brought her had somehow entered his being as well.

He was not aware of being over-confident. In the plans he had laid against the spring investment by Siward and Malcolm, he had taken account of all that Hrolf had been able to tell him and more. To petition King Svein for his missing money when the seas opened in April or May was the kind of gesture he liked making, and would do no harm, but there was always the chance that Svein might feel strong enough to refuse, or even feel weak enough to enter into an alliance with Norway himself. One had to try to think of everything.

The event he had not thought of occurred in February, and news of it reached him ten days later in Monymusk, when the hospice was empty except for someone with a sprained knee, and the grass was already beginning to green a little over the death-mounds at Forth-side and by St Cathán's and Scone and on the top of Dunsinane Hill.

The news that the bloody flux, as Bishop Hrolf had predicted, had broken out in the crowded war-camp in York and had spread over the wall.

The news that Earl Siward of Northumbria was dead; and Bishop Malduin of Alba with him.

The man who brought it came from a merchant's family who had traded with Orkney back to Earl Sigurd's day. Groa's steward Breasal brought him straight to the hall, where the King and his mormaers were together. A moment later, Groa herself arrived and dropped to a stool beside Thorfinn, listening silently as he questioned the man.

Thorfinn saw her and knew she was thinking of Siward. A lout of a boy from the pagan household of Egge, posted between Norway and England during the dangerous wars of Olaf and Canute; son of one of the men who had struck down King Olaf, Siward had hewn out the blocks of his fate and built them himself into an earldom, with the descendant of bishop-princes and earls for a wife.

All that he had possessed and more was in his grasp. Yet he had not met the death Kalv had, or Groa's father was preparing to meet, half blind in the bows of his warship. He had lifted himself at last, so it seemed, helpless and stinking and running with filth like an infant, and had them pack his legs with his breeches, and lower the weight of his chain-mail over his shoulders, and fit over his head the polished helm with the thick boar defiant on top.

Then, taking the weight of his shield in one hand and the haft of his gilded axe in the other, he had pulled himself to his full height and stood for a moment, before he hurtled into the great fall that would kill him.

For he was Siward of Northumbria, he said. And would not die like a cow in the straw.

He had left behind him one living infant, Waltheof. And Northumbria, open to the four winds.

Open to the kindred of the other four sisters of Siward's wife: Orm and Ligulf and Forne and Alfgar, and Duncan's older son Malcolm. To the sons of Maldred and Osulf their cousins. To the sons of Carl, even, whose sister had once married Northumbria.

And to Earl Harold of Wessex and his brother Tostig, who were not only cousins of King Svein of Denmark but, like King Svein, were nephews of Eric Hakonsson of Lade. Eric Hakonsson, who had been created Earl of Northumbria by King Canute his brother-in-law, and whose son had once, long ago, collected the Orkney tax from Thorkel Fóstri.

The Anglo-Saxon line then, against the Scandinavian, in the old, old rivalry for Northumbria.

'Who will get it?' said Tuathal.

'Who can oppose Wessex?' Thorfinn said.

'Alfgar,' said Groa.

'He's reckless enough, I grant you,' said Bishop Hrolf. 'But Leofric and Godiva are not. And when his father dies, Alfgar will have all Mercia so long as he keeps Harold's favour. No. Not Alfgar, I'd say.'

'Wessex has no other rival for wealth,' Lulach said. In debate, he could lead, but never, one noticed, drew conclusions.

'But would Northumbria accept Wessex?' said Bishop Jon.

Morgund, who was sometimes shrewd, said, 'Perhaps not, if all the Anglian rivals banded together. But would they?'

'They might, for a short time,' said Bishop Jon. 'Unless Wessex were to provide against it. By appointing one of their number, perhaps, as vassal under Earl Harold. My lord, what do we know of your nephew Malcolm?'

Silence while they all looked at him.

What did he know of young Malcolm?

That he had lived in Dunkeld with his brothers, like a frightened cub in its bolt-hole, after his father King Duncan had died.

No shame to him: he had been ten years old. The flickering eyes and the animated tongue, asking for a bigger horse and a helmet. And not to have to eat seal-meat, like his barbarian uncle from Orkney, who had slaughtered his father.

Then, two years later, Malcolm had been hauled out of Dunkeld and planted in the York household of his other uncle, the Earl Siward, with a suddenness that must have been nearly as frightening. And from there, almost immediately, drawn by the smooth policies of the Lady Emma to some casual harbour at the English court, with a little land set aside somewhere to feed and clothe himself and his servants, and a court officer given the job, when he had time, to complete the training his father had never troubled to give.

Now he was a man of twenty-five, well grown and less than backward, still, with what he thought he should say to an uncle. Two years before, he had received, one must assume, the added support of his brother Donald, brought back from a different exile in Ireland by Earl Harold. And yet, never in all those years had he shown until now a flicker of spirit; the least trace of a desire, never mind an endeavour, to leave his modest shelter in the south and reclaim any part of the home he had once known.

Fosterlings accepted their fate in different ways, as did exiles and hostages. Between the three, the demarcation, it had to be said, was not always clear. There had been a great English monarch called Athelstan who had filled his house with high-born young men who were the seals he required for every alliance. Good or bad, all those he'd heard of had made their mark in some way on leaving their foster-father. King Athelstan's nephew Louis d'Outremer had crossed the sea to make himself King of the Franks. The Breton Alain Barbetorte had landed at Dol with an army and flung out the Normans. Indulf the son of Constantine of Alba had returned to Alba and taken the throne. Hakon son of Harald Fairhair of Norway had gone back to Norway at fifteen and exiled his older brother.

It told you, perhaps, what Athelstan's household had been like.

Until Earl Harold sent him to Siward, the oldest son of King Duncan had done nothing; nor had he been given a wife. Someone had thought less of his chances than the Emperor had thought of Edmund Ironside's son. And yet, once put into the field, he had borne himself, they all said, like a man. Indeed, after St Cathán's he had fought when he had no need to, attacking Dunsinane until he had worn out the company following him.

Thorfinn said, 'Malcolm? I think he thought that other people would make his fortune for him, as they had arranged the rest of his life. I suppose he has only just realised that there is nothing for him in Wessex, and that the Northumbrians will only follow him if they see a promise of fresh lands in Alba. Make him Earl of Northumbria, and he would be dead in a week, from Osulf's knife or Ligulf's poison, and I'm sure Harold of Wessex knows it.

'Alfgar is too powerful to appoint. None of the northern leaders other than Alfgar is strong enough to hold Northumbria on his own, and that includes Thor of Allerdale. Nor could even Harold do very much for a weak leader. I think he will put in someone from the house of Godwin. It would make sense. A barrier against myself and my more inconvenient alliances. And the assurance also that, come the spring, all the most belligerent blood in the north will be moving out of England and into the land in Alba and Lothian earmarked for them last summer by Siward.'

Groa said, 'So Bishop Malduin's death will make no difference? However small Malcolm's following, or whether he is there or not, you think the new Earl of Northumbria will encourage the armies of last year to return in the spring and take possession? Leading them, perhaps, as Siward did?'

They had paid off the mercenaries, the messenger had said. Thorfinn said, 'I don't think anyone new to Northumbria would waste his own energy or that of an army in marching into Alba next month. I do think the new Earl, whoever he is, will encourage those who were promised land to go and take it. If Allerdale does the same, and if the young mormaer-families of Fife and of the late Bishop still follow Malcolm, they might contrive to fill Lothian and Fife after a fashion, with Angus further north left open between us. It is what I should do in their place. No confrontation is possible, with our numbers, and they might not have very much more. We could harry one another, but with Angus between, it wouldn't be very easy, or very profitable. They would need ships, but those they have.'

'What you are saying,' said Tuathal, 'is that this may not be bad news. It lessens the risk of another invasion. It increases the chance of a peaceful occupation of most of Alba, perhaps as far as Scone but not very much further?'

'It's too early to say,' Thorfinn said. 'We can only hold open our minds, and our plans. There is another point. The Fife lands of Kinrimund are not hereditary to Bishop Malduin and his family. They belong to the Bishop of Alba. Lands usurped from me are my affair, and, so soon as I can, I propose to deal with it. But lands usurped from the church are the affair of the church. Any widow, stepson, half-brother, or protégé of the late Bishop Malduin my cousin who touches those lands will confront the full power of whatever authority consecrates the new Bishop of Alba.'

He had reminded them of intention. Malduin son of Gilla Odhrain, Bishop of Alba, appointed to be the glory of the Gaeidhil in this land, had been the son of Thorfinn's father's sister. Trained in Ireland from childhood, and then seduced by Durham and York, there had been nothing left, in the end, worth even hatred. He wished to remind them of that, too.

There was a pause. Then Lulach said cheerfully, 'So there is a decision you churchmen will have to face before the year is very much older. Who is to be the next Bishop of Alba?'

Thorfinn looked at Bishop Hrolf, who looked at Bishop Jon, who inflated his entire face, section by section, round the broad elk-nose, pale with sequestration. 'There seems,' he said, 'little doubt about that. We thought it prudent to take advice before now of our fellows. We have discussed it for some time with the King. I mentioned it myself to Archbishop Herimann, at the King's suggestion. There is no question in the minds of any one of us. The next Bishop of Alba should be Prior Tuathal.'

He gazed at Tuathal's blank face and then in turn, with a touch of anxiety, at the others. 'The only pig of a question, now, is who should consecrate him?'

That was February. March came, and after the winter of death and prostration the land began to stir again, and the people. And every man's eye looked to the south, from which, if they were lucky, the news would come; and if they were unlucky, the marching armies.

The plan made in the first weeks of Thorfinn's convalescence had altered, but from the decision that was its pivot, nothing would shake him. He would lose no more men.

At first, they did not believe him. Peasants and thralls clung to their land, no matter who took the lordship, and survived, unless the new lord wished to set an example or clear the land for some colony of his own.

There were some such settlements in Alba. But there were also hillsides and riverbanks filled with peoples who were all of one blood, and who would fight for their land with their peat-spades; with stones tied to firewood if need be. And for the leadership of a land to recoil from battle, as it seemed this King proposed to recoil, was to deny all the wars of their fathers, and their courage.

Ten years ago, thinking him ignorant, Thorfinn's advisors might have said as much. This time, they listened to what he had to say.

'We defended Lothian when we had a land full of men, and the Normans. Three armies invaded us, and we had no choice but to resist, or what you see in Fife and Lothian and the south part of Atholl would have occurred also in Angus and Moray. And we did not know then that Siward would leave.

'You know what happened. You know how many died. You know how many are no longer active because of their wounds. It is what my lord Lulach and the Lady have spent all winter finding out. And you know how many men it takes to plough, to cut wood, to build, to launch a fishing-boat. I will not lose any more in battle. For, whether the battle is won or lost, Alba will die.'

'So?' had said Bishop Hrolf. 'Next time, you make no stand? They overrun, if they wish, Angus and Moray as well, and you withdraw before them?'

Thorfinn had held that council at his bedside, and he had been very tired; but to Groa, who was there, it had been clear, for once, how much it mattered to him to have this understood and accepted.

He had said, 'The invaders got what they wanted. Booty. Revenge. Ravaged land lying open for them to take when the spring comes. There is no reason for them to want any more. It would be madness for Allerdale or for Northumbria to return and march north. There is no treasure left that they can be sure of. They could never drive cattle or take corn back from such a distance, and they must know that now I should bring back all my ships, and any built over the winter. None of them could settle in safety so far from home. And if they come too near the northern limits of Alba, they threaten the north, and the north is untouched and would descend on them. It has saved us this winter with its granaries and its storehouses, and it will do so again.'

She did not remember who had said, at the point, 'My lord. I would rather see men of the north in Fife and Atholl and Lothian than men of Northumbria.'

She did not remember, because none of those close to Thorfinn would ever have said that again. But he had answered, if with less than total candour. 'To the men of Bernicia, the southern part of Alba is the kind of land they are used to, and in Lothian the same language is spoken. But even among the men of Moray who fought beside us, there is little desire to move out of the lands that they know; and in Caithness it is not only a different tongue, it is a different habit of life. They would be more alien to the south of Alba than any enemy could be.'

The voice had said, 'They accepted you. And the men you brought south. There is Celtic blood, I thought, in Caithness as well. And in Orkney.'

Whoever it was had no sense. And Thorfinn, for his own sake, was going to have to close the discussion. But he had only said, 'Mormaer can speak to mormaer, but to bring down an army would be a different matter. It would in any case lead to little but a fresh arousal of war, and still without prospect of clearing the country. No. There is land here, in Mar and Moray, that has only to be cleared. The refugees who have been with us all winter can stay if they wish. Nor shall I stop anyone who wants to return south, even if the south is held by Northumbria, so long as they understand that they will have no security. But the land cannot begin to live again until the men are replaced. And the land cannot wait for our children to grow.'

It was Morgund, surprisingly, who had said, his face flushed, 'So you would give over Alba to English vassaldom?'

'No,' had said the King. 'I should allow Malcolm my nephew, if he wishes, to plant his standard at Scone and call himself, if he wishes, King of Alba. And then when I had the power, I should expel him.'

The noise round his bed had been like the clashing of cymbals, and she had seen him relax, in spite of the weariness, and knew that he had them convinced. What she did not know was whether he believed it.

So now the spring had come that was to determine their fate, and there was no threadbare army of Thorfinn's poised south of the Forth or the Tay, under whoever was left of his leaders, waiting to confront whatever the new ruler of Northumbria should choose to send against them.

Nothing happened. A hesitant dwindling began to occur among the refugee communities in Mar and on the Angus border. Families, dragging a handcart or riding garrons and leading pack-mules, began circumspectly to drift southwards towards their former homes. The people of Angus, their loyalty still untried since Kineth their Mormaer had gone south and taken his following with him, let most of them through.

Those who did not emerge had been killed by Angus men for their goods as much as for anything else, it was believed. The rule, the achievement of all that golden time after Rome, was already dispersing, thought Groa with bitterness. Soon, without time or men to repair them, the roads and bridges would begin to give way also, that all through the winter had made possible the great accounting, the conveying of food and succour that the defeat had made necessary.

Only in peace was progress possible. The wars of Rognvald had robbed Thorfinn of the profit of the first half of his reign. And now the wars of Northumbria were destroying the fruits of all he had done in the interval.

In Thorfinn himself, there showed no such awareness: no least resentment over his fate, even when, at last, the reports began to come in from his watchers. Malcolm had entered the Lothians with intent, clearly, to settle. But this time, instead of Siward's thousands, he brought only the exiles from Fife and from Angus with their weapons, followed by the wagon-trains of the new occupiers.

His scouts, also, it would appear, had been industrious in what they conveyed to their lord Malcolm. *Your uncle is lying in Mar, sick or dying or discredited, with a broken and leaderless army. From Angus south, the land is yours if you want it.*

'So he will occupy Lothian, at least,' Thorfinn said. 'And then perhaps Fife, when he feels safer. He can still recoil if we move. But why none of Allerdale's people? And why no word yet of Siward's successor?'

Sometimes, after a long meeting, his weariness would show itself as now in impatience, but only when he was alone with her. Daily, his strength had come back. He could walk freely, although he was not yet on horseback, and could hold light things in his hands, and lift his arms, with care, nearly to shoulder-height. She had never seen whatever agonising work had gone into that. One day he could run on the oars of a galley and one day he could lift his arms: it was the same thing.

While the seas were still closed by storms, the absence of free communication with the south was his greatest hazard. With Cumbria lost and Northumbria an enemy, he had to rely on word brought him by spies, and the distance was too great for many to be successful. Later, when his ships could move, it would be different.

But even the fretting was better than the news, thought Groa, when it came.

First, an indication that, at last, Thor of Allerdale was settling the areas he had conquered. And that, like Malcolm, he had contented himself so far with the southernmost lands, and had brought no more men-at-arms than might be needed to protect a new colony. Certainly not enough to constitute an invasion, or to indicate that he meant, in the near future, to move further north.

'What is happening?' Thorfinn had complained. 'What is happening in Northumbria?'

Then next day, he knew.

He had chosen to go hawking, with a company of about a dozen, Groa among them. It was his fourth day on horseback. His second and his third had been spent riding slowly through the camps and farmsteads about Monymusk, talking to whomever he could find, from the saddle. Close to Monymusk and within daily report of him, they felt themselves his friends and showed it. What he wanted to know for himself was the mood of the people further off, Groa well knew, and would test it as soon as he was able, however accurate the reports she and Lulach had already given him. But, meantime, an appearance spread confidence. The King is well and with us again.

So, also, today he was hunting because now he could balance his falcon and cast her. With Anghared and Maire, Groa rode a little apart so that she need not watch him. Lulach, braver than she was, watched him all the time, and would turn for home before the King ordered it.

It was a mettle that neither Paul nor Erlend had. Thorfinn, much though he loved them, had always seen them quite clearly. *'Paulatim*, or little by little,' he had once called his elder son, with rancourless affection. It was perhaps as well. There could only be one man in that mould.

He was fresh, though, when the messenger cantered up, for they had not been out long, and his falcon had made her first kill, which pleased him. Because he was a little apart, he heard what the message was first, and, seeing his face, the others kept back until the interview ended.

Then Bishop Jon said, 'News, my lord?'

'Belatedly,' Thorfinn said. The bird shook her head, attracting his attention. He hooded her and gave her to someone else to hold. He said, 'Who said that Alfgar would never be so foolish as to risk losing the favour of Wessex? You, Hrolf? After Earl Siward died?'

'What has he done?' said Bishop Hrolf. His voice was louder than Thorfinn's had been.

'Poor Alfgar,' Thorfinn said. 'He tried to seize Northumbria, it would appear. Relying on the bribes he had placed out in Ireland.

'He failed. He was taken before the council in London. They stripped Alfgar of his earldom and outlawed him as a traitor to the King and the nation. He fled the country, taking the troops of his household along with him, and is in Ireland now, raising an army.'

His horse, feeling the pressure removed, began to fidget and sidle, and Groa saw him command her, hard, by the flank. The mare stood silent, nostrils wide with indignation. Tuathal said, 'Then who has been given Northumbria?'

'The man meant, I suppose, to have it all along,' Thorfinn said. 'The King has offered the earldom of Northumbria, Huntingdon, and Northamptonshire to Tostig, Earl Harold's younger brother. And Tostig, of course, has accepted.'

Bishop Hrolf said, 'Hence the odd conduct of the two bodies of settlers.'

'Yes,' Thorfinn said. 'My lord Malcolm, I suspect, skipped north as soon as he could, before he became embroiled in any unpleasantness. Allerdale's coast lies towards Ireland. He may have had to await Tostig's leave before he could expand his territory.'

'They say Tostig is greedy for land,' Groa said.

'But Earl Harold is still afraid of Norway,' Thorfinn said. 'I don't think Malcolm will find himself marching north in the van of a mighty army of Northumbrians under Tostig's banner. I think, for one thing, that Tostig will find quite enough on his hands for a while in reconciling the disappointed kindred of the late Siward's wife. But we should talk about it.'

He turned his horse and set it into a trot, back the way they had come. Bishop Jon, jogging alongside, said, 'Again, 'tis not all bad news. A pity for the Earl Alfgar's sake. He would have been a good neighbour, and we'll lose a friend for our shipping in Anglia. What other harm has it done?'

In the open air, one could not say *Be quiet!* unnoticed. Uttering the words in her heart, Groa stayed in the rear, while Thorfinn rode on in silence. Then he said, 'It has locked Malcolm out of Northumbria. I don't think it matters, so long as he continues to sit on the doorstep doing nothing.'

Bishop Jon said, 'He'll have to do more than that if he wants to win a good following.'

'Well,' said Thorfinn, 'we shall just have to see that he doesn't win any more following than he already has. Do you suppose it will be difficult?'

The tone invited no answer, and, in fact, a moment later the King touched his heels to the horse and rode on a good deal more roughly than his powers would warrant.

After a bit, Lulach spurred also and caught him. What did Lulach know about Thorfinn and Alfgar and boyhood?

Enough, it seemed. Groa swallowed and rode on sedately. Recognise it; assimilate it; put it behind you. The pattern has changed again, and you must change accordingly.

April came, and then May, and the seas opened, but there was no further word of what Alfgar of Mercia might be doing in Ireland, and no threatening move came from the English settled in Lothian or the Cumbrians to their west. Malcolm, it was said, had sat down beside the church of St Cuthbert next to the rock of Dunedin, with one or two ships always prudently beached in the estuary.

Thorfinn, too, had brought his ships back from the Western Isles and some from Orkney as well, although he had to leave them a few to protect themselves with. No trading-vessels went out from Orkney or Alba that year, although he needed the silver. The ships they had built in the winter hardly compensated for those he had lost in July.

Instead, the trade came to him, with the news from the Continent. The ships that brought it sailed from Dol round the Pentland Firth to the river Findhorn, where he presently was, and aboard them were two familiar figures.

Thorfinn had been in his hall of Forres only a few hours when word was brought that ships had arrived and were enquiring as to his whereabouts. The day's ride was the longest he had made yet, but, without waiting, he strode down to the wharf, as he had done at the time of his wedding, with Lulach and some of the young captains following.

Coming ashore was not Juhel of Dol, despite the Archbishop's flag at the masthead, but one of the many he had thought to have forfeited life next the burning forest by the Forth crossing. Flodwig the Breton said, 'My lord King? We thought you dead, and perhaps you thought the same of us. I have orders to buy from you, but the chief cargo I am to bear each way is tidings.'

There was no surliness in his face or his voice, and no false lightness either. Thorfinn said, 'I was told you had all died or been captured. I have had no messages since.'

'You were ill. They told me at Inverness. No. I had a leg-wound—it's healed—and Siward's men took me halfway to Durham after I'd told them how wealthy my family was. But then I escaped and got a ship. There is someone else here who knows you. We called at Wareham and the Sheriff insisted on coming aboard. He says you'll recall him from Rome.'

Even had there been no business between them, he would not have forgotten Alfred of Lincoln and the impertinent tilt of the eyebrows that recalled the English hostel, and the polite boredom of Bishop Hermann, and the vast, effortless diplomacy of Bishop Ealdred. They, too, had been looking for the Archbishop of Dol, whom he himself had removed from the wrath of the church. Bishop Ealdred and his party had no grudge against Dol. Only, when petitioning the Pontiff on behalf of one's royal master, it is not wise to be seen openly favouring an excommunié.

The Alfred he remembered had not been as sober as this. Recalling what else had changed, Thorfinn spoke with impatience. 'I should really prefer cries of alarm to a stricken silence. The wound is healed, and I can walk and talk and even offer you hospitality.' Then the irritation went and he said, 'There are few things I could have wanted more than this meeting.'

Afterwards, he wondered whose prayers had been listened to, for it seemed impossible that two people could have presented him with the answers to so much that he wanted to know.

First, that although Viger and Alberic as well as Hugh de Riveire had been killed, Ansfred of Eu had escaped, and his father Osbern himself had been ransomed and was with Duke William in Normandy now.

'Most of them are,' said Alfred sagaciously. 'There's plenty of fighting left to do in Anjou, but it begins to look as if Duke William will end up on top. I can tell you, no one bears you a grudge for ending the contract when you did, whether an act of fate was to blame, or whether you had started a war you never had any prospect of winning.'

'That is, they would have preferred easier odds, but you fought fairly yourselves, and put the Normans to no risk that Osbern hadn't already agreed to. As it is, those that survived are going to be with Duke William, with any luck, when his great moment arrives. And I don't think you'll see Dol far from his side either, with Flodwig here. At least, that's my view as an outsider.'

'So far as I remember,' Thorfinn said, 'although allegedly reared on English soil, there is hardly a party you have mentioned with whom you are not interbred, myself apart. Without the help of your Norman friends, none of us would be living. If, however, you do happen to hear what began the hostilities in the first place, I should be glad if you would make a note of it.'

'And tell you?' said Alfred, who had not yet quite got his bearings.

Beside him, Flodwig caught Alfred's eye and pulled a face of exaggerated abasement. 'No. What he means, although he is too polite to say so, is tell Osbern of Eu,' he said. 'If you have no value for your skin, that is.' He turned to Thorfinn. 'My lord, Duke William has heard of you.'

'And dislikes the waste of his stock?' Thorfinn said.

'And wishes the land and sea between you allowed of a meeting. I was to tell you from the Archbishop,' said Flodwig, 'that the Duke bears no ill-will against men who go to seek their fortune in Spain or Alba or Italy, since, when they are tired, they will bring back their skills and their fortune to the land he will have made ready for them. I am to tell you, my lord, from the Archbishop that the Duke is aware of the long association between yourself and his great-aunt the Lady Emma, to your mutual profit. And says that, since you and he have common ancestors, he hopes the custom of friendship may continue.'

It was all he said, and Alfred did not add to it. So it was all he had been told to say. And Alfred, with his endless kinship with the rich and the famous, had been sent to reinforce its validity. Which meant . . .

Lulach said, 'I have poured wine. Will you have some, my lord?' Lulach, smoothing over the abyss, or the sorcerer's cave that had opened before him. Thorfinn said, 'Thank you. Now tell me, how are the rest of my old friends from Rome? How is Bishop Ealdred? And how is Bishop Hermann?'

And Alfred, settled now, with obvious pleasure, into the tenor of things, smiled mischievously and began to tell him.

They stayed a week only, while Lulach had gathered from all their storehouses the hides and the furs that were wanted, and two cages that had not been asked for and for which Thorfinn would accept no payment, one destined for Rouen and the other for Dol. Of the dangers of this, the slightest of gestures, he was aware. But the borderline of danger had already been crossed when he invited Osbern to come north from Castle Ewias.

The silver he received for the hides was worth several times their value, and Thorfinn accepted it without demur, for the service he had performed for Juhel had been a considerable one. He waited only to see the ships off, and then rode for Deer, where his household awaited him.

His mind was so engaged, arriving, that the presence of Groa was a shock of delight. Surprise, at the start of a long-planned reunion was hardly a compliment, so he did not betray it, so far as he knew. Most of the best men he had were there as well, and in less than an hour he had them at board with him, listening.

There was no need to take all day about it, and it was over in another hour, after he had told them all they needed to know.

'There is a new Pope: another reformer. In the long run, there is reason to believe that both he and the Emperor will listen to any petition we make. But, first, they have to put their own house in order. There would be no point in looking to either for six months at least. So much for that.

'What this means to the Athelings, the Saxon heirs, wherever they are, no one knows yet. It is said, however, that the male child of that family has survived and is flourishing, although the father is not. They did not appear at Cologne, and they have not been heard of in England. Indeed, the moment the Pope was enthroned, Bishop Ealdred and the good Abbot of Ramsay, his companion, declared their intention of returning home.'

'If I were to make an inspired guess,' said Bishop Hrolf, 'I'd say that the Athelings, *consuetudonis peregrinandi*, were still safely somewhere just inside the German border, saying their prayers in Greek until the Emperor decides what best to do with them.'

'And I should agree with you,' Thorfinn said. 'I imagine Bishop Ealdred reached the same conclusion about eleven months ago, as well. While he was abroad, by the way, our old friend Bishop Hermann has not been wasting his talents. His diocese is being enlarged to include Malmesbury.'

'Do you say?' said Bishop Jon. 'Well, that's a blow for the absent Alfgar and his father, and the good church appointments that have been flowing into that family.'

'As you say,' said Thorfinn. 'I don't know how he and Ealdred see themselves. But it looks to me as if the Godwin family are grooming them as a bulwark round the Severn against Mercia. Two things more.'

He could see in their eyes that they hoped he'd forgotten, so he came to it right away.

'It seems that Archbishop Adalbert has been growing in power during the interregnum, and he and King Svein frequently feast one another and exchange vows and gifts. Svein is still at war with Norway, with no great losses or gains either way. There is nothing to show that the double sale of my ships was anything more than a stroke of malice to earn him some silver. It is time, I think, we asked him for our payment back, with proper interest. After all, we have both a stick and a carrot. We need an ally, and we might well unite with Norway. We have a bishop to consecrate, and we might well think to favour Archbishop Adalbert of Hamburg and Bremen, whose goodwill means so very much to King Svein.'

As the Bishop-elect, Tuathal's mottled face did not change, but the sharp eyes were watching his King. Tuathal said, 'I thought you had decided on Archbishop Herimann of Cologne.'

'I had,' said Thorfinn. 'But he died in February. His successor is Anno of Bamberg. Do you remember? The somewhat acid Provost of Goslar. I am told that he would be unlikely to be either protective or tender.

'The Pontiff cannot be much of a shield until he is established. Of the other archbishops who have a kindness for us, Dol of course is ideal, save that he has been excommunicated. To keep Kinrimund out of English hands is what this is all about, so we can't ask the Archbishop of York, and Canterbury, of course, is another gentleman who has been excommunicated. There is Humbert of Sicily, but his power died with Pope Leo. And there are really not many left, except strangers—Magdeburg, Capua, Besançon, Trèves, Rheims, Colocza—who would have even less power than Humbert.'

He waited.

Lulach said, 'What about Maurilius of Rouen? You haven't told them Alfred's Normandy gossip yet.'

He realised he was holding Lulach's eyes, and that Groa had noticed. He said, 'I was keeping the good news for after. But you may as well hear now.' And told them, quickly, the fate, so far as he knew it, of all Osbern's band they had worked with.

Lulach said nothing more, even to remind him of what he had left out. So, to end the debate, Thorfinn called in his arbitrators. 'Bishop Jon? Bishop Hrolf? Who consecrates the Bishop of Alba?'

Bishop Hrolf said, 'May I make a suggestion?'

Thorfinn knew what was coming, and he knew he was going to have to agree to it.

Bishop Hrolf said, 'It is nearly full summer, and no sign that my lord Malcolm or anyone else intends to move into Fife. You've taken the precaution of resettling Prior Tuathal's Culdees from Loch Leven in Kinrimund. They're holy; they ought to be safe.

'Why not allow me to visit King Svein before you decide which metropolitan to patronise? In the Celtic church, archbishops were never thought to be needed if competent bishops were present. You have such bishops. We here, if need be, could consecrate Prior Tuathal, and the people within his ministry will ask no more meantime, I can assure you.'

No one spoke aloud the names of the counters they were playing with. Svein of Denmark. William of Normandy. Adalbert of Hamburg-Bremen with behind him the shadows of all Scandinavia. And the Emperor.

The King said, 'A good suggestion. I agree,' and drew the meeting, as soon as he could, to a close.

To Lulach he said, 'I thought you never meddled.'

'Nor do I,' said Lulach, 'when it makes any difference.'

Because he was going to Groa, he cleared his mind of that cloud; and his body, so far as he could, of the dragging insistence of his physical longing that, without the harshest of masters, would long ago have destroyed the other harmony they had, that was equal and sometimes could be better.

He had seen often enough the men who, strung up by business or war, would go straight to take their relief like a horn of ale tossed back in the saddle, and follow it by a little banter to keep matters easy.

In all the time he and Groa had known each other, he had never imposed himself on her for that kind of indulgence.

So ran the theory.

He did not know, therefore, how, whenever he came thus determined to listen, she would take him in her arms on the threshold and seduce him.

TWELVE

E HAD SAID he intended to lose no more men. It was tempting, that year, to change his mind, as high summer came and departed and still his rebels with Malcolm their leader did no more than lie quiet in the southern fringe of his country, with the colonists from Bernicia pastured around them.

The stillness, he knew, was not quite what it seemed. Thinking of their vacant lands in Angus and Fife, the young lords who had joined Malcolm, and men like Kineth of Angus must be harassing Malcolm daily with their demands, already shocked by Siward's defection and death.

But even to them it must be obvious that their force was not large enough to inhabit the wasted lands further north with any safety. The Northumbrian settlers they had brought with them had achieved what they wanted and were unlikely to march north in anyone else's cause. And Thorfinn believed what Hrolf had told him again in the long talks they had held before the Bishop set sail for Denmark in the handsomest ship he could give him. Thor of Allerdale, too, had all he wanted meantime, and was likely to be far too apprehensive of his new neighbour Tostig Godwinsson to wish to stir far from Cumbria.

It was wholly tempting, therefore, to send out a summons to all the fit and half-fit of Alba to meet him here, on the Mar border, and march south under his standard to fill Fife, and occupy the ashes of Perth and Scone, and bar the banks of the Forth against Malcolm.

Wholly tempting until you thought what would happen. Even if every fit man came with him, they were badly armed. No victor was ever fool enough to leave good enemy axes and swords on his battle-fields, and they had lost most of what they had. And even had they been well armed, their numbers were still inadequate.

Thus challenged, Malcolm's rebel army alone would be enough to damage them. Malcolm's rebel army added to the strength of the settlers, driven to protect their new property, and that of the Cumbrians, roused likewise, would finish them. And, as he had said, with the rest of her manhood destroyed, there would be the end of Alba, for boy-children must be fed and protected before they can become men.

Scone he thought of, and Dunkeld. Far up in the heart of the kingdom, they were out of Malcolm's reach so far. He had seen two or three English ships. They mostly stayed in the Forth estuary, travelling south now and then to bring back provisions, no doubt, and perhaps people and certainly news. But only once or twice had they come nosing north, putting into slight havens that Kineth of Angus might know, to gauge, one supposed, the chances of a quick landing, or even a small party of occupation in the homelands lying untilled.

Faced with the guard-ships he kept on his coast, they had retired each time without offering battle. They would realise, he took it, that not all the lands they had left were waiting to welcome them. As time passed, more and more of the families whose numbers had been spared found their way south and warily set to work in the field-strips and peat-moors, returning at night to a patchwork of hides and timber, of woven-reed wattle and thatching: good enough in summer weather, and no loss if, running, you had to abandon it.

It was natural, too, if they allowed their cattle to drift into the empty grasslands that had once belonged to Fothaid or Cathail or some of their kinsmen. When the time for the hay-cutting came, they would crop theirs as well. And, long before that, would have been through the ruins of every house, picking out what was of value.

As people spread, quarrels broke out. Someone moved without leave into the substantial holding that had been the chief hall of Mormaer Kineth in Angus. It had been empty but for a steward, put in by Lulach to safeguard the kale and the bere and the livestock with some hired men and slaves.

The family who took it over, with their household, ran to a fair number of men and offered no violence, beyond waiting until the steward was out on his business and then simply barring the doors of the main hall against him.

To any attempt to get them out, however, whether by the lawful steward, outraged, or by their less fortunate and equally furious neighbours, they made it clear by the numbers and display of their weapons that violence was what they would offer.

It had to be dealt with, and Thorfinn took what men he had and flushed them out, hanging the ringleader. He had a suspicion, which no one was able to confirm, that the dead man had been a former crony of Kineth's.

He understood, by that time, that a good many of the sudden brawls that would break out in one or other of the half-empty provinces were not entirely due to the heat, or the stresses of war and exile and loss, and anxiety over what was still to come. They were fights between factions.

On the one side, and still by far the larger, he believed, were the men who had fought beside him last summer, and who still supported him.

On the other were those who had not openly defected with Malduin and the rest, and who had not yet opposed him face to face in the field. But Malcolm, one now realised, had not been idle in his new house on the slopes of Dunedin. There was many a man in Alba whose mormaer was dead, and who did not mind who his next lord would be, provided that he had a firm undertaking that his land would not be broached, or his wife raped, and that under Malcolm he could continue to thrive and even grow wealthy without having, this time, to fight for it.

There were some, toisechs or of mormaers' families themselves, who had only accepted himself as their King because he had done exactly this: wasted their land and left them with no alternative but to prostrate themselves and their families in another war.

There were men who resented him for other reasons, some of them old, and some very new. He had heard that kind of grumbling often enough, and knew when to turn a deaf ear to it. But the first time he heard what they were now saying, shouted at him out of a crowd as he made one of his early testing rides out of Mar and into the edges of Angus and Atholl, set his teeth on edge, although he showed nothing of it, he thought.

There was no quick reply that could satisfy, and so it was best to make no answer at all, except what might be conveyed by his presence unarmed among them, and a hard morning's work, dispensing news and justice, advice and practical help.

A week or two later, something happened that he had to take note of as well. He did not speak of it. There was nothing concrete, and certainly no concerted movement against him. To build forts and put Moray men into them, or men from the north, would be the silliest response he could make. But, in the meantime, he put aside any idea of raising Scone or Perth or Dunkeld and setting himself there again, under his banner of Alba. The provocation might cost more than the gesture. And the ribbon-pattern, he now knew, had changed subtly again.

To Groa he said nothing at all, and very little to anyone else. He received his friends from Orkney and Caithness as he normally did when their ships were passing, and collected their news. He learned that the new Pope had honoured the promise made by the old to Isleifr, and that next year Gizur's son was to travel from Iceland to Bremen to receive his staff and his ring as a bishop.

Thorfinn received, and shared with Groa, news of her father and mother in Denmark, and apprehended that the arrival of Bishop Hrolf there had caused great amazement, not to say admiration, and that King Svein, who had a fancy for practical jokers, had announced that he was going to keep the Bishop all summer and make him a sending-home gift of every girl he got demonstrably pregnant.

('Maire will be sorry,' said Groa.

'*What!*' said Thorfinn.)

About King Svein's response on the matter of money, no one had heard even a rumour.

There was no word from or about Alfgar in Ireland. The western islands, once the clearing-house for all such gossip, were no longer so easy of access without a powerful fleet. With Diarmaid's Dublin ships on the look-out on one side and Allerdale's vessels patrolling from Cumbria to the Clyde, not so many knörrs now would sail from the Garonne and the Loire and share their cargo between Dublin and Orkney. Diarmaid did not care for it.

There were exceptions. Among them were two elegant ships from the

Rance who sailed between Orkney and Caithness one day and arrived at Inverness with Odalric aboard, picked up for pilot.

Lulach came for his stepfather, and Thorfinn rode to Inverness himself to look at the cargo. It was everything he could have wished, and he was able to pay for it all, because just then Bishop Hrolf arrived home, with no feminine company, but conveying a box holding three times the silver Thorfinn had paid for the fifteen ships ordered from Denmark.

As well as the cargo, the two ships from the Rance came with presents. Odalric and Lulach were both with Thorfinn when he opened the boxes and unloosed the mouths of the bales.

Inside were such things as he had forgotten just lately to think of. Wine and spices; oil and basalm. And bale upon bale of exquisite silk.

There were no elephants woven into it, but it was not hard to imagine somewhere the lions of Tancred. Or the mark of Coutances, as Bishop Geoffrey paved his way into heaven. Although, of course, the articles had ended up not in his church but at the feet of the terrestrial lord who could serve Bishop Geoffrey's church best.

'And those?' Lulach had said, indicating the chests still unopened in one corner. 'Still more gifts?'

And Thorfinn had said, 'No. Those were paid for. In silver from Bishop Hrolf's hoard.'

'How else would you pay for them?' Lulach had commented.

Thorfinn did not look up or make an answer: Odalric would see nothing in it. But he remembered the very tone of the remark when, many days later, he was back south, and round a council-table somewhere, and the doors were closed and the chests opened.

Inside was what William of Normandy had sent him, and what·he had paid for in silver. There was a top cover of spoiled hide, roughly cured with the scuffed hair still on it, and similar skins between layers, so that when the lid was prised off, it smelt like the shed of a tanner.

Between the layers flashed steel. A great deal of it, neatly arranged and packed with economy. Spearheads and axe-blades. Two-edged swords, some with their handles and some still to be fitted. Knives of the same order. And in another and larger box, helms of a kind they had become familiar with very recently, and suits of mail: just two of them, of the sort boys had pointed and laughed at when they had seen them carried, hung on their poles, into or out of Osbern of Eu's tent.

The dismay, lowering upon him from all round the table, was as ripe as the hides in the box. Thorfinn said, 'This box I shall have taken and buried. It came with the rest, and I have paid for it, but I do not propose to wear the marks of vassaldom yet. It is there, however, and if some day it means safety instead of annihilation, any one of you may dig it up and make use of it. As for the rest, we fought the last war with steel bought in Germany, and so probably did Thor and Siward.'

'My lord . . . ,' said Tuathal. His rugged face looked no different, although he was a bishop now, in the Celtic fashion, without, as yet, the consecration the Roman obedience demanded. The silk in one of Duke William's bales would make him a cope more splendid than any Malduin had had.

Tuathal said, 'My lord, we are grateful to be taken into your confidence.'

Which, one had to admit, was discretion itself. Thorfinn said, 'Whoever follows after me will have no trouble in picking the reins up. What you know is all there is to know. I only showed you so that you may bear it in mind in any negotiations we may have with Earl Tostig. Earl Tostig is married to Judith of Flanders. And Judith of Flanders is aunt of the half-blood to Duke William's wife Matilda.'

Someone had half-worked it out. Gillocher of Mar was illumined. 'Which makes Earl Tostig of Northumbria into Duke William's uncle!' he said. 'So *that's* why there's been no aggression. No attack through the summer. No effort to give Malcolm an army. My lord, do we have an ally in Northumbria now?'

'I should be happy to think so,' said Thorfinn politely. 'But, in that case, who are the spearheads destined for?'

It was Tuathal the realist who answered. 'You. Or Tostig. Or Malcolm. And either end of them, at that. I don't think Normandy minds in the least which.'

'Well, Bishop Tuathal,' Thorfinn said. In Tuathal's clever face he could see every nuance of his voice striking home, and he knew Tuathal would guess already what his next words were going to be. 'Well, Bishop. In that case, whom do we favour for your consecration? Archbishop Maurilius, I think you mentioned?'

The Archbishop of Rouen. Duke William's Archbishop. Whom Tuathal had certainly mentioned.

Another thing he liked about Tuathal was that when he lost a point, which was seldom, he always conceded it freely. Now he said, 'How wrong I was. I suppose, of all the names we discussed, only Adalbert of Bremen or the Pope himself will serve us now. Would you say?'

It was Hrolf, newly back from Svein of Denmark, to whom he appealed. Bishop Hrolf, thinking, put his fingers together in the way in which, in more carefree times, he would prepare to horrify his observers with the double-jointed collapse of each digit.

He did it now, out of habit, and they all watched his thumbs hanging outside his joints without a quiver. He put them all back, abstractedly.

'At first impression, a determinedly frivolous man,' he said. 'King Svein of Denmark. But to repel, for all these years, the attacks of a soldier of international repute such as Harald of Norway argues great skill as well as great perseverance. So one overlooks the juvenalia.'

Gillocher, in what he thought was a whisper, said, 'He wouldn't try any girls? Or he couldn't get any pregnant?'

'My lord Gillocher,' Thorfinn said. 'You are saying that when next I have an embassy for Denmark, you would like me to send you?'

Although, as now, he had sometimes to be kept in order, everyone liked Gillocher. His wife was a different matter.

'My lord King,' said Gillocher. 'No, my lord King. You must have mistaken what I was saying.'

'I hope so,' said Thorfinn. 'My lord Bishop. You found King Svein shrewder than he appears, with which I should agree. And on good terms with the Archbishop of Bremen, you said. And shamefaced, a trifle, over the matter of the alienated ships, in which you could discern no permanent malice?'

'No one could be sure,' Bishop Hrolf said. 'But I think not.'

Thorfinn said, 'Our aim in meeting the Pope was to obtain the services of the best missionary bishops in western Europe, which we now have, in a context that did not associate us necessarily with the Metropolitan of Hamburg and Bremen and his Scandinavian empire.

'We have Bishop Jon and Bishop Hrolf, but we no longer have the same Pope, nor do we know his mind on the subject of Archbishop Adalbert. All we know is that Norway is no longer under Adalbert, because of Adalbert's associations with England.

'Now England's Archbishop is excommunicated, the only risk, so far as we are concerned, is that Norway may again ask to enter Bremen's authority. While Norway and Denmark are at war, I don't think that is likely. And, despite what he did, I think that for us King Svein is still the better ally.

'It would appear that he thinks so, too, or he would never have repaid our silver. Let us cultivate him. Let us appease Adalbert, who is still admired by the Emperor. Let us, in time, try to form with this new Pope the bond we had, or were beginning to have, with Pope Leo. Let us request Archbishop Adalbert to consecrate Bishop Tuathal, and if, Bishop Tuathal, it displeases you, then let us dismiss the idea.'

Tuathal said, 'He is not a man I admire. I don't see who else could do it. Yes. I agree. When and where?'

'I was going to suggest,' Thorfinn said, 'next year, perhaps, with Isleifr?'

The resistance died out of Tuathal's face until it looked smooth as a pool in a rainstorm. He said, 'Isleifr's getting his bishopric? There won't be a sane man on Iceland all winter. My God . . .' He looked at Bishop Jon and back again. 'What will he take to Saxony this time?'

'You,' said Thorfinn peacefully.

Adapt, and adapt. There came news of another conflict, a bad one near Abernethy, with several people killed. As before, it seemed to Thorfinn that agents had been working among the few modest families who had returned there. He found out and tried the aggressors, and again dealt with them summarily. Before it ended, there was some fighting, and this time, he knew, he had been observed.

Tuathal had been there, in a leather jacket and not yet in the Saracen silks. Riding back, Tuathal said, 'If you must do that, my lord King, you will need a left-handed sword.'

He did not intend to discuss the matter. He had said briefly, 'It is only a matter of time. It isn't worth it.'

'Then meantime,' Tuathal had said, 'you had better leave the fighting to others. They tell me at Kinrimund that the trouble in Fife seems to be spreading.'

'Would you like me to take the monks out?' Thorfinn said. They were brave men, and a civilising influence, even though the coastal regions were his and there was always a ship there as safeguard.

'They wouldn't go,' Tuathal said. 'No. It occurred to me that, nuisance though they are, these particular trouble-makers would be unlikely to slaughter a bishop. I thought of returning to Loch Leven, if you would allow me. In full bishop's attire, if such could be managed. Then at least they would have justice of a sort, and someone to appeal to.'

No, said his entrails. His mind ran about, trying to find a reason for him. He said finally, knowing where it would lead, 'What makes you think a bishop sacrosanct?'

'Their hope of heaven?' Tuathal said. 'They wouldn't give that up for Malcolm.'

The King said, 'They nearly killed Bishop Jon.'

'He was leading an army,' said Tuathal. His voice sounded jaunty. 'That's different.'

Thorfinn said, 'A king also is sacrosanct. And I am not leading an army at present.'

The horses' pace did not break. The thud of the canter went on, and nothing disturbed it. Then Tuathal said, 'When was this?'

'The most recent time? In Atholl,' Thorfinn said. 'Ten days ago, maybe. A nice spear, but thrown very badly.'

'Did you get him?' Between thuds, it came like a snap.

Thorfinn said, 'Hardly. Do you expect me to stop my train and announce to the crowds what had happened? Few saw it, and those few thought it an accident. If I knew it was personal to me, then I should have no objection to your going to Fife. But it was more likely his view of us all.'

Tuathal said, 'Do you think none of us knows? It *is* personal to you, because Malcolm is making it so. The disaffected of Fife won't waste time and risk holy wrath by cutting my throat. They'll try to persuade me, like Malduin, to leave you. And that will give you a breathing-space.'

Change, or adapt. He said, 'Yes. You're right.' There was almost nothing he couldn't do, now, at the cost of some small extra weariness. It was a pity that the exception had been noticed. But that would mend. And as his body grew back to his habit, it would be folly to let his thinking soften. He said none the less, 'It will be autumn soon.'

Autumn, the season of home-coming and mellow regrets, that the summer's strand-raids were over, and the sea-fights with the tax-boats, and the evenings that were the crown of the day: kicking the sand in the fire as you wrestled, happy with ale, while the songs and the sea crashed about you, and the salt-smart and blood of the day's wounds were no more troubling than star-dust. Sad autumn and sadder winter, when the fighting was over till next year.

'Yes,' said Tuathal. 'Thanks be to God. It'll be autumn soon, and we shall have peace for a space.'

Tuathal was away in November when the messenger came from Godiva of Mercia to where Thorfinn was staying at Essie.

In fact, Thorfinn was out riding, and it was the Lady to whom the messenger was taken, and who heard him out and herself took him to the guest-cabin where he could refresh himself.

So Thorfinn found, coming back from his ride through the hill-pass between Spey and Don, with a smell of snow in the air from the Cabrach.

Latterly, he had spent a week or two here in the mountains, dividing his time between Mortlach and his little hall at Noth, beside Essie. Soon they would have to move to lower ground, either north to the Moray coast or south to the softer regions of Mar. Further south, he could not ride like this, with two attendants and no weapons to speak of. In Moray, where Lulach's family had always ruled, and Groa ever since her first marriage, every man and woman was loyal.

The day had been a good one. There was a deer laid across the back of one of the garrons, and he had found someone to speak to in all the farmsteads he had passed, but neither had been the main reason for the excursion, which was to have freedom to breathe and to think.

It had seemed to him, that day, that his design for the country might work. It had been different when Duncan died and he himself had arrived south in Alba a conqueror, and had to plant his armed camps amid the smoking ravages of what Duncan's men had done, and then his own. But even then he had had enough sense to dismiss his men of the north when he could; to take only Moray men with him to Scone. To promise the men of Alba, when he asked them which ruler they wanted, that their leaders would be chosen, as always, from the men of Alba and not from the men of the north.

He did not propose to ask them again which ruler they wanted. Once appointed, his kingship rested with him for life, or until he were crazed or blinded. Nor would he confront anarchy by armed camps of alien warriors, and destroy in a moment all he had been working for, to join together what he had inherited. They thought he had saved his men of the north at the cost of the army of Alba. But he had fought beside them: they had seen him. And if they remembered at all, they must have known that they would like the men of the north down here among them as little as the men of Northumbria.

But people shaken by war and by loss did not always, of course, act reasonably, and there was unruliness, with no standing army left to control it. On the other hand, people grew used to their condition. This winter would be better than last for stores and for shelter. And there was no longer the edge of apprehension and danger that clouded men's thoughts and made them violent.

Malcolm's agents were still working, with stealth, on his people's minds, but the opposite was now also true. Tuathal's presence in Fife, brave man that he was, would do more good than anything else one could think of. He could not grow men in a season, but the fleet was building again, and he had silver to help it build quicker. It seemed possible that, in time, dissent might smoulder and die, and the battle-reluctance induced by fatigue transform itself slowly into a genuine peace.

Gradually, he knew, the exiles he sheltered in Moray would find their way south again to the lands they had left. Gradually, there was no doubt that the colonists from the south would consolidate what they had and drift further north before they were finished. At some point, a good deal in the future, he and Tostig would have to meet and reach an agreement of some sort to do with tributes and taxes. It was what he had thought to do with Siward, before Siward's son Osbern was killed.

At the moment, no man in his senses would try to act the overlord in wasted country, where the means for survival were only just possible. It meant the survivors had no protection and no proper law, apart from whatever patchwork he could obtain for them. Malcolm, he supposed, was in the same position. The snatching of land in the Lothians would not all have gone smoothly.

It might work out. Norway and Denmark, locked in their own strife, were unlikely to trouble him. A ship or two, Thorkel Fóstri reported, had found its way to Thurso or Orphir, sometimes with a genuine cargo to trade, but more often looking for gossip and a good sizing-up of his assets. The masters had not all been well mannered, and after one scuffle aboard, a reproachful message had come south from Odalric, asking for the return of one or two of their own ships when Thorfinn might find it convenient.

He had sent two, but he did not want to spare more till the spring. It was the way of Harald of Norway, to keep reminding his neighbours to be afraid of him. One such Norwegian ship—perhaps the same one—had threaded its way into the Lossie one day when Groa was there, and tried the same thing. She had recognised the master. Groa's tongue and what she knew of the master's grandfather and mother had been enough. She had made them unload their goods, at half-price.

But of course all that begged the question of Malcolm, who was still there with, one supposed, some self-pride and would expect a future of sorts that did not shame him.

So long as armies were not marching and Malcolm had no army of any real size to take anywhere, such matters could always be managed by talking, as time went on. He would have to see Malcolm himself and discuss it with Tostig. And, meanwhile, so act that no one in power saw any benefit at all in offering Malcolm the strength to do anything.

Enclosed in sparkling cold, with the russet and white of the hills all about him, and the frost bursting dry from his horse-hooves, he found it easier to plan without impatience. The course that was natural to him was not this one. In Orkney, he would have acted quite differently. In Orkney, they were different people.

Then he got to the stockade, which had already opened for him, and men came forward quickly for his horse, and he became aware of an extra liveliness: a larger number of people in the yard than was usual, and faces glancing at him, and away. A horse he did not know was being led off, he noticed, with the sweat sluicing the mud from its coat. He reached the hall almost before the man who opened the door for him.

Inside were his household: the few men and women he had brought with him, standing together, bright in the light of the fire, leaning on the pillars, talking to each other and to Groa.

Beside Groa, on the board where they had been taking their morning ale, lay a scarf he recognised. Embroidered on the edge were the rosettas of Mercia.

Thorfinn said, 'Alfgar?'

They all turned. Not Alfgar. Or not his death, for the looks on their faces did not speak of death, but of worry.

Groa said, 'Nothing has happened to Alfgar. Except that he has turned raving mad.'

'What has he done?' He walked up and lifted the ale-pitcher. He cared about Alfgar. He cared more, at the moment, about what would affect the nation he was trying to beguile back to its allegiance.

Groa said, 'He has invaded England. With his personal army and eighteen shiploads of hired troops from Ireland.'

But the scarf had been Godiva's, not Alfgar's. Thorfinn poured the ale and said, 'And?'

'And joined Gruffydd, who has just made himself supreme King of Wales. They laid Archenfield flat, on the Hereford side of the Welsh border, and when Earl Ralph the king's nephew rushed up to oppose them, together with all the Normans still holding castles, Alfgar and his Irish and Welsh levies offered battle. Except that it wasn't, apparently, much of a battle. The English had been given horses to fight on for the first time, and used them, with some sense, to run away on.

'Alfgar marched unopposed into Hereford, burned the town to the ground, and plundered the cathedral of its relics and treasures, murdering seven of its canons. After that, he went on to kill or carry off everyone else still left alive in the town and in Earl Ralph's own castle.'

She paused, as he well knew, not because she was breathless but to let him think, and also to assess how he was taking the news. He drank, and said, 'Where was the King?'

'At Gloucester, as usual. Earl Harold's levies were arriving there while Alfgar was still in Hereford. They say Tostig's force had been summoned already.'

Which was why they had enjoyed such tranquillity on the Northumbrian border. What a pity. He said, 'And Harold's army stopped Alfgar?'

'They didn't get the chance,' Groa said. 'Alfgar and Gruffydd withdrew into the hills and waited, and now there's talk of a peace-pact. Alfgar's army killed five hundred in Hereford and outside, but he's untouched and has almost no losses.

'All this news is from Alfgar's mother, the Lady of Mercia. She says that she thinks Earl Harold has realised that Alfgar is stronger and has more friends than he thought, and that he is going to have to propitiate him. She says that the peace won't last, and that it is only fair that all Alfgar's friends should be warned. She says that you may remember that in the matter of allies Alfgar, if unrestrained, can be ruthless. She says that if the Irish army hadn't been enough, he was thinking of an alliance with Norway.'

And there, on the whole, he was glad that she stopped. For this news, of course, was vital to him. And without Godiva, he never would have known, cut off as he was. Until suddenly, whatever Alfgar's personal plans, he himself was either embroiled in them or surrounded.

He said, 'You've met the Lady. Do you think the Earl of Mercia knows about this?'

'I expect so,' said Groa. She hesitated, and then said, 'I think she warns you from friendship. But also she needs to know whether you would join Norway and Alfgar if he were to ask you.'

It was his reading. Without a word, Alfgar's father Leofric had stood aside, holding Mercia for the King while his son tried this step and that and finally got himself outlawed. When you ruled a great province, there was nothing to be gained by associating yourself with another's disgrace, even if he were your only son. Alfgar had sons in his turn. Whatever happened, there must remain Mercia, untouched, and still in the King's favour. You saw it even in wars: a son on one side and his father or brother on the other. So a line could continue.

He said, 'It's November, and too late for an answer. We shall talk at the Christmas meeting, and I shall go to Chester when the seas open. There are some things that are better said face to face.'

Bishop Jon said sharply, 'Sail! Yourself! With Diarmaid's ships and Allerdale's on the sea?'

Without warning, Thorfinn lost his temper. 'What am I?' he said. 'A prisoner in my own kingdom?'

Bishop Jon's face was unmoved. 'A man who cannot be replaced,' he said. 'Traitor that I am, I will say it. If you go, it will only be because we allow it.'

It was not a matter for smiling, either with Bishop Jon or himself.

Then, suddenly, it was. He saw Groa relax a moment before he said, 'Why are we worrying? Alfgar is invincible. They will have him canonised like Olaf by spring.'

It was the last twist of the pattern that year, and nothing else was to matter so much.

THIRTEEN

SO FAR AS Tuathal of Alba was concerned, the winter, despite his expressed hopes, was no more peaceful than the rest of the year had been.

He came home from Fife on two occasions. One was to attend, with his fellow bishops, the celebration of the Yule Mass. In the absence of Tuathal to stop him, the King had elected to hold it in Brechin, south of the safe borderline of the Dee and where the entire household, in Tuathal's opinion, ran a risk that was not at all necessary.

He expressed this view, since nothing in his previous experience of Thorfinn counselled caution. Emerging red-faced from this interview, he went to find Hrolf, whom he discovered in a mess of stone-dust, carving a gargoyle.

'Hah!' said Bishop Hrolf. 'And what did you complain about?'

'It doesn't matter,' said Tuathal. 'What's happened?'

'Nothing serious,' said Bishop Hrolf. 'Winter. The lack of news. Being tied to Alba. He needs to go north, and of course he mustn't. But the main trouble is that all his energy is coming back. Orkney and Alba between them kept him stretched, with as much of the rest of the world as he could cram in as well. Alba isn't enough. At least, the way he has to keep it just now. That is, there are a thousand things he wants done, but not enough people to do them. Be warned.'

'I've had my warning,' said Tuathal.

After Christmas, he left, and the next time he came back, he knew very well the reception he would get. The fact that Thorfinn received him alone in the Deeside hall he was currently occupying was enough.

For Tuathal, it had been a long ride: first to his own monks at Portmoak in Fife, and then round the ruins of Perth and of Scone, through the suspect vales of Angus, and north to where the King was.

He was no longer in full ceremonial, with mitre and staff and attendants, as he had displayed himself when on his mission. But he still had a train of some size, which took a little handling, although Scandlain, now his lieutenant, was a good man. He had stopped at Scone, where the timber house Malcolm had left above the shrine and the inaugural Stone were still intact, in the care of the hermit who tended them. For the rest, there was nothing but rubble, and the burial-mounds of light grass, whose occupants could not even be separated, and the new crosses of wood driven in over them. He knew of no one who passed it without crossing himself, and no churchman who left it without praying.

To brace himself against the King's direct attack was, therefore, an effort. He did not know the changes in Thorfinn's unsmiling face as the Lady did, but he knew well-controlled anger when he saw it.

He received no welcome. 'Where have you been?' said Thorfinn.

'My lord King. May I sit?'

'If you wish. Where have you been?' It was February and still cold. Thorfinn's tunic was of thick hide, long-sleeved, with narrow, sewn trousers below it. He stood, his feet apart, and looked down at his Bishop of Alba.

Tuathal said, 'You have had reports of my movements, I take it. I have been south of the Forth to see my lord Malcolm your nephew.'

'Without my leave?'

'Do I need it?'

'We are not speaking of a church matter,' Thorfinn said. 'We are speaking of a conceit that overrides other men's judgement in concerns that affect the life of this people. Were it necessary, I should sacrifice your life in that cause as readily as you would.' He waited a moment, and then said, 'Or did you imagine I thought you another Malduin?'

'No, my lord King. But I hoped your nephew Malcolm might,' said Tuathal.

The King took two paces past the fire and back again; and constellations glowed red in the peat, and then dimmed again. He said, 'I must be clear. Nothing that you may possibly have gained could have been worth the risk of losing one of our leaders. Also, you have demeaned me. I don't care to be seen either as a man who sends others to do what is dangerous, or as one whose edicts others may flout. Had I known you were capable of such a thing, I would never have made you Bishop of Alba.'

'Had I not been Bishop of Alba, I couldn't have done it,' Tuathal said. 'I am not yet consecrated. You may degrade me.'

The King stood still, looking at him, and slowly began to draw breath. The thick enamels glowed, flattening over his diaphragm: deep blue and purple and green, with the flash of encased gold. In Birsay, in Canisbay perhaps, he would have lifted what was nearest and heaviest—the iron torch-holder at his back, the board of cups, the brazier even, had there been one—and thrown it, to demonstrate and exorcise his anger.

Now, he loosed his breath and, dropping his hands, for the first time sat down. He said, 'The King I should be would degrade you.'

'*Take him out and thrash him,*' Thorfinn had said, sixteen years ago, of the brilliant, beautiful boy who had also tried to deface his credit in the hall that had once been Perth.

A rare anger came in his turn to Tuathal. He said, 'My lord. I am not an unthinking child.'

He saw, in the blue peat-smoke between them, the years thronging past, and the happenings, and the men.

Thorfinn said, 'No. When I speak like that, you need say only one word. Dunsinane.'

Tuathal made no answer.

Presently, the King said, 'Tell me, then.'

Tuathal said, 'It was properly done. I sent Scandlain forward with gifts. He had a priest with him, and a group of monks, and none of them was armed. When my lord Malcolm sent word that he would see me, I rode there myself. He was at Abercorn. I took the banner of Kinrimund and nothing but my household, again all unarmed. I wore the Saracen silks.'

'Was that wise?' said the King.

'I thought so, my lord,' said Tuathal.

'Go on,' said Thorfinn.

'Scandlain and the men were taken elsewhere, and I was led to the door my lord Malcolm was using. He came out to the threshold to greet me himself. Inside were a number of men, among them Gillocher the stepbrother of the late Bishop Malduin, and the two young men of Fife we know of, and a number of others we thought had gone south. I have a list of their names.'

'Yes. That was useful. Go on,' said the King.

'We talked. He asked me if I represented you, my lord King, in coming to him and I said yes. It was necessary. It did not matter whether he believed me. I said that you were concerned about the needless waste caused by the division of the kingdom, and thought the time had come to agree on a proper boundary-line. I said that the Earl Siward had broken the agreement you had made as to the allocation of the lands of Lothian, but that you recognised that my lord Malcolm would find it difficult now to clear such land of those henchmen of the late Earl who had now taken up holdings there. I said that my lord Malcolm would know that north of the Lothians the land was loyal to you and could only be held down by force. I said that you were willing to concede him the whole of the Lothians up to the line of the river Forth.'

He knew now he had the King's mind. There was no expression of outrage. Thorfinn said, 'And what did he say?'

Tuathal said, 'One of the Fife men, Fothaid, I think, laughed and said that if King Macbeth thought Fife was loyal to him, it was surprising that he never held court there, or had it rebuilt since it was wasted. My lord Malcolm signed to him to be quiet, and said to me that he was glad his uncle was good enough to offer him what was already his and he thanked him. About the possession of the lands further north, I could see that his men took a different view from my master, but that he himself was never one to turn down an offer to negotiate, and if the King would come south himself, he would be prepared to discuss matters with him.'

'Did he really expect it? Or . . . No. Continue,' said the King.

'I said that you were careful, and I was not sure if I could persuade you, but I thought in the end that you might. I am sorry, my lord,' Tuathal said, 'but time is what we need.'

'Yes. All right. I understand that,' said Thorfinn.

'So he said that he was not surprised to hear that his uncle preferred to be careful, as he had heard that there was a good deal of unrest in what used to be his kingdom. He also said that he had heard that the King was a sick man who had never fully recovered from his injuries of eighteen months ago, and that he was surprised that you had never thought of retiring in comfort to the lands that were your own in Caithness and Orkney, and of leaving Alba to those who were of the blood and knew how to run it. He said that, indeed, he had sometimes wondered if that was not what the King might have in mind, since he had preserved the men and lands of the north so carefully from damage in the last war.'

Thorfinn did not speak. Tuathal said, 'It is, of course, important for him to try and guess your mind on these matters. I said that, for whatever reason, you were still adamant about not making use of Caithness and Orkney men in the south. I also said that I did not see how he could talk of Alba belonging to anyone else, since your grandfather, my lord King, had been King of Alba, whereas his had not been of royal blood at all. Also that, as inheritor of Moray, which was part of Alba, you would be unlikely to give up what was loyal to you.'

'And he said that the loyalty of the men of Alba was to my wife, through whom my claim to Moray came,' said Thorfinn.

'I reminded him that you were also Findlaech's stepson,' Tuathal said. 'I also said that your health was good. I don't know if he believed me. He asked no more about that, but went on to talk about Bishop Hrolf's visit to Denmark, about which he had heard, and wanted to know what I thought of King Svein. I said I thought he was a man pushed to the limit in his long war with Norway, so that money could be frightened out of him easily.'

'Tuathal,' said Thorfinn, 'the day is brighter already. Don't stop.'

'Then he talked about Earl Alfgar and his attack on Hereford,' Tuathal said. 'The King had called Earl Tostig down to help deal with it, but in the end Earl Alfgar sued for peace from the mountains, and Earl Harold Godwinsson agreed to talk with him. As a result, Earl Alfgar has become reconciled to the King and has been given back his earldom of East Anglia without either punishment or conditions.'

'Alfgar guessed right,' Thorfinn said slowly.

'So it would seem. Earl Harold has had Hereford refortified, but that is all. His brother Tostig, I gathered, was furious. Of course, if Earl Harold and his father hadn't expelled the best of the Normans four years ago, Osbern and the rest would have thrown Alfgar back with no trouble, and Earl Siward would have found his war against you, my lord, a good deal easier. So, apparently, Tostig is saying. I was asked, of course, if you knew what Earl Alfgar was doing.'

'And you made me seem friendless again,' Thorfinn said.

Tuathal said, 'I said, my lord, that, being cut off from the south, you heard little but rumours, and Earl Alfgar had not been in communication. I said that you have been fortunate enough to be able to reopen some trade overseas, and that I was to tell him that you were not short of money or weapons or other things, as he could see from my garments. He smiled and said that it was only right that the most reverend Bishop of the holy church of Alba should have a fragment, at least, of what was due to his rank. He asked me what I felt about my new position, on which he congratulated me.'

'Tuathal—' said Thorfinn.

'So I said, my lord King,' said Tuathal, ignoring it, 'that I had to confess disappointment. I had hoped when in Rome to see some conversion of the spirit, but, although great promises had been made to the Pontiff, none of them had been carried out, and particularly none of those relating to my lord King's personal faith. I said I was unhappy about this. I also said I had awaited this preferment for a long time, and had thought to have a larger see than now, it appeared, was to be available to me. My lord, I am sorry.'

'Stop apologising,' said Thorfinn, 'and go on.'

'We talked of bishops, and the favours they might expect from those in power,' Tuathal said. 'He told me that when Earl Alfgar was reinstated, an order was made revoking the appointment of Bishop Hermann to Malmesbury, which, as you know, would have given him great power south of the Severn and in Sheriff Alfred's area. He did not say if this was a condition of Earl Alfgar's return. But Bishop Hermann, seemingly, was much upset and has abandoned both Ramsbury and his nephew and crossed the seas to take a monk's habit for three years at St Bertin's. Bishop Ealdred is to supervise his Wiltshire see in his absence, in addition to his own. Bishop Ealdred's example, I was given to understand, was one to follow.'

'You seem to be following it,' said the King. 'He didn't speak of Bishop Ealdred's late mission to Cologne?'

'There was a joke,' said Tuathal, 'which I did not entirely follow. Have you ever thought it possible, my lord King, that Bishop Ealdred and the Abbot might have been sent to the Emperor with two sets of orders? One, we know, was to request the return of the family of Saxon heirs, the Athelings, whom Earl Harold thought, clearly, he could make use of. But that might not have suited King Edward.'

'You mean King Edward might be capable of action of his own?' Thorfinn said. 'Certainly, his half-sister married the Emperor.'

'And he has helped the Emperor in the past. It was my impression,' Tuathal said, 'that in private Bishop Ealdred might have asked the Emperor to do something quite different. Such as to temporise agreeably over the return of the Athelings while making quite sure that they remained in obscurity until King Edward wished it. Scandlain, in his chatter with the household, said he received the same impression.'

'Scandlain, too?' Thorfinn said. 'What did Scandlain learn?'

'A good deal,' Tuathal said. 'He says they talked in their cups, and so it's likely to be true. He says Northumbria lost over fifteen hundred men against us last year, and nearly that number again with the flux afterwards. No one wants more fighting at present. They're grumbling already at having to follow Tostig south when he wants them. He says that my lord Malcolm knows that if he is to take Alba, he must do it by winning over the men already in Alba, and he is finding it difficult. He says, my lord, that Malcolm has told them that the only way for every man to get what he wants, without having to fight, is to bring him your head. There is a price of three hundred pounds of gold on it.'

He waited. Thorfinn said, 'He did not say as much to you.'

'No, my lord,' said Tuathal. 'To me he only said that the resignation of Bishop Aethelric of Durham was likely to be asked for within weeks, and that Earl Tostig would be considering whom to appoint in his place. We left very soon afterwards.'

There was a long silence, during which the King did not allow him to drop his eyes.

At last, 'I see,' said Thorfinn. 'You have not only made it possible for me to go to Chester while you are away. You have made it advisable. Will you consider unsaid all that passed between us just now?'

'My lord King,' said Tuathal. 'For anything that may come between us, you, too, have only to speak one word. It is the same one.'

Despite all that, it was not easy to leave the kingdom when the time came. But, whether because of Tuathal's serpentine mission or for other reasons, the country lay overtly placid, with only small twists and upheavals here and there, as before, to indicate what was artificial in the present state of suspension. Malcolm made no move from the south, nor were there any signs that Earl Tostig, with his Godwinsson eyes on his brother, was in the least interested in what happened north of his border.

Thorfinn provided two ships for Tuathal, of no less splendour than the one he had given Bishop Hrolf, and sent him on his way with his entourage, laden with presents for Archbishop Adalbert.

He carried with him also a great many instructions, including one to bring Isleifr back with him. Then, Thorfinn chose a dozen armed men from his household, and enough servants to attend themselves and the pack-mules, and rode west, avoiding the land that was Allerdale's, until he came to the coast and the Orkney ship that was waiting.

Chester had grown since his last visit, both inside and outside of the Roman walls, and the wharves, which extended much further, seemed to be crammed full of shipping. They also seemed, at first glance, to be in a state of unusual disorder.

Since no advance warning to the Earl had been possible, Thorfinn's ship had to wait until the master went ashore for his entry-permit. He came back in a river-boat flying Mercian colours and containing the guest-master of the Earl's household. With the smoothness one remembered from other occasions, a berth was obtained for his ship, and the King of Alba, his entourage, and his possessions were transferred to the boat and taken to where an escort had assembled already to lead him in state to Earl Leofric.

Except that, as usual, Earl Leofric was absent on one of his numberless properties, and it was Godiva his lady who received him, in her own chamber bright with sewn hangings.

He was alone, having left his companions with the guest-master. He took her hand and bent to kiss her lightly, as the custom was, on the mouth. Then, stepping back, he drew from his belt-purse the fine little scarf with the needlework on it.

He said, 'My lady? I hope I see you well. I have been seeking a chance to return this.'

'Ah. I wondered what had happened to it,' she said. Under her eyes, the carved laughter-shelves deepened. She said, 'Did you notice the state of the wharves? It is what happens when you pay off eighteen shiploads of Irish mercenaries.'

She must be sixty-four, and although she was still beautiful, she looked weary. Thorfinn said, 'None of us could ever keep up with Alfgar.'

Her smile acknowledged the sympathy. 'Nothing stays the same for any of us,' she said. 'He has gone to meet some friends. I have sent for him. He may give you a surprise.'

'I've been practising with Bishop Hrolf,' Thorfinn said. He sat, and accepted a cup of wine from one of her ladies. The girl, whoever she was, stared at him and, when he returned the gaze, coloured. He spoke to Godiva. 'I expect you met our good Bishop when he looked after Cumbria and the islands.'

'I remember. He used to play tricks. You're quite right,' Alfgar's mother said. 'I used to think his laugh was even louder than Alfgar's. He's well, then? And your own family?'

She would know all that, from her messenger. So the chamber-ladies were not wholly in her confidence, and Alfgar was going to make trouble for him.

Not, of course, out of malice. If Alfgar took against anyone, he wouldn't wait nearly thirty years to let him know it. To his friends Alfgar was loyal. To his own viewpoint he was spliced, as immutably as hemp in an anchor-rope. Thorfinn and Alfgar's mother talked of nothing while the back of his mind went on thinking, and the girl who had served him wine sat and watched him unblinkingly. By the time the door opened and Alfgar bounded in, he had decided he was going to have to meet Thor of Allerdale.

It wasn't Thor at all. First Alfgar, with his hair wild as a hay-sheaf and a round beard to match, trimming a face harder and redder than it used to be.

Then, stooping a little, another fair-haired man whose hands would not keep perfectly still, and whose obstinacy in spite of it could be felt. He had been half right. Leofwine of Cumbria, whose fingers had trembled like this over the money-bag when he and Cormac stood on the steps of St Peter's. But of course Cormac was dead, and by failing Thorfinn in that war, Leofwine must carry that, as well as other things, on his conscience.

The last man to enter was the one he had not expected: had not even thought of for four years, since Eachmarcach of Dublin died at his hand in a silly Welsh brawl over booty.

Guthorm Gunnhildarson had the stocky build and brown hair of his uncle St Olaf, rather than the Herculean height and fair hair of his uncle King Harald of Norway; but he arranged his moustaches in the willow-fashion King Harald favoured, as was only right in one of King Harald's dearest cronies.

Like Kalv, who had once been his comrade, he was a man whose company you enjoyed and also put up with. Like Kalv, his ways had nothing in common with kingship. Because of him, Eachmarcach had died, so that Diarmaid took Dublin and added his grain to the weight that had tipped the balance of fate against Alba.

Guthorm was the cause, but anger would serve nothing here, even had Guthorm achieved it from malice any more than Alfgar might. Men were what they were. This was your material and you could only do what you could with it. To Alfgar, Thorfinn said, 'I came to see Leofwine and Guthorm: what are *you* doing here?' and saw the hard-drinking face split, like sheaves to the fork, in its joy.

Alfgar bellowed, his fists on his hips. 'You are old! Other men shrink when they are old! You are in your forties and old, and you are high as a ship's mast, and your hair is dyed black. You dye it!'

'Every night,' said Thorfinn. 'And my beard-bristles every morning before I get up. Come and see.'

'I have to give you a bed?' Alfgar said. 'Have I one wide enough? Look at the saucer-eyes of the girl over there! Thorfinn-Macbeth is all they ever talk about. I tell them you have a red-haired concubine you call a wife and, unless they can outmatch that one, they may as well put up with what Mercia has to offer them. Are you winning?'

'I am alive,' said Thorfinn. 'So, it appears, are you.'

'A man of reason,' Alfgar said. He jerked a thumb at Leofwine. 'I told him. He thought you would kill him.'

'My lord is mistaken,' Leofwine said.

'He is not the first to do what he did,' said Thorfinn. 'And perhaps will not be the last. Nevertheless, I suppose there is something you want to say.'

Leofwine put his hands behind his back. 'I did not fight against you,' he said. 'If I did not fight *for* you, then neither did your men of Orkney. Perhaps our reasons were the same.'

'That they expected Earl Siward to defeat me? I don't think so,' said Thorfinn. 'And in fact, as you see, we managed to survive, even lacking your help. It seems a pity. Whatever lands you now hold, you might equally have held under my banner.'

'Oh, I can see how it happened,' Alfgar said. 'I'm not suggesting it was the right thing to do. After all, as you say, Siward didn't take Alba. But Leofwine and Thor hold valuable land, and Northumbria is a powerful neighbour. If they'd refused to help and Siward had won, they would have lost everything. As it is, their position next to Tostig is none too happy. That's why he and Guthorm are here. Let's go and talk.'

Thorfinn stood where he was. He said to Leofwine, 'As it was, you preferred to see Cormac and Ferteth and Eochaid and Malpedar and Gille-crist lose everything.'

'Do you think I don't know it?' Leofwine said. 'I remember Rome. I remember everything. If I let myself think of it, I would be afraid to die. But I had to choose between Cumbria and Alba.'

Thorfinn stood thinking, perhaps for a long time. No one spoke. Then someone said his name, and he lifted his eyes to Leofwine's and said, 'Then I hope you are sure that you made the right choice.' The misery in Leofwine's eyes surprised him.

The Norseman, who had not so far spoken, said, 'Save your wrath for me, cousin. The saddest day of my life was when I realised Eachmarcach lay dead at my feet and I had lost a friend for some silver. I had the silver made into a statue. It stands over St Olaf's shrine. But it won't bring Eachmarcach back.'

'I don't suppose it will do much to turn Diarmaid out of Dublin either,' Thorfinn said. 'But that, I suppose, was not your first thought. Everyone seems to be afraid of dying these days. Perhaps Leofwine should have something fashioned for your St Werburgh, Alfgar? He has the silver. Unless it is all going to Gruffydd?'

Alfgar said, 'You're an uncomfortable devil. Are you going to talk with us, or are you too easily offended?'

'I will talk with anyone,' he said. 'So long as they do not imagine they are speaking to a friend.'

The girl with the wide eyes said, 'My lord! If you will hold your cup, I will fill it again.'

He let her. It was an old ruse. Given enough, men had been known to come flushed from a meeting and follow the first pretty face they could see. And then, with any luck, there was a half-royal son in the world, together with all that implied.

He had been fourteen years old when Thorkel Fóstri had taught him to have to do with no one but thralls and slave-girls who could be sold, child unborn, to another land. He had never told Groa that. But, of course, the same must have been true in Norway, and probably still was.

Norway, as might be expected, was what they talked of in Alfgar's room when the door had been shut and a man posted on guard outside it.

It was not the first thing, of course. Alfgar had to explain what went wrong in Northumbria, and how he had outwitted Earl Ralph outside Hereford, and how much the Godwin family now feared him.

The Godwinssons had needed a lesson, and the fate of Hereford had provided just that. The devastation had been a pity. Once you allied yourself with the Welsh and the Irish, it was, unfortunately, what you let yourself in for. But it had been successful. Whole opposing armies had left the field unhurt when Earl Harold decided to offer him amnesty instead of battle. With Tostig Godwinsson hovering on his borders, Thorfinn must wish he were in the same position himself.

Thorfinn did not rise to it. 'Did you hear of Sulien?' he said.

'Sulien? He was at Llanbadarn when Harold was in the Golden Valley. He sent to ask if he could help either of us. But Harold had already decided on his spokesman,' Alfgar said. 'Sulien is all right. I keep recommending him, but he doesn't want to leave St David's and his family. A mistake, in my view. Your Normans didn't do you much good.'

'On the contrary,' Thorfinn said.

'Oh? Well, the Saxons couldn't work with them here. If they had, we shouldn't have had such an easy time at Archenfield,' Alfgar said. 'Anyway, Duke William must like you about as little as he likes that thick fool Earl Ralph. You killed all his best men for him, and left him to fight for Normandy with what's left. I hear Svein of Denmark let you down as well.'

Thorfinn said, 'Alfgar. I am not going to help you clear Tostig Godwinsson out of Northumbria. I have no men. And the Godwin family are too powerful everywhere else.'

'I know you've no men,' Alfgar said. 'And who said anything about Northumbria? I'd like to have taken it, but it was only a small trial attempt, that was all. No. The attack against Earl Harold has to be made against Earl Harold's land. Leofwine agrees with me, and so does Thor of Allerdale, and so does Guthorm here.'

Thorfinn said, 'You've just got East Anglia back, and your father has never held richer land or been higher in favour. What are you trying to prove?'

'That I can outwit the Godwin family,' Alfgar said. He looked angry. What he was trying to prove, of course, was that he was a greater man than his father. It was a common disease in a family with one son and an elderly father still in the seat of power and admired for it.

Alfgar said, 'What do you take me for? *I'm* not about to provoke Harold Godwinsson, and you may be sure my father does not even remember he has a son somewhere, except when the King takes his arm and consoles him. Next time, the attack will be by somebody else.'

Neither Guthorm nor Leofwine said anything. Thorfinn said, 'You will have to do better than that, if you want my interest.'

Leofwine said, 'Tell him.'

Alfgar said, 'Well, the time has never been better, has it, for an attack on the upper reaches of the Severn? Gruffydd of Wales is still there, with his mountain men, armed and lurking in the passes. Whether anyone helps him or not, he's going to fight the Saxons on his border until he dies. Last time, I brought him my own household and the Irishmen, and it wasn't enough, that's all. Also, they weren't like Eachmarcach's Irish. These were men of the half-blood, kin to the kind that Duncan took out of Cumbria, and that never did him any good, whether at Durham or against you at Tarbatness. I wouldn't advise you to use them, even if they would come, which I doubt.'

'I'll remember. So you looked round for another army to invade Hereford-shire with King Gruffydd, and since Guthorm is here, I don't see there is much of a mystery. You are asking the help of King Harald of Norway? Or you already have it?' said Thorfinn.

Alfgar looked at Guthorm, who smiled. He was not young any more, and his face and neck were white with nicks and scars. Under his hair on one side, you could see that he had only the bit of one ear. He said, 'A fleet is on its way now. It should land before midsummer. Magnús, King Harald's young son, will be on board. I am leaving to join King Gruffydd today to muster and join them.'

'I see,' said Thorfinn. 'And then what? You expect to take Gloucester and march on Winchester and London? Earl Harold can call out all his brothers and the levies of the whole kingdom.'

'Leave me out of it,' Alfgar said. 'This is between King Gruffydd and Norway. But I dare say they will get a lot of booty, and do a lot of damage to Earl Harold's lands, and kill a lot of his men, and even block off his trade for quite a period. The numbers Harald of Norway can spare from his war with Denmark won't be all that big. But it would be an earnest, you might say, of things to come. You're talking of getting what you want by fighting. I'm talking of calm negotiation and really no fighting to speak of.'

He smiled at Thorfinn. 'It's a pity, isn't it, that Siward left you so low? Once the musters are called, Tostig will be out of Northumbria, hurrying south again with his army, and, for the second time, you can win from it no advantage. I don't suppose your Orkneymen would fight for Northumbria.'

'I haven't asked them,' said Thorfinn. 'And don't put your next question. The answer is no.'

Alfgar disliked being hurried. Guthorm had no objection at all. Guthorm said, 'You need men. We need food, shelter, and a station for rest and repairs when we send a fleet west to attack England. We have to pass between Orkney and Caithness on our way from Norway to Wales, and each time our force will be bigger. If men are battle-stirred, it is hard to turn them from what they want, in any case.'

He smiled, and all the scars stretched. 'Help us, and we shall land a Norse army to sweep Alba clean of your enemies.'

'Except those of Cumbria,' Thorfinn said.

Leofwine flushed, but held his eyes. 'You would not find us enemies,' he said.

'No,' said Thorfinn. 'But I imagine I might find you in the Earl's house in Northumbria if things were to go right. Is that the bargain, Alfgar?'

Guthorm answered for him. 'One day, who knows? But at present we can't expect all the Godwinssons to give way before us, and Tostig has other powerful friends. You would, however, have your southern lands cleared and the nephew you have there got rid of. And, with our ships in the sea and our men in the north, I doubt if Tostig would think it worth troubling you when his brother will need him so badly.'

Thorfinn said, 'You disappoint me, Leofwine. I thought you and Thor would have made a firm bargain. Or had you forgotten that Earl Siward's daughter had married an Arnason? The Queen's cousin, in fact. I could remind you as well that Guthorm here is grandson to the man who was grandson to Eric Bloodaxe, King of Northumbria. Offers from King Harald are always worth looking into.'

'John Arnason has no interest in Northumbria,' Guthorm said. He was not smiling any more. 'Ask the Lady your wife. If you thought Finn her father would send help from Denmark, now you know your mistake. You have just heard my lord Alfgar. The Irish will not follow you. They have gone home with their silver, and if they fight for anyone, it will be Cumbria they will choose. You are at the mercy of everyone around you, and we are offering you the way to peace and security. Without, if you wish it, so much as putting a man of Alba in the field, or appearing in it yourself,' He paused. 'I know what Finn's daughter would say.'

'So do I,' said Thorfinn drily. To Alfgar he said, 'He is eloquent. That's why he and Eachmarcach got on so well. Is that all you wanted?'

'You don't understand,' Alfgar said. Lobes of irritation and puzzlement had settled about the root of his nose, as if accustomed to find their way there. He said, 'You'd think we were offering you some horse you didn't much care for. Norway is sparing some men to mount a series of attacks on Earl Harold's western lands. You may have the use of them if you will agree to allot them a station in Caithness or Orkney.'

He would never understand, even when it was explained to him. And every word, of course, would go straight from Guthorm to King Harald his master. Thorfinn said, 'I lost two-thirds of Alba because I would not let my own northmen fight Alba's battles. I spent the first third of my reign neglecting Alba so that I might keep Norway's hands out of Orkney.

'If those were mistakes, I am about to repeat them. There is no prize you could mention that would make me form an alliance with Norway. Even, Alfgar, to help you.'

Guthorm said, 'Perhaps your nephew Malcolm might feel differently.' The temper that had killed Eachmarcach showed now, in the rims of his eyes.

Thorfinn said, 'He might not think it a very good bargain. For he has no more men than I have, and once your Norse army has gone, it's unlikely to get back, isn't it? For if my Orcadians don't fight in Alba, they are very forward indeed when it comes to fighting for Orkney. You would never get your fleet back to Wales. You would never get a ship round north Scotland to Ireland, or trading to France, or for any reason that I didn't agree with. Because I should take every ship I possessed and stop the firth with them.'

He never raised his voice much, except in the open, and he had not raised it now. He made a pause, and said, 'Tell King Harald. I don't advise him to court my lord Malcolm. Harald is not King of England yet.'

Alfgar, pursuing a thought of his own, wasn't listening. Alfgar said, 'It's nonsense. Norway doesn't want Orkney. And what's the objection to Norsemen throwing out Malcolm? The soil of Alba isn't so sacred. You invited Normans there yourself. You settled them, even.'

'On vacant ground, properly allotted. Yes, I did,' Thorfinn said. 'A picked body, highly trained and under full control of their leaders, who lived among the families they were protecting. There is a difference.'

'And you would do it again?' Guthorm said.

Guthorm was dangerous. Thorfinn said, 'If Earl Ralph and Duke William were both to turn aside from their present preoccupations and send more trained men to settle in Alba—yes. I should do it again. Tell me if you manage to persuade them.'

Alfgar was staring at him. Alfgar said, 'Are you crazy? What's wrong with Norway? You're Norse yourself, aren't you? And, anyway, Malcolm's your enemy, not Harald of Norway. You're a king. You use anyone you can get. Look what I had to use against Hereford. But it succeeded.'

'Yes. It succeeded,' Thorfinn said. He got up. 'I know you felt this was a chance for a good alliance between us. I'm sorry to spoil it. Time will tell which is right. But I think you will find the Norse fleets do their work, even without Orkney bases.'

'It would have been like old times,' Alfgar said.

'Yes. Wouldn't it?' Thorfinn said.

Leofwine walked beside him when eventually they left Alfgar's room and made their way over the yard to the hall where his mother was waiting. Guthorm had said nothing more. Leofwine had said very little, but he could feel his thoughts, breathing beside him.

What it was, Thorfinn could guess and, having no desire to be oppressed with it, kept his own silence. After a few steps, he saw that on his other side a girl had appeared, the same pretty girl who had stared at him in the bower. She said, 'My lord King. You left your wine untouched.'

Which was true. He had laid it down unnoticed a little after she had poured it. He saw she held it in her hands now, and said, 'Forgive me. I was no longer thirsty. You kept it?'

She answered the note in his voice with a smile. 'It would not please you now. I poured a fresh cup instead, since the Lady of Mercia asked me. She wished to make you a gift of the goblet.'

Except that it would have been unwise, he would have kept Godiva's scarf. In his life, there was a special place for the Lady of Mercia.

The cup was worth a deal more than the scarf. It was something from long ago, made in bronze with two little handles, and thickly embossed with men and heroes: Odysseus, Heracles, Philoctectus. A lavish gift. A gift that spoke very specially of Godiva's teasing affection.

He could not carry it full of wine. He took the cup and saluted the girl as he lifted it, ready to drain it. Her face loosened and became very soft, like the face of someone asleep, or coaxing the climax of love, or stopped, for the very first time, by the stir of a child in her belly.

He said, 'No. You will drink it for me.'

Had she cared less, she might have brazened it out. But she stood there with hate in her eyes, and then, turning, ran. She made for the gate, not the hall. It would never enter her head but that he would tell the Lady. He doubted if anyone even in Godiva's entourage would know much about it. She would be recommended to the hall, a high-born friend of a friend. He knew with absolute certainty that none of the Mercian family would have been implicated. He wondered, in those few seconds, who her father or lover had been, and how he had killed him. At the ford over the Tay, perhaps, when the horses stamped in the mud and the trees stretched and walked in their greenery.

Leofwine said, 'What did you say to her? If you don't want the wine—'

Thorfinn had begun, slowly, to pour it away. He stopped.

Leofwine said stiffly, 'I beg your pardon, my lord. There will be wine in the hall.'

Thorfinn thought of the longship taking the seas from Cologne, and the talk, and the laughter. He thought of Cormac, the last to die on Dunsinane. He said, 'Yes. The wine in the hall will be better,' and went on pouring until the goblet was empty.

FOURTEEN

THE ATTACK ON Herefordshire by King Gruffydd of Wales, aided by the son of the King of Norway, took place in the middle of June and ran the exact course of its predecessor: destruction, deadlock, and a suing for peace, ending in conciliation on the English side. Orkney was not involved.

By harvest-time, when Tuathal and the new-made Bishop Isleifr arrived back from Bremen, it was long over, although Denmark, when they called there, was still full of gossip about it. Having withstood a feast given by King Svein and visited Finn and Bergljot, the Lady's father and mother, Tuathal took ship and returned as quickly as he might. For all his precautions, it was not a time for one of his few experienced men to be far from Thorfinn's side.

He said as much to the Lady when he found her with the household at Kineddar, by the sand-strewn flats of the Lossie, awaiting the return of the King from some affair that had taken him south.

Already, he noticed, the women about the King's wife were both younger and older than he had been accustomed to find, just as the courtmen were different. Given time, the heirs to the mormaerdoms grew into their training, and if you were lucky, the wise men came out of whatever monastery they had retired to and helped make the bridge from the old war to the new. Unless you found a king who could change men's nature, so that no war ever came.

The Lady said, 'Of course you had to go, when we need the goodwill of Denmark and Saxony more than ever. And if you hadn't been consecrated somewhere, the Archbishop of York would never have stopped meddling.'

Her spirit had not changed, at least, although he saw Isleifr glance at the dark red hair, a little longer now, pinned into its coif. From her welcome of Isleifr and the quick, searching questions about her parents, you could guess how, stranded in Alba, she must sometimes miss her own kind. In the south, she and Thorfinn never spoke other than in one of the Celtic tongues. When they were together, he did not know what language they used. He asked after the King.

'Oh, he is never still,' she said. 'But you know, perhaps, how difficult things are. To protect themselves, the bigger families who have returned to the south have had to surround themselves with stockades and ditches against Malcolm's sympathisers, who have done the same. It means that when fighting does break out, it kills whole families. Thorfinn has been helping Scandlain in Fife, and has been a lot in Angus and Atholl as well.'

'Is that wise?' Tuathal said.

'Add your voice to that of everyone else,' Groa said. 'He doesn't listen.'

'Thorfinn?' said Isleifr. At fifty, and a bishop, he looked little different from the priest Tuathal had first met at Goslar six years before, although the gown hid the horseman's legs and flaxen-furred arms, and his freckled scalp peered with greater success from its encroaching jungle. He was the hairiest man Tuathal had ever met and, in Bremen and after, had been very good company.

Now, evidently, he had stopped to give thought to something. He said, 'When did Thorfinn ever care what sort of figure he cut? Heroics are for heroes, and good luck to the fools. He can't imagine that he can hold together such provinces by his good looks alone. You tell me that Malcolm will pay for his head. Once a king loses his mystery, men will kill him for nothing.'

Tuathal gazed at the new Bishop, who said, 'Ah. That is—'

The Lady said, 'Don't worry. These things get about. There is always someone who thinks one would be the better for knowing. I think you're wrong. I think that it seems to him that to care for them now, when they need help, might well alter things in his favour. And his visit to Chester, there is no doubt, increased the weight of responsibility he feels he must carry.'

'He refused an alliance with Mercia?' Tuathal said.

'He refused an alliance with Norway. More than that, hardly anyone has managed to get out of him. But it would seem that Harald of Norway has offered to help Alfgar get rid of the Godwinssons, and thought to get a foothold in Orkney by offering Thorfinn something similar. As you would hear, Alfgar, who prefers a short view, went ahead with his scheme.'

'We heard in Denmark,' Tuathal said. 'Alfgar prudently kept out of the way. But King Gruffydd and the Norwegians attacked, and killed the Sheriff of Hereford this time, and the new Bishop. Alfgar's father, Earl Harold, and Bishop Ealdred of Worcester led an army against them, and there was a parley, which ended in King Gruffydd submitting to England, and Bishop Ealdred receiving in gift the now vacant bishopric of Hereford. I was told by someone,' Tuathal said, 'to model myself on Bishop Ealdred. But, however long I live, I feel I can never hope to do half as well.'

'Tell that to the King,' the Lady said. 'He needs news. He has been waiting for you. I won't ask you what else he wanted you both to do, other than return blessed by Archbishop Adalbert, because I think I can guess. But could you tell me, because I don't think I can wait any longer, what was the answer?'

He wondered if she really knew, and decided that of course she did, for there was only one way now out of the troubles of Alba.

Tuathal said, 'The answer was yes. I don't see what else he could have done. But I hope he never regrets it.'

*   *   *

It was not an autumn anyone cared to remember. A drought at the wrong time had produced burned grass and a scanty harvest and a shortening of tempers that made the unrest everywhere worse. The harvest was bad, but no one was starving, and the exhaustion of battle was lifting. Where there had been apathy, there was the clash of argument, followed soon enough by the clash of steel, as boys turned to youths and, listening, took up their father's swords.

It could not go on. This autumn, somehow it had to be contained until the winter put its seal on the violence. And then, next year, it would have to be dealt with.

The autumn had passed and the blessed winter was just beginning when the news came to the court where Thorfinn was. He heard it alone, and then brought it to the next gathering of his household. He said, 'That was a ship from Denmark, bringing news out of Saxony. The Emperor Henry died in October. It will make a difference.'

Tuathal watched him. He showed no signs of concern or alarm. He was still considering, clearly, just how big a difference it would make.

Bishop Jon said, 'Now, there's a loss. Would he be forty? I doubt it. And a good man. Before he took a hand in the matter, there was a Pontiff or two whose toe I should have let go without kissing if I could manage it.'

Thorfinn said, 'His last Pope is to step into the Emperor's shoes, it seems, until they can form a proper regency for his heir, who is only five. The Emperor asked for his heart to be buried at Goslar, and his body to be laid by his father at Spires. He died with the Pope by his bedside.'

'Gebhard of Eichstedt,' Bishop Hrolf said. 'He'll manage well enough. When you think of it, there was never a Pope set foot in Germany for a hundred and fifty years before Benedict, and they've hardly been out of the place since, except to shake their fists at the Normans. So the child's mother will be regent?'

'Subject to her councillors,' Thorfinn said. 'I remember Agnes of Aquitaine and Anjou. If she has time for anything other than the immediate problems of the Empire, which I doubt, it won't be to help us in any way. If Bishop Tuathal hadn't been to Bremen so recently, I should have had to send him. That trip may save us.'

The Lady said, 'Adalbert likes consecrating bishops for the north, it's true, and if ever he's going to be a patriarch, he'll have to cultivate them. But he must wonder from time to time if the King of Alba is paying very much heed to the northern half of his property. The cathedral of Birsay may well have fallen down by now, for all the attention it's getting.'

Tuathal kept his gaze on his hands. Bishop Jon, he saw, was doing the same. Thorfinn said, 'Thorkel Fóstri keeps an eye on it. Do you think it matters? We couldn't send anyone north this late in the year. They might not be able to cross back for weeks.'

The Lady said, 'How long is it since either Bishop Jon or Bishop Hrolf was in Orkney? Three years?'

Bishop Jon said, 'In the spring, one or two of us could be there and back before you'd know it. You're right. There they are, tearing their hearts out building more ships than the sea can carry for weight, and no one giving them a kind word. Also, if Harald of Norway changes his mind, there may be some fighting they ought to be prepared for. I'll go, my lord King, if you'll let me. Perhaps you might even find time to come with me.'

Tuathal turned his hands over and examined the other side. Bishop Hrolf, he sensed, was surveying the rafters.

Thorfinn's voice said, rolling a little, 'Soft as lead, like the Sarabites, and known by their tonsure to be lying to God. All right. Whose idea was it?'

'Mine, just now,' said the Lady. 'Otherwise we should be making a better job of it. You won't get an apology from any of us. If Orkney needs a share of your time, you don't need to refuse it just to show how unselfish you can be. None of us has any illusions about your character.'

'Not by the time you have finished with it,' Thorfinn said. His colour had risen, which was unusual, but he did not look angry. He said, 'How could I possibly go?'

'Good,' said the Lady.

Tuathal, who was not married, could not find anything in what the King had said to warrant either that degree of satisfaction or that degree of finality, but he was prepared to believe that somehow an argument had been presented and a case had been won.

He felt, when he thought about it, nothing but the most profound relief.

They had built another *Grágás* for the King and sent it to Caithness to fetch him.

Riding from Canisbay to Thurso, he went down to the shore to inspect the new ships and saw it at once, its prow swooping over its fellows.

It was bigger than *Grágás*, and much more elaborate: built of broad strakes that could only come, through whatever middlemen, from trees felled in Norway. Thorkel Fóstri, waiting beside it for his welcome, was of course the man to arrange that.

The King's orders to all his shipbuilders had been to make ships that were smaller than the custom, and easy to work with in battle, which in turn meant fewer losses. In place of this vehicle, fit for a King who ruled from Orkney to Cumbria, he could have had two useful longships to counter Harald of Norway with. He went towards his foster-father's embrace and was moved by the look on the other man's face to give his thanks as they should be given, and dismiss his ingratitude.

It had been the same, in a way, with the people who had come to greet him everywhere on this journey, round the halls where he stayed and on his way in between. Until the great gale, he had been north almost every year of his life, and of course had met most of the households one way or another, if only settling their quarrels in a meeting for justice, or greeting them at a feast or tribute-time. For the rest, it was leaders like Hlodver and Odalric and their families who served him, and the young men who sailed and fought with him.

It was what he expected, for although he had been only five years old when his father left for the Irish war in which he died, Thorfinn could remember with a child's clarity the talk and the feasting in the weeks beforehand as the captains gathered in the great hundred-foot hall in Birsay over which, now, he had built a better. And the sea before they set off, dancing with gold; and the moment when the sails sprang open, with a sound like forest trees whipping in thunder, and the look of the fleet, like foxgloves thrown on the water.

He did not remember the look on the faces of the women or the old men, although he knew it now. He supposed his father had been no more conscious of how they felt than they, in turn, understood what the Earl did when he crossed the sea. Any more than, in his own time, the people of Orkney and Caithness thought about his summer absences south, visiting his conquered earldoms elsewhere. It was the custom, in summer, for young men to go fighting and raiding and tribute-gathering and quelling those who thought, during the winter, that they would like to change masters. He had kept Orkney free. And he came back in winter. That was all they were concerned about.

But now it was spring, and although three years had passed since he had been north, whole settlements came out to meet him. In Freswick, someone called out to know how it had gone in his wars with the English. He could not tell what they had heard. It looked as if they thought he had gone seeking new honours for his earldom, as his father had gone seeking a kingdom in Ireland. He said what came easily to him, and they seemed pleased.

The new ship had received a name already, and of course he agreed with it. *Skidbladnir*, the name of the legendary vessel that had nothing but fair winds; that was big enough to hold all the Aesir, and yet would fold small enough to put in a bag.

He could imagine Tuathal's cynical stare and was glad, on the whole, that he and Bishop Hrolf had been left behind with his mormaers to strengthen and fortify the Deeside frontier of Mar and Moray, which had been decided on before he left. With him, he had brought only thirty of his own household and Bishop Jon, whose special care the islands were. The company was fewer than the Aesir, and the new dragon-ship carried them with no trouble. Halfway between Thurso and Orkney, standing in the stern between the steersman and Thorkel Fóstri, it came to Thorfinn that he was on the sea in his own ship again.

He turned, and Thorkel Fóstri said, smiling, 'Your mind was on other things. I know that.' A little later, he said, 'Arnór was here, but he left when he heard you were coming. Perhaps it was embarrassment, or perhaps he was afraid of King Harald. He always asks what Irish bard you have now.'

'A dead one,' said Thorfinn. To have Arnór in Alba composing eulogies on the battle-prowess of the Earl of Orkney would have been the quickest way, he supposed, to sever the two halves of the kingdom for good. He said, 'Did Arnór bring some gossip with him?'

Thorkel shrugged. Now the old lameness showed, when he walked quickly, and his hair and beard were quite grey, although well kept, and his dress was fine. After all, he had been given an earl to rear in his household, and had done it properly, despite the Celtic stepfather. As Earl's spokesman and cousin of the Arnasons, he was used to the councils of rulers as well as to the life of a sea-lord. The years of power in Orkney had brought him great authority.

The lightness in his nature had never changed, but, fortified by his other qualities, it had never come to matter. They were going now to his great hall at Sandwick, as had become the custom while their own hall-houses were being prepared, and they would find it, as ever, full of cheerful, well-trained serving-people, some of them slaves and some free; some of them concubines and some Thorkel's sons or daughters by concubines and even small children of the next generation, also of his blood.

In some ways, Thorkel Fóstri had always lived like a Viking lord, as Thorfinn's father had done. You took a wife if policy required it, and policy had never made that demand on Thorkel Fóstri. The only son he was interested in was not of his siring, and to rear a rival would have been purposeless.

Thorkel Fóstri said, 'Gossip? He spent all his time talking about a new verse-form he thinks he's invented. We've had nothing but Hebrew psalms and Norse Kenningar in the hall-house for weeks. I was glad to escape it.'

'Hebrew psalms?' said Bishop Jon. Obedient even in wind, his hair was composed all round his tonsure as if painted. His eyes moved to Thorfinn. 'I've been looking at the oars. And do you see how they've fixed in the mast-fish?'

Thorfinn said, 'Who else is at Sandwick?' He saw Groa turn at the tone of his voice.

The years had taught Thorkel Fóstri something about his foster-son. He said slowly, 'Why? I thought you would welcome him. I didn't mean you to guess. I suppose the Hebrew gave it away.'

'Sulien of Llanbadarn,' Thorfinn said. He knew already, from the surprise in Groa's eyes, that she knew nothing of it, even before she shook her head slightly, guessing what he wanted to know. Thorfinn said, 'Apart from the company I already have, there is no one I'd rather meet. Did you send for him?'

'Send for him? No,' said Thorkel Fóstri. 'He was passing, he said.'

'On his way from Wales to Moville, perhaps. One of Sulien's special circuits,' Thorfinn said. 'The Normans used to have a phrase for it. *I ferait buon l'envier trachi la mort.*'

Thorkel Fóstri knew no Norman-French. He said, 'What does that mean? A man with no sense of time or direction?'

'More or less,' Thorfinn said. 'It means, a good man to send to find death. It's a joke. So what is amazing about the mast-fish . . . ?'

Sulien was smaller and lighter than he remembered, but not in any sense fragile. His first words were, 'You learned of me, sighing. Now you will have to keep the peace between your three lovers who each long to possess you and Orkney together.' He paused. 'No. I am wrong.'

'You are right,' Thorfinn said. 'Why are you here?'

'Forgive me. At Earl Alfgar's suggestion,' Sulien said. 'That is all.' He hesitated, and then said, 'Perhaps you don't know how tired you are.'

He must be, to be as transparent as that. He stepped forward and said and did what he should have done first, and at the end, releasing him, Sulien said, 'Where is your sense? Orkney is your medicine. Forget your planning, disregard your people, and take it.'

It was true that his mind was tired, but his body was not; which was just as well, for the medicine of Orkney was not for weaklings. And although he cleared his mind of his planning, for there was nothing else he could do, he did not disregard the people, either those close to him or those who knew him only as Earl, for that, too, was part of the medicine. In the cold, fresh air smelling of salt and of peat, he raced with them, on shipboard and horseback and foot, and plunged over the little hills, hunting, and watched horse-fights and ate round towering fires in the open, with singing and declaiming and laughter, and drinking not by measure at all, but as if no man had studs to his cup.

If Sulien was with him, he kept from him the ale brewed with kelp-barley, with which southern tastes and southern stomachs did not always agree. Often Sulien was elsewhere, and Thorkel Fóstri rode at his right hand. Sometimes he had only his two sons and Groa. He knew, as Sulien did, what was needed of him and, if he could, did not fail them.

He did not stay on the main island, but went everywhere: to the north islands and the south islands that had once belonged to his brothers. To Westray, where Rognvald's hall was his now. With Paul and Erlend, to Sanday to fish, coming alongside the peat-boats from Eday with their sticky black load, the *torfskeri* rammed in at all angles, like quills on a hedgehog. He stood on the red cliffs that were made like shelves in a book-tower, their green caps cut into fingers of turf, and watched the sea at their base, scribbled and scrawled over with white, and the gulls fleeting below, faster by far than the fishing-boats underneath them.

Because it was spring, everything was covered with flowers: the grassland, the machair, the salt-marshes, the cliffs, the dunes and the wetlands, the moors and the peat-bogs, the shingle and the bare, rocky outcrops, the banks of the streams and the lochs.

Groa knew the names of them all: blue and yellow, purple and white, high and low. He knew the banks of yellow flags, the sky reflected in their broad leaves, and the sharp, sweet pink of the thrift. He knew better the wisps of bog-cotton, or the fleshy star of the insect-eater with its bald violet flower that told you, when running, where not to step.

He liked to see what was practical. The number of foals and suckling calves. The women pacing on a still day through their corn-plots, the straw basket of bere-seed strapped to the neck like the Brecbennoch, and no less full of prayers. The sound of a sledge pulled over wet turf just after dawn as someone went to rake lichen. An open barn-door with, inside, the coils of rope of grass and heather and straw that had made the winter storms pass more quickly. A good horse, Isleifr said, kept itself in tethers from its mane and its tail.

The timber houses, silver-brown, which had weathered the gale, and the bright chestnut brown of new wood where a fresh home had been built. The new roofs, of sealskin and turf, grass and earth, woven reeds. The herring-bone peat-stacks, layered like the red cliffs or like the tooled stones of the burial-mounds. The smell of sweet milk and the sound of a churn. The quack of hazel-rods, splitting for withies. The beehive towers of the brochs, forty feet high and a thousand years old, and still kept in repair for the same reason that they had been built, for the sea that made Orkney safe in winter was the path that led to her doorway all summer.

At a ford, a crossroads, at the neck of a pass, you built a fort. But where the Romans had long gone, or had never been, the only road was the one where a keel could run. Whoever held Orkney had to hold Caithness as well. Hence all the wars of his forefathers. For, unless you held your road by both margins, you had no security.

Hence also, you could not keep Fife without expecting and planning to hold Angus as well. If you possessed Lothian, you must, for safety, try to plant your people in southern Fife, on the opposite shore. If you lived in Brittany, you looked across the Narrow Seas to Dorset and Devon and Cornwall, as Juhel was doing. If you owned Flanders or Normandy, you might think your need was greater still.

Always, peoples had fought until they owned both sides of the road, or both banks of the river. And gave themselves no respite until they did.

That night, Sulien said, 'It is time that we talked.'

They were at Orphir, and all that day Thorkel Fóstri had been talking of crossing to the mountains of Hoy, where the falcons were.

They could catch falcons without him. Thorfinn left them on the shore next morning, arguing about who was going to row, and took Sulien, riding alone, north to Birsay.

They rode in silence, over the hill and into the *staðir* country, where soon, against a low swell of hill, the Ring of Brodgar showed pale.

One of the monoliths had dropped in the gale. The rest still stood, some fifteen feet high; some brown and stooped, and weathered like rotten silk. He chose to ride past them, between the two lochs that had only once frozen, in his experience, and a swan rose in a flurry and, neck and body undulating, flew slowly round in a white, loosened coil. 'The swans of Urd?' he said to Sulien.

The spring of Urd, which also nourished its swans, was the spring of Destiny, and to it each day came the Norns to draw water. *Urðr, Verðandi,* and *Skuld*. Past, Present, and Future.

'Lulach is helpless,' said Sulien. 'Give him love. He doesn't deserve anything else. If you shut your mind to everything that has been said, it cannot hurt you.'

'You mean it cannot alter things,' Thorfinn said. A white hare, that had forgotten the end of winter had come, looked at them with polished eyes and fled over the brown heath that it knew was hiding it.

'I mean I can't talk when I am riding,' Sulien said. 'But it might occur to you that you have always assumed that you had the power to alter things, and you have always been proved right. No one is going to take that power from you, unless you run away from it yourself.'

It was a ride of three hours to his new hall at Birsay, for they stopped now and then, for one reason and another, although they talked of nothing that mattered when they did. Marriage, thought Thorfinn, suited Sulien. He did not speak of his wife, but there were four children growing up near the monastery: Rhygyfarch, Daniel, Jevan, and Arthgen. Love for them all warmed Sulien's voice when he spoke of them, but of the first, most of all.

He was a famous teacher now, the boy who had defied his own teachers to spend five years in Alba before reaching his intended training in Ireland. A great scholar; a composer of Latin verse. A man who divided his time, it would seem, between St David's and Llanbadarn and any other group of pupils who needed him, and for whom the ring of a bishop was something not to be sought, but to be avoided.

It was not hard, when you had been his first pupil, to see why.

They reached the bay opposite the Brough about midday and had something to eat and drink in his mainland hall, along with the manager of the farms and his family. Then, without waiting for the causeway to dry out, he and Sulien took boat across the short distance from the mainland shore to the long slipway that led up through the cliff-rocks to the settlement and his new hall and church.

Once, before the ocean broke through the neck of it, the island of Birsay had been the north horn of this wide bay where the new boats lay trim in their nousts. Like Deerness, it had been a place of safety sought by many peoples. There was a broch still on its far tip, and there had been a Christian church and a Christian cemetery where now stood his new church.

He took Sulien there when he had greeted those people he should, and visited the hall and the house used by the priest when he came there. Outside the church was a grave-marker from the old cemetery, with the spider-drawings you saw by Forres and Glamis, and the disdainful eagle, and three stalking figures in Assyrian robes with their square shields and their spears. If any Pope-Emperor had ordered the implantment of that little church, it was more likely to be the lord of Greekdom than the lord of Rome.

Thorfinn said, 'We built in the same place, since it was holy. As you see, the church is small.'

There were only fifty-five feet of it, in squared stones, carefully mortared. A rectangular nave, and a narrow choir, with an apse on the east side. Since the gale, the tower had never been rebuilt. Inside, it was sweet and clean, with fresh rushes in the nave and the smell of new carpentering. A plain cloth lay on the stone altar, for the gold easily dulled in the sea-air, and the most precious things were in the hall or the priest's house. But those necessary for the Mass were in their places, and within the altar, in the box made to fit it, the first banner Thorfinn had brought back, blessed by the Pope and sanctified at the tomb of St Peter.

'Bishop Jon dedicated the church for us,' he said. 'To Christ and St Peter. The flag lies with others, which we use when they, too, have become potent by contact. A wise precaution, as it turned out. I wonder what happened to the first one? Somewhere a wound has miraculously healed, or a nest is breaking from the weight of eggs in it, or a murderer in his shroud is being admitted to Paradise.'

There was a bench along one wall, with straw matting on it. Sulien sat down and crossed his strong, bare feet in their sandals while the brown wool of his robe fell to the rushes. Except that he was beardless and had no shield and spear, he could have passed for one of the three calm, fierce warriors on the gravestone outside. He said, 'I was foolish, seven years ago. I should never have talked to you of my disappointment at Rheims.'

Thorfinn sat himself on the edge of the choir flagstones and leaned back on his hands. 'It would have made no difference. Pope Leo wanted to make the church stronger and purer, but he knew as well as anybody that he had no power at all unless he helped the Emperor hold down Lombardy and the old duchies and his more boisterous neighbours. And to keep the papal office in being, never mind get rid of the Normans encroaching on it, he needed to get money in every way possible, and especially by pleasing his wealthiest relatives. Then, in turn, his family will supply advisors and lords of the church to the Empire, and Popes to Rome; and very good, too, if the Pope is of the quality of Leo and the Emperor is of the quality of Henry. But it can't always be so.'

'You don't hear me quarrel with you,' said Sulien. 'Although you have done the same here. Three good bishops, chosen by a good king. But it can't always be so.'

Thorfinn said, 'I thought once that the Celtic church could mould itself to the new needs and let us keep the best of the old style of worship. So did Juhel of Dol, I know. But there is too much against it. Even in Ireland . . .'

'Even in Ireland, the Celtic church is failing,' Sulien took his words. 'Because the abbot-families are war-like, and it suits the kings to make them their allies. Your great Duftah of Armagh himself has just fought a pitched battle over relics with the Coarb of Kells and St Finnian. You can't look to Ireland for aid. Nor to the Culdees. They will save your soul, but they won't help you to rule. And you need a church that will do both, as the Emperor does. Even if when you die, as when an Emperor dies, the church holds your people to ransom. Am I right?'

'I wish,' said Thorfinn, 'there was another way. Isleifr is lucky in Iceland. The great priest-families merely send their sons abroad to be trained, and when they return with good alliances, the old ways go on barely modified. . . . No. I am not serious. We are a land of many and disparate peoples. Iceland is not. It will take longer, that's all, to find our solution.'

Silence fell. The smell and the sound of the sea came through the little window behind him, and a drift of incense, very faintly, from the new altar.

Sulien said, 'They say Holy Church always limits the time men stay when they come to the Pontiff, for before very long the marble wearies them, and the gold and the fountains, and they long for their cabins at home.'

Thorfinn said, 'You are asking if I lean towards Rome for other reasons? I suppose that is what is wrong with Bishop Ealdred and Geoffrey of Coutances, with their dreams of gold-laden cathedrals. But if you went to Norway, I don't think you'd find King Harald trying to re-create the splendours of Constantinople.'

Sulien said nothing.

Thorfinn said, 'I am no different. Harald went east to win gold and, when he came back, bought his power with it. I went to Rome to buy, too, what would keep me in power. I even had money. Perhaps I should have built a copy of the Lateran Palace by the sands at the mouth of the Lossie; or another St Mary of the Snows in the bracken by Essie, or even an octagonal baptistry somewhere. I thought it would be foolish.'

Sulien said, 'Why didn't you use the men of the north against Siward?'

Thorfinn got up and wandered through to the apse. Then, returning, he stopped at the window. So far, generalities. Afterwards, this was the part that was going to hurt. He said, 'They might not have come. They might have lost their heads if they did. The division would have been worse afterwards than before.'

'Did your friends in Alba appreciate that?' Sulien said.

'Some of them. For the rest, it worked well enough. I even had some taunts about northmen being afraid to do any fighting.'

'And that was good?' Sulien said.

'No one likes being despised. But it means that they were not thought of as foreign aggressors. And that is something new. Time is all it needs,' Thorfinn said. 'Time to make the joins firm. The north, the northwest, and Moray fixed firmly and easily to Alba. And Cumbria and Strathclyde restored the way my grandfather had it, whether under nominal rule from England or not. Three languages, I know. Three cultures, I know. But it can be done.'

'Yet Duncan gave you the country in two pieces, and now it has fallen in three. Do you regret taking the kingship?' Sulien said.

Thorfinn turned from the window. He leaned on the wall and folded his arms. 'Every year, I might have given you a different answer,' he said. 'I was fairly sure that if I didn't take it, I should lose Moray. It seemed possible that I could refuse, however, and hope to live out my life here and in Caithness, and perhaps in Ireland and the west, in the way I had always done, and with Groa. Although my frontier with Alba would always have been at risk, and I should have had a lifetime of sparring with Norway.'

'You have had that anyway,' Sulien said.

'But mostly from a position of strength. As it was, I should have had exactly the life that my father had.'

'But, instead, you wanted the life of your grandfather?' Sulien said.

'I expect so,' said Thorfinn. 'Although, at the time, I don't suppose I should have said so. I think I thought of it as a challenge of a kind I hadn't yet faced.

Like one of Tuathal's cryptograms, to which there was an answer, if I thought hard enough.'

'I remember the mood,' Sulien said.

'And you didn't like it. I remember, as well. But do I regret it now? I don't know. For a while,' Thorfinn said, 'it seemed a good game. Skill against skill, and skill against luck. But with my grandfather, it was mostly mercenaries who were killed.'

'Luck?' Sulien said.

'Or chance. Or the three ladies at the spring of Urd, if you like,' Thorfinn said. 'If they choose to be unkind now, there are not so many moves I can make in return.'

'Your divided country may be an asset there,' Sulien said. 'If there is trouble in Alba, you can deal with it, knowing the north lies safe behind you, with two grown heirs and Thorkel Fóstri to guide them, and the fleet nearly restored. Is it Alba where you expect your war to be?'

'There is war in Alba already,' he said. 'War among the people, against themselves. It can't go on, and I can't keep the peace with what I have left.' He paused, and reached a decision. 'I have asked William of Normandy to hire me an army, and he has agreed.'

No riposte in answer to that, in the lilting Breton voice. It was a relief to have said it aloud. Moving to the nave, Thorfinn opened the heavy door a little, so that warm air drifted in, and he could see the graveyard, rising to the scatter of longhouses further up, and the green hill against the western sky. The unseen sun on his left struck the grave-marker, picking out the brick plumage and the powerful claws of the eagle. Behind him, Sulien said, 'You think you can control them?'

He shut the door and turned back. 'I did it with a smaller group,' he said. 'Very few of these will want to linger in Alba. Duke William made a pact with the King of France at the end of the year. If Anjou settles, Normandy will be a rich duchy, and it will suit these men to go back and be part of it. All I want are enough men to clear Alba of rebels.'

'You mean kill them,' said Sulien. 'Otherwise, they would come back, once the Normans had gone.'

'Yes. I mean kill them,' said Thorfinn. 'Because of them, the people loyal to me are dying every day and the country is falling to waste.'

'You have another choice,' Sulien said. 'You could reverse your decision of seventeen years ago and be content with your earldom of Orkney and Caithness.'

Thorfinn said, 'It is not quite the same choice. This time, no King of Alba could afford to let me live.'

Sulien did not speak. No enemy he had ever faced had been as hard as Sulien could be. Thorfinn said, 'Do you imagine I think about nothing but games?'

Sulien said, 'You sometimes give that impression.' He was not smiling. He said, 'You didn't ask me why Earl Alfgar asked me to come and see you.'

'No,' Thorfinn said. Sitting below him, Sulien had changed his position.

Looking down on him, he could see nothing but the shaved top of his head, and his down-bent fair lashes, and two long-fingered hands encircling one knee. He had wondered why Alfgar should have done such a thing, but had said nothing. If the matter was urgent, Sulien would tell him. When he did not, he had assumed that there was an embarrassment somewhere. Alfgar—or Godiva—had thought him in need of help, temporal or spiritual, and had sent for Sulien. Or Alfgar had intended to lay on Sulien an embassy he did not care for, such as persuading himself towards an alliance with Norway and Mercia, to lend power to King Gruffydd in driving the Saxons out of Wales.

He had not forgotten that once he himself had allied with King Gruffydd, to their mutual advantage, and then shortly afterwards Gruffydd had sacked Llanbadarn. The last thing Sulien would help sponsor was an invasion. Sulien knew what greed could do. He had said almost nothing about the Norman mercenaries, but his opinions were none the less plain. Thorfinn knew, who had had to weigh the risk over and over before sending to Normandy. In Italy, the Normans had conquered and stayed, and every footmark had become a ladder-rung to the next conquest.

So now he said, 'No,' wondering what Sulien was going to say that could not be said at the beginning but had to be presented to him like canon tables, arcaded about with all the other considerations they had discussed.

And Sulien said, 'Earl Alfgar wanted me to give you a warning. He said that he thought Denmark and Norway were by way of making some temporary peace. And that if that were so, Norway might send much more than a token fleet next time when they wanted to damage Earl Harold on the Welsh border. He said that you had already refused once to league with Norway, and to allow them the supply-base they needed. Earl Alfgar said that he was in no doubt that when and if the King of Norway's fleet came to the firth, he would attack you here in Orkney. That was why I said you were fortunate. Even if you find Alba and the Normans have all your attention in the south, yet you have two good sons and all your powerful leaders to look after the north for you.'

It took Thorfinn's breath, but he would not show it. This had always been one of the risks. He knew what Sulien intended him to feel, and he felt it. But, at the same time, you could say that his invitation to Duke William had been vindicated. Whoever was locked up here, doing battle with Norway, at least Alba would not lie helpless to any invader. He said, 'Did Alfgar know when?'

'No. But he thought it might take King Harald a little time to get his ships back north and in order. Perhaps midsummer or later. You will see why there was no need to tell you earlier. Will you stay in Orkney?' Sulien said. 'When do your men-at-arms come from Normandy?'

'In a month, perhaps. It may be that I have Alba settled before King Harald's fleet comes to the north,' Thorfinn said. 'If it comes. Perhaps I could even sell my used Normans to King Harald to employ against Wessex. After all, they are Wessex's natural enemies. Do you think a new game is about to start? Front to front, shall eagles claw each other?'

Sulien had looked up. 'You mean it,' he said.

'Does it matter?' said Thorfinn. He touched Sulien lightly on the shoulder and then, impatient at the disparity in their heights, dropped to the rushes at his feet and sat cross-legged, looking up at him.

Thorfinn said, 'I am not very good at making promises, and I don't know why you take this trouble with me. But although, yes, I mean it, I also understand what you are saying to me, and I agree with it. Only my opponents and the three ladies do not always let me take the course I should prefer. And in this case I am led to believe that all decisions are out of my hands, whatever I do. So when I say does it matter, that is all I mean.'

Sulien said slowly, 'It is easy to excuse yourself because of a shadow.'

'Then I don't. My fate is in my own hands,' Thorfinn said.

There was another silence. Then Sulien said, 'If you had faith of any kind, I could get rid of this for you.' Then the note of bitterness went, and he said in his musical Breton, 'I think the time has come to say what you fear and see if we can talk about it. If you had no Celtic blood, I suppose you would never have heard the legend of Luloecen the Fool. That is it, isn't it?'

Long ago, Thorfinn had realised that Sulien had read the histories of the man whose name Lulach bore. The Luloecen of centuries past, of whom, to the superstitious, this Lulach might seem a re-embodiment. Only to the superstitious.

Tuathal also knew. Thorfinn had never discussed it with either. To bring it into the open was like laying bare not a scar but a wound. He kept his voice even.

'For a legend, or course, it has turned out remarkably apt. Five hundred years ago, the seer called Luloecen lived at the court of King Ryderch of Strathclyde, and prophesied the death of the King, and of St Kentigern, and of Morcant, St Kentigern's enemy. Both names, Ruaidhrí and Morgan, are in Lulach's family.'

'And in the family of Findlaech your stepfather,' Sulien said. 'What other tales have you heard?'

Suddenly, it was too much. Thorfinn twisted and got to his feet. 'No. This is foolish. We are grown men, if nothing else.'

'Then behave like one,' said Sulien. 'What other versions have you been told?' He paused and said, 'You may be discussing fantasies, but witchcraft is my business.'

Thorfinn turned. 'No. We're not speaking of witchcraft,' he said. 'Lulach is untouched and innocent, and these are matters that stand outside his knowledge, as much as they stand outside mine. Hear it all, then. In this and other tales of the Madman, the Wild Man, the Fool, the prophecy changes and becomes a threefold foretelling of death. Luloecen the Fool foretold his own. The Lulach of our time knows his own fate. And mine.'

He stopped; and then said, 'Seven-eighths Celt or not, I should have found out about it all anyway. Odin was hanged, and pierced by a spear, and suspended over Mimir's well. *Guin, Badud, Loscad.* Wounding, drowning, and burning. The threefold death comes in all languages.'

'Always by slaughter, drowning, and burning?' Sulien asked.

'Nearly always. I have had my burning and slaughter,' Thorfinn said.

'But that was not what Lulach prophesied for you?'

Thorfinn said, 'Lulach never prophesies. He tells you what has already happened, through many eyes. Sometimes it might all be true. Sometimes it is impossible that it should be. He told me of the High King Diarmait mac Cerbaill who gave judgement against St Columba in the matter of the book of St Finnian, and who had to suffer the Threefold Death as was prophesied. He would not die, he was told, until he ate the flesh of a swine that was never farrowed; but of course he was given bacon one day from a piglet cut from a sow, and died with his house burning about him. That was the first.'

'You escaped from the house,' Sulien said. 'What was the second?'

'That men are threatened or die when woods walk,' Thorfinn said. 'And that trees may prophesy death. A German historian and a French poet told such a story of Alexander the Great, and because of another poet called John, a prophecy came to rest against my name. That when the wood of Birnam should come to Dunsinane, then should I make my end.'

'You are alive,' Sulien said.

'The third event has passed, and I am also unharmed by it,' Thorfinn said. 'Who was Hector? I don't know. But he foretold, or recorded, my death at the hand of Macdubh or Malduin.'

'Malduin is dead,' said Sulien.

'But what he set in train is not yet over,' Thorfinn said. 'To take the gloomy view. The sensible view is that it is a mixture of legend and coincidence and fantasy, told by a child and forgotten even by him in his adulthood. Lulach has never repeated or reiterated any one of these warnings, except perhaps when he sent me a twig from the forest. I asked him about that, and he answered me. And that was many years after.'

'A symbol for the wood?' Sulien said.

'I suppose so. A stick can stand for many things. The wand of kingship. The rod of the coffiner. The yew-twig of sterility.'

And now it was time to stop, for he could hear the flatness this time in his own voice. Sulien said, 'You have sons.' And after a moment, 'If he told you of any fate he has heard of, then you must put it from your mind.'

'No. My sons will flourish, he says. Or *did flourish*. But none of their descendants ever reigned, nor did they.'

'That is not sterility,' Sulien said.

'No. It is only vanity,' Thorfinn said. 'Hurt the worse because Malcolm's sons took the throne of Alba, Lulach says. And after them, in a line unbroken for a thousand years and more, kings of the blood of . . . What name would you hate most to hear?'

'I think, Malduin,' Sulien said.

Thorfinn said, 'I think you are right. Well, it's better than that. A little better than that. After the seed of Malcolm, it seems, all Scotia's kings will derive from our late friend Earl Siward of Northumbria. Hear and congratulate us, Thore Hund of Bjarking.'

Sulien got up. He walked to the steps of the choir and, turning, stood in the light, so that Thorfinn could see clearly the steady, judicial gaze. Sulien said, 'Is that where the real canker lies? I thought that immortal fame was the only desire of a Viking. The future they leave to their women.'

No enemy he had ever faced . . .

Thorfinn said, 'I am not a Viking.'

'Are you not, *Thorfinn Hinn Rikr?*' Sulien said. 'With your black goose-mother the sea, and the ghosts at your elbow? Or is Thorkel Fóstri right when he laments the *heljarskinn* strain in the blood-line? What glorious name would you leave to posterity had you ruled Alba Viking-fashion, with an axe, as Harald rules Norway? There is the path to the unity that has escaped you. You would die monarch of a united Scotia, with no need to care what legacy of hate you left behind you. And the fate of your wife would be unaltered.'

Thorfinn turned on his heel. He found himself facing the altar; and after a moment he moved slowly over and touched it, smoothing the edge with one finger. He said, 'You are warning me that my reign will be forgotten.'

'I am telling you,' said Sulien, 'that, whatever Lulach may say, men will look back and see a king who strove to build for his people; and although the gales may still blow and the flood come and cover it all, the foundations will stand.'

'A picture of ringing success,' Thorfinn said.

'Look at me,' Sulien said.

Thorfinn turned.

Sulien said, 'What I am telling you is that the name each man leaves is a small thing compared with the mark he puts on the world. You may succeed, in the end, in creating the good land you have worked for. Had circumstances been kinder, you would have been sure of it: had Pope Leo lived and been less beset with the struggle against the Normans in Italy, with the Saracens, with the enmity of the Eastern Empire. Had the Holy Roman Emperor lived, and been relieved of the wars on his frontiers. Had the Lady Emma been younger, or her barons less wayward . . .'

'Had Canute lived,' Thorfinn said. 'If I may share in the game. Canute might have made himself master of Alba and perhaps even of Ireland, but I have seen worse overlords. Of course, my task might have been easier, but, sooner or later, everyone dies. You sound as if you believe the gales and the floods one day will stop.'

'One day,' Sulien said, 'I think the Throne of St Peter will be as firm as it seemed, for a moment, it might be; I think the Empire will find a design by which to rule that does not break down between one prince and the next. I think the storms will subside and as nation settles by nation, there will be a place for quiet rule, and for building. Till then, it will be the fate of most leaders to die in their prime, and the fate of most women to carry forward their essence; their habit of mind; their spirit; their disciplines. . . . Be grateful for that, whatever Lulach has told you. You have sons. But, through Groa, what there is of your kingship will pass on as in a lamp, where the flame is what matters, not the vessel. And the flame nothing can touch.'

'Yes,' Thorfinn said. After a moment, he heard reeds rustle where Sulien had been standing, and realised that his own eyes were pressed shut. He opened them.

Sulien was standing beside him. He said, 'Your mother married three times. You are not Groa's first husband. She accepts it.'

'As I remember, it was a fairly dim lamp I received from Gillacomghain,' Thorfinn said. He drew breath, but could not find quite the voice he wanted. 'Of course, you are right. Everyone has lists of suitors. Thorkel made one for me; I made one for Lulach. Groa's father got a priest to draw another when she was young. . . . I wonder what names would it contain now? Godfrey of Man? Diarmaid of Dublin? Thor of Allerdale? The sons of Maldred and Crinan? Malcolm? Tostig? Duke William, even, if his wife were to die . . . I suppose Groa has thought of them, too. I have never discussed it with her. That is, she knows that she must carry the kingdom, if she is left, to the man who is able to win it from me. . . . It does not seem a subject to dwell on. I have done enough damage with my hybrid heritage without hurting the friends I have left.'

'As I am doing?' Sulien said.

'You are my conscience,' Thorfinn said. 'When you cease to hurt me, I shall be either perfect or dead. I wish I could repay you better. I wish I could lay my whole heart on your altar-table. It is a bedevilment of my birth. In death, I shall be split, no doubt, also: my heart in the Celtic isle of Iona and my body in Birsay.'

His arms still at his sides, Sulien smiled, the warm, radiant smile that had never changed since his boyhood. He said, 'You were ordained by God when you took your kingdom at Scone. *Mab maeth*, you are blessed. If you don't want to be twice blessed, I shan't force you.'

Thorfinn said, 'What did you call me?'

'Fosterling. It is one of your names,' Sulien said. 'You have so many: Macbethad . . . Son of Life. Why not use the Christian ones? There is even a prayer with your name in it. A quaint one, for simple, frightened people who are not like you at all. You would never hear it in Rome.'

To repay Sulien, since the proper price was not in his means, he let him recite it, and was not sorry.

> 'Hear Thou, O Jesus . . .
> The soul of every Son of Life
> Through Thou has been sanctified.
> Adam's seed that is highest
> By Thou has been freed.

> 'Free me, O Jesus,
> From every ill on earth
> As Thou savedst Noah
> Son of Lamech from the Flood.

'Free me, O Jesus,
Noble, wondrous King,
As Thou savedst Jonas
From the belly of the great whale.

'Free me, O Jesus,
Into Thy many-graced heaven,
As Thou savedst Isaac
From his father's hand.

'Free me, O Jesus,
O Lord Who are divinest,
As Thou savedst Daniel
Of the den of lions.

'Free me, O Jesus,
Who has wrought great marvels
As Thou freedst the children
From the fiery furnace.

'Free me.'

Then they walked to the hall.

FIFTEEN

T WAS THE end of the carefree time, of course, even before Sulien took ship for Wales, for although Thorfinn's plans were already as well made as they could be, and the messenger-ships plying between Orkney and the rest of his kingdom told him how matters were in the south, a warning was a warning, and had better be heeded, whatever weight Thorkel Fóstri put on it.

The truth was that Thorfinn was not sorry to turn from pastimes to what he could exercise his mind on instead. At the end of the winters in Orkney, he could remember feeling the same. There had been enough drinking, enough sport, enough love-making, even, in the damp, tangled bed of infinite leisure.

With Groa supple in his arms as the sixteen-year-old she had been when he took her, he could lose sight, sometimes, of what else she was, and he knew it was the same for her. His father, he supposed, had kept half a dozen women content. Leading the kind of life they all must, most men still found it hard to do as the priests said, and held, rightly, that to put upon one woman the whole burden of service was inconsiderate.

As indeed it was, if you regarded the act of love as an involuntary exercise, automatic as breathing, and subject to no more restraint.

And, having said all that, he still demanded more of Groa than he should, no matter how well he succeeded the rest of the time. And even then the boundary he imposed was of his making and not hers, for he did not remember a time since the first foolish years when she had not received him freely, with gaiety, sweeping aside his resolutions along with his doubts. 'It is how you sail. Every voyage is new. I will not be left on the shore.'

Now he lay awake in the dawn light after one such voyage and thought how she looked at Dunsinane, and at Monymusk, and knew that it was time to go south.

Something to do with the decision must have shown on his face. Or perhaps it was only the particular bustle on shore that made Sulien smile when he left, and say, 'Where would you be without challenge? Eochaid had a phrase for it. He said you were riding your dolphin. And you still are, I see.'

'I suppose,' Thorfinn said, 'It is going where I want to go.'

*　　*　　*

To Thorkel Fóstri one did not say such things, especially since Thorfinn had become King again, and brought back business to the hall, and broken the news about the army he had summoned from Normandy. To be left out of anything was something that angered his foster-father more than most men, and it was hard to get him to believe that even Groa had known nothing of it, so vital to all Thorfinn's plans was complete secrecy.

It was to placate Thorkel, in a sense, that after Sulien had gone he allowed himself at last to be prodded into one of the boyhood excursions that so far he had not chosen to give time to. He rejected out of hand a sail to lift kestrels in Westray because of the distance, nor did he think it a good idea to take his lame-footed foster-father on a fowling-expedition to Copinsay, although he understood the nostalgia behind the suggestion.

When finally, in anger, Thorkel had said that if he had as little time as that to spare, perhaps he would merely consider sailing from Skaill round the headland at Deerness and back again, he had agreed without making more of it. And even when he saw that it was not a crowded fishing-boat full of his sons and nephews that Thorkel had on the shore, but a new little yole of three thwarts with a neat mast stepped amidships, he was not suspicious. *Your three lovers*, Sulien had said of himself, and of Groa, and of this man who had taken the place of the father he had lost when he was five.

Since the occasion was in his gift, he did what he could with it, and made his foster-father laugh, which was not always easy, and allowed him to put the little boat through its paces in a sharp southerly wind that bowled her along until she was on the verge of going sea-loose, planing over the water.

His face under-lit white with the foam, Thorkel stopped her, turning into the wind as he whipped free the rope. A moment later, the sail rattled down. 'Take the oar, will you?' said Thorkel Fóstri.

'What's wrong?' said Thorfinn. The wind, catching the mast, was swinging them with the current round and up to the Gloup, a sea-tunnel half exposed to the sky, and dirty with rocks at its entrance.

Working with sail and spar, the other man did not even look up. He said, 'Well, don't you think it's worth going in there? It'll be full of birds. Now's the time to see what there is. Look, if you don't take that oar, we'll be on the rocks.'

'I thought I was coming for a sail,' Thorfinn said. He took one oar and, sculling and fending, got the boat lined up for the chasm-entrance. He said, 'What's your beam?'

'Between five and six feet. We'll have two feet at least on either side,' said Thorkel Fóstri. 'You might as well take both oars, to begin with. We'll have to scull later.'

He did take both oars then, and three or four strokes were enough. Then they were past the other aprons of grey rock and under the arch of the sea-cave, its fissures hanging with nest-straw. A cormorant fell like a book and disappeared with a wipe of black, stinking satin. Beyond, the sunlight from a long-fallen roof showed how the river of sea flowed surging and slapping between the continuing walls of the chasm: on the left, sheer, towering rock, and on the right, a broken wall nearly as steep, but bearing rock-plants and lichen spilling down to its ledges from the sandy pastures over its rim.

Beyond the opening, the sea-inlet ran on into darkness, for here the roof had not fallen, and, lying down in your boat, sculling as best you could, you could follow its course until, in the end, a shelf of pebbles showed you, if you had a flare, where the way was finally blocked. Once, they said, the sea-tunnel had run through some fault in the rock all the way underneath Deerness.

'Are you dreaming?' said Thorkel Fóstri. 'Bring it over here, boy.'

The sunlit space was, of course, where the bird-ledges were. Thorkel Fóstri had laid down his oar and was gazing upwards. High up, the fulmars and guillemots were still, grey-breasted and white, their heads moving uneasily. The cormorants had left. You could hear the naked young squawking above the hiss and trickle of water, and see their pink beaks, like the insect-eaters, opening and shutting. A rush of tide came into the channel, and the boat lifted and raced, while the water slapped the walls and fell back with the echoing gurgle that had earned the place its name. Thorkel Fóstri, thrown on all fours, turned and shouted at him.

He was pointing, it seemed, to a ledge he wished to get to, and was enquiring if Thorfinn would be handier at climbing than he was at holding the boat still.

Thorfinn said, 'You're not climbing anywhere. Let's get out.'

Whatever joyous expedition this had been intended to be, he was ruining it, and he didn't care. Another surge of sea came in while Thorkel was issuing orders, and the boat did bump, this time, on the side Thorkel Fóstri had been waving at.

Before he could stop him, his foster-father had stepped on to a ledge in the wall.

Thorfinn shouted at him. His voice slapped like the sea on either side of the rock, with a thread of something in it that he hoped would escape Thorkel's notice. Half the birds rose from their nests and began to circle squealing above, so that the light became furred with grey, moving shapes.

The dark moths of Orkney. If Thorkel Fóstri was ever to get back into the boat, it must be kept intact, and steady, and resting just off the base of the bird-rock. He had just made this good resolution when a block of sea reared through the arch like an animal and plunged from wall to wall, bellowing.

The boat went with it. At the entrance to the tunnel, the emptying water met the incoming rush, and the oar he held as a fender jarred and smashed in his grip as the strakes of his foster-father's new little boat ground against the soaking rock wall. Thorfinn hit the wall with his shoulder, in a great smear of green slime and melted bird-droppings and weed, and felt the boat lurch as he struck the thwarts and slid under them. A slap of water jarred into the boat, more solid than rain, and filled his nose and his eyes and his ears, and then another, so that he lay in it.

A very distant part of his mind remarked that if this were so, the boat could not be holed below the water-line. Another part informed him that someone was shouting, and that he had left someone dear to him on a cliffside and in need of his help.

He spread his hand down through the water and laid it flat on the new boards to begin to lever himself upwards. He put his weight on the hand. And this time the animal came through the arch and devoured him.

When he woke, he was still in the Gloup, but in a dry boat with someone's cloak under him. A voice, Thorkel Fóstri's, was saying over and over, 'My son. My son. Thorfinn my son.'

So his foster-father was safe, and he had made an exhibition of himself. He wondered who else, coming to the rescue, had viewed the spectacle and remembered having seen Copsige's boat out fishing as they came by. He felt like swearing, but knew better than to move. As it was, his head was a shell of iron, clanging with pain past and present.

There was pain, hardly less, in Thorkel Fóstri's strained voice. He must open his eyes and reassure him. It was not his fault that all this had happened.

Then he opened his eyes, and saw the three expressions that fled, naked, across his foster-father's white face, and knew exactly where the fault lay.

Although Copsige wanted it, Thorfinn did not choose to cross to the island to make his recovery, nor did he want to return to Sandwick, or to put himself in the care of Bishop Jon's little monastery at Deerness. He lay at the Gloup entrance, leaning back on the rock in the sun while the little yole was bailed out and made shipshape, and then he let Thorkel Fóstri guide the boat round the cliffs to a landing-place where, unseen from land, he could sit propped against grass and wait until the ruined muscles had ceased the worst of their protest.

They had brought meat and wine with them, and, once the pain had stopped making him sick, he was glad of it. Thorkel Fóstri, after the first moments, had said nothing at all except what had to do with his comfort, and in that he never ceased to show the most agonising and abject care.

Sitting with his eyes closed and a cup of good wine beside him, Thorfinn recognised that a good deal of it was his own fault. He should have told his foster-father from the start. He had refrained, to avoid the very scene to which he was now committed.

He had not reckoned on the fact that, through the years, his way of thinking was, also, something that Thorkel Fóstri had studied. When he opened his eyes, his foster-father spoke first.

Thorkel Fóstri said, 'The blame is all mine. I would have made it difficult for you if you had told me. I've seen the wounds. I should have been content when you didn't come rowing or climbing.'

'Oh, that was only part of the reason,' Thorfinn said. 'Kings are supposed to be perfect. And foster-sons like to be, too. I shall answer your other question, if you like. I can hold a sword for a short time. But not for long.'

He paused, and then said, 'And no one knows that. Not even Sulien.'

He closed his eyes again, because it seemed the best thing. After a long time, his foster-father said, 'Have I made it worse?'

'No,' Thorfinn said. He opened his eyes and made them truthful. 'To be able to do what I do, I had to stretch the muscles every day, and it was nearly as bad. You can't make it any worse now.'

Nor, unfortunately, could you make it any better. But he had had a long time to adapt to all that, and Thorkel Fóstri would also, in time. He set himself to talk the thing out and lead his foster-father back to peace with himself.

It had been done from love, in a form that was not Lulach's but entirely human.

If you looked at it in one way, he had, he supposed, today escaped the last of his hazards, if the third death was by drowning.

And he had plenty of strength, still, to ride a dolphin with.

So the King took leave of his two fair sons and returned south, nor, as he left, did he look over his shoulder, any more than he had looked back at Scone.

It was no time, in any case, for nostalgia, but time to pour out once again all the invention and energy restored to him. For there was no word yet of his army of Normandy.

It was understandable. Duke William had not been an unreasonable ally. As May gave way to June, and June to July and then the beginning of August, the messengers passed backwards and forwards from Caen and Falaise and Bayeux. The peace with Duke William's overlord King Henry was breaking. Count Geoffrey of Anjou again threatened hostilities. No men who wished to be thought well of by their Duke could leave Normandy just at present.

'He seems as beleaguered as you,' Tuathal said. 'So long as he doesn't leave it too late. By winter, you couldn't send transports all the way from Normandy to Alba.'

'By winter, there won't be anyone left alive between Moray and Lothian,' Thorfinn had said. 'It would all make the Abbot of Armagh feel quite at home. How can we persuade King Harald to attack Orkney now?'

For Orkney, prepared for her assailants, lay lean and fit and flashing with steel, and hedged about with her new ships as with a stockade of gold set with jewels. Odalric, Otkel, and Hlodver were in the north, with his sons and his foster-father. There was money for it all since Tuathal's journey overseas, although of course a day of reckoning would come. Money for ships and arms, and money for bribes. Thorkel Fóstri's remorse and Crispin money would see that so soon as a ship's master received orders, word would fly from Norway to his ear or Thorfinn's. In summer, ships were always at sea for one reason or another, and a message could be conveyed by no more than the flash of a flag, or the tilt of a silver mirror, or the blaze of a cresset up at the masthead. In a good wind, a ship from Orkney could find Thorfinn at the southernmost limits of his present kingdom in twenty-four hours.

'But not in a bad wind,' Groa remarked. Since hearing about the Normans, she had taken to coming to all the council meetings in case, Thorfinn observed, he had decided next to call in the Arabs. '*Whoever desires a religion apart from Islam, it will not be accepted of him, and in the world to come, he will be among the Losers.'*

'If the Norwegian fleet attacks Orkney at the same time as Malcolm decides to move north from Lothian, then *you* will be among the Losers, Islam or the Aesir,' Groa said.

'Not with Duke William's men with me in Alba,' said Thorfinn.

'Where?' said Groa.

'All right. In Normandy. But, Duke William willing, on their way soon to Alba. And even before they arrive, it's all right. I have as many men in Alba as Malcolm has,' Thorfinn said.

He meant it as well. He was, Groa saw, perfectly cheerful. Nowadays he moved about Mar and Moray so much that hardly one sentence was spoken in the same hall as the next, but it seemed to refresh him, if anything, and the sparkle communicated itself to those about him. He took and shed Bishop Hrolf and Bishop Jon, Gillocher and Morgund, Lulach and Tuathal, and in his company they all became brisker and laughed more and, when he left them, looked busy and successful.

She herself was the only person, apart from his household, who remained with him all the time, ever since a certain moment in Orkney when he had come back to be industriously good company after a day-long sail with Thorkel Fóstri; after which he had made himself, in private, extremely drunk and had slept for eighteen hours without waking.

What had happened she had no idea and, indeed, preferred not to know. She simply concluded that someone ought to be at hand, in case it happened again.

So she was there with him in Buchan when the news came. She saw him receive it, and fall silent for a moment before he put the messenger through his usual thorough inquisition and dismissed him. Then he sent for his mormaers. Of the Bishops, Hrolf was with him and Tuathal, at Deer, only a short ride away.

Groa thought, *What news can be as bad as that?* but said nothing. Then he turned and caught sight of her.

'It's invasion. Malcolm is at Stirling with an army, and on his way north. And not just with the settlers and rebels. Tostig of Northumbria is behind him, with the whole force of Northumbria and extra troops from his brother Earl Harold. They've heard about the Normans. It's the only possible reason. And, please God, they've heard about the Normans because the Normans happen to be on their way.'

Groa said, 'How many Northumbrians?'

'Under Tostig, something like six to eight thousand, including about five hundred mounted. Assuming Fife and Angus let them through, these could be here fairly soon.'

'The Normans are coming by sea,' Groa said. 'They could still come in time, before the footsoldiers arrive.'

'I suppose they could,' Thorfinn said. After the first word, his mind had left the sentence. He stood quite still, thinking, until the door opened and men began to come in, and then he sat down and talked.

Nothing new. The possibility was one of a dozen he had prepared for, even though it was one of the worst. The loyal troops were to be drawn back north to Mar and Moray, to reinforce the line of the Dee, and the armies of Malcolm and Tostig were to be allowed to march north without resistance. He had not enough men to harass them, but distance and the hill-ground would delay them. During which time, perhaps, his hired troops might arrive.

No one was crass enough to say, *What if they don't?* He had placed the alternatives before them, long before. He could allow eight thousand men to engage in formal battle against his bands of survivors. Or he could negotiate. If they would negotiate.

Tuathal said, 'My lord. The footsoldiers could be here in less than five days. The horse might reach the Dee in not much more than two.'

It was the nearest he came to the other thing that everyone there was thinking. Against King Duncan and his fleet and his Irish mercenaries, the men of Orkney and Caithness had stood side by side with the men of Tarbatness seventeen years before.

But Tarbatness had been within Thorfinn's Caithness earldom. And Caithness and Orkney now had a predator of their own on their doorstep. If the King, against all his past record, emptied Orkney and Caithness in favour of Alba, he would do nothing but lose them to Harald of Norway.

Thorfinn said, 'The Caithness men, as you know, are mustered in the far north against Norway. They could not march down in time, even if they were asked.' He paused, and said, 'If Malcolm will not negotiate and his army breaks through Moray and into the north, there is no doubt, of course, that the Caithness men will make a stand against them. It's unlikely that he will: his lines would be far too extended. I take it there is no fresh news from Normandy?'

Bishop Hrolf said, 'Only the same, and it's stale. A lot of coming and going in Anjou, and Count Geoffrey has been seen in the same room with the King of France more than once.'

'Perhaps they are insulting one another,' said Thorfinn. 'But we shouldn't count on it. You know what to do, then. The Dee is our frontier, and as strong as we can make it. Bishop Tuathal and I are leaving for Lumphanan now. The rest of you had better set out as fast as you can. Do with your families as you have arranged. Lulach, a word.'

The hall-house was a small one, and reeked of summer heat and humanity after the men left. Anghared opened the doors and, drawing two chamber-servants with her, moved discreetly to the other end of the room. Lulach, with his hand on his mother's shoulder, said, 'Finnghuala and the children are away already. You need me.'

'Do I?' said Thorfinn.

'For a while,' Lulach said. 'When the time comes to go, I shall make use of it. And my lady mother will stay?'

Both she and Thorfinn spoke at once, saying different things. She was the first to repeat herself. 'I shall stay at Lumphanan. If your front line is the Dee, that's safe enough. At least, it's a good deal safer than Dunsinane.'

'Of course. What am I thinking of?' said Thorfinn. 'Lumphanan is fully two miles from the Dee. A man could hardly walk there in half an hour. Which of your ladies will you bring with you?'

'All of them, I expect,' Groa said. 'Of course I shall forbid them to come, but if they insist, what can I do about it? Or you?'

Lulach touched her shoulder again. 'I shall see you both,' he said, and walked out of the hall.

Thorfinn said, 'We have made him uncomfortable. It must be as hard for him to listen as it is for us to talk.'

'Then there is no need to talk, so far as I can see,' Groa said.

After that, although she rode with his party, she did not see a great deal of him either that day, on the ride south to Monymusk, or the following morning, when he far outpaced her on the ride to Lumphanan.

She hardly lacked for company. For weeks now, foot-levies had been quartered on Deeside to guard against just such a challenge. Now the rest were moving south also, and the purple hills were accosted by striving, sparkling swarms, whiskered in steel. Groa and her servants and the bereaved women of Scone and Dunsinane who wished to keep her company were the only beings in skirts to be seen, but men going to war did not stop to trouble them, or her guard. In any case, most of them were known to her.

When she caught up with Thorfinn, she heard what the scouts were saying. That the Northumbrian foot were coming steadily north from Stirling to the Tay crossing. That the body of Northumbrian horse, racing ahead, was already well on its way: through Scone; through Glamis. Malcolm's banner was with it, and the flag of Durham with the pennant of Forne. Then someone who had seen it in Winchester identified the flag of Tostig, Earl of Northumbria and younger brother of Harold of Wessex.

At Monymusk, she was allowed a rest of five hours. Thorfinn, who had arrived ahead of her, had had perhaps an hour's sleep, she judged from the look of him, and was eating and talking at the same time before riding off south. When she came into the hall, he broke off and got rid of the man he was talking to and, gathering his horn and what was left to eat, opened the door of their chamber with his back and followed her in.

She said, 'It's all right.'

'No,' he said. 'War happens suddenly, but there is time for what has to be said.'

She said, 'You mean Malcolm may be there already when you get to the Dee?'

'Perhaps,' he said. 'I've got another banner, twinned to the one the Pope gave me. Sulien approved.'

'And the Brecbennoch?' she said. 'I thought that was here.'

'Tuathal has it,' he said. He put the pile of food down on a board and said, 'You won't have eaten. I'll get—'

'Finish it,' she said. 'Thorfinn, for the sake of God. I'll eat your company.'

He looked at her then, and picked up the meat. He said, 'Sulien says that

Fothaid is now an ordained priest. He was in Malduin's household.'

She said, 'But Tuathal has been consecrated.'

'No one else can be Bishop of Alba. Also, it seems that, now the Emperor is dead, the Athelings, the Saxon heirs, have been released. They are being sent to Earl Harold, and not to Duke William. It makes Harold of Wessex their guardian, especially if none but the children are left. Duke William is now a greater rival to Earl Harold than Denmark. But Wessex still fears Harald of Norway.'

She said, 'Thorfinn. I know it all.'

There was a little pause. Then he said, his voice quite different, '*Superba*, I believe you do. Do you know the story of the sibyl called Groa? When Thor and the giant Hrungnir fought a duel, Thor came from it with a hone sunk in his head. When Groa recited her spells, the hone worked its way loose.'

'She was married to a man called Aurvandil the Brave,' Groa said. 'Another of your names?'

'Sulien would not approve,' Thorfinn said. 'But at least we began by talking about the Brecbennoch and the Banner of St Peter. I have to go. I will see you at St Finnian's hill at Lumphanan.' He paused. 'What a lot St Finnian has had to do with my affairs lately. A short-tempered man who, I'm sure, continually gave his wife instructions she did not need.'

'Since she wouldn't need them, how could it matter?' said Groa.

So she slept in a cold bed, but very deeply, and had to be wakened to ride on with the rest. There were not so many now, for all the force Thorfinn had was now down on the banks of the Dee.

The scouts' news she listened to, anxiously. The banners of Earl Tostig and Malcolm had moved from Glamis to Forfar to Brechin and were making their way now over the range of the Mounth by the great pass that led to the banks of the Dee between Kincardine and Banchory. The footsoldiers, showing no disposition to spread, seemed to be following, much behind, in their footsteps.

They would reach the Dee, as Thorfinn had once pointed out, something like two miles or perhaps three from Lumphanan. And since they were not spreading out, it would seem that they intended no irresistible attack over the river, where their power would sweep aside the weaker force, thinly spread, that was all Thorfinn could pitch against them.

Arrived at Lumphanan: 'You think they mean to discuss terms?' Groa said to Thorfinn when, at last, he came within her sight late that evening.

He was dirty, but he looked no more tired now than he had the day before. He could snatch sleep, she knew, in the saddle. Even while she spoke to him, men called, smiling, and he waved in return.

He said, 'Groa?' and she knew that he had forgotten she was near, and her eyes filled at the artless softening of his face and his voice. Then he said, 'Yes. They seem to be making camp over the river, and there's no sign that they mean to cross. They couldn't, anyway, until their main force comes up.

Where they are, they're well protected and perfectly safe, with a guard on each flank and a watch on the hills behind them.'

'They must have been confident,' Groa said, 'to outrun the foot by such a distance. What a surprise they would get if your Normans came.'

'What a surprise we should all get,' Thorfinn said. 'And I don't see why we should despair of it. Once the proper messages have been exchanged, and the bishops have visited one another and delivered their warnings and blessings, and Malcolm and Tostig and I have haggled over a meeting-place and conditions and hostages, and once the three of us finally sit down to decide what it's worth not to kill one another, you would be surprised what a long time I intend to keep them talking. They will have time to give birth to my soldiers in Caen and wean them and rear them to puberty. Have they found you a tent, or are you in the hall?'

To the east of two little lochs, on rising ground, was the old timber hall with its palisade in which Paul had been born, with the church of St Finnian beside it. All about, on the wooded slopes rising from the lakes and the marsh, were the summer tents and campfires of Thorfinn's men, some newly erected and bright, but most soiled and worn from the weeks of their waiting. She said, 'I'm in the hall. They put a pallet in your chamber. I don't mind if I don't sleep.'

It was as well, for the room turned out to have nothing to do with sleeping, but to be a kind of meeting-place to which he returned periodically, and to which tired men came in, without knocking, to wait for him. She had not undressed. She put the candle out in her corner and sat curled against the wall, her arms holding each other under her cloak, and her hood masking her hair. Mostly, no one noticed her, but sometimes someone she knew well would come across and bend over and speak.

Then Lulach found she was there and awake, and, when he could, came with news and once a bowl of soup. The hall and cabins were full of men, and the women of the household, she supposed, were long gone. Her own attendants were where she herself ought to be, asleep in a strong tent with a guard to look after them, and old Sinna to heat something over a fire.

Outside, it was never quiet, even when complete darkness came; and the sound of a galloping horse followed by several others did not make the impression it should, until the rising of men's voices showed that something had happened.

Thorfinn was out, and the room was empty except for Gillocher, awaiting him, who had fallen asleep, candle-lit, with his arms on the table. Then Morgund came in. He said, 'My lady?' and came to her corner.

'Yes. What is it?' she said.

Morgund's face was smeared with metal-blackness and wood-smoke, and there were white marks where he had been rubbing his eyes. He said, 'It's ship-news, my lady. Nothing to do with this war. It seems that things are moving in Norway at last, and King Harald has ordered a fleet to put to sea against Orkney and Caithness, to take them in readiness for a big war against England next year. So my lord King was right, and that answers them all, doesn't it? If he'd shipped all those men down from Orkney, he'd have lost more than Orkney and Caithness. In the long run, we'd all be done for.'

He smiled at her and got up, hesitated over whether to waken Gillocher, and then went out, leaving him sleeping. The fate of Orkney and Caithness had nothing to do with this war. The men of Orkney and Caithness would deal with it, with their great fleet and their tough Viking chieftains and the Earl's two fine sons, Paul and Erlend.

Her sons. Her sons who, unlike Lulach, were only human. Erlend, un-touched by trouble at sixteen, and happy in the care of his foster-kindred. Paul, who trod at his father's heels through every visit, but who knew, in his heart, that the world of high power and cunning and lonely kingship was not for him.

Her heart thudded, thinking of them. Then she set her mind to what she had been told, and saw that Morgund was right. Orkney was well prepared for this, and could handle it. And, once and for all, it proved that what Thorfinn had done, as Earl of Orkney and King of Alba, had been right.

You would think it was news to keep her awake all the same, thinking of the two boys she and Thorfinn had left. Instead, she fell sound asleep, propped like an owl in her corner, and missed Gillocher going out and half a dozen people, no doubt, coming in, and even, she found on waking, the presence of Thorfinn himself, whose cloak lay on the other pallet, creased and moulded as if he had been resting there and had suddenly risen.

And that, indeed, was what had probably happened, for outside was the hubbub that she now realised had probably wakened them both. News, again, from the sound of hooves trampling. And news that, on the whole, Thorfinn preferred, it seemed, to hear in private, for in a moment the door opened and he brought the messenger in.

Lulach and Bishop Jon were behind him, and this time she had not been forgotten. Thorfinn said, 'Are you awake? Groa, this is another ship-message. I didn't want the men outside to hear until we are ready.'

He had opened his leather flask as he was speaking and, handing it to the rider he had just brought in, led the man to a stool and sat him down. 'Now. A message came from Duke William of Normandy.'

'Yes, my lord King. It came up north, by the west seas. He sent one by the east coast as well, but it seemed to be waylaid.'

'By whom, I expect we know,' Thorfinn said. 'Drink, don't sit with it in your hand. Now. A message from Duke William to me? Saying what?'

'My lord King, asking your forgiveness. The duke faces a double invasion himself, from King Henry of France and the Count of Anjou. He has no men to spare. He cannot even tell whether he can survive it. But he says to tell you that no men from Normandy can come to your help, my lord, this year.'

'Well, I doubt if we will need them next year,' Thorfinn said. Outside in the darkness, you could hear that more horses were arriving, and the half-open shutters showed the glimmer of torches down the slope, and the flash of ring-mail and helmet.

Thorfinn lifted his head. 'Is this more of your party? What ship brought you here?'

'Has he not told you yet? Mine,' said Thorkel Fóstri from the door.

No one said anything. Bishop Jon, who had dropped to a chest, rose slowly to his feet, the candle-light scanning his crucifix. Lulach looked at his mother. Groa, who had been studying the man on the stool, lifted her gaze to the grey beard and tired face of Thorfinn's foster-father, and then to Thorfinn, tall as a king-post, his face carved in black and white, thinking. He said very quietly, 'What have you done?'

Thorkel Fóstri smiled. 'You were afraid to call on Orkney. You needn't have been. I told them their Earl was down here with no troops to speak of, and an English army of eight thousand against him. I told them that Duke William had failed you. They said, *There are the ships. Here are we, the Earl's men. What are we waiting for?*'

'You've brought them all?' Thorfinn said.

'They'll be at Deemouth tomorrow,' said Thorkel Fóstri. 'And they'll be disembarking.'

Groa covered her face with her hands. If she could have stopped her ears, she would have done so.

Already the contentment on the older man's face had started to change. She could imagine, as the empty moments went by, how it must be fading and altering. She could not imagine what was going to happen.

Thorfinn's voice said, 'My foster-father . . . A message reached us this evening. King Harald's fleet is on its way to attack Orkney.'

Thorkel Fóstri said, 'No. We should have heard.'

'They will know in Orkney by now,' Thorfinn said. 'You have perhaps thirty hours to get back.'

Silence. Thorkel Fóstri said, 'I still say we would have heard. What report had you?'

Thorfinn said, 'Thorkel, there is no doubt about it. How many ships and men did you leave?'

'Almost none. They would be the same to King Harald as you would have been to Earl Tostig,' Thorkel Fóstri said.

Would have been. Groa opened her eyes. She said, 'Thorkel. Where are Erlend and Paul?'

They were all pale in the candle-light, but under Thorkel Fóstri's cheek-bones and within the coigns of his nose great cavities had blackened and sunk. He said, 'I did not think this battle-field was for them. I left them in Orkney.'

'This battle-field is not for you, either,' Thorfinn said. 'You must go back.'

'Run?' said Thorkel Fóstri. 'It was what they said of us, wasn't it? That we were afraid to come and fight against Earl Siward. Your people have come from Orkney to save you. If you want to spurn them, you will have to tell them yourself. I am not going to lead them back home.'

She could see Thorfinn's thoughts turning this way and that. He said, 'Then you have lost Orkney for me, and killed both my sons.'

Thorkel Fóstri said, 'Are you frightening me or yourself? Men such as your sons are not killed: at worst, they are taken hostages. I don't believe King Harald's ships are on their way. But even if they were, we have come to save Alba for you. Is that such a small thing?'

Thorfinn said, 'It is worth a king's ransom, never mind princelings, to know that there are men in Orkney who would do this. I know they will follow you anywhere, but I can't let them pay the price of losing their homes. Anyway, there is no need. We can't fight; we have not the power. Earl Tostig knows it. If we ask him to negotiate, he will.'

He walked across and looked down at the older man. 'Go back. It will do us no harm. It will be better than letting your army run free where they are not understood. They are needed to protect Orkney. And we can settle this very simply round a table.'

'When?' said Thorkel Fóstri.

'Tomorrow morning,' Thorfinn said. Groa, too, could see what was coming.

'You sound confident,' Thorkel Fóstri said. 'What do you have to offer that Earl Tostig and his nephew can't take for themselves?'

Bishop Jon said quickly, 'Is it the May prey you're thinking of, and them jumping about, whirling their axes? The Northumbrians go about things in a cooler way, I'm told, especially if they have Earl Harold behind them. Silver, now, speaks with a very sweet voice. And so does land. The King might have to lose Fife as well as Lothian, and even Angus on top of Fife, but it's not impossible that another year Duke William will have his duchy trim and in order, and Fife and Angus and more will be put back where they belong. On the other hand, once you let Norway into Orkney, you will have lost Orkney for good.'

Thorkel Fóstri had never looked away from the King. He said, 'And you would be content with that? To give away what you have, rather than fight for it?'

'I have fought for it,' Thorfinn said. 'And lost. I don't mean to fight again until I am sure of winning. And to win Alba at the cost of Orkney would be a poor bargain, if by a little guile we can keep both. . . . My foster-father, let me talk to Malcolm tomorrow. Let me send word afterwards to your ships. If there is to be fighting, I shall call on you. I promise it.'

It was the one answer that could have satisfied Thorkel Fóstri. It was an answer, at least, that sent him out of the camp to rejoin his men until morning. Left behind, Lulach said, 'You hadn't asked for a meeting with Malcolm tomorrow?

'No. But I shall now,' said Thorfinn.

Groa said, 'They'll know the Orkney fleet is here. Won't that frighten them?'

'Not a great deal,' said Thorfinn. 'Even with all Thorkel Fóstri has brought, the English army is still much the bigger. They'll try to get what they want without fighting. They may even try to lengthen the talks, if Earl Tostig is on more friendly terms with King Harald of Norway than he is with Earl Harold his brother. But if they don't get what they want, they'll certainly fight for it.'

'It's a south wind,' said Bishop Jon. 'If you were to talk fast, the fleet could still get back to Orkney in time. Now, there is a great man, your foster-father; but whatever, in the name of God Who all can, made him do the like of this?'

'I've no idea,' Thorfinn said. 'Who wants to take a trumpet to my lord Malcolm tomorrow? I suppose it had better be Tuathal. Bishop Jon—'

'I'll tell him to come to your chamber at dawn. Take sleep, my lord King. And you, my lady. We'll leave you.'

The door closed, and on the inside Thorfinn lifted the heavy lever and pushed it home with a thud. He stood and looked at it.

'It would have been enough,' he said, 'merely to apologise. He didn't need to bring the whole Orkney army to make up for it. Whatever I do now, I can't stop it falling on his head. And on mine. And on yours.'

He turned. 'Will you promise me not to hate him for it? No. You won't. How filthy I am. It comes of turning so quickly in so many different directions. What is the proper weekly order for a king? Sunday for drinking ale. Monday for legal business. Tuesday for chess. Wednesday for watching greyhounds hunting. Thursday for marital intercourse. Is it Thursday?'

'I'm sure it's Thursday,' said Groa. She had spread her cloak underneath her on the pallet and was lying, watching him.

'*Regina optima et benigna*,' he said. 'Queen Medb, goddess and giver of drink of the sovereignty of Alba, who slept with many kings. Shall I make submission at sword-point tomorrow, lying flat on the ground with the point of a sword in my teeth? I suppose I could, if the cryptogram demands it. I wonder if I shall ever find out what it spelled.'

He came to the pallet, the ties of his tunic pulled loose, and knelt beside her, resting his elbows. '*I know where stands a hall, brighter than sunlight* . . . I am too dirty, and you are too beautiful. Will I tell you that I love you? It occurred to me today. It occurs to me all the time, and sometimes you are not there, but I think perhaps you know.'

'I know,' she said.

'Then live, my strength, anchor of weary ships. My honour, my strong city, my sure peace.' His head was on her knee, his eyes tight-closed, and she stirred the sooty hair clogged with sweat and dust, and smoothed her hand from ear to neck.

Then he moved and, in turn, she felt the touch of his hand. He said, his lips against her skin, 'I want you. I'm so dirty. Beloved, will you take me?'

It was not, this time, like the lazy, tumbling nights of a northern summer. It came to the first touch, in seconds, and remained sharper than pleasure, like the blazing white wand of a goldsmith. Half-returned, her body vibrated, embroidering its own history of cataclysm, and she knew from his breathing that he, too, had reached the same place.

Before she was struck with sleep, he kept her by him with caresses, and his familiar voice, close to her ear, made a hermit's hut of the little room, sealed off by nothing else from the jangling, half-awake circus of war that lay just outside its walls. Then, she did not remember where she had heard him speak these words before.

> *'O fair woman!*

> *'O Befind! Will you come with me*
> *To a wonderful country which is mine*
> *Where the people's hair is of golden hue*
> *And their bodies the colour of virgin snow?*

> *'There no grief or care is known.*
> *Beautiful people without any blemish*
> *Love without sin, without wickedness.*
> *O woman! Shouldst thou come to my brave land*
> *All this we shall share, O Befind!'*

Then the dawn came, and showed her an empty bed, and the spears flashing red in the sunrise.

The meeting between Thorfinn, King of Alba, and Malcolm his nephew took place, with the prudence of all such events, on an island in the midst of the Dee, the opposing hosts being ranged on each bank.

It did not take long, and the King of Alba, concluding, was not observed to lie flat with a sword in his teeth. On the other hand, those who returned from the meeting to the hall where Groa had remained were remarkably silent and avoided the room where she stood, as did Thorfinn himself. When, finally, there was a knock on the door and a man entered, she did not know what to expect.

It was Bishop Tuathal. He said, 'You have not seen my lord King?'

For Tuathal, his tone was sharp. She said, 'No. No one has told me what happened.'

Tuathal said, 'He will be coming. I thought he was here.'

Groa said, 'Have they made peace?' If they had, the Orkney ships could go. He must know that was the crux.

Tuathal said, 'Maelmuire was there, and Forne and Gillocher. And Aethelwine of Durham, who is bishop there now, like his brother. My lord Malcolm had the Earl Tostig by him all the time, and sometimes one answered, and sometimes another. I went with the King and two mormaers. He had bathed and wore silk trimmed with gold, my lady, and an otter-skin cloak. It made an impression.'

'He would mean it to,' Groa said. 'Bishop Tuathal—did they make peace?'

Tuathal said, 'My lady, the only terms they would consider were total surrender. Alba to belong to my lord Malcolm, and the King to be sent to Northumbria, where he would be treated, they said, like an honoured guest.'

'He offered them other things?' Groa said. There were no possibilities she had not heard discussed, or had not helped with. Everything that had happened had been foreseen and talked out in one way or another. Except that Thorkel Fóstri would bring the fleet and the men of the north. Far-sighted though they had all been, no one had dreamed of that.

'My lady, they would accept nothing else. Surrender the land and his person, or fight.'

She thought of Orphir, and her sons. She said, 'He chose surrender. But they would never let him survive.'

'He knew that, my lady,' said Tuathal. 'No. He spoke of the killing there had been already, and said that he thought that a king or a would-be king who loved his country might spare it by adopting the old customs. He had done it himself with my lord Malcolm's father. That was, he said, that the head of one faction should challenge the other to a duel to the death, as the King of France did to the Emperor. If my lord Malcolm won, then he would have Alba with no royal prisoner to care for. If my lord Thorfinn won, then Alba would be his, and Earl Tostig would retreat south until, no doubt, he could groom one of my lord Malcolm's brothers. The King said that, so far as he was concerned, that was the only offer he would consider. If they failed to accept it, he would land all his northmen and give battle.'

Tuathal spoke most of it looking out of the window. Groa said, 'Bishop Tuathal. Why should he make such a proposal? It offered my lord Malcolm nothing. So why in the world should he agree to it?'

'My lady,' said Tuathal. 'My lord Malcolm has agreed to it.'

Because speed mattered so much, Thorfinn saw people quickly while the flat plot of ground was being roped off. Because, for lack of firm ground elsewhere, a duelling-spot near Lumphanan had been chosen, it had been agreed that the Lady his wife should be hostage for the safety of his nephew and enemy Malcolm.

Having agreed to it, he placed the matter with firmness to one side of his mind and began to look for the people he wanted.

There were not so many. Bishop Jon and Bishop Hrolf, because the disjointed kingdom would not make matters easy, and there were some ways of solving the problem. Gillocher and Morgund and Scandlain and some of the other young men, who would need all the tact they hadn't yet got to survive. Tuathal, whom he had lost temporarily, and Lulach his stepson, who kissed him and said, 'As soon as my mother leaves, I shall be gone. I have nine months. I told you.'

He paused. 'What are you thinking? That I didn't warn you of this? But I am only a river, with all my voices. And no two drops of water reflect the same way.'

'What am I thinking? I was wondering,' said Thorfinn slowly, 'what story the river will carry of me?'

Lulach smiled his sweet smile, and his swan-white hair shone in the sunshine. 'So many stories,' he said, 'that, a thousand years from today, every name from this world will have faded save those of yourself and your lady. That is immortality.'

'The dream of every Viking. Instead of truth, I think today you offer me comfort. You were always kind,' Thorfinn said. 'Help her, Lulach.'

'You know me,' said Lulach. 'You know me now. I will say anything.'

He met Tuathal at the door of the hall, where it was hard to talk because of the excitement, with people pressing about and shouting to him. They appeared to be quite confident that he would defeat and kill Malcolm. He said to Tuathal. 'I'd better talk to them presently, so that they know what to do. And Thorkel Fóstri has to be told. He'll make no effort to stay. The wind is still from the south.'

Tuathal said, 'They'll get to Orkney in time.' His face looked grim and drawn. 'The Lady is wondering why Malcolm accepted the challenge. I must confess, so am I.'

Change, and adapt. Sitting in one's silks in the sunlight and observing, unobtrusive among the servants of Tostig, a familiar face: that of Copsige of Cornholm, who sometimes fished off the Gloup. Thorfinn said, 'Oh, Malcolm knew I would lose. He has that kind of conceit.'

Tuathal said, 'My lord . . . You must prepare her.'

Thorfinn said, 'She is prepared. As she was Gillacomghain to Moray, so she will be Thorfinn to Alba. You, too, will be needed. Under you, the land will hold steady.'

'I cannot care,' Tuathal said. 'This is a day when the priest needs a priest. I cannot feel God's friendship. I cannot accept such an ending.'

'Why not, if I can?' said Thorfinn. 'I failed. I pay the price of my failure. There is no injustice there. As to the good or bad in what I have done, I am content to leave others to judge.'

His face was calm. He said, 'Forget that Scotia ever existed. There will still be Alba. And Orkney.'

To Groa he said, 'They will take you to a tent, and you will not look out.'

'I will not look out,' she said.

He said, 'You have everything there is of me, save a little I gave to my people. Now you hold that as well.'

And last of all, when he had released her and moved to the door, to stand outside where all the sky was enclosed with thick hills and dark, heavy forests, he said, because he could not prevent himself, 'When next you stand by the sea, say goodbye for me.'

She walked quietly to the tent they gave her among the Northumbrians, and her attendants walked with her in silence. Once inside, they left her alone, and although Sinna watched her without cease, Anghared and Maire did not.

When the noise of the crowd became louder and then changed suddenly to rolls of shield-rattling and the blaring of trumpets, she sat with her arms round her knees and stared into the little fire they had built for her, which she was glad of, although it was August.

Looking at it, she hardly heard the single voices declaiming, although you could not ignore the bellow that greeted the speech-maker. During the wave of bustle and expectancy that came after, she stared at the light until her eyes began to sting, and she squeezed them shut and then studied the fire again.

There was a brief chime of sound such as a smith might make, trying an anvil, and then a roar bigger than any that had gone before, which continued.

She continued to stare at the fire.

Not very long afterwards, the door of the tent stirred, and someone held it aside, and shadows moved up and down, of people approaching. One shadow stepped through and became a man, still not very clear, as her eyes, when she looked up, were dazzled and he stood blocking the light.

He was not of any great size, and his voice, when he spoke, was ordinary and rather breathless.

He said, 'Which is Ingibjorg, Bergljot's daughter?'

'I am,' she said.

The man said, 'Ingibjorg, Bergljot's daughter, I have to tell you that Thorfinn your husband is dead.'

There was a silence.

She realised she did not have to think of anything new.

She said, 'Then I suppose I am your prisoner. Will you ransom me?'

'Ransom?' he said. 'I am Malcolm, son of King Duncan. I am going to marry you.'

> *O Befind! Will you come with me*
> *To a wonderful country which is mine . . .*

'Of course,' she said; and, rising, walked out at his side, and faced her stricken peoples, and saw the hope and the pity born together once more in their eyes.

Edinburgh
20th March 1981

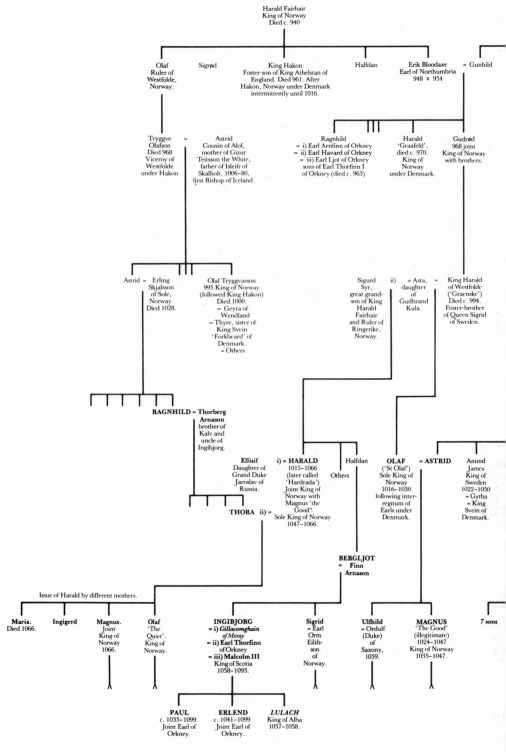

Harald Fairhair
King of Norway
Died c. 940

Olaf
Ruler of
Westfolde,
Norway.

Sigrød

King Hakon
Foster-son of King Athelstan of
England. Died 961. After
Hakon, Norway under Denmark
intermittently until 1016.

Halfdan

Erik Bloodaxe
Earl of Northumbria
948 x 954

= Gunhild

Tryggve
Olafsson
Died 968
Viceroy of
Westfolde
under Hakon

=

Astrid
Cousin of Alof,
mother of Gizur
Teitsson the White,
father of Isleifr of
Skalholt, 1006–80,
first Bishop of Iceland.

Ragnhild
= i) Earl Arnfinn of Orkney
= ii) Earl Havard of Orkney
= iii) Earl Ljot of Orkney
sons of Earl Thorfinn I
of Orkney (died c. 963)

Harald
'Graafeld',
died c. 970.
King of
Norway
under Denmark.

Gudrød
968 joint
King of Norway
with brothers.

Astrid =
Erling
Skjalsson
of Sole,
Norway.
Died 1028.

Olaf Tryggvasson
995 King of Norway
(followed King Hakon)
Died 1000.
= Geyra of
Wendland
= Thyre, sister of
King Svein
'Forkbeard' of
Denmark.
= Others

Sigurd
Syr,
great grand-
son of King
Harald
Fairhair
and Ruler of
Ringerike,
Norway.

ii) = Asta, =
daughter
of
Gudbrand
Kula.

King Harald
of Westfolde
('Graenske')
Died c. 994.
Foster-brother
of Queen Sigrid
of Sweden.

RAGNHILD = Thorberg
Arnason
brother of
Kalv and
uncle of
Ingibjorg.

Ellisif
Daughter of
Grand Duke
Jaroslav of
Russia.

i) = HARALD
1015–1066
(later called
'Hardrada')
Joint King of
Norway with
Magnus 'the
Good'.
Sole King of Norway
1047–1066.

Halfdan

Others

OLAF
('St Olaf')
Sole King of
Norway
1016–1030
following inter-
regnum of
Earls under
Denmark.

= ASTRID

Anund
James
King of
Sweden
1022–1050
= Gytha
= King
Svein of
Denmark.

THORA ii) =

BERGLJOT
= Finn
Arnason

Issue of Harald by different mothers.

Maria.
Died 1066.

Ingigerd

Magnus.
Joint
King of
Norway
1066.

Olaf
'The
Quiet'.
King of
Norway.

INGIBJORG
= i) *Gillacomghain*
of Moray
= ii) Earl Thorfinn
of Orkney
= iii) Malcolm III
King of Scotia
1058–1093.

Sigrid
= Earl
Orm
Eilifs-
son
of
Norway.

Ulfhild
= Ordulf
(Duke)
of
Saxony,
1059.

MAGNUS
'The Good'
(illegitimate)
1024–1047
King of Norway
1035–1047.

7 sons

PAUL
c. 1035–1099.
Joint Earl of
Orkney.

ERLEND
c. 1041–1099
Joint Earl of
Orkney.

LULACH
King of Alba
1057–1058.

Italics represent unsubstantiated data.

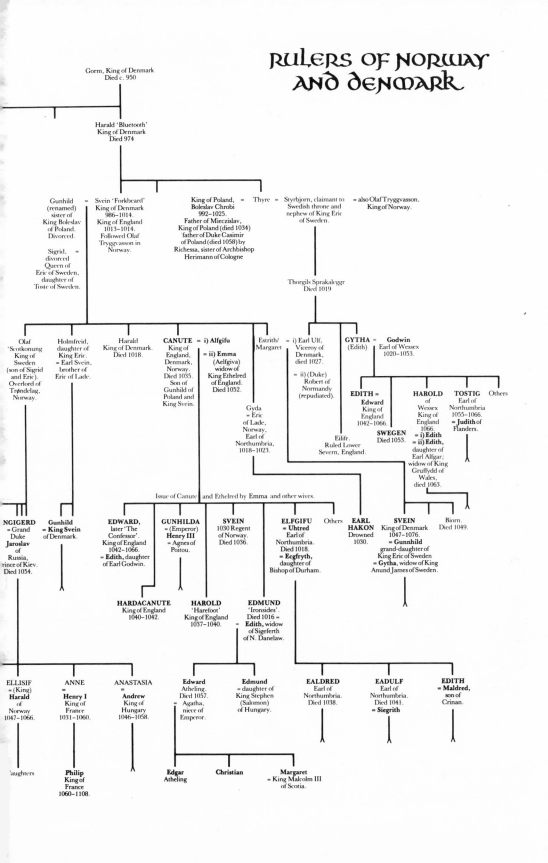

RULERS OF NORWAY AND DENMARK

Gorm, King of Denmark
Died c. 950

Harald 'Bluetooth'
King of Denmark
Died 974

Gunhild
(renamed)
sister of
King Boleslav
of Poland.
Divorced.

Sigrid,
divorced
Queen of
Eric of Sweden,
daughter of
Toste of Sweden.

= Svein 'Forkbeard'
King of Denmark
986–1014.
King of England
1013–1014.
Followed Olaf
Tryggvasson in
Norway.

King of Poland,
Boleslav Chrobi
992–1025.
Father of Mieczislav,
King of Poland (died 1034)
'father of Duke Casimir
of Poland (died 1058) by
Richessa, sister of Archbishop
Herimann of Cologne

= Thyre = Styrbjorn, claimant to
Swedish throne and
nephew of King Eric
of Sweden.

= also Olaf Tryggvasson.
King of Norway.

Thorgils Sprakaleggr
Died 1019

Olaf
'Scotkonung
King of
Sweden
(son of Sigrid
and Eric).
Overlord of
Trøndelag,
Norway.

Holmfreid,
daughter of
King Eric.
= Earl Svein,
brother of
Eric of Lade.

Harald
King of Denmark.
Died 1018.

CANUTE = i) Alfgifu
King of
England,
Denmark,
Norway.
Died 1035.
Son of
Gunhild of
Poland and
King Svein.

= ii) Emma
(Aelfgiva)
widow of
King Ethelred
of England.
Died 1052.

Estrith/
Margaret

= i) Earl Ulf,
Viceroy of
Denmark,
died 1027.

= ii) (Duke)
Robert of
Normandy
(repudiated).

GYTHA
(Edith)

Godwin
Earl of Wessex
1020–1053.

Gyda
= Eric
of Lade,
Norway,
Earl of
Northumbria,
1018–1023.

EDITH =
Edward
King of
England
1042–1066.

Eilifr.
Ruled Lower
Severn, England.

SWEGEN
Died 1053.

HAROLD
of
Wessex
King of
England
1066.
= i) Edith
= ii) Edith,
daughter of
Earl Alfgar;
widow of King
Gruffydd of
Wales,
died 1063.

TOSTIG
Earl of
Northumbria
1055–1066.
= Judith of
Flanders.

Others

Issue of Canute and Ethelred by Emma and other wives.

NGIGERD
= Grand
Duke
Jaroslav
of
Russia,
Prince of Kiev.
Died 1054.

Gunhild
= King Svein
of Denmark.

EDWARD,
later 'The
Confessor'.
King of England
1042–1066.
= Edith, daughter
of Earl Godwin.

GUNHILDA
= (Emperor)
Henry III
= Agnes of
Poitou.

SVEIN
1030 Regent
of Norway.
Died 1036.

ELFGIFU
= Uhtred
Earl of
Northumbria.
Died 1018.
= Ecgfryth,
daughter of
Bishop of Durham.

Others

EARL
HAKON
Drowned
1030.

SVEIN
King of Denmark
1047–1076.
= Gunhild
grand-daughter of
King Eric of Sweden
= Gytha, widow of King
Anund James of Sweden.

Biorn.
Died 1049.

HARDACANUTE
King of England
1040–1042.

HAROLD
'Harefoot'
King of England
1037–1040.

EDMUND
'Ironsides'.
Died 1016 =
Edith, widow
of Sigeferth
of N. Danelaw.

ELLISIF
= (King)
Harald
of
Norway
1047–1066.

ANNE
Henry I
King of
France
1031–1060.

ANASTASIA
Andrew
King of
Hungary
1046–1058.

Edward
Atheling.
Died 1057.
= Agatha,
niece of
Emperor.

Edmund
= daughter of
King Stephen
(Salomon)
of Hungary.

EALDRED
Earl of
Northumbria.
Died 1038.

EADULF
Earl of
Northumbria.
Died 1041.
= Siegrith

EDITH
= Maldred,
son of
Crinan.

Daughters

Philip
King of
France
1060–1108.

Edgar
Atheling

Christian

Margaret
= King Malcolm III
of Scotia.

A NOTE ON THE TYPE

The text of this book was set in Sabon, a type face
created by Jan Tschichold, the well-known German
typographer. Introduced in 1967, Sabon was
loosely patterned on the original designs
of Claude Garamond (ca.1480–1561).

Composed in Great Britain by
Rowland Phototypesetting Ltd, Suffolk

Printed and bound by R. R. Donnelly & Sons,
Harrisonburg, Virginia

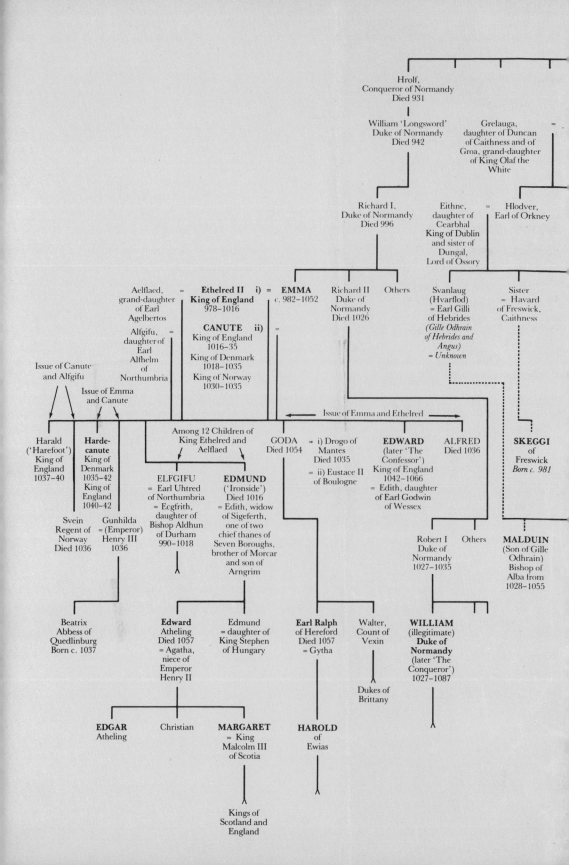

Hrolf,
Conqueror of Normandy
Died 931

William 'Longsword'
Duke of Normandy
Died 942

Grelauga,
daughter of Duncan
of Caithness and of
Groa, grand-daughter
of King Olaf the
White

=

Richard I,
Duke of Normandy
Died 996

Eithne,
daughter of
Cearbhal
King of Dublin
and sister of
Dungal,
Lord of Ossory

=

Hlodver,
Earl of Orkney

Aelflaed,
grand-daughter
of Earl
Agelbertos

=

Ethelred II   i)
King of England
978–1016

=

EMMA
c. 982–1052

Richard II
Duke of
Normandy
Died 1026

Others

Svanlaug
(Hvarflod)
= Earl Gilli
of Hebrides
(Gille Odhrain
of Hebrides and
Angus)
= Unknown

Sister
= Havard
of Freswick,
Caithness

Alfgifu,
daughter of
Earl
Alfhelm
of
Northumbria

=

CANUTE   ii)
King of England
1016–35
King of Denmark
1018–1035
King of Norway
1030–1035

=

Issue of Canute
and Alfgifu

Issue of Emma
and Canute

Among 12 Children of
King Ethelred and
Aelflaed

GODA
Died 1054

= i) Drogo of
Mantes
Died 1035

= ii) Eustace II
of Boulogne

EDWARD
(later 'The
Confessor')
King of England
1042–1066
= Edith, daughter
of Earl Godwin
of Wessex

ALFRED
Died 1036

SKEGGI
of
Freswick
Born c. 981

Issue of Emma and Ethelred

Harald
('Harefoot')
King of
England
1037–40

Harde-
canute
King of
Denmark
1035–42
King of
England
1040–42

ELFGIFU
= Earl Uhtred
of Northumbria
= Ecgfrith,
daughter of
Bishop Aldhun
of Durham
990–1018

EDMUND
('Ironside')
Died 1016
= Edith, widow
of Sigeferth,
one of two
chief thanes of
Seven Boroughs,
brother of Morcar
and son of
Arngrim

Robert I
Duke of
Normandy
1027–1035

Others

MALDUIN
(Son of Gille
Odhrain)
Bishop of
Alba from
1028–1055

Svein
Regent of
Norway
Died 1036

Gunhilda
= (Emperor)
Henry III
1036

Beatrix
Abbess of
Quedlinburg
Born c. 1037

Edward
Atheling
Died 1057
= Agatha,
niece of
Emperor
Henry II

Edmund
= daughter of
King Stephen
of Hungary

Earl Ralph
of Hereford
Died 1057
= Gytha

Walter,
Count of
Vexin

WILLIAM
(illegitimate)
Duke of
Normandy
(later 'The
Conqueror')
1027–1087

Dukes of
Brittany

EDGAR
Atheling

Christian

MARGARET
= King
Malcolm III
of Scotia

HAROLD
of
Ewias

Kings of
Scotland and
England